THE
PRINCE

THE PRINCE

JERRY POURNELLE
S.M. STIRLING

THE PRINCE

Copyright © 2002 by Jerry Pournelle & S.M. Stirling. *Falkenberg's Legion* © 1990 by Jerry Pournelle; *Prince of Mercenaries* © 1989 by Jerry Pournelle; *Go Tell the Spartans* © 1991 by Jerry Pournelle & S.M. Stirling; *Prince of Sparta* © 1993 by Jerry Pournelle & S.M. Stirling.

A Baen Books Original Omnibus

Baen Publishing Enterprises
P.O. Box 1403
Riverdale, NY 10471
www.baen.com

ISBN: 0-7434-3556-7

Cover art by Patrick Turner

First printing, September 2002

Library of Congress Cataloging-in-Publication Data

Pournelle, Jerry, 1933-
   The prince / by Jerry Pournelle & S.M. Stirling.
     p. cm.
   "Previously published in four parts as Falkenberg's legion and Prince of mercenaries by Jerry Pournelle, and Go tell the Spartans and Prince of Sparta by Jerry Pournelle and S.M. Stirling. This is the first complete edition"—Jacket.
   Contents: Falkenberg's legion — Prince of mercenaries — Go tell the Spartans — Prince of Sparta.
   ISBN 0-7434-3556-7
    1. Falkenberg, John Christian (Fictitious character)—Fiction. 2. Life on other planets—Fiction. 3. Science fiction, American. I. Stirling, S. M. II. Title.

PS3566.O815 P75 2002
813'.54—dc21

                2002071122

Distributed by Simon & Schuster
1230 Avenue of the Americas
New York, NY 10020

Production by Windhaven Press, Auburn, NH
Printed in the United States of America

10   9   8   7   6   5   4   3   2   1

CONTENTS

THE
PRINCE

FALKENBERG'S
LEGIONS

TO: Sergeant Herman Leich, Regular Army, U.S.A.;
and Second Lieutenant Zeneke Asfaw,
Kagnew Battalion, Imperial Guard of Ethiopia.

To junior officers
everywhere

Author's Note

This novel is part of the series of "future histories" in which *The Mote in God's Eye* takes place, and it gives the early history of the events in that novel.

The battle in Part II, Chapter XIX is based in large part on the actual experience of Lieutenant Zeneke Asfaw, Ethiopian Imperial Guard, during the Korean War.

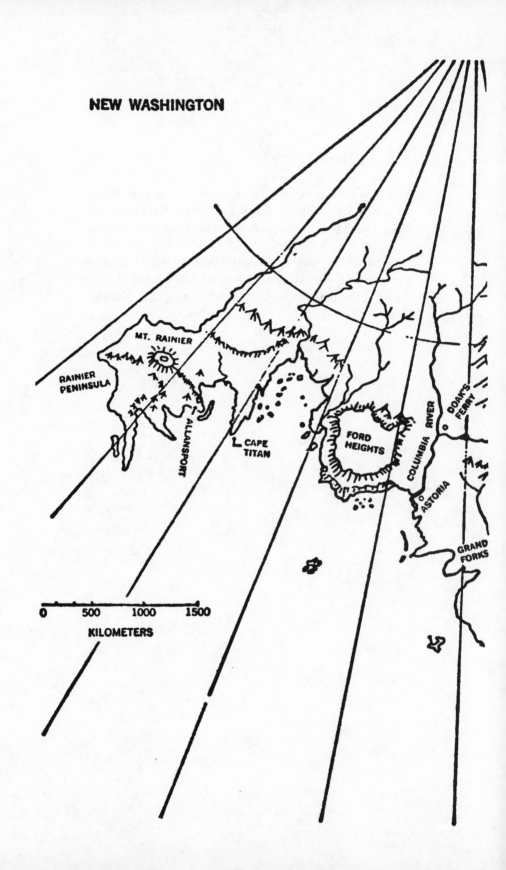

NEW WASHINGTON

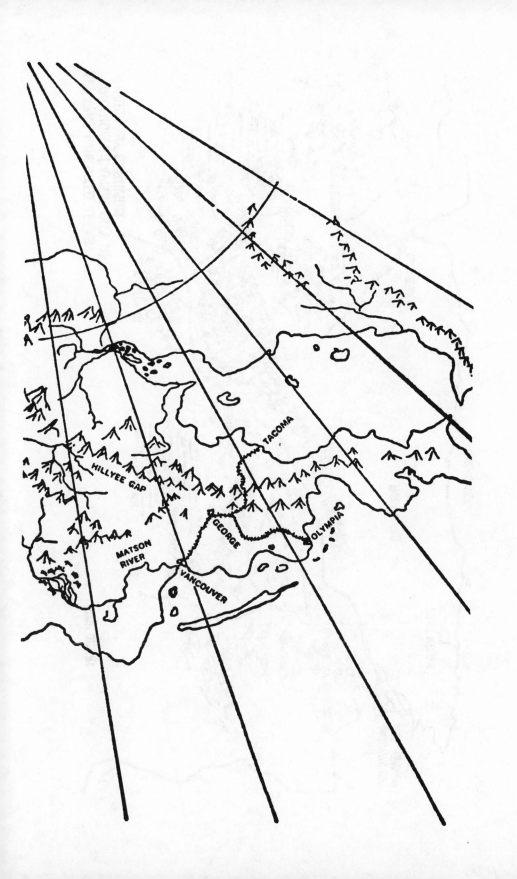

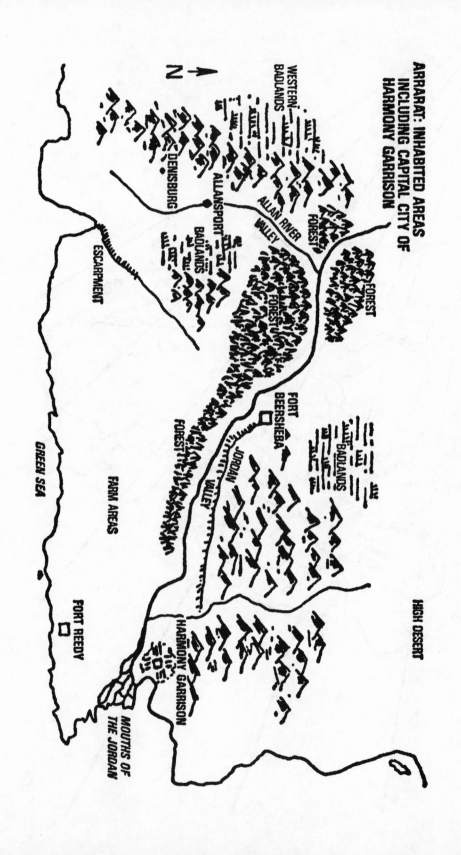

CHRONOLOGY

1969	Neil Armstrong sets foot on Earth's Moon.
1990–2000	Series of treaties between U.S. and Soviet Union creates the CoDominium. Military research and development outlawed.
1995	Nationalist movements intensify.
1996	French Foreign Legion forms the basic element of the CoDominium Armed Services.
2004	Alderson drive perfected at Cal Tech.
2008	First Alderson Drive exploratory ships leave the Solar System.
2010–2100	CoDominium Intelligence Services engage in serious effort to suppress all research into technologies with military applications. They are aided by zero-growth organizations. Most scientific research ceases.
2010	Inhabitable planets discovered. Commercial exploitation begins.
2020	First interstellar colonies are founded. The CoDominium Space Navy and Marines are created, absorbing the original CoDominium Armed Services.
2020	Great Exodus period of colonization begins. First colonists are dissidents, malcontents, and voluntary adventurers.
2030	Sergei Lermontov is born in Moscow.
2040	Bureau of Relocations begins mass outsystem shipment of involuntary colonists.
2043	John Christian Falkenberg III is born in Rome, Italy.
2060	Nationalistic revival movements continue.

PROLOGUE

An oily, acrid smell assaulted him, and the noise was incessant. Hundreds of thousands had passed through the spaceport. Their odor floated through the embarcation hall to blend with the yammer of the current victims crammed into the enclosure.

The room was long and narrow. White painted concrete walls shut out bright Florida sunshine; but the walls were dingy with film and dirt that had been smeared about and not removed by the Bureau of Relocation's convict laborers. Cold luminescent panels glowed brightly above.

The smell and sounds and glare blended with his own fears. He didn't belong here, but no one would listen. No one wanted to. Anything he said was lost in the brutal totality of shouted orders, growls of surly trustee guards in their wire pen running the full length of the long hall; screaming children; the buzz of frightened humanity.

They marched onward, toward the ship that would take them out of the solar system and toward an unknown fate. A few colonists blustered and argued. Some suppressed rage until it might be of use. Most were ashen-faced, shuffling forward without visible emotion, beyond fear.

There were red lines painted on the concrete floor, and the colonists stayed carefully inside them. Even the children had learned to cooperate with BuRelock's guards. The colonists had a sameness about them: shabbily dressed in Welfare Issue clothing mixed with finery cast off by taxpayers and gleaned from Reclamation Stores or by begging or from a Welfare District Mission.

John Christian Falkenberg knew he didn't look much like a typical colonist. He was a gangling youth, already at fifteen approaching six feet in height and thin because he hadn't yet filled out to his latest spurt of growth. No one would take him for a man, no matter how hard he tried to act like one.

A forelock of sand-colored hair fell across his forehead and threatened to blind him, and he automatically brushed it aside with a nervous gesture. His bearing and posture set him apart from the others, as did his almost comically serious expression. His clothing was also unusual: it was new, and fit well, and obviously not reclaimed. He wore a brocaded tunic of real wool and cotton, bright flared trousers, a new belt, and a tooled leather purse at his left hip. His clothes had cost more than his father could afford, but they did him little good here. Still he stood straight and tall, his lips set in defiance.

John stalked forward to keep his place in the long line. His bag, regulation space duffel without tags, lay in front of him and he kicked it forward rather than stoop to pick it up. He thought it would look undignified to bend over, and his dignity was all he had left.

Ahead of him was a family of five, three screaming children and their apathetic parents—or, possibly, he thought, not parents. Citizen families were never very stable. BuRelock agents often farmed out their quotas, and their superiors were seldom concerned about the precise identities of those scooped up.

The disorderly crowds moved inexorably toward the end of the room. Each line terminated at a wire cage containing a plastisteel desk. Each family group moved into a cage, the doors were closed, and their interviews began.

The bored trustee placement officers hardly listened to their clients, and the colonists did not know what to say to them. Most knew nothing about Earth's outsystem worlds. A few had heard that Tanith was hot, Fulson's World cold, and Sparta a hard place to live, but free. Some understood that Hadley had a good climate and was under the benign protection of American Express and the Colonial Office. For those sentenced to transportation without confinement, knowing that little could make a lot of difference to their futures; most didn't know and were shipped off to labor-hungry mining and agricultural worlds, or the hell of Tanith, where their lot would be hard labor, no matter what their sentences might read.

The fifteen-year-old boy—he liked to consider himself a man, but he knew many of his emotions were boyish no matter how hard he tried to control them—had almost reached the interview cage. He felt despair.

Once past the interview, he'd be packed into a BuRelock transportation ship. John turned again toward the gray-uniformed guard standing casually behind the large-mesh protective screen. "I keep trying to tell you, there's been a mistake! I shouldn't—"

"Shut up," the guard answered. He motioned threateningly with the bell-shaped muzzle of his sonic stunner. "It's a mistake for everybody, right? Nobody belongs here. Tell the interview officer, sonny."

John's lip curled, and he wanted to attack the guard, to make him listen. He fought to control the rising flush of hatred. "Damn you, I—"

The guard raised the weapon. The Citizen family in front of John huddled together, shoving forward to get away from this mad kid who could get them all tingled. John subsided and sullenly shuffled forward in the line.

Tri-V commentators said the stunners were painless, but John wasn't eager to have it tried on him. The Tri-V people said a lot of things. They said most colonists were volunteers, and they said transportees were treated with dignity by the Bureau of Relocation.

No one believed them. No one believed anything the government told them. They did not believe in the friendship among nations that had created the CoDominium, or in the election figures, or—

He reached the interview cage. The trustee wore the same uniform as the guards, but his gray coveralls had numbers stenciled across back and chest. There were wide gaps between the man's jaggedly pointed teeth, and the teeth showed yellow stains when he smiled. He smiled often, but there was no warmth in the expression.

"Whatcha got for me?" the trustee asked. "Boy dressed like you can afford anything he wants. Where you want to go, boy?"

"I'm not a colonist," John insisted. His anger rose. The trustee was no more than a prisoner himself—what right had he to speak this way? "I demand to speak with a CoDominium officer."

"One of those, huh?" The trustee's grin vanished. "Tanith for you." He pushed a button and the door on the opposite side of the cage opened. "Get on," he snapped. "Fore I call the guards." His finger poised menacingly over the small console on his desk.

John took papers out of an inner pocket of his tunic. "I have an appointment to CoDominium Navy Service," he said. "I was ordered to report to Canaveral Embarcation Station for transport by BuRelock ship to Luna Base."

"Get movin!—uh?" The trustee stopped himself and the grin reappeared. "Let me see that." He held out a grimy hand.

"No." John was more sure of himself now. "I'll show them

to any CD officer, but you won't get your hands on them. Now call an officer."

"Sure." The trustee didn't move. "Cost you ten credits."

"What?"

"Ten credits. Fifty bucks if you ain't got CD credits. Don't give me that look, kid. You don't pay, you go on the Tanith ship. Maybe they'll put things straight there, maybe they won't, but you'll be late reporting. Best you slip me something."

John held out a twenty-dollar piece. "That all you got?" the trustee demanded. "OK, OK, have to do." He punched a code into the phone, and a minute later a petty officer in blue CoDominium Space Navy coveralls came into the cage.

"What you need, Smiley?"

"Got one of yours. New middy. Got himself mixed up with the colonists." The trustee laughed as John struggled to control himself.

The petty officer eyed Smiley with distaste. "Your orders, sir?" he said.

John handed him the papers, afraid that he would never see them again. The Navy man glanced through them. "John Christian Falkenberg?"

"Yes."

"Thank you, sir." He turned to the trustee. "Gimme."

"Aw, he can afford it."

"Want me to call the Marines, Smiley?"

"Jesus, you hardnosed—" The trustee took the coin from his pocket and handed it over.

"This way, please, sir," the Navy man said. He bent to pick up John's duffel. "And here's your money, sir."

"Thanks. You keep it."

The petty officer nodded. "Thank you, sir. Smiley, you bite one of *our* people again and I'll have the Marines look you up when you're off duty. Let's go, sir."

John followed the spacer out of the cubicle. The petty officer was twice his age, and no one had ever called John "sir" before. It gave John Falkenberg a sense of belonging, a sense of having found something he had searched for all his life. Even the street gangs had been closed to him, and friends he had grown up with had always seemed part of someone else's life, not his own. Now, in seconds, he seemed to have found—found what, he wondered.

They went through narrow whitewashed corridors, then into the bright Florida sunshine. A narrow gangway led to the forward end of an enormous winged landing ship that floated at the end of a long pier crowded with colonists and cursing guards.

The petty officer spoke briefly to the Marine sentries at the officers' gangway, then carefully saluted the officer at the head of the boarding gangway. John wanted to do the same, but he knew that you didn't salute in civilian clothing. His father had made him read books on military history and the customs of the Service as soon as he decided to find John an appointment to the Academy.

Babble from the colonists filled the air until they were inside the ship. As the hatch closed behind him the last sounds he heard were the curses of the guards.

"If you please, sir. This way." The petty officer led him through a maze of steel corridors, airtight bulkheads, ladders, pipes, wire races, and other unfamiliar sights. Although the CD Navy operated it, most of the ship belonged to BuRelock, and she stank. There were no viewports and John was lost after several turns in the corridors.

The petty officer led on at a brisk pace until he came to a door that seemed no different from any other. He pressed a button on a panel outside it.

"Come in," the panel answered.

The compartment held eight tables, but only three men, all seated at a single booth. In contrast to the gray steel corridors outside, the compartment was almost cheerful, with paintings on the walls, padded furniture, and what seemed like carpets.

The CoDominium seal hung from the far wall—American eagle and Soviet sickle and hammer, red, white, and blue, white stars and red stars.

The three men held drinks and seemed relaxed. All wore civilian clothing not much different from John's except that the older man wore a more conservative tunic. The others seemed about John's age, perhaps a year older; no more.

"One of ours, sir," the petty officer announced. "New middy got lost with the colonists."

One of the younger men laughed, but the older cut him off with a curt wave. "All right, Cox'n. Thank you. Come in, we don't bite."

"Thank you, sir," John said. He shuffled uncertainly in the doorway, wondering who these men were. Probably CD officers, he decided. The petty officer wouldn't act that way toward anyone else. Frightened as he was, his analytical mind continued to work, and his eyes darted around the compartment.

Definitely CD officers, he decided. Going back up to Luna Base after leave, or perhaps a duty tour in normal gravity.

Naturally they'd worn civilian clothing. Wearing the CD uniform off duty earthside was an invitation to be murdered.

"Lieutenant Hartmann, at your service," the older man introduced himself. "And Midshipmen Rolnikov and Bates. Your orders, please?"

"John Christian Falkenberg, sir," John said. "Midshipman. Or I guess I'm a midshipman. But I'm not sure. I haven't been sworn in or anything."

All three men laughed at that. "You will be, Mister," Hartmann said. He took John's orders. "But you're one of the damned all the same, swearing in or no."

He examined the plastic sheet, comparing John's face to the photograph, then reading the bottom lines. He whistled. "Grand Senator Martin Grant. Appointed by the Navy's friend, no less. With him to bat for you, I wouldn't be surprised to see you outrank me in a few years."

"Senator Grant is a former student of my father's," John said.

"I see," Hartmann returned the orders and motioned John to sit with them. Then he turned to one of the other midshipmen. "As to you, Mister Bates, I fail to see the humor. What is so funny about one of your brother officers becoming lost among the colonists? You have never been lost?"

Bates squirmed uncomfortably. His voice was high-pitched, and John realized that Bates was no older than himself. "Why didn't he show the guards his taxpayer status card?" Bates demanded. "They would have taken him to an officer. Wouldn't they?"

Hartman shrugged.

"I didn't have one," John said.

"Um." Hartmann seemed to withdraw, although he didn't actually move. "Well," he said. "We don't usually get officers from Citizen families—"

"We are not Citizens," John said quickly. "My father is a CoDominium University professor, and I was born in Rome."

"Ah," Hartman said. "Did you live there long?"

"No, sir. Father prefers to be a visiting faculty member. We have lived in many university towns." The lie came easily now, and John thought that Professor Falkenberg probably believed it after telling it so many times. John knew better: he had seen his father desperate to gain tenure, but always, always making too many enemies.

He is too blunt and too honest. One explanation. He is a revolving S.O.B. and can't get along with anyone. That's another. I've lived with the situation so long I don't care anymore. But, it would have been nice to have a home, I think.

Hartmann relaxed slightly, "Well, whatever the reason, Mister Falkenberg, you would have done better to arrange to be born a United States taxpayer. Or a Soviet party member. Unfortunately, you, like me, are doomed to remain in the lower ranks of the officer corps."

There was a trace of accent to Hartmann's voice, but John couldn't place it exactly. German, certainly; there were many Germans in the CD fighting services. This was not the usual German though; John had lived in Heidelberg long enough to learn many shades of the German speech. East German? Possibly.

He realized the others were waiting for him to say something. "I thought, sir, I thought there was equality within the CD services."

Hartmann shrugged. "In theory, yes. In practice—the generals and admirals, even the captains who command ships, always seem to be Americans or Soviets. It is not the preference of the officer corps, Mister. We have no countries of origin among ourselves and no politics. Ever. The Fleet is our fatherland, and our only fatherland." He glanced at his glass. "Mister Bates, we need more to drink, and a glass for our new comrade. Hop it."

"Aye, aye, sir." The pudgy middy left the compartment, passing the unattended bar in the corner on his way. He returned a moment later with a full bottle of American whiskey and an empty glass.

Hartmann poured the glass full and pushed it toward John. "The Navy will teach you many things, Mister Midshipman John Christian Falkenberg. One of them is to drink. We all drink too much. Another thing we will teach you is why we do, but before you learn why, you must learn to do it."

He lifted the glass. When John raised his and took only a sip, Hartmann frowned. "More," he said. The tone made it an order.

John drank half the whiskey. He had been drinking beer for years, but his father did not often let him drink spirits. It did not taste good, and it burned his throat and stomach.

"Now, why have you joined our noble band of brothers?" Hartmann asked. His voice carried a warning: he used bantering words, but under that was a more serious mood—perhaps he was not mocking the Service at all when he called it a band of brothers.

John hoped he was not. He had never had brothers. He had never had friends, or a home, and his father was a harsh schoolmaster, teaching him many things, but never giving him any affection—or friendship.

"I—"

"Honesty," Hartmann warned. "I will tell you a secret, the secret of the Fleet. We do not lie to our own." He looked at the other two midshipmen, and they nodded, Rolnikov slightly amused, Bates serious, as if in church.

"Out there," Hartmann said, "out there they lie, and they cheat, and they use each other. With us this is not true. We are used, yes. But we know that we are used, and we are honest with each other. That is why the men are loyal to us. And why we are loyal to the Fleet."

And that's significant, John thought, because Hartmann had glanced at the CoDominium banner on the wall, but he said nothing about the CD at all. Only the Fleet. "I'm here because my father wanted me out of the house and was able to get an appointment for me," John blurted.

"You will find another reason, or you will not stay with us," Hartmann said. "Drink up."

"Yes, sir."

"The proper response is 'aye aye, sir.'"

"Aye aye, sir." John drained his glass.

Hartmann smiled. "Very good." He refilled his glass, then the others. "What is the mission of the CoDominium Navy, Mister Falkenberg?"

"Sir? To carry out the will of the Grand Senate—"

"No. It is to exist. And by existing, to keep some measure of peace and order in this corner of the galaxy. To buy enough time for men to get far enough away from Earth that when the damned fools kill themselves they will not have killed the human race. And that is our only mission."

"Sir?" Midshipman Rolnikov spoke quietly and urgently. "Lieutenant, sir, should you drink so much?"

"Yes. I should," Hartmann replied. "I thank you for your concern, Mister Rolnikov. But as you see, I am, at present, a passenger. The Service has no regulation against drinking. None at all, Mister Falkenberg. There is a strong prohibition against being unfit for one's duties, but none against drinking. And I have no duties at the moment." He raised his glass. "Save one. To speak to you, Mister Falkenberg, and to tell you the truth, so that you will either run from us or be damned with us for the rest of your life, for we never lie to our own."

He fell silent for a moment, and Falkenberg wondered just how drunk Hartmann was. The officer seemed to be considering his words more carefully than his father ever had when he was drinking.

"What do you know of the history of the CoDominium Navy, Mister Falkenberg?" Hartmann demanded.

Probably more than you, John thought. Father's lecture on the growth of the CoDominium was famous. "It began with *détente.* That collapsed, but was revived, and soon there was a web of formal treaties between the United States and the Soviet Union. The treaties did not end the basic enmity between these great powers, but their common interest was greater than their differences; for it was obviously better that there be only two great powers, than for there to be . . ." No. Hartmann did not want to hear Professor Falkenberg's lecture. "Very little, sir."

"We were created out of the French Foreign Legion," Hartmann said. "A legion of strangers, to fight for an artificial alliance of nations that hate each other. How can a man give his soul and life to that, Mister Falkenberg? What heart has an alliance? What power to inspire men's loyalty?"

"I don't know, sir."

"Nor do they." Hartmann waved at the other middies, who were carefully leaning back in their seats, acting as if they were listening, as if they were not listening—John couldn't tell. Perhaps they thought Hartmann was crazy drunk. Yet it had been a good question.

"I don't know," John repeated.

"Ah. But no one knows, for there is no answer. Men cannot die for an alliance. Yet we do fight. And we do die."

"At the Senate's orders," Midshipman Rolnikov said quietly.

"But we do not love the Senate," Hartmann said. "Do you love the Grand Senate, Mister Rolnikov? Do you, Mister Bates? We know what the Grand Senate is. Corrupt politicians who lie to each other, and who use us to gather wealth for themselves, power for their own factions. If they can. They do not use us as much as they once did. Drink, gentlemen. *Drink.*"

The whiskey had taken its effect, and John's head buzzed. He felt sweat break out at his temples and in his armpits, and his stomach rebelled, but he lifted the glass and drank again, in unison with Rolnikov and Bates, and it was more meaningful than the Communion cup had ever been. He tried to ask himself why, but there was only emotion, no thought. He belonged here, with this man, with these men, and he was a man with them.

As if he had read John's thoughts, Lieutenant Hartmann put his arms out, across the shoulders of the three boys, two on his left, John alone on his right, and he lowered his voice to speak to all of them. "No. We are here because the Fleet is our only fatherland, and our brothers in the Service are our only family. And if the Fleet should ever demand our lives, we give them as men because we have no other place to go."

PART ONE: THE CODOMINIUM YEARS

I

Princeton, New Jersey, United States of America

The student lounge was noisy as usual. Students in bright tunics sipped coffee paid for by their taxpayer parents, and spoke of the Rights of Man and the Citizen. Others pretended to read while looking to see if anyone interesting had come in. In one corner three young men and a girl—she detested being called a 'young lady'—sat playing bridge. They were typical students, children of taxpayers, well dressed in the latest fashions of subdued colors. Their teeth were straight, their complexions were good. Two of the boys wore contact lenses. The girl, in keeping with fashion, wore large brightly colored glasses with small jewels at the hinges. The remains of their afternoon snack probably contained as many calories as the average Citizen would have for the day.

"Three No Trump, made four. That's game and rubber," Donald Etheridge said. He scribbled for a moment on the score sheet. "Let's see, I owe twenty-two fifty. Moishe, you owe eleven and a quarter. Richie gets nine bucks, and Bonnie wins the rest."

"You always win," Richard Larkin said accusingly.

Bonnie Dalrymple smiled. "Comes of clean living."

"You?" Donald smirked.

"Don't you just wish," Richie said. He glanced at his watch. "Getting on for class time. Visiting lecturer today."

18

Moishe Ellison frowned. "Who?"

"Chap named Falkenberg," Larkin said. "Professor at the CD University in Rome. Going to lecture on problems of the CoDominium. Today it's military leadership."

"Oh, I know him," Bonnie Dalrymple said.

"Is he interesting?" Moishe asked. "I've got a lot to do this afternoon."

"He's dense," Bonnie said. She grinned at the blank looks. "Packs a lot into what he says. Makes every paragraph count. I think you better come listen."

"What did you take from him?" Richard Larkin asked.

"Oh, I wasn't old enough to take his classes. Actually, I didn't know Professor Falkenberg very well, I used to be friends with his son. John Christian Falkenberg the Third. It was when Daddy was stationed at the Embassy in Rome. Johnny Falkenberg and I wandered all over the city. He knew everything about it, it was really fun. The Capitoline Hill, with the statues, and up there is the Tarpeian Rock where they threw traitors off—it's not so high, really. And we'd go to the Via Flaminia. We used to tramp down that and Johnny sang this old Roman marching song. 'When you go by the Via Flaminia, by the Legion's road from Rome—'"

"Fun date."

"Wasn't really dating. He was about fourteen and I was twelve, we were just kids out playing around. But we had fun, really. I guess I was studious, then."

"Heh. You still are. You aced me in that last test," Moishe Ellison said.

"Well, if you'd work more instead of running around with *that* girl—"

Ellison winked, and the others laughed. They got up and walked together toward the lecture hall. The smog was bad outside, but it always was, so they didn't notice. "So how do you know about old man Falkenberg's lectures?"

Bonnie laughed. "Johnny used to take me to his house. Usually there wasn't anyone there but this old black housekeeper, but sometimes the Professor would come home early, and when he did, he'd ask where we'd been. Then he'd tell us all about it. *All* about it, wherever we'd been."

"Oh."

"Actually, it was interesting. Rome was nice then, there were a lot of old buildings I guess they've let fall down now, and the Professor knew about all of them. But he wasn't as interesting as when Johnny told me—I guess I had quite a crush on him." Bonnie laughed.

"That's what's wrong with her," Richie said. "She's never got over her youthful affair with—what was his name?"

"John Christian Falkenberg, the Fourth." Moishe Ellison let the name roll off his tongue.

"Third," Bonnie said. "And maybe you're right."

They reached Smith Hall and went up the marble stairs to the lecture theatre.

Professor Falkenberg was tall and thin, with a surprisingly deep voice that carried authority. Hasn't changed a bit, Bonnie thought. He could read the phone book and make it sound important.

Falkenberg nodded to the students. "Good afternoon. I am pleased to see that there are still a few students in the United States who are interested in history.

"I wish to examine the origins of the CoDominium. To do that, we will have to look at just what happened to the United States and the Soviet Union whose uneasy alliance has produced our modern world. Friends in the Second World War, enemies in the Cold War—how did it happen that these two divided the world between them?

"There are many aspects to this problem. One is the decline of military power in both nations. That in itself has many facets.

"Today we will discuss military leadership, both as a general case and in the specifics of the powers at the time of interest. I begin with a few brief paragraphs by Joseph Maxwell Cameron, a writer of the last century, who said, in his *Anatomy of Military Merit:*"

Professor Falkenberg opened his pocket computer and touched a key, then began to read.

"'Armies are controlled by the actions of two classes of men in authority that are distinct on the surface by levels of rank, but whose significant difference is in the sources of their authority. One class acts on the authority vested in it by the sovereign power. The other acts by authority derived of appointment by the first. This is not a chance relationship but one directed by a natural ruling principle. The 'commissioned' officer acts in the name of sovereign power and, or, by order of its commissioned superiors to himself. The 'non-commissioned' officer exercises equally valid and at times absolute authority, but he holds it from the commissioned officer who appointed him and who can at his discretion remove the office. Few controlling principles are as little understood in current times as these that define the relationships of commissioned and non-commissioned ranks to each other, the government, and to the ordinary soldier. Promotion given as reward, rank seen as caste and pay as incentive in the profession, occupation, or career in arms are the villains that cloud the issues. A private soldier can prove himself of equal value to a general officer, in fact has often done so; and always by being the soldier who knew his business, whatever his immediate motivation. A hierarchy of ranks invented to increase prestige and pay can rob a military body of much of its power while enjoying general approval of what are considered benefits. One of the sure signs of a military system in decay is the appearance of an excess ratio of persons in designated authority over the numbers of those who serve to follow. The optimum ratio may vary a little according to current armaments, but with little else.

"'Because of its specific roles and purposes an army has an optimum design and structure of control mechanisms, instrumentation, and appendages. It is at best simple, devoted to the smooth and graceful application of power to motion and impact. In an almost totally industrial and technocratic time, however, the existence of a natural pattern tends to be forgotten as normal members and appendages are tortured and distorted to conform to the caprices of machines. Military monstrosities analogous to anencephalic and three legged children are born and nursed toward ultimate impotence. They are quite horribly obvious except to minds bemused by the magic of technology. . . .'"

Falkenberg closed his computer and smiled thinly. "Those words were written shortly before the United States acquired, in what was supposed to be peace time, approximately twice as many general officers as it had employed during the conflict known as the Second World War, despite having a much smaller military establishment. Nor was this all. The ratio of officers to men began to creep upward, inexorably; and since the optimum ratio is perhaps five percent, and some elite organizations have done with less, it should be no surprise that as the United States military establishment moved toward one officer for each dozen men—and one general officer for each fifteen hundred—the effectiveness of the system declined accordingly.

"Military managers are easy enough to come by. Real leaders are rare."

"You were right about the density," Moishe Ellison said. Bonnie giggled. "He hasn't changed much, that's for sure."

"And you only heard him at home? Wonder his kid didn't go nuts. Whatever happened to him, anyway?"

"He got in some kind of trouble," Bonnie said.

"And no wonder." Richie chuckled.

"I don't know what it was," Bonnie said. "But the next thing I knew, Johnny was off to the CoDominium Academy. We used to write, but when he graduated and was sent off on a ship, well—"

"You sound like you miss him," Moishe said.

"Yeah, hey, you never get that tone of voice when you talk about me," Richie said.

"That'll be the day," Moishe said. "You ever hear from him?"

Bonnie shook her head.

II

Angela Niles fought for wakefulness. It seemed to take a long time. At one level she knew she was dreaming, but it was still real: the crowded alleys of High Shanghai, thousands of men and women in blue canvas clothing, not quite uniforms but so alike they looked like blue ants. They were shouting, screaming words she could not understand, but what they intended was clear enough. The blue ants were coming to kill her. She ran, and suddenly she wasn't alone, there were blue and gold uniforms, a different blue, CoDominium blue, and the tiny squad of CoDominium troops clustered around her. They pulled her away from the mob, then turned, fired a volley, then another, and the blue ants screamed and halted for a moment.

"Fall back." The Navy lieutenant spoke calmly. "First squad. Fall back toward the harbor. Kewney."

"Sir."

Cousin Harold. How did Cousin Harold get here? But he was here, in the uniform of a Navy middie.

"Can you fly that boat?"

"No, sir."

"The cox'n was killed."

"Yes, sir, I know."

"Right. All right, Midshipman. Fall back with the first squad. Halt while we're still in sight, and take defensive positions. Signal when you're ready. We'll hold here. Miss, you go with him—"

"But, yes, but, Harold, what are you doing here, who is this, what—"

"No time, Angie. Let's go!"

They ran, and now it was certainly a dream, because she couldn't move, her legs wouldn't work, she tried to run and couldn't—

"Try to remember," a voice said. Whose? "What happened then?"

Running. A Marine was holding her arm. Suddenly he stopped. His eyes grew very wide, and he stood, stock still, in the middle of the street. A long thin steel rod grew out of his chest, and blood came out of his mouth, and he crumpled, slowly, slowly—

"Come on Angie, run, dammit!"

Run. Then they were at the end of the block, and turned the corner, and she could see the harbor, not far away, with the long slender shape of the landing craft, and three sailors at the landing with guns, and the turret on top swiveled.

Harold touched his sleeve and spoke rapidly into the communicator card. There was more gunfire, and more people screaming, then the CoDominium lieutenant and his party came running down the street.

"Almost there," Harold said.

"Get her into the ship," the Lieutenant said.

"Sir, you can fly the damn thing. You get her on the ship."

He was very young, that lieutenant, no more than a boy, he looked so thin and so very young, no older than Harold. "Three minutes," he said. "Three minutes, Kewney, then run like hell."

Harold grinned. "You know it. Ready? Go for it!"

And the lieutenant took her hand and ran with her, pulling her along, and the turret guns fired over their heads, and there was more shooting, and noise everywhere. Something exploded close to them and one of the dockside sailors went down. The lieutenant shouted into his sleeve mike, "Mortars! Run for it, Kewney. NOW!" And dragged her on, to the boarding port, threw her into the cabin.

"Sound Board Ship!"

Recorded bugle notes blared into the bright afternoon. The lieutenant ran forward and moments later there were rumbles. Something exploded outside the hatchway, and a swarm of angry bees came through the open hatch, whipped past her and clattered against the bulkheads. There was another explosion.

"We're hulled!" a sailor shouted.

The engine sounds were louder now. She ran to the hatchway to look out, and shouted for Harold. She couldn't see anyone.

"Clear the hatch!" someone shouted. There were whirs and the hatchway began to close. She felt motion as the ship began to move.

"Harold! Harold!" And there was Harold, only he was an old man, and his face was melting, and then he was gone, and there was another man, and the ship began to fade and she was in a white room in bed, a hospital room, and the men beside the bed were a doctor in a white coat and a CoDominium Navy Commander, very thin. She knew them both. How? Who were they? Lermontov. That was his name. How did she know that?

"Did you ever see Midshipman Kewney again?" Commander Lermontov asked.

"No. I never saw him after we left him at the corner, on the street of—the Street of Three Moons." Her throat was dry, and her left arm hurt. She couldn't move it, and when she looked she saw that it was strapped to a board, and there was an IV inserted at the elbow. And she remembered. Pentothal, something like that. They wanted to question her. What had she told them?

"I've told you everything," she said. "Three times, and whatever I said when I was drugged. Why do we have to go over this again?"

"Your Uncle has demanded thorough investigation," Commander Lermontov said. "And that he will have." He used his stylus on the screen of his pocket computer. "So. You last saw Midshipman Kewney at corner, where he was ordered by Lieutenant Falkenberg to hold for three minutes before retreating."

"Actually Harold volunteered—"

"Yes. Thank you. How long after that order was given did ship begin to move?"

"I don't know—"

"Doctor says you believe was less than three minutes."

"How does he know?"

"I don't know," the white-coated man said. "I can only try to construct events from your memories. Based on what we heard, I conclude that you don't really know, but you suspect that Falkenberg took off as soon as he got you to the ship."

"What does he say?" Angela asked.

"You already know that," Doctor Wittgenstein said.

"He told me Harold was hit by mortar fire before we got to the boat."

"But you don't believe him."

"I don't—I don't know what to believe," she said.

"Boat lifted," Lermontov said. "It had not enough fuel to go to orbit, and was damaged."

Angela shuddered. "More damage than—I was shocked when

we landed and I could look. It was amazing that it would fly."

"*Buna* class boat is designed to take damage. So. Falkenberg landed boat at offshore island. What happened there?"

"Nothing. It was perfectly safe there, the people were Thai, no Chinese. Very friendly. It was—nice there, safe and peaceful. So we waited, three weeks until the Navy could send another ship down with a repair crew. Then I was taken to Government House, and John—Lieutenant Falkenberg was sent to his ship. Nothing happened."

"Something happened," Lermontov said.

She frowned at his tone. "What do you mean?"

"Doctor—"

"Miss Niles, you are a month pregnant."

"Oh."

"You do not seem surprised. You took no precautions?"

She felt herself blushing.

"Miss Niles, I have daughter nearly your age," Lermontov said. "You took no precautions?"

She tried to sound casual. "I wasn't thinking about that at the time."

"Nor, apparently, was Lieutenant," Lermontov said. "In this era of disease you were perhaps foolhardy."

Angela shrugged. "Actually, there were no precautions to take—"

"On Navy ship there will always be kits," Lermontov said. "But you are in fact correct. Medical cabinet was damaged along with much other equipment."

"Commander, I fail to see how my condition is relevant—"

"Your uncle will not fail to see," Lermontov said. "Foolhardy young Falkenberg, sacrifices promising Midshipman grandson of Grand Senator, in order to save himself. Then seduces Grand Senator's niece." Lermontov stared pointedly at her midriff. "Evidence will be unmistakable in few weeks."

"Oh. Do you— I guess Uncle Adrian would see it that way."

"At least you're safe," Dr. Wittgenstein said. "That ought to make him grateful."

Angela shook her head. "I'm afraid he won't be, not very. He doesn't like my mother much, and Harold was special. A niece is not a grandson, Doctor. He'd have gladly traded me for Harold." She shrugged. "I think he planned for Harold to become Grand Admiral one day."

"So. What will you do now?" Lermontov asked.

"About—" She rubbed her belly. "It takes getting used to. Does John—does Lieutenant Falkenberg know?"

"Not unless you told him," Dr. Wittgenstein said.

But I didn't know— "You mean, he won't learn unless I tell him?"

Lermontov nodded. "I was told you are intelligent."

"What is that supposed to mean?"

"I think I need not explain. What will Lieutenant Falkenberg do if he learns?"

She blushed again. "I suppose—I suppose he'd marry me, if I wanted him to."

"Is my prediction also," Lermontov said. "Under other circumstances would be good thing for young man's career, marriage to Bronson family. Now—"

"Now it would be ruin for both of us," Angela said. "What—what should I do?"

"You don't have to be pregnant," Dr. Wittgenstein said.

"Damn you! I was waiting for that! Why didn't—while I was still under, while you had me out, why didn't you just do it then, and I'd never have known? But no, you had to wake me up and tell me—"

"You want us to make decision for you?" Lermontov said. When she didn't answer, he turned to Wittgenstein. "Doctor, prepare operating room."

"Wait—no, wait—" She felt tears welling up in her eyes. "What is it?"

"What is what— Oh," Wittgenstein said. "A girl."

"Commander—I want to see John Falkenberg."

"I cannot prevent," Lermontov said. "But I ask you do not. Not until you have decided what you will do. He is not stupid—"

"Do you know him?" she asked. "That's a strange thing to ask, isn't it? Do you know the—father of my unborn daughter? We had three weeks. A lifetime. I think I know him, but do I? I—oh, damn."

Lermontov's expression softened. "He is—was—considered promising young officer. Well regarded." He shrugged. "Pity no one sees Midshipman Kewney die. Now I do not know what we can do for Falkenberg."

"And I can't help—I can only make it worse," she said. "Oh, damn—what should I do?"

"Get rid of it," Lermontov said. "Then, in year, two years, when Senator has forgotten, you will meet again—"

"He'll never forget. And we'll never meet again."

Lermontov was going to speak but she cut him off. "You can't be sure, and I can't be sure," she said. "The only thing that is sure is that—we can kill my daughter."

"Fetus," Wittgenstein said. "Not—"

"I've studied embryology," Angela said. "You don't need to tell me the details." She was silent for a long time. Then she brushed the tears from her eyes and looked directly at Lermontov. "Commander, can you get me passage to Churchill?"

"Yes, but why Churchill?"

"I have relatives there. My branch of the family didn't get the big money, but we're not broke, you know. I'll get by—"

"If you do this, I cannot permit you to see Falkenberg again."

"You couldn't stop me if I demanded it, and you know it," she said. "But—maybe it's better this way. Tell him—" The words caught in her throat, and she felt the tears welling up again. "Tell him I thank him for saving my life, and I wish him well."

The young man marched stiffly into the compartment and saluted. "Lieutenant Falkenberg reporting to Commander Lermontov as ordered, sir."

The thin man behind the desk returned the salute. "Thank you. Have a seat."

"Sir?"

"I said, Sit Down."

"Aye, aye, sir." Falkenberg sat stiffly.

"You believe I am calling you in for punishment?"

Falkenberg fingered the dispatch case under his left arm. "I have orders—"

"I know," Lermontov interrupted. "Not orders I wished to issue, but there is nothing to be done."

"So I'm leaving the Fleet."

"No. Only Navy," Lermontov said. "Unless you prefer to leave Fleet entirely." The older man leaned forward and examined Falkenberg minutely. "I could not blame you if you did, but I hope you will not. I have arranged to transfer you to Marines. As lieutenant with seniority and brevet captain. Also, I have sent message to Senator Grant recommending that he obtain Grand Senate confirmation of Order of Merit, First Class, for you. I expect that will ensure permanent promotion to Marine captain." Lermontov sighed. "If we had better communications, if I could speak to Grant directly, perhaps none of this will be necessary. Perhaps. I do not gauge well the politics of Grand Senate."

Falkenberg glanced at his dispatch case. "Clearly I don't either. Sir."

"This is obvious," Lermontov said. "Yet you did right. Losing one squad of landing party to save others is difficult, but we are all satisfied there was nothing else to be done." He shrugged. "Is unfortunate that squad you lose is commanded by Bronson grandson, but you cannot know this."

"He was a good troop," Falkenberg said. "And actually I did know his connection to—"

Lermontov held up a hand, cutting him off. He glanced involuntarily around the room, then eyed Falkenberg narrowly. "You will never admit that to anyone else," he said. "That your actions cause this young man to be killed is regrettable but justified, and perhaps Bronson will forget. But if Grand Senator Bronson is reminded that you knew of his interest in Midshipman Kewney, it will be much more serious. He will never forget that. I suggest you avoid Senator in future."

"Yes, sir. Only—"

"Yes?"

"Sir, I have asked about Miss Niles, and no one seems to know where she is."

"She requested that she be sent to Churchill, where she has money and relatives. She left two days ago on message boat to rendezvous with ship bound for Churchill."

"Oh—I'd have thought—Did she have a message for me?"

"She says she is very grateful that you have saved her life."

"I see." He was silent for a moment. "Sir, what is my assignment?"

Lermontov smiled thinly. "You have several choices. As usual there is no end of trouble which must be attended to."

III

Crofton's Encyclopedia of Contemporary History
and Social Issues (1st Edition)

THE EXODUS

THE era of exploration following the development of
the Alderson Drive was predictably followed by a wave
of colonization. The initial colonists tended to be both
wealthy and discontented with Earth's civilization. Many
were motivated by religion: both the more traditional
religions, and the secular religion that grew out of what
was known in the Twentieth Century as "The Ecology
Movement, or "The Greens."

Many of the early colonists were quite sophisticated,
and had good reason to expect success in establishing
their cultures on new planets. Unfortunately, they did not
reckon with the intense pressures on the governments of
Earth . . .

2064 AD.

The bright future she sang of was already stiffened in blood,
but Kathryn Malcolm didn't know that, any more than she
knew that the sun was orange-red and too bright, or that the
gravity was too low.

She had lived all of her sixteen standard years on Arrarat,
and although her grandfather often spoke of Earth, humanity's
birthplace was no home to her. Earth was a place of machines
and concrete roads and automobiles and great cities, a place
where people crowded together far from the land. When she

30

thought of Earth at all, it seemed an ugly place, hardly fit for people to live on.

Mostly she wondered how Earth would smell. With all those people huddled together—certainly it must be different from Arrarat. She inhaled deeply, filling her lungs with the pleasing smell of newly turned soil. The land here was good. It felt right beneath her feet. Dark and crumbly, moist enough to take hold of the seeds and nurture them, but not wet and full of clods: good land, perfect land for the late-season crop she was planting.

She walked steadily behind the plow, using a long whip to guide the oxen. She flicked the whip near the leaders, but never close enough to touch them. There was no need for that. Horace and Star knew what she wanted. The whip guided them and assured them that she was watching, but they knew the spiral path as well as she did. The plow turned the soil inward so that the center of the field would be higher than the edges. That helped to drain the field and made it easier to harvest two crops each year.

The early harvest was already gathered into the stone barn. Wheat and corn, genetically adapted for Arrarat; and in another part of the barn were Arrarat's native breadfruit melons, full of sugar and ready to begin fermentation. It had been a good year, with more than enough for the family to eat. There would be a surplus to sell in town, and Kathryn's mother had promised to buy a bolt of printed cloth for a new dress that Kathryn could wear for Emil.

At the moment, though, she wore coveralls and high boots, and she was glad enough that Emil couldn't see her. He should know that she could plow as straight a furrow as any man, and that she could ride as well as her brother—but knowing it and seeing her here on the fields were two different things entirely, and she was glad that he couldn't see her just now. She laughed at herself when she thought this, but that didn't stop the thoughts.

She twitched the whip to move the oxen slightly outward, then frowned imperceptibly. The second pair in the string had never pulled a wagon across the plains, and Kathryn thought that she could no longer put off their training. Emil would not want to live with Kathryn's grandfather. A man wanted land of his own, even though there were more than a thousand hectares in the Malcolm station.

The land here was taken. If she and Emil were to have land of their own, they would have to move westward, toward the other sea, where the satellite pictures showed good land. We could go, she thought; go so far that the convicts will never find us, and the city will be a place to see once in a lifetime. It would be exciting, although she would hate to leave this valley.

The field she plowed lay among low hills. A small stream meandered along one edge. Most of the crops and trees that she could see had come from Earth as seeds, and they had few predators. Most crop-eaters left Earth plants alone, especially if the fields were bordered with spearmints and marigolds to give off odors that even Earth insects detested.

She thought of what she would need if they struck west to found a new settlement. Seeds they would have; and a mare and stallion, and two pairs of oxen; chickens and swine; her grandfather was rich by local standards. There would be her father's blacksmithing tools, which Emil could learn to use.

They would need a television. Those were rare. A television, and solar cells, and a generator for the windmill; such manufactured goods had to be bought in the city, and that took money. The second crop would be needed this year, and a large one next spring, as well—and they would have to keep all the money they earned. She thrust that thought away, but her hand strayed toward the big sheath knife she wore on her belt.

We will manage, she thought. We will find the money. Children should not go without education. Television was not for entertainment. The programs relayed by the satellites gave weather reports and taught farming, ecology, engineering, metalwork—all the skills needed to live on Arrarat. They also taught reading and mathematics. Most of Kathryn's neighbors despised television and wouldn't have it in their houses, but their children had to learn from others who watched the screen.

And yet, Kathryn thought, there is cause for concern. First it is television. Then light industry. Soon there is more. Mines are opened. Larger factories are built, and around them grow cities. She thought of Arrarat covered with cities and concrete, the animals replaced by tractors and automobiles, the small villages grown into cities; people packed together the way they were in Harmony and Garrison; streams dammed and lakes dirty with sewage; and she shuddered. Not in my time, or my grandchildren's. And perhaps we will be smarter than they were on Earth, and it will never happen here. We know better now. We know how to live with the land.

Her grandfather had been a volunteer colonist, an engineer with enough money to bring tools and equipment to Arrarat, and he was trying to show others how to live with technology. He had a windmill for electricity. It furnished power for the television and the radio. He had radio communications with Denisburg, forty kilometers away, and although the neighbors said they despised all technology, they were not too proud to ask Amos Malcolm to send messages for them.

The Malcolm farm had running water and an efficient system for converting sewage to fertilizer. To Amos, technology was something to be used so long as it did not use you, and he tried to teach his neighbors that.

The phone buzzed to interrupt her thoughts, and Kathryn halted the team. The phone was in the center of the plowed land, where it was plugged into a portable solar reflector that kept its batteries charged. There were very few radio-phones in the valley. They cost a great deal and could only be bought in Harmony. Even her grandfather Amos couldn't manufacture the phone's microcircuits, although he often muttered about buying the proper tools and making something that would be as good. "After all," he was fond of saying, "we do not need the very latest. Only something that will do."

Before she reached the phone, she heard the gunshots. They sounded far away, but they came from the direction of her home. She looked toward the hill that hid the ranch from her, and a red trail streaked skyward. It exploded in a cloud of bright smoke. Amos had sent up a distress rocket. "God, no!" Kathryn screamed. She ran for the phone, but she dropped it in her haste. She scrabbled it up from the freshly plowed dirt and shouted into it. "Yes!"

"Go straight to the village, child," her grandfather's voice told her. He sounded very old and tired. "Do not come home. Go quickly."

"Grandfather—"

"Do as I say! The neighbors will come, and you cannot help."

"But—"

"Kathryn." He spoke urgently, but there were centuries in the voice. "They are here. Many of them."

"Who?" she demanded.

"Convicts. They claim to be sheriffs, executing a writ for collection of taxes. I will not pay. My house is strong, Kathryn, and the neighbors will come. The convicts will not get in, and if they kill me now it is no great matter—"

"And mother!" Kathryn shouted.

"They will not take her alive," Amos Malcolm said. "We have talked of this, and you know what I will do. Please. Do not make my whole life meaningless by letting them get you as well. Go to the village, and God go with you. I must fight now."

There were more sounds of firing in the distance. The phone was silent. Then there were rifle shots, plus the harsh stammer of a machine gun. Amos had good defenses for his stone ranch house.

Kathryn heard grenades, sharp explosions, but not loud, and she prayed that she would not hear the final explosion that meant Amos had set off the dynamite under his house. He had often sworn that before he would let anyone take his home, he would blow it and them to hell.

Kathryn ran back to unhitch the oxen. They would be safe enough. The sounds of firing would keep them from going home until the next day, and here on the plains there were no animals large enough to be a threat to healthy oxen. None except men.

She left the team standing beside the plow, their eyes puzzled because the sun was high and the field was not yet plowed, and she ran to the shade trees by the creek. A horse and dog waited patiently there. The dog jumped up playfully, but he sank onto the ground and cringed as he sensed her mood.

Kathryn hurled the saddle onto the horse and fumbled with the leather straps. Her hands were moving so quickly that even familiar motions were difficult, and she was clumsy in her haste. She tied the phone and solar reflector in place behind the saddle and mounted. There was a rifle in the saddle scabbard, and she took it out and fingered it longingly.

Then she hesitated. The guns were still firing. She still heard her grandfather's machine gun and more grenades, and that meant that Amos was alive. *I should help,* she thought. *I should go.*

Emil will be there. He was to plow the field next to our boundary, and he will have heard. He will be there. She turned the horse toward the ranch.

One rider can do no good, she realized. But though she knew that, she knew she must go to her home before it was too late. They would have a good chance, Emil and her grandfather. The house was strong, made of good stone, low to the ground, much of it buried in the earth, sod roof above waterproof plastic. It would withstand raiders. It had before, many times, but there were very many rifles firing now and she could not remember that large a raid before. Not here, and not anywhere.

The phone buzzed again. "Yes!" she shouted. "What is happening?"

"Ride, girl! Ride! Do not disobey my last command. You are all I have—" The voice broke off before Amos said more, and Kathryn held the silent phone and stared at it.

"All I have," Amos had said. Her mother and her brother were dead, then.

She screamed words of hatred and rode toward the sound of the guns. As she crossed over the creek she heard mortars firing, then louder explosions.

Two hundred riders converged on the Malcolm ranch. They rode hard, their horses drenched in sweat, and they came by families, some with their women, all with their oldest boys. Brown dogs ran ahead of them. Their panting tongues hung out between bared fangs as the dogs sensed the anger their masters projected. As the families of riders saw each other, they waved and kicked their horses into an even faster pace.

The riders approached the final rise before the Malcolm ranch and slowed to a trot. There were no sounds from over the hill. Shouted commands sent the dogs ahead. When the loping brown forms went over the hill without halting, the riders kicked their horses back to the gallop and rode on.

"He didn't use the dynamite," George Woodrow said. "I heard explosions, but not Amos's magazines." His neighbors didn't answer. They rode down the hill toward the ranch house.

There was the smell of explosives in the air, mixed with the bright copper smell of fresh blood. The dogs loped among dead men who lay around the stone house. The big front door stood open, and more dead lay in front of that. A girl in bloodstained coveralls and muddy boots sat in the dirt by the open door. She cradled a boy's head in her arms. She rocked gently, not aware of the motion, and her eyes were dry and bright.

"My God!" George Woodrow shouted. He dismounted and knelt beside her. His hand reached out toward the boy, but he couldn't touch him. "Kathryn—"

"They're all dead," Kathryn said. "Grandfather, mother, my brother, and Emil. They're all dead." She spoke calmly, telling George Woodrow of his son's death as she might tell him that there would be a dance at the church next Saturday.

George looked at his dead son and the girl who would have borne his grandchildren. Then he stood and leaned his face against his saddle. He remained that way for a long time. Gradually he became aware that others were talking.

"—caught them all outside except Amos," Harry Seeton said. He kept his voice low, hoping that Kathryn and George Woodrow wouldn't hear. "I think Amos shot Jeanine after they'd grabbed her. How in hell did anyone sneak up on old Amos?"

"Found a dog with an arrow in him back there," Wan Loo said. "A crossbow bolt. Perhaps that is how."

"I still don't understand it," Seeton insisted.

"Go after them!" Kathryn stood beside her dead fiancé. "Ride!"

"We will ride," Wan Loo said. "When it is time."

"Ride now!" Kathryn demanded.

"No." Harry Seeton shook his head sadly. "Do you think this was the only place raided today? A dozen more. Most did not even fight. There are hundreds more raiders, and they will have joined together by now. We cannot ride until there are more of us."

"And then what?" George Woodrow asked. His voice was bitter. "By the time there are enough of us, they will be in the hills again." He looked helplessly at the line of high foothills just at the horizon. "God! Why?"

"Do not blaspheme." The voice was strident. Roger Dornan wore dark clothing, and his face was lean and narrow. *He looks like an undertaker,* Kathryn thought. "The ways of the Lord are not to be questioned," Dornan intoned.

"We don't need that talk, Brother Dornan," Kathryn said. "We need revenge! I thought we had *men* here! George, will you ride with me to hunt your son's murderer?"

"Put your trust in the Lord," Dornan said. "Lay this burden on His shoulders."

"I cannot allow you to ride," Wan Loo said. "You and George would be killed, and for what? You gain no revenge by throwing yourself at their guns." He motioned, and two of his sons went to hold Kathryn's horse. Another took George Woodrow's mount and led it away. "We need all our farmers," Wan Loo said. "And what would become of George's other children? And his wife with the unborn child? You cannot go."

"Got a live one," a rider called. Two men lifted a still figure from the ground. They carried him over to where the others had gathered around Kathryn and George Woodrow, then dropped him into the dirt. Wan Loo knelt and felt for the pulse. Then he seized the raider's hair and lifted the head. Methodically he slapped the face. His fingers left vivid red marks on the too-white flesh. Smack, smack! Forehand, backhand, methodically, and the raider's head rocked with each blow.

"He's about gone," Harry Seeton said.

"All the more reason he should be awakened," Wan Loo said. He ignored the spreading bloodstains on the raider's leather jacket, and turned him face down into the dirt. He seized an arm and twisted violently. The raider grunted.

The raider was no older than twenty. He had a short scraggly beard, not well developed. He wore dark trousers and a leather jacket and soft leather boots much like Kathryn's. There were marks on his fingers, discolorations where rings had been, and his left earlobe was torn.

"They stripped their own dead and wounded," Woodrow grunted. "What all did they get?"

"The windmill generator," Harry Seeton reported. "And all the livestock, and some of the electronics. The phone's gone, too. Wonder why Amos didn't blow the place?"

"Shaped charge penetrated the wall," one of the riders said. "Killed Amos at his gun."

"Leggo. Stop." The young raider moaned. "That hurts."

"He is coming awake," Wan Loo told them. "But he will not last long."

"Pity," George Woodrow said. He bent down and slapped the boy's face. "Wake up, damn you! I want you to feel the rope around your neck! Harry, get a rope."

"You must not," Brother Dornan said. "Vengeance is the Lord's—"

"We'll just help the Lord out a bit," Woodrow said. "Get a rope!"

"Yeah," Seeton said. "I guess. Kathryn?"

"Get it. Give it to me. I want to put it around his neck." She looked down at the raider. "Why?" she demanded. "Why?"

For a moment the boy's eyes met hers. "Why not?"

Three men dug graves on the knoll above the valley. Kathryn came up the hill silently, and they did not see her at first. When they did they stopped working, but she said nothing, and after a while they dug again. Their shovels bit into the rich soil.

"You're digging too many graves," Kathryn said. "Fill one in."

"But—"

"My grandfather will not be buried here," Kathryn said.

The men stopped digging. They looked at the girl and her bloodstained coveralls, then glanced out at the horizon where the rest of the commandos had gone. There was dust out there. The riders were coming home. They wouldn't have caught the raiders before they went into the hills.

One of the gravediggers made a silent decision. Next spring he would take his family and find new lands. It would be better than this. But he wondered if the convicts would not follow wherever he went. When men work the earth, others will come to kill and steal.

"Where?" he asked finally.

"Bury Amos in his doorway," Kathryn said.

"That is a terrible thing, to bury a man in his own door. He will not rest—"

"I don't want him to rest," Kathryn said. "I want him to walk! I want him to walk and remind us all of what Earth has done to us!"

IV

"Hear this. All hands brace for reentry. Hear this."

"Seat straps, Lieutenant," Sergeant Cernan said.

"Right." I pulled the shoulder straps down into place and latched them, then looked out at Arrarat.

The planet had a bleak look, not like Earth. There were few clouds, and lots of desert. There were also heavy jungle forests near the equator. The only cultivated lands I could see were on a narrow strip at the northern edge of a nearly landlocked sea. South of the sea was another continent. It looked dry and dusty, desert land where men had left no mark in passing—if anyone had ever been there at all.

Northward and westward from the cultivated strip were hills and forests, high desert plateaus, high mountains, and ragged canyons. There were streaks through the forests and across the hills, narrow roads not much more than tracks. When the troopship got lower I could see villages and towns, and every one of them had walls or a stockade and ditch. They looked like tiny fortresses.

The ship circled until it had lost enough speed to make a landing approach. Then it ran eastward, and we could see the city. My briefing folio said it was the only city on Arrarat. It stood on a high bluff above the sea, and it seemed huddled in on itself. It looked like a medieval walled town, but it was made of modern concrete, and adobe with plastic waterproofing, and other materials medieval craftsmen probably wouldn't have used if they'd had them.

As the ship passed over the city at two thousand meters, it became obvious that there were really two cities run together, with only a wall between them. Neither was very large. The oldest part of the city, Harmony, showed little evidence of planning: there were little narrow streets running at all angles, and the public squares were randomly placed. The northern part, Garrison, was smaller, but it had streets at precise right angles, and a big public plaza stood opposite the square fort at the northern edge.

All the buildings were low, with only a couple more than two stories high. The roofs were red tile, and the walls were whitewashed. Harmony reminded me of towns I'd seen in Mexico. Bright sun shone off the bay below the city bluff. Garrison was a harsher place, all right angles, neat and orderly, but everything strictly functional. There was a square fortress at its northern edge. My new home.

I was a very junior lieutenant of CoDominium Marines, only three months out of the Academy and green as grass. It was Academy practice to commission the top thirty graduates in each class. The rest went out as cadets and midshipmen for more training. I was proud of the bars on my epaulets, but I was also a bit scared. I'd never been with troops before, and I'd never had any friends from the working classes, so I didn't know much about the kind of people who enlist in the Line Marines. I knew plenty of stories, of course. Men join to get away from their wives, or because some judge gives them a chance to enlist before passing sentence. Others are recruited out of Bureau of Relocation ships. Most come from Citizen classes, and my family's always been taxpayer.

It was just as well for me that my father was a taxpayer. I grew up in the American Southwest, where things haven't changed so much since the CoDominium. We still think we're free men. When my father died, Mom and I tried to run the ranch the way he had, as if it still belonged to us. It did, on paper, but we didn't have his contacts in the bureaucracy. We didn't understand all the regulations and labor restrictions, and we didn't know who to bribe when we broke the rules. When we got in real trouble, I tried to keep the government people from taking possession, and that wasn't too good an idea. The judge was an old friend of my father's and offered to get me into the Academy. U.S. courts don't have jurisdiction over CoDominium officers.

I didn't have a lot of choices, and CD Fleet service looked pretty good just then. I'd not only get out of trouble; I'd leave Earth. Mom was getting married again, so she'd be all right. The government had the ranch and we'd never get it back. I was young enough to think soldiering was a romantic idea, and Judge Hamilton made it pretty clear I was going to have to do something.

"Look, Hal," he told me, "your dad should have left. There's no place for people like us. They want people who want security, who'll obey the rules—people who *like* the welfare state, not ornery cusses like you and your father. Even if I can get you off this time, you'll get in trouble again. You're going to have to leave, and you'll be better off as a CD officer than as a colonist."

He was right. I wondered why he stayed. Same reason my father did, I supposed. Getting older, used to his home, not ready to go make a new start somewhere else. I hadn't said anything, but he must have guessed what I was thinking.

"I can still do some good here. I'm a judge for life—they can't take that away from me without damned good reasons—and I can still help kids like you. There's nothing here for you, Hal. The future's out there. New worlds, new ones found every year. Serve out a hitch in the Fleet service. See what's out there, and decide where you want your kids to grow up. Someplace free."

I couldn't think of anything else to do, so I let him get me into the Academy. It had been all right there. The Fleet has its own brotherhood. I'd been a loner most of my life, not because I wanted to be—God knows I would have liked to have friends!—but because I didn't fit in anywhere. The Academy was different. It's hard to say how. One thing, though, there aren't any incompetents whining to have the world take care of them. Not that we didn't look out for each other. If a classmate's soft on math, you help him, and if somebody has trouble with electronics—I did—a sharper classmate sits up nights boning up with him. But if after all that he can't cut it, he's out. There's more to it than that, though. I can't explain the Fleet's sense of brotherhood, but it's real enough, and it was what I'd been looking for all my life.

I was there two and a half years, and we worked all the time, cramming everything from weapons maintenance to basic science to civil engineering and road construction. I finished seventh in the class and got my commission. After a month's leave to say goodbye to my mother and my girl—only I didn't really have a girl; I just liked to pretend I did—I was on an Olympic Lines passenger ship headed for another star system.

And now I'm here, I thought. I looked down at the planet, trying to spot places I'd seen on the maps in our briefing kit. I was also listening to the troopers in the compartment. The instructors at the Academy had told us that officers could learn a lot by listening to the men, and I hadn't had much opportunity to listen to these. Three weeks before I'd been on the passenger ship, and now I was at the end of nowhere on an ancient troop carrier, with a detachment commander who'd kept us training so hard there'd been no time for talk or anything else.

There were only a few viewports in the compartment,
and those were taken by officers and senior enlisted men.
Behind me, Sergeant Cernan was describing what he saw.
A number of younger Marines, recruits mostly, were crowded
around him. The older troopers were catching naps in their
seats.

"Not much outside the city walls," Cernan said. "Trees, look
like scrub oaks. And I think those others are olives. There's
palms, too. Must be from Earth. Never saw palm trees that
didn't come from Earth."

"Hey, Sarge, can you see the fort?" Corporal Roff asked.

"Yeah. Looks like any CD post. You'll be right at home."

"Sure we will," Roff said. "Sure. Christ, why us?"

"Your birthday present," Cernan said. "Just be damned glad
you'll be leavin' someday. Think of them poor bastards back
aft in the can."

The ship circled the harbor, then glided in on its stubby
wings to settle into the chop outside the breakwater. The waves
were two meters high and more, and the ship rolled badly.
One of the new recruits was sick. His seatmate handed him
a plastic bag.

"Hey, Dietz!" Roff called. "Want some fried bacon? A little
salt pork?" He grinned. "Maybe some sow belly—"

"Sergeant Cernan."

"Sir!"

The captain didn't say anything else. He sat forward, a dozen
rows in front of me, and I hadn't expected him to be listening, but I wasn't surprised. I'd learned in the past three weeks
that not much went on without Captain John Christian
Falkenberg finding out.

Behind me, Cernan said, very tight-lipped, "Roff, one more
word out of you—"

Dietz's buddy found another bag. No one else kidded the
sick recruits. Soon the shuttle moved into the inner harbor,
where there were no waves, and everyone felt better. A lone
tugboat came alongside and eased the spacecraft toward a
concrete pier. There was no other traffic in the harbor except
for a few small fishing boats.

A Navy officer came into the compartment and looked
around until he found Falkenberg. "Sir, the Governor requests
that you turn your men out under arms to assist in the prisoner
formation."

Falkenberg turned toward the Navy man and raised an
eyebrow. Then he nodded. "Sergeant Major!"

"Sir!" Ogilvie shouted from the rear of the compartment.

"Personal weapons for all troops. Rifles and cartridge belts. And bayonets, Sergeant Major. Bayonets, by all means."

"Sir." There was a bustle of activity as Sergeant Major Ogilvie and his weapons sergeants unlocked the arms chest and began passing out rifles.

"What about our other gear?" Falkenberg asked.

"You'll have to make arrangements with the garrison," the ship's officer said.

"Right. That's all, then?"

"Yes. That's all, Major."

I grinned as the Navyman left the compartment. To the Navy there's only one captain aboard ship, and that's the skipper. Marine captains in transit get a very temporary and utterly meaningless "promotion" to major for the duration of the voyage.

Falkenberg went to the forward hatchway. "Lieutenant Slater. A moment, please."

"Sir." I went forward to join him. I hadn't really noticed the low gravity until I stood up, but now it was obvious. It was only eighty-five-percent Earth standard, and on the trip out, Falkenberg had insisted the Navy skipper keep the outer rim of the old troopship at 110 percent spin gravity for as much of the trip as possible. The Navy hadn't liked it, but they'd done it, and Falkenberg had trained us in the high-gravity areas. Now we felt as if we could float away with no trouble.

I didn't know much about Falkenberg. The Service List showed he'd had Navy experience, then transferred to Fleet Marines. Now he was with a Line outfit. Moving around like that, two transfers, should have meant he was being run out, but then there was his rank. He also had a Military Cross, but the List hadn't said what it was for. It did tell me he'd gone into the Academy at fifteen and left as a midshipman.

I first saw him at Betio Transfer Station, which is an airless rock the Fleet keeps as a repair base and supply depot. It's convenient to several important star systems, but there's nothing there. I'd been on my way from graduation to Crucis Sector Headquarters, with assignment to the Fleet Marines. I was proud of that. Of the three Marine branches, Fleet is supposed to be the technical elite. Garrison outfits are mostly for riot suppression. The Line Marines get the dirty jobs left over. Line troops say theirs is the real elite, and they certainly do more than their share of the actual fighting when things are tough. I didn't know if we'd be fighting on Arrarat. I didn't even know why we were sent here. I just knew that Falkenberg had authority to change orders for all unassigned officers, and

I'd been yanked off my comfortable berth—first class, damn it!—to report to him at Betio. If he knew what was up, he wasn't telling the junior officers.

Falkenberg wasn't a lot older than I was. I was a few weeks past my twenty-first birthday, and he was maybe five years older, a captain with the Military Cross. He must have had something going for him—influence, possibly, but if that was it, why was he with the Line Marines and not on staff at headquarters? I couldn't ask him. He didn't talk very much. He wasn't unfriendly, but he seemed cold and distant and didn't encourage anyone to get close to him.

Falkenberg was tall, but he didn't reach my height, which is 193 centimeters according to my ID card. We called it six-four where I grew up. Falkenberg was maybe two inches shorter. His eyes were indeterminate in color, sometimes gray and sometimes green, depending on the light, and they seemed very bright when he looked at you. He had short hair the color of sand, and no moustache. Most officers grow them after they make captain, but he hadn't.

His uniforms always fit perfectly. I thought I cut a good military figure, but I found myself studying the way Falkenberg dressed. I also studied his mannerisms, wondering if I could copy any of them. I wasn't sure I liked him or that I really wanted to imitate him, but I told myself that anybody who could make captain before he was thirty was worth at least a bit of study. There are plenty of forty-year-old lieutenants in the service.

He didn't look big or particularly strong, but I knew better. I'm no forty-four-kilo weakling, but he threw me easily in unarmed combat practice, and that was in 100 percent gravity.

He was grinning when I joined him at the forward hatchway. "Ever think, Lieutenant, that every military generation since World War One has thought theirs would be the last to carry bayonets?" He waved toward where Ogilvie was still passing out rifles.

"No, sir, I never did."

"Few do," Falkenberg said. "My old man was a CoDominium University professor, and he thought I ought to learn military history. Think about it: a weapon originally designed to convert a musket into a pike, and it's still around when we're going to war in starships."

"Yes, sir—"

"Because it's useful, Lieutenant—as you'll find out someday." The grin faded, and Falkenberg lowered his voice. "I didn't call you up here to discuss military history, of course. I want the men to see us in conference. Give them something to worry about. They know they're going ashore armed."

"Yes, sir—"

"Tell me, Harlan Slater, what do they call you?"

"Hal, sir." We had been aboard ship for twenty-one days, and this was the first time Falkenberg had asked. It says a lot about him.

"You're senior lieutenant," Falkenberg said.

"Yes, sir." Which wasn't saying much: the other lieutenants had all been classmates at the Academy, and I outranked them only because I'd graduated higher in the class.

"You'll collect the other officers and stay here at the gangway while we go through this prisoner formation. Then bring up the rear as we take the troops up the hill to the fort. I doubt there's transport, so we'll have to march."

"Yes, sir."

"You don't understand. If you don't understand something, ask about it. Have you noticed our troopers, Mr. Slater?"

"Frankly, Captain, I haven't had enough experience to make any kind of judgment," I said. "We have a lot of recruits—"

"Yes. I'm not worried about them. Nor about the regulars I brought with me to Betio. But for the rest, we've got the scrapings out of half the guardhouses in the Sector. I doubt they'll desert during their first hours ashore, but I'm going to make damned sure. Their gear will stay aboard this ship, and we'll march them up in formation. By dark I'll have turned this command over to Colonel Harrington and it will be his worry, but until then I'm responsible, and I'll see that every man gets to the fort."

"I see. Yes, sir." And that's why he's a captain at his age, on independent assignment at that. Efficient. I wanted to be like that, or thought I did. I wasn't quite sure what I really wanted. The CD Armed Services wasn't my idea, but now that I was in it, I wanted to do it right if I could. I had my doubts about some of the things the CoDominium did—I was glad that I hadn't been assigned to one of the regiments that puts down riots on Earth—but I didn't know what ought to replace the CD and the Grand Senate, either. After all, we did keep the peace, and that has to be worth a lot.

"They're opening the gangway," Falkenberg said. "Sergeant Major."

"Sir!"

"Column of fours in company order, please."

"Sir." Ogilvie began shouting orders. The troops marched

down the gangway and onto the concrete pier below. I went out onto the gangway to watch.

It was hot outside and within minutes I was sweating. The sun seemed red-orange, and very bright. After the smells of the troopship, with men confined with too little water for adequate washing, the planetary smells were a relief. Arrarat had a peculiar odor, slightly sweet, like flowers, with an undertone of wet vegetation. All that was mixed with the stronger smells of a salt sea and the harbor.

There were few buildings down at sea level. The city wall stood high above the harbor at the top of its bluff. Down on the level strip just above the sea were piers and warehouses, but the streets were wide and there were large spaces between buildings.

My first alien world. It didn't seem all that strange. I looked for something exotic, like sea creatures, or strange plants, but there weren't any visible from the gangway. I told myself all that would come later.

There was one larger structure at sea level. It was two stories high, with no windows facing us. It had big gates in the center of the wall facing the ship, with a guard tower at each of its corners. It looked like a prison, and I knew that was what it had to be, but there seemed no point in that. The whole planet was a prison.

There was a squad of local militiamen on the pier. They wore drab coveralls, which made quite a contrast to the blue and scarlet undress of the CoDominium Marines marching down the pier. Falkenberg talked with the locals for a moment, and then Sergeant Major Ogilvie shouted orders, and the Marines formed up in a double line that stretched up the dock to the aft gangway. The line went from the gangway to the big gates in the prison building. Ogilvie shouted more orders, and the Marines fixed bayonets.

They did it well. You'd never have known most of them were recruits. Even in the cramped quarters of the troop carrier, Falkenberg had drilled them into a smart-looking unit. The cost had been high. There were twenty-eight suicides among the recruits, and another hundred had been washed out and sent back among the convicts. They told us at the Academy that the only way to make a good Marine is to work him in training until he can have some pride in surviving it, and God knows Falkenberg must have believed that. It had seemed reasonable enough back in the lecture theater at Luna Base.

One morning we had four suicides, and one had been an

old Line regular, not a recruit at all. I'd been duty officer when the troops found the body. It had been cut down from where he'd hanged himself to a light fixture, and the rope was missing. I tried to find the rope and even paraded all the men in that compartment, but nobody was saying anything.

Later Sergeant Major Ogilvie came to me in confidence. "You'll never find the rope, Lieutenant," he said. "It's cut up in a dozen pieces by now. That man had won the military medal. The rope he hanged himself with? That's lucky, sir. They'll keep the pieces."

All of which convinced me I had a lot to learn about Line Marines.

The forward companionway opened, and the convicts came out. Officially they were all convicts, or families of transportees who had voluntarily accompanied a convict; but when we'd gone recruiting in the prison section of the ship, we found a number of prisoners who'd never been convicted of any-thing at all. They'd been scooped up in one of Bureau of Relocation's periodic sweeps and put on the involuntary colonist list.

The prisoners were ragged and unwashed. Most wore BuRelock coveralls. Some carried pathetically small bundles, everything they owned. They milled around in confusion in the bright sunlight until ship's petty officers screamed at them and they shuffled down the gangway and along the pier. They tended to huddle together, shrinking away from the bayonets of the lines of troops on either side. Eventually they were herded through the big square gates of the prison building. I wondered what would happen to them in there.

There were more men than women, but there were plenty of women and girls. There were also far more children than I liked to see in that condition. I didn't like this. I hadn't joined the CoDominium Armed Services for this kind of duty.

"Heavy price, isn't it?" a voice said behind me. It was Deane Knowles. He'd been a classmate at the Academy. He was a short chap, not much above the minimum height for a com-mission, and had features so fine that he was almost pretty. I had reason to know that women liked him, and Deane liked them. He should have graduated second in the class, but he'd accumulated so many demerits for sneaking off bounds to see his girlfriends that he was dropped twenty-five places in class rank, which was why I outranked him and would until one of us was promoted above the other. I figured he'd make captain before I did.

"Heavy price for what?" I asked.

"For clean air and lower population and all the other goodies they have back on Earth. Sometimes I wonder if it's worth it."

"But what choices do we have?" I asked.

"None. Zero. Nothing else to do. Ship out the surplus and let 'em make their own way somewhere. In the long run it's not only all to the good, it's all there is; but the run doesn't look so long when you're watching the results. Look out. Here comes Louis."

Louis Bonneyman, another classmate, joined us. Louis had finished a genuine twenty-fourth in class rank. He was part French-Canadian, although he'd been raised in the U.S. most of his life. Louis was a fanatic CD loyalist and didn't like to hear any of us question CD policy, although, like the rest of us in the service, it didn't really matter what the policies were. "No politics in the Fleet" was beaten into our heads at the Academy, and later the instructors made it clear that what that really translated to was: "The Fleet is Our Fatherland." We could question anything the Grand Senate did—as long as we stood by our comrades and obeyed orders.

We stood there watching as the colonists were herded into the prison building. It took nearly an hour to get all two thousand of them inside. Finally the gates were closed. Ogilvie gave more orders and the Marines scabbarded their bayonets, then formed into a column of eight and marched down the road.

"Well, fellow musketeers," I said, "here we go. We're to follow up the hill, and there's apparently no transport."

"What about my ordnance?" Deane asked.

I shrugged. "Apparently arrangements will be made. In any event, it's John Christian Falkenberg's problem. Ours not to reason why—"

"Ours but to watch for deserters," Louis Bonneyman said. "And we'd best get at it. Is your sidearm loaded?"

"Oh, come on, Louis," Deane said.

"Notice," Louis said. "See how Falkenberg has formed up the troops. Recall that their baggage is still aboard. You may not like Falkenberg, Deane, but you will admit that he is thorough."

"As it happens, Louis is right," I said. "Falkenberg did say something about deserters. But he didn't think there'd be any."

"There you are," Louis said. "He takes no chances, that one."

"Except with us," Deane Knowles said.

"What do you mean by that?" Louis let the smile fade and lifted an eyebrow at Deane.

"Oh, nothing," Deane said. "Not much Falkenberg could do about it, anyway. But I don't suppose you chaps know what the local garrison commander asked for?"

"No, of course not," Louis said.

"How did you find out?" I asked.

"Simple. When you want to know something military, talk to the sergeants."

"Well?" Louis demanded.

Deane grinned. "Come on, we'll get too far behind. Looks as if we really will march all the way up the hill, doesn't it? Not even transport for officers. Shameful."

"Damn your eyes, Deane!" I said.

Knowles shrugged. "Well, the Governor asked for a full regiment and a destroyer. Instead of a regiment and a warship, he got us. Might be interesting if he really needed a regiment, eh? Coming, fellows?"

V

"I've a head like a concertina,
  And I think I'm going to die,
  And I'm here in the clink for a thunderin' drink,
  And blackin' the corporal's eye. . . ."

"Picturesque," Louis said. "They sing well, don't they?"
"Shut up and walk," Deane told him. "It's bloody hot."
I didn't find it so bad. It was hot. No question about that, and undress blues were never designed for route marches on hot planets. Still, it could have been worse. We might have turned out in body armor.

There was no problem with the troops. They marched and sang like regulars, even if half of them were recruits and the rest were guardhouse cases. If any of them had ideas of running, they never showed them.

"With another man's cloak underneath of my head,
  And a beautiful view of the yard,
  It's thirty day's fine,
  With bread and no wine,
  For Drunk and Resistin' the Guard!
  Mad-drunk and Resistin' the Guard!"

"Curious," Louis said. "Half of them have never seen a guardhouse."
"I expect they'll find out soon enough," Deane said. "Lord love us, will you look at that?"
He gestured at a row of cheap adobe houses along the riverbank. There wasn't much doubt about what they sold. The girls were dressed for hot weather, and they sat on the windowsills and waved at the troopers going by.
"I thought Arrarat was full of holy Joes," Louis Bonneyman

50

said. "Well, we will have no difficulty finding any troopers who run—not for the first night, anyway."

The harbor area was just north of a wide river that fanned into a delta east of the city. The road was just inland from the harbor, with the city a high bluff to our right as we marched inland. It seemed a long way before we got to the turnoff to the city gate.

There were facilities for servicing the space shuttle, and some riverboat docks and warehouses, but it seemed to me there wasn't a lot of activity, and I wondered why. As far as I could remember, there weren't any railroads on Arrarat, nor many highways, and I couldn't remember seeing any airfields, either.

After a kilometer of marching inland, we turned sharply right and followed another road up the bluff. There was a rabbit warren of crumbling houses and alleys along the bluff, then a clear area in front of the high city wall. Militiamen in drab coveralls manned a guardhouse at the city gate. Other militiamen patrolled the wall. Inside the gate was Harmony, another warren of houses and shops not a lot different from those outside, but a little better kept up.

The main road had clear area for thirty meters on each side, and beyond that was chaos. Market stalls, houses, tailor shops, electronics shops, a smithy with hand bellows and forge, a shop that wound electric motors and another that sold solar cells, a pottery with kick-wheel where a woman shaped cups from clay, a silversmith, a scissors grinder—the variety was overwhelming, and so was the contrast of modern and the kinds of things you might see in Frontierland.

There were anachronisms everywhere, but 1 was used to them. The military services were shot through with contrasts. Part of it was the state of development out in the colonies— many of them had no industrial base, and some didn't want any to begin with. If you didn't bring it with you, you wouldn't have it. There was another reason, too. CoDominium Intelligence licensed all scientific research and tried to suppress anything that could have military value. The U.S.-Soviet alliance was on top and wasn't about to let any new discoveries upset the balance. They couldn't stop everything, but they didn't have to, so long as the Grand Senate controlled everyone's R&D budget and could tinker with the patent laws.

We all knew it couldn't last, but we didn't want to think about that. Back on Earth the U.S. and Soviet governments hated each other. The only thing they hated more was the idea that someone else—like the Chinese or Japanese or United

Emirates—would get strong enough to tell them what to do. The Fleet guards an uneasy peace built on an uneasy alliance.

The people of Harmony came in all races and colors, and I heard a dozen languages shouted from shop to shop. Everyone either worked outside his house or had market stalls there. When we marched past, people stopped work and waved at us. One old man came out of a tailor shop and took off his broad-brimmed hat. "God bless you, soldiers!" he shouted. "We love you!"

"Now, that's what we joined up for," Deane said. "Not to herd a bunch of losers halfway across the Galaxy."

"Twenty parsecs isn't halfway across the Galaxy," I told him. He made faces at me.

"I wonder why they're all so glad to see us?" Louis asked. "And they look hungry. How does one become so thin in an agricultural paradise?"

"Incredible," Deane said. "Louis, you really must learn to pay attention to important details. Such as reading the station roster of the garrison here."

"And when could I have done that?" Bonneyman demanded. "Falkenberg had us working twelve hours a day—"

"So you use the other twelve," Deane said.

"And what, O brilliant one, didst thou learn from the station roster?" I asked.

"That the garrison commander is over seventy, and he has one sixty-three-year-old major on his staff, as well as a sixty-two-year-old captain. Also, the youngest Marine officer on Arrarat is over sixty, and the only junior officers are militia."

"Bah. A retirement post," Bonneyman said. "So why did they ask for a regiment?"

"Don't be silly, Louis," Deane said. "Because they've run into something they can't handle with their militia and their superannuated officers, of course."

"Meaning we'll have to," I said. Only, of course, we didn't have a regiment, only less than a thousand Marines, three junior officers, a captain with the Military Cross, and—well, and nothing, unless the local militia were capable of something. "The heroes have arrived."

"Yes. Nice, isn't it?" Deane said. "I expect the women will be friendly."

"And is that all you ever think about?" Louis demanded.

"What else is there? Marching in the sun?"

A younger townman in dark clerical clothing stood at his table under the awning of a sidewalk café. He raised a hand in a gesture of blessing. There were more cheers from a group of children.

"Nice to be loved," Deane said.

Despite the way he said it, Deane meant that. It was nice to be loved. I remembered my last visit to Earth. There were a lot of places where CD officers didn't dare go without a squad of troopers. Out here the people wanted us. The paladins, I thought, and I laughed at myself because I could imagine what Deane and Louis would say if I'd said that aloud, but I wondered if they didn't think it, too.

"They don't seem to have much transport," Louis said.

"Unless you count those." Deane pointed to a watering trough where five horses were tied. There were also two camels, and an animal that looked like a clumsy combination of camel, moose, and mule, with big splayed feet and silly antlers.

That had to be an alien beast, the first thing I was certain was native to this planet. I wondered what they called it, and how it had been domesticated.

There was almost no motor transport: a few pickup trucks, and one old ground-effects car with no top; everything else was animal transport. There were wagons, and men on horseback, and two women dressed in coveralls and mounted on mules.

Bonneyman shook his head. "Looks as if they stirred up a brew from the American Wild West, medieval Paris, and threw in scenes from the Arabian Nights."

We all laughed, but Louis wasn't far wrong.

Arrarat was discovered soon after the first private exploration ships went out from Earth. It was an inhabitable planet, and although there are a number of those in the regions near Earth, they aren't all that common. A survey team was sent to find out what riches could be taken.

There weren't any. Earth crops would grow, and men could live on the planet, but no one was going to invest money in agriculture. Shipping foodstuffs through interstellar space is a simple way of going bankrupt unless there are nearby markets with valuable minerals and no agriculture. This planet had no nearby market at all.

The American Express Company owned settlement rights through discovery. AmEx sold the planet to a combine of churches. The World Federation of Churches named it Arrarat and advertised it as "a place of refuge for the unwanted of Earth." They began to raise money for its development, and since this was before the Bureau of Relocation began involuntary colonies, they had a lot of help. Charity, tithes, government grants, all helped, and then the church groups hit on the idea of a lottery. Prizes were free transportation to Arrarat for winners and their families; and there were plenty of people willing to trade Earth for a place where there was free land, plenty to eat, hard work, no government harrassment, and no pollution. The World Federation of Churches sold tens of millions of one-credit lottery tickets. They soon had enough money to charter ships and sent people out.

There was plenty of room for colonists, even though the inhabitable portion of Arrarat is comparatively small. The planet has a higher mean temperature than Earth, and the regions near the equator are far too hot for men to live in. At the very poles it is too cold. The southern hemisphere is nearly all water. Even so, there is plenty of land in the north temperate zone. The delta area where Harmony was founded was chosen as the best of the lot. It had a climate like the Mediterranean region of Earth. Rainfall was erratic, but the colony thrived.

The churches had very little money, but the planet didn't need heavy industry. Animals were shipped instead of tractors, on the theory that horses and oxen can make other horses and oxen, but tractors make only oil refineries and smog. Industry wasn't wanted; Arrarat was to be a place where each man could prune his own vineyard and sit in the shade of his fig tree. Some of the Federation of Churches' governing board actively hated industrial technology, and none loved it; and there was no need, anyway. The planet could easily support far more than the half to three-quarters of a million people the churches sent out as colonists.

Then the disaster struck. A survey ship found thorium and other valuable metals in the asteroid belt of Arrarat's system. It wasn't a disaster for everyone, of course. American Express was happy enough, and so was Kennicott Metals after they bought mining rights; but for the church groups it was disaster enough. The miners came, and with them came trouble. The only convenient place for the miners to go for recreation was Arrarat, and the kinds of establishments asteroid miners liked weren't what the Federation of Churches had in mind. The "Holy Joes" and the "Goddamns" shouted at each other and petitioned the Grand Senate for help, while the madams and gamblers and distillers set up for business.

That wasn't the worst of it. The Federation of Churches' petition to the CoDominium Grand Senate ended up in the CD bureaucracy, and an official in Bureau of Corrections noticed that a lot of empty ships were going from Earth to Arrarat. They came back full of refined thorium, but they went out deadhead . . . and BuCorrect had plenty of prisoners they didn't know what to do with. It cost money to keep them. Why not, BuCorrect reasoned, send the prisoners to Arrarat and turn them loose? Earth would be free of them. It was humane. Better yet, the churches could hardly object to setting captives free. . . .

The BuCorrect official got a promotion, and Arrarat got over half a million criminals and convicts, most of whom had never lived outside a city. They knew nothing of farming, and they drifted to Harmony, where they tried to live as best they could. The result was predictable. Harmony soon had the highest crime rate in the history of man.

The situation was intolerable for Kennicott Metals. Miners wouldn't work without planet leave, but they didn't dare go to Harmony. Their union demanded that someone do something, and Kennicott appealed to the Grand Senate. A regiment of CoDominium Marines was sent to Arrarat. They couldn't stay long, but they didn't have to. They built walls around the city of Harmony, and for good measure they built the town of Garrison adjacent to it. Then the Marines put all the convicts outside the walls.

It wasn't intended to be a permanent solution. A CoDominium Governor was appointed, over the objections of the World Federation of Churches. The Colonial Bureau began preparations for sending a government team of judges and police and technicians and industrial-development specialists so that Arrarat could support the streams of people BuCorrect had sent. Before they arrived, Kennicott found an even more valuable source of thorium in a system nearer to Earth, the Arrarat mines were put into reserve, and there was no longer any reason for the CoDominium Grand Senate to be interested in Arrarat. The Marine garrison pulled out, leaving a cadre to help train colonial militia to defend the walls of Harmony-Garrison.

"What are you so moody about?" Deane asked.

"Just remembering what was in the briefing they gave us. You aren't the only one who studies up," I said.

"And what have you concluded?"

"Not a lot. I wonder how the people here like living in a prison. It's got to be that way, convicts outside and citizens inside. Marvelous."

"Perhaps they have a city jail," Louis said. "That would be a prison within a prison."

"Fun-ny," Deane said.

We walked along in silence, listening to the tramp of the boots ahead of us, until we came to another wall. There were guards at that gate, too. We passed through into the smaller city of Garrison.

"And why couldn't they have had transportation for officers?" Louis Bonneyman said. "There are trucks here."

There weren't many, but there were more than in Harmony. Most of the vehicles were surplus military ground-effects troop carriers. There were also more wagons.

"March or die, Louis. March or die." Deane grinned.

Louis said something under his breath. "March or Die" was a slogan of the old French Foreign Legion, and the Line Marines were direct descendants of the Legion, with a lot of their traditions. Bonneyman couldn't stand the idea that he wasn't living up to the service's standards.

Commands rattled down the ranks of marching men. "Look like Marines, damn you!" Ogilvie shouted.

"Falkenberg's showing off," Deane said.

"About time, too," Louis told him. "The fort is just ahead."

"Sound off!" Ogilvie ordered.

"We've left blood in the dirt of twenty-five worlds,
　We've built roads on a dozen more,
　And all that we have at the end of our hitch
　Buys a night with a second-class whore.
　The Senate decrees, the Grand Admiral calls,
　The orders come down from on high.
　It's 'On Full Kits' and 'Sound Board Ships,'
　We're sending you where you can die."

Another Legion tradition, I thought. Over every orderly room door in Line regiments is a brass plaque. It says: YOU ARE LINE MARINES IN ORDER TO DIE, AND THE FLEET WILL SEND YOU WHERE YOU CAN DIE. An inheritance from La Légion Etrangère. The first time I saw it, I thought it was dashing and romantic, but now I wondered if they meant it.

The troops marched in the slow cadence of the Line Marines. It wasn't a fast pace, but we could keep it up long after quick-marching troops keeled over from exhaustion.

"The lands that we take, the Senate gives back,
　Rather more often than not,
　But the more that are killed, the less share the loot,
　And we won't be back to this spot.

We'll break the hearts of your women and girls,
We may break your arse, as well,
Then the Line Marines with their banners unfurled
Will follow those banners to hell.
We know the devil, his pomps, and his works,
Ah, yes! We know them well!
When you've served out your hitch in the Line Marines,
You can bugger the Senate of Hell!"

"An opportunity we may all have," Deane said. "Rather sooner than I'd like. What *do* they want with us here?"
"I expect we'll find out soon enough," I said.

"Then we'll drink with our comrades and throw
    down our packs,
We'll rest ten years on the flat of our backs,
Then it's 'On Full Kits' and out of your racks,
You must build a new road through Hell!
The Fleet is our country, we sleep with a rifle,
No man ever begot a son on his rifle,
They pay us in gin and curse when we sin,
There's not one that can stand us unless we're downwind,
We're shot when we lose and turned out when we win,
But we bury our comrades wherever they fall,
And there's none that can face us, though we've
    nothing at all."

VI

Officers' Row stretched along the east side of the parade ground. The fort was nothing special. It hadn't been built to withstand modern weapons, and it looked a bit like something out of *Beau Geste,* which was reasonable, since it was built of local materials by officers with no better engineering education than mine. It's simple enough to lay out a rectangular walled fort, and if that's enough for the job, why make it more complicated?

The officers' quarters seemed empty. The fort had been built to house a regimental combat team with plenty of support groups, and now there were fewer than a dozen Marine officers on the planet. Most of them lived in family quarters, and the militia officers generally lived in homes in the city. It left the rest of us with lots of room to rattle around in. Falkenberg drew a suite meant for the regimental adjutant, and I got a major's rooms myself.

After a work party brought our personal gear up from the landing boat, I got busy and unpacked, but when I finished, the place still looked empty. A lieutenant's travel allowance isn't very large, and the rooms were too big. I stowed my gear and wondered what to do next. It seemed a depressing way to spend my first night on an alien world. Of course, I'd been to the Moon, and Mars, but those are different. They aren't worlds. You can't go outside, and you might as well be in a ship. I wondered if we'd be permitted off post—I was still thinking like a cadet, not an officer on field duty—and what I could do if we were. We'd had no instructions, and I decided I'd better wait for a briefing.

There was a quick knock on my door, and then it opened. An old Line private came in. He might have been my father. His uniform was tailored perfectly, but worn in places. There were hash marks from wrist to elbow.

"Private Hartz reporting, zur." He had a thick accent, but

it wasn't pure anything; a lot of different accents blended together. "Sergeant Major sent me to be the lieutenant's dog-robber."

And what the hell do I do with him? I wondered. It wouldn't do to be indecisive. I couldn't remember if he'd been part of the detachment in the ship, or if he was one of the garrison. Falkenberg would never be in that situation. He'd know. The trooper was standing at attention in the doorway. "At ease, Hartz," I said. "What ought I to know about this place?"

"I don't know, zur."

Which meant he was a newcomer, or he wasn't spilling anything to officers, and I wasn't about to guess which. "Do you want a drink?"

"Thank you, yes, zur."

I found a bottle and put it out on the dressing stand. "Always leave two for me. Otherwise, help yourself," I told him.

He went to the latrine for glasses. I hadn't known there were any there, but then I wasn't all that familiar with senior officers' quarters. Maybe Hartz was, so I'd gained no information about him. He poured a shot for himself. "Is the lieutenant drinking?"

"Sure, I'll have one." I took the glass from him. "Cheers."

"Prosit." He poured the whiskey down in one gulp. "I see the lieutenant has unpacked. I will straighten up now. By your leave, zur."

He wandered around the room, moving my spare boots two inches to the left, switching my combat armor from one side of the closet to the other, taking out my dress uniform and staring at it inch by inch.

I didn't need an orderly, but I couldn't just turn him out. I was supposed to get to know him, since he'd be with me on field duty. If any, I thought. To hell with it. "I'm going down to the officers' mess," I told him. "Help yourself to the bottle, but leave me two shots for tonight."

"Zur."

I felt like an idiot, chased out of my own quarters by my own batman, but I couldn't see what else to do. He was clearly not going to be satisfied until he'd gone over every piece of gear I had. Probably trying to impress me with how thorough he was. They pay dog-robbers extra, and it's always good duty for a drinking man. I was pretty sure I could trust him. I'd never crossed Ogilvie that I knew of. It takes a particularly stupid officer to get on the wrong side of the sergeant major.

It wasn't hard to find the officers' club. Like everything else, it had been built for a regiment, and it was a big building. I got a surprise inside. I was met by a Marine corporal I recognized as one of the detachment we'd brought with us. I started to go into the bar, where I saw a number of militia officers, and the corporal stopped me.

"Excuse me, sir. Marine club is that way." He pointed down the hall.

"I think I'd rather drink with the militiamen, Corporal."

"Yes, sir. Sergeant Major told me to be sure to tell all officers, sir."

"I see." I didn't see, but I wasn't going to get into an argument with a corporal, and there wasn't any point in being bullheaded. I went down the hall to the Marine club. Deane Knowles was already there. He was alone except for a waiter—another trooper from our detachment. In the militia bar the waiters were civilians.

"Welcome to the gay and merry life," Deane said. "Will you have whiskey? Or there's a peach brandy that's endurable. For God's sake, sit down and talk to me!"

"I take it you were intercepted by Corporal Hansner," I said.

"Quite efficiently. Now I know it is Fleet practice to carry the military caste system to extremes, but this seems a bit much, even so. There are, what, a dozen Marine officers here, even including our august selves. So we immediately form our own club."

I shrugged. "Maybe it's the militiamen who don't care for us?"

"Nonsense. Even if they hated our guts, they'd want news from Earth. Meanwhile, we find out nothing about the situation here. What's yours?"

"I'll try your brandy," I told the waiter. "And who's the bartender when you're not on duty?"

"Don't know, sir. Sergeant Major sent me over—"

"Yes, of course." I waited for the trooper to leave. "And Sergeant Major takes care of us, he does, indeed. I have a truly formidable orderly—"

Deane was laughing. "One of the ancients? Yes. I thought so. As is mine. Monitor Armand Kubiak, at my service, sir."

"I only drew a private," I said.

"Well, at least Ogilvie has some sense of propriety," Deane said. "Cheers."

"Cheers. That's quite good, actually." I put the glass down and started to say something else, but Deane wasn't listening to me. He was staring at the door, and after a moment I turned to follow his gaze. "You know, I think that's the prettiest girl I ever saw."

"Certainly a contender," Deane said. "She's coming to our table."

"Obviously." We got to our feet.

She was definitely worth looking at. She wasn't very tall. Her head came about to my chin, so that with the slight heels on her sandals she was just taller than Deane. She wore a linen dress, blue to match her eyes, and it looked as if she'd never been out in the sun at all. The dress was crisp and looked cool. Few of the women we'd seen on the march in had worn skirts, and those had been long, drab cotton things. Her hair was curled into wisps around her shoulders. She had a big golden seal ring on her right hand.

She walked in as if she owned the place. She was obviously used to getting her own way.

"I hope you're looking for us," Deane said.

"As a matter of fact, I am." She had a very nice smile. An expensive smile, I decided.

"Well, you've excellent taste, anyway," Deane said.

I don't know how he gets away with it. I think it's telepathy. There's no particular cleverness to what he says to girls. I know, because I made a study of his technique when we were in the Academy. I thought I could learn it the way I was learning tactics, but it didn't work. What Deane says doesn't matter, and how he says it doesn't seem important. He'll chatter along, saving nothing, even being offensive, and the next thing you know the girl's leaving with him. If she has to ditch a date, that can happen, too.

I was damned if it was going to happen this time, but I had a sinking feeling, because I'd been determined before and it hadn't done me any good. I couldn't think of one thing to say to her.

"I'm Deane Knowles. And this is Lieutenant Slater," Deane said.

You rotten swine, I thought. I tried to smile as she offered her hand.

"And I'm Irina Swale."

"Surely you're the Governor's daughter, then," Deane said.

"That's right. May I sit down?"

"Please do." Deane held her chair before I could get to it. It made me feel awkward. We managed to get seated, and Private Donnelley came over.

"Jericho, please," Irina said.

Donnelley looked blankly at her.

"He came in with us," I said. "He doesn't know what you've ordered."

"It's a wine," she said. "I'm sure there will be several bottles. It isn't usually chilled."

"Yes, ma'am," Donnelley said. He went over to the bar and began looking at bottles.

"We were just wondering what to do," Deane said. "You've rescued us from terminal ennui."

She smiled at that, but there was a shadow behind the smile. She didn't seem offended by us, but she wasn't really very amused. I wondered what she wanted.

Donnelley brought over a bottle and a wineglass. "Is this it, ma'am?"

"Yes. Thank you."

He put the glass on the table and poured. "If you'll excuse me a moment, Lieutenant Knowles?"

"Sure, Donnelley. Don't leave us alone too long, or we'll raid your bar."

"Yes, sir." Donnelley went out into the hall.

"Cheers," Deane said. "Tell us about the night life on Arrarat."

"It's not very pleasant," Irina said.

"Rather dull. Well, I guess we expected that—"

"It's not so much dull as horrible," Irina said. "I'm sorry. It's just that . . . I feel guilty when I think about my own problems. They're so petty. Tell me, when are the others coming?"

Deane and I exchanged glances. I started to say something, but Deane spoke first. "They don't tell us very much, you know."

"Then it's true—you're the only ones coming," she said.

"Now, I didn't say that," Deane protested. "I said I didn't know—"

"You needn't lie," she said. "I'm hardly a spy. You're all they sent, aren't you? No warship, and no regiment. Just a few hundred men and some junior officers."

"I'd have thought you'd know more than we do," I said.

"I just don't give up hope quite as quickly as my father does."

"I don't understand any of this," I said. "The Governor sent for a regiment, but nobody's told us what that regiment was supposed to do."

"Clean up the mess we've made of this planet," Irina said. "And I really thought they'd do something. The CoDominium has turned Arrarat into sheer hell, and I thought they'd have enough . . . what? Pride? Shame? Enough elementary decency to put things right before we pull out entirely. I see I was wrong."

"I take it things are pretty bad outside the walls," Deane said.

"Bad? They're horrible!" Irina said. "You can't even imagine what's happening out there. Criminal gangs setting themselves up as governments. And my father recognizes them as governments! We make treaties with them. And the colonists are ground to pieces. Murder's the least of it. A whole planet going to barbarism, and we don't even *try* to help them."

"But surely your militia can do something," Deane said.

"Not really." She shook her head, slowly, and stared into the empty wineglass. "In the first place, the militia won't go outside the walls. I don't suppose I blame them. They aren't soldiers. Shopkeepers, mostly. Once in a while they'll go as far as the big river bend, or down to the nearest farmlands, but that doesn't do any good. We tried doing something more permanent, but it didn't work. We couldn't protect the colonists from the convict gangs. And now we recognize convict gangsters as legal governments!"

Donnelley came back in and went to the bar. Deane signaled for refills.

"I noticed people came out to cheer us as we marched through the city," I said.

Irina's smile was bitter. "Yes. They think you're going to open up trade with the interior, rescue their relatives out there. I wish you could."

Before we could say anything else, Captain Falkenberg came in. "Good afternoon," he said. "May I join you?"

"Certainly, sir," Deane said. "This is Captain Falkenberg. Irina Swale, Captain, the Governor's daughter."

"I see. Good afternoon. Brandy, please, Donnelley. And will the rest of you join me? Excellent. Another round, please. Incidentally, my name is John. First names in the mess, Deane—except for the colonel."

"Yes, sir. Excuse me. John. Miss Swale has been telling us about conditions outside the walls. They're pretty bad."

"I gather. I've just spent the afternoon with the colonel. Perhaps we can do something, Miss Swale."

"Irina. First names in the mess." She laughed. It was a very nice laugh. "I wish you could do something for those people, but—well, you only have a thousand men."

"A thousand Line Marines," Falkenberg said. "That's not quite the same thing."

And we don't even have a thousand Marines, I told myself. Lot of recruits with us. I wondered what Falkenberg had in mind. Was he just trying to impress the Governor's daughter? I hoped not, because the way he'd said it made me feel proud.

"I gather you sympathize with the farmers out there," Falkenberg said.

"I'd have to, wouldn't I?" Irina said. "Even if they didn't come to me after Hugo—my father—says he can't help them. And I've tried to do something for the children. Do you really think—" She let her voice trail off.

Falkenberg shrugged. "Doubtless we'll try. We can put detachments out in some of the critical areas. As you said, there's only so much a thousand men can do, even a thousand Marines."

"And after you leave?" Irina said. Her voice was bitter. "They are pulling out, aren't they? You've come to evacuate us."

"The Grand Senate doesn't generally discuss high policy with junior captains," Falkenberg said.

"No, I suppose not. But I do know you brought orders from the Colonial Office, and Hugo took them into his office to read them—and he hasn't spoken to anyone since. All day he's been in there. It isn't hard to guess what they say." Irina sipped at the wine and stared moodily at the oak table. "Of course it's necessary to understand the big picture. What's one little planet with fewer than a million people? Arrarat is no threat to the peace, is it? But they are people, and they deserve something better than— Sorry. I'm not always like this."

"We'll have to think of something to cheer you up," Deane said. "Tell me about the gay social life of Arrarat."

She gave a half smile. "Wild. One continuous whirl of grand balls and lewd parties. Just what you'd expect on a church-settled planet."

"Dullsville," Deane said. "But now that we're here—"

"I expect we can manage something," Irina said. "I tend to be Dad's social secretary. John, isn't it customary to welcome new troops with a formal party? We'll have to have one in the Governor's palace."

"It's customary," Falkenberg said. "But that's generally to welcome a regiment, not a random collection of replacements. On the other hand, since the replacements are the only military unit here—"

"Well, we do have our militia," Irina said.

"Sorry. I meant the only Line unit. I'm certain everyone would be pleased if you'd invite us to a formal ball. Can you arrange it for, say, five days from now?"

"Of course," she said. She looked at him curiously. So did the rest of us. It hadn't occurred to me that Falkenberg would be interested in something like that. "I'll have to get started right away, though."

"If that's cutting it too close," Falkenberg said, "we—"

"No, that will be all right."

Falkenberg glanced at his watch, then drained his glass. "One more round, gentlemen, and I fear I have to take you away. Staff briefing. Irina, will you need an escort?"

"No, of course not."

We chatted for a few minutes more, then Falkenberg stood. "Sorry to leave you alone, Irina, but we do have work to do."

"Yes. I quite understand."

"And I'll appreciate it if you can get that invitation made official as soon as possible," Falkenberg said. "Otherwise, we're likely to have conflicting duties, but, of course, we could hardly refuse the Governor's invitation."

"Yes, I'll get started right now," she said.

"Good. Gentlemen? We've a bit of work. Administration of the new troops and such. Dull, but necessary."

VII

The conference room had a long table large enough for a dozen officers, with chairs at the end for twice that many more. There were briefing screens on two walls. The others were paneled in some kind of rich wood native to Arrarat. There were scars on the paneling where pictures and banners had hung. Now the panels were bare, and the room looked empty and cold. The only decoration was the CoDominium flag, American eagle and Soviet hammer and sickle. It stood between an empty trophy case and a bare corner.

Louis Bonneyman was already there. He got up as we came in.

"There won't be many here," Falkenberg said. "You may as well take places near the head of the table."

"Will you be regimental adjutant or a battalion commander?" Deane asked me. He pointed to senior officers' places.

"Battalion commander, by all means," I said. "Line over staff any day. Louis, you can be intelligence officer."

"That may not seem quite so amusing in a few minutes," Falkenberg said. "Take your places, gentlemen." He punched a button on the table's console. "And give some thought to what you say."

I wondered what the hell he meant by that. It hadn't escaped me that he'd known where to find us. Donnelley must have called him. The question was, why?

"Ten-hut!"

We got up as Colonel Harrington came in. Deane had told me Harrington was over seventy, but I hadn't really believed it. There wasn't any doubt about it now. Harrington was short and his face had a pinched look. The little hair he had left was white.

Sergeant Major Ogilvie came in with him. He looked enormous when he stood next to the Colonel. He was almost as tall as Falkenberg, anyway, and a lot more massive, a big man to begin with. Standing next to Harrington, he looked liked a giant.

The third man was a major who couldn't have been much younger than the Colonel.

"Be seated, gentlemen," Harrington said. "Welcome to Arrarat. I'm Harrington, of course. This is Major Lorca, my Chief of Staff. We already know who you are."

We muttered some kind of response while Harrington took his seat. He sat carefully, the way you might in high gravity, only, of course, Arrarat isn't a high-gravity planet. Old, I thought. Old and past retirement, even with regeneration therapy and geriatric drugs.

"You're quite a problem for me," the Colonel said. "We asked for a regiment of military police. Garrison Marines. I didn't think we'd get a full regiment, but I certainly didn't ask for Line troops. Now what am I to do with you?"

Nobody said anything.

"I cannot integrate Line Marines into the militia," the Colonel said. "It would be a disaster for both units. I don't even want your troops in this city! That's all I need, to have Line troopers practicing system D in Harmony!"

Deane looked blankly at me, and I grinned. It was nice to know something he didn't. System D is a Line troop tradition. The men organize themselves into small units and go into a section of town where they all drink until they can't hold any more. Then they tell the saloon owners they can't pay. If any of them causes trouble, they wreck his place, with the others converging onto the troublesome bar while more units delay the guard.

"I'm sorry, but I want your Line troopers out of this city as soon as possible," Harrington said. "And I can't give you any officers. There's no way I can put Marines under militia officers, and I can't spare any of the few Fleet people I have. That's a break for you, gentlemen, because the four of you will be the only officers in the 501st Provisional Battalion. Captain Falkenberg will command, of course. Mr. Slater, as senior lieutenant you will be his second, and I expect you'll have to take a company, as well. You others will also be company commanders. Major Lorca will be able to assist with logistics and maintenance services, but for the rest of it, you'll be on your own."

Harrington paused to let that sink in. Deane was grinning at me, and I answered it with one of my own. With any luck we'd do pretty well out of this miserable place. Experience as company commanders could cut years off our time as lieutenants.

"The next problem is, what the hell can I do with you after you're organized?" Harrington demanded. "Major Lorca, if you'll give them the background?"

Lorca got up and went to the briefing stand. He used the console to project a city map on the briefing screen. "As you can see, the city is strongly defended," he said. "We have no difficulty in holding it with our militia. However, it is the only part of Arrarat that we have ever been required to hold, and as a result there are a number of competing gangs operating pretty well as they please in the interior. Lately a group calling itself the River Pack has taken a long stretch along the river-banks and is levying such high passage fees that they have effectively cut this city off from supply. River traffic is the only feasible way to move agricultural goods from the farm-lands to the city."

Lorca projected another map showing the river stretching northwestward from Harmony-Garrison. It ran through a line of hills; then upriver of that were more farmlands. Beyond them was another mountain chain. "In addition," Lorca said, "the raw materials for whatever industries we have on this planet come from these mines." A light pointer indicated the distant mountains. "It leaves us with a delicate political situation."

The Colonel growled like a dog. "Delicate. Hell, it's impossible!" he said. "Tell 'em the rest of it, Lorca."

"Yes, Colonel. The political responsibilities on this planet have never been carefully defined. Few jurisdictions are clear-cut. For example, the city of Garrison is under direct military authority, and Colonel Harrington is both civil and military commander within its walls. The city of Harmony is under direct CoDominium rule, with Governor Swale as its head. That is clear, but Governor Swale also holds a commission as planetary executive, which in theory subordinates Colonel Harrington to him. In practice they work together well enough, with the Governor taking civil authority and Colonel Harrington exercising military authority. In effect we have integrated Garrison and Harmony."

"And that's about all we've agreed on," Harrington said. "There's one other thing that's bloody clear. Our orders say we're to hold Garrison at all costs. That, in practice, means we have to defend Harmony as well, so we've an integrated militia force. There's plenty enough strength to defend both cities against direct attack. Supply's another matter."

"As I said, a delicate situation," Major Lorca said. "We cannot hold the city without supply, and we cannot supply the city without keeping the river transport lines open. In the past, Governor Swale and Colonel Harrington were agreed that the only way to do that was to extend CoDominium rule to these areas along the river." The light pointer moved again, indicating the area marked as held by the River Pack.

"They resisted us," Lorca said. "Not only the convicts, but the original colonists as well. Our convoys were attacked. Our militiamen were shot down by snipers. Bombs were thrown into the homes of militia officers—the hostiles don't have many sympathizers inside the city, but it doesn't take many to employ terror tactics. The Governor would not submit to military rule in the city of Harmony, and the militia could not sustain the effort needed to hold the riverbanks. On orders from the Governor, all CoDominium-controlled forces were withdrawn to within the walls of Harmony-Garrison."

"We abandoned those people," Harrington said. "Well, they got what they deserved. As you'd expect, there was a minor civil war out there. When it was over, the River Pack was in control. Swale recognized them as a legal government. Thought he could negotiate with them. Horse puckey. Go on, Lorca. Give 'em the bottom line."

"Yes, sir. As the Colonel said, the River Pack was recognized as a legal government, and negotiations were started. They have not been successful. The River Pack has made unacceptable demands as a condition of opening the river supply lines. Since it is obvious to the Governor that we cannot hold these cities without secure supplies, the Governor directed Colonel Harrington to reopen the supply lines by military force. The attempt was not successful."

"They beat our arses," Harrington said. His lips were tightly drawn. "I've got plenty of explanations for it. Militia are just the wrong kind of troops for the job. That's all burned hydrogen anyway. The fact is, they beat us, and we had to send back to Headquarters for Marine reinforcements. I asked for a destroyer and a regiment of military police. The warship and the Marines would have taken the goddam riverbanks, and the MPs could hold it for us. Instead, I got you people."

"Which seems to have turned the trick," Major Lorca said. "At 1630 hours this afternoon, Governor Swale received word that the River Pack wishes to reopen negotiations. Apparently they have information sources within the city—"

"In the city, hell!" Harrington said. "In the Governor's palace, if you ask me. Some of his clerks have sold out."

"Yes, sir," Lorca said. "In any event, they have heard that reinforcements have come, and they wish to negotiate a settlement."

"Bastards," Colonel Harrington said. "Bloody criminal butchers. You can't imagine what those swine have done out there. And His Excellency will certainly negotiate a settlement that leaves them in control. I guess he has to. There's not much doubt that with the 501st as a spearhead we could retake that area, but we can't hold it with Line Marines! Hell, Line troops aren't any use as military government. They aren't trained for it and they won't do it."

Falkenberg cleared his throat. Harrington glared at him for a moment. "Yes?"

"Question, sir."

"Ask it."

"What would happen if the negotiations failed so that the 501st was required to clear the area by force? Would that produce a more desirable result?"

Harrington nodded, and the glare faded. "I like the way you think. Actually, Captain, it wouldn't, not really. The gangs would try to fight, but when they saw it was hopeless, they'd take their weapons and run. Melt into the bush and wait. Then we'd be back where we were a couple of years ago, fighting a long guerrilla war with no prospect for ending it. I had something like that in mind, Captain, but that was when I was expecting MPs. I think we could govern with a regiment of MPs."

"Yes, sir," Falkenberg said. "But even if we must negotiate a settlement with the River Pack, surely we would like to be in as strong a bargaining position as possible."

"What do you have in mind, Falkenberg?" Harrington asked. He sounded puzzled, but there was genuine interest in his voice.

"If I may, sir." Falkenberg got up and went to the briefing screen. "At the moment I take it we are technically in a state of war with the River Pack?"

"It's not that formal," Major Lorca said. "But, yes, that's about the situation."

"I noticed that there was an abandoned CD fort about 240 kilometers upriver," Falkenberg said. He used the screen controls to show that section of the river. "You've said that you don't want Line Marines in the city. It seemed to me that the old fort would make a good base for the 501st, and our presence there would certainly help keep river traffic open."

"All right. Go on," Harrington said.

"Now we have not yet organized the 501st Battalion, but no one here knows that. I have carefully isolated my officers and troops from the militia. Sergeant Major, have any of the enlisted men talked with anyone on this post?"

"No, sir. Your orders were pretty clear, sir."

"And I know the officers have not," Falkenberg said. He glanced at us and we nodded. "Therefore, I think it highly unlikely that we will run into any serious opposition if we march immediately to our new base," Falkenberg said. "We may be able to do some good on the way. If we move fast, we may catch some River Pack gangsters. Whatever happens, we'll disrupt them and make it simpler to negotiate favorable terms."

"Immediately," Harrington said. "What do you mean by immediately?"

"Tonight, sir. Why not? The troops haven't got settled in. They're prepared to march. Our gear is all packed for travel. If Major Lorca can supply us with a few trucks for heavy equipment, we'll have no other difficulties."

"By God," Harrington said. He looked thoughtful. "It's taking a hell of a risk—" He looked thoughtful again. "But not so big a risk as we'd have if you stayed around here. As you say. Right now nobody knows what we've got. Let the troops get to talking, and it'll get all over this planet that you've brought a random collection of recruits, guardhouse soldiers, and newlies. That wouldn't be so obvious if you hit the road."

"You'd be pretty much on your own until we get the river traffic established again," Major Lorca said.

"Yes, sir," Falkenberg answered. "But we'd be closer to food supply than you are. I've got three helicopters and a couple of Skyhooks. We can bring in military stores with those."

"By God, I like it," Harrington said. "Right now those bastards have beaten us. I wouldn't mind paying them out." He looked at us, then shook his head. "What do you chaps think? I can spare only the four of you. That stands. Can you do it?"

We all nodded. I had my doubts, but I was cocky enough to think I could do anything. "It will be a cakewalk, sir," I said. "I can't think a gang of criminals wants to face a battalion of Line Marines."

"Honor of the corps and all that," Harrington said. "I was never with Line troops. You haven't been with 'em long enough to know anything about them, and here you're talking like one of them already. All right. Captain Falkenberg, you are authorized to take your battalion to Fort Beersheba at your earliest convenience. Tell 'em what you can give 'em, Lorca." The Colonel sounded ten years younger. That defeat had hurt him, and he was looking forward to showing the River Pack what regular troops could do.

Major Lorca told us about logistics and transport. There

weren't enough trucks to carry more than a bare minimum of supplies. We could tow the artillery, and there were two tanks we could have. For most of us it would be march or die, but it didn't look to me as if there'd be very much dying.

Finally Lorca finished. "Questions?" he said. He looked at Falkenberg.

"I'll reserve mine for the moment, sir." Falkenberg was already talking like a battalion commander.

"Sir, why is there so little motor transport?" Louis Bonneyman asked.

"No fuel facilities," Lorca told him. "No petroleum refineries. We have a small supply of crude oil and a couple of very primitive distillation plants, but nowhere near enough to support any large number of motor vehicles. The original colonists were quite happy about that. They didn't want them." Lorca reminded me of one of the instructor officers at the Academy.

"What weapons are we facing?" Deane Knowles asked.

Lorca shrugged. "They're better armed than you think. Good rifles. Some rocket launchers. A few mortars. Nothing heavy, and they tend to be deficient in communications, in electronics in general, but there are exceptions to that. They've captured gear from our militia"—Colonel Harrington winced at that— "and, of course, anything we sell to the farmers eventually ends up in the hands of the gangs. If we refuse to let the farmers buy weapons, we condemn them. If we do sell weapons, we arm more convicts. A vicious circle."

I studied the map problem. It didn't look difficult. A thousand men need just over a metric ton of dried food every day. There was plenty of water along the route, though, and we could probably get local forage, as well. We could do it, even with the inadequate transport Lorca could give us. It did look like a cakewalk.

I worried with the figures until I was satisfied, then suddenly realized it wasn't an exercise for a class. This was real. In a few hours we'd be marching into hostile territory. I looked over at my classmates. Deane was punching numbers into his pocket computer and frowning at the result. Louis Bonneyman was grinning like a thief. He caught my eye and winked. I grinned back at him, and it made me feel better. Whatever happened, I could count on them.

Lorca went through a few more details on stores and equipment available from the garrison, plus other logistic support available from the fort. We all took notes, and of course the briefing was recorded. "That about sums it up," he said.

Harrington stood, and we got up. "I expect you'll want to organize the 501st before you'll have any meaningful questions," Harrington said. "I'll leave you to that. You may consider this meeting your formal call on the commanding officer, although I'll be glad to see any of you in my office if you've anything to say to me. That's all."

"Ten-hut!" Ogilvie said. He stayed in the briefing room as Colonel Harrington and Major Lorca left.

"Well. We've work to do," Falkenberg said. "Sergeant Major."

"Sir!"

"Please run through the organization we worked out."

"Sir!" Ogilvie used the screen controls to flash charts onto the screens. As the Colonel had said, I was second in command of the battalion, and also A Company commander. My company was a rifle outfit. I noticed it was heavy with experienced Line troopers, and I had less than my share of recruits.

Deane had drawn the weapons company, which figured. Deane had taken top marks in weapons technology at the Academy, and he was always reading up on artillery tactics. Louis Bonneyman had another rifle company with a heavy proportion of recruits to worry about. Falkenberg had kept a large headquarters platoon under his personal command.

"There are reasons for this structure," Falkenberg said. "I'll explain them later. For the moment, have any of you objections?"

"Don't know enough to object, sir," I said. I was studying the organization chart.

"All of you will have to rely heavily on your NCOs," Falkenberg said. "Fortunately, there are some good ones. I've given the best, Centurion Lieberman, to A Company. Bonneyman gets Sergeant Cernan. If he works out, we can get him a Centurion's badges. Knowles has already worked with Gunner-Centurion Pniff. Sergeant Major Ogilvie stays with Headquarters Platoon, of course. In addition to your command duties, each of you will have to fill some staff slots. Bonneyman will be intelligence." Falkenberg grinned slightly. "I told you it might not seem such a joke."

Louis answered his grin. He was already sitting in the regimental intelligence officer's chair at the table. I wondered why Falkenberg had given that job to Louis. Of the four of us, Louis had paid the least attention to his briefing packet, and he didn't seem cut out for the job.

"Supply and logistics stay with Knowles, of course," Falkenberg said. "I'll keep training myself. Now, I have a proposition for you. The Colonel has ordered us to occupy

Fort Beersheba at the earliest feasible moment. If we simply march there with no fighting and without accomplishing much beyond getting there, the Governor will negotiate a peace. We will be stationed out in the middle of nowhere, with few duties beyond patrols. Does anyone see any problems with that?"

"Damned dull," Louis Bonneyman said.

"And not just for us. What have you to say, Sergeant Major?"

Ogilvie shook his head. "Don't like it, sir. Might be all right for the recruits, but wouldn't recommend it for the old hands. Especially the ones you took out of the brig. Be a lot of the bug, sir."

The bug. The Foreign Legion called it *le cafard*, which means the same thing. It had been the biggest single cause of death in the Legion, and it was still that among Line Marines. Men with nothing to do. Armed men, warriors, bored stiff. They get obsessed with the bug until they commit suicide, or murder, or desert, or plot mutiny. The textbook remedy for *le cafard* is a rifle and plenty of chances to use it. Combat. Line troops on garrison duty lose more men to *cafard* than active outfits lose in combat. So my instructors had told us, anyway.

"It will be doubly bad in this case," Falkenberg said. "No regimental pride. No accomplishments to brag about. No battles. I'd like to avoid that."

"How, sir?" Bonneyman asked.

Falkenberg seemed to ignore him. He adjusted the map until the section between the city and Fort Beersheba filled the screen. "We march up the Jordan," he said. "I suppose it was inevitable that the Federation of Churches would call the planet's most important river 'Jordan,' wasn't it? We march northwest, and what happens, Mr. Slater?"

I thought about it. "They run, I suppose. I can't think they'll want to fight. We've much better equipment than they have."

"Equipment and men," Falkenberg said. "And a damned frightening reputation. They already know we've landed, and they've asked for negotiations. They've got sources inside the palace. You heard me arrange for a social invitation for five days from now."

We all laughed. Falkenberg nodded. "Which means that if we march tonight, we'll achieve *real* surprise. We can catch a number of them unaware and disarm them. What I'd like to do, though, is disarm the lot of them."

I was studying the map, and I thought I saw what he meant. "They'll just about have to retreat right past Fort Beersheba," I said. "Everything narrows down there."

"Precisely," Falkenberg said. "If we held the fort, we could disarm everyone coming through. Furthermore, it is our fort, and we've orders to occupy it quickly. I remind you also that we're technically at war with the River Pack."

"Yes, but how do we get there?" I asked. "Also, Captain, if we're holding the bottleneck, the rest of them will fight. They can't retreat."

"Not without losing their weapons," Falkenberg said. "I don't think the Colonel would be unhappy if we *really* pacified that area. Nor do I think the militia would have all that much trouble holding it if we defeated the River Pack and disarmed their survivors."

"But as Hal asked, how do we get there?" Louis demanded.

Falkenberg said, "I mentioned helicopters. Sergeant Major has found enough fuel to keep them flying for a while."

"Sir, I believe there was something in the briefing kit about losses from the militia arsenal," Deane said. "Specifically including Skyhawk missiles. Choppers wouldn't stand a chance against those."

"Not if anyone with a Skyhawk knew they were coming," Falkenberg agreed. "But why should they expect us? The gear's at the landing dock. Nothing suspicious about a work party going down there tonight. Nothing suspicious about getting the choppers set up and working. I can't believe they expect us to take Beersheba tonight, not when they've every reason to believe we'll be attending a grand ball in five days."

"Yes, sir," Deane agreed. "But we can't put enough equipment into three choppers! The men who take Beersheba will be doomed. Nobody can march up that road fast enough to relieve them."

Falkenberg's voice was conversational. He looked up at the ceiling. "I did mention Skyhooks, didn't I? Two of them. Lifting capacity in this gravity and atmosphere, six metric tons each. That's forty-five men with full rations and ammunition. Gentlemen, by dawn we could have ninety combat Marines in position at Fort Beersheba, with the rest of the 501st marching to their relief. Are you game?"

VIII

It was cold down by the docks. A chill wind had blown in just after sundown, and despite the previous heat of the day I was shivering. Maybe, I thought, it isn't the cold.

The night sky was clear, with what seemed like millions of stars. I could recognize most of the constellations, and that seemed strange. It reminded me that although we were so far from Earth that a man who began walking in the time of the dinosaurs wouldn't have gotten here yet, it was still an insignificant distance to the universe. That made me feel small, and I didn't like it.

The troops were turned out in work fatigues. Our combat clothing and armor were still tucked away in the packs we were loading onto the Skyhook platforms. We worked under bright lights, and anyone watching would never have known we were anything but a work party. Falkenberg was sure that at least one pair of night glasses was trained on us from the bluff above.

The Skyhook platforms were light aluminum affairs, just a flat plate eight meters on a side with a meter-high railing around the perimeter. We stowed packs onto them. We also piled on other objects: light machine guns, recoilless cannon, mortars, and boxes of shells and grenades. Some of the boxes had false labels on them, stenciled on by troops working inside the warehouse, so that watchers would see what looked like office supplies and spare clothing going aboard.

A truck came down from the fort and went into the warehouse. It seemed to be empty, but it carried rifles for ninety men. The rifles went into bags and were stowed on the Skyhooks.

Arrarat has only one moon, smaller than Earth's and closer. It was a bloody crescent sinking into the highlands to the west, and it didn't give much light. It would be gone in an hour. I wandered over to where Deane was supervising the work on the helicopters.

"Sure you have those things put together right?" I asked him.

"Nothing to it."

"Yeah. I hope not. It's going to be hard to find those landing areas."

"You'll be all right." He wasn't really listening to me. He had two communications specialists working on the navigation computers, and he kept glaring at the squiggles on their scopes. "That's good," he said. "Now feed in the test problem."

When I left to go find Falkenberg, Deane didn't notice I'd gone. Captain Falkenberg was inside the warehouse. "We've about got the gear loaded, sir," I told him.

"Good. Come have some coffee." One of the mess sergeants had set up the makings for coffee in one corner of the big high-bay building. There was also a map table, and Sergeant Major Ogilvie had a communications center set up there. Falkenberg poured two cups of coffee and handed one to me. "Nervous?" he asked me.

"Some."

"You can still call it off. No discredit. I'll tell the others there were technical problems. We'll still march in the morning."

"It'll be all right, sir."

He looked at me over the lip of his coffee cup. "I expect you will be. I don't like sending you into this, but there's no other way we can do it."

"Yes, sir," I said.

"You'll be all right. You've got steady troopers."

"Yes, sir." I didn't know any of the men, of course. They were only names and service records, not even that, just a statistical summary of service records, a tape spewed out by the personnel computer. Thirty had been let out of the brig for voluntary service in Arrarat. Another twenty were recruits. The rest were Line Marines, long service volunteers.

Falkenberg used the controls to project a map of the area around Beersheba onto the map table. "Expect you've got this memorized," he said.

"Pretty well, sir."

He leaned over the table and looked at the fort, then at the line of hills north of it. "You've some margin for error, I think. I'll have to leave to you the final decision on using the chopper in the actual assault. You can risk one helicopter. Not both. I must have one helicopter back, even if that costs you the mission. Is that understood?"

"Yes, sir." I could feel a sharp ball in my guts, and I didn't like it. I hoped it wouldn't show.

"Getting on for time," Falkenberg said. "You'll need all the time you can get. We could wait a day to get better prepared, but I think surprise is your best edge."

I nodded. We'd been through all this before. Was he talking because he was nervous, too? Or to keep me talking so I wouldn't brood?

"You may get a commendation out of this."

"If it's all the same to you, I'd rather have a guarantee that you'll show up on time." I grinned when I said it, to show I didn't mean it, but I did. Why the hell wasn't he leading this assault? The whole damned idea was his, and so was the battle plan. It was his show, and he wasn't going. I didn't want to think about the reasons. I had to depend on him to bail me out, and I couldn't even let myself think the word "coward."

"Time to load up," Falkenberg said.

I nodded and drained the coffee cup. It tasted good. I wondered if that would be the last coffee I'd ever drink. It was certain that some of us wouldn't be coming back.

Falkenberg clapped his hand on my shoulder. "You'll give them a hell of a shock, Hal. Let's get on with it."

"Right." But I sure wish you were coming with me.

I found Centurion Lieberman. We'd spent several hours together since Falkenberg's briefing, and I was sure I could trust him. Lieberman was about Falkenberg's height, built somewhere between wiry and skinny. He was about forty-five, and there were scars on his neck. The scars ran down under his tunic. He'd had a lot of regeneration therapy in his time.

His campaign ribbons made two neat rows on his undress blues. From his folder I knew he was entitled to another row he didn't bother to wear.

"Load 'em up," I told him.

"Sir." He spoke in a quiet voice, but it carried through the warehouse. "First and second platoons A Company, take positions on the Skyhook platforms."

The men piled in on top of the gear. It was crowded on the platforms. I got in with one group, and Lieberman boarded the other platform. I'd rather have been up in the helicopter, flying it or sitting next to the pilot, but I thought I was needed down here. Louis Bonneyman was flying my chopper. Sergeant Doty of Headquarters Platoon had the other.

"Bags in position," Gunner-Centurion Pniff said. "Stand ready to inflate Number One." He walked around the platform looking critically at the lines that led from it to the amorphous shape that lay next to it. "Looks good. Inflate Number One."

There was a loud hiss, and a great ghostly bag formed. It began to rise until it was above my platform. The plastic gleamed in the artificial light streaming from inside the warehouse. The bag billowed up until it was huge above us, and still it grew as the compressed helium poured out of the inflating cylinders. It looked bigger than the warehouse before Pniff was satisfied. "Good," he said. "Belay! Stand by to inflate Number Two."

"Jeez," one of the recruits said. "We going up in this balloon? Christ, we don't have parachutes! We can't go up in a balloon!"

Some of the others began to chatter. "Sergeant Ardwain," I said.

"Sir!"

I didn't say anything else. Ardwain cursed and crawled over to the recruits. "No chutes means we don't have to jump," he said. "Now shut up."

Number Two Skyhook was growing huge. It looked even larger than our own, because I could see all of it, and all I could see of the bag above us was this bloated thing filling the sky above me. The choppers started up, and after a moment they lifted. One rose directly above us. The other went to hover above the other Skyhook. The chopper looked dwarfed next to that huge bag.

The choppers settled onto the bags. Up on top the helicopter crews were floundering around on the billowing stuff to make certain the fastenings were set right. I could hear their reports in my helmet phones. Finally they had it all right.

"Everything ready aboard?" Falkenberg asked me. His voice was unemotional in the phones. I could see him standing by the warehouse doors, and I waved. "All correct, sir," I said.

"Good. Send Number One along, Gunner."

"Sir!" Pniff said. "Ground crews stand by. Let go Number One."

The troops outside were grinning at us as they cut loose the tethers holding the balloons. Nothing happened, of course; the idea of Skyhook is to have almost neutral buoyancy, so that the lift from the gas bags just balances the weight of the load. The helicopters provide all the motive power.

The chopper engines rose in pitch, and we lifted off. A gust of wind caught us and we swayed badly as we lifted. Some of the troops cursed, and their non-coms glared at them. Then we were above the harbor, rising to the level of the city bluff, then higher than that. We moved northward toward the fort, staying high above the city until we got to Garrison's north edge, then dipping low at the fortress wall.

Anyone watching from the harbor area would think we'd just ferried a lot of supplies up onto the bluff. They might wonder about carrying men as well, but we could be pretty sure they wouldn't suspect we were doing anything but ferrying them.

We dropped low over the fields north of the city and continued moving. Then we rose again, getting higher and higher until we were at thirty-three hundred meters.

The men looked at me nervously. They watched the city lights dwindle behind us.

"All right," I said. It was strange how quiet it was. The choppers were ultra-quiet, and what little noise they made was shielded by the gas bag above us. The railings cut off most of the wind. "I want every man to get his combat helmet on."

There was some confused rooting around as the men found their own packs and got their helmets swapped around. We'd been cautioned not to shift weight on the platforms, and nobody wanted to make any sudden moves.

I switched my command set to lowest power so it couldn't be intercepted more than a kilometer away. We were over three klicks high, so I wasn't much worried that anyone was listening. "By now you've figured that we aren't going straight back to the fort," I said.

There were laughs from the recruits. The older hands looked bored.

"We've got a combat mission," I said. "We're going 250 klicks west of the city. When we get there, we take a former CD fort, dig in, and wait for the rest of the battalion to march out and bring us home."

A couple of troopers perked up at that. I heard one tell his buddy, "Sure beats hell out of marching 250 klicks."

"You'll get to march, though," I said. "The plan is to land about eight klicks from the fort and march overland to take it by surprise. I doubt anyone is expecting us."

"Christ Johnny strikes again," someone muttered. I couldn't see who had said that.

"Sir?" a corporal asked. I recognized him: Roff, the man who'd been riding the seasick recruit in the landing boat.

"Yes, Corporal Roff?"

"Question, sir."

"Ask it."

"How long will we be there, Lieutenant?"

"Until Captain Falkenberg comes for us," I said.

"Aye, aye, sir."

There weren't any other questions. I thought that was strange. They must want to know more. Some of you will get killed tonight, I thought. Why don't you want to know more about it?

They were more interested in the balloon. Now that it didn't look as if it would fall, they wanted to look out over the edge. I had the non-coms rotate the men so everyone got a chance.

I'd had my look over the edge, and I didn't like it. Below the level of the railing it wasn't so bad, but looking down was horrible. Besides, there wasn't really anything to see, except a few lights, way down below, and far behind us a dark shape that sometimes blotted out stars: Number Two, about a klick away.

"Would the lieutenant care for coffee?" a voice asked me. "I have brought the flask."

I looked up to see Hartz with my Thermos and a mess-hall cup. I'd seen him get aboard with his communications gear, but I'd forgotten him after that. "Thanks, I'll have some," I said.

It was about half brandy. I nearly choked. Hartz didn't even crack a smile.

We took a roundabout way so that we wouldn't pass over any of the river encampments. The way led far north of the river, then angled southwest to our landing zone. I turned to look over the edge again, and I hoped that Deane had gotten the navigation computers tuned up properly, because there wasn't anything to navigate by down there. Once in a while there was an orange-yellow light, probably a farmhouse, possibly an outlaw encampment, but otherwise all the hills looked the same.

This has got to be the dumbest stunt in military history, I told myself, but I didn't really believe it. The Line Marines had a long reputation for going into battle in newly formed outfits with strange officers. Even so, I doubted if any expedition had ever had so little going for it: a newlie commander, men who'd never served together, and a captain who'd plan the mission but wouldn't go on it. I told myself the time to object had been back in the briefing. It was a bit late now.

I looked at my watch. Another hour of flying time. "Sergeant Ardwain."

"Sir?"

"Get them out of those work clothes and into combat leathers and armor. Weapons check after everyone's dressed." Dressed to kill, I thought, but I didn't say it. It was an old joke, never funny to begin with. I wondered who thought of it first. Possibly some trooper outside the walls of Troy.

Hartz already had my leathers out of my pack. He helped me squirm out of my undress blues and into the synthi-leather tunic and trousers. The platform rocked as men tried to pull on their pants without standing up. It was hard to dress because we were sprawled out on our packs and other equipment. There was a lot of cursing as troopers moved around to find their own packs and rifles.

"Get your goddam foot out of my eye!"

"Shut up, Traeger."

Finally everyone had his armor on and his fatigues packed away. The troopers sat quietly now. Even the old hands weren't joking. There's something about combat armor that makes everything seem real.

They looked dangerous in their bulky leathers and armor, and they were. The armor alone gave us a big edge on anything we'd meet here. It also gives a feeling of safety, and that can be dangerous. Nemourlon will stop most fragments and even pistol bullets, but it won't stop a high-velocity rifle slug.

"How you doing down there?" Louis's voice in my phones startled me for a moment.

"We're all armored up," I told him. "You still think you know where you're going?"

"Nope. But the computer does. Got a radar check five minutes ago. Forking stream that shows on the map. We're right on the button."

"What's our ETA?" I asked.

"About twenty minutes. Wind's nice and steady, not too strong. Piece of cake."

"Fuel supply?" I asked.

"We're hip-deep in spare cans. Not exactly a surplus, but there's enough. Quit worrying."

"Yeah."

"You know," Louis said, "I never flew a chopper with one of those things hanging off it."

"Now you tell me."

"Nothing to it," Louis said. "Handles a bit funny, but I got used to it."

"You'd better have."

"Just leave the driving to us. Out."

The next twenty minutes seemed like a week. I guarantee one way to stretch time is to sit on an open platform at thirty-three hundred meters and watch the night sky while you wait to command your first combat mission. I tried to think of something cheerful to say, but I couldn't, and I thought it was better just to be quiet. The more I talked, the more chance I'd show some kind of strain in my voice.

"Your job is to look confident," Falkenberg had told me. I hoped I was doing that.

"Okay, you can get your first look now," Louis said.

"Rojj." I got my night glasses from Hartz. They were better than issue equipment, a pair of ten-cm Leica light-amplifying glasses I bought myself when I left the Academy. A lot of officers do, because Leica makes a special offer for graduating cadets. I clipped them onto my helmet and scanned the hillside. The landing zone was the top of a peak which was the highest point on a ridge leading from the river. I turned the glasses to full power and examined the area carefully.

It looked deserted. There was some kind of scrubby chaparral growing all over it, and it didn't look as if anybody had ever been to the peak.

"Looks good to me," I told Louis. "What do you have?"

"Nothing on IR, nothing on low-light TV," he said. "Nothing barring a few small animals and some birds roosting in the trees. I like that. If there're animals and birds, there's probably no people."

"Yeah—"

"Okay, that's passive sensors. Should I take a sweep with K-band?"

I thought about it. If there were anyone down there, and that theoretical someone had a radar receiver, the chopper would give itself away with the first pulse. Maybe that would be better. "Yes."

"Rojj," Louis said. He was silent a moment. "Hal, I get nothing. If there's anybody down there, he's dug in good and expecting us."

"Let's go in," I said.

And now, I thought, I'm committed.

IX

"Over the side!" Ardwain shouted. "Get those tethers planted! First squad take perimeter guard! Move, damn you!"

The men scrambled off the platform. Some of them had tether stakes, big aluminum corkscrews, which they planted in the ground. Others lashed the platform to the stakes. The first squad, two maniples, fanned out around the area with their rifles ready.

There wasn't much wind, but that big gas bag had a lot of surface area, and I was worried about it. I got off and moved away to look at it. It didn't seem to be too much strain on the tether stakes. The hillside was quiet and dark. We'd set down on top of some low bushes with stiff branches. The leaves felt greasy when they were crushed. I listened, then turned my surveillance amplifier to high gain. Still nothing, not even a bird. Nothing but my own troops moving about. I switched to general command frequency. "Freeze," I said.

The noise stopped. There was silence except for the low "whump!" of the chopper blades, and a fainter sound from Number Two out there somewhere.

"Carry on," I said.

Ardwain came up to me. "Nobody here, sir. Area secure."

"Thank you." I thumbed my command set onto the chopper's frequency. "You can cut yourself loose, and bring in Number Two."

"Aye, aye, sir," Louis said.

We began pulling gear off the platform. After a few moments, Number Two chopper came in. We couldn't see the helicopter at all, only the huge gas bag with its platform dangling below it. The Skyhook settled onto the chaparral and men bailed out with tether stakes. Centurion Lieberman watched until he was sure the platform was secure, then ran over to me.

"All's well?" I asked him.

"Yes, sir." His tone made it obvious he'd wanted to say "of course."

"Get 'em saddled up," I said. "We're moving out."

"Aye, aye, sir. I still think Ardwain would be all right here, sir."

"No. I'll want an experienced man in case something happens. If we don't send for the heavy equipment, or if something happens to me, call Falkenberg for instructions."

"Aye, aye, sir."' He still didn't like it. He wanted to come with us. For that matter, I wanted him along, but I had to leave a crew with the Skyhooks and choppers. If the wind came up so tethers wouldn't hold, those things had to get airborne fast, and the rest of us would be without packs and supplies. There were all kinds of contingencies, and I wanted a reliable man I could trust to deal with them.

"We're ready, sir," Ardwain said.

"Right. Let's move out." I switched channels. "Here we go, Louis."

"I'll be ready," Bonneyman said.

"Thanks. Out." I moved up toward the head of the column. Ardwain had already gone up. "Let's get rolling," I said.

"Sir. Question, sir," Ardwain said.

"Yeah?"

"Men would rather take their packs, sir. Don't like to leave their gear behind."

"Sergeant, we've got eight kilometers to cover in less than three hours. No way."

"Yes, sir. Could we take our cloaks? Gets cold without 'em—"

"Sergeant Ardwain, we're leaving Centurion Lieberman and four maniples of troops here. Just what's going to happen to your gear? Get them marching."

"Sir. All right, you bastards, move out."

I could hear grumbling as they started along the ridge. Crazy, I thought. They want to carry packs in this.

The brush was thick, and we weren't making any progress at all. Then the scouts found a dry stream bed, and we moved into that. It was filled with boulders the size of a desk, and we hopped from one to another, moving slightly downhill. It was pitch-black, the boulders no more than shapes I could barely see. This wasn't going to work. I was already terrified.

But thank God for all that exercise in high gravity, I thought. We'll make it, but we've got to have light. I turned my set to low-power command frequency. "NCOs turn on lowest-power infrared illumination," I said. "No visible light."

I pulled the IR screen down in front of my eyes and snapped on my own IR helmet light. The boulders became pale green shapes in front of me, and I could just see them well enough to hop from one to another. Ahead of me the screen showed bright green moving splotches, my scouts and NCOs with their illuminators.

I didn't think anybody would be watching this hill with IR equipment. It didn't seem likely, and we were far from the fort where the only equipment would be—if the River Pack had any to begin with. I told myself it would take extremely good gear to spot us from farther than a klick.

Eight klicks to go and three hours to do it. Shouldn't be hard. Men are in good condition, no packs—damned fools wanted to carry them!—only rifles and ammunition. And the weapons troops, of course. They'd be slowest. Mortarmen with twenty-two kilos each to carry, and the recoilless riflemen with twenty-four.

We were sweating in no time. I opened all the vents in my armor and leathers and wondered if I ought to tell the troops to do the same. Don't be stupid, I told myself. Most of them have done this a dozen times. I can't tell them anything they don't know.

But it's my command, I kept thinking. Anything goes wrong, it's your responsibility, Hal Slater. You asked for it, too, when you took the commission.

I kept thinking of the millions of things that could go wrong. The plan didn't look nearly so good from here as it had when we were studying maps. Here we are, seventy-six men, about to try to take a fort that probably has us outnumbered. Falkenberg estimated 125 men in there. I'd asked him how he got the number.

"Privies, Mr. Slater. Privies. Count the number of outhouses, guess the number of bottoms per hole, and you've got a good estimate of the number of men." He hadn't even cracked a grin.

One hell of a way to guess, and Falkenberg wasn't coming along. We'd find out the hard way how accurate his estimate was.

I kept telling myself what we had going for us. The satellite photos showed nobody lived on this ridge. No privies, I thought, and grinned in the dark. But I'd gone over the pix, and I hadn't seen any signs that people were ever here. Why should they be? There was no water except for the spring inside the fort itself. There was nothing up here, not even proper firewood, only these pesky shrubs that stab at your ankles.

I came around a bend in the stream bed and found a monitor waiting. His maniple stood behind him. He had three recruits in it: one NCO, one long-term private, and three recruits. The usual organization is only one or two recruits to a maniple, and I wondered why Lieberman had set this one up this way.

The monitor motioned uphill. We had to leave the stream bed here. Far ahead of me I could see the dull green glow of my lead men's lanterns. They were pulling ahead of me, and I strained to keep up with them. I left the stream, and after a few meters the only man near me was Hartz. He struggled along with twenty kilos of communications gear on his back and a rifle in his right hand, but if he had any trouble keeping up with me, he didn't say anything. I was glad I didn't have to carry all that load.

The ridge flattened out after a hundred meters. The cover was only about waist-high. The green lights went out on my IR screen as up ahead the scouts cut their illuminators. I ordered the others turned off, as well. Then I crouched under a bush and used the map projector to show me where we were. The helmet projected the map onto the ground, a dim patch of light that couldn't have been seen except from close up and directly above.

I was surprised to see we'd come better than halfway.

Fort Beersheba hadn't been much to start with. It had a rectangle of low walls with guard towers in the corners, a miniature of the larger fort at Garrison. Then somebody had improved it, with a ditch and parapet out in front of the walls, and a concertina of rusting barbed wire outside of that. I couldn't see inside the walls, but I knew there were four above-ground buildings and three large bunkers. The buildings were adobe. The bunkers were logs and earth. They wouldn't burn. The logs were a local wood with a high metallic content.

The bunkers were going to be a problem, but they'd have to wait. Right now we had to get inside the walls of the fort. There was a gate in the wall in front of me. It was made of the same wood as the bunkers. It had a ramp across the ditch, and it looked like our best bet, except that inside the fort one of the bunkers faced the gate, and it would be able to fire through the opening once the gate was gone.

I had seventy-five men lying flat in the scrub brush three hundred meters from the fort. The place looked deserted. My IR pickups didn't show anyone in the guard towers or on the walls. Nothing. I glanced at my watch. Less than an hour before dawn.

I hadn't the faintest idea of what to do, but it was time to make up my mind.

"Don't get fancy," Falkenberg had told me. "Get the men to the fort and turn them loose. They'll take it for you."

Sure, I thought. Sure. You're not here, you bloody coward, and I am, and it's my problem, and I don't know what the hell I'm doing.

I didn't like the looks of that ditch and barbed-wire concertina. It would take a while getting through it. If we crawled up to the ditch, we'd be spotted. They couldn't be that sloppy; if there weren't any guards, there had to be a surveillance system. Body capacitance, maybe. Or radar. Something. They'd have guards posted unless they had reason to believe nobody could sneak up on them.

To hell with it. We've got to do something, I thought. I nodded to Hartz and he handed me a mike. His radio was set to a narrow-beam directional antenna, and we'd left relays along the line of sight back to the landing area. I could talk to the choppers without alerting the fort's electronic watch-dogs.

"Nighthawk, this is Blackeagle," I said.

"Blackeagle go."

"We can see the place, Louis. Nothing moving at all. I'd say it was deserted if I didn't know better."

"Want me to come take a look?"

It was a thought. The chopper could circle high above the fort and scan with IR and low-light TV. We'd know who was in the open. But there was a good chance it would be spotted, and we'd throw away our best shot.

"Don't get fancy," Falkenberg had said. "Surprise—that's your big advantage. Don't blow it."

But he wasn't here. There didn't seem to be any right decision. "No," I told Louis. "That's a negative. Load up with troops and get airborne, but stay out of line of sight. Be ready to dash. When I want you, I'll want you bad."

"Aye, aye, sir."

"Blackeagle out." I gave Hartz the mike. Okay, I told myself, this is it. I waved forward to Sergeant Ardwain.

He half rose from the ground and waved. The line moved ahead, slowly. Behind us the mortar and recoilless rifle teams had set up their weapons and lay next to them waiting for orders.

Corporal Roff was just to my left. He was directly in front

of the gate. He waved his troops on and we crawled toward the gate.

We'd gotten to within a hundred meters when there appeared a light at the top of the wall by the gate. Someone up there was shining a spot out onto the field. There was another light, and then another, all hand-held spotlights, powerful, but not very wide beams.

Corporal Roff stood up and waved at them "Hello, there!" he shouted. "Whatcha doin'?" He sounded drunk. I wanted to tell him to get down, but it was too late.

"You guys okay in there?" Roff shouted. "Got anything to drink?"

The others were crouched now, up from a crawl, and running forward.

"Who the hell are you?" someone on the wall demanded.

"Who the flippin' hell are you?" Roff answered. "Gimme a drink!" The lights converged toward him.

I thumbed on my command set. "Nighthawk, this is Blackeagle. Come a-runnin'!"

"Roger dodger."

I switched to the general channel. "Roff, hit the dirt! Fire at will. Charge!" I was shouting into the helmet radio loud enough to deafen half the command.

Roff dove sideways into the dirt. There were orange spurts from all over the field as the troopers opened fire. The lights tumbled off the walls. Two went out. One stayed on. It lay in the dirt just outside the gate.

Troopers rose from the field and ran screaming toward the fort. They sounded like madmen. Then a light machine gun opened from behind me, then another.

Trumpet notes sounded. I hadn't ordered it. I didn't even know we had a trumpet with us. The sound seemed to spur the men on. They ran toward the wire as the mortars fired their first rounds. Seconds later I saw spurts of fire from inside the walls as the shells hit. Just as they did, the recoilless opened behind me and I heard the shell pass not more than a couple of meters to my left. It hit the gates and there was a flash, then another hit the gates, and another. The trumpeter was sounding the charge over and over again, while mortars dropped more V.T. fused to go off a meter above ground into the fort itself. The recoilless fired again.

The gates couldn't take that punishment and fell open. There was smoke inside. One of the mortarmen must have dropped smoke rounds between the gates and the bunker. Streams of tracers came out of the gates, but the men avoided them easily. They ran up on either side of the gates.

Others charged directly at the wire. The first troopers threw themselves onto the concertina. The next wave stepped on their backs and dived into the ditch. More waves followed, and men in the ditches heaved their comrades up onto the narrow strip between the ditch and the walls.

They stopped just long enough to throw grenades over the wall. Then two men grabbed a third and flung him up to where he could catch the top of the wall. They stood and boosted him on until he pulled himself up and could stand on top of it. More men followed, then leaned down to pull up their mates from below. I couldn't believe it was happening so quickly.

The men on the wire were struggling to get loose before there was no one below to boost them over. Those were recruits, I thought. Of course. The monitors had sent the recruits first, with a simple job. Lie down and get walked on.

The helicopter came roaring in, pouring streams of twenty-mm cannon fire into the fort. The tracers were bright against the night sky.

And I was still standing there, watching, amazed at how fast it was all happening. I shook myself and turned on my command set. "I.F.F. beacons on! General order, turn on I.F.F. beacons." I changed channels. "Nighthawk, this is Blackeagle. For God's sake, Louis, be careful! Some of ours are already inside!"

"I see the beacons," Louis said. "Relax, Hal, we watched them going in."

The chopper looped around the fort in a tight orbit, still firing into the fort. Then it plunged downward.

"Mortarmen, hold up on that stuff," Sergeant Ardwain's voice said. "We're inside the fort now and the chopper's going in."

Christ, I thought, something else I forgot. One hell of a commander I've made. I can't even remember the most elementary things.

The chopper dropped low and even before it vanished behind the walls it was spewing men.

I ran up to the gate, staying to one side to avoid the tracers that were still coming out. Corporal Roff was there ahead of me. "Careful here, sir." He ducked around the gatepost and vanished. I followed him into the smoke, running around to my right, where other troopers had gone over the wall.

The scene inside was chaotic. There were unarmored bodies everywhere, probably cut down by the mortars. Men were running and firing in all directions. I didn't think any of the defenders had helmets. "Anybody without a helmet is a hostile," I said into the command set. Stupid. They know that. "Give 'em hell, lads!" That was another silly thing to say, but at least it was a better reason for shouting in their ears than telling them something they already knew.

A satchel charge went off at one of the bunkers. A squad rushed the entrance and threw grenades into it. That was all I could see from where I stood, but there was firing all over the enclosure.

Now what? I wondered. Even as I did, the firing died out until there were only a few rifle shots now and then, and the futile fire of the machine gun in the bunker covering the gate.

"Lieutenant?" It was Ardwain's voice.

"Yes, Sergeant."

"There's some people in that main bunker, sir. You can hear 'em talking in there. Sound like women. We didn't want to blow it in, not just yet, anyway."

"What about the rest of the fort?"

"Cleared out, sir. Bunkers and barracks, too. We got about twenty prisoners."

That quick. Like automatic magic. "Sergeant, make sure there's nothing that can fire onto the area northwest of the fort. I want to bring the Skyhook in there."

"Aye, aye, sir."

I thumbed my command set to the chopper frequency. "We've got the place, all except one bunker, and it'll be no problem. Bring Number Two in to land in the area northwest of the fort, about three hundred meters out from the wall. I want you to stay up there and cover Number Two. Anything that might hit it, you take care of. Keep scanning. I can't believe somebody won't come up here to see what's happening."

X

That was my first fire fight. I wasn't too proud of my part in it. I hadn't given a single order once the rush started, and I was very nearly the last man into the fort. Some leader.

But there was no time to brood. Dawn was a bright smear off in the east. The first thing was to check on the butcher's bill. Four men killed, two of them recruits. Eleven wounded. After a quick conference with our paramedic I sent three to the helicopters. The others could fight, or said they could. Then I sent the two choppers east toward Harmony, while we ferried the rest of our gear into the fort. We were on our own.

Sergeant Doc Crisp had another dozen patients, defenders who'd been wounded in the assault. We had thirty prisoners, thirty-seven wounded, and over fifty dead. One of the wounded was the former commander of the fort.

"Got bashed with a rifle butt outside his quarters," Ardwain told me. "He's able to talk now."

"I'll see him."

"Sir." Ardwain went into the hospital bunker and brought out a man about fifty, dark hair in a ring around a bald head. He had thin, watery eyes. He didn't look like a soldier or an outlaw.

"He says his name's Flawn, sir," Ardwain told me.

"Marines," Flawn said. "CoDominium Marines. Didn't know there were any on the planet. Just why the hell is this place worth the Grand Senate's attention again?"

"Shut up," Ardwain said.

"I've got a problem, Flawn," I said. We were standing in the open area in the center of the fort. "That bunker over there's still got some of your people in it. It'd be no problem to blast it open, but the troopers think they heard women talking in there."

"They did," Flawn said. "Our wives."

"Can you talk them into coming out, or do we set fire to it?"

"Christ!" he said. "What happens to us now?"

Machts nichts to me," I told him. "My orders are to disarm you people. You're free to go anywhere you want to without weapons. Northwest if you like."

"Without weapons. You know what'll happen to us out there without weapons?"

"No, and I don't really care."

"I know," Flawn said. "You bastards never have cared—"

"Mind how you talk to the lieutenant," Ardwain said. He ground his rifle on the man's instep. Flawn gasped in pain.

"Enough of that, Sergeant," I said. "Flawn, you outlaws—"

"Outlaws. Crap!" Flawn said. "Excuse me. Sir, you are mistaken." He eyed Ardwain warily, his lip curled in contempt. "You brought me here as a convict for no reason other than my opposition to the CoDominium. You turned me loose with nothing. Nothing at all, Lieutenant. So we try to build something. Politics here aren't like at home. Or maybe they are, same thing, really, but here it's all out in the open. I managed something, and now you've come to take it away and send me off unarmed, with no more than the clothes on my back, and you expect me to be respectful." He glanced up at the CoDominium banner that flew high above the fort. "You'll excuse me if I don't show more enthusiasm."

"My orders are to disarm you, I said. "Now, will you talk your friends out of that bunker, or do we blow it in?"

"You'll let us go?"

"Yes."

"Your word of honor, Lieutenant?"

I nodded. "Certainly."

"I guess I can't ask for any other guarantees." Flawn looked at Sergeant Ardwain and grimaced. "I wish I dared. All right, let me talk to them."

By noon we had Fort Beersheba to ourselves. Flawn and the others had left. They insisted on carrying their wounded with them, even when Doc Crisp told them most would probably die on the road. The women had been a varied assortment, from teenagers to older women. All had gone with Flawn, to my relief and the troopers' disappointment.

Centurion Lieberman organized the defenses. He put men into the bunkers, set up revetments for the mortars, found material to repair the destroyed gates, stationed more men on the walls, got the mess tents put up, put the liquor we'd found into a strong room and posted guards over it—

I was feeling useless again.

In another hour there were parties coming up the road. I
sent Sergeant Ardwain and a squad down there to set up a
roadblock. We could cover them from the fort, and the mortars
were set up to spray the road. The river was about three
hundred meters away and one hundred meters below us, and
the fort had a good field of fire all along the road for a klick
in either direction. It was easy to see why this bluff had been
chosen for a strong point.

As parties of refugees came through, Ardwain disarmed them.
At first they went through, anyway, but after a while they
began to turn back rather than surrender their weapons. None
of them caused any problems, and I wouldn't let Ardwain
pursue any that turned away. We had far too few men to risk
any in something senseless like that.

"Good work," Falkenberg told me when I made the afternoon report. "We've made forty kilometers so far, and we've
got a couple of hours of daylight left. It's a bit hard to estimate how fast we'll be able to march."

"Yes, sir. The first party we disarmed had three Skyhawk
missiles. There were five here at the fort, but nobody got them
out in time to use them. Couple of guys who tried were killed
by the mortars. It doesn't look good for helicopters in this
area, though, not now that they're warned."

"Yes," Falkenberg said. "I suspected as much. We'll retire
the choppers for a while. You've done well, Slater. I caution
you not to relax, though. At the moment we've had no opposition worth mentioning, but that will change soon enough, and
after that there may be an effort to break past your position.
They don't seem to want to give up their weapons."

"No, sir." And who can blame them? I thought. Eric Flawn
had worried me. He hadn't seemed like an outlaw. I don't
know what I'd expected here at Beersheba. Kidnapped girls.
Scenes of rape and debauchery, I suppose. I'd never seen a
thieves' government in operation. Certainly I hadn't expected
what I'd found, a group of middle-aged men in control of
troops who looked a lot like ours, only theirs weren't very
well equipped.

"I understand you liberated some wine," Falkenberg said.

"Yes, sir."

"That'll help. Daily ration of no more than half a liter per
man, though."

"Sir? I wasn't planning on giving them any of it until you
got here."

"It's theirs, Slater," Falkenberg said. "You could get away

with holding on to it, but it wouldn't be best. It's your command. Do as you think you should, but if you want advice, give the troops half a liter each."

"Yes, sir." There's no regulation against drinking in the Line Marines, not even on duty. There are severe penalties for rendering yourself unfit for duty. Men have even been shot for it. "Half a liter with supper, then."

"I think it's wise," Falkenberg said. "Well, sounds as if you're doing well. We'll be along in a few days. Out."

There were a million other details. At noon I'd been startled to hear a trumpet sound mess call, and I went out to see who was doing it. A corporal I didn't recognize had a polished brass trumpet.

"Take me a few days to get everyone's name straight, Corporal," I said. "Yours?"

"Corporal Brady, sir."

"You play that well."

"Thank you, sir."

I looked at him again. I was sure his face was familiar. I thought I remembered that he'd been on Tri-v. Had his own band and singing group. Nightclub performances, at least one Tri-v special. I wondered what he was doing as an enlisted man in the Line Marines, but I couldn't ask. I tried to remember his real name, but that escaped me, too. It hadn't been Brady, I was sure of that. "You'll be sounding all calls here?"

"Yes, sir. Centurion says I'm to do it."

"Right. Carry on, Brady."

All through the afternoon the trumpet calls sent men to other duties. An hour before the evening meal there was a formal retreat. The CoDominium banner was hauled down by a color guard while all the men not on sentry watch stood in formation and Brady played Colors. As they folded the banner I remembered a lecture in Leadership class back at the Academy.

The instructor had been a dried-up Marine major with one real and one artificial arm. We were supposed to guess which was which, but we never did. The lecture I remembered had been on ceremonials. "Always remember," he'd said, "the difference between an army and a mob is tradition and discipline. You cannot enforce discipline on troops who do not feel that they are being justly treated. Even the man who is wrongly punished must feel that what he is accused of deserves punishment. You cannot enforce discipline on a mob, and so your men must be reminded that they are soldiers. Ceremonial is one of your most powerful tools for doing that. It is true that we are perpetually accused of wasting money. The Grand Senate annually wishes to take away our dress uniforms, our badges and colors, and all the so-called nonfunctional items we employ. They are fortunate, because they have never been able to do that. The day that they do, they will find themselves with an army that cannot defend them.

"Soldiers will complain about ceremonials and spit-and-polish, and such like, but they cannot live as an army without them. Men fight for pride, not for money, and no service that does not give them pride will last very long."

Maybe, I thought. But with a thousand things to do, I could have passed up a formal retreat on our first day at Fort Beersheba. I hadn't been asked about it. By the time I knew it was to happen, Lieberman had made all the arrangements and given the orders.

By suppertime we were organized for the night. Ardwain had collected about a hundred weapons, mostly obsolete rifles— there were even muzzle-loaders, handmade here on Arrarat— and passed nearly three hundred people through the roadblock.

We closed the road at dusk. Searchlights played along it, and we had a series of roadblocks made of log stacks. Ardwain and his troops were dug in where they could cover the whole road area, and we could cover them from the fort. It looked pretty good.

Tattoo sounded, and Fort Beersheba began to settle in for the night.

I made my rounds, looking into everything. The body-capacitance system the previous occupants had relied on was smashed when we blew open their bunker, but we'd brought our own surveillance gear. I didn't really trust passive systems, but I needn't have worried. Lieberman had guards in each of the towers. They were equipped with light-amplifying binoculars. There were more men to watch the IR screens.

"We're safe enough," Lieberman said. "If the lieutenant would care to turn in, I'll see the guard's changed properly."

He followed me back to my quarters. Hartz had already fixed the place up. There were fresh adobe patches over the bullet holes in the walls. My gear was laid out where I could get it quickly. Hartz had his cloak and pack spread out in the anteroom.

There was even coffee. A pot was kept warm over an alcohol lamp.

"You can leave it to us," Lieberman said.

Hartz grinned. "Sure. Lieutenants come out of the Academy without any calluses, and we make generals out of them."

"That may take some doing," I said. I invited Lieberman into my sitting room. There was a table there, with a scale model of the fort on it. Flawn had made it, but it hadn't done him much good. "Have a seat, Centurion. Coffee?"

"Just a little, sir. I'd best get back to my duties."

"Call me for the next watch, Centurion."

"If the lieutenant orders it."

"I just—what the hell, Lieberman, why don't you want me to take my turn on guard?"

"No need, sir. May I make a suggestion?"

"Sure."

"Leave it to us, sir. We know what we're doing."

I nodded and stared into my coffee cup. I didn't feel I was really in command here. They tell you everything in the Academy: leadership, communications, the precise form of a regimental parade, laser range-finding systems, placement of patches on uniforms, how to compute firing patterns for mortars, wine rations for the troops, how to polish a pair of boots, servicing recoilless rifles, delivery of calling cards to all senior officers within twenty-four hours of reporting to a new post, assembly and maintenance of helicopters, survival on rocks with poisonous atmosphere or no atmosphere at all, shipboard routines, and a million other details. You have to learn them all, and they get mixed up until you don't know what's trivial and what's important. They're just things you have to know to pass examinations. "You know what you're doing, Centurion, but I'm not sure I do."

"Sir, I've noticed something about young officers," Lieberman said. "They all take things too serious."

"Command's a serious business." Damn, I thought. That's pompous. Especially from a young kid to an older soldier.

He didn't take it that way. "Yes, sir. Too damned serious to let details get in the way. Lieutenant, if it was just things like posting the guard and organizing the defense of this place, the service wouldn't need officers. We can take care of that. What we need is somebody to tell us what the hell to do. Once that's done, we know *how*."

I didn't say anything. He looked at me closely, probably trying to figure out if I was angry. He didn't seem very worried.

"Take me, for instance," he said. "I don't know why the hell we came to this place, and I don't care. Everybody's got his reasons for joining up. Me, I don't know what else to do. I've found something I'm good at, and I can do it. Officers tell me where to fight, and that's one less damn thing to worry about."

The trumpet sounded outside. Last Post. It was the second time we'd heard it today. The first was when we'd buried our dead.

"Got my rounds to make," Lieberman said. "By your leave, sir."

"Carry on, Centurion." A few minutes later Hartz came in to help me get my boots off. He wouldn't hear of letting me turn in wearing them.

"We'll hold 'em off long enough to get your boots on, zur. Nobody's going to catch a Marine officer in the sack."

He'd sleep with his boots on so that I could take mine off. It didn't make a lot of sense, but I wasn't going to win any arguments with him about it. I rolled into the sack and stared at the ceiling. My first day of command. I was still thinking about that when I went to sleep.

The attacks started the next day. At first it was just small parties trying to force the roadblock, and they never came close to doing that. We could put too much fire onto them from the fort.

That night they tried the fort itself. There were a dozen mortars out there. They weren't very accurate, and our radar system worked fine. They would get off a couple of rounds, and then we'd have them backtracked to the origin point and our whole battery would drop in on them. We couldn't silence them completely, but we could make it unhealthy for the crews servicing their mortars, and after a while the fire slackened. There were rifle attacks all through the night, but nothing in strength.

"Just testing you," Falkenberg said in the morning when I reported to him. "We're pressing hard from this end. They'll make a serious try before long."

"Yes, sir. How are things at your end?"

"We're moving," Falkenberg said. "There's more resistance than the colonel expected, of course. With you stopping up their bolt hole, they've got no route to retreat through. Fight or give up—that's all the choice we left them. You can look for their real effort to break past you in a couple of days. By then we'll be close enough to really worry them."

He was right. By the fourth day we were under continuous attack from more than a thousand hostiles.

It was a strange situation. No one was really worried. We were holding them off. Our ammunition stocks were running low, but Lieberman's answer to that was to order the recruits to stop using their weapons. They were put to serving mortars and recoilless rifles, with an experienced NCO in charge to make sure there was a target worth the effort before they fired. The riflemen waited for good shots and made each one count.

As long as the ammunition held out, we were in no serious danger. The fort had a clear field of fire, and we weren't faced by heavy artillery. The best the enemy had was mortars, and our counterbattery radar and computer system was more than a match for that.

"No discipline," Lieberman said. "They got no discipline. Come in waves, run in waves, but they never press the attack. Damned glad there's no Marine deserters in that outfit. They'd have broke through if they'd had good leadership."

"I'm worried about our ammunition supplies," I said.

"Hell, Lieutenant, Cap'n Falkenberg will get here. He's never let anybody down yet."

"You've served with him before?"

"Yes, sir, in that affair on Domingo. Christian Johnny, we called him. He'll be here."

Everyone acted that way. It made the situation unreal. We were under fire. You couldn't put your head above the wall or outside the gate. Mortars dropped in at random intervals, sometimes catching men in the open and wounding them despite their body armor. We had four dead and nine more in the hospital bunker. We were running low on ammunition, and we faced better than ten-to-one odds, and nobody was worried.

"Your job is to look confident," Falkenberg had told me. Sure.

On the fifth day things were getting serious for Sergeant Ardwain and his men at the roadblock. They were running out of ammunition and water.

"Abandon it, Ardwain," I told him. "Bring your troops up here. We can keep the road closed with fire from the fort."

"Sir. I have six casualties that can't walk, sir."

"How many total?"

"Nine, sir—two walking and one dead."

Nine out of a total of twelve men. "Hold fast, Sergeant. We'll come get you."

"Aye, aye, sir."

I wondered who I could spare. There wasn't much doubt as to who was the most useless man on the post. I sent for Lieberman.

"Centurion, I want a dozen volunteers to go with me to relieve Ardwain's group. We'll take full packs and extra ammunition and supplies."

"Lieutenant—"

"Damn it, don't tell me you don't want me to go. You're capable enough. You told me that you need officers to tell you what to do, not how to do it. Fine. Your orders are to hold this post until Falkenberg comes. One last thing— you will not send or take any relief forces down the hill. I won't have this command further weakened. Is that understood?"

"Sir."

"Fine. Now get me a dozen volunteers."

I decided to go down the hill just after moonset. We got the packs loaded and waited at the gate. One of my volunteers was Corporal Brady. He stood at the gate, chatting with the sentry there.

"Quiet tonight," Brady said.

"They're still there, though," the sentry said. "You'll know soon enough. Bet you tomorrow's wine ration you don't make it down the hill."

"Done. Remember, you said *down* the hill. I expect you to save that wine for me."

"Yeah. Hey, this is a funny place, Brady."

"How's that?"

"A holy Joe planet, and no Marine chaplain."

"You want a chaplain?"

The sentry shrugged. He had a huge black beard that he fingered, as if feeling for lice. "Good idea, isn't it?"

"They're all right, but we don't need a chaplain. What we need is a good Satanist. No Satanist in this battalion."

"What do you need one of them for?"

Brady laughed. "Stands to reason, don't it? God's good, right? He'll treat you okay. It's the other guy you have to watch out for." He laughed again. "Got three days on bread and no wine for saying that once. Told it to Chaplain Major McCrory, back at Sector H.Q. He didn't appreciate it."

"Time to move out," I said. I shouldered my heavy pack.

"Do we run or walk, zur?" Hartz asked.

"Walk until they know we're there. And be quiet about it."

"Zur."

"Move out, Brady. Quietly."

"Sir." The sentry opened the gate, just a crack. Brady went through, then another trooper, and another. Nothing happened, and finally it was my turn. Hartz was last in the line.

The trail led steeply down the side of the cliff. It was about two meters wide, just a slanting ledge, really. We were halfway down when there was a burst of machine-gun fire. One of the troopers went down.

"Move like hell!" I said.

Two men grabbed the fallen trooper and hauled him along. We ran down the cliff face, jumping across shortcuts at the switchbacks. There was nothing we could see to shoot at, but more bullets sent chips flying from the granite cliff.

The walls above us spurted flame. It looked like the whole company was up there covering us. I hoped not. One of our recoilless men found a target and for a few moments we weren't under fire. Then the rifles opened up. Something zinged past my ear. Then I felt a hard punch in the gut and went down.

I lay there sucking air. Hartz grabbed one arm and shouted to another private. "Jersey! Lieutenant's down. Give me a hand."

"I'm all right," I said. I felt my stomach area. There wasn't any blood. "Armor stopped it. Just knocked the wind out of me." I was still gasping, and I couldn't get my breath.

They dragged me along to Ardwain's command post. "How would we explain to the Centurion if we didn't get you down?" Hartz asked.

The CP was a trench roofed over with ironwood logs. There were three wounded men at one end. Brady took our wounded trooper there. He'd been hit in both legs. Brady put tourniquets on them.

Hartz had his own ideas about first aid. He had a brandy flask. It was supposed to be a universal cure. After he poured two shots down me, he went over to the other end of the bunker to pass the bottle among the other wounded.

"Only three of them, Ardwain?" I said. I was still gasping for air. "I thought you had six."

"Six who cannot walk, sir. But three of them can still fight."

XI

"We're not going to get up that bluff. Not carrying wounded," I said.

"No, sir." Ardwain had runners carrying ammunition to his troopers. "We're dug in good, sir. With the reinforcements you brought, we'll hold out."

"We damned well have to," I said.

"Not so bad, sir. Most of our casualties came from recoilless and mortars. They've stopped using them. Probably low on ammunition."

"Let's hope they stay that way." I had another problem. The main defense for the roadblock was mortar fire from the fort. Up above they were running low on mortar shells. In another day we'd be on our own. No point in worrying about it, I decided. We'll just have to do the best we can.

The next day was the sixth we'd been in the fort. We were low on rations. Down at the roadblock we had nothing to eat but a dried meat that the men called "monkey." It didn't taste bad, but it had the peculiar property of expanding when you chewed it, so that after a while it seemed as if you had a mouthful of rubber bands. It was said that Line Marines could march a thousand kilometers if they had coffee, wine, and monkey.

We reached Falkenberg by radio at noon. He was still forty kilometers away, and facing the hardest fighting yet. They had to go through villages practically house by house.

"Can you hold?" he asked me.

"The rest of today and tonight, easily. By noon tomorrow we'll be out of mortar shells. Sooner, maybe. When that happens, our outpost down at the roadblock will be without support." I hadn't told him where I was.

"Can you hold until 1500 hours tomorrow?" he asked.

"The fort will hold. Don't know about the roadblock."

"We'll see what we can do," Falkenberg said. "Good luck."

"Christian Johnny'll get us out," Brady said.

"You know him?"

"Yes, sir. He'll get us out."

I wished I was as sure as he was.

They tried infiltrating during the night. I don't know how many crept up along the riverbank, but there were a lot of them. Some went on past us. The others moved in on our bunkers. The fighting was hand to hand, with knives and bayonets and grenades doing most of the work, until we got our foxholes clear and I was able to order the men down into them. Then I had Lieberman drop mortar fire in on our own positions for ten minutes. When it lifted, we went out to clear the area.

When morning came we had three more dead, and every man in the section was wounded. I'd got a grenade fragment in my left upper arm just below where the armor left off. It was painful, but nothing to worry about.

There were twenty dead in our area, and bloody trails were leading off where more enemies had crawled away.

An hour after dawn they rushed us again. The fort had few mortar shells left. We called each one in carefully. They couldn't spare us too much attention, though, because there was a general attack on the fort, as well. When there were moments of quiet in the firing around Fort Beersheba, we could hear more distant sounds to the east. Falkenberg's column was blasting its way through another village.

Ardwain got it just at noon. A rifle bullet in the neck. It looked bad. Brady dragged him into the main bunker and put a compress on. Ardwain's breath rattled in his throat, and his mouth oozed blood. That left Roff and Brady as NCOs, and Roff was immobile, with fragments through his left leg.

At 1230 hours we had four effectives, and no fire support from the fort. We'd lost the troops down by the riverbank, and we could hear movement there.

"They're getting past us, damn it!" I shouted. "All this for nothing! Hartz, get me Lieberman."

"Zur." Hartz was working one-handed. His right arm was in shreds. He insisted on staying with me, but I didn't count him as one of my effectives.

"Sergeant Roszak," the radio said.

"Where's Lieberman?"

"Dead, sir. I'm senior NCO."

"What mortar ammunition have you?"

"Fourteen rounds, sir."

"Drop three onto the riverbank just beyond us, and stand by to use more."

"Aye, aye, sir. One moment. There was silence. Then he said, "On the way."

"How is it up there?"

"We're fighting at the walls, sir. We've lost the north section, but the bunkers are covering that area."

"Christ. You'll need the mortars to hold the fort. But there's no point in holding that fort if the roadblock goes. Stand by to use the last mortar rounds at my command."

"Aye, aye, sir. We can hold."

"Sure you can." Sure.

I looked out through the bunker's firing slit. There were men coming up the road. Dozens of them. I had one clip left in my rifle, and I began trying to pick them off with slow fire. Hartz used his rifle with his left hand, firing one shot every two seconds, slow, aimed fire.

There were more shots from off to my left. Corporal Brady was in a bunker over there, but his radio wasn't working. Attackers moved toward his position. I couldn't hear any others of my command.

Suddenly Brady's trumpet sounded. The brassy notes cut through the battle noises. He played "To Arms!," then settled into the Line Marine march. "We've left blood in the dirt of twenty-five worlds—"

There was a movement in the bunker. Recruit Dietz, hit twice in the stomach, had dragged himself over to Sergeant Ardwain and found Ardwain's pistol. He crawled up to the firing slit and began shooting. He coughed blood with each round. Another trooper staggered out of the bush. He reeled like a drunk as he lurched toward the road. He carried a rack of grenades strung around his neck and threw them mechanically, staggering forward and throwing grenades. He had only one arm. He was hit a dozen times and fell, but his arm moved to throw the last grenade before he died.

More attackers moved toward Brady's bunker. The trumpet call wavered for a moment as Brady fired, and then the notes came as clear as ever.

"Roszak! I've got a fire mission," I said.

"Sir."

"Let me describe the situation down here." I gave him the positions of my CP, Brady's bunker, and the only other one I thought might have any of our troops in it. "Everyplace else is full of hostiles, and they're getting past us along the riverbank. I want you to drop a couple of mortar rounds forty meters down the road from the CP, just north of the road, but not too far north. Corporal Brady's in there and it would be a shame to spoil his concert."

"We hear him up here, sir. Wait one." There was silence. "On the way."

The mortar shells came in seconds later. Brady was still playing. I remembered his name now. It was ten years ago on Earth. He'd been a famous man until he dropped out of sight. Roszak had left his mike open, and in the background I could hear the men in the fort cheering wildly.

Roszak's voice came in my ears. "General order from battalion headquarters, sir. You're to stay in your bunkers. No one to expose himself. Urgent general order, sir."

I wondered what the hell Falkenberg was doing giving me general orders, but I used my command set to pass them along. I doubted if anyone heard, but it didn't matter. No one was going anywhere.

Suddenly the road exploded. The whole distance from fifty meters away down as far as I could see vanished in a line of explosions. They kept coming, pounding the road; then the riverbank was lifted in great clods of mud. The road ahead was torn to bits; then the pieces were lifted by another salvo, and another. I drove into the bottom of the bunker and held my ears while shells dropped all around me.

Finally it lifted. I could hear noises in my phones, but my ears were ringing, and I couldn't understand. It wasn't Roszak's voice. Finally it came through. "Do you need more fire support, Mr. Slater?"

"No. Lord, what shooting—"

"I'll tell the gunners that," Falkenberg said. "Hang on, Hal. We'll be another hour, but you'll have fire support from now on."

Outside, Brady's trumpet sang out another march.

XII

They sent me back to Garrison to get my arm fixed. There's a fungus infection on Arrarat that makes even minor wounds dangerous. I spent a week in surgery getting chunks cut out of my arm, then another week in regeneration stimulation. I wanted to get back to my outfit, but the surgeon wouldn't hear of it. He wanted me around to check up on the regrowth.

Sergeant Ardwain was in the next bay. It was going to take a while to get him back together, but he'd be all right. With Lieberman dead, Ardwain would be up for a Centurion's badges.

It drove me crazy to be in Garrison while my company, minus its only officer and both its senior NCOs, was out at Fort Beersheba. The day they let me out of sick bay I was ready to mutiny, but there wasn't any transportation, and Major Lorca made it clear that I was to stay in Garrison until the surgeon released me. I went to my quarters in a blue funk.

The place was all fixed up. Private Hartz was there grinning at me. His right arm was in an enormous cast, bound to his chest with what seemed like a mile of gauze.

"How did you get out before I did?" I asked him.

"No infection, zur. I poured brandy on the wounds." He winced. "It was a waste, but there was more than enough for the few of us left."

There was another surprise. Irina Swale came out of my bedroom.

"Miss Swale has been kind enough to help with the work here, zur," Hartz said. He seemed embarrassed. "She insisted, zur. If the lieutenant will excuse me, I have laundry to pick up, zur."

I grinned at him and he left. Now what? I wondered. "Thanks."

"It's the least I could do for Arrarat's biggest hero," Irina said.

"Hero? Nonsense—"

"I suppose it's nonsense that my father is giving you the military medal, and that Colonel Harrington has put in for something else; I forget what, but it can't be approved here—it has to come from Sector Headquarters."

"News to me," I said. "And I still don't think—"

"You don't have to. Aren't you going to ask me to sit down? Would you like something to drink? We have everything here. Private Hartz is terribly efficient."

"So are you. I'm not doing well, am I? Please have a seat. I'd get you a drink, but I don't know where anything is."

"And you couldn't handle the bottles, anyway. I'll get it." She went into the other room and came out with two glasses. Brandy for me and that Jericho wine she liked. Hartz at work, I thought. I'll be drinking that damned brandy the rest of my life.

"It was pretty bad, wasn't it?" she said. She sat on the couch that had appeared while I was gone.

"Bad enough." Out of my original ninety, there were only twelve who hadn't been wounded. Twenty-eight dead, and another dozen who wouldn't be back on duty for a long time. "But we held." I shook my head. "Not bragging, Irina. Amazed, mostly. We held."

"I've been wondering about something," she said. "I asked Louis Bonneyman, and he wouldn't answer me. Why did you have to hold the fort? It was much the hardest part of the campaign, wasn't it? Why didn't Captain Falkenberg do it?"

"Had other things to do, I suppose. They haven't let me off drugs long enough to learn anything over in sick bay. What's happening out there?"

"It went splendidly," she said. "The Harmony militia are in control of the whole river. The boats are running again, grain prices have fallen here in the city—"

"You don't sound too happy."

"Is it that obvious?" She sat quietly for a moment. She seemed to be trying to control her face. Her lips were trembling. "My father says you've accomplished your mission. He won't let Colonel Harrington send you out to help the other farmers. And the River Pack weren't the worst of the convict governments! In a lot of ways they weren't even so bad. I thought . . . I'd hoped you could go south, to the farmlands, where things are really bad, but Hugo has negotiated a steady supply of grain and he says it's none of our business."

"You're certainly anxious to get us killed."

She looked at me furiously. Then she saw my grin. "By the

way," she said, "you're expected at the palace for dinner tonight. I've already cleared it with the surgeon. And this time I expect you to come! All those plans for my big party, and it was nothing but a trick your Captain Falkenberg had planned! You will come, won't you? Please?"

We ate alone. Governor Swale was out in the newly taken territory trying to set up a government that would last. Irina's mother had left him years before, and her only brother was a Navy officer somewhere in Pleiades Sector.

After dinner I did what she probably expected me to. I kissed her, then held her close to me and hoped to go to something a bit more intimate. She pushed me away. "Hal, please."

"Sorry."

"Don't be. I like you, Hal. It's just that—"

"Deane Knowles," I said.

She gave me a puzzled look. "No, of course not. But . . . I do like your friend Louis. Can't we be friends, Hal? Do we have to—"

"Of course we can be friends."

I saw a lot of her in the next three weeks. Friends. I found myself thinking about her when I wasn't with her, and I didn't like that. The whole thing's silly, I told myself. Junior officers have no business getting involved with Governors' daughters. Nothing can come of it, and you don't want anything to come of it to begin with. Your life's complicated enough as it is.

I kept telling myself that right up to the day the surgeon told me I could rejoin my outfit. I was glad to go.

It was still my company. I hadn't been with most of them at all, and I'd been with the team at the fort only a few days, but A Company was mine. Every man in the outfit thought so. I wondered what I'd done right. It didn't seem to me that I'd made any good decisions, or really any at all.

"Luck," Deane told me. "They think you're lucky."

That explained it. Line Marines are probably the most superstitious soldiers in history. And we'd certainly had plenty of luck.

I spent the next six weeks honing the troops into shape. By that time Ardwain was back, with Centurion's badges. He was posted for light duty only, but that didn't stop him from working the troops until they were ready to drop. We had more recruits, recently arrived convicts, probably men who'd been part of the River Pack at one time. It didn't matter. The Marine

Machine takes over, and if it doesn't break you, you come out a Marine.

Falkenberg had a simple solution to the problem of deserters. He offered a reward, no questions asked, to anyone who brought in a deserter—and a larger reward for anyone bringing in the deserter's head. It wasn't an original idea, but it was effective.

Or had been effective. As more weeks went by with nothing to do but make patrols along the river, drill and train, stand formal retreat and parades and inspections, men began to think of running.

They also went berserk. They'd get drunk and shoot a comrade. Steal. We couldn't drill them forever, and when we gave them any time off, they'd get the bug.

The day the main body had reached Fort Beersheba, the 501st had been combat-weary, with a quarter of its men on the casualty list. It was an exhausted battalion, but it had high spirits. Now, a few months later, it was up to strength, trained to perfection, well-organized and well-fed—and unhappy.

I found a trooper painting I.H.T.F.P. on the orderly room wall. He dropped the paint bucket and stood to attention as I came up.

"And what does that mean, Hora?"

He stood straight as a ramrod. "Sir, it means 'I Have Truly Found Paradise.'"

"And what's going to happen to you if Sergeant Major truly finds Private Hora painting on the orderly room wall?"

"Cells, Lieutenant."

"If you're lucky. More likely you'll get to dig a hole and live in it a week. Hora, I'm going to the club for a drink. I don't expect to see any paint on that wall when I come back."

Deane laughed when I told him about it. "So they're doing that already. 'I hate this fucking place.' He means it, too."

"Give us another six weeks and I'll be painting walls," I said. "Only I'll put mine on the Governor's palace."

"You'll have to wait your turn," Deane said.

"Goddamn it, Deane, what can we do? The NCOs have gotten so rough I think I'll have to start noticing it, but if we relax discipline at all, things will really come apart."

"Yeah. Have you spoken to Falkenberg about it?"

"Sure I have," I told him. "But what can he do? What we need is some combat, Deane. I never thought I'd say that. I thought that was all garbage that they gave us at the Academy, that business about *le cafard* and losing more men to it than to an enemy, but I believe it now."

"Cheer up," Deane said. "Louis is officer of the day, and I just heard the word from him. We've got a break in the routine. Tomorrow Governor Hugo Swale, Hisself, is coming to pay a visit to the gallant troops of the 501st. He's bringing your medal, I make no doubt."

"How truly good," I said. "I'd rather he brought us a good war."

"Give him time," Deane said. "The way those damned merchants from Harmony are squeezing the farmers, they're all ready to revolt."

"Just what we need. A campaign to put down the farmers," I said. "Poor bastards. They get it from everybody, don't they? Convicts that call themselves tax collectors. Now you say the Harmony merchants—"

"Yeah," Deane said. "Welcome to the glory of CoDominium Service."

Sergeant Major Ogilvie's baritone rang out across the Fort Beersheba parade ground. "Battalion, *attenhut!* A Company color guard, front and center, *march!*"

That was a surprise. Governor Swale had just presented me with the military medal, which isn't the Earth, but I was a bit proud of it. Now our color guard marched across the hard adobe field to the reviewing stand.

"Attention to orders," Ogilvie said. "For conspicuous gallantry in the face of the enemy, A Company, 501st Provisional Battalion, is awarded the Unit Citation of Merit. By order of Rear Admiral Sergei Lermontov, Captain of the Fleet, Crucis Sector Headquarters.

"Company, *pass in review!*"

Bits of cloth and metal, and men will die for them, I thought. The old military game. It's all silly. And we held our heads high as we marched past the reviewing stand.

Falkenberg had found five men who could play bagpipes, or claimed they could—how can you tell if they're doing it right?—and they had made their own pipes. Now they marched around the table in the officers' mess at Fort Beersheba. Stewards brought whiskey and brandy.

Governor Hugo Swale sat politely, trying not to show any distress as the pipers thundered past him. Eventually they stopped. "I think we should join the ladies," Swale said. He looked relieved when Falkenberg stood.

We went into the lounge. Irina had brought another girl, a visitor from one of the farm areas. She was about nineteen,

I thought, with red-brown hair and blue eyes. She would have been beautiful if she didn't have a perpetual haunted look. Irina had introduced her as Kathryn Malcolm.

Governor Swale was obviously embarrassed to have her around. He was a strange little man. There was no resemblance between him and Irina, nothing that would make you think he was her father. He was short and dumpy, almost completely bald, with wrinkles on his high forehead. He had a quick nervous manner of speaking and gesturing. He so obviously disliked Kathryn that I think only the bagpipes could have driven him to want to get back to her company. I wondered why. There'd been no chance to talk to any of them at dinner.

We sat around the fireplace. Falkenberg gave a curt nod, and all the stewards left except Monitor Lazar, Falkenberg's own orderly. Lazar brought a round of drinks and went off into the pantry.

"Well. Here's to A Company and its commander," Falkenberg said. I sat embarrassed as the others stood and lifted their glasses.

"Good work, indeed," Hugo Swale said. "Thanks to this young man, the Jordan Valley is completely pacified. It will take a long time before there's any buildup of arms here again. I want to thank you gentlemen for doing such a thorough job."

I'd had a bit too much to drink with dinner, and there'd been brandy afterward, and the pipers with their wild war sounds. My head was buzzing. "Perhaps too thorough," I muttered as the others sat down. I honestly don't know whether I wanted the others to hear me or not. Deane and Louis threw me sharp looks.

"What do you mean, Hal?" Irina asked.

"Nothing."

"Spit it out," Falkenberg said. The tone made it an order.

"I've a dozen good men in cells and three more in a worse kind of punishment, half my company is on extra duty, and the rest of them are going slowly mad," I said. "If we'd left a bit of the fighting to do, we'd at least have employment." I tried to make it a joke.

Governor Swale took it seriously. "It's as much a soldier's job to prevent trouble as to fight," he said.

You pompous ass, I thought. But of course he was right.

"There's plenty that needs doing," Kathryn Malcolm said. "If your men are spoiling to fight somebody, loan them to us for a while." She wasn't joking at all.

Governor Swale wasn't pleased at all. "That will do, Kathryn. You know we can't do that."

"And why not?" she demanded. "You're supposed to be Governor of this whole planet, but the only people you care about are the merchants in Harmony—those sanctimonious hymn-singers! You know the grain they're buying is stolen. Stolen from us, by gangsters who claim to be our government, and if we don't give them what they want, they take it anyway, and kill everyone who tries to stop them. And then you buy it from them!"

"There is nothing I can do," Swale protested. "I don't have enough troops to govern the whole planet. The Grand Senate explicitly instructed me to deal with local governments—"

"The way you did with the River Pack," Kathryn said. Her voice was bitter. "All they did was try to make some money by charging tolls for river traffic. They wouldn't deal with your damned merchants, so you sent the Marines to bargain with them. Just how many people in the Jordan Valley thanked you for that, Governor? Do they think you're their liberator?"

"Kathryn, that's not fair," Irina protested. "There are plenty of people glad to be free of the River Pack. You shouldn't say things like that."

"All I meant was that the River Pack wasn't so bad. Not compared to what *we* have to live with. But his Excellency isn't concerned about us, because his merchants can buy their grain at low prices. He doesn't care that we've become slaves."

Swale's lips tightened, but he didn't say anything.

"Local governments," Kathryn said. "What you've done, Governor, is recognize one gang. There's another gang, too, and both of them collect taxes from us! It's bad enough with just one, but it can't even protect us from the other! If you won't give us our land back, can't you at least put down the rival gangsters so we only have one set of crooks stealing from us?"

Swale kept his voice under control. He was elaborately polite as he said, "There is nothing we can do, Miss Malcolm. I wish there were. I suggest you people help yourselves."

"That isn't fair, either," Irina said. "You know it isn't. They didn't ask for all those convicts to be sent here. I think Kathryn has a very good idea. Loan her the 501st. Once those hills are cleaned out and the gangsters are disarmed, the farmers can protect themselves. Can't they, Kathryn?"

"I think so. We'd be ready, this time."

"See? And Hal says his men are spoiling for a good fight. Why not let them do it?"

"Irina, I have to put up with that from Miss Malcolm because she is a guest, but I do not have to take it from you, and I will not. Captain, I thought I was an invited guest on this post."

Falkenberg nodded. "I think we'd best change the subject," he said.

There was an embarrassed silence. Then Kathryn got up and went angrily to the door. "You needn't bother to see me to my room," she said. "I can take care of myself. I've had to do it often enough. I'm not surprised that Captain Falkenberg isn't eager to lead his troops into the hills. I notice that he sent a newly commissioned lieutenant to do the tough part of Governor Swale's dirty work. I'm not surprised at all that he doesn't want any more fighting." She left, slamming the door behind her.

Falkenberg acted as if he hadn't heard her. I don't suppose there was anything else he could do. The party didn't last much longer.

I went to my rooms alone. Deane and Louis offered to stay with me, but I didn't want them. I told them I'd had enough celebrating.

Hartz had left the brandy bottle on the table, and I poured myself another drink, although I didn't want it. The table was Arrarat ironwood, and God knows how the troops had managed to cut planks out of it. My company had built it, and a desk, and some other furniture, and put them in my rooms while I was in hospital. I ran my hand along the polished tabletop.

She should never have said that, I thought. And I expect it's my fault. I remembered Irina saying much the same thing back in Garrison, and I hadn't protested. My damned fault. Falkenberg never explained anything about himself, and I'd never learned why he hadn't come with us the night we attacked the fort, but I was damned sure it wasn't cowardice. Louis and Deane had straightened me out about that. No one who'd been with him on the march up the river could even suspect it.

And why the hell didn't I tell Irina that? I wondered. Cocky kid, trying to impress the girl. Too busy being proud of himself to—

There was a knock on the door. "Come in," I said.

It was Sergeant Major Ogilvie. There were some others in the hall. "Yes, Sergeant Major?"

"If we could have a word with the lieutenant. We have a problem, sir."

"Come in."

Ogilvie came inside. When his huge shoulders were out of the doorway, I saw Monitor Lazar and Kathryn Malcolm behind him. They all came in, and Kathryn stood nervously, her hands twisted together. "It's all my fault," she said.

Ogilvie ignored her. "Sir, I have to report that Monitor Lazar has removed certain orders from the battalion files without authorization."

"Why tell me?" I asked. "He's Captain Falkenberg's orderly."

"Sir, if you'll look at the papers. He showed them to this civilian. If you say we should report it to the captain, we'll have to." Ogilvie's voice was carefully controlled. He handed me a bound stack of papers.

They were orders from Colonel Harrington to Falkenberg as commander of the 501st, and they were dated the first day we'd arrived on Arrarat. I'd never seen them myself. No reason I should, unless Falkenberg were killed and I had to take over as his deputy.

Lazar stood at rigid attention. He wasn't looking at me, but seemed fascinated with a spot on the wall above me.

"You say Miss Malcolm has read these, Sergeant Major?"

"Yes, sir."

"Then it will do no harm if I read them, I suppose." I opened the order book. The first pages were general orders commanding Falkenberg to organize the 501st. There was more, about procedures for liaison with Major Lorca and the Garrison supply depot. I'd seen copies of all those. "Why the devil did you think Miss Malcolm would be interested in this stuff, Lazar?" I asked.

"Not that, sir," Ogilvie said. "Next page."

I thumbed through the book again. There it was.

Captain John Christian Falkenberg, Commanding Officer, 501st Provisional Battalion of Line Marines:

These orders are written confirmation of verbal orders issued in conference with above-named officer.

2. The 501st Bn. is ordered to occupy Fort Beersheba at earliest possible moment consistent with safety of the command and at the discretion of Bn. C.O.

Immediate airborne assault on Fort Beersheba is authorized, provided that assault risks no more than 10% of effective strength of 501st Bn.

Any assault on Fort Beersheba in advance of main body of 501st Bn. shall be commanded by officer other than

CO 501st Bn., and request of Captain Falkenberg to accompany assault and return to Bn. after Fort Beersheba is taken is expressly denied.

NOTE: It is the considered judgment of undersigned that officers assigned to 501st would not be competent to organize Bn. and accomplish main objective of pacification of Jordan Valley without supervision of experienced officer. It is further considered judgment of undersigned that secondary objective of early capture of Fort Beersheba does not justify endangering main mission of occupation of Jordan Valley. Captain Falkenberg is therefore ordered to refrain from exposing himself to combat risks until such time as primary mission is assured.

By Order of Planetary Military Commander

Nicholas Harrington, Colonel
CoDominium Marines

"Lazar, I take it you were listening to our conversation earlier," I said.

"No way to avoid it, sir. The lady was shouting." Lazar's expression didn't change.

I turned the book over and over in my hands. "Sergeant Major."

"Sir."

"I'm finished with this order book. Would you please see that it's returned to the battalion safe? Also, I think I forgot to log it out. You may do as you see fit about that."

"Sir."

"Thank you. You and Lazar may go now. I see no reason why the captain should be disturbed because I wanted a look at the order book."

"Yes, sir. Let's go, Monitor." Ogilvie started to say something else, but he stopped himself. They left, closing the door behind them.

"That was nice of you," Kathryn said.

"About all I could do," I said. "Would you like a drink?"

"No, thank you. I feel like a fool—"

"You're not the only one. I was just thinking the same thing, and for about the same reasons, when Ogilvie knocked. Won't you sit down? I suppose we should open the door."

"Don't be silly." She pulled a chair up to the big table. She was wearing a long plaid skirt, like a very long kilt, with a shiny blouse of some local fabric, and a wool jacket that didn't close at the front. Her hair was long, brown with red in it, but I thought it might be a wig. A damned pretty girl, I thought. But there was that haunted look in her eyes, and her hands were scarred, tiny scars that showed regeneration therapy by unskilled surgeons.

"I think Irina said you're a farmer. You don't look like a farmer."

She didn't smile. "I own a farm . . . or did. It's been confiscated by the government—one of our governments." Her voice was bitter. "The Mission Hills Protective Association. A gang of convicts. We used to fight them. My grandfather and my mother and my brother and my fiancé were all killed fighting them. Now we don't do anything at all."

"How many of these gangsters are there?"

She shrugged. "I guess the Protectionists have about four thousand. Something like that, anyway. Then there is the True Brotherhood. They have only a few hundred, maybe a thousand. No one really knows. They aren't really very well organized."

"Seems like they'd be no problem."

"They wouldn't be, if we could deal with them, but the Protective Association keeps our farmers disarmed and won't let us go on commando against the Brotherhood. They're afraid we'll throw the Association out, as well. The Brotherhood isn't anything real—they're closer to savages than human beings—but we can't do anything about them because the Association won't let us."

"And how many of you are there?"

"There are twenty thousand farmers in the Valley," she said. "And don't tell me we ought to be able to run both gangs off. I know we should be able to. But we tried it, and it didn't work. Whenever they raided one of our places, we'd turn out to chase them down, but they'd run into the hills, where it would take weeks to find them. Then they'd wait until we came down to grow crops again, then come down and kill everyone who resisted them, families and all."

"Is that what happened to your grandfather?"

"Yes. He'd been one of the Valley leaders. They weren't really trying to loot his place; they just wanted to kill him. I tried to organize resistance after that, and then—" She looked at her hands. "They caught me. I guess I will have that drink, after all."

"There's only brandy, I'm afraid. Or coffee."

"Brandy is all right."

I got another glass and poured. Her hands didn't shake as she lifted it.

"Aren't you going to ask?" she said. "Everyone wants to know, but they're afraid to ask." She shuddered. "They don't want to embarrass me. Embarrass!"

"Look, you don't want to talk about—"

"I don't want to, but I have to. Can you understand that?"

"Yes."

"Hal, there's very little you can imagine that they didn't do to me. The only reason I lived through it was that they wanted me to live. Afterward, they put me in a cage in the village square. As an example. A warning."

"I'd have thought that would have the opposite effect." I was trying to speak calmly, but inside I was boiling with hatred.

"No. I wish it had. It would have been worth it. Maybe— I don't know. The second night I was there, two men who'd been neighbors killed one of their guards and got me out. The Protectionists shot thirty people the next day in reprisal." She looked down at her hands. "My friends got me to a safe place. The doctor wasn't very well trained, they tell me. He left scars. If they could see what I was like when I got to him, they wouldn't say that."

I didn't know what to say. I didn't trust myself to say anything. I wanted to take her in my arms and hold her, not anything else, just hold her and protect her. And I wanted to get my hands on the people who'd done this, and on anyone who could have stopped it and didn't. My God, what are soldiers for, if not to put a stop to things like that? But all I could do was pour her another drink. I tried to keep my voice calm. "What will you do now?"

"I don't know. When Father Reedy finally let me leave his place, I went to Harmony. I guess I hoped I could get help. But . . . Hal, why won't Governor Swale do something? Anything?"

"More a matter of why should he," I said. "God, Kathryn, how can I say it? From his view, things are quiet. He can report that all's well here. They don't promote troublemakers in BuColonial, and Hugo Swale doesn't strike me as the kind of man who wants to retire on Ararat." I drained my brandy glass. "Maybe I'm not being fair to him. Somehow I don't even want to be."

"But you'd help us if you could. Wouldn't you?"

"My God, yes. At least you're safe now."

She had a sad little smile. "Yes, nothing but a few scars.

Come here. Please." She stood. I went to her. "Put your hands on my shoulders," she said.

I reached out to her. She stood rigidly. I could feel her trembling as I touched her.

"It happens every time," she said. "Even now, and I like you. I . . . Hal, I'd give anything if I could just relax and let you hold me. But I can't. It's all I can do to sit here and talk to you."

"Then I'd better let you go."

"No. Please. Please understand. I like you. I want to talk with you. I want to show myself there are men I can trust. Just . . . don't expect too much . . . not for a while. I keep telling myself I'm going to get over it. I don't want to be alone, but I'm afraid to be with anyone, and I'm going to get over that."

XIII

We had more weeks of parades and training. Falkenberg had a new scheme. He bought two hundred mules and assigned my company the job of learning to live with them. The idea was to increase our marching capability by using pack mules, and to teach the men to hang on to the pack saddles so they could cover more kilometers each day. It worked fine, but it only increased the frustration because there was nothing to march toward.

Governor Swale had gone back to Garrison, but Irina and Kathryn stayed as guests of the battalion. The men were pleased to have them on the post, and there was much less of a problem with discipline. They particularly adopted Kathryn. She was interested in everything they did, and the troops thought of her as a mascot. She was young and vulnerable, and she didn't talk down to them, and they were half in love with her.

I was more than that. I saw so much of her that Falkenberg thought it worthwhile to remind me that the service does not permit lieutenants to marry. That isn't strictly true, of course, but it might as well be. There's no travel allowance and it takes an appeal to Saint Peter or perhaps an even higher level to get married quarters. The rule is, "Captains may marry, Majors should marry, Colonels must marry," and there aren't many exceptions to it.

"Not much danger of that," I told him.

"Yes?" He raised an eyebrow. It was an infuriating gesture. I blurted out her story.

He only nodded. "I was aware of most of it, Mr. Slater."

"How in God's name can you be so cool about it?" I demanded. "I know you don't like her after that outburst—"

"Miss Malcolm has been very careful to apologize and to credit you with the explanation," Falkenberg said. "And the next time you take the order book out of the safe, I'll expect you to log

119

it properly. Now tell me why we have three men of your company sleeping under their bunks without blankets."

He didn't really want an explanation, of course, and for that matter he probably already knew. There wasn't much about the battalion that he didn't know. It made a smooth change of subject, but I wasn't having any. I told him, off the record, what the charges would have been if I'd officially heard what the men had done. "Centurion Ardwain preferred not to report it," I said. "Captain, I still cannot understand how you can be so calm when you know that not two hundred kilometers from here—"

"Mr. Slater, I remain calm because at the moment there is very little I can do. What do you want? That we lead the 501st in a mutiny? If it is any comfort to you, I do not think the situation will last. It is my belief that Governor Swale is living in a fool's paradise. You cannot deal with criminal gangs on any permanent basis, and I believe the situation will explode. Until it does, there is not one damned thing we can do, and I prefer not to be reminded of my helplessness."

"But, sir—"

"But nothing, Mr. Slater. Shut up and soldier."

Falkenberg had guessed right. Although we didn't know it, about the time we had that conversation the Protective Association had decided to raise the price of grain. Two weeks later they hiked the price again and held up the shipments to show the Governor they meant it.

It wasn't long after that the Governor paid another visit to Fort Beersheba.

Deane Knowles found me in the club. "His Excellency has arrived," he said. "He's really come with full kit this time. He's brought Colonel Harrington and a whole company of militia."

"What the devil are they for?" I asked.

"Search me."

"I thought you knew everything, well, well. I suppose we will know soon enough. There's Officers' Call."

The Governor, Colonel Harrington, and Falkenberg were all in the staff conference room. There was also a colonel of militia. He didn't look very soldierly. His uniform was baggy, and he had a bulge around his middle. The Governor introduced him as Colonel Trevor.

"I'll come right to the point, gentlemen," Swale said. "Due to certain developments in the southern areas, I am no longer confident that food supply for the cities of Harmony and

Garrison is assured. The local government down there has not negotiated in good faith. It's time to put some pressure on them."

"In other words," Colonel Harrington said, "he wants to send the Marines down to bash heads so the Harmony merchants won't have to pay so much."

"Colonel, that remark was not called for," Governor Swale said.

"Certainly it was." There was no humor in Harrington's voice. "If we can send my lads down to get themselves killed, we can tell them why they're going. It's hardly a new mission for the Line Marines."

"Your orders are to hold the cities," Swale said. "That cannot be done without adequate food supplies. I think that justifies using your troops for this campaign."

"Sure it does," Harrington said. "And after the CD pulls both of us out of here, what happens? Doesn't that worry you a bit, Colonel Trevor?"

"The CoDominium won't abandon Arrarat." Trevor sounded very positive.

"You're betting a lot on that," Colonel Harrington told him.

"If you two are quite through," Swale said. "Captain, how soon can your battalion be ready to march?"

Falkenberg looked to Colonel Harrington. "Are we to hold the Jordan area, as well, sir?"

"You won't need much here," Harrington said. "The militia can take over now."

"And what precisely are we to accomplish in the southern farm area?" Falkenberg asked.

"I just told you," Swale said. "Go down and put some pressure on the Protective Association so they'll see reason."

"And how am I to do that?"

"For heaven's sake, Falkenberg, it's a punitive expedition. Go hurt them until they're ready to give in."

"Burn farms and towns. Shoot livestock. Destroy transport systems. That sort of thing?"

"Well . . . I'd rather you didn't do it that way."

"Then, Governor, exactly what am I to do?" Falkenberg demanded. "I remind you that the Protective Association is itself an occupying power. They don't really care what we do to the farmers. They don't work that land; they merely expropriate from those who do."

"Then confine your punitive actions to the Protective Association—" Swale's voice trailed off.

"I do not even know how to identify them, sir. I presume

that anyone I find actually working the land is probably not one of the criminal element, but I can hardly shoot everyone who happens to be idle at the moment I pass through."

"You needn't be sarcastic with me, *Captain.*"

"Sir, I am trying to point out the difficulties inherent in the orders you gave me. If I have been impertinent, you have my apology."

Sure you do, I thought. Deane and Louis grinned at each other and at me. Then we managed to get our faces straight. I wondered what Falkenberg was trying to do. I found out soon enough.

"Then what the devil do you suggest?" Swale demanded.

"Governor, there is a way I can assure you a reasonable and adequate grain supply. It requires your cooperation. Specifically, you must withdraw recognition from the Protective Association."

"And recognize whom? An unorganized bunch of farmers who couldn't hold on to the territory in the first place? Captain, I have sympathy for those people, even if all of you here do suspect me of being a monster with no feelings. My sympathy is of no matter. I must feed the people of Harmony, and to do that I'll deal with the devil himself if that's what it takes."

"And you very nearly have," I muttered.

"What's that, Lieutenant Slater?"

"Nothing, Governor. Excuse me."

"I expect I know what you said. Captain, let's suppose I do what you ask and withdraw recognition from the Protective Association. Now what do I do? We are not in the democracy-building business. My personal sympathies may well lie with what we are pleased to call 'free and democratic institutions,' but I happen to be an official of the CoDominium, not of the United States. So, by the way, do you. If this planet had been settled by Soviets, we wouldn't even be having this conversation. There would be an assured grain supply, and no nonsense about it."

"I hardly think the situations are comparable," Colonel Harrington said.

"Nor I," Trevor added. That surprised me.

"I ask again, what do we do?" the Governor said.

"Extend CoDominium protection to the area," Harrington said. "It needn't be permanent. I make no doubt that Colonel Trevor's people have friends among the farmers. *We* may not be in the democracy-building business, but there are plenty who'd like to try."

"You are asking for all-out war on the Protective Association," Swale said. "Colonel Harrington, have you any idea of what that will cost? The Senate is very reluctantly paying the basic costs of keeping these Marines on Arrarat. They have not sent one deci-credit to pay for combat actions. How am I supposed to *pay* for this war?"

"You'll just have to tax the grain transactions, that's all," Harrington said.

"I can't do that."

"You're going to have to do it. Captain Falkenberg is right. We can drive out the Protective Association—with enough local cooperation—but we sure as hell can't grow wheat for you. I suppose we could exterminate everyone in the whole damned valley and repopulate it—

"Now *you're* being impertinent."

"My apologies," Harrington said. "Governor, just what *do* you want? Those farmers aren't going to grow crops just to have a bunch of gangsters take the profits. They'll move out first, or take the land out of cultivation. Then what happens to your grain supply?"

"The situation is more complex than you think, Colonel. Believe me, it is. Your business is war and violence. Mine is politics, and I tell you that things aren't always what they seem. The Protective Association can keep Harmony supplied with grain at a reasonable price. That's what we must have, and it's what you're going to get for me. Now you tell me that my only alternatives are a war I can't pay for, or starvation in the city. Neither is acceptable. I order you to send an expeditionary force to Allansport. It will have the limited objective of demonstrating our intent and putting sufficient pressure on the Protective Association to make them reasonable, and that is the whole objective."

Harrington studied his fingernails for a moment. "Sir, I cannot accept the responsibility."

"Damn you. Captain Falkenberg, you will—"

"I can't accept the responsibility, either, Governor."

"Then, by God, I'll have Colonel Trevor lead it. Trevor, if you say you can't accept responsibility, I damned well know a dozen militia officers who can."

"Yes, sir. Who'll command the Marines sir? They won't take orders from me. Not directly."

"The lieutenants will—" He stopped, because one by one, Deane, Louis, and I all shook our heads.

"This is blackmail! I'll have every one of you cashiered!"

Colonel Harrington laughed. "Now, you know, I really doubt

that. Me you might manage to get at. But junior officers for refusing an assignment their colonel turned down? Try peddling that to Admiral Lermontov and he'll laugh like hell."

Swale sat down. He struggled for a moment until he was in control of his voice. "Why are you doing this?"

Colonel Harrington shook his head slowly. "Governor, everything you said about the service is true. We're used. They use us to bash heads so that some senator's nephew can make a mega-credit. They hand people a raw deal and then call on us to make the victims stay in the game. Most of the time we have to take it. It doesn't mean we like it much. Once in a while, just every now and then, the Fleet gets a chance to put something right after you civilians mess it up. We don't pass up such chances." Harrington's voice had been quiet, but now he let it rise slightly. "Governor, just what the hell do you think men become soldiers for? So that you can get promoted to a cushy job?"

"I have told you, I would like to help those farmers. I can't do it. Cannot you understand? We can't *pay* for a long campaign. *Can't.* Not won't. Can't."

"Yes, sir," Colonel Harrington said. "I expect I'd better get back to Garrison. The staff's going to have to work out a pretty strict rationing plan."

"You think you have won," the Governor said. "Not yet, Colonel. Not yet. Colonel Trevor, I asked you to put a battalion of militia on riverboats. How long will it take for them to get here?"

"Be here tomorrow, sir."

"When they arrive, I want you to have made arrangements for more fuel and supplies. We are taking that battalion to Allansport, where I will personally direct operations. I've no doubt we can make the Protective Association see reason. As to the rest of you, you will sit in this fort and rot for all I care. Good afternoon, gentlemen."

I told Kathryn about the conference when I met her for supper that night. She listened with bewilderment.

"I don't understand, Hal," she finally blurted. "All that fuss about costs. *We'd* pay for the campaign and be happy to do it."

"Do you think the Governor knows that?" I asked.

"Of course he knows it. I've told him, and I've brought him offers from some of the other farmers. Don't you remember I asked him to loan us the 501st?"

"Sure, but you weren't serious."

"I wasn't then, but it sounded like such a good idea that later on we really tried to hire you. He wasn't interested."

"Wasn't interested in what?" Louis Bonneyman asked. "Is this an intimate conversation, or may I join you?"

"Please do," Kathryn said. "We're just finishing—"

"I've had my dinner, also," Louis said. "But I'll buy you a drink. Hal, did you ever think old Harrington had that kind of guts?"

"No. Surprised me. So what happens next?"

"Beats me," Louis said. "But I'll give you a hint. I just finished helping Sergeant Major cut orders putting this whole outfit on full field alert as of reveille tomorrow."

"Figures. I wonder just how much trouble His Excellency will get himself into."

Louis grinned. "With any luck, he'll get himself killed and Colonel Harrington becomes Acting Governor. Then we can really clean house."

"You can't wish that on Irina's father," Kathryn protested. "I thought you liked her, Louis."

"Her, yes. Her old man I can live without. I'd have thought you'd share the sentiment."

"He was kind enough to let me live in his home," Kathryn said. "I don't understand him at all. He seems like a good man. It's only when—"

"When he puts on his Governor's hat," I said. "I keep wondering if we blew it, Kathryn. If we'd taken the Governor up on his offer, we could at least have gotten down there to do *something*. I might even have caught the bastard that— You know who I mean."

"I'm glad you didn't, Hal. It would have been horrible. Anything you did to those gangsters they'd take out on my friends as soon as you'd left. I wouldn't have helped you, and I don't think anyone else would, because anybody that did would be signing death warrants for his whole family, and all his friends, too."

"Sounds like a rough gang," Louis said. "Thorough. If you're going to use terror, go all the way. Unfortunately, it works."

Kathryn nodded. "Yes. I've tried to explain it to Governor Swale. If he sends an expedition there, a lot of my friends will try to help. They'll be killed if he leaves those hoodlums in control when it's over. It would be better if none of you ever went there."

"But the Harmony merchants don't like the prices," Louis said. "They want their grain cheaper, and Swale's got to worry about them, too. A complaint from the Harmony city council wouldn't look too good on his record. Somebody at BuColonial might take it seriously."

"Politics," Kathryn said. "Why can't—"

"Be your age," Louis said. "There's politics in the CoDominium, sure, but we still keep the peace. And it's not all that bad, anyway. Swale was appointed by Grand Senator Bronson's people."

"An unsavory lot," I said.

"Maybe," Louis admitted. "Anyway, of course that means that Bronson's enemies will be looking for reasons to discredit Swale. He's got to be careful. The Harmony merchants still have friends at American Express—and AmEx hates Bronson with a passion."

"I'd say our Governor has problems, then," I said. "From the looks of the troops he took with him, he won't scare the Association much. The militia have pretty uniforms, but they're all city kids. All right for holding walls and cruising along the Jordan now that we've disarmed everybody here, but they're unlikely to scare anybody with real combat experience."

XIV

We put the entire battalion on ready alert, but nothing happened for a week. Colonel Harrington stayed at Fort Beersheba and joined us in the officers' mess in the evenings. Like Falkenberg, he liked bagpipes. To my horror, so did Kathryn. I suppose every woman has some major failing.

"What the hell is he doing?" Colonel Harrington demanded. "I'd have sworn he'd have gotten himself into trouble by now. Maybe we've overestimated the Mission Hills Protective Association. Why the hell did they come up with that name? There aren't any Mission Hills on this planet, to the best of my knowledge."

"They brought the name with them, Colonel," Louis told him. "There's a Southern California gang with that name. Been around for two or three generations. A number of them happened to be on the same prison ship, and they stuck together when they got there."

"How the hell did you find that out?" Harrington demanded.

"Captain Falkenberg insists that his people be thorough," Louis said. "It was a matter of sifting through enough convicts until I found one who knew, and then finding some corroboration."

"Well, congratulations, Louis," Harrington said. "John, you've done well with your collection of newlies."

"Thank you, Colonel."

"Real test's coming up now, though. What the hell is happening down there? Steward, another whiskey, all around. If we can't fight, we can still drink."

"Maybe Governor Swale will come to terms with them," I said.

The colonel gave me a sour look. "Doubt it, Hal. He's between a rock and a hard place. The merchants won't stand for the prices those goons want, and they think they've got him by the balls. They're not afraid of us, you know. They've got a good idea of what's going on in Harmony. They know damned well that Fleet isn't sending any more support to Arrarat, and what the hell can a thousand men do? Even a thousand Line Marines?"

"I hope they think that way," Deane said. "If they'll stand and fight, they're finished—"

"But they won't," John Falkenberg said. "They're no fools. They won't stand and fight, they'll run like hell as soon as we get close to them. They've only to sit up in the hills and avoid us. Eventually we'll have to leave, but they won't."

Harrington nodded. "Yeah. In the long run those poor damned farmers will have to cut it for themselves. Maybe they'll make it. At least we can try to set things right for them. John, do you think the pipers have had their drink by now?"

"I'm certain of it, Colonel. Lazar! Have Pipe Major bring us a tune!"

Eight days after the Governor left Fort Beersheba, we still had no word. That night there was the usual drinking with the pipers in the mess. I excused myself early and went up to my rooms with Kathryn. I still couldn't touch her without setting her to trembling, but we were working on it. I'd decided I was in love with her, and I could wait for the physical aspects to develop. I didn't dare think very far ahead. We had no real future that I could see, but for the moment just being together was enough. It wasn't a situation either of us enjoyed, but we hated to be separated.

The phone buzzed. "Slater," I told it.

"Sergeant Major Ogilvie, sir. You're wanted in the staff room immediately."

"Hallelujah. Be right there, Sergeant Major." As I hung up, Brady's trumpet sounded "On Full Kits." I turned to Kathryn. We were both grinning like idiots. "This is it, sweetheart."

"Yes. Now that it's happened, I'm scared."

"So am I. As Falkenberg says, we're all scared, but it's an officer's job not to show it. Be back when I can—"

"Just a second." She came to me and put her hands on my shoulders. Her arms went around me, and she pulled me against herself. "See? I'm hardly shaking at all." She kissed me, quickly, then a long, lingering kiss.

"This is one hell of a time for a miraculous psychiatric cure," I said.

"Shut up and get out of here."

"Aye, aye, ma'am." I went out quickly.

Hartz was in the hallway. "I will have our gear ready, zur," he said. "And now we fight."

"I hope so."

As I walked across the parade ground, I wondered why I felt so good. We were about to go kill and maim a lot of people, and give them the chance to do it to us. For a million reasons we ought to have been afraid, and we ought to dread what was coming, but we didn't.

Is it that what we think we ought to do is so thoroughly alien to what we really feel? I couldn't kid myself that this time was different because our cause was just. We say we love peace, but it doesn't excite us. Even pacifists talk more about the horrors of war than about the glories of peace.

And you're not supposed to solve the problems of the universe, I told myself. But you do get to kill the man that raped your girl.

The others were already in the conference room, with Colonel Harrington at the head of the table.

"The expected has happened," Harrington said. I knew for a fact that he'd drunk four double whiskeys since supper, but there wasn't a trace of it in his speech. I'd swallowed two quick-sober pills on the way over. I really hadn't needed them. I was sure they hadn't had time to dissolve, but I felt fine.

"Our Governor has managed to get himself besieged in Allansport," Harrington said. "With half of his force outside the town. He wants us to bail him out. I have told him we will march immediately—for a price."

"Then he's agreed to withdraw recognition of the Association?" Deane asked.

"Agreed to, yes. He hasn't done it yet. I think he's afraid that the instant he does, they will get really nasty. However, I have his word on it, and I will hold him to it. Captain Falkenberg, the 501st is hereby ordered to drive the Mission Hills Protective Association out of the Allan River Valley by whatever means you think best. You may cooperate with local partisan forces in the area and make reasonable agreements with them. The entire valley is to be placed under CoDominium protection."

"Aye, aye, sir." Falkenberg's detached calm broke for a moment and he let a note of triumph get into his voice.

"Now, Captain, if you will be kind enough to review your battle plan," Harrington said.

"Sir." Falkenberg used the console to project a map onto the briefing screen.

I'd already memorized the area, but I examined it again. About ten kilometers upriver from Beersheba, the Jordan was joined by a tributary known as the Allan River. The Allan runs southwest through forest lands for about fifty kilometers, then turns and widens in a valley that lies almost due north-south. The east side of the Allan Valley is narrow, because no more than twenty klicks from the river there's a high mountain range and east of that is high desert. Nobody lives there and nobody would want to. The west side, though, is some of the most fertile land on Arrarat. The valley is irregularly shaped, narrowing to no more than twenty-five klicks wide in places, but opening out to more than one hundred klicks in others. It reminded me of the San Joaquin Valley of California, a big fertile bowl with rugged mountains on both sides of it.

Allansport is 125 klicks upriver from where the Allan runs into the Jordan. Falkenberg left the big valley map on one screen and projected a detail onto the other. He fiddled with the console to bring red and green lines representing friendly and hostile forces onto the map.

"As you can see, Governor Swale and one company of militia have taken a defensive position in Allansport," Falkenberg said. "The other two militia companies are south of him, actually upriver. How the devil he ever got himself into such a stupid situation, I cannot say."

"Natural talent," Colonel Harrington muttered.

"No doubt," Falkenberg said. "We have two objectives. The minor, but most urgent, is to rescue Governor Swale. The major objective is pacification of the area. It seems very unlikely that we can accomplish that without a general uprising of the locals in our favor. Agreed?"

We were all silent for a moment. "Mr. Bonneyman, I believe you're the junior," Colonel Harrington said.

"Agreed, sir," Louis said.

Deane and I spoke at once. "Agreed."

"Excellent. I remind you that this conference is recorded," Falkenberg said.

Of course, I thought. All staff conferences are. It didn't seem like Falkenberg and Harrington to spread responsibility around by getting our opinions on record, but I was sure they had their reasons.

"The best way to stimulate a general uprising would be to inflict an immediate and major defeat on the Protective Association," Falkenberg said. "A defeat, not merely driving them away, but bringing them to battle and eliminating a large number of them. It is my view that this is sufficiently important to justify considerable risks. Is that agreed to?"

Aha! I thought. Starting with Louis, we all stated our agreements.

"Then we can proceed to the battle plan," Falkenberg said. "It is complex, but I think it is worth a try. You will notice that there is a pass into the hills west of Allensport. Our informants tell us that this is the route the Association forces will take if they are forced to retreat. Furthermore, there is a sizable militia force south of Allansport. If the militia were strengthened with local partisans, and if we can take the pass before the besieging hostiles realize their danger, we will have them trapped. The main body of the battalion will march upriver, approach from the north, and engage them. We won't get them all, but we should be able to eliminate quite a lot of them. With that kind of victory behind us, persuading the other ranchers to rise up and join us should not be difficult."

As he talked he illustrated the battle plan with lights on the map. He was right. It was complex.

"Questions?" Falkenberg asked.

"Sir," I said, "I don't believe those two militia companies can take the pass. I certainly wouldn't count on it."

"They can't," Harrington said. "But they're pretty steady on defense. Give 'em a strong position to hold and those lads will give a good account of themselves."

"Yes," Falkenberg said. "I propose to stiffen the militia outside the city with two sections of Marines. We still have our Skyhooks, and I see no reason why we can't use them again."

"Here we go again," I muttered. "Even so, sir, it all depends on how strongly that pass is held, and we don't know that. Or do we?"

"Only that it will be defended," Falkenberg said. "The attack on the pass will have to be in the nature of a probe, ready to be withdrawn if the opposition is too stiff."

"I see." I thought about that for a while. I'd never done anything like that, of course. I might have a military medal, but I couldn't kid myself about my combat experience. "I think I can manage that, sir," I said.

Falkenberg gave me his half grin, the expression he used when he was springing one of his surprises. "I'm afraid you won't have all the fun this time, Mr. Slater. I intend to lead the Skyhook force myself. You'll have command of the main body."

There was more to his plan, including a part I didn't like at all. He was taking Kathryn with him on the Skyhook. I couldn't really object. She'd already volunteered. Falkenberg had called her in my rooms while I was on the way over to the conference.

"I really have little choice," Falkenberg said. "We must have someone reliable who is known to the locals. The whole plan depends on getting enough local assistance to seal off the valley to the south of Allansport. Otherwise, there's no point to it."

I had to agree. I didn't have to like it. I could imagine what she'd say if I tried to stop her.

Falkenberg finished with the briefing. "Any more questions? No? Then once again I'll ask for your opinions."

"Looks all right to me," Louis said. Of course he would. He was going with Falkenberg in the Skyhooks.

"No problem with heavy weapons," Deane said. "I like it."

"Mr. Slater?"

"My operation looks straightforward enough. No problems."

"It's straightforward," Colonel Harrington said, "but not trivial. You've got the trickiest part of the job. You have to seal off the northern escape route, engage the enemy, rescue the Governor, and then swing around like a hammer to smash the hostiles against the anvil Captain Falkenberg will erect at the passes. The timing is critical."

"I have confidence in Lieutenant Slater," Falkenberg said.

"So have I, or I wouldn't approve this plan," Harrington said. "But don't ignore what we're doing here. In order to carry out the major objective of clearing the hostiles from the whole valley, we're leaving Governor Swale in a rather delicate situation. If something goes wrong, Sector will have our heads—with justice, I might add." He stood, and we all got to our feet. "But I like it. No doubt the Association thinks we'll be rushing directly to the Governor's aid, and their people are prepared for that. I hate to be obvious."

"So do I," Falkenberg said.

Harrington nodded curtly. "Gentlemen, you have your orders."

The riverboats looked like something out of the American Civil War as they puffed their way down the dark river. We'd had a rainstorm when we left the fort, but now the sky was clear and dark, with bright stars overhead. My rivercraft were really nothing more than barges with steam engines and enough superstructure to get cargo under cover. They were made of wood, of course; there wasn't enough of a metal industry on Arrarat to build steel hulls, and not much reason to want to.

I had three barges, each about fifty meters long and twenty wide, big rectangular floating platforms with cabins whose roofs served as raised decks, and a central bridge to control them.

Every centimeter of available space was covered with troops, mules, guns, supply wagons, ammunition, tentage, and rations. The 501st was going to the Allan Valley to stay.

The barges burned wood, which we had to stop and cut with chain saws. In addition, I had one amphibious hovercraft with light armor. It could make fifty-five kilometers an hour compared to the eleven kilometers an hour the barges got under full steam. Perched on top of the third barge was Number Three helicopter, which could make a couple of hundred kilometers an hour. The discrepancies in speeds would have been amusing if they weren't so frustrating.

"One goddamned DC-45," Deane said. "One. That's all, one Starlifter, and we could be there in an hour."

"We make do with what we got," I told him. "Besides, think how romantic it all is. Pity we don't have a leadsman up in the bows singing out the river depth, instead of a sonar depth finder."

The hovercraft ran interference to be sure there weren't any nasty surprises waiting for us. As we got closer to Allansport, I sent up the chopper to make a high-altitude survey of the landing area. We were landing a good twenty klicks downriver from Allansport. Not only were the banks a lot steeper farther upriver, but we didn't want to scare the Association off by landing too close. Governor Swale was screaming at me hourly, of course. He wanted us in Allansport right now. When I told him where we were putting ashore, he was almost hysterical.

"What the hell are you doing?" he demanded. "All you have to do is show up! They won't stand and fight you. This is all a political maneuver. Put heavy pressure on them and they'll come to terms."

I didn't point out that we didn't intend to come to terms with the Association. "Sir, Colonel Harrington approved the battle plan."

"I don't care if God the Father approved it!" Swale shouted. "What are you doing? I know Falkenberg is south of here with troops he brought in by helicopter, but he won't tell me what he's doing! And now he's withdrawn the militia! I'm trapped in here, and you're playing some kind of game! I demand to know what you intend!"

"Governor, I don't know myself," I said. "I just know what my orders are. We'll have you out of there in a few hours. Out." I switched off the set and turned to Deane.

"Well," I said, "we know Louis and Falkenberg are doing something down south of us. Wish I knew how they're making out."

"If there's something we need to know, they'll tell us," Deane said. "Worried about Kathryn?"

"Some."

"Never get so attached to anyone that you worry about her. Saves a lot of skull sweat."

"Yeah, sure. Helmsman, that looks like our landing area. Look sharp."

"Aye, aye, sir."

"Hartz, get me the chopper pilot."

"Zur." Hartz fiddled with the radio for a moment, then handed me the mike.

"Sergeant Stragoff, sir."

"Stragoff, I want you to make a complete sweep of our landing area. There should be two unarmed people there to meet us. They'll show you a blue light. If they show any other color, spray the whole area and get the hell out of there. If they show blue, tell me about it, but I still want a complete survey."

"Aye, aye, sir."

"And just who is meeting us?" Deane asked.

"Don't know their names," I said. "Falkenberg said he'd try to set up a welcoming committee of local resistance types. If we're satisfied with them, we help 'em arm some of their neighbors. That's why we brought those extra rifles."

The radio came to life again. "Two people with a blue light, sir. Nothing else on radar or IR."

"Good. Okay, now make a wider sweep. I don't want to find out there's an artillery battery registered on our landing area."

"Sir."

"Sergeant Major," I said.

"Sir."

"You can take the hovercraft in to occupy the landing area. Treat the welcoming committee politely, but keep an eye on them. When the area's secure, we'll all go ashore."

"Sir."

I looked up at the stars. There was no moon. About five hours to dawn. With any luck we'd be deployed and ready for combat by first light. "Okay, Deane, you're in charge," I said. "Hartz, you stay with him."

"If the lieutenant orders it."

"Damn it, I did order it. Belay that. All right, come with me."

We went to the deck level. The river was less than a meter below us. It wasn't a river to swim in; there are aquatic snakes on Arrarat, and their poison will finish off anything that has protein in it. It acts as a catalyst to coagulate cell bodies. I had no real desire to be a hard rubber lump.

We had one canoe on board. I'd already found troopers who knew something about handling them. We had a dozen men familiar with the screwy watercraft, which didn't surprise me. The story is that you can find *any* skill in a Line Marine regiment, and it seems to be true. In my own company I had two master masons, an artist, a couple of electronic techs (possibly engineers, but they weren't saying), at least one disbarred lawyer, a drunken psychiatrist, and a chap the men claimed was a defrocked preacher.

Corporal Anuraro showed me how to get into the canoe without swamping it. We don't have those things in Arizona. As they paddled me ashore, I thought about how silly the situation was. I was being paddled in a canoe, a device invented at least ten thousand years ago. I was carrying a pair of light-amplifying field glasses based on a principle not discovered until after I was born. Behind me was a steamboat that might have been moving up the Missouri River at the time of Custer's last stand, and I got to this planet in a starship.

The current was swift, and I was glad to have experienced men at the paddles. The water flowed smoothly alongside. Sometimes an unseen creature made riffles in it. Over on the shore the hovercraft had already landed, and someone was signaling us with a light. When we got to the bank I was glad to be on dry land.

"Where are our visitors, Roszak?" I asked.

"Over here, sir."

Two men, both ranchers or farmers. One was Oriental. They looked to be about fifty years old. As agreed, they weren't armed.

"I'm Lieutenant Slater," I said.

The Oriental answered. "I am Wan Loo. This is Harry Seeton."

"I've heard of you. Kathryn says you helped her, once."

"Yes. To escape from a cage," Wan Loo said.

"You're supposed to prove something," I said.

Wan Loo smiled softly. "You have a scar on your left arm. It is shaped like a scimitar. When you were a boy you had a favorite horse named Candybar."

"You've seen Kathryn," I said. "Where is she?"

"South of Allansport. She is trying to raise a force of ranchers to reinforce Captain Falkenberg. We were sent here to assist you."

"We've done pretty well," Harry Seeton added. "A lot of

ranchers will fight if you can furnish weapons. But there's something else."

"Yes?"

"Please do not think we are not grateful," Wan Loo said. "But you must understand. We have fought for years, and we cannot fight any longer. We have an uneasy peace in this valley. It is the peace of submission, and we do not care for it, but we will not throw it away simply to help you. If you have not come to stay, please take your soldiers, rescue your Governor, and go away without involving us."

"That's blunt enough," I said.

"We have to be blunt," Harry Seeton said. "Wan Loo isn't talking for us. We're outlaws, anyway. We're with you no matter what happens. But we can't go ask our friends to join if you people don't mean it when you say you'll stay and protect them."

"It is an old story," Wan Loo said. "You cannot blame the farmers. They would rather have you than the Association, but if you are here only for a little while, and the Association is here forever, what can they do? My ancestors were faced with the same problem on Earth. They chose to support the West, and when the Americans, who had little stake in the war, withdrew their forces, my great-grandfather gave up land his family had held for a thousand years to go with them. He had no choice. Do you think he would have chosen the American side if he had known that would happen?"

"The CoDominium has extended protection to this valley," I said.

"Governments have no honor," Wan Loo said. "Many people have none, either, but at least it is possible for a man to have honor. It is not possible for a government. Do you pledge that *you* will not abandon our friends if we arouse them for you?"

"Yes."

"Then we have your word. Kathryn says you are an honorable man. If you will help us with transportation and radio, by noon tomorrow I believe we will have five hundred people to assist you."

"And God help 'em if we lose," Seeton said. "God help 'em."

"We won't lose," I said.

"A battle is not a war," Wan Loo said. "And wars are not won by weapons, but by the will to win them. We will go now."

XV

It is a basic military maxim that no battle plan ever survives contact with the enemy, but by noon it looked as if this operation would be an exception. Falkenberg's combat team—two platoons of B Company, brought down by Skyhook after we were aboard our barges—struck at the passes just before dawn and in three hours of sharp fighting had taken them over. He brought up two companies of militia to dig in and hold them.

Meanwhile, the ranchers in the south were armed and turned out on command to block any southward retreat. I had only scattered reports from that sector, but all seemed under control. Kathryn had raised a force of nearly five hundred, which ought to be enough to hold the southern defensive line.

Then it was my turn. Two hours after dawn I had a skirmish line stretching eight kilometers into the valley. My left flank was anchored on the river. There'd be no problem there. The right flank was a different story.

"It bothers me," I told Falkenberg when I reported by radio. "My right flank is hanging in thin air. The only thing protecting us is Wan Loo's ranchers, and there's no more than three hundred of them—if that many." Wan Loo hadn't been as successful as Kathryn had been. Of course, he'd had a lot less time.

"And just what do you expect to hit you in the flank?" Falkenberg asked.

"I don't know. I just don't like it when we have to depend on other people—and on the enemy doing what we want them to do."

"Neither do I, but do you have an alternative to suggest?"

"No, sir."

"Then carry out your orders, Mr. Slater. Advance on Allansport."

"Aye, aye, sir."

✧   ✧   ✧

It wasn't an easy battle line to control. I had units strung all across the valley, with the major strength on the left wing that advanced along the river. The terrain was open, gently rolling hills with lines of hedges and eucalyptus trees planted as windbreaks. The fields were recently harvested, and swine had been turned loose in the wheat stubble. The fields were muddy, but spread as we were, we didn't churn them up much.

The farmhouses were scattered at wide intervals. These had been huge farm holdings. The smallest were over a kilometer square, and some were much larger. A lot of the land was unworked. The houses were stone and earth, partly underground, built like miniature fortresses. Some had sections of wall blown out by explosives.

Harry Seeton was with me in my ground-effects caravan. When we came to a farmhouse, he'd try to persuade the owner and his children and relatives to join us. If they agreed, he'd send them off to join the growing number on our right wing.

"Something bothers me," I told Seeton. "Sure, you have big families and everybody works, but how did you cultivate all this land? That last place was at least five hundred hectares."

"Rainfall here's tricky," Seeton said. "Half the time we've got swamp, and the other half we have drought. The only fertilizer is manure. We've got to leave a lot of the land fallow, or planted in legumes to be plowed under."

"It still seems like a lot of work for just one family."

"Well, we had hired help. Convicts, mostly. Ungrateful bastards joined the Association gangs first chance they got. Tell me something, Lieutenant."

"Yes?"

"Are your men afraid they'll starve to death? I never saw anything like it, the way they pick up anything they can find." He pointed to one B Company trooper who was just ahead of us. He wasn't a large man to begin with, and he had his pockets stuffed with at least three chickens, several ears of corn, and a bottle he'd liberated somewhere. There were bulges in his pack that couldn't have come from regulation equipment, and he'd even strapped firewood on top of it so that we couldn't see his helmet from behind him. "They're like a plague of locusts," Seeton said.

"Not much I can do about it," I said. "I can't be everywhere, and the Line Marines figure anything that's not actually penned up and watched is fair game. They'll eat well for a few days—it beats monkey and greasy rice." I didn't add that if he thought things were bad now, with the troops on the way to a battle, he'd really be horrified after the troops had been in the field a few weeks.

There were shots from ahead. "It's started," I said. "How many of these farm areas are still inhabited by your people?"

"Not many, this close to Allansport. The town itself is almost all Association people. Or goddamned collaborators, which is the same thing. I expect that's why they haven't blasted it down. They outnumber your Governor's escort by quite a lot."

"Yeah." That bothered me. Why hadn't the Association forces simply walked in and taken Governor Swale? As Seeton said, Swale had only a couple of companies of militia with him, yet the siege had been a stalemate. As if they hadn't really wanted to capture him.

Of course, they had problems no matter what they did. If they killed the Governor, Colonel Harrington would be in control. I had to assume the Protective Association had friends in Harmony, possibly even inside the palace. Certainly there were plenty of leaks. They'd know that Harrington was a tougher nut than Swale.

The resistance was stronger as we approached Allansport. The Association forces were far better armed than we'd expected them to be. They had mortars and light artillery, and plenty of ammunition for both.

We had two close calls with the helicopters. I'd sent them forward as gunships to support the advancing infantry. We found out the Association had target-seeking missiles, and the only reason they didn't get the choppers was that their gunners were too eager. They fired while the helicopters still had time to maneuver. I pulled the choppers back to headquarters. I could use them for reconnaissance, but I wasn't going to risk them in combat.

We silenced their artillery batteries one by one. They had plenty of guns, but their electronics were ineffective. Their counterbattery fire was pathetic. We'd have a couple of exchanges, our radars would backtrack their guns, and that would be the end of it.

"Where the hell did they get all that stuff?" I asked Seeton.

"They've always had a lot of equipment. Since the first time they came out of the hills, they've been pretty well armed. Lately it's gotten a lot worse. One reason we gave up."

"It had to come from off-planet," I said. "How?"

"I don't know. Ask your governor."

"I intend to. That stuff had to come through the spaceport. Somebody's getting rich selling guns to the Protective Association."

We moved up to the outer fringes of Allensport. The town
was spread across low hills next to the river. It had a protective wall made of brick and adobe, like the houses. Deane's
artillery tore huge gaps in the wall and the troops moved into
the streets beyond. The fighting was fierce. Seeton was right
about the sentiments of the townspeople. They fought from
house to house, and the Marines had to move cautiously, with
plenty of artillery support. We were flattening the town as we
moved into it.

Governor Swale and two companies of Harmony militia were
dug in on the bluffs overlooking the river, very nearly in the
center of the semicircular town. They held the riverfront almost
to the steel bridge that crossed the Allan. I'd hoped to reach
the Governor by dark, but the fighting in the town was too
severe. At dusk I called to report that I wouldn't reach him
for another day.

"However, we're within artillery range of your position," I
told him. "We can give you fire support if there's any serious attempt to take your position by storm."

"Yes. You've done well," he told me.

That was a surprise. I'd expected him to read me off for
not getting there sooner. Live and learn, I told myself. "I'm
bringing the right flank around in an envelopment," I told
Swale. "By morning we'll have every one of them penned in
Allansport, and we can deal with them at our leisure."

"Excellent," Swale said. "My militia officers tell me the
Association forces have very little strength in the southern part
of the town. You may be able to take many of the streets
during the night."

We halted at dark. I sent Ardwain forward with orders to
take A Company around the edges of the town and occupy
sections at the southern end. Then I had supper with the
troops. As Seeton had noticed, they'd provisioned themselves
pretty well. No monkey and rice tonight! We had roast chicken
and fresh corn.

After dark I went back to my map table. I'd parked the
caravan next to a stone farmhouse two klicks from the outskirts of Allansport. Headquarters platoon set up the C. P.,
and there were a million details to attend to: supply, field
hospitals, plans to evacuate wounded by helicopter, shuffling
ammunition around to make sure each unit had enough of
the right kind. The computers could handle a lot of it, but
there were decisions to be made and no one to make them
but me. Finally I had time to set up our positions into the
map table computer and make new plans. By feeding the

computer the proper inputs, it would show the units on the map, fight battles and display the probable outcomes, move units around under fire and subtract our casualties. . . .

It reminded me of the afternoon's battles. There'd been fighting going on, but I'd seen almost none of it. Just more lines on the map table, and later the bloody survivors brought back to the field hospital. Tri-V war, none of it real. The observation satellite had made a pass over the Allan Valley just before dark, and the new pictures were relayed from Garrison. They weren't very clear. There'd been low clouds, enough to cut down the resolution and leave big gaps in my data about the Association forces.

"Number One chopper's coming in, sir," Sergeant Jaski reported. He was a headquarters platoon communications expert, an elderly wizened chap who ran the electronics section with smiles and affection until something went wrong. Then he could be as rough as any NCO in the Fleet.

Number One was Falkenberg's. I wasn't surprised when the captain came in a few minutes later. He'd said he might join the main body if things were quiet up at the pass. I got up from the map table to give him the command seat. It hadn't fit me too well, anyway; I was glad to have someone else take charge.

"Just going over the satellite pix," I told him.

"One reason I came by. Things are going well. When that happens I wonder what I've overlooked." He keyed the map table to give him the current positions of our troops. "Ardwain having any problem with the envelopment?" he asked.

"No, sir."

He grunted and played with the console keys. Then he stared at the satellite pictures. "Mr. Slater, why haven't the Association troops taken the riverbank areas behind the Governor?"

"I don't know, sir."

"Any why didn't His Excellency withdraw by water? He could certainly have gotten out, himself and a few men."

"Didn't want to abandon the militia, sir?"

"Possibly."

I looked at the time. Two hours after dark. The troops were well dug in along the perimeter, except for Ardwain's mobile force moving toward the southern edge of the town.

Falkenberg went through the day's reports and looked up, frowning. "Mr. Slater, why do I have the impression that there's something phony about this whole situation?"

"In what way, sir?"

"It's been too easy. We've been told the Association is a

tough outfit, but so far the only opposition has been some infantry screens that withdrew before you made real contact, and the first actual hard fighting was when you reached the town."

"There were the artillery duels, sir."

"Yes. All won by a few exchanges of fire. Doesn't that seem strange?"

"No, sir." I had good reason to know that Deane's lads could do some great shooting. After the support they gave me at the roadblock below Beersheba, I was ready to believe they could do anything. "I hadn't thought about it, sir, but now that you ask—well, it was easy. A couple of exchanges and their guns are quiet."

Falkenberg was nodding. "Knocked out, or merely taken out of action? Looking at this map, I'd say you aren't ready for the second alternative."

"I—"

"You've done well, Lieutenant. It's my nasty suspicious mind. I don't like surprises. Furthermore, why hasn't the Governor asked to be evacuated by water? Why is he sitting there in Allansport?"

"Sir—"

He wouldn't let me finish. "I presume you've reported your positions and plans to the Governor?"

"Certainly, sir."

"And we took the pass with very little effort. Next to no casualties. Yet the Association is certainly aware that we hold it. Why haven't their town forces done something? Run, storm the bluffs and take the Governor for a hostage—*something!*" He straightened in decision. "Sergeant Major!"

"Sir!"

"I want a message taken to Centurion Ardwain. I don't want any possibility of it being intercepted."

"Sir."

"He's to hold up on the envelopment. Send a couple of patrols forward to dig in where they can observe, but keep our forces out of Allansport. He can move around out there and make a lot of noise. I want them to think we've continued the envelopment, but, in fact, Ardwain is to take his troops northwest and dig in no closer than two klicks to the town. They're to do that as quietly and invisibly as possible."

"Yes, sir." Ogilvie went out.

"Insurance, Mr. Slater," Falkenberg said. "Insurance. We didn't need your envelopment."

"Yes, sir."

"Confused, Mister?"

"Yes, sir."

"Just preserving options, Lieutenant. I don't like to commit my forces until I'm certain of my objectives."

"But the objective is to trap the Association forces and neutralize them," I said. "The envelopment would have done that. We wouldn't have to trust to the ranchers to keep them from escaping to the south."

"I understood that, Lieutenant. Now, if you'll excuse me, we've both got work to do."

"Yes, sir." I left the caravan to find another place to work. There was plenty to do. I set up shop in one of the farmhouse rooms and went back to shuffling papers. About an hour later Deane Knowles came in.

"I got the change of orders," he said. "What's up?"

"Damfino. Have a seat? Coffee's over there."

"I'll have some, thanks." He poured himself a cup and sat across from me. The room had a big wooden table, roughhewn from a single tree. That table would have been worth a fortune on Earth. Except for a few protected redwoods, I doubted there was a tree that size in the United States.

"Don't you think I ought to know what's going on?" Deane asked. His voice was friendly, but there was a touch of sarcasm in it.

"Bug Falkenberg if you really want answers," I said. "He doesn't tell me anything, either. All I know is he's sent A Company out into the boonies, and when I asked him to let me join my company, he said I was needed here."

"Tell me about it," Deane said.

I described what had happened.

Deane blew on the hot coffee, then took a sip. "You're telling me that Falkenberg thinks we've put our heads in a trap."

"Yes. What do you think?"

"Good point about the artillery. I thought things were going too well myself. Let's adopt his theory and see where it leads."

"You do understand there's only one person who could have set this theoretical trap," I said.

"Yes."

"What possible motive could he have?" I demanded.

Deane shrugged. "Even so, let's see where it leads. We assume for the purposes of discussion that Governor Hugo Swale has entered into a conspiracy with a criminal gang to inflict anything from a defeat to a disaster on the 501st—"

"And you see how silly it sounds," I said. "Too silly to discuss."

"Assume it," Deane insisted. "That means that the Protective Association is fully aware of our positions and our plans. What could they do with that information?"

"That's why it's so stupid," I said. "So what if they know where we are? If they come out and fight, they'll still get a licking. They can't possibly expect to grind up professional troops! They may be great against ranchers and women and children, but this is a battalion of Line Marines."

"A provisional battalion."

"Same thing."

"Is it? Be realistic, Hal. We've had one campaign, a short one. Otherwise, we're still what came here—a random assortment of troops, half of them recruits, another quarter scraped out of guardhouses, commanded by three newlie lieutenants and the youngest captain in the Fleet. Our colonel's a superannuated military policeman, and we've not a quarter of the equipment a regular line battalion carries."

"We're a match for anything a criminal gang can put in the field—"

"A well-armed criminal gang," Deane said. "Hold onto your regimental pride, Hal. I'm not downgrading the 501st. The point is that we may know we're a damned good outfit, but there's not much reason for anyone else to believe it."

"They'll soon have reason to think differently."

"Maybe." Deane continued to study the maps. "Maybe."

XVI

The night was quiet. I went on patrol about midnight, not to inspect the guard—we could depend on the NCOs for all that—but mostly to see what it was like out there. The troops were cheerful, looking forward to the next day's battles. Even the recruits grinned wolfishly. They were facing a disorganized mob, and we had artillery superiority. They'd pitched tents by maniples, and inside each tent they'd set up their tiny field stoves so there was hot coffee and chicken stew—and they'd found wine in some of the farmhouses. Our bivouac had more the atmosphere of a campout than an army just before a battle.

Underneath it all was the edge that men have when they're going to fight, but it was well hidden. You're sure it's the other guy who'll buy the farm. Never you. Deep down you know better, but you never talk about that.

An hour before dawn every house along the southern edge of Allansport exploded in red fire. In almost the next instant a time-on-target salvo fell just outside the walls. The bombardment continued, sharp thunder in the night, with red flashes barely visible through the thick mist rising up off the river. I ran to the command caravan.

Falkenberg was already there, of course. I doubt if he'd ever gone to bed. Sergeant Jaski had gotten communications with one of the forward patrols.

"Corporal Levine, sir. I'm dug in about five hundred meters outside the walls. Looks like it was mines in the houses, Captain. Then they dropped a hell of a load onto where we'd have been if we'd moved up last night."

"What's your situation, Levine?" Falkenberg demanded.

"Dug in deep, sir. They killed a couple of my squad even so. It's thick out here, sir. Big stuff. Not just mortars."

That was obvious from the sound, even as far away as we were. No light artillery makes that kind of booming sound.

145

"A moment, Captain," Levine said. There was a long silence. "Can't keep my head up long, Captain. They're still pounding the area. I see movement in the town. Looks like assault troops coming out the gate. The fire's lifting now. Yeah, those are assault troops. A lot of 'em."

"Sergeant Major, put the battalion on alert for immediate advance," Falkenberg said. "Jaski, when's the next daylight pass of the spy satellite over this area?"

"Seventy minutes after daylight, sir."

"Thank you. Levine, you still there?"

"Yes, Captain. There's more troops moving out of Allansport. Goddamn, there's a couple of tanks. Medium jobs. Suslov class, I'd say. I didn't know them bastards had tanks! Where'd they get them?"

"Good question. Levine, keep your head down and stay out of sight. I want you to stay alive."

"Won't fight over those orders, Captain."

"They're breaking out toward the south," Falkenberg said. "Jaski, get me Lieutenant Bonneyman."

"Sir."

"While you're at it, see if you can raise Centurion Cernan at the pass."

"Aye, aye, sir." Jaski worked at the radio for a moment. "No answer from Mr. Bonneyman, sir. Here's Cernan."

"Thank you." Falkenberg paused. "Mr. Slater, stay here for a moment. You'll need instructions. Centurion Cernan, report."

"Not much to report, Captain. Some movement up above us."

"Above you. Hostiles coming *down* the pass?"

"Could be, Captain, but I don't know. I have patrols up that way, but they haven't reported yet."

"Dig in, Cernan," Falkenberg said. "I'll try to send you some reinforcements. You've got to hold that pass no matter which direction it's attacked from."

"Aye, aye, sir."

Falkenberg nodded. The map board was crawling with symbols and lights as reports came in to Jaski's people and they were programmed onto the display. "Wish I had some satellite pix," Falkenberg said. "There's only one logical move the Association can be making at this point."

He was talking to himself. Maybe he wasn't. Maybe he thought I understood him, but I didn't.

"In any event, we have the only sizable military force on the entire planet," Falkenberg said. "We can't risk its destruction."

"But we've got to relieve Bonneyman and the ranchers," I protested. I didn't mention Kathryn. Falkenberg might think it was just a personal problem. Maybe it was. "Those tanks are headed south, right for their lines."

"I know. Jaski, keep trying to get Bonneyman."

"Sir!"

Outside the trumpets were sounding. "On Full Kits." Brady's sang louder than the rest.

"And we must rescue the Governor," Falkenberg said. "Indeed, we must." He came to a decision. "Jaski, get me Mr. Wan Loo."

While Jaski used the radio, Falkenberg said, "I want you to talk to him, Mr. Slater. He has met you and he has never met me. His first impulse will be to rush to the aid of his friends in the south. He must not do that. His forces, what there are of them, will be far more useful as reinforcements for Centurion Cernan at the pass."

"Mr. Wan Loo, sir," Jaski said.

Falkenberg handed me the mike.

"I don't have time to explain," I said. "You're to take everything you've got and move up to the pass. There are mixed Marine and militia units holding it, and there's a chance Association forces are moving down the pass toward them. Centurion Cernan is in command up there, and he'll need help."

"But what is happening?" Wan Loo asked.

"The Association forces in Allansport have broken loose and are heading south," I said.

"But our friends to the south—"

Falkenberg took the mike. "This is Captain John Christian Falkenberg. We'll assist your friends, but we can do nothing if the forces coming down the pass are not contained. The best way you can help your friends is to see that no fresh Association troops get into this valley."

There was a long pause. "You would not abandon us, Captain?"

"No. We won't abandon you," Falkenberg said.

"Then I have assurances from two honorable men. We will help your friends. Captain. And go with God."

"Thank you. Out." He gave the mike back to Jaski. "Me, I'd rather have a couple of anti-tank guns—or, better still, tanks of our own. How's Old Beastly?"

"Still running, sir." Old Beastly was the 50lst's only tank, a relic of the days when CD regulars had come to Arrarat. It was kept going by constant maintenance.

"Where the devil are the Protective Association people getting fuel for tanks?" Falkenberg said. "To hell with it. Sergeant Major, I want Centurion Ardwain to take two platoons of A Company and Old Beastly. Their mission is to link up with Governor Swale. They're to attack through the north end of the town along the riverbank, and they're to move cautiously."

"Captain, that's my company," I said. "Shouldn't I go with them?"

"No. I have a number of operations to perform, and I'll need help. Don't you trust Ardwain?"

"Of course I trust him, sir—"

"Then let him do his job. Sergeant Major, Ardwain's mission is to simulate at least a company. He's to keep the men spread out and moving around. The longer it takes for the enemy to tumble to how small his force is, the better. And he's not to take chances. If they gang up on him, he can run like hell."

"Sir," Ogilvie said. He turned to a waiting runner.

"Ardwain's got a radio, sir," I said.

"Sure he has." Falkenberg's voice was conversational. "Know much about the theory of the scrambler codes we use, Mr. Slater?"

"Well, no, sir—"

"You know this much: in theory any message can be recorded off the air and unscrambled with a good enough computer."

"Yes, sir. But the only computer on Arrarat that could do that is ours, in Garrison."

"And the Governor's in the palace at Harmony," Falkenberg said. "And those two are the ones we know about."

"Sir, you're saying that Governor—"

"No," he interrupted. "I have said nothing at all. I merely choose to be certain that my orders are not intercepted. Jaski, where the hell is Bonneyman?"

"Still trying to raise him, sir."

"Any word from Miss Malcolm or the other ranchers in the southern area?"

"No, sir."

More information appeared on the map board. Levine was still reporting. There were only the two tanks, but a sizable infantry force had come out of Allansport and was headed south along the riverbank. If Levine was right, there'd been more troops in Allansport than we'd ever suspected.

"I have Lieutenant Bonneyman, sir."

"Thank God." Falkenberg grabbed the mike. "Mr. Bonneyman, nearly one thousand hostiles have broken free from Allansport and are moving south. They have with them at least two medium tanks and an appreciable artillery train. Are you well dug in?"

"Yes, sir. We'll hold them."

"The devil, you will. Not with riflemen against that."

"We have to hold, sir," Louis said. "Miss Malcolm and an escort moved about twenty kilometers south during the night in the hopes of raising more reinforcements. She was not successful, but she has reports of hostile activities south of us. At least two, possibly more, groups of Association forces are moving north. We must hold them or they'll break through and link up with the Allansport groups."

"One moment," Falkenberg said. "Sergeant Major, I want helicopter observation of the area to the south of Lieutenant Bonneyman and his ranchers. Send Stragoff. He's to stay at high altitude, but it's vital that I find out what's coming north at us out of Denisburg. All right, Mr. Bonneyman. At the moment you don't know what you're facing."

"No, sir, but I'm in a pretty good position. Rifle pits, and we're strengthening the southern perimeter."

"All right. You're probably safer there than anywhere else. If you get into trouble, your escape route is east, toward the river. I'm bringing the 501st around the town. We'll skirt it wide to stay away from their artillery. Then we'll cut in toward the river and stay right along the bank until we reach your position. If necessary, our engineers can throw up a pontoon bridge and we'll go out across the river to escape."

"Do we need to run, Captain?" Louis sounded dismayed.

"As I have explained to Mr. Slater, our prime objective is to retain the 501st as a fighting unit. Be prepared to withdraw eastward on command, Mr. Bonneyman. Until then, you're to hold that position no matter what happens, and it's likely to be rough."

"Can do, Captain."

"Excellent. Now, what about Miss Malcolm?"

"I don't know where she is, sir. I can send a patrol—"

"No. You have no forces to spare. If you can get a message to her, have her rejoin you if that's possible. Otherwise, she's on her own. You understand your orders, Mister?"

"Yes, sir."

"Excellent. Out."

"So Kathryn's expendable," I said.

"Anyone is expendable, Mister. Sergeant Major, have Stragoff listen on Miss Malcolm's frequency. If he can locate her, he can try to evacuate her from the southern area, but he is not to compromise the reconnaissance mission in doing it."

"Sir."

"You are one hard-nosed son-of-a-bitch," I said.

His voice was calm as he said, "Mister, I get paid to take responsibilities, and at the moment I'm earning my keep. I'll overlook that remark. Once."

And if I say anything else, I'll be in arrest while my troops are fighting. Got you. "What are my orders, sir?"

"For the moment you're to lead the forward elements of the 501st. I want the battalion to move in column around the town, staying outside artillery range. When you've reached a point directly southwest of Allansport, halt the lead elements and gather up the battalion as I send it to you. I'll stay here until this has been accomplished. I still must report to the Governor and I want the daylight satellite pictures."

I looked at my watch. Incredibly, it was still a quarter-hour before dawn. A lot had happened in the last forty-five minutes. When I left the caravan, Falkenberg was playing games on the map board. More bloodless battles, with glowing lights and wriggling lines crawling across the map at lightning speed, simulations of hours of bloody combat and death and agony.

And what the hell are you accomplishing? I thought. The computer can't give better results than the input data, and your intelligence about the hostiles is plain lousy. How many Association troops are coming down the pass toward Centurion Cernan? No data. How many more are in those converging columns moving toward Louis and Kathryn and their ranchers? Make a guess. What are their objectives? Another guess. Guess and guess again, and Kathryn's out there, and instead of rescuing her, we're keeping the battalion intact. I wanted to mutiny, to go to Kathryn with all the men I could get to follow me, but I wasn't going to do that. I blinked back tears. We had a mission, and Falkenberg was probably right. He was going to the aid of the ranchers, and that's what Kathryn would want. She'd pledged her honor to those people, and it was up to us to make that good. Maybe Stragoff will find her, I thought. Maybe.

I went to my room and let Hartz hang equipment onto my uniform. It was time to move out, and I was glad of something, anything, to do.

XVII

The valley was filled with a thick white mist. The fog boiled out of the river and flowed across the valley floor. In the two hours since dawn, the 501st had covered nine kilometers. The battalion was strung out in a long column of men and mules and wagons on muddy tracks that had once been roads and now had turned into sloppy gunk. The men strained at ropes to pull the guns and ammunition wagons along, and when we found oxen or mules in the fields, we hitched them up as well. The rainstorm that had soaked us two days before at Beersheba had passed across the Allan Valley, and the fields were squishy marshlands.

Out in the distance we could hear the sound of guns: Ardwain's column, the Allansport garrison trying to get through Louis's position—or someone else a world away. In the fog we couldn't know. The sound had no direction, and out here there was no battle, only mud.

There were no enemies here in the valley. There weren't any friends, either. There were only refugees, pathetic families with possessions piled on their mules and oxen, or carried in their arms. They didn't know where they were going, and I had no place to send them. Sometimes we passed farms, and we could see women and children staring at us from the partly open doors or from behind shuttered windows. Their eyes had no expression in them. The sound of the guns over the horizon, and the curses of the men as they fought to move our equipment through the mud; more curses as men whipped oxen we'd found and hitched to the wagons; shrill cries from farmers protesting the loss of their stock; everything dripping wet in white swirling fog, all blended together into a long nightmare of outraged feelings and senselessness. I felt completely alone, alien to all this. Where were the people we'd come to set free?

We reached the map point Falkenberg had designated, and

the troops rested in place while the rest of the column caught up with us. The guns were just moving in when Falkenberg's command caravan roared up. The ground-effects machine could move across the muddy fields with no problems, while we had to sweat through them.

He sent for Deane Knowles and had us both come into the caravan. Then he sent out all the NCOs and enlisted men. The three of us were alone with the map table.

"I've held off explaining what I've been doing until the last minute," he said. "As it is, this is for your ears only. If something happens, I want someone to know I haven't lost my mind."

"Yes, sir," I said. Deane and I looked at each other.

"Some background," Falkenberg said. "There's been something peculiar about the Allan Valley situation for years. The convict groups have been too well armed, for a beginning. Governor Swale was too eager to recognize them as a legitimate local government. I think both of you have remarked on that before."

Deane and I looked at each other again.

"This morning's satellite pictures," Falkenberg said. "There's too much mist to show any great details, but there are some clear patches. This strip was taken in the area south of Mr. Bonneyman. I invite your comments."

He handed us the photos. Most were of patches of mist, with the ground below completely invisible. Others showed patches where the mist was thin, or there wasn't any. "Nothing at all," Deane said.

"Precisely," Falkenberg said. "Yet we have reports of troop movements in that area. It is as if the hostiles knew when the satellite would be overhead, and avoided clear patches."

"As well they might," Deane said. "It shouldn't be hard to work out the ephemeris of the spy-eye."

"Correct. Now look at the high resolution enlargements of those clear areas."

We looked again. "The roads are chewed up," I said. "Mud and ruts. A lot of people and wagons have passed over them."

"And recently, I'd say." Falkenberg nodded in satisfaction. If this had been a test, we'd passed. "Now another datum. I have had Sergeant Jaski's people monitoring all transmissions from Allansport. It may or may not be significant that shortly after every communication between 501st headquarters and outlying commands, there has been a transmission from the Governor to the palace at Harmony—and, within half an hour, a reply. Not an immediate reply, gentlemen, but a reply within half an hour. And shortly after that, there is traffic on the frequencies the Association forces use."

There wasn't anything to say to that. The only explanation made no sense.

"Now, let's see what the hostiles have in mind," Falkenberg said. "They besiege the Governor in Allansport. Our initial orders are to send a force to relieve him. We don't know what they would have done, but instead we devised a complex plan to trap them. We take the initial steps, and what happens? The hostiles invite us to continue. They do nothing. Later we learn that a considerable force, possibly the major part of their strength, is marching northward. Their evident objective is Mr. Bonneyman's mixed group of Marines and ranchers. I point out that the elimination of those ranchers would be significant to the Association. They would not only be rid of potential opposition to their rule, but I think it would in future be impossible to persuade any significant group of ranchers to rise against them. The Association would be the only possible government in the Allan Valley."

"Yes, sir, but why?" Deane said. "What could be . . . why would Governor Swale cooperate with them?"

"We'll leave that for the moment, Mr. Knowles. One thing at a time. Now for the present situation. Centurion Ardwain has done an excellent job of simulating a large force cautiously advancing into Allansport from the north. Governor Swale seems convinced that we've committed at least half our strength there. I have further informed him that we will now bring the balance of the 501st from its present position directly east to the riverbank, where we will once again divide out troops, half going south to aid Mr. Bonneyman, the other half moving into the town. The Governor thought that a splendid plan. Have you an opinion, Mr. Slater?"

"It's the dumbest thing I ever heard of," I said. "Especially if he thinks you've already divided the force! If you do that, you'll be inviting defeat in detail."

"Precisely," Falkenberg said. "Of course Governor Swale has no military background."

"He doesn't need one to know that plan's a bust," I said. "Lousy traitor—"

"No accusations," Falkenberg said. "We've no proof of anything. In any event, I am making the assumption that the Association is getting decoded copies of all my transmissions. I don't need to know how they get them. You'll remember that whenever you use radio signals that might be overheard."

"Yes, sir." Deane looked thoughtful. "That limits our communications somewhat."

"Yes. I hope that won't matter. Next problem. Under my assumption, the hostiles expect me to send a force eastward toward the river. That expectation must be met. I need Mr. Knowles to handle the artillery. It leaves you, Mr. Slater. I want you to take a platoon and simulate two companies with it. You'll send back a stream of reports, as if you're the main body of the battalion reporting to me at a headquarters left safely out of the combat zone." Falkenberg grinned slightly. "To the best of my knowledge, Irina's opinion of me is shared by her father. He won't find it at all hard to believe that I'm avoiding a combat area."

"But what if I really have a message?" I asked.

"You're familiar with O'Grady drill?" Falkenberg asked.

"Yes, sir." O'Grady drill is a form of torture devised by drill sergeants. You're supposed to obey only the commands that begin with "O'Grady says:." Then the sergeant snaps out a string of orders.

"We'll play that little game," Falkenberg said. "Now your mission is to get to the river, make a short demonstration, as if you're about to attack the southern edge of Allansport. and then move directly south, away from the town, until you link up with Mr. Bonneyman. You will then aid in his defense until you are relieved."

"But—Captain, you're assuming they know your orders."

He nodded. "Of course they'll put out an ambush. In this fog it will be a natural thing for them to do. Since they'll assume you have a much larger force with you, they'll probably use all the force that left Allansport this morning. I can't think they're stupid enough to try it with less."

"And we're to walk into it," I said.

"Yes. With your eyes open, but walk into it. You're bait, Mr. Slater. Get out there and wiggle."

I remembered an old comic strip. I quoted a line from it. "Don't much matter whether you catch a fish or not; once you been used for bait, you ain't much good for nothing else nohow."

"Maybe," Falkenberg said. "Maybe. But I remind you that you'll be keeping a major column of Association forces off Mr. Bonneyman's back."

"We will so long as we survive—"

"Yes. So I'll expect you to survive as long as possible."

"Can't quarrel with those orders, Captain."

❖   ❖   ❖

The fog was thicker when we reached the river. The troops were strung out along almost a full kilometer route, each maniple isolated from the others in the dripping-white blanket that lay across the valley. The troops were enjoying themselves, with monitors reporting as if they were platoon sergeants, and corporals playing centurion. They kept up a steady stream of chatter on the radio, while two men back at Falkenberg's headquarters sent orders that we paid no attention to. So far it was easy enough, because we hadn't run into anything at all.

"There's the city wall." Roszak pointed leftward. I could barely see a darker shape in the fog. "We'll take a quick look over. All right, Lieutenant?"

"Yes. Be careful."

"Always am, sir. Brady, bring your squad. Let's see what's over there." They vanished into the fog.

It seemed like hours, but it was only a few minutes before Brady returned. "Nothing, sir. Nothing and nobody, at least not close to the walls. May be a lot of them farther in. I got a feeling."

Roszak's voice came into my command set. "Moved fifty meters in. No change from what Brady reported."

"Did he have your feeling, Brady?" I asked.

"Yes, sir."

I switched the set back on. "Thank you, Roszak. Rejoin your company."

"Aye, aye, sir."

There were distant sounds of firing from the north. Ardwain's group was doing a good job of simulating a company. They were still moving into the town house by house. I wondered if he was running into opposition, or if that was all his own doing. He was supposed to go cautiously, and his men might be shooting up everything in sight. They were making a lot of noise. "Get me Falkenberg," I told Hartz.

"Yes, Mr. Slater?"

"Captain, Monitor O'Grady reports the south end of the town has been abandoned. I can hear the A Company combat team up at the north end, but I don't know what opposition they've encountered."

"Very light, Mister. You leave a company to assist A Company just in case, and continue south. Exactly as planned, Mr. Slater. No change. Got that?"

"Yes, sir."

"Having any trouble with the guns?"

"A little, sir. Roads are muddy. It's tough going, but we're moving."

"Excellent. Carry on, then. Out."

And that, I told myself, is that. I told off a monitor to dig in just outside the town and continue making reports. "You've just become B Company centurion," I said.

He grinned. "Yes, sir. Save a few of 'em for me."

"I'll do that, Yokura. Good luck." I waved the rest of my command down the road. We were strung out in a long column. The fog was a little thinner. Now I could see over twenty meters before the world was blotted out in swirling white mist.

What's the safest way to walk into an ambush? I asked myself. The safest way is not to do it. Bar that solution and you don't have a lot of choices. I used the helmet projector to show me a map of the route.

The first test was a hill just outside of town: Hill 509, called the Rockpile, a warren of jumbled boulders and flinty ledges. It dominated the road into the southern gate of Allansport. Whoever owned it controlled traffic into and out of the town.

If the Association only wanted to block us from moving south, that's where they'd have their strong point. If they were out to ambush the whole battalion, they'd leave it bare and set the trap farther on. Either way, they'd never expected me to go past it without having a look.

Four kilometers past the Rockpile there was a string of low hills. The road ran through a valley below them. It was an ideal place for an ambush. That's where they'll be, I decided. Only they must know we'll expect them to be along there somewhere. Bait should wiggle, but it shouldn't too obviously be bait. How would I act if I really had most of a battalion with me?

Send a strong advance guard, of course. An advance guard about as strong as the whole force I've got. Anything less won't make any sense.

"Roszak, start closing them up. Leave the wagons and half a dozen men with radios strung out along the line of march, and get everyone else up here. We'll form up as an advance guard and move south."

"Aye, aye, sir."

When I had the troops assembled, I led them up on the Rockpile. Nothing there, of course. I'd gauged it right. They were waiting for us up ahead.

Roszak nudged me and turned his head slightly to the right. I nodded, carefully. "Don't point, Sergeant. I saw something move up there myself."

We had reached the hills.

"Christ, what are they waiting for?" Roszak muttered.

"For the rest of the battalion. They don't want us; they want the whole 501st."

"Yes, sir."

We moved on ahead. The fog was lifting; visibility was over fifty meters already. It wouldn't be long before it would be obvious there weren't any troops following me, despite the loud curses and the squeals of wagon wheels back there. It's amazing how much noise a couple of wagons can make if the troops work at it.

To hell with it, I thought. We've got to find a good position and try to hold it. It'll do no good to keep walking farther into their trap. There was a rocky area ahead. It wasn't perfect, but it was the best spot I'd seen in half an hour. I nudged Roszak. "When we get up to there, start waving the men off into the rocks. The fog's thicker there."

"What if there's hostiles there already?" Roszak demanded.

"Then we'll fight for the ground, but I doubt they'll be there. I expect they've been moving out of our way as we advance. They still think there's a column a whole klick long behind us." Sound confident, I told myself. "We'll take up a defensive perimeter in there and wait the war out."

"Sure." Roszak moved to his right and spoke to the next man. The orders were passed along the line.

Three more minutes, I told myself. Three minutes and we'll at least have some cover. The area I'd chosen was a saddle, a low pass between the hills to either side of us. Not good, but better than the road. I could feel rifles aimed at me from the rocks above, but I saw nothing but grotesque shapes, boulders dripping in the fog. We climbed higher, moving steadily toward the place I'd chosen.

Maybe there's nobody up there watching at all. They may be on the other side of the valley. You only saw one man. Maybe not even a man. Just something moving. A wild animal. A dog. A blowing patch of fog.

Whatever it was, I can't take this much longer. You don't have to. Another minute. That boulder up there, the big one. When you reach it, you've finished. Don't run. Keep it slow—

"All right, you can fall out and take a break!" I shouted. "Hartz, tell the column to rest in place. We'll take ten. Companies should close up and gather in the stragglers. They'll assemble here after the break."

"Zur."

"Better get a perimeter guard out, Sergeant."

"Sir," Roszak called.

"Corporal Brady, how about a little coffee? You can set up the stove in the lee of that rock."

"Right, Lieutenant."

The men vanished into the fog. There were scrambling noises as they found hiding places. I moved out of the open and hunkered down in the rocks with Corporal Brady. "You didn't really have to make coffee," I said.

"Why not, Lieutenant? We have a while to wait, don't we?"

"I hope so, Corporal. I hope so. But that fog's lifting fast."

Ten minutes later we heard the guns. It was difficult to tell the direction of the sound in the thick fog, but I thought they were ahead of us, far to the south. There was no way to estimate the range.

"O'Grady message from Captain Falkenberg," Hartz said. "Lieutenant Bonneyman's group is under heavy attack from the south."

"Acknowledge." From the south. That meant the columns coming north out of Denisburg had made contact with Louis's ranchers. Falkenberg had guessed that much right. Maybe this whole screwy plan would work, after all. "Anything new on Ardwain's situation?"

"No messages, zur."

I thumbed my command set to the general frequency. "All units of the 501st, there is heavy fighting to the south. Assemble immediately. We'll be moving south to provide fire support. Get those guns rolling right now."

There was a chorus of radio answers. Only a dozen men, but they sounded like hundreds. I'd have been convinced it was a battalion combat team. I was congratulating myself when a shaft of sunlight broke through the mist and fell on the ground at my feet.

XVIII

Once the sun had broken through, the fog lifted fast. In seconds visibility went from fifty meters to a hundred, then two hundred. In minutes the road for a kilometer north of us was visible—and empty. One wagon struggled along it, and far back in the distance a single man carried a radio.

"O'Grady says hit the dirt!" I yelled. "Hartz, tell Falkenberg the deception's over."

And still there was nothing. I took out my glasses and examined the rocks above and behind us. They were boiling with activity. "Christ," I said. "Roszak, we've run into the whole Allansport outfit. Damned near a thousand men! Dig in and get your heads down!"

A mortar shell exploded on the road below. Then another, and then a salvo. Not bad shooting, I said to myself. Of course it didn't hit anything, because there was nothing to hit except the one wagon, but they had it registered properly. If we'd been down there, we'd have had it.

Rifle bullets zinged overhead. The Association troops were firing at last. I tried to imagine the feelings of the enemy commander, and I found myself laughing. He'd waited patiently all this time for us to walk into his trap, and all he'd caught was something less than a platoon. He was going to be mad.

He was also going to chew up my sixty men, two mortars, and four light machine guns. It would take him a little time, though. I'd picked a good spot to wait for him. Now that the fog had cleared, I saw it was a better place than I'd guessed from the map. We had reasonably clear fields of fire, and the rocks were large and sturdy. They'd have to come in and get us. All we had to do was keep our heads down.

No point in deception anymore. "O'Grady says stay loose and let 'em come to us."

There was a chorus of shouted responses. Then Brady's trumpet sounded, beginning with "On Full Kits" and running

159

through half the calls in the book before he settled onto the Line Marines' March. A favorite, I thought. Damned right. Then I heard the whistle of incoming artillery, and I dove for the tiny shelter between my rocks as barrage after barrage of heavy artillery dropped onto our position.

Riflemen swarmed down onto the road behind me. My radiomen and the two wagoneers were cut down in seconds. At least a company of Association troops started up the gentle slope toward us.

The Association commander made his first mistake then. His artillery had been effective enough for making us keep our heads down, but the rocks gave us good cover and we weren't taking many casualties. When the Association charged us, their troops held back until the artillery fire lifted. It takes experienced non-coms and a lot of discipline to get troops to take casualties from their own artillery. It pays off, but our attackers didn't know or believe it.

They were too far away when the artillery fire lifted. My lads were out of their hiding places in an instant. They poured fire on the advancing troops—rifles and the light machine guns, then both mortars. Few of the enemy had combat armor, and our fire was devastating.

"Good men," Hartz grunted. "They keep coming."

They were, but not for long. Too many of them were cut down. They swept to within fifty meters, wavered, and dropped back, some dragging their wounded with them, others running for it. When the attack was broken, we dropped back into the rocks to wait for the next barrage. "Score one for the Line Marines," I called.

Brady answered with the final fanfare from the March. "And there's none that can face us—"

"They won't try that again," Roszak said. He grinned with satisfaction. "Lads are doing right well, Mr. Slater."

"Well, indeed."

Our area was quiet, but there were sounds of heavy fighting in the south: artillery, rifle and machine gun fire, mortars and grenades. It sounded louder, as if it were coming closer to us. Louis and his commando of ranchers were facing big odds. I wondered if Kathryn were with him.

"They'll try infiltration next," Roszak predicted.

"What makes you think so?" Hartz asked.

"No discipline. After what happened last time, they'll never get a full attack going."

"No, they will have one more try in force. Perhaps two," Hartz argued.

"Never. Bet on it? Tomorrow's wine ration."

"Done," Hartz said. He was quiet for a moment, then handed me the handset. "Captain Falkenberg."

"Thank you. Yes, Captain?"

"O'Grady says the O'Grady drill is over. Understood?"

"Yes, sir."

"What's your situation?"

"We're in the saddle notch of Hill 239, seven klicks south of Allansport," I said. "Holding all right for now, but we're surrounded. Most of the hostiles are between us and Allansport. They let us right through for the ambush. They've tried one all-out attack and that didn't work. Roszak and Hartz are arguing over what they'll try next."

"How long can you hold?"

"Depends on what losses they're willing to take to get us out of here."

"You don't have to hold long," Falkenberg said. "A lot has happened. Ardwain broke through to the Governor and brought him out, but he ran into a strong force in Allansport. There's more coming over the bridge from the east side of the river."

"Sounds like they're bringing up everything they have."

"They are, and we're beating all of it. The column that moved north from Denisburg ran into Bonneyman's group. They deployed to break through that, and we circled around to their west and hit them in the flank. They didn't expect us. Your maneuver fooled them completely. They thought the 501st was with you until it was too late. They know better now, but we've broken them. Of course, there's a lot more of them than of us, and we couldn't hold them. They've broken through between Bonneyman and the river, and you're right in their path."

"How truly good."

"I think you'd do well to get out of their way," Falkenberg said. "I doubt you can stop them."

"If they link up with the Allansport force, they'll get away across the bridge. I can't hold them, but if you can get some artillery support here, I can spot for the guns. We might delay them."

"I was going to suggest that," Falkenberg said. "I've sent Ardwain and the Governor's escort toward that hill outside Allansport—the Rockpile. It looks like a dominant position."

"It is, sir. I've seen it. If we held that, we could keep this lot from getting into Allansport. We might bag the whole lot."

"Worth a try, anyway," Falkenberg said. "Provided you can hold on. It will be nearly an hour before I can get artillery support to you."

"We'll hold, sir."

"Good luck."

Roszak lost his wine ration. They tried one more assault. Two squads of Association troops got within twenty meters of our position before we threw them back. Of my sixty men, I had fewer than thirty effectives when it was over.

That was their last try, though. Shortly after, they regrouped. The elements which had been south of us had already skirted around the hills to join the main body, and now the whole group was moving north. They were headed for Allansport.

The sounds of fighting to the south were coming closer all the time. Falkenberg had Deane moving parallel to the Association troops, racing to get close enough to give us support, but it wouldn't arrive in time.

I sent our wounded up the hill away from the road with orders to dig in and lie low. The rest of us followed the retreating force. We were now sandwiched between the group ahead of us and the Denisburg column behind.

The first elements of Association forces were headed up the Rockpile when Deane came in range. He was still six kilometers southeast of us, long range and long time of flight, but we were in a good position to spot for him. I called in the first salvo on the advancing Association troops. The shells went beyond their target, and before I could walk them back down the hill, the Association forces retreated.

"They'll send another group around behind the hill," Roszak said. "We'll never stop them."

"No." So damned near. A few minutes' difference and we'd have bagged them all. The column Falkenberg was chasing was now no more than two kilometers south of us and moving fast.

"Hold one," Deane said. "I've got a Corporal Dangier calling in. Claims to be in position to spot targets for me."

"He's one of the wounded we left behind," I said. "He can see the road from his position, all right, but he won't last long once they know we've got a spotter in position to observe them."

"Do I fire the mission?" Deane demanded.

"Yes." Scratch Corporal Dangier, who had a girl in Harmony and a wife on Earth.

"I'll leave one gun at your disposal," Deane said. "I'm putting the rest on Dangier's mission."

A few minutes later we heard the artillery falling on the road behind us. That would play hell with the Association retreat. It kept up for ten minutes; then Deane called in again. "Can't raise Dangier any longer."

"No. There's nothing we can do here. They're staying out of sight. I'll call in some fire in places that might do some good, but it's shooting blind."

I amused myself with that for a while. It was frustrating. Once that force got to the top of the Rockpile, the route into Allansport would be secure. I was still cursing when Hartz shouted urgently.

"Centurion Ardwain on the line, sir."

"Ardwain, where are you?"

"Less than a klick west of you, Lieutenant. We moved around the edge of the town. Can't get inside without support. Militia won't try it, anyway."

"How many Marines do you have?" I demanded.

"About eighty effective. And Old Beastly."

"By God! Ardwain, move in fast. We'll join you as you come by. We're going right up to the top of the Rockpile and sit there until Falkenberg gets here. With Deane's artillery support we can hold that hill."

"Aye, aye, sir. We're coming."

"Let's go!" I shouted. "Who's been hit and can't run?"

No one answered. "Sergeant Roszak took one in the leg an hour ago, Lieutenant," Hartz said.

"I can still travel," Roszak said.

"Bullshit. You'll stay here and spot artillery for us. All the walking wounded stay with him. The rest of you get moving. We want to be in position when Centurion Ardwain comes."

"But—"

"Shut up and soldier, Roszak." I waved and we moved down from our low hilltop. We were panting when we got to the base of the Rockpile. There were already Association forces up there. I didn't know how many. We had to get up there before more joined them. The way up just ahead of me was clear, because it was in direct view of Roszak and his artillery spotters. We could use it and they couldn't.

I waved the men forward. Even a dozen of us on top of the Rockpile might be enough if Ardwain came up fast. We started up. Two men went down, then another, and my troops began to look around for shelter. I couldn't blame them, but I couldn't let them do it. Getting up that hill had become the only thing in my life. I had to get them moving again.

"Brady!" I shouted. "Corporal, sound the charge!"

The trumpet notes sang out. A monitor whipped out a

banner and waved it above his head. I shouted, "Follow me!" and ran up the hill. Then a mortar shell exploded two meters away. I had time to see bright red blotches spurt across my trousers legs and to wonder if that was my own blood; then I fell. The battle noises dimmed out.

"Lieutenant! Mr. Slater!"

I was in the bottom of a well. It was dark down there, and it hurt to look up at the light. I wanted to sink back into the well, but someone at the top was shouting at me. "Mr. Slater!"

"He's coming around, Centurion."

"He's got to, Crisp! Mr. Slater!"

There were people all around me. I couldn't see them very clearly, but I could recognize the voice. "Yes, Centurion."

"Mr. Slater," Ardwain said. "The Governor says we shouldn't take the hill! What do we do, sir?"

It didn't make sense. Where am I? I wondered. I had just sense enough not to ask. Everybody asks that, I thought. Why does everybody ask that? But I don't know—

I was pulled to a sitting position. My eyes managed to focus again, just for a moment. I was surrounded by people and rocks. Big rocks. Then I knew where I was. I'd passed these rocks before. They were at the base of the hill. Rocks below the Rockpile.

"What's that? Don't take the hill?" I said.

"Yes, sir—"

"Lieutenant, I have ordered your men to pull back. There are not enough to take this hill, and there's no point in wasting them."

That wasn't the Governor, but I'd heard the voice before. Trevor. Colonel Trevor of the militia. He'd been with Swale at the staff meeting back at Beersheba. Bits of the staff meeting came back to me, and I tried to remember more of them. Then I realized that was silly. The staff meeting wasn't important, but I couldn't think. What was important? There was something I had to do.

Get up the hill. I had to get up the hill. "Get me on my feet, Centurion."

"Sir—"

"Do it!" I was screaming. "I'm going up there. We have to take the Rockpile."

"You heard the company commander!" Ardwain shouted. "Move out!"

"Slater, you don't know what you're saying!" Trevor shouted.

I ignored him. "I've got to see," I said. I tried to get up, but my legs weren't working. Nothing happened when I tried to move them. "Lift me where I can see," I said.

"Sir—"

"Crisp, don't argue with me. Do it."

"You're crazy, Slater!" Trevor shouted. "Delirious. Sergeant Crisp, put him down. You'll kill him."

The medics hauled me to the edge of the boulder patch. Ardwain was leading men up the hill. Not just Marines, I saw. The militia had followed, as well. Insane, something whispered in the back of my mind. All insane. It's a disease, and they've caught it, too. I pushed the thought away.

They were falling, but they were still moving forward as they fell. I didn't know if they'd get to the top.

"You wanted to see!" Trevor shouted. "Now you've seen it! You can't send them up there. It's suicide, and they won't even listen to me! You've got to call them back, Slater. Make them retreat."

I looked at the fallen men. Some were just ahead of me. They hadn't even gotten twenty meters. There was one body blown in half. Something bright lay near it. I saw what it was and turned to Trevor.

"Retreat, Colonel? See that? Our trumpeter was killed sounding the charge. I don't know how to order a retreat."

XIX

I was deep in the well again, and it was dark, and I was afraid. They reached down into it after me, trying to pull me up, and I wanted to come. I knew I'd been in there a long time, and I wanted out, because I could hear Kathryn calling for me. I reached for her hand, but I couldn't find it. I remember shouting, but I don't know what I said. The nightmare went on for a long time.

Then it was daytime. The light was orange-red, very bright, and the walls were splashed with the orange light. I tried to move my head.

"Doc!" someone shouted. His voice was very loud.

"Hal?"

"I can't see you," I said. "Where are you, Kathryn? Where are you?"

"I'm here, Hal. I'll always be here."

And then it was dark again, but it wasn't so lonely in there.

I woke up several times after that. I couldn't talk much, and when I did I don't suppose I made much sense, but finally things were clear. I was in the hospital in Garrison, and I'd been there for weeks. I wasn't sure just how long. Nobody would tell me anything, and they talked in hushed tones so that I was sure I was dying, but I didn't.

"What the hell's wrong with me?" I demanded.

"Just take it easy, young fellow." He had a white coat, thick glasses, and a brown beard with white hairs in it.

"Who the hell are you?"

"That's Dr. Cechi," Kathryn told me.

"Well, why won't he tell me what's wrong with me?"

"He doesn't want to worry you."

"Worry me? Do you think not knowing gives peace of mind? Tell me."

"All right," Cechi said. "Nothing permanent. Understand that

166

first. Nothing permanent, although it's going to take a while
to fix you up. We almost lost you a couple of times, you know.
Multiple perforations of the gut, two broken vertebrae, compound fracture of the left femur, and assorted scrapes, punc-
tures, bruises, abrasions, and contusions. Not to mention almost
complete exsanguination when they brought you in. It's nothing
we can't fix, but you're going to be here a while, Captain."
He was holding my arm, and I felt pressure there, a hypospray. "You just go to sleep and we'll tell you the rest tomorrow."

"But—" Whatever I was going to say never got out. I sank
back, but it wasn't into the well. It was just sleep, and I could
tell the difference.

The next time I awoke, Falkenberg was there. He grinned
at me.

I grinned back. "Hi, Captain."

"Major. You're the captain."

"Uh? Run that past—"

"Just brevet promotions, but Harrington thinks they'll stick."

"We must have won."

"Oh, yeah." He sat where I could see him. His eyes looked
pale blue in that light. "Lieutenant Ardwain took the Rockpile,
but he said it was all your doing."

"Lieutenant Ardwain. Lot of promotions out of this," I said.

"Some. The Association no longer exists as an organized
military force. Your girl's friends are in control. Wan Loo is
the acting president, or supervisor, or whatever they call him.
Governor Swale's not too happy about it, but officially he has
to be. He didn't like endorsing Harrington's report, either, but
he had no choice."

"But he's a lousy traitor. Why's he still governor?"

"Act your age, Captain." There wasn't any humor in
Falkenberg's voice now. "We have no proof. I know the story,
if you'd like to hear it. In fact, you'd better. You're popular
enough with the Fleet, but there'll be elements of the Grand
Senate that'll hate your guts."

"Tell me."

"Swale has always been part of the Bronson faction,"
Falkenberg said. "The Bronson family is big in Dover Mineral Development Inc. Seems there's more to this place than
either American Express or Kennicott ever knew. Dover found
out and tried to buy mineral rights. The holy Joes wouldn't
sell—especially the farmers like Wan Loo and Seeton. They
don't want industrial development here, and it was obvious

to Swale that they wouldn't sell any mining rights to Dover. Swale's policy has been to help groups like the Association in return for their signatures on mining rights contracts. If enough of those outfits are recognized as legitimate local governments, there won't be any trouble over the contracts. You can probably figure out the rest."

"Maybe it's my head," I told him, "but I can't. What the devil did he let us into the valley for, then? Why did he go down there at all?"

"Just because they signed over some mining rights didn't make them his slaves. They were trying to jack up the grain prices. If the Harmony merchants complained loud enough, Swale wouldn't be governor here, and what use would he be to Dover then? He had to put some pressure on them—enough to make them sell, not so much that they'd be thrown out."

"Only we threw them out," I said.

"Only we threw them out. This time. Don't imagine that it's over."

"It has to be over," I said. "He couldn't pull that again."

"Probably he won't. Bronson hasn't much use for failures. I expect Governor Swale will shortly be on his way to a post as First Secretary on a mining asteroid. There'll be another governor, and if he's not a Bronson client, he'll be someone else's. I'm not supposed to depress you. You've got a decision to make. I've been assigned to a regular Line Regiment as adjutant. The 42nd. It's on Kennicott. Tough duty. Probably a lot of fighting, good opportunities, regular troops. I've got room on the staff. Want to come along? They tell me you'll be fit to move by the time the next ship gets here."

"I'll think about it."

"Do that. You've got a good career ahead of you. Now *you're* the youngest captain in the Fleet. Couldn't swing the Military Star, but you'll get another medal."

"I'll think about it. I have to talk with Kathryn—"

He shrugged. "Certainly, Captain." He grinned and went out.

Captain. Captains may marry, Majors should marry, Colonels must marry—

But that was soldier talk, and I wasn't sure I was a soldier. Strange, I thought. Everyone says I am. I've done well, and I have a great career, and it all seems like a fit of madness. Corporal Brady won't be playing his trumpet any longer because of me. Dangier, wounded but alive, until he volunteered to be an artillery spotter. And all the others, Levine and Lieberman and recruit—no, Private—Dietz, and the rest, dead and blended together in my memory until

I can't remember where they died or what for, only that I killed them.

But we won. It was a glorious victory. That was enough for Falkenberg. He had done his job and done it well. Was it enough for me? Would it be in the future?

When I was up and around, I couldn't avoid meeting Governor Swale. Irina was nursing Louis Bonneyman. Louis was worse off than I was. Sometimes they can grow you a new leg, but it takes time, and it's painful. Irina saw him every day, and when I could leave the hospital she insisted that I come to the palace. It was inevitable that I would meet the Governor.

"I hope you're proud of yourself," Swale said. "Everyone else is."

"Hugo, that's not fair," Irina protested.

"Not fair?" Swale said. "How isn't it fair?"

"I did the job I was paid to do, sir," I said.

"Yes. You did, indeed—and thereby made it impossible for me to do mine. Sit down, Captain Slater. Your Major Falkenberg has told you plenty of stories about me. Now let me tell you my side of it."

"There's no need, Governor," I said.

"No, there isn't. Are you afraid to find out just what you've done?"

"No. I've helped throw out a gang of convicts who pretended to be a government. And I'm proud enough of that."

"Are you? Have you been to the Allan Valley lately, Captain? Of course you haven't. And I doubt Kathryn Malcolm has told you what's happening there—how Wan Loo and Harry Seeton and a religious fanatic named Brother Dornan have established commissions of deacons to inquire into the morals and loyalties of everyone in the valley; how anyone they find deficient is turned off the land to make room for their own people. No, I don't suppose she told you any of that."

"I don't believe you."

"Don't you? Ask Miss Malcolm. Or would you believe Irina? She knows it's true."

I looked to Irina. The pain in her eyes was enough. She didn't have to speak.

"I was governor of the whole planet, Slater. Not just Harmony, not just the Jordan and Allan valleys, but all of the planet. Only they gave me responsibilities and no authority, and no means to govern. What am I supposed to do with the convicts, Slater? They ship them here by the thousands, but they give me nothing to feed them with. You've seen them. How are they supposed to live?"

"They can work—"

"At what? As farmhands on ranches of five hundred hectares? The best land on the planet, doled out as huge ranches with half the land not worked because there's no fertilizer, no irrigation, not even decent drainage systems. They sure as hell can't work in our nonexistent industries. Don't you see that Arrarat *must* industrialize? It doesn't matter what Allan Valley farmers want, or what the other holy Joes want. It's industrialize or face famine, and, by God, there'll be no famines while I can do something about them."

"So you were willing to sell out the 501st. Help the Association defeat us. An honorable way to achieve an honorable end."

"As honorable as yours. Yours is to kill and destroy. War is honorable, but deceit isn't. I prefer my way, Captain."

"I expect you do."

Swale nodded vigorously, to himself, not to me. "Smug. Proud and smug. Tell me, Captain, just how are you better than the Protective Association? They fought. Not for the honor of the corps, but for their land, their families, for friends. They lost. You had better men, better officers, better training. A lot better equipment. If you'd lost, you'd have been returned to Garrison under terms. The Association troops were shot out of hand. All of them. Be proud, Slater. But you make me sick. I'll leave you now. I don't care to argue with my daughter's guests."

"That's true also, isn't it?" I asked Irina. "They shot all the Association troops?"

"Not all," Irina said. "The ones that surrendered to Captain Falkenberg are still alive. He even recruited some of them."

He would. The battalion would need men after those battles. "What's happened to the rest?"

"They're under guard at Beersheba. It was after your Marines left the valley that the real slaughter began."

"Sure. People who wouldn't turn out to fight for their homes when we needed their help got real patriotic after it was over," I said. "I'm going back to my quarters, Irina. Thank you for having me over."

"But Kathryn is coming. She'll be here—"

"I don't want to see anyone just now. Excuse me." I left quickly and wandered through the streets of Harmony. People nodded and smiled as I passed. The Marines were still popular. Of course. We'd opened the trade route up the Jordan, and we'd cleared out the Allan Valley. Grain was cheap, and we'd held the convicts at bay. Why shouldn't the people love us?

Tattoo sounded as I entered the fort. The trumpets and drums sounded through the night, martial and complex and the notes were sweet. Sentries saluted as I passed. Life here was orderly and there was no need to think.

Hartz had left a full bottle of brandy where I could find it. It was his theory that the reason I wasn't healing fast was that I didn't drink enough. The surgeons didn't share his opinion. They were chopping away at me, then using the regeneration stimulators to make me grow better parts. It was a painful process, and they didn't think liquor helped it much.

To hell with them, I thought, and poured a double. I hadn't finished it when Kathryn came in.

"Irina said—Hal, you shouldn't be drinking."

"I doubt that Irina said that."

"You know—what's the matter with you, Hal?"

"Why didn't you tell me?" I asked.

"I was going to. Later. But there never was a right time."

"And it's all true? Your friends are driving the families of everyone who cooperated with the Association out into the hills? And they've shot all the prisoners?"

"It's—yes. It's true."

"Why didn't you stop them?"

"Should I have wanted to?" She looked at the scars on her hands. "Should I?"

There was a knock at the door. "Come in," I said.

It was Falkenberg. "Thought you were alone," he said.

"Come in. I'm confused."

"I expect you are. Got any more of that brandy?"

"Sure. What did you mean by that?"

"I understand you've just learned what's happening out in the Allan Valley."

"Crapdoodle! Has Irina been talking to everyone in Garrison? I don't need a convention of people to cheer me up."

"You don't eh?" He made no move to leave. "Spit it out, Mister."

"You don't call Captains 'Mister.'"

He grinned. "No. Sorry. What's the problem, Hal? Finding out that things aren't as simple as you'd like them to be?"

"John, what the hell were we fighting for out there? What good do we do?" •

He stretched a long arm toward the brandy bottle and poured for both of us. "We threw a gang of criminals out. Do you doubt that's what they were? Do you insist that the people we helped be saints?"

"But the women. And children. What will happen to them? And the Governor's right—something's got to be done for the convicts. Poor bastards are sent here, and we can't just drown them."

"There's land to the west," Kathryn said. "They can have that. My grandfather had to start from the beginning. Why can't the new arrivals?"

"The Governor's right about a lot of things," Falkenberg said. "Industry's got to come to Arrarat someday. Should it come just to make the Bronson family rich? At the expense of a bunch of farmers who bought their land with one hell of a lot of hard work and blood? Hal, if you're having second thoughts about the action here on Arrarat, what'll you do when the Fleet's ordered to do something completely raw?"

"I don't know. That's what bothers me."

"You asked what good we do," Falkenberg said. "We buy time. Back on Earth they're ready to start a war that won't end until billions are dead. The Fleet's the only thing preventing that. The only thing, Hal. Be as cynical about the CoDominium as you like. Be contemptuous of Grand Senator Bronson and his friends—yes, and most of his enemies, too, damn it. But remember that the Fleet keeps the peace, and as long as we do, Earth still lives. If the price of that is getting our hands dirty out here on the frontiers, then it's a price we have to pay. And while we're paying it, just once in a while we do something right. I think we did that here. For all that they've been vicious enough now that the battle's over, Wan Loo and his people aren't evil. I'd rather trust the future to them than to people who'd do . . . that." He took Kathryn's hand and turned it over in his. "We can't make things perfect, Hal. But we can damned sure end some of the worst things people do to each other. If that's not enough, we have our own honor, even if our masters have none. The Fleet is our country, Hal, and it's an honorable fatherland." Then he laughed and drained his glass. "Talking's dry work. Pipe Major's learned three new tunes. Come and hear them. You deserve a night in the club, and the drinks are on the battalion. You've friends here, and you've not seen much of them."

He stood, the half smile still on his lips. "Good evening, Hal. Kathryn."

"You're going with him, aren't you?" Kathryn said when he'd closed the door.

"You know I don't care all that much for bagpipes—"

"Don't be flippant with me. He's offered you a place with his new regiment, and you're going to take it."

"I don't know. I've been thinking about it—"

"I know. I didn't before, but I do now. I watched you while he was talking. You're going."

"I guess I am. Will you come with me?"

"If you'll have me, yes. I can't go back to the ranch. I'll have to sell it. I couldn't ever live there now. I'm not the same girl I was when this started."

"I'll always have doubts," I said. "I'll need—" I couldn't finish the thought, but I didn't have to. She came to me, and she wasn't trembling at all, not the way she'd been before, anyway. I held her for a long time.

"We should go now," she said finally. "They'll be expecting you."

"But—"

"We've plenty of time, Hal. A long time."

As we left the room, Last Post sounded across the fort.

Command is the comprehensive responsibility of a
soldier assigned a military mission by the sovereign
authority and given the human and material means he
needs to accomplish it. It is also the sole instrument of
his authority to use and expend at his own discretion any
or all elements of the means at his disposal

Command must wield authority to an absolute degree
within the scope of its charge. It brings into being a
complex of forces emanating from a focal point that keeps
a number of complexes of force integrated and the
manifold power of the whole directed to the desired end.
It is both the binding and the driving force of every
military endeavor. It has no substitute. It is not divisible
in parts. No possible arrangement of organized effort that
lacks it can be called military nor be of any martial value.

Every soul in his earliest stages of untutored awareness feels that the center of the universe resides within
himself. To learn that we exist and move for the most
part in orbits, rather than preside at the focal point of
even a minor cosmic system is a painful and difficult
process for most of us . . .

Joseph Maxwell Cameron
The Anatomy of Military Merit

"Shuttle landing in twenty-six minutes, sir." Centurion
Calvin's tone was flat and unemotional, but he couldn't keep
a questioning edge from his voice. "Pilot says a Rear Admiral is aboard."

Acting Colonel John Christian Falkenberg nodded. "Turn out
a guard to render proper honors. I'll meet him myself."

"Sir." It was clear that Calvin wanted to know more, and
that he might have asked if there hadn't been others in the
Colonel's office. Instead he stiffened to attention and saluted,
got a return, and turned on his heel to stride from the office.

"A Rear Admiral," Captain Harlan Slater said. "You didn't
seem surprised, sir."

"It's Lermontov and I've been expecting him, Hal,"
Falkenberg said.

"The devil you have." Captain Jeremy Savage was incredulous. Despite years in the Line Marines he still spoke with the crisp accents of his native Churchill. "How long has he been in this sector?" Savage looked thoughtful, and said aloud but mostly to himself, "Long enough." He gave Falkenberg a knowing look. "I take it he's sector commander, then?"

Falkenberg nodded. "As you surmise."

Slater looked puzzled. "All right, I give up, what's the big secret here?"

Jeremy Savage smiled thinly. "A newly commissioned major arrives on Kennicott. A bit more than a year later, after a spectacularly successful campaign in which the regimental colonel is killed, that major is now acting colonel of the regiment. Not major in command waiting for a new colonel, Hal, but Acting Colonel, entitled to the rank and pay unless it's rescinded. That kind of appointment can only come from the sector commander, and since that kind of patronage isn't accidental, I have already asked myself who might bestow such an appointment to John Christian Falkenberg." He shrugged. "Now a name comes to mind, and I hear that he's on his way down to this planet . . ."

Falkenberg cut the conversation short by standing. "And he'll be here shortly. We don't want to be late meeting him. Gentlemen?"

Rear Admiral Sergei Lermontov looked around the opulent facilities and nodded. "I need not ask if this office is secure," he said.

"To the best Centurion Calvin can manage, and I checked myself as well, sir," Falkenberg said. He shrugged. "Admiral, is anything secure in these times?"

"You ask correct question," Lermontov said. "And answer is no, despite all we can do." He looked significantly at the golden pips on Falkenberg's epaulettes. "At least we are gathering tools. There is much can be done with a regiment under proper command. Yours."

"You're saying I can keep the 42nd?"

"Unlikely as this seems. We have unusual situation in Grand Senate, coalition in our favor together with urgent need for regiment commanded by one of us. You become colonel and keep regiment. I become Vice Admiral." He nodded. "And perhaps more, if you are successful. But we must act quickly."

"Act quickly? Sir?"

"Yes. Transport brings battalion of Fleet Marines to take up duties here. That will be sufficient, now, I believe? Your report indicates there is no opposition remaining that would strain such resources."

"That's true enough, sir. Provided that the local militia stays loyal."

"This is problem?"

Falkenberg shook his head slowly. "Not a big problem. The local militia leader is my wife's father, which is to say, my wife, given Tobias's failing health. As long as Grace is here, the situation is stable, sir." Falkenberg's face held no expression. "Of course that may present a problem for me. You haven't said where you intend sending the 42nd."

"Far, and probably for long time," Lermontov said. "Two years at least. This will be permanent change, there is transportation for all dependents." He paused. "I must be honest. You will not come back to Kennicott in any case. There is other work for 42nd Line Marines under your command."

"The situation here won't change, Admiral," Falkenberg said. "The miners trust Tobias and Grace. So do the owners. Without them the peace here falls apart."

"I know."

"You ask a lot. Sir." Falkenberg said.

"I offer much," Lermontov said. "Regiment to officer who was captain before Ararat campaign."

Falkenberg shook his head. "Colonel of 42nd, against commander of planetary militia. My wife's family is rich, Admiral. Why would a colonel's pay be tempting? We both know I'll never be anything more than a Line Marine colonel no matter what your influence."

"True enough. There is no question that if you choose to leave service, I cannot prevent, and you will certainly have more pleasant life."

Falkenberg nodded. "So."

"So I need you," Lermontov said. "Shall I be dramatic? Human race needs you."

"That's dramatic enough. Unlikely to be true, but dramatic enough."

"Is quite true," Lermontov said. "Shall I explain?"

PART TWO: MERCENARY

From the last West Point lecture by Professor John Christian Falkenberg, II, delivered at the United States Military Academy immediately prior to the reorganization of the Academy. After the Academy was restructured to reflect rising nationalism in the United States, Falkenberg as a CoDominium Professor was unwelcome in any event; but the content of this lecture would have assured that anyway. *Crofton's Essays and Lectures in Military History, 2nd Edition.*

"All large and important institutions change slowly. It is probably as well that this is true for the military; but well or not, it is inevitable. It takes time to build history and traditions, and military organizations with no history and traditions are generally ineffective.

"There are of course notable exceptions to this rule, although some of the more popular cases do not bear examination. For example, Colonel Michael Hoare's Fifth Commando in Katanga in the 1960s, while rightly studied as a harbinger of the growth of mercenary organizations in this century, owed much of its justly celebrated success to the incompetence—including frequent drunkenness—of its opposition. Moreover, Hoare, by recruiting most of his officers and non-coms, and many of his troopers, from British veterans, was able to draw on the long history and tradition of the British Army.

"I dare say something of this sort will happen in the future, as many CoDominium military units are disbanded. It is conceivable that entire units will be hired on by one or another patron. Certainly a small cohesive unit accustomed to working together would be preferable to a larger group of mercenaries.

"The building of the CoDominium military forces is itself an illustrative case; once again, by incorporating disbanded units such as the French *Légion Étrangére*, the Cameron Highlanders, and the Cossack Adventurers, a fighting force was able to appropriate to itself considerable history and tradition. Even so, it has taken decades to build the CoDominium Line Marines into the formidable force they have become.

"However, I bring up the subject of changing institutions for another reason. We are seeing, I believe, the completion of yet another full cycle in the history of violence and civilization. As late as the turn of the Millennium, most military organizations were motivated by national patriotism, and the 'Laws of War' were treated either as a joke, as unwanted restrictions on military action, or, as in the case of the infamous 'War Crimes' trials following World War II, as a means of retaliation against a defeated enemy.

"Then, during the course of this century, the Laws of War have become quite important, and have often been observed; and where they are not observed there is a good chance that the CoDominium Fleet will punish those who violate them—particularly if the violation involves CoDominium citizens, and inevitably if it involves a member of the Fleet.

"Now I believe we are entering a new period; one in which the nationalist forces will pursue a new policy of expediency, while the CoDominium and mercenary units continue to observe and insist on the Laws of War. Now it would appear that the outcome of such a conflict is predictable: that the organizations which recognize no limitations save expediency will always triumph over those which restrict their uses of military power. This is not impossible. I do not believe it will be inevitable.

However, many do believe that the Laws of War will go the way of the Rights of Neutrals in the last century. After all, the United States, having entered World War I ostensibly to protect the rights of neutral vessels on the high seas, within days of entering World War II declared unrestricted submarine warfare against Germany and Japan; while the Allied powers, having denounced Japanese actions against Nanking in the 1930s, had no scruples about bombing civilians and open cities as the war progressed, culminating in Hiroshima, Nagasaki, and the fire raids against Tokyo.

"By the end of World War II, few observed any limits on the use of military power. Allied units regularly took civilian hostages and exposed civilian officials to danger as a means of discouraging partisan activity. Most of these actions had been taken by the German Army and of course had been denounced at the time.

"That expedient view became so widespread that for decades no one could conceive of another.

"However, it has not always been thus. Prior to the present era there were at least three periods in which war became stylized and subject to rules. These eras have been described well enough by Martin Van Creveld in his definitive *Technology and War*.

"The first such era was the Hellenistic period from about 300 to 200 B.C. During that time there were essentially no differences among the successor states. Each was ruled by despotism built around a dynasty and generally ruled by a single man. The ordinary citizen had no stake in this government, and cared not a whit whether this man or that held the throne. The military units were composed of professionals who had no personal stake in the outcome of a campaign. As Creveld says:

"'Accordingly, there applied among those states a fairly strict code which dictated what was and was not permissible in regard to the treatment of prisoners, the enslavement of captured cities, the robbery for military purposes of temples dedicated to the gods (this was legitimate provided that restitution was subsequently made, or at any rate promised), and so on.

"'The application of rules to warfare was, however, extended further than this. While it would be imprecise to say that there existed an explicit international agreement concerning the types of military technology that might or might not be used, the various contestants shared a common material civilization and knew what to expect of each other. Since they fielded much the same weapons and equipment, but also because commanders and technical experts frequently transferred from one army to another, they found themselves operating on broadly similar tactical and strategic codes . . .'

"The second period of warfare treated as a game with rules was, of course, the period of feudal chivalry, and probably quite enough has been said about it in previous lectures. For the third, I quote again from Creveld:

"'The play-element often present in armed conflict was, however, probably never as pronounced as in the eighteenth century, when war become popularly known as the game of kings. It was an age in which, according to Voltaire, all Europeans lived under the same kind of institutions, believed in the same kind of ideas, and fornicated with the same kind of women. Most states were ruled by absolute monarchs. Even those who were not so ruled neither expected nor demanded the lump-in-the-throat type of allegiance later to be associated with the nationalist states. Armies were commanded by members of an international nobility who spoke French as their *lingua franca* and switched sides as they saw fit. They were manned by personnel who, often enlisted by trickery and kept in the ranks by main force, cared nothing for honor, duty, or country . . .

"'In each of the three above periods, as well as in many others which witnessed the same phenomenon, the transformation of war into something akin to a game did not pass without comment. What some people took as a sign of piety or reason or progress, others saw as proof of stupidity, effeminacy, and degeneration. During the last years before the French Revolution, Gibbon praised war for its moderation and expressed the hope that it would soon disappear altogether. Simultaneously, a French nobleman, the Comte de Guibet, was cutting a figure among the ladies of the *salons* by denouncing the prevailing military practices as degenerate and calling for a commander and a people who, to use his own words, would tear apart the feeble constitution of Europe like the north wind bending the reeds . . .'

"Gentlemen and ladies, I invite you to reflect on this. We live in a time when the major powers of the Earth are governed by what can only be called self perpetuating oligarchies. While there is more ostensible turnover in the compositions of the Congress of the United States and the Supreme Soviet than there was in the last decade of the twentieth century, there is not a lot more, and what turnover there is happens to be meaningless; the new master is indistinguishable from the old.

"Nor is it important that these oligarchs think themselves important doing important work—indeed that they *are* important and *do* important work. The effect has been to alienate the Citizen entirely; while the taxpayer supports the present system only because he fears the loss of his privileges—because he fears he will be cast into the lot of the Citizen. The same is true in the Soviet system, where Party Members have long ago lost confidence in the possibility of reform, and now do no more than jealously hold onto their privileges.

"Yet—while it is easy to denounce the CoDominium and its endless cynicism, it is not so certain that whatever replaces it will be better. Indeed, we must wonder just what would survive the collapse of the CoDominium . . ."

I

Twenty years later . . .

Earth floated eternally lovely above bleak lunar mountains. Daylight lay across California and most of the Pacific, and the glowing ocean made an impossibly blue background for a vortex of bright clouds swirling in a massive tropical storm. Beyond the lunar crags, man's home was a fragile ball amidst the black star-studded velvet of space; a ball that a man might reach out to grasp and crush in his bare hands.

Grand Admiral Sergei Lermontov looked at the bright viewscreen image and thought how easy it would be for Earth to die. He kept her image on the viewscreen to remind himself of that every time he looked up.

"That's all we can get you, Sergei." His visitor sat with hands carefully folded in his lap. A photograph would have shown him in a relaxed position, seated comfortably in the big visitor's chair covered with leathers from animals that grew on planets a hundred light years from Earth. Seen closer, the real man was not relaxed at all. He looked that way from his long experience as a politician.

"I wish it could be more." Grand Senator Martin Grant shook his head slowly from side to side. "At least it's something."

"We will lose ships and disband regiments. I cannot operate the Fleet on that budget." Lermontov's voice was flat and precise. He adjusted his rimless spectacles to a comfortable position on his thin nose. His gestures, like his voice, were precise and correct, and it was said in Navy wardrooms that the Grand Admiral practiced in front of a mirror.

"You'll have to do the best you can. It's not even certain the United Party can survive the next election. God knows we won't be able to if we give any more to the Fleet."

"But there is enough money for national armies." Lermontov looked significantly at Earth's image on the viewscreen. "Armies that can destroy earth. Martin, how can we keep the peace if you will not let us have ships and men?"

"You can't keep the peace if there's no CoDominium."

Lermontov frowned. "Is there a real chance that the United Party will lose, then?"

Martin Grant's head bobbed in an almost imperceptible movement. "Yes."

"And the United States will withdraw from the CD." Lermontov thought of all that would mean, for Earth and for the nearly hundred worlds where men lived. "Not many of the colonies will survive without us. It is too soon. If we did not suppress science and research it might be different, but there are so few independent worlds—Martin, we are spread thin across the colony worlds. The CoDominium must help them. We created their problems with our colonial governments. We gave them no chances at all to live without us. We cannot let them go suddenly."

Grant sat motionless, saying nothing.

"Yes, I am preaching to the converted. But it is the Navy that gave the Grand Senate this power over the colonies. I cannot help feeling responsible."

Senator Grant's head moved slightly again, either a nod or a tremor. "I would have thought there was a lot you could do, Sergei. The Fleet obeys you, not the Senate. I know my nephew has made that clear enough. The warriors respect another warrior, but they've only contempt for us politicians."

"You are inviting treason?"

"No. Certainly I'm not suggesting that the Fleet try running the show. Military rule hasn't worked very well for us, has it?" Senator Grant turned his head slightly to indicate the globe behind him. Twenty nations on Earth were governed by armies, none of them very well.

On the other hand, the politicians aren't doing a much better job, he thought. Nobody is. "We don't seem to have any goals, Sergei. We just hang on, hoping that things will get better. Why should they?"

"I have almost ceased to hope for better conditions," Lermontov replied. "Now I only pray they do not get worse." His lips twitched slightly in a thin smile. "Those prayers are seldom answered."

"I spoke with my brother yesterday," Grant said. "He's threatening to retire again. I think he means it this time."

"But he cannot do that!" Lermontov shuddered. "Your brother is one of the few men in the U. S. government who understands how desperate is our need for time."

"I told him that."

"And?"

Grant shook his head. "It's the rat race, Sergei. John doesn't see any end to it. It's all very well to play rear guard, but for what?"

"Isn't the survival of civilization a worthwhile goal?"

"If that's where we're headed, yes. But what assurance do we have that we'll achieve even that?"

The Grand Admiral's smile was wintry. "None, of course. But we may be sure that *nothing* will survive if we do not have more time. A few years of peace, Martin. Much can happen in a few years. And if nothing does—why, we will have had a few years."

The wall behind Lermontov was covered with banners and plaques. Centered among them was the CoDominium Seal: American eagle, Soviet sickle and hammer, red stars and white stars. Beneath it was the Navy's official motto: PEACE IS OUR PROFESSION.

We chose that motto for them, Grant thought. The Senate made the Navy adopt it. Except for Lermontov I wonder how many Fleet officers believe it? What would they have chosen if left to themselves?

There are always the warriors, and if you don't give them something worthwhile to fight for . . . But we can't live without them, because there comes a time when you have to have warriors. Like Sergei Lermontov.

But do we have to have politicians like me? "I'll talk to John again. I've never been sure how serious he is about retiring anyway. You get used to power, and it's hard to lay it down. It only takes a little persuasion, some argument to let you justify keeping it. Power's more addicting than opiates."

"But you can do nothing about our budget."

"No. Fact is, there's more problems. We need Bronson's votes, and he's got demands."

Lermontov's eyes narrowed, and his voice was thick with distaste. "At least we know how to deal with men like Bronson." And it was strange, Lermontov thought, that despicable creatures like Bronson should be so small as problems. They could be bribed. They expected to be bought.

It was the men of honor who created the real problems. Men like Harmon in the United States and Kaslov in the Soviet Union, men with causes they would die for—they had brought mankind to this.

But I would rather know Kaslov and Harmon and their friends than Bronson's people who support us.

"You won't like some of what he's asked for," Grant said. "Isn't Colonel Falkenberg a special favorite of yours?"

"He is one of our best men. I use him when the situation seems desperate. His men will follow him anywhere, and he does not waste lives in achieving our objectives."

"He's apparently stepped on Bronson's toes once too often. They want him cashiered."

"No." Lermontov's voice was firm.

Martin Grant shook his head. Suddenly he felt very tired, despite the low gravity of the moon. "There's no choice, Sergei. It's not just personal dislike, although there's a lot of that too. Bronson's making up to Harmon, and Harmon thinks Falkenberg's dangerous."

"Of course he is dangerous. He is a warrior. But he is a danger only to enemies of the CoDominium. . . ."

"Precisely." Grant sighed again. "Sergei, I *know*. We're robbing you of your best tools and then expecting you to do the work without them."

"It is more than that, Martin. How do you control warriors?"

"I beg your pardon?"

"I asked, 'How do you control warriors?'" Lermontov adjusted his spectacles with the tips of the fingers of both hands. "By earning their respect, of course. But what happens if that respect is forfeit? There will be no controlling him; and you are speaking of one of the best military minds alive. You may live to regret this decision, Martin."

"Can't be helped. Sergei, do you think I like telling you to dump a good man for a snake like Bronson? But it doesn't matter. The Patriot Party's ready to make a big thing out of this, and Falkenberg couldn't survive that kind of political pressure anyway, you know that. No officer can. His career's finished no matter what."

"You have always supported him in the past."

"Goddamn it, Sergei, I appointed him to the Academy in the first place. I cannot support him, and you can't either. He goes, or we lose Bronson's vote on the budget."

"But why?" Lermontov demanded. "The real reason."

Grant shrugged. "Bronson's or Harmon's? Bronson has hated Colonel Falkenberg ever since that business on Kennicott. The Bronson family lost a lot of money there, and it didn't help that Bronson had to vote in favor of giving Falkenberg his medals either. I doubt there's any more to it than that.

"Harmon's a different matter. He really believes that Falkenberg might lead his troops against Earth. And once he asks for Falkenberg's scalp as a favor from Bronson—"

"I see. But Harmon's reasons are ludicrous. At least at the moment they are ludicrous—"

"If he's that damned dangerous, kill him," Grant said. He saw the look on Lermontov's face. "I don't really mean that, Sergei, but you'll have to do something."

"I will."

"Harmon thinks you might order Falkenberg to march on Earth."

Lermontov looked up in surprise.

"Yes. It's come to that. Not even Bronson's ready to ask for *your* scalp. Yet. But it's another reason why your special favorites have to take a low profile right now."

"You speak of our best men."

Grant's look was full of pain and sadness. "Sure. Anyone who's effective scares hell out of the Patriots. They want the CD eliminated entirely, and if they can't get that, they'll weaken it. They'll keep chewing away, too, getting rid of our most competent officers, and there's not a lot we can do. Maybe in a few years things will be better."

"And perhaps they will be worse," Lermontov said.

"Yeah. There's always that, too."

Sergei Lermontov stared at the viewscreen long after Grand Senator Grant had left the office. Darkness crept slowly across the Pacific, leaving Hawaii in shadow, and still Lermontov sat without moving, his fingers drumming restlessly on the polished wood desktop.

I knew it would come to this, he thought. Not so soon, though, not so soon. There is still so much to do before we can let go.

And yet it will not be long before we have no choice. Perhaps we should act now.

Lermontov recalled his youth in Moscow, when the Generals controlled the Presidium, and shuddered. No, he thought. The military virtues are useless for governing civilians. But the politicians are doing no better.

If we had not suppressed scientific research. But that was done in the name of the peace. Prevent development of new weapons. Keep control of technology in the hands of the government, prevent technology from dictating policy to all of us; it had seemed so reasonable, and besides, the policy was very old now. There were few trained scientists, because no one wanted to live under the restrictions of the Bureau of Technology.

What is done is done, he thought, and looked around the

office. Open cabinets held shelves covered with the mementos of a dozen worlds. Exotic shells lay next to reptilian stuffed figures and were framed by gleaming rocks that could bring fabulous prices if he cared to sell.

Impulsively he reached toward the desk console and turned the selector switch. Images flashed across the viewscreen until he saw a column of men marching through a great open bubble of rock. They seemed dwarfed by the enormous cave.

A detachment of CoDominium Marines marching through the central area of Luna Base. Senate chamber and government offices were far below the cavern, buried so deeply into rock that no weapon could destroy the CoDominium's leaders by surprise. Above them were the warriors who guarded, and this group was marching to relieve the guard.

Lermontov turned the sound pickup but heard no more than the precise measured tramp of marching boots. They walked carefully in low gravity, their pace modified to accommodate their low weight; and they would, he knew, be just as precise on a high-gravity world.

They wore uniforms of blue and scarlet, with gleaming buttons of gold, badges of the dark rich bronze alloys found on Kennicott, berets made from some reptile that swam in Tanith's seas. Like the Grand Admiral's office, the CoDominium Marines showed the influence of worlds light years away.

"Sound off."

The order came through the pickup so loud that it startled the Admiral, and he turned down the volume as the men began to sing.

Lermontov smiled to himself. That song was officially forbidden, and it was certainly not an appropriate choice for the guard mount about to take posts outside the Grand Senate chambers. It was also very nearly the official marching song of the Marines. And that, Admiral Lermontov thought, ought to tell something to any Senator listening.

If Senators ever listened to anything from the military people.

The measured verses came through, slowly, in time with the sinister gliding step of the troops.

"We've left blood in the dirt of twenty-five worlds,
we've built roads on a dozen more,
and all that we have at the end our hitch,
buys a night with a second-class whore.

"The Senate decrees, the Grand Admiral calls,
the orders come down from on high,
It's 'On Full Kits' and sound 'Board Ships,'
We're sending you where you can die.

"The lands that we take, the Senate gives back,
rather more often than not,
so the more that are killed, the less share the loot,
and we won't be back to this spot.

"We'll break the hearts of your women and girls,
we may break your arse as well,
Then the Line Marines with their banners unfurled,
will follow those banners to Hell.

"We know the devil, his pomps and his works,
Ah yes! we know them well!
When we've served out our hitch as Line Marines,
we can bugger the Senate of Hell!

"Then we'll drink with our comrades and lay
   down our packs,
we'll rest ten years on the flat of our backs,
then it's 'On Full Kits' and 'Out of Your Racks,'
you must build a new road through Hell!

"The Fleet is our country, we sleep with a rifle,
no one ever begot a son on his rifle,
they pay us in gin and curse when we sin,
there's not one that can stand us unless we're
   down wind,
we're shot when we lose and turned out when
   we win,
but we bury our comrades wherever they fall,
and there's none that can face us though we've
   nothing at all."

The verse ended with a flurry of drums, and Lermontov
gently changed the selector back to the turning Earth.

Perhaps, he thought. Perhaps there's hope, but only if we
have time.

Can the politicians buy enough time?

II

The honorable John Rogers Grant laid a palm across a winking light on his desk console and it went out, shutting off the security phone to Luna Base. His face held an expression of pleasure and distaste, as it always did when he was through talking with his brother.

I don't think I've ever won an argument with Martin, he thought. Maybe it's because he knows me better than I know myself.

Grant turned toward the Tri-V, where the speaker was in full form. The speech had begun quietly as Harmon's speeches always did, full of resonant tones and appeals to reason. The quiet voice had asked for attention, but now it had grown louder and demanded it.

The background behind him changed as well, so that Harmon stood before the stars and stripes covering the hemisphere, with an American eagle splendid over the Capitol. Harmon was working himself into one of his famous frenzies, and his face was contorted with emotion.

"Honor? It is a word that Lipscomb no longer understands! Whatever he might have been—and my friends, we all know how great he once was—he is no longer one of us! His cronies, the dark little men who whisper to him, have corrupted even as great a man as President Lipscomb!

"And our nation bleeds! She bleeds from a thousand wounds! People of America, hear me! She bleeds from the running sores of these men and their CoDominium!

"They say that if we leave the CoDominium it will mean war. I pray God it will not, but if it does, why these are hard times. Many of us will be killed, but we would die as men! Today our friends and allies, the people of Hungary, the people of Rumania, the Czechs, the Slovaks, the Poles, all of them groan under the oppression of their Communist masters. Who keeps them there? We do! Our CoDominium!

"We have become no more than slavemasters. Better to die as men.

"But it will not come to that. The Russians will never fight. They are soft, as soft as we, their government is riddled with the same corruptions as ours. People of America, hear me! People of America, listen!"

Grant spoke softly and the Tri-V turned itself off. A walnut panel slid over the darkened screen, and Grant spoke again.

The desk opened to offer a small bottle of milk. There was nothing he could do for his ulcer despite the advances in medical science. Money was no problem, but there was never time for surgery and weeks with the regeneration stimulators.

He leafed through papers on his desk. Most were reports with bright red security covers, and Grant closed his eyes for a moment. Harmon's speech was important and would probably affect the upcoming elections. The man is getting to be a nuisance, Grant thought.

I should do something about him.

He put the thought aside with a shudder. Harmon had been a friend, once. Lord, what have we come to? He opened the first report.

There had been a riot at the International Federation of Labor convention. Three killed and the smooth plans for the reelection of Matt Brady thrown into confusion. Grant grimaced again and drank more milk. The Intelligence people had assured him this one would be easy.

He dug through the reports and found that three of Harvey Bertram's child crusaders were responsible. They'd bugged Brady's suite. The idiot hadn't known better than to make deals in his room. Now Bertram's people had enough evidence of sellouts to inflame floor sentiment in a dozen conventions.

The report ended with a recommendation that the government drop Brady and concentrate support on MacKnight, who had a good reputation and whose file in the CIA building bulged with information. MacKnight would be easy to control. Grant nodded to himself and scrawled his signature on the action form.

He threw it into the "Top Secret: Out" tray and watched it vanish. There was no point in wasting time. Then he wondered idly what would happen to Brady. Matt Brady had been a good United Party man; blast Bertram's people anyway.

He took up the next file, but before he could open it his secretary came in. Grant looked up and smiled, glad of his decision to ignore the electronics. Some executives never saw their secretaries for weeks at a time.

"Your appointment, sir," she said. "And it's time for your nerve tonic."

He grunted. "I'd rather die." But he let her pour a shot glass of evil-tasting stuff, and he tossed it off and chased it with milk. Then he glanced at his watch, but that wasn't neces-sary. Miss Ackridge knew the travel time to every Washing-ton office. There'd be no time to start another report, which suited Grant fine.

He let her help him into his black coat and brush off a few silver hairs. He didn't feel sixty-five, but he looked it now. It happened all at once. Five years ago he could pass for forty. John saw the girl in the mirror behind him and knew that she loved him, but it wouldn't work.

And why the hell not? he wondered. It isn't as if you're pining away for Priscilla. By the time she died you were praying it would happen, and we married late to begin with. So why the hell do you act as if the great love of your life has gone out forever? All you'd have to do is turn around, say five words, and—and what? She wouldn't be the perfect secretary any longer, and secretaries are harder to find than mistresses. Let it alone.

She stood there a moment longer, then moved away. "Your daughter wants to see you this evening," she told him. "She's driving down this afternoon and says it's important."

"Know why?" Grant asked. Ackridge knew more about Sharon than Grant did. Possibly a lot more.

"I can guess. I think her young man has asked her."

John nodded. It wasn't unexpected, but still it hurt. So soon, so soon. They grow so fast when you're an old man. John Jr. was a commander in the CoDominium Navy, soon to be a captain with a ship of his own. Frederick was dead in the same accident as his mother. And now Sharon, the baby, had found another life . . . not that they'd been close since he'd taken this job.

"Run his name through CIA, Flora, I meant to do that months ago. They won't find anything, but we'll need it for the records."

"Yes, sir. You'd better be on your way now. Your drivers are outside."

He scooped up his briefcase. "I won't be back tonight. Have my car sent around to the White House, will you? I'll drive myself home tonight."

He acknowledged the salutes of the driver and armed mechanic with a cheery wave and followed them to the elevator at the end of the long corridor. Paintings and photographs of ancient battles hung along both sides of the hall, and there was carpet on the floor, but otherwise it was like a cave. Blasted Pentagon, he thought for the hundredth time. Silliest building ever constructed. Nobody can find anything, and it can't be guarded at any price. Why couldn't someone have bombed it?

They took a surface car to the White House. A flight would have been another detail to worry about, and besides, this way he got to see the cherry trees and flower beds around the Jefferson. The Potomac was a sludgy brown mess. You could swim in it if you had a strong stomach, but the Army Engineers had "improved" it a few administrations back. They'd given it concrete banks. Now they were ripping them out, and it brought down mudslides.

They drove through rows of government buildings, some abandoned. Urban renewal had given Washington all the office space the Government would ever need, and more, so that there were these empty buildings as relics of the time when D.C. was the most crime-ridden city in the world. Sometime in Grant's youth, though, they'd hustled everyone out of Washington who didn't work there, with bulldozers quickly following to demolish the tenements. For political reasons the offices had gone in as quickly as the other buildings were torn down.

They passed the Population Control Bureau and drove around the Elipse and past Old State to the gate. The guard carefully checked his identity and made him put his palm on the little scanning plate. Then they entered the tunnel to the White House basement.

The President stood when Grant entered the Oval Office, and the others shot to their feet as if they had ejection charges under them. Grant shook hands around but looked closely at Lipscomb. The President was feeling the strain, no question about it. Well, they all were.

The Secretary of Defense wasn't there, but then he never was. The Secretary was a political hack who controlled a bloc of Aerospace Guild votes and an even larger bloc of aerospace industry stocks. As long as government contracts kept his companies busy employing his men, he didn't give a damn about policy. He could sit in on formal Cabinet sessions where nothing was ever said, and no one would know the difference. John Grant was Defense as much as he was CIA.

Few of the men in the Oval Office were well known to the public. Except for the President any one of them could have walked the streets of any city except Washington without fear of recognition. But the power they controlled, as assistants and deputies, was immense, and they all knew it. There was no need to pretend here.

The servitor brought drinks and Grant accepted Scotch. Some of the others didn't trust a man who wouldn't drink with them. His ulcer would give him hell, and his doctor more, but doctors and ulcers didn't understand the realities of power. Neither, thought Grant, do I or any of us, but we've got it.

"Mr. Karins, would you begin?" the President asked. Heads swiveled to the west wall where Karins stood at the briefing screen. To his right a polar projection of Earth glowed with lights showing the status of the forces that the President ordered, but Grant controlled.

Karins stood confidently, his paunch spilling out over his belt. The fat was an obscenity in so young a man. Herman Karins was the second youngest man in the room, Assistant Director of the Office of Management and Budget, and said to be one of the most brilliant economists Yale had ever produced. He was also the best political technician in the country, but he hadn't learned that at Yale.

He activated the screen to show a set of figures. "I have the latest poll results," Karins said too loudly. "This is the real stuff, not the slop we give the press. It stinks."

Grant nodded. It certainly did. The Unity Party was hovering around thirty-eight percent, just about evenly divided between the Republican and Democratic wings. Harmon's Patriot Party had just over twenty-five. Millington's violently left wing Liberation Party had its usual ten, but the real shocker was Bertram's Freedom Party. Bertram's popularity stood at an unbelievable twenty percent of the population.

"These are figures for those who have an opinion and might vote," Karins said. "Of course there's the usual gang that doesn't give a damn, but we know how they split off. They go to whomever got to 'em last anyway. You see the bad news."

"You're sure of this?" the Assistant Postmaster General asked. He was the leader of the Republican wing of Unity, and it hadn't been six months since he had told them they could forget Bertram.

"Yes, sir," Karins said. "And it's growing. Those riots at the labor convention probably gave 'em another five points we don't show. Give Bertram six months and he'll be ahead of us. How you like them apples, boys and girls?"

"There is no need to be flippant, Mr. Karins," the President said.

"Sorry, Mr. President." Karins wasn't sorry at all and he grinned at the Assistant Postmaster General with triumph. Then he flipped the switches to show new charts.

"Soft and hard," Karins said. "You'll notice Bertram's vote is pretty soft, but solidifying. Harmon's is so hard you couldn't get 'em away from him without you use nukes. And ours is a little like butter. Mr. President, I can't even guarantee we'll be the largest party after the election, much less that we can hold a majority."

"Incredible," the Chairman of the Joint Chiefs muttered.

"Worse than incredible." The Commerce rep shook her head in disbelief. "A disaster. Who will win?"

Karins shrugged. "Toss-up, but if I had to say, I'd pick Bertram. He's getting more of our vote than Harmon."

"You've been quiet, John," the President said. "What are your thoughts here?"

"Well, sir, it's fairly obvious what the result will be no matter who wins as long as it isn't us." Grant lifted his Scotch and sipped with relish. He decided to have another and to hell with the ulcer. "If Harmon wins, he pulls out of the CoDominium, and we have war. If Bertram takes over, he relaxes security, Harmon drives him out with his storm troopers, and we have war anyway."

Karins nodded. "I don't figure Bertram could hold power more'n a year, probably not that long. Man's too honest."

The President sighed loudly. "I can recall a time when men said that about me, Mr. Karins."

"It's still true, Mr. President." Karins spoke hurriedly. "But you're realistic enough to let us do what we have to do. Bertram wouldn't."

"So what do we do about it?" the President asked gently.

"Rig the election," Karins answered quickly. "I give out the popularity figures here." He produced a chart indicating a majority popularity for Unity. "Then we keep pumping out more faked stuff while Mr. Grant's people work on the vote-counting computers. Hell, it's been done before."

"Won't work this time." They turned to look at the youngest man in the room. Larry Moriarty, assistant to the President, and sometimes called the "resident heretic," blushed at the attention. "The people know better. Bertram's people are already taking jobs in the computer centers, aren't they, Mr. Grant? They'll see it in a minute."

Grant nodded. He'd sent the report over the day before; interesting that Moriarty had already digested it.

"You make this a straight rigged election, and you'll have

to use CoDominium Marines to keep order," Moriarty continued.

"The day I need CoDominium Marines to put down riots in the United States is the day I resign," the President said coldly. "I may be a realist, but there are limits to what I will do. You'll need a new chief, gentlemen."

"That's easy to say, Mr. President," Grant said. He wanted his pipe, but the doctors had forbidden it. To hell with them, he thought, and took a cigarette from a pack on the table. "It's easy to say, but you can't do it."

The President frowned. "Why not?"

Grant shook his head. "The Unity Party supports the CoDominium, and the CoDominium keeps the peace. An ugly peace, but by God, peace. I wish we hadn't got support for the CoDominium treaties tied so thoroughly to the Unity Party, but it is and that's that. And you know damn well that even in the Party it's only a thin majority that supports the CoDominium. Right, Harry?"

The Assistant Postmaster General nodded. "But don't forget, there's support for the CD in Bertram's group."

"Sure, but they hate our guts," Moriarty said. "They say we're corrupt. And they're right."

"So flipping what if they're right?" Karins snapped. "We're in, they're out. Anybody who's in for long is corrupt. If he isn't, he's not in."

"I fail to see the point of this discussion," the President interrupted. "I for one do not enjoy being reminded of all the things I have done to keep this office. The question is, what are we going to do? I feel it only fair to warn you that nothing could make me happier than to have Mr. Bertram sit in this chair. I've been President for a long time, and I'm tired. I don't want the job anymore."

III

Everyone spoke at once, shouting to the President, murmuring to their neighbors, until Grant cleared his throat loudly. "Mr. President," he said using the tone of command he'd been taught during his brief tour in the Army Reserve. "Mr. President, if you will pardon me, that is a ludicrous suggestion. There is no one else in the Unity Party who has even a ghost of a chance of winning. You alone remain popular. Even Mr. Harmon speaks as well of you as he does of anyone not in his group. You cannot resign without dragging the Unity Party with you, and you cannot give that chair to Mr. Bertram because he couldn't hold it six months."

"Would that be so bad?" President Lipscomb leaned toward Grant with the confidential manner he used in his fireside chats to the people. "Are we really so sure that only we can save the human race, John? Or do we only wish to keep power?"

"Both, I suppose," Grant said. "Not that I'd mind retiring myself."

"Retire!" Karins snorted. "You let Bertram's clean babies in the files for two hours, and none of us will retire to anything better'n a CD prison planet. You got to be kidding, retire."

"That may be true," the President said.

"There's other ways," Karins suggested. "General, what happens if Harmon takes power and starts his war?"

"Mr. Grant knows better than I do," General Carpenter said. When the others stared at him, Carpenter continued. "No one has ever fought a nuclear war. Why should the uniform make me more of an expert than you? Maybe we could win. Heavy casualties, very heavy, but our defenses are good."

Carpenter gestured at the moving lights on the wall projection. "We have better technology than the Russki's. Our laser guns ought to get most of their missiles. CD Fleet won't let either of us use space weapons. We might win."

"We might." Lipscomb was grim. "John?"

"We might not win. We might kill more than half the human race. We might get more. How in God's name do I know what happens when we throw nuclear weapons around?"

"But the Russians aren't prepared," Commerce said. "If we hit them without warning—people never change governments in the middle of a war."

President Lipscomb sighed. "I am not going to start a nuclear war to retain power. Whatever I have done, I have done to keep peace. That is my last excuse. I could not live with myself if I sacrifice peace to keep power."

Grant cleared his throat gently. "We couldn't do it anyway. If we start converting defensive missiles to offensive, CoDominium Intelligence would hear about it in ten days. The Treaty prevents that, you know."

He lit another cigarette. "We aren't the only threat to the CD, anyway. There's always Kaslov."

Kaslov was a pure Stalinist, who wanted to liberate Earth for Communism. Some called him the last Communist, but of course he wasn't the last. He had plenty of followers. Grant could remember a secret conference with Ambassador Chernikov only weeks ago.

The Soviet was a polished diplomat, but it was obvious that he wanted something desperately. He wanted the United States to keep the pressure on, not relax her defenses at the borders of the U.S. sphere of influence, because if the Communist probes ever took anything from the U.S. without a hard fight, Kaslov would gain more influence at home. He might even win control of the Presidium.

"Nationalism everywhere," the President sighed. "Why?"

No one had an answer to that. Harmon gained power in the U.S. and Kaslov in the Soviet Union; while a dozen petty nationalist leaders gained power in a dozen other countries. Some thought it started with Japan's nationalistic revival.

"This is all nonsense," said the Assistant Postmaster General. "We aren't going to quit and we aren't starting any wars. Now what does it take to get the support away from Mr. Clean Bertram and funnel it back to us where it belongs? A good scandal, right? Find Bertram's dirtier than we are, right? Worked plenty of times before. You can steal people blind if you scream loud enough about how the other guy's a crook."

"Such as?" Karins prompted.

"Working with the Japs. Giving the Japs nukes, maybe. Supporting Meiji's independence movement. I'm sure Mr. Grant can arrange something."

Karins nodded vigorously. "That might do it. Disillusion his organizers. The pro-CoDominium people in his outfit would come to us like a shot."

Karins paused and chuckled. "Course some of them will head for Millington's bunch, too."

They all laughed. No one worried about Millington's Liberation Party. His madmen caused riots and kept the taxpayers afraid, and made a number of security arrangements highly popular. The Liberation Party gave the police some heads to crack, nice riots for Tri-V to keep the Citizens amused and the taxpayers happy.

"I think we can safely leave the details to Mr. Grant." Karins grinned broadly.

"What will you do, John?" the President asked.

"Do you really want to know, Mr. President?" Moriarty interrupted. "I don't."

"Nor do I, but if I can condone it, I can at least find out what it is. What will you do, John?"

"Frame-up, I suppose. Get a plot going, then uncover it."

"That?" Moriarty shook his head. "It's got to be good. The people are beginning to wonder about all these plots."

Grant nodded. "There will be evidence. Hard-core evidence. A secret arsenal of nuclear weapons."'

There was a gasp. Then Karins grinned widely again. "Oh, man, that's tore it. Hidden nukes. Real ones, I suppose?"

"Of course." Grant looked with distaste at the fat youth. What would be the point of fake nuclear weapons? But Karins lived in a world of deception, so much so that fake weapons might be appropriate in it.

"Better have lots of cops when you break that story," Karins said. "People hear that, they'll tear Bertram apart."

True enough, Grant thought. It was a point he'd have to remember. Protection of those kids wouldn't be easy. Not since one militant group atom-bombed Bakersfield, California, and a criminal syndicate tried to hold Seattle for a hundred million ransom. People no longer thought of private stocks of atomic weapons as something to laugh at.

"We won't involve Mr. Bertram personally," the President said grimly. "Not under any circumstances. Is that understood?"

"Yes, sir," John answered quickly. He hadn't liked the idea either. "Just some of his top aides." Grant stubbed out the cigarette. It, or something, had left a foul taste in his mouth. "I'll have them end up with the CD for final custody. Sentenced to transportation. My brother can arrange it so they don't have hard sentences."

"Sure. They can be independent planters on Tanith if they'll cooperate," Karins said. "You can see they don't suffer."

Like hell, Grant thought. Life on Tanith was no joy under the best conditions.

"There's one more thing," the President said. "I understand Grand Senator Bronson wants something from the CD. Some officer was a little too efficient at uncovering the Bronson family deals, and they want him removed." The President looked as if he'd tasted sour milk. "I hate this, John. I hate it, but we need Bronson's support. Can you speak to your brother?"

"I already have," Grant said. "It will be arranged."

Grant left the meeting a few minutes later. The others could continue in endless discussion, but Grant saw no point to it. The action needed was clear, and the longer they waited the more time Bertram would have to assemble his supporters and harden his support. If something were to be done, it should be now.

Grant had found all his life that the wrong action taken decisively and in time was better than the right action taken later. After he reached the Pentagon he summoned his deputies and issued orders. It took no more than an hour to set the machinery in motion.

Grant's colleagues always said he was rash, too quick to take action without examining the consequences. They also conceded that he was lucky. To Grant it wasn't luck, and he did consider the consequences; but he anticipated events rather than reacted to crisis. He had known that Bertram's support was growing alarmingly for weeks and had made contingency plans long before going to the conference with the President.

Now it was clear that action must be taken immediately. Within days there would be leaks from the conference. Nothing about the actions to be taken, but there would be rumors about the alarm and concern. A secretary would notice that Grant had come back to the Pentagon after dismissing his driver. Another would see that Karins chuckled more than usual when he left the Oval Office, or that two political enemies came out together and went off to have a drink. Another would hear talk about Bertram, and soon it would be all over Washington: the President was worried about Bertram's popularity.

Since the leaks were inevitable, he should act while this might work. Grant dismissed his aides with a sense of satisfaction. He had been ready, and the crisis would be over before it began. It was only after he was alone that he crossed the paneled room to the teak cabinet and poured a double Scotch.

✧   ✧   ✧

The Maryland countryside slipped past far below as the Cadillac cruised on autopilot. A ribbon antenna ran almost to Grant's house, and he watched the twilight scene with as much relaxation as he ever achieved lately. House lights blinked below, and a few surface cars ran along the roads. Behind him was the sprawling mass of Columbia Welfare Island where most of those displaced from Washington had gone. Now the inhabitants were third generation and had never known any other life.

He grimaced. Welfare Islands were lumps of concrete buildings and roof parks, containers for the seething resentment of useless lives kept placid by Government furnished supplies of Tanith hashpot and borloi and American cheap booze. A man born in one of those complexes could stay there all his life, and many did.

Grant tried to imagine what it would be like there, but he couldn't. Reports from his agents gave an intellectual picture, but there was no way to identify with those people. He could not feel the hopelessness and dulled senses, burning hatreds, terrors, bitter pride of street gangs.

Karins knew, though. Karins had begun his life in a Welfare Island somewhere in the Midwest. Karins clawed his way through the schools to a scholarship and a ticket out forever. He'd resisted stimulants and dope and Tri-V. Was it worth it? Grant wondered. And of course there was another way out of Welfare, as a voluntary colonist; but so few took that route now. Once there had been a lot of them.

The speaker on the dash suddenly came to life cutting off Beethoven in mid bar. "WARNING. YOU ARE APPROACHING A GUARDED AREA. UNAUTHORIZED CRAFT WILL BE DESTROYED WITHOUT FURTHER WARNING. IF YOU HAVE LEGITIMATE ERRANDS IN THIS RESTRICTED AREA, FOLLOW THE GUIDE BEAM TO THE POLICE CHECK STATION. THIS IS A FINAL WARNING."

The Cadillac automatically turned off course to ride the beam down to State Police headquarters, and Grant cursed. He activated the mike and spoke softly. "This is John Grant of Peachem's Bay. Something seems to be wrong with my transponder."

There was a short pause, then a soft feminine voice came from the dash speaker. "We are very sorry, Mr. Grant. Your signal is correct. Our identification unit is out of order. Please proceed to your home."

"Get that damned thing fixed before it shoots down a taxpayer," Grant said. Ann Arundel County was a Unity stronghold. How long would that last after an accident like that?

He took the manual controls and cut across country, ignoring regulations. They could only give him a ticket now that they knew who he was, and his banking computer would pay it without bothering to tell him of it.

It brought a grim smile to his face. Traffic regulations were broken, computers noted it and levied fines, other computers paid them, and no human ever became aware of them. It was only if there were enough tickets accumulated to bring a warning of license suspension that a taxpayer learned of the things— unless he liked checking his bank statements himself.

His home lay ahead, a big rambling early twentieth-century place on the cove. His yacht was anchored offshore, and it gave him a guilty twinge. She wasn't neglected, but she was too much in the hands of paid crew, too long without attention from her owner.

Carver, the chauffeur, rushed out to help Grant down from the Cadillac. Hapwood was waiting in the big library with a glass of sherry. Prince Bismark, shivering in the presence of his god, put his Doberman head on Grant's lap, ready to leap into the fire at command.

There was irony in the situation, Grant thought. At home he enjoyed the power of a feudal lord, but it was limited by how strongly the staff wanted to stay out of Welfare. But he only had to lift the Security phone in the corner, and his real power, completely invisible and limited only by what the President wanted to find out, would operate. Money gave him the visible power, heredity gave him the power over the dog; what gave him the real power of the Security phone?

"What time would you like dinner, sir?" Hapwood asked. "And Miss Sharon is here with a guest."

"A guest?"

"Yes, sir. A young man, Mr. Allan Torrey, sir."

"Have they eaten?"

"Yes, sir. Miss Ackridge called to say that you would be late for dinner."

"All right, Hapwood. I'll eat now and see Miss Grant and her guest afterwards."

"Very good, sir. I will inform the cook." Hapwood left the room invisibly.

Grant smiled again. Hapwood was another figure from Welfare and had grown up speaking a dialect Grant would never recognize. For some reason he had been impressed by English butlers he'd seen on Tri-V and cultivated their manner—and now he was known all over the county as the perfect household manager.

Hapwood didn't know it, but Grant had a record of every cent his butler took in: kickbacks from grocers and caterers, contributions from the gardeners, and the surprisingly well-managed investment portfolio. Hapwood could easily retire to his own house and live the life of a taxpayer investor.

Why? Grant wondered idly. Why does he stay on? It makes life easier for me, but why? It had intrigued Grant enough to have his agents look into Hapwood, but the man had no politics other than staunch support for Unity. The only suspicious thing about his contacts was the refinement with which he extracted money from every transaction involving Grant's house. Hapwood had no children, and his sexual needs were satisfied by infrequent visits to the fringe areas around Welfare.

Grant ate mechanically, hurrying to be through and see his daughter, yet he was afraid to meet the boy she had brought home. For a moment he thought of using the Security phone to find out more about him, but he shook his head angrily. Too much security thinking wasn't good. For once he was going to be a parent, meeting his daughter's intended and nothing more.

He left his dinner unfinished without thinking how much the remnants of steak would have cost, or that Hapwood would probably sell them somewhere, and went to the library. He sat behind the massive Oriental fruitwood desk and had a brandy.

Behind him and to both sides the walls were lined with book shelves, immaculate dust-free accounts of the people of dead empires. It had been years since he had read one. Now all his reading was confined to reports with bright red covers. The reports told live stories about living people, but sometimes, late at night, Grant wondered if his country was not as dead as the empires in his books.

Grant loved his country but hated her people, all of them: Karins and the new breed, the tranquilized Citizens in their Welfare Islands, the smug taxpayers grimly holding onto their privileges. What, then, do I love? he wondered. Only our history, and the greatness that once was the United States, and that's found only in those books and in old buildings, never in the security reports.

Where are the patriots? All of them have become Patriots, stupid men and women following a leader toward nothing. Not even glory.

Then Sharon came in. She was a lovely girl, far prettier than her mother had ever been, but she lacked her mother's poise. She ushered in a tall boy in his early twenties.

Grant studied the newcomer as they came toward him. Nice-looking boy. Long hair, neatly trimmed, conservative mustache for these times. Blue and violet tunic, red scarf . . . a little flashy, but even John Jr. went in for flashy clothes when he got out of CD uniform.

The boy walked hesitantly, almost timidly, and Grant wondered if it were fear of him and his position in the government, or only the natural nervousness of a young man about to meet his fiancée's wealthy father. The tiny diamond on Sharon's hand sparkled in the yellow light from the fireplace, and she held the hand in an unnatural position.

"Daddy, I . . . I've talked so much about him, this is Allan. He's just asked me to marry him!" She sparkled, Grant saw; and she spoke trustingly, sure of his approval, never thinking he might object. Grant wondered if Sharon weren't the only person in the country who didn't fear him. Except for John Jr., who didn't have to be afraid. John was out of the reach of Grant's Security phone. The CD Fleet takes care of its own.

At least he's asked her to marry him. He might have simply moved in with her. Or has he already? Grant stood and extended his hand. "Hello, Allan."

Torrey's grip was firm, but his eyes avoided Grant's. "So you want to marry my daughter." Grant glanced pointedly at her left hand. "It appears that she approves the idea."

"Yes, sir. Uh, sir, she wanted to wait and ask you, but I insisted. It's my fault, sir." Torrey looked up at him this time, almost in defiance.

"Yes." Grant sat again. "Well, Sharon, as long as you're home for the evening, I wish you'd speak to Hapwood about Prince Bismark. I do not think the animal is properly fed."

"You mean right now?" she asked. She tightened her small mouth into a pout. "Really, Daddy, this is Victorian! Sending me out of the room while you talk to my fiancé!"

"Yes, it is, isn't it?" Grant said nothing else, and finally she turned away.

Then: "Don't let him frighten you, Allan. He's about as dangerous as that—as that moosehead in the trophy room!" She fled before there could be any reply.

IV

They sat awkwardly. Grant left his desk to sit near the fire with Torrey. Drinks, offer of a smoke, all the usual amenities—he did them all; but finally Hapwood had brought their refreshments and the door was closed.

"All right, Allan," John Grant began. "Let us be trite and get it over with. How do you intend to support her?"

Torrey looked straight at him this time. His eyes danced with what Grant was certain was concealed amusement. "I expect to be appointed to a good post in the Department of the Interior. I'm a trained engineer."

"Interior?" Grant thought for a second. The answer surprised him—he hadn't thought the boy was another office seeker. "I suppose it can be arranged."

Torrey grinned. It was an infectious grin, and Grant liked it. "Well, sir, it's already arranged. I wasn't asking for a job."

"Oh?" Grant shrugged. "I hadn't heard."

"Deputy Assistant Secretary for Natural Resources. I took a master's in ecology."

"That's interesting, but I would have thought I'd have heard of your coming appointment."

"It won't be official yet, sir. Not until Mr. Bertram is elected President. For the moment I'm on his staff." The grin was still there, and it was friendly, not hostile. The boy thought politics was a game. He wanted to win, but it was only a game.

And he's seen real polls, Grant thought. "Just what do you do for Mr. Bertram, then?"

Allan shrugged. "Write speeches, carry the mail, run the Xerox—you've been in campaign headquarters. I'm the guy who gets the jobs no one else wants."

Grant laughed. "I did start as a gopher, but I soon hired my own out of what I once contributed to the Party. They did not try that trick again with me. I don't suppose that course is open to you."

"No, sir. My father's a taxpayer, but paying taxes is pretty tough just now—

"Yes." Well, at least he wasn't from a Citizen family. Grant would learn the details from Ackridge tomorrow, for now the important thing was to get to know the boy.

It was difficult. Allan was frank and relaxed, and Grant was pleased to see that he refused a third drink, but there was little to talk about. Torrey had no conception of the realities of politics. He was one of Bertram's child crusaders, and he was out to save the United States from people like John Grant, although he was too polite to say so.

And I was once that young, Grant thought. I wanted to save the world, but it was so different then. No one wanted to end the CoDominium when I was young. We were too happy to have the Second Cold War over with. What happened to the great sense of relief when we could stop worrying about atomic wars? When I was young that was all we thought of, that we would be the last generation. Now they take it for granted that we'll have peace forever. Is peace such a little thing?

"There's so much to do," Torrey was saying. "The Baja Project, thermal pollution of the Sea of Cortez! They're killing off a whole ecology just to create estates for the taxpayers.

"I know it isn't your department, sir, you probably don't even know what they're doing. But Lipscomb has been in office too long! Corruption, special interests, it's time we had a genuine two-party system again instead of things going back and forth between the wings of Unity. It's time for a change, and Mr. Bertram's the right man, I know he is."

Grant's smile was thin, but he managed it. "You'll hardly expect me to agree with you," Grant said.

"No, sir."

Grant sighed. "But perhaps you're right at that. I must say I wouldn't mind retiring, so that I could live in this house instead of merely visiting it on weekends."

What was the point? Grant wondered. He'd never convince this boy, and Sharon wanted him. Torrey would drop Bertram after the scandals broke.

And what explanations were there anyway? The Baja Project was developed to aid a syndicate of taxpayers in the six states of the old former Republic of Mexico. The Government needed them, and they didn't care about whales and fish. Shortsighted, yes, and Grant had tried to argue them into changing the project, but they wouldn't, and politics is the art of the possible.

Finally, painfully, the interview ended. Sharon came in, grinning sheepishly because she was engaged to one of Bertram's people, but she understood that no better than Allan Torrey. It was only a game. Bertram would win and Grant would retire, and no one would be hurt.

How could he tell them that it didn't work that way any longer? Unity wasn't the cleanest party in the world, but at least it had no fanatics—and all over the world the causes were rising again. The Friends of the People were on the move, and it had all happened before, it was all told time and again in those aseptically clean books on the shelves above him.

BERTRAM AIDES ARRESTED BY INTERCONTINENTAL BUREAU OF INVESTIGATION!! IBI RAIDS SECRET WEAPONS CACHE IN BERTRAM HEADQUARTERS. NUCLEAR WEAPONS HINTED!!!

Chicago, May 15, (UPI)—IBI agents here have arrested five top aides to Senator Harvey Bertram in what government officials call one of the most despicable plots ever discovered. . . .

Grant read the transcript on his desk screen without satisfaction. It had all gone according to plan, and there was nothing left to do, but he hated it.

At least it was clean. The evidence was there. Bertram's people could have their trial, challenge jurors, challenge judges. The Government would waive its rights under the Thirty-first Amendment and let the case be tried under the old adversary rules. It wouldn't matter.

Then he read the small type below. "Arrested were Gregory Kalamintor, nineteen, press secretary to Bertram; Timothy Giordano, twenty-two, secretary; Allan Torrey, twenty-two, executive assistant—" The page blurred, and Grant dropped his face into his hands.

"My God, what have we done?"

He hadn't moved when Miss Ackridge buzzed. "Your daughter on four, sir. She seems upset."

"Yes." Grant punched savagely at the button. Sharon's face swam into view. Her makeup was ruined by long streaks of tears. She looked older, much like her mother during one of their—

"Daddy! They've arrested Allan! And I know it isn't true, he wouldn't have anything to do with nuclear weapons! A lot of Mr. Bertram's people said there would never be an honest election in this country. They said John Grant would see to that! I told him they were wrong, but they weren't, were they? You've done this to stop the election, haven't you?"

There was nothing to say because she was right. But who might be listening? "I don't know what you're talking about. I've only seen the Tri-V casts about Allan's arrest, nothing more. Come home, kitten, and we'll talk about it."

"Oh no! You're not getting me where Dr. Pollard can give me a nice friendly little shot and make me forget about Allan! No! I'm staying with my friends, and I won't be home, Daddy. And when I go to the newspapers, I think they'll listen to me. I don't know what to tell them yet, but I'm sure Mr. Bertram's people will think of something. How do you like that, Mr. God?"

"Anything you tell the press will be lies, Sharon. You know nothing." One of his assistants had come in and now left the office.

"Lies? Where did I learn to lie?" The screen went blank.

And is it that thin? he wondered. All the trust and love, could it vanish that fast, was it that thin?

"Sir?" It was Hartman, his assistant.

"Yes?"

"She was calling from Champaign, Illinois. A Bertram headquarters they think we don't know about. The phone had one of those guaranteed no-trace devices."

"Trusting lot, aren't they?" Grant said. "Have some good men watch that house, but leave her alone." He stood and felt a wave of nausea so strong that he had to hold the edge of the desk. "MAKE DAMNED SURE THEY LEAVE HER ALONE. DO YOU UNDERSTAND?" he shouted.

Hartman went as pale as Grant. The chief hadn't raised his voice to one of his own people in five years. "Yes, sir, I understand."

"Then get out of here." Grant spoke carefully, in low tones, and the cold mechanical voice was more terrifying than the shout.

He sat alone and stared at the telephone. What use was its power now?

What can we do? It wasn't generally known that Sharon was engaged to the boy. He'd talked them out of a formal engagement until the banns could be announced in the National Cathedral and they could hold a big social party. It had been something to do for them at the time, but . . .

But what? He couldn't have the boy released. Not that boy. He wouldn't keep silent as the price of his own freedom. He'd take Sharon to a newspaper within five minutes of his release, and the resulting headlines would bring down Lipscomb, Unity, the CoDominium—and the peace. Newsmen would listen to the daughter of the top secret policeman in the country.

Grant punched a code on the communicator, then another. Grand Admiral Lermontov appeared on the screen.

"Yes, Mr. Grant?"

"Are you alone?"

"Yes."

The conversation was painful, and the long delay while the signals reached the moon and returned didn't make it easier.

"When is the next CD warship going outsystem? Not a colony ship, and most especially not a prison ship. A warship."

Another long pause, longer even than the delay. "I suppose anything could be arranged," the Admiral said. "What do you need?"

"I want . . ." Grant hesitated, but there was no time to be lost. No time at all. "I want space for two very important political prisoners. A married couple. The crew is not to know their identity, and anyone who does learn their identity must stay outsystem for at least five years. And I want them set down on a good colony world, a decent place. Sparta, perhaps. No one ever returns from Sparta. Can you arrange that?"

Grant could see the changes in Lermontov's face as the words reached him. The Admiral frowned. "It can be done if it is important enough. It will not be easy."

"It's important enough. My brother Martin will explain everything you'll need to know later. The prisoners will be delivered tonight, Sergei. Please have the ship ready. And— and it better not be *Saratoga*. My son's in that one and he— he will know one of the prisoners." Grant swallowed hard. "There should be a chaplain aboard. The kids will be getting married."

Lermontov frowned again, as if wondering if John Grant had gone insane. Yet he needed the Grants, both of them, and certainly John Grant would not ask such a favor if it were not vital.

"It will be done," Lermontov said.

"Thank you. I'll also appreciate it if you will see they have a good estate on Sparta. They are not to know who arranged it. Just have it taken care of and send the bill to me."

It was all so very simple. Direct his agents to arrest Sharon and conduct her to CD Intelligence. He wouldn't want to see her first. The attorney general would send Torrey to the same place and announce that he had escaped.

It wasn't as neat as having all of them convicted in open court, but it would do, and having one of them a fugitive from justice would even help. It would be an admission of guilt.

Something inside him screamed again and again that this was his little girl, the only person in the world who wasn't afraid of him, but Grant refused to listen. He leaned back in the chair and almost calmly dictated his orders.

He took the flimsy sheet from the writer and his hand didn't tremble at all as he signed it.

All right, Martin, he thought. All right. I've bought the time you asked for, you and Sergei Lermontov. Now can you do something with it?

V

2087 A.D.

The landing boat fell away from the orbiting warship. When it had drifted to a safe distance, retros fired, and after it had entered the thin reaches of the planet's upper atmosphere, scoops opened in the bows. The thin air was drawn in and compressed until the stagnation temperature in the ramjet chamber was high enough for ignition.

The engines lit with a roar of flame. Wings swung out to provide lift at hypersonic speeds, and the spaceplane turned to streak over empty ocean toward the continental land mass two thousand kilometers away.

The ship circled over craggy mountains twelve kilometers high, then dropped low over thickly forested plains. It slowed until it was no longer a danger to the thin strip of inhabited lands along the ocean shores. The planet's great ocean was joined to a smaller sea by a nearly landlocked channel no more than five kilometers across at its widest point, and nearly all of the colonists lived near the junction of the waters.

Hadley's capital city nestled on a long peninsula at the mouth of that channel, and the two natural harbors, one in the sea, the other in the ocean, gave the city the fitting name of Refuge. The name suggested a tranquility the city no longer possessed.

The ship extended its wings to their fullest reach and floated low over the calm water of the channel harbor. It touched and settled in. Tugboats raced across clear blue water. Sweating seamen threw lines and towed the landing craft to the dock where they secured it.

A long line of CoDominium Marines in garrison uniform marched out of the boat. They gathered on the gray concrete piers into neat brightly colored lines. Two men in civilian clothing followed the Marines from the flyer.

They blinked at the unaccustomed blue-white of Hadley's

sun. The sun was so far away that it would have been only a small point if either of them were foolish enough to look directly at it. The apparent small size was only an illusion caused by distance; Hadley received as much illumination from its hotter sun as Earth does from Sol.

Both men were tall and stood as straight as the Marines in front of them, so that except for their clothing they might have been mistaken for a part of the disembarking battalion. The shorter of the two carried luggage for both of them, and stood respectfully behind; although older he was obviously a subordinate. They watched as two younger men came uncertainly along the pier. The newcomers' unadorned blue uniforms contrasted sharply with the bright reds and golds of the CoDominium Marines milling around them. Already the Marines were scurrying back into the flyer to carry out barracks bags, weapons, and all the other personal gear of a light infantry battalion.

The taller of the two civilians faced the uniformed newcomers. "I take it you're here to meet us?" he asked pleasantly. His voice rang through the noise on the pier, and it carried easily although he had not shouted. His accent was neutral, the nearly universal English of non-Russian officers in the CoDominium Service, and it marked his profession almost as certainly as did his posture and the tone of command.

The newcomers were uncertain even so. There were a lot of ex-officers of the CoDominium Space Navy on the beach lately. CD budgets were lower every year. "I think so," one finally said. "Are you John Christian Falkenberg?"

His name was actually John Christian Falkenberg III, and he suspected that his grandfather would have insisted on the distinction. "Right. And Sergeant Major Calvin."

"Pleasure to meet you, sir. I'm Lieutenant Banners, and this is Ensign Mowrer. We're on President Budreau's staff." Banners looked around as if expecting other men, but there were none except the uniformed Marines. He gave Falkenberg a slightly puzzled look, then added, "We have transportation for you, but I'm afraid your men will have to walk. It's about eleven miles."

"Miles." Falkenberg smiled to himself. This *was* out in the boondocks. "I see no reason why ten healthy mercenaries can't march eighteen kilometers, Lieutenant. He turned to face the black shape of the landing boat's entry port and called to someone inside. "Captain Fast. There is no transportation, but someone will show you where to march the men. Have them carry all gear."

"Uh, sir, that won't be necessary," the lieutenant protested. "We can get—well, we have horse-drawn transport for baggage." He looked at Falkenberg as if he expected him to laugh.

"That's hardly unusual on colony worlds," Falkenberg said. Horses and mules could be carried as frozen embryos, and they didn't require high-technology industries to produce more, nor did they need an industrial base to fuel them.

"Ensign Mowrer will attend to it," Lieutenant Banners said. He paused again and looked thoughtful as if uncertain how to tell Falkenberg something. Finally he shook his head. "I think it would be wise if you issued your men their personal weapons, sir. There shouldn't be any trouble on their way to barracks, but—anyway, ten armed men certainly won't have any problems."

"I see. Perhaps I should go with my troops, Lieutenant. I hadn't known things were quite this bad on Hadley." Falkenberg's voice was calm and even, but he watched the junior officers carefully.

"No, sir. They aren't, really. . . . But there's no point in taking chances." He waved Ensign Mowrer to the landing craft and turned back to Falkenberg. A large black shape rose from the water outboard of the landing craft. It splashed and vanished. Banners seemed not to notice, but the Marines shouted excitedly. "I'm sure the ensign and your officers can handle the disembarkation, and the President would like to see you immediately, sir."

"No doubt. All right, Banners, lead on. I'll bring Sergeant Major Calvin with me." He followed Banners down the pier.

There's no point to this farce, Falkenberg thought. Anyone seeing ten armed men conducted by a Presidential ensign will know they're mercenary troops, civilian clothes or not. Another case of wrong information.

Falkenberg had been told to keep the status of himself and his men a secret, but it wasn't going to work. He wondered if this would make it more difficult to keep his own secrets.

Banners ushered them quickly through the bustling CoDominium Marine barracks, past bored guards who half-saluted the Presidential Guard uniform. The Marine fortress was a blur of activity, every open space crammed with packs and weapons; the signs of a military force about to move on to another station.

As they were leaving the building, Falkenberg saw an elderly Naval officer. "Excuse me a moment, Banners." He turned to the CoDominium Navy captain. "They sent someone for me. Thanks, Ed."

"No problem. I'll report your arrival to the Admiral. He wants to keep track of you. Unofficially, of course. Good luck, John. God knows you need some right now. It was a rotten deal."

"It's the way it goes."

"Yeah, but the Fleet used to take better care of its own than that. I'm beginning to wonder if anyone is safe. Damn Senator—"

"Forget it," Falkenberg interrupted. He glanced back to be sure Lieutenant Banners was out of earshot. "Pay my respects to the rest of your officers. You run a good ship."

The captain smiled thinly. "Thanks. From you that's quite a compliment." He held out his hand and gripped John's firmly. "Look, we pull out in a couple of days, no more than that. If you need a ride on somewhere I can arrange it. The goddam Senate won't have to know. We can fix you a hitch to anywhere in CD territory."

"Thanks, but I guess I'll stay."

"Could be rough here," the captain said.

"And it won't be everywhere else in the CoDominium?" Falkenberg asked. "Thanks again, Ed." He gave a half-salute and checked himself.

Banners and Calvin were waiting for him, and Falkenberg turned away. Calvin lifted three personal effects bags as if they were empty and pushed the door open in a smooth motion. The CD captain watched until they had left the building, but Falkenberg did not look back.

"Damn them," the captain muttered. "Damn the lot of them."

"The car's here." Banners opened the rear door of a battered ground effects vehicle of no discoverable make. It had been cannibalized from a dozen other machines, and some parts were obviously cut-and-try jobs done by an uncertain machinist. Banners climbed into the driver's seat and started the engine. It coughed twice, then ran smoothly, and they drove away in a cloud of black smoke.

They drove past another dock where a landing craft with wings as large as the entire Marine landing boat was unloading an endless stream of civilian passengers. Children screamed, and long lines of men and women stared about uncertainly until they were ungently hustled along by guards in uniforms matching Banners'. The sour smell of unwashed humanity mingled with the crisp clean salt air from the ocean beyond. Banners rolled up the windows with an expression of distaste.

"Always like that," Calvin commented to no one in particular. "Water discipline in them CoDominium prison ships bein' what it is, takes weeks dirtside to get clean again."

"Have you ever been in one of those ships?" Banners asked.

"No, sir," Calvin replied. "Been in Marine assault boats just about as bad, I reckon. But I can't say I fancy being stuffed into no cubicle with ten, fifteen thousand civilians for six months."

"We may all see the inside of one of those," Falkenberg said. "And be glad of the chance. Tell me about the situation here, Banners."

"I don't even know where to start, sir," the lieutenant answered. "I—do you know about Hadley?"

"Assume I don't," Falkenberg said. May as well see what kind of estimate of the situation the President's officers can make, he thought. He could feel the Fleet Intelligence report bulging in an inner pocket of his tunic, but those reports always left out important details; and the attitudes of the Presidential Guard could be important to his plans.

"Yes, sir. Well, to begin with, we're a long way from the nearest shipping lanes—but I guess you knew that. The only real reason we had any merchant trade was the mines. Thorium, richest veins known anywhere for a while, until they started to run out.

"For the first few years that's all we had. The mines are up in the hills, about eighty miles over that way." He pointed to a thin blue line just visible at the horizon.

"Must be pretty high mountains," Falkenberg said. "What's the diameter of Hadley? About eighty percent of Earth? Something like that. The horizon ought to be pretty close."

"Yes, sir. They are high mountains. Hadley is small, but we've got bigger and better everything here." There was pride in the young officer's voice.

"Them bags seem pretty heavy for a planet this small," Calvin said.

"Hadley's very dense," Banners answered. "Gravity nearly ninety percent standard. Anyway, the mines are over there, and they have their own spaceport at a lake nearby. Refuge—that's this city—was founded by the American Express Company. They brought in the first colonists, quite a lot of them."

"Volunteers?" Falkenberg asked.

"Yes. All volunteers. The usual misfits. I suppose my father was typical enough, an engineer who couldn't keep up with the rat race and was tired of Bureau of Technology restrictions on what he could learn. They were the first wave, and they took the best land. They founded the city and got an economy going. American Express was paid back all advances within twenty years." Banners' pride was evident, and Falkenberg knew it had been a difficult job.

"That was, what, fifty years ago?" Falkenberg asked.

"Yes."

They were driving through crowded streets lined with wooden houses and a few stone buildings. There were rooming houses, bars, sailors' brothels, all the usual establishments of a dock street, but there were no other cars on the road. Instead the traffic was all horses and oxen pulling carts, bicycles, and pedestrians.

The sky above Refuge was clear. There was no trace of smog or industrial wastes. Out in the harbor tugboats moved with the silent efficiency of electric power, and there were also wind-driven sailing ships, lobster boats powered by oars, even a topsail schooner lovely against clean blue water. She threw up white spume as she raced out to sea. A three-masted, full-rigged ship was drawn up to a wharf where men loaded her by hand with huge bales of what might have been cotton.

They passed a wagonload of melons. A gaily dressed young couple waved cheerfully at them, then the man snapped a long whip at the team of horses that pulled their wagon. Falkenberg studied the primitive scene and said, "It doesn't look like you've been here fifty years."

"No." Banners gave them a bitter look. Then he swerved to avoid a group of shapeless teenagers lounging in the dockside street. He had to swerve again to avoid the barricade of paving stones that they had masked. The car jounced wildly. Banners gunned it to lift it higher and headed for a low place in the barricade. It scraped as it went over the top, then he accelerated away.

Falkenberg took his hand from inside his shirt jacket.

Behind him Calvin was inspecting a submachine gun that had appeared from the oversized barracks bag he'd brought into the car with him. When Banners said nothing about the incident, Falkenberg frowned and leaned back in his seat, listening. The Intelligence reports mentioned lawlessness, but this was as bad as a Welfare Island on Earth.

"No, we're not much industrialized," Banners continued. "At first there wasn't any need to develop basic industries. The mines made everyone rich, so we imported everything we needed. The farmers sold fresh produce to the miners for enormous prices. Refuge was a service industry town. People who worked here could soon afford farm animals, and they scattered out across the plains and into the forests."

Falkenberg nodded. "Many of them wouldn't care for cities."

"Precisely. They didn't want industry, they'd come here to escape it." Banners drove in silence for a moment. "Then some blasted CoDominium bureaucrat read the ecology reports about Hadley. The Population Control Bureau in Washington decided this was a perfect place for involuntary colonization. The ships were coming here for the thorium anyway, so instead of luxuries and machinery they were ordered to carry convicts. Hundreds of thousands of them, Colonel Falkenberg. For the last ten years there have been better than fifty thousand people a year dumped in on us."

"And you couldn't support them all," Falkenberg said gently.

"No, sir." Banners' face tightened. He seemed to be fighting tears. "God knows we try. Every erg the fusion generators can make goes into converting petroleum into basic protocarb just to feed them. But they're not like the original colonists! They don't know anything, they won't *do* anything! Oh, not really, of course. Some of them work. Some of our best citizens are transportees. But there are so many of the other kind."

"Why'n't you tell 'em to work or starve?" Calvin asked bluntly. Falkenberg gave him a cold look, and the sergeant nodded slightly and sank back into his seat.

"Because the CD wouldn't let us!" Banners shouted. "Damn it, we didn't have self-government. The CD Bureau of Relocation people told us what to do. They ran everything . . ."

"We know," Falkenberg said gently. "We've seen the results of Humanity League influence over BuRelock. My sergeant major wasn't asking you a question, he was expressing an opinion. Nevertheless, I am surprised. I would have thought your farms could support the urban population."

"They should be able to, sir." Banners drove in grim silence for a long minute. "But there's no transportation. The people are here, and most of the agricultural land is five hundred miles inland. There's arable land closer, but it isn't cleared. Our settlers wanted to get away from Refuge and BuRelock. We have a railroad, but bandit gangs keep blowing it up. We can't rely on Hadley's produce to keep Refuge alive. There are a million people on Hadley, and half of them are crammed into this one ungovernable city."

They were approaching an enormous bowl-shaped structure attached to a massive square stone fortress. Falkenberg studied the buildings carefully, them asked what they were.

"Our stadium," Banners replied. There was no pride in his voice now. "The CD built it for us. We'd rather have had a new fusion plant, but we got a stadium that can hold a hundred thousand people."

"Built by the GLC Construction and Development Company, I presume," Falkenberg said.

"Yes . . . how did you know?"

"I think I saw it somewhere." He hadn't, but it was an easy guess: GLC was owned by a holding company that was in turn owned by the Bronson family. It was easy enough to understand why aid sent by the CD Grand Senate would end up used for something GLC might participate in.

"We have very fine sports teams and racehorses," Banners said bitterly. "The building next to it is the Presidential Palace. Its architecture is quite functional."

The Palace loomed up before them, squat and massive; it looked more fortress than capital building.

The city was more thickly populated as they approached the Palace. The buildings here were mostly stone and poured concrete instead of wood. Few were more than three stories high, so that Refuge sprawled far along the shore. The population density increased rapidly beyond the stadium-palace complex. Banners was watchful as he drove along the wide streets, but he seemed less nervous than he had been at dockside.

Refuge was a city of contrasts. The streets were straight and wide, and there was evidently a good waste-disposal system, but the lower floors of the buildings were open shops, and the sidewalks were clogged with market stalls. Clouds of pedestrians moved through the kiosks and shops.

There was still no motor traffic and no moving pedways. Horse troughs and hitching posts had been constructed at frequent intervals along with starkly functional street lights and water distribution towers. The few signs of technology contrasted strongly with the general primitive air of the city.

A contingent of uniformed men thrust their way through the crowd at a street crossing. Falkenberg looked at them closely, then at Banners. "Your troops?"

"No, sir. That's the livery of Glenn Foster's household. Officially they're unorganized reserves of the President's Guard, but they're household troops all the same." Banners laughed bitterly. "Sounds like something out of a history book, doesn't it? We're nearly back to feudalism, Colonel Falkenberg. Anyone rich enough keeps hired bodyguards. They *have* to. The criminal gangs are so strong the police don't try to catch anyone under organized protection, and the judges wouldn't punish them if they were caught."

"And the private bodyguards become gangs in their own right, I suppose."

Banners looked at him sharply. "Yes, sir. Have you seen it before?"

"Yes. I've seen it before." Banners was unable to make out the expression on Falkenberg's lips.

VI

They drove into the Presidential Palace and received the salutes of the blue uniformed troopers. Falkenberg noted the polished weapons and precise drill of the Presidential Guard. There were well-trained men on duty here, but the unit was small. Falkenberg wondered if they could fight as well as stand guard. They were local citizens, loyal to Hadley, and would be unlike the CoDominium Marines he was accustomed to.

He was conducted through a series of rooms in the stone fortress. Each had heavy metal doors, and several were guard-rooms. Falkenberg saw no signs of government activity until they had passed through the outer layers of the enormous palace into an open courtyard, and through that to an inner building.

Here there was plenty of activity. Clerks bustled through the halls, and girls in the draped togas fashionable years before on Earth sat at desks in offices. Most seemed to be packing desk contents into boxes, and other people scurried through the corridors. Some offices were empty, their desks covered with fine dust, and there were plastiboard moving boxes stacked outside them.

There were two anterooms to the President's office. President Budreau was a tall, thin man with a red pencil mustache and quick gestures. As they were ushered into the overly ornate room the President looked up from a sheaf of papers, but his eyes did not focus immediately on his visitors. His face was a mask of worry and concentration.

"Colonel John Christian Falkenberg, sir," Lieutenant Banners said. "And Sergeant Major Calvin."

Budreau got to his feet. "Pleased to see you, Falkenberg." His expression told them differently; he looked at his visitors with faint distaste and motioned Banners out of the room. When the door closed he asked, "How many men did you bring with you?"

"Ten, Mr. President. All we could bring aboard the carrier without arousing suspicion. We were lucky to get that many. The Grand Senate had an inspector at the loading docks to check for violation of the anti-mercenary codes. If we hadn't bribed a port official to distract him we wouldn't be here at all. Calvin and I would be on Tanith as involuntary colonists."

"I see." From his expression he wasn't surprised. John thought Budreau would have been more pleased if the inspector had caught them. The President tapped the desk nervously. "Perhaps that will be enough. I understand the ship you came with also brought the Marines who have volunteered to settle on Hadley. They should provide the nucleus of an excellent constabulary. Good troops?"

"It was a demobilized battalion," Falkenberg replied. "Those are the troops the CD didn't want anymore. Could be the scrapings of every guardhouse on twenty planets. We'll be lucky if there's a real trooper in the lot."

Budreau's face relaxed into its former mask of depression. Hope visibly drained from him.

"Surely you have troops of your own," Falkenberg said.

Budreau picked up a sheaf of papers. "It's all here. I was just looking it over when you came in." He handed the report to Falkenberg. "There's little encouragement in it, Colonel. I have never thought there was any military solution to Hadley's problems, and this confirms that fear. If you have only ten men plus a battalion of forced-labor Marines, the military answer isn't even worth considering."

Budreau returned to his seat. His hands moved restlessly over the sea of papers on his desk. "If I were you, Falkenberg, I'd get back on that Navy boat and forget Hadley."

"Why don't you?"

"Because Hadley's my home! No rabble is going to drive me off the plantation my grandfather built with his own hands. They will not make me run out." Budreau clasped his hands together until the knuckles were white with the strain, but when he spoke again his voice was calm. "You have no stake here. I do."

Falkenberg took the report from the desk and leafed through the pages before handing it to Calvin. "We've come a long way, Mr. President. You may as well tell me what the problem is before I leave."

Budreau nodded sourly. The red mustache twitched and he ran the back of his hand across it. "It's simple enough. The ostensible reason you're here, the reason we gave the Colonial Office for letting us recruit a planetary constabulary, is the bandit gangs out in the hills. No one knows how many of them there are, but they are strong enough to raid farms. They also cut communications between Refuge and the countryside whenever they want to."

"Yes." Falkenberg stood in front of the desk because he hadn't been invited to sit. If that bothered him it did not show. "Guerrilla gangsters have no real chance if they've no political base."

Budreau nodded. "But, as I am sure Vice President Bradford told you, they are not the real problem." The President's voice was strong, but there was a querulous note in it, as if he was accustomed to having his conclusions argued against and was waiting for Falkenberg to begin. "Actually, we could live with the bandits, but they get political support from the Freedom Party. My Progressive Party is larger than the Freedom Party, but the Progressives are scattered all over the planet. The FP is concentrated right here in Refuge, and they have God knows how many voters and about forty thousand loyalists they can concentrate whenever they want to stage a riot."

"Do you have riots very often?" John asked.

"Too often. There's not much to control them with. I have three hundred men in the Presidential Guard, but they're CD recruited and trained like young Banners. They're not much use at riot control, and they're loyal to the job, not to me, anyway. The FP's got men inside the guard."

"So we can scratch the President's Guard when it comes to controlling the Freedom Party," John observed.

"Yes." Budreau smiled without amusement. "Then there's my police force. My police were all commanded by CD officers who are pulling out. My administrative staff was recruited and trained by BuRelock, and all the competent people have been recalled to Earth."

"I can see that would create a problem."

"Problem? It's impossible," Budreau said. "There's nobody left with skill enough to govern, but I've got the job and everybody else wants it. I might be able to scrape up a thousand Progressive partisans and another fifteen thousand party workers who would fight for us in a pinch, but they have no training. How can they face the FP's forty thousand?"

"You seriously believe the Freedom Party will revolt?"

"As soon as the CD's out, you can count on it. They've demanded a new constitutional convention to assemble just after the CoDominium Governor leaves. If we don't give them the convention they'll rebel and carry a lot of undecided with them. After all, what's unreasonable about a convention when the colonial governor has gone?"

"I see."

"And if we do give them the convention they want, they'll drag things out until there's nobody left in it but their people. My Party is composed of working voters. How can they stay on day after day? The FR's unemployed will sit it out until they can throw the Progressives out of office. Once they get in they'll ruin the planet. Under the circumstances I don't see what a military man can do for us, but Vice President Bradford insisted that we hire you."

"Perhaps we can think of something," Falkenberg said smoothly. "I've no experience in administration as such, but Hadley is not unique. I take it the Progressive Party is mostly old settlers?"

"Yes and no. The Progressive Party wants to industrialize Hadley, and some of our farm families oppose that. But we want to do it slowly. We'll close most of the mines and take out only as much thorium as we have to sell to get the basic industrial equipment. I want to keep the rest for our own fusion generators, because we'll need it later.

"We want to develop agriculture and transport, and cut the basic citizen ration so that we'll have the fusion power available for our new industries. I want to close out convenience and consumer manufacturing and keep it closed until we can afford it." Budreau's voice rose and his eyes shone; it was easier to see why he had become popular. He believed in his cause.

"We want to build the tools of a self-sustaining world and get along without the CoDominium until we can rejoin the human race as equals!" Budreau caught himself and frowned. "Sorry. Didn't mean to make a speech. Have a seat, won't you?"

"Thank you." Falkenberg sat in a heavy leather chair and looked around the room. The furnishings were ornate, and the office decor had cost a fortune to bring from Earth; but most of it was tasteless—spectacular rather than elegant. The Colonial Office did that sort of thing a lot, and Falkenberg wondered which Grand Senator owned the firm that supplied office furnishings. "What does the opposition want?"

"I suppose you really do need to know all this." Budreau frowned and his mustache twitched nervously. He made an effort to relax, and John thought the President had probably been an impressive man once. "The Freedom Party's slogan is 'Service to the People.' Service to them means consumer goods now. They want strip mining. That's got the miners' support, you can bet. The FP will rape this planet to buy goods from other systems, and to hell with how they're paid for. Runaway inflation will be only one of the problems they'll create."

"They sound ambitious."

"Yes. They even want to introduce internal combustion engine economy. God knows how, there's no support technology here, but there's oil. We'd have to buy all that from off planet, there's no heavy industry here to make engines even if the ecology could absorb them, but that doesn't matter to the FP. They promise cars for everyone. Instant modernization. More food, robotic factories, entertainment . . . in short, paradise and right now."

"Do they mean it, or is that just slogans?"

"I think most of them mean it," Budreau answered. "It's hard to believe, but I think they do."

"Where do they *say* they'll get the money?"

"Soaking the rich, as if there were enough wealthy people here to matter. Total confiscation of everything everyone owns wouldn't pay for all they promise. Those people have no idea of the realities of our situation, and their leaders are ready to blame anything that's wrong on the Progressive Party, CoDominium administrators, anything but admit that what they promise just isn't possible. Some of the Party leaders may know better, but they don't admit it if they do."

"I take it that program has gathered support."

"Of course it has," Budreau fumed. "And every BuRelock ship brings thousands more ready to vote the FP line."

Budreau got up from his desk and went to a cabinet on the opposite wall. He took out a bottle of brandy and three glasses and poured, handing them to Calvin and Falkenberg. Then he ignored the sergeant but waited for Falkenberg to lift his glass.

"Cheers." Budreau drained the glass at one gulp. "Some of the oldest families on Hadley have joined the damned Freedom Party. They're worried about the taxes *I've* proposed! The FP won't leave them anything at all, but they still join the opposition in hopes of making deals. You don't look surprised."

"No, sir. It's a story as old as history, and a military man reads history."

Budreau looked up in surprise. "Really?"

"A smart soldier wants to know the causes of wars. Also how to end them. After all, war is the normal state of affairs, isn't it? Peace is the name of the ideal we deduce from the fact that there have been interludes between wars." Before Budreau could answer, Falkenberg said, "No matter. I take it you expect armed resistance immediately after the CD pulls out."

"I hoped to prevent it. Bradford thought you might be able to do something, and I'm gifted at the art of persuasion." The President sighed. "But it seems hopeless. They don't want to compromise. They think they can get a total victory."

"I wouldn't think they'd have much of a record to run on," Falkenberg said.

Budreau laughed. "The FP partisans claim credit for driving the CoDominium out, Colonel."

They laughed together. The CoDominium was leaving because the mines were no longer worth enough to make it pay to govern Hadley. If the mines were as productive as they'd been in the past, no partisans would drive the Marines away.

Budreau nodded as if reading his thoughts. "Well, they have people believing it anyway. There was a campaign of terrorism for years, nothing very serious. It didn't threaten the mine shipments, or the Marines would have put a stop to it. But they have demoralized the capital police. Out in the bush people administer their own justice, but here in Refuge the FP gangs control a lot of the city."

Budreau pointed to a stack of papers on one corner of the desk. "Those are resignations from the force. I don't even know how many police I'll have left when the CD pulls out." Budreau's fist tightened as if he wanted to pound on the desk, but he sat rigidly still. "Pulls out. For years they ran everything, and now they're leaving us to clean up. I'm President by courtesy of the CoDominium. They put me in office, and now they're leaving."

"At least you're in charge," Falkenberg said. "The BuRelock people wanted someone else. Bradford talked them out of it."

"Sure. And it cost us a lot of money. For what? Maybe it would have been better the other way."

"I thought you said their policies would ruin Hadley."

"I did say that. I believe it. But the policy issues came after the split, I think." Budreau was talking to himself as much as to John. "Now they hate us so much they oppose anything we want out of pure spite. And we do the same thing."

"Sounds like CoDominium politics. Russkis and U.S. in the Grand Senate. Just like home." There was no humor in the polite laugh that followed.

Budreau opened a desk drawer and took out a parchment. "I'll keep the agreement, of course. Here's your commission as commander of the constabulary. But I still think you might be better off taking the next ship out. Hadley's problems can't be solved by military consultants."

Sergeant Major Calvin snorted. The sound was almost

inaudible, but Falkenberg knew what he was thinking. Budreau shrank from the bald term "mercenary," as if "military consultant" were easier on his conscience. John finished his drink and stood.

"Mr. Bradford wants to see you," Budreau said. "Lieutenant Banners will be outside to show you to his office."

"Thank you, sir." Falkenberg strode from the big room. As he closed the door he saw Budreau going back to the liquor cabinet.

Vice President Ernest Bradford was a small man with a smile that never seemed to fade. He worked at being liked, but it didn't always work. Still, he had gathered a following of dedicated party workers, and he fancied himself an accomplished politician.

When Banners showed Falkenberg into the office, Bradford smiled even more broadly, but he suggested that Banners should take Calvin on a tour of the Palace guardrooms. Falkenberg nodded and let them go.

The Vice President's office was starkly functional. The desks and chairs were made of local woods with an indifferent finish, and a solitary rose in a crystal vase provided the only color. Bradford was dressed in the same manner, shapeless clothing bought from a cheap store.

"Thank God you're here," Bradford said when the door was closed. "But I'm told you only brought ten men. We can't do anything with just ten men! You were supposed to bring over a hundred men loyal to us!" He bounced up excitedly from his chair, then sat again. "Can you do something?"

"There were ten men in the Navy ship with me," Falkenberg said. "When you show me where I'm to train the regiment I'll find the rest of the mercenaries."

Bradford gave him a broad wink and beamed. "Then you did bring more! We'll show them—all of them. We'll win yet. What did you think of Budreau?"

"He seems sincere enough. Worried, of course. I think I would be in his place."

Bradford shook his head. "He can't make up his mind. About anything! He wasn't so bad before, but lately he's had to be forced into making every decision. Why did the Colonial Office pick him? I thought you were going to arrange for me to be President. We gave you enough money."

"One thing at a time," Falkenberg said. "The Undersecretary couldn't justify you to the Minister. We can't get to everyone, you know. It was hard enough for Professor Whitlock to get them to approve Budreau, let alone you. We sweated blood just getting them to let go of having a Freedom Party President."

Bradford's head bobbed up and down like a puppet's. "I knew I could trust you," he said. His smile was warm, but despite all his efforts to be sincere it did not come through. "You have kept your part of the bargain, anyway. And once the CD is gone—"

"We'll have a free hand, of course,"

Bradford smiled again. "You are a very strange man, Colonel Falkenberg. The talk was that you were utterly loyal to the CoDominium. When Dr. Whitlock suggested that you might be available I was astounded."

"I had very little choice," Falkenberg reminded him.

"Yes." Bradford didn't say that Falkenberg had little more now, but it was obvious that he thought it. His smile expanded confidentially. "Well, we have to let Mr. Hamner meet you now. He's the Second Vice President. Then we can go to the Warner estate. I've arranged for your troops to be quartered there, it's what you wanted for a training ground. No one will bother you. You can say your other men are local volunteers."

Falkenberg nodded. "I'll manage. I'm getting rather good at cover stories lately."

"Sure." Bradford beamed again. "By God, we'll win this yet." He touched a button on his desk. "Ask Mr. Hamner to come in, please." He winked at Falkenberg and said, "Can't spend too long alone. Might give someone the idea that we have a conspiracy."

"How does Hamner fit in?" Falkenberg asked.

"Wait until you see him. Budreau trusts him, and he's dangerous. He represents the technology people in the Progressive Party. We can't do without him, but his policies are ridiculous. He wants to turn loose of everything. If he has his way, there won't be any government. And his people take credit for everything—as if technology was all there was to government. He doesn't know the first thing about governing. All the people we have to keep happy, the meetings, he thinks that's all silly, that you can build a party by working like an engineer."

"In other words, he doesn't understand the political realities," Falkenberg said. "Just so. I suppose he has to go, then."

Bradford nodded, smiling again. "Eventually. But we do need his influence with the technicians at the moment. And of course, he knows nothing about any arrangements you and I have made."

"Of course." Falkenberg sat easily and studied maps until the intercom announced that Hamner was outside. He wondered idly if the office was safe to talk in. Bradford was the most likely man to plant devices in other people's offices, but he couldn't be the only one who'd benefit from eavesdropping, and no place could be absolutely safe.

There isn't much I can do if it is, Falkenberg decided. And it's probably clean.

George Hamner was a large man, taller than Falkenberg and even heavier than Sergeant Major Calvin. He had the relaxed movements of a big man, and much of the easy confidence that massive size usually wins. People didn't pick fights with George Hamner. His grip was gentle when they shook hands, but he closed his fist relentlessly, testing Falkenberg carefully. As he felt answering pressure he looked surprised, and the two men stood in silence for a long moment before Hamner relaxed and waved to Bradford.

"So you're our new colonel of constabulary," Hamner said. "Hope you know what you're getting into. I should say I hope you *don't* know. If you know about our problems and take the job anyway, we'll have to wonder if you're sane."

"I keep hearing about how severe Hadley's problems are," Falkenberg said. "If enough of you keep saying it, maybe I'll believe it's hopeless, but right now I don't see it. So we're outnumbered by the Freedom Party people. What kind of weapons do they have to make trouble with?"

Hamner laughed. "Direct sort of guy, aren't you? I like that. There's nothing spectacular about their weapons, just a lot of them. Enough small problems make a big problem, right? But the CD hasn't permitted any big stuff. No tanks or armored cars, hell, there aren't enough cars of any kind to make any difference. No fuel or power distribution net ever built, so no way cars would be useful. We've got a subway, couple of monorails for in-city stuff, and what's left of the railroad . . . you didn't ask for a lecture on transportation, did you?"

"No."

Hamner laughed. "It's my pet worry at the moment. We don't have enough. Let's see, weapons . . ." The big man sprawled into a chair. He hooked one leg over the arm and ran his fingers through thick hair just receding from his large brows. "No military aircraft, hardly any aircraft at all except for a few choppers. No artillery, machine guns, heavy weapons in general. Mostly light-caliber hunting rifles and shotguns. Some police weapons. Military rifles and bayonets, a few, and we have almost all of them. Out in the streets you can find anything, Colonel, and I mean literally anything. Bows and arrows, knives, swords, axes, hammers, you name it."

"He doesn't need to know about obsolete things like that," Bradford said. His voice was heavy with contempt, but he still wore his smile.

"No weapon is ever really obsolete," Falkenberg said. "Not in the hands of a man who'll use it. What about body armor? How good a supply of Nemourlon do you have?"

Hamner looked thoughtful for a second. "There's some body armor in the streets, and the police have some. The President's Guard doesn't use the stuff. I can supply you with Nemourlon, but you'll have to make your own armor out of it. Can you do that?"

Falkenberg nodded. "Yes. I brought an excellent technician and some tools. Gentlemen, the situation's about what I expected. I can't see why everyone is so worried. We have a battalion of CD Marines, not the best Marines perhaps, but they're trained soldiers. With the weapons of a light infantry battalion and the training I can give the recruits we'll add to the battalion, I'll undertake to face your forty thousand Freedom Party people. The guerrilla problem will be somewhat more severe, but we control all the food distribution in the city. With ration cards and identity papers it should not be difficult to set up controls."

Hamner laughed. It was a bitter laugh. "You want to tell him, Ernie?"

Bradford looked confused. "Tell him what?"

Hamner laughed again. "Not doing your homework. It's in the morning report for a couple of days ago. The Colonial Office has decided, on the advice of BuRelock, that Hadley does not need any military weapons. The CD Marines will be lucky to keep their rifles and bayonets. All the rest of their gear goes out with the CD ships."

"But this is insane." Bradford protested. He turned to Falkenberg. "Why would they do that?"

Falkenberg shrugged. "Perhaps some Freedom Party manager got to a Colonial Office official. I assume they are not above bribery?"

"Of course not," Bradford said. "We've got to do something!"

"If we can. I suspect it will not be easy." Falkenberg pursed his lips into a tight line. "I hadn't counted on this. It means that if we tighten up control through food rationing and identity documents, we face armed rebellion. How well organized are these FP partisans, anyway?"

"Well organized and well financed," Hamner said. "And I'm

not so sure about ration cards being the answer to the guerrilla problem anyway. The CoDominium was able to put up with a lot of sabotage because they weren't interested in anything but the mines, but we can't live with the level of terror we have right now in this city. Some way or other we have to restore order—and justice, for that matter."

"Justice isn't something soldiers ordinarily deal with," Falkenberg said. "Order's another matter. *That* I think we can supply."

"With a few hundred men?" Hamner's voice was incredulous. "But I like your attitude. At least you don't sit around and whine for somebody to help you. Or sit and think and never make up your mind."

"We will see what we can do," Falkenberg said.

"Yeah." Hamner got up and went to the door. "Well, I wanted to meet you, Colonel. Now I have. *I've* got work to do. I'd think Ernie does too, but I don't notice him doing much of it." He didn't look at them again, but went out, leaving the door open.

"You see," Bradford said. He closed the door gently. His smile was knowing. "He is useless. We'll find someone to deal with the technicians as soon as you've got everything else under control."

"He seemed to be right on some points," Falkenberg said. "For example, he knows it won't be easy to get proper police protection established. I saw an example of what goes on in Refuge on the way here, and if it's that bad all over—

"You'll find a way," Bradford said. He seemed certain. "You can recruit quite a large force, you know. And a lot of the lawlessness is nothing more than teenage street gangs. They're not loyal to anything. Freedom Party, us, the CD, or anything else. They merely want to control the block they live on."

"Sure. But they're hardly the whole problem."

"No. But you'll find a way. And forget Hamner. His whole group is rotten. They're not real Progressives, that's all." His voice was emphatic, and his eyes seemed to shine. Bradford lowered his voice and leaned forward. "Hamner used to be in the Freedom Party, you know. He claims to have broken with them over technology policies, but you can never trust a man like that."

"I see. Fortunately, I don't have to trust him."

Bradford beamed. "Precisely. Now let's get you started. You have a lot of work, and don't forget now, you've already agreed to train some party troops for me."

VII

The estate was large, nearly five kilometers on a side, located in low hills a day's march from the city of Refuge. There was a central house and barns, all made of local wood that resembled oak. The buildings nestled in a wooded bowl in the center of the estate.

"You're sure you won't need anything more?" Lieutenant Banners asked.

"No, thank you," Falkenberg said. "The few men we have with us carry their own gear. We'll have to arrange for food and fuel when the others come, but for now we'll make do."

"All right, sir," Banners said. "I'll go back with Mowrer and leave you the car, then. And you've the animals. . . ."

"Yes. Thank you, Lieutenant."

Banners saluted and got into the car. He started to say something else, but Falkenberg had turned away and Banners drove off the estate.

Calvin watched him leave. "That's a curious one," he said. "Reckon he'd like to know more about what we're doing."

Falkenberg's lips twitched into a thin smile. "I expect he would at that. You will see to it that he learns no more than we want him to."

"Aye aye, sir. Colonel, what was that Mr. Bradford was saying about Party troopers? We going to have many of them?"

"I think so." Falkenberg walked up the wide lawn toward the big ranch house. Captain Fast and several of the others were waiting on the porch, and there was a bottle of whiskey on the table.

Falkenberg poured a drink and tossed it off. "I think we'll have quite a few Progressive Party loyalists here once we start, Calvin. I'm not looking forward to it, but they were inevitable."

"Sir?" Captain Fast had been listening quietly.

Falkenberg gave him a half-smile. "Do you really think the

governing authorities are going to hand over a monopoly of military force to us?"

"You think they don't trust us."

"Amos, would *you* trust us?"

"No sir," Captain Fast said. "But we could hope."

"We will not accomplish our mission on hope, Captain. Sergeant Major."

"Sir."

"I have an errand for you later this evening. For the moment, find someone to take me to my quarters and then see about our dinner."

"Sir."

Falkenberg woke to a soft rapping on the door of his room. He opened his eyes and put his hand on the pistol under his pillow, but made no other movement.

The rap came again. "Yes," Falkenberg called softly.

"I'm back, Colonel," Calvin answered.

"Right. Come in." Falkenberg swung his feet out of his bunk and pulled on his boots. He was fully dressed otherwise.

Sergeant Major Calvin came in. He was dressed in the light synthetic leather tunic and trousers of the CD Marine battledress. The total black of a night combat coverall protruded from the war bag slung over his shoulder. He wore a pistol on his belt and a heavy trench knife was slung in a holster on his left breast.

A short wiry man with a thin brown mustache came in with Calvin.

"Glad to see you," Falkenberg said. "Have any trouble?"

"Gang of toughs tried to stir up something as we was coming through the city, Colonel," Calvin replied. He grinned wolfishly. "Didn't last long enough to set any records."

"Anyone hurt?"

"None that couldn't walk away."

"Good. Any problem at the relocation barracks?"

"No, sir," Calvin replied. "They don't guard them places. Anybody wants to get away from BuRelock's charity, they let 'em go. Without ration cards, of course. This was just involuntary colonists, not convicts."

As he took Calvin's report, Falkenberg was inspecting the man who had come in with him. Major Jeremy Savage looked tired and much older than his forty-five years. He was thinner than John remembered him.

"Bad as I've heard?" Falkenberg asked him.

"No picnic," Savage replied in the clipped accents he'd

learned when he grew up on Churchill. "Didn't expect it to
be. We're here, John Christian."

"Yes, and thank God. Nobody spotted you? The men behave
all right?"

"Yes, sir. We were treated no differently from any other
involuntary colonists. The men behaved splendidly, and a week
or two of hard exercise should get us all back in shape.
Sergeant Major tells me the battalion arrived intact."

"Yes. They're still at Marine barracks. That's our weak link,
Jeremy. I want them out here where we control who they talk
to, and as soon as possible."

"You've got the best ones. I think they'll be all right."

Falkenberg nodded. "But keep your eyes open, Jerry, and
be careful with the men until the CD pulls out. I've hired Dr.
Whitlock to check things for us. He hasn't reported in yet,
but I assume he's on Hadley."

Savage acknowledged Falkenberg's wave and sat in the
room's single chair. He took a glass of whiskey from Calvin
with a nod of thanks.

"Going all out hiring experts, eh? He's said to be the best
available. . . . My, that's good. They don't have anything to
drink on those BuRelock ships."

"When Whitlock reports in we'll have a full staff meeting,"
Falkenberg said. "Until then, stay with the plan. Bradford is
supposed to send the battalion out tomorrow, and soon after
that he'll begin collecting volunteers from his party. We're
supposed to train them. Of course, they'll all be loyal to
Bradford. Not to the Party and certainly not to us."

Savage nodded and held out the glass to Calvin for a refill.

"Now tell me a bit about those toughs you fought on the
way here, Sergeant Major," Falkenberg said.

"Street gang, Colonel. Not bad at individual fightin', but
no organization. Hardly no match for near a hundred of us."

"Street gang." John pulled his lower lip speculatively, then
grinned. "How many of our battalion used to be punks just
like them, Sergeant Major?"

"Half anyway, sir. Includin' me."

Falkenberg nodded. "I think it might be a good thing if the
Marines got to meet some of those kids, Sergeant Major.
Informally, you know."

"Sir!" Calvin's square face beamed with anticipation.

"Now," Falkenberg continued. "Recruits will be our real
problem. You can bet some of them will try to get chummy
with the troops. They'll want to pump the men about their
backgrounds and outfits. And the men will drink, and when

they drink they talk. How will you handle that, Top Soldier?"

Calvin looked thoughtful. "Won't be no trick for a while. We'll keep the recruits away from the men except drill instructors, and DIs don't talk to recruits. Once they've passed basic it'll get a bit stickier, but hell, Colonel, troops like to lie about their campaigns. We'll just encourage 'em to fluff it up a bit. The stories'll be so tall nobody'll believe 'em."

"Right. I don't have to tell both of you we're skating on pretty thin ice for a while."

"We'll manage, Colonel." Calvin was positive. He'd been with Falkenberg a long time, and although any man can make mistakes, it was Calvin's experience that Falkenberg would find a way out of any hole they dropped into.

And if they didn't—well, over every CD orderly room door was a sign. It said, "You are Marines in order to die, and the Fleet will send you where you can die." Calvin had walked under that sign to enlist, and thousands of times since.

"That's it, then, Jeremy," Falkenberg said.

"Yes, sir," Savage said crisply. He stood and saluted. "Damned if it doesn't feel good to be doing this again, sir." Years fell away from his face.

"Good to have you back aboard," Falkenberg replied. He stood to return the salute. "And thanks, Jerry. For everything. . . ."

The Marine battalion arrived the next day. They were marched to the camp by regular CD Marine officers, who turned them over to Falkenberg. The captain in charge of the detail wanted to stay around and watch, but Falkenberg found an errand for him and sent Major Savage along to keep him company. An hour later there was no one in the camp but Falkenberg's people.

Two hours later the troops were at work constructing their own base camp.

Falkenberg watched from the porch of the ranch house. "Any problems, Sergeant Major?" he asked.

Calvin fingered the stubble on his square jaw. He shaved twice a day on garrison duty, and at the moment he was wondering if he needed his second. "Nothing a trooper's blast won't cure, Colonel. With your permission I'll draw a few barrels of whiskey tonight and let 'em tie one on before the recruits come in."

"Granted."

"They won't be fit for much before noon tomorrow, but we're on schedule now. The extra work'll be good for 'em."

"How many will run?"

Calvin shrugged. "Maybe none, Colonel. We got enough to keep 'em busy, and they don't know this place very well. Recruits'll be a different story, and once they get in we may have a couple take off."

"Yes. Well, see what you can do. We're going to need every man. You heard President Budreau's assessment of the situation."

"Yes, sir. That'll make the troops happy. Sounds like a good fight comin' up."

"I think you can safely promise the men some hard fighting, Sergeant Major. They'd also better understand that there's no place to go if we don't win this one. No pickups on this tour."

"No pickups on half the missions we've been on, Colonel. I better see Cap'n Fast about the brandy. Join us about midnight, sir? The men would like that."

"I'll be along, Sergeant Major."

Calvin's prediction was wrong: the troops were useless throughout the entire next day. The recruits arrived the day after.

The camp was a flurry of activity. The Marines relearned lessons of basic training. Each maniple of five men cooked for itself, did its own laundry, made its own shelters from woven synthetics and rope, and contributed men for work on the encampment revetments and palisades.

The recruits did the same kind of work under the supervision of Falkenberg's mercenary officers and NCOs. Most of the men who had come with Savage on the BuRelock colony transport were officers, centurions, sergeants, and technicians, while there was an unusual number of monitors and corporals within the Marine battalion. Between the two groups there were enough leaders for an entire regiment.

The recruits learned to sleep in their military great-cloaks, and to live under field conditions with no uniform but synthileather battledress and boots. They cooked their own food and constructed their own quarters and depended on no one outside the regiment. After two weeks they were taught to fashion their own body armor from Nemourlon. When it was completed they lived in it, and any man who neglected his duties found his armor weighted with lead. Maniples, squads, and whole sections of recruits and veterans on punishment marches became a common sight after dark.

The volunteers had little time to fraternize with the Marine veterans. Savage and Calvin and the other cadres relentlessly drove them through drills, field problems, combat exercises, and maintenance work. The recruit formations were smaller each day as men were driven to leave the service, but from somewhere there was a steady supply of new troops.

These were all younger men who came in small groups directly to the camp. They would appear before the regimental orderly room at reveille, and often they were accompanied by Marine veterans. There was attrition in their formations as well as among the Party volunteers, but far fewer left the service— and they were eager for combat training.

After six weeks Vice President Bradford visited the camp. He arrived to find the entire regiment in formation, the recruits on one side of a square, the veterans on the other.

Sergeant Major Calvin was reading to the men.

"Today is April 30 on Earth." Calvin's voice boomed out; he had no need for a bullhorn. "It is Camerone Day. On April 30, 1863, Captain Jean Danjou of the Foreign Legion, with two officers and sixty-two legionnaires, faced two thousand Mexicans at the farmhouse of Camerone.

"The battle lasted all day. The legionnaires had no food or water, and their ammunition was low. Captain Danjou was killed. His place was taken by Lieutenant Villain. He also was killed.

"At five in the afternoon all that remained were Lieutenant Clement Maudet and four men. They had one cartridge each. At the command each man fired his last round and charged the enemy with the bayonet.

"There were no survivors."

The troops were silent. Calvin looked at the recruits. They stood at rigid attention in the hot sun. Finally Calvin spoke. "I don't expect none of you to ever get it. Not the likes of you. But maybe one of you'll someday know what Camerone is all about.

"Every man will draw an extra wine ration tonight. Combat veterans will also get a half-liter of brandy. Now attention to orders."

Falkenberg took Bradford inside the ranch house. It was now fitted out as the Officers' Mess, and they sat in one corner of the lounge. A steward brought drinks.

"And what was all that for?" Bradford demanded. "These aren't Foreign Legionnaires! You're supposed to be training a planetary constabulary."

"A constabulary that has one hell of a fight on its hands," Falkenberg reminded him. "True, we don't have any continuity with the Legion in this outfit, but you have to remember that our basic cadre are CD Marines. Or were. If we skipped Camerone Day, we'd have a mutiny."

"I suppose you know what you're doing." Bradford sniffed. His face had almost lost the perpetual half-smile he wore, but there were still traces of it. "Colonel, I have a complaint from the men we've assigned as officers. My Progressive Party people have been totally segregated from the other troops, and they don't like it. I don't like it."

Falkenberg shrugged. "You chose to commission them before training, Mr. Bradford. That makes them officers by courtesy, but they don't know anything. They would look ridiculous if I mixed them with the veterans, or even the recruits, until they've learned military basics."

"You've got rid of a lot of them, too—"

"Same reason, sir. You have given us a difficult assignment. We're outnumbered and there's no chance of outside support. In a few weeks we'll face forty thousand Freedom Party men, and I won't answer for the consequences if we hamper the troops with incompetent officers."

"All right. I expected that. But it isn't just the officers, Colonel. The Progressive volunteers are being driven out as well. Your training is too hard. Those are loyal men, and loyalty is important here!"

Falkenberg smiled softly. "Agreed. But I'd rather have one battalion of good men I can trust than a regiment of troops who might break under fire. After I've a bare minimum of first-class troops, I'll consider taking on others for garrison duties. Right now the need is for men who can fight."

"And you don't have them yet—those Marines seemed well disciplined."

"In ranks, certainly. But do you really think the CD would let go of reliable troops?"

"Maybe not," Bradford conceded. "OK. You're the expert. But where the hell are you getting the other recruits? Jailbirds, kids with police records. You keep them while you let my Progressives run!"

"Yes, sir." Falkenberg signaled for another round of drinks. "Mr. Vice President—"

"Since when have we become that formal?" Bradford asked. His smile was back.

"Sorry. I thought you were here to read me out."

"No, of course not. But I've got to answer to President Budreau, you know. And Hamner. I've managed to get your activities assigned to my department, but it doesn't mean I can tell the Cabinet to blow it."

"Right," Falkenberg said. "Well, about the recruits. We take what we can get. It takes time to train green men, and if the street warriors stand up better than your party toughs, I can't help it. You can tell the Cabinet that when we've a cadre we can trust, we'll be easier on volunteers. We can even form some kind of part-time militia. But right now the need is for men tough enough to win this fight coming up, and I don't know any better way to do it."

After that Falkenberg found himself summoned to report to the Palace every week. Usually he met only Bradford and Hamner; President Budreau had made it clear that he considered the military force as an evil whose necessity was not established, and only Bradford's insistence kept the regiment supplied.

At one conference Falkenberg met Chief Horgan of the Refuge police.

"The Chief's got a complaint, Colonel," President Budreau said.

"Yes sir?" Falkenberg asked.

"It's those damned Marines," Horgan said. He rubbed the point of his chin. "They're raising hell in the city at night. We've never hauled any of them in because Mr. Bradford wants us to go easy, but it's getting rough."

"What are they doing?" Falkenberg asked.

"You name it. They've taken over a couple of taverns and won't let anybody in without their permission, for one thing. And they have fights with street gangs every night.

"We could live with all that, but they go to other parts of town, too. Lots of them. They go into taverns and drink all night, then say they can't pay. If the owner gets sticky, they wreck the place. . . ."

"And they're gone before your patrols get there," Falkenberg finished for him. "It's an old tradition. They call it System D, and more planning effort goes into that operation than I can ever get them to put out in combat. I'll try to put a stop to System D, anyway."

"It would help. Another thing. Your guys go into the roughest parts of town and start fights whenever they can find anyone to mix with."

"How are they doing?" Falkenberg asked interestedly.

Horgan grinned, then caught himself after a stern look from Budreau. "Pretty well. I understand they've never been beaten. But it raises hell with the citizens, Colonel. And another trick of theirs is driving people crazy! They march through the streets fifty strong at all hours of the night playing bagpipes!

Bagpipes in the wee hours, Colonel, can be a frightening thing."

Falkenberg thought he saw a tiny flutter in Horgan's left eye, and the police chief was holding back a wry smile.

"I wanted to ask you about that, Colonel," Second Vice President Hamner said. "This is hardly a Scots outfit, why do they have bagpipes anyway?"

Falkenberg shrugged. "Pipes are standard with many Marine regiments. Since the Russki CD outfits started taking up Cossack customs, the Western bloc regiments adopted their own. After all, the Marines were formed out of a number of old military units. Foreign Legion, Highlanders—a lot of men like the pipes. I'll confess I do myself."

"Sure, but not in my city in the middle of the night," Horgan said.

John grinned openly at the chief of police. "I'll try to keep the pipers off the streets at night. I can imagine they're not good for civilian morale. But as to keeping the Marines in camp, how do I do it? We need every one of them, and they're volunteers. They can get on the CD carrier and ship out when the rest go, and there's not one damned thing we can do about it."

"There's less than a month until they haul down that CoDominium flag," Bradford added with satisfaction. He glanced at the CD banner on its staff outside. Eagle with red shield and black sickle and hammer on its breast; red stars and blue stars around it. Bradford nodded in satisfaction. It wouldn't be long.

That flag meant little to the people of Hadley. On Earth it was enough to cause riots in nationalistic cities in both the U.S. and the Soviet Union, while in other countries it was a symbol of the alliance that kept any other nation from rising above second-class status. To Earth the CoDominium Alliance represented peace at a high price, too high for many.

For Falkenberg it represented nearly thirty years of service ended by court martial.

Two weeks to go. Then the CoDominium governor would leave, and Hadley would be officially independent. Vice President Bradley visited the camp to speak to the recruits.

He told them of the value of loyalty to the government, and the rewards they would all have as soon as the Progressive Party was officially in power. Better pay, more liberties, and the opportunity for promotion in an expanding army; bonuses and soft duty. His speech was full of promises, and Bradford was quite proud of it.

When he had finished, Falkenberg took the Vice President into a private room in the Officers' Mess and slammed the door.

"Damn you, you don't *ever* make offers to my troops without my permission." John Falkenberg's face was cold with anger.

"I'll do as I please with my army, Colonel," Bradford replied smugly. The little smile on his face was completely without warmth. "Don't get snappy with me, *Colonel* Falkenberg. Without my influence Budreau would dismiss you in an instant."

Then his mood changed, and Bradford took a flask of brandy from his pocket. "Here, Colonel, have a drink." The little smile was replaced with something more genuine. "We have to work together, John. There's too much to do, even with both of us working it won't all get done. Sorry, I'll ask your advice in future, but don't you think the troops should get to know me? I'll be President soon." He looked to Falkenberg for confirmation.

"Yes, sir," John took the flask and held it up for a toast. "To the new president of Hadley. I shouldn't have snapped at you, but don't make offers to troops who haven't proved themselves. If you give men reason to think they're good when they're not, you'll never have an army worth its pay."

"But they've done well in training. You said so."

"Sure, but you don't tell *them* that. Work them until they've nothing more to give, and let them know that's just barely satisfactory. Then one day they'll give you more than they knew they had in them. That's the day you can offer rewards, only by then you won't need to."

Bradford nodded grudging agreement. "If you say so. But I wouldn't have thought—"

"Listen," Falkenberg said.

A party of recruits and their drill masters marched past outside. They were singing and their words came in the open window.

> "When you've blue'd your last tosser,
>   on the brothel and the booze,
>   and you're out in the cold on your ear,
>   you hump your bundle on the rough,
>   and tell the sergeant that you're tough,
>   and you'll do him the favor of his life.
>   He will cry and he will scream,
>   and he'll curse his rotten luck,
>   and he'll ask why he was ever born.
>   If you're lucky he will take you,

and he'll do his best to break you,
and they'll feed you rotten monkey on a knife."

"Double time, heaow!" The song broke off as the men ran
across the central parade ground.

Bradford turned away from the window. "That sort of thing
is all very well for the jailbirds, Colonel, but I insist on keeping
my loyalists as well. In future you will dismiss no Progressive without my approval. Is that understood?"

Falkenberg nodded. He'd seen this coming for some time.
"In that case, sir, it might be better to form a separate battalion. I will transfer all of your people into the Fourth Battalion and put them under the officers you've appointed. Will
that be satisfactory?"

"If you'll supervise their training, yes."

"Certainly," Falkenberg said.

"Good." Bradford's smile broadened, but it wasn't meant
for Falkenberg. "I will also expect you to consult me about
any promotions in that battalion. You agree to that, of course."

"Yes, sir. There may be some problems about finding locals
to fill the senior NCO slots. You've got potential monitors and
corporals, but they've not the experience to be sergeants and
centurions."

"You'll find a way, I'm sure," Bradford said carefully. "I have
some rather, uh, special duties for the Fourth Battalion, Colonel.
I'd prefer it to be entirely staffed by Party loyalists of my
choosing. Your men should only be there to supervise training, not as their commanders. Is this agreed?"

"Yes, sir."

Bradford's smile was genuine as he left the camp.

Day after day the troops sweated in the bright blue-tinted
sunlight. Riot control, bayonet drill, use of armor in defense
and attacks against men with body armor; and more complex
exercises as well. There were forced marches under the relentless direction of Major Savage, the harsh shouts of sergeants
and centurions, Captain Amos Fast with his tiny swagger stick
and biting sarcasm. . . .

Yet the number leaving the regiment was smaller now, and
there was still a flow of recruits from the Marine's noctur-
nal expeditions. The recruiting officers could even be selective, although they seldom were. The Marines, like the Legion
before it, took anyone willing to fight; and Falkenberg's officers were all Marine trained.

Each night groups of Marines sneaked past sentries to drink

and carouse with the field hands of nearby ranchers. They gambled and shouted in local taverns, and they paid little attention to their officers. There were many complaints, and Bradford's protests became stronger.

Falkenberg always gave the same answer. "They always come back, and they don't have to stay here. How do you suggest I control them? Flogging?"

The constabulary army had a definite split personality, with recruits treated harsher than veterans. Meanwhile the Fourth Battalion grew larger each day.

VIII

George Hamner tried to get home for dinner every night, no matter what it might cost him in night work later. He thought he owed at least that to his family.

His walled estate was just outside the Palace district. It had been built by his grandfather with money borrowed from American Express. The old man had been proud of paying back every cent before it was due. It was a big comfortable place which cunningly combined local materials and imported luxuries, and George was always glad to return there.

At home he felt he was master of something, that at least one thing was under his control. It was the only place in Refuge where he could feel that way.

In less than a week the CoDominium Governor would leave. Independence was near, and it should be a time of hope, but George Hamner felt only dread. Problems of public order were not officially his problem. He held the Ministry of Technology, but the breakdown in law and order couldn't be ignored. Already half of Refuge was untouched by government.

There were large areas where the police went only in squads or not at all, and maintenance crews had to be protected or they couldn't enter. For now the CoDominium Marines escorted George's men, but what would it be like when the Marines were gone?

George sat in the paneled study and watched lengthening shadows in the groves outside. They made dancing patterns through the trees and across neatly clipped lawns. The outside walls spoiled the view of Raceway Channel below, and Hamner cursed them.

Why must we have walls? Walls and a dozen armed men to patrol them. I can remember when I sat in this room with my father, I was no more than six, and we could watch boats in the Channel. And later, we had such big dreams for Hadley. Grandfather telling why he had left Earth, and what we could

242

do here. Freedom and plenty. We had a paradise, and Lord, Lord, what have we done with it?

He worked for an hour, but accomplished little. There weren't any solutions, only chains of problems that led back into a circle. Solve one and all would fall into place, but none were soluble without the others. And yet, if we had a few years, he thought. A few years, but we aren't going to get them.

In a few years the farms will support the urban population if we can move people out to the agricultural interior and get them working—but they won't leave Refuge, and we can't make them do it.

If we could, though. If the city's population could be thinned, the power we divert to food manufacture can be used to build a transport net. Then we can get more to live in the interior, and we can get more food into the city. We could make enough things to keep country life pleasant, and people will want to leave Refuge. But there's no way to the first step. The people don't want to move and the Freedom Party promises they won't have to.

George shook his head. Can Falkenberg's army make them leave? If he gets enough soldiers can he forcibly evacuate part of the city? Hamner shuddered at the thought. There would be resistance, slaughter, civil war. Hadley's independence can't be built on a foundation of blood. No.

His other problems were similar. The government was bandaging Hadley's wounds, but no more. Treating symptoms because there was never enough control over events to treat causes.

He picked up a report on the fusion generators. They needed spare parts, and he wondered how long even this crazy standoff would last. He couldn't really expect more than a few years even if everything went well. A few years, and then famine because the transport net couldn't be built fast enough. And when the generators failed, the city's food supplies would be gone, sanitation services crippled . . . famine and plague. Were those horsemen better than conquest and war?

He thought of his interview with the Freedom Party leaders. They didn't care about the generators because they were sure that Earth wouldn't allow famines on Hadley. They thought Hadley could use her own helplessness as a weapon to extract payments from the CoDominium.

George cursed under his breath. They were wrong. Earth didn't care, and Hadley was too far away to interest anyone. But even if they were right they were selling Hadley's independence, and for what? Didn't real independence mean anything to them?

Laura came in with a pack of shouting children.

"Already time for bed?" he asked. The four-year-old picked up his pocket calculator and sat on his lap, punching buttons and watching the numbers and lights flash.

George kissed them all and sent them out, wondering as he did what kind of future they had.

I should get out of politics, he told himself. I'm not doing any good, and I'll get Laura and the kids finished along with me. But what happens if we let go? What future will they have then?

"You look worried." Laura was back after putting the children to bed. "It's only a few days—"

"Yeah."

"And what really happens then?" she asked. "Not the promises we keep hearing. What really happens when the CD leaves? It's going to be bad, isn't it?"

He pulled her to him, feeling her warmth, and tried to draw comfort from her nearness. She huddled against him for a moment, then pulled away.

"George, shouldn't we take what we can and go east? We wouldn't have much, but you'd be alive."

"It won't be *that* bad," he told her. He tried to chuckle, as if she'd made a joke, but the sound was hollow. She didn't laugh with him.

"There'll be time for that later," he told her. "If things don't work. But it should be all right at first. We've got a planetary constabulary. It should be enough to protect the government—but I'm moving all of you into the palace in a couple of days."

"The army," she said with plenty of contempt. "Some army, Georgie. Bradford's volunteers who'd kill you—and don't think he wouldn't like to see you dead, either. And those Marines! You said yourself they were the scum of space."

"I said it. I wonder if I believe it. There's something strange happening here, Laura. Something I don't understand."

She sat on the couch near his desk and curled her legs under herself. He'd always liked that pose. She looked up, her eyes wide with interest. She never looked at anyone else that way.

"I went to see Major Karantov today," George said. "Thought I'd presume on an old friend to get a little information about this man Falkenberg. Boris wasn't in his office, but one of the junior lieutenants, fellow named Kleist—"

"I've met him," Laura said. "Nice boy. A little young."

"Yes. Anyway, we got into a conversation about what happens after independence. We discussed street fighting, and the mob riots, you know, and I said I wished we had some reliable Marines instead of the demobilized outfit they were leaving here. He looked funny and asked just what did I want, the Grand Admiral's Guard?"

"That's strange."

"Yes, and when Boris came in and I asked what Kleist meant, Boris said the kid was new and didn't know what he was talking about."

"And you think he did?" Laura asked. "Boris wouldn't lie to you. Stop that!" she added hastily. "You have an appointment."

"It can wait."

"With only a couple of dozen cars on this whole planet and one of them coming for you, you will not keep it waiting while you make love to your wife, George Hamner!" Her eyes flashed, but not with anger. "Besides, I want to know what Boris told you." She danced away from him, and he went back to the desk.

"It's not just that," George said. "I've been thinking about it. Those troops don't look like misfits to me. Off duty they drink, and they've got the field hands locking their wives and daughters up, but you know, come morning they're out on that drill field. And Falkenberg doesn't strike me as the type who'd put up with undisciplined men."

"But—"

He nodded. "But it doesn't make sense. And there's the matter of the officers. He's got too many, and they're not from Hadley. That's why I'm going out there tonight, without Bradford."

"Have you asked Ernie about it?"

"Sure. He says he's got some Party loyalists training as officers. I'm a little slow, Laura, but I'm not that stupid. I may not notice everything, but if there were fifty Progressives with military experience I'd know. Bradford is lying, and why?"

Laura looked thoughtful and pulled her lower lip in a gesture that Hamner hardly noticed now, although he'd kidded her about it before they were married. "He lies for practice," she said. "But his wife has been talking about independence, and she let something slip about when Ernie would be President she'd make some changes."

"Well, Ernie expects to succeed Budreau."

"No," Laura said. "She acted like it would be soon. Very soon."

George Hamner shook his massive head. "He hasn't the guts

for a coup," he said firmly. "And the technicians would walk out in a second. They can't stand him and he knows it."

"Ernest Bradford has never recognized any limitations," Laura said. "He really believes he can make anyone like him if he'll just put out the effort. No matter how many times he's kicked a man, he thinks a few smiles and apologies will fix it. But what did Boris tell you about Falkenberg?"

"Said he was as good as we can get. A top Marine commander, started as a Navy man and went over to Marines because he couldn't get fast enough promotions in the Navy."

"An ambitious man. How ambitious?"

"Don't know."

"Is he married?"

"I gather he once was, but not for a long time. I got the scoop on the court martial. There weren't any slots open for promotion. But when a review board passed Falkenberg over for a promotion that the admiral couldn't have given him in the first place, Falkenberg made such a fuss about it that he was dismissed for insubordination."

"Can you trust him, then?" Laura asked. "His men may be the only thing keeping you alive—"

"I know. And you, and Jimmy, and Christie, and Peter. . . . I asked Boris that, and he said there's no better man available. You can't hire CD men from active duty. Boris recommends him highly. Says troops love him, he's a brilliant tactician, has experience in troop command and staff work as well—"

"Sounds like quite a catch."

"Yes. But Laura, if he's all that valuable, why did they boot him out? My God, it all sounds so trivial—"

The interphone buzzed, and Hamner answered it absently. It was the butler to announce that his car and driver were waiting. "I'll be late, sweetheart. Don't wait up for me. But you might think about it . . . I swear Falkenberg is the key to something, and I wish I knew what."

"Do you like him?" Laura asked.

"He isn't a man who tries to be liked."

"I asked if *you* like him."

"Yes. And there's no reason to. I like him, but can I trust him?"

As he went out he thought about that. Could he trust Falkenberg? With Laura's life . . . and the kids . . . and for that matter, with a whole planet that seemed headed for hell and no way out.

The troops were camped in an orderly square. Earth ramparts had been thrown up around the perimeter, and the tents were pitched in lines that might have been laid with a transit.

The equipment was scrubbed and polished, blanket rolls were tight, each item in the same place inside the two-man tents . . . but the men were milling about, shouting, gambling openly in front of the campfires. There were plenty of bottles in evidence even from the outer gates.

"Halt! Who's there?"

Hamner started. The car had stopped at the barricaded gate, but Hamner hadn't seen the sentry. This was his first visit to the camp at night, and he was edgy. "Vice President Hamner," he answered.

A strong light played on his face from the opposite side of the car. Two sentries, then, and both invisible until he'd come on them. "Good evening, sir," the first sentry said. "I'll pass the word you're here."

He raised a small communicator to his lips. "Corporal of the Guard. Post Number Five." Then he shouted the same thing, the call ringing clear in the night. A few heads around campfires turned toward the gate, then went back to their other activities.

Hamner was escorted across the camp to officers' row. The huts and tent stood across a wide parade ground from the densely packed company streets of the troops and had their own guards.

Over in the company area the men were singing, and Hamner paused to listen.

> "I've a head like a concertina, and I think I'm ready
>   to die,
> and I'm here in the clink for a thundrin' drink and
>   blacking the Corporal's eye,
> With another man's cloak underneath of my head
>   and a beautiful view of the yard,
> it's the crapaud for me, and no more System D,
> I was Drunk and Resistin' the Guard!
> Mad drunk and resistin' the guard!
> It's the crapaud for me, and no more System D,
> I was Drunk and Resistin' the Guard."

Falkenberg came out of his hut. "Good evening, sir. What brings you here?"

I'll just bet you'd like to know, Hamner thought. "I have a few things to discuss with you, Colonel. About the organization of the constabulary."

"Certainly." Falkenberg was crisp and seemed slightly nervous. Hamner wondered if he were drunk. "Shall we go to the Mess?" Falkenberg asked. "More comfortable there, and I haven't got my quarters made up for visitors."

Or you've got something here I shouldn't see, George thought. Something or someone. Local girl? What difference does it make? God, I wish I could trust this man.

Falkenberg led the way to the ranch house in the center of officers' row. The troops were still shouting and singing, and a group was chasing each other on the parade ground. Most were dressed in the blue and yellow garrison uniforms Falkenberg had designed, but others trotted past in synthi-leather battledress. They carried rifles and heavy packs.

"Punishment detail," Falkenberg explained. "Not as many of those as there used to be."

Sound crashed from the Officers' Mess building: drums and bagpipes, a wild sound of war mingled with shouted laughter. Inside, two dozen men sat at a long table as white-coated stewards moved briskly about with whiskey bottles and glasses.

Kilted bandsmen marched around the table with pipes. Drummers stood in one corner. The deafening noise stopped as Falkenberg entered, and everyone got to his feet. Some were quite unsteady.

"Carry on," Falkenberg said, but no one did. They eyed Hamner nervously, and at a wave from the mess president at the head of the table the pipers and drummers went outside. Several stewards with bottles followed them. The other officers sat and talked in low tones. After all the noise the room seemed very quiet.

"We'll sit over here, shall we?" the colonel asked. He led Hamner to a small table in one corner. A steward brought two glasses of whiskey and set them down.

The room seemed curiously bare to Hamner. A few banners, some paintings; very little else. Somehow, he thought, there ought to be more. As if they're waiting. But that's ridiculous.

Most of the officers were strangers, but George recognized half a dozen Progressives, the highest rank a first lieutenant. He waved at the ones he knew and received brief smiles that seemed almost guilty before the Party volunteers turned back to their companions.

"Yes, sir?" Falkenberg prompted.

"Just who are these men?" George demanded. "I know they're not native to Hadley. Where did they come from?"

"CoDominium officers on the beach," Falkenberg answered

promptly. "Reduction in force. Lots of good men got riffed into early retirement. Some of them heard I was coming here and chose to give up their reserve ranks. They came out on the colony ship on the chance I'd hire them."

"And you did."

"Naturally I jumped at the chance to get experienced men at prices we could afford."

"But why all the secrecy? Why haven't I heard about them before?"

Falkenberg shrugged. "We've violated several of the Grand Senate's regulations on mercenaries, you know. It's best not to talk about these things until the CD has definitely gone. After that, the men are committed. They'll have to stay loyal to Hadley." Falkenberg lifted his whiskey glass. "Vice President Bradford knew all about it."

"I'll bet he did." Hamner lifted his own glass. "Cheers."

"Cheers."

And I wonder what else that little snake knows about, Hamner wondered. Without his support Falkenberg would be out of here in a minute . . . and what then?

"Colonel, your organization charts came to my office yesterday. You've kept all the Marines in one battalion with these newly hired officers. Then you've got three battalions of locals, but all the Party stalwarts are in the Fourth. The Second and Third are local recruits, but under your own men."

"That's a fair enough description, yes, sir," Falkenberg said.

And you know my question, George thought. "Why, Colonel? A suspicious man would say that you've got your own little army here, with a structure set so that you can take complete control if there's ever a difference of opinion between you and the government."

"A suspicious man might say that," Falkenberg agreed. He drained his glass and waited for George to do the same. A steward came over with freshly filled glasses.

"But a practical man might say something else," Falkenberg continued. "Do you expect me to put green officers in command of those guardhouse troops? Or your good-hearted Progressives in command of green recruits?"

"But you've done just that—"

"On Mr. Bradford's orders I've kept the Fourth Battalion as free of my mercenaries as possible. That isn't helping their training, either. But Mr. Bradford seems to have the same complaint as you."

"I haven't complained."

"I thought you had," Falkenberg said. "In any event, you

have your Party force, if you wish to use it to control me. Actually you have all the control you need anyway. You hold the purse strings. Without supplies to feed these men and money to pay them, I couldn't hold them an hour."

"Troops have found it easier to rob the paymaster than fight for him before now," Hamner observed. "Cheers." He drained the glass, then suppressed a cough. The stuff was strong, and he wasn't used to drinking neat whiskey. He wondered what would happen if he ordered something else, beer, or a mixed drink. Somehow it didn't seem to go with the party.

"I might have expected that remark from Bradford," Falkenberg said.

Hamner nodded. Bradford was always suspicious of something. There were times when George wondered if the First Vice President were quite sane, but that was silly. Still, when the pressure was on, Ernie Bradford did manage to get on people's nerves with his suspicions, and he would rather see nothing done than give up control of anything.

"How am I supposed to organize this coup?" Falkenberg demanded. "I have a handful of men loyal to me. The rest are mercenaries, or your locals. You've paid a lot to bring me and my staff here. You want us to fight impossible odds with nonexistent equipment. If you also insist on your own organization of forces, I cannot accept the responsibility."

"I didn't say that."

Falkenberg shrugged. "If President Budreau so orders, and he would on your recommendation, I'll turn command over to anyone he names."

And he'd name Bradford, Hamner thought. I'd rather trust Falkenberg. Whatever Falkenberg does will at least be competently done; with Ernie there was no assurance he wasn't up to something, and none that he'd be able to accomplish anything if he wasn't.

But. "What do you want out of this, Colonel Falkenberg?"

The question seemed to surprise the colonel. "Money, of course." Falkenberg answered. "A little glory, perhaps, although that's not a word much used nowadays. A position of responsibility commensurate with my abilities. I've always been a soldier, and I know nothing else."

"And why didn't you stay with the CD?"

"It is in the record," Falkenberg said coldly. "Surely you know."

"But I don't." Hamner was calm, but the whiskey was enough to make him bolder than he'd intended to be, even in this camp surrounded by Falkenberg's men. "I don't know at all. It makes no sense as I've been told it. You had no reason to complain about promotions, and the admiral had no reason to prefer charges. It looks as if you had yourself cashiered."

Falkenberg nodded. "You're nearly correct. Astute of you." The soldier's lips were tight and his gray eyes bored into Hamner. "I suppose you are entitled to an answer. Grand Senator Bronson has sworn to ruin me for reasons you needn't know. If I hadn't been dismissed for a trivial charge of technical insubordination, I'd have faced a series of trumped-up charges. At least this way I'm out with a clean record."

A clean record and a lot of bitterness. "And that's all there is to it?"

"That's all."

It was plausible. So was everything else Falkenberg said. Yet Hamner was sure that Falkenberg was lying. Not lying directly, but not telling everything either. Hamner felt that if he knew the right questions he could get the answers, but there weren't any questions to ask.

And, Hamner thought, I must either trust this man or get rid of him; and to irritate him while keeping him is the stupidest policy of all.

The pipers came back in, and the mess president looked to Falkenberg. "Something more?" Falkenberg asked.

"No."

"Thank you." The colonel nodded to the junior officer. The mess president waved approval to the pipe major. Pipe major raised his mace, and the drums crashed. The pipers began, standing in place at first, then marching around the table. Officers shouted, and the room was filled with martial cries. The party was on again.

George looked for one of his own appointees and discovered that every Progressive officer in the room was one of his own. There wasn't a single man from Bradford's wing of the Party. Was that significant?

He rose and caught the eye of a Progressive lieutenant. "I'll let Farquhar escort me out, Colonel," Hamner said.

"As you please."

The noise followed them out of the building and along the regimental street. There were more sounds from the parade ground and the camp beyond. Fires burned brightly in the night.

"All right, Jamie, what's going on here?" Hamner demanded.

"Going on, sir? Nothing that I know of. If you mean the party, we're celebrating the men's graduation from basic training. Tomorrow they'll start advanced work."

"Maybe I meant the party," Hamner said. "You seem pretty friendly with the other officers."

"Yes, sir." Hamner noted the enthusiasm in Jamie Farquhar's voice. The boy was young enough to be caught up in the military mystique, and George felt sorry for him. "They're good men," Jamie said.

"Yes, I suppose so. Where are the others? Mr. Bradford's people?"

"They had a field problem that kept them out of camp until late," Farquhar said. "Mr. Bradford came around about dinner time and asked that they be sent to a meeting somewhere. He spends a lot of time with them."

"I expect he does," Hamner said. "Look, you've been around the Marines, Jamie. Where are those men from? What CD outfits?"

"I really don't know, sir. Colonel Falkenberg has forbidden us to ask. He says that the men start with a clean record here."

Hamner noted the tone Farquhar used when he mentioned Falkenberg. More than respect. Awe, perhaps. "Have any of them served with the colonel before?"

"I think so, yes, sir. They don't like him. Curse the colonel quite openly. But they're afraid of that big sergeant major of his. Calvin has offered to whip any two men in the camp, and they can choose the rules. A few of the newcomers tried it, but none of the Marines would. Not one."

"And you say the colonel's not popular with the men?"

Farquhar was thoughtful for a moment. "I wouldn't say he was *popular,* no sir."

Yet, Hamner thought, Boris had said he was. Whiskey buzzed in George's head. "Who is popular?"

"Major Savage, sir. The men like him. And Captain Fast, the Marines particularly respect him. He's the adjutant."

"All right. Look, can this outfit fight? Have we got a chance after the CD leaves?" They stood and watched the scenes around the campfires. Men were drinking heavily, shouting and singing and chasing each other through the camp. There was a fist fight in front of one tent, and no officer moved to stop it.

"Do you allow that?" Hamner demanded.

"We try not to interfere too much." Farquhar said. "The colonel says half an officer's training is learning what *not* to see. Anyway, the sergeants have broken up the fight, see?"

"But you let the men drink."

"Sir, there's no regulation against drinking. Only against being unfit for duty. And these men are tough. They obey orders and they can fight. I think we'll do rather well."

Pride. They've put some pride into Jamie Farquhar, and maybe into some of those jailbirds out there too. "All right, Jamie. Go back to your party. I'll find my driver."

As he was driven away, George Hamner felt better about Hadley's future, but he was still convinced something was wrong; and he had no idea what it was.

IX

The stadium had been built to hold one hundred thousand people. There were at least that many jammed inside it now, and an equal number swarmed about the market squares and streets adjacent to it. The full CoDominium Marine garrison was on duty to keep order, but it wasn't needed.

The celebration was boisterous, but there wouldn't be any trouble today. The Freedom Party was as anxious to avoid an incident as the Marines on this, the greatest day for Hadley since Discovery. The CoDominium was turning over power to local authority and getting out; and nothing must spoil that.

Hamner and Falkenberg watched from the upper tiers of the Stadium. Row after row of plastisteel seats cascaded like a giant staircase down from their perch to the central grassy field below. Every seat was filled, so that the Stadium was a riot of color.

President Budreau and Governor Flaherty stood in the Presidential box directly across from Falkenberg and Hamner. The President's Guard, in blue uniforms, and the CoDominium Marines, in their scarlet and gold, stood at rigid attention around the officials.

The President's box was shared by Vice President Bradford, the Freedom Party opposition leaders, Progressive officials, officers of the retiring CoDominium government, and everyone else who could beg an invitation. George knew that some of them were wondering where he had got off to.

Bradford would particularly notice Hamner's absence. He might, George thought, even think the Second Vice President was out stirring up opposition or rebellion. Ernie Bradford had lately been accusing Hamner of every kind of disloyalty to the Progressive Party, and it wouldn't be long before he demanded that Budreau dismiss him.

To the devil with the little man! George thought. He hated crowds, and the thought of standing there and listening to all those speeches, of being polite to party officials whom he detested, was just too much. When he'd suggested watching from another vantage point, Falkenberg had quickly agreed. The soldier didn't seem to care too much for formal ceremonies either. Civilian ceremonies, Hamner corrected himself; Falkenberg seemed to like military parades.

The ritual was almost over. The CD Marine bands had marched through the field, the speeches had been made, presents delivered and accepted. A hundred thousand people had cheered, and it was an awesome sound. The raw power was frightening.

Hamner glanced at his watch. As he did the Marine band broke into a roar of drums. The massed drummers ceased to beat one by one until there was but a single drum roll that went on and on and on, until finally it too stopped. The entire Stadium waited.

One trumpet, no more. A clear call, plaintive but triumphant, the final salute to the CoDominium banner above the Palace. The notes hung in Hadley's air like something tangible, and slowly, deliberately, the crimson and blue banner floated down from the flagpole as Hadley's blazing gold and green arose.

Across the city uniformed men saluted these flags, one rising, the other setting. The blue uniforms of Hadley saluted with smiles, the red-uniformed Marines with indifference. The CoDominium banner rose and fell across two hundred light years and seventy worlds in this year of Grace; what difference would one minor planet make?

Hamner glanced at John Falkenberg. The colonel had no eyes for the rising banners of Hadley. His rigid salute was given to the CD flag, and as the last note of the final trumpet salute died away Hamner thought he saw Falkenberg wipe his eyes.

The gesture was so startling that George looked again, but there was nothing more to see, and he decided that he had been mistaken.

"That's it, then," Falkenberg snapped. His voice was strained. "I suppose we ought to join the party. Can't keep His Nibs waiting."

Hamner nodded. The Presidential box connected directly to the Palace, and the officials would arrive at the reception quickly while Falkenberg and Hamner had the entire width of the crowded Stadium to traverse. People were already streaming out to join the festive crowds on the grass in the center of the bowl.

"Let's go this way," George said. He led Falkenberg to the top of the Stadium and into a small alcove where he used a key to open an inconspicuous door. "Tunnel system takes us right into the Palace, across and under the Stadium," he told Falkenberg. "Not exactly secret, but we don't want the people to know about it because they'd demand we open it to the public. Built for maintenance crews, mostly." He locked the door behind them and waved expressively at the wide interior corridor. "Place was pretty well designed, actually."

The grudging tone of admiration wasn't natural to him. If a thing was well done, it was well done . . . but lately he found himself talking that way about CoDominium projects. He resented the whole CD administration and the men who'd dumped the job of governing after creating problems no one could solve.

They wound down stairways and through more passages, then up to another set of locked doors. Through those was the Palace courtyard. The celebrations were already under way, and it would be a long night.

George wondered what would come now. In the morning the last CD boat would rise, and the CoDominium would be gone. Tomorrow, Hadley would be alone with her problems.

"Tensh-Hut!" Sergeant Major Calvin's crisp command cut through the babble.

"Please be seated, gentlemen." Falkenberg took his place at the head of the long table in the command room of what had been the central headquarters for the CoDominium Marines.

Except for the uniforms and banners there were few changes from what people already called "the old days." The officers were seated in the usual places for a regimental staff meeting. Maps hung along one wall, and a computer output screen dominated another. Stewards in white coats brought coffee and discreetly retired behind the armed sentries outside.

Falkenberg looked at the familiar scene and knew the constabulary had occupied the Marine barracks for two days; the Marines had been there twenty years.

A civilian lounged in the seat reserved for the regimental intelligence officer. His tunic was a riot of colors; he was dressed in current Earth fashions, with a brilliant cravat and baggy sleeves. A long sash took the place of a belt and concealed his pocket calculator. Hadley's upper classes were only just beginning to wear such finery.

"You all know why we're here," Falkenberg told the assembled officers. "Those of you who've served with me before know I don't hold many staff councils. They are customary among mercenary units, however. Sergeant Major Calvin will represent the enlisted personnel of the regiment."

There were faint titters. Calvin had been associated with John Falkenberg for twenty standard years. Presumably they had differences of opinion, but no one ever saw them. The idea of the RSM opposing his colonel in the name of the troops was amusing. On the other hand, no colonel could afford to ignore the views of his sergeants' mess.

Falkenberg's frozen features relaxed slightly as if he appreciated his own joke. His eyes went from face to face. Everyone in the room was a former Marine, and all but a very few had served with him before. The Progressive officers were on duty elsewhere—and it had taken careful planning by the adjutant to accomplish that without suspicion.

Falkenberg turned to the civilian. "Dr. Whitlock, you've been on Hadley for sixty-seven days. That's not very long to make a planetary study, but it's about all the time we have. Have you reached any conclusions?"

"Yeah." Whitlock spoke with an exaggerated drawl that most agreed was affected. "Not much different from Fleet's evaluation, Colonel. Can't think why you went to the expense of bringin' me out here. Your Intelligence people know their jobs about as well as I know mine."

Whitlock sprawled back in his seat and looked very relaxed and casual in the midst of the others' military formality. There was no contempt in his manner. The military had one set of rules and he had another, and he worked well with soldiers.

"Your conclusions are similar to Fleet's, then," Falkenberg said.

"With the limits of analysis, yes, sir. Doubt any competent man could reach a different conclusion. This planet's headed for barbarism within a generation."

There was no sound from the other officers but several were startled. Good training kept them from showing it.

Whitlock produced a cigar from a sleeve pocket and inspected it carefully. "You want the analysis?" he asked.

"A summary, please." Falkenberg looked at each face again. Major Savage and Captain Fast weren't surprised; they'd known before they came to Hadley. Some of the junior officers and company commanders had obviously guessed.

"Simple enough," Whitlock said. "There's no self-sustaining technology for a population half this size. Without imports the standard of livin's bound to fall. Some places they could take that, but not here.

"Here, when they can't get their pretty gadgets, 'stead of

workin' the people here in Refuge will demand the Government do something about it. Guv'mint's in no position to refuse, either. Not strong enough.

"So they'll have to divert investment capital into consumer goods. There'll be a decrease in technological efficiency, and then fewer goods, leadin' to more demands, and another cycle just like before. Hard to predict just what comes after that, but it can't be good.

"Afore long, then, they won't have the technological resources to cope even if they could get better organized. It's not a new pattern, Colonel. Fleet saw it comin' a while back. I'm surprised you didn't take their word for it."

Falkenberg nodded. "I did, but with something this important I thought I better get another opinion. You've met the Freedom Party leaders, Dr. Whitlock. Is there any chance they could keep civilization if they governed?"

Whitlock laughed. It was a long drawn-out laugh, relaxed, totally out of place in a military council. "'Bout as much chance as for a 'gator to turn loose of a hog, Colonel. Even assumin' they know what to do, how can they do it? Suppose they get a vision and try to change their policies? Somebody'll start a new party along the lines of the Freedom Party's present thinkin'.

"Colonel, you will *never* convince all them people there's things the Guv'mint just *cain't* do. They don't want to believe it, and there's always goin' to be slick talkers willin' to say it's all a plot. Now, if the Progressive Party, which has the right ideas already, was to set up to rule strong, they might be able to keep something goin' a while longer."

"Do you think they can?" Major Savage asked.

"Nope. They might have fun tryin'," Whitlock answered. "Problem is that independent countryside. There's not enough support for what they'd have to do in city or country. Eventually that's all got to change, but the revolution that gives this country a real powerful government's going to be one bloody mess, I can tell you. A long drawn-out bloody mess at that."

"Haven't they any hope at all?" The questioner was a junior officer newly promoted to company commander.

Whitlock sighed. "Every place you look, you see problems. City's vulnerable to any sabotage that stops the food plants, for instance. And the fusion generators ain't exactly eternal, either. They're runnin' 'em hard without enough time off for maintenance. Hadley's operating on its capital, not its income, and pretty soon there's not goin' to be any capital to operate off of."

"And that's your conclusion," Falkenberg said. "It doesn't sound precisely like the perfect place for us to retire to."

"Sure doesn't," Whitlock agreed. He stretched elaborately. "Cut it any way you want to, this place isn't going to be self-sufficient without a lot of blood spilled."

"Could they ask for help from American Express?" the junior officer asked.

"They could ask, but they won't get it," Whitlock said. "Son, this planet was neutralized by agreement way back when the CD Governor came aboard. Now the Russians aren't going to let a U.S. company like AmEx take it back into the U.S. sphere, same as the U.S. won't let the Commies come in and set up shop. Grand Senate would order a quarantine on this system just like that." The historian snapped his fingers. "Whole purpose of the CoDominium."

"One thing bothers me," Captain Fast said. "You've been assuming that the CD will simply let Hadley revert to barbarism. Won't BuRelock and the Colonial Office come back if things get that desperate?"

"No."

"You seem rather positive," Major Savage observed.

"I'm positive." Dr. Whitlock said. "Budgets got cut again this year. They don't have the resources to take on a place like Hadley. BuRelock's got its own worries."

"But—" The lieutenant who'd asked the questions earlier sounded worried. "Colonel, what could happen to the Bureau of Relocation?"

"As Dr. Whitlock says, no budget," Falkenberg answered. "Gentlemen, I shouldn't have to tell you about that. You've seen what the Grand Senate did to the Fleet. That's why you're demobilized. And Kaslov's people have several new seats on the Presidium next year, just as Harmon's gang has won some minor elections in the States. Both those outfits want to abolish the CD, and they've had enough influence to get everyone's appropriations cut to the bone."

"But population control has to ship people out, sir," the lieutenant protested.

"Yes." Falkenberg's face was grim; perhaps he was recalling his own experiences with population control's methods. "But they have to employ worlds closer to Earth, regardless of the problems that may cause for the colonists. Marginal exploitation ventures like Hadley's mines are being shut down. This isn't the only planet the CD's abandoning this year." His voice took on a note of thick irony. "Excuse me. Granting independence."

"So they can't rely on CoDominium help," Captain Fast said.

"No. If Hadley's going to reach takeoff, it's got to do it on its own."

"Which Dr. Whitlock says is impossible," Major Savage observed. "John, we've got ourselves into a cleft stick, haven't we?"

"I said it was unlikely, not that it was impossible," Whitlock reminded them. "It'll take a government stronger than anything Hadley's liable to get, though. And some smart people making the right moves. Or maybe there'll be some luck. Like a good, selective plague. Now that'd do it. Plague to kill off the right people—but if it got too many, there wouldn't be enough left to take advantage of the technology, so I don't suppose that's the answer either."

Falkenberg nodded grimly. "Thank you, Dr. Whitlock. Now, gentlemen, I want battalion commanders and headquarters officers to read Dr. Whitlock's report. Meanwhile, we have another item. Major Savage will shortly make a report to the Progressive Party Cabinet, and I want you to pay attention. We will have a critique after his presentation. Major?"

Savage stood and went to the readout screen. "Gentlemen." He used the wall console to bring an organization chart onto the screen.

"The regiment consists of approximately two thousand officers and men. Of these, five hundred are former Marines, and another five hundred are Progressive partisans organized under officers appointed by Mr. Vice President Bradford.

"The other thousand are general recruits. Some of them are passable mercenaries, and some are local youngsters who want to play soldier and would be better off in a national guard. All recruits have received basic training comparable to CD Marine ground basic without assault, fleet, or jump schooling. Their performance has been somewhat better than we might expect from a comparable number of Marine recruits in CD service.

"This morning, Mr. Bradford ordered the Colonel to remove the last of our officers and noncoms from the Fourth Battalion, and as of this P.M. the Fourth will be totally under the control of officers appointed by First Vice President Bradford. He has not informed us of the reason for this order."

Falkenberg nodded. "In your estimate, Major, are the troops ready for combat duties?" Falkenberg listened idly as he drank coffee. The briefing was rehearsed, and he knew what Savage would answer. The men were trained, but they did not as yet make up a combat unit. Falkenberg waited until Savage had finished the presentation. "Recommendations?"

"Recommended that the Second Battalion be integrated with the First, sir. Normal practice is to form each maniple with one recruit, three privates, and a monitor in charge. With equal numbers of new men and veterans we will have a higher proportion of recruits, but this will give us two battalions of men under our veteran NCOs, with Marine privates for leavening.

"We will thus break up the provisional training organization and set up the regiment with a new permanent structure, First and Second Battalions for combat duties, Third composed of locals with former Marine officers to be held in reserve. The Fourth will not be under our command."

"Your reasons for this organization?" Falkenberg asked.

"Morale, sir. The new troops feel discriminated against. They're under harsher discipline than the former Marines, and they resent it. Putting them in the same maniples with the Marines will stop that."

"Let's see the new structure."

Savage manipulated the input console and charts swam across the screen. The administrative structure was standard, based in part on the CD Marines and the rest on the national armies of Churchill. That wasn't the important part. It wasn't obvious, but the structure demanded that all the key posts be held by Falkenberg's mercenaries.

The best Progressive appointees were either in the Third or Fourth Battalions, and there were no locals with the proper command experience; so went the justification. It looked good to Falkenberg, and there was no sound military reason to question it. Bradford would be so pleased about his new control of the Fourth that he wouldn't look at the rest; not yet, anyway. The others didn't know enough to question it.

Yes, Falkenberg thought. It ought to work. He waited until Savage was finished and thanked him, then addressed the others. "Gentlemen, if you have criticisms, let's hear them now. I want a solid front when we get to the Cabinet meeting tomorrow, and I want every one of you ready to answer any question. I don't have to tell you how important it is that they buy this."

They all nodded.

"And another thing," Falkenberg said. "Sergeant Major."

"Sir!"

"As soon as the Cabinet has bought off on this new organization plan, I want this regiment under normal discipline."

"Sir!"

"Break it to 'em hard, Top Soldier. Tell the Forty-second the act's over. From here on recruits and old hands get treated alike, and the next man who gives me trouble will wish he hadn't been born."

"Sir!" Calvin smiled happily. The last months had been a strain for everyone. Now the colonel was taking over again, thank God. The men had lost some of the edge, but he'd soon put it back again. It was time to take off the masks, and Calvin for one was glad of it.

X

The sound of fifty thousand people shouting in unison can be terrifying. It raises fears at a level below thought; creates a panic older than the fear of nuclear weapons and the whole panoply of technology. It is raw, naked power from a cauldron of sound.

Everyone in the Palace listened to the chanting crowd. The Government people were outwardly calm, but they moved quietly through the halls, and spoke in low tones—or shouted for no reason. The Palace was filled with a nameless fear.

The Cabinet meeting started at dawn and continued until late in the morning. It had gone on and on without settling anything. Just before noon Vice President Bradford stood at his place at the council table with his lips tight in rage. He pointed a trembling finger at George Hamner.

"It's your fault!" Bradford shouted. "Now the technicians have joined in the demand for a new constitution, and you control them. I've always said you were a traitor to the Progressive Party!"

"Gentlemen, please," President Budreau insisted. His voice held infinite weariness. "Come now, that sort of language—"

"Traitor?" Hamner demanded. "If your blasted officials would pay a little attention to the technicians, this wouldn't have happened. In three months you've managed to convert the techs from the staunchest supporters of this Party into allies of the rebels despite everything I could do."

"We need strong government," Bradford said. His voice was contemptuous, and the little half-smile had returned.

George Hamner made a strong effort to control his anger. "You won't get it this way. You've herded my techs around like cattle, worked them overtime for no extra pay, and set those damned soldiers of yours onto them when they protested. It's worth a man's life to have your constabulary mad at him."

"Resisting the police," Bradford said. "We can't permit that."

"You don't know what government is!" Hamner said. His control vanished and he stood, towering above Bradford. The little man retreated a step, and his smile froze. "You've got the nerve to call me a traitor after all you've done! I ought to break your neck!"

"Gentlemen!" Budreau stood at his place at the head of the table. "Stop it!" There was a roar from the Stadium. The Palace seemed to vibrate to the shouts of the constitutional convention.

The Cabinet room became silent for a moment. Wearily, Budreau continued. "This isn't getting us anywhere. I suggest we adjourn for half an hour to allow tempers to cool."

There was murmured agreement from the others.

"And I want no more of these accusations and threats when we convene again," President Budreau said. "Is that understood?"

Grudgingly the others agreed. Budreau left alone. Then Bradford, followed by a handful of his closest supporters. Other ministers rushed to be seen leaving with him, as if it might be dangerous to be thought in opposition to the First Vice President.

George Hamner found himself alone in the room. He shrugged, and went out. Ernest Bradford had been joined by a man in uniform. Hamner recognized Lieutenant Colonel Cordova, commander of the Fourth Battalion of constabulary, and a fanatic Bradford supporter. Hamner remembered when Bradford had first proposed a commission for Cordova, and how unimportant it had seemed then.

Bradford's group went down the hall. They seemed to be whispering something together and making a point of excluding the Second Vice President. Hamner merely shrugged.

"Buy you a coffee?" The voice came from behind and startled George. He turned to see Falkenberg.

"Sure. Not that it's going to do any good. We're in trouble, Colonel."

"Anything decided?" Falkenberg asked. "It's been a long wait."

"And a useless one. They ought to invite you into the Cabinet meetings. You might have some good advice. There's sure as hell no reason to keep you waiting in an anteroom while we yell at each other. I've tried to change that policy, but I'm not too popular right now." There was another shout from the Stadium.

"Whole government's not too popular," Falkenberg said. "And when that convention gets through . . ."

"Another thing I tried to stop last week," George told him. "But Budreau didn't have the guts to stand up to them. So now we've got fifty thousand drifters, with nothing better to do, sitting as an assembly of the people. That ought to produce quite a constitution."

Falkenberg shrugged. He might have been about to say something, George thought, but if he were, he changed his mind. They reached the executive dining room and took seats near one wall. Bradford's group had a table across the room from them, and all of Bradford's people looked at them with suspicion.

"You'll get tagged as a traitor for sitting with me, Colonel." Hamner laughed, but his voice was serious. "I think I meant that, you know. Bradford's blaming me for our problems with the techs, and between us he's also insisting that you aren't doing enough to restore order in the city."

Falkenberg ordered coffee. "Do I need to explain to you why we haven't?"

"No." George Hamner's huge hand engulfed a water glass. "God knows you've been given almost no support the last couple of months. Impossible orders, and you've never been allowed to do anything decisive. I see you've stopped the raids on rebel headquarters."

Falkenberg nodded. "We weren't catching anyone. Too many leaks in the Palace. And most of the time the Fourth Battalion had already muddied the water. If they'd let us do our job instead of having to ask permission through channels for every operation we undertake, maybe the enemy wouldn't know as much about what we're going to do. Now I've quit asking."

"You've done pretty well with the railroad."

"Yes. That's one success, anyway. Things are pretty quiet out in the country where we're on our own. Odd, isn't it, that the closer we are to the expert supervision of the government, the less effective my men seem to be?"

"But can't you control Cordova's men? They're causing more people to desert us for the rebels than you can count. I can't believe unrestrained brutality is useful."

"Nor I. Unless there's a purpose to it, force isn't a very effective instrument of government. But surely you know, Mr. Hamner, that I have no control over the Fourth. Mr. Bradford has been expanding it since he took control, and it's now almost as large as the rest of the regiment—and totally under his control, not mine."

"Bradford accused me of being a traitor," Hamner said

carefully. "With his own army, he might have something planned. . . ."

"You once thought that of me," Falkenberg said.

"This is very serious," Hamner said. "Ernie Bradford has built an army only he controls, and he's making wild accusations."

Falkenberg smiled grimly. "I wouldn't worry about it too much."

"You wouldn't? No. You wouldn't. But I'm scared, Colonel. I've got my family to think of, and I'm plenty scared." Well, George thought, now it's out in the open; can I trust him not to be Ernie Bradford's man?

"You believe Bradford is planning an illegal move?" Falkenberg asked.

"I don't know." Suddenly George was afraid again. He saw no sympathy in the other man's eyes. And just who can I trust? Who? Anyone?

"Would you feel safer if your family were in our regimental barracks?" Falkenberg asked. "It could be arranged."

"It's about time we had something out," George said at last. "Yes, I'd feel safer with my wife and children under protection. But I'd feel safer yet if you'd level with me."

"About what?" Falkenberg's expression didn't change.

"Those Marines of yours, to begin with," George said. "Those aren't penal battalion men. I've watched them, they're too well disciplined. And the battle banners they carry weren't won in any peanut actions, on this planet or anywhere else. Just who are those men, Colonel?"

John Falkenberg smiled thinly. "I've been wondering when you'd ask. Why haven't you brought this up with President Budreau?"

"I don't know. I think because I trust you more than Bradford, and the President would only ask him . . . besides, if the President dismissed you there'd be nobody able to oppose Ernie. If you will oppose him that is—but you can stand up to him, anyway."

"What makes you think I would?" Falkenberg asked. "I obey the lawful orders of the civilian government—"

"Yeah, sure. Hadley's going downhill so fast another conspiracy more or less can't make any difference anyway . . . you haven't answered my question."

"The battle banners are from the Forty-second CD Marine Regiment," Falkenberg answered slowly. "It was decommissioned as part of the budget cuts."

Forty-second, Hamner thought for a second. He searched

through his mental files to find the information he'd seen on Falkenberg. "That was your regiment."

"Certainly."

"You brought it with you."

"A battalion of it," John Falkenberg agreed. "Their women are waiting to join them when we get settled. When the Forty-second was decommissioned, the men decided to stay together if they could."

"So you brought not only the officers, but the men as well."

"Yes." There was still no change in Falkenberg's expression, although Hamner searched the other man's face closely.

George felt both fear and relief. If those were Falkenberg's men—"What is your game, Colonel? You want more than just pay for your troops. I wonder if I shouldn't be more afraid of you than of Bradford."

Falkenberg shrugged. "Decisions you have to make, Mr. Hamner. I could give you my word that we mean you no harm, but what would that be worth? I will pledge to take care of your family. If you want us to."

There was another shout from the Stadium, louder this time. Bradford and Lieutenant Colonel Cordova left their table, still talking in low tones. The conversation was animated, with violent gestures, as if Cordova were trying to talk Bradford into something. As they left, Bradford agreed.

George watched them leave the room. The mob shouted again, making up his mind for him. "I'll send Laura and the kids over to your headquarters this afternoon."

"Better make it immediately," Falkenberg said calmly.

George frowned. "You mean there's not much time? Whatever you've got planned, it'll have to be quick, but this afternoon?"

John shook his head. "You seem to think I have some kind of master plan, Mr. Vice President. No. I suggest you get your wife to our barracks before I'm ordered not to undertake her protection, that's all. For the rest, I'm only a soldier in a political situation."

"With Professor Whitlock to advise you," Hamner said. He looked closely at Falkenberg.

"Surprised you with that one, didn't I?" Hamner demanded. "I've seen Whitlock moving around and wondered why he didn't come to the President. He must have fifty political agents in the convention right now."

"You do seem observant," Falkenberg said.

"Sure." Hamner was bitter. "What the hell good does it do me? I don't understand anything that's going on, and I don't trust anybody. I see pieces of the puzzle, but I can't put them together. Sometimes I think I should use what influence I've got left to get *you* out of the picture anyway."

"As you will." Falkenberg's smile was coldly polite. "Whom do you suggest as guards for your family after that? The Chief of Police? Listen."

The Stadium roared again in an angry sound that swelled in volume.

"You win," Hamner left the table and walked slowly back to the council room. His head swirled.

Only one thing stood out clearly. John Christian Falkenberg controlled the only military force on Hadley that could oppose Bradford's people—and the Freedom Party gangsters, who were the original enemies in the first place. Can't forget them just because I'm getting scared of Ernie, George thought.

He turned away from the council room and went downstairs to the apartment he'd been assigned. The sooner Laura was in the Marine barracks, the safer he'd feel.

But am I sending her to my enemies? O God, can I trust anyone at all? Boris said he was an honorable man. Keep remembering that, keep remembering that. Honor. Falkenberg has honor, and Ernie Bradford has none.

And me? What have I got for leaving the Freedom Party and bringing my technicians over to the Progressives? A meaningless title as Second Vice President, and—

The crowd screamed again. "POWER TO THE PEOPLE!"

George heard and walked faster.

Bradford's grin was back. It was the first thing George noticed as he came into the council chamber. The little man stood at the table with an amused smile. It seemed quite genuine, and more than a little frightening.

"Ah, here is our noble Minister of Technology and Second Vice President," Bradford grinned. "Just in time, Mr. President, that gang out there is threatening the city. I am sure you will all be pleased to know that I've taken steps to end the situation."

"What have you done?" George demanded.

Bradford's smile broadened even more. "At this moment, Colonel Cordova is arresting the leaders of the opposition. Including, Mr. President, the leaders of the Engineers' and Technicians' Association who have joined them. This rebellion will be over within the hour."

Hamner stared at the man. "You fool! You'll have every technician in the city joining the Freedom Party gang! And the techs control the power plants, our last influence over the crowd. You bloody damned fool!"

Bradford spoke with exaggerated politeness. "I thought you would be pleased, George, to see the rebellion end so easily. Naturally I've sent men to secure the power plants. Ah, listen."

The crowd outside wasn't chanting anymore. There was a confused babble, then a welling of sound that turned ugly. No coherent words reached them, only the ugly, angry roars. Then there was a rapid fusillade of shots.

"My God!" President Budreau stared wildly in confusion. "What's happening? Who are they shooting at? Have you started open war?"

"It takes stern measures, Mr. President," Bradford said. "Perhaps too stern for you?" He shook his head slightly. "The time has come for harsh measures, Mr. President. Hadley cannot be governed by weak-willed men. Our future belongs to those who have the will to grasp it!"

George Hamner turned toward the door. Before he could reach it, Bradford called to him. "Please, George." His voice was filled with concern. "I'm afraid you can't leave just yet. It wouldn't be safe for you. I took the liberty of ordering Colonel Cordova's men to, uh, guard this room while my troops restore order."

An uneasy quiet had settled on the Stadium, and they waited for a long time. Then there were screams and more shots.

The sounds moved closer, as if they were outside the Stadium as well as in it. Bradford frowned, but no one said anything. They waited for what seemed a lifetime as the firing continued. Guns, shouts, screams, sirens, and alarms—those and more, all in confusion.

The door burst open. Cordova came in. He now wore the insignia of a full colonel. He looked around the room until he found Bradford. "Sir, could you come outside a moment, please?"

"You will make your report to the Cabinet," President Budreau ordered. Cordova glanced at Bradford. "Now, sir."

Cordova still looked to Bradford. The Vice President nodded slightly.

"Very well, sir," the young officer said. "As directed by the Vice President, elements of the Fourth Battalion proceeded to the Stadium and arrested some fifty leaders of the so-called constitutional convention.

"Our plan was to enter quickly and take the men out through the Presidential box and into the Palace. However, when we attempted to make the arrests we were opposed by armed men, many in the uniforms of household guards. We were told there were no weapons in the Stadium, but this was in error.

"The crowd overpowered my officers and released their prisoners. When we attempted to recover them, we were attacked by the mob and forced to fight our way out of the Stadium."

"Good Lord," Budreau sighed. "How many hurt?"

"The power plants! Did you secure them?" Hamner demanded.

Cordova looked miserable. "No, sir. My men were not admitted. A council of technicians and engineers holds the power plants, and they threaten to destroy them if we attempt forcible entry. We have tried to seal them off from outside support, but I don't think we can keep order with only my battalion. We will need all the constabulary army to—"

"Idiot." Hamner clutched at his left fist with his right, and squeezed until it hurt. A council of technicians. I'll know most of them. My friends. Or they used to be. Will any of them trust me now? At least Bradford didn't control the fusion plants.

"What is the current status outside?" President Budreau demanded. They could still hear firing in the streets.

"Uh, there's a mob barricaded in the market, and another in the theater across from the Palace, sir. My troops are trying to dislodge them." Cordova's voice was apologetic.

"Trying. I take it they aren't likely to succeed." Budreau rose and went to the anteroom door. "Colonel Falkenberg?" he called.

"Yes, sir?" Falkenberg entered the room as the President beckoned.

"Colonel, are you familiar with the situation outside?"

"Yes, Mr. President."

"Damn it, man, can you do something?"

"What does the President suggest I do?" Falkenberg looked at the Cabinet members. "For three months we have attempted to preserve order in this city. We were not able to do so even with the cooperation of the technicians."

"It wasn't my fault—" Lieutenant Colonel Cordova began.

"I did not invite you to speak." Falkenberg's lips were set in a grim line. "Gentlemen, you now have open rebellion and simultaneously have alienated one of the most powerful blocs within your Party. We no longer control either the power plants or the food processing centers. I repeat, what does the President suggest I do?"

Budreau nodded. "A fair enough criticism."

He was interrupted by Bradford. "Drive that mob off the

streets! Use those precious troops of yours to fight, that's what you're here for."

"Certainly," Falkenberg said. "Will the President sign a proclamation of martial law?"

Budreau nodded reluctantly. "I suppose I have to."

"Very well," Falkenberg said.

Hamner looked up suddenly. What had he detected in Falkenberg's voice and manner? Something important?

"It is standard for politicians to get themselves into a situation that only the military can get them out of. It is also standard for them to blame the military afterwards," Falkenberg said. "I am willing to accept responsibility for enforcing martial law, but I must have command of all government forces. I will not attempt to restore order when some of the troops are not responsive to my policies."

"No!" Bradford leaped to his feet. The chair crashed to the floor behind him. "I see what you're doing! You're against me too! That's why it was never time to move, never time for me to be President, you want control of this planet for yourself! Well, you won't get away with it, you cheap dictator. Cordova, arrest that man!"

Cordova licked his lips and looked at Falkenberg. Both soldiers were armed. Cordova decided not to chance it. "Lieutenant Hargreave!" he called. The door to the anteroom opened wide.

No one came in. "Hargreave!" Cordova shouted again. He put his hand on the pistol holstered at his belt. "You're under arrest, Colonel Falkenberg."

"Indeed?"

"This is absurd," Budreau shouted. "Colonel Cordova, take your hand off that weapon! I will not have my Cabinet meeting turned into a farce."

For a moment nothing happened. The room was very still, and Cordova looked from Budreau to Bradford, wondering what to do now.

Then Bradford faced the President. "You too, old man? Arrest Mr. Budreau as well, Colonel Cordova. As for you, Mr. Traitor George Hamner, you'll get what's coming to you. I have men all through this Palace. I knew I might have to do this."

"You knew—what is this, Ernest?" President Budreau seemed bewildered, and his voice was plaintive. "What are you doing?"

"Oh, shut up, old man," Bradford snarled. "I suppose you'll have to be shot as well."

"I think we have heard enough," Falkenberg said distinctly. His voice rang through the room although he hadn't shouted. "And I refuse to be arrested."

"Kill him!" Bradford shouted. He reached under his tunic.

Cordova drew his pistol. It had not cleared the holster when there were shots from the doorway. Their sharp barks filled the room, and Hamner's ears rang from the muzzle blast.

Bradford spun toward the door with a surprised look. Then his eyes glazed and he slid to the floor, the half-smile still on his lips. There were more shots and the crash of automatic weapons, and Cordova was flung against the wall of the council chamber. He was held there by the smashing bullets. Bright red blotches spurted across his uniform.

Sergeant Major Calvin came into the room with three Marines in battle dress, leather over bulging body armor. Their helmets were dull in the bright blue-tinted sunlight streaming through the chamber's windows.

Falkenberg nodded and holstered his pistol. "All secure, Sergeant Major?"

"Sir!"

Falkenberg nodded again. "To quote Mr. Bradford, I took the liberty of securing the corridors, Mr. President. Now, sir, if you will issue that proclamation, I'll see to the situation in the streets outside. Sergeant Major."

"Sir!"

"Do you have the proclamation of martial law that Captain Fast drew up?"

"Sir." Calvin removed a rolled document from a pocket of his leather tunic. Falkenberg took it and laid it on the table in front of President Budreau.

"But—" Budreau's tone was hopeless. "All right. Not that there's much chance." He looked at Bradford's body and shuddered. "He was ready to kill me." Budreau muttered. The President seemed confused. Too much had happened, and there was too much to do.

The battle sounds outside were louder, and the council room was filled with the sharp copper odor of fresh blood. Budreau drew the parchment toward himself and glanced at it, then took out a pen from his pocket. He scrawled his signature across it and handed it to Hamner to witness.

"You'd better speak to the President's Guard," Falkenberg said. "They won't know what to do."

"Aren't you going to use them in the street fight?" Hamner asked.

Falkenberg shook his head. "I doubt if they'd fight. They have too many friends among the rebels. They'll protect the Palace, but they won't be reliable for anything else."

"Have we got a chance?" Hamner asked.

Budreau looked up from his reverie at the head of the table. "Yes. Have we?"

"Possibly," Falkenberg said. "Depends on how good the people we're fighting are. If their commander is half as good as I think he is, we won't win this battle."

XI

"Goddamn it, we won't do it!" Lieutenant Martin Latham stared in horror at Captain Fast. "That market's a death trap. These men didn't join to attack across open streets against rioters in safe positions—"

"No. You joined to be glorified police," Captain Fast said calmly. "Now you've let things get out of hand. Who better to put them right again?"

"The Fourth Battalion takes orders from Colonel Cordova, not you." Latham looked around for support. Several squads of the Fourth were within hearing, and he felt reassured.

They stood in a deep indentation of the Palace wall. Just outside and around the corner of the indentation they could hear sporadic firing as the other units of the regiment kept the rebels occupied. Latham felt safe here, but out there—

"No," he repeated. "It's suicide."

"So is refusal to obey orders," Amos Fast said quietly. "Don't look around and don't raise your voice. Now, glance behind me at the Palace walls."

Latham saw them. A flash from a gun barrel; blurs as leather-clad figures settled in on the walls and in the windows overlooking the niche.

"If you don't make the attack, you will be disarmed and tried for cowardice in the face of the enemy," Fast said quietly. "There can be only one outcome of that trial. And only one penalty. You're better off making the assault. We'll support you in that."

"Why are you doing this?" Martin Latham demanded.

"You caused the problem," Fast said. "Now get ready. When you've entered the market square the rest of the outfit will move up in support."

The assault was successful, but it cost the Fourth heavily. After that came another series of fierce attacks. When they were finished the rioters had been driven from the immediate area of the Palace, but Falkenberg's regiment paid for every meter gained.

Whenever they took a building, the enemy left it blazing. When the regiment trapped one large group of rebels, Falkenberg was forced to abandon the assault to aid in evacuating a hospital that the enemy put to the torch. Within three hours, fires were raging all around the Palace.

There was no one in the council chamber with Budreau and Hamner. The bodies had been removed, and the floor mopped, but it seemed to George Hamner that the room would always smell of death; and he could not keep his eyes from straying from time to time, from staring at the neat line of holes stitched at chest height along the rich wood paneling.

Falkenberg came in. "Your family is safe, Mr. Hamner." He turned to the President. "Ready to report, sir.

Budreau looked up with haunted eyes. The sound of gunfire was faint, but still audible.

"They have good leaders," Falkenberg reported, "When they left the Stadium they went immediately to the police barracks. They took the weapons and distributed them to their allies, after butchering the police."

"They murdered—"

"Certainly," Falkenberg said. "They wanted the police building as a fortress. And we are not fighting a mere mob out there, Mr. President. We have repeatedly run against well-armed men with training. Household forces. I will attempt another assault in the morning, but for now, Mr. President, we don't hold much more than a kilometer around the Palace."

The fires burned all night, but there was little fighting. The regiment held the Palace, with bivouac in the courtyard; and if anyone questioned why the Fourth was encamped in the center of the courtyard with other troops all around them, they did so silently.

Lieutenant Martin Latham might have had an answer for any such questioner, but he lay under Hadley's flag in the honor hall outside the hospital.

In the morning the assaults began again. The regiment moved out in thin streams, infiltrating weak spots, bypassing strong, until it had cleared a large area outside the Palace again. Then it came against another well-fortified position.

An hour later the regiment was heavily engaged against rooftop snipers, barricaded streets, and everywhere burning buildings. Maniples and squads attempted to get through and into the buildings beyond but were turned back.

The Fourth was decimated in repeated assaults against the barricades.

George Hamner had come with Falkenberg and stood in the field headquarters. He watched another platoon assault of the Fourth beaten back. "They're pretty good men," he mused.

"They'll do. Now," Falkenberg said.

"But you've used them up pretty fast."

"Not entirely by choice," Falkenberg said. "The President has ordered me to break the enemy resistance. That squanders soldiers. I'd as soon use the Fourth as blunt the fighting edge of the rest of the regiment."

"But we're not getting anywhere."

"No. The opposition's too good, and there are too many of them. We can't get them concentrated for a set battle, and when we do catch them they set fire to part of the city and retreat under cover of the flames."

A communications corporal beckoned urgently, and Falkenberg went to the low table with its array of electronics. He took the offered earphone and listened, then raised a mike.

"Fall back to the Palace," Falkenberg ordered.

"You're retreating?" Hamner demanded.

Falkenberg shrugged. "I have no choice. I can't hold this thin a perimeter, and I have only two battalions. Plus what's left of the Fourth."

"Where's the Third? The Progressive partisans? My people?"

"Out at the power plants and food centers," Falkenberg answered. "We can't break in without giving the techs time to wreck the place, but we can keep any more rebels from getting in. The Third isn't as well trained as the rest of the regiment—and besides, the techs may trust them."

They walked back through burned-out streets. The sounds of fighting followed them as the regiment retreated. Civilian workers fought the fires and cared for the wounded and dead.

Hopeless, George Hamner thought. Hopeless. I don't know why I thought Falkenberg would pull some kind of rabbit out of the hat once Bradford was gone. What could he do? What can anyone do?

Worried-looking Presidential Guards let them into the Palace and swung the heavy doors shut behind them. The guards held the Palace, but would not go outside.

President Budreau was in his ornate office with Lieutenant Banners. "I was going to send for you," Budreau said. "We can't win this, can we?"

"Not the way it's going," Falkenberg answered. Hamner nodded agreement.

Budreau nodded rapidly, as if to himself. His face was a mask of lost hopes. "That's what I thought. Pull your men back to barracks, Colonel. I'm going to surrender."

"But you can't," George protested. "Everything we've dreamed of . . . You'll doom Hadley. The Freedom Party can't govern."

"Precisely. And you see it too, don't you, George? How much governing are we doing? Before it came to an open break, perhaps we had a chance. Not now. Bring your men back to the Palace, Colonel Falkenberg. Or are you going to refuse?"

"No, sir. The men are retreating already. They'll be here in half an hour."

Budreau sighed loudly. "I told you the military answer wouldn't work here, Falkenberg."

"We might have accomplished something in the past months if we'd been given the chance."

"You might." The President was too tired to argue. "But putting the blame on poor Ernie won't help. He must have been insane.

"But this isn't three months ago. Colonel. It's not even yesterday. I might have reached a compromise before the fighting started, but I didn't, and you've lost. You're not doing much besides burning down the city . . . at least I can spare Hadley that. Banners, go tell the Freedom Party leaders I can't take anymore."

The Guard officer saluted and left, his face an unreadable mask. Budreau watched him leave the office. His eyes focused far beyond the walls with their Earth decorations.

"So you're resigning," Falkenberg said slowly.

Budreau nodded.

"Have you resigned, sir?" Falkenberg demanded.

"Yes, blast you. Banners has my resignation."

"And what will you do now?" George Hamner asked. His voice held both contempt and amazement. He had always admired and respected Budreau. And now what had Hadley's great leader left them?

"Banners has promised to get me out of here," Budreau said. "He has a boat in the harbor. We'll sail up the coast and land, then go inland to the mines. There'll be a starship there next week, and I can get out on that with my family. You'd better come with me, George." The President put both hands over his face, then looked up. "There's a lot of relief in giving in, did you know? What will you do, Colonel Falkenberg?"

"We'll manage. There are plenty of boats in the harbor if we need one. But it is very likely that the new government will need trained soldiers."

"The perfect mercenary," Budreau said with contempt. He sighed, then sent his eyes searching around the office, lingering on familiar objects. "It's a relief. I don't have to decide things anymore." He stood and his shoulders were no longer stooped. "I'll get the family. You'd better be moving too, George."

"I'll be along, sir. Don't wait for us. As the Colonel says, there are plenty of boats." He waited until Budreau had left the office, then turned to Falkenberg. "All right, what now?"

"Now we do what we came here to do," Falkenberg said. He went to the President's desk and examined the phones, but rejected them for a pocket communicator. He lifted it and spoke at length.

"Just what are you doing?" Hamner demanded.

"You're not president yet," Falkenberg said. "You won't be until you're sworn in, and that won't happen until I've finished. And there's nobody to accept your resignation, either."

"What the hell?" Hamner looked closely at Falkenberg, but he could not read the officer's expression. "You do have an idea. Let's hear it."

"You're not president yet," Falkenberg said. "Under Budreau's proclamation of martial law, I am to take whatever actions I think are required to restore order in Refuge. That order is valid until a new President removes it. And at the moment there's no President."

"But Budreau's surrendered! The Freedom Party will elect a President."

"Under Hadley's constitution only the Senate and Assembly in joint session can alter the order of succession. They're scattered across the city and their meeting chambers have been burned."

Sergeant Major Calvin and several of Falkenberg's aides came to the door. They stood, waiting.

"I'm playing guardhouse lawyer," Falkenberg said. "But President Budreau doesn't have the authority to appoint a new president. With Bradford dead, you're in charge here, but not until you appear before a magistrate and take the oath of office."

"This doesn't make sense," Hamner protested. "How long do you think you can stay in control here, anyway?"

"As long as I have to." Falkenberg turned to an aide. "Corporal, I want Mr. Hamner to stay with me and you with him. You will treat him with respect, but he goes nowhere and sees no one without my permission. Understood?"

"Sir!"

"And now what?" Hamner asked.

"And now we wait," John Falkenberg said softly. "But not too long . . ."

George Hamner sat in the council chambers with his back to the stained and punctured wall. He tried to forget those stains, but he couldn't.

Falkenberg was across from him, and his aides sat at the far end of the table. Communications gear had been spread across one side table, but there was no situation map; Falkenberg had not moved his command post here.

From time to time officers brought him battle reports, but Falkenberg hardly listened to them. However, when one of the aides reported that Dr. Whitlock was calling, Falkenberg took the earphones immediately.

George couldn't hear what Whitlock was saying and Falkenberg's end of the conversation consisted of monosyllables. The only thing George was sure of was that Falkenberg was very interested in what his political agent was doing.

The regiment had fought its way back to the Palace and was now in the courtyard. The Palace entrances were held by the Presidential Guard, and the fighting had stopped. The rebels left the guardsmen alone, and an uneasy truce settled across the city of Refuge.

"They're going into the Stadium, sir," Captain Fast reported. "That cheer you heard was when Banners gave 'em the President's resignation."

"I see. Thank you, Captain." Falkenberg motioned for more coffee. He offered a cup to George, but the Vice President didn't want any.

"How long does this go on?" George demanded.

"Not much longer. Hear them cheering?"

They sat for another hour, Falkenberg with outward calm, Hamner with growing tension. Then Dr. Whitlock came to the council room.

The tall civilian looked at Falkenberg and Hamner, then sat easily in the President's chair. "Don't reckon I'll have another chance to sit in the seat of the mighty," he grinned.

"But what is happening?" Hamner demanded.

Whitlock shrugged. "It's 'bout like Colonel Falkenberg figured. Mob's moved right into the Stadium. Nobody wants to be left out now they think they've won. They've rounded up what senators they could find and now they're fixin' to elect themselves a new president."

"But that election won't be valid," Hamner said.

"No, suh, but that don't seem to slow 'em down a bit. They figure they won the right, I guess. And the Guard has already said they're goin' to honor the people's choice." Whitlock smiled ironically.

"How many of my technicians are out there in that mob?" Hamner asked. "They'd listen to me, I know they would."

"They might at that," Whitlock said. "But there's not so many as there used to be. Most of 'em couldn't stomach the burnin' and looting. Still, there's a fair number."

"Can you get them out?" Falkenberg asked.

"Doin' that right now," Whitlock grinned. "One reason I come up here was to get Mr. Hamner to help with that. I got my people goin' round tellin' the technicians they already got Mr. Hamner as President, so why they want somebody else? It's workin' too, but a few words from their leader here might help."

"Right," Falkenberg said. "Well, sir?"

"I don't know what to say," George protested.

Falkenberg went to the wall control panel. "Mr. Vice President, I can't give you orders, but I'd suggest you simply make a few promises. Tell them you will shortly assume command, and that things will be different. Then order them to go home or face charges as rebels. Or ask them to go home as a favor to you. Whatever you think will work."

It wasn't much of a speech, and from the roar outside the crowd did not hear much of it anyway. George promised amnesty for anyone who left the Stadium and tried to appeal to the Progressives who were caught up in the rebellion. When he put down the microphone, Falkenberg seemed pleased.

"Half an hour, Dr. Whitlock?" Falkenberg asked.

"About that," the historian agreed. "All that's leavin' will be gone by then."

"Let's go, Mr. President." Falkenberg was insistent.

"Where?" Hamner asked.

"To see the end of this. Do you want to watch, or would you rather join your family? You can go anywhere you like except to a magistrate—or to someone who might accept your resignation."

"Colonel, this is ridiculous! You can't force me to be president, and I don't understand what's going on."

Falkenberg's smile was grim. "Nor do I want you to understand. Yet. You'll have enough trouble living with yourself as it is. Let's go."

George Hamner followed. His throat was dry, and his guts felt as if they'd knotted themselves into a tight ball.

The First and Second Battalions were assembled in the Palace courtyard. The men stood in ranks. Their synthi-leather battledress was stained with dirt and smoke from the street fighting. Armor bulged under their uniforms.

The men were silent, and Hamner thought they might have been carved from stone.

"Follow me," Falkenberg ordered. He led the way to the Stadium entrance. Lieutenant Banners stood in the doorway.

"Halt," Banners commanded.

"Really, Lieutenant? Would you fight my troops?" Falkenberg indicated the grim lines behind him.

Lieutenant Banners gulped. Hamner thought the Guard officer looked very young. "No, sir," Banners protested. "But we have barred the doors. The emergency meeting of the Assembly and Senate is electing a new President out there, and we will not permit your mercenaries to interfere."

"They have not elected anyone," Falkenberg said.

"No, sir, but when they do, the Guard will be under his command."

"I have orders from Vice President Hamner to arrest the leaders of the rebellion, and a valid proclamation of martial law," Falkenberg insisted.

"I'm sorry, sir." Banners seemed to mean it. "Our Council of officers has decided that President Budreau's surrender is valid. We intend to honor it."

"I see," Falkenberg withdrew. He motioned to his aides, and Hamner joined the group. No one objected.

"Hadn't expected this," Falkenberg said. "It would take a week to fight through those guardrooms." He thought for a moment. "Give me your keys," he snapped at Hamner.

Bewildered, George took them out. Falkenberg grinned widely. "There's another way into there, you know. Major Savage! Take G and H Companies of Second Battalion to secure the Stadium exits. Dig yourselves in and set up all weapons. Arrest anyone who comes out."

"Sir."

"Dig in pretty good, Jeremy. They may be coming out fighting. But I don't expect them to be well organized."

"Do we fire on armed men?"

"Without warning, Major. Without warning. Sergeant Major, bring the rest of the troops with me. Major, you'll have twenty minutes."

Falkenberg led his troops across the courtyard to the tunnel entrance and used Hamner's keys to unlock the doors.

Falkenberg ignored him. He led the troops down the stairway and across, under the field.

George Hamner stayed close to Falkenberg. He could hear the long column of armed men tramp behind him. They moved up stairways on the other side, marching briskly until George was panting. The men didn't seem to notice. Gravity difference, Hamner thought. And training.

They reached the top and deployed along the passageways. Falkenberg stationed men at each exit and came back to the center doors. Then he waited. The tension grew.

"But—"

Falkenberg shook his head. His look demanded silence. He stood, waiting, while the seconds ticked past.

"MOVE OUT!" Falkenberg commanded.

The doors burst open. The armed troopers moved quickly across the top of the Stadium. Most of the mob was below, and a few unarmed men were struck down when they tried to oppose the regiment. Rifle butts swung, then there was a moment of calm. Falkenberg took a speaker from his corporal attendant.

"ATTENTION. ATTENTION. YOU ARE UNDER ARREST BY THE AUTHORITY OF THE MARTIAL LAW PROCLAMATION OF PRESIDENT BUDREAU. LAY DOWN ALL WEAPONS AND YOU WILL NOT BE HARMED. IF YOU RESIST, YOU WILL BE KILLED."

There was a moment of silence, then shouts as the mob realized what Falkenberg had said. Some laughed. Then shots came from the field and the lower seats of the Stadium. Hamner heard the flat snap of a bullet as it rushed past his ear. Then he heard the crack of the rifle.

One of the leaders on the field below had a speaker. He shouted to the others. "ATTACK THEM! THERE AREN'T MORE THAN A THOUSAND OF THEM, WE'RE THIRTY THOUSAND STRONG. ATTACK, KILL THEM!" There were more shots. Some of Falkenberg's men fell. The others stood immobile, waiting for orders.

Falkenberg raised the speaker again. "PREPARE FOR VOLLEY FIRE. MAKE READY. TAKE AIM. IN VOLLEY, FIRE!"

Seven hundred rifles crashed as one.

"FIRE!" Someone screamed, a long drawn-out cry, a plea without words.

"FIRE!"

The line of men clambering up the seats toward them wavered and broke. Men screamed, some pushed back, dove under seats, tried to hide behind their friends, tried to get anywhere but under the unwavering muzzles of the rifles.

"FIRE!"

It was like one shot, very loud, lasting far longer than a rifle shot ought to, but it was impossible to hear individual weapons. "FIRE!"

There were more screams from below. "In the name of God—"

"THE FORTY-SECOND WILL ADVANCE. FIX BAYONETS. FORWARD, MOVE. FIRE. FIRE AT WILL."

Now there was a continuous crackle of weapons. The leather-clad lines moved forward and down, over the stadium seats, flowing down inexorably toward the press below on the field.

"Sergeant Major!"

"SIR!"

"Marksmen and experts will fall out and take station. They will fire on all armed men."

"Sir!"

Calvin spoke into his communicator. Men dropped out of each section and took position behind seats. They began to fire, carefully but rapidly. Anyone below who raised a weapon died. The regiment advanced onward.

Hamner was sick. The screams of wounded could be heard everywhere. God, make it stop, make it stop, he prayed.

"GRENADIERS WILL PREPARE TO THROW." Falkenberg's voice boomed from the speaker. "THROW!"

A hundred grenades arched out from the advancing line. They fell into the milling crowds below. The muffled explosions were masked by screams of terror.

"IN VOLLEY, FIRE!"

The regiment advanced until it made contact with the mob. There was a brief struggle. Rifles fired, and bayonets flashed red. The line halted but momentarily. Then it moved on, leaving behind a ghastly trail.

Men and women jammed in the Stadium exits. Others frantically tried to get out, clambering over the fallen, tearing women out of their way to push past, trampling each other in their scramble to escape. There was a rattle of gunfire from outside. Those in the gates recoiled, to be crushed beneath others trying to get out.

"You won't even let them out!" Hamner screamed at Falkenberg.

"Not armed. And not to escape." The Colonel's face was hard and cold, the eyes narrowed to slits. He watched the slaughter impassively, looking at the entire scene without expression.

"Are you going to kill them all?"

"All who resist."

"But they don't deserve this!" George Hamner felt his voice breaking. "They don't!"

"No one does, George. SERGEANT MAJOR!"

"SIR!"

"Half the marksmen may concentrate on the leaders now."

"SIR!" Calvin spoke quietly into his command set. The snipers concentrated their fire on the Presidential box across from them. Centurions ran up and down the line of hidden troops, pointing out targets. The marksmen kept up a steady fire.

The leather lines of armored men advanced inexorably. They had almost reached the lower tier of seats. There was less firing now, but the scarlet-painted bayonets flashed in the afternoon sun.

Another section fell out of line and moved to guard a tiny number of prisoners at the end of the Stadium. The rest of the line moved on, advancing over seats made slick with blood.

When the regiment reached ground level their progress was slower. There was little opposition, but the sheer mass of people in front of them held up the troopers. There were a few pockets of active resistance, and flying squads rushed there to reinforce the line.

More grenades were thrown. Falkenberg watched the battle calmly, and seldom spoke into his communicator. Below, more men died.

A company of troopers formed and rushed up a stairway on the opposite side of the Stadium. They fanned out across the top. Then their rifles leveled and crashed in another terrible series of volleys.

Suddenly it was over. There was no opposition. There were only screaming crowds. Men threw away weapons to run with their hands in the air. Others fell to their knees to beg for their lives. There was one final volley, then a deathly stillness fell over the Stadium.

But it wasn't quiet, Hamner discovered. The guns were silent, men no longer shouted orders, but there was sound. There were screams from the wounded. There were pleas for help, whimpers, a racking cough that went on and on as someone tried to clear punctured lungs.

Falkenberg nodded grimly. "Now we can find a magistrate, Mr. President. Now."

"I—Oh my God!" Hamner stood at the top of the Stadium. He clutched a column to steady his weakened legs. The scene below seemed unreal. There was too much blood, rivers of blood, blood cascading down the steps, blood pouring down stairwells to soak the grassy field below.

"It's over," Falkenberg said gently. "For all of us. The regiment will be leaving as soon as you're properly in command. You shouldn't have any trouble with your power plants. Your technicians will trust you now that Bradford's gone. And without their leaders, the city people won't resist.

"You can ship as many as you have to out to the interior. Disperse them among the loyalists where they won't do you any harm. That amnesty of yours—it's only a suggestion, but I'd renew it."

Hamner turned dazed eyes toward Falkenberg. "Yes. There's been too much slaughter today. Who are you, Falkenberg?"

"A mercenary soldier, Mr. President. Nothing more."

"But—then who are you working for?"

"That's the question nobody asked before. Grand Admiral Lermontov."

"Lermontov? But you were drummed out of the CoDominium! You mean that you were hired—by the admiral? As a mercenary?"

"More or less." Falkenberg nodded coldly. "The Fleet's a little sick of being used to mess up people's lives without having a chance to—to leave things in working order."

"And now you're leaving?"

"Yes. We couldn't stay here, George. Nobody is going to forget today. You couldn't keep us on and build a government that works. I'll take First and Second Battalions, and what's left of the Fourth. There's more work for us."

"And the others?"

"Third will stay on to help you," Falkenberg said. "We put all the married locals, the solid people, in Third, and sent it off to the power plants. They weren't involved in the fighting." He looked across the Stadium, then back to Hamner. "Blame it all on us, George. You weren't in command. You can say Bradford ordered this slaughter and killed himself in remorse. People will want to believe that. They'll want to think somebody was punished for—for this." He waved toward the field below. A child was sobbing out there somewhere.

"It had to be done," Falkenberg insisted. "Didn't it? There was no way out, nothing you could do to keep civilization. . . . Dr. Whitlock estimated a third of the population would die when things collapsed. Fleet Intelligence put it higher than that. Now you have a chance."

Falkenberg was speaking rapidly, and George wondered whom he was trying to convince.

"Move them out," Falkenberg said. "Move them out while they're still dazed. You won't need much help for that. They won't resist now. And we got the railroads running for you. Use the railroads and ship people out to the farms. It'll be rough with no preparation, but it's a long time until winter—"

"I know what to do," Hamner interrupted. He leaned against the column, and seemed to gather new strength from the thought. Yes. I do know what to do. Now. "I've known all along what had to be done. Now we can get to it. We won't thank you for it, but—you've saved a whole world, John."

Falkenberg looked at him grimly, then pointed to the bodies below. "Damn you, don't say that!" he shouted. His voice was almost shrill. "I haven't saved anything. All a soldier can do is buy time. I haven't saved Hadley. You have to do that. God help you if you don't."

XII

Crofton's Encyclopedia of Contemporary History
and Social Issues (2nd Edition)

MERCENARY FORCES

Perhaps the most disturbing development arising from CoDominium withdrawal from most distant colony worlds (see *Independence Movements)* has been the rapid growth of purely mercenary military units. The trend was predictable and perhaps inevitable, although the extent has exceeded expectations.

Many of the former colony worlds do not have planetary governments. Consequently, these new nations do not possess sufficient population or industrial resources to maintain large and effective national military forces. The disbanding of numerous CoDominium Marine units left a surplus of trained soldiers without employment, and it was inevitable that some of them would band together into mercenary units.

The colony governments are thus faced with a cruel and impossible dilemma. Faced with mercenary troops specializing in violence, they have had little choice but to reply in kind. A few colonies have broken this cycle by creating their own national armies, but have then been unable to pay for them.

Thus, in addition to the purely private mercenary organizations such as Falkenberg's Mercenary Legion, there are now national forces hired out to reduce expenses to their parent governments. A few former colonies have found this practice so lucrative that the export of mercenaries has become their principal source of income, and the recruiting and training of soldiers their major industry.

The CoDominium Grand Senate has attempted to maintain its presence in the former colonial areas through promulgation of the so-called *Laws of War (q. v.)*, which purport to regulate the weapons and tactics mercenary units may employ. Enforcement of these regulations is sporadic. When the Senate orders Fleet intervention to enforce the Laws of War the suspicion inevitably arises that other CoDominium interests are at stake, or that one or more Senators have undisclosed reasons for their interest.

Mercenary units generally draw their recruits from the same sources as the CoDominium Marines, and training stresses loyalty to comrades and commanders rather than to any government. The extent to which mercenary commanders have successfully separated their troops from all normal social intercourse is both surprising and alarming.

The best-known mercenary forces are described in separate articles. See: *Covenant; Friedland; Xanadu; Falkenberg's Mercenary Legion; Nouveau Legion Etrangere; Katanga Gendarmerie; Moolman's Commandos . . .*

FALKENBERG'S MERCENARY LEGION

Purely private military organization formed from the former Forty-second CoDominium Line Marines under Colonel John Christian Falkenberg III. Falkenberg was cashiered from the CoDominium Fleet under questionable circumstances, and his regiment disbanded shortly thereafter. A large proportion of former Forty-second officers and men chose to remain with Falkenberg.

Falkenberg's Legion appears to have been first employed by the government of the then newly independent former colony of Hadley *(q.v.)* for suppression of civil disturbances. There have been numerous complaints that excessive violence was used by both sides in the unsuccessful rebellion following CoDominium withdrawal, but the government of Hadley has expressed satisfaction with Falkenberg's efforts there.

Following its employment on Hadley, Falkenberg's Legion took part in numerous small wars of defense and conquest on at least five planets, and in the process gained a reputation as one of the best-trained and most effective small military units in existence.

It was then engaged by the CoDominium Governor on the CD prison planet of Tanith.

This latter employment caused great controversy in the Grand Senate, as Tanith remains under CD control. However, Grand Admiral Lermontov pointed out that his budget did not permit his stationing regular Marine forces on Tanith owing to other commitments mandated by the Grand Senate; after lengthy debate the employment was approved as an alternative to raising a new regiment of CD Marines.

Tanith's bright image had replaced Earth's on Grand Admiral Lermontov's view screen. The planet might have been Earth: it had bright clouds obscuring the outlines of land and sea, and they swirled in typical cyclonic patterns.

A closer look showed differences. The sun was yellow: Tanith's star was not as hot as Sol, but Tanith was closer to it. There were fewer mountains, and more swamplands steaming in the yellow-orange glare.

Despite its miserable climate, Tanith was an important world. It was first and foremost a convenient dumping ground for Earth's disinherited. There was no better way to deal with criminals than to send them off to hard—and useful—labor on another planet. Tanith received them all: the rebels, the criminals, the malcontents, victims of administrative hatred; all the refuse of a civilization that could no longer afford misfits.

Tanith was also the main source of borloi, which the World Pharmaceutical Society called "the perfect intoxicating drug." Given large supplies of borloi the lid could be kept on the Citizens in their Welfare Islands. The happiness the drug induced was artificial, but it was none the less real.

"And so I am trading in drugs," Lermontov told his visitor. "It is hardly what I expected when I became Grand Admiral."

"I'm sorry, Sergei." Grand Senator Martin Grant had aged; in ten years he had come to look forty years older. "The fact is, though, you're better off with Fleet ownership of some of the borloi plantations than you are relying on what I can get for you out of the Senate."

Lermontov nodded in disgust. "It must end, Martin. Somehow, somewhere, it must end. I cannot keep a fighting service together on the proceeds of drug sales—drugs grown by slaves! Soldiers do not make good slavemasters."

Grant merely shrugged.

"Yes, it is easy to think, is it not?" The admiral shook his head in disgust. "But there are vices natural to the soldier and the sailor. We have those, in plenty, but they are not vices that corrupt his ability as a fighting man. Slaving is a vice that corrupts everything it touches."

"If you feel that way, what can I say?" Martin Grant asked. "I can't give you an alternative."

"And I cannot let go," Lermontov said. He punched viciously at the console controls and Tanith faded from the screen. Earth, bluer and to Lermontov far more lovely, swam out of the momentary blackness. "They are fools down there," Sergei Lermontov muttered. "And we are no better. Martin, I ask myself again and again, why can we not control—anything? Why are we caught like chips in a rushing stream? Men can guide their destinies. I know that. So why are we so helpless?"

"You don't ask yourself more often than I do," Senator Grant said. His voice was low and weary. "At least we still try. Hell, you've got more power than I have. You've got the Fleet, and you've got the secret funds you get from Tanith—Christ, Sergei, if you can't do something with that—"

"I can urinate on fires," Lermontov said. "And little else." He shrugged. "So, if that is all I can do, then I will continue to make water. Will you have a drink?"

"Thanks."

Lermontov went to the sideboard and took out bottles. His conversations with Grand Senator Grant were never heard by anyone else, not even his orderlies who had been with him for years.

"Prosit."

"Prosit!"

They drank. Grant took out a cigar. "By the way, Sergei, what are you going to do with Falkenberg now that the trouble on Tanith is finished?"

Lermontov smiled coldly. "I was hoping that you would have a solution to that. I have no more funds—"

"The Tanith money—"

"Needed elsewhere, just to keep the Fleet together," Lermontov said positively.

"Then Falkenberg'll just have to find his own way. Shouldn't be any problem, with his reputation," Grant said. "And even if it is, he's got no more troubles than we have."

PRINCE OF MERCENARIES

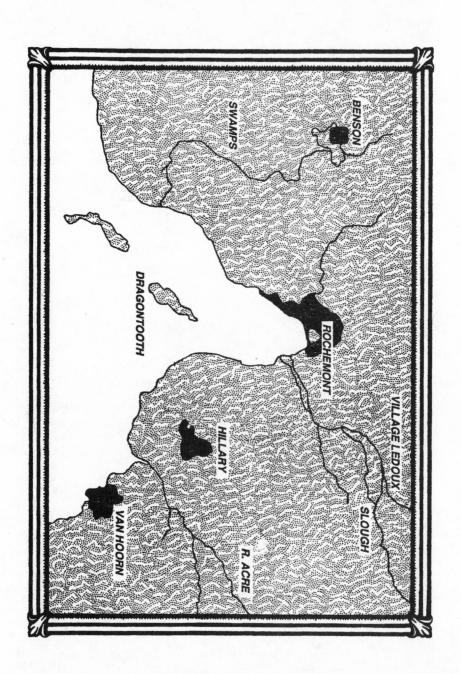

I

Lysander peered down through orange clouds. The ground was invisible, but cloud wisps streaked past, and stress diamonds formed near the wingtips of the landing ship. It was eerily quiet in the passenger cabin. Lysander turned from the viewport to his companion, a young man about twenty and much like himself. "Mach 25, I'd guess," Lysander said, then caught himself. "Fast. Faster than sound, Harv. A lot faster."

Harv leaned across to try to look through the port. "I can't see the ground."

"We won't for a while. The book says most of Tanith has clouds all the time. And it's hot."

"Oh. I don't like hot much." Harv smiled briefly and leaned back in his seat.

The landing ship banked sharply, then banked again. Strange accelerations lifted the more than two hundred passengers from their seats, then slammed them down again. The ship turned, banked, turned again in the opposite direction. Lysander remembered the dry voice of his ground school instructor explaining that delta wing ships lose energy in turns. Lysander had certainly learned that on the flight simulator and later in his practice re-entry landings. He glanced outside. The landing boat had a lot of energy to lose before it could settle on one of Tanith's protected bays.

A dozen turns later the ship slipped below the cloud cover, and he could see Tanith below.

It didn't look any different from the veedisk pictures. Green and yellow seas, with inlets jutting far into the bright green of the land areas. Land and sea were mixed together in a crazy quilt.

Harv leaned over to look out. "Looks—looks flat."

"It is flat. The whole planet."

"No mountains, Prince?"

"None. Like Earth during the Carboniferous. No mountains, no snow, no glaciers. That's why it's hot everywhere."

"Oh." Harv strained to see out the port. "Am I in your way?"

"No, it's all right." Lysander didn't really like having Harv lean over him like that, but he would never say so. Harv Middleton would be devastated by any criticism from his prince, Brotherhood or no.

The landing ship streaked over the swamps and lowlands, losing speed at each turn. Finally it banked over a series of hills that rose above an inlet of the sea. The hills were covered with low buildings set in a grid of broad, straight streets. The city was left behind as the ship went beyond and out over the green and yellow sea. Then it turned sharply.

"Taxpayers, we are on final approach to Lederle, the capital city of Tanith. Please keep your seat and shoulder belts securely fastened until we have docked at the landing port. Tovarisches . . ." The message was repeated in Russian, then in several other languages.

They came in over the water. The low ridges that held Lederle and its suburbs rose on their left. The ship settled in closer, then touched down. Spray flew up by the port.

We're here, Lysander thought. Tanith. The CoDominium prison planet.

Heat lay over the dock area in moist waves, doubly unpleasant after the air conditioned landing ship. The Customs shed was corrugated iron, manned by three bored workers in grimy white canvass jackets, supervised by a clerk who wore a blue guayabera shirt with CoDominium badges sewed to the epaulettes. The clerk checked identifications carefully, making each passenger stare into a retinal pattern reader, but his subordinates were content with hasty X-ray scans of the baggage.

Makes sense, Lysander thought. What in the name of Dracon would anyone smuggle *into* Tanith?

The helicopter that waited beyond the Customs shed was an ancient Nissan with an unpleasant tick in the engine. It would hold twenty friendly people. Lysander shamelessly used his rank to get a seat up in the cockpit and left Harv in the rear to deal with the baggage. The pilot wasn't a lot older than Lysander. He eyed Lysander skeptically, then glanced at the passenger list. "Lysander Collins. They tell me you're to sit up here with me. You bribed someone. Who?"

Lysander shrugged. "Does it matter?"

"Not a lot, since it wasn't me. I'm Joe Arabis." He pulled down a folding seat. "Here, this is the flight inspector's seat."

Arabis cocked his head to listen to the engine, then laughed. "Not that I ever saw an inspector. Oh, the heck with it, take the left-hand seat, there's no co-pilot this trip. So. Welcome to Tanith, mate."

"Thanks." Lysander sat and strapped himself in. "I've heard there are some big critters in the oceans. Big enough to give the landing ships problems?"

Arabis shrugged. "Well, they *say* the dam the CoDominium put in across the inlet keeps the nessies out. Me, I don't fly out there any more than I have to."

Lysander lifted an eyebrow.

"Yeah. Well, mate, if you ever pilot a chopper over the real oceans here, be damned sure you stay thirty meters up. Not twenty, thirty."

And I can believe as much of that as I want to, Lysander thought. Newcomers are always fair game. Of course sometimes the tallest tales are real. . . . "Thanks." Lysander pointed to the stub-winged landing ship at the end of the wharf. "Are your nessies really big enough to be a problem for those?"

"That's sure one reason for the dam," Arabis said. "Other stuff, too. I wouldn't want to set one of those shuttles down anywhere but here. Christ, I wouldn't want to ride a Fleet Marine assault boat down to some random stretch of water on Tanith. Ah. There's our clearance."

Arabis gunned the engines and lifted off from the floating dock. In seconds they were a hundred meters about the city. They circled, then headed in a direct line. The diffuse light from the eternal cloud cover cast no real shadows, so that Lysander found it impossible to get his bearings. The compass showed they were flying northwest.

"Looks like rain." Lysander said.

Arabis glanced upward and shrugged. "It generally does look like rain." He laughed. "Naturally. It's generally going to rain. At least there's no storms coming."

"Get bad ones?"

"Lots of storms. Also hurricanes like you wouldn't believe, mate. You ever do any flying here, you damn well check with the weather people early and often. Tanith can brew up a storm in a couple of hours."

"You do have weather satellites?"

"Sure. And like most stuff on Tanith they work most of the time. The ground net works most of the time, too. And most of the time the convicts they've got watching the screens remember to tell somebody, and most of the time the CD clerks remember to broadcast a general alert, and—"

"I see." Lysander examined the city below. Most buildings here were low, one story, covered with white or pastel stucco and roofed with broad slabs of what seemed to be light-colored rock. The city was laid out in a standard grid, broad streets, some divided with strips planted in fantastic colors and shapes. Most of the buildings were very much alike. Off the major streets there were jumbles of what were no more than shacks built of some kind of wood and roofed with wilting green thatch. Far down past the landing area was what looked like a separate city dominated by a massive concrete building.

The neighborhoods became more colorful as they went north. Soon they were in an area where the buildings had two stories. Wide verandas circled them at the second floor level. "Rich people," Arabis shouted above the engine noise. "Like to get up out of the mud. Can't say I blame them."

They crossed a large park, and now the city was cut across with broad diagonal avenues converging toward a complex of taller buildings dominated by one at least six stories tall.

Government House Square, Lysander thought. Lederle was laid out much like the capital city of the United States, where avenues too broad to be easily barricaded converged on the Capitol. Like Washington, Lederle was designed to let a small band of soldiers keep the mob at bay.

Tanith didn't have any magnificent public buildings to match Washington's. Government House shared the Square with a branch of Harrod's and a Hilton, none of them more than five stories high. At the far corner of the square was Lederle House, Tanith headquarters for the ethical drug company that sponsored the first colonies on Tanith, and easily the finest building Lysander had seen in the city. It had terraces and fountains, and a rooftop botanical garden that blazed with colors.

They landed in the center of the square. A handful of men in dirty white canvass coats came up to help with the baggage, but Harv waved them away when one reached for Lysander's trunk.

Lysander watched long enough to be sure that no one objected when Harv lifted a large footlocker on each shoulder and staggered across the square in Tanith's high gravity. Harv claimed the privilege of looking after his prince, but it wasn't worth making a scene over. They were already conspicuous enough. Not that his mission required much secrecy, but it was best not to attract attention.

The Hilton was no more than fifty meters away. The rain began before he got to the entrance.

The small lobby was up a flight of broad stairs from the street level. A ceiling fan turned endlessly above the registration counter. Opposite the registration desk was a wide door leading into a bar on a large screened and roofed porch. Half a dozen men and two women sat at tables in the bar room, but there was no one at the registration desk. Lysander tapped impatiently on the counter. Eventually a small Eurasian woman in a clean white canvass jacket came out from a back room. She wore a necklace of bright blue stones, and matching earrings.

"Yes, sir?" She was polite but seemed distracted.

"Lysander Collins and Harvey Middleton, of Sparta."

"Ah." She tapped keys on the console. "Yes, Your Highness. Two rooms. Right away, sir. We've put you in the Governor's Suite. I'm sure you'll find it satisfactory. Taxpayer Middleton's room is just across the hall. Your suite is fully furnished; I'm sure everything will be to your liking, but if there's anything else we can do, just call the desk."

"Thanks. Right now what I most want is a hot shower."

She nodded in sympathy. "Not much water on those liners, even in first class. That's one thing we have here. Plenty of water. Thumbprint here, please—thank you." She tapped the bell on the counter. "Joaquin will show you to your room."

Joaquin was short and stocky. His white canvass jacket had sweat stains under the arms.

"Uniform?" Harv asked.

"Sir?"

"White jackets. Uniforms?"

"Yes, sir. Trustees. Let me take your trunks—"

Harv looked at Lysander.

"It's OK, Harv."

Joaquin loaded the trunks onto a cart and led the way to the elevator. "The service elevator isn't working, sir. Please go up to the fifth floor, and I'll follow you."

"There's room." Lysander flattened himself against the elevator wall. It was crowded with the three of them and two footlockers.

The fifth-floor corridor was carpeted with some bright synthetic. The walls held plastic decorative panels depicting strange animals in bas relief. One of the creatures looked very like a giant woodchuck with three short horns. "Wouldn't want to see him in the dark," Harv said.

The Governor's Suite was bright and airy, and the air conditioning had been turned on long enough to cool the room before they arrived. There were a dozen plastic pots of brilliantly flowered plants, and baskets of fruit, some familiar like oranges and kiwi, and others that Lysander didn't recognize.

"Very nice," Lysander said. He handed Joaquin three five-credit bills. "Please see that the receptionist gets one of these."

"Yes, sir. May I help you unpack, sir?"

"Thank you. No, but you might see if Citizen Middleton needs anything."

"Citizen." The bellman frowned. "Yes, sir."

I'll need to watch that, Lysander thought. Citizen isn't a title of respect on Earth. Or here. He chuckled as he thought of the tests to pass and obligations to assume before one became a Citizen of Sparta. Different worlds, in every way.

When the bellman left, Lysander carefully bolted the door. It was the first time he had been alone in the weeks since they left Sparta, and he welcomed the feeling. He stretched elaborately, and sought out the shower.

The bathroom was large. The floor was tile inlaid in intricate designs. Most of the fittings were gold plated. Lysander felt like a Sybarite. *And I'm probably the only one on this planet who knows who the Sybarites were!* The room held both shower and a round tub already filled and liberally furnished with water jets. The water was cold, but there were instructions on heating it and starting the jets. The instructions were written in a dozen languages and five alphabets, and there were diagrams for anyone left out.

Lysander chose the circular shower. There were five shower heads around three quarters of a circle. Each had separate hot and cold controls. The control handles were shaped like sea creatures, the cold water tap like a fish, hot something like a dragon. Lysander frowned at them. "I'd hate to meet that—"

"Meet what, sir?"

He turned, startled. A girl, younger than himself but definitely a woman, stood naked at the shower entrance. Her dark red hair was beginning to curl from the steam of the hot water. Lysander dropped momentarily into fighting stance, then relaxed. "Who the devil are you?" he demanded.

"Ursula, sir. I'll be your hostess. I thought you might like to have me scrub your back."

"Hostess." He nodded to himself. He'd heard of such customs. "Thank you, I can shower by myself."

She smiled slightly. "As you wish. Would you like me to turn on the hot tub? Or do you care for a cold plunge? Afterward I can massage your back."

"That's a fairly tempting offer. Cold plunge and back rub."

She knelt to feel the water in the tub. "Cold enough, I think. I'll wait for you—"

"No, you needn't do that. I'll come out when I'm ready for a back rub."

She shrugged slightly and smiled again. He retreated into the shower compartment to sort out his thoughts.

Ursula. He liked the name, and he liked her smile. It was clear that she was offering herself to him. That was exciting. He hadn't had much experience with women.

Melissa will never know. And the Hilton won't have a diseased hostess.

She was definitely available, even eager, but what were the conditions? What obligations would he have—

He chuckled mirthlessly. None, of course. The girl was clearly a whore.

Ugly word. He didn't like "prostitute" much more. Ursula looked altogether too young, and her eyes—were they really as green as they had seemed in this light? Whatever color, they didn't have the hardness he associated with the women of Minetown's dance halls.

He had tried to read up on Tanith customs, but the veedisks on the passenger liner only gave him standard tourist spiels. Visit exotic Tanith. Gorgeous flowers, bright plumaged birds, the thrill of hunting real dinosaurs. Not much about Tanith's principal industry, which was hardly surprising.

And almost nothing about local customs.

Ursula had put on a rose-colored short-skirted one-piece garment that tied in front. It reminded him of the stola worn by hetaera in classical Greece. *That's a custom we could have revived with some profit. Maybe it's not too late.* He glanced around, half expecting to see a white canvass jacket somewhere, but if she had any other clothes here they had been put away. She was seated on a big easy chair with her legs tucked appealingly under her, and was staring at the big room screen. Words flowed swiftly across the veedisk reader screen, and she leaned forward in total concentration. Lysander walked up quietly behind her.

"The primary economic conflict, I think, is between people whose interests are with already well-established economic activities, and those whose interests are with the emergence of new economic activities. This is a conflict that can never be put to rest except by economic stagnation. For the new economic activities of today are the well-established economic activities of tomorrow which will be threatened in turn by further economic development. In this conflict, other things being equal, the well-established activities and those whose interests are attached to them must win. They are, by definition, the stronger. The only possible way to keep open the economic opportunities for new activities is for a 'third force' to protect their weak and still incipient interests. Only governments can play this economic role. And sometimes, for pitifully brief intervals, they do. . . ."

He read the status line. Page 249, Jane Jacobs. *The Economy of Cities,* first publication New York, 1970. Volume: Grolier's Collection of Classics in Social Science, Catalog 236G-65t—

She looked up, startled, flinched away from him, and quickly switched the screen to bring a local news program. "I'm sorry—"

"Whatever for? You're further in that book than I am." He chuckled. "Actually, I haven't started, but it's on the list my tutor gave me. Were you reading my copy?"

"On, no, the whole Grolier's collection is in the Hilton's library." She stood, and the tunic draped itself in interesting ways. She had good legs, with well-articulated calves. Her finger and toe nails were carefully painted in a light pink that contrasted sharply with the startling green of her eyes. "Ready?" she asked.

For what? Of course I'm ready, but— "Uh—I have an appointment with the governor. I'd better get dressed."

"Oh. Well—"

"Will you be here when I get back?"

"I come with the suite. I'll be here if you want me, and if I'm not here call 787."

"Do you have a reader in your room?"

"Well, yes—it's not as big as yours."

"Then stay here. And I'll be looking forward to that back rub."

II

"We have some time before our appointment with Governor Blaine," Lysander said. "Let's walk."

Harv nodded agreement. "Be good to stretch our legs, and the rain's stopped. Shouldn't go too far, Prince. Better early than late."

"Right." Not this early, Lysander thought. If he'd stayed in the suite he'd have had to do something about Ursula, and he wasn't ready to decide what that should be. "Were you alone in your room?"

"Sure, Prince."

Another data point. Maybe only the Governor's Suite came automatically—equipped. Guests in other rooms call the desk. I'll have to ask Ursula how many girls work for the hotel. Wonder if the Hilton heirs on Earth know what kind of services the Lederle Hilton provides? Or maybe the stories about Earth's decadence are true. . . .

He knew he wasn't ready for this mission, didn't know enough about Earth or Tanith or anywhere else, but that didn't really matter. There wasn't anyone else to do it. *If I just had a better idea of what I'm supposed to do!*

They walked past the Lederle Building. A riot of color hung from the balcony. A woman in bright pink leaned over the veranda railing. Others moved behind her, obviously enjoying the fresh air after the tropical rain. The building had clearly been inspired by the legends of Babylon's Hanging Gardens. "Maybe not the only thing this place has in common with Babylon."

"Oh. OK," Harv said.

Irrationally he wished that Ursula were walking with him. She'd have understood. Harv was competent and reliable and one of the Brotherhood, but sometimes it was a little trying to spend so much time with a man who—didn't care much for intellectual matters.

Beyond the square were several blocks of the two-story homes with verandas. Generally the ground floor was windowless, with few doors, giving the houses a fortress-like appearance. Most were surrounded by gardens of the ubiquitous Tanith flowering shrubs. One had only Earth hibiscus. They looked dull and prosaic in this setting. A kilometer further north the houses changed to single-story dwellings of dull-colored stucco. A few people sat on porches or strolled through the streets, but nowhere near as many as there had been nearer Government Square.

They came to a broad concrete highway. There were few vehicles, but it was wider than anything yet built on Sparta. It reminded Lysander of the veedisk pictures of freeways that ran the whole length of the California coast on Earth. A monorail supported on massive concrete columns ran down the highway's center.

In contrast, a horse and wagon trotted down the empty street past them. The bearded driver was dressed in black and wore a black hat. He gave them a cheery wave as he rode past.

They went under the highway through a pedestrian tunnel that smelled sourly of urine. The tunnel was deserted, and so was the area beyond.

The stucco houses went one more block beyond the highway, then gave way to a tangle of wooden shacks. Nothing was neat or well kept here. Discarded furniture rotted at the street corner. Litter and garbage were scattered through gardens that looked more like untended jungle than anything planned or deliberate.

"It's like Minetown, only it's wet," Harv said.

"Sort of," Lysander agreed. Except that Minetown wasn't walking distance from Government House Square, and the government of Sparta would never have permitted any place *this* unsanitary to exist anywhere on the planet. "We'd better—"

Three young men were coming toward them, and when Lysander turned to go back toward the pedestrian tunnel he saw two more had moved in behind them. All five walked arrogantly toward him.

"Trouble, Prince," Harv said. He smiled.

Lysander examined them carefully for weapons. They weren't wearing jackets, white or otherwise, and their jeans and shirts were formfitted over their muscled chests and hips leaving no room to conceal anything. They carried nothing except a length of chain and a couple of knives. Lysander's Walther rested comfortable in its holster under his guayabera, but he didn't reach for it. "Maybe they just want the time of day."

"Sure, Prince." The five came closer.

"Prince," one of the men said. "What kind of prince?"

"Jimmy, maybe he is," one of the others whined. "Maybe we—"

"Fuck off, Mario. Hey, Prince, you got any money? We'd sure like five credits."

They were not much younger than Lysander and Harv. Drop them outside the capital city of Sparta and you might not notice them, Lysander thought. They dress a bit sloppily, but there's little else different about them. "What will you do to earn the money?" Lysander asked.

Harv laughed.

One of the men giggled. Jimmy, their leader, said "Oh, well, like this is a bad place, you know? You're lost, right? And we can show you how to get out of here, you know? Ten credits. That's all we want. Ten."

"Thank you, but I know the way out," Lysander said.

"Have it your way—"

Harv had all the time in the world. He struck as the gang leader was still speaking. His upthrust palm took the leader under the nose and rocked him back on his heels as the stiffened fingers of the other hand stabbed at the boy's abdomen. Harv's foot darted out in a snap kick to the knee. Jimmy fell as if shot. Before he hit the ground, Harv was standing relaxed as if he had never moved.

"Jesus Christ!" One of the two who had come up behind reached toward Lysander. His hand drew back and dangled uselessly, and he stared in amazement at bright blood welling from elbow to wrist. Harv carefully shifted the knife to his left hand. He still hadn't said a word, but his grin was broad.

"Who the fuck *are* you?" The one the leader had called Mario backed away. "Who?" He looked at his companions. "Fellows, maybe—"

"Maybe you made a mistake," Lysander said. "Please leave us alone."

The third one thought he had studied martial arts. He kicked at Harv, then pivoted to swing a three foot length of chain. Lysander swayed back to let the chain miss. Harv moved just behind the chain until he was close to the boy. His right hand moved upward as his left foot landed on the youth's instep. The boy fell groaning.

"Please," Lysander said.

"Yeah, sure, man. Sure," Mario said. He helped the third boy to his feet.

Harv looked disappointed when they all turned and walked away, walking, carefully not running, but not looking back at their fallen leader.

Governor Carleton Blaine was just under forty standard years old. Lysander's uncle had said Blaine was crazy: with his family connections he had enough political clout to get nearly any post he wanted, and he'd chosen Tanith. Every previous governor of Tanith had found himself on the prison planet because he had *lost* a power struggle.

He came out to meet them in the anteroom. The reception area was paneled in some exotic wood that might have been imported from Earth, although Lysander was sure it hadn't been. Tanith didn't merit that kind of expense. When Lysander unobtrusively touched one wall, the panels felt like wood, but the new plastics often did.

Blaine was noticeably taller than Lysander's 180 centimeters, and thinner. His sandy brown hair looked to have been combed with his fingers. He wore the CoDominium seal on the left pocket of his light blue guayabera shirt. His handshake was firm. "Glad to see you, Prince Lysander. Taxpayer Middleton."

"Thank you."

"It's Citizen," Harv said proudly.

"Oh. Er, Your Highness, we were told this is an unofficial visit."

"Yes. Quite."

Blaine nodded. "I also have a message from the Chairman of Lederle A.G. requesting us to cooperate with you. Of course we will. What can we do for you?" Blaine ushered them toward his office door.

"You might find someone to show Citizen Middleton around and perhaps buy him a drink."

Blaine raised one eyebrow, then turned to his receptionist. "Ann, ask Mr. Kim to come up and take Prince Lysander's friend to the club room. Thank you." He led the way into his private office.

The office was paneled in the same stuff as the reception room. The desk was much more spectacular, banded in exotic woods framing thin panels of highly polished stone. It dominated the room, and invited questions. "That's really handsome. I've never seen anything like it," Lysander said.

Blaine smiled broadly. "Thank you. All native materials. Snakewood, and Grey Howlite. Of course the electronic innards were made on Earth by Viasyn. It will take us a few years before we can make anything like that here. Drink?"

"Thank you."

"We have an excellent liqueur, rum based with flavoring from the Tanith Passion Fruit, but perhaps it's a bit early in the day for something so sweet. Tanith whiskey, perhaps?"

"Thank you." Lysander sipped gingerly at the dark whiskey. "That's quite good."

"Glad you like it. Bit like Scotch only more so. Some find it strong."

"Sparta's whiskey is descended from Irish," Lysander said. "We think it's better than Earth's best. We had a master distiller from Cork—"

"Much the same story here," Blaine said. "Whole family from near Inverary. Can't imagine what they did to annoy BuRelock, but up they came; Tanith's benefit and Earth's loss. One of my predecessors set them up in the distilling business. So. I trust your stay on Tanith has been pleasant?"

"It *began* pleasantly enough—may I ask you about local customs?"

"Please do."

"There was a girl in my suite—"

"Ah. Blonde or red hair?"

"Red."

"That would be Ursula Gordon. Bright girl. I believe you when you say things began pleasantly—"

"What the hell is she doing there?"

"I beg your pardon?"

"Isn't she a bit young for prostitution?"

Blaine looked embarrassed. "Actually, she had no choice in the matter."

"I thought not. We don't have slavery on Sparta."

"Ah. Yes, and we do on Tanith. Something I'm trying to change. Takes longer than you might think."

"Yes, we've had much the same experience, everything takes longer and costs more, but slavery! Can't you stop that?"

"It's not slavery. Not precisely. Indentured," Blaine said. "Children born to convicts are indentured to the owner of the mother's contract. The theory is that since the owner has been burdened with the child's upbringing and education, he's entitled to something out of the arrangement. The Hilton bought her contract when she was quite young, and paid for her education. Now they expect some return. It's a nasty practice, and I've put an end to it for the future. Unfortunately I can't do anything retroactively. Tried. CoDominium arbitrator held for the contracts." Blaine was talking very fast. He went to the bar and brought the bottle back. "Shoot you in the other hip?"

"Thank you—how long will she be indentured?"

"Until she turns nineteen. That's Earth years. Tanith years are longer. The days are a bit shorter, but we measure 365 Tanith days as an Earth year. Too much trouble to measure hours." Blaine tapped keys on a console by his desk. "She'd be free in 209 local days."

"What will she do then?" Lysander asked.

Blaine took a deep breath. "If she's lucky she'll keep that job with the Hilton."

"And that's the best she can do?"

"I suppose it depends on which friends she makes. Or has made. This is a hard world, Your Highness." The governor went back to his desk. "You said things *began* pleasantly. Any problems?"

"Actually, yes." Lysander told Blaine about the five young men who'd approached him. "They ran away. Their leader was lucky. Harv only broke his nose. Possibly his leg as well, but I don't think so. I wondered if I ought to report it, but I didn't see any police—"

Blaine's smile had vanished. "In theory, of course you should have reported it, but in practice no one ever does. I'd stay out of that section of the city in future—"

"We will."

"But you said you were still among the stucco houses. You hadn't actually crossed into the Wattletown area?"

"No."

"I see. Excuse me, please." Blaine touched buttons on his desk. "Ann, please ask the chief of police to send a squad into Wattletown and round up the usual suspects. They can pass the word that Jimmy and Mario have stirred the soup."

"No need for that," Lysander protested.

"But there is," Blaine said. "We can't police everything, but we certainly can't put up with attacks on tourists in parts of town where they should be safe," He sighed. "I've posted signs at the tunnels under the Bronson Highway but the people on the other side tear them down. Can't say I blame them. Wouldn't want to live in an abandoned area myself."

"We don't have abandoned areas on Sparta. Not yet."

"I take it your chap is quite an experienced bodyguard."

"He's not precisely a bodyguard. I doubt you have anything like the Phraetries on Tanith."

"Phraetries?"

"Brotherhoods. Every potential Citizen of Sparta is potentially assigned to one at birth. We try to mix the social classes and backgrounds. It's a bit hard to explain—we're all brothers in our Phraetrie. Harv is my traveling companion, and I pity anyone who tries to give me trouble, but he's my Brother, and a full Citizen, not my bodyguard. Incidentally, 'Citizen' is an honorific on Sparta. We don't have 'taxpayers.'"

"Oh. Quite. Now, Your Highness, what else can I do for you?"

"I need to see Colonel Falkenberg."

"Ah. Good man. Ordinarily it would be no trouble, but just now I have him out suppressing the last of the escapee pirate gangs. There's a bit of other work for him here as well."

"It's very important."

Blaine cocked his head to one side. "I make no doubt it's important. I've heard a story or two myself. Care to tell me anything?" When Lysander didn't answer, Blaine nodded. "Right. Look, I'll do what I can, but it will take a while. Meanwhile, we're having a small dinner party here next week, nothing fancy, informal in fact. Falkenberg is invited, should be there if he's not altogether tied up with the Free State mess. If you like you could bring Miss Gordon."

"That would be appropriate for a dinner at Government House?"

"Yes— Well, no, in fact. And I'd like to change that. You could help me. No one is going to be rude to *you*. Or your guest."

"My father told me not to interfere in foreign affairs."

"Good advice," Blaine said.

"But surely this can't do any harm. I'll be glad to come. With the young lady."

"Thank you. Your Highness, I'm convinced that the future of this planet lies with the convicts and involuntary colonists. Some of the original settlers, the planters and pharmaceutical processing officials, understand that. Many don't, and want to hang on to meaningless aristocratic privileges."

"We've had something of the same problem," Lysander said. "Of course it helps that we get—many of the convicts brought to Sparta have bribed their way there—"

"Giving you a slightly better grade of convict?" Blaine smiled. "Happens here, too, but of course on a lower scale. Still, anyone who can will pay to come here rather than be sent to Fulson's world. And once in a while we get a really bright one."

III

One Year Earlier . . .

The California sky was bright blue above eight thousand young bodies writhing to the maddening beat of an electronic bass. Some danced while others lay back on the grass and drank or smoked. None could ignore the music, although they were only barely aware of the nasal tenor whose voice was not strong enough to carry over the wild squeals of the theremin and the twang of a dozen steel-stringed guitars. Other musical groups waited their turn on the gray wooden platform erected among the twentieth-century Gothic buildings of Los Angeles University.

Some of the musicians were so anxious to begin that they pounded their instruments. This produced nothing audible because their amplifiers were turned off, but it allowed them to join in the frenzied spirit of the festival on the campus green.

The concert was a happy affair. Citizens from a nearby Welfare Island joined the students in the college park. Enterprising dealers hawked liquor and pot and borloi. Catering trucks brought food. The Daughters of Lilith played original works while Slime waited their turn, and after those would come even more famous groups. An air of peace and fellowship engulfed the crowd.

"Lumpen proletariat." The speaker was a young woman. She stood at a window in a classroom overlooking the common green and the mad scene below. "Lumpen," she said again.

"Aw, come off the bolshi talk. Communism's no answer. Look at the Sovworld—"

"Revolution betrayed! Betrayed!" the girl said. She faced her challenger. "There will be no peace and freedom until—"

"Can it." The meeting chairman banged his fist on the desk. "We've got work to do. This is no time for ideology."

"Without the proper revolutionary theory, nothing can be accomplished." This came from a bearded man in a leather jacket. He looked first at the chairman, then at the dozen others in the classroom. "First there must be a proper understanding of the problem. Then we can act!"

The chairman banged his fist again, but someone else spoke. "Deeds, not words. We came here to plan some action. What the hell's all the talking about? You goddamned theorists give me a pain in the ass! What we need is action. The Underground's done more for the Movement than you'll ever—"

"Balls." The man in the leather jacket snorted contempt. Then he stood. His voice projected well. "You act, all right. You shut down the L.A. transport system for three days. Real clever. And what did it accomplish? Made the taxpayers scared enough to fork over pay raises to the cops. You ended the goddamn pig strike, that's what you did!"

There was a general babble, and the Underground spokesman tried to answer, but the leather-jacketed man continued. "You started food riots in the Citizen areas. Big deal. It's results that count, and your result was the CoDominium Marines! You brought in the Marines, that's what you did!"

"Damned right! We exposed this regime for what it really is! The Revolution can't come until the people understand—"

"Revolution, my ass. Get it through your heads, technology's the only thing that's going to save us. Turn technology loose, free the scientists, and we'll be—"

He was shouted down by the others. There was more babble.

Mark Fuller sat at the student desk and drank it all in. The wild music outside. Talk of revolution. Plans for action, for making something happen, for making the Establishment notice them; it was all new, and he was here in this room, where the real power of the university lay. God, how I love it! he thought. I've never had any kind of power before. Not even over my own life. And now we can show them all!

He felt more alive than he ever had in all his twenty years. He looked at the girl next to him and smiled. She grinned and patted his thigh. Tension rose in his loins until it was almost unbearable. He remembered their yesterdays and imagined their tomorrows. The quiet world of taxpayer country where he had grown up seemed very far away.

The others continued their argument. Mark listened, but his thoughts kept straying to Shirley; to the warmth of her hand on his thigh, to the places where her sweater was stretched out of shape, to the remembered feel of her heels against his back and her cries of passion. He knew he ought to listen more carefully to the discussion. He didn't really belong in this room at all. If Shirley hadn't brought him, he'd never have known the meeting was happening.

But I'll earn a place here, he thought. In my own right. Power. That's what they have, and I'll learn how to be a part of it.

The jacketed technocracy man was speaking again. "You see too many devils," he said. "Get the CoDominium Intelligence people off the scientists' backs and it won't be twenty years before *all* of the earth's a paradise. All of it, not just taxpayer country."

"A polluted paradise! What do you want, to go back to the smog? Oil slicks, dead fish, animals exterminated, that's what—"

"Bullshit. Technology can get us *out* of—"

"That's what caused the problems in the first place!"

"Because we didn't get far enough! There hasn't been a new scientific idea since the goddamn space drive! You're so damned proud because there's no pollution. None here, anyway. But it's not because of conservation, It's because they ship people out to hellholes like Tanith, because of triage, because—"

"He's right, people starve while we—"

"Damn right! Free thoughts, freedom to think, to plan, to do research, to publish without censorship, that's what will liberate the world."

The arguments went on until the chairman tired of them. He banged his fist again. "We are here to *do* something," he said. "Not to settle the world's problems this afternoon. That was agreed."

The babble finally died away and the chairman spoke meaningfully. "This is our chance. A peaceful demonstration of power. Show what we think of their goddamn rules and their status cards. But we've got to be careful. It mustn't get out of hand."

Mark sprawled on the grass a dozen meters from the platform. He stretched luxuriantly in the California sun while Shirley stroked his back. Excitement poured in through all his senses. College had been like this in imagination. The boys at the expensive private schools where his father had sent him used to whisper about festivals, demonstrations, and confrontations, but it hadn't been real. Now it was. He'd hardly ever mingled with Citizens before, and now they were all around him. They wore Welfare-issue clothing and talked in strange dialects that Mark only half understood. Everyone,

Citizens and students, writhed to the music that washed across them.

Mark's father had wanted to send him to a college in taxpayer country, but there hadn't been enough money. He might have won a scholarship, but he hadn't. Mark told himself it was deliberate. Competition was no way to live. His two best friends in high school had refused to compete in the rat race. Neither ended here, though; they'd had the money to get to Princeton and Yale.

More Citizens poured in. The festival was supposed to be open only to those with tickets, and Citizens weren't supposed to come onto the campus in the first place, but the student group had opened the gates and cut the fences. It had all been planned in the meeting. Now the gate-control shack was on fire, and everyone who lived nearby could get in.

Shirley was ecstatic. "Look at them!" she shouted. "This is the way it used to be! Citizens should be able to go wherever they want to. Equality forever!"

Mark smiled. It was all new to him. He hadn't thought much about the division between Citizen and taxpayer, and had accepted his privileges without noticing them. He had learned a lot from Shirley and his new friends, but there was so much more that he didn't know. I'll find out, though, he thought. We know what we're doing. We can make the world so much better—we can do anything! Time for the stupid old bastards to move over and let some fresh ideas in.

Shirley passed him a pipe of borloi. That was another new thing for him; it was a Citizen habit, something Mark's father despised. Mark couldn't understand why. He inhaled deeply and relished the wave of contentment it brought. Then he reached for Shirley and held her in his warm bath of concern and love, knowing she was as happy as he was.

She smiled gently at him, her hand resting on his thigh, and they writhed to the music, the beat thundering through them, faces glowing with anticipation of what would come, of what they would accomplish this day. The pipe came around again and Mark seized it eagerly.

"Pigs! The pigs are coming!" The cry went up from the fringes of the crowd.

Shirley turned to her followers. "Just stay here. Don't provoke the bastards. Make sure you don't do anything but sit tight."

There were murmurs of agreement. Mark felt excitement flash through him. This was it. And he was right there in front with the leaders; even if all his status did come from being Shirley's current boyfriend, he was one of the leaders, one of the people who made things happen. . . .

The police were trying to get through the crowd so they could stop the festival. The university president was with them, and he was shouting something Mark couldn't understand. Over at the edge of the common green there was a lot of smoke. Was a building on fire? That didn't make sense. There weren't supposed to be any fires, nothing was to be harmed; just ignore the cops and the university people, show how Citizens and students could mingle in peace; show how stupid the damned rules were, and how needless—

There *was* a fire. Maybe more than one. Police and firemen tried to get through the crowd. Someone kicked a cop and the bluecoat went down. A dozen of his buddies waded into the group. Their sticks rose and fell.

The peaceful dream vanished. Mark stared in confusion. There was a man screaming somewhere, where was he? In the burning building? A group began chanting: "Equality now! Equality now!"

Another group was building a barricade across the green.

"They aren't supposed to do that!" Mark shouted. Shirley grinned at him. Her eyes shone with excitement. More police came, then more and a group headed toward Mark. They raised aluminum shields as rocks flew across the green. The police came closer. One of the cops raised his club.

He was going to hit Shirley! Mark grabbed at the nightstick and deflected it. Citizens and students clustered around. Some threw themselves at the cops. A big man, well-dressed, too old to be a student, kicked at the leading policeman. The cop went down.

Mark pulled Shirley away as a dozen black-jacketed Lampburners joined the melee. The Lampburners would deal with the cops, but Mark didn't want to watch. The boys in his school had talked contemptuously about pigs, but the only police Mark had ever met had been polite and deferential; this was ugly, and—

His head swam in confusion. One minute he'd been lying in Shirley's arms with music and fellowship and everything was wonderful. Now there were police, and groups shouting "Kill the pigs!" and fires burning. The Lampburners were swarming everywhere. They hadn't been at the meeting. Most claimed to be wanted by the police. But they'd had a representative at the planning session, they'd agreed this would be a peaceful demonstration—

A man jumped off the roof of the burning building. There was no one below to catch him, and he sprawled on the steps like a broken doll. Blood poured from his mouth, a bright-red splash against the pink marble steps. Another building shot flames skyward. More police arrived and set up electrified barriers around the crowd.

A civilian, his bright clothing a contrast with the dull police blue, got out of a cruiser and stood atop it as police held their shields in front of him. He began to shout through a bull horn:

"I read you the Act of 2018 as amended. Whenever there shall be an assembly likely to endanger public or private property or the lives of Citizens and taxpayers, the lawful magistrates shall command all persons assembled to disperse and shall warn them that failure to disperse shall be considered a declaration of rebellion. The magistrates shall give sufficient time . . ."

Mark knew the act. He'd heard it discussed in school. It was time to get away. The local mayor would soon have more than enough authority to deal with this mad scene. He could even call on the military, US or CoDominium. The barriers were up around two sides of the green, but the cops hadn't closed off all the buildings. There was a doorway ahead, and Mark pulled Shirley toward it. "Come on!"

Shirley wouldn't come. She stood defiant, grinning wildly, shaking her fist at the police, shouting curses at them. Then she turned to Mark. "If you're scared, just go on, baby. Bug off."

Someone handed a bottle around. Shirley drank and gave it to Mark. He raised it to his lips but didn't drink any. His head pounded and he was afraid. I should run, he thought. I should run like hell. The mayor's finished reading the act.

"*Equality now! Equality now!*" The chant was contagious. Half the crowd was shouting.

The police waited impassively. An officer glanced at his watch from time to time. Then the officer nodded, and the police advanced. Four technicians took hoses from one of the cruises and directed streams of foam above the heads of the advancing blue line. The slimy liquid fell in a spray around Mark.

Mark fell. He tried to stand and couldn't. Everyone around him fell. Whatever the liquid touched became so slippery that no one could hold onto it. It didn't seem to affect the police.

Instant banana peel, Mark thought. He'd seen it used on tri-v. Everyone laughed when they saw it used on tri-v. Now

it didn't seem so funny. A couple of attempts showed Mark
that he couldn't get away; he could barely crawl. The police
moved rapidly toward him. Rocks and bottles clanged against
their shields.

The black-jacketed Lampburners took spray cans from their
pockets. They sprayed their shoes and hands and then got up.
They began to move away through the helpless crowd, away
from the police, toward an empty building—

The police line reached the group around Mark. The cops
fondled their nightsticks. They spoke in low tones, too low
to be heard any distance away. "Stick time," one said. "Yeah,
our turn," his partner answered.

"Does anyone here claim taxpayer status?" The cop eyed
the group coldly. "Speak up."

"Yes. Here." One boy tried to get up. He fell again, but he
held up his ID card. "Here." Mark reached for his own.

"Fink!" Shirley shouted. She threw something at the other
boy. "Hypocrite! Pig! Fink!" Others were shouting as well. Mark
saw Shirley's look of hatred and put his card back into his
pocket. There'd be time later.

Two police grabbed him. One lifted his feet, the other lifted
his shoulders. They carried him to the sidewalk. Then they
lifted him waist high, and the one holding his shoulders let
go. The last thing Mark heard as his head hit the pavement
was the mocking laughter of the cop.

The bailiff was grotesque, with mustaches like Wyatt Earp
and an enormous paunch that hung over his equipment belt.
In a bored voice he read, "Case 457-984. People against Mark
Fuller. Rebellion, aggravated assault, resisting arrest."

The judge looked down from the bench. "How do you
plead?"

"Guilty, Your Honor," Mark's lawyer said. His name was
Zower, and he wasn't expensive. Mark's father couldn't afford
an expensive lawyer.

But I didn't, Mark thought. I didn't. When he'd said that
earlier, though, the attorney had been contemptuous. "Shut
up or you'll make it worse," the lawyer had said. "I had trouble
enough getting the conspiracy charges dropped. Just stand there
looking innocent and don't say a goddamn thing."

The judge nodded. "Have you anything to say in mitiga-
tion?"

Zower put his hand on Mark's shoulder. "My client throws
himself on the mercy of the court," he said. "Mark has never
been in trouble before. He acted under the influence of evil

companions and intoxicants. There was no real intent to commit crimes. Just very bad judgment."

The judge didn't look impressed. "What have the people to say about this?"

"Your Honor," the prosecutor began, "the people have had more than enough of these student riots. This was no high-jinks stunt by young taxpayers. This was a deliberate rebellion, planned in advance.

"We have recordings of this hoodlum striking a police officer. That officer subsequently suffered a severe beating with three fractures, a ruptured kidney, and other personal injuries. It is a wonder the officer is alive. We can also show that after the mayor's proclamations, the accused made no attempt to leave. If the defense disputed these facts . . ."

"No, no." Zower spoke hastily. "We stipulate, Your Honor." He muttered to himself, just loud enough that Mark could hear. "Can't let them run those pix. That'd get the judge *really* upset."

Zower stood. "Your Honor, we stipulate Mark's bad judgement, but remember, he was intoxicated. He did not actually strike the policeman, he merely gripped the officer's nightstick. Mark was with new friends, friends he didn't know very well. His father is a respected taxpayer, manager of General Foods in Santa Maria. Mark has never been arrested before. I'm sure he's learned a lesson from all this."

And where is Shirley? Mark wondered. Somehow her politician father had kept her from even being charged.

The judge was nodding. Zower smiled and whispered to Mark, "I stroked him pretty good in chambers. We'll get probation."

"Mister Fuller, what have you to say for yourself?" the judge demanded.

Mark stood eagerly. He wasn't sure what he was going to say. Plead? Beg for mercy? Tell him to stick it? Not that. Mark breathed hard. I'm scared, he thought. He walked nervously toward the bench.

The judge's face exploded in a cloud of red. There was wild laughter in the court. Another balloon of red ink sailed across the courtroom to burst on the high bench. Mark laughed hysterically, completely out of control, as the spectators shouted.

"*Equality now!*" Eight voices speaking in unison cut through the babble. "*Justice! Equality! Citizen judges, not taxpayers! Equality now! Equality now! Equality now! All power to the Liberation Party!*"

The last stung like a blow. The judge's face turned even

redder. He stood in fury. The fat bailiff and his companions moved decisively through the crowd. Two of the demonstrators escaped, but the bailiff was much faster than his bulk made him look. After a time the court was silent.

The judge stood, ink dripping from his face and robes. He was not smiling. "This amused you?" he demanded.

"No," Mark said. "It was none of my doing."

"I do not believe the outlawed Liberation Party would trouble itself for anyone not one of their own. Mark Fuller, you have pleaded guilty to serious crimes. We would normally send a taxpayer's son to rehabilitation school, but you and your friends have demanded equality. Very well. You shall have it.

"Mark Fuller, I sentence you to three years at hard labor. Since you renounced your allegiance to the United States by participating in a deliberate act of rebellion, such participation stipulated by your attorney's admission that you made no move to depart after the reading of the act, you have no claim upon the United States. The United States therefore renounces you. It is hereby ordered that you be delivered to the CoDominium authorities to serve your sentence wherever they shall find convenient." The gavel fell to the bench. It didn't sound very loud at all.

IV

The low gravity of Luna Base was better than the endless nightmare of the flight up. Mark had been trapped in a narrow compartment with berths so close together that the sagging bunk above his pressed against him at high acceleration. The ship had stunk with the putrid smell of vomit and stale wine.

Now he stood under the glaring lights in a bare concrete room. The concrete was the gray-green color of moon rock. They hadn't been given an outside view, and except for the low gravity he might have been in a basement on Earth. There were a thousand others standing with him under the glaring bright fluorescent lights. Most of them had the dull look of terror. A few glared defiantly, but they kept their opinions to themselves.

Gray-coveralled trustees with bell-mouthed sonic stunners patrolled the room. It wouldn't have been worthwhile trying to take one of the weapons from the trustees, though; at each entrance was a knot of CoDominium Marines in blue and scarlet. The Marines leaned idly on weapons which were not harmless at all.

"Segregate us," Mark's companion said. "Divide and rule."

Mark nodded. Bill Halpern was the only person Mark knew. Halpern had been the technocrat spokesman in the meeting on the campus.

"Divide and rule," Halpern said again. It was true enough. The prisoners had been sorted by sex, race and language, so that everyone around Mark was white male and either North American or from some other English-speaking place. "What the hell are we waiting for?" Halpern wondered. There was no possible answer, and they stood for what seemed like hours.

Then the door opened and a small group came in. Three CoDominium Navy petty officers, and a midshipman. The middie was no more than seventeen, younger than Mark. He used a bullhorn to speak to the assembled group. "Volunteers for the Navy?"

There were several shouts, and some of the prisoners stepped forward.

"Traitors," Halpern said.

Mark nodded agreement. Although he meant it in a different way from Halpern, Mark's father had always said the same thing. "Traitors!" he'd thundered. "Dupes of the goddamn Soviets. One of these days that Navy will take over this country and hand us to the Kremlin."

Mark's teachers at school had different ideas. The Navy wasn't needed at all. Nor was the CD. Men no longer made war, at least not on Earth. Colony squabbles were of no interest to the people on Earth anyway. Military services, they'd told him, were a wasteful joke.

His new friends at college said the purpose of the CoDominium was to keep the United States and the Soviet Union rich while suppressing everyone else. Then they'd begun using the CD fleet and Marines to shore up their domestic governments. The whole CD was no more than a part of the machinery of oppression.

And yet—on tri-v the CD Navy was glamorous. It fought pirates (only Mark knew there were no real space pirates) and restored order in the colonies (only his college friends told him that wasn't restoring order, it was oppression of free people). The spacers wore uniforms and explored new planets.

The CD midshipman walked along the line of prisoners. Two older petty officers followed. They walked proudly—contemptuously, even. They saw the prisoners as another race, not as fellow humans at all.

A convict not far from Mark stepped out of line. "Mister Blaine," the man said. "Please, sir."

The midshipman stopped. "Yes?"

"Don't you know me, Mister Blaine? Able Spacer Johnson, sir. In Mister Leary's division in *Magog*."

The middie nodded with all the gravity of a seventeen-year-old who has important duties and knows it. "I recall you, Johnson."

"Let me back in, sir. Six years I served, never up for defaulters."

The midshipman fingered his clipboard console. "Drunk and disorderly, assault on a taxpayer, armed robbery. Mandatory transportation. I shouldn't wonder that you prefer the Navy, Johnson."

"Not like that at all, sir. I shouldn't ever have took my musterin'-out pay. Shouldn't have left the Fleet, sir. Couldn't find my place with civilians, sir. God knows I drank too much, but I was never drunk on duty, sir, you look up my records—"

"Kiss the middie's bum, you whining asshole," Halpern said.

One of the petty officers glanced up. "Silence in the ranks." He put his hand on his nightstick and glared at Halpern.

The midshipman thought for a moment. "All right, Johnson. You'll come in as ordinary. Have to work for the stripe."

"Yes, sir, sure thing, sir." Johnson strode toward the area reserved for recruits. His manner changed with each step he took. He began in a cringing walk, but by the time he reached the end of the room, he had straightened and walked tall.

The midshipman went down the line. Twenty men volunteered, but he took only three.

An hour later a CoDominium Marine sergeant came looking for men. "No rebels and no degenerates!" he said. He took six young men sentenced for street rioting, arson, mayhem, resisting arrest, assault on police and numerous other crimes.

"Street gang," Halpern said. "Perfect for Marines."

Eventually they were herded back into a detention pen and left to themselves. "You really hate the CD, don't you?" Mark asked his companion.

"I hate what they do."

Mark nodded, but Halpern only sneered. "You don't know anything at all," Halpern said. "Oppression? Shooting rioters? Sure that's part of what the CD does, but it's not the worst part. Symptom, not cause. The case is their goddamn so-called intelligence service. Suppression of scientific research. Censorship of technical journals. They've even stopped the pretense of basic research. When was the last time a licensed physicist had a decent idea?"

Mark shrugged. He knew nothing about physics.

Halpern grinned. There was no warmth in the expression. His voice had a bitter edge. "Keeping the peace, they say. Only discourage new weapons, new military technology. Bullshit, they've stopped everything for fear somebody somewhere will come up with—"

"Shut the fuck up." The man was big, hairy like a bear, with a big paunch jutting out over the belt of his coveralls. "If I hear that goddamn whining once more, I'll stomp your goddamn head in."

"Hey, easy," Halpern said. "We're all in this together. We have to join against the class enemy—" The big man's hand swung up without warning. He hit Halpern on the mouth. Halpern staggered and fell. His head struck the concrete floor.

"Told you to shut up." He turned to Mark. "You got anything to say?"

Mark was terrified. I ought to do something, he thought. Say something. Anything. He tried to speak, but no words came out.

The big man grinned at him, then deliberately kicked Halpern in the ribs. "Didn't think so. Hey, you're not bad-lookin', kid. Six months we'll be on that goddamn ship, with no women. Want to be my bunkmate? I'll take good care of you. See nobody hurts you. You'll like that."

"Leave the kid alone." Mark couldn't see who spoke. "I said let go of him."

"Who says so?" The hairy man shoved Mark against the wall and turned to the newcomer.

"I do." The newcomer didn't look like much, Mark thought. At least forty, and slim. Not thin though, Mark realized. The man stood with his hands thrust into the pockets of his coveralls. "Let him be, Karper."

Karper grinned and charged at the newcomer. As he rushed forward, his opponent pivoted and sent a kick to Karper's head. As Karper reeled back, two more kicks slammed his head against the wall. Then the newcomer moved forward and deliberately kneed Karper in the kidney. The big man went down and rolled beside Halpern.

"Come on, kid, it stinks over here." He grinned at Mark.

"But my buddy—"

"Forget him." The man pointed. Five trustees were coming into the pen. They lifted Halpern and Karper and carried them away. One of the trustees winked as they went past Mark and the other man. "See? Maybe you'll see your friend again, maybe not. They don't like troublemakers."

"Bill's not a troublemaker! That other man started it! It's not fair!"

"Kid, you better forget that word 'fair.' It could cause you no end of problems. Got any smokes?" He accepted Mark's cigarette with a glance at the label. "Thanks. Name?"

"Mark Fuller."

"Dugan. Call me Biff."

"Thanks, Biff. I guess I needed some help."

"That you did. Hell, it was fun. Karper was gettin' on my nerves, anyway. How old are you, kid?"

"Twenty." And what does he want? Lord God, is he looking for a bunkmate, too?

"You don't look twenty. Taxpayer, aren't you?"

"Yes—how did you know?"

"It shows. What's a taxpayer's kid doing here?"

Mark told him. "It wasn't fair," he finished.

"There's that word again. You were in college, eh? Can you read?"

"Well, sure, everyone can read."

Dugan laughed. "I can't. Not very well. And I bet you're the only one in this pen who ever read a whole book. Where'd you learn?"

"Well—in school. Maybe a little at home."

Dugan blew a careful smoke ring. It hung in the air between them. "Me, I never even saw a veedisk screen until they dragged me off to school, and nobody gave a shit whether we looked at 'em or not. Had to pick up some of it, but—look, maybe you know things I don't. Want to stick with me a while?"

Mark eyed him suspiciously. Dugan laughed. "Hell, I don't bugger kids. Not until I've been locked up a lot longer than this, anyway. Man needs a buddy, though, and you just lost yours."

"Yeah. Okay. Want another cigarette?"

"We better save 'em. We'll need all you got."

A petty officer opened the door to the pen. "Classification," he shouted. "Move out this door."

"Got to it pretty fast," Dugan said. "Come on." They followed the others out and through a long corridor until they reached another large room. There were tables at the end, and trustees sat at each table. Eventually Mark and Dugan got to one.

The trusty barely looked at them. When they gave their names, he punched them into a console on the table. The printer made tiny clicking noises and two sheets of paper fell out. "Any choice?" the trusty asked.

"What's open, shipmate?" Dugan asked.

"I'm no shipmate of yours," the trusty sneered. "Tanith, Sparta, and Fulson's World."

Dugan shuddered. "Well, we sure don't want Fulson's World." He reached into Mark's pocket and took out the pack of cigarettes, then laid them on the table. They vanished into the trusty's coveralls.

"Not Fulson's," the trusty said. "Now, I hear they're lettin' the convicts run loose on Sparta." He said nothing more but looked at them closely.

Mark remembered that Sparta was founded by a group of intellectuals. They were trying some kind of social experiment. Unlike Tanith with its CoDominium governor, Sparta was independent. They'd have a better chance there. "We'll take Sparta," Mark said.

"Sparta's pretty popular," the trusty said. He waited for a moment. "Well, too bad." He scrawled "Tanith" across their papers and handed them over. "Move along." A petty officer waved them through a door behind the table.

"But we wanted Sparta," Mark protested.

"Get your ass out of here," the CD petty officer said. "Move it." Then it was too late and they were through the door.

"Wish I'd had some credits," Dugan muttered. "We bought off Fulson's though. That's something."

"But—I have some money. I didn't know—"

Dugan gave him a curious look. "Kid, they didn't teach you much in that school of yours. Well, come on, we'll make out. But you better let me take care of that money."

CDSS *Vladivostok* hurtled toward the orbit of Jupiter. The converted assault troop carrier was crammed with thousands of men jammed into temporary berths welded into the troop bays. There were more men than bunks; many of the convicts had to trade off half the time.

Dugan took over a corner. Corners were desirable territory, and two men disputed his choice. After they were carried away, no one else thought it worth trying. Biff used Mark's money to finance a crap game in the area near their berths, and in a few days he had trebled their capital.

"Too bad," Dugan said. "If we'd had this much back on Luna, we'd be headed for Sparta. Anyway, we bought our way into this ship, and that's worth something." He grinned at Mark's lack of response. "Hey, kid, it could be worse. We could be with BuRelock. You think this Navy ship's bad, try a BuRelock hellhole."

Mark wondered how Bureau of Relocation ships could be worse, but he didn't want to find out. The newscasters back on Earth had documentary specials about BuRelock. They all said that conditions were tough but bearable. They also told of the glory: mankind settling other worlds circling other stars. Mark felt none of the glory now.

Back home Zower would be making an appeal. Or at least he'd be billing Mark's father for one. And so what? Mark thought. Nothing would come of it. But something might! Jason Fuller had some political favors coming. He might pull a few strings. Mark could be headed back home within a year. . . .

He knew better, but he had no other hope. He lived in misery, brooding about the low spin gravity, starchy food, the constant stench of the other convicts; all that was bad, but the water was the worst thing. He knew it was recycled. Water on Earth was recycled, too, but there you didn't know that it had been used to bathe the foul sores of the man two bays to starboard.

Sometimes a convict would rush screaming through the compartment, smashing at bunks and flinging his fellow prisoners about like matchsticks, until a dozen men would beat him to the deck. Eventually the guards would take him away. None ever came back.

The ship reached the orbit of Jupiter and took on fuel from the scoopship tankers that waited for her. Then she moved to the featureless point in space that marked the Alderson jump tramline. Alarms rang; then everything blurred. They sat on their bunks in confusion, unable to move or even think. That lasted long after the instantaneous Jump. The ship had covered light-years in a single instant; now they had to cross another star's gravity well to reach the next Jump point.

Two weeks later a petty officer entered the compartment. "Two men needed for cleanup in the crew area. Chance for Navy chow. Volunteers?"

"Sure," Dugan said. "My buddy and me. Anybody object?"

No one did. The petty officer grinned. "Looks like you're elected." He led them through corridors and passageways to the forward end of the ship, where they were put to scrubbing the bulkheads. A bored Marine watched idly.

"I thought you said never volunteer," Mark told Dugan.

"Good general rule. But what else we got to do? Gets us better chow. Always take a chance on something when it can't be no worse than what you've got."

The lunch was good and the work was not hard. Even the smell of disinfectant was a relief, and scrubbing off the bulkheads and decks got their hands clean for the first time since they'd been put aboard. In mid-afternoon a crewman came by. He stopped and stared at them for a moment.

"Dugan! Biff Dugan, by God!"

"Horrigan, you slut. When'd you join up?"

"Aw, you know how it is, Biff, they moved in on the racket and what could I do? I see they got you—"

"Clean got me. Sarah blew the whistle on me."

"Told you she wouldn't put up with you messing around. Who's your chum?"

"Name's Mark. He's learning. Hey, Goober, what can you do for me?"

"Funny you should ask. Maybe I got something. Want to enlist?"

"Hell, they don't want me. I tried back on Luna. Too old."

Horrigan nodded. "Yeah, but the Purser's gang needs men. Freakie killed twenty crewmen yesterday. Recruits. This geek opened an air lock and nobody stopped him. That's why you're out here swabbing. Look, Biff, we're headed for a long patrol after we drop you guys on Tanith. Maybe I can fix it."

"No harm in trying. Mark, you lost anything on Tanith?"

"No." But I don't want to join the CD Navy, either. Only why not? He tried to copy his friend's easy indifference. "Can't be worse than where we are."

"Right," Horrigan said. "We'll go see the Purser's middie. That okay, mate?" he asked the Marine.

The Marine shrugged. "Okay by me."

Horrigan led the way forward. Mark felt sick with excitement. Getting out of the prison compartment suddenly became the most important thing in his life.

Midshipman Greschin was not surprised to find two prisoners ready to join the Navy. He questioned them for a few minutes. Then he studied Dugan's records on the readout screen. "You have been in space before, but there is nothing on your record—"

"I never said I'd been out."

"No, but you have. Are you a deserter?"

"No," Dugan said.

Greschin shrugged. "If you are, we'll find out. If not, we don't care. We are short of hands, and I see no reason why you cannot be enlisted. I will call Lieutenant Breslov."

Breslov was fifteen years older than his midshipman. He looked over Dugan's print-out. Then he examined Mark's. "I can take Dugan," he said. "Not you, Fuller."

"But why?" Mark asked.

Breslov shrugged. "You are a rebel, and you have high intelligence. So it says here. There are officers who will take the risk of recruiting those like you, but I am not one of them. We cannot use you in this ship."

"Oh." Mark turned to go.

"Wait a minute, kid." Dugan looked at the officer. "Thanks, Lieutenant, but maybe I better stick with my buddy—"

"No, don't do that," Mark said. He felt a wave of gratitude toward the older man. Dugan's offer seemed the finest thing anyone had ever tried to do for him.

"Who'll look out for ya? You'll get your throat cut."

"Maybe not. I've learned a lot."

Breslov stood. "Your sentiment for your friends is admirable, but you are wasting my time. Are you enlisting?"

"He is," Mark said. "Thank you, Lieutenant." He followed

the Marine guard back to the corridor and began washing the bulkhead, scrubbing savagely, trying to forget his misery and despair. It was all so unfair!

V

Tanith was hot, steaming jungle under a perpetual orange and gray cloud cover. The gravity was too high and the humidity was almost unbearable. Mark had no chance to see the planet. The ship landed at night, and the convicts were marched between tall fences into a concrete building with no outside windows. It was sparsely furnished and clearly intended only for short-term occupancy.

The exercise yard was a square in the center of the massive building. It was a relief to have space to move around in after the crowded ship, but shortly after they were allowed in the yard a violent rainstorm drove them inside the prison building. Even with the storm the place was sweltering. Tanith's gravity seemed ready to crush him.

The next day he was herded through medical processing, immunization, identification, a meaningless classification interview, and both psychological and aptitude tests. They ran from one task to the next, then stood in long lines or simply waited around. On the fourth day he was taken from the detention pen to an empty adobe-walled room with rough wooden furniture. The guards left him there. The sensation of being alone was exhilarating.

He looked up warily when the door opened. "Biff!"

"Hi, kid. Got something for you." Dugan was dressed in the blue dungarees of the CD Navy. He glanced around guiltily. "You left this with me and I run it up a bit." He held out a fistful of CoDominium scrip. "Go on, take it, I can get more and you can't. Look we're pullin' out pretty soon, and . . ."

"It's all right," Mark said. But it wasn't all right. He hadn't known how much friendship meant to him until he'd been separated from Dugan; now, seeing him in the Navy uniform and knowing that Dugan was headed away from this horrible place, Mark hated his former friend. "I'll get along."

"Damned right you will! Stop sniffing about how unfair

everything is and wait your chance. You'll get one. Look, you're a young kid and everything seems like it's forever, but—" Dugan fell silent and shook his head ruefully. "Not that you need fatherly advice from me. Or that it'd do any good. But things end, Mark. The day ends. So do weeks and months."

"Yeah. Sure." They said more meaningless things, and Dugan left. Now I'm completely alone, Mark thought. It was a crushing thought. Some of the speeches he'd heard in his few days in college kept rising up to haunt him. *"Die Gedanken, Sie sind frei."* Yeah. Sure. A man's thoughts were always free, and no one could enslave a free man, and the heaviest chains and darkest dungeons could never cage the spirit. Bullshit. I'm a slave. If I don't do what they tell me, they'll hurt me until I do. And I'm too damned scared of them. But something else he'd heard was more comforting. "Slaves have no rights, and thus have no obligations."

That, by God, fits. I don't owe anybody a thing. Nobody here, and none of those bastards on Earth. I do what I have to do and I look out for number-one and rape the rest of 'em.

There was no prison, or rather the entire planet was a prison. As he'd suspected, the main CD penal building was intended only for classification and assignment, a holding pen to keep prisoners until they were sold off to wealthy planters. There were a lot of rumors about the different places you might be sent to: big company farms run like factories, where it was said that few convicts ever lived to finish out their terms; industrial plants near cities, which was supposed to be soft duty because as soon as you got trusty status, you could get passes into town; town work, the best assignment of all; and the biggest category, lonely plantations out in the sticks where owners could do anything they wanted and generally did.

The pen began to empty as the men were shipped out. Then came Mark's turn. He was escorted into an interview room and given a seat. It was the second time in months that he'd been alone and he enjoyed the solitude. There were voices from the next room.

"Why do you not keep him, *hein?*"

"Immature. No reason to be loyal to the CD."

"Or to me."

"Or to you. And too smart to be a dumb cop. You might make a foreman out of him. The governor's interested in this one, Ludwig. He keeps track of all the high-IQ types. Look, you take this one, I owe you. I'll see you get good hands."

"Okay. *Ja.* Just remember that when you get in some

with muscles and no brains, *hein?* Okay, we look at your genius."

Who the hell were they talking about? Mark wondered. Me? Compared to most of the others in the ship, I guess you could call me a genius, but—

The door opened. Mark stood quickly. The guards liked you to do that.

"Fuller," the captain said. "This is Herr Ewigfeuer. You'll work for him. His place is a country club."

The planter was heavy-set, with thick jowls. He needed a shave, and his shorts and khaki shirt were stained with sweat. "So you are the new convict I take to my nice farm." He eyed Mark coldly. "He will do, he will do. Okay, we go now, *ja?*"

"Now?" Mark said.

"Now, *ja,* you think all day I have? I can stay in Whiskeytown while my foreman lets the hands eat everything and lay around not working? Give me the papers, Captain."

The captain took a sheaf of papers from a folder. He scrawled across the bottom, then handed Mark a pen. "Sign here."

Mark started to read the documents. The captain laughed. "Sign it, goddamit. We don't have all day."

Mark shrugged and scribbled his name. The captain handed Ewigfeuer two copies and indicated a door. They went through the adobe corridors to a guardroom at the end. The planter handed the guards a copy of the document and the door was opened.

The heat outside struck Mark like a physical blow. It had been hot enough inside, but the thick earthen walls had protected him from the worst; now it was almost unbearable. There was no sun, but the clouds were bright enough to hurt his eyes. Ewigfeuer put on dark glasses. He led the way to a shop across from the prison and bought Mark a pair of dark glasses and a cap with a visor. "Put these on," he commanded. "You are no use if you are blind. Now come."

They walked through busy streets. The sky hung dull orange, an eternal sunset. Sweat sprang from Mark's brow and trickled down inside his coveralls. He wished he had shorts. Nearly everyone in town wore them.

They passed grimy shops and open stalls. There were sidewalk displays of goods for sale, nearly all crudely made or Navy surplus or black-marketed goods stolen from CD storerooms. Strange animals pulled carts through the streets and there were no automobiles at all.

A team of horses splashed mud on Ewigfeuer's legs. The fat planter shook his fist at the driver. The teamster ignored him.

"Have you owned horses?" Ewigfeuer demanded.

"No," Mark said. "I hadn't expected to see any here."

"Horses make more horses. Tractors do not," the planter said. "Also, with horses and jackasses you get mules. Better than tractors. Better than the damned stormand beasts. Stormands do not like men." He pointed to one of the unlikely animals. It looked like a cross between a mule and a moose, with wide, splayed feet and a sad look that turned vicious whenever anyone got near it. It was tied to a rail outside one of the shops.

There were more people than Mark had expected. They seemed to divide into three classes. There were those who tended the shops and stalls and who smiled unctuously when the planter passed. Most of those wore white canvass jackets. Then there were others, some with white canvass jackets and some without, who strode purposefully through the muddy streets and finally there were those who wandered aimlessly or sat on the street corners staring vacantly.

"What are they waiting for?" Mark said. He hadn't meant to say it aloud, but Ewigfeuer heard him.

"They wait to die," the planter said. "*Ja,* they think something else will come to save them. They will find something to steal, maybe, so they live another week, another month, a year even; but they are waiting to die. And they are white men!" This seemed their ultimate crime to Ewigfeuer.

"You might expect this of the blacks," the planter said. "But no, the blacks work, or they go to the bush and live there—not like civilized men, perhaps, but they live. Not these. They wait to die. It was a cruel day when their sentences ended."

"Yeah, sure," Mark said, but he made sure the planter didn't hear him. There was another group sitting on benches near a small open square. They looked as if they had not moved since morning, since the day before, or ever; that when the orange sky fell dark, they would be there yet. Mark mopped his brow with his sleeve. Heat lay across Whiskeytown so that it was an effort to move, but the planter hustled him along the street, his short legs moving rapidly through the mud patches.

"And what happens if I just run?" Mark asked.

Ewigfeuer laughed. "Go ahead. You think they will not catch you? Where will you go? You have no papers. Perhaps you buy some if you have money. Perhaps what you buy is not good enough. And when they catch you, it is not to my nice farm they send you. It will be to some awful place. Run, I will not chase you. I am too old and too fat."

Mark shrugged and walked along with Ewigfeuer. He noticed

that for all his careless manner, the fat man did not let Mark get behind him.

They rounded a corner and came to a large empty space. A helicopter stood at the near edge. There were others in the lot. A white jacketed man with a rifle sat under an umbrella watching them. Ewigfeuer threw the man some money and climbed into the nearest chopper.

He strapped himself in and waited for Mark to do the same. Then he used the radio.

"Weather service, Ewigfeuer 351." Ewigfeuer listened, nodded in satisfaction, and gunned the engines. The helicopter lifted them high above the city.

Whiskeytown was an ugly sprawl across a plateau. The broad streets of Tanith's capital lay on another low hill beyond it. Both hills rose directly out of the jungle. When they were higher, Mark could see that the plateau was part of a ridge on a peninsula; the sea around it was green with yellow streaks. The buildings on the other hill looked cleaner and better made than those in Whiskeytown. In the distance was a large square surrounded by buildings taller than the others.

"Government House," Ewigfeuer shouted above the engine roar. "Where the governor dreams up new ways to make it impossible for honest planters to make a profit."

Beyond the town were brown hills rising above ugly green jungles. Hours later there was no change—jungle to the right and the green and yellow sea to the left. Mark had seen no roads and only a few houses; all of those were in clusters, low adobe buildings atop low brown hills. "Is the whole planet jungle?" he asked.

"*Ja,* jungles, marshes, bad stuff. People can live in the hills. Below is green hell. Weem's beast, killer things like tortoises, crocodiles so big you don't believe them and they run faster than you. Nobody runs far in that."

A perfect prison, Mark thought. He stared out at the sea. There were boats out there. Ewigfeuer followed his gaze and laughed.

"Some damn fools try to make a few credits fishing. Maybe smart at that, they get killed fast, they don't wait for tax farmers to take everything they make. You heard of Loch Ness monster? On Tanith we got something makes Earth nessies look like an earthworm."

They flew over another cluster of adobe buildings. Ewigfeuer used the radio to talk to the people below. They spoke a language Mark didn't know. It didn't seem like German, but he wasn't sure. Then they crossed another seemingly endless stretch of jungle. Finally a new group of buildings was in sight ahead.

The plantation was no different from the others they had seen. There was a cluster of brown adobe buildings around one larger whitewashed wooden house at the very top of the hill. Cultivated fields lay around that on smaller hills. The fields blended into jungle at the edges. Men were working in the fields.

It would be easy to run away, Mark thought. Too easy. It must be stupid to try, or there would be fences. Wait, he thought. Wait and learn. I owe nothing. To anyone. Wait for a chance—

—a chance for what? He pushed the thought away.

The foreman was tall and crudely handsome. He wore dirty white shorts and a sun helmet, and there was a pistol buckled on his belt.

"You look after this one, *ja*," Ewigfeuer said. "One of the governor's pets. They say he has brains enough to make supervisor. We will see. Mark Fuller, three years."

"Yes, sir. Come on, Mark Fuller, three years." The foreman turned and walked away. After a moment Mark followed. They went past rammed earth buildings and across a sea of mud. The buildings had been sprayed with some kind of plastic and shone dully. "You'll need boots," the foreman said. "And a new outfit. I'm Curt Morgan. Get along with me and you'll be happy. Cross me and you're in trouble. Got that?"

"Yes, sir."

"You don't call me sir unless I tell you to. Right now you call me Curt. If you need help, ask me. Maybe I can give you good advice. If it don't cost me much, I will." They reached a rectangular one-story building like the others. "This'll be your bunkie."

The inside was a long room with places for thirty men. Each place had a bunk, a locker and an area two meters by three of clear space. After the ship, it seemed palatial. The inside walls were sprayed with the same plastic material as the outside; it kept insects from living in the dirt walls. Some of the men had cheap pictures hung above their bunks: pinups, mostly, but one had the Virgin of Guadalupe, and in one corner area there were charcoal sketches of men and women working, and an unfinished oil painting.

There were a dozen men in the room. Some were sprawled on their bunks. One was knitting something elaborate, and a small group at the end were playing cards. One of the card players, a small ferret-faced man, left the game.

"Your new man," Curt said. "Mark Fuller, three years. Fuller, this is your bunkie leader. His name is Lewis. Lew, get the kid bunked and out of those prison slops."

"Sure, Curt." Lewis eyed Mark carefully. "About the right size for Jose's old outfit. The gear's all clean."

"Want to do that?" Curt asked. "Save you some money."

Mark stared helplessly.

The two men laughed. "You better give him the word, Lew," Curt Morgan said. "Fuller, I'd take him up on the gear. Let me know what he charges you, right? He won't squeeze you too bad." There was laughter from the other men in the bunkie as the foreman left.

Lewis pointed out a bunk in the center. "Jose was there, kid. Left his whole outfit when he took the green way out. Give you the whole lot for, uh, fifty credits."

And now what? Mark wondered. Best not to show him I've got any money. "I don't have that much—"

"Hell, you sign a chit fur it," Lewis said. "The old man pays a credit a day and found."

"Who do I get a chit from?"

"You get it from me." Lewis narrowed watery eyes. They looked enormous through his thick glasses. "You thinking about something, kid? You don't want to try it."

"I'm not trying anything. I just don't understand—"

"Sure. You just remember I'm in charge. Anybody skips out, I get their gear. Me. Nobody else. Jose had a good outfit, worth fifty credits easy—"

"Bullshit," one of the cardplayers said. "Not worth more'n thirty and you know it."

"Shut up. Sure, you could do better in Whiskeytown, but not here. Look, Morgan said take care of you. I'll sell you the gear for forty. Deal?"

"Sure."

Lewis gave him a broad smile. "You'll get by, kid. Here's your key." He handed Mark a magnokey and went back to the card game.

Mark wondered who had copies. It wasn't something you could duplicate without special equipment; the magnetic spots had to be in just the right places. Ewigfeuer would have one, of course. Who else? No use worrying about it.

He inspected his new possessions. Two pairs of shorts. Tee shirts, underwear, socks, all made of some synthetic. Comb, razor and blades. Soap. Used toothbrush. Mark scowled at it, then laughed to himself. No point in being squeamish.

Some of the clothes were dirty. Others seemed clean, but Mark decided he would have to wash them all. Not now, though. He tucked his money into the toe of a sock and threw the rest of his clothes on top of it, then locked the whole works into the locker. He wondered what he should do with the money; he had nearly three hundred credits, ten month's wages at a credit a day—enough to be killed for.

It bothered him all the way to the shower, but after that, the unlimited water, new bar of soap, and a good razor were such pleasures that he didn't think about anything else.

VI

The borshite plant resembles an artichoke in appearance: tall, spiky leaves rising from a central crown, with one flowerbearing stalk jutting upward to a height of a meter and a half. It is propagated by bulbs; in spring the previous year's crop is dug up and the delicate bulbs carefully separated, then each replanted. Weeds grow in abundance and must be pulled out by hand. The jungle constantly grows inward to reclaim the high ground that men cultivate. Herbivores eat the crops unless the fields are patrolled.

Mark learned that and more within a week. The work was difficult and the weather was hot, but neither was unbearable. The rumors were true: compared to most places you could be sent, Ewigfeuer's plantation was a country club. Convicts schemed to get there. Ewigfeuer demanded hard work, but he was fair.

That made it all the more depressing for Mark. If this was the easy way to do time, what horrors waited if he made a mistake? Ewigfeuer held transfer as his ultimate threat, and Mark found himself looking for ways to keep his master pleased. He disgusted himself—but there was nothing else to do.

He had never been more alone. He had nothing in common with the other men. His jokes were never funny. He had no interest in their stories. He learned to play poker so well that he was resented when he played. They didn't want a tight player who could take their money. Once he was accused of cheating and although everyone knew he hadn't, he was beaten and his winnings taken. After that he avoided the games.

The work occupied only his hands, not his mind. There were no veedisk readers in the barracks. A few convicts had small radios but the only station they could tune in played nothing but sad country western music. Mark shuddered at the thought of getting to like it.

There was little to do but brood. I wanted power, he thought.

We were playing at it. A game. But the police weren't playing, and now I've become a slave. When I get back, I'll know more of how this game is played. I'll show them.

But he knew he wouldn't, not really. He was learning nothing here.

Some of the convicts spent their entire days and nights stoned into tranquility. Borshite plants were the source of borloi, and half the Citizens of the United States depended on borloi to get through each day; the government supplied it to them, and any government that failed in the shipments would not last long. It worked as well on Tanith, and Herr Ewigfeuer was generous with both pipes and borloi. You could be stoned for half a credit a day. Mark tried that route, but he did not like what it did to him. They were stealing three years of his life, but he wouldn't cooperate and make it easier.

His college friends had talked a lot about the dignity of labor. Mark didn't find it dignified at all. Why not get stoned and stay that way? What am I doing that's important? Why not go out of being and get it over? Let the routine wash over me, drown in it—

There were frequent fights. They had rules. If a man got hurt so that he couldn't work, both he and the man he fought with had to make up the lost work time. It tended to keep the injuries down and discouraged broken bones. Whenever there was a fight, everyone turned out to watch.

It gave Mark time to himself. He didn't like being alone, but he didn't like watching fights, especially since he might be drawn into one himself—

The men shouted encouragement to the fighters. Mark lay on his bunk. He had liquor but didn't want to drink. He kept thinking about taking a drink, just one, it will help me get to sleep—and you know what you're doing to yourself—and why not?

The man was small and elderly. Mark knew he lived in quarters near the big house. He came into the bunkie and glanced around. The lights had not been turned on, and he failed to see Mark. He looked furtively about again, then stooped to try locker lids, looking for one that was open. He reached Mark's locker, opened it, and felt inside. His hand found cigarettes and the bottle—

He felt or heard Mark and looked up. "Uh, good evening."

"Good evening." The man seemed cool enough, although he risked the usual punishments men mete out to thieves in barracks.

"Are you bent on calling your mates?" The watery eyes darted around looking for an escape. "I don't seem to have any defense."

"If you did have one, what would it be?"

"When you are as old as I am and in for life, you take what you can. I am an alcoholic, and I steal to buy drink."

"Why not smoke borloi?"

"It does little for me." The old man's hands were shaking. He looked lovingly at the bottle of gin that he'd taken from Mark's locker.

"Oh, hell, have a drink," Mark said.

"Thank you." He drank eagerly, in gulps.

Mark retrieved his bottle. "I don't see you in the fields."

"No. I work with the accounts. Herr Ewigfeuer has been kind enough to keep me, but not so kind as to pay enough to—"

"If you will keep the work records, you could sell favors."

"Certainly. For a time. Until I was caught. And then what? It is not much of a life that I have, but I want to keep it." He stood for a moment. "Surprising, isn't it? But I do."

"You talk rather strangely," Mark said.

"The stigmata of education. You see Richard Henry Tappinger, Ph.D., generally called Taps. Formerly holder of the Bates Chair of History and Sociology at Yale University."

"And why are you on Tanith?" Prisoners do not ask that question, but Mark could do as he liked. He held the man's life in his hands: a word, a call, and the others would amuse themselves with Tappinger. And why don't I call them? Mark shuddered at the notion, but it didn't quite leave his consciousness.

Tappinger didn't seem annoyed. "Liquor, young girls, their lovers, and an old fool are an explosive combination. You don't mind if I am more specific? I spend a good part of my life being ashamed of myself. Could I have another drink?"

"I suppose."

"You have the stigmata about you as well. You were a student?"

"Not for long."

"But worthy of education. And generous as well. Your name is Fuller. I have the records, and I recall your case."

The fight outside ground to a close, and the men came back into the barracks. Lewis was carrying an unconscious man to the showers. He handed him over to others when he saw Tappinger.

"You sneaky bastard, I told you what'd happen if I found you in my bunkie! What'd he steal, Fuller?"

"Nothing. I gave him a drink."

"Yeah? Well, keep him out of here. You want to talk to him, you do it outside."

"Right." Mark took his bottle and followed Tappinger out. It was hot inside and the men were talking about the fight. Mark followed Tappinger across the quad. They stayed away from the women's barracks. Mark had no friends in there and couldn't afford any other kind of visit—at least not very often, and he was always disturbed afterwards. None of the women seemed attractive or to care about themselves.

"So. The two outcasts gather together," Tappinger said. "Two pink monkeys among the browns."

"Maybe I should resent that."

"Why? Do you have much in common with them? Or do you resent the implication that you have more in common with me?"

"I don't know. I don't know anything. I'm just passing time. Waiting until this is over."

"And what will you do then?"

They found a place to sit. The local insects didn't bother them; the taste was wrong. There was a faint breeze from the west. The jungle noises came with it, snorts and grunts and weird calls.

"What can I do?" Mark asked. "Get back to Earth and—"

"You will never get back to Earth," Tappinger said. "Or if you do, you will be one of the first ever. Unless you have someone to buy your passage?"

"That's expensive."

"Precisely."

"But they're supposed to take us back!" Mark felt all his carefully built defenses begin to crumble. He lived for the end of the three years—and now—

"The regulations say so, and the convicts talk about going home, but it does not happen. Earth does not want rebels. It would disturb the comfortable life most have. No, you are unlikely to leave here, and if you do ship out, it will be to another colony. Unless you are very rich."

So I am here forever. "So what else is there? What do ex-cons do here?"

Tappinger shrugged. "Sign up as laborers. Start their own plantations. Go into government service. Start a small business. You see Tanith as a slave world, which it is, but it will not always be that. Some of you, people like you, will build it into something else, something better or worse, but certainly different."

"Yeah. Sure. The Junior Pioneers have arrived."

"What do you think happens to involuntary colonists?" Tappinger asked. "Or did you never think of them? Most people on Earth don't look very hard at the price of keeping their wealth and their clean air and clean oceans. But the only difference between you and someone shipped by BuRelock is that you came in a slightly more comfortable ship, and you will put in three years here before they turn you out to fend for yourself. Yes, I definitely suggest the government services for you. You could rise quite high."

"Work for those slaving bastards? I'd rather starve!"

"No, you wouldn't. Nor would many others. It is easier to say that than to do it."

Mark stared into the darkness.

"Why so grim? There are opportunities here. The new governor is trying to reform some of the abuses. Of course he is caught in the system just as we are. He must export his quota of borloi and miracle drugs, and pay the taxes demanded of him. He must keep up production. The Navy demands it."

"The Navy?"

Tappinger smiled in the dark. "You would be surprised at just how much of the CD Navy's operations are paid for by the profits from the Tanith drug trade."

"It doesn't surprise me at all. Thieves. Bastards. But it's stupid. A treadmill, with prisons to pay for themselves and the damned fleet—"

"Neither stupid nor new. The Soviets have done it for nearly two hundred years, with the proceeds of labor camps paying for the secret police. And our tax farming scheme is even older. It dates back to old Rome. Profits from other planets support BuRelock. Tanith supports the Navy."

"Damn the Navy."

"Ah, no, don't do that. Bless it instead. Without the CD Fleet, the Earth governments would be at each other's throats in a moment. They very nearly are now. And since they won't pay for the Navy, and the Navy is very much needed to keep peace on Earth, why, we must continue to work. See what a noble task we perform as we weed the borloi fields?"

Unbearably hot spring became intolerably hot summer, and the work decreased steadily. The borshite plants were nearly as high as a man's waist and were able to defend themselves against most weeds and predators. The fields needed watching but little else.

To compensate for the easier work, the weather was sticky hot, with warm fog rolling in from the coast. The skies turned from orange to dull gray. Twice the plantations and fields were lashed by hurricanes. The borshite plants lay flattened, but soon recovered; and after each hurricane came a few brief hours of clear skies when Mark could see the stars.

With summer came easy sex. Men and women could visit in the evenings, and with suitable financial arrangements with bunkie leaders, all night. The pressures of the barracks eased. Mark found the easier work more attractive than the women. When he couldn't stand it any longer, he'd pay for a few minutes of frantic relief, then try not to think about sex for as long as he could.

His duties were simple. Crownears, muskrat-sized animals that resembled large shrews, would eat unprotected borshite plants. They had to be driven away. They were stupid animals, and ravenous, but not very dangerous unless a swarm of them could catch a man mired down in the mud. A man with a spear could keep them out of the crops.

There were other animals to watch for. Weem's Beast, named for the first man to survive a meeting with one, was the worst. The crownears were its natural prey, but it would attack almost anything that moved. Weem's Beast looked like a mole but was over a meter long. Instead of a prehensile snout, it had a fully articulated grasping member with talons and pseudo-eyes. Man approached holes very carefully on Tanith; the Beast was fond of lying just below the surface and came out with astonishing speed.

It wouldn't usually leave the jungle to attack a man on high ground.

Mark patrolled the fields, and Curt Morgan made rounds on horseback. In the afternoons Morgan would sit with Mark and share his beer ration, and the cold beer and lack of work was almost enough to make life worth living again.

Sometimes there was a break in the weather, and a cooler breeze would blow across the fields. Mark sat with his back to a tree, enjoying the comparatively cool day, drinking his beer ration. Morgan sat next to him.

"Curt, what will you do when you finish your sentence?" Mark asked.

"Finished two years ago. Two Tanith, three Earth."

"Then why are you still here?"

Morgan shrugged. "What else do I know how to do? I'm saving some money; one day I'll have a place of my own." He shifted his position and fired his carbine toward the jungle.

"I swear them things get more nerve every summer. This is all I know. I can't save enough to buy into the tax farm syndicate."

"Could you squeeze people that way?"

"If I had to. Them or me. Tax collectors get rich."

"Sure. Jesus, there's no goddamn hope for anything, is there? The whole deck's stacked." Mark finished his beer.

"Where isn't it?" Morgan demanded. "You think it's tough now, you ought to have been here before the new governor came. Place they stuck me—my sweet lord, they worked us! Charged for everything we ate or wore, and you open your mouth, it's another month on your sentence. Enough to drive a man into the green."

"Uh—Curt—are there—"

"Don't get ideas. I'd hate to take the dogs and come find you. Find your corpse, more likely. Yeah, there's men out in the green. Live like rats. I'd rather be under sentence again than live like the Free Staters."

The thought excited Mark. A Free State! It would have to be like the places Shirley and her friends had talked about, with equality, and there'd be no tax farmers in a free society. He thought of the needs of free men. They would live hard and be poor because they were fugitives, but they would be free! He built the Free State in his imagination until it was more real than Ewigfeuer's plantation.

The next day the crownears were very active, and Curt Morgan brought another worker to Mark's field. They rode up together on the big Percheron horses brought as frozen embryos from Earth and repeatedly bred for even wider feet to keep them above the eternal mud. The newcomer was a girl. Mark had seen her before, but never met her.

"Brought you a treat," Curt said. "This is Juanita. Juanny, if this clown gives you trouble, I'll break him in half. Be back in an hour. Got your trumpet?"

Mark indicated the instrument.

"Keep it handy. Them things are restless out there. I think there's a croc around. And porkers. Keep your eyes open." Curt rode off toward the next field.

Mark stood in embarrassed silence. The girl was younger than Mark, and sweaty. Her hair hung down in loose blonde strings. Her eyes had dark circles under them, and her face was dirty. She was built more like a wiry boy than a girl. She was also the most beautiful girl he'd ever seen.

"Hi," Mark said. He cursed himself. Shyness went with civilization, not a prison!

"Hi yourself. You're in Lewis's bunkie."

"Yes. I haven't seen you before. Except at Mass." Each month a priest of the Ecumenical Church came to the plantation. Mark had never attended services, but he'd watched idly from a distance.

"Usually work in the big house. Sure hot, isn't it?"

He agreed it was hot and was lost again. What should I say? "You're lovely" is obvious, even if I do think it's true. "Let's go talk to your bunkie leader" isn't too good an idea even if it's what I want to say. Besides, if she lives in the big house, she won't have one. "How long do you have?"

"Another two. Until I'm nineteen. They still run sentences on Earth time. I'm eleven, really." There was more silence. "You don't talk much, do you?"

"I don't know what to say. I'm sorry—"

"It's okay. Most of the men jabber away like porshons. Trying to talk me into something, you know?"

"Oh."

"Yeah. But I never have. I'm a member of the Church. Confirmed and everything." She looked at him and grinned impishly. "So that makes me a dumb hymn singer, and what's left to talk about?"

"I remember wishing I was you," Mark said. He laughed. "Not quite what I meant to say. I mean, I watched you at Masses. You looked happy. Like you had something to live for."

"Well, of course. We all have something to live for. Must have, people sure try hard to stay alive. When I get out of here, I'm going to ask the padre to let me help him. Be a nun, maybe."

"Don't you want to marry?"

"Who? A Con? That's what my mother did, and look. I got 'apprenticed' until I was nineteen Earth years old because I was born to convicts. No kids of mine'll have that happen to 'em!"

"You could marry a free man."

"They're all pretty old by the time they finish. And not worth much. To themselves or anybody else. You proposin' to me?"

He laughed and she laughed with him, and the afternoon was more pleasant than any he could remember since leaving Earth.

"I was lucky," she told him. "Old man Ewigfeuer traded for me. Place I was born on, the planter'd be selling tickets for me now." She stared at the dirt. "I've seen girls they did that with. They don't like themselves much after a while."

They heard the shrill trumpets in other fields. Mark scanned the jungle in front of him. Nothing moved. Juanita continued to talk. She asked him about Earth. "It's hard to think about that place," she said. "I hear people live all bunched up."

He told her about cities. "There are twenty million people in the city I come from." He told her of the concrete Welfare Islands at the edges of the cities.

She shuddered. "I'd rather live on Tanith than like that. It's a wonder all the people on Earth don't burn it down and live in the swamps."

Evening came sooner than he expected. After supper he fell into an introspective mood. He hadn't wanted a day to last for a long time. It's silly to think this way, he told himself.

But he was twenty years old, she was nearly seventeen, and there wasn't anyone else to think about. That night he dreamed about her.

He saw her often as the summer wore on. She had no education, and Mark began teaching her to read. He scratched letters in the ground and used some of his money to buy lurid adventure stories. He had no access to veedisk screens, and the only printed works available in the barracks were sex magazines and adventure novels printed on paper so cheap that it soon went limp in the damp Tanith heat.

Juanita learned quickly. She seemed to enjoy Mark's company and often arranged to be assigned to the same field that he was. They talked about everything: Earth, and how it wasn't covered with swamps. He told her of personal fliers in blue skies, and sailing on the Pacific, and the island coves he'd explored. She thought he was making most of it up.

Their only quarrels came when he complained of how unfair life was. She laughed at him. "I was born with a sentence," she told him. "You lived in a fine house and had your own 'copter and a boat, and you went to school. If I'm not whining, why should you, Mr. Taxpayer?"

He wanted to tell her she was unfair too, but stopped himself. Instead he told her of smog and polluted waters, and sprawling cities. "They've got the pollution licked, though," he said. "And the population's going down. What with the licensing, and BuRelock—"

She said nothing, and Mark couldn't finish the sentence. Juanita stared at the empty jungles. "Wish I could see a blue sky some day. I can't even imagine that, so you must be tellin' the truth."

He did not often see her in the evenings. She kept to herself or worked in the big house. Sometimes, though, she would walk with Curt Morgan or sit with him on the porch of the big house, and when she did, Mark would buy a bottle of gin and find Tappinger. It was no good being alone then.

The old man would deliver long lectures in a dry monotone that nearly put Mark to sleep, but then he'd ask questions that upset any view of the universe that Mark had ever had.

"You might make a passable sociologist some day," Tappinger said. "Ah, well, they say the best university is a log with a student at one end and a professor at the other. I doubt they had me in mind, but we have that, anyway."

"All I seem to learn is that things are rotten. Everything's set up wrong," Mark said.

Tappinger shook his head. "There has never been a society in which someone did not think there had to be a better deal—for himself. The trick is to see that those who want a better way enough to do something about it can either rise within the system or are rendered harmless by it. Which, of course, Earth does—warriors join the Navy. Malcontents are shipped to the colonies. The cycle is closed. Drugs for the Citizens, privileges for the taxpayers, peace for all thanks to the Fleet—and slavery for malcontents. Or death. The colonies use up people."

"I guess it's stable, then."

"Hardly. If Earth does not destroy herself—and from the rumors I hear, the nations are at each other's throats despite all the Navy can do—why, they have built a pressure cooker out here that will one day destroy the old home world. Look at what we have. Fortune hunters, adventurers, criminals, rebels—and all selected for survival abilities. The lid cannot stay on."

They saw Juanita and Curt Morgan walking around the big house, and Mark winced. Juanita had grown during the summer. Now, with her hair combed and in clean clothes, she was so lovely that it hurt to look at her. Taps smiled. "I see my star pupil has found another interest. Cheer up, lad, when you finish here, you will find employment. You can have your pick of convict girls. Rent them, or buy one outright."

"I hate slavery!"

Taps shrugged. "As you should. Although you might be surprised what men who say that will do when given the chance. But calm yourself, I meant buy a wife, not a whore."

"But damn it, you don't buy wives! Women aren't things!"

Tappinger smiled softly. "I tend to forget just what a blow it is to you young people. You expect everything to be as it was on Earth. Yet you are here because you were not satisfied with your world."

"It was rotten."

"Possibly. But you had to search for the rot. Here you cannot avoid it."

On such nights it took Mark a long time to get to sleep.

VII

The harvest season was approaching. The borshite plants stood in full flower, dull-red splashes against brown hills and green jungles, and the field buzzed with insects. Nature had solved the problem of propagation without inbreeding on Tanith and fifty other worlds in the same way as on Earth.

The buzzing insects attracted insectivores, and predators chased those; close to harvest time there was little work, but the fields had to be watched constantly. Once again house and processing-shed workers joined the field hands, and Mark had many days with Juanita.

She was slowly driving him insane. He knew she couldn't be as naive as she pretended to be. She had to know how he felt and what he wanted to do, but she gave him no opportunities.

Sometimes he was sure she was teasing him. "Why don't you ever come to see me in the evenings?" she asked one day.

"You know why. Curt is always there."

"Well, sure, but he don't—doesn't own my contract. 'Course, if you're scared of him—"

"You're bloody right I'm scared of him. He could fold me up for glue. Not to mention what happens when the foreman's mad at a con. Besides, I thought you liked him."

"Sure. So what?"

"He told me he was going to marry you one day."

"He tells everybody that. He never told me, though."

Mark noted glumly that she'd stopped talking about becoming a nun.

"Of course, Curt's the only man who even says he's going to—Mark, *look out!*"

Mark saw a blur at the edge of his vision and whirled with his spear. Something was charging toward him. "Get behind me and run!" he shouted. "Keep me in line with it and get out of here."

She moved behind him and he heard her trumpet blare, but she wasn't running. Mark had no more time to think about her. The animal was nearly a meter and a half long, built square on thick legs and splayed feet. The snout resembled an earth wart-hog's, with four upthrusting tusks, and it had a thin tail that lashed as it ran.

"Porker," Juanita said softly. She was just behind him. "Sometimes they'll charge a man. Like this. Don't get it excited, maybe it'll go away."

Mark was perfectly willing to let the thing alone. It looked as if it weighed as much as he did. Its broad feet and small claws gave it a better footing than hobnails would give a man. It circled them warily at a distance of three meters. Mark turned carefully to keep facing it. He held the spear aimed at its throat. "I told you to get out of here," Mark said.

"Sure. There's usually two of those things." She spoke very softly. "I'm scared to blow this trumpet again. Wish Curt would get here with his gun." As she spoke, they heard gunshots. They sounded very far away.

"Mark," Juanita whispered urgently. "There is another one. I'm getting back to back with you."

"All right." He didn't dare look away from the beast in front of him. What did it want? It moved slowly toward him, halting just beyond the thrusting range of the spear. Then it dashed forward, screaming a sound that could never have come from an Earthly pig.

Mark jabbed at it with his spear. It flinched from the point and ran past. Mark turned to follow it and saw the other beast advancing on Juanita. She had slipped in the mud and was down, trying frantically to get to her feet, and the porker was running toward her.

Mark gave an animal scream of pure fury. He slid in the mud but kept his feet and charged forward, screaming again as he stabbed with his spear and felt it slip into the thick hide. The porker shoved against him, and Mark fell into the mud. He desperately held the spear, but the beast walked steadily forward. The point went through the hide on the back, and came out again, the shaft sliding between skin and meat, and the impaled animal advancing inexorably up the shaft. The tusks neared his manhood. Mark heard himself whimpering in fear. "I can't hold him!" he shouted. "Run!"

She didn't run. She got to her feet and shoved her spear down the snarling throat, then thrust forward, forcing the head toward the mud. Mark scrambled to his feet. He looked wildly around for the other animal. It was nowhere in sight, but the pinned porker snarled horribly.

"Mark, honey, take that spear of yours out of him while I hold him," Juanita shouted. "I can't hold long—quick, now."

Mark shook himself out of the trembling fear that paralyzed him. The tusks were moving wickedly. They were nowhere near him, but he could still feel them tearing at his groin.

"Please, honey," Juanita said.

He tugged at the spear, but it wouldn't come free, so he thrust it forward, then ran behind the animal to pull the spear through the loose skin on the porker's back. The shaft came through bloody. His hands slipped but he held the spear and thrust it into the animal, thrust again and again, stabbing in insane fury and shouting, "Die, die, die!"

Morgan didn't come for another half an hour. When he galloped up, they were standing with their arms around each other. Juanita moved slowly away from Mark when Morgan dismounted, but she looked possessively at him.

"That way now?" Morgan asked.

She didn't answer.

"There was a herd of those things in the next field over," Curt said. His voice was apologetic. "Killed three men and a woman. I came as quick as I could."

"Mark killed this one."

"She did. It would have had me—"

"Hold on," Curt said.

"It walked right up the spear," Mark said.

"I've seen 'em do that, all right." Morgan seemed to be choosing his words very carefully. "You two will have to stay on here for awhile. We've lost four hands, and—"

"We'll be all right," Juanita said.

"Yeah." Morgan went back to his mount. "Yeah, I guess you will." He rode off quickly.

Tradition gave Mark and Juanita the carcass, and they feasted with their friends that night. Afterwards Mark and Juanita walked away from the barracks area, and they were gone for a long time.

"Taps, what the hell am I going to do?" Mark demanded. They were outside, in the unexpected cool of a late summer evening. Mark had thought he would never be cool again; now it was almost harvest time. The fall and winter would be short, but Tanith was almost comfortable during those months.

"What is the problem?"

"She's pregnant."

"Hardly surprising. Nor the end of the world. There are many ways to—"

"No. She won't even talk about it. Says it's murder. It's that damned padre. Goddamn church, no wonder they bring that joker around. Makes the slaves contented."

"This is hardly the only activity of the church, but it does have that effect. Well, what is it to you? As you have often pointed out, you have no responsibilities. And certainly you have no legal obligations in this case."

"That's my kid! And she's my—I mean, damn it, I can't just—"

Tappinger smiled grimly. "I remind you that conscience and a sense of ethics are expensive luxuries. But if you are determined to burden yourself with them, let us review your alternatives.

"You can ask Ewigfeuer for permission to marry her. It is likely to be granted. The new governor has ended the mandatory so-called apprenticeship for children born to convicts after next year. Your sentence is not all that long. When it ends, you will be free—"

"To do what? I saw the time-expired men in Whiskeytown."

"There are jobs. There is a whole planetary economy to be built."

"Yeah. Sure. Sweat my balls off for some storekeeper. Or work like Curt Morgan, sweating cons."

Tappinger shrugged. "There are alternatives. Civil service. Or learn the business yourself and become a planter. There is always financing available for those who can produce."

"I'd still be a slaver. I want out of the system. Out of the whole damned thing!"

Tappinger sighed and lifted the bottle to drink. He paused to say, "There are many things we all want. So what?" Then he drained the pint.

"There's another way," Mark said. "A way out of all this."

Tappinger looked up quickly. "Don't even think it! Mark, the Free State you believe in is no more than a dream. The reality is much less, no more than a gang of lawless men who live like animals off what they can steal. Lawless. Men cannot live without laws."

I can damned well live without the kind of laws they have here, Mark thought. And of course they steal. Why shouldn't they? How else can they live?

"And it is unlikely to last in any event. The governor has

brought in a regiment of mercenaries to deal with the Free State."

About what I'd expect, Mark thought. "Why not CD Marines?"

Tappinger shook his head. "A complex issue. The simplest answer is financial. There are not enough CD forces to keep the peace everywhere because the Grand Senate will not appropriate enough money."

"But you said Tanith drug profits go to the Navy—"

"In large part they do. And since that is a lot of money, do you not think others want some of it? The Grand Senate itself envies the Navy's share, for it is money the Senate doesn't control. The Senate sends the Navy anywhere but Tanith, so the planters are squeezed again, to pay for their protection."

And that's fine with me, Mark thought. "Mercenaries can't be much use. They'd rather lie around in barracks and collect their pay." His teachers had told him that.

"Have you ever known any?"

"No, of course not. Look, Taps, I'm tired. I think I better get to bed." He turned and left the old man. To hell with him, Mark thought. Old man, old woman, that's what he is. Not enough guts to get away from here and strike out on his own.

Well, that's fine for him. But I've got bigger things in mind.

The harvest began at the end of the hurricane season. The borshite pods formed and were cut, and the sticky sap collected. The sap was boiled, skimmed, boiled again until it was reduced to a tiny fraction of the bulky plants they had worked all summer to guard.

And Ewigfeuer collapsed on the steps of the big house. Morgan flew him to the Lederle hospital. Curt returned with a young man: Ewigfeuer's son, on leave from his administrative post in the city.

"That old bastard wants to see you outside," Lewis said.

Mark sighed. He was tired from a long day in the fields. He was also tired of Tappinger's eternal lectures on the horrors of the Free State. Still, the man was his only friend. Mark took his bottle and went outside.

Tappinger seized the bottle eagerly. He downed several swallows. His hands shook. "Come with me," he whispered.

Mark followed in confusion. Taps led the way to the shadows near the big house. Juanita was there.

"Mark, honey, I'm scared."

Tappinger took another drink. "The Ewigfeuer boy is trying to raise money," he said. "He storms through the house complaining of all the useless people his father keeps on, and shouts that his father is ruining himself. The hospital bills are very high, it seems. And this place is heavily in debt. He has been selling contracts. He sold hers. For nearly two thousand credits."

"Sold?" Mark said stupidly. "But she has less than two years to go!"

"Yes," Taps said. "There is only one way a planter could expect to make that much back from the purchase of a young and pretty girl."

"God damn them," Mark said. "All right. We've got to get out of here."

"No," Tappinger said. "I've told you why. No, I have a better way. I can forge the old man's signature to a permission form. You can marry Juanita. The forgery will be discovered, but by then—"

"No," Mark said. "Do you think I'll stay to be part of this system? A free society will need good people."

"Mark, please," Tappinger said. "Believe me, it is not what you think it is! How can you live in a place with no rules, you with your ideas of what is fair and what is—"

"Crap. From now on, I take care of myself. And my woman and my child. We're wasting time." He moved toward the stables. Juanita followed.

"Mark, you do not understand," Tappinger protested.

"Shut up. I have to find the guard."

"He's right behind you." Morgan's voice was low and grim. "Don't do anything funny, Mark."

"Where did you come from?"

"I've been watching you for ten minutes. Did you think you could get up to the big house without being seen? You damned fool. I ought to let you go into the green and get killed. But you can't go alone—no, you have to take Juanny with you. I thought you had more sense. We haven't used the whipping post here for a year, but a couple of dozen might wake you up to—" Morgan started to turn as something moved behind him. Then he crumpled. Juanita hit him again with a billet of wood. Morgan fell to the ground.

"I hope he'll be all right," Juanita said. "When he wakes up, Taps, please tell him why we had to run off."

"Yeah, take care of him," Mark said. He was busy stripping the weapons belt from Morgan. Mark noted the compass and grinned.

"You're a fool," Tappinger said. "Men like Curt Morgan take care of themselves. It's people like you that need help."

Tappinger was still talking, but Mark paid no attention. He broke the lock on the stable and then opened the storage room inside. He found canteens in the harness room. There was also a plastic can of kerosene. Mark and Juanita saddled two horses. They led them out to the edge of the compound. Tappinger stood by the broken stable door.

They looked back for a second, then waved and rode into the jungle. Before they were gone, Tappinger had finished the last of Mark's gin.

They fled southward. Every sound seemed to be Morgan and a chase party following with dogs. Then there were the nameless sounds of the jungle. The horses were as frightened as they were.

In the morning they found a small clump of brown grass, a minuscule clearing of high ground. They did not dare make a fire, and they had only some biscuit and grain to eat. A Weem's Beast charged out of a small clump of trees near the top of the clearing, and Mark shot it, wasting ammunition by firing again and again until he was certain that it was dead. They then were too afraid to stay and had to move on.

They kept moving southward. Mark had overheard convicts talking about the Free State. On an arm of the sea, south, in the jungle. It was all he had to direct him. A crocodile menaced them, but they rode past, Mark holding the pistol tightly, while the beast stared at them. It wasn't a real crocodile, of course; but it looked much like the Earthly variety. Parallel evolution, Mark thought. What shape would be better adapted to life in this jungle?

On the eighth day they came to a narrow inlet and followed it to the left, deeper into the jungle, the sea on their right and green hell to the left. It twisted its way along a forgotten river dried by geological shifts a long time before. Tiny streams had bored through the cliff faces on both sides, and plunged thirty meters across etched rock faces into the green froth at the bottom. They were the highest cliffs Mark had seen in his limited travels on Tanith.

At dark on the second day after they found the inlet Mark risked a fire. He shot a crownears and they roasted it. "The worst is over," Mark said. "We're free now. Free."

She crept into his arms. Her face was worried but contented, and it had lines that made her seem older than Mark. "You never asked me," she said.

He smiled. "Will you marry me?"

"Sure."

They laughed together. The jungle seemed very close and the horses were nickering in nervous fear. Mark built up the fire. "Free," he said. He held her tightly, and they were very happy.

VIII

Lysander set down his fork and turned to his hostess. Ann Hollis Chang looked much more elegant here in the dining room of the governor's private apartments than she had when Lysander had seen her in the governor's office. Her silver grey hair was down in loose waves and held by a bright blue jeweled comb, and her gown was simply cut but clung in ways that flattered her somewhat bony figure. Still there was much of the senior bureaucrat about her. She was attentive to the guests at her end of the table, but she was also thoroughly aware of everything Governor Blaine said at the far end. She had mentioned earlier that her husband was a senior chemist with the Lederle company, and never came to government functions, official or not.

Lysander smiled. "Madame Chang, this roast is excellent."

"Thank you. But the real thanks should go to Mrs. Reilly."

"Oh?" He turned to his right. "Indeed?"

"Not really." Alma Reilly was a small woman, expensively dressed, but her hands were square and competent. Lysander guessed that she was in her mid-forties, a few years younger than her husband. The Reillys had been chemical engineers but were now planters. They held one of the largest and most productive stations. Alma Reilly's gown was sequined and she wore a large opal brooch, but her only ring was a plain gold band. "Actually, our foreman shot the porker three days ago, and we knew the dinner was coming up, and I knew the governor likes marinated porker so—" She laughed. "I know I talk too much."

"No, please go on," Lysander assured her. "Is there much wild game here?"

"More than we like," Alma said. "Henry—our son—had a fight with a Weem's beast last week and he's still in the hospital."

"Oh—"

"Nothing the regenners can't handle, but Henry's furious. He loves riding, and he won't be able to compete this year at all."

"I'm sorry to hear that. I take it you've had no trouble with the rebels, then?"

Alma Reilly glanced nervously up and down the table. "Trouble? We'd hardly have trouble with them, Your Highness. Most of them are our friends."

"Oh. But clearly you're not with them." He looked significantly at Colonel John Christian Falkenberg, who was seated near Governor Blaine at the head of the table.

"No, we've sent our crop in. Chris and I are agreed, Carleton Blaine is the best thing that has happened to Tanith since we got here. But it's not simple. Some of the reforms have been very hard on our friends." She looked across the table at Ursula Gordon. "Not that Governor Blaine wasn't right about many things, you understand. But it's very hard. There's precious little profit to be made on Tanith."

At the mention of profits, Dr. Phon Nol looked up from his plate and nodded. "Little enough before, and now we must make a further investment in—militia," he said. "More than worth the money once the escapees and pirates are killed, but I must say that Colonel Falkenberg's services are more expensive than I had hoped."

Captain Jesus Alana smiled thinly. "I appreciate your difficulties, Dr. Nol, but you of all people on Tanith must understand the economics. Without munitions we'd be useless, and we have to import most of our supplies and just about all our equipment."

"I understand, I sympathize," Nol said. "But permit me not to care much for the expenses."

Both Captains Alana, Jesus and Catherine, laughed at that. "Permit us to dislike them just as much," Catherine said. "I can't imagine the colonel is much happier than you." She looked at Ursula on her right. "That's a very nice gown. From Harrod's?"

"Actually, no. Ly—Prince Lysander bought it for me at a little shop in the garden district. He was looking for something made here."

"Ah, very astute," Dr. Nol said. "Tell me, Your Highness, did you know our governor before you came to Tanith?"

"Not at all. We'd heard about him of course. Seems very dedicated to his work."

"He is that," Hendrik ten Koop said from Alma Reilly's right. "Too dedicated for some."

✧   ✧   ✧

White-jacketed servants cleared the table and brought an elaborate three-tiered compote of sherbets and ices. After desert they brought crystal decanters of a rose-colored liqueur. Governor Blaine stood to offer the first toast.

"To our guest, Prince Lysander of Sparta. May there always be friendship between Tanith and Sparta."

That's a bold toast, Lysander thought. Considering that Sparta is sovereign and Tanith isn't. Not yet.

Lysander acknowledged the toast with a bow. "Our thanks. May we always be friends, and your enemies be ours." There was silence for a moment. Lysander looked across the table to smile reassurance at Ursula, then up toward the governor. Colonel Falkenberg caught his eye, and might have smiled. Lysander turned back to his left. "And if I may offer a toast to our charming hostess. Madame Chang."

Hendrik ten Koop laughed aloud. The portly Dutch planter had already drunk four glasses of port, but it hadn't seemed to affect him at all. "Good, good. May I second? To the real governor of Tanith."

"Why, thank you," Mrs. Chang said. "And in response—to the new order on Tanith." She looked significantly at Ursula Gordon. "But I can't quite let Mynheer ten Koop get away with that. To the best governor Tanith will ever have." She raised her glass toward Blaine.

Another moment of silence, even longer than the first. Then Falkenberg lifted his glass. "Well said," Captain Ian Frazer and both Captains Alana instantly lifted theirs. Dr. Nol smiled, a tiny smile at just the corners of his mouth. "If Colonel Falkenberg agrees, then it must be so."

Christopher Reilly was next. "Indeed. Thank you, Dr. Nol." He sipped at his liqueur.

"I see," Hendrik ten Koop said. "I see indeed." He drained his glass in one gulp.

The outside walls of Government House were bleak and fortified, with few windows. The building's roofed verandas all lined its inner walls, which enclosed a large courtyard dotted with fountain pools and crowned with a large illuminated aviary. Sprays of water traced sparkling paths through the multicolored spotlight beams, and the patter of the fountains was punctuated by the occasional cries of the birds.

There were ceiling fans out here as well as inside. Lysander watched a pair of brilliant blue-and-red hens strut in their cage, then turned to the others who had gathered around him at the veranda railing. "I'd thought Tanith was a young planet," Lysander said. "But surely birds are a late stage of evolution?"

"Quite late, Highness," Catherine Alana said. "Even though this planet looks like it's still in the Cretaceous, it's actually in an era beyond Earth's present period."

"Ah. I hadn't known that. And no intelligent life evolved. Not here, not anywhere—"

Ursula smiled. "Except on Earth, of course."

"Sometimes I wonder," Christopher Reilly said. He looked out over the fountains below. "If we're so intelligent, why do we act so stupid?"

"You're not being stupid," Captain Alana said. Her smile faded. "It's those others. They aren't going to win, so why are they making us fight? It will be expensive for everyone." She looked across the veranda where her husband stood with Colonel Falkenberg. "It could be very expensive."

"She ought to know," Beatrice Frazer said. "Catherine is the regiment's chief accountant."

"I see. Captain Alana is in uniform, but you're not, Madame Frazer," Lysander prompted.

"No, I'm a civilian." She laughed. "As much as we have civilians in Falkenberg's Legion. I teach in the regimental schools."

"Are there many women in your regiment?" Ursula asked.

"A fair number if you count the dependents," Beatrice said. "Most of the men are married, so there are nearly as many women as men. I expect Catherine could tell you exactly how many of us are in uniform. Actually, we don't make too strong a distinction between those in ranks and the dependents. We take care of our own."

"Do you fight?" Lysander asked Catherine Alana. He glanced at her holstered pistol.

"I presume you mean the women? Only if we have to. The regiment is organized so that it can take the field without us, and we manage the rear areas, so to speak. Sometimes things don't work the way they're planned." Captain Alana's blue eyes danced. "I should tell you? You've a whole planet to run. Or will have."

"It's not quite cut and dried," Lysander said. "Sparta has a dual monarchy, and the throne is elective in each royal house. Then there's the Senate, and the Council."

"How could they pass you over?" Catherine said.

"Well, it would be pretty stupid, wouldn't it?" Lysander grinned and turned so that he faced her, with his back to the others. "You seem to know everything, Captain. Tell me, please: What *is* all this about a revolt of the planters?"

"I expect you'll find out soon enough," Catherine said. "Very soon, in fact. Here's the governor, and if no one's already told you, he's revived the custom of inviting the menfolk into his office for after-dinner cigars."

Governor Blaine had brought Falkenberg down to join them. Like his officers, Falkenberg wore dress whites. Lysander smiled to himself. He'd already noticed that the colonel and his staff were the only guests wearing white upper garments.

"Your Highness, Colonel Falkenberg has asked me to provide you transport to his regimental compound tomorrow," Blaine said. "Easy enough to do, if you like."

"Oh, please," Lysander said. "Good of you to invite me, Colonel."

"My pleasure. I'll ask the mess president to come up with something special for dinner. Lunch as well?"

"Certainly, if it's not an inconvenience."

"Not at all."

Blaine turned to Ursula. "Meanwhile, if the ladies would excuse us? Gentlemen, if you'd care to join me in my office, I can offer you genuine Havana cigars. Rolled on Tanith, of course, but the tobacco is imported from Cuba. It'll be another few years before we can grow our own."

"Not too long, I hope," Lysander said. "I confess I've never smoked a genuine Havana. Thank you." He looked to Ursula. "You'll excuse me?"

She glanced nervously around. Beatrice Frazer caught Falkenberg's eye, then smiled at Lysander. "Your Highness, with your permission we'll bore your young lady with tales of life in the regiment."

"Ah. Yes. Thank you." He squeezed Ursula's hand and turned to Blaine. "Governor, I would very much like a taste of your tobacco."

A detailed map swam up on the monitor screen. Blaine pointed at an inlet of the sea. The view zoomed in until Government House Square filled the screen, then zoomed back out to show an area of several hundred kilometers around the city. The screen held the display for a moment, then the view zoomed out once more.

"The last pirates are down here, between us and the southern province," Blaine said. "They call themselves the Free State."

Hendrik ten Koop drained his glass of port and poured another. "Free State. Yes, that's what they called themselves.

Last month they killed five of my people and kidnapped three women on my south station. Then they burned what they could not carry away."

"Yes. Well, it shouldn't take Colonel Falkenberg long to root them out." Blaine zoomed the map to an area a few hundred kilometers west of Lederle. "It's the rebel planters who're likely to be more trouble to us all. Most of them are in this area here." He pointed.

"I would not go so far as to call them rebels," Dr. Nol said. He drew delicately on his cigar. "Excellent tobacco. Thank you. Governor, is it wise to think of our friends as rebels?"

"Perhaps not." Blaine looked thoughtful. "Think rebel and drive them to rebellion. Note taken. Still—what should we call them?"

"The opposition?" Christopher Reilly asked.

"Hardly a loyal opposition," Blaine said. "But very well. 'Opposition' it is."

"Your pardon, Governor," Lysander said. "If they're not rebels, what have they done that you're about to send some of the best troops in the galaxy against them?"

"Withheld their crops," Blaine said.

"They won't pay taxes," ten Koop said. "Often I wonder why I do not join them."

"For the same reason I don't," Reilly said. "The Navy will have our crops, or someone else will. Better we keep something than nothing."

"Will they kill all the geese?" ten Koop demanded.

"I expect that'd depend on the goose supply," Falkenberg said carefully. "Fifty geese laying silver eggs might be worth as much as one that lays gold, if the one that lays gold eats too much."

"Now, there's an unsettling notion for you," Christopher Reilly said. "Colonel, I'm very glad it's our side you're on."

"Oh, indeed. I am also," ten Koop said. He turned to Lysander. "I expect this is nothing new for a prince of Sparta. I understand you have rebels there also."

"Unfortunately, yes. I wish things were different."

"So," ten Koop said. "Tell us, Colonel, once you have killed the last of the pirates, what will you do about the— opposition?"

"Are you sure the Legion needs to do anything?" Falkenberg asked. Ten Koop opened his mouth to speak but Falkenberg went on. "They must know just how little military force they can field. No, this is a political problem, gentlemen. With any luck you'll find it has a political solution."

"I certainly hope so," Blaine said.

Ten Koop shut his mouth. "Yes, yes. Much better that way," he muttered.

Lysander couldn't be sure, but he thought one or two of the others gave the Dutch planter a sidelong look. He filed the impression and turned back to the maps on the monitor screen. "Just how much force does this opposition group command? I shouldn't think much compared to Falkenberg's Legion."

"Precisely," Christopher Reilly said. "I'm sure they'll see reason."

Falkenberg nodded. "That's as it may be. Meanwhile we have the pirates to deal with."

"Out of bed, sleepy bunnies."

Ursula moaned and pulled the bedclothes over her head. "Noooo . . . Five minutes more—"

"Not another second!" Lysander threw the covers to the foot of the bed and got to his feet. He turned the air conditioner to full cold.

Ursula shivered visibly. "Not fair. I don't have to get up yet!"

"Yes you do. I told you, you're coming with me."

She sat up and tucked her knees under her chin. "Lysander, I wasn't invited."

"Not your worry. I want you with me. What's wrong now?"

"Take Harv."

"He wasn't invited either. One unexpected guest is enough." She turned away from him.

"Ursula—"

"You'll lose me my job, and then where will I be?"

"Oh, come now—"

"You will. One word from Colonel Falkenberg to the governor, and I'll be doing tours of worker barracks at the plantations."

"That's a horrible thought!"

"It happens."

"Besides, Colonel Falkenberg wouldn't do that, and even if he did I can't think the governor would let that happen."

"Why not?"

"I just don't think so—after all, you were the star of his reconciliation dinner last night."

"That was a nice dinner." She stretched her arms toward him. "Don't we have a few more minutes?"

"No, Miss Minx. Now get your clothes. Traveling clothes."

✧   ✧   ✧

The Legion's encampment covered the top of a low hill thirty kilometers from the capital city. It was laid out much like the classical Roman camp, except that it was much larger, with more space between tents and houses. There were other differences. Radar dishes pivoted ceaselessly at every corner of the encampment. The spaces between the rows of tents were dotted with low bunkers, personnel shelters, revetments for air defenses.

As the helicopter circled well away from the camp, the governor's pilot spoke carefully into his headset, and seemed relieved to be acknowledged. They flew straight in. As they got close Lysander saw three battle tanks and two infantry fighting vehicles. He knew there were many others, but they were nowhere in sight. At the landing area there were two helicopter gun ships and one small fixed-wing observation plane.

Soldiers in jungle camouflage moved between the orderly lines of tents. None of them seemed interested in the approaching helicopter.

A young officer greeted them at the landing pad. "I'm Lieutenant Bates, sir. Colonel Falkenberg is expecting you." He indicated a waiting jeep. "I hadn't been told the lady was coming. The ride may be a bit bumpy."

"I'll manage." Ursula smiled. "Thank you."

Muddy water stood in the unpaved tracks around the perimeter of the camp. Sentries saluted with a wave as they passed through the gates and splashed toward the headquarters area. As they entered Lysander heard trumpets sound. In seconds men rushed out of the tents, spread groundcloths, and began laying out equipment. Sergeants and centurions moved along the neat lines to inspect the gear.

"Moving out?" Lysander asked. "Or is this for me?"

"Don't know," Bates said.

Ursula stifled a giggle.

Headquarters was a low stucco building. Falkenberg and Beatrice Frazer stood waiting on the porch. "Glad you could come," Falkenberg said.

"Thank you. I hope you won't mind if Miss Gordon has a look around—"

"Not at all." He nodded slightly at Ursula. "Pleased to have you, Miss Gordon. I've asked Mrs. Frazer to see that you're comfortable. You'll join us for lunch, of course."

"Thank you," Ursula said.

"Excellent. Now if you'll excuse us, the regiment is going into the field tomorrow, and I've a few matters to discuss with Prince Lysander."

✧　　✧　　✧

The office was dominated by an elaborately carved wooden desk. Other wooden furniture matched it. The walls were decorated with photographs and banners.

"Well. You've come a long way, Your Highness." Falkenberg indicated a chair, and sat at his desk. "Drink?"

"No, thank you. Impressive show out there."

"It was meant to be. I take it you have bad news."

"Not entirely bad."

"Not entirely bad," Falkenberg said. "But not good either. You haven't come to take us to Sparta." He looked up with a slight smile. "Despite the show we put on for you."

"I truly wish I could, but we don't have the resources yet. We still want you. We certainly want your good will."

"Thank you," Falkenberg said. "I'm afraid good will doesn't buy many munitions."

"No, of course not."

"Rather sudden change of plans?" Falkenberg said.

"Well, yes, sir, I suppose so," Lysander said. *Damned sudden. One day Father was eager to get Falkenberg to Sparta, and the next he was worried about money. The budget's tight, but not that tight. I really don't understand. I guess I don't have to.* "Colonel, I've brought a sight draft as a retainer against future need. Sort of an option on your services."

"Services when?"

Lysander glanced around the room. Falkenberg smiled thinly. "Your Highness, if this room's bugged, there's no place safe on the planet."

"I well believe it. Very well, I was told to be honest with you. We won't be ready to move for another four or five standard years. Admiral Lermontov agrees with that. Provided—" He let his voice trail off.

"Provided that things on Earth don't come apart on their own before then," Falkenberg said. "Yes. Now, how real is that Tanith-Sparta friendship Governor Blaine was hinting at?"

"I think very real. As real as my father and I can make it, in any event."

"I thought so. Good. But does your father control Spartan foreign policy?"

Lysander looked thoughtful. "Just how much do you know about our Constitution?"

"Assume nothing," Falkenberg said.

"Well, I won't do quite that," Lysander said. "Do you know my father?"

"Met him once. Long ago," Falkenberg said.

"Yes. Well, Sparta's government was designed by—well, by intellectuals. Intellectuals who were disgusted with what happened to the United States, where by the year 2000 both houses of the Congress for all practical purposes held office for life, and the only really elective office was held by a president who had to spend so much time learning how to get the job that he never learned how to do it."

"An interesting way of putting things."

Lysander grinned. "Actually I'm quoting my grandfather. Who was, of course, one of those disgusted intellectuals. Anyway, Sparta was designed differently. The dual monarchy controls foreign policy. The two kings are supposed to be a check on each other, but my father and his colleague are very much in agreement. If something happens to Father, it's nearly certain that I'll take his place. As the junior king, of course. Really, Colonel, I don't think you need to worry too much about changes in Spartan policy."

"Who controls the money? Your legislature?"

"We don't exactly have a legislature," Lysander said. "But yes, the Senate and Council control most of Sparta's budget. Not all of it, though. Control of some revenues is built into the Constitution. There are funds reserved for the monarchy, and others controlled by the Senate, and the Senate—well, it's pretty complicated. Some seats are elected in districts and some are virtually hereditary. Others are appointed by the unions and the trade associations. I'd hate to have to explain it."

"The bottom line, though, is that you can't get the money right now."

"The bottom line, Colonel, is that we don't *have* the money right now. But we're pretty sure we know where to get it."

Falkenberg sat impassively.

"If it's any consolation, Admiral Lermontov agrees with us," Lysander said. "I'm surprised he hasn't made you party to his views."

"He has," Falkenberg said.

"Ah. I see. Then you know his ultimate goal hasn't changed." Lysander frowned. "One thing concerns me, Colonel. This—Blaine doesn't want to call it a rebellion, but we may as well. If they're holding back their crops, what does that do to Admiral Lermontov's budget?"

"It could be grim. Which is why Blaine can't let them get away with it."

"Yes. I thought as much. There's more at stake here than Blaine and his reforms. Just how much of the crop has been withheld?"

"At least a quarter. Maybe as much as a third."

Lysander whistled softly. "Colonel, that—that could mean—what? Half the Fleet's operations budget?"

"Not quite that. The Grand Senate still appropriates *something* for operations. But it would certainly wipe out Grand Admiral Lermontov's discretionary funds."

"I can't say I care for that. Still, Colonel, what can they *do* with their crop if they don't sell it to the government? Surely they won't carry out their threat to destroy it."

Falkenberg laughed. "With that much money at stake? Hardly. I'm afraid there are a lot of markets, Prince Lysander. Some will pay more than the government."

"But—"

"The most likely customer is a company owned by the Bronson family."

"Oh. I see. Grand Senator Bronson. With his protection—"

"Precisely. His faction doesn't control a majority in the Grand Senate, but he doesn't have to, does he? No one else has a majority either. Lots of horse trading, I'm told."

"Yes," Lysander looked at the far wall. It was covered with holographs. One showed the Legion in formal parade with battle banners and victory streamers. "Still, I gather you don't anticipate any trouble recovering the crops?"

"I always anticipate trouble, Your Highness."

"Colonel, let me be frank. You're very heavily involved in Admiral Lermontov's plan, but we are even more so. Anything that changes or delays it—well, we would have to take that very seriously back on Sparta." He spread his hands wide. "Of course I'm only a message carrier. I'm not empowered to negotiate."

Falkenberg raised an eyebrow. "Well, if you say so. But you do carry messages to high places. Your Highness, you have to appreciate my situation. I'm certain this mess with the opposition planters will be cleared up in weeks, months at most. It will have to be. After that the regiment won't be able to stay on Tanith very long. Certainly not five years. The economy won't support us, and besides, I can't condemn my people to five years in this place."

"What will you do?"

"We have offers. I'll have to take one of them."

"Preferably something that doesn't tie you down for too long—"

"Preferably," Falkenberg agreed. "But the Regimental Council makes that decision."

"Colonel, my father—all of us regret putting you in this situation."

"I'm sure you do," Falkenberg said. "How long will you be on Tanith?"

"It's not definite, but—let's say weeks. Months at most."

Falkenberg smiled and nodded. "Right. I expect you'll want to see a bit of the country beyond the capital while you're here. I'll have Captain Rottermill draw up a travel guide if you like."

"Very kind of you. Should be helpful." Lysander frowned. "Colonel, what is your impression of Governor Blaine?"

Falkenberg chuckled. "At the risk of being offensive, he seems much like the people who established your government. Let's hope he learns as much from experience as your father and grandfather did."

"I see. Do you think he will?"

"He has held on quite well so far."

"Colonel, I have reasons for asking your opinion. I'm authorized to tell Governor Blaine certain things about Lermontov's plans, provided you agree."

Falkenberg touched a button on the side of his desk. "Whiskey and soda. Ice. Two glasses, please." He turned back to Lysander. "I repeat. He has managed quite well so far."

"With your Legion at his back. What happens when you leave?"

"That is the question, isn't it?" Falkenberg touched controls in a desk drawer. The gray of the desktop flashed into a brightly colored map of the region around Lederle. "The main opposition to Blaine's new policies is out here in the bush. Until recently they were unable to form any effective organization. Now they have done so. They've even hired a battalion of mercenaries. Light infantry, mostly."

"I hadn't heard that," Lysander said.

"Governor Blaine isn't particularly proud of having let things go that far."

There was a tap at the door. An orderly brought in a tray and set it down. "Anything else, sir?"

"Thank you. No." Falkenberg poured for both of them. "Cheers."

"Cheers. Colonel, I notice that *you* haven't told the governor anything—or if you have, he's very discreet."

"He is discreet, but in fact I was waiting for your father's views. Incidentally, I'd be careful when and where you told him anything. This room is secure, but I wouldn't bet that the governor's office is. Or the study in his apartments, for that matter."

"Who?"

Falkenberg shrugged. "When was a politician's office ever

secure? In this case it's even more likely to be leaky. You will remember Mynheer ten Koop?"

"Certainly."

"I don't recall it was mentioned at Blaine's dinner, but ten Koop's oldest daughter is married to one Hiram Girerd—who just happens to be one of the leaders of the planters' boycott. That's just one of the odd mixtures you can find at Government House."

"Hah. Then perhaps it would be best to wait until this boycott affair is settled before we come to any decisions about Tanith's role in—" He shrugged. "We've no name for Lermontov's grand scheme."

"Just as well."

"I suppose. In any event, Colonel, I can't think that even with their mercenary battalion the planters could muster much force against your Legion."

"Military, no. But they've hired Barton's Bastards, and Major Barton is no fool." Falkenberg chuckled. "If he were, I'd hardly say so. He was once a captain in the 42nd."

"Oh? Why did he leave?"

"His hitch ran out and he got a better offer," Falkenberg said. "After that we were allies for a while."

"I see." Classic situation? Lysander wondered. Two condottiere captains facing each other, neither willing to fight a battle because the losses would be too costly. A long confrontation but no fighting. Mercenary paradise. Surely not Falkenberg's game? "What will you do?"

"That rather depends on what the opposition intends, doesn't it?" Falkenberg studied the map table. "One thing is certain. They'll have to deliver that crop to someone, presumably a Bronson agent. Major Barton will see to that. It's the only way he can be paid, and he needs the money."

"So if you can intercept the delivery—"

"The conflict is ended, of course. Governor Blaine will have his taxes, the Navy will have its drugs, and Lermontov will have his secret funds." Falkenberg glanced at his watch and stood. "But first things first. This week we have to clean out that nest of pirates in the south."

"Of course. Colonel, I don't want to keep you from your work, but there is one thing. May—I would very much like to accompany your troops on this campaign."

Falkenberg considered it for a moment. "I think not this time. Ordinarily I wouldn't mind having a volunteer subaltern along, but this looks like a job for specialists. Hostage situations generally are."

"Another time, then?"

Falkenberg looked thoughtful again. "It makes sense. In fact, it's as good a way as any for you to get the intelligence your father will need. When we get back from this mission, you'll be welcome aboard."

IX

Mark Fuller awoke with a knife at his throat. A big, ugly man, burned dark and with scars crisscrossing his bare chest, squatted in front of them. He eyed Mark and Juanita, then grinned. "What have we got ourselves?" he said. "A couple of runaways?"

"I got everything, Art," someone said from behind them.

"Yeah. Okay, mates, up and at 'em. Move out. I ain't got all day."

Mark helped Juanita to her feet. One arm was asleep from holding her. As Mark stood, the ugly man expertly took the gun from Mark's belt. "Who are you?" Mark asked.

"Call me Art. Sergeant to the Boss. Come on, let's go."

There were five others, all mounted. Art led the way through the jungle. When Mark tried to say something to Juanita, Art turned. "I'm going to tell you once. Shut up. Say another word to anybody but me, and I kill you. Say anything to me that I don't want to hear, and I'll cut you. Got that?"

"Yes, sir," Mark said.

Art laughed. "Now you've got the idea."

They rode on in silence.

The Free State was mostly caves in hillsides above the sea. It held over five hundred men and women. There were other encampments of escapees out in the jungles, Art said. "But we've got the biggest. Been pretty careful—when we raid the planters, we can usually make it look like one of the other outfits did it. Governor don't have much army anyway. They won't follow us here."

Mark started to say something about the mercenaries that the governor was hiring. Then he thought better of it.

The boss was a heavy man with long, colorless hair growing to below his shoulders. He had a handlebar mustache and staring blue eyes. He sat in the mouth of a cave on a big carved chair as if it were a throne, and he held a rifle across his knees. A big black man stood behind the chair, watching everyone, saying nothing.

"Escapees, eh?"

"Yes," Mark said.

"Yes, boss. Don't forget that."

"Yes, boss."

"What can you do? Can you fight?"

When Mark didn't answer, the Boss pointed to a smaller man in the crowd that had gathered around. "Take him, Choam."

The small man moved toward Mark. His foot lashed upward and hit Mark in the ribs. Then he moved closer. Mark tried to hit him, but the man dodged away and slapped Mark across the face. "Enough," the boss said. "You can't fight. What can you do?"

"I—"

"Yeah." He looked backward over his shoulder to the black man. "You want him, George?"

"No."

"Right. Art, you found him. He's yours. I'll take the girl."

"But you can't!" Mark shouted.

"No!" Juanita said.

The other men looked at the boss. They saw he was laughing. They all laughed. Art and the two others took Mark's arms and began to drag him away. Two more led Juanita into the cave behind the boss.

"But this isn't right!" Mark shouted.

There was more laughter. The boss stood. "Maybe I'll give her back when I'm through. Unless Art wants her. Art?"

"I got a woman."

"Yeah." The boss turned toward the cave. Then he turned back to Mark and the men holding him. "Leave the kid here, Art. I'd like to talk to him. Get the girl cleaned up," he shouted behind him. "The rest of you get out of here."

The others left, all but the black man who stood behind the boss's throne. The black man went a few meters away and sat under a rock ledge. It looked cool in there. He took out a pipe and began stuffing it.

"Come here, kid. What's your name?"

"Fuller," Mark said. "Mark Fuller."

"Come over here. Sit down." The boss indicated a flat rock bench just inside the cave mouth. The cave seemed to go in a long way; he could hear women talking. "Sit, I said. Tell me how you got here." The boss's tone was conversational, almost friendly.

"I was in a student riot." Mark strained to hear, but there were no more sounds from inside the cave.

"Student, eh. Relax, Fuller. Nobody's hurting your girlfriend. Your concern is touching. Don't see much of that out here. Tell me about your riot. Where was it?"

The boss was a good listener. When Mark fell silent, the man would ask questions—probing questions, as if he were interested in Mark's story. Sometimes he smiled.

Outside were work parties: wood details; a group incomprehensibly digging a ditch in the flinty ground out in front of the caves; women carrying water. None of them seemed interested in the boss's conversation. Instead, they seemed almost afraid to look into the cave—all but the black man, who sat in his cool niche and never seemed to look away.

Bit by bit Mark told of his arrest and sentence, and of Ewigfeuer's plantation. The boss nodded. "So you came looking for the Free States. And what did you expect to find?"

"Free men! Freedom, not—"

"Not despotism." There was something like kindness in the words. The boss chuckled. "You know, Fuller, it's remarkable how much your story is like mine. Except that I've always known how to fight. And how to make friends. Good friends." He tilted his head toward the black man. "George, here, for instance. Between us there's nothing we can't handle. You poor fool, what the hell did you think you'd do out here? What good are you? You can't fight, you whine about what's right and fair, and you don't know how to take care of yourself, and you come off into the bush to find us. You knew who we were."

"But—"

"And now you're all broken up about your woman. I'm not going to take anything she hasn't got plenty of. It doesn't get used up." He stood and shouted to one of the men in the yard. "Send Art over."

"So you're going to rape Juanita." Mark looked around for a weapon, for anything. There was a rifle near the boss's chair. His eyes flickered toward it.

The boss laughed. "Try it. But you won't. Aw, hell, Fuller, you'll be all right. Maybe you'll even learn something. Now I've got a date."

"But—" If there was something I could say, Mark thought. "Why are you doing this?"

"Why not? Because I'll lose your valuable loyalty? Get something straight, Fuller. This is it. There's no place left to go. Live here and learn our ways, or go jump over the cliff there. Or take off into the green and see how far you get.

You think you're pretty sharp. Maybe you are. We'll see. Maybe you'll learn to be some use to us. Maybe. Art, take the kid into your squad and see if he can fit in."

"Right, boss. Come on." Art took Mark's arm. "Look, if you're going try something, do it and get it over with. I don't want to watch you all the time."

Mark turned and followed the other man. Helpless. Damn fool, and helpless. He laughed.

"Yeah?" Art said. "What's funny?"

"The Free State. Freedom. Free men—"

"We're free," Art said. "More'n the losers in Whiskeytown. Maybe one day you will be. When we think we can trust you." He pointed to the cliff edge. The sea inlet was beyond it. "Anybody we can't trust goes over that. The fall don't always kill 'em, but I never saw anybody make it to shore."

Art found him a place in his cave. There were six other men and four women there. The others looked at Mark for a moment, then went back to whatever they had been doing. Mark sat staring at the cave floor and thought he heard, off toward the Boss's cave, a man laughing and a girl crying. For the first time since he was twelve, Mark tried to pray.

Pray for what? he asked himself. He didn't know. I hate them. All of them.

Just when, Mark Fuller, are you going to get some control over your life? But that doesn't just happen. I have to do it for myself. Somehow.

A week went past. It was a meaningless existence. He cooked for the squad, gathered wood and washed dishes, and listened to the sounds of the other men and their women at night. They never left him alone.

The crying from the boss's cave stopped, but he didn't see Juanita. When he gathered wood, there were sometimes women from the boss's area, and he overheard them talking about what a relief it was that Chambliss—that seemed to be the boss's name—had a new playmate. They did not seem at all jealous of the new arrival.

Play along with them, Mark thought. Play along until—until what? What can I do? Escape? Get back to the plantation? How? And what happens then? But I won't join them, I won't become a part of this! I won't!

After a week they took Mark on hunting parties. He was unarmed—his job was to carry the game. They had to walk several kilometers away from the caves. Chambliss didn't permit hunting near the encampment.

Mark was paired with Art. The older man was neither friendly nor unfriendly; he treated Mark as a useful tool, someone to carry and do work.

"Is this all there is?" Mark asked. "Hunting, sitting around the camp, eating and—"

"—a little screwing," Art said. "What the hell do you want us to do? Set up farms so the governor'll know where we are? We're doin' all right. Nobody tells us what to do."

"Except the boss."

"Yeah. Except the boss. But nobody hassles us. We can live for ourselves. Cheer up, kid, you'll feel better when you get your woman back. He'll get tired of her one of these days. Or maybe we'll get some more when we go raiding. Only thing is, you have to fight for a woman. You better do it better'n you did the other day."

"Doesn't she—don't the women have anything to say about who they pair up with?" Mark asked.

"Why should they?"

On the tenth day there was an alarm. Someone thought he heard a helicopter. The boss ordered night guards.

Mark was paired with a man named Cal. They sat among the rocks at the edge of the clearing. Cal had a rifle and a knife, but Mark was unarmed. The jungle was black dark, without even stars above.

Finally the smaller man took tobacco and paper from his pocket. "Smoke?"

"Thanks, I'd like one."

"Sure." He rolled two cigarettes. "Maybe you'll do, huh? Had my doubts about you when you first come. You know, it's a wonder the boss didn't have you tossed over the side, the way you yelled at him like that. No woman's worth that, you know."

"Yeah."

"She mean much to you?" Cal asked.

"Some," Mark swallowed hard. His mouth tasted bitter. "'Course, they get the idea they own you, there's not much you can do."

Cal laughed. "Yeah. Had an old lady like that in Baltimore. Stabbed me one night for messing around with her sister. Where you from, kid?"

"Santa Maria. Part of San-San."

"I been there once. North San-San, not the part where you come from. Here." He handed Mark the cigarette and struck a match to light both.

They smoked in silence. It wasn't all tobacco, Mark found; there was a good shot of borloi in the cigarette. Mark avoided inhaling but spoke as if holding his breath. Cal sucked and packed.

"Good weed," Cal said. "You should have brought some when you ran off."

"Had to get out fast."

"Yeah." They listened to the sounds of the jungle. "Hell of a life," Cal said. "Wish I could get back to Earth. Some Welfare Island, anyplace where it's not so damned hot. I'd like to live in Alaska. You ever been there?"

"No. Isn't there—don't you have any plans? Some way to make things better?"

"Well, the boss talks about it, but nothing happens," Cal said. "Every now and then we go raid a place, get some new women. We got a still in not long ago, that's something."

Mark shuddered. "Cal?"

"Yah?"

"Got another cigarette?"

"You'll owe me for it."

"Sure."

"Okay." Cal took out paper and tobacco and rolled two more smokes. He handed one to Mark. "Been thinking. There ought to be something better'n this, but I sure don't see what it'll be." As Cal struck his match, Mark shut his eyes so he wouldn't be blinded. Then he lifted the rock he'd found in the darkness and brought it down hard onto Cal's head. The man slumped, but Mark hit him again. He felt something wet and sticky warming his fingers and shuddered.

Then he was sick, but he had to work fast. He took Cal's rifle and knife and his matches. There wasn't anything else useful. Mark moved from the rocks onto the narrow strip of flinty ground. No one challenged him. He ran into the jungle with no idea of where to go.

He tried to think. Hiding out until morning wouldn't help. They'd find Cal and come looking. And Juanita was back there. Mark ran through the squishy mud. Tears came and he fought them back, but then he was sobbing. Where am I going? Where? And why bother?

He ran on until he felt something moving beside him. He drew in a breath to cry out, but a hand clamped over his mouth. Another grasped his wrist. He felt a knifepoint at his throat. "One sound and you're dead," a voice whispered. "Got that?"

Mark nodded.

"Right. Just keep remembering that. Okay, Ardway, let's go."

"Roger," a voice answered.

He was half-carried through the jungle from the camp. There were several men. He did not know how many. They moved silently. "Ready to walk?" someone asked.

"Yes," Mark whispered. "Who are—"

"Shut up. One more sound and we cut your kidneys out. You'll take a week dying. Now follow the man ahead of you."

Mark made more noise than all the others combined, although he tried to walk silently. They went a long way through knee-deep water and thick mud, then over harder ground. He thought they were going slightly uphill. Then he no longer felt the loom of the trees. They were in a clearing.

The night was pitch black. How do they see? Mark wondered. And who are they? He thought he could make out a darker shape ahead of him. It was more a feeling than anything else, but then he touched something soft. "Through that," one of his captors said.

It was a curtain. Another was brought down behind him as he went through, and still another was lifted ahead of him. Light blinded him. He stood blinking.

He was inside a tent. Half a dozen uniformed men stood around a map table. At the end of the tent opposite Mark was a tall, slender man. Mark could not guess how old he was, but there were thin streaks of gray in his hair. His jungle camouflage uniform was neatly pressed. He looked at Mark without expression. "Well, Sergeant Major?"

"Strange, Colonel. This man was sitting guard with another guy. Neither one of them knew what he was doing. We watched them a couple of hours. Then this one beats the other one's brains out with a rock and runs right into the jungle."

Mercenaries, Mark thought. They've come to—"I need help," Mark said. "They've got my—my wife in there."

"Your name?" the colonel asked.

"Mark Fuller."

The colonel looked to his right. Another officer had a small desk console. He punched Mark's name into it, and words flashed across the screen. The Colonel read for a moment. "Escaped convict. Juanita Corlee escaped with you. That is your wife?"

"Yes."

"And you had a falling-out with the Free Staters."

"No. It wasn't that way at all." Mark blurted out his story.

The colonel looked back to the readout screen. "And you are surprised." He nodded to himself. "I knew the schools on Earth were of little use. It says here that you are an intelligent man, Fuller. So far you haven't shown many signs of it."

"No. Lord God, no. Who—who are you? Please."

"I am Colonel John Christian Falkenberg. This regiment has been retained by the Tanith governor to suppress these so-called Free States. You were captured by Sergeant Major Calvin, and these are my officers. Now, Fuller, what can you tell me about the camp layout? What weapons have they?"

"I don't know much," Mark said. "Sir." Now why did I say that?

"There are other women captives in that camp," Falkenberg said.

"Here," one of the other officers said. "Show us what you do know, Fuller. How good is this satellite photo map?"

"Christ, Rottermill," a third officer said. "Let the lad be for a moment."

"Major Savage, intelligence is my job."

"So is human compassion. Ian, do you think you can find this boy a drink?" Major Savage beckoned to Falkenberg and led him to the far corner of the tent. Another officer brought a nylon musette bag from under the table and took out a bottle. He handed the brandy to Mark.

Falkenberg listened to Savage. Then he nodded. "We can only try. Fuller, did you see any signs of power supplies in that camp?"

"No, sir. There was no electricity at all. Only flashlights."

"Any special armament?"

"Colonel, I only saw rifles and pistols, but I heard talk of machine guns. I don't know how many."

"I see. Still, it is unlikely that they have laser weapons. Rottermill, have any target seekers turned up missing from armories? What are the chances that they have air defense missiles?"

"Slim, Colonel. Practically none. None stolen I know of."

"Check that out, please. Jeremy, you may be right," Falkenberg said. "I believe we can use the helicopters as fighting vehicles."

There was a moment of silence; then the officer who'd given Mark the brandy said, "Colonel, that's damned risky. There's precious little armor on those things."

"Machines not much better than ours were major fighting vehicles less than a hundred years ago, Captain Frazer." Falkenberg studied the map. "You see, Fuller, we could have wiped out this lot any time. The hostages are our real problem. Because of them we have kept Aviation Company back and brought in our troops on foot. We've not been able to carry heavy equipment or even much personal body armor across these swamps."

No, I don't expect you would, Mark thought. He tried to imagine a large group traveling silently through the swamps. It seemed impossible. What had they done when animals attacked? Certainly no one in the Free State had heard any gunfire. Why would an armed man let himself be killed when he could shoot?

"I expect they will threaten their prisoners when they know we are here," Falkenberg said. "Of course we will negotiate as long as possible. How long do you think it will take for them to act when they know that we will not actually make any concessions?"

"I don't know," Mark said. It was something he could not have imagined two years before: men who'd kill and torture, sometimes for no reason at all. No. Not men. Beasts.

"Well, you've precipitated the action," Falkenberg said. "They'll find your dead companion within hours. Captain Frazer."

"Sir."

"You have been studying this map. If you held this encampment, what defenses would you set up?"

"I'd dig in around this open area and hope someone was fool enough to come at us through it, Colonel."

"Yes. Sergeant Major."

"Sir!"

"Show me where they have placed their sentries." Falkenberg watched as Calvin sketched in outposts. Then he nodded. "It seems this Chambliss has some rudimentary military sense. Rings of sentries. In-depth defense. Can you infiltrate that, Sergeant Major?"

"Not likely, sir."

"Yes." Falkenberg stood for a moment. Then he turned to Captain Frazer. "Ian, you will take your scouts and half the infantry. Make preparations for an attack on the open area. We will code that Green A. This is not precisely a feint, Ian. It would be a good thing if you could punch through. However, I do not expect you to succeed, so conserve your men."

Frazer straightened to attention. "Sir."

"We won't abandon you, Ian. When the enemy is well committed there, we'll use the helicopters to take you out. Then we will move on both their flanks and roll them up." Falkenberg pointed to the map again. "This depression seems secure enough as a landing area. Code that Green A-one."

Major Jeremy Savage held a match over the bowl of his
pipe and inhaled carefully. When he was satisfied with the
light, he said, "Close timing needed, John Christian. Ian's in
a spot of trouble if we lose the choppers."

"Have a better way, Jerry?" Falkenberg asked.

"No."

"Right. Fuller, can you navigate a helicopter?"

"Yes, sir. I can even fly one."

Falkenberg nodded again. "Yes. You are a taxpayer's son,
aren't you? Fuller, you will go with Number 3 chopper. Captain Owensford."

"Sir."

"I want you to lead the rescue of the hostages. Sergeant
Major, I want a squad of headquarters assault guards, full body
armor, in Number 3. Fuller will guide the pilot as close as
possible to the cave where the women are held. Captain
Owensford will follow in Number 2 with another assault squad.
Every effort will be made to secure the hostages alive."

"Yes, sir," Owensford said.

"Fuller, is this understood?"

"Yes, sir."

"Very good. You won't have time to go in with them. When
the troops are off, those choppers must move out fast. We'll
need them to rescue Ian's lot."

"Colonel?" Mark said.

"Yes?"

"Not all women are hostages. Some of them will fight, I
think. I don't know how many. And not all the men are—
not everybody wants to be in there. Some would run off if
they could."

"And what do you expect me to do about it?"

"I don't know, sir."

"Neither do I, but Captain Owensford will be aware of the
situation. Sergeant Major, we will move this command post
in one hour. Until then, Fuller, I'll ask you to show Captain
Rottermill everything you know about that camp."

It isn't going to work, Mark thought. I prayed for her to
die. Only I don't know if she wants to die. And now she will.
He took another pull from the bottle and felt it taken from
his hand.

"Later," Rottermill said. "For now, tell me what you know
about this lot."

X

"They've found that dead guard." The radio sergeant adjusted his earphones. "Seem pretty stirred up about it."

Falkenberg looked at his watch. There was a good hour before sunrise. "Took them long enough."

"Pity Fuller couldn't guide that chopper in the dark," Jeremy Savage said.

"Yes. Sergeant Major, ask Captain Frazer to ready his men, and have your trail ambush party alerted."

"Sir."

"I have a good feeling about this one, John Christian." Savage tapped his pipe against the heel of his boot. "A good feeling."

"Hope you're right, Jeremy. Fuller doesn't believe it will work."

"No, but he knows this is her best chance. He's steady enough now. Realistic assessment of probabilities. Holding up well, all things considered."

"For a married man." Married men make the kinds of promises no man can keep, Falkenberg thought. His lips twitched slightly at the memory, and for a moment Grace's smile loomed in the darkness of the jungle outside. "Sergeant Major, have the chopper teams get into their armor."

"Is it always like this?" Mark said. He sat in the left hand seat of the helicopter. Unlike fixed wing craft, the right hand seat is the command pilot's position in a helicopter.

Body armor and helmet were an unfamiliar weight, and he sweated inside the thick clothing. The phones in his helmet crackled with commands meant for others. Outside the helmet there were sounds of firing. Captain Frazer's assault had started a quarter of an hour before; now there was a faint reddish gray glow in the eastern skies over the jungle.

Lieutenant Bates grinned and wiggled the control stick.

"Usually it's worse. We'll get her out, Fuller. You just put us next to the right cave."

"I'll do that, but it won't work."

"Sure it will."

"You don't need to cheer me up, Bates."

"I don't?" Bates grinned again. He was not much older than Mark. "Maybe I need cheering up. I'm always scared about now."

"Really? You don't look it."

"All we're expected to do. Not look it." He thumbed the mike button. "Chief, everything set back there?"

"Aye-aye, sir."

The chatter in Mark's helmet grew still. A voice said "Missiles away." Seconds later a new and sterner voice said *"All helicopters, start your engines. I say again, start engines."*

"That's us," Bates reached for the starting controls and the turbines whined. "Not very much light."

"Helicopters, report when ready."

"Ready aye-aye," Bates said.

"Aye-aye?" Mark asked.

"We're an old CD Marine regiment," Bates said. "Lot of us, anyway. Stayed with the old man when the Senate disbanded his regiment."

"You don't look old enough."

"Me? Not hardly. This was Falkenberg's Mercenary Legion long before I came aboard."

"Why? Why join mercenaries?"

Bates shrugged. "I like being part of the regiment. The pay's good. What's the matter, don't you think the work's worth doing?"

"Lift off. Begin helicopter assault."

Lift-off aye-aye." The turbine whine increased and the ship lifted in a rising, looping circle. Bates took the right hand position in the three-craft formation.

Mark could dimly see the green below, and the visibility increased every minute. Now he could make out the shapes of small clearings among the endless green marshes.

"You take her," Bates said. His hands hovered over the controls, ready to take his darling away from this stranger.

Mark grasped the unfamiliar stick. It was different from the family machine he'd learned on, but the principles were the same. The chopper was not much more than a big airborne truck, and he'd driven one of those on a vacation in the Yukon. The Canadian lakes seemed endlessly far away, in time as well as in space.

Flying came back easily. He remembered the wild stunts he'd tried when he was first licensed. Once a group from his school had gone on a picnic to San Miguel Island and Mark had landed in a cove, dropping onto a narrow, inaccessible beach between high cliffs during a windstorm. It had been stupid, but wildly exciting. After that, they always let him drive when they wanted to do something unusual. Good practice for this, he thought. And I'm scared stiff, and what do I do after this is over? Will Falkenberg turn me in? They'll sell me to a mining company. Or worse.

There were low hills ahead, dull brown in the early morning light. Men huddled in the rocky areas. Some lay sprawled, victims of the bomblets released by the first salvo of rockets. Gatlings in the compartment behind Mark crackled like frying bacon. The shots were impossibly close together, like a steady stream of noise. The helicopter raked the Free State. The small slugs sent chips flying from the rocks. The other choppers opened up, and six tracer streams twisted in crazy patterns intertwining like some courtship dance.

Men and women died on that flinty ground. They lay in broken heaps, red blood staining the dirt around them, exactly like a scene on tri-v. It's not fake, Mark thought. They won't get up when the cameras go away. Did they deserve this? Does anyone?

Then he was too busy piloting the helicopter to think about anything else. The area in front of the cave was small, very small—would the rotors clear it? A strong gust from the sea struck them and the chopper rocked dangerously.

"Watch her—" Whatever Bates had intended to say, he never finished it. He slumped forward over the stick, held just above it by his shoulder straps. Something wet and sticky splashed across Mark's left hand and arm. Brains. A large slug had come angling upward to hit Bates in the jaw, then ricochet around in his helmet. The young lieutenant had almost no face. Get her down, Mark chanted, easy baby, down you go, level now, here's another gust, easy baby. . . .

Men poured out of the descending chopper. Mark had time to be surprised: they jumped down and ran into the cave even as their friends fell around them.

Then something stabbed Mark's left arm, and he saw neat holes in the Plexiglas windscreen in front of him. The men went into the cave. They were faceless in their big helmets, identical robots moving forward or falling in heaps. . . .

Lord God, they're magnificent. I've got to get this thing down! Suddenly it was the most important thing in his life.

Get down and get out, go into the cave with those men. Find Juanita, yes, of course, but go with them, do something for myself because I want to do it—

"*Bates, stop wasting time and get to green A-one urgent.*"

God damn it! Mark fumbled with the communications gear. "Bates is dead. This is Fuller. I'm putting the chopper down."

The voice in the phones changed. Someone else spoke. "Are the troops still aboard?"

"No. They're off."

"Then take that craft to Green A-one immediately."

"My—my wife's in there!"

The colonel's aware of that." Jeremy Savage's voice was calm. "That machine is required, and now."

"But—"

"Fuller, this regiment has risked a great deal for those hostages. The requirement is urgent. Or do you seriously suppose you would be much use inside?"

Oh, Christ! There was firing inside the cave, and someone was screaming. I want to kill him, Mark thought. Kill that blond-haired bastard. I want to watch him die. A babble filled the helmet phones. Crisp commands and reports were jumbled together as a background noise. Frazer's voice. "We're pinned. I'm sending them back to A-one as fast as I can."

There was more firing from inside the cave.

"Aye-aye," Mark said. He gunned the engine and lifted out in a whirling loop to confuse the ground fire. Someone was still aboard; the Gatlings chattered and their bright streams raked the rocks around the open area below.

Where was Green A-one? Mark glanced at the screen in front of the control stick. There was gray and white matter, and bright red blood in a long smear across the glass surface. Mark had to lift Bates's head to get a bearing. More blood ran across his fingers, and something warm trickled down his left arm.

Then the area was ahead, a clear depression surrounded by hills and rocks. Men lay around the top of the bowl. A mortar team worked mechanically, dropping the shells down the tube, leaning back, lifting, dropping another. There were bright flashes everywhere. Mark dropped into the bowl and the flashes vanished. There were sounds; gunfire, and the whump! whump! of the mortar. A squad rushed over and began loading wounded men into the machine. Then the sergeant waved him off, and Mark raced for the rear area where the surgeon waited. Another helicopter passed, headed into the combat area.

The medics off-loaded the men.

"Stand by, Fuller, we'll get another pilot over there," Savage's calm voice said in the phones.

"No, I'll keep it. I know the way."

There was a pause. "Right. Get to it, then."

"Aye-aye, sir."

The entrance to the boss's cave was cool, and the surgeon had moved the field hospital there. A steady stream of men came out of the depths of the cave: prisoners carrying their own dead, and Falkenberg's men carrying their comrades. The Free State dead were piled in heaps near the cliff edge. When they were identified, they were tossed over the side. The regiment's dead were carried to a cleared area, where they lay covered. Armed soldiers guarded the corpses.

Do the dead give a damn? Mark wondered. Why should they? What's the point of all the ceremony over dead mercenaries? He looked back at the still figure on the bed. She seemed small and helpless, and her breath rasped in her throat. An IV unit dripped endlessly.

"She'll live."

Mark turned to see the regimental surgeon.

"We couldn't save the baby, but there's no reason she can't have more."

"What happened to her?" Mark demanded.

The surgeon shrugged. "Bullet in the lower abdomen. Ours, theirs, who knows? Jacketed slug, it didn't do a lot of damage. The colonel wants to see you, Fuller. And you can't do any good here." The surgeon took him by the elbow and ushered him out into the steaming daylight. "That way."

There were more work parties in the open space outside. Prisoners were still carrying away dead men. Insects buzzed around dark red stains on the flinty rocks. They look so dead, Mark thought. So damned dead. Somewhere a woman was crying.

Falkenberg sat with his officers under an open tent in the clearing. There was another man with them, a prisoner under guard. "So they took you alive," Mark said.

"I seem to have survived. They killed George." The boss's lips curled in a sneer. "And you helped them. Fine way to thank us for taking you in."

"Taking us in! You raped—"

"How do you know it was rape?" the boss demanded. "Not that you were any great help, were you? You're no damned good, Fuller. Your help didn't make a damned bit of difference. Has anything you ever did made any difference?"

"That will do, Chambliss," Falkenberg said.

"Sure. You're in charge now, Colonel. Well, you beat us, so you give the orders. We're pretty much alike, you and me."

"Possibly," Falkenberg said. "Corporal, take Chambliss to the guard area. And make certain he does not escape."

"Sir." The troopers gestured with their rifles. The boss walked ahead of them. He seemed to be leading them.

"What will happen to him?" Mark asked.

"We will turn him over to the governor. I expect he'll hang. The problem, Fuller, is what to do with you. You were of some help to us, and I don't like unpaid debts."

"What choices do I have?" Mark asked.

Falkenberg shrugged. "We could give you a mount and weapons. It is a long journey to the farmlands in the south, but once there, you could probably avoid recapture. Probably. If that is not attractive, we could put in a good word with the governor."

"Which would get me what?"

"At the least he would agree to forget about your escape and persuade your patron not to prosecute for theft of animals and weapons."

"But I'd be back under sentence. A slave again. What happens to Juanita?"

"The regiment will take care of her."

"What the hell does that mean?" Mark demanded.

Falkenberg's expression did not change. Mark could not tell what the colonel was thinking. "I mean, Fuller, that is unlikely that the troops would approve turning her over to the governor. She can stay with us until her apprenticeship has expired."

Emotions raged through him. Mark opened his mouth, then bit off the words. *So you're no better than the boss!*

"What Colonel Falkenberg means," Major Savage said, "is that she will be permitted to stay with us as long as she wishes. We don't lack for women, and there are other differences between us and your Free State. Colonel Falkenberg commands a regiment. He does not rule a mob."

"Sure. What if she wants to come with me?"

"Then we will see that she does. When she recovers," Savage said. "That will be her choice. Now what is it you want to do? We don't have all day."

What do I want to do? Lord God, I want to go home, but that's not possible. Dirt farmer, fugitive forever. Or slave for at least two more years. "You haven't given me a very pleasant set of alternatives."

"You had fewer when you came here," Savage said.

A party of prisoners was herded toward the tent. They stood looking nervously at the seated officers, while their guards stood at ease with their weapons. Mark licked his lips. "I heard you were enlisting some of the Free Staters."

Falkenberg nodded. "A few. Not many."

"Could you use a helicopter pilot?"

Major Savage chuckled. "Told you he'd ask, John Christian."

"He was steady enough this morning," Captain Frazer said. "And we do need pilots."

"Do you know what you're getting into?" Falkenberg asked. "Soldiers are not slaves, but they must obey orders. All of them."

"Slaves have to obey, too."

"It's five years," Major Savage said. "And we track down deserters."

"Yes, sir." Mark looked at each of the officers in turn. They sat impassively. They said nothing; they did not look at each other, but they belonged to each other. And to their men. Mark remembered the clubs that children in his neighborhood had formed. Belonging to them had been important, although he could never have said why.

"You see the regiment as merely another unpleasant alternative," Falkenberg said. "If it is never more than that, it will not be enough."

"He came for us, colonel," Frazer said. "He didn't have to."

"I take it you are sponsoring him."

"Yes, sir."

"Very well," Falkenberg said. "I doubt, Mister Fuller, if you realize just how you have been honored. Sergeant Major, is he acceptable to the men?"

"No objections, sir."

"Jeremy?"

"No objection, John Christian."

"Adjutant?"

"I've got his records, Colonel," Captain Fast indicated the console readout. "He'd make a terrible enlisted man."

"But not necessarily a terrible aviation officer?"

"No, sir. He scores out high enough. But I've got my doubts about his motivations."

"Yes. But we do not generally worry about men's motives. We only require that they act like soldiers. Are you objecting, Amos?"

"No, Colonel."

"Then that's that. Fuller, you will be on trial. It will not be the easiest experience of your life. Men earn their way into this regiment." He smiled suddenly. "The lot of a junior warrant officer is not always enviable."

"Yes, sir."

"You may go. There will be a formal swearing in when we return to our own camp. And doubtless Captain Fast will need information for his data base. Dismissed."

"Yes, sir." Mark left the command tent. The times are out of joint, he thought. Is that the right line? Whatever. Does anyone control his own life? I couldn't. The police, the Marines, the boss, now these mercenaries—they tell us all what to do. Who tells them?

Now I'm one of them. Mercenary soldier. It sounds ugly, but I don't have any choices at all. It's no career. Just a way out of slavery.

And yet—

He remembered the morning's combat and felt guilty at the memory. He had felt alive then. Men and women died all around him, but he'd felt more alive than he'd ever been.

He passed the graves. The honor guard stood at rigid attention, ignoring the buzzing insects, ignoring everything around them as they stood over the banner-draped figures laid out in neat rows. I'm one of them now, he thought, but whether he meant the guards or the corpses he couldn't say.

XI

"Mr. President!"

"Mr. Vice!"

"I regret to report that, contrary to the rules of the mess, Captain Owensford brought his drink to his table. Sir!"

Captain Jesus Alana stood at the end of the head table and fixed Owensford with a chilly stare. "Captain Owensford!"

Owensford stood. "Mr. President."

"What have you to say in defense of your heinous crime?"

"It was a good drink, sir!"

"Unconscionable, Captain. You will report to the grog bucket."

"Sir!" Owensford marched to the end of the room.

"I presume you do this sort of thing on Sparta," Major Savage said.

"Perhaps we don't follow *all* of the old traditions," Lysander said. Then he grinned. "Actually, very little of this, but I may change that when I get back."

Owensford used fireman's tongs to remove a smoking flask from within a container marked with radiation trefoils. He carefully poured a metal cup full of the smoking brew, then put on welders' gloves and lifted the cup. "To our guest, to the mess president, and to the 42nd!" He drank, set the cup upside down on his head, and saluted.

"Mr. President!"

"Mr. Vice!"

"I regret to report that Captain Owensford neglected to salute the mess prior to imbibing. Sir!"

"Captain Owensford, what have you to say for yourself?"

"Previous drink was a *very* good drink, sir!"

"We'll excuse you. Once. Take your seat!"

"*Thank* you, sir!"

The ladies, except those in uniform, had long since retired from the dining hall. Catherine Alana had worn a civilian gown,

385

and didn't return after escorting Ursula to her room in the
regiment's guest quarters. *And I sleep alone tonight.* Lysander
looked down to the far end of the table where Falkenberg sat
impassively. *Interesting that he arranged our rooms that way.
Or does he even know?*

Guests were excused from following the customs of the mess,
but even without visiting the grog bucket Lysander had drunk
more than he usually did. There had been cocktails before dinner, wine during dinner, port after dinner, and brandy after the
port. Then Falkenberg had signaled, and the stewards brought
whiskey, Scotch so smooth that it was more like brandy.

Now the colonel caught Alana's eye. The mess president
nodded. "Pipe Major!"

"Sir!" A dozen pipers marched into the hall. Stewards
brought more whiskey.

"Good God, Major," Lysander said. "Do you do this often?"

"Only when we've a good excuse."

And I expect you can always find one. "Of course, your
victory last week needed celebrating."

"Right. We already did that, you know. You're the excuse
tonight." Savage glanced at his watch. "Actually, I expect things
will end soon enough. Staff meetings in the morning." He
stood. "And on that score, if you'll excuse me, I have some
preparations."

"I don't suppose you need help?"

Savage grinned. "It can be a bit much. Tell you what, I'll
have a word with the mess president on my way out."

Ten minutes later the pipers paused for refreshments, and
Captain Alana announced the formal end of the dining-out.
Lysander got unsteadily to his feet.

Captain Owensford came over and spoke quietly. "Some of
them will stay at it all night. Would you like a guide to your
room?"

"Yes. Please!"

It was almost cool outside, and Lysander felt a little less
drunk.

"Actually, the noise gets to me as much as the whisky,"
Owensford said. "I've never been crazy about pipers myself.
Feeling all right now?"

"Not too bad—"

"I know a way to feel better."

"Yes?"

"We have a concoction. Vitamins. Tonic. Other stuff. Works
every time. Would you care for some?"

"Captain, I would *kill* for a glass of that. Or two glasses. Please?"

Owensford grinned. "This way." He led Lysander to a small bar at the far end of the officers' mess, and ushered him to a table. "Billings, two Night Befores, please."

"Sir." The bartender was an old man, but he carried himself like a soldier. His left hand was a prosthetic adapted to bartending. He grinned and set two tall glasses on the table, went back, and brought a pitcher of water.

"You sip it," Owensford said. "Then down at least two glasses of water. Works like a charm."

Lysander sipped, and grimaced.

"I didn't say it *tasted* good," Owensford said. "Cheers." He sipped at his drink. "Understand you see the governor fairly often."

"Yes. Things heated up a bit while you were out in the field."

Owensford's eyes narrowed. "How so?"

"More plantation owners have joined the combine. Several dozen more. The boycott is working better than anyone expected."

"Damn. But I'm not surprised."

"Why not?"

"I've known Ace Barton for a while."

"Barton. The major in charge of the opposition's mercenaries."

"That's Ace."

"How did you get to know him?"

"Well—actually he was responsible for my being recruited into the Legion. It's a long story."

Lysander sipped at the drink and grimaced again. "I may be a while getting this down—"

Owensford leaned back and stared at the ceiling. "It was quite a long time ago, long enough that it's almost as if it happened to someone else. I was much younger then. . . ."

XII

"As He died to make men holy, let us die to make men free. . . ."

The song echoed through the ship, along gray corridors stained with the greasy handprints of the thousands who had traveled in her before; through the stench of the thousands aboard, and the remembered smells of previous shiploads of convicts.

Peter Owensford looked up from the steel desk that hung from the wall of his tiny stateroom. The men weren't singing very well, but they sang from their hearts. There was a faint buzzing from a loose rivet vibrating to a strong bass voice. Owensford nodded to himself. The singer was Allan Roach, onetime professional wrestler, and Peter had marked him for promotion to noncom once they reached Santiago.

The trip from Earth to Thurstone takes three months in a Bureau of Relocation transport ship, and it had been wasted time for all of them. It was obvious to Peter that the CoDominium authorities aboard the ship knew that they were volunteers for the war. Why else would ninety-seven men voluntarily ship out for Santiago? It didn't matter, though. Political Officer Stromand was afraid of a trap. Stromand was always suspecting traps.

In all the three months Peter Owensford had held only a dozen classes. He'd found an empty compartment near the garbage disposal and assembled the men there; but Stromand had caught them. There had been a scene, with Stromand insisting that Peter call him "Commissar" and the men address him as "Sir." Instead, Peter addressed him as "Mister" and the men made it come out like "Comics-star." Stromand had been livid, and he'd stopped Peter's classes.

Now Peter had ninety-six men who knew nothing of war. They were educated men. He had students, workers, idealists; but it might have been better if they'd all been zapouts with a long history of juvenile gangsterism.

388

He went back to his papers, jotting notes on what must be done when they landed. At least he'd have some time to train them before they got into combat.

He'd need it.

Thurstone is usually described as a hot, dry copy of Earth and Peter found no reason to dispute that. The CoDominium Island is legally part of Earth, but Thurstone is twenty parsecs away, and travelers go through customs. Peter's ragged group packed away whatever military equipment they had brought privately, and dressed in the knee breeches and tunics popular with businessmen in New York. Peter found himself just behind Allan Roach in the line to debark.

Allan was laughing.

"What's the joke?" Peter asked.

Roach turned and gestured at the men behind him. All ninety-six scattered through the first two hundred passengers leaving the BuRelock ship, and they were all dressed identically. "Humanity League decided to save money," Roach said. "What do you reckon the CD makes of our comic-opera army?"

Whatever the CoDominium inspectors thought, they did nothing, hardly glancing inside the baggage, and the volunteers were hustled out of the CD building to the docks. A small Russian in baggy pants sidled up to them.

"Freedom," he said. He had a thick accent.

"No passaran!" Commissar Stromand answered.

"I have tickets for you," the Russian said. "You will go on the boat." He pointed to an excursion ship with peeling paint and faded gilt handrails.

"Man, he looks like he's lettin' go his last credit," Allan Roach muttered to Owensford.

Peter nodded. "At that, I'd rather pay for the tickets than ride the boat. Must have been built when Thurstone was first settled."

Roach shrugged and lifted his bags. Then, as an afterthought, he lifted Peter's as well.

"You don't have to carry my goddamn baggage," Peter protested.

"That's why I'm doing it, Lieutenant. I wouldn't carry Stromand's." They went aboard the boat and stood at the rails to stare at Thurstone's bright skies. The volunteers were the only passengers, and the ship left the dock to lumber across shallow seas. It was less than fifty kilometers to the mainland, and before the men really believed they were out of space and onto a planet again, they were in Free Santiago.

They marched through the streets. People cheered, but a lot of volunteers had come through these streets and they didn't cheer very loud. Owensford's men were no good at marching and they had no weapons; so Stromand ordered them to sing war songs.

They didn't know very many songs, so they always sang the Battle Hymn of the Republic. It said everything they were feeling, anyway.

The ragged group straggled to the local parish church. Someone had broken the cross and spire off the building, and turned the altar into a lecture desk. It was nearly dark by the time Owensford's troops were bedded down in the pews.

"Lieutenant?"

Allan Roach and another volunteer stood in front of him. "Yes?"

"Some of the men don't like bein' in here, lieutenant. We got church members in the outfit."

"I see. What do you expect me to do about it?" Peter asked. "This is where we were sent." And why didn't someone meet us instead of having a kid hand me a note down at the docks? But it wouldn't do to upset the men.

"We could bed down outside," Roach suggested.

"Nonsense. Superstitious garbage." The strident, bookish voice came from behind him, but Peter didn't need to look around. "Free men have no need for that kind of belief. Tell me who is disturbed."

Allan Roach set his lips tightly together.

"I insist," Stromand demanded. "Those men need education, and I will provide it. We cannot have superstition within our company."

"Superstition be damned," Peter said. "It's dark and gloomy and uncomfortable in here. If the men want to sleep outside, let them."

"No."

"I remind you that I am in command here." Peter's voice was rising despite his effort to control it. He was twenty-three standard years old, while Stromand was forty, and this was Peter's first command. He knew this was an important issue, and the men were all listening.

"I remind *you* that political education is totally up to me," Stromand said. "It is good indoctrination for the men to stay in here."

"Crap." Peter stood abruptly. "All right, everybody outside. Camp in the churchyard. Roach, set up a night guard around the camp."

"Yes, sir!" Allan Roach grinned.

Commissar Stromand watched his men melt away. A few minutes later he followed them outside.

They were awakened by an officer in synthileather trousers and tunic. He wore no badges of rank, but it was obvious to Peter that the man was a professional soldier. Someday, Peter thought, I'll look like that. The thought was cheering.

"Who's in charge here?"

Stromand and Owensford answered simultaneously. The officer looked at them for a moment, then turned to Peter. "Name?"

"Lieutenant Peter Owensford."

"Lieutenant. And why might you be a lieutenant?"

"I'm a graduate of West Point, sir. And your rank?"

"Captain, sonny. Captain Anselm Barton, at your service, God help you. The lot of you have been posted to the Twelfth Brigade, second battalion, of which battalion I have the misfortune to be adjutant. Any more questions?" He glared at Peter and the commissar. Before either of them could answer there was a roar and the wind whipped red dust around them. A moment later a fleet of ground-effects trucks rounded the corner and stopped in front of the church.

"Okay," Barton shouted. "Into the trucks. You, too, Mister Comics-Star. Lieutenant, you ride in the cab with me. Come on, come on, we haven't all day. Can't you get them to hop it, Owensford?"

No two of the trucks were alike. One Mercedes stood out proudly from the lesser breeds, and Barton went to it. After a moment Stromand took the unoccupied seat in the cab of the second truck, an old Fiat. Despite the early hour, the sun was hot and bright, and it was good to get inside.

The Mercedes ran smoothly, but had to halt frequently while the drivers worked on the other trucks. The Fiat could only get ten centimeters above the road. Peter noted the ruts in the dirt track.

"Sure," Barton said. "We've got wheeled transport. Lots of it. Animal-drawn wagons too. Tracked railroads. How much do you know about this place?"

"Not very much," Peter admitted.

"At least you know that," Barton said. He gunned the engine to get the Mercedes over a deeply pitted section of the road and the convoy climbed up onto a ridge. Peter could look back and see the tiny port town, with its almost empty streets, and the blowing red dust.

"See that ridge over there?" Barton asked. He pointed to

a thin blue line beyond the far lip of the saucer on the other side of the ridge. The air was so clear that Peter could see for sixty kilometers or more. Distances were hard to judge.

"Yes, sir."

"That's it. Dons territory beyond that line."

"We're not going straight there, are we? The men need training."

"You might as well be going to the lines, for all the training they'll get. They teach you anything at the Point?"

"I learned something, I think." Peter didn't know what to answer. The Point had been "humanized" and he knew he hadn't had the military instruction that graduates had once received. "What I was taught, and a lot from books."

"We'll see." Barton took a plastic toothpick out of one pocket and stuck it into his mouth. Later, Peter would learn that many men developed that habit. "No hay tobacco" was a common notice on stores in Santiago. The first time he saw it, Allan Roach said that if they made their tobacco out of hay he didn't want any. "Long out of the Point?" Barton asked.

"Class of '77."

"Just out. U.S. Army didn't want you?"

"That's pretty personal," Peter said. The toothpick danced across smiling lips. Peter stared out at the rivers of dust blowing around them. "There's a new rule now. You have to opt for CoDominium in your junior year. I did. But they didn't have any room for me in the CD service."

Barton grunted. "And the U.S. Army doesn't want any commie-coddling officers who'd take the CD over their own country."

"That's about it."

They drove on in silence. Barton hummed something under his breath, a tune that Peter thought he would recognize if only Barton would make it loud enough to hear. Then he caught a murmured refrain. "Let's hope he brings our godson up, to don the Armay blue . . ."

Barton looked around at his passenger and grinned. "How many lights in Cullem Hall, Mister Dumbjohn?"

"Three hundred and forty lights, sir," Peter answered automatically. He looked for the ring, but Barton wore none. "What was your class, sir?"

"Sixty-two. Okay, so the U.S. didn't want you, and the CD's disbanding regiments. There's other outfits. Falkenberg's recruiting. . . ."

"I'm not a mercenary," Peter said stiffly.

"Oh, Lord. So you're here to help the downtrodden masses throw off the yoke of oppression. I might have known."

"But of course I'm here to fight slavery! Everyone knows about Santiago."

"Everyone knows about other places, too." The toothpick danced again. "Okay, you're a liberator of suffering humanity. God knows, anything makes a man feel better out here is okay. But to help *me* feel better, remember that you're a professional officer."

"I won't forget." They drove over another ridge. The valley beyond was no different from the one behind them, and there was another ridge at its end.

"What do you think those people out there want?" Barton said.

"Freedom."

"Maybe to be left alone. Maybe they'd be happy if we all went away."

"They'd be slaves. Somebody's got to help them—" Peter caught himself. There was no point to this, and he was sure Barton was laughing at him.

Instead, the older man's expression softened from his usual sardonic grin to a wry smile. "Nothing to be ashamed of, Pete. Most of us read those books about knighthood. We wouldn't be in the services if we didn't have that streak in us. But remember, you get over most of that or you won't last."

"Maybe without something like that I wouldn't want to last."

"Suit yourself. Just don't let it break your heart."

"If you feel that way about everything, why are you here? Why aren't you in one of the mercenary outfits?"

"Commissars ask that kind of question," Barton said. He gunned the motor viciously and the Mercedes screamed forward.

It was late afternoon when they got to Tarazona. The town was an architectural hodgepodge, as if a dozen amateurs had designed it. The church, now a hospital, was Elizabeth III modern; the post office was American Gothic; and most of the houses were white stucco. The volunteers unloaded at a plasteel barracks that was a bad copy of the quad at West Point. It had sally ports, phony portcullis and all, and plastic medieval shields decorated the cornices.

Inside there was trash in the corridors and blood on the floors. Peter set the men to cleaning up.

"About that blood," Captain Barton said. "Your men seem interested."

"First blood some of 'em have seen," Peter told him. Barton was still watching him closely. "All right. For me, too."

Barton nodded. "Two stories about that blood. The Dons had a garrison here. They made a stand when the Revolutionaries took the town. Some say the Dons slaughtered their prisoners here. Others say when the Republic took the barracks, our troops slaughtered the garrison."

Peter looked across the dusty courtyard and beyond the hills where the fighting was. It seemed a long way off. There was no sound, and the afternoon sun was unbearably hot. "Which do you think is true?"

"Both." Barton turned away toward the town. Then he stopped for a moment. "I'll be in the bistro after dinner. Join me if you get a chance." He walked on, his feet kicking up little clouds of dust that blew across the road.

Peter stood a long time in the courtyard, staring across fields that stretched fifty kilometers to the hills. The soil was red, and a hot wind blew dust into every crevice and hollow. The country seemed far too barren to be a focal point in the struggle for freedom in the known galaxy.

Thurstone had been colonized early in the CoDominium period, but the planet was too poor to attract wealthy corporations. The third Thurstone expedition was financed by the Carlist branch of the Spanish monarchy, and eventually Carlos XII and a group of supporters—malcontents, like most voluntary colonists—founded Santiago.

Some of the Santiago colonists were protesting the Bourbon restoration in Spain. Others were unhappy with John XXVI's reunification of Christendom. Others still protested the cruel fates, unhappy love affairs, nagging wives, and impossible gambling debts. The Carlists got the smallest and poorest of Thurstone's three continents, but they did well enough with it.

For thirty years Santiago received only voluntary immigrants from Spanish Catholic cultures. The Carlists were careful who they let in, and there was plenty of good land for everyone. The Kingdom of St. James had little modern technology, and no one was very rich, but few were very poor either.

Eventually the Population Control Commission designated Thurstone as a recipient planet, and the Bureau of Relocation began moving people there. All three governments on Thurstone protested, but unlike Xanadu or Danube, Thurstone had never developed a navy; a single frigate from the CoDominium Fleet convinced them they had no choice.

BuRelock ships carried two million involuntary colonists to Thurstone. Convicts, welfare frauds, criminals, revolutionaries, rioters, street gangsters, men who'd offended a BuRelock clerk, men with the wrong color eyes, and those who were just plain unlucky; all of them bundled into unsanitary transport ships and hustled away from Earth. The other nations on Thurstone had friends in BuRelock and money to pay for favors; Santiago got the bulk of the new immigrants.

The Carlists tried. They provided transportation to unclaimed lands for all who wanted it and most who did not. The original Santiago settlers had fled from industry and had built very little; and now, suddenly, they were swamped with city dwellers from a different culture who had no thought of the land and less love for it.

·In less than a decade the capital grew from a sleepy town to a sprawling heap of shacks. The Carlists demolished the worst of the shacks. Others appeared on the other side of town. New cities grew from small towns.

When industries appeared in the new cities, the original settlers revolted. They had fled from industrialized life, and wanted no more of it. A king was deposed and an infant prince placed on his father's throne. The Cortes took government into its own hands, and enslaved everyone who did not pay his own way.

It was not called slavery, but "indebtedness for welfare service"; but debts were inheritable and transferable. Debts could be bought and sold on speculation, and everyone had to work them off.

In a generation half the population was in debt. In another the slaves outnumbered the free men. Finally the slaves revolted, and overnight Santiago became a *cause celebre.*

In the CoDominium Grand Senate, the U.S., with a nudge from the other governments on Thurstone and the corporations who bought agricultural products from Santiago, supported the Carlists, but not strongly. The Soviet senators supported the Republic, but not strongly. The CD Navy was ordered to quarantine the war area.

The fleet had few ships to spare for that task. The Navy grounded all military air and spacecraft in Santiago, and prohibited the import of any kind of heavy weapons. Otherwise Santiago was left alone.

It was never difficult for the Humanity League to send volunteers to Santiago as long as they brought no weapons. Because the volunteers had no experience, the League also searched for trained officers to lead them.

The League rejected mercenaries, of course.

XIII

Peter Owensford sat in the pleasant cool of the Santiago evening at a scarred table that might have been oak, but wasn't. Captain Ace Barton brought a pitcher of dark red wine and joined him.

"I thought they'd put me in the technical corps," Peter said.

"Speak Mandarin?" Peter looked up in surprise. Barton grinned. "The Republicans hired Xanadu techs. What with the quarantine we don't have much high tech equipment. Plenty of Chinese for what little we've got."

"So I'm infantry."

Barton shrugged. "You fight, Pete. Just like me. They'll give you a company. The ones you brought in, and maybe another hundred recruits. All yours. You'll get Stromand for political officer, too."

Peter grimaced. "What use is he?"

Barton made a show of looking around. "Careful." His grin stayed, but his voice was serious. "Political officers are a lot more popular with the high command than we are. Don't forget that."

"From what I've seen the high command isn't very competent. . . ."

"Jesus," Barton said. "Look, Pete, they can have you shot for talking like that. This isn't a merc outfit under the Mercenary Code, you know. This is a patriotic war, and you'd better not forget it."

Peter stared at the packed clay floor. He'd sat at this table every night for a week now, and he was beginning to understand Barton's cynicism. "There's not enough body armor for my men. The ones I've got. You say they'll give me more men?"

"New group coming in tomorrow. No officer with them. Sure, they'll put 'em with you. Where else? Troops have to be trained."

"Trained!" Peter snorted. "We have enough Nemourlon to

396

make armor for about half the troops, but I'm the only one in the company who knows how to do it. We've got no weapons, no optics, no communications—"

"Yeah, things are tough all over," Barton poured another glass of wine. "What'd you expect in a non-industrial society quarantined by the CD?"

Peter slumped back into the hard wooden chair. "Yeah, I know. But—I can't even train them on what we do have. Whenever I get the men assembled, Stromand starts making speeches."

Barton smiled. "International Brigade Commander Cermak thinks the American troops have lousy morale. Obviously, the way to fix that is to make speeches."

"Their morale is lousy because they don't know how to fight."

"Another of Cermak's solutions to the morale problem is to shoot defeatists," Barton said softly. "I've warned you, kid."

"The only damn thing my men have learned in the last week is how to sing and which red-light houses are safe."

"More'n some do. Have another drink."

"Thanks." Peter nodded in resignation. "That's not bad wine."

"Right. Pretty good, but not good enough to export," Barton said. "Whole goddamn country's that way, you know. Pretty good, but not quite good enough."

The next day they gave Peter Owensford 107 new men fresh from Earth. A week later Peter found Ace Barton at his favorite table in the bistro.

Barton poured a glass of wine as Peter sat down. "You look like you need a drink. I thought you were ordered to stay on nights to train the troops."

Peter drank. "Same story, Ace. Speeches. More speeches. I walked out. It was obvious I wasn't going to have anything to do."

"Risky," Barton said. They sat in silence as Barton looked thoughtful. Finally he spoke. "Ever think you're not needed, Pete?"

"They act that way, but I'm still the only man in the company with any military training."

"So what? The Republic doesn't need your troops. Not the way you think. The main purpose of the volunteers is to see the right party stays in control."

Peter sat stiffly silent. He'd promised himself that he wouldn't react quickly to anything Barton said. "I can't believe that," he said finally. "The volunteers come from everywhere. They're not fighting to help any political party, they're here to set people free."

Barton said nothing. A red toothpick danced across his face, and a sly grin broke across his square features.

"See, you don't even believe it yourself," Peter said.

"Could be. Pete, you ever think how much money they raise back in the States? Money from people who feel guilty about not volunteerin'?"

"No. There's no money here. You've seen that."

"There's money, but it goes to the techs," Barton said. "That at least makes sense. Xanadu isn't sending their sharp boys for nothing, and without them, what's the use of mudcrawlers like us?"

Peter leaned back. "Then we've got pretty good technical support. . . ."

"About as good as the Dons have. Which means neither side has a goddamn thing. Either group gets a real edge that way, the war's over, right? But nobody's going to get past the CD quarantine, so all the Dons and the Republicans can do is kill each other with rifles and knives and grenades. Not very damn many grenades, either."

"We don't even have rifles."

"You'll get them. Meantime, relax. You've told Brigade your men aren't ready to fight. You've asked for weapons and more Nemourlon. You've complained about Stromand. You've done it all. Now shut up before they shoot you for a defeatist. That's an order, Pete."

"Yes, sir."

The trucks came back to Tarazona a week later. They carried coffin-shaped boxes full of rifles and bayonets from New Aberdeen, Thurstone's largest city. The rifles were covered with grease, and there wasn't any solvent to clean them with. Most were copies of Remington 2045 model automatics, but there were some Krupps and Skodas. Most of the men didn't know which ammunition fit their rifles.

"Not bad gear." Barton turned one of the rifles over in his hands. "We've had worse."

"But I don't have much training in rifle tactics," Peter said.

Barton shrugged. "No power supplies, no maintenance ships. Damn few mortars and rockets. No fancy munitions. There's no base to support anything more complicated than chemical slug-throwers, Peter. Forget the rest of the crap you learned and remember that."

"Yes, sir."

Whistles blew, and someone shouted from the trucks. "Get your gear and get aboard!"

"What?" Owensford turned to Barton. "Get aboard for where?"

Barton shrugged. "I'd better get back to my area. Maybe they're moving the whole battalion up while we've got the trucks."

They were. Men who had armor put it on, and everyone dressed in combat synthileather. Most had helmets, ugly hemispheric models with a stiff spine over the most vulnerable areas. A few men had lost theirs, and they boarded the trucks without them.

The convoy rolled across the plains and into a greener farm area. After dark the air chilled fast under clear, cloudless sides. The drivers pushed on, driving too fast without lights. Peter sat in the back of the lead truck, his knees clamped tightly together, his teeth unconsciously beating out a rhythm he'd learned years before. No one talked.

At dawn they unloaded in another valley. Trampled crops lay all around them.

"Good land," Private Lunster said. He lifted a clod and crumbled it between his fingers. "Very good land."

Somehow that made Peter feel better. He formed the men into ranks and made sure each knew how to load his weapon. Then he had each of them fire at a crumbling adobe wall. He chose a large target that they couldn't miss. More trucks pulled in and unloaded heavy generators and antitank lasers. When Owensford's men tried to get close to the heavy weapons the gunners shouted them away. The gunners seemed familiar with their equipment, and that was encouraging.

Everyone spoke softly, and when anyone raised his voice it was like a shout. Stromand tried to get the men to sing, but they wouldn't.

"Not long now, eh?" Sergeant Roach said.

"I expect not," Peter told him, but he didn't know, and went off to find the commissary truck. He wanted to be sure the men got a good meal that evening.

Orders to move up came during the night. A guide whispered to Peter to follow him, and they moved out across the unfamiliar land. Somewhere out there were the Dons with their army of peasant conscripts and mercenaries and family retainers. Peter and his company hadn't gone fifty meters before they passed an old tree and someone whispered to them.

"Everything will be fine," Stromand's voice said from the

shadows. "All of the enemy are politically immature. Their vaqueros will run away and their peasant conscripts will throw away their weapons. They have no reason to be loyal."

"Why the hell has the war gone on three years?" someone whispered behind Peter.

He waited until they were long past the tree. "Roach, that wasn't smart. Stromand will have you shot for defeatism."

"He'll play hell doing it, lieutenant. You, man, pick up your feet. Want to fall down that gully?"

"Quiet," the guide whispered urgently. They went on through the dark night, down a slope, then up another, past men dug into the hillside. No one spoke.

Peter found himself walking along the remains of a railroad. Most of the ties were gone, and the rails had been taken away. Eventually his guide halted. "Dig in here," he whispered. "Long live freedom."

"No pasaran!" Stromand answered.

"Please be quiet," the guide urged. "We are within earshot of the enemy."

"Ah," Stromand answered. The guide turned away and the political officer began to follow him.

"Where are you going?" Corporal Grant asked in a loud whisper.

"To report to Major Harris," Stromand answered. "The battalion commander ought to know where we are."

"So should we," a voice said.

"Who was that?" Stromand demanded. The only answer was a juicy raspberry.

"That bastard's got no right," a voice said close to Peter. "Who's there?"

"Rotwasser, sir." Rotwasser was the company runner. The job gave him the nominal rank of monitor but he had no maniple to command. Instead he carried complaints from the men to Owensford.

"I can spare the P.O. better than anyone else," Peter whispered. "I'll need you here, not back at battalion. Now start digging us in."

It was cold on the hillside, but digging kept the men warm. Dawn came slowly and brought no warmth. Peter took out his light-amplifying binoculars and cautiously looked out ahead. The binoculars had been a present from his mother, and were the only good optical equipment in the company.

The countryside was cut into small, steep-sided ridges and valleys. Allan Roach lay beside Owensford and whistled softly. "We take that ridge in front of us, there's another just like it after that. And another. Nobody's goin' to win this war that way. . . ."

Owensford nodded silently. There were trees in the valley below, oranges and dates imported from Earth mixed in with native fruit trees as if a giant had spilled seeds across the ground. The fire-gutted remains of a whitewashed adobe peasant house stood among the trees.

Zing! Something that might have been a hornet but wasn't buzzed angrily over Peter's head. There was a flat crack from across the valley, then more angry buzzes. Dust puffs sprouted from the earthworks.

"Down!" Peter ordered.

"What are they trying to do, kill us?" Allan Roach shouted. There was a chorus of laughs. "Sir, why didn't they use IR on us in the dark? We should have stood out in this cold—"

Peter shrugged. "Maybe they don't have any. We don't."

The men who'd skimped on their holes dug in deeper, throwing the dirt out onto the ramparts in front of them. They laughed as they worked. It was very poor technique, and Peter worried about artillery, but nothing happened. The enemy was about four hundred meters away, across the valley, stretched out along a ridge identical to the one Peter held. No infantry that ever lived could have taken either ridge by charging across the valley. Both sides were safe until something heavier was brought up.

One large-caliber gun was trained on their position. It fired on anything that moved. There was also a laser, with several mirrors that could be moved about between flashes. The laser itself was safe. So were the mirrors, because the monarchists never fired twice from the same position.

The men shot at the guns and at where they thought the mirror was anyway until Peter ordered them to stop wasting ammunition. It wasn't good for morale to lie there and not fight back, though.

"I bet I can locate that goddamn gun," Corporal Bassinger told Peter. "I got the best eyesight in the company."

Peter mentally called up Bassinger's records. Two ex-wives and an acknowledged child by each. Volunteered after being an insurance man in Brooklyn for years. "You can't spot that thing."

"Sure I can, Lieutenant. Loan me your glasses, I'll spot it sure."

"All right. Be careful. They're shooting at anything they can see."

"I'm careful."

"Let me see, man!" someone shouted. Three men clustered in the trench around Bassinger. "Let us look!" "Don't be a hog, we want to see too." "Comrade, let us look—"

"Get away from here," Bassinger shouted. "You heard the lieutenant, it's dangerous to look over the ramparts."

"What about you?"

"I'm an observer. Besides, I'm careful." He crawled into position and looked out through the little slot he'd cut away in the dirt in front of him. "See, it's safe enough. I think I see—"

Bassinger was thrown back into the trench. The shattered glass fell on top of him, and he had already ceased breathing by the time they heard the shot that hit him in the eye.

That day two men had toes shot off and had to be evacuated.

They lay on a hill for a week. Each night they lost a few more men to minor casualties that could not possibly have been inflicted by the enemy. Then Stromand had two men with foot injuries shot by a squad of military police from staff headquarters.

The injuries ceased, and the men lay sullenly in the trenches until the company was relieved.

They had two days in a small town near the front, then the officers were called to a meeting. The briefing officer had a thick accent, but it was German, not Spanish. The briefing was for the Americans and it was held in English.

"We vill have a full assault. All international volunteers vill move out at once. We vill use infiltration tactics."

"What does that mean?" Captain Barton demanded.

The staff officer looked pained. "Ven you break through their lines, go straight to their technical areas and disrupt them. Ven that is done, the war is over."

"Where are their technical corpsmen?"

"You vill be told after you have broken through their lines."

The rest of the briefing made no more sense to Peter. He walked out with Barton after they were dismissed. "Looked at your section of the line?" Barton asked.

"As much as I can," Peter answered. "Do you have a decent map?"

"No. Old CD orbital photographs, and some sketches. No better than what you have."

"What I did see looks bad," Peter said. "There's an olive grove, then a hollow I can't see into. Is there cover in there?"

"You better patrol and find out."

"You will ask the battalion commander for permission to conduct patrols," a stern voice said from behind them.

"You better watch that habit of walking up on people, Stromand," Barton said. "One of these days somebody's not going to realize it's you." He gave Peter a pained look. "Better ask."

Major Harris told Peter that Brigade had forbidden patrols. Surprise was needed, and patrols might alert the enemy of the coming attack.

As he walked back to his company area, Peter reflected that Harris had been an attorney for the Liberation Party before he volunteered to go to Santiago.

They were to move out the next morning. The night was long. The men cleaned their weapons and talked in whispers. Some drew meaningless diagrams in the mud of the dugouts. About halfway through the night forty new volunteers joined the company. They had no equipment other than rifles, and they had left the port city only two days before. Most came from Churchill, and because they spoke English and the trucks were coming to this section, they had been sent along.

Major Harris called the officers together at dawn. "The Xanadu techs have managed to acquire some rockets," he told them. "They'll drop them on the Dons before we move out. Owensford, you will move out last. You will shoot any man who hasn't gone before you do."

"That's my job," Stromand protested.

"I want you to lead," Harris said. "The bombardment will come at 0815 hours. Do you all have proper timepieces?"

"No, sir," Peter said. "I've only got a watch that counts Earth time. . . ."

"Hell," Harris muttered. "Okay, Thurstone's hours are 1.08 Earth hours long. You'll have to work it out from that. . . ." He looked confused.

"No problem," Peter assured him.

"Okay, back to your areas."

Zero hour went past with no signals. Another hour passed. Then a Republican brigade to the north began firing, and a few men left their dugouts and moved onto the valley floor.

A ripple of fire and flashing mirrors colored the ridge beyond as the enemy began firing. The Republican troops were cut down, and the few who were not hit scurried back into their shelters.

"Fire support!" Harris shouted. Owensford's squawk box made unintelligible sounds, effectively jammed as were all electronics Peter had seen on Santiago, but he heard the order passed down the line. His company fired at the enemy, and the monarchists fired back.

Within minutes it was clear that the enemy dominated the valley. A few large rockets rose from behind the enemy lines and crashed randomly into the Republican positions. There were more flashes across the sky as the Xanadu technicians backtracked the enemy rockets and returned counterfire. Eventually the shooting stopped for lack of targets.

It was 1100 by Peter's watch when a series of explosions lit the lip of the monarchist ramparts. Another wave of rockets fell among the enemy, and the Republicans to the north began to charge forward.

"Ready to move out!" Peter shouted. He waited for orders.

There was nearly a minute of silence. No more rockets fell on the enemy. Then the ridge opposite rippled with fire again, and the Republicans began to go down or scramble back to their positions.

The alert tone sounded on Peter's squawk box and he lifted it to his ear. Amazingly, he could hear intelligible speech. Someone at headquarters was speaking to Major Harris.

"The Republicans have already advanced half a kilometer. They are being slaughtered because you have not moved your precious Americans in support."

"Bullshit!" Harris's voice had no tones in the tiny speaker. "The Republicans are already back in their dugouts. The attack has failed."

"It has not failed. You must show what high morale can do. Your men are all volunteers. Many Republicans are conscripts. Set an example for them."

"But I tell you the attack has failed."

"Major Harris, if your men have not moved out in five minutes I will send the military police to arrest you as a traitor."

The box went back to random squeals and growls; then the whistles blew and orders were passed down the line. "Move out."

Peter went from dugout to dugout. "Up and at them. Jarvis, if you don't get out of there I'll shoot you. You three, get going." He saw that Allan Roach was doing the same thing.

When they reached the end of the line, Roach grinned at Peter. "We're all that's left, now what?"

"Now we move out, too." They crawled forward, past the lip of the hollow that had sheltered them. Ten meters beyond that they saw Major Harris lying very still.

"Captain Barton's in command of the battalion," Peter said.

"Wonder if he knows it? I'll take the left side, sir, and keep 'em going, shall I?"

"Yes." Now he was more alone than ever. He went on through the olive groves, finding men and keeping them moving ahead of him. There was very little fire from the enemy. They advanced fifty meters, a hundred, and reached the slope down into the hollow beyond. It was an old vineyard. The stumps of the vines reached out of the ground like old women's hands.

They were well into the hollow when the Dons fired.

Four of the newcomers from Churchill were just ahead of Owensford. When the volley lashed their hollow they hit the dirt in perfect formation. Peter crawled forward to compliment them on how well they'd learned the training-book exercises. All four were dead.

He was thirty meters into the hollow. In front of him was a network of red stripes woven through the air a meter above the ground. He'd seen it at the Point: an interlocking network of crossfire guided by laser beams. Theoretically the Xanadu technicians should be able to locate the mirrors, or even the power plants, but the network hung there motionless.

Some of the men didn't know what it was and charged into it. After a while there was a little wall of dead men and boys at its edge. No one could advance. Snipers began to pick off any of the still figures that tried to move. Peter lay there, wondering if any of the other companies were making progress. Most of his men tried to find shelter behind the bodies of dead comrades. One by one his troops died as they lay there in the open, in the bright sunshine of a dying vineyard.

Late in the afternoon it began to rain: first a few drops, then harder, finally a storm that cut off all visibility. The men who could crawl made their way back to their dugouts. There were no orders for a retreat.

Peter found small groups of men and sent them out to bring back the wounded. It was hard to get men to go back into the hollow, even in the driving rainstorm, and he had to go with them or they would vanish in the mud and gloom. Eventually there were no more wounded to find.

The scene in the trenches was a shambled hell of bloody mud. Men fell into the dugouts and lay where they fell, too tired and scared to move. Some of the wounded died there in the mud, and others fell on top of them, trampling the bodies down and out of sight because no one had the strength to move them. For several hours Peter was the only officer

in the battalion. The company was his, and the men were
calling him "Captain."

In mid afternoon Stromand came into the trenches carrying a bundle.

Incredibly, Allan Roach was unhurt. The huge wrestler stood
in Stromand's path. "What is that?" he demanded.

"For morale." Stromand showed papers.

Roach didn't move. "While we were out there you were off
printing leaflets?"

"I had orders," Stromand said. He backed nervously away
from the big sergeant. His hand rested on a pistol butt.

"Roach," Peter said calmly. "Help me with the wounded,
please."

Roach stood in indecision. Finally he turned to Peter. "Yes,
sir."

At dawn Peter had eighty effectives to hold the lines. The
Dons would have had no trouble taking his position, but they
were strangely quiet. Peter went from dugout to dugout trying to get a count of his men. Two hundred wounded sent
to rear areas.

He could count one-hundred-thirteen dead. That left ninety-
four vanished. Died, deserted, ground into the mud; he didn't
know.

There hadn't been any general attack. The international
volunteer commander had thought that even without it, this
would be a splendid opportunity to show what morale could
do. It had done that, all right.

The Republican command was frantic. The war was stale-
mated, which meant the superior forces of the Dons were
slowly grinding the Republicans down.

In desperation they sent a large group to the stable front
in the south. The previous attack had been planned to the
last detail; this one was to depend entirely on surprise. Peter's
remnants were reinforced with pieces of other outfits and fresh
volunteers, and sent against the enemy.

The objective was an agricultural center called Zaragoza,
a small town set among olive groves and vineyards. Peter's
column moved through the groves to the edge of town.

Surprise was complete, and the battle was short. A flurry
of firing, quick advances, and the enemy retreated. Communications were sporadic, but it looked as if Peter's group had
advanced farther than any other. They were the spearhead of
freedom in the south.

They marched in to cheering crowds. His army looked like

scarecrows, but women held their children up to see their liberators. It made it all worthwhile: the stupidity of the generals, the heat and mud and cold and dirt and lice—all of it forgotten in their victory.

More troops came in behind them, but Peter's company camped at the edge of their town. The next day the army would advance again; if the war could be made fluid, fought in quick battles of fast-moving men, it might yet be won. Certainly, Peter thought, certainly the people of Santiago were waiting for them. They'd have support from the population. How long could the Dons hold?

Just before dark they heard shots in the town.

He brought his duty squad on the run, dashing through the dusty streets, past the pockmarked adobe walls to the town square. The military police were there.

"Never saw such pretty soldiers," Allan Roach said.

Peter nodded.

"Captain, where do you think they got those shiny boots? And the new rifles? Seems we never have good equipment for the troops, but the police always have more than enough. . . ."

A small group of bodies lay like broken dolls at the foot of the churchyard wall. The priest, the mayor, and three young men. "Monarchists. Carlists," someone whispered. Some of the townspeople spat on the bodies.

An old man was crouched beside one of the dead. He cradled the youthful head in his hands, and blood poured through his fingers. He looked at Peter with dull eyes. "Why are you here?" he asked. "Are there not richer worlds for you to conquer?"

Peter turned away without answering. He could think of nothing to say.

"Captain!"

Peter woke to Allan Roach's urgent whisper.

"Cap'n, there's something moving down by the stream. Not the Dons. Mister Stromand's with 'em, about five men. Officers, I think, from headquarters."

Peter sat upright. He hadn't seen Stromand since the disastrous attack three hundred kilometers to the north. The man wouldn't have lasted five minutes in combat among his former comrades. "Anyone else know?"

"Albers, nobody else. He called me."

"Let's go find out what they want. Quietly, Allan." They walked silently in the hot night. What were staff officers doing in his company area, near the vanguard of the advancing Republican forces? And why hadn't they called him?

They followed the small group down the nearly dry creek bed to the town wall. When their quarry halted, they stole closer until they could hear.

"About here," Stromand's bookish voice said. "This will be perfect."

"How long do we have?" Peter recognized the German accent of the staff officer who'd briefed them. The next voice was even more of a shock.

"Two hours. Enough time, but we must go quickly." It was Brigadier Cermak, second in command of the volunteer forces. "It is set?"

"Yes."

"Hold it." Peter stepped out from the shadows. He covered the small group with his rifle. Allan Roach moved quickly away from him so that he also threatened them. "Identify yourselves."

"You know who we are, Owensford," Stromand snapped.

"Yes. What are you doing here?"

"That is none of your business, Captain," Cermak answered. "I order you to return to your company area and say nothing about seeing us."

"In a minute. Major, if you continue moving your hand toward your pistol, Sergeant Roach will cut you in half. Allan, I'm going to have a look at what they were carrying. Cover me."

"Right."

"You can't!" The German staff officer moved toward Peter. Owensford reacted automatically. His rifle swung in an uppercut that caught the German under the chin. The man fell with a strangled cry and lay still. Everyone stood frozen.

"Interestin', Captain," Allan Roach said. "I think they're more scared of bein' heard by our side than by the enemy."

Peter squatted over the device they'd set by the wall. "A bomb of some kind, from the timers—Jesus!"

"What is it, Cap'n?"

"A fission bomb," Peter said slowly. "They were going to leave a fission bomb here. To detonate in two hours, did you say?" he asked conversationally. His thoughts whirled, but he could find no explanation; and he was very surprised at how calm he felt. "Why?"

No one answered.

"Why blow up the only advancing force in the Republican army?" Peter asked wonderingly. "They can't be traitors. The Dons wouldn't have these on a platter—but—Stromand, is there a new CD warship in orbit here? New fleet forces to stop this war?"

More silence.

"What does it mean?" Allan Roach asked. His rifle was steady, and there was an edge to his voice. "Why use an atom bomb on their own men?"

"The ban," Peter said. "One thing the CD does enforce. No nukes." He was hardly aware that he spoke aloud. "The CD inspectors will see the spearhead of the Republican army destroyed by nukes, and think the Dons did it. They're the only ones who could benefit from it. So the CD cleans up the Carlists, and these bastards end up in charge when the fleet pulls out. That's it, isn't it? Cermak? Stromand?"

"Of course," Stromand said. "You fool, come with us, then. Leave the weapons in place. We're sorry we didn't think we could trust you with the plan, but it was just too important . . . it means winning the war."

"At what price?"

"A low price. A battalion of soldiers and one village. More are killed every week. A comparatively bloodless victory."

Allan Roach spat viciously. "If that's freedom, I don't want it. You ask any of them?" He waved toward the village.

Peter remembered the cheering crowds. He stooped down to the weapon and examined it closely. "Any secret to disarming this? If there is, you're standing as close to it as I am."

"Wait," Stromand shouted. "Don't touch it, leave it, come with us. You'll be promoted, you'll be a hero of the movement—"

"Disarm it or I'll have a try," Peter said. He retrieved his rifle and waited.

After a moment Stromand bent down to the bomb. It was no larger than a small suitcase. He took a key from his pocket and inserted it, then turned dials. "It is safe now."

"I'll have another look," Peter said. He bent over the weapon. Yes, a large iron bar had been moved through the center of the device, and the fissionables couldn't come together. As he examined it there was a flurry of activity behind him.

"Hold it!" Roach commanded. He raised his rifle, but Political Officer Stromand had already vanished into the darkness. "I'll go after him, Cap'n." They could hear thrashing among the olive trees nearby.

"No. You'd never catch him. Not without making a big stir. And if this story gets out, the whole Republican cause is finished."

"You are growing more intelligent," Cermak said. "Why not let us carry out our plan now?"

"I'll be damned," Peter said. "Get out of here, Cermak. Take your staff carrion with you. And if you send the military police after me or Sergeant Roach, you can be damned sure this story—and the bomb—will get to the CD inspectors. Don't think I can't arrange it."

Cermak shook his head. "You are making a mistake—"

"The mistake is lettin' you go," Roach said. "Why don't I shoot him? Or cut his throat?"

"There'd be no point in it," Peter said. "If Cermak doesn't stop him, Stromand will be back with the MPs. No, let them go."

XIV

Peter's company advanced thirty kilometers in the next three days. They crossed the valley with its dry river of sand and moved swiftly into the low brush on the other side. They were halted at the top of the ridge.

Rockets and artillery fire exploded all around them. There was no one to fight, only unseen enemies on the next ridge, and the fire poured into their positions for three days.

The enemy fire held them while the glare and heat of Thurstone's sun punished them. Men became snowblind, and wherever they looked there was only one color: fiery yellow. When grass and trees caught fire they hardly noticed the difference.

When the water ran out they retreated. There was nothing else to do. They fled back across the valley, past the positions they'd won, halting to let other units pass while they held the road. On the seventh day after they'd left it, they were back on the road where they'd jumped off into the valley.

There was no organization. Peter was the only officer among 172 men of a battalion that had neither command nor staff; just 172 men too tired to care.

"We've the night, anyway," Roach said. He sat next to Peter and took out a cigarette. "Last tobacco in the battalion, Cap'n. Share?"

"No, thanks. Keep it all."

"One night to rest," Roach said again. "Seems like forever, a whole night without anybody shooting at us."

Fifteen minutes later Peter's radio squawked. He strained to hear the commands through the static and jamming. "Call the men together," Peter ordered when he'd heard it out.

"It's this way," he told them. "We still hold Zaragoza. There's a narrow corridor into the town, and unless somebody gets down there to hold it open, we'll lose the village. If that goes, our whole position in the valley's lost."

"Cap'n, you can't ask it!" The men were incredulous. "Go back down into there? You can't make us do that!"

"No. I can't make you. But remember Zaragoza? Remember how the people cheered us when we marched in? It's our town. Nobody else set those people free. We did. And there's nobody else who can go help keep them free, either. No other reinforcements. Will we let them down?"

"We can't," Allan Roach said. "It needs doing. I'll come with you, Cap'n."

One by one the others got to their feet. The ragged column marched down the side of the ridge, out of the cool heights where their water was assured, down into the valley of the river of sand.

By dawn they were half a kilometer from the town. Republican troops streamed down the road toward them. Others ran through the olive groves that lined both sides of the road.

"Tanks!" someone shouted. "Tanks coming!"

It was too late. The enemy armor had bypassed Zaragoza and was closing on them fast. The Dons' infantry came right behind the tanks. Peter swallowed the bitter taste in his mouth, and ordered his men to dig in among the olive trees. It would be their last battle.

An hour later they were surrounded. Two hours passed as they fought to hold the useless groves. The tanks had long since passed their position, but the enemy was still all around them. Then the shooting stopped, and silence lay over the grove.

Peter crawled around the perimeter of his command: a hundred meters, no more. He had fewer than fifty men.

Allan Roach lay in a shallow hole at one edge. He was partially covered by ripe olives shaken from the trees, and when Peter came close, the sergeant laughed. "Makes you feel like a salad," he said, brushing away more olives. "What do we do, Cap'n? Why do you think they quit shooting?"

"Wait and see."

It didn't take long. "Will you surrender?" a voice called.

"To whom?" Peter demanded.

"Captain Hans Ort, Second Friedland Armored Infantry."

"Mercenaries," Peter hissed. "How did they get here? The CD was supposed to have a quarantine. . . ."

"Your position is hopeless, and you are not helping your comrades by holding it," the voice shouted.

"We're keeping you from entering the town!" Peter shouted back.

"For a while. We can go in any time, from the other side. Will you surrender?"

Peter looked helplessly at Roach. He could hear the silence among the men. They didn't say anything, and Peter was proud of them. But, he thought, I don't have any choice. "Yes," he shouted.

The Friedlanders wore dark green uniforms, and looked very military compared to Peter's scarecrows. "Mercenaries?" Captain Ort asked.

Peter opened his mouth to answer defiance. A voice interrupted him. "Of course they're mercenaries." Ace Barton limped up to them.

Ort looked at them suspiciously. "Very well. You wish to speak with them, Captain Barton?"

"Sure. I'll get some of 'em out of your hair," Barton said. He waited until the Friedlander was gone. "You almost blew it, Pete. If you'd said you were volunteers, Ort would have turned you over to the Dons. This way, he keeps you. And believe me, you'd rather be with him."

"What are you doing here?" Peter demanded.

"Captured up north," Barton said. "By these guys. There's a recruiter for Falkenberg's outfit back in the rear area. I signed up, and they've got me out looking for a few more good men. You want to join, you can. We'll be off this planet next week; and of course you won't be doing any fighting here."

"I told you, I'm not a mercenary—"

"What are you?" Barton asked. "What have you got to go back to? Best you can hope for here is to be interned. But you don't have to make up your mind just yet. Come on back to town." They walked through the olive groves toward the Zaragoza town wall. "You opted for CD service, didn't you." Barton said. It wasn't a question.

"Yes. Not to be one of Falkenberg's—"

"You think everything's going to be peaceful out here when the CoDominium fleet pulls out?"

"No. But I like to choose my wars."

"You want a cause. So did I, once. Now I'll settle for what I've got. Two things to remember, Pete. In an outfit like Falkenberg's, you don't choose your enemies, but you'll never have to break your word. And just what will you do for a living now?"

He had no answer to that. They walked on.

"Somebody's got to keep order out here," Barton said. "Think about it."

They had reached the town. The Friedland mercenaries hadn't

entered it; now a column of monarchist soldiers approached. Their boots were dusty and their uniforms torn, so that they looked little different from the remnants of Peter's command.

As the monarchists reached the town gates, the village people ran out of their houses. They lined both sides of the streets. As the Carlists entered the public square, the cheering began.

Lysander drained his glass. The water pitcher was empty. "That's quite a story, captain. One thing—what did you do with that fission bomb?"

"Turned it over to Falkenberg."

"And he—?"

"Damned if I know."

"In any event Major Barton doesn't have it," Lysander said.

"Remember, that all happened twelve years ago. If Ace Barton thinks he needs a nuke, he'll have one."

"Twelve years, and you still think quite highly of him."

"Obviously. I'm not looking forward to this fight."

"Maybe there won't be one," Lysander said. "Colonel Falkenberg told Governor Blaine this was a political matter, and should be settled by political means."

"I hope he's right, but Ace won't give up easily."

"Of course there's one simple solution. . . ."

"Yes?"

"Just get control of the harvest they've been holding back."

"That would do it, all right." Owensford chuckled. "But Ace knows that as well as we do. He's been damned clever about hiding the stuff. Rottermill has his people sweating blood over the satellite photos, but so far they've got damn all."

"You can't bribe one of the planters?"

"It's been tried. They don't know either. Apparently Barton tells them the delivery point, and his troops take it from there."

Lysander's mental concentration wasn't helped by the residual effects of the evening's liquor. He frowned. "It has to be a pretty big place. Even if it's concentrated there has to be tons of the stuff. Not easy to hide."

"Maybe not. But they've done it."

Lysander closed the door and leaned against it. He didn't bother with the room lights. Gray dawn let him see well enough to move without bumping into the furniture, and despite Owensford's nostrum, bright light was more than he wanted to deal with. "Sleep," he muttered. He stripped off his tunic and trousers and threw them over a chair, then staggered to the bed.

There was someone in it. "Who the hell?"

"Umm? Lynn?"

"Ursula?"

"Oh my God, what time is it?"

"Quarter past five. What the hell are you doing here?"

"I didn't want to sleep alone. Why are you just standing there? It's cold in here."

"Not for long." He slid in beside her and settled himself against the curve of her body. A few moments later he gently but firmly folded her hands together in front of her. "Not now, Ursa. Please."

"Aww. Head hurt?"

"Not as much as it did."

"You should drink water—"

"Good God, darling, what do you think I've been doing?"

"You've been drinking *water* for four hours? Uh— Your Highness—"

He laughed, but that hurt his head. "Water. Vitamin gunk. Listening to Captain Owensford's story."

"Must have been quite a story!"

"It was. Also trying to figure out where those damned ranchers are hiding gallons and gallons of drugs. But we didn't get anywhere."

"Oh. All right. Good night."

"Ursa—what the hell will you do in the morning?"

"Have breakfast with you. Good night."

The Officers' Mess was empty. Lysander and Ursula chose a table in the corner, out of earshot of the steward, and set down their breakfast trays.

"Sorry about the selection," Lysander said, grimacing at his bowl of what looked like green oatmeal.

"This late, we're lucky to get anything at all. Anyway, you look a lot more chipper than you did half an hour ago."

"I'm going to take the formula for that vitamin gunk back to Sparta. We'll make it a government monopoly and after five years we'll be able to abolish taxes." He clinked his coffee mug against hers. "Now suppose you tell me what's been on *your* mind since we woke up."

She sipped her coffee. "Lynn—they'd have to move those drugs by helicopter, wouldn't they?"

"Uh?"

"The planters. The rebels."

"Oh. Yes, I suppose they would. Why have you been brooding about that?"

"Shouldn't I be interested? Or is this purely a man's problem?"

"Come on, Ursa. I don't deserve that."

She sighed. "No. I guess you don't."

"What is it, then? Do you have an idea?"

"Maybe. I don't know."

"Well, tell me."

"I—I'm ashamed to."

"What? This is me, remember?" He set down his coffee mug and put his arm around her shoulders. "Whatever it is—"

"Of course. Very well. It happened about six weeks before you came to Tanith. Before we met."

"Yes?"

"Remember I told you that some of us, some of the hotel girls, got sent on tours of the plantations?"

"Good God! You mean you—"

"No, not me. Not exactly. I was luckier. I was—don't look at me while I tell you this."

"Whatever this is, you'd better tell me. Now, what was it?"

"I was—it was a birthday party for a planter's son. His sixteenth birthday. I was—you've read Mead and Benedict, haven't you? This was, well, Coming of Age On Tanith." She laughed dryly.

"Ursa—" His arm tightened around her.

"Never mind that. That was—business. There was something else. It didn't mean anything to me at the time, but now—"

Lysander set down his spoon. "Tell me."

XV

"Attention, please," Captain Fast said formally. Everyone stood as Falkenberg came in and took his place at the head of the long table.

"Mr. Mess President, is the Regimental Council assembled?"

"Yes, sir," Captain Alana said.

"Thank you. Sergeant Major, has the room been secured? Thank you. I declare this meeting opened. Be seated, please."

Falkenberg looked down the twin rows of familiar faces, senior officers in descending rank to his right, Sergeant Major Calvin at the far end with the senior NCOs. Beatrice Frazer and Laura Bryant were present as representatives for the civilian women. Faces came and went but the basic structure of the Regimental Council hadn't changed since the 42nd CoDominium Line Marines had been disbanded and had chosen to stay together as Falkenberg's Mercenary Legion.

"First item. Congratulations to you all on ending the Free State campaign with so few casualties. Well done. Of course, it was rather an expensive operation, which brings us to our second item. Treasurer's report." Papers rustled as they picked up their printouts. "In the past month we have expended over seven hundred cluster bombs and forty thousand rounds of small-arms ammunition. We used thirty Bearpaw rockets and sixty mortar bombs in the Free State operation alone. All necessary, of course, but we have to replace them. Captain Alana has made substantial economies in routine operations, but I'm afraid that's not enough. Further cutbacks will be necessary. Comments?"

"We can hardly cut back on SAS operations against the rebel planters. Or the air support for them," Ian Frazer said.

"Of course not. I think I speak for us all on that? Thank you. Other suggestions?"

"Pay cuts, sir?" Sergeant Major Calvin asked.

"Possibly. Last resort, of course, but it may come to that."

"Not a good time for that, sir."

Falkenberg smiled grimly. "Sergeant Major, if any of the troops want to desert on Tanith, I wish them well. I expect we can find more recruits here if we have to."

"Sir."

"Next item," Falkenberg said. "We've received a sight draft for one point five million credits as a stand-by retainer from Sparta. It should clear the Tanith banks within the month. If the coming campaign doesn't get too expensive that will ease the economic situation a little."

"Stand-by," Major Savage said. "I gather we needn't rush packing up."

"That's right. The retainer gives them priority on our services for five years, but we'll have to find other work in the meantime."

There was a moment of silence. Beatrice Frazer looked unhappy. "I must say we were all looking forward to permanent homes," she said.

"This doesn't rule out a permanent home for the regiment. It just means we may have to wait longer than we thought. First question: do we accept Sparta's retainer?"

"On what terms?" Centurion Bryant asked.

"First choice on our services, with the usual provisions for letting us finish any active job."

"We certainly can use the money," Catherine Alana said.

"As I see it, turning down this retainer would play hob with our long-term plans," Jeremy Savage said. "I move we allow the colonel full discretion in this matter."

"Second," Sergeant Major Calvin said.

"Discussion?" Falkenberg prompted.

"What's to discuss?" Ian Frazer said.

"Quite a lot, if we refuse this offer," Jeremy Savage said dryly. "Since we won't have the slightest idea where we're going."

"That's what I mean," Frazer said. "Question, Colonel. If we do take the retainer, what are our chances of salvaging the plan?"

"Good, I'd say."

"Thank you, sir."

"Further discussion?" Falkenberg nodded. "There being none, those in favor? Opposed? Thank you. Off the record, I'm going to quibble about the terms, but I'll accept the Spartan retainer.

"Next item. Captain Fast, what offers do we have?"

"There's a prisoners' rebellion on Fulson's World—"

Several officers laughed. Laura Bryant looked horrified. "That's worse than here!" she said.

Falkenberg nodded. "It happens that the offer from Fulson's World is likely to be the most profitable, but I take it Laura speaks for us all?"

Everyone nodded vigorously.

"New Washington," Captain Fast said. "A dissident group wants help breaking loose from Franklin. The Franklin government has brought in Friedlanders and some other mercenary outfits, and has a pretty good army of its own."

"That one's dicey," Major Savage said. "Likely to take time. Good living on New Washington, though. Cool."

A senior battalion commander looked thoughtful. "What have these dissidents got in the way of an army?"

Falkenberg smiled thinly. "Lots of troops. Hardly an army."

Centurion Bryant frowned, then grinned. "Colonel—if they don't have an army, and we do, and we win—"

"The thought had crossed my mind," Falkenberg said. "We might well be the only organized militia on a wealthy—well, relatively wealthy—world."

"No drug trade," Beatrice Frazer said. "We might not be under so much pressure from the Grand Senate. Or Admiral Lermontov. I know you love him, Colonel, but some of us wouldn't mind being free of him."

There were murmurs of approval.

"It would be a while before we could bring in the families," Falkenberg said. "You'd have to make do here."

Beatrice shuddered slightly. "Better here than Fulson's World. Or rattling all around the galaxy."

"We're agreed, then," Falkenberg said. "We'll look further into the New Washington situation. In favor—"

There was a chorus of ayes.

"I see none opposed. Captain Fast."

"Colonel, there are situations in three other places, but no firm offers. Worth discussing now?"

"Get us more information on them first, I think," Falkenberg said. "We don't want to pin all our hopes on New Washington. All agree? Thank you. Next item. Mrs. Frazer."

"The school equipment is breaking down in the heat and wet," she said. "About half our veedisk readers are on the fritz, and we're only keeping the rest together by overworking the technicians. When you take the hardware into the field, everything comes apart."

"That sounds like the right place to put part of the Spartans' retainer," Falkenberg said. "Ladies and gentlemen? Discussion?"

"How much are we talking about?" Jesus Alana asked. "Oerlikon has a new smart rocket out. Coded laser target designators. Countermeasures aren't going to be cheap. And we might want some of the offensive munitions. They're damned expensive, but they could be the edge against that Friedland armor in New Washington. And we'll certainly need new chaff shells."

"It would be nice if the children could read," Captain Catherine Alana said. "Sixteen thousand credits would buy milspec readers for the school. Then we could stop worrying about them."

"They'd make a difference," Beatrice Frazer agreed. "Of course if it's a choice between making do and winning the next campaign there's no choice at all. Classes have been taught with paper and chalkboards, and even less."

"Sixteen thousand. It's not that much," Centurion Tamago said. "I move we appropriate it for the readers." He grinned. "With luck we'll get much more than that out of this operation against the planters."

Falkenberg frowned slightly. Loot was an unpleasant subject, and chancy as well. He never let it enter formal discussions. "Is there a second?"

"Second," Catherine Alana said.

"Ayes? Thank you. I believe I hear a majority. Does anyone wish no votes recorded? I hear none. Captain Alana, you will consult with Mrs. Frazer and order the necessary equipment, not to exceed sixteen thousand credits' worth. Next item?"

"Thank you, Amos." Falkenberg looked down the long table. "That concludes the agenda. Are there any other items to bring before the Council? There being none, do I hear a motion to adjourn? Thank you. Those in favor. Thank you. This meeting is adjourned." He stood and strode out of the meeting chamber.

"Attention," Amos Fast said. All stood until Falkenberg had left the room. The Adjutant looked at his watch. "There will be a staff meeting in ten minutes. Thank you. Dismissed."

The meeting dissolved in babble. "Jesus, Sergeant Major," Centurion Bryant said. "Fulson's World? We ain't *never* going to be that broke."

"I sure hope not, Alf."

Catherine Alana and Beatrice Frazer went out together, deep in a discussion of brand names and shipping schedules. Ian Frazer took Jesus Alana by the elbow. "Tell me more about this Oerlikon missile."

"Just saw the write-up in *Military Technology*," Alana said.
"Eh? Where—"

"I'll show you. Catherine brought it. She had lunch in the wardroom of that CD cruiser that came through here last week. Anyway, the missile looks like something new, not just a reshuffle of the same old stuff."

Orderlies came in to clear the table and bring fresh coffee cups.

"Ten-hut!" Sergeant Major Calvin said as Falkenberg entered and again took his place at the head of the table.

"At ease," he said automatically and sat. There were fewer people around the table. No enlisted personnel except Sergeant Major Calvin. The only woman was First Lieutenant Leigh Swensen, the senior photo interpreter and one of Rottermill's deputies.

Her fingers moved rapidly over the keyboard. The tabletop turned translucent and the crystals below its surface swarmed together to form the map of the areas held by the rebels.

"Jesus, there's a sight I'm sick of," someone muttered.

Major Savage smiled. "Tiresome, isn't it."

Swensen moved the joystick, and military unit symbols appeared on the map: dark and solid for enemy units located with certainty, fading to ghostly outlines for those whose positions were only guessed at. The outlined symbols far outnumbered the solid ones.

"I see Major Barton's lost none of his skills at camouflage," Falkenberg observed.

"Ian's lads are doing their best," Savage said.

A dozen small blue dots crawled across the map. "Captain Frazer's Special Air Services teams," Lieutenant Swensen said. As they watched, three of the dots were replaced by red splotches.

"Christ," Captain Fast muttered. "Battles. Isn't there a better way to locate Barton's gang?"

"Those weren't battles!" Frazer protested.

"Casualties, Captain?" Falkenberg prompted.

"Very light, sir. Three men killed. Seven wounded, all extracted by air. Hardly what anyone would call battles."

"Sorry, Ian," Fast said. He glanced at Falkenberg, then at Captain Rottermill. "Is it fair to say we don't know where most of Barton's troops are, and we've no idea at all where the planters are hiding the borloi?"

Rottermill nodded reluctantly, "You could put it that way. I don't like it, but it's fair."

"Also," Captain Fast continued, "we face unroaded terrain. Worse than unroaded. Swamp and jungle. The only possible transportation is by air, and the enemy has effective infantry carried anti-aircraft missiles. We can smuggle a few troops behind their lines, but effective strikes deep into their territory are impossible."

"Fair summary," Rottermill said. "You can add that their satellite observation security is excellent, and the governor's office leaks like a sieve."

"Suggestions?" Captain Fast asked.

Rottermill shrugged.

"Occupy their bloody plantations," one of the senior battalion commanders said. "Start with the close ones and roll them up. There aren't more than a couple of hundred—"

"Sure. And garrison them how?" Rottermill demanded. "Two maniples per farm? Why don't we just wrap up the troops with ribbons and tell Barton to come get them? Christ, Larry—"

"Burn the damn farms! I've got troops ready to do that. The rebels can't stand that, they'll *make* Barton fight."

"I'm afraid we don't have proper transport to set up the necessary ambuscades," Falkenberg said. "And there are political considerations. I doubt Governor Blaine will let us kill his geese."

"Yeah. So what the hell can we do?"

"Let Ian's lads carry on scouting," Major Savage said.

"I could go out myself," Ian Frazer offered.

"No," Falkenberg said. "This is hardly our favorite kind of campaign, but it's going as well as we can expect. The—opposition—has to hand the merchandise over to Bronson's people. Or someone else, never mind who. All we need do is keep them from delivering it. Major Barton can't operate on credit and he won't fight on promises."

"If we can take the borloi, he won't fight at all," Captain Fast said.

"Yes, sir," Lieutenant Swensen said. "We're trying—"

"All my people are trying," Rottermill said.

"So are mine," Ian Frazer said.

Sergeant Taras Hamilton Miscowsky shut down the flame on the nearly buried mini-stove. "Tea time."

The other four members of his SAS team huddled under the basha formed by Miscowsky's poncho. Automatically they cradled the warm tea cups in their hands, even though the fine rain would limit IR scanning ranges to less than a hundred meters. Miscowsky looked at the tangle of vines, tree trunks, exotic flowers, and weirdly shaped leaves. He'd never heard of anything that could detect a hot teacup under this much jungle foliage, but good habits were always worth developing.

The jungle didn't look like anything that ever grew on Earth, but that didn't bother Miscowsky. He'd never been on Earth, and jungles there would have been just as strange as Tanith's. Miscowsky had been recruited from Haven, and his primary training was for mountain operations.

He'd had to learn fast. Everyone did. On Tanith you learned fast or you didn't live long. The insects didn't bother humans much, but there were plenty of big things that did. And fungus never much cared where it grew. He looked at his troops.

Two new faces. *I screwed the pooch this time.* Kauffman dead, Hwang off to the regenners and fucking just in time, new shave or not that goddamn Fuller can sure fly a chopper. High wind and rain pissing down, and Cloudwalker's chain saw dull as shit, that damn little patch we cleared was too small for the bird to land in . . . Howie lying there next to his leg. Son of a bitch that Fuller kid can fly! And he shouldn't have had to, 'cause I shouldn't have let the Bastards find us. Shit.

It wasn't Cloudwalker's turn to sit guard, but he liked doing it. He took his cup and moved out from under the basha, picking up his rifle and slinging it over his shoulder. As Cloudwalker padded down the trail Miscowksy surveyed the rest of the maniple. One of the new men was Andy Owassee. Miscowsky knew him; he'd been trying to get into the Special Air Service for years. The other—

Miscowsky raised his steel Sierra cup. As he drank he studied the new man's face. Buford Purdy. Mulatto, by the look of him. "Cap'n Frazer doesn't usually send recruits out with SAS patrols," Miscowsky said.

"Hell, Sarge, he *lives* out here," Owassee said. "Used to, anyway."

"Yeah, I heard that."

There was a long silence. Rain pattered down and dripped off the edges of the basha. Finally Purdy said, "I've got a lot to learn, don't I?"

"Looks that way," Miscowsky said, and set down his cup. "All right. Gimme your poncho." He folded the poncho twice and laid it flat on the ground. Tandon and Owassee moved closer. Miscowsky adjusted the controls on his helmet and the outlines of the area appeared, faint against the mottled green of the poncho. "OK. We're here." He ignored the red splotch that showed where Barton's Bastards had ambushed him. "Sat recon says there's a village over west of us. Twelve klicks. Standard procedure. We go set up to watch, be sure they're not working with Barton—"

"They not," Purdy said.

"Eh? How do you—"

"It's my Uncle Etienne's village," Purdy said.

"No shit?"

"No shit, Sarge."

"So where exactly do you come from, kid?"

"Village about ninety klicks south of here," Purdy said. "On a branch of the slough that goes through Etienne's village. Catfish don't like it this far downstream. Little nessies get them. We bring our catches down five, six times a year to trade for salt-water stuff."

"I will be dipped in shit. Okay, Purdy, what do they talk down in that village?"

"Cooney."

"What's that?"

Purdy cut loose with a string of musical but unintelligible words. He grinned. "It's more like Anglic than you think."

"Has to be more like it than I think," Corporal Tandon muttered.

"You really speak that stuff?" Miscowsky looked skeptical.

"Sure. Grew up with it."

"So how'd you learn real talk?" Tandon asked.

"From my mother. Most of us out here speak some Anglic." He coughed. "Spare some of that hot water, Sarge?"

"Sure." Miscowsky poured the last of the water from the tiny kettle and started dismantling the mini-stove. "Okay, trooper. Looks like we're in your territory. Lead off?"

"Sure, Sarge!" Purdy finished his tea while the others shouldered their packs and struck the basha. Then he moved noiselessly into the thick jungle. In seconds he had disappeared.

"Jesus Christ," Tandon said. "Sarge, that kid's all right."

"Yeah."

XVI

Ann Chang stared out the window of her office at Government House, then back at her computer screen. The request was still there, and it was routine enough; but who the hell was Geoffrey Niles, and why was he asking permission to hunt a dinosaur? Actually, the why wasn't a problem; Governor Blaine's new regulations required his personal approval of every license to kill or capture one of the huge saurians that inhabited Tanith's northeastern island complex. Ann thought Blaine was carrying environmentalism a bit far, because all the reports showed there were plenty of dinosaurs; but it wasn't a burdensome regulation because there were so few would-be hunters these days.

But who was Geoffrey Niles? And where was he? A search through the Customs and Immigration files showed no sign that he had ever landed on Tanith.

She looked at the entry again. The Honorable Geoffrey Niles, Wimbledon, Surrey, United Kingdom, Earth; local address care of Amalgamated Foundries, Ltd. She didn't have to look that one up. AF was a conglomerate that dealt mostly in chemicals. Most of their operations were in Dagon; mining, and processing of Tanith fauna. If they still owned foundries, they didn't advertise it. Certainly there were none on Tanith.

Why would a Geoffrey Niles, who apparently had never landed on Tanith in the first place, give AF as an address? The computer wouldn't know, but it couldn't hurt to see what data they had. She keyed in the company name, waited for the screen to fill with the usual trivia, and typed in the code for details.

RESTRICTED DATA.

What the hell? She typed in her own access code.

RESTRICTED DATA.

That does it, she thought. She entered Carleton Blaine's override code.

425

AMALGAMATED FOUNDRIES, LTD. CHAIRMAN AND CHIEF EXECUTIVE OFFICER LORD HARVEY NILES, SURREY, UNITED KINGDOM, EARTH. WHOLLY OWNED SUBSIDIARY OF CONSOLIDATED EUGENICS, INC. OUTSTANDING SHARES ZERO. ESTIMATED WORTH: UNEVALUTED.

There followed several pages of listed assets. Warehouses, chemical processing plants. A drug store chain in North America. An item at the bottom of the third screenful caught her eye. Amalgamated Foundries, Ltd. owned three interstellar class merchant ships.

"Curiouser and curiouser," she muttered, and typed again.

DATA DETAILS CONSOLIDATED EUGENICS.

RESTRICTED DATA.

OVERRIDE BLAINE 124C41 + HUGO.

WHOLLY OWNED SUBSIDIARY OF BRONSON AND TYNDALL CONSTRUCTION ENTERPRISES, INC . . .

Fine, she thought. Which probably makes The Honorable Geoffrey Niles a twig on the old Bronson family tree. And still doesn't explain why he wants a dinosaur license. Why ask for one unless he's on Tanith? Only he's not on Tanith. In orbit, maybe? But then he'd have turned up on the Customs list, and that showed no new traffic since last week's visit by the CoDominium warship.

Ann frowned and touched more keys.

AIR/SPACE TRAFFIC CONTROL.

ONLINE.

HOW MANY SHIPS IN ORBIT NOW?

ONE.

SHIP NAME.

FILE NOT FOUND.

OVERRIDE BLAINE 124C41 + HUGO.

FILE NOT FOUND.

That made no sense at all. Still frowning, she clicked back to the Amalgamated Foundries data window and called up more details. Of the company's three ships, two were noted as being on scheduled runs. The third was CDMS *Norton Star.*

Not likely. But—Ann touched buttons on the speakerphone. Government House had once had vidphones, but Tanith's climate had long since sent them to the scrap bin.

"Air/Space Commissioner's Office."

"Chief Administrator Chang here. Deputy Commissioner Paulik, please." A moment later she was put through to him. "Hello, Don. It's Ann. Quick question for you. The Governor has friends aboard the *Norton Star.* Everything all right up there?"

"Sure is." Her speakerphone deepened his familiar reedy voice. "Amalgamated chartered one of our landing boats to send up supplies just this morning. Rather a lot of stuff, actually. Looks like they're planning to be there a while."

"Ah. Thanks. Don, there's something screwy with my data system this morning. I can't seem to find their landing request."

"Oh? Hold on a moment. Yes, here it is. They've got a standby for a remote-area water landing. Location to be named later. Seems a bit unusual . . . Are you sure you don't have it, Ann? It looks like it was approved by your office."

"Oh, I'm sure it was," she said. *Just what is our fearless leader up to? And why didn't he tell me about it? I could have upset his plans—* "Just to help me sort this out, who does it say approved the request?"

"It says here that Everett did."

Everett. Everett Mardon. Her son-in-law. "Oh. Thanks."

"Look, Ann, there's nothing irregular about this, is there?"

"No, I'm sure it's all in order. Thanks, Don. Will we see you at the Lederle party next week?"

"Sure thing. Bye, Chief."

Her hand trembled slightly as she turned off the speakerphone.

"Good work, boss."

She turned, startled. "Everett—"

"Let's take a break, Ann. You look like you could use one."

"Everett, what the hell's going on?"

He came around her desk and put his hand on her shoulder. "Like I said. You need a break. Let's take a walk."

She waited until they were outside Government House and halfway across the square. "All right, Ev," she said. "What's this all about, and why would the governor tell you and not me?"

"Governor—oh. Ann, Governor Blaine doesn't know anything about this. He can't find out, either."

"What?" She stopped, then turned and started back toward the building. Everett reached out and caught her by the sleeve.

"Really, Ann. Stop a minute and listen."

"No." She jerked her sleeve free and faced him. "Listen, Ev. Whatever you've done to my database access, you fix it, and now. Then I'll try to keep the governor from firing you."

"Not good enough."

Her eyes narrowed. "Everett, you may be able to treat my daughter like this—"

"The hell I can, and you know it! Now just for one lousy minute, will you *listen?*"

She took a deep breath. "All right. Alicia's sake. But this had better be good."

"Where do I start? Start at the beginning, go on to the end, then stop. That's what you told Philip—"

"And you needn't keep bringing Alicia and my grandson into this—"

"I'm not the one who brought up Alicia. Look, I'm trying to—" He stopped. "Sorry, Ann. I didn't mean to bite. Okay, let's start at the beginning. Where does the borloi go?"

"The borloi? What's that got to do with—"

"Just listen, would you, please?"

She raised one eyebrow at him. "Very well. Lederle AG buys the borloi."

"Right. Lederle. At least that's the theory. But we all know that most of it actually goes to the Navy. They sell it, and that gives them money over and above what they get from the Grand Senate. Lets them do whatever they want, no matter what the Senate says they should do. The fact is, every single person on Tanith is party to a conspiracy against the CoDominium Treaty."

"Well . . ." She reflected. "Yes, I suppose technically that's true, but—"

"But nothing! It's not just technically true. It *is* true. So far we've gotten away with it, but that can't last. Did you know that Grand Senator Bronson is starting an investigation? By the time he's done, your precious governor will be in jail. So will you, if we don't cooperate with Bronson's people."

"Cooperate." Her face turned stony. "How, cooperate?"

"You don't have to do anything. Not one thing. Just forget you ever heard about the *Norton Star*. How did you tumble to it, anyway? I installed a flag to alert me if you or Blaine asked for any space-traffic info, but it didn't tell me how you found out."

Ann glanced at him, and found she was smiling in spite of herself. "Geoffrey Niles asked for a dinosaur hunting permit."

"What!" Everett spluttered a guffaw. "That fathead! He would."

"But you're working for him—"

"Not for him. For his father. Lord Niles is one of Bronson's key people, and Captain Yoshino is plenty sharp—"

"Yoshino?"

"*Norton* Star's skipper. Bronson bought him away from the Meiji navy. Geoff Niles is supposed to be Purser."

"I see now. I suppose they're planning to land a boat in the planters' territory and cart away the crop."

"But of course. What else?"

"When?"

"No idea."

"Soon?"

"What's soon? I don't really know, but I don't think it'll be tomorrow or anything near it."

"No, I suppose not. If Niles thinks he has time to collect a dino—" She stopped and leaned against a tree. Everett looked quickly at her.

"Are you all right?"

"No. Yes, of course I'm all right. I just have to think. Everett, the governor trusts me."

"I know. And this is a lousy thing to do to him. But damn it, Ann, he's on the wrong side—"

"He's not! He's ending the slave trade, he's going to put up power satellites as soon as he gets the money, he's—"

"Sure, sure . . . All that's fine. But what about the other things he's doing? I know you weren't happy having that whore at your table in Government House last week."

"Well—maybe he is moving a little fast in some directions—"

"But that wasn't what I meant," Everett cut in. "Maybe I shouldn't have said the wrong side. Maybe I should have said the losing side. Because, Ann, everybody who fights Bronson loses. Always."

"Now that's not true. Governor Blaine's got the support of Grand Senator Grant—"

"It's true in the long run. Grant's losing support. Bronson's going to win this one, and where will that leave us? Look, it's not as though I'm asking you to *do* anything—"

"I don't know, Ev. I just don't know. I have to talk to Satay."

"I thought he was out of town."

"He'll be back at the end of the week."

"Good. I didn't know he cared about politics."

"He doesn't, but—I still think I ought to talk to him."

"All right. Talk to him. But promise me one thing, will you? Before you tell Blaine, will you come see me first?"

Ann took a deep breath. *Nothing makes sense anymore. Still, family has to count for something.* "All right, Ev. I will."

Ursula walked so slowly Lysander was afraid she might stop. He kept his arm around her waist as they entered Falkenberg's office.

"Good of you to see us, Colonel."

"Not at all, Your Highness." Falkenberg stood at his desk. "Miss Gordon. Please sit down. Would either of you care for a drink?"

"Thank you, no," Lysander said.

"Sherry?" Ursula said faintly.

"Of course." Falkenberg took a decanter and glasses from the credenza behind his desk. "Your Highness?"

"Well, since everyone else is. Thank you."

Falkenberg poured, then sat down facing them across his desk. "Cheers."

"Cheers," Lysander said automatically.

Ursula drained her glass. Lysander glanced at Falkenberg, then refilled her glass from the decanter.

"So," Falkenberg prompted.

"Colonel, Ursula has a story I think you should hear. It happens that six weeks ago she was an overnight guest at one of the Girerd family's establishments. The main one, I think, given the circumstances of her visit. Can you find it on your map there?"

"Should," Falkenberg said. He moved a stack of papers to the side table and pulled out the keyboard drawer. "Hmm. Girard. G-I-R-A-R-D-?"

"No, it ends in 'ERD,'" Ursula said.

"Ah. There are three villas. Let's see—" The map appeared and zoomed in.

"Not that one," Ursula said. "There was a sea inlet to the south."

"Was there? Ah. Here we are. 'Rochemont Manor.' Grand name for a drug farm on a prison planet." A satellite photograph replaced the map. "Nine hundred kilometers southwest of here."

"That's it, I'm sure it is," Ursula said.

"Good." Falkenberg refilled her glass and waited.

"It was about four in the morning," Ursula said. "I was— the party was over, and it was hot, and I couldn't sleep. The room was on a balcony, and I thought I heard something. More like thunder than wind, but there wasn't any thunder. No wind either. I got up. I told myself it was to go look, but really I just wanted to walk around. While I was getting my robe I heard a helicopter land."

"At four A.M.," Lysander said.

Falkenberg nodded.

"When I got outside, I swear I heard some people talking down below somewhere, but I couldn't see anyone, and there wasn't any helicopter."

"And you should have seen it?" Falkenberg asked.

"Yes. The helipad was down the hill from the balcony."

"But they hadn't put her in a room facing it," Lysander said. Falkenberg frowned.

"The veranda runs all the way around the house." Ursula pointed to the satellite photo. "See, there it is. The room was over here, and the helipad is down there. I don't know why I walked around to the north side. I suppose I was curious about the helicopter. It did seem a little unusual—"

Falkenberg waited, but she was staring at the map. "I see," he said. "You were in a room on the east side."

"Yes, I thought that was strange, because the best rooms are always on the north side. But that's where we were. And they would have given us—I mean—"

"It's all right, Ursa," Lysander said, and squeezed her hand.

"You were in an east room," Falkenberg repeated. "You heard sounds. As you got up, you heard a helicopter land. By the time you were above the helipad, there wasn't any helicopter. How long did it take you to get around to the north side?"

"Not very long at all. Well, a minute or two," Ursula said. "I had to find my robe. And the bedroom isn't really off the veranda. It has a little balcony of its own, with steps that go down to the veranda. It was still dark, and the veranda lights were out, so it took a little time getting down the steps. And I wasn't in any hurry. Really, Colonel—"

"So you walked around the veranda until you could see the helipad, but there was no helicopter. What happened then?"

"Not much at all. There was nothing there, so I walked back around to the balcony. My—Oskar was waiting for me there and we went back inside."

"I see. And you say the noise that woke you sounded like thunder?"

"Well, at first I thought it was thunder. But it wasn't anywhere near as loud, and it lasted a lot longer than thunder does."

"And there was no storm."

"None at all. The night was quite calm."

Falkenberg took out a pair of rimless spectacles and put them on. He leaned over the map for a minute. "This party. Who were the guests?"

"Uh, Colonel, is this relevant?" Lysander asked.

"I think so."

"It's all right," Ursula said. "It was—Oskar Girerd's sixteenth birthday party. There were about a dozen planters and their sons. Most of the boys were about Oskar's age. But they all left about midnight."

"All? No overnight guests?"

"Well, let's see. There was quite a crowd at breakfast. Supervisors and overseers and—of course. Jonkheer van Hoorn and his son were still there."

"Supervisors and overseers," Falkenberg said. "Any military people?"

"I don't think so—well, there were the Girerds' own guards. At least that's who I thought they were."

"Uniforms?"

She shrugged. "Standard camouflage coveralls. Nothing I'd recognize."

"Think hard," Falkenberg said. "Badges? Patches?"

She shook her head. "None I remember."

"Did any of them wear earrings?"

"Why—well, yes, now that you mention it. Not exactly rings. Cuffs. Two of the security people—"

"Wore bulldog ear cuffs," Falkenberg said.

"How did you know that?" Lysander began. "Ah. Of course. Barton's Bulldogs—"

"Was once their official name," Falkenberg said. "May still be. What would you engrave on a 'bastard' earring?" He shook his head. "One or two things puzzle me. Miss Gordon, what was the weather like the day before this party?"

"Terrible. It was one of the last big storms of the harvest season, and it rained all week. We weren't sure I'd be able to get there."

Falkenberg typed rapidly. "And more bad weather was forecast."

"I don't know. I guess so—"

"I'm not guessing," Falkenberg said. He gestured toward the data screen. "So. They knew they had exactly one night of good weather for at least several days to come. Still, it seems exceedingly stupid of them to have run the operation with strangers on the premises. Just what were—just how did you come to be invited to that party, Miss Gordon?"

"Colonel, really, I don't think—"

"Your Highness, Miss Gordon, I am not asking out of idle curiosity."

"I was—invited—by Jonkheer van Hoorn."

"Directly?"

"No, sir." She set her lips. "They bought me for the night from the Hilton."

"I see. Could—would they do this without consulting the Girerd family?"

"It's not the way it's usually done, but it does happen." She glanced quickly at Lysander and went on. "This wasn't the first time."

"Thank you."

"Colonel—"

"I'm sorry, Your Highness. I had to establish whether the Girerds were incredibly stupid or had no choice in the matter. Miss Gordon, the one thing that surprises me is that you were allowed to leave that house alive."

"I—" She shivered. "I never thought of that."

"Doubtless there were reasons. You would have been missed by your employers and—"

"And others," Ursula finished for him.

"Yes. Well. You may have done us quite a service," Falkenberg said. He took off his spectacles and turned to Lysander. "Your Highness. Under the circumstances, I suggest that Miss Gordon remain a guest of the Regiment. She might not be safe at the Hilton."

"But I have to go back!" Ursula protested. "My contract—"

"I doubt you need concern yourself with your contract any longer," Falkenberg said. "We'll buy what's left of it."

"But—I need the job. Not that it matters, I guess. The Hilton won't keep a girl who talks about her clients."

"I think you'll find no lack of alternatives," Falkenberg said. "If need be, we can discuss the matter with Governor Blaine." He stood. "Now, if you'll both excuse me—"

"Certainly, Colonel." Lysander stood. As he opened the door for Ursula he heard Falkenberg talking rapidly into the intercom.

XVII

Corporal Tandon heard a faint chirp in his left ear. He touched the control in his breast pocket. "Sarge," he whispered into his throat mike. "Stand by. Message coming in."

Sergeant Miscowsky acknowledged with a tiny shrug. He didn't look around to where Tandon was standing behind him, but went on talking with the village headman. Etienne Ledoux was the blackest man Miscowsky had ever seen. Although clearly past his forties, he had slim hips and a solid barrel chest. He spoke excellent Anglic, sometimes breaking into the Cooney patois to shout something to a villager or make a point with Purdy, then switching back to Anglic without a pause. His voice was musical and surprisingly high. Tough-looking, though, Miscowsky thought. Could have been a good boxer.

"Yeah, we can leave some of the penicillin, no problem," Miscowsky said. "Fungus powder, too. We carry lots."

"So do Major Barton's men," Ledoux said. He set his tea cup down on the table between them and grinned broadly. "For my people's sake I am not sorry you both are trying to bribe us."

Miscowsky grinned back. "And I'm glad we've got your nephew with us."

"Buford was ambitious," Ledoux said. "Not that this place could do much to keep an ambitious boy." His grin faded as he surveyed the oblong clearing from the open thatched pavilion where they sat. Miscowsky followed his gaze. Thatch-and-wicker houses stood on two-meter stilts. A long house on a low platform occupied the side of the village square opposite them. There was a well in one corner of the square, and the brick-lined fire pit in the center was surrounded by benches and tables much like picnic tables.

"Looks pretty good to me," Miscowsky said. "I've seen pictures of jungle living on Earth. This doesn't seem so bad."

"If you like the jungle it is not bad at all," Ledoux said.

He paused, and Miscowsky thought he seemed to come to a decision. "Sergeant, let me be frank with you. We cannot help you. Whatever your quarrel is with Major Barton, we want no part of it. We hold no title to this land. In truth, we own nothing. We survive because the planters don't think we're worth the trouble to evict us—"

"I know," Miscowsky said. "The Old Man—Cap'n Frazer— told us. Maybe he could talk to the governor about it."

Ledoux laughed. "You are kind, Sergeant. But I cannot quite believe your governor would make enemies for our sake."

"Maybe not." Miscowsky sipped tea. Behind him Corporal Tandon excused himself and went off to the privy behind the long house. "Cap'n Frazer says the governor's a pretty good guy, though. And the local planters here are already his enemies. They hired Barton."

Ledoux poured more tea and Miscowsky waited. They'd stressed patience in his training. You don't ask too many questions on a prison planet, and anyway Purdy had told him most of the story. Ledoux, and Purdy's father, and some others like them had led a band of time-expired convicts into the jungle, as far from the plantations as they could get and still be able to get back to a road if they had to. By now most of the villagers didn't need or want anything to do with roads or what was at the end of them; but they'd done too much work, clearing jungle and damming streams, to move on.

Nobody knew how many villages like this existed. Satellite photos said several hundred, but most of those were a lot smaller: two or three families, no more. Purdy said his uncle's compound was one of the largest, with almost two hundred people, counting the children.

"Heck, a few more years and you folks will outnumber the planters," Miscowksy said.

He missed Ledoux's reply. Tandon's voice spoke in his ear. "Sarge, we've got new orders. There's a plantation about fifty klicks southwest, on the sea. Cap'n wants us to haul ass down there. Top priority."

Shit fire. Miscowsky visualized the map. Cut straight across the jungle, just about due southwest. No trails mapped. Maybe they'd find one. Have to find something. He gave hand signals to the others. Leave the supplies and get moving, and hope Ledoux didn't think they were being impolite.

"Sure ain't much for a trail," Miscowsky muttered. "They want somebody up there in a hurry, they'd do better to drop a new team in closer."

"Cap'n Frazer said they couldn't do that," Tandon said. "Regiment thinks they'll be watching that place real close."

"What's up there anyway?" Cloudwalker asked.

"I couldn't ask, could I? Only transmission we made was a click to acknowledge orders. One thing, we're supposed to report helicopter traffic, day or night. Break radio silence on that one."

"Won't the rebels be waiting for us?" Purdy asked. "I mean, if we can hear headquarters, they can too, right?"

Miscowsky waved to shush them while they went through a thicket. Then the underbrush thinned and it was safe to talk again. "Nope," Tandon said. "Look, what happens is they send up a chopper so it can see us. Not really see us, but we're in the line of sight, right? Then they aim a beam where they think we are. When I hear it, I click the set. That sends back a signal they can home in on. They narrow the beam down so it's no bigger'n ten meters when it gets to us. Anybody wants to listen to that, he's got to be between us and the chopper. Not much chance of that."

"Besides, it's all in code," Miscowsky said.

"Oh." Purdy peered ahead into the jungle and automatically veered around to the right. "Watch it up ahead. Something in the mud."

"Weems?" Cloudwalker asked.

"Maybe just a log," Purdy said. "Sure rather not find out, though."

Miscowsky shuddered and held his bayonetted rifle warily at chest level. "Tell you, kid, I'm getting right glad you're along."

They were quiet until they were past the small open mud flat. "If it works so well, how come we can't talk back to them the same way?" Purdy asked.

"We don't carry enough gear. Can't aim close enough," Tandon said. "Sure, give me a stable platform and enough time to set things up, I can lock on to the chopper, but it sure ain't any use trying from the crapper in your uncle's village."

They slogged on, Purdy in the lead. Thick mud dragged at their boots but the spiny underbrush slid harmlessly off the nylon of their tunics. After an hour, Purdy stopped and let Miscowsky catch up.

"Sarge, it's getting thicker. We won't make much time."

"Shit fire. We're not making any time now."

"Going to be slower yet."

"Yeah, I can see that. Nothing we can do."

"Well, there's one thing, Sarge. There's water off east of

us. Don't remember just how far, but it can't be more than about five klicks. Slough. It runs past the village, and down to the sea. We could get over there and use boats."

"Boats, huh? And where are these boats gonna come from?"

"I can go back and borrow them while you cut over to the water. Then I pole down and pick you up."

"Shit, I don't know," Miscowsky said. "Tandon, just how'd they say that part about the place being watched?"

"Just like that, Serge. Barton's guys'll probably be watching the whole area around the plantation. Chopper patrols, too, maybe, but probably not."

"Purdy, how close does this stream—"

"Not a stream, Sarge. More like a slough—"

"Stream, slough, whatever. How close does it get to the plantation?"

"Lets out into open water about six klicks southeast of there, but we don't want to follow it that far. Gets too deep. But we can get out straight east of the plantation and cut across. It'll be thick, thick as this, but we won't have more'n a klick of it."

"Kid's got a point, Sarge," Cloudwalker said. "No way we'll make more than twenty klicks a day in this stuff no matter how hard we try. Maybe not even that."

"That's right," Purdy said. "The boats would save a day, maybe two."

Miscowsky stared hard at Purdy. "Well . . . Okay. Cloudwalker, you go with him—"

"He'd just slow me down, Sarge," Purdy said.

"Yeah. So how'll you know where to meet us?"

"You cut straight across, due east," Purdy said. "You'll hit the slough by dark. You can't miss it, the water's over your waist. Camp there. I'll start at first light. Can't take me more than two hours. Watch for me."

"Okay, but don't start at first light. Give us a couple hours in case we don't get through this stuff as fast as you do. Got that?"

"Right, Sarge!"

Miscowsky and the others watched as Purdy disappeared back into the underbrush they'd just come through.

"Not too shabby," Owassee said.

"Yeah, the kid just might do. Okay, let's hump it."

Captain Rottermill's light pointer swept around the image projected on the situation room wall. "Good location, all right," he said. "Deep water to the south. Low hills on three sides.

Thick jungle for a hundred kilometers in all directions. One narrow road runs northwest to hit the main road to Dagon. Big plantation, six registered helicopters, lots of chopper traffic."

"Did you see anything new in the survsat photos?" Ian Frazer asked.

"Not a thing," Lieutenant Swensen answered.

"Nothing real," Rottermill said. "But I did some fooling around. Watch."

The map table projected the satellite photograph of Rochemont Manor, then dissolved into a computerized drawing of the building and the hill it stood on. An outline formed on the side of the hill next to the helipad, solidified, and opened.

"It's big enough," Rottermill said. "Not one shred of evidence, of course. If there's a door they were careful to use material that gives off the same IR signature as the rocks around it. There's probably not a straight line anywhere in it. Not easy, but not all that difficult either."

"Deep water," Falkenberg said. "How deep?"

"Twenty, thirty meters," Rottermill said. "Maybe more. Charts aren't that accurate for that region. Less than fifty meters, more than twenty."

"Enough," Falkenberg said quietly. He bent over to study the photograph. "These structures here. Docks?"

"Well, some kind of floating platform, sir," Lieutenant Swensen said. "It could be used as a pier. Colonel, do you think—"

"Exactly," Rottermill said.

"It certainly is odd," Falkenberg said. "Only fools regularly go out in deep water on Tanith. Could a landing ship actually operate in that water, Captain?"

"Tough question, sir," Rottermill said. "The inlet's long enough. Bit short for takeoff, maybe. It would depend on the landing ship."

"Could any of Tanith's landing craft operate there?"

"No way, Colonel. Those crates shouldn't be allowed out of a wading pool. You just might get one in but you'd sure never get it out again."

"But military craft could land and take off," Falkenberg said. "Especially if the takeoff load wasn't too heavy."

"Yes, sir. I thought of that, but there aren't any CD Marine landing boats on Tanith," Rottermill said. "I checked. None here to start with, and that cruiser took all hers with her when she left last week."

"You're certain of that?"

"Yes, sir."

"Good work. I doubt Captain Andreyev would be involved in a plot against the Fleet, but it's well to be sure. No other ships have arrived since the *Kuryev* left?"

"No, sir. At least the governor's office hasn't reported any, and they're supposed to advise us of all space traffic."

Falkenberg frowned. "The harvest season's nearly over and more than ninety percent of the crop is in. Tell me, Captain Rottermill, is Ace Barton a fool?"

"No, sir."

"Precisely. So just what does he expect to *do* with that— merchandise?"

"We've known all along there had to be a ship coming for it," Major Savage said.

"No question about it, Major," Rottermill said. "There's sure no other way to turn the drugs into cash." He slid the keyboard tray out of the side of the map table and began typing.

"She should be coming soon, too," Captain Fast said. "The longer they wait, the more things can go wrong for them. Such as an assault on Rochemont. Colonel, shall I order an alert?"

Falkenberg frowned. "Jeremy?"

"Stage One. Get ready to move," Major Savage said. "But don't go in there just yet. Whatever else Barton is planning, you may be sure he'll have air defenses ringing that plantation."

"Agreed," Falkenberg said. "Amos, if you please . . ."

"Yes, sir." Captain Fast typed rapidly at his computer console.

"Pity we don't have a Fleet Marine assault boat," Jeremy Savage said. "That would give Barton a surprise."

"Sir, could we borrow one from *Kuryev*?" Lieutenant Swensen asked.

Falkenberg chuckled. "Ingenious, Lieutenant, but I'm afraid we'd never get that much cooperation from Captain Andreyev. Besides, by now they'll be halfway to the Alderson point."

Rottermill looked up from his keyboard. "No incoming shipping scheduled for a month, Colonel."

"Not good." Falkenberg ran one hand through his thinning straw-colored hair. "Damn it, they must have plans for what to *do* with the blasted drugs once they've collected them— Captain Fast, would you please get the governor on the line. Use the scrambler."

"Sir."

"Ian, when do your lads reach the plantation?" Major Savage asked.

"Be surprised if they're anywhere near the place before Wednesday night."

"Four days," Rottermill said. "Sounds about right. It's thick out there."

"Governor Blaine's office, sir."

"Thank you. Falkenberg here. Good afternoon, Mrs. Chang. I really do need to speak to the governor. Yes, thank you, I'll wait—Ah. Good afternoon, Governor. Yes. Yes, possibly something significant. I'd rather not discuss it on the telephone. Perhaps you'd care to join us for dinner tonight?" He glanced at Captain Fast and got a nod. "The Mess would be honored—Well, yes, it may be important. I'd like to show you. Excellent. Eighteen thirty, then. One other matter, not your concern of course, but we need a complete schedule of all ships expected for the rest of the year. Well, as soon as possible—Yes, of course. Perhaps I should speak to her directly? Good. I'll wait." Falkenberg touched the mute switch on the telephone. "Should have asked Mrs. Chang when I had her on the line. I'll put this on the speaker."

Lieutenant Swensen opened her notebook and unclipped her pen.

"Yes, Colonel?" Ann Chang's amplified voice filled the room. "What can we do for you?"

"We need a full shipping schedule as soon as possible," Falkenberg said. "All space traffic from now through the end of the year."

"Of—of course, Colonel. But you know not all traffic is scheduled—"

"Yes, of course," Falkenberg said impatiently.

Captain Rottermill frowned and reached under the table for his briefcase.

"I'll send you a copy of everything we have at the moment. If you'll wait just a moment. It'll take a few minutes to search the files."

Rottermill set his briefcase on the table in front of him and lifted out a small plastic box. He pressed a switch on it and placed it facing Falkenberg's speaker-phone.

"We can wait," Falkenberg said. He glanced at Rottermill and raised one eyebrow. Rottermill nodded curtly.

"Colonel, the computers are doing odd things with the data base," Ann Chang said. "Let—let me call you back, please."

Falkenberg glanced at Rottermill. The intelligence officer nodded again. "Very well," Falkenberg said. "We really do need that schedule. We'll wait for your call."

"Thank you, Colonel," Ann Chang said. "It'll be just a few minutes. I appreciate your patience—"

"Not at all. Goodbye." Falkenberg punched the off button, looked to make sure the connection was broken, and looked back to Rottermill. "Well?"

Rottermill turned the Voice Stress Analyzer so that Falkenberg could see the readout. A line of X's reached far into the red zone. "Colonel, she's scared stiff."

"What put you onto her?" Ian Frazer asked.

Rottermill shrugged. "Do enough interrogations and you get a feel for it. Mind you, this isn't certain. That damn scrambler could affect the patterns. But I'll bet dinner for a week that woman's hiding something. Three days' dinners it's something to do with shipping schedules."

Jeremy Savage laughed. "Rottermill, I doubt anyone will take your bets no matter how you dress them up. I certainly won't."

Rottermill made a wry face. "Colonel, if we could have the next call without the scrambler?"

"Of course."

Captain Fast scratched his head. "Colonel, if the Chief Administrator is in league with the rebels—"

"We don't know that," Rottermill said.

"But it's not unlikely?" Amos Fast asked.

"With Rottermill willing to bet?" Ian Frazer said. "Christ, do you think she's been feeding Barton satellite data? No wonder they keep finding my patrols!"

Captain Fast whistled softly. "Colonel, shouldn't we send some of the Headquarters Squad to see she doesn't run away?"

"A bit hasty, perhaps," Major Savage said. "Still, if this proves out—"

"I'll ask the governor to bring her to dinner tonight," Falkenberg said.

XVIII

Ann Chang sipped at an unremarkable port while the mess stewards silently cleared away. She half-listened as Falkenberg went through a meaningless ritual of thanking the Acting Mess President, as if Captain Fast weren't Falkenberg's adjutant and chief assistant. *Come to that, this whole dinner has been pretty unremarkable.* Nothing wrong with it, really: there'd been four courses and two kinds of game, and nothing was overcooked; but you could dine on the same fare in a dozen restaurants within two kilometers of Government House. Certainly the meal wasn't anything worth inviting the governor to—and there was even less about it to have made Carleton Blaine insist that she change her dinner plans and come with him. *Funny. I don't think I've ever heard him so insistent about anything. Odd.*

Not a lot of people here. Colonel Falkenberg and Major Savage—apparently neither of them married, was there something strange about that? Captain Frazer's wife seemed to be the official hostess. And of course Prince Lysander had brought that hotel girl. Captain Catherine Alana had come in late. Odd. Didn't I see her in town, outside Government House, just this afternoon?

A trivial dinner, and that didn't make sense. Why would Falkenberg invite the governor and his Chief Administrator to a very ordinary meal on such short notice? But Blaine had seemed pleased, even eager; almost as if he were anticipating something— She gasped involuntarily.

Could he know? No. Certainly not. He wasn't that good an actor. "The guilty flee where no man pursueth." Who said that? It certainly applies to me, Ann thought.

The toasts were over. All at once Falkenberg, the governor, and Captain Rottermill were standing at her chair.

"Excuse me for a few minutes, would you, Ann?" Blaine said. "The colonel has some news for me. Apparently it's sensitive enough that I mustn't share it with anyone, even you. Can't imagine what it might be, but there it is. We shouldn't be long. Perhaps you'll join Prince Lysander and his young lady for a while?"

"I'm sure I'll be fine," Ann said automatically.

"Of course you will," Blaine said. He walked away with Colonel Falkenberg.

Captain Rottermill stayed behind. "It's really not all that complicated, Mrs. Chang," he said. "Something to do with shipping schedules, I think."

"I—shipping schedules?"

"A minor discrepancy somewhere," Rottermill said. "Ah. Here's Prince Lysander. I'll leave you in his good hands." Rottermill bowed and followed Falkenberg and Blaine.

What is this? Ann looked around wildly. Nothing seemed to have changed. No one was watching her. But— *Something's wrong. Terribly wrong.* She fled to the women's room.

No one else was inside. She stayed there as long as she thought she decently could. When she came out, Captain Alana was waiting for her. Captain Catherine Alana, and five soldiers in combat fatigues. Three were women. They all carried weapons and wore "MP" brassards.

"I'm sorry, Mrs. Chang," Catherine Alana said. She didn't seem at all like the young lady who'd been at the governor's dinner party only two weeks before. "I must ask you to come with us."

"What? But I'm supposed to be with Prince Lysander—"

"We'll explain to His Highness," Captain Alana said. "I'm sorry, but I really must insist." Catherine gestured, and her soldiers surrounded Ann Chang.

No one had touched her, or even been impolite, but Ann knew better than to resist. She nodded helplessly and followed her captor.

They took her to a bare, unadorned room. A folding plastic table and two folding chairs stood on the plastic floor. They ushered her inside and left her there alone.

They can't do this! Inside, she knew they could. There were special laws and regulations for officials of very high rank. Governor Blaine had plenty of authority to deal with suspected treason.

Treason. But it wasn't. *I'm no traitor—*

The door opened, and a young man about thirty years old came in. He wore sergeant's stripes on his undress khaki uniform. "Good evening," he said perfunctorily. "I am Special Investigator Andrew Bielskis. For the record, are you Ann Hollis Chang, Chief Administrator of Tanith?"

"Yes. Yes, I am. And by what right are you talking to me like this?"

"Just routine, Ma'am."

A sergeant. Not even an officer. Ann set her lips in a thin line. "I see no reason why I should speak to you at all. Please inform Governor Blaine that I want to go home now."

"The governor's busy with the colonel, Ma'am." Sergeant Bielskis said. "Now, we understand you're saying there are no ships in orbit around Tanith at present. Is this correct?"

"I don't have to answer that!"

"No, Ma'am. We have the tapes of your conversation with Colonel Falkenberg this afternoon. I'll play them if you like."

"This is none of your business!" Ann shouted. "I want to see the governor!"

"I'm afraid it is my business, Ma'am," Sergeant Bielskis said. "Colonel Falkenberg's contract stipulates the neutralization and suppression of all organizations and persons dedicated to the overthrow of the lawful authorities of Tanith. Do you deny cooperating with the rebels?"

"What? But—"

The door opened and Captain Rottermill came in. His face was slightly red, as if he'd been running. "Sergeant Bielskis, what is this? Madame Chang, my apologies!"

Thank God! "No harm done, Captain. Thank you."

"Now, Bielskis, just what do you think you're doing?"

"Preliminary interrogation of detainee, sir," Bielskis said.

"Sergeant, for heaven's sake, this is the Chief Administrator of this planet!"

"Makes no difference, sir. We have solid evidence—"

"Evidence, Sergeant?"

"Yes, sir. At 1548 P.M., suspect having been instructed by the governor to inform this Regiment of all space traffic at present and for the future, personally stated to Colonel Falkenberg that there were no ships in orbit around Tanith and none expected. At approximately 0845 two days ago a Tanith landing ship under contract to Amalgamated Foundries, Inc. delivered supplies, liquid hydrogen, and liquid oxygen to CDMS *Norton Star,* which ship was then and is now in orbit around this planet. The landing ship requested and received clearance from the governor's office. Sir."

"Good Lord. But surely Mrs. Chang was not aware—"

"You can spare me the act, Captain," Ann said. "Although I must say you're very good at it. Tell me, Sergeant, what do you do when you're not intimidating middle-aged grandmothers?"

Bielskis shrugged. "Pull the wings off flies, Ma'am?"

Ann chuckled. "All right, Captain, what's going on here?"

"We've got you, you know," Rottermill said. "Voice Stress Analyzers this afternoon, and this room is equipped with a full battery of remote physiological sensors."

"Got me—"

"That may not be the best way to put it," Rottermill said. "If we were concerned with legalities, we'd have you. But of course that's not part of our job here. Sergeant, why don't you find us something to drink? Would you care for a brandy, Mrs. Chang?"

"Captain Rottermill, I would *love* a brandy."

"Good. Now let's get square with each other. So far the only people who know about this conversation are you, me, Sergeant Bielskis, and Captain Alana."

"Captain Catherine Alana?"

"Of course. She's a witness. Would you like her to join us?"

"Why not, if she's going to listen?"

"Very well. Now, as I say, this hasn't gone very far yet. There's no reason for it to reach the governor unless you want it to."

"Well—I'd really rather not disturb him," Ann said.

Rottermill smiled briefly. "Precisely. So why don't you just tell us all about it."

"All about what?" Ann said.

"Mrs. Chang, I can't turn you over to Sergeant Bielskis without the governor's consent, and I'd really hate to go ask him for that, but I will if I have to."

The door opened and Catherine Alana came in. She carried a tray with a brandy decanter and glasses.

"I used to think you were nice," Ann Chang said. "That was you I saw outside Government House today, wasn't it?"

"Oh, dear, you weren't supposed to recognize me," Catherine said.

"So you knew, even then," Ann mused. "All right, what do you want to know?"

"To start with, how long you've been cooperating with the rebels," Rottermill said.

Ann laughed. "That's easy. Since about three o'clock yesterday afternoon."

Rottermill was shocked.

That got him! "I do believe your boss is nonplussed," Ann said to Captain Alana. "But it's true. I'm afraid if you want to 'turn' me and use me as a double agent, it won't work. You see, I'm not a rebel."

Rottermill glanced down at his oversized wristwatch and frowned. "I believe you. So why were you withholding important information from the governor?"

"Yes, of course, that is the question. I'd really rather not say—"

"Mrs. Chang," Rottermill said. "We can find out. But if my OSI people start moving around Government House, we won't be able to keep anything a secret. Won't it be better for all of us if we keep it among ourselves?"

Ann sighed. "Oh, I suppose so. May I have that brandy now? Thank you. Well, it started with a request for a dinosaur permit. . . ."

Everett Mardon stared at the uniformed men on his doorstep. "Let me get this straight. Mrs. Chang wants me to come with you to Colonel Falkenberg's camp?"

"Yes, sir," the sergeant said. "Here's her note, and she sent this compact along. Said you'd recognize it. Said to tell you it's something to do with keeping a promise she recently made to you."

Alicia called from the other room. "Who is it, Ev?"

"Some people your mother sent," Everett said. "She wants to see me tonight."

"What? But we're playing bridge at the Hendersons'!"

The sergeant coughed. "I was told to keep this as informal as possible, sir."

"Meaning I don't really have a choice?" Everett demanded.

The soldier shrugged.

"I see. Alicia, you'll have to call Brenda and tell her we can't make it. I really do have to go."

"Good thinking," Sergeant Bielskis said.

Alicia Mardon tried to telephone Brenda Henderson but the phone was dead. A few minutes later a very helpful young technician arrived. It would take a while to get the phone working, he said; but he'd be sure to see the Hendersons got the message.

Half a dozen men were clustered around the map table in the regiment's conference room. When Lysander was ushered in, Governor Blaine raised a questioning eyebrow at Falkenberg.

"Prince Lysander located the enemy's headquarters," Falkenberg said.

Lysander opened his mouth to correct Falkenberg, then thought better of it.

"Did he? Congratulations, Your Highness." Blaine turned back to his inspection of the map table. "Rochemont. I knew the Girerds had a major hand in this mess, but I hadn't thought they'd get them this dirty." He shrugged. "So now we know where they're probably storing the borloi. But—as I understand it, Colonel, you haven't the ability simply to take the place by storm."

"That's about the size of it," Falkenberg said. "Not even if we commandeered every air-transport vehicle on the planet. Barton's got more than enough anti-air defenses to hold that place long enough to get the stuff out." Falkenberg smiled faintly. "Of course we could very likely manage to destroy it."

"Good Lord," Blaine said. "Colonel, please! Assure me that won't happen. It's all Bronson's people would need to put Grand Admiral Lermontov in a cleft stick. Not to mention the whole Grant faction in the Senate."

"We'll take every precaution, Governor," Falkenberg said. "So, I imagine, will Barton's Bulldogs."

"That's certain," Amos Fast said. "If that crop's lost, there's nothing to pay him with."

"It occurs to me," Major Savage said, "that Major Barton must have made contingency plans. Specifically, he must have a way to remove the merchandise on short notice."

"Well, now that his ship's here, he can just send for the landing boats, can't he?" Captain Fast said.

Governor Blaine frowned. "Ship? What—"

"CDMS *Norton Star.* An asset of Amalgamated Foundries, Inc."

"Here now? In orbit? Why the devil wasn't I told?" Blaine demanded.

"We'll get to that," Falkenberg said. "Amos, you've got a firm ID on the ship? Good. What do we have on her?"

"Unscheduled merchantman," Fast said. He tapped keys on the control console. "Carries her own landing boat. One moment, sir—there's more coming in. Ahah. She's commanded by one Captain Nakata, formerly of the Imperial Meiji fleet. Let's see what we have on him . . . Hmm. As of last spring there was a Lieutenant Commander Yoshino Nakata on the rolls. Four standard years' service as skipper of an assault carrier."

Major Savage whistled softly.

"Good Lord." Blaine stared at the map. "An assault carrier commander, an experienced one at that, skippering a tramp merchantman with her own landing ship. My God, Colonel! I've been at Rochemont. It's on an inlet, you know—the deep water runs almost all the way to the main compound. A landing ship could—"

"Exactly," Falkenberg said. "That's the assumption we're working on."

"Well, damn it, Colonel, what are you going to do about it?"

"That's what we're here to decide, sir," Falkenberg said.

"Governor," Captain Fast said, "The *Kuryev's* still in the system. You could recall her—"

"To do what?" Blaine asked.

"Recover the cargo from Nakata," Fast said. "If *Kuryev* gets here before *Norton Star*'s boat takes the stuff off planet, there's no harm done—we just borrow *Kuryev's* assault boats and go in ourselves."

"Captain, that's absurd," Blaine said. "First, I've no authority whatever to order a CD warship to board a CD merchantman—"

"Not even to seize contraband, sir?" Fast suggested.

"Borloi's not contraband, Captain. And you can be sure *Norton Star* will have a perfectly legal bill of sale for any-thing anyone might find on board," Blaine said. "I suppose I could claim we're sequestering goods against payment of taxes, but I don't for a minute think the CD Council would back me up. Sure, they might order Amalgamated Foundries to pay taxes and imposts, but I have no doubt the Council will turn the cargo right back over to them."

"Excuse me, Governor," Prince Lysander said. "I'm a little confused. Aren't the planters committing a crime—even an act of rebellion—by keeping back their crops?"

"Of course they are. But it's only a crime on Tanith," Blaine said. "The regulation that says all borloi has to be sold to the Lederle Trust is a perfectly legal Order in Coun-cil; but it's an internal matter, quite outside the jurisdic-tion of the CD. Surely the circumstances are similar on Sparta. The CoDominium isn't likely to enforce your domestic regulations."

"Yes, of course. But somehow I thought it might be differ-ent here, since this is a CD planet—"

"I take it then," Major Savage said carefully, "that in this case possession is considerably more than nine points of the law."

"Which leaves us exactly where we started," Captain Fast growled. "We can't just take Rochemont because we don't have transport to get enough troops there fast enough. Meanwhile, any minute now they could just drop in and pick up the stuff."

"At least the governor can refuse to give them a landing permit," Lysander said.

"Not that it would do any good," Blaine said. "Tanith doesn't have planetary defenses or warships. If they want to land, there's nothing to stop them."

"Besides, they already have a landing permit," Captain Fast said.

"What! How—"

"Approved by your office, Governor," Fast replied.

"How the—Colonel—"

"Later, please, Governor. At the moment we seem to have ourselves a problem."

"Christ on a crutch," Sergeant Miscowsky muttered. He glared at his watch, then back at the tangle of vines and bright flowers hanging over the brackish water. "I think I just screwed the pooch again."

"Nah," Corporal Tandon said. "You told him to start late, so he did. He'll get here."

"Shit, how's he going to *find* us?" Miscowsky demanded. "There's ten channels to this fucking excuse for a river."

"He'll find us," Owassee said.

"If he can get the boats. I didn't get the idea that uncle of his was all set to help us."

"Hell, Sarge, you worry too much."

"I get paid to worry." Miscowsky looked again at his watch. "He gets here or not, we still have to report our position. Better get set up, Nick."

"Right." Tandon took gear out of his knapsack. He set the point of what looked like a large corkscrew against a goshee tree trunk and drove it in, turning the handles until it was seated solidly in the corky wood. When he had the horn-shaped antenna firmly in place, he unpacked the hand-cranked generator and plugged the radio set into it. "Okay, Owassee, you're junior man now."

"One bad thing about letting the kid go," Owassee muttered, but he took the generator and strapped it to a log, attached the handles, and gave it an experimental turn. "Ready when you are, C.B."

Miscowsky consulted his watch. "Not long now. Maybe ten minutes. Wish that kid—"

There was a low whistle from upstream.

"Goddam," Miscowsky muttered.

Another whistle, then what might have been an answering one.

"Sumbitch! That's Cloudwalker all right," Tandon said.

A minute later two flatbottomed skiffs came into sight. Jimmie Cloudwalker was perched in the bow of the first. Buford Purdy stood in the back with a long pole. The second skiff was poled by Etienne Ledoux. They piloted the boats to the bank and tied them to low branches of the overhanging trees.

"Good to see you," Miscowsky said, as his troops and Ledoux jumped onto solid ground. "Wondered if you might have trouble borrowing a boat."

"I am still not certain this is wise," Ledoux said. "You have told me the Girerds are already enemies of the governor."

"That's for sure," Miscowsky said.

"I have considered. They claim this land. It is no real use to them—few can live and work here—but still they claim it." Ledoux shrugged. "Eh, bien. I can take you within three kilometers of the Girerd hills. We will be there by midnight. Then I will take my boats and go. With God's help the Girerds will not know the—guests on their land gave you aid. But if you should find our assistance of value—perhaps you will remember us. No one cares to be a guest forever."

"We won't forget you."

"Time to check in, Sarge," Tandon said. He plugged his helmet set into the radio and began speaking in a low voice. After a few moments he made adjustments with the control wheels on the antenna, listened, and adjusted again. Then he smiled and motioned to Owassee to begin cranking.

"My nephew has explained why you are not likely to be overheard," Ledoux said. "I confess I am still concerned—"

"So are we," Miscowsky said. "We don't want trouble any more than you do."

Tandon continued to speak in a low voice. Suddenly he straightened. "Sarge! The colonel wants to talk to you."

XIX

Lysander wondered if he would be allowed in the situation room, but when he went there after breakfast the sentries saluted and let him pass. Despite the best efforts of the stewards and the air conditioning system, the conference room stank. Fear and excitement blended with stale tobacco and spilled coffee.

The scene inside hadn't changed from the night before. Intelligence NCOs bent over the big map table. The Officer of the Day sat in a high chair at one end of the room. Senior officers came in, examined the maps and spoke to the sergeants, and went out shaking their heads.

One thing had changed: now the map table showed the actual location of Frazer's patrols in green. In most cases that was all there was, but some patrols had shadow locations shown in yellow. Lysander frowned at the display, then finally asked one of the plot sergeants.

"That's what we're telling Barton, sir." The sergeant grunted in disgust. "'Cause of those traitors in the Governor's office, the rebels have been getting satellite reports all along. Mostly those'll just show big troop movements, they won't see the patrols, but once in a while they get lucky and see some of Captain Frazer's specials." The sergeant grinned. "Our turn now. Cap'n Alana fed in a program to jigger things so when the satellite does get a reading, the Government House computer reports the location a little off from where they really are. Can't hurt."

"No, I don't suppose it can. Thank you, Sergeant." Lysander leaned over the map and frowned. It couldn't be that simple. If they cut off all data, the rebels would get suspicious, but what if they sent patrols of their own to verify the satellite information? Rottermill must have thought all that out. Or Falkenberg himself.

Probably it didn't matter. Things would get settled soon or

not at all. The basic situation was thoroughly simple: they knew where the borloi was kept. The problem was what to do about it. So far no one seemed to have thought of anything.

Someone's watch chirped the hour. In the next few minutes most of the senior staff came in to stare at the map table. The plot didn't tell them anything they hadn't known twelve hours earlier, but if anything was going to happen, they'd know it in the chart room before anyone else did.

"Do you all a world of good to go for a walk," Rottermill said.

"Sure would." Ian Frazer bent over the map table and eyed the distances between Rochemont and the nearest airfields.

"Report time," Rottermill said. "Swenson."

"Sir." Lieutenant Swensen adjusted her headset and nodded to the communications sergeants. It took nearly an hour for Frazer's SAS teams to make all their reports. As they did, Lieutenant Swensen fed their present and anticipated positions into the map computer. All twenty-three teams would converge on Rochemont, but not for several days.

There was a sudden hush as the projected position of Miscowsky's team appeared on the map.

"Get a confirmation on that," Captain Rottermill said automatically.

"Confirmed," Captain Frazer said. "Looks like the lads have found themselves river transport. Cooperation from the locals."

Captain Fast leaned down for another look. Then he straightened in decision. "Swensen, hang onto that contact." He touched buttons on the intercom. "Colonel, there's something here you ought to see."

Falkenberg was grinning when he came into the staff room. It was infectious. Soon everyone in the room was smiling.

"We've made several promises in the governor's name," Falkenberg said. "All worth it, I think. Headman Ledoux swears he can put twenty troopers and a fair amount of equipment in the Rochemont hills by dawn if we get them to the river early tonight. I've sent Miscowsky on ahead with Purdy as guide, so we'll have some forces on the spot no matter what happens. Of course they won't be able to do very much without reinforcements."

"I like it, John Christian," Major Savage said. "A good mortar team with complete surprise might just be able to take out a landing boat."

"I can see some problems," Captain Fast said carefully. He looked at Falkenberg. "With your permission, I'll reserve my comments for later, though."

"Looks better than anything else I've seen," Ian Frazer said. "Only problem is, I don't have twenty SAS troops left. In fact, I don't have any."

"Your regular scouts will do for this, Ian," Captain Fast said. "It's not like they'd have to stay out there for weeks."

"Harv and I will go," Lysander said quietly.

Everyone turned to look at him. There was silence for a moment. "Well, Your Highness, it could get a bit—" Frazer cut himself off.

Lysander smiled, not unkindly. "Captain, I don't know what notion you have of how princes of Sparta are brought up, but you might reflect on the name we've given our planet. Harv Middleton has spent the last couple of weeks teaching unarmed combat to your special forces troops, right?"

"Yes—"

"And they've learned from him, haven't they. Well, not to boast, but I can take him three falls in four."

"I—see," Frazer said.

"So that's settled," Lysander said. He thought he saw Falkenberg grin momentarily.

"Ian, I expect you ought to round up the other volunteers," Major Savage said. "Mortars and recoilless teams particularly wanted."

"You know, this just ought to work," Rottermill said. He grinned. "Legal, too. Provided they've put the borloi aboard the boat before we fire on it."

"Hadn't occurred to me," Major Savage said. "But yes, that could be important."

Falkenberg nodded slowly. "It could be critical. You can be sure Bronson's agents will file piracy charges. Let's make that an order, Ian. No one fires on the landing boat until we're certain a significant portion of the borloi is on board. If nothing else we'll make the governor's job a lot easier."

"Maybe we better reserve that decision for headquarters," Amos Fast said.

"Bit tricky," Rottermill said. "The field commander might not be able to communicate with headquarters."

"No, leave the authority in the field," Falkenberg said. "Just be sure the order's understood."

"Sir, why are you so sure they'll bring in the landing ship?" Captain Jesus Alana asked. "Mightn't they just transfer that crop to someplace else?"

Falkenberg smiled thinly. "Now that the observation satellites really belong to us, I hope they do."

"They're waiting for the harvest to finish," Rottermill said. "I don't know how long that will be."

"I don't either," Falkenberg said. "Time to help them decide. As soon as Captain Frazer's battle group is in place, we'll start an all-out assault on Rochemont." He pointed to a small island some fifty kilometers due south of the plantation. "Dragontooth Island. Appropriate name. This will be our assault base. Amos, we'll need all the transport we can get. Everything the governor can commandeer. We can't risk civilian craft in combat, of course; we'll use them to ferry gasoline and supplies for this operation. Rottermill, get your people started finding beaches, clearings—anything we can use as staging areas to move Second and Aviation Battalions to the island. From there Second will be well within striking range of Rochemont. Wait for final orders, but plan on starting the ferry operations not long after first light tomorrow. When this is done we'll have Aviation Battalion poised to run right down their throats."

"That should do it nicely," Captain Rottermill said. "Barton won't be able to stand just sitting back and watching us get into striking distance. He'll have to make his move. What's nice is that our troops won't have to hide—"

"I think it would be wise if they tried," Falkenberg said. "Barton will certainly see what we're doing. He'll know we can't possibly have thought we could hide an operation this size. He also knows we'd try our best to hide it anyway unless it's a feint, so that's what we'll do now. Best security you can manage. Act like this is all we can do."

Major Savage nodded. "Which it very nearly is. If we hadn't known about the landing ship, we wouldn't have had much choice."

"The one thing we do hide, of course, is that the whole operation is aimed straight at Rochemont," Falkenberg said. "What I want Barton to believe is that we're trying to outmaneuver him by placing a sizable force behind his lines. Given that strategy, Rochemont is an obvious target, but there are others." He indicated ranches dotted along the bay. "We don't single out Rochemont."

Captain Fast nodded. "Yes, sir."

Falkenberg turned to Major Savage. "Jeremy, I want you to do a second operation for cover. Overland assault with swamp boogies in the southeastern sector. This one really is a feint. After the first few hours we don't mind if they know that, but at the start it has to look real. Just look real, mind you, we don't want casualties. Steady troops on this, you'll roll through some of the most productive land on Tanith, and I don't want needless damage. I'd prefer none at all."

"There shouldn't be much," Captain Fast said. "That part's all right, Barton will fall back to regroup. If it goes on very long there could be some hard fighting, but we'll control that."

"If it goes on very long, we'll all be broke," Captain Alana said.

"So will Barton," Major Savage said. "I'll try to be frugal, Jesus."

"All right, Amos," Falkenberg said. "You say this part's all right. You don't like the rest."

"No, sir, I don't. And I'm not dead sure why."

Falkenberg looked around the table. "Who else doesn't like it?"

"I don't, sir," Peter Owensford said. "The problem is that the whole thing hangs on Ace Barton's cooperation."

"I'm afraid that's true," Major Savage said. "But have we any choice? Everything else we've thought of is a sure loss. This operation has surprise, and that means it has a chance. Barton can't possibly know we've found out about his ship, and he certainly has no reason to believe we know about Rochemont."

"How about this?" Captain Owensford said. "We go in. Barton calls in a landing boat and starts loading it up. You can be damned sure he'll put every last one of his troops on alert. He knows we have SAS teams out in the bush."

The others nodded agreement.

"He gets the stuff aboard. Or he gets *something* aboard. No way for our people to tell what. Eventually there's enough that we get worried, and our mortar teams open up. Say they're lucky. They cripple the landing boat without sinking it—"

"That's not luck," Ian Frazer said. "Just good shooting."

"Okay, Ian, and I believe your scouts are up to that," Owensford said. "But Barton will be ready for them. He's got to be. First salvo, he'll have his counterbatteries working."

"Well, we know that," Frazer said. "So our lads shoot and duck fast. Won't be a picnic—"

"Picnic be damned," Owensford said. "The troops can take care of themselves. Most of them should survive. Their mortars won't. Now what happens when the second landing boat comes in?"

"Second boat," Ian Frazer said, nodding slowly.

"Is that what was bothering you, Amos?" Falkenberg asked.

"Yes, sir. Except I hadn't thought it through as well as

Captain Owensford did. But he's got it. We won't have any way at all to knock out a second boat."

"We don't know there is a second boat," someone muttered.

"We sure as hell don't know there isn't one," Amos Fast said. "It's not usual for a tramp freighter, but *Norton Star's* hardly an ordinary tramp."

The others watched as Ian Frazer bent over the map table. Finally he straightened. "It's close all right, but it's not hopeless. Stash some helicopters in Ledoux's village. When the first lander comes in, we send in the choppers. Time it right and one of them will be in position to knock out the second lander—"

"If it gets through. It certainly will never get out," Captain Alana said. "And it'll take every credit we have to replace Aviation Battalion."

"It's worse than that," Amos Fast said. "We can't just start shooting at the second lander. It won't have any borloi aboard."

"It will by the time a CD inspector sees it," Rottermill muttered.

"You know," Frazer said, "maybe it would make sense to reverse things. Try to knock out the *first* landing ship with the choppers, and leave the recoilless teams as a surprise for the second. We do have those Sea Skimmer missiles. Maybe it's time to use them."

"Makes sense," Rottermill said. "But—"

"But—" Captain Jesus Alana repeated firmly. "Do you know what those birds cost?"

"What the hell good are they if we never use them?" Frazer demanded. "We've been saving them for the right mission. This is it."

"I agree. Hang the expense. Sometimes there's no choice," Peter Owensford said.

"Sometimes there isn't," Major Savage agreed. "Colonel, shall we send the Skimmers out to Dragontooth? Thank you. All right, Jesus, you've got the word."

"Yes, sir," Alana's voice held no enthusiasm.

"We may not need them," Savage said. "Let's not concede anything just yet. Especially since Barton knows we have those missiles. He just may have set up defenses. We'll know when Miscowsky's lads get in place."

"I've seen situations I like better," Owensford said.

"But maybe this is the best we can do."

There was a long silence. "Anyone else have suggestions?" Falkenberg asked.

"Not just now," Savage said. He tamped tobacco into a large

pipe. "Seems to me that Ian is on the right track. The mortar and recoilless teams will be our biggest surprise. We ought to save that surprise until it's needed most. What we need is a cheaper way to knock out the first assault boat."

"Of course there may not be a second one," Lysander said softly.

Falkenberg put on his spectacles and bent over the map table. "Amos, what time is our next contact with Miscowsky's group?"

"Well, they're supposed to stop and listen for messages every two hours—about forty minutes."

"Good. I want to talk to Etienne Ledoux."

"Got an idea, John Christian?"

"Just may, Jeremy. I just may. Meanwhile, someone find me the best expert on local conditions we have here at the base."

"Fuller, I'd think," Amos Fast said.

"Right. Fuller it is. Although if we have anyone who's lived near the coast—wasn't there a recruit from the jungle villages?"

"Purdy. Ledoux's nephew," Ian Savage said. "He's out with Miscowsky's team."

"Yes, of course. Anyone else like that? Anyway, send Fuller to my office, and then ask McClaren to pick three men and come see me about equipment."

"McClaren? Colonel, you're not going in there—" Ian Frazer was shocked.

"I think I will," Falkenberg said.

"But Colonel—"

Falkenberg's smile was cold. "Your concern is noted, Captain."

"Yes, sir."

"Mr. Prince, I'd be pleased if you would accompany me as my aide. And your *korpsbruder*, of course."

"Thank you, sir."

"Right. Amos, I'll be in my office in five minutes. Carry on." Falkenberg strode to the door.

"Christ, that's torn it," Ian Frazer muttered. He lifted his personal communicator card. "Centurion Yaguchi. Get my orderly. We'll be going into the field tonight."

"I doubt that, Ian," Major Savage said.

"Sir?"

"He isn't going to let you go out there."

"Damn it, Jeremy— Look, you talked me out of it before, but this time I'm going to do it, I swear, next Regimental Council I'm going to—"

"No you won't," Savage said. "You'd lose, and the colonel wouldn't accept that kind of restriction if you won the vote.

Be logical, Ian. Everything's cut and dried now. We're needed here to handle the details. The key command decisions will be made out there." Major Savage shrugged. "If the colonel weren't going, I would be. Rather nice of him to spare me that."

"Yeah. Look, you don't mind if I worry about him?"

"We can all do that. If you think you're upset, imagine what Sergeant Major is going to say. I doubt John Christian will be taking him, either." Savage nodded to Lysander. "Sorry you had to hear all this—"

"Glad I did, sir. Now if you'll excuse me, I've some arrangements I'd best see to."

"Carry on, Mr. Prince."

XX

The Officers' Open Mess was a blur of activity. There weren't any customers, but the staff had folded up most of the tables and chairs, and stacked the rest of the chairs on the tables. Two privates were enthusiastically mopping the floor. Another was behind the bar packing the bottles into boxes.

"Chance of dinner?" Lysander asked the mess steward.

"Yes, sir, but there's not much choice. Catfish and sweet potatoes—"

"Hum." Ursula smiled thinly. "Tanith standard fare—"

Sergeant Albright looked pained. "Yes, Ma'am, not up to the standards of the Mess, but we've got an alert on, you see."

"It's also all we'll get," Lysander said. "Please, Sergeant, I'd love some catfish and sweet potatoes. With beer, please."

"Yes, sir. Alieri, set up a table for Mr. Prince. Excuse me, sir, I'm needed in the kitchen."

"We don't have to eat," Ursula said. "I'd rather—"

"Of course we have to eat," Lysander said. "Certainly I do." He worked to keep his voice calm, and hoped he'd succeeded. Conflicting emotions boiled within him. He was eager to get away from Ursula, to get on with the mission and show Falkenberg what he could do. Odd, he thought; he liked being with Ursula. He even wondered if he might be in love with her, and what kinds of problems that would make for him. Certainly he felt guilty for being ready to leave her to go with Falkenberg. Mostly, though, he was more afraid that he wouldn't meet Falkenberg's expectations than anything else. He wanted to please Falkenberg more than he'd ever wanted to please his own father, and he didn't really understand that. Deep under all his emotions was the elemental fear of death, or worse, dismemberment.

Meanwhile, Ursula was being very understanding about his volunteering to go with Falkenberg, and while Lysander appreciated that, it was getting a bit hard to take.

They sat and waited for drinks. "I've made some arrangements," he said. "If I don't come back. The Regiment will take care of you—"

"If they'll give me my contract, I can take care of myself," Ursula said. "You won't be back, will you?"

"Don't be silly. I'm the colonel's aide. I'll have the best bodyguards in the galaxy. And besides all that, there's Harv."

"Sure. When are you leaving Tanith?"

"I'm not sure."

They sat in awkward silence for a moment. Then she smiled and said, "It's all right. I'll miss you."

I'll miss you, he thought. He wanted to say something, but he couldn't. The silence stretched on.

He was relieved when Sergeant Albright came over to their table. "Excuse me, sir, we're short handed, and the tables are packed. Would you mind if Captain Svoboda and Mrs. Fuller joined you? Thank you, sir." Albright left without waiting for an answer. A moment later a lanky officer limped up to the table.

"I'm Anton Svoboda. Headquarters Commandant. Your Highness, we've been told you've no objection to our joining you—"

"No, of course not, sir." Lysander stood. "I expect things will go better if you call me Lysander." He touched the cornet's insignia on his collar. "They told me the rule was first names in the mess. And this is Ursula Gordon."

"Pleased to meet you. Ursula. Lysander. Right." Svoboda said. "Juanita Fuller, Prince Lysander Collins of Sparta, at present a volunteer cornet of the regiment. Which means that your husband is no longer the junior comet. And Miss Ursula Gordon."

Captain Svoboda held out his arm to help Juanita sit, then sat down carefully. His left leg was encased in what looked like a large pillow. "Couple of crocks," he said. "Actually, they just let us both out of hospital this afternoon. Juanita's husband is in conference—"

"Ah," Lysander said. "Cornet Mark Fuller? I met him this afternoon in the Colonel's office. Apparently he's the colonel's pilot tonight."

"I hope they get done with him pretty soon," Juanita said.

"Yes, that can't be much fun, first day out of hospital and no one to welcome you home," Ursula said.

Juanita shook her head. "We don't have a home—"

"I'll take care of that," Svoboda said. "We'll find something. Although I'm not sure what I can do for right now." Svoboda shook his head. "Maybe you ought to stay in the hospital tonight."

"I'd sure rather not," Juanita said.

"What's the problem?" Lysander asked.

"Well, Cornet Fuller just joined the regiment," Svoboda said. "Hasn't been assigned quarters. He's been staying in the BOQ. Juanita was hit in the rescue operation, so she was sent directly to hospital when she got here, and no one thought to assign them married quarters. Usually it would be my job to take care of that sort of thing, but—" He pointed to his leg. "I haven't been at my desk since we rescued Mrs. Fuller." He shrugged. "Wouldn't be a problem if they hadn't let us out in the middle of a general alert. Which reminds me." Svoboda raised his voice slightly. "Albright."

"Sir!" The mess steward came over to the table.

"Sergeant, it looks like you're packing up to pull out."

"Yes, sir."

"May I see your orders?"

"They're in the kitchen, sir."

"Please bring them. Along with a bottle of wine. Anything that's open."

"Yes, sir."

They waited until Albright returned carrying a large jug of red wine. "Not officer quality, sir," Albright said apologetically.

"It will do," Svoboda said absently. "Pour me a glass, please." He took the message flimsy Albright handed him and read for a moment. "Bloody hell."

"Problem, sir?" Lysander asked.

"You could say that. Sergeant, you've been given the wrong orders. The regiment itself isn't moving out, just most of the battalions. Regimental headquarters will stay right here. You shouldn't be packing up."

"Cap'n, the orders say right there—"

"I see they do," Svoboda said. "But someone has punched in the wrong codes on the computer. I'll straighten it out, but meanwhile, you can stand down. You're not going anywhere." Svoboda looked down at his leg. "Neither one of us is."

"Yes, sir."

"So. I'll take care of this nonsense. You go find us something decent to drink. And see what you can scare up to make the catfish a bit more palatable."

Albright grinned. "Yes, sir. I think I can unpack something."

Svoboda reached beneath the table and lifted a portable

computer console onto the place in front of him. "If you'll excuse me for just a moment," he said.

"Certainly," Lysander said. "But I confess some confusion—"

"Well," Svoboda said, "we have a data base of detailed order sets for nearly anything the Regiment might want to do. The colonel has ordered a general alert, and is shipping quite a lot of the regiment's strength out to—well, to various places. It sounds simple, but actually it's pretty complicated to move a battalion and all its gear and all the supplies it will need. There are thousands of items to worry about, stuff from battalion headquarters, stuff that has to be drawn from central supply—now suppose a battalion is to be reinforced with units that don't belong to it. More orders. Believe me, it can get sticky."

"Oh," Ursula said. "Yes, of course—"

"Computers handle most of it," Svoboda said. "We keep canned order sets for nearly every contingency. All it takes is calling out the proper ones. Only in this case, someone punched in the wrong code, so Sergeant Albright got the wrong orders." Svoboda bent over the bright blue screen, then typed quickly. "Hah. And here they were. Hmmm."

"Who did it?" Ursula asked.

"Little hard to tell," Svoboda said. He shrugged. "Won't take long to straighten out." He looked thoughtful, then shrugged again. "Can't think Barton will be foolish enough to attack this headquarters, but I expect I ought to buck this over to Rottermill, just in case it wasn't a mistake." He typed furiously for a moment.

"Attack?" Ursula asked. "How?"

"Bombs. Missiles," Svoboda said. "Not likely any would get through. We have a few nasty surprises for anyone who tries. Less likely that Barton would try it."

"Why wouldn't he?" Juanita asked.

"What would—Ah. Here's Sergeant Albright with something more fit to drink." Svoboda waited until the steward had poured a sparkling wine for everyone. "Cheers. As I was saying, what would it get Major Barton to attack regimental headquarters? Besides making everyone mad at him? It's not strictly in the Code, but the tradition is strong that you don't do that until you've warned the other chap."

"But we're about to—" Lysander caught himself. "Aren't we about to attack Barton's headquarters?"

"Certainly not," Svoboda said. "We don't make war on women and children. Barton's Bulldogs have their base near Dagon. We won't go near that. Why should we?"

"Wouldn't it help win this war?" Ursula asked.

"Not really," Svoboda said. "Oh, we'd get his computers, and a lot of his central stores, all right. As against that, we'd make this place a legitimate target. We'd have to detail more troops and equipment to defend our headquarters. Our troops in the field would have to worry about their families." The captain shrugged. "It's making war on civilians, and we just don't do that sort of thing. Not without good reason."

"It would be expensive, too," Ursula said.

Svoboda looked at her through drooping eyelids. "Aye. Should we not be concerned wi' expenses, lassie?"

"You'd do better to adopt a Latin accent," Lysander said.

"One mimics Captain Alana at considerable risk," Svoboda said. "The Mess President has ways of getting his own back."

"I suppose a mercenary regiment is in business to make money," Ursula said. "I guess I just never thought that through."

"Well, yes, we are," Svoboda said. "Which means we keep the costs down. That includes troops, of course. Good people are the most expensive item we have." His voice had a bantering tone, but there was an edge of menace in it as well.

"But your business is winning," Ursula said.

"Ursa—"

"Actually, she has a point," Svoboda said. "Our business is winning. But at what cost? Some games aren't worth the candle— Excuse me." Svoboda's computer console gave out several soft bleeps. Svoboda typed an acknowledgment, then frowned at the screen. "As I thought, we won't be moving the Mess—but it looks like we'll have to forego its pleasures, Mr. Prince. We're both wanted in conference." He gripped the edge of the table and stood carefully.

"When will you be back?" Ursula demanded.

Svoboda glanced at his watch. "Lysander may not be back at all this evening."

"But—"

"I'll try to get away for a minute," Lysander said.

"But—Mark—" Juanita protested.

"Ah. And Cornet Fuller is flying the colonel's helicopter. Not likely he'll have much time off for the next few days. I'll try to remind the colonel that your husband will need a few minutes before they take off—O Lor'; we haven't found you a place to stay, either!"

"Would you like to stay with me?" Ursula asked. "There's plenty of room."

"Oh—well I wouldn't like—"

"No trouble at all," Ursula said. "His Highness has other interests—"

"Well, thank you."

The computer console beeped more insistently.

"That's all right, then?" Svoboda asked. "Good. I'd best be going. Juanita. Ursula. Pleased to have met you." He bowed slightly and limped toward the door.

Lysander stood. "I'll try to see they give your husband a moment." He looked to Ursula. "Where will you be?"

"Here for dinner, then your rooms," Ursula said. "And—be careful."

"I wish I could be calm like you," Juanita said. "But I'm scared. You do this much?"

Ursula laughed. "Send my man off to war? First time. You too?"

"Yes, we haven't been married long—actually, we was never married at all, not in a church. Mark's from Earth. Sent here as a rebel. I was born to convicts on a borshite plantation. You from Sparta too?"

Ursula chuckled. "No-oo, not quite. I was born with a contract too. Except I had the good fortune to be owned by the Hilton, and they sent me to a good school. As an investment." Ursula smiled musingly. "You're luckier than me. At least the man you're sending off will come back to you. Mine won't."

"I don't understand—"

"I was contracted to a hotel. As a hostess. A hotel where Lysander, Prince of Sparta happened to stay."

"Oh. But—I think he likes you," Juanita said.

"He likes me all right. And so what? I doubt that a future king has any large place in his future for a hotel girl."

"Oh. But that's awful. You like him—"

"Is it that easy to see?"

"Yes. Ursula—what will you do?"

"I'll get by." Ursula laughed suddenly. "After all, I've been ruined."

"Ruined?"

"A poem I ran across in the hotel library," Ursula said. "Written a hundred years ago on Earth by Thomas Hardy. I liked it enough to memorize it."

"Oh. My mother used to read poems to me. Do you really remember it? Tell me."

"Well—all right. Two girls from the country meet—

"Oh, 'Melia, my dear, this does everything crown!
Who could have supposed I should meet you in Town?
And whence such fair garments, such prosperi-ty?

"Oh, didn't you know I'd been ruined? said she.

—"You left us in tatters, without shoes or socks,
Tired of digging potatoes, and spudding up docks;
And now you've gay bracelets and bright feathers three!"

"Yes: That's how we dress when we're ruined," said she.

—"At home in the barton you said 'thee' and 'thou',
And 'thik oon' and 'theas oon' and 't'other'; but now
Your talking quite fits 'ee for high compa-ny!"

"Some polish is gained with one's ruin," said she.

—"Your hands were like paws then, your face blue and bleak
But now I'm bewitched by your delicate cheek,
And your little gloves fit as on any la-dy!"

"We never do work when we're ruined," said she.

—"You used to call home-life a hag-ridden dream,
And you'd sigh, and you'd sock; but at present you seem
To know not of megrims or melancho-ly!"

"True. One's pretty lively when ruined," said she.

—"I wish I had feathers, a fine sweeping gown,
And a delicate face, and could strut about Town!"

"My dear—a raw country girl, such as you be,
Cannot quite expect that. You ain't ruined," said she.

"That's—" Juanita turned away with tears in her eyes.

"Hey, no need to get upset," Ursula said. "Don't cry over me! I'll get by—"

"Not you," Juanita said. "I suppose I should be thinking about you, but—that poem is about me, too. What'd it say, 'raw country girl'? That's me! I'm supposed to be an officer's wife, and I don't know anything. I could dream, about—about marrying a foreman, or maybe a planter; I know plantation life, but what am I goin' to do here? I can do farming, and take in washing. I did some house work in the big house. I don't know anything else. You're educated—"

"And ruined," Ursula said. "Don't forget that."

XXI

Pipe Major Douglas raised his baton and brought it down sharply to cut the pipes off in mid skirl. Lysander, feeling bulky in combat leathers and Nemourlon armor, followed Falkenberg into the first of the four waiting helicopters. Harv Middleton climbed in behind them.

"Prince, I like those," Harv said. He gestured to indicate the pipers. "We ought to do that at home."

Lysander nodded thoughtfully. He had been surprised to find pipers at the airfield, and had been ready to laugh at the needless ceremony. Why should they pipe troops aboard helicopters? Then they began to play the stirring old marches that had sent men to a thousand battles, and he knew.

They did nothing like that on Sparta. Why not? Leonidas and his Three Hundred had marched to Thermopylae to the sound of flutes. Something to mention to the Council . . .

The helicopter was surprisingly quiet even without combat helmets. When Lysander and the others put their helmets on in obedience to Falkenberg's gesture, every bit of the helicopter motor noise was gone. Instinctively Lysander adjusted the gain on the helmet's pickup until he could dimly hear the chopper motors again.

The helicopter held ten men in addition to its own crew, two rows of five on each side of the ship. The deck between them was covered with their equipment. The helicopter's crew chief inspected the equipment lashings. "Looks good, Mr. Fuller."

Lysander strapped himself into his seat. Falkenberg sat to Lysander's right. Harv was to his left, with two Scouts beyond him. Andrew Mace, the senior Scout lieutenant, sat across from Falkenberg, with second Lieutenant Harry Janowitz next to him. Then came Corporal McClaren, who seemed to be Falkenberg's bodyguard, and two others of the Headquarters Guard. The guards were all big men, and looked strangely alike. Harv had said they were pretty good troops, which was a lot for Harv to concede to anyone but Spartans.

"All correct, chief?" the pilot called.

"All correct, sir." The crew chief took his seat forward of the passengers. "Let 'er rip."

The motor sounds rose in pitch and the helicopter lifted. Lysander was surprised at how quiet it was even in flight.

"It had better be quiet," he muttered. "And what in hell am I doing here?"

"Good question." Falkenberg's voice startled him.

"Sir?"

"Your mike is on, Mister Prince."

Lysander looked around in dismay. No one was staring at him.

"You needn't be alarmed. You're switched to my frequency," Falkenberg said.

"Oh." Lysander touched a stud on the side of his helmet to activate the status displays. There were five communication channels, each with a diagram showing its connections. Channel One was a link directly to Falkenberg. Channel Two showed links to Falkenberg, Mace, and Janowitz. The other three had not been configured. "I'll turn it off, sir."

"No need," Falkenberg said. "It was a good question. What the devil *are* you doing here?"

"Sir?"

"Not that we're ungrateful, but this isn't your fight," Falkenberg said. "And you don't strike me as a glory hunter."

"No, sir. If you—I was told that if I got a chance to watch you in action, I should take it."

"Good enough."

"Sir—why are you here?"

"We're paid to be here, Mr. Prince."

"Yes, sir."

"You can hardly say that protecting the Grand Admiral's secret funds isn't my fight," Falkenberg said.

"No, sir, but on that scoring it's my fight too."

"So it is, Mr. Prince."

Lysander listened to the thrum of the helicopter motors.

"Very well, Mr. Prince. You asked a question. Verbal games aside, you asked why we were here."

"Yes, sir."

"I may have an answer."

"I'd like to hear it."

There was another long silence. "I don't generally care much for preachers," Falkenberg said. "But I don't often get an opportunity to preach to a future king.

"We are here, Mr. Prince, because it is our job to be here. Have you ever read a book called *La Peste*?"

"*The Plague*. Albert Camus," Lysander said. "No sir. It's on the reading list my tutor prepared."

"Along with a hundred other books you don't particularly want to read, I make no doubt," Falkenberg said. "Read that one. You won't enjoy it, but you'll be glad for having read it."

"Yes, sir."

"Camus tells us that life consists of doing one's job. As I get older, I find that more and more profound. Mr. Prince, I have tried to live up to that notion. I believe that the sum total of your life is what you have accomplished. Some of us don't get to accomplish much."

"Sir? Some may not, but you have. You've changed the history of whole planets!"

"True enough. Whether for better or worse, whether anything I've done has any significance for the future, is another matter, and doesn't depend on me. Everything I've done could be made irrelevant by events I can't control. I like to think I have done what I could with the opportunities I had, but I do not delude myself. I have never had any great weight in the cosmic balance."

"Who does?"

"You may have. Statesmen and kings sometimes have. I once thought I might. That was easy to think as a boy in Rome, tramping the Via Flaminia and looking down the Tarpian Rock on the Capitolean. The ruins of glory. Do you know that for over two thousand years the Romans kept a female wolf in a cage on the Capitolean? During the Republic, in the Civil Wars, in the great days of the Empire. During the dark ages after the fall, during the Renaissance, the Papal States, the Risorgimento. Mussolini. But after the Second World War they couldn't do it any more. They couldn't protect the wolf from vandals. Modern vandals. I don't know what the original Vandals did."

Falkenberg laughed. "Enough of that. I've had no great weight in the cosmic balance because for better or worse, Mr. Prince, I chose the profession of arms."

"Surely you're not saying that violence never settled anything?"

"Hardly. But soldiers do not often get to choose what issues their actions settle. I suppose it's irrelevant in my case. I said I chose the profession of arms, but in fact it chose me."

"A good profession, sir."

Lysander felt Falkenberg's shrug. "Perhaps. Certainly a much misunderstood profession. In my case, as I was not born an American taxpayer or a Soviet Party Member, there was no chance I would rise high enough in the CoDominium service to have any great influence. Of course, we soldiers seldom have as much influence as we like to believe. It is true that what we do is necessary and often can be decisive, but we are not often asked to make the crucial decisions. War and peace. We don't make wars, and we seldom control the peace."

"Is peace the goal?" Lysander asked.

"What is peace?" Falkenberg asked. "On historical grounds I could argue that it is no more than an ideal whose existence we deduce from the fact that there have been intervals between wars. Not very many such intervals, or very long ones, either. But let's assume we know what peace is, and that we want it. At what price? Patrick Henry demanded liberty or death. Others say nothing is worth dying for. Again those are issues soldiers are seldom asked to deal with."

"Then what do we—"

"If you think of war and oppression and violence as a plague like the Red Death, then soldiers are the sanitation crew. We bury the dead. We sterilize regions, and try to keep the plague from spreading. Sometimes we spread plague, even when we try not to. Sometimes, not often, we are allowed to eliminate the causes of the plague. We are seldom asked to treat the victims, although good soldiers often do. The politicians are the physicians and surgeons, the ones who are supposed to find a cure."

"They never have—"

"They never have. There may not be one, which makes the sanitation crew even more necessary. You were born a politician, Mr. Prince. If you live, remember the sanitation crew. You need us. Interestingly, we need you as well. We need to believe that there are physicians and surgeons."

"It's a fascinating analogy, sir, but haven't you carried it too far? You say you have no weight, but you've certainly influenced events."

"And will again," Falkenberg said. "Sometimes we find the scales are balanced. Each pan holds enormous weight, far more than anything we control—but at times like that, a small weight can tip the balance. It's that way now."

The helicopter banked sharply. Lysander caught a glimpse of lights far below. The pilot's voice came through the intercom.

"Coming down now. It'll be rough when we get to the deck. Be sure you're fastened in."

Lysander inspected his straps. Then he turned to Falkenberg. "Yes, sir. How do you know which side to choose?" Lysander demanded.

"The key question. I can tell you what I do. Which side will leave the human race with the greatest potential?" Falkenberg asked. "Find that out and the answer is clear enough. Mr. Prince, every man is born with a potential. Life consists of using that potential as well as possible. To hurt as few people as possible—but understand that to do nothing may be far worse than any harm you can possibly do."

"The greatest happiness for the greatest number?"

"No. That goal is often used to justify doing people good whether they like it or not. No, Mr. Prince, it's not that simple. You have to ask people what they want. You have to ask the experts what humanity needs. And you must listen to the answers. But having done all that you still must make your own decisions.

"You can't just count noses. You have to weigh them, but you can't just weigh opinions either. Numbers do count," Falkenberg laughed suddenly. "We're flying over a jungle toward a battle. If we're lucky we'll rescue a huge supply of drugs. Drugs that will keep Earth's hordes docile for a while longer. They may well think they are happy. Is that good? Or would Earth be a better place if we destroyed the crop? And that's only one question, because there is more at stake than borloi. Our job, Mr. Prince, is to give Admiral Lermontov his secret funds—and hope that he does more good than harm, more good than the borloi does harm. Will he?"

"We can't know," Lysander said. "My father supports Lermontov. I don't think he likes him."

"He doesn't have to. So, Mr. Prince, what do you fight for?"

"Freedom, Colonel. The rights of free men."

"And what are those? Where do they come from?"

"Sir?"

"Consider, Mr. Prince. The soldiers of the 42nd are under rigid discipline. Most would say they are not free—yet we are under no government. We may be the most free people in the galaxy. Of course, that kind of freedom has a damned high cost."

"Yes, sir, we're finding that out on Sparta."

Falkenberg chuckled. "I expect you are, Mr. Prince. I expect you are." He was silent for a moment. "Mr. Prince, would you like to know the most significant event in the history of freedom?"

"The American revolution?"

"A defensible choice, a close second even, but not mine. I would choose the moment when the Roman plebians required the patricians to write down the twelve tables of the law and put them where everyone could see them—and thereby proclaimed the law supreme over the politicians. The rule of law is the essence of freedom."

"I'll think about that, sir."

Lysander felt Colonel Falkenberg's shrug. "Please do. My apologies, Mr. Prince. When I have a politician for a captive audience it's tempting to lecture, but I suspect a young man brought up on a planet settled by professors of political science has heard enough of this to last a lifetime."

Not from you. Lysander wanted to ask Falkenberg to go on, but the colonel had already changed channels on his helmet radio.

"Gentlemen," Falkenberg said. "You were all introduced, so we can dispense with that." The two lieutenants across the aisle nodded agreement. "It's school time." The helicopter maneuvered violently. "We're close to the jungle top now, so we won't distract Cornet Fuller from his piloting. That leaves the four of us. Lieutenant Mace, I believe you are senior. Please explain to Mr. Prince."

"Yes, sir." Mace looked at Lysander. "The Colonel means that it's time for what he calls his school for captains. Since there aren't any captains aboard I guess we'll have to do. The colonel states a problem, then we say what we'd do about the situation, then we all discuss it. Ready? Good. Colonel—"

"Gentlemen, we have a decision to make," Falkenberg said. He pointed to the heavy gear lashed to the deck of the helicopter.

"Our objective is to get ourselves and that equipment from the Ledoux village to a point close to Rochemont. We can presume that we will reach Village Ledoux undetected. From there we load onto small boats. Propulsion will be provided by the villagers, with paddles and poles. They are experts and have made this journey many times. The boats are wooden, not large. As I understand it, each can carry two men and their personal gear, or an equivalent amount of equipment. There are some twenty boats, enough to carry all of us as well as our heavy equipment in one trip. Naturally we'll space the boats out somewhat. Clear so far? Good. The problem is, how do we load the boats, and in what order do we send them?

"Mr. Prince, as junior man you're first. What's in the first boat we send down river?"

"Two Scouts, sir?"

"Don't *ask*," Lieutenant Mace said.

"Scouts," Falkenberg said. "And in the second?"

"I guess I want to think about it," Lysander said.

"Lieutenant Janowitz has recently been promoted from cornet to second lieutenant," Falkenberg said. "Congratulations. What's in the first boat, Mr. Janowitz?"

"Two Scouts," Janowitz said. He sounded older than Lysander, and quite positive. "Officers in the second. We send the boats in waves, with the personnel first, then the heavy equipment following, the colonel and his guard in the last boat."

"I see. Why?" Falkenberg asked.

"Radar, Colonel. They may not be able to see into the jungle, but if they can, there's less chance of being spotted—"

"Yes. Lieutenant Mace? Do you agree?"

"I don't know, Colonel. I see Harry's point. The heavy stuff will show up on radar better than troops. A lot better, so there's more chance some scope dope will see the blips. Easier to sneak the men through. Less chance of alerting Barton's people. But—"

"You have reservations," Falkenberg said. "Noted. Mr. Prince?"

"I have some reservations too, now that I think about it," Lysander said. "If the troops are spotted, if they even raise suspicions, then the heavy weapons are much more likely to be spotted."

"They may think they're Ledoux's people," Janowitz said. "Probably will."

"It's possible," Mace said. "Especially if all they see is people. Suppose they don't believe it's natives?"

"Calculated risk," Lieutenant Janowitz said. "The probabilities favor sending the troops first."

"Sure of that?" Falkenberg asked. "Mr. Mace?"

"It's the other way," Mace said. "We send the heavy stuff first, because if it gets through, then the troops will, and if Barton's people are alerted we'll never get the weapons through."

"And?" Falkenberg prompted.

"Well—I don't know, sir."

"Mr. Prince?"

"We can't do the mission without the heavy guns?"

"Precisely," Falkenberg said. "Our whole mission depends on getting our heavy equipment into place. If we fail in that, we're not likely to accomplish much. Well done, gentlemen. Now I have an entirely different problem for your consideration. . . ."

The clearing was small, and utterly dark except for tiny pencil beams of red light from the crews' flashlights. Four helicopters had come here. Two, refueled by the others, would go on. The other two would keep just enough fuel to get back to the last staging point.

Cornet Fuller squatted on the ground and used his helmet to project a map. "Fuel's going to be close," he said.

Falkenberg pointed to Village Ledoux. "Once we're there, what will be your operating radius?"

"Maybe a hundred klicks," Fuller said. "Depends on the winds for the rest of the way."

"That should be enough," Falkenberg said. "One way or another, you won't need more." He got up and strolled to the edge of the clearing.

"Now why does the way he says that scare hell out of me?" Fuller asked.

Lysander chuckled. "You too? Good."

"I never got a chance to thank you for putting Juanita up."

"It was Ursula's notion," Lysander said.

"Yeah. Thanks anyway. And for talking the colonel into giving me five minutes with her." Fuller wiped his forehead. "Sure hot."

"It is that."

"What's it like on Sparta?" Fuller asked.

"Well, it's much cooler—"

"Yeah. I heard that. I meant for convicts."

"We don't have contract labor like Tanith," Lysander said. "New chums from Earth can choose their employment."

"You just turn convicts loose?"

"Well, not precisely, but anyone willing to work won't find the restrictions onerous. The CoDominium doesn't like our giving citizenship to anyone still under formal sentence, but that doesn't come up often anyway. Not many try to become citizens."

"Uh? People want to be citizens?"

"Some do," Lysander said.

"Oh. Perks? Welfare?"

"Not precisely. Everyone on Sparta has political rights, but citizens have more. More obligations, too, of course."

"Oh. Sort of like taxpayers."

"No, not quite—"

The crew chief materialized next to them. "Fuel's aboard, Mr. Fuller."

"Thanks, Chief. Load 'em up." Fuller chuckled in the dark. "If I'd been a little smarter, I'd have got to Sparta. Had a chance, but I didn't know what to do. Maybe it's just as well."

XXII

The school was over, and there was no more conversation with Falkenberg. The helicopter flew low over the jungle, sometimes maneuvering between the trees. Tanith's small moon came up, but was no more than a blur above the clouds. Sometimes when the helicopter banked sharply Lysander could see the jungle below, but as no more than a darkness even blacker than the clouds above.

After one violent maneuver, Lysander felt Harv's nudge. He gestured toward his helmet. Lysander set one of the channels to Harv's headset frequency.

"How does he see?" Harv said.

"Radar, I suppose," Lysander said, but he wondered, since radar might be detected from a distance. "IR? I don't know, but I'm glad I'm not flying it."

"He's pretty good," Harv conceded.

"Yes." I suppose he is, Lysander thought, and wondered what would have happened if Fuller had bribed his way to Sparta. Where would he have gone? His natural talents as a pilot might have brought him to an airline, or a wealthy mine owner in need of a chauffeur. He'd never have had a chance to become a Spartan officer.

The helicopter flew on, and despite its violent maneuverings, Lysander fell asleep.

Village Ledoux seemed crowded. The villagers had already prepared shelters for the helicopters. As soon as the passengers were out of the planes, a hundred men grabbed each one and carried it under a thatch-roofed structure. Mats were unrolled to form walls, and the helicopter vanished.

In moments the equipment was unloaded, and they followed the villagers into the dense jungle. Lysander felt rather than saw the thick growth around him. Then he was at the water's edge. A score of small flat-bottomed boats were pulled up against the shore.

Falkenberg's NCOs gestured. The recoilless rifle was loaded into the first boat. After a moment, Lieutenant Mace climbed in with it and lay flat on the bottom of the boat. A tall, dark civilian gestured, and the boatman poled the boat away from the shore. In seconds it vanished into the underbrush.

The next boat held lumpy gear, including what Lysander thought was a sea sled. It was sent into the night. Boat after boat was loaded and sent off. Mortars and mortar bombs. Communications gear. Radar antennae. Everything went swiftly and soon the equipment was gone. Then came the soldiers. Then it was Lysander's turn. He and Harv lay flat in the boat, and waited.

The boatman's pole had a sort of paddle blade so that it could be used as a scull as well as to pole the boat. There was so little light that Lysander couldn't see the boatman's face.

He knew it would be a long way, and tried to sleep, but despite his training he couldn't. Thoughts came and went. Pictures of himself killed, or wounded. Harv falling. Falkenberg lying bleeding on the ground. What if I'm left in charge? Lysander wondered. No chance of that, or was there?

Ursula. What would happen to her? He thought of Melissa back on Sparta. Everyone assumed they'd marry. So had he. Now he wasn't so sure. Melissa was his friend, he could talk to her. They'd been a lot of places together, and twice they'd made love. The first time for both of them. He liked her a lot. She was easy to be with, and of course she was a full citizen. She'd be a good mother, and a good partner in government. That's not love, he thought. And so what? What is love? Am I in love with Ursula? I want her. I want to be with her.

What would Melissa think if he brought Ursula to Sparta? Would she understand? No. Neither would his father. No, it was ridiculous. There was no place for Ursula in the palace.

And why not? Kings in history books had mistresses. But the kings of Sparta weren't real kings, not like the old kings of France. There wasn't any Divine Right in the Spartan constitution. The kings of Sparta didn't have to grub for office by kissing babies, but they were supposed to be better trained, and better qualified than anyone else. Or at least as well qualified. They were also supposed to have children, legitimate children, children who would inherit positions of leadership. That way Sparta's leaders would have a long view of things, look to the next generation and not just the next election.

And we're supposed to be moral, whatever that means. Set an example for the people. Keeping a mistress isn't much of an example. The Council would find out, and there'd be hell to pay. And even if the Council would accept Ursula, Melissa never would.

So? Give up Melissa. Marry Ursula. He chuckled aloud, and felt a quick pressure from Harv's foot to remind him to be quiet.

It really was impossible. The Council would want genetic tables and family history, information Ursula probably didn't have, and they wouldn't be likely to approve if she did have it. Suppose they liked her ancestry? She'd still have to qualify for citizenship. Even as bright as she is, starting at her age it could take years. If she'd do it at all. No. Ursula won't be going back to Sparta with me.

He didn't like that thought.

Change the subject.

He could hear the water streaming past beneath the hull of the pirogue. It was pitch dark in the jungle. Dark in here, but we're not invisible. Not to radar. Is someone looking at us right now? Falkenberg must have detection equipment. What if he does? What can we do? If they find us, they can take us. We don't have enough people or ammunition to hold out very long.

This isn't getting me anywhere. What is? Why am I here? Life consists of doing one's job. Is this my job? What is? The thoughts whirled through his head until he forced them away.

"Prince." Harv's voice was low and urgent. "We're here."

It was still dark, but there was faint grey light in the clouds above. Lysander climbed out of the boat. His left leg was asleep, and he rubbed it gently.

As soon as he was off the boat, the boatman backed it away from the shore, turned, and poled upstream. In moments the boat had vanished.

"This way," someone whispered. A shadowy figure led the way. Their footsteps squished in soft mud. Once Lysander's boot went in above the ankle, and there was a loud sucking noise when he pulled it out. There still wasn't enough light to see anything, only flint grey directly above the jungle canopy. Harv followed silently.

Lysander thought they'd walked half a kilometer when his guide stopped.

"Over here, sir. Under the tarp," the trooper whispered.

Lysander knelt to feel the edge of a tarp directly in front

of him. He crawled under. It was stifling hot under there. When he was all the way under he felt the ground sloping down slightly. The tiny glow of a map projector was blinding.

Falkenberg, Lieutenant Mace, and a sergeant lay under the tarp, all facing a central area where the sergeant had projected a chart.

"Sergeant Miscowsky, my aide, Cornet Prince," Falkenberg said. His voice was low but unstrained. "Mr. Prince, you will study this chart. Sergeant—"

"Sir." Miscowsky reached out into the holographic image. "This is the coast. We're back inland, here. The stream we came in on is behind us. It runs south some more before it turns west into the bay." He touched his helmet and the view changed. "OK, this is us again, coast there. The jungle ends about a klick to the west here. Then there's just over three klicks of cleared hills, farmlands mostly, and Rochemont Manor. That sits on what passes for a big hill here, sort of a low mound. We were able to pick up lots of details on that area. Antenna farms here, and here. Some sheds here, I think they have heavy mortars under them but I can't be sure. They went to a lot of effort to hide everything from the satellites."

"How about the antennas?" Mace asked.

"Got a break on those, sir," Miscowsky said. "Leastwise this set of 'em. About two hours ago, after the satellite was past maybe twenty minutes, they peeled back the roof of this shed here. This thing that looks like a grape arbor is a frame the roof slides onto. Inside are search and surveillance antennas, no question about it, they showed up good in passive IR, and they put out a strong K-band search pattern too. Good thing we was dug in good." Miscowsky touched his helmet and the projected scene changed to a dark outline. "I got a good camera set up at the edge of the jungle, but there's not enough light to see anything yet."

"We have about an hour before Captain Fast starts Operation Hijack," Falkenberg said. "Call it another ten minutes after that for Barton to find out we're on the move. You'll want to get your observations fast, because after that we'll want to be dug in good. We don't want them to suspect we're here. Without surprise we might as well not be."

"Yes, sir," Mace said. "Shouldn't be a problem. Miscowsky, tell us what you've done for emergency shelters."

"Sir. We can't dig in without them seeing us, but I figure it's going to get thick when they do find out we're here. Seemed to me we'll need some shelter, so I rigged primacord around trees, here, and here. Soon as it's sure they know we're here, we'll drop those trees in a box pattern. Got a couple of shells dug in just in the center of the box, they'll help make it deeper. Not what I like, but it ought to make a storm cellar. I've got another crew doing the same thing over here." He pointed again, and a second area turned red in the hologram.

"Good work," Mace said. "Be sure all troops are warned."

Lysander studied the red areas in the projection. "I'll tell Middleton," he said.

"Right," Falkenberg said. "Pity we don't know what they're using to protect their guns. Sergeant, when they opened that antenna shed, did you get any estimate on what it's made of?"

"IR signature says wood, Colonel. Maybe there's something under it, but I don't think it's armor."

"Right. Probably nothing but wood. Mr. Mace, what's your opinion? Can we take those antennas out in the first salvo?"

"Yes, sir, I think we can."

"Of course we don't know where they keep their spares," Falkenberg said. "Even so, they'll be blind for a while. Mr. Mace, it's your tactical command, but my recommendation is to give target priority to the antennas. Hit them, then the CP if we can find it. Then go for the guns when they start shooting at us."

"Yes, sir."

"That's assuming you don't have a higher priority target," Falkenberg said. He leaned closer to the holographic projection. "Show me the docking area. Thank you. What is this structure?"

"Pretty big for a boat house," Mace said.

"Not likely a boat house, not on Tanith, sir," Miscowsky said. "Colonel, I never noticed until we got here and took a good look, but they've got solar screens all over that place, more than a farm that size would have. Lots of juice. I think they're making hydrogen and LOX, and where else would they store it but near the docks?"

"Hmm. As far as we can tell, *Norton Star* carries Talin class landers," Falkenberg said. "Just barely have the legs to make orbit from a sea launch. They'll need all the fuel they can get—all right, Miscowsky, I'll buy that, you've located the fuel facility." Falkenberg studied the hologram again. "And these will be barns?"

"Yes, sir. These two are cattle barns. This one's for horses. The ones set up above are farm worker barracks."

"The horses have better facilities. All right." Falkenberg studied the holographic display another few moments, then looked up. "Mr. Prince, you and Mace look as if you're melting.

Come to that, I find it pretty warm myself. All right, everyone take ten minutes to cool off. Get outside and loosen up
your equipment. Ventilate properly. Then I'll want you again.
Under here, I'm afraid. We've gone to this much trouble to
keep Barton's troops from knowing about us, no point in taking
chances now. Ten minutes, gentlemen. Meanwhile, Sergeant,
I have a task for your SAS team."

The sky was dull grey. There still wasn't enough light to
see objects, but when he knelt Lysander could just tell where
the lumpy tarp was, and he thought he could see someone
approaching from the other side. He winced at the thought
of the stifling heat, then crawled under. Mace and Janowitz
were already there. A moment later Falkenberg joined them.
"Gentlemen. No doubt you're wondering what I'm doing here
when I could be back at headquarters." He waited a moment,
and when there was no answer, Falkenberg chuckled. "Only
you're too polite to say so. To begin, Lieutenant Mace, I did
not come here because of any lack of confidence in your ability
to control the situation."
"Thank you, sir." Mace's voice was flat.
"In fact, there's not a lot for you to control," Falkenberg
said. "We've laid our plans. The headquarters staff can carry
out their end. You and Janowitz are more than competent to
bring off your part. It's a good plan, and we have sufficient
forces. With no more than ordinary luck we'll accomplish the
objective. Cripple the landing ship and take Rochemont."
"Yes, sir." Mace said.
Falkenberg touched his helmet and the holographic image
of the Rochemont area sprang up between them. "Unfortunately, given the enemy's position here, doing that is likely
to be expensive, in lives and money. Anyone disagree?"
Lysander frowned at the projected map. "No, sir. And there's
a chance it won't work at all. Or that they'll destroy the borloi."
"Exactly. So," Falkenberg said. "We have the best plan we
can think of, but it's hardly an elegant solution to our problem. I've come to see if we can pass a miracle."
"Sir?"
"No battle plan survives contact with the enemy," Falkenberg
said. "That's the elder Moltke, but the principle had been
known for a long time when he said it."
"Wasn't Cannae according to plan?" Lysander asked.
"Yes, Mr. Prince. Of course Cannae required the Romans'
cooperation. Commanders have been trying to duplicate
Hannibal's success ever since. Most haven't done so, because

the enemy generally won't be as obliging as Gaius Terentius Varro was. Certainly Major Barton won't be. On the other hand, Hannibal was in Italy in the first place because the Romans believed it impossible to cross the Alps with an army. Surprise can do a very great deal."

"Yes sir?"

"Let's look at the situation. First, the objective. What is our objective, Mr. Mace?"

"Sir? Ah. To capture the borloi."

"Correct," Falkenberg said. "Not to capture Rochemont, but to get possession of several tons of borshite juice. What's the first requirement for that, Mr. Janowitz?"

"Well, to keep them from moving it somewhere else while we get enough troops in place to take Rochemont," Lieutenant Janowitz said. "Which is where we come in."

"Right. That's the plan. Of course, it's the expensive way. Is there another?"

The officers peered at the maps and photographs. "I sure don't see how we can get the stuff without taking Rochemont," Lieutenant Mace said.

"Yet we think they are going to pack it into a landing boat," Falkenberg said. "If we could take that boat after they've loaded it—"

"Yes, sir, we've all been thinking of that all the way here, but there's no way," Lieutenant Mace said. "Colonel, the minute that landing boat comes in, they won't try to hide anything. They'll have those radars sweeping every inch of ground around Rochemont. They probably already have trip wires. Mine fields too."

"Besides," Lieutenant Janowitz said. "Even if we could take the landing boat, what would we do with it?"

"One thing at a time," Falkenberg said. "If you had that boat, Mr. Prince, what would you do with it?"

"Fly it to the capital," Lysander said.

"Fly? And who'd do that?" Mace demanded.

"I could."

"Precisely," Falkenberg said. "As it happens, Mr. Prince has had quite extensive training. He is one of the three qualified landing boat pilots in the Regiment."

"Sir? I'm hardly qualified. I've done the training, yes, sir—"

"Three flights, I believe? Takeoff, atmosphere flying, and landing from orbit. You're the best qualified pilot we have, actually."

"Well, if you say so, sir. Uh—Colonel, who are the other two?"

"Captain Svoboda. And me."

"Colonel—" Lieutenant Mace drew in his breath. "Colonel, just what do you have in mind?"

"About what you think, Mr. Mace. A miracle. A small change in Major Barton's plans."

Lysander looked at the projected charts of Rochemont's defenses. "With respect, Colonel, it would take a miracle. Granted I—we could fly that boat out of here, how do we capture it? We can't even get to it."

"That's certainly what Barton thinks," Falkenberg said. "Just as the Romans believed Hannibal couldn't get to them from North Africa."

"Colonel, the Alps is one thing, that field's another. They're bound to have radars sweeping that whole area right now."

"They do," Miscowsky said. "Random intervals, but often enough to keep anyone from getting across those fields. Even my squad couldn't make it."

"Precisely," Falkenberg said. "They're watching the fields. Makes them feel safe. But I doubt they have sonars—"

"Sonar?" Miscowsky said. "Colonel, you ain't thinking of swimming over there? Colonel, everybody knows you don't swim on Tanith! You'd be breakfast for a nessie before you got halfway!"

"Everyone agrees? You can't get past the nessies?" Falkenberg asked. "Good. I'm sure Barton believes it as well."

"Believes it because it's true, Colonel," Miscowsky said. "I don't know much about this crazy planet, but I know that! Sir, it ain't a matter of guts, or firepower. It wouldn't be easy to fight off a nessie, but maybe you could do that, only Barton's people would sure as hell know you did it! And the damn nessie might win the fight anyway."

"My analysis precisely, Sergeant," Falkenberg said. "I came to that conclusion before we left headquarters." He reached into his battle armor and produced a tape cassette. "We can't fight nessies, but perhaps we can avoid them. I had an advantage over you, Sergeant. Being at headquarters I could do some research. More precisely, find out who has already done the research. I called in Mrs. Chang and asked who knew the most about nessies. It turns out there is one team that does nothing but study them."

Falkenberg slapped the tape against his palm. "I got the reports and read them, then I had Mrs. Chang download this from the governor's data banks. It's a tape of nessie calls."

Lysander frowned. "Sir?"

"Feeding calls, mostly. As it happens, there were two deep

diving sea sleds in the regimental quartermaster stores. When we loaded the choppers I brought them, and two scuba outfits," Falkenberg said. "Now suppose that we put this tape into an amplifier on a sea sled. I also have tapes of the sounds of crippled prey. Calls and swimming sounds. Put those in the sled, too. Now suppose we send that sea sled on autopilot out into the bay. Make part of that sled's load a dead porker. A bleeding dead porker. When it gets out a way, turn on the tapes."

Lysander nodded to himself. "And while the nessies are following that, we take the other sled over to the dock area. It might work, but won't the landing boat cause problems? How do nessies react to something like that? Will they even hear the tapes?"

"I don't know, Mr. Prince," Falkenberg said. "I don't propose to wait that long. My notion was to get over there while it's still dark. There seem to be ample places to hide."

"A porker isn't all that big," Lieutenant Mace said. "What happens when the nessies finish yours off?"

"Minigrenades," Falkenberg said. "Several of them in the porker, and more outside on the sled. They may not kill any nessies, but they'll wound a couple."

"And nessies are cannibals," Mace said. "Feeding frenzy. You sure don't want to be near that—"

"And won't be," Falkenberg said. "That will happen a couple of klicks out in the bay. We'll be much nearer the shore."

"We," Lysander said.

"I had presumed you'd volunteer," Falkenberg said. "If not, it's no discredit. The notion of swimming out among those creatures isn't exactly pleasant. McClaren will volunteer."

"Oh, I'm going, Colonel. That's not the problem."

"What is?"

"Harv will have to come."

"We only have two sets of scuba gear."

"That's enough. Colonel, you're needed here."

"That's for sure," Lieutenant Mace said.

"Mr. Prince—"

"Colonel, for God's sake! We're talking about swimming three klicks, then hiding out to wait for the landing boat. After that we have to take the boat. With all respect, Colonel, that's stuff Harv and I can do a lot better than you."

"Mr. Prince—"

"Colonel, you're twice my age. More. How long has it been since you took out a sentry? I'd never have thought this up, but Harv and I can sure do it better than you can."

"He's right, Colonel," Miscowsky said. "Only, about this Harv, maybe I ought to go instead—"

Falkenberg laughed softly. "Leave it, Sergeant. Mr. Prince, your point is made. Good luck."

XXIII

Lysander stood waist deep in the soupy warm water. Here at one of the slough outlets the surf was mild, but he could hear crashing waves out beyond the stream mouth. There was just enough grey light to see the small whitecaps three meters away. When he put his head beneath the surface he had to strain to see the luminous dial of the compass even when he held it close to his face.

The water was warm, but cooler than the jungle had been. It felt good, but he couldn't forget that this wasn't the friendly Aegean on Sparta. This was Tanith, home to nessies. They'd already chased some small eel-like carnivores away.

"Good sign," Private Purdy said. "If there's little ones, the big ones aren't around. Take 'em a while to chew through Nemourlon, too. Take little ones a while, anyway."

They loaded the other sled and sent it on its way. Falkenberg's listening gear told them when the amplifiers began playing the taped nessie calls, and shortly after they heard large creatures moving. Certainly some of them had been attracted to the sled. Some. But had all? It only took one—

"One way to find out," Lysander muttered to himself. He splashed ashore to the stream edge. "Guess I'm off," he said softly.

He felt Falkenberg's hand on his shoulder. "Break a leg," Falkenberg said.

"Sir?"

"Good luck, Mr. Prince."

"Sir," Lysander hesitated. The colonel's hand was still on his shoulder. Lysander stood another moment, then sat in the warm water to put on his flippers. Harv followed close behind when Lysander dove forward into the chop. The second sea sled was waiting on the bottom.

Lysander guided the electric sled under the surf at the stream outlet, then out. When he estimated that he was thirty meters offshore, he turned west to parallel the shoreline. Tension on the tow line told him that Harv was right behind him. No need to worry about Harv. There never was.

Something large loomed ahead and he felt a moment of panic. Nothing happened. A log? Seacow? Whatever it was didn't follow him. He guided the sea sled downward until the gauge showed twenty meters. It was pitch black, murky water and no light above, so that he could barely see the dials.

Lysander concentrated on the compass and the water speed gauge. It was difficult holding a steady course and speed with no visibility, but that was the only way to verify the position he got from the tiny inertial navigation system built into the sled. The system gave him the direction and distance of the Rochemont docking area. It seemed to be working fine.

Sparta had introduced dolphins and orcas into the planet's seas. Both were domesticated, nearly tame, accustomed to swimming with humans. They liked being with people, swimming with them, towing them, and they were more than a match for the native Spartan sea life. Lysander wished he had orcas with him now. Lots of them for preference. A school of killer whales might be able to fend off nessies, at least for a little while. . . .

The seconds ticked away. Somewhere off to his left the other sled would be slowing. The nessies would begin to feed. He listened for the mini grenades, even though he knew they'd be too far away to detect. If the trick didn't work—

Lysander fingered the high pressure lance. In theory you stabbed something—it was designed for sharks—with the long hollow needle, and that would release carbon dioxide under high pressure, rupturing the innards of whatever you'd stabbed. In theory it would be instantly fatal, and the victim, inflated, would float to the surface. An ugly death from an ugly weapon. Lysander hoped he'd never have to test it. There was also the question of whether the needle would penetrate a nessie's armored hide—and what would happen if you killed a nessie and the others went into a frenzy.

After twenty minutes on course, Lysander tugged the tow line. Harv swam up beside him and took control of the sea sled. Lysander checked his tether line and let it reel out as he swam upward toward the surface.

The wind was onshore and there were whitecaps in the bay, nothing for a landing boat to worry about but quite enough chop to make it impossible to see the shoreline in the dim grey light. Instead he looked behind him. After a while there was a tiny blink from the shore as Sergeant Miscowsky briefly

clicked a hooded flash. Lysander waited, and when it flashed
again he was ready to take a bearing.

There wasn't any navigation satellite system on Tanith.
Governor Blaine wanted to install one, but the CD wouldn't
finance it. Sparta's system wasn't complete, but it was good
enough to locate your position to a few meters, much better
than he could do taking visual bearings in choppy seas. Here
he had no choice.

The bearing was one more check on the sled's navigator.
More importantly, the flash told him that the listening gear
hadn't picked up any nessies near the shore, and none following him. Not yet . . .

After he had taken the bearing on Miscowsky's light he
couldn't keep himself from staring off southward toward the
place the other sled had gone. He couldn't see anything. A
wave broke over his head.

Enough. He thumbed his buoyancy valve to let out air, and
sank slowly toward the sled.

Concentrate, he thought. Stick to your job. The sled and
its tapes and dead porker would attract all the nessies or it
wouldn't. Worrying about it couldn't change that. He ignored
the tight knot in his gut, and tried not to remember vivid
images of nessies tearing at each other.

Once he was below the surface he used the helmet display
to get his position from the inertial system. It agreed with
his visual bearings. When be was sure, he pulled himself to
the sled and tapped Harv. Middleton dropped back to let
Lysander take the controls.

He held his course. More images of nessies came unwanted.
He tried to dismiss them, and when that didn't work he began
to recite slowly to himself. Leonidas. Megistias. Dieneces.
Alpheus. Maro. Eurytus. Demaratus the lesser. Denoates. Three
hundred names, the heroes of Thermopylae.

He was well into the second hundred when it was time to
change course and angle in toward the Rochemont dock area.

"Major Barton!" Ace Barton woke to find his orderly calling from the bedroom door. "Major!"

"Yeah, Carruthers?"

"Cap'n Honistu said you're needed in the staff room, sir.
Looks like Falkenberg's making his move."

"Oh shit. Right. I'll be right there. Have coffee ready." There
was bright light outside. The bedside clock showed an hour
after sunrise. Not enough sleep, he thought.

When he stood his head pounded. *Shouldn't drink so*

damned much. He found vitamins and headache powder and swallowed them, poured a second glass of water and drank that. *I don't even like to drink. Rather drink than talk to those rancher types.*

He dressed quickly. By the time he was done his head felt better.

The staff room had formerly been the Rochemont study, and was the kind of room that Barton would have wanted if he had been a wealthy rancher, although most of the books were ones he wouldn't be interested in reading. He wondered what it had cost to have leather-bound volumes brought from wherever they had been made. Earth? Someday he'd have the servants unlock one of the glass-fronted book cases and see just where those had been printed. They didn't look as if they'd ever been opened.

Anton Girerd stood at the foot of the big conference and map table. He always seemed to be there. Barton wondered when the rancher leader ever slept. He was certainly conscientious enough. Or just worried. Chandos Wichasta, Senator Bronson's representative, sat quietly in a far corner of the room. He acknowledged Barton with a raised eyebrow.

Captain Honistu looked up from the map table. "They're moving, Major."

Barton went to his place at the center of the table. His coffee mug was already there, and he drank a heavy swallow. *Someday Carruthers is going to slip up and I'll scald myself.* "Tell me about it, Wally."

"Two fronts. One's obvious, they're moving in force along the southeastern front. Almost no casualties. As you ordered, we're firing off our long-range weapons and getting the hell out. We've knocked out half a dozen of their swamp boogies, but we'll lose four ranches in the next hour."

"And another fifty in a week, and so what?" Barton mused. "They could have had those anytime they really wanted. OK, try to make them pay *something* for the land, but it ain't worth many casualties. Christian Johnny knows that, it won't be worth many to him, either. So what's he covering up?"

"Not exactly sure," Honistu said. "Reports are still coming in. Looks big enough, Major. Aircraft commandeered. Commercial, even ranchers' private planes. It looks like they're after every airplane on the planet. And some of their air assault troops have been consolidating ranch lands, bringing in engineers."

"Where?"

"Here's the places we know about." Blue lights came on across the map display. "And probables." More lights, in light blue.

"Moving southwest," Barton said.

"Yes, sir. We don't *know* anything, but the pattern makes me think they're after something in this area. Rochemont, even."

"Makes more sense than his other operation. Think they're on to us, Wally?"

"No data."

"What does our man in the governor's office say?"

"He can't be reached, sir."

"Can't be reached." Barton drank another heavy swallow of coffee. "As of when?"

"This morning, I guess. He went home at the usual time last night."

"What happens when you call his home?"

Anton Girerd said, "A stranger answers. A woman who claims to be Alicia Chang Mardon's visiting cousin. But Alicia has no cousin."

"Sure of that?"

"We are quite aware of our relatives, Major."

"I expect you are. Sorry."

"He's not the only one," Honistu said. "We can't reach any of our people in the governor's office."

"None. I see. OK. We're sure none of them knew about this place?"

"We told none of them," Girerd said. His voice was filled with disdain.

"And none of my troops who know ever talked to them," Barton said. "All right, Falkenberg's closed out our sources. We knew it would happen some day. Now he's on the move, possibly directed at Rochemont, possibly just getting a staging base in the southern area. Sure would be bad luck if he wanted Rochemont as a staging base."

"Wouldn't make a bad one," Honistu said.

"Yeah." Barton let the toothpick dance across his mouth again. "Especially if they look at the fuel facilities here. Mr. Girerd, Mardon may not have known about Rochemont, but he did know about *Norton Star.*"

"Yes."

"Should we be worried?"

Girerd shrugged. "I have been considering that. I don't know, because I can't guess what pressures Falkenberg might put on him."

"Me either. So. We assume Falkenberg has learned we have a ship in orbit. What will he do?"

"As long as he doesn't know where it lands, nothing,"

Captain Honistu said. "There are no space defense forces on Tanith, and that CD warship is a long way off."

"Yeah. OK, Captain, what have you done about all this?"

"Put our people on full alert with orders to maintain security from satellite and air surveillance. Upped the frequency of our surveillance sweeps. Alerted *Norton Star* to stand by," Honistu said. "And sent for you."

"Right." Barton studied the situation map for another minute. Then he turned to Anton Girerd. "Sir, I recommend that we bring in the landing ship and get the stuff out of here."

Girerd sighed. "I thought you would decide that." He sighed again. "A few more days. Van Hoorn has had an excellent year. A few more days—but of course you are correct, Major. Better this much than nothing. I will notify Jonkheer Van Hoorn to make the best arrangement he can with the governor."

"You'll do nothing of the kind." Chandos Wichasta spoke quietly, his voice barely carrying through the library. "He must take his chances like everyone else."

"Now wait—" Girerd protested.

"Wait for what?" Wichasta asked. He got up from his place at the far corner of the room and came over to the big staff table. His voice remained low and persuasive. "All this is a strain, and I am sorry, but surely it is clear to you? The more of the crop the governor takes in, the lower the price we will get for what you have gathered. While it would be better if Jonkheer Van Hoorn's crops were added to our collection, we gain nearly as much if they are merely destroyed. If this disturbs you, pay the Jonkheer from your increased profits."

"What will you contribute?" Girerd demanded.

Wichasta looked thoughtful. "We will pay twenty-five percent of the value of Van Hoorn's crop if none of it reaches Falkenberg and Blaine. We will accept any reasonable estimate of its value."

"Not enough."

Wichasta shrugged. "It is all I have authority to give. Perhaps I can persuade my principals to pay more, but I would not be honest with you if I promised they would. They are hard men. I suggest that if you wish Van Hoorn to receive further compensation, you must provide it yourself. Major Barton, I take it you are requesting that we send down the landing boat?"

"Yes, sir."

"I shall arrange it. Immediately?"

"As soon as convenient," Barton said.

"Very well. I will call *Norton Star*." Wichasta left the room.

"Arrogant bastard," Girerd said.

"Yes, sir," Barton said. *Bronson's people usually are. And from here on you'll spend a lot of your life in debt to people like Wichasta.* "OK, Wally, satellite surveillance security can go hang. Full alert for everyone. Deploy air defenses. Full radar search. Get ready to transfer the borloi, and have the fuel people stand by. I want that damn thing in and out fast."

Sergeant Manuel Fuentes was taking a leak against the side of the horse barn when Private Hapworth found him.

"Corporal Hardy says tell you two things, Sarge. Full alert and stand by. Just got the word," Hapworth said.

"Another damn drill. Shit."

"No drill, Sarge. Leastwise the comm room people sure don't act like it's a drill. Falkenberg's on the move. The major's bringing in that landing boat."

"Oh, ho. Be glad of that. This duty's soft enough, but I'm gettin' tired of it. Time we was out of here," Fuentes said. "What's the other thing?"

"Sarge?"

"You said there was two things Hardy wanted you to tell me."

"Oh. Yeah, I did. Other thing is, the nessies are freaking out."

"Eh?"

"Whole shit pot of them, less than a mile off shore. Eatin' something. Eatin' each other, too."

Sergeant Fuentes shuddered. "Saw that once. They got a seacow, and by the time they were finished with it one of the nessies was wounded, and—" He shuddered again. Corporal Hardy knew about Fuentes's interest in nessies. When they'd first landed on Tanith, Fuentes took a dip in the ocean. Then the officers told them about nessies. Thinking about that incident still gave him the willies, but it had also given him a fanatical interest in the big sea carnivores. He wanted to go see what they were doing.

And Hardy wants my job. "Nessies will wait," he said. "We better go check on the fuel supply." He was halfway to the fuel shed when the alarms began to sound.

Sergeant Miscowsky lay in the goopy mud at the edge of the jungle and cursed whatever tiny thing had got inside his pants leg. He hoped it wasn't one of the thin red worms that passed for leeches on Tanith, but he was afraid it was. As long as it didn't climb up to his crotch— He ignored the crawly feeling and carefully panned his binoculars across the Rochemont scene for the tenth time in as many minutes. There was just enough light to see, and the sky was brightening by the minute. Miscowsky scanned slowly, from the docking area on his left to the big house in the center, then across fields and barns—

He'd just focused on a barn when its roof opened down the middle and the two halves dropped to the sides. A radar dish popped up and began to rotate.

Holy shit. He thumbed a button on the small console on his left sleeve. "Get the colonel. They're doing something," he said.

Even at lowest power a radio signal might be detected. Miscowsky was linked to the central communications computer through an optical fibre phone line, as thin and flexible as a thread. The fibre optic system was totally undetectable. It was also incomplete, since not everyone was wired into it. Miscowsky panned his binoculars across Rochemont again. There was more activity.

"Falkenberg."

"Colonel, they've opened the roofs on most of their buildings," Miscowsky said. "Antennas everywhere, sweeping everything. They don't care if somebody detects them. Field strength here's pretty amazing."

"Will they spot you?"

"Not me, Colonel."

"Sorry I asked. Do you think they've spotted Mr. Prince?"

"Colonel, I can't tell. All I know is all of a sudden they popped the roofs, and they're sweeping like hell."

"Right. How many observers do we have, and can you pipe any of it back here?"

"Five lookouts, and yes, sir, the cameras ought to be picking stuff up now."

"Thanks. I'll have a look, but keep talking."

"Yes, sir. OK, they're opening the rest of the sheds. I see guns. Couple on the roof of the manor house. More in the sheds. AA and dual purpose stuff mostly. Christ, Colonel, they've got damn near everything Barton owns here! There goes a Leopard. Nasty little bugger." The Leopard was a self-propelled twin rapid-fire gun system mounted on a tank chassis. Used in connection with long-range smart missiles, it was highly effective against helicopters. It could also deliver high volume direct fire against ground targets. "They're moving it this way. Still coming. My guess is they'll put it on the rise about a klick west of here."

"Right. Make sure the computer knows where it is."

"Aye aye, sir. There goes another Leopard, and a couple of

missile launchers. I sure wouldn't want to try getting in here with a chopper. Colonel—hah. One whole goddam side of Rochemont hill is opening up! Chopper coming out. Two of them. Two choppers revving up."

"Command override, command override." Lieutenant Mace's voice broke into Miscowsky's helmet phones. "All personnel, secure against aerial observation. Choppers on the rise. I say again, all personnel, take cover, conceal from aerial observation. Choppers coming. Do not fire. I say again, do not fire."

Miscowsky touched the ACKNOWLEDGE button. The computer would collect the responses and tell Mace who hadn't answered.

"Anything else?" Falkenberg asked.

"Well, yes, sir, there's just a lot of activity. People milling around. Last time I looked, the dock area was empty, but there's lots of people there now. Bunch more going into the hill. Looks like a truck coming out of there— Must be a big cave. Truck coming out, heading for the dock area. Bunch of guys hanging on the running boards. Not Barton people, not most of 'em anyway. Different cammies, like what the ranchers wear."

"Any sign of Mr. Prince?"

"No, sir, none at all. Barton's troops still don't act like they've seen anybody, though."

"Carry on, Sergeant."

Miscowsky nestled closer to the squishy ground and adjusted his binoculars. They were definitely moving stuff from the house down to the dock area. Lots of stuff. "Has to be the drugs," he reported to Lieutenant Mace at communications central. "What else could it be?"

"No attempt at concealment?" Lieutenant Mace asked.

"No, sir, none at all. Like they don't care who sees—Holy shit."

They all heard it. A double sonic boom that crackled across the jungle. Then the roar of a hypersonic jet overhead.

"I think we can guess why they don't care who sees them," Mace said. "Command override, command override. Landing ship approaching. Full alert, I say again full alert. Battle plan Alfa, battle plan Alfa."

It was still grey dark when Lysander and Harv came ashore. They took off their flippers and moved silently toward the building Miscowsky had identified as a fueling station. Part of the building was an open-roofed area. Two tractors and a large harrow were parked there. They slipped into the shed area and toward the door to the building itself.

"Those tractors run on hydrogen," Harv whispered.

Lysander nodded. It made sense. It was easier to make hydrogen from seawater than to ship other kinds of fuel on a primitive world. It also made for less trouble with the various ecology groups. And if you could make liquid hydrogen, you could certainly make LOX. "Tanks are probably underground."

The main entrance to the building was a double door wide enough for vehicles. The long corridor beyond was dimly lit with overhead bulbs. There were a number of doors off the corridor.

They could hear soft voices inside, voices too low to be understood. This went on for a few minutes. Lysander looked around the shed area for a place to hide. Nothing looked very promising. The area was too open. He had decided they'd have to risk going inside when the nearest door off the long interior corridor opened.

A man and a woman came out. They leaned on each other and were obviously drunk. The man wore the faded camouflage uniforms favored by the Tanith rancher militia. The woman wore grey coveralls opened to the waist. They giggled as they walked past Lysander and Harv.

"Of course I love you," the man said. "Couple more years, I'll have enough saved, we can buy out—" He looked around furtively. "Best be quiet." They went out of the shed and toward the worker barracks.

Lysander waved Harv forward and pointed to the door the two had come out. The lock was a simple one that took Harv only seconds to open.

The room inside was filled with crates of spare parts for tractors and farm machinery. Lysander locked the door behind him, then risked using a flash held hooded in his fingers. He found a narrow passage through the crates. It led to a small compartment not high enough to stand in. There was a mattress and several empty beer and whiskey bulbs. A heavy air of sweat filled the compartment.

Harv wrinkled his nose in disgust.

"Yeah, but it looks OK for us." Lysander looked around the small area again. "Looks fine. Now we wait."

Their compartment was against the east wall of the shed. Lysander used his knife to make a tiny peephole in the corrugated sheet plastic wall. When there was enough light outside he could see part of the docking area. Perfect, he thought. We've been lucky.

Luck counts, Falkenberg once told him. But it's no use at all if you don't know enough to take advantage of good luck.

They waited. Harv dozed like a cat, his eyes opening whenever Lysander shifted weight or anyone moved outside. After a while Lysander let himself drift to the edge of sleep.

They heard the alarms first, then voices.

"Get them lines laid out, Hapworth," someone shouted. "Hardy, get the wrenches. Come on, come on, we ain't got all damn day!"

Sonic booms shook them, then there was the roar of the landing ship.

XXIV

Ace Barton listened to staff reports as long as he could stand it, then left Captain Guilford in charge and took Honistu out to find some fresh air on Rochemont's wide veranda. The breeze off the sea felt heavy, laden with moisture, but it was better than the atmosphere in the staff room.

Honistu pointed out to sea. Barton scanned the area with his binoculars. About two kilometers out, the whitecaps were tinged with scarlet, and the water roiled with dark shapes. "Worst I ever saw them things," Honistu said.

Barton nodded. "Maybe so." There had been feeding frenzies before. Once the battalion cook had stimulated a frenzy by dumping garbage off the pier. The nessies had come for the garbage, and one rose out of the sea and grabbed the cook's assistant. Troops came running up to help, but it was too late to save the recruit. One of the man's messmates shot the nessie, and half a dozen other nessies attacked the wounded one. The resulting frenzy almost destroyed the docks.

After that they were more careful where they threw the garbage . . . .

There was a sharp double sonic boom.

"Right on time," Honistu said.

Barton's binoculars gave him an excellent view of the stubby-winged craft as it settled in on the choppy water. It skirted the crimson waves where the nessies were fighting and sped across to the dock area at too high a speed, turning just in time. It had come full speed close enough to the pier to make Barton wince.

"Hotshot," he muttered. Most landing boat pilots were.

"Worried about nessies. I would be too," Honistu said.

The Talin class was the smallest of the CD's assault/pickup boats. It looked fairly large, but most of its bulk was tankage and engines behind a small cabin and cargo area. The Talin class was designed to carry a marine assault section, two metric

496

tonnes, to orbit, or bring twice that mass from orbit to ground. Its mission was to land troops in unexpected places.

And that we've done, Ace Barton thought.

Crewmen appeared at the aft hatches and caught lines thrown from the docks. The landing boat was winched in until it lay against the pier. The broad landing hatch opened.

"What the hell?" Barton said. A light armored vehicle rolled out. It was followed by a dozen armed men in dark cammies. "Command override," Barton shouted. "Cover the dock area."

Alarms hooted.

"Major, Guilford here."

"Yeah."

"Mr. Wichasta says that's ours. A present from Senator Bronson."

"Tell the son of a bitch—Captain, put me through to him."

"This is Chandos Wichasta."

"Mr. Wichasta, you damned near started a battle."

"I deeply regret any difficulties we may have caused," Wichasta said. "I did not know they were coming. I have the captain of *Norton Star* on line now. He says they were conducting an exercise, and could not unload the assault boat and still land during this orbit."

"And didn't have any way to tell us."

"I know nothing of that."

"Yeah. And I can believe as much of that as I want to. All right, Mr. Wichasta, but those troops are under my command. Mine, not yours."

"Of course."

"Guilford, get me the officer in charge of that assault team."

"Roger." There was a pause. "Lieutenant Commander Geoffrey Niles here."

"Niles, what the hell do you think you're doing here?"

"Sir, I'm sure Captain Nakata has explained. We were conducting an exercise."

"Yeah. OK, Niles, I want your people off that boat. All of them, except the pilot and crew. That damned thing's going to be overloaded as it is."

"But of course, sir."

"Good. Second, I want them out of the way. Take your vehicle up to the field on the east side of the house, and keep them there. *All* of them. Guilford, notify security we've got strangers among us." He thumbed off the mike. "Wally, that's all we bloody need."

"Watchdogs," Honistu said. "Looks like Bronson doesn't trust us."

"Yeah. And I don't trust him, either." He thumbed his mike again. "Get me Anderson on a secure circuit."

"Captain Anderson here."

"Barton. Bobby, I want you to have a Leopard where it can cover Bronson's people."

"Sir?"

"You heard me. He don't trust us, I guess, but come to that I don't trust him."

"Yes, sir. Anything else?"

"No. Just be sure to do that."

"Yes, sir. Anderson out."

"Want me to assign someone in addition?" Honistu said.

"Oh, Bobby's all right," Barton said. "Maybe you ought to, though. OK, let's get that damn ship loaded and out of here."

Honistu gave orders. As soon as Bronson's troops were clear, the waiting trucks drove out onto the docks.

Barton's crew helped the ranch hands pull fuel lines out and connect them up to the landing craft. Rancher militia began unloading the trucks and carrying crates aboard.

"Well, Wally, this is what it was all for," Barton said.

"Yeah. And none too soon, Major."

"Come on, it was soft duty."

"Sure, but—Hell, Major, you must have felt it. Wondering what Falkenberg was going to do. Not that there was much he *could* do, but it doesn't stop the troops from worrying. He's pulled rabbits out of empty hats before."

"Yeah," Barton said. "But it does look like we've stymied him this time." He touched buttons on his sleeve console. "Patch me to the pilot of that landing boat."

"Aye aye," the comm sergeant said.

"Commander Perkins here."

"Major Barton. Have a good trip?"

"Yes, sir, uneventful. Understand we surprised you with the troops aboard. Sorry about that."

"Yeah, sure. When will you be ready to take off?"

"Assuming fuel and cargo are aboard, the next launch window for rendezvous with *Norton Star* will open at 0930," Perkins said.

"Seventy minutes. OK, you'll make that," Barton said. He touched more buttons on his sleeve console. "Sergeant major, move it out," he said. "You got fifty minutes to refuel and get that cargo aboard. Hop it."

He turned his binoculars on the Bronson group and watched as they went up the hill. Then he took a toothpick from his pocket and chewed thoughtfully.

"Nagging doubts, Wally. I keep thinking Falkenberg has an ace up his sleeve." He lifted his binoculars and swept them across the jungle edge. "But what the hell, he doesn't know everything."

Lysander could just see the assault boat through his peephole. It was the center of a flurry of activity. First the assault crew came ashore, weapons ready, and for a moment it looked like there might be a fight right there on the pier. Then they went northwards out of sight.

A crew snaked fuel lines out. A minute after they were connected up, they glistened with condensing frost. The fuel and oxygen lines crossed the road to the pier, and the ranch hands had put up a steel crossover to allow trucks to drive over them without pinching them off. Now a mixed crew of ranch hands and Barton Bulldogs was unloading crates from the trucks and carrying them aboard the landing craft. There were ranch hands in soiled coveralls; rancher militia in their jungle stripes; Barton Bulldogs in darker cammies; and in addition, there were darker blue coveralls which Lysander thought must be the landing ship crew. They were all mixed together. Can't possibly know each other, he thought. And there were the troops from the assault boat itself.

"Harv. Get the insignia off our cammies," he whispered. "May give us an edge." Falkenberg's legion wore a tiger-stripe camouflage uniform that wasn't like either Barton's or the rancher militia. With all those others mixed in, each group might think he belonged to some other. It was worth a try.

"We got a jackpot," he whispered, and gestured for Harv to come look through the peephole. "Get the layout. When the time comes, we walk out there like we've got jobs to do. When we get into the ship, you handle the doors. Get the hatches closed and the lines cast off. I'll get it off the water."

"Right." Harv grinned. "Be something to tell the phraetrie."

"May be." *Of course I'll also have to explain to Mother what the hell I was doing here.*

He let Harv study the situation outside while he tuned one channel of his receiver to Falkenberg's communications frequency, and slaved the other to his pocket computer. Then he called up a program to listen for and analyze electronic signals.

There were a *lot* of them. Apparently Barton wasn't worried about electronic security any longer. There was energy in all the radar frequencies, and widely across the communications bands. The communications signals were not strong and couldn't have been intercepted from very far away, but most of them were in plain English.

"—fifty minutes, you bastards! Move goddamit, that bird flies on schedule!" someone shouted.

Lysander tuned across the bands, and heard "Not now. Wait an hour and you got all the people you need, but let it wait."

Fifty minutes. Wait an hour. It was an easy inference that the landing ship would fly then. Lysander frowned in concentration on *Norton Star*'s ephemeris, then nodded in satisfaction. It would be about fifty minutes before the ship was in the proper position for orbital rendezvous with a minimum-energy landing boat. They'd fly then, about 0930.

He tapped Harv on the shoulder and took over the peephole. Should have made two, he thought. Too late now.

Another truck rolled down to the dock.

Lysander tuned his transmitter to the frequency Falkenberg's troops would be monitoring. He hesitated a moment, then keyed the microphone. "Yeah, this is Lion. We'll be ready for liftoff in fifty minutes." He cut off the transmitter and listened. There was a faint click. Lysander winked, and Harv grinned wolfishly.

"That was him, all right," Corporal Tandon said. "Right on our frequency. I didn't acknowledge except to key in a click, sir."

"Good," Falkenberg said. "That's enough to let him know we heard him. Any sign they know about him, or us?"

"Not one damn thing, Colonel," Tandon said. "They're chattering away like nobody's listening. Sir, Mr. Prince is a little off on the launch time; I've heard a dozen people say it goes up at oh-nine-thirty, and that squares with the ephemeris. Fifty minutes from his message is 0920."

"I see. I think you underestimate him, Corporal. Lieutenant Mace."

"Sir."

"I want you to be ready to start your bombardment at 0915. Tandon, five minutes before that you will use the code we worked out to alert Mr. Prince. Be prepared to notify Lieutenant Mace to change that schedule if Mr. Prince requests it."

"Aye aye, sir."

Falkenberg studied the time readout on his sleeve console. "And now we wait. Lieutenant Mace, I think we should discuss your target priorities."

At precisely 0910 Lysander heard Corporal Tandon's voice

in his earpiece. "Oh, hell, Lion, hold your horses, we'll have the stuff on the way in five minutes flat."

And what will Barton's communications monitors make of that? Lysander wondered. Assuming they heard it at all. He gestured to Harv and led the way through the passage between the packing crates. They unlocked the door and stepped into the corridor. There were two people there, one close, the other an armed Bulldog near the main door.

"What the hell are you doing in there?" the closest man demanded.

Lysander thought he recognized him as the man who'd come out of the store room earlier that morning. It hardly mattered. Lysander gestured toward the further man. Harv moved ten feet in a single flowing motion. As he did, Lysander spun the rancher around and brought his hand down in a sharp blow to the base of the skull. The man dropped. When Lysander looked up, Harv was dragging the soldier toward the store room.

They pushed both men inside. The rancher was still breathing. Harv thought the soldier was dead but he didn't really want to know. He locked the door. "Let's go."

There was no one in the tractor shed. They walked through that and toward the dock, striding briskly as if they had an errand there. No one stopped them.

The fuel lines were still rigged. There was no way to tell how much hydrogen and LOX had been pumped into the ship. Probably not enough to make orbit. What would happen if they took off with the fuel lines still in place? Presumably there were automatic shutoffs, but were there? Lysander tried to remember if they'd told him in training, and decided they'd never mentioned it. Why should they?

Just before they reached the pier there were sounds of mortar fire from the jungle edge. Several of Barton's people froze in their tracks. Someone shouted, "Incoming!" Several of Barton's troops hit the dirt.

There was a series of explosions up the hill near the house. Then the rattle of small arms fire, and more mortars fired. Several rounds hit the house itself. Part of the veranda was blown away, and the roof was on fire. A nearby shed was also burning. At the dock area people began to run, toward the ship or away from it, while others lay on the ground, or stared, or ran in circles.

There were more explosions from up the hill. The Leopard swivelled its guns to aim at the jungle edge and began to fire. Trees fell at the jungle's edge.

Lysander and Harv reached the dock and broke into a run

toward the landing ship. A crewman was just beginning to close the hatch. Lysander leaped across the loading gangplank and pushed past the man, leaving him to Harv. Inside were narrow passageways.

"Who the hell are you?" someone called.

"Get the damn crates lashed in!" Lysander shouted. "Secure for immediate takeoff!"

"Holy shit!" the crewman shouted. "Sir, goddamit—"

"Hop to it! We'll be under fire in a second," Lysander said. He rushed forward to the pilot compartment. There was no one in the right hand seat.

The pilot turned with a frown. "What's going on?"

"Immediate takeoff," Lysander said.

"We're not fueled for takeoff, you idiot!"

"We'll be blown away if we don't get off now. I mean *now.*"

"Off and go wh—uff."

Lysander unclipped the lap belt and heaved the pilot over into the copilot's seat. As he was securing the man's pistol, a crewman put his head into the compartment. Lysander kicked him and pushed him out, then slammed the cockpit door and locked it. He climbed into the left hand seat and inspected the control panel.

Ace Barton took a final look at the map table and turned to Anton Girerd. He grinned widely. "All done here. We can watch the takeoff from the veranda. Wally—"

He was interrupted by mortar fire. There was the sound of crashing glass. The house shook, then shook again. The door to the next room smashed open. Another explosion shook them and his staff dived under the heavy table. A third explosion nearby knocked him off his feet.

"Fire! Fire!" one of the servants shouted.

Barton got to his feet. Something was burning in the next room, and he gestured toward the fire in annoyance. "Carruthers! Deal with that!" He punched in code on his sleeve console. "Comm room, report!"

There was nothing but static. Barton switched to speakers so that Honistu could hear, and methodically punched in codes for emergency communication channels. "Comm Central, report!"

Surprise. Barton recalled Falkenberg's dry voice in the officers mess. "Surprise is an event that takes place in the mind of an opposing commander." *You son of a bitch.*

"Comm Central, Centurion Martino here, sir." The Centurion spoke slowly and carefully as he'd been trained to do.

"We are under heavy mortar and recoilless fire from a battery in the jungle approximately four klicks to the east. There was no warning. The first salvo took out the power plant and damn near every antenna we have. I've got damage control and power crews out now. I have no estimate of the time required to restore power. Captain Anderson is switching control of his units to auxiliary antennas."

Barton heard the sharp crump! of his own mortar units. "What's he shooting at?"

"Stand by one," Martino said. There was a long silence. "Counterbattery. Captain Anderson got some backtrack info with the secondary antennas. Is your plot table powered?"

Barton looked the question at Honistu. "Yes."

"Stand by, Major, I'll try to feed a report to the plot table now—plot responds. Successful feed."

Lights blinked on the liquid crystal map table. Bright orange bordered in blue for his disabled units. Antennas and power plants, and now guns. Too many. More orange blotches on the house itself. Barton could hear frantic sounds from the next room, but he ignored them. The air smelled of smoke, but less now than before.

Red squares for suspected enemy installations. Four guns for sure, all in the jungle. The squares were large, indicating uncertainty in locating them. "There'll be spotters," Barton said. "Have the Leopards chew up the jungle edge. Mortar fire on the probable enemy locations. And have the choppers stand by for target information."

Choppers. How had Falkenberg got troops into that jungle? They sure didn't walk. "They may have some new kind of stealthy chopper," Barton said. "Watch out for it. All AA units stand by."

"Yes, sir."

So what the hell did Falkenberg intend? "Martino, have they hit the landing ship?"'

"Stand by one, sir." Another silence. "No, sir, they haven't been shooting at it."

Haven't been shooting at it. Barton's head hurt. He put his hands to the back of his neck and willed himself to relax. Slow. Send the pain away. Ignore the ringing. Forget the smoke. Forget everything, relax, concentrate. Surprise is an event that takes place in the mind of an enemy commander. Me.

They haven't been shooting at the landing ship. Why haven't they been shooting at it? Why didn't they disable it first thing? "Patch me through to the assault boat pilot."

"Stand by."

It seemed like an eternity.

"I'm still trying, but there's no answer, Major."

"No answer. No communications, or no answer?"

"Don't know, sir. Tried four channels."

"Keep trying. Sound a full security alert in the dock area. Then get somebody down there on line."

"Aye aye, sir."

"Wally, there's something damned wrong out there," Barton said. "Get your butt down to that ship and see what it is. Stay with Martino on Red Four. Martino, reserve Channel Red Four. You, me, and Captain Honistu."

"Aye, aye, sir."

"Major?" Honistu asked.

"Damn it, get down there! Secure that ship! I won't be happy until you're sitting in the pilot compartment. Take whatever troops you need."

"Right. I'm on my way."

Barton thumbed his mike again. "Get me Anderson."

"Aye aye, sir."

Another long wait. *That son of a bitch. Power plants, antennas, comm shack, damn near got me. Two salvoes and we're damn near out of business. That son of a bitch. He's out there—*

"Captain Anderson."

"Bobby, aim something at that assault boat. Do that now, then stand by to disable it on my command."

"Disable? With the fuel lines pumping? Not bloody likely, Major. We can blow it to hell, but I don't know how to disable it."

"Holy shit. Stand by anyway. Martino! Keep track of Captain Honistu's group. I want security forces in that boat *now!*"

"Major, you must not, you must not destroy—" Anton Girerd's hands fluttered frantically. "Major—"

"On the contrary," Chandos Wichasta said. "You must arrange to destroy it before Governor Blaine can capture it."

"He cannot capture—"

"Anton, of course he can," Wichasta said. "Clearly their objective is to disable the landing ship. Major Barton has told us of the buildup on Dragontooth Island. Once that is complete we can't hold Rochemont. It is obvious they know this is the central storage place. If they did not know before, the landing ship told them that. I wonder if—but no, they had soldiers in the jungle. They must have come before the landing ship. Or did they?"

"They did," Barton said. "They're good, but they're not that good. Bobby, you sure you can't disable that assault boat without blowing it up?"

"Wouldn't want the responsibility, sir. Not till they get the fuel lines disconnected and capped. I've got artillery, not magic."

"Bring in another assault boat!" Girerd shouted.

"Right. Mr. Wichasta, do you have communications with *Norton Star*?"

"I will see."

"Please do. So. Martino, where the hell's the pilot of that boat?"

"Still no answer, Major."

"God damn it—"

"Captain Anderson," Wichasta said. "This is Chandos Wichasta. I speak for Senator Bronson. Captain, that landing boat must not be recovered by Governor Blaine. If there is any chance of that boat falling into the hands of the governor, destroy it."

"No!" Anton Girerd screamed.

"Captain, I am authorized to offer you wealth beyond your wildest dreams," Wichasta said. "Major Barton, we will pay your expenses and fees in full, with a bonus, provided that the borloi does not come into Governor Blaine's possession. An extra bonus for delivering the crop to us, but we will pay even if it is destroyed."

"Major." Centurion Martino's voice took on the deadly calm note professional soldiers use when things get serious. "The landing boat has started its engines. I still have no contact with the pilot."

"Wally!"

"All true," Honistu said. His voice sounded strained. "I'm running like hell—"

"Captain Anderson," Wichasta shouted. "Destroy that ship now!" Then he turned away and spoke into his microphone. Barton heard nothing of what he said.

Ace Barton touched buttons on his sleeve console. "Martino, keep this secure. Bobby, belay that instruction."

Anderson's voice was in his earpiece. "Ace, how much is wealth beyond our wildest dreams? Enough to get out of this racket?"

"What do you care? Belay that order!"

"Honistu here. Bronson's tank is firing at the landing boat."

XXV

Lysander examined the landing ship's control panel. All the test circuits glowed green except fuel line security. *Nothing I can do about that. No point in communications security, either.* "Harv."

"Right here, Prince."

"Mooring lines."

"Done, Prince. You all right up there?"

"Fine here. Watch my back." He thumbed the ship intercom button. *"Hear this. Secure for immediate liftoff. Hear this. Secure for immediate suborbital flight."* He punched in the code for Falkenberg's alert frequency. "Schoolmaster, this is Lion. I've got her. Attempting to move now."

Then he said a silent prayer and hit the startup sequencer. Displays flashed.

FUEL LINES NOT SECURE.

Lysander punched in **OVERRIDE. IMMEDIATE STARTUP. OVERRIDE. IMMEDIATE STARTUP. CONFIRM? CONFIRM.**

There was a loud whine of pumps, then the roar of the engines. Lysander steered to port, away from the dock. The ship began to move.

A geyser erupted in front of him. Someone was firing at him. Falkenberg?

"Schoolmaster, this is Lion. I say again, I have control. Attempting takeoff." Steer at the splashes, he thought. And hit the throttles. Accelerate. Moving target. Damned *big* moving target . . .

The pilot struggled into wakefulness. "What the hell are you doing?" he shouted.

"Getting us out of here! They're shooting at us."

"I'll be damned if—"

"Look, I haven't time to discuss this. If you touch the controls, I'll shoot you, provided that we live through it, which we probably won't. They're shelling us."

506

"Close the refueling valves, you moron! Christ, where did you learn to fly?"

"On Sparta. But I don't know how to do that."

"I'll get it—"

"Right. Be careful." Another geyser rose just to starboard. "If we slow down they'll hit us."

"Christ, I didn't contract to get killed." The pilot threw two switches. Red lights changed to green.

"Thanks," Lysander said.

"Jesus! Look, you'll never make it, there's not enough fuel—"

"I'm not trying for orbit. Just up and back down again."

"Down where?"

"Lederle for preference. Otherwise, anywhere I can set down."

"Did you ever fly one of these boats?"

"Landed once," Lysander said.

"Jesus Christ," the pilot said.

There was a scream of rage. Ace Barton turned to see Anton Girerd struggling with Chandos Wichasta. "He's ordered that tank to fire on the landing ship!" Girerd shouted. "We're ruined! Major, you must stop him!"

"Do not be a fool," Wichasta said. "Senator Bronson will pay your expenses. These wretches can pay nothing. As Girerd says, they are ruined."

"Yeah, you're right about that," Barton said. "All the same, I give the orders here. Corporal, see that Mr. Wichasta doesn't talk to anyone until I say he can."

"Sir." Barton's orderly moved up behind Wichasta.

"Get me Anderson," Barton said. "Bobby, concentrate on the enemy artillery. Ignore that landing boat."

"Sure you know what you're doing, Ace?"

"I think so. No time for discussion. Carry out your orders."

"He's talking real money, Major. And who's going to pay our fees if we lose the crop?"

"Captain Anderson, you have your orders."

There was a long pause. "All right. There goes wealth beyond my wildest dreams."

There goes a life of looking over your shoulder. "Channel Red Four. Wally!"

"Yeah."

"Tell whoever you put to covering Bronson's tank to take it out. *Now.*"

"Aye aye. Leopard Three, this is Honistu. Command override.

Sergeant Billings, Fire Mission Dead Muskrat. Execute. I say again, command override, execute Dead Muskrat."

"You are a fool," Wichasta said.

"Yeah," Barton said. "I expect I am. But I do know who hired me."

"Corpsman!" someone shouted. "The lieutenant's down!"

"Coming."

Alf Tandon hunkered down as low as possible. The Leopard was chewing up the edge of the jungle, and if you stuck your head up you'd get it blown off. Then abruptly the firing stopped. Tandon waited. Still nothing. He lifted his head warily, then took a chance and used his binoculars. "Holy shit. Sarge!"

Nothing. The fibre optic lines were down. Maybe the computer was gone too. Lieutenant is down. Can't reach Miscowsky. Who's in charge? Maybe it's me. Hell with it. They sure as shit know we're here. He thumbed the radio switch. "Sarge, this is Alf."

The damned thing definitely was a leechworm, and it was crawling up his right leg toward his crotch, but right now the other leg was Miscowsky's biggest problem. His left thigh hurt like hell above the knee, and he couldn't feel a thing below that. His trouser leg was soaked with blood, and the last mortar round had been close enough to rattle his teeth. Stuff was whizzing overhead and all around so he didn't dare sit up to look at how bad he was hit. *It don't seem too much for the regenners. Not yet. If I just don't fucking run out of blood—*

"Sarge, this is Alf."

It was an effort, but Miscowsky punched buttons on the big radio box that lay next to him. *Fuckers are probably homing in on the set. My turn in the fucking barrel.* "Go ahead, Alf."

"Lieutenant's down. Corpsmen on the way."

"Roger that." *And not much I can do about it.*

"The Leopard's changed targets. It's shooting hell out of the light tank they brought in on the landing boat."

"Repeat that."

"The Leopard is firing at the troops brought in on the assault carrier. It has disabled the light tank."

"I'll be damned. OK, keep watching. Out."

Miscowsky felt himself getting weaker. There was enough of a lull in the firing that he could sit up and look at his leg— *In a damn minute.* He thumbed the mike switch on his helmet. "Command information. Lieutenant Mace is down. Orders. All units report status." He listened, then changed frequencies. "Colonel, Lieutenant Mace is out of action. You're in tactical charge, only there ain't much here. No more than ten effectives including wounded, and no working guns."

"I heard the reports."

"Any orders, sir?"

"I relieve you. Have you heard from Mr. Prince?"

"Nothing you didn't hear, sir."

"We'll have to hang on until we do hear from him. Are you hit?"

"Yes, sir."

"Take care of yourself, Sergeant. I'll mind the store."

"Aye aye, Colonel." *Hang on. Rather run for it. Only where the hell can we run? With this leg I ain't running anyway.* He wriggled painfully across the jungle floor, dragging the radio, his wounded leg dragging uselessly behind him, until there was a thick tree trunk between him and the jungle edge. Then he sat up with his back to the tree.

His left leg was broken and there were jagged holes in his Nemourlon armor. A thin shiny sliver stuck out halfway down his shin. The upper part of his leg hurt like hell, but the numbness in the lower half worried him more. *Tourniquet time. I can get that on, but . . .* "Medic. Any medic. This is Miscowsky. I'm hit. Need help."

"Kamaria here. I can get over there after I finish with the lieutenant. Five minutes. Can you hang on that long?"

"I'll have to." He tuned back to the general command frequency.

"That Leopard's finished with the tank," Tandon reported. "Guns swiveling. Looks like he's got us in mind."

Oh, shit. Nothing we can hit him with, either.

"Can you see the landing boat?" Falkenberg asked.

"Not without sticking my head out of the bush!"

"Is there anyone in position to report on the landing boat?" Falkenberg asked.

"Colonel, I can look."

Jesus. Colonel, for God's sake don't make Alf stick his head up there. Oh, God, Damn, It.

"Thank you, Corporal, but hold off a moment," Falkenberg said.

The Leopard began firing again. Miscowsky wriggled down to get as close to the ground as he could. *Kamaria won't get to me through that. Better tell him not to try.*

The shellfire moved closer. Miscowsky didn't think his tree

would last much longer. Then there was a roar louder than the cannon fire. A long sustained roar.

"That's the engines," Falkenberg said. "Tandon, keep your head down. Wait."

The roar got louder, then held steady.

"Schoolmaster, the Lion is aloft. Schoolmaster, this is Lion, the Lion is aloft."

"Colonel," Miscowsky shouted. "Goddamn, sir, he did it!"

"Right. Now can you get me Major Barton?"

"Sir? Well, I can try—I can use full power and try to cut in on a frequency I've heard him on."

"Do it, and patch me in."

"Aye, aye, sir. Stand by—" Miscowsky tuned his set and turned the dial to full power. "Done. Go ahead, Colonel."

"Major Barton, this is John Christian Falkenberg."

There was a long pause. "This is Barton."

"We surrender," Falkenberg said.

"Surrender. You've just won the damn war and you surrender. All right, Colonel, I accept. Wally, you heard him. All units cease fire."

"Yes, sir."

"Thank you," Falkenberg said. "We have wounded."

"So do we," Barton said.

XXVI

"Bloody hell," Mark Fuller said. He sat at a small table under the canopy of leaves and vines that concealed his helicopter and sipped tea. He'd been there for hours, far too long, the ship ready to go at a second's notice. Now they heard the distant sound of artillery. "Bloody hell."

Crew Chief Hal Jordan nodded in sympathy. "The waitin's always hardest. But I wouldn't be too anxious for orders, was I you. Goin' after Barton'll be a little different from storming them pirates that had your lady."

"I know, Chief. It doesn't make waiting any easier." He glanced at his sleeve console. The time was 0935. "Listen to that. Something sure as hell is going on."

"Yeah," Jordan agreed. "Only from the sound of it they're not likely to have time to tell us about it."

"But maybe they'll want us. Better be sure we're ready."

"Mr. Fuller, If I get the damn thing any more ready, she'll fly off by herself! Relax, sir."

One of the villagers brought more tea. What they called tea here, anyway. Some kind of orange flavored grass. It didn't taste bad, just very different. Mark sipped and tried to look patient. There was a loud roar, loud enough to drown out the gunfire.

"Holy shit!" Jordan said. "Landing ship taking off!" Something large flashed overhead, low above the village clearing. "Look at it go!"

"I never saw one take off before," Mark said.

"Yeah, mostly I was *in* the damn things when they went up. There she goes—ain't going to make orbit, that's for damn sure! Hope the poor bastards know what they're doing."

The landing ship vanished. Mark sipped tea and waited. "Guns are quiet," he said.

"Yeah," Jordan said. "Too damn quiet."

There was a chirp from the helicopter radio. Mark stood quickly, but restrained himself. Let Jordan answer it.

511

"It's someone claims to be the colonel," Jordan said. "He's sending authentication codes—It checks out, sir. He want us to answer."

"Crap doodle. The radio silence orders are damned clear."

"Yes, sir, I know, but I'm pretty sure it's the colonel," Jordan said. "Sounds like him, and the authentication codes check. And they knew what frequency to call on, and who to ask for."

"What the hell should I do?"

"They pay you to decide, Mr. Fuller. Not me."

"I keep forgetting that. All right. Acknowledge," Fuller said.

"Yes, sir." Jordan spoke briefly, then handed the phones and mike out.

"Cornet Fuller here, sir," Mark said.

"Falkenberg. Stand by to check authentication." He read a string of numbers, which Fuller punched into his console.

"Yes, sir. Authentication acknowledged. Standing by."

"Orders, Mister Fuller. Hostilities are ended. You may defend yourself if fired upon, but you are to take no aggressive action unless directly ordered by Regiment. Is this understood?"

"Yes, sir. Did we win?"

"We can discuss that later. I am a prisoner of war."

"Sir?"

"I have surrendered this small command, and this will be my last transmission to you. You will make contact with regimental headquarters for further orders."

"Yes, sir—Colonel—"

"That's all Mr. Fuller. Out."

"Oh, boy," Mark said.

"Problems, Mr. Fuller?" Jordan asked.

"You might say that. We've surrendered. Or Falkenberg has."

"Sir?"

Mark explained. "He said we could defend ourselves, so I guess he didn't surrender us. Only now what do I do?"

"Well, sir, we've already broken radio security by answering that transmission. Maybe we ought to try to get headquarters?"

Mark thought that over and nodded. "Right. See if you can raise them."

It took well over an hour. Finally Mark was speaking with Captain Frazer.

"Yes, we heard that the Colonel surrendered his force," Frazer said. "Understand that our transmissions to you are not secure, but yours to us should be all right. What is your situation?"

"Well, I've got fuel for maybe a hundred klicks if I'm careful.

The other chopper's bone dry, and the crew went down the river with Colonel Falkenberg so there's nobody to fly it. Sergeant Jordan and I are the only ones here."

"Right. Well, just sit put, Mark. We'll send someone in for you when we get the chance."

"Yes, sir, but—I know the colonel said hostilities were over, but shouldn't we be doing something?"

"It's all right, lad," Frazer said. "We've won. Didn't the colonel tell you?"

"No, sir."

"Oh. Of course he wouldn't. It's a bit complex. Prince Lysander hijacked their landing boat. They'd loaded the drugs into it. Mr. Prince brought over ninety percent of the hold-out crops into Lederle harbor twenty minutes ago. Some of the ranchers are still trying to continue the revolt, but they don't have much to bargain with. They can't pay Barton, either. Stay alert and stay sober, there may be someone out there who didn't get the word, but this campaign's over."

"I see. Thank you sir. Could someone tell Mrs. Fuller I'm all right?"

"Of course. Right away. Fuller, it may be a couple of days before we get you out. When I've got transport we'll get some fuel and crew in there. Tell Mr. Ledoux the governor won't forget him. Otherwise, relax."

"But what happens to the colonel?"

"I wouldn't worry about it," Frazer said. "It's likely to cost us a bit, that's all. Relax, lad."

Everyone stood when Lysander came into the staff room. Major Savage nodded approval. "Well done, Mr. Prince."

"Thank you, sir."

"Sorry to hear about your corps brother."

"Surgeon says he'll be all right," Lysander said. "He won't like the inactivity, but a good rest won't hurt him. The colonel's all right, then?"

"So they tell me," Savage said. "We're expecting Barton's people to call with their terms. Shouldn't be too severe, they've little enough to bargain with, thanks to you." He shrugged. "Of course none of us will be sorry to see all our people back where they belong. For one thing, we've much better hospital facilities than Barton has."

The atmosphere was jovial, more like a luncheon in the Officers' Mess than duty in the staff room. Everyone was friendly.

Lysander studied the map table. The familiar lines were all

changed. Instead of neat areas held by ranchers and other places held by Falkenberg's Legion or Governor Blaine's militia, there were mixed splotches, mutually penetrating lines, scattered bases and staging areas. One long pseudopod stretched out toward Rochemont. Another slashed into the former rebel territory in the southeast. As he watched one large block went from hostile orange to secure blue.

"Bit of a mess, actually," Major Savage said. "But that won't last. Ah. Is that our call, Amos?"

"Yes." Amos Fast frowned. "It's not Barton, it's a rancher. Anton Girerd. Wants to talk to you and no one else."

Savage shrugged. "No reason not to. Put him on the speaker phone. Mynheer Girerd? Jeremy Savage here. What can we do for you?"

"You can give our property back," Girerd said. His voice was very tense. Everyone in the staff room fell silent.

"I beg your pardon?"

"Our crop," Girerd said. "The harvest. Give it back."

"I'm afraid I don't quite follow. We don't have your crop. That was turned over to the governor."

"I don't care what you did with it. You took it from us, and you can take it back from Governor Blaine. I'm telling you, if you want to see Colonel Falkenberg and those others again, get our crops back to us!"

"Come now, we can't do that," Savage said. "We're prepared to pay a reasonable ransom for the colonel, of course. And if you haven't heard, the governor's offering amnesty on very reasonable terms."

"No terms," Girerd said. "No negotiations. The crop. All of it."

"I think you'd better put Major Barton on."

"Barton's got nothing to do with this," Girerd said. "Damn you people! It's all a game to you. Nothing but a lousy stinking game! Well, it's no game to us. It's our lives, and our fortunes, and our honor."

"Honor from a dope peddler," Captain Rottermill said *sotto voce.*

Savage held up a hand for silence. "Do I understand that you've taken Colonel Falkenberg from Major Barton's custody?"

"Damn right we have."

"And where is Major Barton now?"

"In hell for all I know!"

Jeremy Savage touched the button to cut off the mike on the phone. His voice was low and clear, almost pleasant. "Amos, perhaps we'd better resume operations against Dragontooth. And please see what else you can muster to the southern area. We may need to assault Rochemont after all."

"Yes, sir." Amos Fast began typing furiously on his keyboard.

Savage activated the phone again. "Be reasonable, Mr. Girerd—"

"No. No, I will not be reasonable," Girerd said. "I have been ruined by being reasonable."

"You are hardly ruined. The governor's terms are quite generous."

"It's ruin."

"I assure you that's not the case," Savage said. "A number of your friends have already accepted. I do think you should reconsider while you have a choice."

"No. You've finished me, and I won't go alone."

"What possible good could it do you to harm your prisoners?" Savage asked.

"None. But I'll get the satisfaction. You get my property back, or your colonel's dead."

"It might take some time."

"It better not take long. After 1700 today I will start executing prisoners. One per hour. Beginning with the youngest. Your colonel can watch them die. Goodbye."

There was a moment of silence.

"Well, that's torn it," Major Savage said. "You are all familiar with the colonel's standing orders on negotiating with terrorists."

"How serious are they?" Captain Fast asked. "Anyone know this Girerd?"

"Governor's office will know him," Rottermill said.

"Ursula has met him," Lysander said. "Major—Major, we have to *do* something!"

"Yes, of course we must. Ian, if you'd be kind enough to get those choppers in Ledoux's village ready? They'll need fuel, a pilot, guns and gun crews. Perhaps you could pick up any of your SAS troops who might be along the way there?"

"Right away, sir. I'll be going myself, of course." Captain Frazer lifted his phone and spoke urgently.

"Captain Rottermill, I would very much like to know what has become of Major Barton."

"Yes, sir."

"Mr. Prince, we'll speak to the governor's office, but if you would be kind enough to bring your friend here, it might be helpful to speak with someone who knows Mynheer Girerd."

"I don't know that she actually *knows* him—"

"I really would appreciate it, Mr. Prince."

Savage hadn't changed his tone, and his smile was pleasant, but Lysander felt a moment of fear. "Yes, sir. I'll get her."

"Thank you. Now, if you please. Captain Fast, perhaps it would be well to tell sergeant major about this latest development."

"Yes, sir."

Lysander felt relieved to get out of the staff room.

"You could have come to see me first."

"Ursula, be reasonable. They brought me here by helicopter. I had to go to the hospital with Harv, and then I had to report! This is the first chance I've had."

"I suppose. You don't act very glad to see me." She grinned. "Here you come back a genuine hero, and I'd already planned to give you a hero's welcome just for getting back alive."

"I'm looking forward to it. A lot. But just now—Ursa, the colonel's in trouble."

"What do you mean?"

"Girerd's threatening to kill him if we don't recapture their crop from the governor and turn it over to them."

"That's crazy. Falkenberg's soldiers won't do that. If they did, and the colonel got out of it alive, he'd have them shot! Even I know that!"

"Yes. And I'm scared." He took her arm and led her to the staff room.

"Miss Gordon," Major Savage said. "Kind of you to come. I was wondering if you could help with a problem that seems to have developed."

"If I can—"

"I'm told you know Anton Girerd."

"Not really," Ursula said. "I did get to know his son Oskar—briefly but quite well—but I don't really know Mynheer Girerd."

"Still, you've met him. I'd be grateful for an opinion. Is he likely to carry out his threat?"

"Yes."

"You sound quite positive. Why?"

"Things Oskar told me. Sometimes he was afraid of his father."

"Sometimes?"

"When his father had been drinking. I imagine he has been now. He drinks under stress."

"I see. So we dare not assume he is bluffing. Well, it won't be the first time alcoholism proved fatal. Thank you. Captain Rottermill, I'd appreciate that report. You may go, Miss Gordon."

"May I see Ursula to her rooms?"

"Certainly, Mr. Prince, but I would appreciate it if you'd come right back."

"Yes, sir."

Ursula shuddered when they were outside. "I won't try to keep you," she said.

"Thanks. You felt it too?"

"He's so calm and careful and polite, and I don't think I've ever been quite so frightened of anyone in my life," she said. "And he isn't even mad at *me*." They walked in silence for a moment. "I suppose you have to go with them?" Ursula asked.

"If they'll let me."

"Why?"

"Why? Because—damn it, it's obvious."

"No. No, Lysander, it's not obvious that you should risk getting yourself killed in order to rescue a man who has already manipulated you into doing his work for him."

"What? But he didn't do that—"

She laughed. "Didn't he? Think about it. Not much happens around him that he hasn't planned."

"Ursula, he was ready to do it himself. Without me."

"Sure."

"Well, he was."

She smiled and shook her head. "Lynn, Lynn my darling, you really don't understand him, do you? I wasn't even there, and I know what happened. He was ready to go himself. Of course he was. Him and one of his Headquarters Company guards. Be only too glad to, and of course he understood. No discredit for not volunteering, none at all. Only he didn't have to go himself because you were right there to talk him out of it. Isn't that what happened?"

"Well—"

"See? But no, you don't see. Forget that. But whatever happened doesn't obligate you to go get killed for him now."

"I won't get killed."

"Oh probably you won't, they won't even let you get close to the action now, but that isn't the point."

"What is the point?"

"One you'll never understand. When are you going back to Sparta?"

"What? I don't know. It will be a while. Have to wait for Harv to get out of the regeneration stimulators—"

"But not long after that."

"I don't know. I suppose not, father will be anxious for my report, Ursa, we have to discuss this . . ."

"I wish I could go with you."

"Ursula—"

"I know. You wish it too, but it won't happen." She smiled thinly. "It's all right. It would never work. It's all wishes. Serves us both right for forgetting the rules. Goodbye, Lysander."

"We'll talk about this—I won't be long—"

"No. No, my dear it's hard enough this way." She stood on tiptoe to kiss him, very lightly and very quickly. "I won't be here when you get back."

"Where will you go?"

"I'll find something. I own my contract, you know. Colonel Falkenberg saw to that. Maybe I'll look up Oskar Girerd. He really was sweet, and even with his father acting like an idiot, he's likely to keep some of his wealth—"

"Ursula, stop, please stop—"

"I'm sorry. Maybe it wasn't funny. Maybe I wasn't trying to be funny."

"How can you be so—so damned calm about it?"

"Probably caught it from Major Savage." They had reached the door to her room. Not his. She went inside, making it clear she didn't want him to follow. She was already closing the door when she looked up at him and said, "I do love you, you know. Goodbye, my dear."

"I've got Barton," Rottermill said.

Major Savage gestured to indicate the speaker phone. "Good afternoon, Major. Jeremy Savage here."

"Good afternoon."

"Sorry to trouble you, but I doubt I must explain why I have called," Savage said.

"No, of course not."

"Will you need our help?"

"No. We're going in now. Sorry to have been so long. They surprised us, and it took this long to get the forces together."

"Yes, of course," Major Savage said. "Still, I hope you won't be long about it."

"No, Major Savage, I won't be long about it. You'll hear from me in an hour. Barton out."

"Will someone please explain what's happening?" Lysander asked.

"What's to explain?" Captain Fast asked. "Ace Barton's meeting his obligations."

"He's going to rescue the colonel?"

"Certainly. Who else should?"

"Well—us."

"Oh, sure, we'd give it a try," Amos Fast said. "We're moving

in backup units. But our motives wouldn't be quite the same
as Barton's, would they?"

"So we're not going to rescue the colonel?"

"If we must, we will," Major Savage said. "As Amos says,
we continue to make preparations. But I can't think it will
be necessary. Barton's lot are thoroughly competent."

"But—they may kill Colonel Falkenberg."

Jeremy Savage's smile didn't change. "That really would be
a mistake, you know. Hard to believe they'd be that stupid."

"But they might try! Major, our people are more competent than Barton's! We have to go in there!"

"I do think that's needlessly hard on Ace Barton," Savage
said. "Let's give him a chance, shall we?"

"I don't think I'll ever understand you people," Lysander
said.

"Politicians seldom do," Major Savage said.

The helicopter turned a tight spiral around Rochemont before
landing on the helipad outside.

The roof of the eastern wing had collapsed, and all the glass
was broken out. Smoke blackened the walls outside two rooms.
The rest of the house seemed repairable.

Ace Barton got out of the helicopter and strode toward the
front door. Now's the time he shoots me, Barton thought. I'm
getting too damned old for this.

He was nearly to the door when it opened. Anton Girerd
came out. He had a small automatic pistol in his hand, but
he held it barrel down. "What the devil do you want?"

"You know what I want," Barton said.

"No. I meant what I told that Savage—"

"I'm sure you did," Barton said. "But do the rest of your
people understand what you've got them into?"

Barton waved to indicate the fleet of helicopters coming in
around the house. "First there's my troops. You know what
they can do. Let me show you." Barton waved in a complex
gesture.

One of the helicopters circled the horse barn. A stream of
fire poured from the gunship's door. Horses screamed in agony
as tracers riddled the barn, then set it on fire. One of the
horse herders staggered out of the barn door. He was covered in blood.

Barton waved again. A dozen cattle burst from another barn.
A helicopter circled and came in behind them, sending them
in wild flight out into grain fields. The chopper's gatling opened
fire. Tracers chewed the ground just behind the cattle, and

the beasts ran faster in blind panic. The tracers moved slowly
into the herd. Blood and meat and smoke mingled on the
trampled grain.

Girerd screamed and aimed his pistol at Barton. "Stop! Stop
it!"

Barton gestured again and the choppers ceased firing.
"Okay. But my troops aren't your real problem. I'm a sweetheart compared to what you get if you shoot me. First off,
my troops will be pissed. Maybe you can take them all out
before they level this place. I doubt it, but suppose you can?
After us, you damned fool, there's the whole Forty-second!
Man, you've got yourself on the shit list of the toughest
bastards in the galaxy! Don't you know what they're doing?
They're not getting ready to negotiate. They don't negotiate with people like you. They're getting ready to come here
and sterilize this place."

"They can't do that, I've got their colonel—"

Barton laughed. "Girerd, don't you think Falkenberg thought
this might happen someday? His troops have standing orders.
They won't negotiate." He spoke louder, so that everyone
nearby could hear. "They'll never negotiate. They'll just see
that nothing survives here. Nothing. Not you, not your animals, not your troops. Not even women and kids. Nobody and
nothing. Then they'll burn everything. It's their colonel! They'll
sow the ground with salt, Girerd. Hell, that's exactly what
they'll do. Girerd, you're in trouble, and so is everyone here.
You're all fucking *dead.*" Ace kept his face turned toward
Girerd, but he let his eyes look to the side. Several Girerd
ranch hands were slinking away.

"You're just trying to frighten me—"

"Trying? I sure as hell hope I've done better than try! I hope
I've scared the shit out of you." He waved again. One of the
helicopters darted down.

"Wait, wait, don't!" someone screamed.

"But—they wouldn't—my children? My wife?" Girerd demanded.

"Every man, woman, and child," Barton said. "What the
hell did you expect?" He waved again. The chopper opened
up on the chicken house. In moments the ground outside it
was strewn with flaming, squawking chickens. The building
spewed out black smoke.

Girerd raised the pistol again.

"For God's sake, man, the next time you raise that damned
piece, you're going to eat it, use it or not. I'm getting damned
tired of this." Barton raised his hand again. The choppers
circled closer.

"Mynheer," one of the ranch hands shouted. "Mynheer, please, Mynheer—"

Girerd looked at the pistol and shook his head. "I don't know what I expected. A miracle, perhaps," Girerd said.

"Not my department," Barton said.

"But what can I do?"

"You were talking pretty rough when you threw me out of here," Barton said. "Have you actually killed anyone?"

"No."

"Any of them die?"

"Two, but they were not expected to live."

"Yeah, those. No one else?"

"No."

"You're a lucky man," Barton said. He turned and waved to his helicopters. They rose slightly but continued to circle. He touched his sleeve console. "Wally, bring in the rest of the troops."

Girerd examined the pistol as if he'd never seen it before.

"Use it or give up," Barton said.

Girerd looked at the pistol, then tossed it underhanded down the stairs.

Barton winced as it hit the dirt. *Be a hell of a thing to be shot by accident just now.* "All right." He went up the stairs and took Girerd by the arm to lead him into the house. "Now you're getting smart."

"No. I am a fool." He led the way into the big study. Falkenberg and three of his men sat there. There were also four ranchers in militia uniform standing stiffly against the far wall. One of the doors lay twisted off its hinges, and seven Barton Bulldogs in full armor menaced the ranchers.

"Mynheer," one of the ranchers said. "While the guns fired outside they came—" The man simpered in terror. "Mynheer, we heard these men say—Mynheer, we have families."

Girerd shuddered. "I see. Major Barton rules here, as elsewhere. Odd. I thought he worked for me."

"I did," Barton said.

"And do again," Falkenberg said. "Mynheer, he's done you better service than you know."

"Colonel—"

"All correct, Major."

"Thank you, sir." Barton saluted.

"Rules, Codes. What good are they?" Girerd demanded.

Barton and Falkenberg exchanged glances. Then they both looked at Anton Girerd. Their eyes were filled with pity.

XXVII

Waves of sound from the open door of the Officers' Mess battered Lysander with enough force to make him take a step backward. Skirl of pipes and stamp of marching feet. Songs of glory, songs of betrayal. "McPherson's time will nay be long, on yonder gallows tree . . ."

"Welcome aboard, Mr. Prince. They've saved a place for you."

Lysander didn't recognize the mess steward, but it hardly mattered. He breasted the waves of sound to get inside. The large room was crowded. Men in the blue and gold of Falkenberg's Legion mingled with the green of Tanith's militia. There was also a scattering of officers in blue and tan with silver bulldog badges.

Lysander let the corporal lead him to a table for four near the wall. Falkenberg sat alone at the far side. To his right was a man who wore oak leaves on the shoulder boards of his blue and tan uniform. Governor Blaine sat on Falkenberg's left.

Captain Jesus Alana got up from the next table and came over to clap Lysander on the back. "Good to have you," Alana shouted over the din.

"Welcome aboard," Falkenberg said. "We've saved you a place. You've already met Governor Blaine."

"Your Highness," Governor Blaine said.

"Your Highness, may I present Major Anselm Barton. Prince Lysander of Sparta."

Barton stood to shake hands. "An honor. One I would prefer under different circumstances, I think."

Lysander took the seat opposite Falkenberg. A steward brought him a glass of Tanith whiskey.

"Heard about what you did at Rochemont, Major Barton," Governor Blaine said. It was hard to hear him over the din from the party. "Good work, that. Must have been a bit tricky facing Girerd like that."

"Not as dangerous as it looked," Barton said. "I doubt that pistol of his would penetrate Nemourlon."

"Yes, well, good work anyway. Of course you do know Girerd has a trophy case of medals for his shooting."

And Barton wasn't wearing a face mask. On the other hand, how many Bulldog marksmen had Girerd in their sights? Wheels within wheels. But you couldn't fault Barton's success just because he took precautions.

"Is that what that tin in the study was about? Hmm. Well, I did need him alive. He's stupid, but killing him wouldn't make it easier to get the others to call off the revolt."

"Indeed. Most helpful, the way you managed things. Still, it is a bit odd you'd be concerned about our problems," Blaine said.

"Odd? No, sir," Barton said. "Seemed clear enough to me. Girerd's people can't pay me, and Bronson sure won't." He shrugged. "You and Falkenberg are the only ones on the planet who might hire me. Making your life difficult can't help me at all."

"Ah," Blaine said. He sipped at his whiskey.

"What will happen to Girerd?" Lysander asked.

"Oh, he's earned a stiff lesson," Blaine said. "But after all, I did proclaim a partial amnesty. No criminal penalties for the rebels, but some stiff civil fines. I'll use the money for a better satellite system, that kind of thing. I expect we ought to let the amnesty cover Girerd. Assuming it's all right with Colonel Falkenberg."

"I won't object," Falkenberg said. "I expect his lesson will be stiff enough. Among other things, he owes Major Barton quite a lot."

Barton looked glum, "I wish he had it to pay. Or someone did. We could use the money."

"You could have gone with Bronson," Falkenberg said.

"So I could," Barton said. "And from what I hear is happening in the Grand Senate, I might have been joining the winning side." He shrugged. "Never quite seemed to get around to it."

Falkenberg nodded. "You're available, then."

Barton chuckled. "Colonel, I doubt you've ever seen anyone as available as me."

"What makes you believe Bronson's faction is going to win?" Governor Blaine asked.

"Well, that investigation—"

"Will be quashed," Blaine said. "Bronson doesn't have the votes. If this borloi maneuver had worked it might have been a different story."

"Well, well," Barton said. "So nobody has a majority. Puts things back to what they were a year ago. Except that Falkenberg and I have both of us done ourselves out of a job. Governor, I may as well ask for the record. Are any of my people going to be charged? For that matter, am I under arrest?"

"I think that's what we're here to discuss. You certainly could be charged," Blaine said. "Arson, murder, aiding and abetting rebellion . . ."

"All done strictly in accord with the Laws of War," Barton said.

"Yes, certainly," Blaine said. "That's the only reason we have anything to discuss. Still, there is some question about the legitimacy of the group that hired you. Bona fide political group or criminal gang?"

"I guess it all depends on whether you want to put my arse in a sling."

"Actually," Blaine said, "I don't have much choice in the matter. If I charge you, I have to rule they're criminals, and that makes hash out of my political settlement."

"That's about how I read it, too," Barton said. "So?"

"So I would greatly prefer not to do that," Blaine said. "On the other hand, you have enemies. Some of the loyal ranchers were hit pretty hard. Many would be happy to see you hanged."

"I can live with their wanting it. Not so keen to see them get their wish."

"Indeed. It would be easier if you were no longer here. Remove the reminder, so to speak."

Barton shrugged. "Sure. How do we arrange that?"

"There might be a way," Falkenberg said.

"Ha. You have an offer?"

"I may have."

"Ah. But you're not quite prepared to make it?"

"We'll see. Time for another duty." Falkenberg caught the Mess President's eye, then stood. The pipers and singers fell quiet, and the babble in the room faded out. "Mr. President," Falkenberg said.

"Colonel!"

"A toast and a welcome. To Cornet Prince, once and future Prince of Sparta. He has earned the thanks of the Regiment."

Everyone stood. "Mr. Prince," Captain Alana said. The others echoed, "Mr. Prince."

Not quite everyone, Lysander saw. Barton stood when the others did, but he didn't say anything or raise his drink. *Can't really blame him.*

He saw a flash of green three tables away, and recognized

the gown he'd bought in the local shop. *Of course she wore it. What else would she have?*

Ursula stood next to Captain Peter Owensford. Her eyes met Lysander's briefly as she raised her glass. Then she looked away, toward her escort.

He didn't have time to think about that. The toast was done. *My turn now. What do I say?* He waited until the others were seated, and stood. "Mr. President?"

"Mr. Prince."

"My thanks to the Regiment. A toast: May we be comrades in arms again."

"Hear, hear," someone shouted. Falkenberg nodded approval.

Ursula was leaning toward Captain Owensford. Whatever she said made him laugh. Then Mark and Juanita Fuller came over to sit beside her. They all seemed very happy.

There were more toasts, then Governor Blaine stood. "I can do no better than echo Prince Lysander," he said. "To Sparta and Tanith and Falkenberg's Legion, and a time when we will be comrades again. A time more likely now."

A few more minutes, then the pipers resumed. Someone started a song. *"The Knight came back from the quest, muddied and sore he came. Battered of shield and crest, bannerless, bruised and lame . . ."*

"Governor, Major, if you'll excuse me? Thank you. Mr. Prince, if you'd care to join me?" Falkenberg stood and gestured toward the door. "Perhaps we have a few items worth discussion."

"Thank you, sir, I'd love to." Lysander followed Falkenberg out. As he reached the door he heard Ursula's laugh.

The song continued. *"Fighting we take no shame, better is man for a fall. Merrily borne, the bugle-horn answered the warder's call.*

"Here is my lance to mend, Haro! Here is my horse to be shot! Aye, they were strong, and the fight was long, but I paid as good as I got! Haro! I paid as good as I got!"

Falkenberg's rooms were in a severely square detached building of sheet plastic that stood centered at the north end of the open area used as the regimental parade ground. They were met at the door by Corporal McClaren, who wore a very functional pistol over undress blues. Two more Headquarters Company troops were at the end of the hall.

The small study in Falkenberg's quarters had the look of a monk's cell. *Spartan,* Lysander thought. Actually, we go in for more decoration than this. He lives as the old Spartans must have.

There was one book case, of a wood native to Tanith. The desk was bare except for a screen set at a comfortable angle for reading. The keyboard was evidently concealed in a drawer. Lysander had once looked into the Regiment's electronic library, and had been amazed: tens of thousands of volumes, histories and world literature, atlantes, art, and technology, philosophy and cook books and travelogues, all available in an instant. *As long as the computers work he doesn't need real books. So why does he have any at all?* Lysander edged closer to the book case. The books were a jumbled collection, anthropology and military history mixed with biographies and novels. Most were cheaply bound, and they all looked as if Falkenberg had had them for a long time.

Falkenberg touched a hidden button. Music began, soft enough not to disturb conversation, loud enough to hear. Lysander frowned.

"Sir Hamilton Harty," Falkenberg said. "It's called 'With The Wild Geese.'"

The room's big central table was functional duraplast, with a top of clear Plexiglas over the liquid crystal display. Snifters and a decanter of brandy were already in place on the table. Corporal McClaren waited until Lysander and the Colonel were inside, then went out, closing the door behind him.

"Welcome," Falkenberg said perfunctorily. "I won't keep you long."

As long as you like, Lysander thought. I doubt I'll ever get used to that kind of party. Too much noise. He tried not to think of Ursula's hand laid lightly on Captain Owensford's arm. What was he to her? New lover? A date for the evening? Both? He squirmed as pictures came uninvited.

They sat and Falkenberg waved to indicate the brandy. "Help yourself."

"I think I've had enough," Lysander said.

"Perhaps. You don't mind if I do? Thank you. You'll be leaving soon."

"I thought so. Now I'm not so sure. And you?"

"New Washington."

"That's a long way out from earth. What's there?"

Falkenberg looked thoughtful. "What are your plans, Mr. Prince? I suppose I'd best return to using your proper title."

"What's proper? I've earned being Cornet Prince. I think I'd rather be Mr. Prince than Prince Lysander."

"Certain of that?"

"No. Not certain."

"You have no real choice, you know."

"Sir?"

Falkenberg chuckled. "The stakes are too high, Your Highness. I won't say it never happened that someone as prominent as you joined the Legion, but in your case it won't work. If you choose to remain Cornet Prince, your orders will be to return to Sparta and become King. We need friends there."

"We?"

"That's the second time you've asked for information I can't give to Cornet Prince."

"But Prince Lysander—"

"Is an ally. Potentially a great deal more."

More. What's more than an ally? "What makes you think Prince Lysander can keep secrets?"

"We have our ways."

"I guess you do. All those friendly people buying me drinks and asking me questions—"

"That was part of it. Mostly, there comes a point when you have to trust someone, because if you don't, you can't accomplish the mission."

"Like sending the heavy weapons first?"

"Something like that. So. Who are you, Lysander Collins?"

"Colonel—Oh, damn it, Colonel, what will happen to her?"

"Her choice. She has choices now. You've given her that," Falkenberg said. "The governor has offered to hire her. I doubt she'll take that offer, because we'll make her a better one. The Regiment can always use toughminded bright people. Captain Alana has a post for her. Or—well, there are entirely too many bachelors and widowers among my officers. Women with the temperament for a soldier's life aren't easily found."

Who gets her? You? She's too damned young for you. Or—

"None of which answers the question I asked you."

"No, sir."

"Odd," Falkenberg mused. "A couple of hundred years ago it was a standard situation. Prince or Princess involved with commoner, conflict of love and duty. Lots of stories about that. None now, of course. How could there be? Not many people with a sense of duty."

Not a lot of love, either. What's more rare, love or duty?

"Damn it all, Colonel. Mr. Fuller has his Juanita to take care of him. Someone—else—gets Ursula. I have Harv. It's not fair!"

"I can also point out that Mr. Cornet Prince would never have met her."

"Whereas Prince Lysander of Sparta could take her to dinner in the Governor's Palace. You would remind me of that, you son of a bitch."

Falkenberg's smile was thin but triumphant. "Your Highness, when junior officers get to feeling sorry for themselves, we tell them to shut up and soldier. In your case—"

"Shut up and princify. Especially if I'm going to talk to you like that. Hardly appropriate for Cornet Prince. Yes, sir. Bloody hell." Lysander smiled wistfully. "I don't suppose anything has to be fair. At least you're not telling me to count my blessings."

There was a long pause. Finally Lysander reached up and took off the shoulder boards from his blues. "Colonel Falkenberg, I believe you were going to tell me something about New Washington."

It was well past midnight, and the sounds of the party were fading away. Lysander stared at the sketches and maps on Falkenberg's table screen. "God knows it's ambitious enough. There's a lot that can go wrong."

"Of course. There always is, when the stakes are high enough."

And these can't get a lot higher. "Let me be blunt about this. I've known something about Lermontov's plan for a year, but this is a lot more. You, the Blaine family, and half the senior officers of the Fleet are part of a conspiracy led by Grand Admiral Lermontov. You want Sparta to join that conspiracy."

"It's what I *want.* I do realize that you haven't the authority to commit your government."

"I can't even commit my *father* to this!"

"Your Highness, he joined us years ago."

"Oh, I'll be damned—yes, of course that would explain a lot of things I didn't understand. Colonel, this is going to take getting used to."

"You'll have time. While you're digesting that, get used to this: the only person who outranks your father in this—conspiracy—is Lermontov himself."

"What? But—Colonel, what are you saying?"

"Your Highness, the CoDominium is finished. Dr. Whitlock and Vice Admiral Harris of Fleet Intelligence don't give it ten years."

"Yes, of course, Sparta sees it coming too."

"Without the CoDominium there won't be any order at all. Not even the laws of war. Your Highness, I don't know what will—what can replace the CoDominium. I just know something has to, and it will need a secure base."

"Ten years," Lysander mused.

"Maybe longer. The Grand Admiral believes we can hold

on for twenty, and we might get a miracle after that."
Falkenberg shook his head. "I think it will take a miracle just
to keep things together for twenty years, and I don't believe
in miracles."

"But you're going to New Washington anyway."

"I've told Lermontov about my doubts. Perhaps you can
guess what he said."

"Shut up and soldier."

"Precisely," Falkenberg shrugged. "Actually, it makes sense.
If things don't come apart too soon, we can keep the balance of power. If it all collapses, New Washington is a
potentially valuable addition to the Alliance."

"But we need your troops as cadre for the new Spartan army.
You're going to New Washington! How—?"

"You'll get your cadres. I'm merging Barton's troops into
the 42nd. That frees up men to send home with you. Not as
many as we'd like, but enough. We all make sacrifices, Mr.
Prince. Pardon me. Your Highness."

"Who will you send?"

"I haven't thought about it."

"Owensford?"

"A good candidate, actually. Good teacher." Falkenberg stood.
"And now, Your Highness, it's probably time I make a quick
appearance at the party, then get some sleep. Major Barton
and I have a number of details to iron out in the morning."

"Yes, sir. Thank you for your confidence."

Falkenberg's look said nothing. Or everything. "Just don't
forget the sanitation workers," he said. "Goodbye, Mr. Prince."

The night outside was cool. Lysander left Falkenberg's
quarters and went to the Officer's Mess. He stood outside the
door. Inside he heard laughter. After a long while he turned
and went to his empty room.

SWORD AND SCEPTRE

Military authority has no parts. It can be delegated but it cannot be divided without in the doing it be shattered. Euphemisms for its hopeless fragments obscure truth and invite supervention of the natural forces that destroy nations. It is safer to allow that the few victims of injustice resulting from the fallibilities of even the best of human commanders pay the penalties than that the whole should come to ruin in the hope of saving them. The great pandemarchic cultures that seethe and ferment in the cadavers of empires are foremost in their concern for the weak, the stupid, the unlucky, and see the hope of aiding them only through the destruction of all official authoritarian systems (more often than not in order to exploit them privately for greater personal gain). Such governments have therein been also foremost in expediting their own extinction, both from within and without. The concerted power of the common man is formidable; but the power is not concerted by men who are common. Born of the efforts of common men to rationalize mediocrity into decisive roles without whole authority to play them are the modern concepts of leadership and management.

Leadership, management and command are terms too often confused by mistaking the similar for the synonymous.

James Maxwell Cameron
The Anatomy of Military Merit

The purpose of surprise is to generate uncertainty in the mind of the opponent. Surprise may result from technology, but the actual surprise is not in the weapon system. It is the mind of the commander and staff that surprise really takes place. Military commanders, not weapons systems, are surprised.

It is probably worth repeating that: Surprise is an event that takes place in the mind of an enemy commander.

Stefan T. Possony and Jerry E. Pournelle
The Strategy of Technology

I

Tanith

Heat beat down on sodden fields. Two hours before the noon of Tanith's fifteen plus hours of sunshine the day was already hot; but all of Tanith's days are hot. Even in midwinter the jungle steams in late afternoon.

The skies above the regiment's camp were yellow-gray. The ground sloped off to the west into inevitable swamp, where Weem's Beasts snorted as they burrowed deeper into protective mud. In the camp itself the air hung hot and wet, heavy, with a thick smell of yeast and decay.

The regiment's camp was an island of geometrical precision in the random tumble of jungles and hilltops. Each yellow rammed-earth barrack was set in an exact relationship with every other, each company set in line from its centurion's hut at one end to the senior platoon sergeant's at the other.

A wide street separated Centurion's Row from the Company Officers Line, and beyond that was the shorter Field Officers Line, the pyramid narrowing inevitably until at its apex stood a single building where the colonel lived. Other officers lived with their ladies, and married enlisted men's quarters formed one side of the compound; but the colonel lived alone.

The visitor stood with the colonel to watch a mustering ceremony evolved in the days of Queen Anne's England when regimental commanders were paid according to the strength of their regiments, and the Queen's muster masters had to determine that each man drawing pay could indeed pass muster—or even existed.

The visitor was an amateur historian and viewed the parade with wry humor. War had changed and men no longer marched in rigid lines to deliver volleys at word of command—but colonels were again paid according to the forces they could bring into battle.

"Report!" The adjutant's command carried easily across the open parade field to the rigidly immobile blue and gold squares.

"First Battalion, B Company on patrol. Battalion present or accounted for, sir!"

"Second Battalion present or accounted for, sir." "Third Battalion present or accounted for, sir!"

"Fourth Battalion, four men absent without leave, sir."

"How embarrassing," the visitor said *sotto voce*. The colonel tried to smile but made a bad job of it.

"Artillery present or accounted for, sir!" "Scout Troop all present, sir!" "Sappers all present, sir!"

"Weapons Battalion, Aviation Troop on patrol. Battalion present or accounted for, sir!"

"Headquarters Company present or on guard, sir!"

The adjutant returned each salute, then wheeled crisply to salute the colonel. "Regiment has four men absent without leave, sir."

Colonel Falkenberg returned the salute. "Take your post."

Captain Fast pivoted and marched to his place. "Pass in review!"

"Sound off!"

The band played a military march that must have been old in the twentieth century as the regiment formed column to march around the field. As each company reached the reviewing stand and men snapped their heads in unison, guidons and banners lowered in salute, and officers and centurions whirled sabers with flourishes.

The visitor nodded to himself. No longer very appropriate. In the eighteenth century, demonstrations of the men's ability to march in ranks, and of the noncoms and officers to use a sword with skill, were relevant to battle capabilities. Not now. Still, it made an impressive ceremony.

"Attention to orders!" The sergeant major read from his clipboard. Promotions, duty schedules, the daily activities of the regiment, while the visitor sweated.

"Very impressive, Colonel," he said. "Our Washingtonians couldn't look that sharp on their best day."

John Christian Falkenberg nodded coldly. "Implying that they mightn't be as good in the field. Mr. Secretary? Would you like another kind of demonstration?"

Howard Bannister shrugged. "What would it prove, Colonel? You need employment before your regiment goes to hell. I can't imagine chasing escapees on the CoDominium prison planet has much attraction for good soldiers."

"It doesn't. When we first came things weren't that simple."

"I know that too. The Forty-second was one of the best outfits of the CD Marine—I've never understood why it was disbanded instead of one of the others. I'm speaking of your present situation with your troops stuck here without transport—surely you're not intending to make Tanith your lifetime headquarters?"

Sergeant Major Calvin finished the orders of the day and waited patiently for instructions. Colonel Falkenberg studied his bright-uniformed men as they stood rigidly in the blazing noon of Tanith. A faint smile might have played across his face for a moment. There were few of the four thousand whose names and histories he didn't know.

Lieutenant Farquhar was a party hack forced on him when the Forty-second was hired to police Hadley. He became a good officer and elected to ship out after the action. Private Alcazar was a brooding giant with a raging thirst, the slowest man in K Company, but he could lift five times his own mass and hide in any terrain. Dozens, thousands of men, each with his own strengths and weaknesses, adding up to a regiment of mercenary soldiers with no chance of going home, and an unpleasant future if they didn't get off Tanith.

"Sergeant Major."

"Sir!"

"You will stay with me and time the men. Trumpeter, sound Boots and Saddles, On Full Kits, and Ready to Board Ship."

"Sir!" The trumpeter was a grizzled veteran with corporal's stripes. He lifted the gleaming instrument with its blue and gold tassels, and martial notes poured across the parade ground. Before they died away the orderly lines dissolved into masses of running men.

There was less confusion than Howard Bannister had expected. It seemed an incredibly short time before the first men fell back in. They came from their barracks in small groups, some in each company, then more, a rush, and finally knots of stragglers. Now in place of bright colors there was the dull drab of synthetic leather bulging over Nemourlon body armor. The bright polish was gone from the weapons. Dress caps were replaced by bulging combat helmets, shining boots by softer leathers. As the regiment formed, Bannister turned to the colonel.

"Why trumpets? I'd think that's rather out of date."

Falkenberg shrugged. "Would you prefer shouted orders? You must remember, Mr. Secretary, mercenaries live in garrison as well as in combat. Trumpets remind them that they're soldiers."

"I suppose."

"Time, Sergeant Major," the adjutant demanded.

"Eleven minutes, eighteen seconds, sir."

"Are you trying to tell me the men are ready to ship out now?" Bannister asked. His expression showed polite disbelief.

"It would take longer to get the weapons and artillery battalion equipment together, but the infantry could board ship right now."

"I find that hard to believe—of course the men know this is only a drill."

"How would they know that?"

Bannister laughed. He was a stout man, dressed in expensive business clothes with cigar ashes down the front. Some of the ash floated free when he laughed. "Well, you and the sergeant major are still in parade uniform."

"Look behind you," Falkenberg said.

Bannister turned. Falkenberg's guards and trumpeter were still in their places, their blue and gold dress contrasting wildly with the grim synthi-leathers of the others who had formed up with them. "The headquarters squad has our gear," Falkenberg explained. "Sergeant Major."

"Sir!"

"Mr. Bannister and I will inspect the troops."

"Sir!" As Falkenberg and his visitor left the reviewing stand Calvin fell in with the duty squad behind him.

"Pick a couple at random," Falkenberg advised. "It's hot out here. Forty degrees anyway."

Bannister was thinking the same thing. "Yes. No point in being too hard on the men. It must be unbearable in their armor."

"I wasn't thinking of the men," Falkenberg said.

The Secretary for War chose L Company of Third Battalion for review. The men all looked alike, except for size. He looked for something to stand out—a strap not buckled, something to indicate an individual difference—but he found none. Bannister approached a scarred private who looked forty years old. With regeneration therapy he might have been half that again. "This one."

"Fall out, Wiszorik!" Calvin ordered. "Lay out your kit."

"Sir!" Private Wiszorik might have smiled thinly, but if he did Bannister missed it. He swung the packframe easily off his shoulders and stood it on the ground. The headquarters squad helped him lay out his nylon shelter cloth, and Wiszorik emptied the pack, placing each item just so.

Rifle: a New Aberdeen seven-mm semi-automatic with ten-shot clip and fifty-round box magazine, both full and spotlessly clean like the rifle. A bandolier of cartridges. Five grenades. Nylon belt with bayonets, canteen, spoon, and stainless cup that served as a private's entire mess kit. Great-cloak and poncho, string net underwear, layers of clothing—

"You'll note he's equipped for any climate," Falkenberg commented. "He'd expect to be issued special gear for a non-Terran environment, but he can live on any inhabitable world with what he's got."

"Yes." Bannister watched interestedly. The pack hadn't seemed heavy, but Wiszorik kept withdrawing gear from it. First aid kit, chemical warfare protection drugs and equipment, concentrated field rations, soup and beverage powders, a tiny gasoline-burning field stove—"What's that?" Bannister asked. "Do all the men carry them?"

"One to each maniple, sir," Wiszorik answered.

"His share of five men's community equipment," Falkenberg explained. "A monitor, three privates, and a recruit make up the basic combat unit of this outfit, and we try to keep the maniples self-sufficient."

More gear came from the pack. Much of it was light alloys or plastic, but Bannister wondered about the total weight. Trowel, tent pegs, nylon cordage, a miniature cutting torch, more group equipment for field repairs to both machinery and the woven Nemourlon armor, night sights for the rifle, a small plastic tube half a meter long and eight centimeters in diameter—"And that?" Bannister asked.

"Anti-aircraft rocket," Falkenberg told him. "Not effective against fast jets, but it'll knock out a chopper ninety-five percent of the time. Has some capability against tanks, too. We don't like the men too dependent on heavy weapons units."

"I see. Your men seem well equipped, Colonel," Bannister commented. "It must weight them down badly."

"Twenty-one kilograms in standard g field," Falkenberg answered. "More here, less by a lot on Washington. Every man carries a week's rations, ammunition for a short engagement, and enough equipment to live in the field."

"What's the little pouch on his belt?" Bannister asked interestedly.

Falkenberg shrugged. "Personal possessions. Probably everything he owns. You'll have to ask Wiszorik's permission if you want to examine that."

"Never mind. Thank you, Private Wiszorik." Howard Bannister produced a brightly colored bandanna from an inner pocket and mopped his brow. "All right, Colonel. You're convincing—or your men are. Let's go to your office and talk about money."

As they left, Wiszorik and Sergeant Major Calvin exchanged knowing winks, while Monitor Hartzinger breathed a sigh of relief. Just suppose that visiting panjandrum had picked Recruit Latterby! Hell, the kid couldn't find his arse with both hands.

II

Falkenberg's office was hot. It was a large room, and a ceiling fan tried without success to stir up a breeze. Everything was damp from Tanith's wet jungle air. Howard Bannister thought he saw fungus growing in the narrow space between a file cabinet and the wall.

In contrast to the room itself, the furniture was elaborate. It had been hand carved and was the product of hundreds of hours' labor by soldiers who had little else but time to give their commanding officer. They'd taken Sergeant Major Calvin into a conspiracy, getting him to talk Falkenberg into going on an inspection tour while they scrapped his functional old field gear and replaced it with equipment as light and useful, but hand carved with battle scenes.

The desk was large and entirely bare. To one side a table, in easy reach, was covered with papers. On the other side a one-meter star cube portrayed the known stars with inhabited planets. Communication equipment was built into a spindly legged sideboard that also held whiskey. Falkenberg offered his visitor a drink.

"Could we have something with ice?"

"Certainly." Falkenberg turned toward his sideboard and raised his voice, speaking with a distinct change in tone. "Orderly, two gin and tonics, with much ice, if you please. Will that be satisfactory, Mr. Secretary?"

"Yes, thank you." Bannister wasn't accustomed to electronics being so common. "Look, we needn't spar about. I need soldiers and you need to get off this planet. It's as simple as that."

"Hardly," Falkenberg replied. "You've yet to mention money."

Howard shrugged. "I don't have much. Washington has damned few exports. Franklin's dried those up with the blockade. Your transport and salaries will use up most of what we've got. But you already know this, I suppose—I'm told you have access to Fleet Intelligence sources."

Falkenberg shrugged. "I have my ways. You're prepared to put our return fare on deposit with Dayan, of course."

"Yes." Bannister was startled. "Dayan? You do have sources. I thought our negotiations with New Jerusalem were secret. All right—we have arrangements with Dayan to furnish transportation. It took all our cash, so everything else is contingency money. We can offer you something you need, though. Land, good land, and a permanent base that's a lot more pleasant than Tanith. We can also offer—well, the chance to be part of a free and independent nation, though I'm not expecting that to mean much to you."

Falkenberg nodded. "That's why you—excuse me." He paused as the orderly brought in a tray with tinkling glasses. The trooper wore battledress, and his rifle was slung across his shoulder.

"Will you be wanting the men to perform again?" Falkenberg asked.

Bannister hesitated. "I think not."

"Orderly, ask Sergeant Major to sound recall. Dismissed." He looked back to Bannister. "Now. You chose us because you've nothing to offer. The New Democrats on Friedland are happy enough with their base, as are the Scots on Covenant. Xanadu wants hard cash before they throw troops into action. You could find some scrapings on Earth, but we're the only first-class outfit down on its luck at the moment—what makes you think we're *that* hard up, Mr. Secretary? Your cause in Washington is lost, isn't it?"

"Not for us." Howard Bannister sighed. Despite his bulk he seemed deflated. "All right. Franklin's mercenaries have defeated the last organized field army we had. The resistance is all guerrilla operations, and we both know that won't win. We need an organized force to rally around, and we haven't got one."

Dear God, we haven't got one. Bannister remembered rugged hills and forests, weathered mountains with snow on their tops, and in the valleys were ranches with the air crisp and cool. He remembered plains golden with mutated wheat and the swaying tassels of Washington's native corn plant rippling in the wind. The Patriot army marched again to the final battle.

They'd marched with songs in their hearts. The cause was just and they faced only mercenaries after defeating Franklin's regular army. Free men against hirelings in one last campaign.

The Patriots entered the plains outside the capital city, confident that the mercenaries could never stand against them—and the enemy didn't run. The humorless Covenant Scots regiments chewed through their infantry, while Friedland armor squadrons cut across the flank and far into the rear, destroying their supply lines and capturing the headquarters. Washington's army had not so much been defeated as dissolved, turned into isolated groups of men whose enthusiasm was no match for the iron discipline of the mercenaries. In three weeks they'd lost everything gained in two years of war.

But yet—the planet was still only thinly settled. The Franklin Confederacy had few soldiers and couldn't afford to keep large groups of mercenaries on occupation duty. Out in the mountains and across the plains the settlements were seething, and ready to revolt again. It would only take a tiny spark to arouse them.

"We've a chance, Colonel. I wouldn't waste our money and risk my people's lives if I didn't think so. Let me show you. I've a map in my gear."

"Show me on this one." Falkenberg opened a desk drawer to reveal a small input panel. He touched keys and the translucent gray of his desk top dissolved into colors. A polar projection of Washington formed.

There was only one continent, an irregular mass squatting at the top of the planet. From 25° North to the South Pole there was nothing but water. The land above that was cut by huge bays and nearly landlocked seas. Towns showed as a network of red dots across a narrow band of land jutting down to the 30° to 50° level.

"You sure don't have much land to live on," Falkenberg observed. "A strip a thousand kilometers wide by four thousand long—why Washington, anyway?"

"Original settlers had ancestors in Washington state. The climate's similar too. Franklin's the companion planet. It's got more industry than we do, but even less agricultural land. Settled mostly by Southern U.S. people—they call themselves the Confederacy. Washington's a secondary colony from Franklin."

Falkenberg chuckled. "Dissidents from a dissident colony. You must be damned independent chaps."

"So independent that we're not going to let Franklin run our lives! They treat us like a wholly owned subsidiary, and we are not going to take it!"

"You'll take it if you can't get somebody to fight for you," Falkenberg reminded him brutally. "Now, you are offering us transport out, a deposit against our return, minimum troop pay, and land to settle on?"

"Yes, that's right. You can use the return deposit to

transport your noncombatants later. Or cash it in. But it's all the money we can offer, Colonel." And be damned to you. You don't care at all, but I have to deal with you. For now.

"Yeah." Falkenberg regarded the map sourly. "Are we facing nukes?"

"They've got some but so do we. We concealed ours in Franklin's capital to make it a standoff."

"Uh-huh." Falkenberg nodded. The situation wasn't that unusual. The CD Fleet still tried to enforce the ban for that matter. "Do they still have those Covenant Highlanders that whipped you last time?"

Bannister winced at the reminder. "Goddamn it, good men were killed in that fight, and you've got no right to—"

"Do they still have the Covenanters, Mr. Secretary?" Falkenberg repeated.

"Yes. Plus a brigade of Friedland armor and another ten thousand Earth mercenaries on garrison duty."

Falkenberg snorted. No one thought much of Earth's cannon fodder. The best Earth recruits joined the growing national armies. Bannister nodded agreement. "Then there are about eight thousand Confederate troops, native Franklin soldiers who'd be no match for our Washingtonians."

"You hope. Don't play Franklin down. They're putting together the nucleus of a damned good fighting force, Mr. Bannister— as you know. It is my understanding that they have plans for further conquests once they've consolidated their hold on New Washington."

Bannister agreed carefully. "That's the main reason we're so desperate, Colonel. We won't buy peace by giving in to the Confederacy because they're set to defy the CoDominium when they can build a fleet. I don't understand why the CD Navy hasn't put paid to Franklin's little scheme, but it's obvious Earth isn't going to do anything. In a few years the Confederates will have their fleet and be as strong as Xanadu or Danube, strong enough to give the CD a *real* fight."

"You're too damn isolated," Falkenberg replied. "The Grand Senate won't even keep the Fleet up to enough strength to protect what the CD's already got—let alone find the money to interfere in your sector. The shortsighted bastards run around putting out fires, and the few Senators who look ten years ahead don't have any influence." He shook his head suddenly. "But that's not our problem. Okay, what about landing security? I don't have any assault boats, and I doubt you've the money to hire those from Dayan."

"It's tough," Bannister admitted. "But blockade runners can get through. Tides on New Washington are enormous, but we know our coasts. The Dayan captain can put you down at night here, or along there . . ." The rebel war secretary indicated a number of deep bays and fiords on the jagged coast, bright blue spatters on the desk map. "You'll have about two hours of slack water. That's all the time you'd have anyway before the Confederate spy satellites detect the ship."

III

New Washington

Roger Hastings drew his pretty brunette wife close to him and leaned against the barbecue pit. It made a nice pose and the photographers took several shots. They begged for more, but Hastings shook his head. "Enough, boys, enough! I've only been sworn in as mayor of Allansport—you'd think I was Governor General of the whole planet!"

"But give us a statement," the reporters begged. "Will you support the Confederacy's rearmament plans? I understand the smelter is tooling up to produce naval armament alloys—"

"I said *enough*," Roger commanded. "Go have a drink." The reporters reluctantly scattered. "Eager chaps," Hastings told his wife. "Pity there's only the one little paper."

Juanita laughed. "You'd make the capital city *Times* if there was a way to get the pictures there. But it was a fair question, Roger. What are you going to do about Franklin's war policies? What will happen to Harley when they start expanding the Confederacy?" The amusement died from her face as she thought of their son in the army.

"There isn't much I can do. The mayor of Allansport isn't consulted on matters of high policy. Damn it, sweetheart, don't you start in on me too. It's too nice a day."

Hastings' quarried stone house stood high on a hill above Nanaimo Bay. The city of Allansport sprawled across the hills below them, stretching almost to the high water mark running irregularly along the sandy beaches washed by endless surf. At night they could hear the waves crashing.

They held hands and watched the sea beyond the island that formed Allansport Harbor. "Here it comes!" Roger said. He pointed to a wall of rushing water two meters high. The tide bore swept around the end of Waada Island, then curled back toward the city.

"Pity the poor sailors," Juanita said.

Roger shrugged. "The packet ship's anchored well enough."

They watched the 150-meter cargo vessel tossed about by the tidal force. The tide bore caught her nearly abeam and she rolled dangerously before swinging on her chains to head into the flowing tide water. It seemed nothing could hold her, but those chains had been made in Roger's foundries, and he knew their strength.

"It has been a nice day." Juanita sighed. Their house was on one of the large greensward commons running up the hill from Allansport, and the celebrations had spilled out of their yard, across the greens, and into their neighbors' yards as well. Portable bars manned by Roger's campaign workers dispensed an endless supply of local wines and brandies.

To the west New Washington's twin companion, Franklin, hung in its eternal place. When sunset brought New Washington's twenty hours of daylight to an end it passed from a glowing ball in the bright day sky to a gibbous sliver in the darkness, then rapidly widened. Reddish shadows danced on Franklin's cloudy face.

Roger and Juanita stood in silent appreciation of the stars, the planet, the sunset. Allansport was a frontier town on an unimportant planet, but it was home and they loved it.

The inauguration party had been exhaustingly successful. Roger gratefully went to the drawing room while Juanita climbed the stairs to put their sleepy children to bed. As manager of the smelter and foundry, Roger had a home that was one of the finest on all the Ranier Peninsula. It stood tall and proud—a big stone Georgian mansion with wide entry hall and paneled rooms. Now, he was joined by Martine Ardway in his favorite, the small conversation-sized drawing room.

"Congratulations again, Roger," Colonel Ardway boomed. "We'll all be behind you." The words were more than the usual inauguration day patter. Although Ardway's son Johann was married to Roger's daughter, the Colonel had opposed Hastings' election, and Ardway had a large following among the hard-line Loyalists in Allansport. He was also commander of the local militia. Johann held a captain's commission. Roger's own boy Harley was only a lieutenant, but in the Regulars.

"Have you told Harley about your winning?" Ardway asked.

"Can't. The communications to Vancouver are out. As a matter of fact, all our communications are out right now."

Ardway nodded phlegmatically. Allansport was the only town on a peninsula well over a thousand kilometers from the nearest settlements. New Washington was so close to its red dwarf sun that loss of communications was standard through much of the planet's fifty-two standard-day year. An undersea cable to Preston Bay had been planned when the rebellion broke out, and now that it was over work could start again.

"I mean it about being with you," Ardway repeated. "I still think you're wrong, but there can't be more than one policy about this. I just hope it works."

"Look, Martine, we can't go on treating the rebels like traitors. We need 'em too much. There aren't many rebels here, but if I enforce the confiscation laws it'll cause resentment in the East. We've had enough bloody war." Roger stretched and yawned. "Excuse me. It's been a hard day and it's a while since I was a rock miner. There was once a time when I could dig all day and drink all night."

Ardway shrugged. Like Hastings, he had once been a miner, but unlike the mayor he hadn't kept in shape. He wasn't fat, but he had become a large, balding, round man with a paunch that spilled over his wide garrison belt. It spoiled his looks when he wore military uniform, which he did whenever possible. "You're in charge, Roger. I won't get in your way. Maybe you can even get the old rebel families on your side against this stupid imperialistic venture Franklin's pushing. God knows we've enough problems at home without looking for more. I think. What in hell's going on out there?"

Someone was yelling in the town below. "Good God, were those shots?" Roger asked. "We better find out." Reluctantly he pushed himself up from the leather easy chair. "Hello— hello—what's this? The phone is out, Martine. Dead."

"Those *were* shots," Colonel Ardway said. "I don't like this— rebels? The packet came in this afternoon, but you don't suppose there were rebels on board her? We better go down and see to this. You sure the phone's dead?"

"Very dead," Hastings said quietly. "Lord, I hope it's not a new rebellion. Get your troops called out, though."

"Right." Ardway took a pocket communicator from his belt pouch. He spoke into it with increasing agitation. "Roger, there is something wrong! I'm getting nothing but static. Somebody's jamming the whole communications band."

"Nonsense. We're near periastron. The sunspots are causing it." Hastings sounded confident, but he was praying silently. Not more war. It wouldn't be a threat to Allansport and the Peninsula—there weren't more than a handful of rebels out here, but they'd be called on for troops to go east and fight in rebel areas like Ford Heights and the Columbia Valley. It was so damn rotten! He remembered burning ranches and plantations during the last flareup.

"Goddamn it, don't those people know they lose more in the wars than Franklin's merchants are costing them?" But he was already speaking to an empty room. Colonel Ardway had dashed outside and was calling to the neighbors to fall out with military equipment.

Roger followed him outside. To the west Franklin flooded the night with ten thousand times Luna's best efforts on Earth. There were soldiers coming up the broad street from the main section of town.

"Who in hell—those aren't rebels," Hastings shouted. They were men in synthi-leather battledress, and they moved too deliberately. Those were Regulars.

There was a roar of motors. A wave of helicopters passed overhead. Roger heard ground effects cars on the greensward, and at least two hundred soldiers were running purposefully up the street toward his house. At each house below a knot of five men fell out of the open formation.

"Turn out! Militia turn out! Rebels!" Colonel Ardway was shouting. He had a dozen men, none in armor, and their best weapons were rifles.

"Take cover! Fire at will!" Ardway screamed. His voice carried determination but it had an edge of fear. "Roger, get the hell inside, you damn fool!"

"But—" The advancing troops were no more than a hundred meters away. One of Ardway's militia fired an automatic rifle from the house next door. The leather-clad troops scattered and someone shouted orders.

Fire lashed out to rake the house. Roger stood in his front yard, dazed, unbelieving, as under Franklin's bright reddish light the nightmare went on. The troops advanced steadily again and there was no more resistance from the militia.

It all happened so quickly. Even as Roger had that thought, the leather lines of men reached him. An officer raised a megaphone.

"I CALL ON YOU TO SURRENDER IN THE NAME OF THE FREE STATES OF WASHINGTON. STAY IN YOUR HOMES AND DO NOT TRY TO RESIST. ARMED MEN WILL BE SHOT WITHOUT WARNING."

A five-man detachment ran past Roger Hastings and through the front door of his home. It brought him from his daze. "Juanita!" He screamed and ran toward his house.

"HALT! HALT OR WE FIRE! YOU MAN, HALT!"

Roger ran on heedlessly.

"SQUAD FIRE."

"BELAY THAT ORDER!"

As Roger reached the door he was grabbed by one of the soldiers and flung against the wall. "Hold it right there," the trooper said grimly. "Monitor, I have a prisoner."

Another soldier came into the broad entryway. He held a clipboard and looked up at the address of the house, checking it against his papers. "Mr. Roger Hastings?" he asked.

Roger nodded dazedly. Then he thought better of it. "No. I'm—"

"Won't do," the soldier said. "I've your picture, Mr. Mayor." Roger nodded again. Who was this man? There had been many accents, and the officer with the clipboard had yet another. "Who are you?" he demanded.

"Lieutenant Jaimie Farquhar of Falkenberg's Mercenary Legion, acting under authority of the Free States of Washington. You're under military detention, Mr. Mayor."

There was more firing outside. Roger's house hadn't been touched. Everything looked so absolutely ordinary. Somehow that added to the horror.

A voice called from upstairs. "His wife and kids are up here, Lieutenant."

"Thank you, Monitor. Ask the lady to come down, please. Mr. Mayor, please don't be concerned for your family. We do not make war on civilians." There were more shots from the street.

A thousand questions boiled in Roger's mind. He stood dazedly trying to sort them into some order. "Have you shot Colonel Ardway? Who's fighting out there?"

"If you mean the fat man in uniform, he's safe enough. We've got him in custody. Unfortunately, some of your militia have ignored the order to surrender, and it's going to be hard on them."

As if in emphasis there was the muffled blast of a grenade, then a burst from a machine pistol answered by the slow deliberate fire of an automatic rifle. The battle noises swept away across the brow of the hill, but sounds of firing and shouted orders carried over the pounding surf.

Farquhar studied his clipboard. "Mayor Hastings and Colonel Ardway. Yes, thank you for identifying him. I've orders to take you both to the command post. Monitor!"

"Sir!"

"Your maniple will remain here on guard. You will allow no one to enter this house. Be polite to Mrs. Hastings, but keep her and the children here. If there is any attempt at looting you will prevent it. This street is under the protection of the Regiment. Understood?"

"Sir!"

The slim officer nodded in satisfaction. "If you'll come with me, Mr. Mayor, there's a car on the greensward." As Roger followed numbly he saw the hall clock. He had been sworn in as mayor less than eleven hours ago.

The Regimental Command Post was in the city council meeting chambers, with Falkenberg's office in a small connecting room. The council room itself was filled with electronic gear and bustled with runners, while Major Savage and Captain Fast controlled the military conquest of Allansport. Falkenberg watched the situation develop in the maps displayed on his desk top.

"It was so fast!" Howard Bannister said. The pudgy secretary of war shook his head in disbelief. "I never thought you could do it."

Falkenberg shrugged. "Light infantry can move, Mr. Secretary. But it cost us. We had to leave the artillery train in orbit with most of our vehicles. I can equip with captured stuff, but we're a bit short on transport." He watched lights flash confusedly for a second on the display before the steady march of red lights blinking to green resumed.

"But now you're without artillery," Bannister said. "And the Patriot army's got none."

"Can't have it both ways. We had less than an hour to offload and get the Dayan boats off planet before the spy satellites came over. Now we've got the town and nobody knows we've landed. If this goes right the first the Confederates'll know about us is when their spy snooper stops working."

"We had some luck," Bannister said. "Boat in harbor, communications out to the mainland—"

"Don't confuse luck with decision factors," Falkenberg answered. "Why would I take an isolated hole full of Loyalists if there weren't some advantages?" Privately he knew better. The telephone exchange taken by infiltrating scouts, the power plant almost unguarded and falling to three minutes' brief combat—it was all luck you could count on with good men, but it was luck. "Excuse me." He touched a stud in response to a low humming note. "Yes?"

"Train coming in from the mines, John Christian," Major Savage reported. "We have the station secured, shall we let it go past the block outside town?"

"Sure, stick with the plan, Jerry. Thanks." The miners coming home after a week's work on the sides of Ranier Crater were due for a surprise.

They waited until all the lights changed to green. Every objective was taken. Power plants, communications, homes of leading citizens, public buildings, railway station and airport, police station . . . Allansport and its eleven thousand citizens were under control. A timer display ticked off the minutes until the spy satellite would be overhead.

Falkenberg spoke to the intercom. "Sergeant Major, we have twenty-nine minutes to get this place looking normal for this time of night. See to it."

"Sir!" Calvin's unemotional voice was reassuring.

"I don't think the Confederates spend much time examining pictures of the boondocks anyway," Falkenberg told Bannister. "But it's best not to take any chances." Motors roared as ground cars and choppers were put under cover. Another helicopter flew overhead looking for telltales.

"As soon as that thing's past get the troops on the packet ship," Falkenberg ordered. "And send in Captain Svoboda, Mayor Hastings, and the local militia colonel—Ardway, wasn't it?"

"Yes, sir," Calvin answered. "Colonel Martine Ardway. I'll see if he's up to it, Colonel."

"Up to it, Sergeant Major? Was he hurt?"

"He had a pistol. Colonel. Twelve millimeter thing, big slug, slow bullet, couldn't penetrate armor but he bruised hell out of two troopers. Monitor Badnikov laid him out with a rifle butt. Surgeon says he'll be all right."

"Good enough. If he's able to come I want him here."

"Sir."

Falkenberg turned back to the desk and used the computer to produce a planetary map. "Where would the supply ship go from here, Mr. Bannister?"

The secretary traced a course. "It would—and will—stay inside this island chain. Nobody but a suicide takes ships into open water on this planet. With no land to interrupt them the seas go sixty meters in storms." He indicated a route from Allansport to Cape Titan, then through an island chain in the Sea of Mariners. "Most ships stop at Preston Bay to deliver metalshop goods for the ranches up on Ford Heights Plateau. The whole area's Patriot territory and you could liberate it with one stroke."

Falkenberg studied the map, then said, "No. So most ships stop there—do some go directly to Astoria?" He pointed to a city eighteen hundred kilometers east of Preston Bay.

"Yes, sometimes—but the Confederates keep a big garrison in Astoria, Colonel. Much larger than the one in Preston Bay. Why go twenty-five hundred kilometers to fight a larger enemy force when there's good Patriot country at half the distance?"

"For the same reason the Confederates don't put much strength at Preston Bay. It's isolated. The Ford Heights ranches are scattered—look, Mr. Secretary, if we take Astoria we have the key to the whole Columbia River Valley. The Confederates won't know if we're going north to Doak's Ferry, east to Grand Forks and on into the capital plains, or west to Ford Heights. If I take Preston Bay first they'll know what I intend because there's only one thing a sane man could do from there."

"But the Columbia Valley people aren't reliable! You won't get good recruits—"

They were interrupted by a knock. Sergeant Major Calvin ushered in Roger Hastings and Martine Ardway. The militiaman had a lump over his left eye, and his cheek was bandaged.

Falkenberg stood to be introduced and offered his hand, which Roger Hastings ignored. Ardway stood rigid for a second, then extended his own. "I won't say I'm pleased to meet you, Colonel Falkenberg, but my compliments on an operation well conducted."

"Thank you, Colonel. Gentlemen, please be seated. You have met Captain Svoboda, my Provost?" Falkenberg indicated a lanky officer in battledress who'd come in with them. "Captain Svoboda will be in command of this town when the Forty-second moves out."

Ardway's eyes narrowed with interest. Falkenberg smiled. "You'll see it soon enough, Colonel. Now, the rules of occupation are simple. As mercenaries, gentlemen, we are subject to the CoDominium's Laws of War. Public property is seized in the name of the Free States. Private holdings are secure, and any property requisitioned will be paid for. Any property used to aid resistance, whether directly or as a place to make conspiracy, will be instantly confiscated."

Ardway and Hastings shrugged. They'd heard all this before. At one time the CD tried to suppress mercenaries. When that failed the Fleet rigidly enforced the Grand Senate's Laws of War, but now the Fleet was weakened by budget cuts and a new outbreak of U.S.-Soviet hatred. New Washington was isolated and it might be years before CD Marines appeared to enforce rules the Grand Senate no longer cared about.

"I have a problem, gentlemen," Falkenberg said. "This city is Loyalist, and I must withdraw my regiment. There aren't any Patriot soldiers yet. I'm leaving enough force to complete the conquest of this peninsula, but Captain Svoboda will have few troops in Allansport itself. Since we cannot occupy the city, it can legitimately be destroyed to prevent it from becoming a base against me."

"You can't!" Hastings protested, jumping to his feet, shattering a glass ashtray. "I was sure all that talk about preserving private property was a lot of crap!" He turned to Bannister. "Howard, I told you last time all you'd succeed in doing was burning down the whole goddamn planet! Now you import soldiers to do it for you! What in God's name can you get from this war?"

"Freedom," Bannister said proudly. "Allansport is a nest of traitors anyway."

"Hold it," Falkenberg said gently.

"Traitors!" Bannister repeated. "You'll get what you deserve, you—"

"TENSH-HUT!" Sergeant Major Calvin's command startled them. "The Colonel said you was to hold it."

"Thank you," Falkenberg said quietly. The silence was louder than the shouts had been. "I said I could burn the city, not that I intended to. However, since I won't I must have hostages." He handed Roger Hastings a computer typescript. "Troops are quartered in homes of these persons. You will note that you and Colonel Ardway are at the top of my list. All will be detained, and anyone who escapes will be replaced by members of his family. Your property and ultimately your lives are dependent on your cooperation with Captain Svoboda until I send a regular garrison here. Is this understood?"

Colonel Ardway nodded grimly. "Yes, sir. I agree to it."

"Thank you," Falkenberg said. "And you, Mr. Mayor?"

"I understand."

"And?" Falkenberg prompted.

"And what? You want me to like it? What kind of sadist are you?"

"I don't care if you like it, Mr. Mayor. I am waiting for you to agree."

"He doesn't understand, Colonel," Martine Ardway said. "Roger, he's asking if you agree to serve as a hostage for the city. The others will be asked as well. If he doesn't get enough to agree he'll burn the city to the ground."

"Oh." Roger felt a cold knife of fear. What a hell of a choice.

"The question is," Falkenberg said, "will you accept the responsibilities of the office you hold and keep your damn people from making trouble?"

Roger swallowed hard. *I wanted to be mayor so I could erase the hatreds of the rebellion.* "Yes. I agree."

"Excellent. Captain Svoboda."

"Sir."

"Take the mayor and Colonel Ardway to your office and interview the others. Notify me when you have enough hostages to ensure security."

"Yes, sir. Gentlemen?" It was hard to read his expression as he showed them to the door. The visor of his helmet was up, but Svoboda's angular face remained in shadow. As he escorted them from the room the intercom buzzed.

"The satellite's overhead," Major Savage reported. "All correct, John Christian. And we've secured the passengers off that train."

The office door closed. Roger Hastings moved like a robot across the bustling city council chamber room, only dimly aware of the bustle of headquarters activities around him. The damn war, the fools, the bloody damned fools—couldn't they ever leave things alone?

IV

A dozen men in camouflage battledress led a slim pretty girl across hard-packed sands to the water's edge. They were glad to get away from the softer sands above the highwater mark nearly a kilometer from the pounding surf. Walking in that had been hell, with shifting powder sands infested with small burrowing carnivores too stupid not to attack a booted man.

The squad climbed wordlessly into the waiting boat while their leader tried to assist the girl. She needed no help. Glenda Ruth wore tan nylon coveralls and an equipment belt, and she knew this planet and its dangers better than the soldiers. Glenda Ruth Horton had been taking care of herself for twenty-four of her twenty-six years.

White sandy beaches dotted with marine life exposed by the low tide stretched in both directions as far as they could see. Only the boat and its crew showed that the planet had human life. When the coxswain started the boat's water jet the whirr sent clouds of tiny sea birds into frantic activity.

The fast packet *Maribell* lay twelve kilometers offshore, well beyond the horizon. When the boat arrived deck cranes dipped to seize her and haul the flatbottomed craft to her davits. Captain Ian Frazer escorted Glenda Ruth to the chart room.

Falkenberg's battle staff waited there impatiently, some sipping whiskey, others staring at charts whose information they had long since absorbed. Many showed signs of seasickness: the eighty-hour voyage from Allansport had been rough, and it hadn't helped that the ship pushed along at thirty-three kilometers an hour, plowing into big swells among the islands.

Ian saluted, then took a glass from the steward and offered it to Glenda Ruth. "Colonel Falkenberg, Miss Horton. Glenda Ruth is the patriot leader in the Columbia Valley. Glenda Ruth, you'll know Secretary Bannister."

She nodded coldly as if she did not care for the rebel

minister, but she put out her hand to Falkenberg and shook his in a thoroughly masculine way. She had other masculine gestures, but even with her brown hair tucked neatly under a visored cap no one would mistake her for a man. She had a heart-shaped face and large green eyes, and her weathered tan might have been envied by the great ladies of the CoDominium.

"My pleasure, Miss Horton," Falkenberg said perfunctorily. "Were you seen?"

Ian Frazer looked pained. "No, sir. We met the rebel group and it seemed safe enough, so Centurion Michaels and I borrowed some clothing from the ranchers and let Glenda Ruth take us to town for our own look." Ian moved to the chart table.

"The fort's up here on the heights." Frazer pointed to the coastal chart. "Typical wall and trench system. Mostly they depend on the Friedlander artillery to control the city and river mouth."

"What's in there, Ian?" Major Savage asked.

"Worst thing is artillery," the Scout Troop commander answered. "Two batteries of 105's and a battery of 155's, all self-propelled. As near as we can figure it's a standard Friedland detached battalion."

"About six hundred Friedlanders, then," Captain Rottermill said thoughtfully. "And we're told there's a regiment of Earth mercenaries. Anything else?"

Ian glanced at Glenda Ruth. "They moved in a squadron of Confederate Regular Cavalry last week," she said. "Light armored cars. We think they're due to move on, because there's nothing for them to do here, but nobody knows where they're going."

"That is odd," Rottermill said. "There's not a proper petrol supply for them here—where would they go?"

Glenda Ruth regarded him thoughtfully. She had little use for mercenaries. Freedom was something to be won, not bought and paid for. But they needed these men, and at least this one had done his homework. "Probably to the Snake Valley. They've got wells and refineries there." She indicated the flatlands where the Snake and Columbia merged at Doak's Ferry six hundred kilometers to the north. "That's Patriot country and cavalry could be useful to supplement the big fortress at the Ferry."

"Damn bad luck all the same, Colonel," Rottermill said. "Nearly three thousand men in that damned fortress and we've not a lot more. How's the security, Ian?"

Frazer shrugged. "Not tight. The Earth goons patrol the city, doing MP duty, checking papers. No trouble avoiding them."

"The Earthies make up most of the guard details too," Glenda Ruth added. "They've got a whole rifle regiment of them."

"We'll not take that place by storm, John Christian," Major Savage said carefully. "Not without losing half the regiment."

"And just what are your soldiers for?" Glenda Ruth demanded. "Do they fight sometimes?"

"Sometimes." Falkenberg studied the sketch his scout commander was making. "Do they have sentries posted, Captain?"

"Yes, sir. Pairs in towers and walking guards. There are radar dishes every hundred meters, and I expect there are body capacitance wires strung outside as well."

"I told you," Secretary Bannister said smugly. There was triumph in his voice, in contrast to the grim concern of Falkenberg and his officers. "You'll have to raise an army to take that place. Ford Heights is our only chance, Colonel. Astoria's too strong for you."

"No!" Glenda Ruth's strong, low-pitched voice commanded attention. "We've risked everything to gather the Columbia Valley Patriots. If you don't take Astoria now, they'll go back to their ranches. I was opposed to starting a new revolution, Howard Bannister. I don't think we can stand another long war like the last one. But I've organized my father's friends, and in two days I'll command a fighting force. If we scatter now I'll never get them to fight again."

"Where is your army—and how large is it?" Falkenberg asked.

"The assembly area is two hundred kilometers north of here. I have six hundred riflemen now and another five thousand coming. A force that size can't hide!" She regarded Falkenberg without enthusiasm. They needed a strong organized nucleus to win, but she was trusting her friends' lives to a man she'd never met. "Colonel, my ranchers can't face Confederate Regulars or Friedland armor without support, but if you take Astoria we'll have a base we can hold."

"Yes." Falkenberg studied the maps as he thought about the girl. She had a more realistic appreciation of irregular forces than Bannister—but how reliable was she? "Mr. Bannister, we can't take Astoria without artillery even with your Ford Heights ranchers. I need Astoria's guns, and the city's the key to the whole campaign anyway.

With it in hand there's a chance to win this war quickly."

"But it can't be done!" Bannister insisted.

"Yet it must be done," Falkenberg reminded him. "And we do have surprise. No Confederate knows we're on this planet and won't for—" he glanced at his pocket computer—"twenty-seven hours, when Weapons Detachment knocks down the snooper. Miss Horton, have you made trouble for Astoria lately?"

"Not for months," she said. Was this mercenary, this man Falkenberg, different? "I only came this far south to meet you."

Captain Frazer's sketch of the fort lay on the table like a death warrant. Falkenberg watched in silence as the scout drew in machine-gun emplacements along the walls.

"I forbid you to risk the revolution on some mad scheme!" Bannister shouted. "Astoria's far too strong. You said so yourself."

Glenda Ruth's rising hopes died again. Bannister was giving the mercenaries a perfect out.

Falkenberg straightened and took a brimming glass from the steward. "Who's junior man here?" He looked around the steel-riveted chart room until he saw an officer near the bulkhead. "Excellent. Lieutenant Fuller was a prisoner on Tanith, Mr. Bannister. Until we caught him—Mark, give us a toast."

"A toast, Colonel?"

"Montrose's toast, Mister. Montrose's toast."

Fear clutched Bannister's guts into a hard ball. Montrose! And Glenda Ruth stared uncomprehendingly, but there was reborn hope in her eyes. . . .

"Aye aye, Colonel." Fuller raised his glass. "He either fears his fate too much, or his deserts are small, who dares not put it to the touch, to win or lose it all."

Bannister's hands shook as the officers drank. Falkenberg's wry smile, Glenda Ruth's answering look of comprehension and admiration—they were all crazy! The lives of all the patriots were at stake, and the man and the girl, both of them, they were insane!

Maribell swung to her anchors three kilometers offshore from Astoria. The fast-moving waters of the Columbia swept around her toward the ocean some nine kilometers downstream, where waves crashed in a line of breakers five meters high. Getting across the harbor bar was a tricky business, and even in the harbor itself the tides were too fierce for the ship to dock.

Maribell's cranes hummed as they swung cargo lighters off her decks. The air-cushion vehicles moved gracelessly across the water and over the sandy beaches to the corrugated aluminum warehouses, where they left cargo containers and picked up empties.

In the fortress above Astoria the officer of the guard dutifully logged the ship's arrival into his journal. It was the most exciting event in two weeks. Since the rebellion had ended there was little for his men to do.

He turned from the tower to look around the encampment. Blasted waste of good armor, he thought. No point in having self-propelled guns as harbor guards. The armor wasn't used, since the guns were in concrete revetments. The lieutenant had been trained in mobile war, and though he could appreciate the need for control over the mouth of New Washington's largest river, he didn't like this duty. There was no glory in manning an impregnable fortress.

Retreat sounded and all over the fort men stopped to face the flags. The Franklin Confederacy colors fluttered down the staff to the salutes of the garrison. Although as guard officer he wasn't supposed to, the lieutenant saluted as the trumpets sang.

Over by the guns men stood at attention, but *they* didn't salute. Friedland mercenaries, they owed the Confederacy no loyalty that hadn't been bought and paid for. The lieutenant admired them as soldiers, but they were not likable. It was worth knowing them, though, since nobody else could handle armor like them. He had managed to make friends with a few. Someday, when the Confederacy was stronger, they would dispense with mercenaries, and until then he wanted to learn all he could. There were rich planets in this sector of space, planets that Franklin could add to the Confederacy now that the rebellion was over. With the CD Fleet weaker every year, opportunities at the edges of inhabited space grew, but only for those ready for them.

When retreat ended he turned back to the harbor. An ugly cargo lighter was coming up the broad roadway to the fort. He frowned, puzzled, and climbed down from the tower.

When he reached the gate the lighter had halted there. Its engine roared, and it was very difficult to understand the driver, a broad-shouldered seaman-stevedore who was insisting on something.

"I got no orders," the Earth mercenary guardsman was protesting. He turned to the lieutenant in relief. "Sir, they say they have a shipment for us on that thing."

"What is it?" the lieutenant shouted. He had to say it again to be heard over the roar of the motors. "What is the cargo?"

"Damned if I know," the driver said cheerfully. "Says on the manifest 'Astoria Fortress, attention supply officer.' Look, Lieutenant, we got to be moving. If the captain don't catch the tide he can't cross the harbor bar tonight and he'll skin me for squawrk bait! Where's the supply officer?"

The lieutenant looked at his watch. After retreat the men dispersed rapidly and supply officers kept short hours. "There's nobody to offload," he shouted.

"Got a crane and crew here," the driver said. "Look, just show me where to put this stuff. We got to sail at slack water."

"Put it out here," the lieutenant said.

"Right. You'll have a hell of a job moving it though." He turned to his companion in the cab. "OK, Charlie, dump it!"

The lieutenant thought of what the supply officer would say when he found he'd have to move the ten-by-five-meter containers. He climbed into the bed of the cargo lighter. In the manifest pocket of each container was a ticket reading "COMMISSARY SUPPLIES."

"Wait," he ordered. "Private, open the gates. Driver, take this over there." He indicated a warehouse near the center of the camp. "Offload at the big doors."

"Right. Hold it, Charlie," Sergeant Major Calvin said cheerfully. "The lieutenant wants the stuff inside." He gave his full attention to driving the ungainly GEM.

The lighter crew worked the crane efficiently, stacking the cargo containers by the warehouse doors. "Sign here," the driver said.

"I—perhaps I better get someone to inventory the cargo."

"Aw, for Christ's sake," the driver protested. "Look, you can see the seals ain't broke—here, I'll write it in. 'Seals intact, but cargo not inspected by recip—' How you spell 'recipient,' Lieutenant?"

"Here, I'll write it for you." He did, and signed with his name and rank. "Have a good voyage?"

"Naw. Rough out there, and getting worse. We got to scoot, more cargo to offload."

"Not for us!"

"Naw, for the town. Thanks, Lieutenant." The GEM pivoted and roared away as the guard lieutenant shook his head. What a mess. He climbed into the tower to write the incident up in the day book. As he wrote he sighed. One hour to dark, and three until he was off duty. It had been a long, dull day.

Three hours before dawn the cargo containers silently opened, and Captain Ian Frazer led his scouts onto the darkened parade ground. Wordlessly they moved toward the revetted guns. One squad formed ranks and marched toward the gates, rifles at slope arms.

The sentries turned. "What the hell?" one said. "It's not time for our relief, who's there?"

"Can it," the corporal of the squad said. "We got orders to go out on some goddam perimeter patrol. Didn't you get the word?"

"Nobody tells me anythin'—uh." The sentry grunted as the corporal struck him with a leather bag of shot. His companion turned quickly, but too late. The squad had already reached him.

Two men stood erect in the starlight at the posts abandoned by the sentries. Astoria was far over the horizon from Franklin, and only a faint red glow to the west indicated the companion planet.

The rest of the squad entered the guardhouse. They moved efficiently among the sleeping relief men, and when they finished the corporal took a communicator from his belt. "Laertes."

On the other side of the parade ground, Captain Frazer led a group of picked men to the radar control center. There was a silent flurry of bayonets and rifle butts. When the brief struggle ended Ian spoke into his communicator. "Hamlet."

There was no answer, but he hadn't expected one.

Down in the city other cargo containers opened in darkened warehouses. Armed men formed into platoons and marched through the dockside streets. The few civilians who saw them scurried for cover; no one had much use for the Earthling mercenaries the Confederates employed.

A full company marched up the hill to the fort. On the other side, away from the city, the rest of the regiment crawled across plowed fields, heedless of radar alarms but careful of the sentries on the walls above. They passed the first line of capacitance wires and Major Savage held his breath. Ten seconds, twenty. He sighed in relief and motioned the troops to advance.

The marching company reached the gate. Sentries challenged them while others in guard towers watched in curiosity. When the gates swung open the tower guards relaxed. The officer of the watch must have had special orders . . .

The company moved into the armored car park. Across the parade ground a sentry peered into the night. Something out there? "Halt! Who's there?" There was only silence.

"See something, Jack?" his companion asked.

"Dunno—look out there. By the bushes. Somethin'—My God, Harry! The field's full of men! CORPORAL OF THE GUARD! Turn out the Guard!" He hesitated before taking the final step, but he was sure enough to risk his sergeant's scathing displeasure. A stabbing finger hit the red alarm button, and lights blazed around the camp perimeter. The sirens hooted, and he had time to see a thousand men in the field near the camp; then a burst of fire caught him, and he fell.

The camp erupted into confusion. The Friedland gunners woke first. They wasted less than a minute before their officers realized the alarm was real. Then the gunners boiled out of the barracks to save their precious armor, but from each revetment, bursts of machine-gun fire cut into them. Gunners fell in heaps as the rest scurried for cover. Many had not brought personal weapons in their haste to serve the guns, and they lost time going back for them.

Major Savage's men reached the walls and clambered over. Alternate sections kept the walls under a ripple of fire, and despite their heavy battle armor the men climbed easily in Washington's lower gravity. Officers sent them to the parade ground where they added their fire to that of the men in the revetments. Hastily set machine guns isolated the artillery emplacements with a curtain of fire.

That artillery was the fort's main defense. Once he was certain it was secure, Major Savage sent his invaders by waves into the camp barracks. They burst in with grenades and rifles ready, taking whole companies before their officers could arrive with the keys to their weapons racks. Savage took the Confederate Regulars that way, and only the Friedlanders had come out fighting; but their efforts were directed toward their guns, and there they had no chance.

Meanwhile the Earth mercenaries, never very steady troops at best, called for quarter; many had not fired a shot. The camp defenders fought as disorganized groups against a disciplined force whose communications worked perfectly.

At the fortress headquarters building the alarms woke Commandant Albert Morris. He listened in disbelief to the sounds of battle, and although he rushed out half-dressed, he was too late. His command was engulfed by nearly four thousand screaming men. Morris stood a moment in indecision, torn by the desire to run to the nearest barracks and rally what forces he could, but he decided his duty was in the communications room. The Capital must be told. Desperately he ran to the radio shack.

Everything seemed normal inside, and he shouted orders to the duty sergeant before he realized he had never seen the man before. He turned to face a squad of leveled rifles. A bright light stabbed from a darker corner of the room.

"Good morning, sir," an even voice said.

Commandant Morris blinked, then carefully raised his hands in surrender. "I've no sidearms. Who the hell are you, anyway?"

"Colonel John Christian Falkenberg, at your service. Will you surrender this base and save your men?"

Morris nodded grimly. He'd seen enough outside to know the battle was hopeless. His career was finished too, no matter what he did, and there was no point in letting the Friedlanders be slaughtered. "Surrender to whom?"

The light flicked off and Morris saw Falkenberg. There was a grim smile on the Colonel's lips. "Why, to the Great Jehovah and the Free States of Washington, Commandant. . . ."

Albert Morris, who was no historian, did not understand the reference. He took the public address mike the grim troopers handed him. Fortress Astoria had fallen.

Twenty-three hundred kilometers to the west at Allansport, Sergeant Sherman White slapped the keys to launch three small solid rockets. They weren't very powerful birds, but they could be set up quickly, and they had the ability to loft a hundred kilos of tiny steel cubes to 140 kilometers. White had very good information on the Confederate satellite's ephemeris; he'd observed it for its past twenty orbits.

The target was invisible over the horizon when Sergeant White launched his interceptors. As it came overhead the small rockets had climbed to meet it. Their radar fuses sought the precise moment, then they exploded in a cloud of shot that rose as it spread. It continued to climb, halted, and began to fall back toward the ground. The satellite detected the attack and beeped alarms to its masters. Then it passed through the cloud at fourteen hundred meters per second relative to the shot. Four of the steel cubes were in its path.

V

Falkenberg studied the manuals on the equipment in the Confederate command car as it raced northward along the Columbia Valley road toward Doak's Ferry. Captain Frazer's scouts were somewhere ahead with the captured cavalry equipment and behind Falkenberg the regiment was strung out piecemeal. There were men on motorcycles, in private trucks, horse-drawn wagons, and on foot.

There'd be more walking soon. The captured cavalry gear was a lucky break, but the Columbia Valley wasn't technologically developed. Most local transport was by animal power, and the farmers relied on the river to ship produce to the deepwater port at Astoria. The river boats and motor fuel were the key to the operation. There wasn't enough of either.

Glenda Ruth Horton had surprised Falkenberg by not arguing about the need for haste, and her ranchers were converging on all the river ports, taking heavy casualties in order to seize boats and fuel before the scattered Confederate occupation forces could destroy them. Meanwhile Falkenberg had recklessly flung the regiment northward.

"Firefight ahead," his driver said. "Another of them one battery posts."

"Right." Falkenberg fiddled with the unfamiliar controls until the map came into sharper focus, then activated the comm circuit.

"Sir," Captain Frazer answered. "They've got a battery of 105's and an MG Company in there. More than I can handle."

"Right, pass it by. Let Miss Horton's ranchers keep it under siege. Found any more fuel?"

Frazer laughed unpleasantly. "Colonel, you can adjust the carburetors in these things to handle a lot, but Christ, they bloody well won't run on paraffin. There's not even farm machinery out here! We're running on fumes now, and damned low-grade fumes at that."

"Yeah." The Confederates were getting smarter. For the first hundred kilometers they took fueling stations intact, but now, unless the patriots were already in control, the fuel was torched before Frazer's fast-moving scouts arrived. "Keep going as best you can, Captain."

"Sir. Out."

"We got some reserve fuel with the guns," Sergeant Major Calvin reminded him. The big RSM sat in the turret of the command caravan and at frequent intervals fondled the thirty-mm cannon there. It wasn't much of a weapon, but it had been a long time since the RSM was gunner in an armored vehicle. He was hoping to get in some fighting.

"No. Those guns have to move east to the passes. They're sure to send a reaction force from the capital, Top Soldier."

But would they? Falkenberg wondered. Instead of moving northwest from the capital to reinforce the fortress at Doak's Ferry, they might send troops by sea to retake Astoria. It would be a stupid move, and Falkenberg counted on the Confederates acting intelligently. As far as anyone knew, the Astoria Fortress guns dominated the river mouth.

A detachment of Weapons Battalion remained there with antiaircraft rockets to keep reconnaissance at a distance, but otherwise Astoria was held only by a hastily raised Patriot force stiffened with a handful of mercenaries. The Friedlander guns had been taken out at night.

If Falkenberg's plan worked, by the time the Confederates knew what they faced, Astoria would be strongly held by Valley Patriot armies, and other Patriot forces would have crossed the water to hold Allansport. It was a risky battle plan, but it had one merit: it was the only one that could succeed.

Leading elements of the regiment covered half the six hundred kilometers north to Doak's Ferry in ten hours. Behind Falkenberg's racing lead groups the main body of the regiment moved more ponderously, pausing to blast out pockets of resistance where that could be quickly done, otherwise bypassing them for the Patriot irregulars to starve into submission. The whole Valley was rising, and the further north Falkenberg went the greater the number of Patriots he encountered. When they reached the four-hundred-kilometer point, he sent Glenda Ruth Horton eastward toward the passes to join Major Savage and the Friedland artillery. Like the regiment, the ranchers moved by a variety of means: helicopters, GEM's, trucks, mules, and on foot.

"Real boot straps," Hiram Black said. Black was a short, wind-browned rancher commissioned colonel by the Free States

Council and sent with Falkenberg to aid in controlling rebel forces. Falkenberg liked the man's dry humor and hard realism. "General Falkenberg, we got the damnedest collection in the history of warfare."

"Yes." There was nothing more to say. In addition to the confused transport situation, there was no standardization of weapons: they had hunting pieces, weapons taken from the enemy, the regiment's own equipment, and stockpiles of arms smuggled in by the Free States before Falkenberg's arrival. "That's what computers are for," Falkenberg said.

"Crossroad coming up," the driver warned. "Hang on." The crossing was probably registered by the guns of an untaken post eight kilometers ahead. Frazer's cavalry had blinded its hilltop observation radars before passing it by, but the battery would have had brief sights of the command car.

The driver suddenly halted. There was a sharp whistle, and an explosion rocked the caravan. Shrapnel rattled off the armored sides. The car bounded into life and accelerated.

"Ten credits you owe me, Sergeant Major," the driver said. "Told you they'd expect me to speed up."

"Think I wanted to win the bet, Carpenter?" Calvin asked.

They drove through rolling hills covered with the golden tassels of corn plants. Genetic engineering had made New Washington's native grain one of the most valuable food crops in space. Superficially similar to Earth maize, this corn had a growing cycle of two local years. Toward the end of the cycle hydrostatic pressures built up until it exploded, but if harvested in the dry period New Washington corn was high-protein dehydrated food energy, palatable when cooked in water, and good fodder for animals as well.

"Ought to be getting past the opposition now," Hiram Black said. "Expect the Feddies'll be pulling back to the fort at Doak's Ferry from here on."

His estimate was confirmed a half hour later when Falkenberg's comm set squawked into action. "We're in a little town called Madselin, Colonel," Frazer said. "Used to be a garrison here, but they're running up the road. There's a citizen's committee to welcome us."

"To hell with the citizen's committee," Falkenberg snapped. "Pursue the enemy!"

"Colonel, I'd be very pleased to do so, but I've no petrol at all."

Falkenberg nodded grimly. "Captain Frazer, I want the scouts as far north as they can get. Isn't there *any* transport?"

There was a long silence. "Well, sir, there are bicycles . . ."

"Then use bicycles, by God! Use whatever you have to, Captain, but until you are stopped by the enemy you will continue the advance, bypassing concentrations. Snap at their heels. Ian, they're scared. They don't know what's chasing them, and if you keep the pressure on they won't stop to find out. Keep going, laddie. I'll bail you out if you get in trouble."

"Aye, aye, Colonel. See you in Doak's Ferry."

"Correct. Out."

"Can you keep that promise, General?" Hiram Black asked.

Falkenberg's pale blue eyes stared through the rancher. "That depends on how reliable your Glenda Ruth Horton is, Colonel Black. Your ranchers are supposed to be gathering along the Valley. With that threat to their flanks the Confederates will not dare form a defense line south of Doak's Ferry. If your Patriots don't show up then it's another story entirely." He shrugged. Behind him the Regiment was strung out along three hundred kilometers of roads, its only flank protection its speed and the enemy's uncertainties. "It's up to her in more ways than one," Falkenberg continued. "She said the main body of Friedland armor was in the capital area."

Hiram Black sucked his teeth in a very unmilitary way. "General, if Glenda Ruth's sure of something, you can damn well count on it."

Sergeant Major Calvin grunted. The noise spoke his thoughts better than words. It was a hell of a thing when the life of the Forty-second had to depend on a young colonial girl.

"How did she come to command the Valley ranchers, anyway?" Falkenberg asked.

"Inherited it," Black answered. "Her father was one hell of a man, General. Got himself killed in the last battle of the first revolution. She'd been his chief of staff. Old Josh trusted her more'n he did most of his officers. So would I, if I was you, General."

"I already do." To Falkenberg the regiment was more than a mercenary force. Like any work of art, it was an instrument perfectly forged—its existence and perfection its own reason for existence.

But unlike any work of art, because the regiment was a military unit, it had to fight battles and take casualties. The men who died in battle were mourned. They weren't the regiment, though, and it would exist when every man now in it was dead. The Forty-second had faced defeat before and might find it again—but this time the regiment itself was at hazard. Falkenberg was gambling not merely their lives, but the Forty-second itself.

He studied the battle maps as they raced northward. By keeping the enemy off balance, one regiment could do the work of five. Eventually, though, the Confederates would no longer retreat. They were falling back on their fortress at Doak's Ferry, gathering strength and concentrating for a battle that Falkenberg could never win. Therefore that battle must not be fought until the ranchers had concentrated. Meanwhile, the regiment must bypass Doak's Ferry and turn east to the mountain passes, closing them before the Friedland armor and Covenant Highlanders could debauch onto the western plains.

"Think you'll make it?" Hiram Black asked. He watched as Falkenberg manipulated controls to move symbols across the map tank in the command car. "Seems to me the Friedlanders will reach the pass before you can."

"They will," Falkenberg said. "And if they get through, we're lost." He twirled a knob, sending a bright blip representing Major Savage with the artillery racing diagonally from Astoria to Hillyer Gap, while the main force of the regiment continued up the Columbia, then turned east to the mountains, covering two legs of a triangle. "Jerry Savage could be there first, but he won't have enough force to stop them." Another set of symbols crawled across the map. Instead of a distinctly formed body, this was a series of rivulets coming together at the pass. "Miss Horton has also promised to be there with reinforcements and supplies—enough to hold in the first battle, anyway. If they delay the Friedlanders long enough for the rest of us to get there, we'll own the entire agricultural area of New Washington. The revolution will be better than half over."

"And what if she can't get there—or they can't hold the Friedlanders and Covenant boys?" Hiram Black asked.

Sergeant Major Calvin grunted again.

VI

Hillyer Gap was a six-kilometer-wide hilly notch in the high mountain chain. The Aldine Mountains ran roughly northwest to southeast, and were joined at their midpoint by the southward stretching Temblors. Just at the join was the Gap that connected the capital city plain to the east with the Columbia Valley to the west.

Major Jeremy Savage regarded his position with satisfaction. He not only had the twenty-six guns taken from the Friedlanders at Astoria, but another dozen captured in scattered outposts along the lower Columbia, and all were securely dug in behind hills overlooking the Gap. Forward of the guns were six companies of infantry, Second Battalion and half of Third, with a thousand ranchers behind in reserve.

"We won't be outflanked, anyway," Centurion Bryant observed. "Ought to hold just fine, sir."

"We've a chance," Major Savage agreed. "Thanks to Miss Horton. You must have driven your men right along."

Glenda Ruth shrugged. Her irregulars had run low on fuel 180 kilometers west of the Gap, and she'd brought them on foot in one forced march of thirty hours, after sending her ammunition supplies ahead with the last drops of gasoline. "I just came on myself, Major. Wasn't a question of driving them, the men followed right enough."

Jeremy Savage looked at her quickly. The slender girl was not very pretty at the moment, with her coveralls streaked with mud and grease, her hair falling in strings from under her cap, but he'd rather have seen her just then than the current Miss Universe. With her troops and ammunition supplies he had a chance to hold this position. "I suppose they did at that." Centurion Bryant turned away quickly with something caught in his throat.

"Can we hold until Colonel Falkenberg gets here?" Glenda Ruth asked. "I expect them to send everything they've got."

"We sincerely hope they do," Jeremy Savage answered. "It's our only chance, you know. If that armor gets onto open ground . . ."

"There's no other way onto the plains, Major," she replied. "The Temblors go right on down to the Matson swamplands, and nobody's fool enough to risk armor there. Great Bend's Patriot country. Between the swamps and the Patriot irregulars it'd take a week to cross the Matson. If they're comin' by land, they're comin' through here."

"And they'll be coming," Savage finished for her. "They'll want to relieve the Doak's Ferry fortress before we can get it under close siege. At least that was John Christian's plan, and he's usually right."

Glenda Ruth used her binoculars to examine the road. There was nothing out there—yet. "This colonel of yours. What's in this for him? Nobody gets rich on what we can pay."

"I should think you'd be glad enough we're here," Jeremy said.

"Oh, I'm glad all right. In 240 hours Falkenberg's isolated every Confederate garrison west of the Temblors. The capital city forces are the only army left to fight—you've almost liberated the planet in one campaign."

"Luck," Jeremy Savage murmured. "Lots of it, all good."

"Heh." Glenda Ruth was contemptuous. "I don't believe in that, no more do you. Sure, with the Confederates scattered out on occupation duty anybody who could get troops to move fast enough could cut the Feddies up before they got into big enough formations to resist. The fact is, Major, nobody believed that could be done except on maps. Not with real troops—and he did it. That's not luck, that's genius."

Savage shrugged. "I wouldn't dispute that."

"No more would I. Now answer this—just what is a real military genius doing commanding mercenaries on a jerkwater agricultural planet? A man like that should be Lieutenant General of the CoDominium."

"The CD isn't interested in military genius, Miss Horton. The Grand Senate wants obedience, not brilliance."

"Maybe. I hadn't heard Lermontov was a fool, and they made him Grand Admiral. O. K, the CoDominium had no use for Falkenberg. But why Washington, Major? With that regiment you could take anyplace but Sparta and give the Brotherhoods a run for it there." She swept the horizon with the binoculars, and Savage could not see her eyes.

This girl disturbed him. No other Free State official questioned the good fortune of hiring Falkenberg. "The regimental council voted to come here because we were sick of Tanith, Miss Horton."

"Sure." She continued to scan the bleak foothills in front of them. "Look, I'd better get some rest if we've got a fight coming—and we do. Look just at the horizon on the left side of the road." As she turned away Centurion Bryant's communicator buzzed. The outposts had spotted the scout elements of an armored task force.

As Glenda Ruth walked back to her bunker, her head felt as if it would begin spinning. She had been born on New Washington and was used to the planet's forty-hour rotation period, but lack of sleep made her almost intoxicated even so.

Walking on pillows, she told herself. That had been Harley Hastings' description of how they felt when they didn't come in until dawn.

Is Harley out there with the armor? she wondered. She hoped not. It would never have worked, but he's such a good boy. Too much of a boy though, trying to act like a man. While it's nice to be treated like a lady sometimes, he could never believe I could do anything for myself at all. . . .

Two ranchers stood guard with one of Falkenberg's corporals at her bunker. The corporal came to a rigid present; the ranchers called a greeting. Glenda Ruth made a gesture, halfway between a wave and a return of the corporal's salute and went inside. The contrast couldn't have been greater, she thought. Her ranchers weren't about to make themselves look silly, with present arms, and salutes, and the rest of it.

She stumbled inside and wrapped herself in a thin blanket without undressing. Somehow the incident outside bothered her. Falkenberg's men were military professionals. All of them. What were they doing on New Washington?

Howard Bannister asked them here. He even offered them land for a permanent settlement and he had no right to do that. There's no way to control a military force like that without keeping a big standing army, and the cure is worse than the disease.

But without Falkenberg the revolution's doomed.

And what happens if we win it? What will Falkenberg do after it's over? Leave? I'm afraid of him because he's not the type to just leave.

And, she thought, to be honest Falkenberg's a very attractive man. I liked just the way he toasted. Howard gave him the perfect out, but he didn't take it.

She could still remember him with his glass lifted, an

enigmatic smile on his lips—and then he went into the packing crates himself, along with Ian and his men.

But courage isn't anything special. What we need here is loyalty, and that he's never promised at all . . .

There was no one to advise her. Her father was the only man she'd ever really respected. Before he was killed, he'd tried to tell her that winning the war was only a small part of the problem. There were countries on Earth that had gone through fifty bloody revolutions before they were lucky enough to have a tyrant gain control and stop them. Revolution's the easy part, as her father used to say. Ruling afterwards—that's something else entirely.

As she fell asleep she saw Falkenberg in a dream. What if Falkenberg wouldn't let them keep their revolution? His hard features softened in a swirling mist. He was wearing military uniform and sat at a desk, Sergeant Major Calvin at his side.

"These can live. Kill those. Send these to the mines," Falkenberg ordered.

The big sergeant moved tiny figures that looked like model soldiers, but they weren't all troops. One was her father. Another was a group of her ranchers. And they weren't models at all. They were real people reduced to miniatures whose screams could barely be heard as the stern voice continued to pronounce their dooms. . . .

Brigadier Wilfred von Mellenthin looked up the hill toward the rebel troop emplacements, then climbed back down into his command caravan to wait for his scouts to report. He had insisted that the Confederacy send his armor west immediately after the news arrived that Astoria had fallen, but the General Staff wouldn't let him go.

Fools, he thought. The staff said it was too big a risk. Von Mellenthin's Friedlander armored task force was the Confederacy's best military unit, and it couldn't be risked in a trap.

Now the General Staff was convinced that they faced only one regiment of mercenaries. One regiment, and that must have taken heavy casualties in storming Astoria. So the staff said. Von Mellenthin studied the map table and shrugged.

Someone was holding the Gap, and he had plenty of respect for the New Washington ranchers. Given rugged terrain like that in front of him, they could put up a good fight. A good enough fight to blunt his force. But, he decided, it was worth it. Beyond the Gap was open terrain, and the ranchers would have no chance there.

The map changed and flowed as he watched. Scouts reported, and von Mellenthin's staff officers checked the reports, correlated the data, and fed it onto his displays. The map showed well-dug-in infantry, far more of it than von Mellenthin had expected. That damned Falkenberg. The man had an uncanny ability to move troops.

Von Mellenthin turned to the Chief of Staff. "Horst, do you think he has heavy guns here already?"

Oberst Carnap shrugged. "*Weiss nicht,* Brigadier. Every hour gives Falkenberg time to dig in at the Gap, and we have lost many hours."

"Not Falkenberg," von Mellenthin corrected. "He is now investing the fortress at Doak's Ferry. We have reports from the commandant there. Most of Falkenberg's force must be far to the west."

He turned back to his maps. They were as complete as they could be without closer observation.

As if reading his mind, Carnap asked, "Shall I send scouting forces, Brigadier?"

Von Mellenthin stared at the map as if it might tell him one more detail, but it would not. "No. We go through with everything," he said in sudden decision. "Kick their arses, don't pee on them."

"*Jawohl.*" Carnap spoke quietly into the command circuit. Then he looked up again. "It is my duty to point out the risk, Brigadier. We will take heavy losses if they have brought up artillery."

"I know. But if we fail to get through now, we may never relieve the fortress in time. Half the war is lost when Doak's Ferry is taken. Better heavy casualties immediately than a long war. I will lead the attack myself. You will remain with the command caravan."

"*Jawohl,* Brigadier."

Von Mellenthin climbed out of the heavy caravan and into a medium tank. He took his place in the turret, then spoke quietly to the driver. "Forward."

The armor brushed the infantry screens aside as if they had not been there. Von Mellenthin's tanks and their supporting infantry cooperated perfectly to pin down and root out the opposition. The column moved swiftly forward to cut the enemy into disorganized fragments for the following Covenanter infantry to mop up.

Von Mellenthin was chewing up the blocking force piecemeal as his brigade rushed deeper into the Gap. It was all too easy, and he thought he knew why.

The sweating tankers approached the irregular ridge at the very top of the pass. Suddenly a fury of small arms and mortar fire swept across them. The tanks moved on, but the infantry scrambled for cover. Armor and infantry were separated for a moment, and at that instant his lead tanks reached the mine fields.

Brigadier von Mellenthin began to worry. Logic told him the mine fields couldn't be wide or dense, and if he punched through he would reach the soft headquarters areas of his enemies. Once there his tanks would make short work of the headquarters and depots, the Covenanter infantry would secure the pass, and his brigade could charge across the open fields beyond.

But—if the defenders had better transport than the General Staff believed, and thus had thousands of mines, he was dooming his armor.

"Evaluation," he demanded. The repeater screen in his command tank swam, then showed the updated maps. His force was bunched up, and his supporting infantry was pinned and taking casualties. "Recommendation?"

"Send scouting forces," Oberst Carnap's voice urged.

Von Mellenthin considered it for a moment. Compromises in war are often worse than either course of action. A small force could be lost without gaining anything. Divided forces can be defeated in detail. He had only moments to reach a decision. "Boot, don't spatter," he said. "We go forward."

They reached the narrowest part of the Gap. His force now bunched together even more, and his drivers, up to now automatically avoiding terrain features that might be registered by artillery, had to approach conspicuous landmarks. Brigadier von Mellenthin gritted his teeth.

The artillery salvo was perfectly delivered. The brigade had less than a quarter-minute warning as the radars picked up the incoming projectiles. Then the shells exploded all at once, dropping among his tanks to brush away the last of the covering infantry.

As the barrage lifted, hundreds of men appeared from the ground itself. A near perfect volley of infantry-carried anti-tank rockets slammed into his tanks. Then the radars showed more incoming mail—and swam in confusion.

"*Ja*, that too," von Mellenthin muttered. His counter-battery screens showed a shower of gunk.

The defenders were firing chaff, hundreds of thousands of tiny metal chips which slowly drifted to the ground. Neither side could use radar to aim indirect fire, but Von Mellenthin's armor was under visual observation, while the enemy guns had never been precisely located.

Another time-on-target salvo landed. "Damned good shooting," von Mellenthin muttered to his driver. There weren't more than five seconds between the first and the last shell's arrival.

The brigade was being torn apart on this killing ground. The lead elements ran into more mine fields. Defending infantry crouched in holes and ditches, tiny little groups that his covering infantry could sweep aside in a moment if it could get forward, but the infantry was cut off by the barrages falling behind and around the tanks.

There was no room to maneuver and no infantry support, the classic nightmare of an armor commander. The already rough ground was strewn with pits and ditches. High explosive antitank shells fell all around his force. There were not many hits yet, but any disabled tanks could be pounded to pieces, and there was nothing to shoot back at. The lead tanks were under steady fire, and the assault slowed.

The enemy expended shells at a prodigal rate. Could they keep it up? If they ran out of shells it was all over. Von Mellenthin hesitated. Every moment kept his armor in hell.

Doubts undermined his determination. Only the Confederate General Staff told him he faced no more than Falkenberg's Legion, and the staff had been wrong before. Whatever was out there had taken Astoria before the commandant could send a single message. At almost the same moment the observation satellite was killed over Allansport. Every fortress along the Columbia was invested within hours. Surely not even Falkenberg could do that with no more than one regiment!

What was he fighting? If he faced a well-supplied force with transport enough to continue this bombardment for hours, not minutes, the brigade was lost. His brigade, the finest armor in the worlds, lost to the faulty intelligence of these damned colonials!

"Recall the force. Consolidate at Station Hildebrand." The orders flashed out, and the tanks fell back, rescuing the pinned infantry and covering their withdrawal. When the brigade assembled east of the Gap, von Mellenthin had lost an eighth of his tanks, and he doubted if he would recover any of them.

VII

The honor guard presented arms as the command caravan unbuttoned. Falkenberg acknowledged their salutes and strode briskly into the staff bunker. "Tensh-Hut!" Sergeant Major Calvin commanded.

"Carry on, gentlemen. Major Savage, you'll be pleased to know I've brought the regimental artillery. We landed it yesterday. Getting a bit thin, wasn't it?"

"That it was, John Christian," Jeremy Savage answered grimly. "If the battle had lasted another hour we'd have been out of everything. Miss Horton, you can relax now—the colonel said carry on."

"I wasn't sure," Glenda Ruth huffed. She glanced outside where the honor guard was dispersing and scowled in disapproval. "I'd hate to be shot for not bowing properly."

Officers and troopers in the CP tensed, but nothing happened. Falkenberg turned to Major Savage. "What were the casualties, Major?"

"Heavy, sir. We have 283 effectives remaining in Second Battalion."

Falkenberg's face was impassive. "And how many walking wounded?"

"Sir, that includes the walking wounded."

"I see." Sixty-five percent casualties, not including the walking wounded. "And Third?"

"I couldn't put together a corporal's guard from the two companies. The survivors are assigned to headquarters duties."

"What's holding the line out there, Jerry?" Falkenberg demanded.

"Irregulars and what's left of Second Battalion, Colonel. We are rather glad to see you, don't you know?"

Glenda Ruth Horton had a momentary struggle with herself. Whatever she might think about all the senseless militaristic rituals Falkenberg was addicted to, honesty demanded

576

that she say something. "Colonel, I owe you an apology. I'm sorry I implied that your men wouldn't fight at Astoria."

"The question is, Miss Horton, will yours? I have two batteries of the Forty-second's artillery, but I can add nothing to the line itself. My troops are investing Doaks Ferry, my cavalry and First Battalion are on Ford Heights, and the regiment will be scattered for three more days. Are you saying your ranchers can't do as well as my mercenaries?"

She nodded unhappily. "Colonel, we could never have stood up to that attack. The Second's senior centurion told me many of his mortars were served by only one man before the battle ended. We'll never have men that steady."

Falkenberg looked relieved. "Centurion Bryant survived, then."

"Why—yes."

"Then the Second still lives." Falkenberg nodded to himself in satisfaction.

"But we can't stop another attack by that armor!" Glenda Ruth protested.

"But maybe we won't have to," Falkenberg said. "Miss Horton, I'm betting that von Mellenthin won't risk his armor until the infantry has cleared a hole. From his view he's tried and run into something he can't handle. He doesn't know how close it was.

"Meanwhile, thanks to your efforts in locating transport, we have the artillery partly resupplied. Let's see what we can do with what we've got."

Three hours later they looked up from the maps. "That's it, then," Falkenberg said.

"Yes." Glenda Ruth looked over the troop dispositions. "Those forward patrols are the key to it all," she said carefully.

"Of course." He reached into his kit bag. "Have a drink?"

"Now?" But why not? "Thank you, I will." He poured two mess cups partly full of whiskey and handed her one. "I can't stay long, though," she said.

He shrugged and raised the glass. "A willing foe. But not too willing," he said.

She hesitated a moment, then drank. "It's a game to you, isn't it?"

"Perhaps. And to you?"

"I hate it. I hate all of it. I didn't want to start the rebellion again." She shuddered. "I've had enough of killing and crippled men and burned farms—"

"Then why are you here?" he asked. There was no mockery in his voice—and no contempt. The question was genuine.

"My friends asked me to lead them, and I couldn't let them down."

"A good reason," Falkenberg said.

"Thank you." She drained the cup. "I've got to go now. I have to get into my battle armor."

"That seems reasonable, although the bunkers are well built."

"I won't be in a bunker, Colonel. I'm going on patrol with my ranchers."

Falkenberg regarded her critically. "I wouldn't think that wise, Miss Horton. Personal courage in a commanding officer is an admirable trait, but—"

"I know." She smiled softly. "But it needn't be demonstrated because it is assumed, right? Not with us. I can't order the ranchers, and I don't have years of tradition to keep them— that's the reason for all the ceremonials, isn't it?" she asked in surprise.

Falkenberg ignored the question. "The point is, the men follow you. I doubt they'd fight as hard for me if you're killed."

"Irrelevant, Colonel. Believe me, I don't want to take this patrol out, but if I don't take the first one, there may never be another. We're not used to holding lines, and it's taking some doing to keep my troops steady."

"And so you have to shame them into going out."

She shrugged. "If I go, they will."

"I'll lend you a Centurion and some headquarters guards."

"No. Send the same troops with me that you'll send with any other Patriot force." She swayed for a moment. Lack of sleep and the whiskey and the knot of fear in her guts combined for a moment. She held the edge of the desk for a second while Falkenberg looked at her.

"Oh damn," she said. Then she smiled slightly. "John Christian Falkenberg, don't you see why it has to be this way?"

He nodded. "I don't have to like it. All right, get your final briefing from the sergeant major in thirty-five minutes. Good luck, Miss Horton."

"Thank you." She hesitated but there was nothing more to say.

The patrol moved silently through low scrub brush. Something fluttered past her face; a flying squirrel, she thought. There were a lot of gliding creatures on New Washington.

The low hill smelled of toluenes from the shells and mortars that had fallen there in the last battle. The night was pitch dark, with only Franklin's dull red loom at the far western horizon, so faint that it was sensed, not seen. Another flying fox chittered past, darting after insects and screeching into the night.

A dozen ranchers followed in single file. Behind them came a communications maniple from the Forty-second's band. Glenda wondered what they did with their instruments when they went onto combat duty, and wished she'd asked. The last man on the trail was a Sergeant Hruska, who'd been sent along by Sergeant Major Calvin at the last minute. Glenda Ruth had been glad to see him, although she felt guilty about having him along.

And that's silly, she told herself. Men think that way. I don't have to. I'm not trying to prove anything.

The ranchers carried rifles. Three of Falkenberg's men did also. The other two had communications gear, and Sergeant Hruska had a submachine gun. It seemed a pitifully small force to contest ground with Covenant Highlanders.

They passed through the final outposts of her nervous ranchers and moved into the valleys between the hills. Glenda Ruth felt completely alone in the silence of the night. She wondered if the others felt it too. Certainly the ranchers did. They were all afraid. What of the mercenaries? she wondered. They weren't alone, anyway. They were with comrades who shared their meals and their bunkers.

As long as one of Falkenberg's men was alive, there would be someone to care about those lost. And they do care, she told herself. Sergeant Major Calvin, with his gruff dismissal of casualty reports. "Bah. Another trooper," he'd said when they told him an old messmate had bought it in the fight with the armor. Men.

She tried to imagine the thoughts of a mercenary soldier, but it was impossible. They were too alien.

Was Falkenberg like the rest of them?

They were nearly a kilometer beyond the lines when she found a narrow gulley two meters deep. It meandered down the hillsides along the approaches to the outposts behind her, and any attacking force assaulting her sector would have to pass it. She motioned the men into the ditch.

Waiting was hardest of all. The ranchers continually moved about, and she had to crawl along the gulley to whisper them into silence. Hours went by, each an agony of waiting. She glanced at her watch to see that no time had elapsed since the last time she'd looked, and resolved not to look again for a full fifteen minutes.

After what seemed fifteen minutes, she waited for what was

surely another ten, then looked to see that only eleven minutes had passed altogether. She turned in disgust to stare into the night, blinking against the shapes that formed; shapes that couldn't be real.

Why do I keep thinking about Falkenberg? And why did I call him by his first name?

The vision of him in her dream still haunted her as well. In the starlit gloom she could almost see the miniature figures again. Falkenberg's impassive orders rang in her ears. "Kill this one. Send this one to the mines." He could do that, she thought. He could—

The miniatures were joined by larger figures in battle armor. With a sudden start she knew they were real. Two men stood motionless in the draw below her.

She touched Sergeant Hruska and pointed. The trooper looked carefully and nodded. As they watched, more figures joined the pair of scouts, until soon there were nearly fifty of them in the fold of the hill two hundred meters away. They were too far for her squad's weapons to have much effect, and a whispered command sent Hruska crawling along the gulley to order the men to stay down and be silent.

The group continued to grow. She couldn't see them all, and since she could count nearly a hundred she must be observing the assembly area of a full company. Were these the dreaded Highlanders? Memories of her father's defeat came unwanted, and she brushed them away. They were only hired men—but they fought for glory, and somehow that was enough to make them terrible.

After a long time the enemy began moving toward her.

They formed a V-shape with the point aimed almost directly at her position, and she searched for the ends of the formation. What she saw made her gasp.

Four hundred meters to her left was another company of soldiers in double file. They moved silently and swiftly up the hill, and the lead elements were already far beyond her position. Frantically she looked to the right, focusing the big electronic light-amplifying glasses—and saw another company of men half a kilometer away. A full Highlander Battalion was moving right up her hill in an inverted M, and the group in front of her was the connecting sweep to link the assault columns. In minutes they would be among the ranchers in the defense line.

Still she waited, until the dozen Highlanders of the point were ten meters from her. She shouted commands. "Up and at them! Fire!" From both ends of her ditch the mercenaries' automatic weapons chattered, then their fire was joined by her riflemen. The point was cut down to a man, and Sergeant Hruska directed fire on the main body, while Glenda Ruth shouted into her communicator.

"Fire Mission. Flash Uncle Four!"

There was a moment's delay which seemed like years. "Flash Uncle Four." Another long pause. "On the way," an unemotional voice answered. She thought it sounded like Falkenberg, but she was too busy to care.

"Reporting," she said. "At least one battalion of light infantry in assault columns is moving up Hill 905 along ridges Uncle and Zebra."

"They're shifting left." She looked up to see Hruska. The noncom pointed to the company in front of her position. Small knots of men curled leftward. They hugged the ground and were visible only for seconds.

"Move some men to that end of the gulley," she ordered. It was too late to shift artillery fire. Anyway, if the Highlanders ever got to the top of the ridge, the ranchers wouldn't hold them. She held her breath and waited.

There was the scream of incoming artillery, then the night was lit by bright flashes. VT shells fell among the distant enemy on the left flank. "Pour it on!" she shouted into the communicator. "On target!"

"Right. On the way."

She was sure it was Falkenberg himself at the other end. Catlike she grinned in the dark. What was a colonel doing as a telephone orderly? Was he worried about her? She almost laughed at the thought. Certainly he was, the ranchers would be hard to handle without her.

The ridge above erupted in fire. Mortars and grenades joined the artillery pounding the leftward assault column. Glenda Ruth paused to examine the critical situation to the right. The assault force five hundred meters away was untouched and continued to advance toward the top of the ridge. it was going to be close.

She let the artillery hold its target another five minutes while her riflemen engaged the company in front of her, then took up the radio again. The right-hand column had nearly reached the ridges, and she wondered if she had waited too long.

"Fire mission. Flash Zebra Nine."

"Zebra Nine," the emotionless voice replied. There was a short delay, then, "On the way." The fire lifted from the left flank almost immediately, and two minutes later began to fall five hundred meters to the right.

"They're flanking us, Miss," Sergeant Hruska reported. She'd been so busy directing artillery at the assaults against the ridge line that she'd actually forgotten her twenty men were engaged in a firefight with over a hundred enemies. "Shall we pull back?" Hruska asked.

She tried to think, but it was impossible in the noise and confusion. The assault columns were still moving ahead, and she had the only group that could observe the entire attack, Every precious shell had to count "No. We'll hold on here."

"Right, Miss." The sergeant seemed to be enjoying himself. He moved away to direct the automatic weapons and rifle fire. How long can we hold? Glenda Ruth wondered.

She let the artillery continue to pound the right-hand assault force for twenty minutes. By then the Highlanders had nearly surrounded her and were ready to assault from the rear. Prayerfully she lifted the radio again.

"Fire Mission. Give me everything you can on Jack Five—and for God's sake don't go over. We're at Jack Six."

"Flash Jack Five," the voice acknowledged immediately. There was a pause. "On the way." They were the most beautiful words she'd ever heard.

Now they waited. The Highlanders rose to charge. A wild sound filled the night. MY GOD, PIPES! She thought. But even as the infantry moved the pipes were drowned by the whistle of artillery. Glenda Ruth dove to the bottom of the gulley and saw that the rest of her command had done the same.

The world erupted in sound. Millions of tiny fragments at enormous velocity filled the night with death. Cautiously she lifted a small periscope to look behind her.

The Highlander company had dissolved. Shells were falling among dead men, lifting them to be torn apart again and again as the radar-fused shells fell among them. Glenda Ruth swallowed hard and swept the glass around. The left assault company had reformed and was turning back to attack the ridge. "Fire Flash Uncle Four," she said softly.

"Interrogative."

"FLASH UNCLE FOUR!"

"Uncle Four. On the way."

As soon as the fire lifted from behind them her men returned to the lip of the gulley and resumed firing, but the sounds began to die away.

"We're down to the ammo in the guns now, Miss," Hruska reported. "May I have your spare magazines?"

She realized with a sudden start that she had yet to fire a single shot.

✧ ✧ ✧

The night wore on. Whenever the enemy formed up to assault her position he was cut apart by the merciless artillery. Once she asked for a box barrage all around her gulley— by that time the men were down to three shots in each rifle, and the automatic weapons had no ammo at all. The toneless voice simply answered, "On the way."

An hour before dawn nothing moved on the hill.

VIII

The thin notes of a military trumpet sounded across the barren hills of the Gap. The ridges east of Falkenberg's battle line lay dead, their foliage cut to shreds by shell fragments, the very earth thrown into crazy-quilt craters partly burying the dead. A cool wind blew through the Gap, but it couldn't dispel the smells of nitro and death.

The trumpet sounded again. Falkenberg's glasses showed three unarmed Highlander officers carrying a white flag. An ensign was dispatched to meet them, and the young officer returned with a blindfolded Highlander major.

"Major MacRae, Fourth Covenant Infantry," the officer introduced himself after the blindfold was removed. He blinked at the bright lights of the bunker. "You'll be Colonel Falkenberg."

"Yes. What can we do for you, Major?"

"I've orders to offer a truce for burying the dead. Twenty hours, Colonel, if that's agreeable."

"No. Four days and nights—160 hours, Major," Falkenberg said.

"A hundred sixty hours, Colonel?" The burly Highlander regarded Falkenberg suspiciously. "You'll want that time to complete your defenses."

"Perhaps. But twenty hours is not enough time to transfer the wounded men. I'll return all of yours—under parole, of course. It's no secret I'm short of medical supplies, and they'll receive better care from their own surgeons."

The Highlander's face showed nothing, but he paused. "You wouldn't tell me how many there be?" He was silent for a moment, then speaking very fast, he said, "The time you set is within my discretion, Colonel." He held out a bulky dispatch case. "My credentials and instructions. 'Twas a bloody battle, Colonel. How many of my laddies have ye killed?"

Falkenberg and Glenda Ruth glanced at each other. There is a bond between those who have been in combat together, and it can include those of the other side. The Covenant officer stood impassively, unwilling to say more, but his eyes pleaded with them.

"We counted 409 bodies, Major," Glenda Ruth told him gently. "And—" she looked at Falkenberg, who nodded. "We brought in another 370 wounded." The usual combat ratio is four men wounded to each killed; nearly sixteen hundred Covenanters must have been taken out of action in the assault. Toward the end the Highlanders were losing men in their efforts to recover their dead and wounded.

"Less than four hundred," the major said sadly. He stood to rigid attention. "Hae your men search the ground well, Colonel. There's aye more o' my lads out there." He saluted and waited for the blindfold to be fixed again. "I thank you, Colonel."

As the mercenary officer was led away Falkenberg turned to Glenda Ruth with a wistful smile. "Try to bribe him with money and he'd challenge me, but when I offer him his men back—" He shook his head sadly.

"Have they really given up?" Glenda Ruth asked.

"Yes. The truce finishes it. Their only chance was to break through before we brought up more ammunition and reserves, and they know it."

"But why? In the last revolution they were so terrible, and now—why?"

"It's the weakness of mercenaries," Falkenberg explained crisply. "The fruits of victory belong to our employers, not us. Friedland can't lose her armor and Covenant can't lose her men, or they've nothing more to sell."

"But they fought before!"

"Sure, in a fluid battle of maneuver. A frontal assault is always the most costly kind of battle. They tried to force the passage, and we beat them fairly. Honor is satisfied. Now the Confederacy will have to bring up its own Regulars if they want to force a way through the Gap. I don't think they'll squander men like that, and anyway it takes time. Meanwhile we've got to go to Allansport and deal with a crisis."

"What's wrong there?" she asked.

This came in regimental code this morning." He handed her a message flimsy.

FALKENBERG FROM SVOBODA BREAK PATRIOT ARMY LOOTING ALLANSPORT STOP REQUEST COURT OF INQUIRY INVESTIGATE POSSIBLE VIOLATIONS OF LAWS OF WAR STOP EXTREMELY INADVISABLE FOR ME TO

COMPLY WITH YOUR ORDERS TO JOIN REGIMENT STOP
PATRIOT ARMY ACTIONS PROVOKING SABOTAGE AND
REVOLT AMONG TOWNSPEOPLE AND MINERS STOP MY
SECURITY FORCES MAY BE REQUIRED TO HOLD THE
CITY STOP AWAIT YOUR ORDERS STOP RESPECTFULLY
ANTON SVOBODA BREAK BREAK MESSAGE ENDSXXX

She read it twice. "My God, Colonel—what's going on there?"

"I don't know," he said grimly. "I intend to find out. Will
you come with me as a representative of the Patriot Council?"

"Of course—but shouldn't we send for Howard Bannister?
The Council elected him President."

"If we need him we'll get him. Sergeant Major."

"Sir!"

"Put Miss Horton's things on the troop carrier with mine.
I'll take the Headquarters Guard platoon to Allansport."

"Sir. Colonel, you'll want me along."

"Will I? I suppose so, Sergeant Major. Get your gear aboard."

"Sir."

"It's probably already there, of course. Let's move out."

The personnel carrier took them to a small airfield where
a jet waited. It was one of forty on the planet, and it would
carry a hundred men; but it burned fuel needed for ammunition transport. Until the oil fields around Doak's Ferry could
be secured it was fuel they could hardly afford.

The plane flew across Patriot-held areas, staying well away
from the isolated Confederate strongpoints remaining west of
the Gap. Aircraft had little chance of surviving in a combat
environment when any infantryman could carry target-seeking
rockets, while trucks could carry equipment to defeat airborne
countermeasures. They crossed the Columbia Valley and turned
southwest over the broad forests of Ford Heights Plateau, then
west again to avoid Preston Bay where pockets of Confederates remained after the fall of the main fortress.

"You do the same thing, don't you?" Glenda Ruth said
suddenly. "When we assaulted Preston Bay you let my people
take the casualties."

Falkenberg nodded. "For two reasons. I'm as reluctant to
lose troops as the Highlanders—and without the regiment you'd
not hold the Patriot areas a thousand hours. You need us as
an intact force, not a pile of corpses."

"Yes." It was true enough, but those were her friends who'd
died in the assault. Would the outcome be worth it? Would
Falkenberg *let* it be worth it?

Captain Svoboda met them at the Allansport field. "Glad to see you, sir. It's pretty bad in town."

"Just what happened, Captain?" Svoboda looked critically at Glenda Ruth, but Falkenberg said, "Report."

"Yes, sir. When the provisional governor arrived I turned over administration of the city as ordered. At that time the peninsula was pacified, largely due to the efforts of Mayor Hastings, who wants to avoid damage to the city. Hastings believes Franklin will send a large army from the home planet and says he sees no point in getting Loyalists killed and the city burned in resistance that won't change the final outcome anyway."

"Poor Roger—he always tries to be reasonable, and it never works," Glenda Ruth said. "But Franklin will send troops."

"Possibly," Falkenberg said. "But it takes time for them to mobilize and organize transport. Continue, Captain Svoboda."

"Sir. The Governor posted a list of proscribed persons whose property was forfeit. If that wasn't enough, he told his troops that if they found any Confederate government property, they could keep half its value. You'll see the results when we get to town, Colonel. There was looting and fire that my security forces and the local fire people only barely managed to control."

"Oh, Lord," Glenda Ruth murmured. "Why?"

Svoboda curled his lip. "Looters often do that, Miss Horton. You can't let troops sack a city and not expect damage. The outcome was predictable, Colonel. Many townspeople took to the hills, particularly the miners. They've taken several of the mining towns back."

Captain Svoboda shrugged helplessly. "The railway is cut. The city itself is secure, but I can't say how long. You only left me 150 troops to control eleven thousand people, which I did with hostages. The Governor brought another nine hundred men and that's not enough to rule *their* way. He's asked Preston Bay for more soldiers."

"Is that where the first group came from?" Glenda Ruth asked.

"Yes, Miss. A number of them, anyway."

"Then its understandable if not excusable, Colonel," she said. "Many ranches on Ford Heights were burned out by Loyalists in the first revolution. I suppose they think they're paying the Loyalists back."

Falkenberg nodded. "Sergeant Major!"

"Sir!"

"Put the Guard in battle armor and combat weapons. Captain, we are going to pay a call on your provisional governor. Alert your men."

"Colonel!" Glenda Ruth protested. "You—what are you going to do?"

"Miss Horton, I left an undamaged town, which is now a nest of opposition. I'd like to know why. Let's go, Svoboda."

City Hall stood undamaged among burned-out streets. The town smelled of scorched wood and death, as if there'd been a major battle fought in the downtown area. Falkenberg sat impassive as Glenda Ruth stared unbelievingly at what had been the richest city outside the capital area.

"I tried, Colonel," Svoboda muttered. He blamed himself anyway. "I'd have had to fire on the Patriots and arrest the governor. You were out of communication, and I didn't want to take that responsibility without orders. Should I have, sir?"

Falkenberg didn't answer. Possible violations of mercenary contracts were always delicate situations. Finally he said, "I can hardly blame you for not wanting to involve the regiment in war with our sponsors."

The Patriot irregular guards at City Hall protested as Falkenberg strode briskly toward the Governor's office. They tried to bar the way, but when they saw his forty guardsmen in battle armor they moved aside.

The governor was a broad-shouldered former rancher who'd done well in commodities speculation. He was a skilled salesman, master of the friendly grip on the elbow and pat on the shoulder, the casual words in the right places, but he had no experience in military command. He glanced nervously at Sergeant Major Calvin and the grimfaced guards outside his office as Glenda introduced Falkenberg.

"Governor Jack Silana," she said. "The governor was active in the first revolution, and without his financial help we'd never have been able to pay your passage here, Colonel."

"I see." Falkenberg ignored the governor's offered hand. "Did you authorize more looting, Governor?" he asked. "I see some's still going on."

"Your mercenaries have all the tax money," Silana protested. He tried to grin. "My troops are being ruined to pay you. Why shouldn't the Fedsymps contribute to the war? Anyway, the real trouble began when a town girl insulted one of my soldiers. He struck her. Some townspeople interfered, and his comrades came to help. A riot started and someone called out the garrison to stop it—"

"And you lost control," Falkenberg said.

"The traitors got no more than they deserve anyway! Don't think *they* didn't loot cities when they won, Colonel. These men have seen ranches burned out, and they know Allansport's a nest of Fedsymp traitors."

"I see." Falkenberg turned to his Provost. "Captain, had you formally relinquished control to Governor Silana before this happened?"

"Yes, sir. As ordered."

"Then it's none of the regiment's concern. Were any of our troops involved?"

Svoboda nodded unhappily. "I have seven troopers and Sergeant Magee in arrest, sir. I've held summary court on six others myself."

"What charges are you preferring against Magee?" Falkenberg had personally promoted Magee once. The man had a mean streak, but he was a good soldier.

"Looting. Drunk on duty. Theft. And conduct prejudicial."

"And the others?"

"Three rapes, four grand theft, and one murder, sir. They're being held for a court. I also request an inquiry into my conduct as commander."

"Granted. Sergeant Major."

"Sir!"

"Take custody of the prisoners and convene a General Court. What officers have we for an investigation?"

"Captain Greenwood's posted for light duty only by the surgeon, sir."

"Excellent. Have him conduct a formal inquiry into Captain Svoboda's administration of the city."

"Sir."

"What will happen to those men?" Glenda Ruth asked.

"The rapists and murderer will be hanged if convicted. Hard duty for the rest."

"You'd hang your own men?" she asked. She didn't believe it, and her voice showed it.

"I cannot allow rot in my regiment," Falkenberg snapped. "In any event the Confederacy will protest this violation of the Laws of War to the CD."

Governor Silana laughed. "We protested often enough in the last revolution, and nothing came of it. I think we can chance it."

"Perhaps. I take it you will do nothing about this?"

"I'll issue orders for the looting to stop."

"Haven't you done so already?"

"Well, yes, Colonel—but the men, well, they're about over their mad now, I think."

"If previous orders haven't stopped it, more won't. You'll have to be prepared to punish violators. Are you?'

"I'll be damned if I'll hang my own soldiers to protect traitors!"

"I see. Governor, how do you propose to pacify this area?"

"I've sent for reinforcements—"

"Yes. Thank you. If you'll excuse us, Governor, Miss Horton and I have an errand." He hustled Glenda Ruth out of the office. "Sergeant Major, bring Mayor Hastings and Colonel Ardway to Captain Svoboda's office."

"They shot Colonel Ardway," Svoboda said. "The mayor's in the city jail."

"Jail?" Falkenberg muttered.

"Yes, sir. I had the hostages in the hotel, but Governor Silana—"

"I see. Carry on, Sergeant Major."

"Sir!"

"What do you want now, you bloody bastard?" Hastings demanded ten minutes later. The mayor was haggard, with several days' growth of stubble, and his face and hands showed the grime of confinement without proper hygiene facilities.

"One thing at a time, Mr. Mayor. Any trouble, Sergeant Major?"

Calvin grinned. "Not much, sir. The officer didn't want no problems with the Guard—Colonel, they got all them hostages crammed into cells."

"What have you done with my wife and children?" Roger Hastings demanded frantically. "1 haven't heard anything for days."

Falkenberg looked inquiringly at Svoboda but got only a headshake. "See to the mayor's family, Sergeant Major. Bring them here. Mr. Hastings, do I understand that you believe this is my doing?"

"If you hadn't taken this city . . . ."

"That was a legitimate military operation. Have you charges to bring against my troops?"

"How would I know?" Hastings felt weak. He hadn't been fed properly for days, and he was sick with worry about his family. As he leaned against the desk he saw Glenda Ruth for the first time. "You too, eh?"

"It was none of my doing, Roger." He had almost become her father-in-law. She wondered where young Lieutenant Harley

Hastings was. Although she'd broken their engagement long ago, their disagreements had mostly been political, and they were still friends. "I'm sorry."

"It was your doing, you and the damned rebels. Oh, sure, you don't like burning cities and killing civilians, but it happens all the same—and you started the war. You can't shed the responsibility."

Falkenberg interrupted him. "Mr. Mayor, we have mutual interests still. This peninsula raises little food, and your people cannot survive without supplies. I'm told over a thousand of your people were killed in the riots, and nearly that many are in the hills. Can you get the automated factories and smelters operating with what's left?"

"After all this you expect me to—I won't do one damn thing for you, Falkenberg!"

"I didn't ask if you would, only if it could be done."

"What difference does it make?"

"I doubt you want to see the rest of your people starving, Mr. Mayor. Captain, take the mayor to your quarters and get him cleaned up. By the time you've done that Sergeant Major Calvin will know what happened to his family." Falkenberg nodded dismissal and turned to Glenda Ruth. "Well, Miss Horton? Have you seen enough?"

"I don't understand."

"I am requesting you to relieve Silana of his post and return administration of this city to the regiment. Will you do it?"

Good Lord! she thought. "I haven't the authority."

"You've got more influence in the Patriot army than anyone else. The Council may not like it, but they'll take it from you. Meanwhile, I'm sending for the Sappers to rebuild this city and get the foundries going."

Everything moves so fast. Not even Joshua Horton had made things happen like this man. "Colonel, what is your interest in Allansport?"

"It's the only industrial area we control. There will be no more military supplies from off planet. We hold everything west of the Temblors. The Matson Valley is rising in support of the revolution, and we'll have it soon. We can follow the Matson to Vancouver and take that—and then what?"

"Why—then we take the capital city! The revolution's over!"

"No. That was the mistake you made last time. Do you really think your farmers, even with the Forty-second, can move onto level, roaded ground and fight set-piece battles? We've no chance under those conditions."

"But—" He was right. She'd always known it. When they

defeated the Friedlanders at the Gap she'd dared hope, but the capital plains were not Hillyer Gap. "So it's back to attrition."

Falkenberg nodded. "We do hold all the agricultural areas. The Confederates will begin to feel the pinch soon enough. Meanwhile we chew around the edges. Franklin will have to let go—there's no profit in keeping colonies that cost money. They may try landing armies from the home world, but they'll not take us by surprise and they don't have *that* big an army. Eventually we'll wear them down."

She nodded sadly. It would be a long war after all, and she'd have to be in it, always raising fresh troops as the ranchers began to go home again—it would be tough enough holding what they had when people realized what they were in for. "But how do we pay your troops in a long war?"

"Perhaps you'll have to do without us."

"You know we can't. And you've always known it. What do you want?"

"Right now I want you to relieve Silana. Immediately."

"What's the hurry? As you say, it's going to be a long war."

"It'll be longer if more of the city is burned." He almost told her more, and cursed himself for the weakness of temptation. She was only a girl, and he'd known thousands of them since Grace left him all those years ago. The bond of combat wouldn't explain it, he'd known other girls who were competent officers, many of them—so why was he tempted at all? "I'm sorry," he said gruffly. "I must insist. As you say, you can't do without us."

Glenda Ruth had grown up among politicians and for four years had been a revolutionary leader herself. She knew Falkenberg's momentary hesitation was important, and that she'd never find out what it meant.

What was under that mask? Was there a man in there making all those whirlwind decisions? Falkenberg dominated every situation he fell into, and a man like that wanted more than money. The vision of Falkenberg seated at a desk pronouncing dooms on her people haunted her still.

And yet. There was more. A warrior leader of warriors who had won the adoration of uneducated privates—and men like Jeremy Savage as well. She'd never met anyone like him.

"I'll do it." She smiled and walked across the room to stand next to him. "I don't know why, but I'll do it. Have you got any friends, John Christian Falkenberg?"

The question startled him. Automatically he answered. "Command can have no friends, Miss Horton."

She smiled again. "You have one now. There's a condition to my offer. From now on, you call me Glenda Ruth. Please?"

A curious smile formed on the soldier's face. He regarded her with amusement, but there was something more as well. "It doesn't work, you know."

"What doesn't work?"

"Whatever you're trying. Like me, you've command responsibilities. It's lonely, and you don't like that. The reason command has no friends, Glenda Ruth, is not merely to spare the commander the pain of sending friends to their death. If you haven't learned the rest of it, learn it now, because some day you'll have to betray either your friends or your command, and that's a choice worth avoiding."

What am I doing? Am I trying to protect the revolution by getting to know him better—or is he right, I've no friends either, and he's the only man I ever met who could be— She let the thought fade out, and laid her hand on his for a brief second. "Let's go tell Governor Silana, John Christian. And let the little girl worry about her own emotions, will you? She knows what she's doing."

He stood next to her. They were very close and for a moment she thought he intended to kiss her. "No, you don't."

She wanted to answer, but he was already leaving the room and she had to hurry to catch him.

IX

"I say we only gave the Fedsymp traitors what they deserved!" Jack Silana shouted. There was a mutter of approval from the delegates, and open cheers in the bleachers overlooking the gymnasium floor. "I have great respect for Glenda Ruth, but she is not old Joshua," Silana continued. "Her action in removing me from a post given by President Bannister was without authority. I demand that the Council repudiate it." There was more applause as Silana took his seat.

Glenda Ruth remained at her seat for a moment. She looked carefully at each of the thirty men and women at the horseshoe table, trying to estimate just how many votes she had. Not a majority, certainly, but perhaps a dozen. She wouldn't have to persuade more than three or four to abandon the Bannister-Silana faction, but what then? The bloc she led was no more solid than Bannister's coalition. Just who would govern the Free States?

More men were seated on the gymnasium floor beyond the council table. They were witnesses, but their placement at the focus of the Council's attention made it look as if Falkenberg and his impassive officers might be in the dock. Mayor Hastings sat with Falkenberg, and the illusion was heightened by the signs of harsh treatment he'd received. Some of his friends looked even worse.

Beyond the witnesses the spectators chattered among themselves as if this were a basketball game rather than a solemn meeting of the supreme authority for three-quarters of New Washington. A gymnasium didn't seem a very dignified place to meet anyway, but there was no larger hall in Astoria Fortress.

Finally she stood. "No, I am not my father," she began. "He would have had Jack Silana shot for his actions!"

"Give it to 'em, Glenda Ruth!" someone shouted from the balcony.

594

Howard Bannister looked up in surprise. "We will have order here!"

"Hump it, you Preston Bay bastard!" the voice replied. The elderly rancher was joined by someone below. "Damn right, Ford Heights don't control the Valley!" There were cheers at that.

"Order! Order!" Bannister's commands drowned the shouting as the technicians turned up the amplifiers to full volume. "Miss Horton, you have the floor."

"Thank you. What I was trying to say is that we did not start this revolution to destroy New Washington! We must live with the Loyalists once it is over, and—"

"Fedsymp! She was engaged to a Feddie soldier!" "Shut up and let her talk!" "Order! ORDER!"

Falkenberg sat motionless as the hall returned to silence, and Glenda Ruth tried to speak again. "Bloody noisy lot," Jeremy Savage murmured.

Falkenberg shrugged. "Victory does that to politicians."

Glenda Ruth described the conditions she'd seen in Allansport. She told of the burned-out city, hostages herded into jail cells—

"Serves the Fedsymps right!" someone interrupted, but she managed to continue before her supporters could answer.

"Certainly they are Loyalists. Over a third of the people in the territory we control are. Loyalists are a majority in the capital city. Will it help if we persecute their friends here?"

"We won't ever take the capital the way we're fighting!" "Damn right! Time we moved on the Feddies." "Send the mercenaries in there, let 'em earn the taxes we pay!"

This time Bannister made little effort to control the crowd. They were saying what he had proposed to the Council, and one reason he supported Silana was because he needed the governor's merchant bloc with him on the war issue. After the crowd had shouted enough about renewing the war, Bannister used the microphone to restore order and let Glenda Ruth speak.

The Council adjourned for the day without deciding anything. Falkenberg waited for Glenda Ruth and walked out with her. "I'm glad we didn't get a vote today," she told him. "I don't think we'd have won."

"Noisy beggars," Major Savage observed again.

"Democracy at work," Falkenberg said coldly. "What do you need to convince the Council that Silana is unfit as a governor?"

"That's not the real issue, John," she answered. "It's really the war. No one is satisfied with what's being done."

"I should have thought we were doing splendidly," Savage retorted. "The last Confederate thrust into the Matson ran into your ambush as planned."

"Yes, that was brilliant," Glenda Ruth said.

"Hardly. It was the only possible attack route," Falkenberg answered. "You're very quiet, Mayor Hastings." They had left the gymnasium and were crossing the parade ground to the barracks where the Friedlanders had been quartered. Falkenberg's troops had it now, and they kept the Allansport officials with them.

"I'm afraid of that vote," Hastings said. "If they send Silana back, we'll lose everything."

"Then support me!" Falkenberg snapped. "My engineers already have the automated factories and mills in reasonable shape. With some help from you they'd be running again. Then I'd have real arguments against Silana's policies."

"But that's treason," Hastings protested. "You need the Allansport industry for your war effort. Colonel, it's a hell of a way to thank you for rescuing my family from that butcher. but I can't do it."

"I suppose you're expecting a miracle to save you?" Falkenberg asked.

"No. But what happens if you win? How long will you stay on the Ranier Peninsula? Bannister's people will be there one of these days—Colonel, my only chance is for the Confederacy to bring in Franklin troops and crush the lot of you!"

"And you'll be ruled from Franklin," Glenda Ruth said. "They won't give you as much home rule as you had last time."

"I know," Roger said miserably. "But what can I do? This revolt ruined our best chance. Franklin might have been reasonable in time—I was going to give good government to everyone. But you finished that."

"All of Franklin's satraps weren't like you, Roger," Glenda Ruth said. "And don't forget their war policies! They'd have got us sucked into their schemes and eventually we'd have been fighting the CoDominium itself. Colonel Falkenberg can tell you what it's like to be victim of a CD punitive expedition!"

"Christ, I don't know what to do," Roger said unhappily.

Falkenberg muttered something which the others didn't catch, then said, "Glenda Ruth, if you will excuse me, Major Savage and I have administrative matters to discuss. I would be pleased if you'd join me for dinner in the Officers' Mess at nineteen hundred hours."

"Why—thank you, John. I'd like to, but I must see the other delegates tonight. We may be able to win that vote tomorrow."

Falkenberg shrugged. "I doubt it. If you can't win it, can you delay it?"

"For a few days, perhaps—why?"

"It might help, that's all. If you can't make dinner, the regiment's officers are entertaining guests in the mess until quite late. Will you join us when you're done with politics?"

"Thank you. Yes, I will." As she crossed the parade ground to her own quarters, she wished she knew what Falkenberg and Savage were discussing. It wouldn't be administration—did it matter what the Council decided?

She looked forward to seeing John later, and the anticipation made her feel guilt. What is there about the man that does this to me? He's handsome enough, broad shoulders and thoroughly military—nonsense. I am damned if I'll believe in some atavistic compulsion to fall in love with warriors, I don't care what the anthropologists say. So why do I want to be with him? She pushed the thought away. There was something more important to think about. What would Falkenberg do if the Council voted against him? And beyond that, what would she do when he did it?

Falkenberg led Roger Hastings into his office. "Please be seated, Mr. Mayor."

Roger sat uncomfortably. "Look, Colonel, I'd like to help, but—"

"Mayor Hastings, would the owners of the Allansport industries rather have half of a going concern, or all of nothing?"

"What's that supposed to mean?"

"I will guarantee protection of the foundries and smelters in return for a half interest in them." When Hastings looked up in astonishment, Falkenberg continued. "Why not? Silana will seize them anyway. If my regiment is part owner, I may be able to stop him."

"It wouldn't mean anything if I granted it," Hastings protested. "The owners are on Franklin."

"You are the ranking Confederate official for the entire Ranier Peninsula," Falkenberg said carefully. "Legal or not, I want your signature on this grant." He handed Roger a sheaf of papers.

Hastings read them carefully. "Colonel, this also confirms a land grant given by the rebel government! I can't do that!"

"Why not? It's all public land—and that *is* in your power. The document states that in exchange for protection of lives and property of the citizens of Allansport you are awarding certain lands to my regiment. It notes that you don't consider a previous grant by the Patriot Government to be valid. There's no question of treason—you do want Allansport protected against Silana, don't you?"

"Are you offering to double-cross the Patriots?"

"No. My contract with Bannister specifically states that I cannot be made party to violations of the Laws of War. This document hires me to enforce them in an area already pacified. It doesn't state who might violate them."

"You're skating on damned thin ice, Colonel. If the Council ever saw this paper they'd hang you for treason!" Roger read it again. "I see no harm in signing, but I tell you in advance the Confederacy won't honor it. If Franklin wins this they'll throw you off this planet—if they don't have you shot."

"Let me worry about the future, Mr. Mayor. Right now *your* problem is protecting your people. You can help with that by signing."

"I doubt it," Hastings said. He reached for a pen. "So long as you know there isn't a shadow of validity to this because I'll be countermanded from the home world—" he scrawled his name and title across the papers and handed them back to Falkenberg.

Glenda Ruth could hear the regimental party across the wide parade ground. As she approached with Hiram Black they seemed to be breasting their way upstream through waves of sound, the crash of drums, throbbing, wailing bagpipes, mixed with off-key songs from intoxicated male baritones.

It was worse inside. As they entered a flashing saber swept within inches of her face. A junior captain saluted and apologized in a stream of words. "I was showing Oberleutnant Marcks a new parry I learned on Sparta, Miss. Please forgive me?" When she nodded the captain drew his companion to one side and the saber whirled again.

"That's a Friedland officer—all the Friedlanders are here," Glenda Ruth said. Hiram Black nodded grimly. The captured mercenaries wore dress uniform, green and gold contrasting with the blue and gold of Falkenberg's men. Medals flashed in the bright overhead lights. She looked across the glittering room and saw the colonel at a table on the far side.

Falkenberg and his companion stood when she reached the table after a perilous journey across the crowded floor. Pipers marched past pouring out more sound.

Falkenberg's face was flushed, and she wondered if he were drunk. "Miss Horton, may I present Major Oscar von Thoma," he said formally. "Major von Thoma commands the Friedland artillery battalion."

"I—" She didn't know what to say. The Friedlanders were enemies, and Falkenberg was introducing her to the officer as his guest. "My pleasure," she stammered. "And this is Colonel Hiram Black."

Von Thoma clicked his heels. The men stood stiffly until she was seated next to Falkenberg. That kind of chivalry had almost vanished, but somehow it seemed appropriate here. As the stewards brought glasses von Thoma turned to Falkenberg. "You ask too much," he said. "Besides, you may have fired the lands from the barrels by then."

"If we have we'll reduce the price," Falkenberg said cheerfully. He noted Glenda Ruth's puzzled expression. "Major von Thoma has asked if he can buy his guns back when the campaign is ended. He doesn't care for my terms."

Hiram Black observed drily, "Seems to me the Council's goin' to want a say in fixin' that price, General Falkenberg."

Falkenberg snorted contemptuously. "No."

He is drunk, Glenda Ruth thought. It doesn't show much, but—do I know him that well already?

"Those guns were taken by the Forty-second without Council help. I will see to it that they aren't used against Patriots, and the Council has no further interest in the matter." Falkenberg turned to Glenda Ruth. "Will you win the vote tomorrow?"

"There won't be a vote tomorrow."

"So you can't win," Falkenberg muttered. "Expected that. What about the war policy vote?"

"They'll be debating for the next two days—" she looked nervously at Major von Thoma. "I don't want to be impolite, but should we discuss that with him at the table?"

"I understand." Von Thoma got unsteadily to his feet. "We will speak of this again, Colonel. It has been my pleasure, Miss Horton. Colonel Black." He bowed stiffly to each and went to the big center table where a number of Friedland officers were drinking with Falkenberg's.

"John, is this wise?" she asked. "Some of the Councillors are already accusing you of not wanting to fight—"

"Hell, they're callin' him a traitor," Black interrupted. "Soft on Fedsymps, consortin' with the enemy—they don't even like you recruitin' new men to replace your losses." Black hoisted a glass of whiskey and drained it at one gulp. "I wish some of 'em had been ridin' up the Valley with us! Glenda Ruth, that was some ride. And when Captain Frazer runs out of fuel, Falkenberg tells him, cool as you please, to use bicycles!" Black chuckled in rememberance.

"I'm serious!" Glenda Ruth protested. "John, Bannister hates you. I think he always has." The stewards brought whiskey for Falkenberg. "Wine or whiskey, Miss?" one asked.

"Wine—John, please, they're going to order you to attack the capital!"

"Interesting." His features tightened suddenly, and his eyes became alert. Then he relaxed and let the whiskey take effect. "If we obey those orders I'll need Major von Thoma's good offices to get *my* equipment back. Doesn't Bannister know what will happen if we let them catch us on those open plains?"

"Howie Bannister knows his way 'round a conspiracy better'n he does a battlefield, General," Black observed. "We give him the secretary of war title 'cause we thought he'd drive a hard bargain with you, but he's not much on battles."

"I've noticed," Falkenberg said. He laid his hand on Glenda Ruth's arm and gently stroked it. It was the first time he'd ever touched her, and she sat very still. "This is supposed to be a party," Falkenberg laughed. He looked up and caught the mess president's eye. "Lieutenant, have Pipe Major give us a song!"

The room was instantly still. Glenda Ruth felt the warmth of Falkenberg's hand. The soft caress promised much more, and she was suddenly glad, but there was a stab of fear as well. He'd spoken so softly, yet all those people had stopped their drinking, the drums ceased, the pipes, everything, at his one careless nod. Power like that was frightening.

The burly Pipe Major selected a young tenor. One pipe and a snare drum played as he began to sing. "Oh Hae ye nae heard o' the false Sakeld, Hae ye nae heard o' the keen Lord Scroop? For he ha' ta'en the Kinmont Willie, to Haribee for to hang him up . . ."

"John, please listen," she pleaded.

> "They hae ta'en the news to the Bold Bacleugh,
> in Branksome Ha where he did lay,
> that Lord Scroop has ta'en the Kinmont Willie,
> between the hours of night and day.
>
> He has ta'en the table wi' his hand,
> he has made the red wine spring on hie.
> Now Christ's curse be on my head, he said,
> but avenged of Lord Scroop I will be."

"John, really."

"Perhaps you should listen," he said gently. He raised his glass as the young voice rose and the tempo gathered.

"O is my basnet a widow's curch?
Or my lance the Wand o' the willow tree?
And is my hand a lady's lilly hand,
That this English lord should lightly me?"

The song ended. Falkenberg signaled to the steward. "We'll have more to drink," he said. "And no more talk of politics."

They spent the rest of the evening enjoying the party. Both the Friedlanders and Falkenberg's mercenary officers were educated men, and it was a very pleasant evening for Glenda Ruth to have a room full of warriors competing to please her. They taught her the dances and wild songs of a dozen cultures, and she drank far too much.

Finally he stood. "I'll see you back to your quarters," Falkenberg told her.

"All right." She took his arm, and they went through the thinning crowd. "Do you often have parties like this?" she asked.

"When we can." They reached the door. A white-coated private appeared from nowhere to open it for them. He had a jagged scar across his face that ran down his neck until it disappeared into his collar, and she thought she would be afraid to meet him anywhere else.

"Good night, Miss," the private said. His voice had a strange quality, almost husky, as if he were very concerned about her.

They crossed the parade ground. The night was clear, and the sky was full of stars. The sounds of the river rushing by came faintly up to the old fortress.

"I didn't want it ever to end," she said.

"Why?"

"Because—you've built an artificial world in there. A wall of glory to shut out the realities of what we do. And when it ends we go back to the war." And back to whatever you meant when you had that boy sing that sinister old border ballad.

"That's well put. A wall of glory. Perhaps that's what we do."

They reached the block of suites assigned to the senior officers. Her door was next to his. She stood in front of it, reluctant to go inside. The room would be empty, and tomorrow there was the Council, and—she turned to him and said bitterly, "Does it have to end? I was happy for a few minutes. Now—"

"It doesn't have to end, but do you know what you're doing?"

"No." She turned away from her own door and opened his. He followed, but didn't go inside. She stood in the doorway for a moment, then laughed. "I was going to say something silly. Something like, 'Let's have a last drink.' But I wouldn't have meant that, and you'd have known it, so what's the point of games?"

"There is no point to games. Not between us. Games are for soldiers' girls and lovers."

"John—my God, John, are you as lonely as I am?"

"Yes. Of course."

"Then we can't let the party end. Not while there's a single moment it can go on." She went inside his room.

After a few moments he followed and closed the door.

During the night she was able to forget the conflict between them, but when she left his quarters in the morning the ballad returned to haunt her.

She knew she must do something, but she couldn't warn Bannister. The Council, the revolution, independence, none of them had lost their importance; but though she would serve those causes she felt apart from them.

"I'm a perfect fool," she told herself. But fool or not, she could not warn Bannister. Finally she persuaded the President to meet John away from the shouting masses of the Council Chamber.

Bannister came directly to the point. "Colonel, we can't keep a large army in the field indefinitely. Miss Horton's Valley ranchers may be willing to pay these taxes, but most of our people can't."

"Just what did you expect when you began this?" Falkenberg asked.

"A long war," Bannister admitted. "But your initial successes raised hopes, and we got a lot of supporters we hadn't expected. They demand an end."

"Fair-weather soldiers." Falkenberg snorted. "Common enough, but why did you let them gain so much influence in your Council?"

"Because there were a lot of them."

And they all support you for President, Glenda Ruth thought. While my friends and I were out at the front, you were back here organizing the newcomers, grabbing for power . . . you're not worth the life of one of those soldiers. John's or mine.

"After all, this is a democratic government," Bannister said.

"And thus quite unable to accomplish anything that takes sustained effort. Can you afford this egalitarian democracy of yours?"

"You were not hired to restructure our government!" Bannister shouted.

Falkenberg activated his desktop map. "Look. We have the plains ringed with troops. The irregulars can hold the passes and swamps practically forever. Any real threat of a breakthrough can be held by my regiment in mobile reserve. The Confederates can't get at us—but we can't risk a battle in the open with them."

"So what can we do?" Bannister demanded. "Franklin is sure to send reinforcements. If we wait, we lose."

"I doubt that. They've no assault boats either. They can't land in any real force on our side of the line, and what good does it do them to add to their force in the capital? Eventually we starve them out. Franklin itself must be hurt by the loss of the corn shipments. They won't be able to feed their army forever."

"A mercenary paradise," Bannister muttered. "A long war and no fighting. Damn it, you've got to attack while we've still got troops! I tell you, our support is melting away."

"If we put our troops out where von Mellenthin's armor can get at them with room to maneuver, they won't melt, they'll burn."

"You tell him, Glenda Ruth," Bannister said. "He won't listen to me."

She looked at Falkenberg's impassive face and wanted to cry. "John, he may be right. I know my people, they can't hold on forever. Even if they could, the Council is going to insist . . ."

His look didn't change. There's nothing I can say, she thought, nothing I know that he doesn't, because he's right but he's wrong too. These are only civilians in arms. They're not iron men. All the time my people are guarding those passes their ranches are going to ruin.

Is Howard right? Is this a mercenary paradise, and you're not even trying? But she didn't want to believe that.

Unwanted, the vision she'd had that lonely night at the pass returned. She fought it with the memory of the party, and afterwards . . .

"Just what the hell are you waiting on, *Colonel* Falkenberg?" Bannister demanded.

Falkenberg said nothing, and Glenda Ruth wanted to cry; but she did not.

X

The Council had not voted six days later. Glenda Ruth used every parliamentary trick her father had taught her during the meetings, and after they adjourned each day she hustled from delegate to delegate. She made promises she couldn't keep, exploited old friends and made new ones, and every morning she was sure only that she could delay a little longer.

She wasn't sure herself why she did it. The war vote was linked to the reappointment of Silana as governor in Allansport, and she did know that the man was incompetent; but mostly, after the debates and political meetings, Falkenberg would come for her, or send a junior officer to escort her to his quarters— and she was glad to go. They seldom spoke of politics, or even talked much at all. It was enough to be with him—but when she left in the mornings, she was afraid again. He'd never promised her anything.

On the sixth night she joined him for a late supper. When the orderlies had taken the dinner cart she sat moodily at the table. "This is what you meant, isn't it?" she asked.

"About what?"

"That I'd have to betray either my friends or my command— but I don't even know if you're my friend. John, what am I going to do?"

Very gently he laid his hand against her cheek. "You're going to talk sense—and keep them from appointing Silana in Allansport."

"But what are we waiting for?"

He shrugged. "Would you rather it came to an open break? There'll be no stopping them if we lose this vote. The mob's demanding your arrest right now—for the past three days Calvin has had the Headquarters Guard on full alert in case they're fool enough to try it."

She shuddered, but before she could say more he lifted her gently to her feet and pressed her close to him. Once again her doubts vanished but she knew they'd be back. Who was she betraying? And for what?

The crowd shouted before she could speak. "Mercenary's whore!" someone called. Her friends answered with more epithets, and it was five minutes before Bannister could restore order.

How long can I keep it up? At least another day or so, I suppose. Am I his whore? If I'm not, I don't know what I am. He's never told me. She carefully took papers from her briefcase, but there was another interruption. A messenger strode quickly, almost running, across the floor to hand a flimsy message to Howard Bannister. The pudgy President glanced at it, then began to read more carefully.

The hall fell silent as everyone watched Bannister's face. The President showed a gamut of emotions: surprise, bewilderment, then carefully controlled rage. He read the message again and whispered to the messenger, who nodded. Bannister lifted the microphone.

"Councillors, I have—I suppose it would be simpler to read this to you. 'PROVISIONAL GOVERNMENT FREE STATES OF WASHINGTON FROM CDSN CRUISER INTREPID BREAK BREAK WE ARE IN RECEIPT OF DOCUMENTED COMPLAINT FROM CONFEDERATE GOVERNMENT THAT FREE STATES ARE IN VIOLATION OF LAWS OF WAR STOP THIS VESSEL ORDERED TO INVESTIGATE STOP LANDING BOAT ARRIVES ASTORIA SIXTEEN HUNDRED HOURS THIS DAY STOP PROVISIONAL GOVERNMENT MUST BE PREPARED TO DISPATCH ARMISTICE COMMISSION TO MEET WITH DELEGATES FROM CONFEDERACY AND CODOMINIUM INVESTIGATING OFFICERS IMMEDIATELY UPON ARRIVAL OF LANDING BOAT STOP COMMANDING OFFICERS ALL MERCENARY FORCES ORDERED TO BE PRESENT TO GIVE EVIDENCE STOP BREAK BREAK JOHN GRANT CAPTAIN CODOMINIUM SPACE NAVY BREAK MESSAGE ENDS'"

There was a moment of hushed silence, then the gymnasium erupted in sound. "Investigate us?" "Goddamn CD is—" "Armistice hell!"

Falkenberg caught Glenda Ruth's eye. He gestured toward the outside and left the hall. She joined him minutes later. "I really ought to stay, John. We've got to decide what to do."

"What you decide has just become unimportant," Falkenberg said. "Your Council doesn't hold as many cards as it used to."

"John, what will they do?"

He shrugged. "Try to stop the war now that they're here.

I suppose it never occurred to Silana that a complaint from Franklin industrialists is more likely to get CD attention than a similar squawk from a bunch of farmers. . . ."

"You expected this! Was this what you were waiting for?"

"Something like this."

"You know more than you're saying! John, why won't you tell me? I know you don't love me, but haven't I a right to know?"

He stood at stiff attention in the bright reddish-tinted sunlight for a long time. Finally he said, "Glenda Ruth, nothing's certain in politics and war. I once promised something to a girl, and I couldn't deliver it."

"But—"

"We've each command responsibilities—and each other. Will you believe me when I say I've tried to keep you from having to choose—and keep myself from the same choice? You'd better get ready. A CD Court of Inquiry isn't in the habit of waiting for people, and they're due in little more than an hour."

The Court was to be held aboard *Intrepid.* The four-hundred-meter bottle-shaped warship in orbit around New Washington was the only neutral territory available. When the Patriot delegates were piped aboard, the Marines in the landing dock gave Bannister the exact honors they'd given the Confederate Governor General, then hustled the delegation through gray steel corridors to a petty officer's lounge reserved for them.

"Governor General Forrest of the Confederacy is already aboard, sir," the Marine sergeant escort told them. "Captain would like to see Colonel Falkenberg in his cabin in ten minutes."

Bannister looked around the small lounge. "I suppose it's bugged," he said. "Colonel, what happens now?"

Falkenberg noted the artificially friendly tone Bannister had adopted. "The Captain and his advisors will hear each of us privately. If you want witnesses summoned, he'll take care of that. When the Court thinks the time proper, he'll bring both parties together. The CD usually tries to get everyone to agree rather than impose some kind of settlement."

"And if we can't agree?"

Falkenberg shrugged. "They might let you fight it out. They might order mercenaries off planet and impose a blockade. They could even draw up their own settlement and order you to accept it."

"What happens if we just tell them to go away? What can they do?" Bannister demanded.

Falkenberg smiled tightly. "They can't conquer the planet because they haven't enough Marines to occupy it—but there's not a lot else they can't do, Mr. President. There's enough power aboard this cruiser to make New Washington uninhabitable.

"You don't have either planetary defenses or a fleet. I'd think a long time before I made Captain Grant angry—and on that score, I've been summoned to his cabin." Falkenberg saluted. There was no trace of mockery in the gesture, but Bannister grimaced as the soldier left the lounge.

Falkenberg was conducted past Marine sentries to the captain's cabin. The orderly opened the door and let him in, then withdrew.

John Grant was a tall, thin officer with premature graying hair that made him look older than he was. As Falkenberg entered, Grant stood and greeted him with genuine warmth. "Good to see you, John Christian." He extended his hand and looked over his visitor with pleasure. "You're keeping fit enough."

"So are you, Johnny." Falkenberg's smile was equally genuine. "And the family's well?"

"Inez and the kids are fine. My father's dead."

"Sorry to hear that."

Captain Grant brought his chair from behind his desk and placed it facing Falkenberg's. Unconsciously he dogged it into place. "It was a release for him, I think. Single-passenger flier accident."

Falkenberg frowned, and Grant nodded. "Coroner said accident," the Captain said. "But it could have been suicide. He was pretty broken up about Sharon. But you don't know that story, do you? No matter. My kid sister's fine. They've got a good place on Sparta."

Grant reached to his desk to touch a button. A steward brought brandy and glasses. The Marine set up a collapsible table between them, then left.

"The Grand Admiral all right?" Falkenberg asked.

"He's hanging on." Grant drew in a deep breath and let it out quickly. "Just barely, though. Despite everything Uncle Martin could do the budget's lower again this year. I can't stay here long, John. Another patrol, and it's getting harder to cover these unauthorized missions in the log. Have you accomplished your job?"

"Yeah. Went quicker than I thought. I've spent the last hundred hours wishing we'd arranged to have you arrive sooner." He went to the screen controls on the cabin bulkhead.

"Got that complaint signaled by a merchantman as we came in," Grant said. "Surprised hell out of me. Here, let me get that, they've improved the damned thing and it's tricky." He played with the controls until New Washington's inhabited areas showed on the screen. "OK?"

"Right." Falkenberg spun dials to show the current military situation on the planet below. "Stalemate," he said. "As it stands. But once you order all mercenaries off planet, we won't have much trouble taking the capital area."

"Christ, John, I can't do anything as raw as that! If the Friedlanders go, you have to go as well. Hell, you've accomplished the mission. The rebels may have a hell of a time taking the capital without you, but it doesn't really matter who wins. Neither one of 'em's going to build a fleet for a while after this war's over. Good work."

Falkenberg nodded. "That was Sergei Lermontov's plan. Neutralize this planet with minimum CD investment and without destroying the industries. Something came up, though, Johnny, and I've decided to change it a bit. The regiment's staying."

"But I—"

"Just hold on," Falkenberg said. He grinned broadly. "I'm not a mercenary within the meaning of the act. We've got a land grant, Johnny. You can leave us as settlers, not mercenaries."

"Oh, come off it." Grant's voice showed irritation. "A land grant by a rebel government not in control? Look, nobody's going to look *too* close at what I do, but Franklin can buy one Grand Senator anyway. I can't risk it, John. Wish I could."

"What if the grant's confirmed by the local Loyalist government?" Falkenberg asked impishly.

"Well, then it'd be OK—how in hell did you manage *that?*" Grant was grinning again. "Have a drink and tell me about it." He poured for both of them. "And where do you fit in?"

Falkenberg looked up at Grant and his expression changed to something like astonishment. "You won't believe this, Johnny."

"From the look on your face you don't either."

"Not sure I do. Johnny, I've got a girl. A soldier's girl, and I'm going to marry her. She's leader of most of the rebel army. There are a lot of politicians around who think they count for something, but—" He made a sharp gesture with his right hand.

"Marry the queen and become king, uh?"

"She's more like a princess. Anyway, the Loyalists aren't

going to surrender to the rebels without a fight. That complaint they sent was quite genuine. There's no rebel the Loyalists will trust, not even Glenda Ruth."

Grant nodded comprehension. "Enter the soldier who enforced the Laws of War. He's married to the princess and commands the only army around. What's your *real* stake here, John Christian?"

Falkenberg shrugged. "Maybe the princess won't leave the kingdom. Anyway. Lermontov's trying to keep the balance of power. God knows, somebody's got to. Fine. The Grand Admiral looks ten years ahead—but I'm not sure the CoDominium's going to *last* ten years, Johnny."

Grant slowly nodded agreement. His voice fell and took on a note of awe. "Neither am I. It's worse just in the last few weeks. The Old Man's going out of his mind. One thing, though. There are some Grand Senators trying to hold it together. Some of them have given up the Russki-American fights to stand together against their own governments."

"Enough? Can they do it?"

"I wish I knew." Grant shook his head in bewilderment. "I always thought the CoDominium was the one stable thing on old Earth," he said wonderingly. "Now it's all we can do to hold it together. The nationalists keep winning, John, and nobody knows how to stop them." He drained his glass. "The Old Man's going to hate losing you."

"Yeah. We've worked together a long time." Falkenberg looked wistfully around the cabin. Once he'd thought this would be the high point of his life, to be captain of a CD warship. Now he might never see one again.

Then he shrugged. "There's worse places to be, Johnny," Falkenberg said. "Do me a favor, will you? When you get back to Luna Base, ask the admiral to see that all copies of that New Washington mineral survey are destroyed. I'd hate for somebody to learn there really is something here worth grabbing."

"OK. You're a long way from anything, John."

"I know. But if things break up around Earth, this may be the best place to be. Look, Johnny, if you need a safe base some day, we'll be here. Tell the Old Man that."

"Sure." Grant gave Falkenberg a twisted grin. "Can't get over it. Going to marry the girl are you? I'm glad for both of you."

"Thanks."

"King John I. What kind of government will you set up, anyway?"

"Hadn't thought. Myths change. Maybe people are ready for

monarchy again at that. We'll think of something, Glenda Ruth and I."

"I just bet you will. She must be one hell of a girl."

"She is that."

"A toast to the bride, then." They drank, and Grant refilled their glasses. Then he stood. "One last, eh? To the CoDominium."

Falkenberg stood and raised his glass. They drank the toast while below them New Washington turned, and a hundred parsecs away Earth armed for her last battle.

GO TELL
THE SPARTANS

FOR THE THREE HUNDRED

Go tell the Spartans, passerby,
That here obedient to their laws we lie.

PROLOGUE

The history of the 21st century was dominated by two developments, one technical and one social.

The technical development was, of course, the discovery of the Alderson Drive a decade after the century began. Faster-than-light travel released mankind from the prison of Earth, and the subsequent discovery of inhabitable planets made interstellar colonization well nigh inevitable; but the development of interstellar colonies threatened great social and political instability at a time when the international political system was peculiarly vulnerable. Whether through some hidden mechanism or a cruel coincidence, mankind's greatest technical achievements came at a time when the educational system of the United States was in collapse; at a time when scientists at Johns Hopkins and the California Institute of Technology were discovering the fundamental secrets of the universe, scarcely a mile from these institutions over a third of the population was unable to read and write, and another third was most charitably described as under-educated.

The key social development was the rise and fall of the U.S./U.S.S.R. CoDominium. Begun before the turn of the Millennium, the CoDominium was a natural outgrowth of the Cold War between the Superpowers. When the Cold War ended, the European nations once known in International Law as "Great Powers" retained some of the trappings of international sovereignty, but had become client states of the U.S.; while the Soviet Union, shorn of its external empire, retained both its internal empire and great military power, including the world's largest land army, fleet, and inventory of nuclear warheads and delivery systems.

In the last decade of the 20th century both the United States and the Soviet Union experimented with foreign policies that left the rest of the world free to compete with the former Superpowers. It soon became clear, if not to the world's

613

peoples, at least to political leaders of the U.S. and U.S.S.R., that the resulting disorder was worse than the Cold War had ever been. It was certainly more unpredictable, and thus more dangerous for the politicians, who had, under the Cold War, evolved systems to ensure their tenure of power and office. The political masters of the two nations did not at first openly state that it would be far better to divide the world into spheres of influence than to allow smaller powers to rise to prominence; but the former United Nations Security Council easily evolved into a structure which could not only keep the peace, but prevent any third party from challenging the principle of superpower supremacy. . . .

The 20th century social analyst and philosopher Herman Kahn would hardly have been surprised by this evolution. One of Kahn's speculations had been that the natural form of human government was empire, and the natural tendency of an empire was to expand, there being no natural limit to that expansion save running up against another empire of equal or greater strength.

There had been exceptions to that rule, the most notable being the United States of America, which, after the "manifest destiny" period of imperial expansion, attempted to settle into peaceful isolation. That repose was shattered by the latter half of the 20th century, when the United States was called upon to change its very nature, first to meet the threat of National Socialism, then of Soviet Imperialism. Kahn postulated in 1959 that in order to resist the Soviet Empire, the United States would be required to make such fundamental transformations of its republican structure as virtually to become an empire itself; and that having made the transformation, the end of the Cold War would not be sufficient to undo the change. He was, of course, not alone in that prediction, which proved largely to be true. Kahn did not live to see the CoDominium, but it would hardly have surprised him.

Of course no one predicted that the rapid development of faster-than-light space travel would rapidly follow the formation of the CoDominium. However, once the Alderson Drive was perfected, few disputed that there had to be some kind of universal government; and while few would, given free choice, have chosen the CoDominium for that role, there was a surprising consensus that the CoDominium was better than anarchy.

As the 21st century came to a close, it was obvious to most analysts that the CoDominium was doomed. There was widespread speculation on what would replace it. Astute observers looked to the CoDominium Fleet to provide the nucleus of stability around which a new order might be built, and they were not disappointed. What was surprising, though, was the role played by the Dual Monarchy of Sparta.

Sparta was not founded as an imperial power, and indeed its rulers explicitly rejected the notion of either ambitions or responsibilities extending beyond their own planetary system; yet when the CoDominium finally collapsed, no planetary nation was more important in building the new order.

As with any complex event, many factors were important in the transformation of Sparta from a nation founded by university professors seeking to establish the good society to the nucleus of what is formally called the Spartan Hegemony and which in all but name is the first interstellar empire; but analysts are universally agreed that much of the change can be traced to the will and intent of one man, Lysander I, Collins King of Sparta. It remains for us to examine how Lysander, originally very much in agreement with the Spartan Founders that the best policy for Sparta would be an armed neutrality on the Swiss model, came to embrace the necessity of empire.

—From the preface to *From Utopia to Imperium: A History of Sparta from Alexander I to the Accession of Lysander,* by Caldwell C. Whitlock, Ph.D. (University of Sparta Press, 2120).

CHAPTER ONE

Crofton's Essays and Lectures in Military History
(2nd Edition)

Professor John Christian Falkenberg II:
Delivered at Sandhurst, August 22nd, 2087

In the last decades of the 20th century, many predicted
that the battlefield of the future would be one of swift
and annihilating violence, ruled by an elaborate technology.
Instead, in one of history's many illustrations of the Law
of Unintended Consequences, the 21st century saw military technology enter an era of stalemate. Cheap and
accurate handheld missiles swept the air above the battlefield clear of manned aircraft; railguns, lasers and larger
rockets did likewise for the upper atmosphere and near
space.

The elaborate dance of countermeasures made many
sophisticated electronic devices so much waste weight;
tailored viruses made networks of linked computers a
recipe for battlefield chaos. Paradoxically, many of the most
sophisticated weapons could only be used against opponents who were virtually unarmed. By freezing technological research, the CoDominium preserved this situation
like a fly in amber.

Beyond Earth, the rarity and patchy development of
industry exaggerated these trends in the colony worlds.
CoDominium Marine expeditionary forces often operated
at the end of supply lines many months long, with shipping space too limited for heavy equipment, on thinly
settled planets where a paddle-wheel steamboat might
represent high technology. The Marines—and still more
the independent mercenary companies—have been forced

to become virtually self-sufficient. Troops travel scores of light-years by starship, then march to battle on their own feet, and their supplies may be carted by mules. Artillery is priceless but scarce, and tanks so rare a luxury that the intervention of half a dozen might well decide a campaign. Infantry and the weapons they carry on their backs; machine guns and mortars and light rockets, have come into their own once more. Apart from a few flourishes, body armor and passive nightsight goggles, the recent campaigns on Thurstone and Diego showed little that would have puzzled soldiers of the British Empire fighting the Boer War two centuries ago.

TANITH:

"Battalions, Attention!"

The noon sun of Tanith beat down unmercifully as Falkenberg's Mercenary Legion stood to parade in the great central square of the regiment's camp; the stabilized earth was a dun red-brown under the orange haze above. Behind the reviewing stand stood the Colonel's quarters; behind that the houses of the Company Officer's Line, then the wide street that separated them from Centurion's Row and the yellow rammed-earth barracks beyond. The jungle began just outside the dirt berm that surrounded the camp; a jungle that would reclaim the parade ground and all the huts in a single growing season once the hand of man was removed. The smell of that jungle filled the air, like spoiled bread and brewing beer and compost, heavy with life and rot. A thick gobbling roar boomed through the still muggy air, the cry of a Weems Beast in the swamps below the hill.

"Report!"

"First Battalion all present or accounted for, sir!"

"Second Battalion all present, sir!"

Men and women stood to rigid attention as the ritual continued. There had been a time when Peter Owensford found it difficult not to laugh at the parade ceremonies, originally intended to show Queen Anne's Mustermasters that the colonels had in fact raised and equipped regiments that could pass muster; but he had learned better. In those days colonels owned their regiments as property. *And it's not much different now. . . .*

"Sound Officer's Call," the Adjutant ordered. Trumpet notes pealed, and the Legion's officers, accompanied by guidon bearers, trooped forward to the reviewing stand. This too was ritual, once designed to show that the officers were properly uniformed and equipped. *And I may be the only one here who knows that,* Owensford thought. *Except for Falkenberg.*

"Attention to orders!" Sergeant Major Calvin's voice sounded even more gravelly through the amplifier pickup in his collar. He read through routine orders. Then: "Captain Peter Owensford, front and center!"

And this is it. Peter marched out to face the Adjutant. Sweat trickled down his flanks under the blue and gold parade tunic, from his forehead beneath the white kepi with its neck-flap.

"Sir."

Captain Amos Fast returned Owensford's salute. "By order of the Regimental Council of the Legion, Captain Peter Owensford is hereby promoted to the rank of major and assigned command of Fifth Battalion."

Peter Owensford felt his stomach clench as he stepped forward another pace and saluted again. Colonel Falkenberg returned the salute and held out his hand. It was impossible to read his expression.

"Congratulations," Falkenberg said. A slight smile creased the thin line of Falkenberg's mouth below the neatly clipped mustache. Peter had long ago learned that it was a smile that could indicate anything. *But Oh, beware my Colonel, when my Colonel grows polite. . . .* Owensford took the proffered hand in his.

"Thank you, sir," he said. Captain Fast stepped forward with the new rank-tabs on a cloth-covered board. Owensford felt the regimental adjutant's fingers remove the Captain's pips from his shoulderboards, replace the five small company-grade stars of a senior captain with the single larger star of a major. It felt heavier, somehow . . . absurd.

"Congratulations, sir," Fast said, smiling as well.

It felt odd to outrank him; Fast had been with the Colonel back when the Legion was the 42nd CoDominium Marines. *Not that I really do. He's still Adjutant, whatever the pay grades. And Falkenberg's friend.*

Owensford swallowed and stepped back a precise two paces; saluted the Colonel, did a quarter-turn and repeated the gesture to the Legion's banner in the midst of the color-party, trumpeter and standard-bearer and honor guard. He swallowed again at the lump in his throat as he did a quick about-face. It was the sudden shout from the ranks ahead that surprised him into missing a half-step.

"Fifth! Three cheers for Major Owensford!"

"HIP-HIP *HOORAY!*"

The sound crashed back from the walls of the buildings surrounding the parade square, and Owensford felt the top of his ears reddening. When he found out who was responsible for this he'd—*do absolutely nothing.* He grinned to himself behind a poker face, taking up his position in front of the battalion. *His* battalion, now. Not as captain-in-command of a provisional unit, but *his.*

His responsibility. The weight on his epaulets turned crushing.

Sergeant Major Calvin's voice continued:

"Attention to orders. Fifth Battalion will be ready for transport to embarkation at 0900 hours tomorrow. Remainder of Regiment will continue preparations for departure as per schedule." There was a quiet flurry of activity around the command group.

"Regiment—"

The command echoed from the subordinate units:

"Battalion—"

"Company—"

"Ten' *'hut!*"

"Pass in Review!"

The pipe band struck up "Black Dougal's Lament." The color party followed them out into the cleared lane between the ranked troops and the Colonel, marching at the slow double longstep that the CoDominium Marines had inherited from the French Foreign Legion . . . and now Falkenberg's Mercenary Legion had inherited from *them.* How many of the forty-four hundred soldiers on this square had been with the Colonel in the 42nd, he wondered? Perhaps a thousand, the core of senior commanders and NCOs. A few specialists and technicians. And of course some long service privates who had been up and back down the ladder of rank a dozen times. Not Peter Owensford; he had been recruited out of the losing side on Thurstone, another planet the CoDominium had abandoned. Not Fuller, the Colonel's pilot. New men and old, the Regiment went on; the traditions remained, just as the Regiment remained. Would after the last trooper in it now was dead or retired—

Even after the Colonel was gone?

The color party had passed the Colonel, dipping the banner to the commander's salute, then turned at the far end of the parade ground to pass before the assembled battalions. It swung by in jaunty blue and gold, the campaign ribbons and medals fluttering from the crossbar, the gilt eagle flaring its wings above. Hadley, Thurstone, Makassar, Haven . . . Tanith as well, now.

Owensford came to attention and saluted the colors; behind him the noncom's voices rang out:

"*Pree*-sent *arms!*"

Five thousand boots lifted and crashed down, an earthquake sound. Owensford had heard people sneer at a soldier's readiness to die for pieces of cloth. *For symbols,* he thought. *For what they symbolize.*

"Battalion Commanders, retire your battalions."

SPARTA:

The moon Cythera had set, and the Spartan night was cool; it smelled of turned earth and growing things, the breeze blowing up from the fields below. Skida Thibodeau snapped down the face shield of her helmet, and the landscape sprang out in silvery brightness. The two-story adobe ranchhouse set in its lawn, barns, stables, outbuildings and bunkhouse; cultivated fields beyond, watered by the same stream that turned the turbine of the microhydro station. Very successful for a fairly new spread in the mountain and basin country of the upper Eurotas Valley. Shearing and holding pens for sheep and beefalo, although the vaqueros would be mostly out with the herds this time of year. Irrigated alfalfa, fields of wheat and New Washington cornplant, and a big vineyard just coming into bearing.

The owners had put up the extra bunkhouse for the laborers needed, hired right off the landing shuttles in Sparta City because they were cheap and a start-up ranch like this needed to watch the pennies. *A mistake,* Skida thought. And they had taken on a dozen guards, because things had gotten a little rough up here in the hills. She grinned beneath the face shield; that was an even worse mistake.

Trusting, she thought, reaching back for the signal lamp and looking at the chronometer on her left wrist.

0058, nearly time.

Very trusting they were here on Sparta, compared to someone who had grown up in the slums of Belize City, a country and a place forgotten and rotting in its Caribbean backwater. Even more trusting than the nuns at the Catholic orphanage who had taught her to read; she had been only nine when she realized there was nothing for her there. Runner for a gang at ten, mistress to the gang leader at twelve . . . the look on his face the day she shopped him to a rival was one of her happier memories.

That deal had given her enough capital to skip to Mayopan on the border and set up on her own, running anything that needed moving—drugs, stolen antiquities from the Mayan cities, the few timber trees left in the cut-over jungle—while managing a hotel and cathouse in town.

0100. She pointed the narrow-beam lantern at the squat corner tower of the ranchhouse and clicked it twice. With the shield, she could see the figure who waved an arm there.

"Two-knife," she said to the man beside her. The big Mayan grunted and disappeared down the slope to ready the others. *Good man,* she thought. The only one who had stayed with her when Garcia sold her out and she ended up on a CoDo convict ship. Well worth the extra bribe money to get him onto Sparta with her.

Whump. The transmitter dish on the tower went over with a rending crash. No radio alarm to the Royal Spartan Mounted Police. *Whump.* The faint lights that shone through the windows went out as the transformer blew up in a spectacular shower of sparks. That would take out the electrified wire, searchlights and alarm.

Men boiled out of the guard barracks—to drop as muzzle flashes stabbed from behind; it had been more economical to buy only half of them. No need to use the mortar or the other fancy stuff.

"Follow me! ¡*Vámonos, compadres!*" Skida shouted, rising and leaping down the slope with her rifle held across her chest.

Her followers rose behind her and flung themselves forward with a howl. *Fools,* she thought. All men were fools, and fought for foolish things. Words, words like *macho* or *honor* or *liberty.*

They were into the house grounds before rifle muzzles spat fire from the second-story windows. Some of the attackers fell, and others went to ground to return fire. Squads fanned out to their assigned targets, dark figures against darkness. Skida dove up the stairs to the veranda and rolled across to slap a stickymine against the boards of the main door, then rose to flatten herself against the wall beside it. Two-knife was on the other side; they waited while the plastique blew the door in with a flash and *crump,* then leaped through to land in a crouch. Her rifle and his light machine gun probed at the corners. The entrance chamber was empty; it was a big room, a hallway with stairs leading up. Pictures on the walls, books, couches and carpets and smell of cleanliness and wax under the sharp chemical stink of explosives.

Skida Thibodeau is no fool, she thought, motioning Two-knife toward the stairs. The firing was coming from the upper level; she covered him, ready to snap-shoot as he padded forward readying a grenade. *No fool who fights for words.*

Someday *she* was going to have a house even finer than this, and a good deal else besides. And it would all be nice and legal.

Because she would be making the laws.

TANITH:

"I still think I should be going with you, Colonel," Owensford said.

Falkenberg's office was hot. There was precious little air conditioning within the Legion's encampment: a few units for the hospital, another for essential equipment. The command center, because it might be important to think clearly and quickly without distractions. None for the Colonel's home, study or office.

The overhead fan stirred the wet air into languid motion, and Major Peter Owensford gratefully accepted the glass of gin and tonic proffered by Falkenberg's orderly. Ice tinkled; the sound was a little different with most of the familiar office furniture gone. All that remained was the field-desk, the elaborate carvings of battle scenes disguising highly functional electronics. Without the filing cabinets the fungus growing in the corners showed acid green and livid purple, with a wet sheen like the innards of a slaughtered beast.

"I'd like nothing better," Falkenberg said. "But the men will feel a lot better about going to New Washington, knowing the families are safe on Sparta. They trust you. One thing, Major. Nothing is ever as easy as it looks."

He looked up. "You're anticipating trouble?" The Colonel's face was as unreadable as ever, but Falkenberg did not waste words. Theoretically, the Fifth Battalion's mission was training Field Force regiments of regular troops for the embryonic Royal Spartan Army. There were said to be some bandits on Sparta, but not enough to be a real threat. "Any special reason for that, sir? I thought this was a training command. Troop exercises, staff colleges. Cakewalk."

Falkenberg shrugged. "No battle plan ever survives contact with the enemy. And don't kid yourself, Major. The Spartans have enemies, even if they're not telling us much about them."

"Has Rottermill—"

"Intelligence has nothing you don't know about," Falkenberg

said. "But the Spartans aren't paying our prices without good reasons." He shrugged. "And maybe I'm suspicious over nothing. We do have a good reputation; hiring us to set up their national forces makes sense. Still, I have an odd feeling—pay attention to your hunches, Peter Owensford. Like as not, if you get a strong hunch, your subconscious is trying to tell you something."

"Yes—sir." *First names in the mess, except for the Colonel, but Major Savage calls him John Christian. I never heard anyone call him John. His wife must have—maybe not in public.* Peter had never met Grace Falkenberg, and none of the Colonel's oldest friends ever spoke of her.

Falkenberg touched a control in a drawer and the pearly gray surface of the desk blinked into a holographic relief map of Sparta's inhabited continent. "The latest word."

Owensford leaned forward to stare at the maps, hoping they'd tell him something he didn't already know. He'd memorized everything in the Legion's data base, and spent countless evenings with Prince Lysander. Not that it was so difficult spending time with the Prince. Lysander was a good lad, a bit naive, but he'd outgrow that. *And how does it feel to know that one day your word will be law to a whole planet?*

Sparta. A desirable planet. Gravity too high, day too short, but more comfortable than Tanith. One big serpentine-shaped major continent, three times the area of North America, and a scattering of islands ranging from the size of Australia down to flyspecks. The inhabited portions were around a major inland sea about the size of the Mediterranean, in the south. Originally slated as a CoDominium prison-planet, then leased out to a rather eccentric group of American political idealists on condition that they take in involuntary colonists swept up by BuReloc.

"Colonel, I am surprised at how much rebel activity there is," Owensford said. "It's much better run than the average autonomous planet these days. At least I get that impression from Prince Lysander."

Falkenberg sipped at his drink. "Problems of success." His finger tapped Sparta City, on a bay toward the eastern end of the Aegean Sea. "They've managed to keep the population of their capital down."

About two hundred fifty thousand, out of a total three million. They had both seen planets where ninety percent of the people were crammed into ungovernable slum-settlements around the primary spaceport.

"But that means a lot of population in the outback." Falkenberg swept his hand across the map. "It's pretty easy to live there, too. Not much native land-life, so the Package worked quite well. All too well, perhaps." The Standard Terraforming Package included everything from soil-bacteria and grass seeds to rabbits and foxes; where the native ecology was suitable it could colonize whole continents in a generation. "There's even a fairly substantial trade in hides and tallow from feral cattle and such. Scattered ranches, small mines—plentiful minerals, but no large concentrations—poor communications, not enough money for good satellite surveillance, even."

Owensford nodded. "About like the Old West, sans Indians," he said. "You think some of the bandit activity is political?"

"Of course it's political. By definition, any large coordinated action is political. But if you mean connected with off-planet forces, possibly not. Fleet intelligence says no, anyway. Of course Sparta is a long way away." The Legion had strong, if clandestine, links to Sergei Lermontov, Grand Admiral of the CoDominium Fleet.

"Mostly it's insurrection, which can't be too big a surprise. The involuntary colonists and convicts Sparta gets are a cut above the usual scrapings. They'll be unhappy about being sent to Sparta. Ripe for political organization, and when there's an opportunity, a politician will find it."

BuReloc had been shipping the worst troublemakers off Earth for two generations now . . . *except for the Grand Senators,* Owensford thought mordantly. Earth could not afford more trouble. The CoDominium had kept the peace since before his grandfather's birth, the United States and Soviet Union acting in concert to police a restive planet. The cost had been heavy; an end to technological progress, as the CoDo Intelligence services suppressed research with military implications . . . which turned out to be all research.

For the United States the price of empire had proved to be internal decay; the dwindling core of taxpayers grimly entrenched against the swelling misery of the Citizens in their Welfare Islands, kept pacified by arbitrary police action and subsidized drugs. Convergence with the Soviets even as nationalist hatred between the two ruling states paralyzed the CoDominium.

By the time they destroy each other, there won't be any real difference at all.

They. Them. The thought startled him; he had been born American and graduated from West Point. *Legio Patria Nostra,* he quoted to himself. *The Legion is our Fatherland.*

"Yes, I expect most of the deportees who make it to Sparta bribed the assignment officers," Owensford said. Which indicated better than average resources, of money or determination or intelligence. There were planets like Thurstone or Frystaat or Tanith where incoming deportees ended up in debt-peonage that was virtual slavery. A few like Dalarna where the Welfare provisions were as generous as on Earth, though God alone knew how long *that* would last. On Sparta able-bodied newcomers had the same civil rights as the old voluntary settlers, and the same options of working or starving.

"So," Falkenberg said, "I don't have anything specific, but something doesn't feel right. And Sparta is just too damned important to Lermontov's plan."

"Our plan," Owensford said carefully.

Falkenberg shrugged. "If you like."

"I thought you were an enthusiast—the Regimental Council approved it, mostly on your insistence."

"Correct. Don't misunderstand," Falkenberg said. "Lermontov is our patron. Whatever the problems with this scheme, we don't have anything better—so we act as if it's going to work and do what we have to do for it."

"But you're not happy even so."

Falkenberg shrugged. "We don't control Sparta, and it isn't our home. I'd be happier with a base we do control—but we don't have one. So we go on putting out fires for the Grand Admiral."

Owensford made a noncommittal sound; Grand Admiral Lermontov's private policy-making was a dangerous game. Essential when the Russki-American clashes paralyzed the Grand Senate, but dangerous nonetheless. Falkenberg's Legion had defended Lermontov's interests for decades, and that too was dangerous.

"Unfortunately, putting out fires isn't enough anymore," Falkenberg said. "The CoDominium is dying. When it dies, Earth will die with it; but I like to think we've bought enough time for civilization to live outside the Solar System. The Fleet can't protect civilization and order without a base."

"And Sparta looks to be it."

"It's the best we have," Falkenberg said. He shrugged. "Who knows, we may find a home on Sparta. People don't usually have much use for the mercenaries they hire, but the Spartans may be different. Given time, who knows? Lermontov doesn't expect things to come apart for ten years, twenty if we're lucky. When the crash comes it's important to have Sparta in good shape."

He paused, finished his drink and frowned at the rapidly melting ice cubes in the bottom of the glass. "I suspect it will take luck to keep things going ten more years."

Peter nodded slowly. "Whitlock's report. You put a lot of confidence in him—"

"It's been justified so far. Peter, what's important is that Sparta stays committed to the Plan, that they see us—the Regiment, and the Fleet, and the rest of us—as part of their solution and not more problems. Otherwise we'd end up with another insular regional power like Frystaat or Dayan or Xanadu, not a seed-crystal of . . . call it Empire for lack of anything better."

Owensford chuckled. "Colonel, are you saying the future of civilization is in my hands?"

Falkenberg grinned slightly, but he didn't answer.

"All right, why me?"

"An honest question," Falkenberg said. "Because you'll get the job done. You won't be ashamed to take advice. Just remember, you won't be alone in this."

"I hope not—John Christian. Who else is in on this conspiracy?"

"Not so much a conspiracy as people who think alike. An alliance. Incidentally, including some people from our side. I've just got word, Colonel Slater will reach Sparta about the same time you do. You'll remember him."

"Yes, sir."

Falkenberg smiled thinly. "Don't worry, he's not there to outrank you. Hal's mission is to set up the Spartan War College."

"He's recovered, then?" Lt. Col. Hal Slater had been shot up badly enough that he'd been forced to retire from the Legion and go back to Earth for therapy.

"Well, maybe not completely," Falkenberg said. "But enough that he can command a war academy. Hal even managed to get himself a Ph.D. in military history from Johns Hopkins while the medicos were putting him back together."

"He was with you a long time—"

Falkenberg nodded. "Since Arrarat. Before I was posted to the Forty-second. I have a request."

"Request, sir?"

"I'd like to swap you a company commander. George Slater for Brainerd. Only you'll have to ask, I wouldn't want it thought I'd set this up myself."

"No problem. I'd rather have Hal Slater's son than Henry in a training command anyway."

"Right. Thank you."

Owensford looked away in embarrassment. Falkenberg didn't often ask for favors. *Hal Slater must be his oldest friend, now that I think of it.*

"As to the conspiracy," Falkenberg said, "there aren't any secret passwords, nothing like that. Just people who think alike. Lermontov and his immediate staff. Most of the Grant family. The Blaines, although they hope the CoDominium will survive the collapse, and they work in that direction. The Leontins." Falkenberg took a message cube out of a drawer. "The file name is BIGPLAN. The password is 'carnelian.' Don't forget that the file erases itself if you try to access it with the wrong password. Study it on your way. Then erase it."

"Yes, sir. Carnelian."

"The most important allies from your point of view are Prince Lysander and his father. His Majesty Alexander Collins First was one of Admiral Lermontov's first partners."

Owensford nodded. Sparta had a dual monarchy like the ancient Greek state. There were two royal families, the Collinses and the Freedmans; three generations away from being ordinary families of American college professors, but any royal line had to start somewhere. It was a change from the usual lucky soldier as a founder, anyway.

"But the Freedmans are inclined to isolationism. So you see it's not *just* a training command I'm giving you."

"Well," Owensford said, finishing his drink and picking up his swagger stick. "At least we won't have the Bronsons to worry about."

EARTH:

" . . . and we both know you're a pompous, spoiled, inbred, insufferable *fool*," Grand Senator Adrian Bronson concluded. He was a tall man, still erect in his eighty-fifth year; the blue eyes were very cold on his grandnephew. "Did you have to make it known to the entire *universe?*"

A hint of Midwestern rasp roughened the normally smooth generic-North-American accent. The Grand Senator represented a district that included Michigan and several other states in the CoDominium Senate, and led a faction whose votes were the subject of frantic bidding in that perpetually deadlocked body. That was power, even more power than the Bronson family's wealth could buy. The quarter-million acres centered around this Wisconsin estate were more symbol of that authority than its source, but on this land Adrian Bronson governed more absolutely than any feudal lord. A man who angered him sufficiently here could disappear and never be heard of again.

The Honorable Geoffrey Niles swallowed and unconsciously

braced to attention, a legacy of Sandhurst. He was sixty years younger than the man on the other side of the table, blondly handsome and muscular, but there was no doubt about who was dominant here.

"Really, Great-Uncle—"

"*Don't remind me!*" Bronson shouted, slamming a fist down on the polished teak of the table. The crystal and silver of the decanter set jumped and jingled. "Don't remind me that my little sister's daughter managed to produce *you*! *I* won't die of the grief, but by *God* you may!"

He turned to the other men present; there were three, one in the plain blue overall of a starship captain, the other in a trim brown uniform with a pistol at his belt, a third elaborately inconspicuous.

"Captain Nakata," he said. "Report in this matter."

The spacer was Nipponese, from Meiji; Bronson had hired him away from that newly independent planet's expanding space navy. His loyalty was expensively bought and paid for, but would be absolute for the duration of his contract.

"Sir," he said, bowing. "While in orbit about Tanith, waiting to receive the shipment of borloi"—the perfect euphoric drug, and vastly profitable—"Lieutenant Commander Niles, on his own authority, contacted the authorities in Lederle for, ah, a hunting permit."

"A hunting permit." Bronson waited a moment, meeting his grandnephew's eyes. They were steady. *No coward, at least,* he thought grudgingly.

"Mr. Wichasta," Bronson continued. Chandos Wichasta coughed discreetly into a hand; he was a small brown man, a confidential agent for many years.

"Senator, until this communication—apparently a bureaucrat flagged it as a routine measure and grew curious—until this communication, our agents in Governor Blaine's office had kept the Governor and Colonel Falkenberg in complete ignorance of *Norton Star's* presence. Apparently, the request began a chain of discoveries which led to Governor Blaine and Falkenberg's mercenaries discovering that Rochemont plantation was the headquarters of the rebel planters and *their* mercenaries. And that we were in contact with the rebels and planning to lift the borloi they had denied the official Lederle monopoly. The timing was very close; if your grandnephew had not made that call, we would in all probability have been able to secure the drugs, and we certainly could have destroyed them."

"Captain Hertzimer," Bronson said. The man in the brown uniform saluted smartly. Officially he was an employee of

Middleford Security Services; in fact, he was an officer of Bronson's household troops.

Household troops, Bronson thought sourly. *Recruited from my estates. God, how did America come to this?* The tenants here knew they owed their farms to him; if the Bronson family had not been prepared to keep them on the land, this area would be corporate latifundia like the rest of the Midwest. No independent farmer had the resources or the political clout to survive on good land, these days; without the Bronsons, the farmers would have been lucky to get enough to emigrate off-planet. Quite likely to have ended upon a Welfare Island.

"Sir," Hertzimer said. "On Lieutenant Commander Niles's instructions, I loaded the security platoon and the Suslov class armored vehicle on the shuttle that was to fetch the borloi. When we arrived unexpectedly, there was nearly fighting with the plantation troops and mercenaries."

"Barton's Bulldogs," Wichasta said.

"When the shuttle was hijacked by Falkenberg's infiltrators, Mr. Niles ordered the tank to open fire on it. Unfortunately—"

"He *missed,* to top it all off." Bronson sighed, and poured himself a small brandy. "You're all dismissed. Not you, Geoffrey."

The big room grew quiet as the three employees took their leave; snow beat with feather paws at the windows behind the curtains, and the fire crackled as it cast its light over the pictures and the spines of the books. Pictures by Thomas Hart Benton and Norman Rockwell and Maxfield Parrish, visions of a people and a way of life vanished almost as thoroughly as Rome. And the books, his oldest friends: *The Federalist Papers,* Sandburg's monumental *Lincoln,* Twain's *Life on the Mississippi.*

The brandy bit his tongue gently, aromatic and comforting. *My world is dying,* Bronson thought, looking at the younger man. *Nothing left but a few remnants.* He had known all his life that the Earth was turning to slime beneath his feet; once he had wanted to do something about it, to halt the process, reverse it. When had he realized that no man could? But the death of a world is a gradual process, longer than the lifetime of a man. . . . *And perhaps something can be saved. The Bronsons, at least.*

"Geoffrey, what am I to do with you? Unless you'd rather go back to England and take a post in Amalgamated Foundries with Hugo. Wait a minute." He raised a hand at the younger man's frown and thinned lips. "Your father does good work there, important work. You'd have a decent place. I know you see yourself as a second Lawrence of Arabia and another Selous rolled into one, with a dash of Richard Burton and some Orde Wingate on the side, but this isn't the 19th century . . . or even the 20th."

"No, sir," Geoffrey Niles said. A hesitation: "Does this mean you're . . . going to give me a second chance, Great-Uncle? I say, that *is* decent of you."

Bronson smiled coldly. "No it isn't, Jeff. You see, I *know* there's the making of a man somewhere inside you, under that dilettante surface. They tell me you were steady enough under fire. You didn't miss that landing craft, did you?"

"No, sir. I hulled the ship, but Barton's people hit us before I could get off another round."

"Were you hit?"

"Yes, sir."

"I'm pleased to see you're no braggart." Bronson took papers out of a drawer. "I have the medical reports. Apparently you were three weeks in the regeneration stimulators. And you still want another try?"

"Yes, sir."

"All right. But no more command positions for a while, Jeff. No more relative-of-the-boss. If you want to play with the big boys, you'll have to earn it."

He picked up a pipe from the table and began the comforting ritual of loading it.

"You see," he continued softly, "your little fiasco on Tanith did more than cost me several hundred million CD credits. It gave me a public black eye—oh, not to the chuckleheads who watch the media, but to the people who really know things." His hand closed tightly on the bowl of the corncob.

"That damnable hired gun Falkenberg!" Bronson's eyes went to a picture framed in black: Harold Kewney. Barely twenty, in the uniform of a CoDominium Space Navy midshipman. His daughter's son, the chosen heir. . . dead thirty years ago, holding a rear-guard while then-Lieutenant John Christian Falkenberg escaped. Escaped, and then—

"And the Blaines and the Grants behind *him*, and that Russki bastard Lermontov, God *curse* the day I went along with making him Grand Admiral of the Fleet. They've all of them cost me time and grief before, the hypocrites. . . . Do they think I'm a *fool*, not to know that Tanith drug money's underwriting the Fleet? We all know the CoDominium won't outlast even my lifetime"—he ignored Niles's look of shock—"and I know *their* cure: a coup by the Fleet, with Lermontov calling the shots and the Grants and Blaines providing a civilian cover. And from what happened on Tanith, the Spartans are in it up to their 'idealistic' eyeballs. That so-called Prince Lysander of theirs was the one who hijacked the shuttle from under your nose."

He pressed a control, sourly watching the mixture of hatred and envy flicker across the young Englishman's face. The hijacking had been exactly the sort of exploit Geoffrey Niles dreamed about. *And perhaps could accomplish, if he learned some self-discipline first,* the Senator thought.

The door opened silently, and a man entered. An Oriental like Nakata, but without his stiffness, and dressed in a conspicuously inconspicuous outfit of dark-blue tunic and hose. Geoffrey Niles looked at him and returned the other man's smile, feeling a coldness across his shoulders and back. A little shorter than the Englishman, which made him towering for his race, sharp-featured and broad-shouldered; the hand that held his briefly was like something carved from wood. No more than thirty.

"This is Kenjiro Murasaki," Bronson said. "Owner and manager of Special Tasks, Inc., of New Osaka." The capital city of the planet Meiji.

"Mr. Murasaki has agreed to . . . take care of the Spartan problem for me. New Washington is outside my sphere of operations, but Falkenberg's Legion is *not* going to establish a base on Sparta if I can help it. I've had tentative contacts with the underground opposition on Sparta for some time; now things get serious. And the Spartans, and Grant and Blaine and Lermontov, are going to get an object lesson in what happens to people who try to fuck with Adrian Bronson."

Niles swallowed in shock. It was the first time he had ever heard the Grand Senator use an obscenity, and it was as out-of-place as a knife-fight at a garden party.

"You can join the expedition. I'll let you keep your nominal rank of Lieutenant Commander, but you'll be an aide, subordinate to Mr. Murasaki and under the same discipline as other members of his organization. Or you can return to London tomorrow and never leave Earth again except as a tourist. Take your pick."

There was a long moment of silence. Niles nodded jerkily. "If that's acceptable to you, Mr. Murasaki," he said, with a precisely calculated bow. The Meijian returned it, bowing fractionally less.

"Indeed, Mr. Niles," he said, with the social smile Nipponese used in such situations. "If one thing is understood at the outset. We will be in a situation of conflict with two organizations, the Royal government of Sparta, and Falkenberg's Legion. Capable organizations, which operate according to certain rules, the Spartan Constitution, the Laws of War. We too will operate according to rules. The Hama rules."

Geoffrey Niles frowned. "I'm . . . Please excuse my ignorance of Japanese history," he said, racking his memory.

The smile grew broader. "Not Japanese, Mr. Niles. Hama was a city in . . . the Republic of Syria, then; Northern Israel, since 2009. In the later 20th century, it rebelled against the Syrian government." Geoffrey let one brow rise slightly. "The government made no effort to pacify the city. Instead it was surrounded by armor and artillery and leveled in a week's bombardment. The survivors died by bayonet, or fire when flamethrowers were turned on cellars. Man, woman and child."

Black eyes held blue. "Hama rules. First: *There are no rules.* Second: *Rule or die.* Understood?"

Bronson drew on the pipe. "Something can be made of that young man," he said, glancing at the door Niles had closed behind him.

"Perhaps, excellency. Yet the best steel comes from the hottest fire," Murasaki said politely.

"If you mean, do I want him kept out of harm's way, the answer's no," Bronson said brutally. "I expect that rebellion to do a lot of damage before it's crushed, and that means fighting. It's time to see what young Niles is made of, one way or the other. This isn't a time for the stupid or the weak, and I don't want them in my bloodline. Test him; I'd be delighted if he passes, but if it kills him, so be it."

SPARTA:

Skida Thibodeau blinked as the light-intensifiers in her faceplate cycled down; it was fairly bright in the yard behind the ranch house, with the burning hovertruck not ten meters away.

"Smith!" she shouted. "Get that doused, do you want the RSMP down on us?"

Most of the fifty-odd ranch hands and laborers were gathered in an apprehensive clump, beneath the weapons of the guerrillas. Some wore the rough coveralls of working dress, others no more than a snatched-up blanket; they were a tough-looking lot, the sort you could hire cheap for a place a *long* way from the pleasures of town. Almost all men; there was a severe imbalance between the genders among deportees who made it to Sparta, and most women could find work closer to Sparta City than this. Some glowered at the attackers, others cringed, but none seemed ready to defy the raiders whose nightsight goggles and bandannas made them doubly terrible, anonymous in their outbacker leathers.

Others of the guerrillas were leading spare horses and mules out of the stables, fitting packsaddles and loading them with bundles of loot, everything from weapons to trail-rations and medicine. She was glad to see nobody was trying to hide anything massive anymore, or steal liquor for themselves, but . . .

The tall woman took three quick steps to where the ranch-family stood in a huddle of personal servants and the retainers who had been fighting by their sides. One of the guards had his hand under the skirt of a housemaid, ignoring the girl's squirming and whimpers. The man was one of her old hidehunters; they were nearly as much trouble as that clutch of Liberation Party deportees from Earth Croser had sent along two months back.

No point in wasting words, she thought, and whipped the butt of her rifle around to crack against his elbow. The man gave a wordless snarl of pain and crouched for a moment, before looking aside.

"Ay, Skilly, you said—"

"Keep you hands to youself," she hissed. "That for later. Be *political,* you silly mon. Now bring the haciendado and his woman out. You, Diego, take their children over to the shed and lock them in. Take the nursemaid too. And Diego, Skilly would be *angry* if anything happened to them."

The crowd grew quieter still as the couple who owned this land were prodded out into the trampled earth of the yard. *Velysen,* Skida remembered from the intelligence report. *Harold and Suzanne Velysen, Spartan-born, Citizens.* They were unremarkable. A man in his midthirties, dark and wiry; the woman a little younger, blond and as plump as you got on this heavy-gravity world. Another woman who looked to be the wife's younger sister. Harold Velysen had managed to don pants and boots, but his wife was still in torn silk pajamas that showed a bruise on her right shoulder where a rifle-butt would rest. Skida pitched her voice to carry, standing with legs straddled and thumbs in her belt:

"Now, listen. The Helots has no quarrel with you workers. The Non-Citizens' Liberation Front fights for you aboveboard and legal; we Helots does it with guns. Nobody's been hurt except the ranchero and his gunmen, hey? Not even his children. The Helots fights civ-il-ized."

She turned and extended a finger toward the group of household staff. "Any of you houseboys Citizens. Any of you want to stand over there with the bossman?" A few of the field-workers stirred before they remembered this was Sparta, where Citizen meant member of the ruling class rather than a Welfare Island scut.

Four of the house-workers moved over to stand beside the rancher; an older man and his wife, two of the surviving guards. A boy of about fourteen tried to follow them and was pushed back by the guerrillas, not unkindly. The little band had their hands roughly bound behind their backs.

"These good *Citizens* wouldn't listen when the Helots came calling," Skida continued. "No, they wouldn't listen to such rabble as us. Wouldn't listen to the workers' friends about the low pay and the bad *con*ditions. Wouldn't pay their taxes for the people's cause." She shook her head, making *tsk, tsk,* sounds. "Thought the kings off in Sparta City would help them against such riffraff as us. Thought the Really Shitty Mounted Pimps would protect them."

The guerrillas laughed at the nickname of the Royal Spartan Mounted Police; a few of the farmhands joined in ingratiatingly.

"But then, why should they lift a finger for you?" Skida continued. She freed one hand to wave backward at the house. "Why should the *haciendado* listen to the friends of the poor? Isn't it always the way? They get the big houses and the fancy cars. They ride by and watch while you sweat in the fields? And if you object, if you stand up for your rights—"

She grinned, a glint of white teeth against the matt brown of her skin "—why, they call in the RSMP to beat you down. You aren't *Citizens,* you haven't *earned* the vote." A scornful laugh. "Learn how to pass their exams and tests—" There was a stir; most Welfare Island dwellers were not only illiterate but had what amounted to a cultural taboo against everything about the written word. "—while you're working for a living and they're living off you! Your kids can spend their lives shoveling shit, while the children of the noble *Brotherhoods* get their special schools and fancy—"

"You lying bitch!" It was the older man who had volunteered to stand with the rancher. "Mr. Velysen built this place up from nothing, and anyone can—"

Thunk. The carbon-fiber stock of Two-knife's machine gun

caught him at the base of the skull. *Silly mon*, she thought as he sank to his knees and shook his head dazedly. *Skilly is giving a speech, not arguing.*

"—fancy tutors. But tonight, everyone's equal! Tonight, you see how the rich live."

A working party had been setting out tables. Now they stepped back, showing trestle tables covered with bottles and casks and heaped plates; whatever had been available in the wine cellar and the kitchens. The farm-workers moved hesitantly forward, but most of them snatched at the liquor eagerly enough. Doubly eager from fear, but they would have drunk anyway; Skida watched with carefully hidden contempt. You did not get out of the gutters on booze-dreams, or on cocaine or smack or borloi; those were for fools, like God or the lotteries or the Tri-V with its lying dreams.

Skida waited until the liquor had a little time to work, then rapped on the table with her rifle butt.

"You see who your real friends are," she said, as the guerrillas went up and down the table; they distributed handfuls of cash and jewelry. Most of the workers snatched greedily at the plunder. A few had the sense to think ahead, but nobody wanted to be a holdout.

"The Helots is your friend. The kings and the RSMP couldn't protect their friends, but the Helots can protect and punish. The Helots have its eyes and ears everywhere; here and in Sparta City, in the government, in the police, we know everything. The government is blind, it strikes at the air but it can't catch us; we cut it and turn away, cut it and turn away, and soon it will bleed to death and we be the government. Look around you! We didn't harm a hair on your heads. We didn't touch the tools or workstock or barns . . . because all this will belong to *you* when the people rules."

She smiled broadly. *And if you gallows bait believe all that, Skilly has this card game she could teach you.* "And look what else the Helots gives you!" she said, signaling. Guerrillas pushed the rancher's wife forward, and the two other women who had come to stand with her. The rancher began to shout and struggle as they were stripped and thrown down on the rough planks of the trestles.

Skida signaled to Two-knife as the screaming began, from the women and the men. "The other women, house servants and the workers, give them a shotgun and put them in a room with a lock," she said. "It is *muy importante*, understand. Just before we leave, we lock the other workers back in their barracks."

Two-knife blinked at her. "*Sí*, Skilly, if you say so. The gringo

Croser, he say that?"

Skida sighed. "No, my loyal fool, he has taught Skilly much
of the way of fighting the guerrillero, the little war, but Skilly
put the books to work. See, if we let these animals loose they
will rape all the women, burn down the ranch and then start
killing each other. That makes them just criminals who the
RSMP will hang. This must be a political thing, not a bandit
raid."

The Mayan frowned and pushed back his broad-brimmed
leather hat to scratch his bald scalp. "But the RSMP will hang
them anyway," he said reasonably.

"If all share the crime, then none will talk for a while at
least," she said patiently. "They will themselves kill any who
would. They will say that we did it, that they were helpless
before our guns, but among themselves they will know. They
will feel they must support us, because they are as guilty as
we, and they fear our spies among them."

She made a throwing gesture. "Many will run before the
police come. Some the RSMP will catch and hang; these will
be martyrs for our cause. Others will scatter to rancheros who
ask no questions of a man willing to work. They will talk
in secret in the bunkhouses, and all those who hate their
masters will dream of doing as was done here—perhaps some
will. The haciendados will hear as well, by rumor; they will
fear their workers, and be twice as hard on them, which will
turn more to us. You see?"

The man stood, frowning in concentration. He was far from
stupid, simply not very used to abstract thought. She slapped
him on the shoulder as he nodded agreement. The screams
had died to a broken sobbing. Skida cast a critical eye at the
tables. Unlikely that the haciendados women would survive;
best to have the rancher and all of his supporters shot just
as the guerrillas left, though.

"Two-knife, you will take the first Group and any recruits
we get from here back to Base One," she said. "All the Group
leaders are to make for their drop camps and lie low until I
return. Work the new ones hard, but do not kill more than
is necessary. McMillan may begin their instruction."

Two-knife snorted; Skida nodded agreement; the Liberation Party theorist was something of a bore, but necessary.
She found his cranky neo-Marxism even more ridiculous
than the religion the nuns had taught her, but it was a
lie with power.

"You would do well to learn his words also," she said. "I
must attend a conference of regional leaders. The kings are

bringing in help from off-planet. Mercenaries." *And we will have help as well, but that is a secret even from you for a while,* she thought.

Skida frowned thoughtfully down the rutted dirt road that lead away from the ranch house; it joined a gravel track down toward the Eurotas. Her mind threw a map over the night; the Torrey estate was there, older and larger than this and too formidable to attack as yet. Then came the switchback down into the valley of the upper Eurotas. The guerrillas had a Group there, about the size of a platoon, to serve as a blocking force, and then as her cover for the trip to town.

"And I might as well leave now," she added. "Adios. Meet me in the usual place in three weeks."

CHAPTER TWO

Crofton's Encyclopedia of Contemporary History
and Social Issues (1st Edition):

The CoDominium emerged almost by accident as Earth's
first world government; many of the consequences were
unplanned and unanticipated.

One of the most notable was the emergence of a far
less competitive world society. The founding powers of
the CoDominium had an effective monopoly on military
power, and an absolute monopoly on space-based weapons.
After a series of crises convinced the United States and
the Soviet Union to work together, smaller states could
no longer play the Great Powers off against each other.
Maintaining that power monopoly became a goal in itself.

An early result was CoDominium Intelligence suppression of research; first military and then all technology
began to stagnate. Likewise, private corporations could
no longer escape the power of one state by moving;
instead, the worldwide regulations imposed by the Alliance, later the Grand Senate, came more and more to favor
established economic interests with lobbying power. In
turn, the Grand Senators and their clients accumulated
increasing wealth based on patronage and politically
allocated contracts. Earth of the 21st century saw unprecedented economic concentration in the hands of a dwindling number of oligarchs.

Political-social stasis also settled on the rest of the world.
The CoDominium allowed no international wars after the
final Arab-Israeli conflict of 2009; hence, regimes no longer
needed to win the support of their populations against
outside enemies. Revolt against a government supported
by the CoDominium was impossible; even guerrilla war
was futile without external arms supplies and sanctuaries.

At best, developed states became junior partners. In what was once known as the "Third World" utterly corrupt gangster regimes became the norm (for 20th-century analogies see *Haiti, Liberia, Romania*), presiding over despair and famine. Only the mass deportations of BuReloc, combined with the release of viral contraceptives and the distribution of tranquilizing agents such as borloi, maintain the present situation. . . .

[*This article was removed from the 2nd edition by order of CoDominium Intelligence and its author was last seen in a group of involuntary colonists embarking for Fulson's World.*]

TANITH:

"Soft duty, you lucky bastards."

The words had come from a unit of the First Battalion, trudging in from night patrol past the waiting ranks of the Fifth. It was only an hour past dawn, and already hot enough to make the camouflage paint run in sweat-streaks down the soldiers' faces; the Fifth Battalion were lounging on their personal kits, fresh from the showers and in walking-out khakis, ready for the ground-effect trucks to take them to the shuttle docks. The sun was a yellow-brown glare through the ever-present haze of Tanith's atmosphere. Some of the other remarks were more personal and pointed.

Battalion Sergeant Sergio Guiterrez looked up from his kit and grinned as he jerked one of the hotter-tempered new troopers back; a local kid from a jungle village, with a log-sized chip on his shoulder.

"Cool it, trooper, unless you want to spend the first month on Sparta doing punishment detail," he said genially. "And Purdy," he continued, pointing to the recruit's rifle, "if I *ever* see you let your weapon fall in the dirt like that again, you will *suffer*. ¿Comprende?"

The recruit looked down. His New Aberdeen 7mm semi-automatic had slipped off the lumpy surface of his duffel bag and was lying on the hard-packed dirt of the parade square. Appalled, he hesitated for an instant before scooping it up.

"Sss . . . sorry, Battalion Sergeant," he began, bracing to attention. "I, ah, I was—"

"Is that an *excuse* I'm hearing, Private Purdy?"

"Oh, *no*, Battalion Sergeant."

"Good. Present arms for inspection."

Flick-click-snick. The trooper swung the rifle up, extracted the magazine and held the weapon extended across his palms with the bolt locked open.

The noncom ran a finger over the surface of the bolt head. "See this?" he said, rubbing forefinger and thumb together. "Gun oil picks up dust, and that erodes the working parts. Clean it."

Good kid, he thought, watching the earnest black face. *Plenty of brains, and Mother of God, but he can move through bush.* Purdy was one of several brothers and cousins from a jungle settlement here on Tanith, born to time-expired convicts who'd moved out into the bush to start on their own. They'd all been posted to the Scouts, and would be useful on Sparta.

"Battalion Sergeant?"

Guiterrez turned and saluted. "Ma'am?" he said.

It *did* feel odd to be saluting a redheaded chit only just turned eighteen, but he did it willingly enough. Cornet Ursula Gordon might not have saved the Legion's ass, exactly, but the story was that she *had* furnished the information that let them fulfill their contract with the Governor. What was for certain was that the Legion had bought her contract of indenture from the Hilton Hotel. *Entertainer.* Guiterrez snorted. It had been pretty clear what kind of entertainment she'd provided. Not that she'd had any choice in the matter. They might call it indentured service to repay the Hilton's costs for her education, but it was slavery right enough.

Damned if I know why she wants to go for a soldier, Guiterrez thought. The word was that Governor Blaine had offered her a good job in administration here on Tanith. *Maybe she wants to make a fresh start.* He could understand that; Sergio Guiterrez had started out running with a gang in San Diego, and had been lucky enough to catch the attention of a CD Marine recruiter looking over the newcomers to a relocation center. It was the Marines or a one-way trip to Tanith. *Got me here anyway. But not as a slave.* Smart girl, and a looker too, with that heart-shaped face and enormous green eyes; a little more athletic than he liked, but on a heavy-gravity world like this you got a workout just walking down to the corner.

"Well, it's confirmed I'll be coming to Sparta with the Fifth," she continued, returning his salute. It was a little awkward, like the way she wore the blue and gold of the Legion, but she was trying. "Captain Alana wants me to arrange a cross-training schedule on the Armor Company simulators while we're on shipboard."

"Yes, Ma'am. I'll take care of it. Welcome to the Fifth," Guiterrez said. He liked the smile he got back. *Maybe she'll do.*

Did the Governor have *to hold the going-away party in the Hilton?* Ursula Gordon thought.

She surreptitiously wiped her palms on her pocket handkerchief and smoothed down her dress-white jacket. The Tanith upper-classes never wore white, because white jackets were the uniform of convict trustee laborers; but Falkenberg's Legion wasn't about to change its customs. No one was going to mistake one of Falkenberg's officers for a convict. Not more than once, anyway.

It was only mildly hot in the screened and sunroofed porch of the Lederle Hilton, with the overhead fans whirring and cool water trickling down the vine-grown screens of Gray Howlite stone spaced about. *My palms would be sweaty if it was air-conditioned.* This building had been her home since the Hilton company bought her contract at the age of four; children of convicts had been automatically indentured then, back before the current Governor's reforms. Her place of work from the day she turned fifteen and became a fixture of the luxury suites, until Prince Lysander checked in. Three short months ago, and now she was seeing it for the last time. As a guest.

She sipped at her iced soda water and watched her fellow officers mingle with Governor Blaine's bureaucrats and planters; the planters included some former rebels, here to show their humble gratitude for the amnesty. *Sweating to please*, she thought coldly. *Learn how it feels, you slave-driving bastards.*

Blaine himself was being determinedly friendly to all. . . . It was his main weakness, a desire to be liked. Fortunately, he knew how to control it. He broke free of the circle of former enemies and came over to her. "Good-bye." He gripped both her hands with his.

I think he really will miss me.

Blaine was a tall man, over 190 centimeters, and thin enough to look almost skeletal to someone Tanith-born; his sandy brown hair was thinning on top and tousled as always, and he wore the inevitable blue guayabera shirt with the CoDominium seal on the left pocket.

"I still wish you'd taken my offer," he said. Second Administrative Assistant in the Department of Labor; a glorified executive secretary, but it was in the line of promotion, a good position for someone as young as she was. "I hate to see Tanith lose anyone with your abilities; we need all the smart, tough people we can get. Perhaps something else? Name it." Blaine was eccentric that way; he had *requested* posting to Tanith, when every previous governor had taken it as a punishment post. For that matter most planters and company executives dreamed of making a killing and moving somewhere else.

"No, thank you, sir," she said. Then she smiled; it made her look younger than her eighteen Earth years. "That's the second serious proposition I've declined in the last week; it's refreshing."

"Proposition?" he said, looking protective.

"Well, the other one was of marriage," she said. "Captain . . . ah, an officer of the Legion."

Blaine nodded, looking away slightly.

What romantics men are, she thought. It made them easy to manipulate, if you knew. Women had to; some men learned. Colonel John Christian Falkenberg III was as expert as she; military romanticism was as powerful a way to lead men by the nose as the sexual variety.

"Spare the pity, please, Governor," she said a little sharply. "It wasn't all bad here, and I'm not scarred for life, I assure you." Though there were some memories that still woke her shivering in the night; that couple from California . . . She pushed the memory aside.

"Actually, the worst thing about being a . . ." She considered; prostitute was not exactly accurate. For one thing, *she* had never seen any of the money, except for tips and gifts. For another, she had been carefully trained to offer a number of services besides the sexual. ". . . a geisha was that you had to be so damned *agreeable* and *nice* all the time. In the Legion, nobody gives a tinker's curse if I have the personality of a Weems Beast, as long as I get my job done and stand by my comrades."

"Well—"

"Look, sir, I appreciate your concern—and the gentleman who asked me to marry him—but *I don't need any more rescuing.* Right now, I'm getting a fresh start away from Tanith. I know you'll make Tanith a better place to live, but not for *me.* And I've got a movable home and family going with me, the Legion. It's a tough place, but you *earn* what you get, you don't *wheedle* somebody to *give* it to you." She shrugged. "And if I get a husband someday, it won't be someone who wants to protect me because I'm young and pretty and look vulnerable. Hell, maybe *I'll* rescue *him.*"

Blaine laughed. "I understand," he said. "I hope you like Sparta, too. Bit drier and cooler than you're used to, I hear."

Ursula laughed back at him, still feeling a slight stab of satisfaction that she could laugh because she *wanted* to. "I'm looking forward to it, to getting out of this sauna."

Major Peter Owensford sipped at his drink; it was the perpetual gin-and-bitters of Tanith. There was the rum-based liqueur made with Tanith Passion Fruit, but that was too sweet for lunchtime, and anyway it was rumored to be a mild aphrodisiac. *That's the* last *thing I need right now,* he thought dismally, looking over at Ursula where she stood talking and laughing with Blaine . . . *Cornet Gordon,* he reminded himself. Who had politely but firmly put him in his place; a favored uncle's place . . . *God damn it all.*

"Feeling sorry for yourself?" Ace Barton said.

"Not really, Anselm." *Captain* Anselm Barton, he reminded himself. It was going to be difficult, with Ace along. He had been senior too long; with the Legion, and then an independent merc commander for nearly a decade. *And my commanding officer on Thurstone, a lifetime ago.*

"Now I *know* you're pissed, you never call me that unless something's got your goat."

Owensford relaxed. "Oh, all right, Ace; yes."

"Smart and gorgeous, but too young for you. The problem is," he went on, resting a hand on the younger man's shoulder, "you're getting those settling-down feelings. Endemic, once you turn thirty."

"You don't have them?" Owensford replied.

"Oh, yes, but I lie down until they go away." A wink. "Works fine, provided you lie down with the right woman."

Owensford snorted laughter. "Frankly, Ace, I'm nervous about this command as well. The rest of the Legion's going to be a *long* way away." Then he winced inwardly; he had never had a detached command before, and the older man *had.*

Barton shrugged. "What's to worry about? We go set up schools. Which works fine, because we've got the older troopers. Maybe they can't march fifty klicks and fight when they get there, but they can sure train others to do it."

Besides the raw Tanith recruits, Falkenberg had taken the opportunity to move a lot of men near retirement into the Fifth. Tanith was a good place to recruit, you had to be tough to survive here, and there were plenty of broken and desperate men. The Legion as a whole was over-strength, particularly the rifle companies. His unit would include the standard six hundred or so, but twice or three times the proportion of men over thirty-five. Many of them monitors or sergeants or centurions nearing retirement, rock-steady men but tired. There would be near a thousand women and children and pensioners as well.

"Fine for training," Owensford agreed. "On that score, just got the word. Hal Slater's going to Sparta. To set up their staff college. Which means we'll be taking George as well as Iona."

Barton raised an eyebrow but didn't say anything.

"OK, so we got the old ones," Peter said.

"The old, the halt, and the lame," Barton agreed. "But not the stupid. Given my druthers I'll take what we got. Hell, Pete, it's just a training war anyway."

"Training war?" Lysander Collins said from behind them.

They turned to greet the heir to the Collins throne of Sparta. Prince Lysander was a tall young man, 180 centimeters in his sandals; about twenty, a broad-shouldered youth with cropped brown hair and hazel eyes that looked somehow firmer than they had when he came to Tanith a few months ago.

"We were just discussing the sort of recruits we'll be getting on Sparta, for your new army. We're not used to Taxpayer enlisted men. Sorry," Owensford corrected himself. "Recruits from the Citizen class, I meant." He would have to remember that on Earth, Citizen meant a member of the underclass, the welfare-dependent or casual-laboring lumpenproletariat. Better than half the population of the U.S., and more elsewhere. On Sparta a Citizen was a voter, a member of the political ruling class. Not necessarily socially upper-class, but solidly respectable at least.

"Well, not all the recruits will be Citizens or from Citizen families," Prince Lysander said. "It's a big planet and not many people and there's a lot to do, if you've got some sort of education. A lot of the deportees BuReloc sends us are illiterate and have never held a job; there's plenty of unskilled laboring positions open, but I think some of them will join up for the Field Force as well."

He frowned slightly; a serious young man for the most part, thoughtful. "I'd have thought our Citizens would be easier to train," he added. "The schools on Sparta are pretty good, and there's a lot of paramilitary training through the Brotherhoods' youth-wings."

"True enough," Owensford said. "The Legion's training schedule is pretty much the same as the CoDo Marines, though. With the sort of street-toughs and gang warriors we get, you break the recruit to build the soldier; everything they've learned all their lives is wrong, except for pack loyalty and aggressiveness."

Which was why nine-tenths of Marine recruits had records; the sort who just sat in front of the Tri-V screens and stirred only to get more booze and borloi were little use.

> "*The new recruit is silly,*
> *'e thinks o'suicide*
> *'e's lost 'is gutter-devil*
> *'e hasn't got 'is pride—*"

Lysander quoted softly. "It makes better sense, now. He knew his stuff, didn't he?"

"Certainly did," Owensford replied. He had discovered Kipling on his own. The man had long since been purged from what passed for an educational system in North America, but Lysander had mentioned he was by way of a national poet. Sparta promised to be full of surprises like that.

They all lifted their glasses for a moment to Kipling's memory.

"We'll manage," Ace Barton said. "Soldiers do."

"Not only soldiers," the Prince said quietly; his eyes flicked toward Ursula Gordon and then away.

Owensford felt a brief stab of irritation mixed with pity. Sparta seemed to be a pretty straight-laced sort of place, at least at the upper levels, and Ursula had hit the young man like a ton of cement. First love and first adventure, that daredevil stunt with the Bronson's shuttle and a beautiful damsel in genuine distress, heady stuff. Doubly bitter when he realized that he could have neither; back to the strait confines of duty, and a marriage arranged by his elders.

At least she would have said yes *to you,* Owensford thought ironically.

"You'll probably see more soldiering," he said kindly to the young man. "Don't mean to sound cold-blooded, but this little guerrilla-bandit problem will be perfect for providing on-the-job training for your new Field Force, and it's an old tradition for crown princes to hold commissions."

"Yep." Ace finished his drink; there were times when Arizona sounded clearly in his voice, under the accentless polish an officer acquired in the CoDominium service. "Nothin' like hearing a bullet and realizing there's someone out there trying to *kill* you to put the polish on a soldier."

Lysander grimaced; his own baptism of fire had been quite

recent, and his Phraetrie-brother Harv bad been badly wounded, nearly killed.

"I could do without it," he said.

"That's exactly the point, Prince. Exactly the point."

SPARTA:

"Hey, Skilly, what-a you got for us? Where's Two-knife?"

"Gots good stuff this time, Marco," Skida said genially, walking down the landing ramp with her knapsack, taking a deep lungful of air that held slight traces of smoke and massed humanity, if you concentrated. She had been born a city girl and grown up on streets, however squalid. After a while in the outback the silence and clear air got to you. "Two-knife coming downriver with the bulk product."

The stamped steel treads rang under her boots, and the blimp creaked at its mooring tower above her. The landing field was down by the water, in the East Haven side of Sparta City, along with the fishing fleet and the river barges from up the Eurotas and coastal shipping; the shuttle landing docks and the deep-sea berths were on the other side of the finger of hilly built-up land. The pale sun was high, and crowds of seagulls swarmed noisily over the maze of concrete docks, nets, masts, warehouses and cranes along the waterfront. A good dozen airships were in, long cigar-shapes of inflated synthetic fabric with aluminum gondolas and diesel engine-pods; the one behind her had *Clemens Airways* painted on the envelope. Two more were leaving, turning south and east for the Delta with leisurely grace; out on the water a three-masted schooner was running on auxiliaries. Then the sails went up, lovely clean shapes of white canvas; the ship heeled, and her prow bit the water in a sunlit burst of spray.

"What exactly?" Marco said, as she stepped to the cracked, stained concrete. Five of her hidehunters followed, big shaggy men in sheepskin jackets, open now in the mild heat of the seafront city, their rifles slanted over their backs.

"Got twenty-five tons good clear tallow," she began, as they walked toward the street entrance.

Marco followed beside her, making unconscious hand-washing gestures; he was a stumpy little man, bald but with blue jowls. A fashion designer from Milan in his youth, swept up after the riots against the Sicilian-dominated government and handed over to BuReloc.

"One fifty tons first-grade spicebush-smoked beef jerky," she continued. "One-twenty venison. Twenty-two hundred raw cowhides, two-thousand-fifty horsehides, horns and hooves appropriate, 'bout the same deerhides, some elk. Five hundred twenty good buffalo hides, do for robes. Beaver and capybara, five hundred and seven hundred. One twenty red fox, seventy wolfhides, twenty cougar. One hundred-twenty-two saddle-broken mustangs from the Illyrian Dales, *really* saddle-broke and to pack saddles as well. Holding the horses in Olynthos, but Skilly can get them downriver if you know a better market."

They pushed through the exit gate of the landing field, and into the crowded streets of dockside; it was convenient, how Sparta had no internal checks, no waiting to have your papers cleared every time you got on or off something. There was a row of electric runabouts, little fuel-cell-powered things that ran on alcohol and air; she waved dismissal at the hidehunters and handed the attendant a gold coin. He knew her well, and there was no nonsense with bank machines that recorded where you were and what you did. Another convenient thing about Sparta.

Skida noted these matters; they were all things that would have to change, when *she* was in charge. She paid the hidehunters off in Consolidated Hume Financial Bank script; Thibodeau Animal Products Inc. used them as their bank of deposit. They also handled her modest but growing investment portfolio; under other names, they administered some of the accounts she had on Dayan and Xanadu, as well. *Skilly's just-in-case money,* she thought, dumping her knapsack beside the bundles the hunters had left in the backseat and ushering Marco to the passenger side.

"See you at the Dead Cow in three days," she said to the men. They nodded silently; she had picked them well. "Any of you gets into trouble before then, Skilly bails him out of jail then cuts off his balls, *¿comprende?*"

"Sure, Skilly," the oldest of them said. "I'll watch them."

"I can get you two-fifty crowns for the beef," Marco said, as the car pulled silently out onto the street. He was always a little nervous while the hidehunters were around. She headed uphill, to the Sacred Way, which ran down the ridge-spine of the city from the CoDo enclave to Government House Square. The road went up in switchbacks, through a neighborhood of stucco family homes over embankments planted in rhododendrons. "Standard rate for the tallow, but the hides are up two-tenths. And I can get you six crowns apiece for the horses here in town."

She raised her brows. Those were excellent prices; agricultural produce was usually a glut, and only the low costs of harvesting feral stock made the hidehunting business profitable at all.

"The Crown he's-a buying," Marco explained, then blanched slightly as she cut blindside around a horse-drawn dray loaded with melons, in a curve that lifted two wheels off the pavement. "These soldiers they bring in, and the new army, you hear?"

"Skilly knows," she said. "OK, sounds good, regular commission." She grinned broadly; there was a certain irony to it, after all. Like charging someone for the ammunition you shot them with; the Belizian government had done that when she was a youngster.

The commission would be fair, five percent. Marco was broker for half a dozen hidehunter outfits, although Thibodeau Inc. was his biggest customer. They had had no problems, after the first time she caught him shorting her; obviously he had not expected a deportee to know accounting systems. Unfortunately for him, Skida Thibodeau had been in jail for most of her first eighteen months on Sparta—a little matter of someone hurt in a game of chance she was running for start-up capital—and she had divided her time inside between working out to get used to the heavy gravity and taking correspondence courses from the University. A simple fracture of the forearm had reformed the broker's morals, that and the cheerful warning that next time she would send Two-knife around to start with his kneecaps and work upward.

"What's this good stuff you got for me?" the Italian continued.

Skida pulled the car to the curb on the Sacred Way; Sparta City had plenty of parking, cars still being a rare luxury. This was the medium-rent district, not too close to Government House Square. A few four-story apartment houses, with restaurants and shops on the ground level; there were showrooms, headquarters of shipping or fishing firms, doctors' and lawyers' offices. The broad sidewalk next to their parking spot was set with tables, shaded by the big jacarandas and oaks that fringed the main street: the Blue Mountain Café. Run by a family of Jamaican deportees, and set up with a loan Skilly had guaranteed. It was useful, and she had wanted at least one place in town where you could get a decently spiced meat patty. There were all types on Sparta, but the basic mix was Anglo-Hispanic-Oriental, like the United States.

"Here," she said, pulling a fur from one of the bundles in the rear seat and tossing it across his lap.

"Oh, holy Jesus!" he blurted. It was a meter long and a double handspan broad, a shining lustrous white color, supple and beautiful. The ex-fashion designer ran his hand over it reverently. "What *is* this?"

"Some of Skilly's people were working the country northeast of Lake Ochrid, you know, the Hyborian Tundra?" Remote and desolate, almost never visited. "Turns out those ermine the CoDo turned loose to eat the rabbits been getting *big*, mon."

Marco made a soundless happy whistle. There were excellent markets for furs, even Earth now that the Greens had less influence . . . especially Earth; after they had lost their commercial value nobody had bothered to preserve many of the fur species.

"Seventy-five, maybe eighty each," he said, his voice soft with the pleasure of handling the pelt.

"And this," she continued. What she dumped in his lap next was a kilo-weight silver ingot, stamped with the mark of the Stora Kopparberg mine.

"*Shit!*" he said, in a falsetto shriek. The metal disappeared under the seat. "Oh, no, not again!"

Skida grinned with ruthless amusement. So few people seemed to realize that once you made a single illegal deal you were in for good. Especially a family man like Marco, so concerned for the three children he hoped to see make Citizen someday. Every parent on Sparta got educational vouchers, but there was no law saying a prestige school had to accept the children of non-Citizens. With enough money, everything was possible, of course.

"Yes. But doan worry, this de last time."

"Oh, Mother of God, you mean that? They hang us all, they hang us all!"

"Not unless they catch us, mon," Skilly soothed. "Of course I mean it. All legitimate from now on." Skida Thibodeau believed firmly in never welshing on a business deal; it was too much like peeing in the bathwater. Besides, they were moving into big-time money now, and the fencing would have to be handled through the political side. "Coming downriver nice and safe in the tallow; besides, they never know what happen to that blimp from the mine. Bad weather, maybe."

A stowaway named Skida Tbibodeau with a small leather sack full of lead shot had happened to it, but there was no point in burdening Marco with unnecessary information. Much of the vessel had been useful to the Helots—high-speed diesels were not easy to come by—and the rest had joined the crew in a very deep sinkhole.

"OK," Marco said, wiping his brow with a handkerchief. "You want me to fix you up a place at-a my house?" he said, with insincere hospitality. Skilly had more than enough to rent or buy a place in town for her visits, but that would have offended her sense of thrift. As often as not she dossed down on a cot in Thibodeau Inc.'s single-room office.

"No, Skilly going to catch a curry patty and a beer here and then meet her boyfriend," she said. Take another car out to his place, rather, but there was a mild pleasure in teasing the factor.

Marco shuddered again. "Skilly, he's a Citizen and First Families, and he's in politics and the government don't like him," he said half-pleadingly. "Why?"

"Love be blind, my mon," Skilly said. One reason she avoided it, but an affair was surprisingly good cover. The founders of Sparta had had a privacy fetish that they built into the local culture. She reached over and pinched the Italian's cheek. "You leave a message for Skilly as soon as you find a way to wash the silver money, hey?"

CHAPTER THREE

Crofton's Encyclopedia of Contemporary History
and Social Issues (2nd Edition):

THE EXODUS

The great outburst of interstellar colonization in the early
21st century paradoxically led to the reappearance of economic and social problems which Earth had thought
vanished. Fusion-powered spaceships, mass-driver launchers
and the virtually energy-free Alderson drive brought transport costs between systems down to levels comparable
to those of 20th-century air freight, but they were still
not cheap. New colonies were chronically short of the
hard currency they so desperately needed to pay for
imports of capital equipment. Human labor was plentiful—
the Bureau of Relocation would furnish it whether the
recipient wanted it or not—but everything else, from
transport to machine tools, was chronically scarce.

Earth's markets were jealously guarded by the cartels
which dominated the planetary economy; and there was
a well-founded suspicion that those cartels and the shipping lines they controlled conspired to maintain the colony
worlds as dependent markets. Some metals and drugs
could bear the costs of interstellar transport, along with
extrasolar rarities and luxury goods, but bulk agricultural
produce was shipped only to mining systems without
habitable planets.

The stable elite of colony worlds—Dayan, Xanadu, Meiji,
Friedland, Churchill—were those where wealthy parent governments or corporations provided cash and credit enough
to finance self-sustaining industrialization. With plentiful resources and fewer social problems, by the late 21st
century these planetary states had populations in the

10–50 million range, higher per capita incomes than most Earthly nations, and were taking advantage of the CoDominium's retreat to establish sub-imperialisms and trade spheres of their own. Some planets (see *Haven*) remained mere dumping grounds, sustained by Colonial Bureau largess; *Hadley* was an interesting example of such a world escaping mass die-off after CoDominium withdrawal.

Many of the less well-financed colonies, launched by "Third World" nations or private organizations—some religious, some secular—with only enough funds to pay for transport, lapsed into a virtually pre-industrial existence of peasant farming and handicrafts; see *Arrarat, Zanj, Santiago*. A common pattern on intermediate planets was the emergence of a severely hierarchical society, with a dominant elite using access to interstellar technology to rule an impoverished mass; see *Frystaat, Thurstone, Diego, Novi Kossovo*.

Constant political and social unrest resulted from this situation. See *Sparta* for an interesting case-study of an attempt to deal with these problems through careful planning; while partially successful, it . . .

SPARTA:

Major Peter Owensford looked up from his laptop computer to the viewport of the shuttle. It was a Royal Spartan Airways custom craft, on continuous orbit-to-ground runs; rather different from the assault boats he was accustomed to, which had to be small enough to be carried within a starship's hull. Certainly more comfortable, with the seats in facing pairs and lavishly padded. The orbiter was low enough to switch to turbojet mode, a difference in the subliminal hum that came through the hull. Below, the surface of the Inland Sea was bright-blue, speckled with islands; even from fifteen thousand meters it looked clear and inviting. A welcome change from the livid yellow and green of Tanith's seas, always warm as blood and full of life-forms more active and vicious than anything Earth had bred. You could swim in Sparta's seas.

Both planets had high gravity, twenty percent greater than Earth. Otherwise very little on Sparta was like Tanith. Sparta had little land, but what it had was rugged, with high peaks and active volcanoes. There was hardly a mountain on Tanith.

The hook-shaped peninsula that held Sparta City on its tip came into view; off to the east across Constitution Bay was the vast marshland of the Eurotas Delta, squares of reclaimed cropland visible along its edges. The shuttle made banking turns to shed energy and descend. Most of the city was on a thumb-shaped piece of land that jutted out into the water. Owensford could make out docks at either side of the thumb's base, the characteristic low squares and domes of a fusion plant in the gigawatt range, factory districts more extensive than on most planets. Lots of green, tree-lined streets and gardens, parks, villas and estates along the shores south of the city proper. Very few tall buildings, which was typical even of capital cities off-Earth; an entire planet with barely three million people was rarely crowded. Ships at the docks, everything from schooners and trawlers to surprisingly modern-looking steel-hulled diesels.

And a big section on the western side reserved for shuttles, buoys on the water marking out their landing paths. There were two more at the docks; a big walled compound topped a hill nearby, with the CoDominium flag at the guardhouse by the entrance. That would be the involuntary-colonist holding barracks. The major road ran south from that, to a cluster of parks and public buildings around a large square.

Owensford looked up at the man opposite him and smiled at his attempt to hide the obvious emotion he felt.

"I envy you, Prince Lysander," he said. "Having a home to return to."

"Yours as well, now," Lysander said. His Phraetrie-brother Harv was beside him, staring out the viewport with open longing on his face.

"I hope so, Prince; I sincerely hope so," Owensford said. *Phraetries,* he thought. *Brotherhoods.* It was another thing he'd have to get used to; Spartan Citizens were all members of one; being accepted was a condition of Citizenship. A Phraetrie was everything from a social club and mutual-benefit association to a military unit, and the Spartan militia was organized around them.

"Reminds me of California," Ace Barton said beside him, as the shuttle's wings extended fully and it touched down in twin plumes of spray.

There was a faint rocking sensation, then a *chung* as the tug linked and began towing them toward the docks. Owensford nodded; the houses on the low hills above the quaysides were mostly white stucco over stone or brick or concrete, with red tile roofs. None of them was very large, apart from the old cluster around the CoDominium center; even the colonnaded neoclassic public buildings were only a few stories high.

The style was appropriate enough; the local climate around the Aegean Sea had the same rhythm of warm dry summers and cool moist winters as the Mediterranean basin. And a fair proportion of the original settlers had been from the North American west coast as well.

"Before they mucked it up, Ace, like California before they mucked it up."

"May I ask an awkward question?" Lysander asked.

"Considering that you're paying our bills, you can ask just about anything you like," Owensford said.

"Well—I've never been a mercenary. Maybe this happens a lot, but not long ago Captain Barton—Major Barton then—was the enemy. And outranked you. Now he's your subordinate. Isn't this a little strange?"

Ace Barton shrugged. "Maybe not so unusual as all that. And it's OK by me."

"Ace and I go back a long way," Peter Owensford said. "I guess I told you the story one night."

"I remember some of it, but that had been a long night," Lysander said.

"I remember," Peter said. "Anyway, rank isn't a big deal in Falkenberg's Legion. Hell, nearly everyone is a captain. The chain of command depends on what post you have."

"First names in the mess," Barton said. "Sort of a brotherhood. Like yours, Prince Lysander."

"Ah. Thank you," Lysander said.

Peter nodded thoughtfully. This command would have its problems, but Ace Barton wouldn't be one of them. Ace had recruited Peter Owensford into the Legion. Peter flinched at the memory. It had been after a fiasco in the Santiago civil war on Thurstone, when he had ended up on the losing side. The memory was mildly embarrassing; you expected young men to be stupid, but that had been nearly terminal. Opting for the CoDominium service at West Point, when anyone who read the papers knew the Fleet Marines were disbanding regiments and had forty-year-old lieutenants in some outfits. No chance of a U.S. Army commission when he'd shown he was a commie-coddling CD-lover, either. Then letting the Liberation Party's people recruit him for that blindsided slaughterhouse. . . .

Ace Barton had been in it for his own reasons, and a damned good thing. Without him Owensford would have been shot half a dozen times by the Republican Commissars. Or by the Dons when the Republic went down in defeat; Barton had passed the defeated volunteers off as mercenaries entitled to protection under the Code, and then gotten Christian Johnny to take them on spec. Ace went on to ten successful years skippering his own mercenary outfit before getting smashed by the Legion on Tanith. "So," Peter said. "Another beginning."

"My grandfather said Sparta was a second chance in more ways than one," Lysander said.

Owensford smiled thinly as he stood and adjusted his kepi; the troops back in the belly of the shuttle were in dress blue and gold, and so were the officers. Noncombatants and most of the baggage would be coming later, but it was important to make a good showing for the reception committee. Important for the men as well as impressing the locals . . . and after all, it was not that often that *two* kings came to greet a unit of Falkenberg's Legion when it staged down from orbit. Even on those occasions when they didn't come down in assault boats to a high-firepower reception.

"Odd that you should say that, your Highness," Owensford said. "I was just thinking that a fresh start is the commonest dream of men past their first youth, and the hardest of things to find. We carry too much baggage with us."

Lysander looked past the older man, not quite letting his eyes settle on Cornet Ursula Gordon as she stuffed the printouts and textbooks she had been studying into her carryall. Peter Owensford suspected that both parties would have been much happier if Cornet Gordon had shipped out to New Washington. An untrained and exceedingly junior female staff officer—not much more than an officer candidate, really—did not serve the needs of the Legion on that war-torn planet, and so there was another case of convenience yielding to necessity.

For that matter, he would have preferred to be on New Washington himself. The Legion had been hired on by the secessionist rebels who wanted to free their planet from its neighbor Franklin. A desperate struggle against long odds to begin with, and Franklin had hired mercenaries of their own to boot. Covenant Highlanders and Friedland armor, at that; Christian Johnny's plan would get into the textbooks with a vengeance, if it worked. While Major Peter Owensford built a base camp, trained yokels and chased a few bandits through the hills.

No, there are no clean endings, Owensford thought. *Or fresh beginnings. But we do our jobs.*

Dion Croser leaned back in the armchair and stared into the embers of the coal fire, holding the brandy snifter in one hand, his pipe in the other. Cool air drifted in through the French windows to his left, the ones that opened out on the gardens, smelling of eucalyptus and clipped grass. The study was a big room, paneled with slabs of dark native stone; there had been little wood available when Croser's father built the ranch house, in the early days of settlement on Sparta. A coal fire burned in the big hearth, casting flickering red shadows that caught at the crystal decanters on the sideboard, the holos and pictures amid the bookcases on the walls. One big oil portrait, of Elliot Croser as a young man on Earth, standing before the library of the University in Berkeley. Back when Sparta was a plan, something talked about in student cafés and in the living rooms of the faculty.

He raised his glass, meeting the eyes of the painted figure. *They twisted your dream, father,* he thought. Twisted it, denied him the place he'd earned as one of the founders of Sparta. Drove him into exile on this estate, into drink-sodden futility. *I'm going to set it straight.* The face in the painting might have been his, perhaps not so high in the cheekbones, and without the slanted eyes that were a legacy from Dion's Hawaiian-Japanese mother. Without the weathered look and rangy muscle that forty years spent outside and largely in the saddle brought, either.

A discreet cough brought his attention to the door.

"Miss Thibodeau," the butler said, disapproval plain beneath the smooth politeness of his tone. Chung had worked for his father back on Earth, and his grandfather before that, and Skida Thibodeau was *not* the sort of person a Taxpayer in California would receive.

"Ah, you re*mem*ber Skilly," she said ironically to the servant, handing him her bulky sheepskin jacket and gunbelt, before pushing through into the study and walking over to pour herself a glass of wine.

Dion rose courteously for a moment and nodded to her, feeling his breath catch slightly; they had been political associates for ten years, lovers for five, and it was still pure pleasure to watch her move. Nearly two meters tall—and the tight leather pants and cotton shirt showed every centimeter to advantage, moving the way he imagined a jaguar might in the jungles of her homeland. With a sigh she threw herself into the seat across from him, hooking a leg over one arm; that pushed the high breasts against the thin fabric of her shirt. He swallowed and looked up, to the chocolate-brown face framed in loose-curled hair that glinted blue-black. High cheekbones and full lips, nose slightly curved, eyes tilted and colored hazel, glinting green flecks. Her mother had been Mennonite-German, he remembered, a farmer's daughter from the colonies in northern Belize kidnaped into prostitution during a visit to Belize City. Father a pimp; and both had died young.

"Dion my mon," she said, raising her glass.

"Skida," he replied, not using the nickname.

"Skilly hears Van Horn met with the accident she recommended," she said. "Bobber in line for his job?"

Croser winced slightly; setting up an assassination squad reporting directly to himself had been her idea. Skilly had been eclectically well read even before she arrived on Sparta, but sometimes he regretted introducing her to the classic works on guerrilla warfare and factional politics. Van Horn had been necessary, of course, once he had brought his toughs into the Movement. Head of the Werewolves, the only real street gang in Minetown—gangs were difficult on Sparta, where you went to school or worked as a teenager—but not loyal. Still . . . she saw the expression and smiled indulgently.

"Mon, in this business, you doan fire people," she pointed out. "Retire feet first is the only way."

He nodded; even with the cell-structure, Van Horn could have done the Front too much damage if he had gone to the RSMP; not least because he was one of the links between the NCLF's above-ground organization and the Helots. Discipline had to be enforced, especially now that direct-action work was increasing. Far too many of the recruits were Welfare Island street-gangers, the leaders had to set an example.

"You think Bobber may resent what happened?" he said. "She and Van Horn were . . . close."

Skida laughed. "Bobber de one tell me Van Horn dipping the till excessive," she said. "Bobber and I came in on the same CoDo ship; she a cool one. Van Horn a stepping stone for her, and beside, Bobber likes girls better. Good hater, she a real believer in the Movement." She shrugged indifferently. "And she from Chicago; that useful now we getting so many *gringo* gangers off the transports."

He sipped at the brandy and took another pull at the pipe, the comforting mellow bite at his tongue.

"Congratulations on the Velysen raid," he said. "Ah . . . Skida . . . what happened to his wife and sister-in-law is creating a lot of indignation."

"Just what Skilly wanted; Dion, you know we not getting these ranchers to *like* us, whatever. And just killing them, it make them mad only and want to fight us." She extended a hand palm up, then curled the fingers. "Threaten they families, and we have them by the *balls,* mon."

He sighed again; the basic strategy was his, in any event. "I know; and they'll push for harsher measures on the non-Citizens, which drives them into our camp."

"*The worse, the better,* that what that Russki mon Lenin say, no? Very nice statement you make to the *Herald,* denouncing violent splinter faction and then blaming oppression for driving us to it." She took another slow sip of her wine; he had taught her that, to appreciate a good vintage. "How things going at the University?"

"Slowly, but we've got a structure there now. Particularly in the Sociology and Humanities divisions; there're a lot of scions there who're worried about making their Citizenship tests. Plus the usual hangers-on."

"Many ready to go Helot?" she asked. It was a bother, keeping the other recruits from eating the student types alive, but the survivors were valuable when they'd toughened up. Too many of the rank-and-file NCLF fighters broke into a sweat if they had to think more than a week ahead.

Dion's face creased in a bleak grin. "There will be, after we provoke the next riot. Sore heads and sore tempers, and once they're commited . . ." They toasted each other. "I've gotten another half-dozen CoDo Marine deserters for you, too, and another officer."

Skilly thumped the arm of the chair in delight "Good man!" she said. Trained cadre willing to work for the Helots had always been a problem; there were plenty of CoDo officers up on the beach, but most of them were picky. *Too squeamish to be useful,* she thought. The ones who weren't tended to have other problems that restricted their usefulness.

"Roughly, what else are we going to need in the next year or so?"

She frowned. "Dion, we got as far as we getting without serious outside help, like we discussed. Plenty recruits and enough arms"—Sparta exported the simpler infantry weapons and equipment, and the Movement had been diverting a percentage of that for years—"money coming in steady, but raids and holding up trucks not enough; we need electronics, commo gear, heavy weapons, this precision-guided stuff. Better network in Sparta City and the Valley towns, too. And techs, and a secure conduit off-planet. Not just to those Liberation Party *grisgris,* either. Even *with* help, going to be long time before we can slug it out with the Brotherhoods."

He set down glass and pipe and tapped his fingers together beneath his chin. "We've got it."

Skida raised an eyebrow. "Money?"

"Money, yes."

"Enough to pay your debts? Who we owe for this?"

Croser ignored the first question. Neither he nor his father had been very good at financial management. The Revolution would take care of the situation, but that wasn't any of Skida's business. "A lot more than money. From the Senator." A snort. "It was the Royal government hiring Falkenberg's people that decided him to do more for us than the trickle we've gotten so far. Weapons, shipping out for what the NCLF takes in, loans—*big* loans—technical personnel. . . .

"A group from Meiji is arriving next week." This time his grin was a wolf's. "Full conference of the clandestine branch section heads as soon as the Meijians have been briefed."

Skida's teeth showed dazzling white against her skin. "That my mon!" She raised her wine. "To the Revolution!"

He leaned over to clink his snifter against her glass. "To the Democratic Republic of Sparta!"

"To the first *President* of the Republic, Dion Croser!"

"To the first Minister of Defense"—the Royal government had a Ministry of War—"Skida Thibodeau!" he said.

They emptied their glasses and she uncoiled to her feet, walked over, braced her hands against the armrests of his chair and leaned forward until their faces were almost touching. Lips met; her mouth tasted of wine and mint. The man's nostrils flared, taking in the strong mixed scents from her clothes and skin, woodsmoke and sweat and leather and horse. Dion reached for her.

"No, not yet," Skida said huskily; her eyes glittered in the firelight. "Skilly wants a shower first. And then we lock the door for a day. Skilly has been in the outback too long. Skilly is so horny goats and girls and even my hidehunters were starting to look good."

She drew back with taunting slowness, and looked over her shoulder. "Scrub de back, mon?"

CHAPTER FOUR

Crofton's Essay and Lectures in Military History (2nd Edition)

Professor John Christian Falkenberg II:
Delivered at the CoDominium University, Rome, 2080

"The principal military states 'own' perhaps ninety-five percent of all military expertise, if that can be measured by the number of publications on the subject. They have even managed to turn that expertise into a minor export commodity in its own right. Officers belonging to countries which are not great military powers are regularly sent to attend staff and war colleges in Washington, Moscow, London, and Paris . . . the principal powers themselves have sent thousands upon thousands of military 'experts' to dozens of third-world countries all over Latin America, Africa, and Asia.

"The above notwithstanding, serious doubt exists concerning the ability of developed states—both such as are currently 'liberating' themselves from communist domination and such as are already 'free'—to use armed force as an instrument for attaining meaningful political ends. This situation is not entirely new. In numerous incidents during the last two decades, the inability of developed countries to protect their interests and even their citizens' lives in the face of low-level threats has been demonstrated time and time again. As a result, politicians as well as academics were caught bandying about such phrases as 'the decline of power,' 'the decreasing utility of war,' and—in the case of the United States—'the straw giant.'

"So long as it was only Western society that was becoming 'debellicized' the phenomenon was greeted with anxiety. The Soviet failure in Afghanistan has turned the

scales, however, and now the USSR too is a club member in good standing. In view of these facts, there has been speculation that war itself may not have a future and is about to be replaced by economic competition among the great 'trading blocs' now forming in Europe, North America, and the Far East. This volume will argue that such a view of war is not correct. Large-scale, conventional war—war as understood by today's principal military powers—may indeed be at its last gasp; however, war itself, war as such, is alive and kicking and about to enter a new epoch. . . ."
—*The Transformation of War:* Free Press, 1991

The above was written by Martin van Creveld and published shortly before the United States began the largest conventional military action of the second half of the 20th century. We are now to consider where Creveld, one of the best military historians of the last or indeed any century, was correct—and where he went wrong.

"That was an impressive show, Major," Alexander I said as the last of Filth Battalion clambered aboard the trucks in the square below.

They were locally made, diesel-powered flatbeds with wheels that were balls of spun chrome-steel alloy thread. Primitive compared to ground-effect machines, but better than the horse-drawn wagons found on many worlds. There were plenty of draft animals on the streets of Sparta City, but there were electric runabouts and diesel-engined vans as well, and even a few Earth-made hovercars.

Here in Government House Square where the mercenaries had paraded for their employer's inspection the town looked much like a Californian university campus of the older type, complete with tiled walks, gardens, and neospanish architecture. The Hall of State could have done for a convocation, with its green copper dome and pillars; the Palace was a rambling affair that might have been the Dean's residence.

"I hope you don't mind our detaining you and your officers," Alexander said. He was a tall spare man in his fifties; much like an older Prince Lysander, except that his gray-shot hair was blond and worn ear-length in a cut fashionable on Earth two generations before. And for the infinite weariness around his eyes; Owensford knew it for the look of tension borne too long.

"By no means, sir," Peter said. He bowed slightly, reflecting that the Spartan monarchy was an informal affair, at least so far.

David I, the Freedman king, was already seated at the briefing table. Crown Prince David, actually, but his father Jason was quasi-retired, victim of a debilitating disease, and David was Freedman king for all practical purposes. David was a stocky man, dressed like his colleague in brown tunic and knee-breeches of extremely conservative cut; one of the more elderly bureaucrats near him wore a suit and tie, old-fashioned enough to be bizarre. Another man had a shaven-bald head, monocle, quasi-military tunic and riding crop; that would be *Freiherr* Bernard von Alderheim. His father had been from what was once Königsberg, East Prussia, then Kaliningrad, and now Königsberg again; his daughter was Prince Lysander's fiancée, and he was the most prominent industrialist on the planet. He was also titular head of one of the largest and most important Phraetries.

Considered eccentric, Owensford remembered from the briefing. *All in all, you can certainly tell we're seven months' transit from Earth.* He took his seat among the Legion officers.

Uniforms on one side of the square, civilians on the other, except for the man in the dull-scarlet tunic and blue breeches of the Royal Spartan Mounted Police. From the look of his boots, the "mounted" meant exactly that.

"The junior officers and NCOs can handle encampment easily enough," Owensford said. "You will understand, we're anxious to get the basic facilities in place before our noncombatants and families arrive." Some next week, and the rest over the following months. "The Legion's accustomed to being fairly self-contained, and billeting might create problems."

Alexander cleared his throat. "I don't anticipate any trouble with that," he said. "We've got the first five hundred recruits for the Field Force standing by, and there's earth-moving equipment we can make available."

"And anything else you need, I can find for you," Baron von Alderheim said. "Will you also need workmen?"

"Thank you, no, Baron," Peter said. "Learning camp construction is as good an introduction to military discipline as any."

Ace Barton nodded agreement.

"Very good," von Alderheim said. "Castramentation. The first lessons for a Roman soldier."

Peter smiled slightly, unsure of what to say. "Sire, shall I introduce my officers now?"

"Please do," Alexander said.

"My chief of staff, Captain Anselm Barton. Captain Andrew Lahr, Battalion Adjutant. Captain Jameson Mace, Scouts commander. Captains Jesus and Catherine Alana, Intelligence and Planning and Intelligence and Logistics, respectively. George Slater, our senior company commander."

Alexander I raised an eyebrow. "Slater?"

George Slater grinned. "Yes, Sire. My father will be your War College Director when he gets here."

"Ah. Thank you. Mr. Plummer—"

"Yes, Sire." The speaker was a small man, elderly, conservatively dressed but with a splash of color in his scarf. "I'm Horace Plummer, secretary to the cabinet. This is the Honorable Roland Dawson, Principal Secretary of State. Mr. Eric Respari, Treasury and Finance. Sir Alfred Nathanson, Minister of War. Madame Elayne Rusher, Attorney General. Lord Henry Yamaga, Interior and Development. General Lawrence Desjardins, Commandant of the Royal Spartan Mounted Police."

The gendarmerie chief was a blocky man with a thin mustache, with the heavy-gravity musculature most Spartans shared and a dark tan that must have taken work under a sun this pale; not a desk man by preference, Peter estimated.

"This is the War Council," Plummer said. "In formal meetings the Speaker of the Senate would be present, and others can be invited to attend if their expertise is required, but these are Their Majesties' key advisors. Your military orders will come directly from Their Majesties. For administrative purposes you will report to Sir Alfred. Their Majesties ask that you make your initial presentation now."

"Thank you." Peter stood and went to the display board. "I gather from the reports Mr. Plummer has been sending us ever since we entered the Sparta system that things are not quite what we expected here," he said. "Some of this may need adjustment, but I think it important that we all agree on just what the Legion's mission is."

"Yes, of course," Plummer said.

"With your permission, I'm going to lecture a bit," Peter said. "Sparta has always had an enviable militia system based on the Brotherhoods, but until recently the Kingdom hasn't had any need of a standing army or expeditionary forces. That's changing due to the unstable political situation, and you've thought it wise to acquire both."

"To be blunt," King David Freedman said, "we can only afford the one if we have the other. We'll need to rent out expeditionary troops which we hope we can count on at need, because we certainly can't afford to keep a big standing army."

"Just so," Peter said. "Now, the original plan was to bring the entire legion in, let it clone itself, and hire out the clone. That would take care of an expeditionary force. Meanwhile, we would build the infrastructure for doing that trick several times over. By hiring out some units, and bringing selected experienced units home, Sparta would bootstrap up to having the equivalent of a regiment factory. With any luck they'd hire out for enough to support themselves while remaining loyal to Sparta."

"Put that way, it doesn't sound like a very good deal for the soldiers," Roland Dawson said.

"Actually, it could be," Peter said. "Depending on how it was done. Majesties, my lords, my lady—"

"With Madame Elayne's permission, 'gentlemen' will suffice as a collective," Alexander said.

Peter grinned. "Thank you, Sire. To continue. Sparta has considerable experience with militia, but not so much with long service professionals. The professional soldier, for the early part of his career, is quite different from the citizen soldier. Later, though, the differences tend to vanish. There are exceptions, but for the most part the troops may join for glamour, and fight for their comrades, but their real goal is acceptance and respect from someone they respect. A chance at honor, perhaps a second career, and a decent retirement. Sparta can provide all that."

"Pensions," David I said. "They can be expensive."

"Yes, Sire, they can be, but if you want troops loyal to Sparta, as opposed to freebooters, that's ultimately what you have to offer. I do point out that you have a growing economy, so that by the time the pensions are due you should have more than enough to pay them with. Also, you have land, and community resources. I think you may find that retired long service troopers make a net contribution to your economy even with pension costs."

"Yes, yes, of course—"

"So," Peter continued. "If it is still the goal to build long service expeditionary quality units, there will be a number of intermediate objectives, all interrelated. Take weapons systems as an example. They must be designed to take advantage of Sparta's production facilities, but also the troop capabilities— education, schools, quality of the officer corps. What weapons are available will influence how the men are trained. Naturally all this has to fit into your industrial policy.

"Staff officers. I'm sure you know there's a lot of difference between troop leaders and military managers."

"I'd always thought so until I worked with Falkenberg," Prince Lysander said.

Owensford nodded agreement. "The Legion is a bit special, Highness. Even so, you mostly worked with Colonel Falkenberg's staff, who alternate between planning and troop leadership. We also have officers who never leave their units—don't want to. Some of the best leaders you'll ever find. Soldiers should be ambitious, but not so much so that the troops wonder why they should fight for a man anxious to leave them.

"Also, what you saw was the Legion on campaign, which, I grant you, we seem to be most of the time. What you didn't see was in the background. Schools, technical training, social activities, weapons procurement, financial investments, mostly done by non-combatants. And for all that we're a self-contained force, we're only a regimental combat team. What Sparta needs to build will be considerably larger, and thus more complex."

Peter shrugged. "A lot of that will be in Colonel Slater's department, of course, but I do want you to be aware of it."

"Yes, I see," Alexander said. "It's a bit daunting put all at once, but we knew we were in for a major effort. I think we're still agreed?" He looked around the table and collected nods of assent.

"Yes," David said simply. "Only things are not quite what they were. Perhaps we should let General Desjardins talk about the security situation. General—"

"You knew we had a security problem," the constabulary commander said, touching the controls of a keypad. Everyone shifted in their seats as a three-meter square screen on the wall opposite the windows came to life. "It's gotten considerably worse since the last packet of information we sent your Colonel Falkenberg."

A map of the main inhabited portions of Sparta sprang out; the city, and the valley of the Eurotas and its tributaries, snaking north and west from the delta. A scattering along the shores of the Aegean and Oinos seas, and on islands. Dots showed towns; Melos at the junction of the Eurotas and the Alcimion, Clemens about a third of the way up, Dodona in the Middle Valley and Olynthos at the falls where it left Lake Alexander. That was a *big* river, half again as long as the Amazon. Another river and delta on the west coast opposite the Bay of Islands, with the town of Rhodes at the mouth; that one was about comparable to the Mississippi.

Red spots leapt out across the map; there was a concentration on the upper Eurotas and in the foothill zones flanking it on either side. A lighter speckle stretched west into the plains and mountains of the interior of the Serpentine continent, among the isolated grazing stations and mines and hunters' shacks. There was a clear zone in the lower Eurotas, but a dense scattering in Sparta City itself.

"We've always had some banditry in the outback," Desjardins continued. "Worse lately, and you can imagine why."

"Scattered population," Ace Barton said. "Vulnerable communications."

"In spades," the policeman said grimly. "There's still plenty of good land near the capital—even here on the peninsula— but it takes money to develop it, which we don't have. Agricultural prices so low that there's no profit if you need much capital investment. And a lot's locked up in big grants from the early settlement."

David I stirred. "The government has always had more land than money," he said, in a slightly defensive tone.

"Sir," the police chief said, nodding acknowledgment. "So people swarmed up the Eurotas, and into the side hills. Miners too: there are pockets of good ore, silver and gold, copper, thorium, whatever, over most of the continent. None very big except for up near Olynthos, but enough . . . Everyone in the outback has a horse and a gun, and if you know what you're doing you can live off the land pretty easy. Lot of tempting targets. The RSMP has been able to keep a lid on things, mostly; the Brotherhoods help. Until recently. This is the latest: the Velysen ranch."

A picture sprang out, an overhead shot taken from an aircraft, of the smoldering ruins of a big two-story house amid undamaged outbuildings. The screen blinked down to a ground level receptor with the slight jiggle of a helmet-mounted camera, and men in khaki battledress and nemourlon body-armor moved against the same background. A row of blanket-shrouded shapes lay beside trestle tables. Hands reached into the line of sight and lifted one covering. The corpse was that of a woman, and it was obvious how she had died. The soldiers leaned forward with a rustle of coiled tension, and one of the civilians retched.

"That's Eleanor Velysen," the policeman continued, in a voice taut with suppressed anger. "The other woman's her sister." He paused. "None of the remaining women on the ranch were molested; Arthur Velysen was shot, and his foreman and two other Citizens, and the place was pretty effectively stripped. Not much vandalism, and the Velysen children weren't harmed." The camera panned again, to a wall where HELOTS RULE OK had been spray-painted in letters three meters high.

"Terrorism," Owensford said softly. "Not bandits, terrorists. Helots?"

"What the terrorists call themselves these days. The same graffiti has gone up here in the city. They're *effective* terrorists, though," Desjaidins said with a grim nod. "Over the past year, more than two dozen attacks fitting this pattern. Sixteen in the last two months alone, from south of Clemens to north of Olynthos, and as far west as the upper Meneander. Plus dozens of reports of intimidation, demands for protection money, pamphlets . . . and some of the ranchers and mine owners *are* paying these Helots off, I swear it."

One of the bureaucrats stirred. "If the RSMP were more active—"

Desjardins's fist hit the table. "Madam Minister—with respect—I've got three thousand police, that's *counting* the clerks and forensics people and the ones who maintain the navigation buoys and the technicians and the training cadre. I've got a grand total of *ten* tiltrotors, and *thirty* helicopters, so when we get to road's end everyone walks or rides or takes a steamboat or blimp. If I split the five hundred or so Mobile Force personnel up, the Helots will eat them alive! This gang that attacked the Velysens's place, there were sixty of them—they blew the satellite dish and cut the landlink to the Torrey estate and had an ambush force emplaced to block the road in."

"Classic," Ace Barton said.

"Seems so," Owensford said.

"You've faced this kind of thing?" General Desjardins asked.

"Oh, yes," Peter said. He nodded to Barton.

"So far it's late Phase One guerrilla ops," Barton said. "To stop it, you can't sit and wait for guerrillas to come to you. They'll destroy you in detail. You have to be *more* mobile, and let militia do the positional defense."

Desjardins laughed without humor. "That's what the Velysens thought," he said. "They had a dozen armed guards and electrified wire. My forensics people are pretty sure the six guards who died were killed by their buddies, and the sabotage was an inside job too."

Owensford and Barton exchanged a glance and a thought: *so much for a peaceful training command.*

Alexander spoke. "So you see, gentlemen, we need the Legion more than ever, which is one reason we kept the rest of it on retainer. Unfortunately, we're less able to *pay* for it than ever, as well."

Catherine Alana looked up from her notes. "Your Majesty—sir—surely this hasn't reduced your revenue *that* much?"

"Not yet," his co-monarch answered; the Freedmans had been economists, holders of the professorships at Columbia and the CoDominium University in Rome. "But Captain, the economic justification behind the Field Force—yes, I know the strategic arguments, Alexander, but we have to cut our coat to fit the cloth—the economic rationale is that it will *help* our foreign currency situation."

Peter nodded agreement. Many of the newly independent planets defrayed the costs of their national armies by hiring them out, with a little low-budget imperialism on the side. For some like Covenant and Friedland, it was their major industry. Sparta had planned to get into the game. Foreign exchange aside, it was necessary in order to develop and maintain the kind of military force that would make it *obvious* to the likes of Friedland that here was no easy prey.

David sighed. "Ideologically, we're free traders here, Major Owensford; bureaucracy and regulation were what our parents came here to *avoid*, after all. But—'Needs must when the devil drives.' All foreign currency is allocated through the Ministry of Trade, and luxury imports—anything but capital equipment—are highly taxed. It's one of the slogans the NCLF use to whip up the non-Citizens, they say they want imported luxuries and more welfare."

Captain Jesus Alana smiled thinly; he was a dark man, a few inches shorter than his red-haired wife, with a trimmed black mustache. "There was much the same on Hadley. Your opposition will be the . . . Non-Citizens' Liberation Front?" he said. "Mr. Dion Croser?"

"*Citizen* Dion Croser, and that's half the problem," Desjardins said. "And a son of one of the Founders, which is even worse. Sir, I'm morally certain he's in this up to his well-bred neck. Just let me pull him in, and—"

Alexander made a sharp gesture. "No. Not without evidence linking him to these Helots. Which I don't believe; Dion Croser's misguided, but he *is* Anthony's son, after all. 'Liberty under Law,' General Desjardins." He turned to the soldiers. "Croser's got some following here in Sparta City, mostly among the recent immigrants and unskilled workers; and a few at the University." A wry smile. "Our founders were political scientists and sociologists, but they underestimated the effect of an underemployed intelligentsia when they founded our higher educational system."

"Layabouts," David snorted. "Hanging around the campus and complaining they aren't allowed to mind other people's business in the civil service. Major, our government has only a few thousand employees and contracts most of its limited functions out—" He stopped his impulse to lecture with a visible effort. "The fact remains, that to fully equip the Field Force regiments we must expend hard currency, and that's hard to come by. We need more export earnings. If we have soldiers employed off-world and we collect their pay in Dayan shekels or Friedlander marks, that is one thing. If they have to stay *here* and fight . . ." He shrugged.

"'Opulence must take second place to defense,'" Owensford recited; the Freedman king looked mildly surprised to hear a mercenary quoting Adam Smith. *You'd be surprised what Christian Johnny gets us to do,* Owensford thought. *His father was a history professor after all.* "You have indigenous munitions manufacturing."

"Small arms and mortars, nemourlon under license from DuPont; weapons are one of our main processed exports, along with intermediate-technology equipment for planets even less industrialized than we are. We can make armored cars and tanks, but there won't be a lot of output. No electronics to speak of; we've been negotiating with Xanadu and Meiji for chip fabricators, but . . ." He shrugged again; everyone knew the prices were kept artificially high. "We have the people and the knowledge, energy and resources and opportunity, all the classic requirements, but we're at the tools-to-make-the-tools-to-make-the-machines stage.

"We need *time.*"

"Which is one commodity we can buy you," Owensford said. "Soldiers do a lot of that. Well, the bright side is that if you don't have much in the way of electronics, neither will the enemy. Jesus, I'd be grateful if you'd see to increased security on all the Regiment's equipment. Some of our advanced gear will be very much on the rebel want list."

"Yes, sir." Alana scrawled a note on his pocket computer.

"We are going to need air transport," Peter said. "You can't send aviation into a battle area, but it's very often the key to making battles happen where you want them, rather than where the enemy wants them. I'll ask you to do what you can to ramp up production of helicopters. They needn't be fancy."

"Ja," Baron von Alderheim said.

"And not just in the one firm," Peter said. "Aviation is too important to be a point failure source—uh, for there to be only one supplier."

"I see," von Alderheim said. "You wish me to help my competition?"

"I'm afraid that's exactly what I wish," Peter said. "Understand, we don't need to make everything ourselves, but it sure helps if we're self-sufficient in big ticket items."

"That makes a great deal of sense," the Minister of War said. "If Baron von Alderheim will agree—"

"Oh, I agree," von Alderheim said. "Civic duty and all that. Besides, if Major Owensford is successful, there will be plenty of orders for military equipment, and hard currency as well."

"That is certainly the goal," David I said.

"A goal the enemy may have made easier," Peter said.

"Ah?" Sir Alfred looked puzzled.

"One difficulty in expanding a military force is leadership," Peter said. "Many of our first wave of recruits will have to rather quickly become noncoms and junior officers for the second group. Combat experience, even in a low-intensity war like this, will help a lot."

"I doubt Eleanor Velysen thought it was low intensity," Roland Dawson said.

"No sir, of course not," Peter said. "I don't mean to be flippant." He shrugged. "But that's still what we have here. A training war."

"So far," Desjardins said. "But it has been escalating."

Peter nodded. "Right, but we'll soon be set to deal with that, I think. Now, we're all right on technology. It's not as if we had to worry about off-planet forces with high-tech gear. Eventually we'll want troops capable of taking on a Line Marine regiment, but fortunately we don't have to ask that of them just yet." He looked at the map display. "Lot of water here. I presume we can shut down rebel water traffic."

"Lots of boats out there," Desjardins said. "Fishing, cargo hauling, even some yachts."

"They aren't likely to be smugglers. Nothing worth smuggling, is there? So surely all boat owners are loyalists."

"Or say they are," Desjardins muttered.

"You have reason for suspicion?" Barton asked.

"Fear, sir," Desjardins said. "Terrorism can be an effective recruiting device. Especially when all you're asked to do is look the other way."

"That much we can handle. We won't be recruiting any traitors. Security is Captain Catherine Alana's department and she's good at it."

Catherine smiled acknowledgment of the compliment and said, "General Desjardins, I strongly suggest an armed Coast Guard Auxiliary river and sea. Give it responsibility for seeing that water traffic is ours or neutral."

"It might work," Desjardins said.

"Have them do random sweeps in strength," Ace Barton commented. "And be sure they have good communications, both with the RSMP and the Fifth." He grinned mirthlessly. "It's not likely, but the rebels may be stupid enough to concentrate their forces."

"Precisely," Peter Owensford said. "I doubt General Desjardins is worried about defeating the rebels in battle—"

"Well, there are a fair number of them," Desjardins said. "And the RSMP isn't trained for set piece battles. But no, we're not worried, especially now that you lot are here. It's finding them that's the real problem. Captain Alana, I'll be very happy to work with you in setting up the Coast Guard."

"And I," Baron von Alderheim said. "The fishing village on my estate can furnish the nucleus. They are all armed, they will only need instructions."

"Close off water transport and we'll have a good part of the problem licked," Owensford said. He turned to King Alexander. "Sir, you do understand, we will need some kind of registration system. A way to identify legitimate boats—"

"We have that now," Prince David said. "We believe in freedom, Major, but with freedom come responsibilities." He shook his head. "I presume you want authority for your Coast Guard to intercept vessels and search them at random."

"Yes, sir."

"That won't be popular," David said. "But I believe we can get the Council and Senate to agree. As a temporary measure, of course. I suggest one year, with full debate required before renewal of the law. Alexander?"

"I'll agree to that."

"Thank you. I'll have it drafted," David said. "Major, you said you could assure the loyalty of the Coast Guard Auxiliary. I'd like to know how."

"Ah—we have equipment—"

"Lie detectors?" Alexander asked. There was an edge to his voice.

"Something like that, sir," Prince Lysander said. "They're—" He looked to Peter Owensford. "Perhaps I'd better not say? It's non-intrusive. Nothing anyone can object to."

"Hah." Baron von Alderheim looked thoughtful.

"Sir," Peter said. "I presume everyone here has taken some kind of oath of office? With criminal penalties?"

"Yes, yes, of course, everyone here is sworn to the Privy Council," David said.

"Fine," Peter said. "Then we can begin here. And we may as well start now."

"Start what?" Elayne Rusher asked.

She was a woman of indeterminate age. Peter guessed fifty, but he would have believed anything between forty and sixty. She was attractive but not especially pretty, and gave Peter a feeling of confidence. *Like having a competent big sister.* "Loyalty testing, Madame Attorney General."

She frowned. "How do you propose to do that?"

Peter shrugged. "It's simple enough. What part of Sparta do you come from, madam?"

"I have always lived in the City," Rusher said. "And how will knowing that help?"

"You'd be surprised at what helps, madam," Peter said. "Do you know any rebels?"

"Dion."

"Of course, and his supporters. Who else?"

"No one else—"

Peter looked to Captain Alana. "Catherine?"

Captain Alana had been staring at her oversized wristwatch. "Loyal, but defending someone. She suspects someone. I'd guess a close relative, but perhaps a friend of a relative."

"Why—What in the world makes you think that?"

Catherine smiled. "A good guess, but it's true, isn't it?"

Rusher sighed. "Close enough. My daughter Jennifer is seeing a young man from the University. There's something about him—but it's nothing I could justify investigating. How have you found out all this? You've hardly had time—"

"You just told them," General Desjardins said. "Voice stress analyzers. I've heard about them, but I didn't think anyone but CoDominium Intelligence had them."

"That's what everyone thinks," Peter said. "And we want them to go on thinking it. Mr. Plummer, do you know any rebels?"

"Of course not. Other than Citizen Croser." He smiled thinly. "I take it I'm being tested now? Should I be concerned?"

Just relax, sir," Catherine said. "Would you mind telling me your mother's maiden name?"

❖   ❖   ❖

"All clear," Catherine Alana said. "See, that wasn't so bad."

"I can't say I like the implications," Henry Yamaga said. "As if you suspect us—"

"Sir," Peter began.

"Let me, sir," Ace Barton said. "With all due respect, my lords and ladies, this is a war of information. Determining who is and is not trustworthy is most of the battle. If your rancher—"

"Velysen," Desjardins said.

"If Mr. Velysen had known who among his guards were traitors, he'd be alive, and so would his women. Frankly, I'd think speaking a few sentences into a computer would be a small price to pay for peace of mind. While we're at it— Madame Rusher, I'm sure we'll all feel much better if Catherine were invited to dinner the next time your daughter brings her odd friend home."

"It's a bit distasteful," Rusher said. She paused a moment. "But yes, thank you. Captain, could you and your husband join us for dinner the day after tomorrow?"

"I'd be delighted," Catherine said.

"So. One less thing to worry about," Peter said. "Now, I presume that you were planning on recruiting mostly transportees for the Field Force?"

The civilians looked at each other, embarrassed; it was a little like what BuReloc did to troublemakers on Earth, with the added refinement that Sparta intended to use them as cannon fodder and make a profit on them to boot.

Alexander sighed. "Our Citizens are mostly native-born now, family people, and we have an open land frontier for restless youngsters. The people BuReloc dumps on us are mostly single adults, six-tenths men," he said.

"And many of them come from four, five, six generations who haven't worked, haven't got the *concept* of work anywhere in their mental universe. We tell them to work or starve, and it *takes* starvation to make them work—or military discipline, we presume. Some younger Citizens will be volunteering as well; we'll pass the word through the Brotherhoods, and Prince Lysander's exploits on Tanith have made the Legion pretty glamorous on the video." He looked with fond pride at his son; Lysander had been brooding at the gruesome pictures from the Velysen ranch, but he blushed slightly at his father's words.

Owensford nodded. "It's infiltrators *I'm* worried about," he said frankly, glancing over at the Alanas. They nodded. "One thing has to be understood," Owensford said. "A legionnaire has no *civil* rights."

Freedman raised an eyebrow. "And what does that mean, Major?"

"Literally what I said, Sire. Your Citizens, your non-citizens, your civilians have various civil rights which we'll do what we can to get our troops to respect; but once they've signed up as soldiers, we expect their loyalty, and that loyalty includes cooperating with our investigators to determine that they *are* loyal."

"Yes, of course. And I suppose that includes the RSMP. It doesn't appear that General Desjardins has any objections."

"On the contrary, Majesty," Desjardins said. "I'm quite confident of the loyalty of my men, but it can't hurt for everyone to be certain."

A clock chimed in the background. "Other duties," Alexander said. "We'll continue this tomorrow, but I take it we are all agreed that the primary mission of the Legion has not changed? Thank you. David?" The two kings rose, and the others in the room followed. "Until this evening, Colonel," Alexander said. "We've laid on a welcoming banquet at the Spartosky, that's our local social center." He spread his hands. "Political, I'm afraid, but necessary. The food's decent, at any rate."

Geoffrey Niles leaned back against the rear of the booth and took another sip of his drink, coughing slightly at the taste of the raw cane spirit. The Dead Cow was hopping tonight; it was autumn, after all, and the outbacker hunters were mostly in town with their summer haul of tallow and skins. Money to pay off some of their debts to the banks and the backer-merchants, money to burn in a debauch they could remember when they were freezing and sweating in some forsaken gully in the outback. There was a live band snarling out music, and a few tired-looking women in G-strings bumping and grinding in front of them; more were working the tables. A solid wall of noise made most conversation impossible, although not innumerable card and dice games. The fog of tobacco, hash, and borloi smoke, plus the strong smells of leather and unwashed flesh, went a fair distance toward making breathing impossible, too.

"Interesting, sir, eh, what?" Niles said to the man beside him. Kenjiro Murasaki smiled thinly and kept his eyes on the crowded chaos of the room.

Dammed wet blanket, Niles thought.

You couldn't find a place like this on Earth anymore. Oh, there were dives enough if you had a taste for slumming, but an Earthside slum was a dumping-ground for the useless, the refuse of automation and the gray stagnation of a planet locked in political and economic stasis by its ruling oligarchies. There was a raw energy here, the sort he imagined might have been found on America's western frontier or the outposts of the Raj two centuries ago. These were not idlers, they were hard men who went out and wrested a living from a wilderness still imperfectly adapted to Terran life. He looked at the stuffed longhorn steer on the wall behind the long bar, lying toes-up and flanked by wolf heads, legacy of some demented Green back in the early days.

To adventure, he thought with a tingle of excitement, lifting his glass. Murasaki made a noncommittal noise; he was taciturn at the best of times, and the implants which altered the shape of his face were still a little tender.

A group had walked in, past the bouncers in their military-style nemourlon armor and helmets. *That's them,* he thought. Only one he recognized from the briefing, the tall black woman in scuffed leathers. *Stunner,* he thought admiringly. A big bald Indian-looking man with twin machetes over his back and a bowie down one boot-top, similarly dressed. Several others in the black leather jackets, red tights and metal-studded boots of the Werewolves, the gang whose turf included the Minetown section of Sparta City. Heads turned in their direction, then away; this was not the sort of place an uptown civilian could go safely, but the habitués mostly had a well-developed sense of personal survival.

Not all of them. One raised his head out of a puddle of spilled rum, stared blearily and made a grab for the black woman's crotch. She pivoted on one heel, her hands slapping down; the whinnying scream the hidehunter made was audible even over the background roar of the bar, and that dropped away to relative silence as others noted the byplay.

"Ugly, *ugly* mon," she said; her fingers held his hand in a come-along hold Niles recognized, the wrist twisted to lock the joint and a thumb planted on a nerve-cluster. "Say sorry to Skilly, ugly mon."

The bearded face blinked and twisted up, half in pain and half in astonishment. "Oh, Jesus, Skilly, sure I'm sorry, didn't fuckin' *recognize* you, honest!" He relaxed slightly as she smiled whitely.

"Not sorry enough," she said, grabbing his thumb with her free hand and jerking sharply backward.

His eyes bulged, and his free hand scrabbled for the automatic at his waist. Skilly released his hand, and her elbow moved in a short chopping arc that ended on his temple; there was a *thock,* and another as he collapsed back into the chair and his head dropped limply to the table. There were nervous grins from the other cardplayers, hoots and guffaws from all around; the woman moved through the throng slapping palms and backs, calling greetings and declining offers of drinks as she led the others to the door at the back of the room.

Niles swallowed. "Well, I'm certainly not going to press uninvited attentions on *that* lady," he said, fiddling slightly with the catch of his Jujitsu laptop. It would be ten minutes before they could join the others.

Murasaki looked up from doing calculations on his wristcomp; this time his smile showed real amusement. "Let us hope, Niles-san, that *she* does not choose to press her attentions on *you.*"

Niles took a swallow of his drink. Grand-Uncle had promised him an experience that would show what he was made of. So far, it was living up to the advance billing. Collecting himself, he glanced at the ceiling. Time for the conspirators to meet and plan; he smoothed back his fluffy blond mustache with a finger and practiced his grin.

Adventure, complete with exotic dusky maiden, he thought. *I'll just remember not to offer her a thumb.*

"Excellent," Kenjiro Murasaki said. "As a beginning."

It was a small meeting: Croser and Skida on the one side, the Meijian and his equally stone-faced aide on the other. The small upper room smelled of wine and spilled beer and sweat; there were stains on the blankets that covered the cot in the corner, and a scribble of names knife-carved in the broad pine planks. There were no papers on the table. A first-rate memory was a condition of leadership in work like this.

The Meijian continued. "I am particularly pleased with the slow, careful preparation for overt action, the building of funds and organization."

"Protracted struggle," Croser said. He did not like the Meijian; the man was a mercenary, someone who made war for money, not principle. But there was no doubt of his competence; Grand Senator Bronson—*Earth Prime, remember that*—did not spend good money on incompetents.

"Exactly," Murasaki nodded. "Now, Capital Prime, with the assets I have brought, we may proceed much more rapidly from the phase of organization and low-intensity guerrilla struggle to that of large-scale destabilization. Indeed, I believe we must work quickly. The reports of the War Cabinet meeting today indicate that Major Owensford has already begun mobilization."

"You can overhear War Cabinet meetings?" Croser asked.

Murasaki bowed slightly. "Let us say they are not as secure as they believe. You will understand, Capital Prime, my men are specialists and technicians, not soldiers in the strict sense of the term. What we can do is give you secure communications, subvert the enemy's communications and computer networks, and provide a small but crucial increment of highly advanced weapons to offset those employed by the Spartan government. Occasional direct action of a limited nature."

"That's the *Royal* government," Croser corrected. "The Movement is the legitimate government of Sparta."

"As you say. Now, despite this, the enemy will maintain superior conventional military power almost to the end. As your own plan outlines, we must keep the struggle on a political level as far as possible." He smiled, an expression that went no further than his lips. "In this we are aided by the nature of reality, and the arrow of entropy. It is always easier to tear down than to build, to make chaos rather than order, to render a society ungovernable rather than to govern effectively.

"So. First, we must weaken and immobilize the governing class, the Citizens. Split them along every possible fault line. Next, we must detach as many of the non-Citizens who are loyal to the regime as possible, by driving the *Royal* government into a policy of *ineffective* repression. This will not be difficult; to create an atmosphere of fear through terrorism, we need only a small organization and limited support. The countermeasures, if clumsy or made to appear so, will furnish us with our mass base.

"In conjunction with this, we strike both covertly and overtly at the economy; for example, this planet is desperately short of capital, so capital assets must be destroyed, particularly those which generate foreign exchange. Earth Prime will be assisting, of course, with financial manipulations which the enemy has no effective means of countering. Once the economy is locked in a downward spiral, the NCLF and its Movement will become the only factor to *benefit* from chaos and decay. The Royal government's own diversion of resources to the police and military will work in our favor. In this stage, the NCLF can establish its own shadow regime, its no-go areas, and eat the Royal administration up from below. By then we will have built a guerrilla army capable of denying territory to the Royal forces, which we will infiltrate and subvert as well. Then, victory, and you may proceed to establish your own regime of peace and enlightenment."

The last was delivered deadpan, but Croser stifled a glare. *Easy for you to be sarcastic,* he thought. *Meiji's a rich planet. You can't make an omelet without breaking eggs!* He had to admit there was a certain grisly fascination in hearing his own thoughts mapped out so bluntly.

"Best I keep the above-ground NCLF in operation as long as possible," he said. "In fact, I think I may be representing it in the Senate quite soon. Technically as the delegate of the Dockworkers' Union." Which would give him a position of considerable legal immunity. "We don't have much support there, but there's enough to create considerable deadlock, with a little skillful horsetrading."

"Yes," the Meijian said, warming to his topic; there was almost a tinge of enthusiasm in his voice. "Also for your already-skillful disinformation campaign. If enough plausible lies circulate, truth becomes lost and all men begin to fear and doubt. The easiest environment for conspiracy is one where conspiracies are suspected everywhere. May I suggest that part of the funds I brought with me be used to make additional purchases of media and transport companies?"

Croser nodded. "We'll have to be careful," he said. "The Finance Ministry is already checking my books."

Skida sipped at her fruit-juice; the others were drinking wine, and she had always found it advisable to have her head straighter than the company.

"Skilly likes all this if it works," she said. "But the outback operation is as big as it can get without doing some serious fighting, especially now that the enemy bringing in mercs. Skilly needs to get out from under their spy-eyes, faster communication, and something to counter their aircraft."

"My technoninjas can provide all that," Murasaki said. "Of the two hundred who accompanied me—" many on the BuReloc transports that landed every month "—approximately half will return with you to the outback, Field Prime. From now on, your situation will be very different. For example, on Meiji we have developed a method of long-distance tightbeam communication, bouncing the message off the ionization tracks of meteors."

Of which Sparta had more than its fair share; the hundred-kilometer circle of Constitution Bay was the legacy of one such, millennia ago.

"Soon also, we will be reading the enemy's transmissions as soon as they do. You will have abundant computer power to coordinate your logistics, and we will be able to manipulate the enemy's accounting programs to conceal our own shipments. Also, we can degrade performance of automatic systems, the surveillance satellites the Royal government has put up, similar measures elsewhere."

"Skilly likes, but when we start popping, they going to know we getting stuff from off-planet," she said. "Then they start looking physical."

"Olympian Lines uses the Spartan system for transit to Byer's Star," Murasaki said enigmatically.

The outermost colonized system, reachable only by a complex series of Alderson Point jumps from Sparta and a full year's journey from Earth. It had a quasi-inhabitable planet; Haven, the second moon of a superjovian gas giant, a unique case. Croser remembered reading of it, and nodded to Skida. There was a CoDo relocation colony there, and some minerals.

"Earth Prime controls the Olympian Lines and has interests in the shimmerstone trade with Haven. While transiting this system, parcels can be released on ballistic trajectories. Given stealthing, and some minimal interference with the local surveillance computers, they will appear to be normal meteorites."

Croser clapped his hands together. "Won't *that* be a lovely surprise for Falkenberg's killers," he said. "Speaking of which, how's he doing?" Grand Senator Bronson had excellent intelligence, from his own resources and his leads into the Fleet.

"They are expected to land on New Washington shortly," Murasaki said. "With luck, while we destroy the Fifth Battalion here, the Friedlanders and Covenanters will do the same for the rest there."

Croser grunted skeptically. Falkenberg's Legion were some of the best light infantry in known space. Scum soldiers, but well trained, well equipped and well lead; and Falkenberg had a reputation. Men like that made their own luck. *Men like me*, he thought. Still, New Washington was five months' transit from Sparta; they ought to have ample warning of any move.

"We'll see," he said. "Now, the other half of your people will be integrated into my clandestine operation in the towns?"

"Yes; the companies our sponsors own will provide excellent cover. I myself and my closest aides, with your permission, will form the cadre for the extension of your *Spartacus* organization." The inner-circle hit squads. "We can begin Operations against enemy targets almost immediately."

"A little early for that, surely?" Croser said.

"I think you are underestimating the element of *ju*," Murasaki said.

Croser blinked for a second. *Ah, "go-with,"* he thought. The

Meijian was fond of using martial-arts metaphors for political struggle; only to be expected, of course. The man was a mercenary, with a professional's emotional detachment. *All to the good. You need a cold head.* Anger was like compassion; for afterwards, when the struggle was over and it was time for the softer virtues of peace. You made the decision, you *had* to make the decision, from your heart. Grief at what his father's dream had become; rage at the smug fools who ignored him when he warned, when he pleaded, when he *showed* them and they wouldn't believe. After that everything had to come from the head; anything else was a betrayal of the Cause.

"Granted that it is too early and our network in the towns too incomplete for a comprehensive campaign of terrorism—"

People's justice, damn you, Croser thought, with a well-concealed wince. There was such a thing as taking detachment too far.

"—selective action against the proper figures is possible at once. Indeed, Capital Prime, it will be valuable training for your death-squads and their integration with my specialists."

"Who did you have in mind?" Croser asked, intrigued despite himself.

The books all said the most efficient strategy was to go for the cadres of the government: village mayors, local policemen, sanitation officers. To demonstrate the government's impotence, to blind its eyes among the populace, and to leave a vacuum the insurgents' political apparatus could fill.

"Certain of the Pragmatist leaders."

"Hmmm." Croser frowned. "Won't that just provoke . . . ah, I see."

"Yes. Either they will force through ill-conceived repressive measures, increasing our support, or they will become locked in political conflict with the Loyalist faction. In either case, we benefit."

"I'd better accelerate work on the front organizations, in case the whole NCLF has to go underground," Croser said meditatively. That would not be for a while, but when the Crown proscribed . . . nothing like being declared an outlaw to force people to *commit* themselves.

"I authorize your suggestion," Croser said. Murasaki bowed. *And it takes care of certain other problems,* the Spartan thought. A guardian corps within the Movement was all well and good, but who would guard the guardians? These mercenaries had no local roots, and no possibility of taking over the structure he had built. With them in charge of his enforcers, his back would be safe. "Now, about the computers."

"Croser-san," Murasaki said. "Penetration of the local net has proved surprisingly easy. You will understand, we cannot *use* the data gathered too often, or the enemy will suspect and begin countermeasures. The University has a surprisingly strong software engineering section."

Croser nodded. "Policy," he said. "They wanted to begin basic research in the sciences, but that means counter-sabotage work."

CoDominium Intelligence was tasked with suppressing scientific research; their most effective method had been a generations-long effort to corrupt every data base and research program on Earth. Few of the colony worlds had the time or resources needed to undo the damage. Besides, there were few trained scientists left anywhere after four generations. Nobody wanted to live under the lidless eye of BuInt all their lives, with involuntary transportation to someplace like Fulson's World as the punishment for stepping over the line. Mostly what were left were technicians, cookbook engineers who might make a minor change in a recipe if they were very daring.

"Yes. Similar effort on Meiji is underway."

Croser held up a hand. "We can also use the information to sow suspicion—make them think we have more agents in place than we do." Murasaki smiled, a rare gesture of approval, and rose for a second to make a short bow. "My thoughts exactly, Mr. Croser. We will identify their best operatives, and then . . . for example, incorrectly hidden bank accounts with suspicious funds. Then we reveal by action we know data that this agent has access to. Synergy."

The discussion moved on to technicalities: peoples, places, times. At the last, Skida spoke.

"The Englishman. Skilly wants him."

The men both looked at her. "He a trained officer, isn't he? Skilly is going to need a good staff, and that the hardest type of talent for us to find; Skilly read the books, but got no hands-on training except learn by doing."

Murasaki nodded slowly. "He does have the training," he said slowly. "Sandhurst, and some naval experience as well. Also, he is intelligent if extremely naive. Not suitable for urban operations, I think. Too squeamish. But in the field, yes."

Croser looked at the woman narrowly; she met his gaze with an utterly guileless smile. *And he's nearer your age, and remarkably handsome,* he thought. Then: *No, Skida never does things on impulse.* As passionate as you could want . . . but underneath it the coldest pragmatist he had ever known;

literally unthinkable for her to act without considering the long-term interests involved.

"I authorize it," he said. There was no time wasted on amenities, not among them; they walked through into the adjoining room, where their aides and staff sat in disciplined silence.

"Hope you like riding, English-*mon*," Skilly tossed over her shoulder, as she and Croser paused at the head of the stairs, arms about each other's waists.

Niles was blinking in bewilderment at Murasaki as Skilly's clear laugh drifted back up the stairs.

"Did you not speak of your admiration for the great English explorers and adventurers?" the Meijian asked. Niles nodded. "Consider yourself in my debt, Niles-san. I have found you as close an analog as exists in the universe."

There was something extremely disquieting in the technoninja's grin.

CHAPTER FIVE

Crofton's Essays and Lectures in Military History
(2nd Edition)

Professor John Christian Falkenberg II:
Delivered at Sandhurst, August 22nd, 2087

The main constraint on the size of states is speed of communication. The Empire of Rome rarely stretched more than two weeks' march from the sea or a navigable river, simply because water was the fastest way to ship troops and messengers—force and information, the basic constituents of state power. The Mongol realm established by Genghis Khan and his descendants was a tour de force, a unified state stretching from Poland to Burma; it fell apart in less than two generations, from sheer clumsiness. Where a message might take six months and an army a year to travel from one end of the empire to another, it was simply too difficult to enforce the Khan's will in the border provinces—too difficult for the Khan's officials to collect the data they needed to make effective decisions. With mechanical transport and electronic communications, these constraints were removed; the series of wars and great-power rivalries which racked Earth from the early 20th century on were a recognition of this fact. A planetwide, later solar-system-wide, state had become possible. With the CoDominium we acquired one, in a stumbling and half-blind fashion.

The Alderson Drive gave us access to the stars at super-luminal speeds—but not instantaneous transportation. In addition, there is no faster-than-light equivalent of radio; messages carried by starship are the fastest means of interstellar communication. With the farthest colonies up to a year's travel time from Earth, the CoDominium faces many of the problems encountered by the maritime empires of Western Europe during the era of the sailing ship. Once more, distance and scale limit the effectiveness of the superstate, diffusing its strength. Smaller but more tightly organized and quick-reacting local organizations can bring more power to bear in their own neighborhoods. As long as the CoDominium remained strong and its Fleet held a monopoly of significant space warships, this mattered little.

Now that the Grand Senate is effectively paralyzed and regional powers such as Meiji and Friedland have navies of their own, the CoDominium is faced with insoluble problems. Despite the cutbacks, the Fleet is still stronger than any of its rivals—but it must scatter its strength, while the outplanet navies can concentrate. As always when an empire dies, an era of chaos intervenes until a new equilibrium of forces is born.

Similar effects may be seen on individual planets, as the unity and concentration imposed by initial settlement and CoDominium power are removed. . . .

"Well, *this* looks familiar enough," Peter Owensford said dryly, as they emerged from the front door of the Spartosky Ole. Sparta's twenty-hour cycle had moved far into night while the official banquet continued, and the narrow canyon of street was dimly lit by the fiber-optic marquee of the Spartosky and the glowstrips five stories up on the surrounding buildings. The red and gold light from the signs scattered over the faces of the densely packed demonstrators and mingled with the flamelight of the torches some bore along with their banners.

"Freedom! Freedom!" the crowd chanted; the surf-roar of their noise bounced back from the concrete walls. There were several thousand of them, filling the narrow street outside the line of cars and the cordon of Milice, police reservists from the Brotherhoods called up to keep order. Banners and placards waved over the mob, ranging from a misspelled FUCK THE CITYZENS through DOCKWORKERS' UNION FOR REFORM to a cluster of professional-looking variations on NCLF DEMANDS UNIVERSAL SUFFRAGE NOW. Almost all of them had versions of the NCLF banner, a red = sign in the middle of a black dot against a red background.

Ace Barton chuckled. "I particularly like those two," he said, pointing. One read PRODUCTION FOR THE PEOPLE, while its neighbor proclaimed ECOLOGY YES INDUSTRY NO.

Peter nodded absently as he studied the crowd. The ones with the printed signs seemed to be the heart of the demonstration; they had a quasi-uniform of crash helmets and gloves, and the staves carrying their signs were good solid hardwood. The mob was growing by accretion, like a crystal in a saturated solution; many of the people on the fringes wore what looked like gang colors, or the sort of clothes you saw in an American Welfare Island. A cold knot clenched below his breastbone, and he felt a familiar papery dryness in his mouth. *This isn't a demonstration,* he thought. *It's a riot waiting to happen.*

"Nice to be loved," Owensford added dryly. Some of the signs read MERCENARY KILLER SCUM GO HOME and MONEY FOR THE PEOPLE NOT WAR WHORES. "As you say, Ace, positively homelike."

"It isn't familiar to me," Lysander said grimly. "I've never seen anything like *this* on Sparta before. Melissa, stay back." He was angry; his Phraetrie-brother Harv Middleton had naked fury on his face.

The girl at Lysander's elbow pushed forward to stand by him, studying the crowd.

"I realize you're a hero now, but try to contain it, Lysander," she said. Melissa von Alderheim was a determined-looking person, not pretty but good-looking in a fresh-faced way that suggested horses and tennis; she took after her mother's side of the family, who had been from Oxford. Even in an evening gown, with her seal-brown hair piled under a tiara, there was a suggestion of tweeds and sensible shoes about her. She and the Prince had been seated with the mercenaries and the two kings during the formal dinner and the speeches that followed; she had been coolly polite to all the officers, but teeth had shone a little every time her glance met Ursula Gordon's.

Owensford looked around. The Spartosky Ole was one of a set of fifteen-story fibrocrete buildings not far from the CoDominium compound, part of the oldest section of Sparta City and bordering on the Minetown slums. The others were plain slick-gray, but the Spartosky had a portico of twisted pillars and a marquee of glittering multicolored fiber-optic display panels.

"Who built this neighborhood, anyway?" he said, as a car pushed slowly through the crowd and the police lines, it was a simple local job converted for police use with a hatch on the roof and armor panels. It rocked and lurched as the protesters thundered their signs on the roof or grabbed for the fenders and tried to rock it off its wheels.

The two kings and their party came up beside the mercenaries. "GLC Construction and Development Company," David I said. "Why?"

"I recognize the style," Owensford said. His eyes were on the rooftops. *I'd have cover teams there if this were my operation,* he thought. "Grand Senator Bronson owns it. They never alter the plans; the Colonial Bureau built them on thirty or forty planets." Nothing but a pair of news cameras on the roofs, avid ghoul-vulture eyes drawn to trouble.

A new chant had started, among the helmeted demonstrators. *"Dion the Leader! Down with the Kings! Up the Republic! Dion to Power! Dion to Power!"* Jeers and catcalls rang as the demonstrators saw the royal party; the cleared pavement was growing crowded as more of the guests left the Spartosky.

A Milice officer pushed up out of the roof-hatch of the police car; he was wearing full battle armor, and landed heavily as he slid to the pavement and trotted over to the kings.

"Your Majesties," he said. "Sorry about this, but it . . . they had a permit, we thought it would be just the usual couple of dozen University idiots, and it just *grew.* Sirs, if you'll come this way, we've secured the rear entrance."

"No," Alexander said sharply. "I'm not in the habit of running away from my people, and I don't intend to start now."

"Your people?" a man said, with contempt in his voice. Owensford noted him without turning; Steven Armstrong, leader of the Pragmatist party, the faction in the Legislative Assembly who wanted more restrictions on the convicts and deportees. A bull-necked man, heavily muscled even by Spartan standards, owner of a small fishing fleet he had built up from nothing. The Pragmatists were the loyal opposition, more or less; the kings both backed the Foundation Loyalists. "Your Majesty had better take care your *people* don't assassinate you, since they're allowed to pick up weapons the minute they leave the CoDo prison."

Alexander acknowledged him with a curt nod, then turned back to the police officer. "Saunders, what's your estimate of the crowd?"

"Sir—" the man looked acutely unhappy. "They're pushing, but no more than the usual arms."

The Legion officers had gathered in a loose clump around their commander and the Spartan monarchs; some of them had unobtrusively buckled back the covers of their sidearms. Those were light machine-pistols, Dayan-made Microuzis. Owensford found himself estimating relative firepower; the

Milice were in riot gear, truncheons and shields, but they had auto shotguns or rifles over their backs. Most of the guests had pistols of some sort—it was a Citizen tradition here—and few of the mob seemed to be carrying firearms. That meant little, though. They could be concealed.

"Sir," he said. "I'd advise you to take this officer's advice. Quickly."

Alexander Collins's mouth clenched. "Not quite yet, Major Owensford," he said.

Peter turned and caught Jesus Alana's eye. He jerked his head toward the rear door. Alana nodded and left the group.

Collins turned to the militia officer. "Saunders, this is in violation of the permit, isn't it?"

"Yes, sir," the policeman said. "Excessive numbers, obstructing traffic, half a dozen counts."

"Hand me your 'caster," the king said.

The policeman pulled a hand-unit from his belt; Alexander took it, keying it to the loudspeakers in the police car and stepping up on the base of one of the Spartosky's columns to make himself visible to the crowd.

"Get the crowd-control car ready," he said to the policeman. Then he drew breath to speak to the crowd.

"Two-knife," Skida said. She was lying on her back below the window, studying the crowd through a thin fiber-optics periscope. "Bobber. Now. And Bobber, Skilly would be very happy if you keep the Werewolves from getting too antsy. Important the *cam*eras get good shots of nasty policemons whipping on heads before it starts. We provoke them to provoke us, understand? On the word."

Niles looked over at Bobber. This suite was supposed to be the offices of Universal Exports, and the female gang leader looked wildly out of place in it with her red tights and silver-studded knee boots. The chain-decked black leather jacket was unfastened to her waist, half-baring breasts far too rounded to be natural. Both bore a one-word tattoo: SWEET on the left, SOUR on the right. She stood, the tall fore-and-aft crest of hair on her shaven head nodding with the motion that had given her her street name; the rocket launcher was cradled protectively in her arms.

"Yo, Skilly," she said, wrapping it in cloth and trotting out the door. The squad of feral-eyed youths in Werewolf colors followed at her heels, and then the huge Mayan.

A snarl came from below, and Niles felt the small hairs on his spine try to rise; instinct deeper than thought told him that the pack was on his heels. He grinned past the fear, vision gone ice-clear with the wash of adrenaline, and Skida smiled back at him. Her eyes took him in again, with flattering attentiveness.

"You expect the police to attack the crowd?" he said quietly. They were alone in the room except for one of Murasaki's men, who might have been a statue as he sat at the tiny console of his portable com unit. The Englishman shifted his grip on the silenced scope-sighted carbine. "Rather brutal bunch, eh?"

"Skilly expects the police to be good and frightened, Jeffi," she replied. "They only shopkeepers and clerks, mon. Respectable people, not used to this. Frightened peoples act stupid. We take it from there." A chuckle. "Then the RSMP come kills *us*, if your Nippo friend's toys doan work."

MY PEOPLE," a voice called from the street below, amplified echoes bouncing off the buildings. "WE ARE ALWAYS READY TO HEAR YOUR PETITIONS. REMEMBER THAT LIBERTY CAN COME ONLY TO THOSE READY TO BEAR ITS BURDENS—"

The crowd howled when it saw Alexander; and again, when he began to speak. The sound was huge, almost enough to override the amplifiers. Then another megaphone spoke, from among the demonstrators.

"FUCK THE KINGS! FUCK THE KINGS!"

Owensford was close enough to see Alexander flush, and then his lips move in a prayer or curse as the mob took it up. He was also close enough to see the anger on the faces of the Milice. They began to surge forward, pushing with batons held level, until their officers called them back; hauled them back physically, in some cases.

The twist in his stomach grew; there was more here than met the eye. Peter Owensford had been a soldier for all his adult life, very little of it behind a desk, and he knew the scent of trouble. Events were moving to a plan, a plan laid by somebody who meant no good.

"Saunders," the king said. "Read them the Act and clear the street. Minimal force, but don't endanger lives hesitating."

"*Sir!*" the policeman said with enthusiasm. He took the handunit and began—

"CLEAR THE STREET AND DISPERSE! YOU ARE IN VIOLATION OF THE PUBLIC ORDER AND ASSEMBLIES ACT AND SUBJECT TO ARREST IF YOU DO NOT DISP*SKKREEEEEEEE*—"

The deafening feedback squeal continued until one of the

Milice ripped the wires loose from the speaker on the car's roof. Jeering laughter rippled from the crowd among the chants, and a few bottles and rocks arched forward to bang against the shields. Owensford saw one man stagger out of the police line, hands over a smashed nose. There was a momentary gap; through it he could see two of the helmeted protesters, a man and a woman. Boy and girl rather, in their late teens. Well-dressed in a scruffy sort of way, and grinning as if this was all a game.

It is, he thought bleakly. *But not the sort you imagine.*

"Sir, the unit won't work at all, we've got no commo."

Owensford met his second-in-command's eyes; they nodded.

"Sirs," Peter said to the two kings. He had to shout. "I must insist that you return to the building, otherwise I cannot be responsible."

"The back entrance," Saunders said.

"No. Too risky, it might be covered. Captain Alana has secured the lobby. *Now,* if you please, sirs." Several of the Legion officers grouped around the kings with pistols drawn and began backing towards the entrance, carrying the protesting monarchs along willy-nilly.

"Clear the street," Saunders was screaming in the ears of his officers, who relayed it verbally to the Milice.

They raised their batons and linked shields, pushing forward. The glowstrips blinked out, and the marquee of the Spartosky, and the street was suddenly plunged into darkness. Then another light came on, a narrow-beam illuminator from the news cameras, flicking across the line of Milice and incidentally into their eyes. Owensford shaded his, and saw several of the protesters fling themselves forward on the line of clubs. He bared his teeth; they were not trying to fight, just cowering dramatically and holding up their hands as the police instinctively lashed out with their truncheons. One of the protesters turned as if staggering, and the camera light caught a mask of blood across his agonized face.

Razor cuts, Owensford knew. Flicked open to give the appearance of dramatic wounds. "Get all these people back inside," he shouted to the remaining mercenaries. The guests were milling and shouting on their own. Different from an Earthling crowd, though; many were drawing weapons and pushing their way to the front, and there were few shrieks. A gunfight, *just* what was needed. "You, you, you, get the doors open and start pushing people into the lobby. Move!"

More bottles arched out of the crowd, some of them Molotovs trailing smoke, which burst in puddles of flame on the pavement. The police scattered away, and knots of disciplined rioters burst through, lashing out with the poles of their signs. Again they seemed more interested in being beaten than really fighting. . . .

"Jamming," Ace spoke into his ear; he had one of their own communicators in his hand, they were all carrying one in a pocket of their dress blue and golds. "I'm through to the base camp. Jesus is bringing in some MPs."

"Right. Get everything you can," Owensford said.

"Mission?"

"Cover our retreat," Peter said. "We don't understand the politics, and we sure don't have time to learn. I want everyone out of here alive and unhurt. Preferably without inflicting casualties."

"Roger," Barton said.

"The crowd-control car, thank God," Saunders muttered.

A turbine hum echoed back from the walls, and a vehicle floated into sight. It was Earth-made, a Boeing-Northrup Peacemaker: essentially an upright rectangle, supported by six powerful ducted-fan engines on either side. Nozzles protruded below the control bubble on the forward edge, and they could see the operator in the armored nacelle within. Hot exhaust air washed over them, rippling the clothes of the crowd.

"Hurry up, dammit!" Owensford barked. His men had gotten the guests moving, but it was a painfully slow process, the more when many wanted to stay right where they were.

Fresh howls rose at the eight of the riot-control vehicle; many of the Welfare Island types would recognize it from Earth, where they were used to put down slum riots daily. Shots rang out, and bullets ricocheted from the armor panels in bursts of sparks. The Milice line was buckling, and the gang members from the outside of the crowd had waded in; Owensford saw chains and iron bars whipping through the air in deadly arcs, and then a shotgun went *thump* five times in as many seconds. The riot car turned in midair, ponderously graceful, and a nozzle swiveled. Bright yellow gas shot out, a thick jet under high pressure that bounced from the crowd and dispersed in a dense fog.

"Guiltpuke gas," Ace said. The area behind the police line was finally clearing. Owensford swiveled his head. Lysander, and what *was* his fiancée doing there; she had the back of one hand to her mouth . . . guiltpuke gas, a nausea agent with an indelible dye mixed in, so you could identify the suspects later. The sick-sweet smell of vomitus filled the air, and underlying it came a tang he recognized, the salt-iron-shit smell of violent death.

"Ace, get those troops in here NOW. I don't like this at all."

"Nor me," Barton said. "Only one problem. They've got our frequency too. With better gear than we have."

Better than we have? How? "We'd better—" he began. The world came apart in a slamming roar.

"Field Prime says *now*," Two-knife said. He and Bobber were waiting perilously close, around a corner that gave on a parking lot. The gray fibrocrete wall was pockmarked, and slashed with graffiti; variations on WEREWOLVES FOREVER, mostly. And a new one: HELOTS RULE OK with the red = sign. He shrugged off the fifty-kilo load of rockets and began handing them out to the other gang-members; they seized one each and dashed or crawled off into the darkness.

"Me first," Bobber said. "Remember that, Werewolves."

Better you than me, defiling bitch, Two-knife thought, going down on one knee and drawing the pistol-shaped designator as he lowered the goggles over his eyes. They were nightsight devices and more, also showing the red line of the designator's laser, invisible to the naked eye. He held the communicator to his face and spoke, in Mayan. Not likely anyone else on this world spoke it, beside him and the *señora*.

"All in readiness here," he said.

"*Go.*"

Bobber had unwrapped her launcher, a molded plastic tube with pistol grips and a scope sight; Friedlander-made, a one-shot disposable. Her smile was wide and wet as she pivoted around the corner and raised the launcher to her shoulder. Two-knife dropped flat and scuttled sideways, taking up the slack of the designator's trigger. He could see the Spartosky clearly now; a police groundcar was parked in front of it, with a man in the hatch signaling to the vehicle floating above. The red blip of the designator settled effortlessly on the control bubble: only seventy meters; he could usually put four bullets out of five in a man-sized target at that range.

The first rocket was Bobber's; it *whumped* out of the tube, propelled by a light charge and balanced by the shower of plastic confetti that blasted out of the rear. Then the sustainer motor cut in, with a scream like a retching cat.

"Down!" Owensford yelled. Needlessly for his own men; as he dove to the pavement he saw Cornet Gordon trip Melissa, Lysander's fiancée, and throw herself over the older girl before drawing her pistol. Lysander and Harv hit the dirt and rolled into the gutter in well-trained unison, their sidearms out and eyes searching for targets.

The mob was running now, but that was the least of their problems.

The flight path of the rocket was a bright streak across his retinas. Where it struck the Peacemaker a pancake of fire expanded as the shaped-charge warhead slammed its lance of incandescent plasma through the armor. The big vehicle lurched in the air, then forward. It caromed into the side of the building opposite the Spartosky with an impact that made the paving stones of the forecourt shudder beneath his stomach like the hide of some huge beast shuddering in its sleep. Then it pinwheeled end over end to strike the empty roadway a hundred meters farther down. Fuel tanks ruptured, spraying vaporized kerosene into the air; Owensford buried his head in his arms and held his breath. The curve of the walls protected him from the wash of flame, that and the pillars that ringed the area under the marquee and the stone lip at the end of the roadway.

Savage heat passed over him, and a soft strong *whump* of shockwave that tried to pick him up and roll him; the exposed areas of his skin were tight and painful. He raised his head as soon as it was safe, to see the police groundcar settling back on its springs; it had taken the main force of the blast. Saunders was still in the hatchway, burning and screaming and waving his arms. For a few seconds, and then two more rockets blasted into the groundcar. The top blew off in a vertical gout of fire, metal slashing into the walls and into the backs of those Milice not incapacitated by the burning fuel. Saunders was silhouetted for a moment against the fireball, until he struck the opposite building with enough force to turn his body into a lose sack of ruptured cells and bone fragments inside the armor.

Owensford turned, his vision jumping in snapshots of relevant data. Barton and most of the remaining Legion officers were behind pillars, the stocks of the Microuzis extended as they scanned the windows opposite for movement. Gordon was just pushing Melissa back through the door of the Spartosky; a junior lieutenant was using his uniform coat to smother the flames in the hair and gown of a guest. He staggered, grunted, fell; still moving, but grasping at a bullet wound in his thigh.

"You Milice," Owensford called. Some of them were still on their feet, and they had all abandoned the useless riot gear for the guns on their backs. "Get the wounded in here under cover.

You, Sergeant, get me ten, we've got to secure the building across the way."

The police-militia noncom turned, a look of grateful relief on his face that *someone* was taking charge. His mouth opened; then he staggered, a red splotch opening on the front of his jacket, and dropped bonelessly to the ground.

"Cover, cover!" Owensford called.

"I'll clear the building," Lysander said. He dashed forward, diving and rolling as bullets chipped the pavement at his feet, Harv skipping sideways behind him and snapping off covering shots at the windows. The Milice rallied and followed, driving into the dead ground at the base of the building across the street. The prince kicked in a door and dove through, the militia of the Brotherhoods at his heels.

Ace Barton was firing controlled three-round bursts from behind a pillar. "Fifth floor, second from the right," he shouted as he ducked back behind the stone to reload. Return fire pocked the column; he dodged down and to the other side, snapping off another burst.

"Where the hell is the battalion?"

"Coming."

"¡*Mierda!*" Skilly said, dropping down behind the window ledge.

Light pistol-caliber bullets hammered at the stone below; she rose and squeezed off the five rounds left in the clip, *phut-phut-phut-phut-phut.*

"Somebody down there too good a shot," she said with respect, slapping another magazine into the well in the pistol grip of the carbine and stepping back out of the line of fire. "That enough, everyone out!"

The dark-clad Meijian at the com unit snapped it closed, picked up his personal weapon and darted to the door. "Niles!"

The young Englishman squeezed off another round and turned. "*Got* one, by god!" he said.

"Good," Skilly replied impatiently. "Doan matter, we gots nice pictures, cameras knocked out just before the first rocket. Papers will tell, but people we interested in doan read, is all. Hoped we'd get the kings . . . you take rear, my mon. Go, go, *go.*"

The corridor outside was cool white silence, insanely distant from the fire and blood outside. Niles crouched, his weapon covering the long hallway as the others dashed toward the staircase; the corridors were shaped like a capital "I," with elevators in the middle and stairs at either end. He skipped backward crabwise, conscious of the steadiness of his hands and the bright concentration in his mind. *Read about* this, *Grand-Uncle,* he thought. *Tell me I'm a useless playboy* now, *father.*

They were to the stairs; he could hear the thunder of feet on the metal slats. And the door at the other end of the corridor was opening.

"Hostiles!" Niles shouted, dropping into prone position. Elbows on the ground, and the stock smacked into his shoulder, *squeeze* off two rounds. Star-shaped holes in the frosted glass, and a scream of pain. Then the door opened again, just enough to let a muzzle through. Shots blazed, a military automatic rifle, ugly *crack* sounds above his head, hammering into the plasterwork and leaving stinging dust in the air.

"Come on, mon, we leaving," Skilly said behind him.

Niles shook his head, fired again. "Got to give them something to think about," he said. "Grenade, please?"

She handed one forward to him, a standard plastic concussion-model egg. He waited until the opposite door began to open, then pulled the tab and lobbed it with a cricketer's expert overarm snap; it bounced into the narrow gap between door and wall and exploded, tearing the door from the hinges.

"Another, fragmentation," Niles said. Skilly handed it to him as they scuttled backward into the stairwell; there was something of a surprised look on her face.

Niles let the door close, pulling a roll of electrical tape from a pocket of his new hidehunter leather costume. The door was a simple rectangle of pressed metal, with a frosted glass window and a U-shaped aluminum handle. Moving with careful speed, he taped the grenade inside the metal loop, then ran a strip of the tape from the pin to the top of the stair railing. Finally he drew his knife and used the point to straighten the split ends of the pin, where they bent back on the other side of the grenade's lever; the slightest pressure would strip it out, now.

"Hoo, Skilly *like* that," she said, with new-found respect, slapping him on the shoulder. He found himself smiling back.

A bellow from below. "Skilly! ¡*Vamonos!*"

They turned, taking the stairs a dozen at a time and whooping like children.

"They *didn't* cut the line, sir," the Legion electronics tech said, looking up from her equipment. The glowstrips blinked back on. "Something with the central power control computer; I'd say." They had flown her in in one of the RSMP tiltrotors, along with the reaction company who were securing the area, and Fifth Battalion medics to help with the wounded.

There were enough that they still had to be triaged. Peter Owensford walked over to where someone was bandaging Prince Lysander's shoulder. *A nice romantic wound in the extremities,* he thought. A demonstrator looked up as he passed; he recognized her, the pretty girl who had been grinning when the bottle hit the policeman. She was not smiling now, as she sat with her dead companion's head in her lap, and her face was less pretty for the streaks of blood drying on it.

"Murderer!" she shrilled. "You'll pay for this, you'll *pay*—" Then she slumped, as a passing medic stopped to press a hypospray against the back of her neck.

Lysander had heard the exchange. "Somebody will pay," he promised, looking around the street. Wreckage still smoldered, and bodies were lying in neat rows under blanket covers. "Somebody definitely will."

"Bad?" Owensford said, nodding at the wound.

"Just a flesh wound," he said. "What really hurts is that I was putting a field-dressing on it when the men with me charged down that corridor. The door was booby-trapped. Five of them died, and whoever it was got away. We'll do better the next time, sir."

"*I* call *you* sir, sir," Owensford said. A squad of Legionnaires in synthileather battledress and nemourlon combat armor moved down the street.

"Major, the Field Force is going to be under your command, and right now the best service I can do Sparta is to be part of it. Sir."

"As a beginning," Owensford said. "We'll create a Prince Royal's Own, which you can command in the field long enough that the men learn to trust you. After that, it's staff schools." Peter grinned hollowly when Lysander winced. "Someone has to lead when all this is over."

"Thank you," Melissa said, across the body. "This one's dead."

"You're welcome," Ursula Gordon said, as they moved onto the next.

Pressure bandage, Melissa thought. They ripped the Milice trooper's tunic free and wadded it over the long cut in his thigh, pressing the flesh closed and binding it with twists of cloth. The Spartan found herself breathing through her nose; it was not that the smell was unfamiliar, gralloching deer was pretty much like this, it was just that when she thought of it together with *people*—

"*Out of the way, out of the way!*" the paramedics shouted.

Melissa and Ursula jumped back; the white-coated team from the latest ambulance moved in, one setting up a plasma drip and slapping an antishock hypo on the man's arm.

"I think—" Melissa started to brush a strand of hair back out of her eyes, then stopped; in the glowlight it looked as if she was wearing gloves to the elbow, of something dark and glistening. She swallowed. "I think that's the last; they can handle it now."

"Water," Ursula croaked.

There was a fountain in the center of the Spartosky's lobby. They pushed through the thinning crowd that still milled, some shocked-silent, some hysterical, some getting first aid for minor injuries while the professionals saved those on the edge of death. The kings were in one corner with a communications tech and a knot of uniforms, mercenary and RSMP, grimly busy. Water bubbled clear and cold from the fretted terracotta basin; Melissa and the woman in uniform rinsed their hands until they were clean enough to scoop up a handful. For a long minute they waited, letting stress-exhaustion slump their shoulders.

"Thank you again, for saving my life," Melissa said. She shivered slightly, remembering it again; the roar of fire, the screams, the sudden flat *crack* of bullets.

"It's my job," Ursula said. Her eyes met the other woman's; Melissa wondered how her own looked now. *Glazed, probably. Not as steady as hers.*

"I'm . . . sorry, I've been . . . impolite," she continued. Her skin flushed, embarrassment and anger at having to say what honor demanded; the feeling was welcome, pushing away the sick knot of fear and disgust in her stomach.

"Miss von Alderheim," Ursula said calmly. Her eyes moved to one side, ever so slightly. "It's perfectly understandable. Lys—The Prince—goes to Tanith, nearly gets killed, and nearly gets snatched by a designing whore. Perfectly understandable that you should be angry, especially when she shows up here to remind everyone of it."

"I never said you—"

"Well, I was. A whore, that is, if not designing. Not my career of choice, but there it is. My lady, I never had any slightest belief the Prince would stay with me. I wanted it, yes, but I never believed it. The Prince dreamed about it; he's a romantic to his bones, but he knew better too."

"But that's it, isn't it?" Melissa said with quiet bitterness.

"He loves you, you love him, but he'll *marry* me, out of *duty*." Her mouth twisted in something that might have been a smile. "A designing woman and an infatuated Prince would have been much easier on my pride, I think. I may get what I want, but not the way I want it."

Unexpectedly, Ursula smiled, an almost tender expression, and reached out to touch the Spartan on the shoulder. "He will, if you let him." she said. "Love you, that is; he's that sort of man. Besides, that's not the important thing."

"Easy for you to say."

"Well no, actually, it's rather difficult. But it's true. We were in love, or thought we were, and that's about all we had in common, apart from a few books. My mother was a drug addict and a prostitute and a petty thief, until they sent her to Tanith; who my father is or was, God only knows. I grew up on a prison-planet that lives from drugs grown by slaves, and it's just the sort of place you'd expect it to be. All I was taught was enough to make me pleasant company. You grew up with him, you've got a shared *world* in common, the beliefs and the feelings and the little things like knowing the jokes and songs . . . and something important to work on together. Opposites may attract, but it's the similarities keep people together."

Melissa blinked at her and slowly sat on the coping of the fountain. "Now I really *am* sorry," she said. "I forgot how difficult it must be for you."

"I'll heal," Ursula said. "Mostly I already have. I'd have preferred to go somewhere else, but—" She touched the Legion crest on her shoulder. "There's more choices in this business than in my old trade, but not a whole lot more. The Prince will heal too, if you help him, Miss von Alderheim."

"Melissa," the other said impulsively, holding out her hand. They clasped palms, smiling tentatively. "How old are you, Cornet Gordon?"

"Ursula. Eighteen standard years and six months. Going on fifty."

"You certainly make me feel like a babe in the woods, Ursula!"

"Never had a chance for a childhood," Ursula said. "But look at it this way: you're still more grown-up than most men of fifty." They shared a chuckle. "Not all, of course. Colonel Falkenberg's quite adult—but then, he *is* fifty-odd."

The chuckle grew into a laugh; a quiet one that died away as they grew conscious of a man standing near.

"Why, Lysander," Melissa said, rising and taking his unwounded arm. "Ursula and I were just talking about you."

The Spartan prince looked a little paler as they walked away; Harv followed, giving Ursula a glare as he passed.

The mercenary sighed, rising and looking down at the ruin of her dress uniform. *Amazing,* she thought, suddenly a little nauseated with herself. *Twenty-odd people just killed, and we find time for emotional fiddlefaddle. That's humanity, I guess.* There was a line of caked, crusted blood under her fingernails, where she had had to clamp hard.

"Cornet Gordon?"

A Legion trooper, face anonymous under the bulging combat helmet, body blocky and mechanical in armor and mottled synthileather. He carried a smell with him, of gun oil and metal and burnt powder, impersonal and somehow clean. "Captain Alana wants you in the manager's office, they're setting up debriefing, ma'am."

"Thank you. Carry on." Manager's office would be up the sweeping double stairs, all marble and gilt bronze. She took a deep breath and forced herself to stride briskly, but paused at the top to look back. There was a good view out the big doors; he was holding open the door of a car as Melissa climbed in.

Just like him, she thought. *Shot in the shoulder, and he holds the car door for* her.

There was something in her throat; she coughed and swallowed. *Client number 176, not counting family groups,* she told herself coldly. *After all that, a few years of celibacy and hard work are just what you need, Cornet Gordon.*

You could believe anything, if you repeated it to yourself often enough.

Peter Owensford shuffled the pile of paper from one side of his desk to the other. Most of it was routine, but it could be important to set up the right routines. Or avoid the wrong ones, anyway.

Personnel decisions. Munitions design. Military industrialization with extremely limited resources. Schools for the Legion's children. Commissary, laundry, home construction, perimeter defense, training schedules. Reports for Falkenberg, who wouldn't get them for months. Use of aircraft. Communications. Medical supplies. Much of it had nothing at all to do with strategy or leadership, but it all had to be taken care of, and some of it *did* have an impact on strategic decisions. More important, though, was that strategy had to drive the details, rather than the other way around.

And just now I don't have a strategy. Just objectives.

Captain Lahr knocked at Peter's office door. "Colonel Slater's here, sir," he announced.

"Thanks, Andy. Send him in. Give me a few minutes, then we'll need to see you."

Peter stood to greet his visitor. Hal Slater walked with a cane; there was only so much that regeneration stimulators could do when the same tissues were damaged time after time. Slater's handshake was firm, and his eyes steady.

"Good to see you again, sir," Peter said. "Damned good. Glad to see you recovered so well."

"Yes. Thank you. Surprising how little all that titanium in there bothers me. Of course given my druthers I'd take a low-gravity planet—"

"Sit down, please."

"Thank you, I will."

Peter eyed Slater's conservative suit. "Still in civvies?"

"Well, I wanted to check with you," Slater said. "They say they've made me a major general, though that's more title than rank. And of course I've still got a Legion suit with oak leaves—"

"You'd be welcome here either way," Owensford said. "Of course you knew that."

"Thank you," Slater said. "I figured as much, but it never hurts to touch the bases properly. How is John Christian?"

"A little heavier, hair a little grayer, otherwise much the same," Owensford said. "He said to give you his regards. Care for a drink?"

"Not just now, thank you," Hal said. He looked around the office.

"Pretty bare," Peter said. "But the electronics are here."

"Yes, and so is the paperwork."

"You know it."

"It looks like you've enough to do," Hal Slater said. "I know I'm up to my arse in Weems Beasts. They seem to have given you plenty to work with from what I saw on the way in."

"Quite decent," Peter said. "I think they actually like us."

"Seems that way," Slater agreed. "Certainly they gave me decent facilities, I'll say that for them. Right near the University. Good library. Fair computer, but I brought better. Anyway, we're setting up, and I'll be having some kind of opening ceremony one of these days. I'd appreciate it if you'd come help."

Peter grinned. "Sure. I'll bring Centurion Hanselman. He wears enough fruit salad to impress the yokels." Peter waved at the stack of paper on his desk. "You can't start turning out staff officers soon enough for me!"

"Well, it will still take a bit of time—"

"Yeah." Peter paused for a moment. "Did you get a chance to look over the reports on the riot?"

Dr. Slater nodded. "Yes. Very interesting."

"Interesting."

"Perhaps I should say revealing," Hal said.

"Yeah, well they showed us some unsuspected capabilities all right," Peter said.

"Perhaps a bit more than that," Hal Slater said. "They told us a bit about themselves, too. For instance, what did they expect to accomplish?"

"Eh? I'd have said they did very well," Peter said. "They showed they can disrupt a Royal gathering. Scared the militia, killed some of them. Stood up to us, and got headlines and TV pictures showing them doing it. I'd say they racked up some points."

"Yes, of course," Slater said. "But think about it. They showed us they have far more capability than we suspected. More important, they revealed they have considerable off-planet support—"

"I doubt they intended that we learn that."

"So they underestimated us," Slater said. "All the more interesting. So they gave us all that information, and to what end? They haven't harmed the Legion. They've made the kings furious, and they convinced most of the waverers in the Brotherhoods that the threat is serious. They let us know they have professional competence in crowd manipulation, and that they can assemble a larger and uglier crowd than the RSMP suspected. They told us they have fairly sophisticated military equipment and the ability to use it. And with all that capability they destroyed one crowd-control car and killed no one irreplaceable."

"Hmm. I didn't think of it that way. All right, Hal, what do you make of it?"

"First, since they aren't complete fools, look for them to have a great deal more capability that they didn't show," Hal said.

"Hmm. Yeah. Right. You said they told us about themselves. What?"

"I think they're amateurs," Slater said. "Academics."

"If you'd seen that fighting retreat you wouldn't say that."

"Oh, I grant you they're competent enough," Slater said. "But even so there's a decided flavor of book learning. Peter, I think they're operating right out of the classical guerrilla war theory manuals. People's War, People's Army. Mao's Basic Tactics. Enemy advance, we retreat. Enemy halt, we harass. Enemy retire, we attack."

"All that from one riot?"

"Well, of course I'm guessing."

"Pay attention to your hunches," Falkenberg said. Only I don't have a hunch. Hal Slater has a hunch, and Hal Slater isn't Christian Johnny.

"Ok, I'll think about it," Owensford said. "Now, let's get Andy Lahr in here and go over just what I can do to help you get set up properly. . . ."

CHAPTER SIX

Crofton's Encyclopedia of the Inhabited Planets
(2nd Edition):

> **Eurotas,** river. [E-ur-o-tas], named for river in south-
> ern Greece, Earth. (see *names,* Mythological, Graeco-
> Roman)
> Largest river on the planet *Sparta* [see *Sparta*];
> Length (main stream): 9,600 kilometers
> Drainage basin: 8,225,000 sq. kilometers
> Maximum volume: 860,000,000 liters
> Minimum volume: 475,000,000 liters
> **Description:** The Eurotas is customarily divided into
> the Lower, Middle and Upper Valleys, respectively, and
> the Delta. The Delta proper flows northward into the nearly
> circular Constitution Bay, encompassing an area of approx.
> 25,000 sq. kilometers of silt and peat-soil marshes, under-
> going reclamation for agriculture in some areas. The Lower
> Valley runs north-south between the *Lycourgos Hills*
> fronting on the Aegean Sea in the west, and the twin
> ranges of *Parnassus* and *Pindaros* on the east, separat-
> ing the Eurotas from the Jefferson Ocean (q.v.). Lying
> between the river-ports of *Clemens* and *Olynthos* is the
> Middle Valley, occupying a low-lying fault zone between
> uplifted blocks on the north and south. To the west, the
> upper portion of the Middle Valley is flanked on the south
> and west by the *Illyrian Dales,* a region of limestone
> uplands, and beyond these by the *Drakon Mountains.*
> North of Olynthos the river descends via the *Vulcan Rapids*
> from *Lake Alexander,* a body of water comparable to
> Earth's Lake Ontario. From the Vulcan Rapids the Upper
> Valley runs generally north-south to the slightly smaller
> *Lake Ochrid,* the formal source of the Eurotas.
> The Middle and Lower Valleys are essentially silt-filled

rift depressions, whose drainage link is geologically recent. Gradients are therefore small, and vessels drawing up to 3 meters may navigate the Eurotas as far inland as Olynthos, 6,400 kilometers from the mouth of the river. Flooding, siltation, breaks in the natural levees, marshes and ox-bow lakes are common. The Upper Valley is an area of rejuvenated drainage and exposed basic rock, with frequent steep falls.

Climate and Hydrology: The Delta has a humid-Mediterranean regime, with mild rainy winters, warm dry summers and a nearly year-round growing season. The Lower Valley is similar but slightly more continental with increasing distance from the sea; the Middle Valley is comparable, on a larger scale, to the Po basin of Italy, Earth, with cold damp winters with some snow, and warm summers with occasional convection thunderstorms. Winter cold increases westward and northward, until the Upper Valley ranges from cool-temperate semiarid to subarctic north of Lake Ochrid. Lakes Ochrid and Alexander are both frozen for several months of the year, as is the Upper Valley as a whole. The Eurotas reaches maximum flow in the late winter or early spring; summer flow is largely sustained by snowmelt from flanking mountain ranges. More than half the dry-season flow is derived from the snowmelt of the Drakon Range, and most of this flows underground through the 1,400,000 sq. kilometer area of the Illyrian Dales, with their extensive near-horizontal limestone formations.

"Hunf!" Geoffrey Niles grunted, beginning to regret accepting Skida's offer to spar. His forearms slapped down on the boot just before it hit his midriff, and his hands twisted to lock on the foot. Skilly spun around the axis of the trapped foot, tearing it out of his bands before the grip could solidify and then rolled backward off her shoulder, out of his reach and flicking up, then boring back in. The circle of hidehunter faces around the campfire watched with mild interest, jaws moving stolidly as they scooped up stew.

It's going to be difficult to win this without thumping her, he thought; he had not expected that. The Belizean was a big woman, very strong for her weight, but he had fifteen kilos on her and none of it was fat. *She must have had some training.* There would be bruises on his upper arm, where she had broken a clamp-hold by stabbing at the nerve cluster. . . .

Flick. Snap-kick to his left knee. He let the right relax, and gravity pushed him out of the way; then he punched his fist underarm toward her short ribs. She let the kicking foot drop down and around, spun again with a high slashing heel-blow toward his head; the punch slid off thigh muscle as hard as teak, but his other palm came up hard under her striking leg to throw her backward. *Street-warrior style, those high kicks,* he thought critically.

She went with it, backflipping off her hands and doing a scissor-roll to land upright facing him. Then she surprised him, coming up out of her crouch, shrugging with a grin and turning away toward the fire.

Thank goodness, he thought. She was so damned *fast,* sooner or later he'd have had to hurt her, and that would be unfair, undermining her in front of her people. And—

Even then he almost caught the backkick that lashed out, the long leg seeming to stretch in the dim light. But there had been no warning from her stance.

"Ufff," he croaked, folding around his paralyzed diaphragm. She caught the outstretched hand in both of hers, twisted to lock the arm. A boot-edge thumped with stunning force into his armpit, then the leg swung over to lock around his elbow, and they were both going down. The ground sprang up to meet them with unnatural heavy-world swiftness, jarring every bone from his lower spine up as she landed half across him with a scissor on his right arm.

The Englishman writhed, turning on his left and reaching behind; there were three ways to break that hold, or with strength alone. . . . He froze as a hard thumbnail poked into the corner of one eye.

"Lie still," the liquid voice said from behind his ear; he could smell the sweat that ran down her face, and the mint she chewed. "This heavy planet, a real gentlemon always let de lady get on top."

"Your point!" he said hastily. He had been around the Upper Valley hidehunters long enough now to know why so many were one-eyed.

"Sure, just a friendly match," Skilly said. She rolled off him and stood, offering a hand and pulling him up after her. They dusted themselves off; the campside was a sandy dried riverbed, with little vegetation. "You not bad, Jeff-my-mon, just . . . Skilly hasn't fallen for *that* trick since she was ten. You fight too much like a *rabiblanco,* you know?"

They walked over toward the fire; the fuel was some native plant like a dense orange bamboo, which burned low and hot and gave off a smell of cinnamon. The camp was simple, a ring of saddles and buffalo-hide bedrolls around the hearth. Horses stamped and nickered occasionally where they were tethered a few meters away, and in the distance something howled long and mournfully. Cythera was full, nearly half again as large as Luna, silver-bright against a sky filled with stars in constellations subtly different from Earth's. Meteors streaked across it every few minutes, multicolored fire.

"Rabiblanco?" he said. No Spanish that he recognized.

"Oh, nice clean gym, nice flat mats, pretty little white suits and colored belts, hey?"

Too academic, he translated mentally. *Well, she has a point.* The shoulder felt stiff, and he rotated it gingerly.

"Yes, but what does it *mean?*" he asked. They leaned back against their saddles, nearly side by side, and one of the others handed them plates of stew and metal cups of strong black coffee from the pot resting on the edge of the fire.

"Rabiblanco?" she said. Her teeth showed in a friendly grin. "White-ass."

"You're quiet today, Skilly," Niles said.

"Skilly is thinking," she said. "We nearly there."

That was a bit of a relief. Not that she chattered; it had been more like a continuous interrogation nearly every day, starting two hours after breakfast, once she learned of his background at Sandhurst. A grab bag of everything he had sat through in those interminable lectures: leadership, communications, how to parade a regiment, logistics, laser range-finding systems, how to hand-compute firing patterns for mortars, how to maintain recoilless rifles, tactical use of seeker missiles . . . She had taken notes, too. Afternoons and they were back in the saddle and she was grilling him on how to *use* it, comparing it with things she had heard from others or read in an astonishing number of books, making up hypotheticals and hashing out alternative solutions. Evenings around the fire it had been about *him.* His relations, who knew who, how were you presented at court, what were the rules about giving parties, schools, table manners. . . .

It had been two weeks since they left the Upper Valley plains and rode into the hill country called the Illyrian Dales, and he was feeling pumped dry. It was like being picked over by a mental crow, all the bright shiny things plucked out and sorted into neat heaps and tirelessly fitted together again. He had mentioned the thought to her, and she had given that delightful laugh and said: *Bird that know the ground doan get into stewpot,* and begun again.

What a woman, he thought contentedly. Not exactly what you'd bring home to mother—he blanched inwardly at the thought—but absolutely riffing for this caper. From hints and glances, even more delightful when they had some privacy. *Burton and Selous should have had it so good,* he thought. Although Burton would probably have made more of his chances; the man *had* translated the Kama Sutra, after all.

"Jeffi, you smiling like the jaguar that got the farmer's pig," Skida said, coming out of her brown study.

"Beautiful country," he said contentedly, waving his free arm around.

That was true enough. The Illyrian Dales were limestone hills, big but gently sloped, endlessly varied. Most of the ridgetops were open, in bright swales of tall grass gold-green with the first frosts. The spiderweb of valleys between was deeper-soiled and held denser growth. Sometimes thickets of wild rose or native semibamboo so dense they had to dismount and cut a path with machetes, more often something like the big maples that arched over their heads here.

Those were turning with the frosts too, to fire-gold and scarlet, and there was a rustling bed of leaves that muffled the beat of hooves from the horses and pack-mules. Afternoon light stabbed down in stray flickers into the gloom below, turning the ground into a flaming carpet of embers for brief seconds. Sometimes there would be a hollow sound under the iron-shod feet of the animals, or they would have to detour around sinkholes; the others had told him of giant caves, networks that ran for scores of kilometers underground. Few rivers, but many springs and pools. West and south on the horizon gleamed the peaks of the Drakon Range, higher than the Himalayas and three times as long. The air was mildly chill and intensely clean, smelling of green and rock.

Best game country I've seen, too, he thought happily. Whoever was sent on ahead to make camp could count on finding supper in half an hour; there were usually a couple of fat pheasant or duck or rabbit waiting to be grilled, and the hidehunters had grumbled at having to eat venison four days in a row when one of them snapshot a yearling buck from the saddle.

"Thinking like a *rabiblanco* again," Skilly said, gently teasing. "Outback is bugs and boring, *solamente,* you know? Skilly is here because of her job, then it's city life for her."

"Incorrigible white-ass, that's me," Geoffrey laughed.

Ahead and to their right he could see a herd of bison on a rise in the middle distance, about a kilometer away. A few of the bulls raised their heads at the sound of hooves, and the clump of big shaggy animals began a slow steady movement away, flowing like a carpet over the irregular ground.

"I'm surprised there's so many big grazers after only, what, eighty years?"

"CoDo," Skilly shrugged. "They seeded the plants, did the gene-thing with some of them to grow faster, you know? Then the animals, sent all females and all pregnant, and screwed around with their genes too, so they have only one bull to ten cowbeasts for a while. No diseases and plenty room, grow by ge-o-metric progressive. Only last couple of years the meateaters start to catch up." Those had come from zoos, mostly; the Greens had had a lot of influence back in the 2030s, enough to override local protests and have bears, wolves, dholes, leopards and tigers and whatnot dropped into remote areas. No point in trying that on Earth, the former ranges were jammed with starving people who would gladly beat a lion to death with rocks for the meat on its bones.

"Quiet now."

The valley opened up slightly, glances of blue noon sky and Sparta's pale-yellow sun through the canopy above. Skida halted her mount with a shift of balance, touching its neck with the rein to turn it three-quarters on.

"Skilly sees you," she said in a bored tone of voice.

Niles blinked, as two figures rose from the hillside. Both had been invisible a few minutes earlier; they were covered from head to foot by loose-woven twine cloaks stuck with twigs and leaves, and the scope-sighted rifles cradled in their arms were swaddled in mottled rags. Farther up the hill the ground moved aside under the roots of a pine, and a man vaulted out and skidded down the slope to the mounted party. This one wore leather breeches and boots, a camouflage jacket over that, and webbing gear. A machine-pistol was slung across his chest and there were corporal's stripes on his sleeve; the military effect was a little offset by the black pigtail, bandanna and brass hoop-earring.

"Corporal Hermanez," Skilly said, returning his casual salute.

"Field Prime," he said, obviously pleased that she had remembered his name. "How did you spot my scouts?"

"Leaf piles doan scratch their arse." The guerrilla noncom turned to glare briefly at one of the men, who stiffened. "Two-knife?"

"Off popping the virgins, Field Prime—another fifty recruits in yesterday."

"Carry on."

The valley narrowed again. Alerted, Niles thought he saw movement now and then, once something that *might* be a sonic sensor input mike. The skin on the back of his neck crawled slightly. Then the thickly grown rock flared back on either side of them, into a hummocky clearing of gravel and rock and thin grass several hectares in extent, scattered with medium-sized oaks and big eucalyptus trees with peeling bark. Camouflage nets were rigged between the trees at a little over head-height, mimicking the ground. Across the way was a taller hill where the shell of limestone rock had collapsed inward. Water fell over the lip to a pool at the base, and he could see several dark spaces in the light-colored rock that reached back out of sight.

"Home," Skilly said. "Base One."

Men in the same uniform came and led the horses away at a trot. Niles followed Skida as she ducked under one of the tarpaulins and walked toward the falls, trying not to be too obvious as he looked around. *Not my idea of a rebel encampment,* he thought. There were dug-in air defense missiles, light Skyhawks and frame-mounted Talons; CoDo issue, or copies. Plenty of people moving around; not a spit-and-polish outfit, but they all seemed fairly clean and to know where they were going. Crates and boxes were stacked in neat heaps, and there were half a dozen circles around blackboards or pieces of equipment, familiarization-lectures. A pile of meter-diameter cylinders lay on a timber frame. He stared at them in puzzlement and then recognized a Skysweeper, a simple solid-fuel rocket that could loft a hundred-kilo load of ball bearings into the orbital path of a spy satellite.

His lips shaped a soundless whistle. *Not too shabby,* he thought. A squad jogged by, rifles at port; Skilly returned their leader's salute, the same half-casual wave, and then slapped palms with a figure he recognized: the big Indian he had met briefly in Sparta City, with his twin machetes over his back. Here he also carried a light machine gun, dangling from one hand as if it were no more than a rifle.

"Yo, Two-knife. How it go?"

"Yo, Skilly. Not bad. Your little yellow men got here with their toys, setting up now." He jerked a thumb at the caves.

"Toys may save our asses, Two-knife. Any trouble?"

"Discipline parade for offenders, and taking in the fresh meat. Got them kit, ran them up and down hills all yesterday, usual thing like you say." The blank black eyes turned on Niles, and the Indian said something in a choppy-sounding language, not Spanish.

"He's a trained officer, not just a pretty face," Skilly replied; Niles felt oddly flattered, and returned the bigger man's gaze coolly. She slung her rifle. "Let's go. Niles should see our discipline."

The stench almost made Niles gag as they walked past the row of a half a dozen pits. Each was just wide enough to hold a man and deep enough that only the faces showed; none of them looked up.

"We got this from the CoDo Marines," Skilly said, watching him out of the corner of her eye. "Make them dig a hole and then live in it for a week. Next step up from punishment drill. Lot of our original trainers were ex-Marines"—*mostly gone now*, she thought but did not say—"and we had a bunch of our Movement people do hitches with the CD and some of the other armies."

"Second offense, not cleaning rifle," Two-knife said, kicking dirt in the direction of the first pit and walking on to each in turn. "Stealing. Second offense, refusing to wash. This one didn't want to learn to read. Backtalking his squad leader. Smoking borloi. Lighting fire in the open."

Beyond the row of pits were two upright X-frames made of saplings, with men lashed to them spreadeagled. Odd-looking bruises and dried crusted scabs covered their naked bodies.

"Gauntlet," Skilly explained. Niles kept his face carefully blank; that meant running between lines of your comrades while they flogged you with their belts. You could not have an army without discipline, and a guerrilla army like this had no system of laws and courts to fall back on. Not to mention the type of recruits they would have to depend on, men on the bad side of the law to begin with.

"Asleep on watch," Two-knife said of the first man. "Striking an officer," of the second. "Got an offender among the virgins, too," he went on.

They were near the C-shaped bowl that fronted the clearing; the waterfall was a hundred meters away, at the center of the curve, and its sound was a burr of white noise in the background. Here the ground ran down to the base of the cliff in a natural amphitheater. Fifty or so men and a few women were squatting on the rocky ground, in uniform but looking awkward in it, and groggy with exhaustion where they were not tense with fear. Very out of place, as well; you could tell these were men who had spent their lives in cities, and on their streets. A few armed troops stood by, not quite guarding the recruits; two more flanked a bound prisoner at the base of the slope, very definitely guarding *him*. A short woman stood nearby, glaring at the one under guard.

"The virgin's name is Carter," Two-knife continued. "The other one is Werewolf. He caught Williams in the third back warehouse cave, tried to hump her. She caught him a couple and he whipped on her *muy mal*, then ran when the patrol came."

"Williams . . . Citizen family, University, come in right after we blow the Peacemaker? Her squeeze killed by Milice?"

He nodded and Skilly fell silent, taking in the parties as she walked down toward them. Then she turned to face the recruits, ignoring the judicial matter for the moment.

"This," she said, indicating herself with a thumb, "is Field Prime. Field Prime commands the Spartan People's Liberation Army. We call ourselves the Helots; pretty soon you learn why. Helots are under the direction of the Movement Council and Capital Prime. Field Second," she continued, turning to Two-knife, "repeat the charge."

When he had finished, she turned to the woman. Girl, rather; about nineteen, but it was difficult to tell anything else because of massive purple-and-yellow bruises that covered her face.

"Yes."

"Louder, Helot."

"Yes! I told him to go away and he grabbed me and I kicked him and he started hitting me and—" She turned away, arms tightly crossed over her chest.

"So, Carter," Skida continued, to the prisoner "What you say?"

"Lies," the man said. He was not much older than his victim, still in gang colors, a thin acne-scarred face and darting eyes. "Them University cunts, they'll spread for anything. Stuck-up bitch probably has the crud, anyway."

Skida looked at Two-knife, then took the girl's chin between thumb and forefinger for a moment to examine her injuries. A slight nod and the guards stepped away from Carter, who smiled and stood taller. Skida was wearing a Walther in a cross-draw holster below her left breast, with the butt turned in. Her hand did not seem to move with any particular haste, but the echoing crack of the first shot rang out before Carter's eyes had time to do more than widen. He jerked back, folding as if an invisible horse had kicked him in the gut. The flat slap of the 10mm bullet hitting the muscle of his stomach was just audible under the gunshot, and she held the second until he clapped his hands to the spreading red patch and moaned in shock. The next bullet left a black hole in the middle of his forehead and snapped him erect again for an instant while the back of his skull blew out in a shower of bone-chips and pink-gray jelly.

"Take this shit away and throw it down a hole," she said, holstering the weapon.

"First lesson!" she continued to the recruits. "Only two ways out of this army!" Skida held up a fist. One finger shot up. "One, when we marches down the Sacred Way in the victory parade." Another finger. "Two—feet first. This the Revolution. The Revolution not a tea party; it not so kind, so gentle, so reasonable as that."

She paused to let the recruits absorb that; one was retching, and a few were looking shaky. Most of the rest sat stock-still, but the smell of their fear was rank. After a moment she tapped herself on the chest.

"Skilly—that Field Prime to you—Skilly knows you. Knows all the secret of you dirty little souls. You think you baaad, eh? Think the world give you a hard *time*, think the world *owe* you something. Now you going to go *take* it, eh?" Mutters of approval. The tall woman sneered.

"Well, Skilly tells you something; you half right. Yes, the world shit on you all your lives. The Welfare officers, the CoDo, the rich, the taxpayers back on Earth, Citizens here—all of them fuck you over from the day you born. What does that make you?"

She paused, then spoke in a tone thick with scorn. "Shit yourselves, is what." Another murmur, hostile this time and quickly dying under her glare. "Yes! You everything the bossman ever tell you you are. You *worthless*, you *useless*, no good to yourself or anybody. They *laughing* at you, mon."

"But here"—she tapped a booted toe against the rocky earth—"here, you *maybe* become something. Here you learn how to take what the world owe you." She crossed her arms. "How? Not by sitting in a bar, talking wit' you friends about how you do something *next month*, for sure. Not by rolling drunks and beating up on tourists and cutting each other. Not by pushing shit into your arm or up your nose.

"Here, you learn to *fight*. Here, you learn to be an *army*. That is *power*, mon! Who wants that? Who wants power, who wants to fuck the people that been up your ass all your life?" They cheered at that, a raw savage sound. Niles felt his stomach clench with the sudden realization that it was directed at *him* and people like him.

Alarming, he thought. And exhilarating, the same wild excitement you got on a fast powder-snow slope.

"Shut up! Shouting won't get it for you; lying under a tree won't, nohow. *Work* get it for you." There was dead silence now; Skida's grin was gaunt and knowing. "Yes, *compadres,* here you *work.* You work harder than field-hands cutting cane, you work until the brains run out your nose like sweat. And you *learn.*" She stooped, and caught up a glob of semiliquid gray. A tuft of hair and bone was still attached to the glistening string of matter. Skida swung her arm in an arc, spattering it at the feet of the crowd, grimly amused as they shrank back.

"Look at that! Brains, and never used for anything but holding two deaf ears apart. Brains that wouldn't *learn,* wouldn't *listen.* At least now the ants eat them, get some use out of them. You want to be like that? No? So that the next thing you do here, you learn to *use* the brains. You *stupid,* now. Too stupid to *know* you stupid; now, we fix that.

"One last thing. Look at each other." She waited a moment, until their heads turned uncertainly from side to side. "These people your *compadres.* These are the peoples you live with, eat with, work with, *fight beside* from now. Field Prime isn't your mother; Field Prime doesn't care if you love each other. You can hate each other like brothers. But when we finished with you, you will be tighter than brothers—you will save your *compadre's* ass, because you know he will save *yours.*

"And when you've done all that, *then* you'll have the power. The power of an *army.* Do you understand?"

"Answer, *Yes, Field Prime!*" Two-knife shouted; it was an astonishing sound, loud enough for a powered megaphone.

"*Yes, Field Prime!*"

"Louder, so Field Prime can hear you."

"YES, FIELD PRIME!"

"And this your place, right next to mine," Skilly said.

Niles nodded, a little dazed. The tour had been exhaustive, and combined with a running staff meeting and a series of introductions; he sensed that was a test too, of his ability to assimilate information quickly and not lose his feet. The network of caverns was enormous; on Earth it would have been a famous tourist attraction. Here it was being put to more practical use: stables, armories, kitchens, barracks, infirmary, machine-shop, a hydro-generator running on an underground

stream, classrooms, even a small computer room with a commercial optical-disk system capable of holding almost unlimited data. The Meijians had been setting up shop next to that;
farther back were caves stacked high with hides and tallow
and jerky, part of the operation that provided cover and
additional funds.

"This . . . must have taken years," he said.

"Near ten years. Skilly found it just after she got here"—
over a decade—"but she was *really* running a hide-hunting
business then." She waved a hand into the darkness. This
stretch of corridor was lit by fluorescent tubes stapled to the
rock. "Plenty more place like this in the Dales. About four
hundred Helots here now, most training, and then we push
them out to the other bases, keep everything dispersed.
Duplicate all the *facilities* here, too, stuff in various place, if
we ever have to move out fast. Building up the numbers now,
got the frame*work* and just need the warm bodies."

"Well, ah, yes, Field Prime," he said. She was leaning against
the doorway of her quarters, set into the fissured rock, smiling slightly.

"Field problem in the morning," she said, looking at the
chronometer-compass on her wrist. "Oh," she added, just as
she closed the door. "Connecting door from your place inside.
Not locked."

This is ridiculous, Geoffrey Niles thought, staring at the
doorknob.

His room was a simple bubble in the rock, roughly shaped
with pneumatic hammers; the floor was covered with mats
of woven quasibamboo, and there was simple furniture of wood
and metal that looked as if it had been knocked together in
one of the workshops and doubtless had been. There was a
jug and bowl on the dresser and a field phone beside the bed,
which was covered in furs that would have been worth a
fortune on Earth and were probably what the poor used on
Sparta. Someone had unpacked his gear and stowed it neatly
in the dressers: there were four sets of Helot uniforms in his
size with Senior Group Leader's rank-badges—about equivalent to Major—hanging from the wooden rod that served as
a closet, a complete set of web gear, and boots that fitted
him. No excuse to linger beyond washing up and changing
his clothes.

Also a bottle of brandy and some glasses in a cupboard.
For a moment he considered taking a shot . . . *Don't be ridiculous*, he told himself again. *You're twenty-four years old, not*

some schoolboy virgin. You've had plenty of experience with women. His palms were sweating; he wiped them, and looked at the door again. Saw Skilly's face as she shot the man in the stomach this morning, bored disinterest. Saw it as they ran down the stairs in Sparta city, laughing as the grenade blew and shrapnel licked at their heels amid the screams and curses. He shivered slightly with a complex emotion he could not have named, and wiped the back of his hand across his mouth.

"So she's not a debutante," he muttered.

The door swung open noiselessly. There were two chambers on the other side; the first was an office, tables of neatly stacked papers, filing cabinets, a retrieval system and desk; all dim, lit only by the reflected light of a small lamp in the next. The only ornament was something that looked like an Indian figurine about six inches high, a six-armed goddess dancing.

He walked through. The bedroom was larger than his, but scarcely better furnished, except for one wall that held racked bookcases and a veedisk player. A big Japanese-looking print beside that, but he paid little attention to it. Skilly was lying reading on her bed, the blankets and ermine coverlet folded down to the foot of it. She was entirely naked, and there were two glasses of brandy waiting on the night table. "Well," she said softly, putting aside the book. Some distant part of his brain noted the title: *Seven Pillars of Wisdom.* "Skilly was beginning to think you not mon enough, Jeffi."

She slid down from the pillows and stretched; her chocolate-colored skin rippled in long smooth curves as she linked her hands behind her head. Her breasts were high and rounded, the nipples plum-dark and taut. He felt his hands open and close convulsively, and when he spoke his voice was hoarse with the pulse that hammered painfully in throat and temples and groin.

"I think you'll find me man enough and more."

She laughed, with a child's gleeful malice in the tone. "Come show Skilly, then. Show me what you made of."

The Englishman murmured slightly as Skida slipped out of bed; she waited for a moment until he turned over and burrowed his head into the pillow. Chuckling soundlessly, she pulled the ermine coverlet up around him before slipping into her pajamas and out the door. This was officer country and safe, but she tucked a small automatic into the back of the trouser-band just the same; habit, and good habits kept you alive. She gave a contented yawn as she padded down to the wardroom and over to the cooler unit set against one wall, taking out a tall glass of milk and a plate of her favorite oatmeal cookies before flopping down on a couch. The wardroom's style was deliberately casual, to encourage the command cadre to develop a club spirit. Not very likely anyone would be here at this hour, though; Base One rose with the dawn, and Sparta's nights were short.

She sipped and nibbled contentedly, thinking, smiling to herself.

"Skilly looking happy," Two-knife said. "You going to drop Croser?" He knew she seldom had more than one man at a time; Skida Thibodeau hated mess and confusion and unnecessary trouble.

"Not right now, but it time to put us on a more *professional* footing," she said lightly.

Two-knife walked over to the cooler and fixed himself a plate of cold chicken, popping the cap off a beer bottle with one thumb. He was wearing only cotton-duck trousers, and the faint glowlight emphasized the heavy bands of muscle over shoulders and chest and stomach; he was taller than her, but broad enough to seem squat. She smiled affectionately, remembering the time a pimp in Mayopan had decked her from behind with a crowbar during a negotiation session over territorial rights; Two-knife had grabbed him by wrist and neck and done a straight pull until the man's arm came out at the shoulder socket.

"What joke?" he said.

"Remembering old times," she said; they dropped back into a familiar mixture of Belizean English, Spanish and low-country Mayan. "Remember the time RoBo was going to shoot you?"

Two-knife laughed, a rumbling sound. "Never forget it. The look on his face when you broke his neck! Ah, those were the days, Skilly." There was a companionable silence. "How long you going to keep the Englishman?"

"Permanent, Skilly thinks," she said. At his look of surprise: "Well, Croser not the one I want for keeps. Hard man, him, maybe too much to handle up close. Besides, Skilly don't like cutting throats in the family, and if . . ." She made a gesture, and he nodded: it had long been obvious there would be an endgame after the Revolution, if they won.

"Jeffi perfect; got the right connections, smart enough, make good babies"—she had had several hundred ova frozen a couple of years ago—"just what Skilly need to put on the polish when she move up in the world. Anyway, going to be busy for a while."

Two-knife grunted. "Yes. There's going to be a lot of dead white-asses soon."

"Hey," she said playfully, "no race prejudice in the Helots—that a gauntlet offense!" They both laughed. Of course, there *was* a regulation to that effect; there had to be, given the polyglot nature of the force. Two-knife made a show of despising everyone but Mayans from his home district, anyway, and for that matter, the term meant "naive fool" as much as anything specifically ethnic.

"Besides, Skilly's momma was a white-ass."

"I, Two-knife, will forgive you for that. Even forgive you that your father was a damned Black Carib pimp."

She finished her milk and licked her lips. "Hey, Two-knife, serious, mon; remember after we win, we gots to put this place back together and *run* it." She looked at him from under her eyelids. "Ah! Skilly will find you a nice widow—widows be plentiful then—with yellow hair and big tits and good hips and a big hacienda, she teach you how to take off your boots in bed and eat with a fork, so Skilly won't have to hide you in the closet at the fancy parties."

"You want to *kill* me, woman?" he asked, shaking with laughter again; then his face fell, as he realized she was half-serious. And when Skilly made a plan . . . "You told the Englishman he's getting married?" he said.

"No," she said, dusting her hands as she finished the last cookie. "Skilly will train him up to it gradual."

CHAPTER SEVEN

**Crofton's Encyclopedia of the Inhabited Planets
(2nd Edition):**

Sparta: Sparta (originally Botany Bay) was discovered by Captain Mark Brodin of the CoDominium Exploration Service ship *Lewis and Clark* during the Grand Survey of 2010. Alderson point connections to the Sol system are via Tanith, Markham, Xanadu, GSX-1773, and GSX-2897. Further connections exist to Frystaat, Dayan and Haven. Initial survey indicated a very favorable native ecology but no exceptional mineral or other resources. A Standard Terraforming Package was seeded in 2011, and the Category VI Higher Mammal Package followed in 2022.

Circumference: 13,600 kilometers
Diameter: 13,900 kilometers
Gravity 1.22 standard
Diurnal cycle: 20 hours
Year 1.6 standard
Composition: Nickel-iron, silicates
Satellites: Cythera, mass 1.7 Luna

Atmosphere is basically terrestrial, but with 1.17 standard sea-level pressure. Total land area is approximately half that of Earth, with extensive oceans; much of the land, c. 28,800,000 sq. kilometers (18,000,000 sq. miles), is concentrated in the Serpentine Continent, an equatorial landmass deeply penetrated by inland seas . . . Native life is mainly marine; the high concentration of dissolved oxygen in the oceanic waters, and the extensive shallow seas, permit a very active oceanic ecosystem with many large piscoid species. Land-based forms are limited to primitive vegetation and analogs of simple insects;

terrestrial species have largely replaced the native on the Serpentine continent and adjacent islands. Total illumination is 92% of standard, resulting in a warm-temperate to subtropical climate in the equatorial Serpentine continent, shading to cold-temperate and subarctic conditions on the northern shores.

Initial settlement: A CoDominium research station was established in 2024, and shipment of involuntary transportees began in 2032. In 2036 settlement rights were transferred to the Constitutionalist Society (conditional upon continued receipt of involuntary colonists), a political group centered in the United States, and settlement began in 2038. Internal self-government was granted in 2040, and the Dual Kingdom of Sparta was recognized as a sovereign state by the Grand Senate in 2062; the CoDominium retained an enclave in Sparta City, and involuntary colonization continued per the Treaty of Independence.

"Well, I'm glad we won't be doing a full review just yet, sir." Battalion Sergeant Sergio Guiterrez said. There was heartfelt relief in his tone.

"His Majesty Alexander isn't coming; General Alexander Collins will be here instead, Top," Peter Owensford said. "A useful fiction; Prince Lysander came up with it, some historical thing from Britain." Their vehicle was waiting at the steps of the General Headquarters building, but Owensford stopped for a moment to look at the camp.

The Fifth Battalion's camp was a hundred kilometers south of Sparta City, at the base of the peninsula that held the capital and on the western fringe of the Eurotas delta. The main road from the city ran by along the sea, but that was merely a two-lane gravel strip; most traffic was by barge or river-steamer. Marsh and sandy beach and rocky headlands fronted the water, with a screen of small islands on the horizon. Inland were the Theramenes Hills that ran north to the outskirts, not really mountains but tumbled and rough enough to suit; between hills and sea was a narrow strip of plain. Eight weeks of Sparta's short days ago it had been bare save for a thin covering of grass, a useless stretch of heavy adobe clay.

Now it was the base camp of the Fifth Battalion, Falkenberg's Mercenary Legion—and the newly formed First Royal Spartan Infantry, King Alexander's Own Regiment: Fort Plataia. Men and machines had thrown up a five-meter earth berm around an area a kilometer square; radar towers showed at the corners. The capacitance wire and bunkers and minefields outside did not, but they were there and ready, and beyond them signs warned intruders that the camp was protected by deadly force.

Within was still an orderly chaos. The essential buildings had gone in first: revetments for air defense, bunkers, shelters. Dug-in armories, the generators, stores, roofed with steel beams and sandbags. This HQ building, Officers' and NCOs' mess, kitchens, all of the same adobe bricks and rammed earth stabilized with plastic and roofed with utilitarian asbestos cement. Married quarters were just going up in a separate section in the southeast corner, and there were peg-and-string outlines for barracks.

Many dependents, most of the troopers, and all the continuous inflow of recruits were still in tents. They had *made* the tents, under the direction of the veterans of the Fifth, each maniple of five issued canvas and rope; learning to cook and clean for themselves, to work as a unit. Not that they spent much time in the tents; the recruits lived in their leather and cotton-drill uniforms, out in the field in all weathers with nothing but their greatcloaks for protection. Two weeks of conditioning and close order drill and basic military courtesy, then they learned to make their battle-armor of nemourlon and live in *that,* night and day. Small arms training, maintenance work, unarmed combat; field problems, live fire exercises. The recruit formations shrank under the brutally demanding training, but more flowed in. Street toughs just off the CoDo shuttles, fresh-faced Citizen farmboys from the Valley. . . .

All done quickly, and done well. Peter nodded in satisfaction. Then he caught the Sergeant Major's faint grin. Owensford swung into the jeep. "Let's go," he said.

"Again, I'm rather impressed," King Alexander said, returning Peter Owensford's salute and nodding toward the bustle about them.

He had come by helicopter, and was dressed in the uniform of a General in the Royal Spartan Army, which meant minimal ceremony. It was a new uniform, since Sparta had nothing but the Brotherhood militias and a company-sized Royal Guard until the Legion landed. Melissa had designed it; there was a high-collared tunic and trousers of a dark sand-gray, pipped along the seams in silver, with Sam Browne belt and boots, and a peaked cap. Owensford rather liked it; less showy than the Legion's blue and gold, but sharp, and men needed

to feel like soldiers in garrison situations where battledress
and weapons were ridiculous.

"Thank you, sir. We've been turning adversity to advantage.
I'll fill you in at the briefing. If you'll come this way?" The
Spartan monarch was looking older, and much more tired; his
skin seemed to have coarsened in the weeks since he had
greeted the Legion.

General Desjardins of the RSMP was with him, and some
of his officers; a few civilians, including Melissa von Alderheim.
*I suppose she thinks Lysander could get back to the city more
often,* Owensford thought, a little wistfully. In his thirty-sixth
year he was growing more than a little envious of his married comrades. . . . *Although I suppose any marriage a prince
makes will be more a matter of duty. At least there aren't any
more stories about the Prince and Cornet Gordon.*

The main landing field was outside the kilometer-square
perimeter of the base, but not outside its circle of activity.
A company-sized group of young men in uniform trousers
and T-shirts jogged by down a newly made dirt track behind
a standard-bearer with a pennant, their booted feet striking
the gravel in crunching unison. Their heads were cropped
close, and sweat ran down their faces, made the cotton
singlets cling to their muscled chests despite the cool wind
from the water. The man with the pennant was at least forty,
or possibly half again that with regeneration treatment, but
he showed no strain at keeping up with youngsters raised
in this gravity.

"Heaow, *sound off!*" he barked.

A hundred strong young voices broke into a song that was
half-chant:

"Kiss me good night, Sergeant Major
Tuck me in my little feather-bed,
Kiss me good night, Sergeant Major—
Sergeant Major, be a mother to meeee*!"*

The king smiled. There was a good deal else going on. A
regular *crack . . . crack . . .* came from a firing range further
inland. In the middle distance mortar teams were drilling,
schoomp as the rounds left the barrels, *pumpf* as they burst
several thousand meters to the west. Officers and noncoms in
Legion uniforms stood nearby to supervise mortar crews. Fatigue
parties in gray overalls were at work, digging or repairing heavy
equipment. A column of armored vehicles was leaguered in a
square to one side of the roadway. There were six-wheeled battle
cars, with turrets mounting a 15mm gatling machine gun, or
a single-barreled model and a grenade launcher or mortar.

Turretless versions were parked within the leaguer; hatches and rear ramps showed they were intended as personnel carriers.

"From the von Alderheim works?" Alexander said, as he climbed into Owensford's jeep. It was a safe bet; the AFVs had locally made spun-alloy wheels, and the armor was welded steel rather than composites. "Quick work."

"Yes, sir," Owensford said. "Miss von Alderheim has been most helpful."

Melissa blushed as the two men turned to look at her. "Well, it's the all-terrain truck chassis and engine," she said. "You know, Uncle Alexander, I trained on the CAD-CAM computer Father brought in for the University?" Not really needed, when most of what Sparta's major vehicle company turned out was standard models built to obsolete designs. And there was a waiting list for *them*. "I just . . . ran up something. The machine does most of it, really."

"Which reminds me," Peter said. "Until we get the aircraft construction going, I'll need another way to loft Thoth missiles. Dumb solid rockets should do. Not quite in the von Alderheim line, but shouldn't be too difficult."

"Thoth missiles?"

"Well, that's the code word. Small smart missiles. Usually rolled out of a cargo aircraft just over the horizon from the target, but that's a bit hard to do here without airplanes. A rocket booster system would be trickier, but the Alanas think they can do it."

"I'll get someone on that," Melissa said.

"No point in spreading this around," Peter said. "Who knows, we might surprise someone."

The jeep swept past the gate, as guards in the blue and gold of the Legion and the gray of Sparta brought their rifles to salute. *I'm a damned tour guide,* Owensford thought, as he pointed out the important features. Here too there were endless groups of marching men, most in mottled camouflage fatigues and bulky nemourlon armor. One group of such were double-timing with their rifles over their heads; lead weights were fastened all over their battle harness.

"Punishment detail," Owensford explained. "When you're working men as hard as we are, you have to come up with something a little more severe to act as a deterrent."

The rest of the command group were waiting at the Headquarters building. There was a flurry of salutes and handshakes before they moved into the staff conference room.

Peter Owensford felt an almost eerie sense of *déjà vu* as he took his seat at the head of the table. The room was a long rectangle, one wall dominated by maps, the other by a computer display screen; the officers were in the standard places for a staff meeting. Enlisted stewards brought coffee, then retired behind the guarded door. A Royal Army corporal-stenographer sat in one corner, her hands poised over the keyboard.

"Ten' *'hut!*" Battalion Sergeant Guiterrez said.

"At ease, gentlemen, ladies," Owensford said. *Odd. How often have I seen Christian Johnny do this?* "General Collins is here as a participant observer." Hence not in the chain of command, and seated to his right. "We'll begin with the readiness report. If you please, Captain Barton?"

"Sir." He nodded to the "general." "The Fifth and its noncombatants are now fully settled. Expansion and training is proceeding as follows."

He touched the controls and an organizational chart sprang out on the computer display screen to the left of the table.

"We've received approximately thirty-seven hundred recruits, of which four hundred and eight have proven unsuitable. An unusually low ratio, considering that we're training the cadre for larger units.

"We've shifted the least physically fit members of the Fifth into four training companies, configured as cadre units to handle basic training, and a technician's course largely manned by pensioners and noncombatants. That hasn't presented a major difficulty in unit continuity, because they wouldn't be in combat units to begin with. Four additional rifle and one heavy-weapons company have been formed, using many of our remaining enlisted cadre and local recruits; we've concentrated the, ah, less socially desirable individuals into the new Legion formations."

"Your appraisal?"

"The five new companies are now combat-ready. There's not as much unit cohesion as we'd like, but they'll shake down. The new personnel have received the full basic training except for space assault and non-terrestrial environment practice. We've got the nucleus of a good combat force here."

"So you've cloned your battalion," Alexander said.

"Well, the new units haven't the experience, of course," Owensford said. "Normal Legion procedure is to organize with no more than one recruit in each maniple. In the present situation we may have as many as three, and some of those have monitors who aren't long past being a PFC." He shrugged. "We make do with what we have, but frankly, I'm not so sorry that the rebels have been active lately. Combat's just what we need to make regulars out of these units."

"Ah. And what of our Royal Spartan forces?" Alexander asked. There was eagerness in his voice.

"Approximately five hundred recruits are still in the basic training pipeline," Barton said. "Two thousand three hundred have completed basic and in some cases advanced training, and have been formed into three infantry, one mechanized and one support battalion, plus headquarters units and armored-cavalry squadrons. One of the infantry battalions is the Prince Royal's Own, and we've tried to post some of the best troops into that. When we get more aviation assets we'll turn it into an air assault unit."

Another chart took form. The table of organization was based on the Legion's, essentially similar to a CoDominium Marine regimental combat team: Headquarters company; Scouts; signals platoon; combat engineering platoon; two heavy-weapons companies with mortars and recoilless rifles; transport company—mules, in this case, with some unarmored versions of the von Alderheim 6x6; aviation company, and medical section.

"There are conspicuous gaps, of course," Barton concluded. "No aircraft, so aviation company is only a shell. Light on artillery. Communications aren't what we'd like them to be. However, I can say that the first Field Force regiment of the Royal Spartan Army now exists, and we can add combat battalions as we get them. As you can see"—arrows sprang out, linking the Spartan regiment with the structure of the Fifth—"our primary limiting factor is leaders, both officers and NCOs. Of the two, the shortage of experienced NCOs is more difficult. Junior officers are in sufficient supply; a number of officers from the Brotherhood militia units have enlisted, and more than forty former Line Marine personnel resident on Sparta have offered their services to date."

Sparta was a popular retirement spot for CoDo officers; many of them on early retirement, with the cutbacks. The social atmosphere appealed to them, you could get quite a reasonable estate for very low prices, and even a meager pension in CoDominium credits went a long way here. Much further than on Churchill or Friedland, even, if you were prepared to live without the high-tech gadgetry.

"For the rest, we have filled the senior NCO slots and most of the company, battalion and HQ positions by lateral transfer from the Legion, usually involving brevet promotions. Wearing two hats, as it were."

A temporary promotion, to allow the mercenaries to

command their theoretical equals in the larger Royal Army formation.

"If I may, Major?" General Collins's voice. Owensford nodded.
"Of course, sir."

"My—that is, the two kings have been informed of the matter
of brevet promotions. We have decided that for the duration
of the Legion's stay such personnel will be carried on the Royal
Army rolls and receive the pay and other privileges attendant
on their rank. Which of course will become permanent if any
choose to remain with the Royal forces when at liberty to do
so."

"Thank you, sir, on behalf of my men," Owensford said.
"They'll very much appreciate it." Many of the Legionnaires
were nearing the end of their terms of enlistment, retirement
age, or both. *And if the plan works out, the Legion or part
of it may well be based on Sparta.*

Alexander Collins smiled. "Including Captain Barton and
yourself, of course," he said, holding up a hand. His aide placed
two small wooden boxes in his hands. "Your other hats,
gentlemen." A colonel's eagles for him, and a lieutenant-
colonel's oak leaves for Ace.

"Again, thank you, sir." *And now is not the time to lecture
about rank and brotherhood and ambition. . . .*

"Furthermore, an Order in King and Council has been made
that a full five-year term of service in the Royal army will
constitute fulfillment of the public-service portion of the Citizenship examinations. Three terms of service with honorable
discharge, or award of the *coronea aurea* award for valor during
service, or promotion to commissioned rank, upon honorable
discharge will constitute full qualification for Citizenship."

"We are in your debt." There were murmurs from the other
mercenary officers; not many host-worlds were that hospitable.
Many regarded hired soldiers as in much the same category
as whores: paid professionals filling a necessary but unmen-
tionable service. Offer of citizenship and a home was more
important than rank inflation, and by a lot. *They clearly took
us seriously when we talked about loyalties and incentives. The
Colonel's going to be pleased. I wonder how much of this is
Lysander's doing? Probably a lot.*

"The nominal commander of the First Royal Infantry is, of
course, His Majesty Alexander First," Ace Barton said. "The
professional commander for the moment is Major—Colonel
Owensford, with Lieutenant Colonel Arnold Kistiakowski as
deputy."

Kistiakowski, a militia officer, had been an accountant in

civil life, but did seem to have a flair for military command. He was also the son of one of the First Families, and an elected Senator. He nodded acknowledgment.

"Captain—Major Barton," Owensford said, "is chief of staff to the First Royal as well as to me as nominal chief of staff to the Minister of War." The Spartan chain of command sounded more complex than it was. Peter could hardly blame the Spartans for wanting to retain control over the military machine they were constructing.

"Major, are the First Royals ready for combat?"

"Low-intensity combat only, sir. The First is lacking in battle computers, secure communications gear, nightfighting equipment, range finders, modern artillery—the artillery battalion is using locally made one-twenty-five- and one-sixty-mm mortars—antiaircraft and antitank capacity. It also has no organic air transport, and the combat engineers are underequipped. None of that is fatal, but you wouldn't want to throw them up against experienced troops with full equipment."

"General comments?"

"Sir . . . as recruits, the recruits are of excellent quality; the standard of literacy and general mechanical aptitude was particularly notable. About half the men are of Citizen background and half not." As opposed to seventy-thirty in the general population, and about eighty-twenty in the relevant age groups.

He smiled: "There was some friction at first; they thought of each other as hick sissies and gutter thugs respectively. Going through basic has cured a good deal of that."

At least while they were in ranks. There was a more basic culture clash; the Citizens seemed to be very like what the old middle class of America had been, before it fissured into taxpayer and Welfare Island Citizen. Respectable people, stable personalities from stable families. While the transportees came from a brutally chaotic background of illiteracy, illegitimacy and instant gratification.

"What they need most now is some experience to convince them that they're really soldiers; that would shake them down, solidify unit esprit, and help us identify potential leaders, which is our main restraint on further expansion at the moment."

"Thank you," Peter said. "Next item, logistics and technical support. Captain Alana?"

Catherine Alana touched her own keyboard, and a series of boxed equipment mixes appeared on the computer screen.

"As Captain Barton reported, the main shortage is in high-tech equipment. Local industry makes high-quality gear, but the variety is restricted. We're working with designers to overcome that. Basic equipment is excellent, as are ammunition supplies. We get smart weapons in sufficient quantity for training, and we're building a stockpile, but there are never enough."

"And won't be," Alexander said. "Until we begin earning hard currency. Which will expend those munitions—"

"Yes, sir, bootstrap operations tend to be slow," Catherine agreed. She shrugged. "So we do the best we can. As presently equipped, the First would already be suitable for employment in some off-planet situations. New Washington, for example, if Colonel Falkenberg needs more troops. Particularly as light infantry in unroaded situations, they could already command better contract terms than most Earth-based outfits."

There were a few snorts; nobody thought much of Earthling mercenaries these days. The best recruits were going to the growing national armies, as the CoDominium grip weakened.

"I've shown here four alternate add-on weapons and equipment kits, with their probable price ranges, and the degree to which they'd enhance effectiveness. It's my estimation that with certified combat experience, the First—excuse me, the Royal Army, I'm not used to thinking in these terms—the First could secure an equipment loan from Dayan or Xanadu against a lien on their first few contracts." Those powers offered specialist mercenary units of their own, but also acted as escrow agents and financed turnkey operations. "We've got plenty of technical personnel here, and I've assigned each of them two Royal Army understudies. By the time the equipment comes in, the people to operate it will be there too."

Owensford nodded. "Well done." He meant that. Building a regimental-sized fighting force in such a short time was a considerable accomplishment. "Fortunately, we don't have to provide all the managerial and staff service training. General Slater's War College is doing an excellent job of that.

"What we here must do is develop combat capability. That's more than simply honing individual skills. It's a matter of working with what we have, to blend weapons and skills and capabilities into fighting units. Captain Jesus Alana will elaborate."

"If I may lecture for a moment," Jesus Alana said. "The available weapons, Sparta's industries, and financial limitations all dictate that whatever we eventually add to the mix, Sparta will for some time to come specialize in infantry. This is not necessarily a disadvantage. Infantry has dominated war in many eras, and can be decisive today.

"Since we have little choice but to develop infantry teams,

we need to understand what infantry does. There are two major objectives to infantry action. One is to take ground and hold it. The other is to kill or disable the enemy.

"These are generally achieved in quite different ways. The best way to take ground is to move in when it's not occupied, and get there with enough force that no one wants to dispute it.

"The best way to kill enemy troops is to make him break his teeth assaulting prepared positions. Of course, it doesn't take too bright a commander to know frontal assaults against strong positions aren't a good idea, so it follows that the best tactic is to make him think there aren't many of you out there. No big target for him to shoot at. Then hit him with real firepower he didn't expect. The United States developed that into a fine art in Vietnam just before the politicos closed them down: small patrols able to spot for long-range artillery and missiles. The enemy couldn't fight back because he couldn't get at the artillery and missile bases, and the patrols weren't a very good target because they were small enough to stay dug in. They were also well armed and trained for close combat."

"Doesn't that take high technology we don't have?" Alexander asked.

"Not so high as all that, sir," Catherine Alana said. "And again we make do with what we have. Jesus and I have worked out something. Should be quite a surprise to the enemy."

"That would be a pleasant change," Alexander said. The frowns on the faces of the king and General Desjardins brought Owensford back from the pure professional satisfaction of doing a difficult job, reminding him of exactly why it had been so necessary to hurry.

"So," Jesus continued. "Our goal, then, is to develop light and agile forces accustomed to digging in and defending themselves against close in enemies, while bringing in fire support to deal with everything else. We then tailor our training to that end—and of course that decision affects our weapons procurements, which impact industrial decisions.

"As to the technological skills, first we teach them to be military officers, leaders, then we send them to General Slater's War College, or the University. Or both. In this way we bootstrap up to larger units." Jesus shrugged. "Unit cohesion suffers, of course, but we can stabilize assignments to troop units once we have developed all the skills required. After that it's a matter of sane replacement policies."

"If we live that long," Desjardins said.

Peter Owensford nodded. "I'm coming to that. Captain Alana,

please give us a strategic appreciation. Begin with the political background, if you please."

"Sir. First, the good news," Jesus Alana said. "The Foundation Loyalist and Pragmatist factions—not really parties yet—have agreed on the tax increases necessary for the security program." The Spartan constitution included discretionary funds always at the disposal of the Crown, but new taxes required Council and Senate approval. "As long as they pull together, the situation is serious but not desperate."

"The bad news," he went on, "is that the NCLF is making political hay with the massacre at the Spartosky. They brought criminal charges against the Milice, the kings, the Legion individually and collectively, even Miss von Alderheim here." Somebody laughed down the table, Owensford sent a quelling glance.

General Desjardins snorted. "After twenty police were killed! Cases thrown out of court." Spartan law was quite unequivocal on the subject of deadly self-defense. Grudgingly, he added: "Some of the crowd *were* shot in the back as they ran. The Milice had never been under fire before, and they panicked."

Jesus Alana smiled. "Ah, but General Desjardins, the news cameras were disabled before the rocket attack. To the NCLF's target audience, pictures are truth and written words automatically lies. Street demonstrations have become a daily occurrence. The Dockworkers' Union has staged several sympathy strikes, and there has been loss of produce on the docks to spoilage. And Mr. Dion Croser—let me rephrase that—*Senator* Dion Croser is now their representative in the legislature."

Alexander sighed. "I wouldn't have thought the Citizens in the union would tolerate it," he said.

"They know they're outnumbered, and they know Croser's goons know where their families live," Desjardins said bluntly. "You will not let us use those measures against him, but he is free to use them himself. The end result is, he's now got a perfect platform and Legislative immunity from libel laws. He's spent the last two months up and down the Valley, organizing in the riverport towns. The bastard can make a speech, I'll grant him that. Even got some farm-workers signed up, won't *that* be lovely when he takes them out on strike in the middle of harvest in the sugar country, say."

Jesus Alana coughed. "Yes. Unfortunately, we also have nothing we could take to court to connect the NCLF with serious illegal activity. Of which there has been a steady increase." He touched the controls, calling up a map of the Eurotas Valley, a shape like a horizontal S running four thousand kilometers from northwest to southeast as the crow flew. Much more in terms of river frontage, of course. For most of its length it was an alluvial trough, flanked by hills and mountain ranges; those culminated in the Himalayan-sized Drakon Range in the west.

"More Helot attacks on isolated ranches. Also trucks, transport, economic targets—weirs, power stations—and most recently, a small RSMP post here in the Middle Valley. Most of the troopers were out on patrol, but four were killed and considerable weapons and equipment seized. So far, retaliatory action has not been . . . very effective."

Desjardins stirred. "My men are doing their best, but they're impossibly overstretched," he said. "Just the Valley is over two million square miles! By the time they've gotten to the site of one incident, the trail is cold and there's another alarm somewhere else. What prisoners we've taken are useless, and deny any knowledge of a connection between the Helots and the NCLF."

"Yet it seems conclusive," Owensford said. All eyes turned to him; it was a lonely feeling. "This is not bandit trouble. This is the beginning of a classic two-level guerrilla war, of a pattern quite common on Earth during the Cold War period, before the CoDominium. Quite classic, almost as if it were taken from a book. The directors of this war—it can only be called that— know what they're about. We are facing an able, determined and ruthless enemy."

"One singularly well equipped," Catherine Alana said. "We've been analyzing the jamming signals used during the riot. Highly sophisticated. Definitely off-planet equipment, and probably personnel."

The Spartans looked up quickly. "Who?" Alexander asked.

"Nothing definitive," Catherine said. "But if I had to say for the record, I'd guess one of the Meiji technoninja outfits."

"But you're not sure?" Desjardins said.

"They're blooming expensive," Jesus Alana said. "We can't think who hates Sparta enough to pay that price. This planet doesn't have that sort of enemy."

"Croser does," Alexander said. "So long as his creditors don't call in his debts and ruin him."

"Which perhaps we should arrange," Catherine Alana said quietly.

Jesus grinned. "Then there is another matter."

"Yes?" Desjardins prompted.

"The atrocities," Catherine Alana said. "If the rebels do have off-planet help, it is from an organization that does not recognize the Laws of War. A lot of the Meijian outfits don't, but they're mostly espionage and clandestine-operations oriented. Outside the mercenary structure entirely."

Jesus Alana shrugged. "So. We have guesses as to who, but there is no uncertainty about what: the enemy has high-tech off-planet support. That being true, they probably have other capabilities we have not seen."

"A timely warning," Alexander said.

"Indeed," Jesus Alana agreed. "More timely, I think, than the enemy suspected. Moreover, General Slater has the opinion that these people have been closely studying the classic works on guerrilla warfare. I am inclined to agree. And while the classic patterns are classic because they have been effective, they do have the disadvantage of being well known. From here on, we should have clues as to what the enemy will do next."

"Precisely," Peter Owensford said. "Now. Here's the situation as I see it."

He touched the keys to call up checklists and organization patterns. "The first principle is that political action is as crucial as the strictly military. That is as true for us as for the enemy. Therefore, we will begin counterespionage operations in coordination with the RSMP and General Slater's schools. A first priority will be to prove the links between the NCLF and the Helots. Second, we must learn the means by which they obtain. And tighten customs inspections, of course."

Everyone nodded; the weapons captured after the Spartosky affair were mostly of Friedlander and Xanadu manufacture but that meant little, since both those powers had a cash-and-carry policy and did not require end-user certificates.

"Now, in strictly military terms, the essentials of counter-guerrilla warfare are intelligence, mobility and interdiction. The closest possible coordination of police, militia and military activities in each area is essential. With the Royal government's permission"—a nod from Alexander—"I am appointing Captain Barton as liaison officer and Inspector-General of Militia. Captain Barton, you will see to the organization of a three-tier system in each canton of the affected areas; police, home guard and local reaction forces."

Ace nodded; there was a faraway look in his eyes, the expression of a man marshaling himself for a difficult job.

"This will provide patrols, point-security and raw intelligence data. We will also use this structure to cut off the guerrillas as far as possible from contact with the civilian population, and from their sources of supply."

"The First RS Infantry, and the four available companies of

Legion troops, will be the active military element in our strategy. Using active patrolling, SAS teams"—Special Air Services, the traditional term for deep-intrusion scout forces behind enemy lines; they were a specialty of the Legion—"and the intelligence data funneled through Captain Alana's office, we will find, fix and destroy the guerrilla bands operating in the Middle and Upper Valley districts. Once we have significant aviation assets we can be even more aggressive, but there is no reason why we can't start some operations now." Peter grinned. "If you have one problem, you have a problem. If you have several, they can sometimes be made to solve each other. In our case we need to give combat experience to our troops, and simultaneously we have an enemy trying to initiate classic guerrilla operations against us. Questions, gentlemen?"

There were; mostly technical, directed at the staff. He leaned back in his chair. *No reason it shouldn't work, in theory,* he thought. Falkenberg had required them to study enough examples, from the brilliant successes like Sir Gerald Templar's in Malaysia in the 1950s, through military victories and political defeats like that of the French in Algeria and the Americans in Vietnam, to outright disasters like the First Indochina War. Plenty of rebellions out among the colony worlds as well.

Interesting factors here, he thought: *unique, like every war.* The land-population ratio was higher than any comparable situation he could think of, for example. Nor could he think of another case where the population was mostly rural but of urban origins. Very little in the way of aviation assets, as yet, but what he did have was probably reasonably safe from sophisticated antiaircraft weapons. Very little in the way of mechanical transport at all; mounted infantry would probably be valuable. The enemy would certainly be using them. A cavalry guerrilla. *Interesting.* There were recent precedents; and further back. . . . *The Boer War, of course. And Southern Africa about a century ago, or a little more.*

"I think that's all, then," he said at last, and turned to Alexander Collins. "Comments, sir?"

"Yes, Major." The older man leaned his hands on the table-top; there was a slight tremor in the left. "Two things. First, I have received notification from the CoDominium Bureau of Relocation, through the commandant of the local CD enclave . . . Sparta's quota of involuntary convicts is to be doubled over the coming fiscal year."

That brought everyone bolt upright. "Sir," Jesus Alana said. "We were expecting it to be *reduced.*"

The king nodded. There was a slight sheen of sweat on his

brow although the room was cool. "Yes. Of the planets receiving deportees, only Haven is farther from Earth. BuReloc has been steadily shifting to the closer worlds to cut expenses." Since it was being systematically starved of funds by the deadlocked Grand Senate, outright sale of involuntary convicts on worlds where that was legal had become an important source of BuReloc's budget. "There has been a reversal of policy."

"The fix is in," Jesus Alana said flatly. "The NCLF bought a Grand Senator."

"Or already had one," Catherine added thoughtfully.

"I do not think so," the king said, rubbing a hand across his brow. "I always felt that Earth would not allow the Spartan experiment to succeed, to expose its ancient corruptions, that there were forces moving secretly . . ." He stopped with an effort, then shrugged: "You see, though, what sixty thousand new untrained, unskilled, possibly unemployable refugees carefully trained to hate all authority dropped onto Sparta City will do. Especially with the new taxes restricting employment."

There was silence for a moment. Everyone *did* see; it was a cruelly well-aimed blow. *The CoDominium kept Earth from suicide,* Owensford thought, *but the price is damned high.* Sparta could not refuse, of course. The action was technically within the provisions of the treaty of Independence, and Sparta had no navy and little in the way of planetary defenses. A single Fleet destroyer would compel obedience, and even Sergei Lermontov could not fudge a direct order from the Grand Senate.

The king collected himself, relaxing slightly. "This . . . emergency has come up so quickly that a few of us are inclined to panic. To see conspirators and traitors under every bed."

A wry smile. "I find myself doing so, in the small hours of the night. Nevertheless, we must remember that the vast bulk of the population—including the non-Citizen population—are *not* conspirators, are *not* traitors. Our enemy—the true enemy, the few malignant minds behind this unspeakable thing—will attempt to divide us. Citizen against non-Citizen, employer against employee, outback against city, old settler from new immigrant. Our enemy wants us to hate, to fear, and to lash out blindly. *We must not do so.* Because if we do, we will *create* the divisions the enemy falsely claims exist; we will drive whole segments of our people into the enemy's camp."

"True enough," Owensford said. "The people are on our side, something we have to remember. Guerrilla operations are painful, but they can't win against determination. Even the importation of barbarian elements from Earth can't defeat a strong civilization. Sparta has overwhelming strength in the Citizen militia. It's our job to do as much of the fighting as we can so the nation doesn't have to. We'll do that job."

"*Gracias,*" Jesus Alana said, as Ursula handed him a cup of coffee.

They all had one in front of them, along with their read-out screens and notes. *Husband, wife and protégée,* Ursula thought ironically. *And probably the future teacher for Michael and Maryanne Alana when they're older. . . . However they've managed it, what these two have together is worth learning about . . .*

The Legion was pretty much of a family business, at that. One window in the thick adobe wall was open, and they could hear faint construction sounds and the *heep, heep* sound of someone counting cadence. Intelligence Central was a big office, more than enough for their three desks and filing equipment, with maps and charts pinned to the whitewashed walls.

"Now, let us implement some of the fine theories we talked about to the kings this morning," Jesus Alana said. He called up a map of the western portion of the Middle Valley district, and his finger tapped the Illyrian Dales. "Notice the relative concentration of guerrilla attacks on the south side of the Eurotas, and between the area just above Clemens and around Olynthos. All within striking distance of the Dales, which are themselves little-known and without permanent habitation. And are also larger than all the Spains. Cornet Gordon, what other relevant information do we have about the Dales?"

He only calls me that when he's putting me on the spot, she thought. Then—

"Limestone, sir."

"Limestone. Precisely. Why?"

"Limestone is water-soluble, which means caves, and with the amount of outflow coming down from the Drakons and reaching the Eurotas, there must be a *lot* of caves. Underground river-systems, in fact. Excellent concealment from satellite surveillance."

"And from everything else," Catherine said.

"So that is point one," Jesus said. "Then you let the computers chew on the statistical data, and you get—what?"

Ursula nodded enthusiasm. "Direct correlations between guerrilla activity, length of settlement, percentage of Sparta-born and Citizen population, average size of rural holding and land values."

"Excellent," he said dryly. "In other words, in the Lower Valley there is little guerrilla activity, many Citizens, relatively smaller ranches and farms. In the Middle and Upper Valleys, newer and larger ranches, more non-Citizens, more recent immigrants, and more guerrilla incidents. What exceptions are there to this?"

"Ahh . . . the area of the Upper Valley, between Olynthos and the Cupros Mountains. There've been mining and support settlements around there since the early days, but there's a good deal of guerrilla activity reported there as well."

Jesus Alana relaxed. "Inquisition ended. You should have looked more carefully at the data about the Upper Valley; first, the mines employ many unskilled laborers. Second, there is a new fringe of settlement in adjacent areas, to supply the growing industrial population. *And* it is very close to the Dales, again. Remember, patterns of *detail.*

"Cathy, what does PhotoRecon say about the spysat of the Dales area?"

"Not much, Jesus, but Lieutenant Swenson doesn't think much of the hardware they've got. She says it's basically weather and geosurvey oriented, and badly out of date at that; not very maneuverable, and there are only two eyes. If you know their orbital ephemeris, and you've got good satellite observation security, you could fox them. Mostly what it shows is wildlife, the odd forest or grass fire, and occasional hunting camps. What *should* be hunting camps."

"We should recommend low-level aerial survey," Jesus said. "But with care. Have Swenson set up a team of technicians, and we will borrow some of the RSMP tiltrotors—blimps if we must—and do some intensive sidescan and IR work. Land parties and do seismic mapping at intervals as well."

"I'll coordinate with Major Barton," Catherine said.

"And Captain Mace. His scouts may be glad of the opportunity."

"Right. Anything else?"

"Yes." He touched his controls, and the area around Olynthos sprang out; it was a city of about forty thousand, just below the exit from Lake Alexander. Smelters originally, more recently general industry, and many of the outbacker hunters operated out of there. "The Scout Company of the Prince Royal's Battalion is going to base out of here when they move out. Have Sweeny run some of them through on her depth-sounding equipment, and then issue it to them when they begin practicing their SAS games up in the Dales. If you can pry the stuff loose."

They both smiled; Senior Lieutenant Leigh Swenson guarded her remote reconnaissance equipment with the brooding intensity of a hen with one chick.

"That should turn up some interesting data," he said meditatively, finishing his coffee. "Which leaves the question of the NCLF and Sparta City. On the one hand, that's more the Milice and RSMP's territory. On the other, I agree with Desjardins: the NCLF as a whole may not be with the Helots, but their leadership *is*. Pity this is a constitutionalist planet."

On most worlds—on anywhere directly ruled by the CoDominium Colonial Bureau, or for that matter in the United States—they would simply disappear Mr. Dion Croser and sweat the facts out of him.

"No it isn't, or had you forgotten we were supposed to be based here permanently?" Catherine Alana said. "I wouldn't want our children to grow up on that sort of world, Jesus."

"But if they don't get moving, this may *become* that sort of world," he replied. "Personally, I don't find the NCLF's political program very reassuring."

Ursula cleared her throat " '*If you fight dragons long enough, you become a dragon: if you stare into the Abyss, the Abyss will stare back into* you.' " Nietzsche, and on her required reading list. Along with all the rest of the canon, in case she was bored in her munificent four hours of free time daily.

"The fact remains, the Milice and the RSMP have no political intelligence to speak of," Jesus continued sourly. "They are trying to remedy that lack, but you know the problems."

"Philby," Ursula said. "But isn't your lie detector gear—"

"It's good but not that good," Catherine said. "What we can detect is stress. If we're lucky, and especially when we surprise people, we can get differential stress—stress indications where there shouldn't be so much, that sort of thing. Casual use against well-prepared subjects, that's another matter."

"So we may have infiltrators," Ursula said. She had been doing a good deal of reading in the classical espionage cases. How the West German counterintelligence chief in the 1980s had been a Sovworld plant, and one reason the Israelis had overrun the Levant so quickly in 2009 was a deep-sleeper who was head of Military Intelligence Evaluation for the Greater Syrian Republic.

"Well, not in the Legion itself. Certainly not among the officers. What I would like is a source of information of our own." He called up a map of Sparta city, clicking in on the lower southwestern corner. The spacious grounds of the Royal

University of Sparta filled the screen. "We know that the NCLF has an active student chapter. The usual thing: boredom and guilt and excuses for failure among the spoiled children of success. Not as much here as most places—this is a frontier planet—but enough." A grim smile. "Odd, how guilt is inversely proportional to real culpability. On Santiago"—his home, one of the three nations of Thurstone—"where there is real slavery, most university students are fanatic Carlist reactionaries."

"The ones here probably don't feel really afraid," Ursula said clinically. There had been clients like that, back on Tanith in the Lederle Hilton, who had been sorry for her. They usually expected something extra for it, too.

"Yes. And we also know that there have been disappearances among members of the student chapter of the NCLF. Half a dozen immediately after the Spartosky incident, for example. Educated people would be one of the chokepoints for a guerrilla force recruited mainly from transportees. They will need junior officers."

"Well, then we should obviously try infiltrating through there," Ursula said. "Who did you have in mind—oh."

Catherine Alana reached over and patted her hand. "You *do* need some more formal schooling, dear," she said.

"Oh." She looked down at her hands, with a sinking feeling. The structured, ordered life of the Legion was a little confining sometimes, but wonderfully secure. "Well, I do have acting training," she said dryly. "But Mata Hari I am not, with respect, sir, ma'am."

"Mata Hari we don't want," Catherine said. "You'll be a student on detached duty taking courses in cartography and statistics, both of which are quite relevant to your career. Who you date is your business, not ours. Except that if you meet any of the militants there's no point in being rude to them."

"Oh. But—"

Jesus shook his head. "I am not sure this is a good idea," he said.

"I'll be fine," Ursula insisted.

"Perhaps. But we have no wish to cause you embarrassment. You need not reveal anything at all about your previous experience. Merely tell them that you were recruited on Tanith, and you have been sent to the University for formal training. Then be careful, because you will almost certainly be approached by the enemy in the hopes that you will let slip something of value."

"Only I don't know anything—"

"That is not strictly true," Jesus said. "In any event, I think I can guarantee that at least one of those who pays attention to you will have ulterior reasons. What you do about that is your business, but be certain, we are not asking you to play Mata Hari."

"Would it help if I tried?" Ursula asked.

"My dear," Catherine said, "I should think you know the answer to that. The Legion needs nice, healthy young officers, not psychological wrecks. Learn and observe, that's all. We're soldiers, not spies."

CHAPTER EIGHT

Crofton's Encyclopedia of the Inhabited Planets
(2nd Edition):

> **Aegean,** sea. [Ae-ge-an], named for enclosed portion of eastern Mediterranean, Earth. (see *names,* Mythological, Graeco-Roman)
> One of two linked inland seas on the planet *Sparta* (see *Sparta*];

The Aegean, with the larger *Oinos sea* (q.v.) to the south, forms the great inland embayment which separates the northern and southern lobes of the *Serpentine Continent,* Sparta's principal landmass. Roughly rectangular in shape, the Aegean covers approximately 510,000 sq. kilometers; geological investigation shows that it was formed by a complex process of subsidence, attendant on the crustal plate movements which accompanied the raising of the *Drakon Mountains* (q.v.). In general terms, the Aegean is therefore relatively warm, shallow (few areas over 500 meters depth) and characterized by a rough balance between sediment deposition and subsidence of the sea floor. Characteristic terrain on all sides of the Aegean consists of coastal plains of varying width, backed by hills or mountains; the northeastern corner offers a lowland corridor to the valley of the *Middle Eurotas* (q.v.) The main river draining into the Aegean is the Eurotas, which reverses its lower course and drains northward through its delta into *Constitution Bay* (q.v.), a nearly circular impact crater associated with an asteroid collision of circa 50,000 BCE. The large volcanic islands of *Zakynthos* (q.v.), *Leros* (q.v.), *Keos,* (q.v.) *New Crete* (q.v.) and *Mytilene* (q.v.) are products of the same astrophysical event.

Marine life is abundant, and is based on native equivalents of plankton. Common species include the *grunter,* notable for its great numbers and resemblance to the terrestrial cod, the multiclawed *rockcrawler,* much in demand as a delicacy offworld, and the *torpedofish,* a predatory species up to 10 meters in length, which attacks its prey by ramming with its bone-armored nose. All vertebrate piscoids are gill-breathers but have pseudo-mammalian features such as four-chambered hearts, and are viviparous. The *tangler kelp* is the sole source of Ez-e-Mind™, Lederle AG's vastly profitable "morning after" contraceptive. Introduced terrestrial species include the common dolphin and the orca (killer whale), both wild and domesticated.

> *We have fed our sea for a thousand years*
> *And she calls us, still unfed,*
> *Though there's never a wave of all her waves*
> *But marks our English dead:*
> *We have strawed our best to the weed's unrest,*
> *To the shark and the sheering gull.*
> *If blood be the price of admiralty,*
> *Lord God, we ha' paid in full!*
>
> —Rudyard Kipling

Steven Armstrong pushed his chair back from the table and loosened his belt. *Been doing that a lot lately,* he thought. Growing a bit of a pot, to offset the massive shoulders and bull neck and the barrel chest that bulged out his roll-necked sweater. . . . He grinned and tossed back thick rough-cut hair the color of butter, only lightly streaked with gray. Once he took the *Alicia* out of harbor and north to the Thule Sea, he'd work that off soon enough, no matter how good Cookie's hash was. The air was full of the odors of good solid cooking, with an overtone of pipe tobacco and damp cool air from Constitution Bay below; they were close enough to the docks to hear the gulls, and the clacking sound of the cranes.

"Ladies and gentlemen!" he said, standing and raising his stein. "I give you—the Alicias, both of 'em! The ship, and the lady who made her possible!"

There was a cheer from all the tables he had rented in the Neptune; hearty cheers, though nobody had been drinking more than enough to put a little edge on. Most of them would be sailing with him in an hour or so, after all. All eyes had turned to his wife at the other end of the table. Alicia Armstrong was smiling and wiping at her eyes at the same time, as the guests began to applaud her. She was a round-faced woman with a close-cropped head of tightly curled hair, and eggplant-black skin that set off her gold seashell earrings. Three children from four to ten were seated next to her; they leaped up and began clapping too, with high-pitched shouts of *"Mommy! Mommy!"*

"I—" she began, as cries of "speech, speech" rang through the taproom. Then: "Oh, let Steven make the speech—he *likes* doing it."

More laughter; Steven Armstrong had been Senator-legate of the Maritime Products Trade Association for a year now, and was famous for a rhetorical style that included thumping lecterns hard enough to break the wood at Pragmatist rallies.

"OK, I promise not to damage Mrs. Kekkonen's tables, at least," he began, looking around until he caught the proprietor's eye and winked. She winked back; the Armstrongs and the Neptune Inn went back a long way. It was the sort of place he enjoyed; not fancy, just a taproom and kitchen with an outdoor terrace for summer and some rooms above. A workingman's place, where you could get a good solid mess of grunter fillet and yam or a twenty-ounce steak and potatoes and pie for an honest tenth-crown; the sort of place you could bring your family, too. "Actually, I hate giving speeches."

"Then you must love to suffer, bucko!"

"Shut up, Sven. Where was I . . . Armstrong & Armstrong's come a long way," he said. "When Alicia and I got married, we honeymooned here at the Neptune because we couldn't afford anything else—"

"Well!" the widow Kekkonen said, mock-indignant.

"—and all we had was these hands"—he held them up; massive and reddened, scarred and callused with hooks and nets and lines—"Alicia's brains and one rickety overgrown dory with an engine that worked, sometimes. I busted my butt, and Alicia kept books better than the computer we couldn't afford—found out that the Meijians would pay through their noses for rockcrawler claws—and we saved every penny. Now we've got four trawlers and damned good ones, and best of all—the *Alicia*. You all know what it'll mean, being able to tap the Thule Sea shoals; off-planet exchange, for one thing. No reason to let the Newfies get it all."

Cheers and jeers; nobody much liked the secretive and clannish settlers of New Newfoundland, the big island in the gulf where the Oinos Sea met the outer Jefferson Ocean.

"I'd like to thank everyone who helped make it possible," he went on. "Even Consolidated Hume Financial." More laughter, sheepishly joined in by the representative of the bank in his conservative brown tunic and sash and knee-breeches. *Well, nobody loves a banker,* Armstrong thought. Especially not on a planet starved for capital and with a strict hard-money policy. "And the great people from Huang, Lee and Parkinson." The shipbuilders; his sincerity came through. "My friends from the Association, who paid as the only way to shut me up and get me out of Sparta City"—cries of protest and a few half-eaten rolls flew past his ears, with the odd "damn straight"—"and most of all, my wife. My only regret is she isn't coming with us—but she's got the best excuse I can think of."

Six months of pregnancy, now showing considerably. She put her hand on her stomach and met his eyes.

"Yeah, Armstrong, but when's *yours* due?" Sven Nyqvist said, poking a stubby finger into his captain's midriff. Steven Armstrong's booming voice led the laughter.

"Thank Christ *that's* over," he muttered, standing beside the wheel of the *Alicia*. Dockside was a kilometer to the west now, Sparta City a sprawl of white and pastel and greenery across its hills. And the dockside crowds, and the reporters.

The *Capital Herald's* little newsblimp was still overhead, with the irritating buzz of its twin engines; he was strongly tempted to give it the finger. *No.* The cameras could count the hairs in your nose from 800 meters. *Too many watching,* he thought. *Ignore them.*

As he'd ignored the reporters with their asinine questions. *"Why do you want to enslave the transportees, Senator Armstrong?"*

"Assholes."

"Sir?" from the helmsman.

"Steady as she goes. Just glad to get out of town. If I never see another equals sign, it'll be too soon."

"Amen," said the helmsman.

Enslave the transportees, Armstrong thought disgustedly. *Sweet Christ, I married a transportee, didn't I?* Many of his best workers were transportees, and he had sponsored a half-dozen into the Brotherhood of Poseidon after helping them make Citizen. Even the common ruck of them weren't too bad, once they learned they couldn't sit in the gutter and live on handouts here. He snorted again; anyone who starved on Sparta deserved it; you could eat for a week on two day's wages for casual labor. *Hell, you can walk out of town and throw rocks at the rabbits.* He'd done that himself as a boy, when times were *really* hard.

No, it was the real scum that needed attention. Not those scooped up by BuReloc for being in the wrong place at the wrong time, like Alicia's parents; the real criminals, the pimps and street-gangers and whores. Bad enough they cut each other up down in Minetown, dropped their bastards in the gutters without even caring enough to take them to the nuns. Now they were swarming into that son-of-a-bitch Croser's NCLF, outnumbering the real workingmen in the Dockworkers' and half a dozen other unions. Strikes—only last month he'd lost fifteen tons of rockcrawler while they struck the packing-plant over some idiot political thing. Killings, like that mess at the Spartosky. Thank *God* Alicia hadn't been there.

"Aaah, enough politics," he muttered.

He pushed the captain's cap back on his head and worked the cigar to the corner of his mouth. One of cookie's stewards brought him a cup of coffee the way he liked it, black and sweet, and he cupped his hands around the thick white china. The *Alicia* was making good speed, seven knots; not wise to go much faster. Constitution Bay had enough sandbars and shallow water to give a strong man the willies. She would do better out in the open ocean, though. He looked around with pride: fifteen hundred tons, good von Alderheim steel for the hull, decking and upperworks of redwood. Two thousand-horsepower diesels with electric transmission, burbling their song of power through his feet. Deck-winches, nets, processing-holds and bunkrooms, all the best that Sparta City could make, and that was damned good. Even off-planet electronics, echo-sounder and radar.

The horseshoe bridge with its consoles and dials smelled of paint and seasoned wood and very slightly of the vegetable-oil fuel burned by the engines; he liked it, would like it even better when she'd been battered a little by the ocean swells, and smelled of salt and piscoid. The shallow Aegean and Oinos swarmed with good eating-fish, far more than Sparta's limited population could use. The *Alicia* was bound for bigger game: the huge piscoids of the cold and dangerous Thule Sea; that was what the rocket-harpoon launcher was for. Lustrous metallic-scaled hide, mouth-ivory more beautiful than the vanished elephant herds of Earth. Complex oils with a dozen uses, from perfumes to drugs.

"Sir."

He jerked out of his reverie, looked around: It was the radio watch, Maureen Terwonsky. Looking worried, which was not like her.

"It's a radiotelephone call, sir. They want to speak to you personally. They won't give a name."

He pulled the cigar out of his mouth and considered the chewed wet end. "If it's those news people again, tell them to go bugger themselves," he said. She began to speak into her equipment.

"Captain . . . Captain Armstrong, he says if you don't listen you'll regret it, and your family will too."

Something cold and limp touched his spine. He leaned forward quickly, touching the control that shut off the speaker for a moment.

"Get to the auxiliary in the radio room, *and get the Milice on the line.* Move!"

He took up the handset with a deep breath. "This is Captain Armstrong," he said; his voice was deadly flat with the effort of control. "Who is this?"

"This is the voice of the workers, *Captain* Armstrong," the voice said. "This is the voice of the ones you think are tools to be used and thrown aside to make your riches."

This can't be serious, he thought. A crank call; the voice sounded a little nasal, probably North American. Not a slum dialect; educated, but not Spartan-born either.

"What the hell are you talking about?" he asked, playing for time. With a little luck, the Milice would trace the call back through Broadcast Central. "You can't—"

"Oh, but we can, *Captain.* Hear the voice of the tool. We've heard your voice, making speeches. Trying to grind the common people down, make them suffer even more. Now you're going to feel our anger, now *you're* going to suffer from the just wrath of the people."

"What the fuck—" Static hiss; Terwonsky stuck her head through the hatch at the rear of the bridge.

"Milice got it, they're working on it, Cap," she said.

"Don't worry, probably just a crank—" he began.

The *Alicia* jerked and stopped dead in the water, almost as if she had hit a shoal. Echoing silence fell as the engines cut out, broken only by yells from startled crewfolk. Lights flickered, then came on more dimly as the emergency batteries cut in. Armstrong lunged across the bridge, balance telling him the ship was already down by the stern and to starboard. His hand slapped down on the communicator, and a screen lit with a view of the engine room.

Armstrong's stomach clenched, and he could feel his scrotum contract and try to draw his testicles up against his stomach. Nothing lit the engine compartment but the red emergency

lights, and they shone on a scene out of hell. Water plumed
in through the floor gratings, from a slashing cut that must
run the full length of the compartment; no, beyond it, into
the rear hold. The deck was already awash. The engineering
crew were scrambling around the main hatchway in the
bulkhead just below the pickup, battering and prying with crow-
bars and hand-tools.

"Sven!" Armstrong shouted. "What's going on?"

A desperate face turned up, blood and water running down
it from sodden hair and a cut across the forehead. "Jesus, it
just went like a bomb! Both the hatchways are sprung, she's
flooding, we'll be under in three minutes."

"Hold on!" He slammed the all-stations button, and his
amplified voice bellowed out throughout the *Alicia.*

*"Now hear this! The black gang is trapped in the engine-
room, and it's flooding. McLaren, whoever's near there, gut the
cutting lance down there* now, *d'you hear. Now!"*

"Jesus, Steve, it's flooding faster, we can't budge this bastard." Panting, and an iron *chung* as a prybar broke under the
desperate heaving of three strong men. Some of the others were
shouldering in to try with their bare hands, screaming in panic.

Hurry up, hurry, up, Armstrong pleaded.

"Jesus! *Jeezzzuussss—"*

"Sven's dead," Armstrong said hoarsely, throwing off the
blanket somebody was trying to put around his shoulders. There
were Milice cordoning off the dock; out on the waters he could
see divers jumping from a hovering helicopter.

"Oh, honey, *no,"* Alicia said.

"I saw it," Armstrong mumbled. Then he shook himself,
stood erect. "Come on, we're getting you and the kids home
and then I'm going to get some *answers,* by God."

They pushed through the awestruck crowd toward the family
van: a six-wheeler they used for vacations at their cottage up
in the hills. A cameraman tried to work through to them; one
of the Milice tripped him, then stamped a boot through the
equipment. The sight brought a tiny sliver of chill satisfaction, something to put between himself and the vision of his
oldest friend floating dead before a pickup camera. . . . Soothing
the children was better, forcing him out of himself.

"Honey, you sure I shouldn't stay?"

"No, not in your condition. Get them back to the house,
Fred's sending some of his people over"—his brother-in-law,
and a commander in the police—"and *stay* there until I call.
OK, sweetheart?"

She bit her lip, nodded, kissed him and slid into the driver's seat. He waited until the big vehicle was safely out of the parking lot, before he turned and looked at the death of a lifetime's dream. *Half an hour,* he thought, dazed. *Half a flipping hour. It's impossible.*

The explosion was not quite enough to knock him down; it did send him staggering half a dozen steps forward. Even as he turned and ran, the van blossomed in a circle of fire as the ruptured fuel-tank blew. He could hear his children screaming quite clearly over the roar, as he wrenched at the burning metal.

Steven Armstrong was screaming himself as they pulled him away from the wreckage where nothing lived, although not from the pain of his charred hands or the third-degree burns across most of the front of his body. He was still screaming as the paramedics dragged him back, until they hyposprayed enough sedative into his veins to turn a bull toes-up.

"I am ashamed. I have failed," the Meijian said.

Murasaki nodded; they were alone in the plain white room of his lodgings, which with the equipment he had brought was as secure as any building on Sparta. The floor was covered with local bamboo matting; his futon was neatly rolled in one corner, and beyond that there was only the low table between them, an incense burner, and one spray of willow-buds in a simple jar. Sandalwood perfumed the air; a cricket chirped from its tiny cage of silver wire.

"I must expiate my shame," his follower said.

They knelt facing each other across the table, dressed in dark kimonos. The technoninja drew a knife and laid the smooth curve of it on the lacquered wood before him, then began to tie a handkerchief tightly about the base of the smallest finger of his left hand.

"Wait," Kenjiro Murasaki said. For some time they did only that, moving solely to breathe. At last:

"You are in error. You have not failed."

"*Roshi,*" his follower said, bowing his head to the mats between his palms. "Yet Armstrong lives."

"Beware of the illusions of specificity. Although Armstrong lives, circumstance is such that he will serve our purposes none the less. For the Armstrong we wished to die, has died; in his place is born another.

"So."

"So."

Silence stretched.

CHAPTER NINE

Crofton's Encyclopedia of the Inhabited Planets
(2nd Edition):

Sparta, Royal University of: Institution of postsecondary education, sole university of the *Dual Monarchy of Sparta* (q.v.). Founded in 2040, only a few years after the arrival of the first settlers of the *Constitutionalist Society* (q.v.), the University of Sparta embodies many interesting organizational principles and fulfills a number of functions.

The University is organized as a cooperative corporation, with the Crown, the faculty and individual professors holding shares. Some state revenues are "dedicated" to the University; other sources of income include endowments, extensive property holdings, fees, service charges for research work, and patent revenues. Individual faculty are paid a basic salary, with bonuses determined by number of students enrolled and by a complicated, results-oriented testing process. Some chairs are separately endowed, and the endowing individual or authority may nominate the holder subject to a Dean and Faculty veto.

Enrollment is by two methods; scholarship examination, and fee payment. The scholarship tests are severely selective, but confer free tuition, preference for work-study occupations, and in some cases rent-free student accommodations and a stipend. Those entering via fee payment need not take the entrance exams but may and often are disqualified during their course of study; fees are not refunded. Additional supplements are also offered to those willing to contract for public service work (e.g., primary school teaching in remote locations) after their graduation.

All the common courses are taught, together with some unique to Sparta such as Introductory Military Science;

there is no law school, as formal qualifications are unnecessary for practice on Sparta. The University is affiliated with St. Thomas Royal Hospital and the McGregor Oceanographic Institute; it cooperates closely with the research departments of many private businesses, and undertakes contract and freelance research work on an extensive basis. The University also operates an extensive correspondence degree section, and many students take the academic portions of their courses by mail or Tri-V link, coming to the campus only for laboratory work or oral examinations.

There are no sororities and fraternities, although the Candidate Sections of the *Phraetries* (q.v.) fulfill many of the same functions.

Current enrollment (2090): students, 8,000; post-graduate students and teaching assistants, 2,000; faculty, 998.

"God Almighty, that's gruddy," one of the students said. "Overload gruddy."

Ursula Gordon nodded as she relaxed back into the wicker chair in the student commons. The 'caster himself was obviously shaken as he showed the bodies being recovered from the burnt-out wreckage of the Armstrongs's van.

"I don't know what the planet's coming to," one of the observers said disgustedly, taking another pull at his beer.

Observe, Ursula told herself. *That's what you're here for.* That and the classes, and hers were over for the morning. They had been interesting . . . odd mixture of people, too. Mostly young, but with a solid sprinkling of older types; evidently the University ran extension-courses all over the settled portions of the planet, not difficult with satellite communications. No problems about enrolling, either; if you paid your way, you could sign up for any course that had room for you, although the fees were quite high.

There were plenty of scholarship students as well, often from poorer Citizen or even transportee families. They *did* have to pass entrance exams, stiff ones, but their tuition was free and they got first crack at the service-staff jobs that would let you live with modest comfort while you studied. It was a tempting arrangement: leave the Legion, go to the University and eventually become a citizen of Sparta. *But there's a job to be done first.*

The viewer switched to underwater shots of divers pulling bodies from the wreck of the *Alicia,* with voice-over commentary on the long slash that peeled open her hull for half its length. Ursula looked aside, out the arched windows. You could tell what the priorities of the Spartan Founders had been; the University had been started almost as soon as the prefab shelters went up. It occupied an inordinate stretch of high-value land, too, down on the southwestern shoreline of the city. Georgian-brick dormitories and white neoclassical lecture halls, flagstoned paths and gardens that were quietly spectacular; without the harsh flamboyance she had been accustomed to on Tanith. From here you could see students strolling along the pathways, sitting on stone benches under trees, eating or flirting, people-watching themselves or indulging in the perennial undergraduate arguments about the Nature of Things.

A sailboat was skipped across Sparta Sound, its sails gaily blue and yellow against the forest green of the offshore islands. The air of the winter afternoon was chilly enough to make the walking-out khakis and wooly-pully sweater comfortable; shirtsleeve weather to the others on the verandah.

"Yeah, it's tragic, but . . ." someone was saying. He had a button on his tunic, black with a crimson rim and a red = sign. Then his voice went higher: "Hey, Senator Croser's on!"

The lean Eurasian face filled the screen; that was set into the wall to imitate a crystal display unit, but it was actually a locally made cathode ray set-up with no Tri-V capacity at all.

"Quiet everybody! Listen!" That from Mary Williams, an intense girl who'd taken little part in the earlier discussions.

" . . . NCLF and I, personally, denounce this abhorrent crime, and demand that the Royal administration bring the perpetrators to justice," he was saying.

Sincere looking, Ursula thought judiciously. Being interviewed in his study, from the bookcases and shabby-elegant furniture. Looking very professorial in a dark-blue tunic with leather elbow-patches, knee-breeches, and matching sash. *No. A little too hard-faced,* she decided. An outdoorsman's look, body fit even by Spartan standards; and yes, that was a snow-leopard head on the wall behind him. Beaky Anglo face with slightly tilted blue eyes, gray-streaked black hair.

"At the same time, and without condoning such atrocities or the sick minds that conceive them, this senseless violence is exactly what the Non-Citizens' Liberation Front is doing its best to stop—and which the so-called Pragmatists are fanning. Extremism breeds extremism. A new deal for our oppressed classes is the only way to restore true peace and social harmony to Sparta."

"Are you saying that Senator Armstrong provoked this attack?" the interviewer asked sharply.

Croser shook his head. "Please, I *insist* that you not read words into my mouth." He leaned forward, making a clean, spare gesture with one hand; his voice was deep and sincere, the eyes level and intense.

"I am simply saying that the Pragmatist proposals—to forcibly indenture convicts for the length of the sentence the CoDominium imposes, or involuntary transportees who don't immediately become 'self-sufficient'—this is not only wrong, stupid, a step on the road to slavery—it's a source of the very violence the Pragmatists complain of." His voice grew passionate for a moment: "Our parents and grandparents didn't come here to live in an armed camp, or for cheap labor, they came for *freedom*. We didn't come to be the CoDominium's partners in oppression. We've lost sight of that, and we're paying the price."

"By 'we,' do you mean the Pragmatists, or the Citizen body as a whole?" the interviewer continued.

"Pragmatists and Foundation Loyalists both; the ugly and benign faces of repression. Oh, I grant the good intentions of the most of the Loyalist leadership, even of some Pragmatists, poor Senator Armstrong among them. But look how the Crown and its Senate and Council hangers-on is reacting to the current crisis! Hiring off-planet paid killers and raising armies, when the same funds devoted to the welfare of the less fortunate would buy us *real* peace."

He smiled sadly. "There's a very old joke from Earth. A Minister of State goes to his king and says: 'Sire, in your new budget I notice you spend *billions* for weapons and not one *penny* for the poor.' The king replies: 'Yes, when the revolution comes, I'll be *ready*.'"

There was a chuckle through the common room; even the interviewer's voice seemed more friendly when he continued:

"You don't advocate revolution, then, Senator Croser? Some of your followers seem more radical."

Croser chuckled. "*There go my people; I must hurry to get ahead of them, for I am their leader,*" he quoted. "Mahatma Gandhi. The moderate leadership of the NCLF—of which I am only one—are Sparta's best guarantee *against* revolution. It's the Citizens who obstinately cling to outworn aristocratic privilege, who prate about self-serving and exploded slogans such as the separation of state and economy, who are risking everything. The true radicals look on the NCLF as the greatest obstacle to a bloody revolution, and driving the NCLF underground would be the best gift the Crown could give to the real rebels—to the extent that there are any."

"You don't agree there's a real security threat?"

"Yes! Of course there's a threat: and it is the inequitable distribution of power and wealth on Sparta, not a few extremists in the hills, or the type of fanatic who perpetrated this action today. We won't discuss the ludicrous tales of massive conspiracies the Government is putting about to justify its preparations for war on the people."

"Senator, some have pointed out that you, yourself are a wealthy man with extensive landholdings and mineral interests. . . ."

Croser nodded and began loading a pipe. "Quite true. And if I gave it all away, the process of economic concentration would continue; we're breeding an oligarchy here, based on nothing better than the luck of being born into an old-settler family. If you look at the record, you'll find almost all my income goes into the NCLF, free of charge. And"—he waggled the pipestem admonishingly—"the NCLF stands four-square for private property; we just want more people to have the privilege! John Stuart Mill himself said that excessive concentration of wealth is a provocation to leveling legislation."

"Thank you, Senator. This is Jerric van Damm of the Spartan Herald Service, interviewing Senator Dion Croser, legate of the Dockworkers' Union on today's terrorist attack which resulted in the death of Mrs. Alicia Armstrong and her three children, and the severe injury of her husband, Senator Steven Armstrong. Senator Croser, any closing remarks?"

"Thank you, Citizen van Damm. Just this." The camera panned in, until the blue eyes filled the screen. "I appeal to *you*, my fellow citizens of Sparta, to wake up and realize injustice can never rest secure. In your hands lies the power to avert tragedy—and the price is reform. Act now!"

"Now, *there's* someone who knows what's going on!" one of the students said, pushing his glasses back with his thumb.

"Horseshit," another said. She was sitting with a young man, and they were both in the gray sweatsuit outfits of Brotherhood militia training. "You boil that little speech down, and what it amounts to is that somehow we're all guilty because a bunch of scum-suckers burned a pregnant woman and three children to death; not to mention the sailors on that boat. C'mon, Ahmed, we'll be late for drill."

"Brainless jocks," the student with the glasses muttered; not,

Ursula noticed, until they were gone. "That's the only type the Brotherhoods are letting in these days; I thought Sparta was founded by people like *us*." Glasses was in sociology.

"Ahmed's folks were transportees," someone said.

"Ass-kisser," Glasses sneered. More politely: "What did *you* think of the Leader's speech. Ursula?"

"Well, I'm certainly against slavery," she said sincerely. Many of the others looked embarassed, especially Glasses—*McAlastair,* she thought—who had tried to kiss her in the stairwell at the faculty-student mixer last week. His wrist had healed nicely. *Tanith certainly has a reputation here,* she thought. If possible, worse than the actuality. Interesting that somehow everyone seemed to know all about what she did on Tanith.

"Then why are you in that Legion?" Mary Williams said sharply.

"Because I owe them for rescuing me from slavery."

"I heard the mercenaries owe you," the Williams girl said. This one was altogether more serious than the rest of the crowd of parlor pinks and NCLF-groupies she'd fallen in with. "For helping put down slave revolts on Tanith."

"There weren't any slave revolts on Tanith, just outlaws who robbed and killed convicts because it was easier than attacking the planters. Catching and hanging them did everyone a favor."

McAllistair frowned and made to speak, but Williams laughed and laid a hand across his mouth.

"At least you're honest," she said. "I like that. And not so squeamish as the rest of these crybabies."

"I am *not* squeamish!" McAllistair said. "Look, Croser himself—"

"Croser's heart is in the right place, but he's blind to some things too—that massacre at the Spartosky, people shot down in the streets!" *Ah, yes, she was there with the demonstraters,* Ursula thought. *Dropped out of sight for a while, pretty broken up, her boyfriend was killed.*

Williams was continuing passionately: "Can't you see that the time Croser's warning about, when refusal to reform brings on revolution is . . . oh, forget it, Andy. Anyway, Ursula, we're going down to Ptomaine Heaven to grab some grunter sticks and fries. Want to join us?"

"Love to," Ursula said. *And keep talking, the meter is running.*

Horace Plummer, Secretary to the Council, struck a pose. "His Majesty Jason the First, being unable to attend and having need of the assistance of Prince David, has designated King Alexander the First as his representative at this meeting, which is therefore an official meeting of the Council empowered to approve all measures. All rise."

King Alexander came into the Council chamber and took his seat at the head of the big table. He nodded to the Council and the military staff. "Thank you. You may begin."

Lysander stared at his father as they all took their seats. What he saw was shocking. He had been in the field with his battalion so that this was the first time he had seen the King in a month. *I knew he was working too hard, but this—!* Alexander Collins looked to have aged a decade in the last few months; the lines in his boney face were graven deeper, and there was a disturbing nervous glint in his eyes, a hint of desperation as he looked around the War Council. The meeting was in the Government House chamber where they had held the first briefing by the mercenaries three months ago. Today the chill seemed deeper than the mild seacoast winter beyond the windows could account for. Rain fell steadily from a soft gray sky.

"I gather you've got something for us?" The king was speaking more slowly than usually, as if he were fighting a speech impediment, but there was an edge of impatience in his voice.

"Colonel Owensford, please begin your presentation," Plummer said.

"Your Majesty." Peter stood. "We have a great deal to cover today. First, a summary: The First Royal Infantry is fully qualified to take the field, and I shall shortly recommend that we do so."

"That sounds encouraging," Alexander said.

"Yes, Sire," Peter said. "Captain Alana, please give your report."

Jesus Alana had been trying to hide a frown while looking at King Alexander. Now he stood and took his place at the display screen.

"We have found the satellite systems oddly ineffective," Jesus said. "But yesterday we finally found something worthwhile." Images formed on the screen. "The location is the Rhyndakos river, about twenty kilometers upstream from Dodona." The screen briefly flashed a map, locating the area as a south-bank tributary of the Eurotas, in the western part of the Middle Valley; Dodona was a small town at its juncture with the main stream. "Lieutenant Swenson will explain."

"Sir. Your majesty, we wouldn't have gotten anything if the

leaves weren't off the trees, and there isn't much even so, but look here."

The screen changed. The image outlined in black was something that could be barely made out as the lines of a small river-steamer's hull, a flat wooden rectangle with a rear-mounted paddle wheel. A little out of date now that diesels were becoming more common, but they were cheap and simple to make, able to put in anywhere and hundreds of identical models plied the Eurotas from the Delta to Olynthos.

"Here's the computer enhancement."

The image was still coarse and grainy; even the Legion's computers could do only so much with the data input offered. What did show was glimpses of men in bulky clothing unloading coffin-sized boxes and carrying them down the bow-ramp to waiting animals, pack-horses or mules, where others lifted them on to the carrying saddles.

"Next sequence is interesting," Swenson said; her voice had a technician's satisfaction in getting better performance than could be reasonably expected from second-rate equipment.

This time it was a smaller, square box, and it had broken when it fell. The contents had spilled free, some of them out of the cylindrical wicker containers. Dull-gray metal cylinders about the length of a man's arm, with conical tops and a rod coming out the bottom.

"Mortar bombs," she said, with a prim smile. "Specifically, for your Rojor 125mm rifled medium mortar. There is," she added pedantically, "no stencilling on the crates, but there isn't much doubt where they came from, either."

"Olynthos or Sparta City," Owensford said. Those were the only two places on the planet with forging and machining shops capable of doing the work. "Probably Olynthos, given the location."

Alexander's voice was thin with fury he rose and turned to General Desjardins. *"What is your explanation for this?"*

The constabulary chief stuttered, paling. "Your Majesty, I, ah—"

"And how long has this been going on?" The king's voice rose to a shriek: *"Who is the traitor?"*

"Your Majesty," Owensford said. Then more sharply: *"Your Majesty!"*

Alexander Collins caught himself and wiped a handkerchief over his mouth. "Colonel," he said, sitting again.

"Your Majesty, until quite recently Sparta had only the most cursory controls on weapons movement," Owensford said. His face was blankly expressionless; Lysander had been with him long enough to know what *that* meant. "This could have been going on for quite some time, I'm afraid. With enough money, it wouldn't have been hard to organize."

"Export shipments," Jesus Alana said. "Thurstone has been buying from here for half a decade now." The five-sided civil war there had been going on for twice that length of time. "Mother of God, even the CoDominium Marines on Haven use Spartan-made light arms. Just shaving a few percentage points off each would get you a respectable amount, provided you weren't expending them. You'd have to fiddle the weight allotments, but it could be done if no one was looking hard. Just for an example, you could overweight something else going up with the same load, and it'd look fine."

"Yes, yes," the king said. "What do you propose to do, Colonel Owensford?"

"Treat this as an opportunity, Your Majesty." He called up a map. "We now have two battalions of the Legion. The Fifth is eager for duty, and has already been sent upriver. The First Royal is also on route to the Mandalay-Olynthos area. The seismic-testing teams have begun operations, and scouts can be sent into those hills immediately.

"I propose that we take to the field in full force. Three battalion-sized columns, with Brotherhood first-line militia in support, will move into the Dales on converging vectors."

Worms of colored light writhed into the hills from the Valley.

"This will be a reconnaissance in force. That's often a polite way to say 'we have no objective,' or in this instance 'training war,' but in fact we do have an objective. The enemy has probably been accumulating heavy equipment for years. We also know that they recently acquired off-planet support, which very likely includes computers, radars, possibly considerably more. All that requires a base. I propose to find that base and destroy it."

"Bravo," Alexander said.

"So in this case we really do have a reconnaissance in force," Peter said. "Strong enough to fight anything they can put against us, and mobile enough to cover a lot of ground. We go in searching. Depending on the information we gain, we'll modify the directions of attack, attempting to corral and destroy any Helot forces we contact."

"Do you think you can destroy the . . ." the king was reluctant to use the enemy's own designation, "the guerilla forces?"

"That depends on how mobile and well-organized they are, and their leadership," Owensford said. "Also how many, and how good their reconnaissance and intelligence is. They don't know what we're up to yet, but when we begin to move they'll see us coming." He pursed his lips. "The truth is, I don't know what we will accomplish. At the least we should be able to make them abandon a good part of their heavy equipment, and we will kill some of their cadre. That, I think, is the worst case. General Slater will discuss what else we might accomplish."

Hal Slater stood with some difficulty. Everyone had tried to get him to remain seated when giving his reports and lectures, but he never did. Hal limped to the briefing stand and faced the Council.

"Gentlemen. I believe we are facing amateurs. Of course that's true on the face of it—clearly they haven't brought in any large military professional units without our knowledge. I think they *have* brought in some off-planet consultants, and we're fairly certain they recruited some retired CoDominium officers as advisors, but the important point is that the Helot movement is headed by amateurs."

"Croser," Alexander said.

"Croser for one," Hal Slater said. "And some I can't identify, but I've been studying the patterns of operation, and I think I know those commanders better than they suspect I do. In particular, I am certain I know what books they have studied."

Aha! Lysander thought about the implications of that. *I wouldn't make much of it, but I can see how Slater might.*

"I will be glad to discuss this further if you like, but let me state my conclusion: I believe the Helot organization thinks itself ready to step up to the next phase in the classic guerrilla sequence. If that is so—and the pattern of their terrorist activities makes me quite sure it is—they will be extremely reluctant to abandon their heavy equipment."

"No sanctuary," Ace Barton muttered.

Hal Slater smiled thinly. "No political sanctuary, so they have attempted to build themselves a geographical sanctuary. When we violate that sanctuary, their leaders, following the classic pattern, will say to themselves that they should retreat, abandon their base—but they will not *want* to do that. Far less will their troops want to do so. Even the lowest dregs of humanity has some need for personal space and ownership. Moreover, that heavy equipment is the key to continuing on their schedule.

"Gentlemen, Madam, I believe they will fight on far longer than they should. They will tell themselves they are trying to give us a bloody nose, to punish us, and they will believe that. They will tell themselves they are going to hit us and run, and they will believe that. But they will always be more eager to resist than to run."

"And the upshot?" Peter Owensford prompted.

"They will stand and fight long after they should have quit. They will take more casualties than they expected to. There's another point."

Hal Slater's lecture, or something, had had a visibly relaxing effect on Alexander I. "Yes, General?" he prompted.

"Amateurs make elaborate plans," Slater said. "They concoct schemes. Often quite complex schemes. They rely on gimmicks. Their notion of surprise is sneaking up on someone, hitting him with an unexpected weapon, that sort of thing. It often works—against other amateurs."

"We wouldn't want to underestimate the enemy," Henry Yamaga said.

"No, my lord," Peter said. "But we don't take counsel from our fears, either. This campaign is unlikely to be decisive, but we should do them considerable damage. Throw them well off balance. Pity the transport situation will hinder us so badly, but there it is."

Most of the Middle and Lower Valleys were pretty much a sea of glutinous mud at this time of year, apart from the natural levees and some artificially drained portions. The westernmost end of the Middle Valley where the Eurotas turned northwest toward the Vulcan Falls was just as muddy, with the addition of occasional heavy snows that generally melted within a week or so and added to the saturated ground. The Illyrian Dales were a little better, since the porous limestone was free-draining, but they were very broken, and the rain-laiden winter winds from the east rose and dumped blizzard after blizzard when they met the hills and the mountains behind.

"If we had more air transport, we could drop blocking forces and round more of them up," Owensford said. "As it is, a number of them will escape. If General Slater is correct, not as many as they think, but without aviation we're much hampered." He shrugged. On most planets there would have been a scattering of private helicopters owned by the rich, at least, and available for emergency use; on Tanith, for example, most planters owned at least one. Sparta had forbidden that, with wise forethought, putting the money into importing production goods and relying on lower-tech transport. Now she was seeing the unintended consequences of her planning. The new industrial plan called for production of military helicopters, but they wouldn't have them in quantity for more than a year.

"In any event, the objective is to force them to choose between fighting and abandoning equipment which will be hard to replace now that security's been tightened; and to demonstrate that they have no sanctuary from the Royal government forces."

"Yes, by all means," Alexander said. His shoulders slumped slightly. "I almost envy you, Colonel, taking the field against an open enemy. While I sit here, fighting shadows, shadows." His eyes began flickering from side to side again. "Their spies are everywhere—if not Croser's, then that *fool* Armstrong's! Everywhere! The Royal government leaks like a sieve, trying to get anything done is a nightmare, wading through glue while they close in around me."

His voice was growing shrill again. "But I'll destroy them yet, do you hear me, *destroy* them." He panted slightly as he pushed two folders of documents across the polished black wood of the table to Owensford. "The first's the authorization to raise three more regiments, together with a notification to the Brotherhoads that we're in a state of apprehended insurrection. How soon can the Second RSI be ready?"

"With luck, ten weeks, Your Majesty." Owensford nodded in satisfaction. The notice to the Brotherhoods meant that they were put on formal notice to meet their Obligations to the Crown. Spartan Citizens took that very seriously indeed; he could expect a new flood of recruits, and more importantly men who had military experience or who had been through the excellent Spartan ROC, Reserve Officer Course.

"And here's a Royal Rescript—I had the devil of a time getting David's assent, is he *blind*—anyway, this is a Rescript declaring a State of Emergency in the Province of Olynthos." Owensford nodded again, more grimly. Virtual martial law. "Now get out there and *kill* them, Colonel."

"Yes, Your Majesty. Up to now these Helots have had it their way. They are very experienced in terrorism. We will now show them something they don't know about. We will show them war."

The King stood and waved dismissal. The officers rose and left, leaving the monarch staring moodily at the wall map. Royal Army sentries in the hall outside snapped to salute, and Owensford returned it absently as he pulled on his gloves. When he spoke to the Prince it was in a low murmur.

"My Lord Prince, has your father been seeing a physician?" he said.

"I don't know, sir. I'll certainly look into it."

"Do so, Lynn. Do so." He looked at his chronometer. "Landing ground at 0600, Captain Prince."

"Good *God*, Melissa, what's *happened* to him?" Lysander asked, in a furious whisper.

Melissa von Alderheim looked overworked herself; and she had flung herself into his arms with an enthusiasm that startled him. Especially since the nook they were in was not strictly private. Her father, *Freiherr* Bernard von Alderheim, was notoriously strict.

She snuggled closer within the circle of his arms. "It's the strain," she said. Her voice tickled the underside of his jaw. "Oh, Lynn, I've missed you so!"

A breathless moment later: "Isn't he seeing a doctor?"

"We've had a specialist in, but he couldn't find anything organic wrong."

"It's not like Father," Lysander said stubbornly. "I've never seen him—he isn't the type to crack under pressure."

"There's never been pressure like this before," she said.

"Keep an eye on him, will you? Try to get him to rest more." A thought. "What was that he said about *Armstrong's* spies?"

"You didn't hear? Steven Armstrong got out of regenn two weeks ago—earlier than he should have, the doctors say—and vanished. Until yesterday, of course."

"Darling," he said. "I've haven't slept in twenty hours, we've been planning—what *did* happen yesterday?

"The NCLF offices on North Sacred Way were bombed. Two people were killed, and someone phoned in to the police. They said the Secret Citizen's Army was responsible, that the Secret Army would do what the Royal Army couldn't. The Milice . . . the Milice think Armstrong's behind the Secret Army, Lynn."

Lysander closed his eyes. *Every time I think things are getting better they get* worse *instead,* he thought. *Is this planet under a curse?* It was enough to make *him* start believing in conspiracies.

"Just what we need," he said wearily. Then he smiled down into her face. "Funny, we haven't had much time together, and yet . . . well, we feel a lot closer."

"We've been working together for the same thing, Lynn," she said.

True. Melissa was more than the heir to the von Alderheim works, and future Queen; she was a very talented hand at the computerized design machines. The best they had, and needed more than ever with the sudden demand for new military products.

"Don't work yourself to death over at the War College," he said gently, taking her head between his hands. "And there's only a few hours before we move out. I don't want to spend them talking about the war"—*how naturally we start to use the word*—"or, or anybody else."

"I know," she said. "That's why I had dinner for us sent up to my rooms."

"What will your father say?"

"I don't really care." She took his hands between hers and kissed the palms. "I just . . . want to make sure you have a good solid memory to remind you of your reason for staying alive."

And something to remember you by if you don't come back, went unspoken between them, as they walked toward the stairs hand-in-hand.

CHAPTER TEN

Crofton's Encyclopedia of the Inhabited Planets
(2nd Edition):

Illyrian Dales, The: area of hilly terrain, named for
areas of the Balkan peninsula now part of Serbia, Croatia
and Albania. (see *names*, Mythological, Graeco-Roman)
Notable feature of the planet *Sparta* [see *Sparta*];

The Illyrian Dales cover an area of approximately
1,400,000 sq. kilometers (875,000 sq. miles) between the
western extremity of the Middle Valley of the *Eurotas* river
(q.v.) and the *Drakon Mountains* (q.v.). The Dales take
the shape of a blunt pyramid, with its base pointing
northward and its apex lying along the course of the
Rhyndakos river (q.v.), a south-bank tributary of the
Eurotas.

The Dales are geologically recent, composed of sedimentary marine limestones deposited while the present
Middle Valley was a shallow inland sea, prior to the
collision of crustal plates which produced the Drakon
Range. Buckling and rapid water-erosion has produced a
landscape of low hills and gentle ridges, occasionally
punctuated by intrusions of harder metamorphic or volcanic rock, which form "plugs" remaining above the
peneplain-like surface surrounding them; limited areas of
steeper slope have developed semi-karstic formations. The
Dales' limestones consist essentially of calcium carbon-
ate, with high concentrations of potassium, phosphorus
and other trace elements. Similar formations on Earth
include the Nashville basin of Tennessee, and the central ("Bluegrass") basin of Kentucky. No formation of this
size would be possible on Earth, but the greater liquid-
ity of the Spartan magma and higher internal heat from

gravitational contraction and the decay of radioactives produces more rapid and uniform patterns of deposition and uplift. (Thus accounting for the prevalence of high mountains on a planet with such active erosive forces). Altitude ranges from 300 (in the southeast) to 1,200 meters above sea level in the northwest. After allowing for the 18-month Spartan year the climate is comparable to the mid-latitude temperate zone of Earth's northern hemisphere, having warm to hot summers and cold winters with (depending on area) three to six months of continuous snow cover. There is little surface drainage, but artesian springs and underground water are common, as are sinkholes and caves.

Description: As with much of Sparta, the native vegetation has been largely replaced by introduced Terran varieties. Initially covered with tall-grass prairies (largely greater bluestem, panicum and canegrass) it has increasingly been colonized by broad-leafed trees ranging from tulip poplar and magnolia in the south to rock maple and birch on the northern fringe; forest cover is more plentiful to the south. Rainfall increases from north to south and from east to west, reaching a climax on the lower slopes of the Drakon range; the southernmost areas receive 180 centimeters per annum, dropping to 80 centimeters per annum on the northern fringe where the Dales give way to the level formations of the *Hylas Steppe* (q.v.). Animal life is almost exclusively Terran, and includes feral cattle, sheep, horse and beefalo, wild swine, various deer species, elk, wapiti, European and North American bison, and brown and black bear. Carnivores were a somewhat later introduction and include wolves (Siberian timber wolf varieties), bobcat, wild cat, lynx, leopard, ounce (snow leopard) and Siberian tiger. Ecological conditions are chaotic, as the introduced species eliminate the less-evolved natives and seek a new equilibrium. (see *Planetary Ecology, Terraforming.*) To date, there is no resident human population due to transportation difficulties and superior opportunities elsewhere, and exploitation is limited to harvesting of wildlife, with limited timbering and quarrying on the eastern border.

> *When first under fire an' you're wishful to duck*
> *Don't look nor take 'eed at the man that is struck.*
> *Be thankful you're livin', and trust to your luck*
> *And march to your front like a soldier*

❖   ❖   ❖

"Hey, Top."

Sergio Guiterrez lowered the field glasses; there wasn't anything to see, anyway.

"Yeah, Purdy?"

He'd known it was one of the Legionnaires; the Spartans in the First RSI were calling him Sergeant Major, which was his brevet-transfer rank. To a member of Falkenberg's Mercenary Legion, there was exactly one RSM among Legionnaires; and that was Regimental Sergeant Major Calvin, just as Falkenberg was the only colonel.

"This river ever end?"

"They say so, Purdy; supposed to be today. I can't see much sign of it."

Not *much* of anything to see all the weeks upriver, just the Eurotas getting smaller in stages so tiny you couldn't notice them. Riverbanks with trees, riverbanks *without* trees, views of farm fields, views of grassy prairie and swamp and bare mud and tangled forest. Animals and birds, of course, like something out of the zoo or an old flat Tri-V documentary. Damned few people even the first few days out of Sparta City, so the wildlife was something welcome, something to look at. That and the other troops on the big flat barge, and every now and then some little town where they stopped to take on fuel or run the troops around to keep them from losing their edge. Wet and cool down on the Lower Valley, wetter and colder as they went west along the Middle, which was the same as the Lower except there were fewer people. Wettest and coldest since they'd turned southwest up this tributary, the Rhyndakos.

"Top?"

"Yeah?"

"Something I can't figure," the Tanith-born Legionnaire said.

"Ask away, kid," Guiterrez said. Purdy liked to figure things out, which was one reason he'd made monitor so quick, that and being able to read and having a way with machinery.

"What I can't figure, is why does anyone on this planet want to rebel? It doesn't figure, you know?"

The noncom pushed himself into a sitting position against the pile of supplies and looked around. The barge was a wooden box ten meters by twenty, one of a string pulled along by a puffing little stern-wheeler boat. A dozen more boats and barge-strings further back, where the Brotherhood militia battalions they'd picked up in Dodona were following. About half of this one was taken up by supplies, mostly a battery of heavy 160mm mortars, three-meter tubes on wheeled carriages, and boxed Legion electronics, counterbattery radars and suchlike. The rest was filled with a company or so of the First RSI; they'd rigged up tarps over the hold of the barge, so everyone was pretty dry, and lit low-coal fires in steel drums, so you could get warm. Some of them were cooking things, fish they'd caught or chickens from the last stop, or brewing coffee, and the quality of the wine ration was better than he'd had anywhere else.

He grinned. They had kept the troops busy as possible, classes and even small-arms practice at things passing by, but it was still soft duty. A few of the Spartans had had the gall to complain about conditions, until they saw the Legion veterans laughing at them.

Wait until they're up to their balls in mud and eating monkey, he thought. "You can get rebellions in most places," he said. "They don't like the people running the place, I guess. Your folks moved off into the jungle back on Tanith to get away from the planters and the government, didn't they?"

"Yeah, but Top, they'd have given their right foot to have a place like this. Except it's so cold. No jungle, no Purple Rot, no Weems Beasts or Nessies, lots of good eats, you can pick who you want to work for without slaving your sentence term on some plantation, or hell, just get away from the river a ways and start farming."

Guiterrez laughed softly; there was no sting in it, but Purdy looked slightly abashed.

"It's alright, Purdy, keep thinking that hard and someday you'll be giving *me* orders. See, kid, you're thinking like Tanith. Somebody straight from a Welfare Island on Earth—like I was— it's not so hot. Sure, you don't have to eat protocarb glop, but they *like* glop. Taxpayers eat meat, and they're not taxpayers. There's no Tri-V here, and no Welfare either—no borloi, come to that, or free government booze. Say you're a street-gang warrior like I was, you don't get far here either, the people are all ironed and it's mostly a losing proposition to run in a gang. So it's work for a living or starve, and sure, *you're* used to that—your folks raised you that way, and they learned the hard way—but the convicts aren't. Aren't used to country living, either. Make's 'em feel hard done-by."

One of the First RSI troopers looked up from loading a magazine. "Nah," he said. "It's the girls."

"Girls?" Purdy said, half-turning.

"Sure. Like, I'm a transportee, right? So there's, say, seven pricks to three gashes on those CoDo transports landing here. Studs lined up waiting for them, the transportee gash gets

snapped up damn fast, you bet. And you can't get alongside much Citizen cunt even in Sparta City, and if you're
outback in a bunkhouse, nothin'. So unless you like men,
you might as well get yourself killed 'cause life ain't worth
living, right?"

Purdy looked around. The banks of the Rhyndakos were low
and swampy for the most part, covered in dead brown reeds;
beyond them were thickets of oak and beech, bare and gray-
brown as well; to the south and west, very distant, they could
see the white glaciers of the Drakon range catch the afternoon light. A hawk hovered overhead, and apart from the
chuffing of the tugboats' engines the only sound was wind
in the branches. Thick flakes of damp snow were falling from
a sky mostly clouds, melting almost at once when they touched
the barge. On the shore above the reeds it lay half a meter
deep, and the hills to the north were domes of white. The
last farmhouse had been yesterday.

"There sure aren't any girls out here," he said.

"Nah, but you can kill somebody and take out your mad,
see?" The soldier grinned, showing yellowed teeth. "Me, I figure
on being a hero when I get back, get some fine patriotic Citizen
to give it to me, see?"

Another trooper laughed. "You wish, Michaels. Maybe some
woman *dies*, leaves it to you in her *will*, that's the only way
you ever going to see any isn't bought and paid for."

The steamboat rounded a corner, and sounded three sharp
hoots on its whistle. Guiterrez pushed himself erect; his battle
armor was feeling a little tight around the gut, but a couple
of days humping the boonies ought to cure that. "Fall in, get
ready to disembark! And Purdy," he said.

"Yes, Top?"

"You're lucky. In the Legion, you don't have to know *who*
the enemy are, or *why* they're there. All you have to know
is how to get them in your sights."

The steamboat let go the towing hitch and turned, the
reversed paddlewheel churning the surface of the Rhyndakos
into white foam. On shore, the advance party fired a light
mortar with a special attachment to carry a line; it trailed
coiling through the air and landed across the bows with a
wet *thwack*, scattering troopers.

"Dog that line to the brackets," Guiterrez said.

A dozen hands rove it through metal eyelets along the
notional bow of the barge, and on shore a working party ran
the other end through a block and tackle to a tree and heaved
in unison. The lead barge in the chain grounded on the soft

silt with a shuddering crunch, and the others closed up as the troops on board hauled in the connecting cables.

"Form up!" Guiterrez said, and the company NCOs echoed it. A plank landing ramp splashed over the side. Then there was a whining screech from the shore, as the First's pipe-band prepared to play its soldiers ashore and into the bridgehead.

Operation Scrub Brush was under way.

Geoffrey Niles blew gratefully on the surface of the coffee cup and took a sip. The Command Group post-exercise criticism session had broken up, and he was *still* chilled from the last two days of winter maneuvers. Sighing, he sank back in the chair and looked around the cave, inhaling the scents of wet wool and limestone and coffee.

It's not the cold out there, it's the bloody damp, he thought. Thick snow, and more coming when you least expected it. All made harder by the draining pull of heavy gravity.

The inside of the base was all well back from the entrances, which meant it was not much more dank and chill than it had been in summer. Dimly lit by a few glowtubes stapled to the rock, and if you wanted to get warm you went to your room and moved the heater in under the blankets with you. There were heat sensors all over, and thermal camouflage discipline was enforced with a ferocious disregard for the privileges of rank. The officers were all bundled to the ears . . . *Not a bad lot,* he thought. Friendly enough now that he had proven himself able to keep up and not one to presume on a consort's influence. *Hard men, though,* he decided, studying their faces. *Dangerous men.* Which was all right with The Honorable Geoffrey Niles, since he had always aspired to being a hard and dangerous man himself.

Not exactly top-hole, though, these johnnies. Not gentlemen at all. Except for a couple of the ex-CD types like von Reuter and he suspected they had been broken out of the service. It was the first time he had ever associated with members of the lower classes so intimately, except with servants. Strange, in some ways; rather like being in the monkey-house at the zoo. They were intelligent enough, a few of them even well-read, but they simply had very little in common, from backgrounds so alien.

Still, I feel good, he decided. The past month and a half had been the hardest work he had ever done, physically and mentally. He felt hard and fit from the relentless drill; balanced and confident inside. *For once nobody gives a damn who my pater or Great-Uncle is,* he thought. *They don't even know.* Whatever respect he had won here was his and his alone.

Not to mention, he mused happily, looking over at Skilly. She was talking to von Reuter, the artillery specialist, probably about the latest shipment from offworld and the wonderful surprises it had brought. She felt his gaze and flashed him a smile; he returned it and raised his cup.

"Field Prime," the orderly said. Skilly raised a hand to stay von Reuter. "The consultant"—*mercenary* was not a word the Spartan People's Liberation Army used for its off-planet helpers—"says there's a priority message for you, ma'am."

Skida's stance did not change, but Niles knew her well enough now to see the sudden tension in her leopard gracefulness. Conversation died as she stalked out of the cave and into the next chamber. A thick waiting descended, until a scream rang out.

Niles blinked. He knew that exultant catamount screech very well, and the usual cause for it, but somehow he doubted Skilly was having an orgasm in the radio shack. The others exchanged glances, grins; Two-knife turned and slammed the heel of one palm into the rock, manic exuberance from him. When the guerrilla commander stalked back into the room it fairly crackled from her. "The mountain has moved! *They took the bait!*" She shoved one fist into the air. "Long live the Revolution!"

Niles felt his skin tighten; it was an eerie sensation, as if he was trying to bristle like a mastiff that had caught the scent. Words ran through his mind, ancient words—

> *But word is gane to the land sergeant,*
> *In Askerton where that he lay—*
> *"The deer that ye hae coursed sae lang*
> *Is seen into the Waste this day."*

And perhaps it was wrong to think so of hunting men, but at this moment there was no place in the human universe he would rather be.

The officers stood and cried her hail; out of conviction, or for sheer relief that the waiting was ended. When she spoke again it was with crisp decision.

"General alert. Group Leaders, concentration points as per plan Triphammer. Takadi"—directed at the Meijian liaison and technical expert—"get your surprises ready. Two-knife, we start reeling in their little picnic parties as soon as we sure they not modifying their plan. After that, first thing Skilly wants is to hurry them up a little and put them off-balance. Senior Group Leader Niles, you take—"

✧   ✧   ✧

The militia battalion commanders of Operation Scrub Brush, Task Force Erwin, were gathered around the command caravan with their staffs and the RSI officers; Owensford was using its internal map-projector on the dropped rear ramp of the converted APC.

"And you'll need observation posts here, here and here," he said to Morrentes, the major in charge of the stayback force at the bridgehead, pointing to positions on the map in a semicircle about the landing stage. High ground for calling in fire.

It was nightfall on the Rhyndakos, but there were arc-lights playing on the improvised landing stage, as men surged off the barges and manhandled equipment through roots and mud and onto firm ground; mules were being led down ramps, and their mournful braying echoed along the silent banks of the river. Empty barges were lashed together into makeshift docks covered with planking brought along for the purpose, and in the middle of the hundred-meter width of the river steamboats were maneuvering to bring their strings to the outermost links. Wheels and hooves trundled thunder-hollow as the Brotherhood Citizen-soldiers poured onto the banks. There was an occasional sharp *crack* as someone felled a tree with a string of detcord around the base, and the snarl of chainsaws. Two militia infantry battalions were digging in around the bridgehead; cleared fire zones, trenches, log-and-dirt bunkers, machine gun nests and revetments for their mortars, minefields and wire. A corduroy road had been laid down from the bluff to the water's edge, and the last of the marching column's equipment was being trundled up and loaded onto the waiting mules.

"I'll run a practice-fire program," the Brotherhood officer said thoughtfully. "We'll do some selective felling and booby-trapping out a klick or so from our perimeter."

Behind him a Legion technician squeezed a small plastic bulb. It inflated into a neutral-colored sphere the size of two beachballs; he slung a piece of plastic machinery beneath it, fastened it to a spool of wire the size of thread and let it unreel as the balloon rose.

"That'll give you real-time overhead surveillance," Owensford continued. A small camera-pickup, with the optical processor relatively safe down at the bottom; hence the balloon units were so cheap you could use them prodigally. "Lace the woods around here with communications thread and cameras, it'll make your perimeter security more redundant. We're going to spike camouflaged laser-relays to the trees, so we'll have a way of talking to you without breaking radio silence. This base is absolutely crucial. Keep the drones ready, but don't use them unless you have to."

Major Morrentes was a rancher, a man of medium height with a weathered tan and the bouncy rounded muscularity that second-and third-generation Spartans seemed to have.

"Still wish I was going with you, Colonel," he said ruefully. His lips lost what appeared to be a habitual smile. "My spread's just down from Dodona; they killed two of my vaqueros, good men and Phraetrie brothers, last spring. Not to mention the stock run off and stolen or equipment destroyed, and the convicts who took my boat and came here, I think."

"You may see some action, Major," Owensford said. It was a little disturbing, the sullen anger the Brotherhood soldiers felt toward their opponents. *You've been a mercenary too long,* he thought. *Remember what a grudge-fight is like.* "Just don't forget that your primary tasking here is to keep the river open behind us."

"Sir."

"Now, the rest of us are advancing by battalion columns."

The lead element would be a battalion of the First RSI, heavily reinforced. Twelve of the von Alderheim armored cars, and two dozen of the APCs. Not carrying infantry, but towing heavy mortars, fuel, counterbattery radar and communications gear from the Legion stocks. A command car on the same model, with his staff and gear. Then the rest of the First Battalion, First RSI; eight hundred men, more or less, with their supplies on pack-mules. Six more battalions of first-line militia, seven to nine hundred men each. Enough distance between to give each other room and cover a reasonable amount of space, close enough for immediate mutual support if—when—they ran into something.

"Every half-day's march"—fifteen kilometers, more or less—"we'll drop off one company and two mortar batteries on these locations." Hilltops with good fields of fire, available water, and favorable placing to act as patrol bases. "With rocket-assist, the heavy mortars will give overlapping fields of fire all along the route. As reinforcements come in upriver, we feed them up the line and relieve the dropoff units to rejoin their battalions. Task Forces Wingate and *Till Eulengenspiegel* will be doing likewise."

"By the time we reach here"—he placed a spot of light about three hundred and twenty kilometers north—"the enemy'll have to either fight or run; in either case, our satellite observation will spot them as soon as they're forced to move substantial units and we can reconcentrate and either destroy them or chase them west into the Drakon Range foothills. They've evidently got excellent overhead surveillance security, but the fact they haven't been spotted much puts an upper limit on possible numbers."

Unlikely that the Royalist force would be able to catch the guerrillas, if the insurgents abandoned their heavy equipment, although he had brought enough horses to equip a substantial force of mounted infantry in that event. But of course if they captured or destroyed the enemy equipment, the exercise would be a success no matter what else was accomplished.

"That done, we can convert some of our firebases into permanent patrol outposts, rotate the militia garrisons as needed, and move the First and the other Field Force regiments in to clean more territory." Guerrillas would still be able to infiltrate, but it would be infinitely more difficult and dangerous once they had to start from bases further away from the Eurotas. "Any questions?"

"Sir." Captain Prince Lysander, code name Kicker Six, who would be leading the scout element. "It's unlikely we have tactical or strategic surprise." Impossible, with troops steaming up the river from Sparta City and militia being mobilized all through this part of the Middle Valley. "Why haven't the rebels done anything yet?"

"I don't know, Captain. I expect we will find out presently."

"We are facing a three-pronged attack," von Reuter said, in accented Anglic with the slightly pedantic twist of a CD veteran. "North, center and south, as vas indicated by our preliminary intelligence. Probably due to our disinformation, the main *schwerepunkt* is in the south, with the northerly force acting as a mobile anvil and the central pozzibly as a strike reserve."

His pointer moved from opposite Olynthos in the north to the middle Rhyndakos in the south, stopping on the way to tap at the box-figures representing the Royalist forces' central landing on the right bank of the Eurotas. "Mobilized militia units are standing by on t'Eurotas to act as blocking forces and general reserve, with mobile mechanized reserves in Olynthos and Dodona.

"Zis attack vill take the form of a closing concentric ring, attempting to constrict our movements. The elements are widely spaced—distances of several hundred kilometers—and t' enemy is relying on superior communications and reconnaissance to immobilize us and prevent our timely concentration against any of his columns, and superior artillery and command and control to overpower zose units of our forces he does encounter. Current intelligence indicates the spearheads of each enemy column are composed of troops of Falkenberg's Legion and the First RSI, wit' substantial numbers of Brotherhood militia in support. Total enemy attack forces are in the range of fourteen to seventeen battalions."

He clicked heels and handed the pointer to Skilly. Niles felt a tightly controlled excitement as she leaned forward into the light that shone over the map table; beyond her the caves of Base One were a kicked anthill of activity as the Helots prepared to go to war.

"Thank you, Senior Group Leader," she said seriously. "OK. We know more than the Royalists think we know; they haven't changed their battle plan much and we going implement the first contingency for Triphammer."

The pointer skipped south. "This column under Owensford is most important one. They coming through pretty thick country, not too many ways they can go. Group Leader Niles, you take the fast reaction force and stop their lead elements here." She stabbed the pointer into a spot about five days march from the Rhyndakos. "Day before that, they have to commit to one of three alternative pathways, you got twenty hours or so to get ready. That get them good and far from base; when they hot and bothered dealing with you, Skilly will swing in with the forces from the bases along the route, the Base One elements, and the prepositioned equipment.

"Von Reuter, you has the northern wing. They got more mechanized stuff there and the ground more open, but looks like heavy weather. We wants them in good and deep so we can delay them once the southern column is disposed with. You—"

The briefing continued, the officers mostly silent, scribbling an occasional note on their pads; there was a brief question-and-answer session period.

"So," Skida said at last. "Now, you, Tenjiro." The Meijian mercenary bowed slightly. "When we come in contact, they going know we fudging the recon satellite data if they got reports from their troops and the pictures doan show. You gets the Skysweepers ready. Niles," she continued, "Tenjiro's people feeding you the locations of the Royalist SAS teams as they reports. Niles, everyone, Skilly really upset if those teams make any contacts. Be ready to take them out just before we is engaged. Be sure to send enough stuff to do it right."

"Do it right," Niles said. "I can tell you those people are good." They had driven Barton to distraction on Tanith. "We're not going to take them out with any small units."

"So send big ones. Skilly think they like those people, gonna hurt them when they die."

Niles nodded assent.

"Field Prime," one of the other officers said. "They're going to know we're in their communications link when we silence the SAS people. And once the satellites are down, we're as blind as they are to further movement."

"Balance of advantage to us," Skilly said. She bent the pointer between strong brown fingers, looking down at the map with a hungry expression. "We gots their basic positions, and our fixed sensors. They going to be off-balance and hitting air." She raised her head, met their eyes; Niles felt a slight shiver at the feline intensity of it.

"One last thing Skilly want clear: we not fighting for territory, that *their* game. This going to be a long war; unfair one, too. So long as we doan lose, we win; so long as they doan win, they lose. Hit them hard, hurt them—the Brotherhoods particular—but preserving your force is maximum priority." A deep breath. "Let's do it. Let's *go*."

"Ready to move out, sir," Lysander said.

"All right, Prince Captain," Owensford said, nodding. "Find them, laddie. We'll be right behind if you run into trouble. Good hunting."

Lysander saluted and turned. The men of his company rose to their feet silently, weapons cradled across their chests. One hundred and twenty, a fifth of them seconded Legionnaires, because this was point duty and crucial. Bulky and anonymous, the gray of their fleece-lined parkas and trousers and body-armor hidden by the mottled-white winter camouflage coveralls. Bulbous helmets framed their faces; the mercenaries and officers were wearing Legion gear, with its complex mapping and communications capacity, the sound and light amplifiers; the ordinary First RSI troopers made do with a built-in radio and nightsight goggles. Everyone had heavy packs, half their own mass or more, because no mules were coming with *them*.

Marius's mules, he thought. *That's what Roman soldiers called themselves.* After Gaius Marius reformed the Republic's army around 100 BC, abolishing the cumbersome baggage trains and giving every legionnaire a bone-crushing load. *Some things in war never change.*

The dying didn't change either.

You'll be in tight-beam communication via the aircraft, and you can't get lost, Lysander told himself. With aviation assets so sparse the seismic-mapping units were doing double and triple duty, reconnaissance and forward-supply as well. Still, they had satellite communications and navigation, and good photomaps.

I wonder how Falkenberg felt the first time he led troops out. Was he scared? Interesting. It's worse this time than back on Tanith. On Tanith it was just me and Harv I'd kill if I mucked it up.

"Move it out," he called; the platoon commanders and NCOs echoed him. The first platoon filed into the waiting woods, and in less than a minute were totally invisible. "Follow me. With our shields or on them, brothers." *Nothing ahead of us but the SAS teams,* he thought; it was a lonely feeling, almost as lonely as the weight of command on painfully inexperienced shoulders. *If there was anything big, the satellite's IR scanners or the SAS would have caught it. And you've got a whole battalion of the Regiment behind you.*

Harv closed up beside him, moving easily under the burden of pack and communications gear. He pulled the screen down before his face and keyed it to light-enhancement; they moved off into the deeper darkness under the trees, white shadows against the night.

Sergeant Taras Hamilton Miscowsky handed out the packets of pemmican, and the other members of his SAS squad huddled together in the lee of the fallen oak; his tarp had been rigged over the roots to cover the hollow made where the big tree had toppled. Doctrine said it was possible to light a well-shielded mini-stove buried in the earth, and God knew some coffee or tea would be welcome with the wet cold, but he was taking no chances right now.

He looked out into the night-black woods. *Dark as a tax-farmer's soul,* he thought.

The forest around him would have looked half familiar and oddly strange to someone used to the temperate zone of Earth; the trees were of too uniform an age, none more than seventy or eighty years. Too thickly grown with an undergrowth that included everything from briars to feral rosebushes, and an occasional patch of native pseudomoss with an olive-gray tint fighting its losing battle against the invading grass. Many of the trees had fallen, grown too high and spindly to bear a gravity a fifth again as high as that for which their genes prepared them. *Chaotic ecology,* was what the briefing veedisks had said.

None of it bothered Sergeant Miscowsky; he had been born on Haven, where it was always cold and almost always very dry and all forests were equally alien to him, problems to be learned and solved.

What *was* bothering him was the fact that he had discovered nothing in a week's scouting. Nothing, zip, nada, zilch. He looked at his wrist. 0130 hours, coming upon time to report.

"Andy, rig the tightbeam," he said.

Andy Owassee was a Legion veteran, who'd made the SAS just before they left Tanith. The other two were locals. Good men, outbackers who'd done a lot of hunting, but he wished he had more veterans with him, the men who'd gone with the bulk of the Legion to New Washington.

"Isn't that a risk?" one of the RSI newlies asked; in a whisper, mouth pointed down.

"Not much," Miscowsky said. "Line of sight from the blimp." There were several patrolling along the Eurotas northeast of here. "Nothin' sent back or forth except clicks, until they lock in—feedback loop. And it's all coded anyway." Tightbeam to the blimp, blimp to satellite, then satellite to whoever needed to hear it.

Out in the dark something yowled. *Something big and hungry,* Miscowsky thought. At that, at least the local predators didn't hide in mudholes to sink their fangs in your ass as you stepped over like the ones on Tanith. Earth stock anyway, and Earth carnivores were all descended from a million years of ancestors with the sense to avoid humans.

"Got it, Sarge," Owassee said, handing the noncom a thread-thin optical fiber link; he plugged it into a socket on the inside rim of his helmet, and then ducked back outside to the watch position.

"Close the tarp," Miscowsky ordered. They made sure it was light-tight, and then the sergeant touched the side of his helmet. It projected a low-light map of the terrain on the poncho folded over the uneven dirt floor of the hollow.

"Cap'n Mace? Mic-four-niner, location"—he touched the map his helmet was projecting, automatically sending the coordinates—"over."

"Reading you, Mic-four-niner. Signs of life?"

"Nothin', sir, and I'm stone worried. Plenty of animals"— they had blundered almost into a deeryard with a hundred or so whitetails—"and sign, shod hooves and old fires, might be hunters or if it's enemy then they police up real careful."

They had found a body at the bottom of a sinkhole, about a year dead and looking as if nothing had gotten to it but the ants; the leg bones were broken in four places, and there were a few empty cans around it.

"This place is like a Swiss cheese for caves and holes, sir," Miscowsky went on. He paused. "Yes, sir, I know it's a big search zone but it's as if we're moving in an empty bubble. I think it's a dance, Skipper. They're playing with us."

"What's your situation?"

"Camped high. Dug in. Perimeter gear out. I been running scared all week, and—"

"*Sarge. Sound.*"

All three men froze, only Miscowsky's hand going to the tarp. He touched his helmet to cycle the audio pickups to maximum gain and background filter; the officer at the other end had caught the alarm and waited, silent on the circuit. The noncom closed his eyes to focus his senses.

Creaking, wind, somewhere far off the thud of animal hooves. Then a crackle . . . *might be a branch breaking in the wind.* Rubbing sounds, and a tear of cloth. A muffled metallic click; some dickhead waiting until too late to take off the safety. "Got something on pickup. Three hundred forty meters bearing two-nine-five. There's another. Four hundred forty-five bearing one-seven-five."

"They all around you?"

"May be."

"Stand by one."

"Hartley here," a voice said. "You're sure?"

"Sure enough."

"Call it off."

"Fire mission. Offset three hundred forty, bearing two-niner-five, moving. Offset four hundred forty-five, bearing one-seven-five, stationary. More to come."

"On the way."

A long pause, then a flare of light somewhere off toward battalion. A big rocket flashed high, arced toward them.

"Comin' in, peg 'em."

Miscowsky scanned the area below him. "Goddam," he muttered. There were fifty men closing in. "It's a bloody damned race," he said.

"Think they got us located?" Owassee asked.

"Maybe not." Miscowsky began setting in ranges and offset bearings on his sleeve console. "Gonna be close—ah." A timer glowed softly on his sleeve. Fifty-five seconds. Fifty-four.

"Impact in fifty seconds. Estimate where they'll be when the balloon goes up." He grinned wolfishly.

"Kicker Six," the voice said softly in Lysander's ear. "Third Platoon here. We found a mine."

"Halt," Lysander said, on the unit push. "Perimeter, defensive." The first thing but foot and hoofprints they had found in three days' march.

Ahead of him and to either side, men stopped and melted into invisibility. Behind fallen logs, in the shadow of bushes, simply sinking into snow until only their eyes and the white-painted muzzles of their weapons showed. There was very little noise; the odd crunching sound, a few clicks as the team-served weapons set up. He and Harv went to one knee, waiting until the guide from Third Platoon came. The trooper gave a hand-signal from twenty meters; they followed him in silence, from cover to cover. The last three hundred meters they did on their bellies.

"Sir," the junior lieutenant breathed as they crawled into the lee of a big beech; the snow was thin here, high on the other side of the tree where the prevailing east wind piled it. Ice hung from the thick branches in stalactites, legacy of what had probably been the last thaw of the year, up here in the hills.

"Monitor Andriotti spotted it."

Andriotti was a Legionnaire, a man with a dark face and scars that ran down it into the neckline of his parka. Forty years old, perhaps fifty. Alert, but with a phlegmatic resignation that went deeper than words could reach.

"Zur," he said; there was a thick accent to his words, but it was of no particular place. The accent of a man who has spent his adult life speaking Anglic as a *lingua franca* with others also not born to it. "Tere. Snow is just off the tripwire between t'ose trees."

Lysander cycled his faceplate to IR; nothing, the booby trap was at ambient, which meant it had been here for a while. He risked a brief burst of ultrasound, then froze the image. A curved plate resting on a low tripod in a clump of leafless thorny bush, impossible to spot with the naked eye. The wire ran at ankle-height, in a triangle secured at the corners to two trees five meters apart by plastic eyebolts screwed into the bark. The gap was the obvious route for anyone who didn't want to crash through brush, and anyone who had would have been shredded by thousands of fléchettes.

"All units," he said. "Remain in place and look for mines.

I don't have to tell you to be careful. Dig in. Full perimeter defence." Never a mistake to dig, if you had to stop. The books said minefields and other obstacles were primarily useful to pin a force so that it could be attacked.

"Com, patch me through to Command."

"How many?" Peter Owensford asked as Mace finished. *Contact. This is it.*

"Sir, Miscowsky and his team are under attack by at least a company. Team Z-2 doesn't report. A-1 and A-2 report all nominal. Something coming in—Deighton's under attack. And Laramie."

"Deighton, Laramie and Miscowsky. And Katz doesn't report. Bingo," Owensford said. "Well, we sent them out to find something."

Find it and kill it. Each of the SAS teams carried directional beaming equipment that could feed the team's coordinates, plus an offset, to incoming Thoth missiles. Thoth was normally launched by aircraft kept just at the team's horizon, but in this case there weren't any airplanes for that, so the birds were lofted by solid rockets. That could be expensive if the birds went out and there were no targets, but Peter didn't think that would be the problem here.

"Jamming. We're getting jammed," Mace said.

"Jamming," Owensford acknowledged. "Well, we expected it after the Spartosky. Loft the anti-radiation missiles. And keep lofting Thoth support." Thoth missiles depended on a direct line of sight communication, and employed an autocorrelation system that was nearly impossible to jam, even with brute force.

"Aye aye."

Owensford studied the map. Miscowsky was Z-1, ranging in ahead of the column of Royal troops heading north from the Rhyndakos, Katz with Z-2 likewise. T-1 and T-2 were with the central column, punching in directly west from a convenient bend in the Eurotas. A-1 and A-2 with the northern force, pressing southeast from Olynthos.

"They knew where to look," Peter said aloud. He thought about the implications of that. There was only one way they could have known that well. He turned to his adjutant, Andy Lahr. "Andy, they knew where to look. You agree?"

"Yes, sir."

"Jericho. Get the word out, all units, Jericho."

"Roger."

Peter picked up the microphone. "Mace, broadcast to all of your units. Code Jericho. Repeat, Code Jericho. Got that?"

"Roger. Code Jericho."

"Message, Captain." Communications Sergeant Masterson spoke urgently.

Lysander frowned. "I need to talk to headquarters—"

"They're broadcasting, sir. Jericho. Code Jericho."

"Jericho."

"Yes, sir. I got special orders on that one—"

"I know," Lysander said. "All right. Acknowledge."

"Acknowledge Jericho," the comm sergeant said. "I say again, we acknowledge Jericho. All units Task Force Candle Four, command override, your word is Jericho, Code Jericho. I say again, Code Jericho."

Jericho, Lysander thought. Assume that all transmissions are monitored by enemy. Assume that all ciphers and encryptions are compromised. All communication in future to be by code book, or in clear with enemy presumed listening.

"We're getting another," Masterson said. "This one's just for us. Kicker Six, Code Dove Hill. Code Dove Hill."

"Right. Thank you." Lysander touched his sleeve console and typed rapidly. "DOVE HILL."

"ASSUME ENEMY IN GREATER STRENGTH THAN ANTICIPATED." "Bennington," Masterson said. "Wait a second, that's not for us. Here's ours. Saratoga. Tiger. I say again, saratoga, tiger."

"SARATOGA," Lysander typed.

"DIG IN AND PUNISH THE ENEMY. UNLIMITED FIRE SUPPORT AUTHORIZED."

"TIGER," he typed.

"GOD BLESS US, THERE'S NONE LIKE US."

"All right," Owensford said. "Code books from here on." And thank God for a suspicious mind. Codes were not convenient. You couldn't say anything you hadn't thought of in advance and put in the code book—or personal data base, as the case might be—but they did have the advantage of being unbreakable. You'd have to capture a pocket computer intact, and even that wouldn't help for long, since the code word meanings changed from day to day and unit to unit.

"Code this," Owensford told Andy Lahr. "Teams A-1 and A-2 are to shift position and maintain radio silence unless attacked. Their primary mission is to get home alive. Relay message to Task Force *Till Eulengenspiegel*—" the central column "—entrench in place, stand by to call in Thoth, and hurt the enemy."

That wouldn't take long, since the central column was a feint, a company-strength unit making enough radio noise for a battalion. Of course a feint backed by enough callable fire-power was more trap than feint . . .

"Task Force Wingate is to shift to fallback communications and maintain nominal transmission. Maximum alert; reduce movement, prepare for meeting engagement."

"Righto."

The interlock chimed, and the com technical looked up from his board at the rear of the command-car's hull.

"Sir, priority report from Captain Collins."

"Put him through. Kicker Six, you understand Jericho?"

"Roger Jericho, sir. Sir, I've got multiple detection sensor and tripwire-detonated mine sightings all along my line of advance here."

"Merry times." Owensford looked down at his map; wheeled vehicles could advance through this section of the southern Dales, only about four-tenths of the ground was under for-est, but if you counted that and very broken terrain it chan-neled an attack quite nicely. Channeled it down to about four alternative angles of approach within the fifty klicks on either side of the arms sighting that had started this whole affair.

"Check for command-detonated devices within your perim-eter, Lynn," he said.

"Shit, I never thought—sorry."

"Quite all right," Owensford said with a bleak smile. "We're only four klicks south. You have your orders, Kicker Six. Stand by one." He turned. "Andy, how do I say 'Use explosives to clear mines. Conserve troops.'?"

"GLOSSARY. HILDEBRAND."

"Got it. Captain, your codes are Glossary, I say again Glos-sary. Hildebrand. I say again Hildebrand."

"Roger. Glossary, Hildebrand. And TIGER to you, too. Out."

"Andy, check confirmation all units acknowledge condition Jericho," Peter said. "Then get me Task Force Atlas, Lieutenant-Colonel Barton." They were all wearing their Royal Army hats tonight, that was the central reserve, in Dodona. The line there at least was secure.

A wait of a few minutes. "Barton here. Ready to scramble."

"Ready. Scramble." There was a tell-tale sing-song background in his earpiece. "Scrambled."

"Scrambled," Barton confirmed. "OK. I've been following it."

"You get the same feeling I do, Ace?"

"That joyful, tingling sense of anticipation that comes just before you jam your dick into the garbage grinder? Yeah."

"How do you figure it?"

"Could be either an agent in place, a pirate tap in the satellite, or both. They know more than we thought, and they've got more force than we expected."

There was no visual link, but it took no imagination for Peter to see Barton's face, cynical grin, toothpick moving rapidly from one side of his mouth to the other. "Status of the reserves, Ace?"

"Nominal. Of course we're using up Thoth at a fearful rate, ditto ARM."

"Any effect?"

"Sure. Their jamming's just about stopped, and Miscowsky and Katz are having a field day. Between them, they've taken out the equivalent of a battalion."

"Think we got all their antennas?"

"Hell, no."

"Yeah, I agree," Peter said.

Owensford looked at the map again. Four Brotherhood battalions with his Task Force Erwin column in the south, and the reinforced battalion of the First RSI. The same with Task Force Wingate in the north. One company with the feint. The mechanized battalion of the First outside Olynthos with two squadrons of armored cars, ready to back up Wingate. Four companies of Legion troops in Dodona, with all the ground-effect transport that the Middle Valley could provide, fast enough to reinforce *either* Wingate *or* Erwin. On the map the advancing columns looked like the jaws of a beast, closing around the south-central Dales. On the ground it was fewer than ten thousand men moving through an area of rough terrain larger than many countries back on Earth.

Plenty of troops in reserve, if you counted the militia, Ace had been working miracles with them. Another full brigade of first-line mobilized Brotherhood fighters along the river ready to intervene if it must, and the twenty thousand or so of the second-line were standing to arms on the defensive, giving him a secure base. Five times that number of third-line, women and older men, not field units but ready to fight and doing noncombatant work. None of them very mobile, unfortunately. Sparta's blessing and curse, the Eurotas; it made bulk transport in the settled regions so easy that there was an overwhelming temptation to put off developing a ground-transport infrastructure.

Should I have taken more of the militia in with me? he thought. Then: *no, the reasons are still valid.* Risky enough to have them standing by as emergency reserves.

Good militia were still part-time troops, unpracticed in large-unit maneuvers. The Brotherhood fighters were first-rate in their own neighborhoods. That was one reason nobody had ever taken a serious crack at Sparta, the Brotherhoods could field better than a third of a million at a pinch. The problem with that Swiss Militia system was that if you called everyone to arms, there was no one left to do the work; and Sparta's economy was in bad enough shape as it was.

Losing too many of them could be absolutely fatal; at a pinch, Sparta could stand heavy casualties to its offensive force, but the Brotherhoods were the iron frame that kept this section of the Valley under government control.

"All right, we probe, but *carefully*," he said at last. "This operation is primarily a reconnaissance in force, anyway." The best way to learn about an opponent was to fight him. "It all depends on what they've got and how good it is. We've already learned something about that."

"Yeah; they're pretty good, and they've got a secure communications system in there. Which is more than we do." Owensford nodded thoughtfully; it looked unpleasantly like the enemy had been preparing this for years. The whole of the Dales could be linked together with optical thread-cable and permanent line-of-sight stuff.

"The main thing is not to get hurt," Peter said. "Get that out to all units. If the other guys want to play, dig in and pound them. They're better than we thought they were, but they're still just light infantry.

"Meanwhile, let the SAS teams come home, but keep sending them fire support as long as they can spot targets. After all, it's what they're out there for."

"I ain't worried about them," Barton said. "But there's something sour about this whole operation."

"I got that feeling too."

"And we're blind. Pete, I suggest we wait for new satellite pix before we commit."

"Trust them?" Owensford asked innocently.

"Oh. Now that you mention it, no. Guess I don't."

"So we have to try something else. Bring up the birds; one with me, one with Task Force Wingate. Keep them well back." Tiltrotor VTOL aircraft, commandeered from the RSMP for the seismic-mapping project. They could transport a complete platoon of infantry; right now they were crammed with other stuff. It would not do to put them in harm's way, of course. Aircraft over a battlefield had been an impossibility since good light seeker rockets became common. The enemy certainly had those.

"You're the boss," Barton said.

"Bring up, code—" He did a quick search on his data base. "The code is Babylon."

"Babylon." A pause. "Babylon it is. Anything else?"

"That's it."

"Task Force Atlas, out."

"Out," Peter said.

Next. "Andy, let Heavy Weapons company dig in and prepare to fire support missions. Have Scout company pull all forward units inside artillery support range." Not many proper guns, most of it was big mortars, but still enough range once the scouts drew in.

"Roger. SAS teams report enemy activity slacking off."

Peter glanced at the munitions expenditure readouts. "I should bloody hope so. Haven't you got a better report than that?"

"Miscowsky reports 'DYANAMO.' That translates as 'heavily engaged.' "

"Other teams?"

"Much the same. Heard from Katz finally. His report prior to acknowledging Jericho was 'JESUS CHRIST!' Now reports, 'Heavily engaged, am hurting enemy.' "

"Good." *The SAS teams are doing their job, but I don't like this. Ace doesn't either.* "Bring them home. Send out escort patrols to assist."

"Suggestion," Captain Lahr said.

"Spill it."

"This is all by the book," Lahr said. "They'll set up ambushes for the escorts, sure as hell."

"Gotcha. Yeah, send an SAS Thoth controller along with each escort team. With luck they'll find some targets going in while the teams kick ass coming out."

"Roger that."

"Now get me Collins again."

"Can't guarantee security."

"Understood."

"Coming up," Andy Lahr said.

There was a pause. "Kicker Six here."

"Jericho."

"Understood."

"Captain, I need an estimate of how far that mine obstacle stretches. . . ."

"About five hundred meters to my left, sir; three hundred to the right, and it's anchored in a ravine. About fifty to a hundred meters thick. We estimate a minimum of three hours to clear a path suitable for vehicles."

"Stand by one." Owensford studied the map. The western end of the minefield ran down toward a valley; there was a lip to that hill, a traversable slope beyond the mines, and then broken wooded ground down to the low point.

What was it Ace said about garbage grinders? That gap might as well have a sign on it, "Please insert male generative organ here." *Well, a trap you know is a trap is no trap.*

"Stand by for orders," Peter said.

No point in having Collins waste troops on mines. Use fuel-aid to blast hell out of the area and be done with it. The main thing was to stay out of trouble. Owensford typed orders.

"DIG IN. STAY DUG IN UNTIL MINEFIELDS CLEARED. USE ARTILLERY AND HE TO CLEAR MINE AREA. DONT RISK TROOPS ON MINES. PREPARE TO PUNISH ENEMY ATTACK-ERS."

"Andy, put this through the data base and give me the codes. Thanks."

"OK. Attention to orders. Code DECEMBER. Repeat December. Code TRILOGY. Repeat Trilogy. Code ELK HILL. Repeat Elk Hill."

"DECEMBER, TRILOGY, ELK HILL. Roger."

"Code TIGER."

"Tiger it is."

"Okey Doke. Out." Peter Owensford reached up and undogged the hatch, climbing up to stand with head and shoulders in the chill air. Cythera was up, shedding patchy moonlight through scud clouds. He cycled the facemask until the scene had a depthless brightness. The main body of Task Force Erwin was moving at the equivalent of a quick walk, no more. A dozen armored cars were leapfrogging forward, moving in spurts and then waiting in hull-down positions while the flanking infantry companies swept through the wooded areas to either side in skirmish line; behind both the bulk of the expeditionary force marched in company columns, enclosing their mule-born supply trains.

That changed even as he watched. The APCs halted and spilled their eight-man crews to begin setting up the heavy weapons. Shovels and the 'dozer blade of the engineering vehicle began preparing firing positions for the mortars, well spaced out and downslope from the crest. Still further down, the Headquarters troops were digging in as well, spider-holes and pits for their heavy machine guns and perimeter gatlings.

"Sir, Senior Lieutenant Fissop." The commander of the HQ company. "He requests permission to blow standing timber for entrenchment purposes."

"By all means," Owensford said, studying his map again.
Assume there's a blocking force near that minefield, he
thought. *Can't be too large. Now, what avenues of attack are
there . . . ahh.*

"Message to Third Brotherhood. Close up to two klicks west
of us and advance using this ridge"—his light-pencil traced it—
"having his mortars ready for support"—mule-born 125mms—
"and begin a probe here." That ought to put them right behind
whoever was waiting for him to swing around the mines.

"Twenty-Second is to maintain distance on the Third's left,
ready to move in support. Eighteenth is to close up to within
five klicks to our rear, and Fifty-first to deploy in place for
the moment on the right." A good well-rounded position, ready
to attack, retreat or switch front at need, and capable of
interdicting the low covered ground on all sides.

"Sir, CO Task Force Wingate."

"Patch."

"Slater here," a familiar voice said.

"Copy, George," Owensford said.

"I've run into a spot of trouble."

"Details?"

"Mines, snipers and teams of rocket launchers infiltrating
between my columns. Lost two armored cars and about fifteen casualties; we've counted about five times that in enemy
dead. They're willing to take casualties to hurt us."

"Interesting."

"Isn't it? Also, two of my forward support bases along
the route back report harassing fire from mortars. One twenty-
five millimeter stuff, shoot-and-scoot, they're working
counterbombardment."

With locally made counterbattery radars; Owensford had no
special confidence in them. Single-frequency, and the innards
were positively neolithic, hand-assembled transistors and
chipboards salvaged from imported consumer electronics.

"Stand by for orders." He looked up "Conserve Ammuni-
tion" and "Fire if target under observation and located." "Code
HAWKWOOD. Repeat Hawkwood. Code ARAGON. Repeat
Aragon."

"HAWKWOQD. ARAGON. Roger."

"Stand by one."

"Roger."

"Intelligence. What's on Elint?" Electronic traffic interception.

"Nothing, sir."

There were ways to handle movement without any radio

traffic at all, but not many. One way was to move everything according to a prearranged plan. Like terrorists. That would be interesting. He switched back to the commander of the northern column.

"We'll know more in a bit. Hop to it."

"Roger. Wingate, out."

"Come on, birdie," Owensford murmured to himself. "Because here I sit, bloody blind."

"Senior Group Leader," the communications tech said, "Base One reports there was a three-minute lapse in enemy satellite-link commo immediately after the SAS teams were attacked. They are now using alternates, and code book."

"Thank you," Geoffrey Niles said. "Results?"

"Heavy casualties, sir. The SAS teams are calling down some sort of smart weapon bombardment, and they're all well dug-in. They've shredded our people, some have already cut and run." He touched the earphone of his headset. "The consultants say the weapons are being lofted by short-range rockets from the main enemy columns. Antiradiation missiles are giving our jamming serious problems."

"Damn." He frowned; overrunning the SAS teams would have been a significant blow to the enemy's capacities. Skilly's orders had been quite specific, though. "Break off the attacks. They'll probably try to send someone to pull the scouts out. Have the attack teams set ambushes on the likely approach paths. Otherwise, stay out of visual observation range and harass with mortar fire."

"Counterbattery hits our mortar people every time they fire."

"Poor babies." Niles looked at his chronometer; 0200. "Time to surveillance satellite overpass?"

"One hour twenty-seven minutes, sir." A pause. "Sir, Base One reports two enemy aircraft are lifting off-schedule from Olynthos and Dodona." They had agents in place in both towns. All you needed was someone with binoculars, and a zeroed-in laser transponder aimed at a spot in the hills to the west and south. A negligible chance of someone having detection gear in the path of a tight beam during the few seconds it was in use.

"Tiltrotors. Looks like they're heading for the rear zones to do Elint and remote-sensor interpretation." The pickups would be forward. "ETA forty minutes."

"Very good," he said with a fierce grin, looking back at the map. The enemy were quick on the uptake, but there were still things they didn't know. "I'm moving forward to take personal command of the blocking force. Sutchukil," he continued to his adjutant, "keep me notified of the status of the aircraft."

"Sir," the Thai transportee said; he was a short stocky man with a grin that never reached his eyes, an aristocrat and would-be artist shopped to BuReloc in some local power struggle.

Outside the tarp shelter it was growing rapidly colder in the gully under the light of the sinking moon; Niles stopped for a second to pull on his thin insulated gloves and fasten the top of his parka. Breath puffed white as the headquarters section fell in around him; there was little other movement in the rocky draw where they had left the vehicles. Those were simple frameworks of wood on skis, holding little but a light airship engine with rear-mounted propeller and a fuel tank. The troops' skis and the sleds that carried heavy equipment were stacked nearby, several layers thick against the rough limestone of the cliff wall.

"La joue commence," he murmured to himself.

CHAPTER ELEVEN

Crofton's Essays and Lectures in Military History (2nd Edition)

**Professor John Christian Falkenberg II:
Delivered at Sandhurst, August 22nd, 2087**

The nature of the societies which raise armies, the economic resources available to the state, and the nature and aims of the wars which the state wishes to, or fears it must, wage, are all mutually dependent.

Thus for the last two centuries of its existence, the Roman Republic kept an average of ten percent of its total free citizen population under arms, or half or more its adult males. This was an unprecedented accomplishment, made possible in a preindustrial world only by mass plunder of the whole Mediterranean world—directly, by tribute, and through the importation of slave forced labor—and a very high degree of social cohesion. When Hannibal was at the gates of Rome and fifty thousand of Italy's soldiers lay dead on the field of Cannae, the Republic never even thought of yielding. New armies sprang up as if from the very earth, fueled by the bottomless well of patriotic citizen-yeomen. By contrast, under the Empire a mere three hundred thousand long-service professionals served to guard the frontiers of a defensive-minded state. No longer could the provinces be plundered to support a total-mobilization war effort, and it was precisely the aim of the Principate to depoliticize—and hence demilitarize—the citizenry. By the fifth century, relatively tiny barbarian armies of a few score thousands were wandering at will through the Imperial heartlands.

Eighteenth-century Europe saw another turn of the cycle. The "absolute" monarchies of the period brought limited wars, with limited means for limited aims. They had neither the power nor the wish to tax heavily or conscript; their armies were recruited from the economically marginal—aristocrats and gutter dregs—and waged war in a formalized, ritual minuet. A few years later the French Republic proclaimed the levee en masse, and the largest battle of the Napoleonic Wars involved nearly a million men. The cycle repeated itself with a vengence in the next century; in 1840 the combined armies of Hamburg, Bremen, Lubeck and the Grand Duchy of Oldenburg numbered some three thousand men. In 1914, those same territories contributed in excess of thirty thousand men to the forces of Imperial Germany, and replaced them several times over in the holocaust that followed.

Yet the wheel of history continues to turn. The CoDominium, ruling all Earth and at one time or another over one hundred colonized planets, never had more than five hundred thousand men under arms; during its rule, most national armies on Earth declined to the status of ceremonial guards or glorified riot police. Once more, stagnant oligarchies have nothing to gain by arming the masses; small, professional armies operating according to the Laws of War conduct limited conflicts to maintain a delicate sociopolitical balance. In the colonies and ex-colonies, important campaigns are decided by tiny forces of well-trained mercenaries or professional soldiers; a regiment here, a brigade there.

And now another turn of the wheel seems to be beginning.

If your officer's dead and the sergeants look white,
Remember it's ruin to run from a fight,
So take open order, lie down, and sit tight,
And wait for supports like a soldier.

"Task Force Wingate. Slater here." A buzzing in the background; scrambling, and Ace's people had rerouted the link though a newly laid cable up the riverbed to Olynthos. Everything through Legion equipment.

"Owensford here. What's the story, George?"

"A bit of a dog's breakfast, I'm afraid," the commander of the northern column said; Peter Owensford could hear a dull *crump . . . crump* in the background, and small-arms fire.

Dog's breakfast, he thought. One of Major Jeremy Savage's expressions. *And I wish he and Christian Johnny were in charge here instead of twenty light years away.*

"My central element ran into an infantry screen," Slater said. "Well placed; we had to deploy and put in a full attack, couldn't just brush them aside. Gave us a stiff fight and then moved back sharpish. We cut them up nicely, but then I went forward to try and keep them from breaking contact and we got caught by a mortar and bombardment rocket attack."

"Rockets?"

"One-twenty-seven mm's, the same type the Royals use." A six-tube launcher, in batteries of three. "Four batteries, widely spaced. Proximity fused, time-on-target with the mortars, and cursed well placed. Then the ones we'd been chasing came back at us, right on the heels of it, grenade and bayonet work for a while."

Owensford winced; that was a bad sign, that the enemy had troops willing to take casualties from their own artillery to push in an assault while the fire kept the defenders' heads down.

"Pretty much the same thing happened to the Forty-First Brotherhood." The militia unit on the far left flank of Task Force Wingate.

"They pursued until they were out of reach of the battalion on their right, with more enthusiasm than sense"—Owensford nodded; you wanted aggression, but only experience could temper it with caution—"and now they're leaguered and under attack from all sides. The enemy is trying to infiltrate squad-sized units and recoilless teams down the wooded vales between my units, and it's sopping up my riflemen to stop them, turning into a bloody dog-fight down there. Plus constant harassing fire from eighty-two mm's"—platoon level mortars—"and snipers behind every bush. I'm moving the Seventeenth Brotherhood up from reserve to help pull the Forty-first out of its hole and back to the main body, and putting the Tenth"—the unit on his immediate right—"into the low ground to work their way around the flank of the people ahead of me, while the Seventh drops back and covers us both on the right."

"Appraisal of the enemy?"

"Too damned good for comfort; not up to Legion standards, but good. Their equipment's about the same as the Royals, except their radar and radar countermeasures, which are better, probably as good as ours. Off-planet stuff. Chaff and jamming, so I'm returning the favor; they've got more visual observation right now, I'm working on it."

A gatling six-barrel went off somewhere near to the mike, a savage *brrrrrrrt-brrrrrrt* sound, a hail of bullets that would saw through trees.

"They know how to use their weapons, they've got discipline and good small-unit tactics," Slater continued. A wounded man screamed, a high endless sound suddenly cut off as if with a knife. "Not bothered by armor, either; they've got plenty of light recoilless stuff and unguided antitank rockets, and they're not afraid to get in close and try to use it. I've taken damned few unwounded prisoners."

A pause. "The Brotherhood people don't seem to have taken any prisoners at all, by the way."

Damn, damn, don't they understand it'll make the enemy fight harder? Owensford thought. He would have to do something about that.

"And whoever's in charge knows his hand from a hacksaw too. I'd swear there's a CoDominium Academy mind behind that fire mission."

"How many of them?"

"Difficult to say; they keep shooting down my spyeye balloons as fast as I put them up. At least a thousand, no more than two." Task Force Wingate would outnumber them by at least fifteen hundred men, possibly by twice that.

"I could fight through what's facing me," Slater continued, echoing Owensford's thoughts. "Why don't I think this is a good idea?"

"It's what they want you to do, of course. Bugger that. We're better set for a battle of attrition than they are. The one thing I haven't noticed in all this is logistics troops. They may be able to make infantrymen out of those street gangs, but they seem to be a bit short on supply clerks.

"Consolidate as soon as you've pulled the Forty-first out of its hole, and dig in. The mission's changed, George. To hell with moving across ground. The objective is to kill their cadres. Troops as good as those can't be all that plentiful, not to terrorists, so dig in and break their teeth. Before we're finished they'll have their battalion commanders out fighting like riflemen. And make them use up their munitions. This has just become a logistics war."

"Suppose they won't come at us?"

"They will. 'Enemy advance, we retreat. Enemy halt, we harass.' They'll think you're slowing down because you're beaten just like the Brotherhood troops," Peter said. "Let's encourage that thought. They've got some kind of complicated battle plan, and just for the moment I'd as soon they thought it was working. I particularly don't want them to think that either you or the Brotherhoods can mount an attack. And they'll think they have to attack before they run out of supplies. Or just to get ours."

"Gotcha."

"You're an anvil. Be a good one. When I've got recon I'll put some mobility back in this battle. For now they expect you to advance, so digging in will be a surprise. But be ready to advance again when I need you."

"Understood."

"Godspeed. Out."

"There, Senior Group Leader," the platoon leader of the guerilla advance element said, making a tiny hand motion through the improvised blind of thorny brush. "The rest of them are a thousand meters back, digging in."

Niles slipped up his nightsight goggles and used the glasses instead, switched to x10 magnification and light-enhancement. The hundred-meter gap between the minefield and the steeper slope down to the valley was an expanse of snow stippled with the dry yellow stalks of summer's grass. A few small trees were scattered across it, and the odd bush. Nothing moved but the wind, scudding a thin mist of ice crystals along the surface of the ground. Then a man rose to one knee, motionless with a white-painted rifle across his chest. A full minute's silence, then he made a hand signal; half a dozen others rose out of concealment and moved forward twenty paces, sank to the earth again. Another six rose from behind the lead element's position and passed through, went to ground ten or twenty meters in advance.

Good fieldcraft, Niles thought. Aloud: "Open fire!"

Muzzle-flashes lit the night, twinkling like malignant orange fireflies. Men flopped, screamed, were still; a stitch of tracers curved out toward the Helot positions, and the Royalist riflemen opened return fire as well. Bullets went by over Niles's head with an ugly flat *whack* sound, and bark fell on his helmet and the backs of his gloves. He raised his own rifle and settled the translucent pointer of the optical sight on a suspicious gray rock that jutted up out of the snow.

A head and arms snaked around it, a long finned oval on the muzzle of the weapon they carried; rifle grenade. Niles stroked the trigger gently. *Crack.* The recoil was a surprise, sign of a good shot. The head dropped back and the rifle slipped back into view and landed in the snow.

God, Niles thought as a surge of excitement flowed from throat to gut. He touched the side of his helmet.

"Status of element Icepick."

"Moving out," his adjutant said.

"Execute fire mission Alpha," Niles ordered. "I'll join Icepick with the Headquarters squad. Switch to local band relay." They were moving now. Communications weren't so good. *So what? No commanding from the rear! Get out where the troops could know you weren't afraid.*

"On your own, platoon leader," Niles continued, beginning to worm his way backward. Then the sky overhead glared a violet almost as bright as day.

"*Incoming. Able Company position.*" Owensford watched the battle screen change again.

"Lysander's scouts," Captain Lahr said.

In the background Captain Sastri, the artillery chief, spoke in a monotone. "Multiple incoming. Tracking." Light flickered across the northern horizon. "Computing positions. Preparing for counterbattery shoot . . . countermeasures. Chaff and broad-frequency jamming, decoys."

Peter nodded in satisfaction. "Andy, be sure we record all this for analysis."

"Roger," the adjutant said. "The bad guys are expending a hell of a lot of ordnance, Colonel."

"Yeah. Sort of makes you wonder who paid for it all. Andy, what do you make of this?"

"Well, they had a hell of a lot more gear than we expected. It hasn't been used all that effectively."

"Not too surprising. Most of their training had to be map exercises. Dry fire."

"Yes, sir. Just as well."

"They jumped the gun, too," Peter mused. "They should have waited until we got in deeper."

"Probably scared we'd find their base."

"Could be. I still think there's some kind of plan at work here. Something complicated. Main thing is, keep them using up their heavy stuff until they notice they're running short."

Behind him the 160mm mortars flashed as Sastri sent in anti-radar and counterbattery fire. *Crump. Crump. Crump.* Twelve times repeated, and then the brief winking of rocket-assist at the high points of the shell's trajectories, thousands of meters overhead. The muzzles disappeared behind their raw-earth revetments, as the hydraulics in the recoil-system automatically lowered them to loading position; the bitter smell of burnt propellant settled across the hilltop. Inside the gunpits the two loaders would be dropping the forty-kilo bombs down the barrels . . . the tubes showed again, ten seconds to load and alter the aiming point both. *Crump. Crump. Crump.*

A rumble through the ground, and an edge of satisfaction in Sastri's voice:

"Secondary explosions. Scratch one rocket battery."

Rockets hissed skyward, arcing northward.

"Jamming antennae down. One. Two . . . Active jamming off. Chaff continuing."

"Sir, Second Platoon, we're under fire." A bit superfluous, Lysander thought, since they could all hear the crackling two thousand meters to their left.

"Where's Lieutenant Doorn, sergeant?"

"Dead, sir. Three dead, five wounded. Heavy automatic-weapons fire. Maybe a whole company come after us, we'd have been dead if we hadn't dug in."

Lysander could hear the relief, and more, in the sergeant's voice.

"Incoming!"

Lysander ducked lower into the hole. *At least everyone is dug in.* Explosions all along the line, but a lot fell into the minefield, setting off more mines. *They thought we'd be in there. . . .*

"Alexi's hit, medic, medic!" somebody shouted.

Then the sky screamed, globes of violet light raking through the cloud towards them. The Collins prince dropped to the bottom of his spider pit and tucked his limbs in, standard drill to let the thicker torso armor protect you. A flicker of silence, and then the world came apart in a surf-roar of white noise. The rocket warheads burst apart thirty meters up, showering their rain of hundreds of grenade-sized bomblets to bounce and explode and fill the air with a rain of notched steel wire. The sound was distant as the helmet clamped down on audio input that would have damaged his ears, like a movie on Tri-V in another room of the house, and it seemed to go on forever. Something struck him below the right shoulderblade with sledge-hammer force, driving a grunt out between clenched teeth.

Fragment, but the armor had stopped it. If a bomblet fell into the hole with him, well, Sparta would just need another heir to the Collins throne. He felt sick, a little lightheaded; part of him not believing this was real, a deeper part knowing it was and wanting to run away. Had it been this bad, swimming underwater to hijack the shuttle on Tanith? *No,* he decided. Then he had had one definite task to do, and Falkenberg waiting, and that had been very comforting. *Peter's a good man,* he told himself. *Good soldier. And now there are people looking for* you *to be their rock.*

A lot of the incoming barrage had fallen into the minefield. The enemy had expected to catch troops out in the open, not down in holes.

The rocket fire lifted, to be replaced almost instantly by the whistle of mortar shells; continuous bombardments were luxuries for rich worlds with abundant mechanical transport. Lysander raised his head, automatically sorting through the messages passing through the audio circuits of his helmet. Casualties, more than he liked, but nothing like what there could have been if they'd been out there in the open.

"Shift the wounded to perimeter defense," he said on the company push. *Schoop.* A mortar firing, it might be up to a klick away. *Whunk.* A fountain of snow and vegetation and wet old earth bloomed ahead of him, in among the minefield. *Well that's one way to clear a field. Let the enemy pound it. Bloody good thing we stopped the advance.*

Schoop. Schoop. Whunk. Whunk. The three eighty-two mm's of his own weapons platoon were back in action, firing to the direction of the Second's observers over to the left.

"Fire central," he said, switching to the interunit frequency. "I'm taking medium mortar fire. Counterfire needed."

Far above, points of light winked briefly; heavy mortar shells getting an extra kick at the top arch of their trajectory. Seconds later a heavy *crump . . . crump* echoed from the hills, mingling with the noise of explosions eight or ten thousand meters to the north, wherever the computers thought the rockets had come from.

"Sastri here." The battalion heavy-weapons company CO. "Can you observe the fall of shot?"

"That's negative, Fire Central."

"Not much point, then," the artillery officer said. "With passive sensors, there just isn't enough backtrack on mediums. If you can get drones over the target, let me know." A hint of impatience; the battalion heavy weapons were working hard to supress the enemy's area-bombardment weapons.

Schoop. Schoop. Schoop.

Lysander looked again to his left. "Patch to Colonel Owensford."

"Owensford here."

"Sir. Code JOSHUA, repeat Joshua." Owensford did not have to look up the meaning: "Permission to continue attack."

"Negative. DOVE HILL continues."

"Then give me some fire support! Some of those Thoth missiles—"

"Who's asking?"

"Kicker Six, sir, this is—"

"So long as it's not the Prince Royal, shut up and soldier. We'll know more in a few minutes."

"Aye aye, sir. Out."

Dig in. Dig in and wait, while they drop stuff on our heads. They're out there, Lysander thought. They're out there, those terrorist bastards, they're out there killing my brothers, and we could go kill them. Let me go get them, dammit. *Next time, by God, you just might be talking to the Prince Royal. . . .*

Lieutenant Deborah Lefkowitz frowned at the satellite photo as the engines of the tiltrotor transport built to their humming whirr. There was plenty of room inside, even with the sidescan radar and IR sensors and analysis computers the Legion had installed; this class of craft was originally designed as troop-transports for the CoDominium Marines, capable of carrying a full platoon a thousand kilometers in two hours. Room enough for the six equipment operators and her, and even a cot and coffee machine so that they could take turns on a long trip. The smell of burnt kerosene from the ceramic turbines gave an underlying tang to the warm ozone-tinted air.

That is an odd *snow formation,* she thought, calling up a close-range 3-D screen of the picture. Down a ridgeline bare of trees, through a shallow valley where it vanished under forest cover, then starting up again three hundred meters south. Multiple sharp depressions the width of a man's hand and many meters long, running in pairs. It could be a trick of lighting, shadow played odd games when you were taking optical data through an atmosphere under high magnification. . . . She began to play with gain, then froze the image and rotated it.

Her round heavy-featured face frowned in puzzlement. *Mark it and send it back to the interpreters. But—*

Deborah Lefkowitz had been born on Dayan, a gentle world of many islands in warm seas. She had trained in photo-interpretation as part of her National Service, and followed her husband into the Legion when he grew bored with peacetime soldiering on a planet too shrewd and too feared to have many enemies; he was on New Washington now, commanding an infantry company. Massaging computers was a good second-income job for her, perfectly compatible with looking after two young children. But these odd shapes in the snow tugged at some childhood memory. . . .

The aircraft was rolling forward, no reason for a fuel-expensive vertical lift here. As the wheels left the ground, Lefkowitz touched the communicator. There was a slight pause as the seeker locked on to the relay station in Dodona, and then the status light turned green.

"Commander Task Force Erwin, please."

"Owensford here."

"Major, I will be on target in thirty minutes. In the meantime, I have an anomaly in the last series of satellite photos. What look like . . . well, like ski tracks, sir."

"Ski tracks?"

"Cross-country skis." *That* had been the memory. Jerry and she had spent their honeymoon at Dayan's only winter resort, on one of the subpolar islands. "Moving—" she paused to reference. "From a position three-fifty kilometers north northwest of your present location almost like an arrow towards you, stretching for ten kilometers or so, then vanishing."

Silence for a long moment. "How many? And how long ago?"

"Impossible to say how many, sir. Could be anything from one hundred up, or more if some sort of vehicle on ski-shaped runners was used. How long depends on snow conditions, wet snow freezing and then being covered by fresh falls . . . that could mean anytime since the first firm snowfall."

Her fingers danced over the console. "Say any time in the last three weeks. But, sir, even if they all went to ground every time the satellite came over the horizon . . . very difficult to conceal, sir. The IR scanners and the imaging radar are much less affected by vegetation, and anyway, the leaves are off the trees."

"If the satellites are giving us the real data, lieutenant." Owensford's voice was harsh, and she felt a similar roughness in her own. On Tanith the Legion had fought rebel planters supported by the Bronson interests, and Bronson had suborned personnel in the governor's office, filtering the satellite data.

"But sir, we've had our own people in there from the day we landed! Senior lieutenant Swenson went over it all with a fine-toothed comb; nobody's been allowed past those computers and we take the datadump right into our own equipment."

"Still, it's interesting, isn't it, Lieutenant? And those computers aren't ROM-programmed like ours. It'll be even more interesting when you get some direct confirmation. Meanwhile, I'm not real confident about those satellite pictures. Owensford out."

Lefkowitz looked up. The other's faces were bent over their equipment, underlit by the soft blue light of the display screens, but she could see the sheen of sweat on one face, the lips of another moving in prayer. They had been nibbling at the outskirts of the Dales for a month, even landing and planting sensors; so far, not a hint of enemy activity. Suddenly that seemed a good deal less comforting.

"Relay link," she said.

"Green," the radio technician replied; the tiltrotors had a feedback-aimed link with a blimp circling at five thousand meters over Dodona, ample to keep them in line of sight even when doing nape-of-the-earth flying.

"Set for continuous download, all scanners." Everything the instruments took in would be blipped back to headquarters in Dodona in real time. "Pilot," she said, "I really think we should stay low, perhaps?" Even though they were staying well short of the action, south below the horizon from Task Force Wingate, along the path it had marched.

"Ma'am," the flyer said. "Everyone strap in."

There was a flurry of activity as the technicians secured themselves and anything loose. Silence for long minutes; Lefkowitz caught herself stealing glances out the nearest port. Moonlight traced lighter streaks across dark ploughland and pasture, where the long windbreaks of cypress and eucalyptus caught and shaded snow. The last lights of the widely scattered farmhouses dropped away as they left the settled lands around the confluence of the Eurotas and Rhyndakos. The pilot brought the plane lower still, until the tallest trees blurred by underneath so closely that they would have hit the undercarriage if it had not been retracted. There were trees in plenty, then open grassland where sleeping beasts—she thought they were cattle but could not be sure—fled in bawling panic as the dark quiet shape flashed by. Swamp, where puddles of water cast wind-riffled reflections from stars and moon.

"Relay from Major Owensford. Column's under attack, rocket and mortar fire."

Then they were over hills, the ground rising steadily. More snow appeared, first in patches and then as continuous cover; the reflected light made the night seem brighter. Forest showed black against the open ground, as if the hills were lumpy white pillows rising out of dark water. The lights of the base on the Rhyndakos showed; the tiltrotor circled, then swung north toward the chain of firebases.

"Passive sensors only," Lefkowitz said. "Warm up the IR scanner." A bit of a misnomer, since it was a liquid-nitrogen cooled superconductor in large part. "Prepare for pop-up manouver. Location, pilot."

"Coming up parallel with Task Force Erwin's column of march, one-ten klicks south."

"Major Owensford, I'm making my first run. Stand by."

"Standing by, Lieutenant," the cool voice replied.

"Pilot, now."

Debbie Lefkowitz keyed her own screen into the IR sensor. It had fairly sophisticated electronics, enough to throw a realistic 3-D map and pre-separate anything not the natural temperature of rock or vegetation. Data was pouring into the craft from the sensors with the column and in the firebases along the route, free of the suspect satellite link that lay between the Dales and the Legion's analysis computers back in Fort Plataia.

"Major, you've got about . . . two thousand hostiles in your immediate vicinity," she said, as the machines correlated the fragmentary input. "Grid references follow." And relay this back to Swenson, now!

A machine beeped at her. She looked at it and her stomach clenched.

"Major, I've got multiple readings *south* of your position. South of *my* position. Readings all around," she said. *Calm,* she told herself sternly. This was certainly more hands-on than headquarters duty, but needs must. If the Royalist line of march was a bent I, the troops—they must be troops—were two parallel lines flanking it on either side, with another bar in the north closing the C. *This safe rear zone just became bandit country.* The enemy below *might* not have stinger missiles and detection gear, but they probably did. "Permission to conduct direct scan."

"South—" Owensford began, then snapped: "Denied. Get low and get *out* of there, and do it *now.*"

"Sir." Gravity sagged her into the seat as the pilot turned for home and rammed the throttles to full.

"We're getting out of here soonest," she said on the cockpit link. "Might as well take a look while we're leaving. Prepare for pop-up. Stand by for sidescan."

The rotors screamed as the engine-pods at the ends of the wings tilted, changing the propellors' angle of attack. The aircraft jerked upward as if pulled by a rubber band stretching down from orbit "Scanning . . . down!"

Another freight-elevator drop. "Major, troops, at least two thousand down here heavy weapons probable category follows—"

Alarms squealed. "Detection, detection, multiples, frequency-hoppers—"

"*Jesus Christ missile signatures multiple launch—*"

The pilot's voice overrode it, shouting to his copilot. "Flares and chaff, flares and chaff! Those are Skyhawks!"

The *putputput* of the decoys coughing out of the slots was lost in the scream of the airframe as the pilot looped, twisted and dove almost in the same instant. The cabin whirled around her. For a moment they were upside down and flying in the opposite direction to their course two seconds ealier, and she could see two livid streaks of fire pass through the space she had been occupying. One struck trees and exploded in a globe of magenta fire as they began to turn, but the other did not. "Shit, shit, shit, *shit*," the pilot cursed.

The Lord our God, the Lord is One— Lefkowitz found herself praying, for the first time since girlhood. *Get the data stream out. Send everything we know. Nobody dies for nothing. Let them know what we saw.* Lights flashed as the computers dumped their data.

The tiltrotor was *below* the nape of the earth now, threading its way through narrow passages between trees and rocks, flipping from one wingtip to the other with insane daring as the pilot stretched the machine to its limits. Inspired flying, and very nearly enough; the missile was barely within effective radius when the idiot-savant brain that guided it sensed its fuel was nearly exhausted and detonated.

"Portside engine out, cutting fuel." The copilot's voice, metronome-steady. The aircraft lurched and turned sluggish, barely missed a hilltop.

"Starboard's losing power!" Both pilots' hands moved feverishly on the controls. "Something nicked the turbine casing, she's going to split. Shut it off, Mike, shut her *down.*"

"I *can't,* we're too *low—*"

The plane surged upward, painfully, clawing for enough altitude to pick its landing-spot. The starboard engine's hum turned to a whining shriek that ended in an intolerable squeal of tortured synthetic and an explosion that sent the tiltrotor cartwheeling through the sky. Fragments of fiber-bound ceramic turbine blade sleeted through the walls of the aircraft, and lights and equipment shorted out in a flash of sparks and popping sounds and human screams, of fear or pain it was impossible to say. Lefkowitz felt something like a needle of cold fire rip down the length of one forearm.

They struck.

✧   ✧   ✧

"The observation plane's down," Andy Lahr said. "Lefky bought us a lot of data. Still sending when she augured in."

"Dead?"

"Dunno. Went in from low altitude. Maybe not."

"What can we send to rescue her?" Owensford demanded.

"Not one damn thing. That area's crawling with hostiles. Which we know about only because of her, but they'll get to her long before we do."

"I see. Tell Mace. All right, let's see what she found out."

"It's a lot. One thing's certain, Major. The satellite data is thoroughly corrupted. We didn't get clue one of that force to the south, and it's far too damn big that we wouldn't have seen *something*."

"Right. Get me Jesus Alana."

"Alana here."

"Jesus, we've been snookered."

"Yes, sir, I'm following it."

"Got anything for me?"

"First cut analysis: your upper limit's blown away. The satellite hasn't been reporting properly, and we must ignore all its data. The conclusion is that we do not know what we're facing."

"How truly good," Owensford said. "What else?"

"They're trying for a giant Cannae."

"Hell, we knew that."

"Yes, sir, but they have more in place than you thought. We have been thoroughly deceived from the beginning. The satellite data were not merely incomplete, they were corrupted."

"How?"

"Someone is spending money like water," Alana said. "They have imported gear that we cannot afford, and people who can use it."

"People who didn't come off a BuReloc transport, that's for sure. OK, we have rich enemies off-planet. What do I do this morning? What's vulnerable?"

"The force to the south is not well organized," Alana said. "And they cannot be reliably in communication with their headquarters."

"Not in communication. But they're moving. So they're following a plan."

"Probably."

"OK. A giant Cannae, and they think it's working. I want to think about that. You flog hell out of the data and report when you have something. Out."

After the battle he'd have to send a report to Falkenberg.

And a letter to Jerry Lefkowitz. But just now there were other things to worry about.

"Andy."

"Sir?"

"They want us to move into the jaws. We want them to think we're doing it. Have all the units out there keep up coded chatter, lots of message traffic." He typed furiously. "OPERATION RATFINK, VARIATION THREE. GET YOUR STAFF PEOPLE WORKING ON THAT."

"Senior Group Leader, we have confirmation, they're talking a lot," the headquarters comm sergeant said.

"Acknowledged." Niles grinned, and turned to the company commander. "Right on schedule. The Brotherhood troopers will be coming down there," Niles said quietly, pointing west and to his right as his left hand traced the line on the map. "Get as far upslope as you can, dig in, and hold them. You're going to be heavily outnumbered. Hold while you can, then pull out; but every minute counts."

"They'll have to come to us," the Company Leader said. "Can do, sir."

"Good man. Go to it."

That's G Company gone, the Englishman thought, as they headed into the trees.

A stiff price, but worth it. They had gambled heavily on Skilly's plan. Niles had argued that it was too complicated, and was ordered to stop being negative.

But it's working. It really is.

He had to trot to catch up with his headquarters squad; nobody was stopping now. The three remaining companies of Icepick were moving at better than a fast walk, through the thick snow-laded brush of the swale between the two Royalist forces; you could do that, with a little advance preparation of the ground and a great deal of training. Already past the skirmish at the minefield; he could hear the crackle of small-arms fire half a kilometer away to his left.

God, I hope the rocket batteries are still up. Enough of them, at least; the Royalist counterbattery fire had been better than expected. At least they seemed to have run out of whatever they'd used to support the SAS teams, those horribly accurate rockets. . . .

Violet spheres of light floated across the sky. Six lines of three on the main First RSI position. Another six on the Brotherhood battalion to his right, that ought to give them something to think about. Six more on the unit off on the enemy's western flank. *They'll be out in the open. Should be taking heavy casualties, that will help George company.* Then the crump of mortars and the rattle of small arms; the better part of four companies of Helots putting in their attack on the flanking unit right on the heels of the bombardment *One hour thirty minutes to the satellite,* he thought.

Group Icepick was nearly silent as it moved, only the crunch of feet through the snow and the hiss of the sleds. There were ten of those, each pulled by half a platoon, bending into their rope harnesses. The loads were covered by white sheeting that bid the lumpiness of mortars and heavy machine guns, recoilless rifles, boxes and crates. The men trotting silently through the forest undergrowth in platoon columns were heavily burdened as well, with loads of ammunition and rifle grenades, spare barrels and extra belts for the machine guns, light one-shot rockets in their fiberglass tubes, loops of det cord. They showed little strain and no confusion, only a hard intent concentration.

Well, Skilly was right, he thought; training to the point just short of foundering them was the only way.

There was a sudden burst of small-arms fire and shouting from just ahead and to the left.

"Report!" he snapped.

"Sir, First platoon, E Company, Cit's comin' down off the ridge. 'Bout a platoon of 'em, we're engaging."

Rotten luck, he thought. Still, you couldn't expect the enemy to cooperate with the plan. *Act quickly.*

"Kolnikov," he said, keying his circuit to the E Company leader. "Detach First and Third to me, you're in charge, get Icepick where it's going and *fast,* then set up. Headquarters platoon," he continued to the men around him, "Signalers and techs, accompany Company Leader Kolnikov until I rejoin you. The rest of you, follow me. Move!"

He angled to the left and increased his pace to a pounding lope, all he could manage in this gravity with what he was carrying. The men followed, and all down the column the pace picked up as the orders were relayed. There were no cleared lanes through the brush upslope, but his men wormed through it quickly enough; visibility dropped to five meters or less, and stray rounds began clipping through the branches unpleasantly close. Grenades were going off, and he could hear the hiss of the light rockets the guerillas carried. A glance at his wrist.

0300. One hour twenty minutes.

"Sutchukil here," a voice said in his ear as he went to one

knee and waved the others past him. "The enemy aircraft is
down."

"Good," Niles said. Intelligence would be interested, and
the "consultants" were as eager as their stoneface training
allowed to get their hands on Falkenberg's electronics. A
prisoner would be a bonus too, although Legion people were
said to be very stubborn. *God, it's getting* comfortable *to think
of fifteen things at once, I must getting used to this business.*
"Advise the nearest officer to send a patrol. Out."

"Wake her up."

A cold tingling over the surface of her skin, and Lieutenant Lefkowitz blinked her eyes open. She was lying against
a packing crate, in a gully that was not quite a cave. There
was a strip of faint light thirty meters up, where moonlight
leaked through interlacing branches across the narrow slit in
the stone, a little more from shaded blue-glow lanterns. Below
the walls widened out, vanishing into darkness beyond. To
her right the gully narrowed and made a dog-leg; that must
be to the outside. Men were moving in and out; out with boxes
and crates from the stacks along the walls—*skis and sleds I
knew it, that thing with the propellor must be a powered
snowsled*—and on the other side of the cave she could see
the cots and medical equipment of a forward aid-station.
Nobody in it yet, the medics standing around watching or
helping with the work.

The air was cold enough to make her painfully conscious
of the thinness of her khaki garrison uniform, and smelled
of blood and medicines and gunoil and the mules stamping
and snorting somewhere back in the darkness.

"She's awake." The voice was kneeling at her elbow; a
woman in camouflage jacket and leather pants like all the rest
she could see moving around, with corporal's stripes and a
white capital M on the cuff. The shoulder flashes held nothing she recognized except a red = sign on a black circle.

"Fit to stand rigorous interrogation?" An officer, from his
stance and sidearm; Asian, short and stocky-muscular. In the
same uniform as the others, but without insignia, and he wore
something that was either a long knife or a short sword in
a curved laquered sheath at his side. She felt a slight chill
as his eyes met hers. Complete disinterest, the way a tired
man looked at flies.

The medic nodded. "Bruises, wrenched ankle, cut on the
arm, slight chill, no concussion," she said, as she packed her
equipment and headed back to the tent with the wounded.

"Stand her up."

Hands gripped her and wrenched her to her feet; she bit the inside of her mouth to keep from crying out at the pain in her head. The enemy officer turned to a bank of communications equipment, an odd mixture of modern-looking modules and primitive locally manufactured boxes. *Very odd. None of the advanced equipment are models I could place.* Functions, yes, but not these plain black boxes without maker's marks or even the slightly bulky squared-off look of milspec. His hands skipped across a console, and a printer spat hardcopy. He held it up, looked at her, nodded and raised a microphone.

"Base One, Intelligence, Tetsuko, please."

There was a moment of silence; Debbie Lefkowitz used it to control her breathing, and the throbbing and dizziness in her head receded. Very faintly, the sound of explosions echoed in through the entrance and the opening overhead. The communicator chirped.

"Triphammer Base Beta, Yoshida here," he said. "We have a live survivor from the enemy surveillance plane; Lieutenant Deborah Lefkowitz, one of Falkenberg's people, recon interpretation specialist. Field Prime is with the advance element. Yes. Yes, sir, I'm sending all the equipment we salvaged in an hour or so with the next evacuation sled. Sir, I have no facilities or drugs for—yes, sir." The printer spat more paper with soundless speed, as the officer looked around.

"Sergeant Sikelianos," he called.

"Sir?"

"I don't have time to attend to this, and your guard squad might as well be making themselves useful. Here's a list of information we need from this prisoner: get it out of her, but she's got to be ready to travel in a couple of hours; Tetsuko wants to do a more thorough debriefing. See to it."

"Yes, *sir.*" Sikelianos was a thickset man, you could tell that even through parka and armor, with a rifle slung muzzle-down across his back. Thick close-cropped beard and hair twisted into a braid down his neck, both blue-black. He was grinning, as well, showing white, even teeth with the slightly blueish sheen of implants.

"Remember Field Prime's Rule, Sikelianos. One chance."

"Yessir. Come on, you four."

The four soldiers—*armed men at least, if not soldiers,* she thought with contempt beneath her fear—tied her hands behind her back and hustled her into the dark area where the rock did meet overhead. Past a herd of mules within a rope corral, into echoing silence and chill; the cold was beginning to drain her resources, and she shivered slightly.

"OK, this is good enough," the guerilla noncom said. It was almost absolutely dark to her eyes; they would be using their nightsight goggles. Hands came out of nowhere and threw her back against the wall; she saw an explosion of colored lights behind closed lids. Then real light. Sikelianos had switched on a small hook-shaped flashlight dangling through a loop on his webbing belt. It underlit the men's faces, caught gleams from items of equipment slung about them.

"OK," Sikelianos said; he was smiling, and she could see him wet his lips behind the white puffing of his breath. "We got some questions for you, mercenary bitch. You going to answer?"

"Lieutenant Deborah Lefkowitz, Falkenberg's Mercenary Legion, 11A7782-ze-l *uhhhh.*" He had hit her under the breastbone, fast and very hard. She dropped to the ground, gagging and coughing as she struggled to draw air into paralyzed lungs. They waited until she was merely panting before drawing her up again.

"You going to answer the questions?" Sikelianos said, brushing his knuckles across his lips.

"Under the Mercenary Code and the Laws of War—"

This time the fist struck her almost lightly, so that she was able to keep erect by leaning against the rock. Again he waited; when she straightened up, he had drawn the knife worn hilt-down at his left shoulder. The blade was a dull black curve, but the edge caught the faint light of the shielded torch. His left hand held a pair of pliers. He laughed, putting the point of the knife under her chin; she could feel the skin part, it must be shaving-sharp. A tiny stab of pain, and the warmth of blood on her cold-roughened skin.

"You mercs and the Cits, you deserve each other." The knifepoint rose and she craned upward, head tilted back until the muscles creaked. "Now, by now even a stupid cunt like you ought to realize something. This is the Revolution, we're not playing no stinking game, and we got our *own* rules. Like, everything is either *them* or *us*, you understand? Other rules we sort of make up as we go along."

"But," he went on, "we do got a few real ironclad *laws*. Field Prime's Rule, that's one. You listening?" He leaned closer. "Outsiders get just *one chance* to cooperate. Savvy? You answer our questions, we take you back to the officer and you get a nice warm blanket and a safe trip to Base One, everything real nice, you can sit out the war in a cell. Maybe we even exchange you.

You don't answer . . . well, you will. Up to you, smooth or rough."

"Lieutenant Deborah Lefkowitz, Falkenberg's Mercenary Legion, 11A7732-ze-l," she began. Then she closed her eyes and clamped her mouth tight as he gripped the collar of her jacket and slit it open down the front.

"Hey, Sarge," one of the guerillas laughed. "Goosebumps— maybe she likes it rough."

There was a shark's amusement in his voice. "I always got the pliers to fall back on."

Deborah Lefkowitz remained silent when a boot tripped her. She only began to scream when they stretched her legs wide and slashed the pants off her hips.

"Goddamn it!" Lysander swore to himself in quiet frustration, as the cry of *incoming* echoed across his position. The engineers stayed at their positions long enough to fire the breeching charges, stubby mortars that dragged lines of plastic tubing stuffed with explosives through the air across the minefield. Then they copied everyone else and dove for cover, many of them rolled under the bellies of the six armored cars that had come forward. The assault company of infantry had no such option, nor had there been time for it to dig in. They hugged the earth and prayed or cursed according to inclination; a few managed to roll into already occupied holes dug by the Scout company.

"Overshot," he murmured a moment later; there were mortar rounds falling on them, but the rockets . . . *on Peter,* he thought. *Well, he has those armored cans. . . .*

"Sir." The Legion helmet identified the speaker, Junior Lieutenant Halder, Fourth Platoon, the ones he had sent down to scout the woods. "We're engaged, ran into an enemy unit in the thick bush. They were moving south, sir, hard to tell how many, but they're loaded for bear. I'm getting heavy rifle grenade and antipersonnel rocket fire, sir."

"Calderon, switch the company mortars to support Third Command."

"Owensford here."

"Sir, Code—" he punched at the keyboard woven into his cuff. "Code ALGERNON, repeat Algernon. Code MOSEBY." Enemy forces in large but unknown strength west of my position.

"Copy. The land-line should be connected now; link to Sastri to call in fire support. Hurt them, Kicker Six, that's what you're out there for."

✦　　✦　　✦

Another blast of shrapnel from the antipersonnel bomblets
swept over the command caravan. *Goddamn it, I'm an Infantryman, not a turtle,* Owensford thought. Although there was
a certain comfort to having 20mm of hardened plate between
you and unpleasantness.

Movement in the ravine. Hmmmm. Up north around Slater's
column, the enemy had been using infiltration tactics down
the wooded corridors. Potentially more of a problem here than
there, since the proportion of forest was greater.

He looked at the map; squares were beginning to fill in for
enemy units. The tiltrotor's sacrifice had been worth a lot;
now they knew where to fly their drones, and they were getting
more data.

So. What do we know?

The Fifty-first out on his flank had been hit hard, infantry
attacks in strength right on the heels of the first bombardment; now they were gradually turning front as parties of the
enemy tried to work around their rear. The Third on his left
was moving east and north to cover the flank of his probe
through the minefield, the Second on the far left was getting
hit-and-run skirmishing and snipers and moving slowly to close
up with the 3rd.

"Andy, link me up with Barton and Alana. Can we do that
securely?"

"Sure can. Got a new fiber thread laid five minutes ago.
Stand by one—got it."

"Ace. Jesus. Stand by to trade data sets." Peter slapped the
function keys, and lights blinked. His map screens changed
subtly.

"All right, Jesus," Peter said. "What are they trying to do?"

"It depends upon whether or not they are fools."

"What do you think?"

"Don't look like fools to me," Ace Barton said.

"They are not fools," Alana said. "Their plan is well
executed. The problem is that they have not enough force to
accomplish what clearly they believe they can do."

"Say that again."

"Colonel, they look to be trying to cut through to your base
camp and destroy it. All their movements point to that. Yet
they have not enough force to do it, and the result is that
they expose themselves to attrition, and then to counterattack."

"First they build a pocket for you, now they stick their own
dicks in the garbage grinder," Ace Barton said.

"Not fools but acting like fools."

"That's close enough," Alana said.

"Secret weapon, Jesus? Nukes?"

"It is a possible explanation."

"Damn high cost, using nukes," Peter said. "If anything would unite the CoDominium from the Grand Senate down to the NCO Clubs, that would do it. Ace, do you get the impression that things are not what they seem?"

"I sure do, Boss."

"OK," Peter said. "Here's what I'm seeing. We have three elements, two real attacks and a feint. The feint is left alone, the two real attacks are under fire within a few minutes of each other. Conclusions, Jesus?"

"Our plan, at least in outline, was known to the enemy."

"Sounds right," Barton said.

"Now they are committing major portions of their strength in what appears to be a hopeless attack. It's not a feint, they're in too far for that already."

"Correct again," Alana said.

"All right. New mission for Task Force Wingate: fall back and regroup as mobile reserve. While they're doing that, Ace, you scramble your four companies in the hovertrucks, and get the Dodona militia moving too. I want reinforcements moving toward the Bridgehead Base *soonest*. That's where they're heading. But hang back, don't get in there and make a big target of yourselves. It's time we started playing this according to our own script."

"Aye aye. I don't like this secret weapon deal."

"Nor I. Jesus, put somebody smart to thinking about the situation: what could they have that would justify what they're doing? Use drones as you need them. This is a priority one mission. Report as soon as you've got an idea."

"Aye, aye, sir."

"One thing," Ace Barton said. "We've learned something about the enemy commander."

"Yes?"

"Devious mind, Pete. Devious. Atlas out."

He paused for a second. *Right.* One damned thing after another, like a picador driving spikes under the hide of the bull. Nothing deadly, but designed to disorient and enrage, while the sword stayed hidden in the cloak . . . *or better still, a cat playing with a mouse.* There was an almost feline malice to the whole setup; whoever was in charge on the other side was inflicting damage for its own sake. He looked at the map again. *Particularly on the Brotherhoods.* Who were well-trained troops, but civilians-in-uniform, with families and communities that depended on them.

This is as much a terrorist operation as a battle, he thought, with a slight prickle at the back of his neck. You had to be a bit case-hardened to be a mercenary anyway, but . . .

"Get me Morrentes." Back at the river base-camp.

"Colonel," the militia officer said. "Hear you're having problems. All quiet here, so far. No sign of the force the 'plane reported."

"Yes. I'm sending Lieutenant-Colonel Barton and the Legion companies up to join you," he said. "Possibly I'm being nervous, but I don't think so."

"I see, sir," the rancher said; his voice was slow and thoughtful.

"You're already dug in good," Owensford said. "Stay that way, but now I want you to be ready to move fast. I don't know what they have, but they're acting like it's going to turn the battle around for them. Like they can wipe you out with one blow."

"Nukes?"

"It sure looks like it, but we don't know," Peter said. "We just don't know."

CHAPTER TWELVE

Crofton's Essays and Lectures in Military History
(2nd Edition)

Herr Doktor Professor Hans Dieter von und zu Holbach:
Delivered at the Kriegsakademie, Konigsberg
Planetary Republic of Friedland, October 2nd, 2090

Since the development of the metallic cartridge, smoke-less powder and the self-loading firearm, small-arms development has gone through a number of cycles. The original generation of magazine rifles were the result of a search for range and accuracy; they were bolt-action weapons, capable in skilled hands of accurate fire at up to several thousand meters. In the opening battles of the First War of AntiGerman Encirclement (1914-1918), the professional soldiers of the British Army delivered deadly fire at ranges well in excess of 1000 meters, at the rate of twelve aimed rounds per minute—leading the officers of the opposing Imperial German formations to suppose they were the targets of massed machine guns! By the 1930s, these bolt-action rifles were being replaced by self-loading models firing identical ammunition and of roughly comparable performance.

However, the mass slaughters and hastily trained mass conscript armies of the 20th century rendered the long-range accuracy of such weapons irrelevant. Studies indicated that virtually all infantry combat occurred at ranges of less than 800 meters, and that in any case most casualties were inflicted by crew-served weapons, particularly artillery. Accordingly, beginning with the Wehrmacht in 1942, most armies switched to small-calibre assault rifles capable of fully automatic fire but with effective ranges of as little as 500 meters; in effect, glorified machine pistols.

For a few decades, it appeared that laser designators would provide an easy answer to the problem of accuracy, but as usual with technological solutions countermeasures limited their usefulness to specialist applications.

Two developments brought the return of the long-range semiautomatic infantry rifle. The first was the development of first kevlar and then the much more efficient nemourlon body-armor. Nemourlon armor of reasonable weight resists penetration by most fragments and any bullet that is not both reasonably heavy and fairly high-velocity. Since modern body-armor covers head, neck, torso and most of the limbs, experiment has proven that a cartridge of at least 7x55 mm is necessary for adequate penetration; such a round renders an infantry rifle of acceptable weight uncontrollable if used in a fully automatic mode. The second factor was the gradual decay of the mass, short-term conscript army, as small forces of highly trained professionals once more' became common. Sufficient training-time for real marksmanship was available in these forces—thus increasing their advantage over less well-trained armies still more.

A belligerent with small regard for human life is far less sensitive to taking casualties than one accustomed to cherish life highly—a factor that surely must enter into strategic calculations. The American practice of "body-counting" enemy casualties in the Vietnam War was mindless in innocently assuming that these deaths had a bearing on North Vietnamese capabilities and willpower.

The weight of burdens, up to some unknowable point, is relative, as anyone knows who has ever gazed at the statue in front of Boys' Town, Nebraska: One boy carrying another over the inscription "He ain't heavy, Father. He's my brother." What some consider burdens, for example digging ditches, others consider good sense and the chance to build good morale. Nor will it do to try to calculate the economic costs of each side's losses or efforts. Not only do people put different values on things, but more important, military goods are valuable not for the materials and labor that go into them, but for the strategic gains that can be got out of using them. No one in wartime has ever been struck by a piece of gross national product.

—Paul Seabury and Angelo Codevilla,
WAR: Ends and Means

✧   ✧   ✧

"Field Prime."

Skida Thibodeau woke as she usually did, reaching for the weapon resting beside her head.

"One hour, Field Prime," the orderly said, handing a cup of coffee in through the flap of her field shelter.

She took the cup and sat up, pushing aside the greatcloak and stamping her feet into her boots; all she had taken off was the footwear and the webbing gear and armor. Her eyes were sandy as she sipped. There had been a dream. . . . *Skilly was walking down a fancy marble staircase with Niles. Maybe Niles.* Whoever it was had been in a fancy uniform, and she had been wearing jewels and a sweeping gown. Trumpets blowing, and men and women in expensive clothes and uniforms bowing. The faces had been an odd mixture. The Spartan kings, and Belezian gang leaders she had known back a decade ago. The CoDo assignment clerk who had taken half her credits to get her to Sparta and tried to make her spread for him besides; the "uncle" who had raped her when she was ten. Those tourists who had made her smile for the camera before they'd give her the one-credit note. That was when she was a runner for Dimples, sixteen, no, seventeen years ago; odd she remembered it.

All the faces had been terrified; except Two-knife's and he was grinning at her in a formal suit with the machetes over his back, next to the *haciendado* woman she had promised, or threatened him with. The triumph had been sweet beyond belief. . . . Then the dream had changed, she was in an office that was somehow a bedroom and dining room too. Sitting at a table eating breakfast, with a huge pile of official-looking papers waiting beside the plate, all stamps and seals, while a nursemaid held up a baby that had her skin and hair and huge blue eyes like Niles, or her mother's.

Skilly's mind is telling her to get her ass in gear, she thought, as she buckled the webbing belt and rolled out of the shelter. *Dreams are fine for in-cen-tive.* The air was cold and full of mealy granular snow, flicking down out of a sky like 'wet concrete; the damp chill cut deeper than the hard cold that had settled over the northern Dales these past few weeks. Wind cuffed at her; it was still a little surprising occasionally, how much *push* the air on this planet had.

There was quiet stirring all through the spread-out guerilla camp, men rolling out of their shelter-halves—many had just lain down under them, exhausted by the trek—water cooking on buried stoves covered in improvised log blinds. Slightly risky, even in this steady light snow, but worth it for the boost; she had specified that everyone got a hot drink and some- thing to eat before the action. High energy stuff, candy and sweets, coffee, caffeine pills for a few of the most groggy. Grins, salutes, an occasional thumbs-up greeted her.

They good bunch, she caught herself thinking, slightly startled. Then: *this isn't just like running a gang.* That was more like lion-taming, never knowing when they would turn on you. This trust stuff was infectious, like the clap. *Skilly will have to watch herself or she'll go soft.*

The command staff were waiting under a tarp stretched out from a fallen tree; these were dense woods, down at the edge of the Rhydankos floodplain, huge cottonwoods and oaks and magnolias. Skida walked toward the officers, chewing on a strip of jerky. The sort that the CoDo Marines called *mon- key,* that swelled up in your mouth like rubber bands. She swallowed, followed it with a piece of hard candy, and looked at the situation map.

"Report," she said.

"We recovered a prisoner from the aircraft. She is resist- ing interrogation, but Yoshida reports the enemy have some warning of our location but no precise data."

"Hmm." That was an inconvenience; they would be watch- ing, and there would be more losses from the base's tubes before they closed. Although the prisoner might be valuable later.

"Stragglers?" she continued.

"Fewer than ten percent," Sanjuki said; the Meijians were good at computerized lists. "I am surprised."

She nodded. "You doan understand how powerful a force the need to prove yourself be, mon." *Or think only Meijians can feel it.* "Can they fight?" she continued, to the unit com- manders.

Nods, despite the brutal forced-march pace of the past week; they had all had a few hours rest by now, and there were the pills as a last resort. Amazing how it had not occurred to anybody that it was *easier* to move around the Dales in deep winter. Not to the Royals, although most of them came from the Valley where "winter" meant "mud." Nor to her guerillas, well, most of them were cityfolk, or from hot climates . . . she was from a tropical slum herself, but she read history. Russian history in this case: if Batu Khan could do it, why not Skida Thibodeau? Snow made it *much* easier to carry heavy equipment along, helping with the perennial dilemma of infantry; move slow and you missed the chance,

move light and fast and you didn't have the stuff there when
the shit came down.

She looked at the map, absorbing the latest changes. About
as planned, except that the mercs seemed to have twigged faster
than she hoped.

"OK," she said. "Up to now, we has been biff-baffing
them—" she made a gesture, miming striking for one side
of the face and then another "—because we knew exactly
where they were and they couldn't find us. That about over
after our next surprise. Then it just a matter of fighting,
which they pretty good at when they know where to point
the ends the bullets come out of. Ojinga, Raskolnikov." The
two who were to attack the first firebase north, present by
link rather than personally.

"Field Prime."

"You ready?"

"Green and go."

"Niles."

"Yes, Skilly?" he said, slightly breathless. She could hear
firing in the background.

"0400," Skida said. "Twenty minutes from . . . *mark.*"

"Fuck, am I glad to see *you,* sir," the platoon leader said.
He had a thin brown face, scarred by childhood malnutrition,
desperate with worry now and bleeding from a light fragmentation wound on one cheek. There were slick-shiny scars across
the nemourlon of his body armor and the battle-plastic of his
helmet. "I got thirty percent casualties, more maybe, it hard
to know, and these Cit cocksuckers can *fight.*"

"So can we, platoon leader, so can we," Niles said. "Get
your wounded out now."

A mortar shell exploded in the treetops twenty meters
upslope, a bright flash through the night and *crack* and the
top half of the tree toppled into the forest. They both ducked
reflexively and then grinned at each other.

There was a furious close-range firefight going on in the
brush just ahead and upslope, continuous automatic weapons
fire, thud of grenades, the louder whut-*bang* of rifle-launched
bombs, and an occasional *raaaaak*-thud of shoulder-launched
rockets. Mortar shells from the Royalist forward positions were
landing, beating a pathway through the forest canopy, the
follow-up rounds exploding contact-fused on the floor below.

"Alexandro," he said, to one of the platoon leaders from
Kolnikov's E company. "Reinforce the engaged platoon, but
have your sappers start stringing improvs"—boobytraps rigged

from munitions they were carrying, rockets and grenades—
"right behind your line. Careful, eh? When we fall back, your
people delay the pursuit while the engaged platoon passes
through you and moves south. Martins," he went on to the
other of Kolnikov's subordinates. "You come in on their left."
From the south. "I'm going in on the other side. Hit hard,
hit fast, then get the hell out when they reinforce."

He turned to the headquarters platoon around him; two
dozen, spread out in small clumps. "Sergeant," he continued
crisply, "deploy into skirmish line. We're going south and
upslope, and be careful you don't get the end of the line visible
from the top of the ridge. When I give the word, a volley of
rifle grenades, then attack. Oh, and fix bayonets." A rattle as
the blades went on, then another as the finned bombs were
attached to the launcher clips built into the muzzles. "Follow me, *compadres!*"

"Sir, *sir!*" the desperate voice in Lysander's earphones said.
He could hear the cause already, a fourfold increase in the
firing to his left, down in the woods. "Sergeant Ruark here,
Lieutenant Halder's dead, we lost the recoilless, they're coming
in on both sides of us!"

"Steady, Brother," Lysander said, feeling an almost physical effort as he tried to pour strength down the circuit link.
"Help's on the way. Call the positions. Weapons," he continued, "switch the rest of the mortars and the recoilless to
support 4th. All headquarters rifle squads, prepare to move
downslope. Company Sergeant Hertzmeier, you're in charge
here." He waited until the next stick of enemy mortars landed.
"Let's go!"

"They told us to stay in place." Harv said.

"They told Captain Collins to stay in place," Lysander said.
"Those are our Brothers down there!"

Harv grinned wolfishly. "Welcome back, Prince."

"Incoming!"

"For what we are about to receive, may the Lord make us
truly thankful," the driver of the command caravan muttered.

What the hell *are they doing?* Peter Owensford thought,
clanging the hatch shut as another volley of rockets came
howling in. Only two batteries on his position now, the 160mm's
had caught several, unmistakable seismic indications of secondary explosions.

"Andy, get me Jesus Alana."

"Stand by one—go."

"Jesus, what the hell are they doing?"

"I truly do not know, Colonel," Alana said. "They are sending a major force through the valley between you and the Third Brotherhood."

"Isn't that suicide?"

"It is suicide if they do not win big. Which is to say, they must expect to defeat the entire First Royal Infantry, plus the Brotherhood forces holding the river camp."

"And that's not going to happen. All right, Jesus, they think they've got something decisive. What? Nukes?"

"No, they have moved far too many troops far too close for that."

"Then what in the hell—" He was interrupted by two close explosions that rattled the caravan.

"Hah."

"You have something, Jesus?"

"Yes, sir. As you ordered, I have been prodigal in expenditures of drones. One has sent back photographs that show enemy troops, several hundred. Colonel, every one of them is carrying a gas mask. A few are wearing them."

"Gas mask. *Wearing* them?"

"Three men only. That we have seen."

"Three scared men. Gas masks. Chemical weapons. Poison gas. Is *that* what they're counting on?"

"Quien sabe? But it explains all the data we have."

"OK. Go look again while I think." An enemy willing to use poison gas. Prima facie violation of the Laws of War. You got hanged for using chemical weapons. Unless you won, of course.

The Helots expected to win. Expected to win big.

"Close in, close in, the bastid sumbitches can't mortar us if we close in!" the sergeant of Niles's headquarters squad was shouting.

Good advice, he thought sardonically, dashing forward to roll over a convenient log. Very convenient, and a Royalist machine gunner had thought so too; two of the crew sprawled around the weapon were dead or unconscious from the rifle grenade that had destroyed their position. The third was just rising; there was blood all down one leg, but his hands were steady on the machine pistol.

I'm bloody dead, Niles had time to think, before two massive impacts sledged him back sprawling against the log. Then the Royalist was twisting sideways against something that shouted and lunged behind a glint of metal. Too late, and the

Helot's bayonet grated into his lower chest; nemourlon was excellent protection from fragments, moderate against blast and no good at all against cold steel. The return stroke with the rifle butt laid him out beside his comrades, and the rifle poised.

"No," Niles wheezed. "Don't kill him."

He looked around, fighting the savage pain when he breathed, feeling at his stomach and chest. The covering of the armor was ripped, and he could feel the heat of the flattened disks of lead alloy embedded in it, digging into his skin where the tough material had dimpled inside as it came close to parting. One of his ribs might be—was—cracked, but the nemourlon had stopped both rounds. It was *supposed* to be proof against pistol-calibre, but that had been awfully close . . . *a good thing the local arms industry doesn't run to tungsten.*

"Sir, you all right?" the guerilla trooper said, flat on the ground and scanning upslope.

"Yes," Niles lied. "Here, pull the straps on my chest armor tighter. Lieutenant," he went on, touching the side of his helmet, "you have any prisoners?"

"Yeah, sir. Five anyways, all cut up pretty bad. You want I should slag 'em?"

"Negative!" Niles said sharply. *Not gentlemen at all,* he reminded himself. *But they're brave lads, and they can learn.* "I'm going to buy us a little time with them, Lieutenant. Pass the word to be ready to pull out sharpish." He looked over at the three wounded Royalists, two were still breathing. At his watch: 0410. "Man that machine gun, soldier," he said to the trooper who had saved him. It was the same type the Helots used, a Remington M-72 model 2050, and familiar enough.

"More Cits comin'!" from upslope, as the trooper wrestled the bipod-mounted weapon around.

CrashCrashCrashCrash of mortars, the soft coughing *thump* of a medium recoilless, followed by whirrrrrrr-*whomp!* as the shell landed and blasted dirt into the air uncomfortably close; a thirty-meter oak toppled back and downslope, rolling and bounding in the heavy pull of Sparta's gravity. A deep cheer, and firing. Niles touched his helmet in another combination, switching to a frequency the enemy used and broadcasting in clear.

"Royalist commander! White flag, parley!"

"Push 'em back, Brothers! Kings and Country!" Lysander shouted.

The line of RSI infantry was dodging forward; yelling like

madmen and firing from the hip as they ran on the heels of their mortar fire. They were coming in on the south side of the trapped Royalist platoon, flanking the enemy flankers; well-aimed machine gun fire lashed out at the rescuers, but the forest made it impossible to keep much ground under fire. A trumpet sounded from the Royal Army line, high and sweet over the crackling of burning trees and brush.

"By squads," Lysander said. His automatic weapons were opening up, covering the short dashes of the infantrymen who then covered the forward movement of the machine gun teams. Grenades arched through the woods toward the rebels, the RSI troops taking advantage of their higher position on the hillside, white flashes that faded on nightsight goggles like blinking at the sun and then away. Suddenly it was the guerillas who were under fire from both sides.

"Royalist commander! White flag, parley!"

Lysander started violently, almost breaking stride. He went to cover with practiced skill.

"You want to surrender?" he said, switching to clear on the same band. The firefight grew in intensity as men blasted at each other from point-blank range.

"No, do you?" the voice said coolly; Lysander gritted his teeth in fury. Two of his men were dragging a third back upslope, and the wounded man's legs glistened black in the amplified light of the prince's face shield.

Recorder. Turn on the recorder, Lysander thought.

"Actually," the rebel continued—his voice was incongruously cultivated, a British accent like Melissa's grandfather— "I've got eight or ten of your men down here, badly wounded I'm afraid. Ten minutes truce to pull out our wounded, and you can have them back. This immediate area only, of course. One thousand meters radius from your position."

"Who's this?" he asked, playing out the scenarios in his mind.

"Senior Group Leader Graham, Spartan People's Liberation Army," the rebel said. "Who might you be?"

"It hardly matters." Lysander made hand signals. Continue the attack.

"It's their funeral. Your Brothers."

"No deal," Lysander said. "Harm my men and you'll hang, if you live that long." Switch to command channel. "Let's go kill that smug son of a bitch! Go, go—" He thumbed the command set again. "Get me the Colonel."

"All units, WIPERS, I say again, WIPERS," Owensford broadcast. "WIPERS, TRILOGY, WESTWOOD." Don protective equipment and prepare for chemical attack. All troops without protective gear withdraw from present positions. Fall back and regroup for counter attack.

"Andy, who's mobile with chemical protection?"

"Prince Royal's Own, sir."

"Where are they dug in?"

"On— They're not dug in. They're moving, in support of one of the Brotherhood units."

"Son of a bitch."

"You aren't surprised?"

"Should I be? Andy, make sure Collins acknowledges WIPERS, TRILOGY, WESTWOOD."

"Aye aye."

"Sparks, get me Morrentes."

"Morrentes." That line, at least, was secure.

"Sir."

"They're coming right at you, and it's clear they believe they'll win. We can't figure how unless they use gas, and so far as we can tell, every one of theirs has chemical protection gear."

"Holy shit, Colonel, most of my lads—"

"Right. So bug out, and now."

"Where to?"

"High ground. Group toward Barton's force. And don't get lost. We'll need you again."

"Well—Colonel are you sure about this?"

"No. If I'm wrong, I'll have let them sucker you out of a good position. That's not fatal. They may be able to raid your camp, but looting the baggage has got more than one army killed. You'll still outnumber them, and you'll be ready to counter attack. And if they are using gas, Major, if they are—"

"Yes, sir. OK, here I go."

"Barton."

"Right here, Boss."

"You been following this?"

"Better than that," Ace said. "I sent out a couple of my own drones. Jesus is right, they all got gas gear. A few have already put their masks on."

"Scared," Peter said. "Can't blame them. All right. They'll send in their gas, then what? Jump Morrentes's position, I'd guess."

"Me too. Devious mind, Colonel. Devious mind."

"It isn't going to work."

"Didn't say smart, said devious. Amateur's plan. Terrorists rehearse everything fifty times and think being prepared for friction and bad luck means you don't expect *everything* to go right. In the real world—"

"In the real world, no battle plan survives contact with the enemy," Peter said. Falkenberg's favorite military aphorism.

"Eggszactly. So I'm sending my chemical protected troops up to take good positions. When the rebels overrun Morrentes's camp, we pound hell out of them, then while they're figuring that out, we'll be in position to counter-attack."

"That sounds right. I'll leave you to it, then. Hurt the bastards, Ace."

"I'll do that little thing. Out."

"Andy, get me Captain Mace."

"Mace here."

"How are your SAS units?"

"As you requested, I have four operational and standing by."

"Good. Jamey, they're about to bite off more than they can chew. When that happens they'll figure to fade off into the hills."

"Yes, sir—"

"So I want your SAS teams standing by to vector Thoth in on them when they run. Use what air transport we've got to inject those lads into good positions to cover retreat areas."

"Roger. Can do. Colonel, I have a problem. Miscowsky wants to go after Lieutenant Lefkowitz."

"Yeah, he's served with Jerry, that figures. What is that situation? Can Miscowsky's team do any good?"

"Colonel, I don't know, and that's a fact. We've got the crash site pinpointed, but there doesn't look to be anyone there. It's just damned hard to know."

"Assume she's alive. Which way will they take her if they break and run?"

"You really expect them to break, Skipper?"

"Good chance of it. They're gambling a lot on this gas attack. Or whatever they're aiming down my throat." Peter watched as his screens showed updates on the enemy positions. "And they're still at it, trying to run right down our throats like there's no tomorrow. Jamey, what the hell else could it be that would make them act like this?"

"Yeah. I expect you've hit on it. Suppose they stop and pull back now?"

"Let 'em. They've still got to run a gauntlet to get out of there. Jamey, use your own judgment on trying to rescue

Lefkowitz." *Which means he'll send a team, of course.* "But have teams ready to pound on 'em when they run.

"Next. I want as many of your scouts as you can organize set up and ready to run in amongst them when they break. This battle is by God going to end with pursuit."

"Right on. I'll see what I can get ready."

"Andy, what communications are secure?"

"Everything local. If it's not on a fiber line, you'll hear the warning wail."

"Right. Thanks."

"And D Company reports contact."

Owensford nodded. That was the blocking force down in the ravine to the west, and now he would learn for sure why the enemy seemed bent on committing suicide.

"Put McLaren on." Another secure channel. The signals people all deserved medals.

"Captain McLaren here," a thickly accented voice said; from New Newfoundland, the island settlement in the Oinos Gulf. "There's a force of at least three companies comin' doon the valley at me, Colonel. They're carrying heavy weapons, but they'll nae get past if we get fire support."

"On its way, Captain," Owensford said. "Are you ready for chemical attack?"

"As ready as I'll ever be. The lads that hae the gear ha' put it oon, the rest hae moved back to hasty shelters."

"That *ought* to do it. We don't know what they have, or how much, but with luck it can't be *that much.*"

"Luck goes both ways, Colonel. We're warned noo, the lads know which side of the turf goes up."

"Right. Captain, I don't mind if they get past you."

"Sir?"

"I want them to think they fought past you, but I don't want you taking casualties. When they move in, probably under cover of that gas attack, punish them as they go past, but mostly fall back on your reserves, regroup, and wait for the signal to counter attack. They're putting themselves into the bag, Captain, and I wouldn't want to stop them."

"I see. We'll be ready, then."

"Incoming," Sastri's voice said on the Heavy Weapons line. "New pattern. Incoming on *all* positions, single batteries to each of our battalions. Impact in thirty seconds."

"Looks like this is it, Captain. Godspeed."

✧   ✧   ✧

"Sir, Morrentes calling, urgent."

"Owensford here." There was a faint but unmistakable background sound, a rising and falling wail: the line was radio line of sight, possibly secure, possibly not.

"Colonel, FAIROAK." Owensford whistled silently; *radars inoperative due to enemy antiradiation missiles.* "Ditto Firebase One, we've got movement all around. I'm lofting some of the Thoths, but there isn't enough target data to—"

"Gas!" An automatic alarm squeal, and then Sastri's voice screaming on the override push: "*GAS! ALL UNITS ARE UNDER GAS ATTACK, PROTECTIVE MEASURES IMMEDIATELY GAS GAS GAS!*"

"Morrentes here, the camp's under gas attack."

"Loft your birds high, then drop them onto your old camp, sector fiver," Owensford said. "That's where they'll be coming in."

"GAS, GAS, GAS . . ."

A long chilling scream from someone, that ended in retching coughs. Owensford's hands were moving in drilled reflex, as a ring of plastic popped loose around the base of his Legion-issue helmet. *Open* the armor at the neck *strip* it back *pull* the tab; a sudden hiss as the seal inflated tight to his skin and the lower rim of his faceplate. Strip the hypnospray out of its pocket in the fabric of his sleeve and press it to the neck below the seal; antidote, if it was a nerve agent.

But the Brotherhood troops and the RSI don't have Legion equipment. Except the Prince Royal's Own. And everyone has masks. It was still in the training. One reason gas wasn't used much. They have the masks, if they didn't ditch them as useless weight. Think of that as a way to weed out stupid troops. We had warning, not enough, but why am I surprised that terrorists use terror weapons? One thing for sure, they haven't any more experience with war gasses than we do.

"Command override," he said. That put him on the universal push. There was no emotion now; everything felt ice-clear. "All units, gas counter-measures." He turned to Captain Lahr. "OK, that's their big move. Stop them now, and we've won. Andy, make sure we preserve records of this. Make damned sure of that. I want evidence that will stand up in every hearing room from here to the Grand Senate."

"Now," Skilly said, looking at her watch. 0420. Her hand stabbed down, one finger extended.

The Meijian touched a control. The antiradiation missiles lept skyward and looped over down toward the Royalist river-base.

"Now," Skilly repeated. A second finger.

The sky lit with violet as the bombardment rockets drew their streaks across the sky. Two hundred meters above the earth they burst, and a colorless, odorless liquid volatized into gas and floated downward.

"Now." A third time. Nothing visible here, but hundreds of kilometers to the north another of Murasaki's technoninjas touched the controls before him. Two solid-fuel rockets leaped aloft and arched west as they rose; they were not capable of reaching orbital velocity, but they had more than enough power to spew their loads of ballbearings into the path of the observation satellite. The steel would meet the orbiter at a combined velocity of better than sixteen thousand meters per second.

"Now." Fourth and last. From all around the Royalist base, men rose and rushed forward, even as the alarm klaxons wailed.

CHAPTER THIRTEEN

Crofton's Essays and Lectures in Military History
(2nd Edition)

Herr Doktor Professor Hans Dieter von und zu Holbach:
*Delivered at the Kriegsakademie, Konigsberg
Planetary Republic of Friedland, October 2nd, 2090.*

War among the interstellar colonies is a relatively new
phenomenon, although civil disturbance is not. Only since
the emergence of strongly independent planetary states
in the 2060s has a new balance of power begun to
manifest itself, with the traditional accompanying features:
armaments races, offensive and defensive alliances, puppet
governments and spheres of influence. This process is still
incomplete, as the significant powers—Dayan, our own
Friedland, Meiji, Xanadu—are still somewhat deterred by
the enormous although declining and semi-paralytic power
of Earth's CoDominium Fleet. Space combat remains an
almost exclusively theoretical exercise. Ground warfare has
been limited, with intervention in the disputes of worlds
without unified planetary governments, or undergoing civil
war, the characteristic form. The independent planets seek
to defray the costs of raising armies and to gain combat experience by following the example of the autonomous mercenary formations and hiring out their elite
troops; political influence often follows automatically, as
in, for example, the close links now existing between the
Republic of Friedland and the restored Carlist monarchy
of Santiago on Thurstone.

As one consequence of this pattern, the significant
armies have continued to be small and usually based on
voluntary recruitment, intended for deployment outside

their native systems. The strong, industrialized and unified worlds have no use for mass armies, and the planets which need such have not the resources to maintain
them. Thus reserves of trained manpower, and still more
the organizational and social structures needed to support universal mobilization, have become virtually nonexistent. Some planets, of which Sparta is an excellent
example, have attempted to raise well-trained and widely
based militia systems. The primary weakness of this
approach is the lack of standing forces, and hence of the
infrastructure of higher command and administration; also,
the lack of fighting experience, the only true method of
testing the efficiency of a military system. . . .

We was rotten 'for we started—
  we was never disciplined;
We made it out a favor if an order was obeyed.
Yes, every little drummer 'ad 'is
  rights and wrongs to mind,
So we had to pay for teachin'—an' we paid!

There was thirty dead and wounded
  on the ground we wouldn't keep—
No, there wasn't more than twenty
  when the front began to go—
But Christ! Along the line o' flight they
  cut us up like sheep,
An' that was all we gained by doin' so!

"Faster!" Niles hissed at the two guerillas who were supporting him on either side.
  "Niles." Skilly's voice.
  "Getting into position," he gasped. "Will be there."
  "You'd better."
  He could move, but there were limits on how fast a man
with a hairline rib fracture could run. The hypnospray was
beginning to take effect, pain receding and the band around
his chest loosening.
  They had caught up with the bulk of the Icepick column;
men were crouched next to their loads of explosive death,
looking forward to the firing ahead at the enemy infantry's
blocking position, or up to where the forty-kilo loads of the
Royalist heavy mortars would drop on their heads from only
three thousand meters away.

We're here. The cost had been high. All of his headquarters and special guards, dead or left behind to block that hard-nosed Spartan bastard who wouldn't parley. *Can't blame him, but it was worth a try.*

"Drill A, Drill A!" Niles gasped, over the command push. Maximum gain. "*DRILL A!*" His escort stopped, and he pulled open the throat of his own armor to seal the ring around his neck; the Helot senior commanders had offworld helmets with all the trimmings, for obvious reasons.

Stasis dissolved into action; nobody had explained why Drill A was practiced so often, but the movements were automatic. Helmet off. Pull the plastic bag out of its case on the belt, drag it over the head, yank the tab. Disconcerting how it plastered itself to the face and neck, but the areas that touched mouth and nose turned permeable instantly; permeable to air molecules, and nothing else. Helmet on . . . even the men probing with fire at the Royalist line ahead stopped the necessary few seconds. Or most did, from the way the sound dropped off for a few seconds, and anybody who didn't . . .

Rockets burst overhead; there were cries of alarm from the Helot columns, but no rain of bomblets followed.

. . . anybody who didn't, deserved what was about to happen to them.

"Kolnikov!" he snapped, as they came to the head of the column. "Hit them, hit them *now.*"

It was quiet ahead. All quiet. The gas must have acted more quickly than he thought. The Helots were already surging forward through the woods; their screams no less chilling for being muffled through their gas filters. Niles drove forward himself, the pain in his side was distant, he would pay for it later, no *time* to think of that. Past the enemy line, past gunners sprawled shot or bayonetted around their machine gun, helmets off and gas filters in their hands. Firing, screaming; the company behind him deploying and charging uphill, at right angles to the Royalist blockforce's position, rolling it up from the downslope flank, throwing them back toward the top of the ridge.

Grenades crumped and rifles chattered; he could see figures darting through the woods. Firing, falling; not all the enemy were down, the RSI's training was recent and the response to the gas alert quick . . . but it was enough. They were getting past the enemy. Losing troops, but they were getting past, moving faster now. . . .

"Keep moving, Kolnikov!" he said, turning from the fight and loping up to one of the sleds. The men pulling it were sprinting now, their breath harsh and rasping through the filters, faces red and contorted into gorgon-shapes. One stumbled and went down as a bullet punched into his side. His comrades ripped him free almost without breaking stride, and Niles snatched up the rope and put it over his shoulder.

"We're through, everyone move, this is *it, do* it, lads, go, go, *go.*"

Ahead was the knoll where the weakest of the Brotherhood forces waited; the Eighteenth, the one that had been dropping off men for the firebases. Men and weapons . . .

"Go, go, go!" The sky screamed as the follow-on bombardment launched. He had lost a third of his frames to the Royalist counterbattery fire, but there were enough for these two targets.

The knoll lit with a surf-wall of flame.

"They're past us, Colonel," McLaren said. "I thank you for the warning. I've lost aye more o' my laddies than I like, but 'tis no what would hae happened if we hadna known."

"Can you see the enemy?"

"Aye, they're past and running up toward the Eighteenth's encampment."

"Excellent. Regroup and get ready to go kill them." Owensford switched channels. "Stand by to Flash Blue Peter Four," he said quietly.

"Standing by."

"Let me know when they go to ground, McLaren," Owensford said.

"Aye, that I will, Colonel. That I will, the murtherin' bastards."

"Warning."

"Go ahead, Guns."

"Colonel, incoming, our position and the Eighteenth's, *all* their batteries on those targets. Thirty seconds to impact." A second's pause. "Second launch. I should have better counterbattery after this, but we're going to be buttoned up in our holes until they run out of rockets." The mortar crews had no overhead protection, and the submunitions would slaughter them if they stood to their weapons.

"Right. Button up and stay buttoned. Andy, get me the Eighteenth."

"Eighteenth Brotherhood, Wilson."

"Wilson, they'll be battering hell out of your old position. Get down and stay down. When the bombardment's over, continue your withdrawal."

"Sir, we'd like to go after them."

"Negative. Your mission is to stay intact and stay alive. Just by existing you keep the bastards in the sack they put themselves in. They thought they'd fight through you. They don't know you're still organized and on their flank."

"Aye, aye, sir."

"Good man. Hang in there."

WhumpWhumpWhumpWhump—the bursting charges of the rockets went on longer this time, much longer. The aching moment of comparative silence, and then the long roar of white noise. The sound of the wire shrapnel hitting the sides of the command car was like being inside a steel bucket that was being sandblasted. The seven tons of armor rocked back and forward as the bomblets cascaded off its hull.

A much louder explosion, and for a moment he thought the command van *would* turn over.

"Sastri here. We lost one of the one-sixty-mm's, something hit the ready ammunition in the pit with the tube," he said. A hint of real pain this time; like most gunners, the officer from Krishna loved his artillery pieces. "Priorities?"

"Stand by to flash the Eighteenth's former area. They'll learn in a minute that they aren't the only ones who can be clever."

"Sir, I have the Third Brotherhood on the push. Secure."

"Owensford here."

"Colonel, they—there was at least a company of them, we ran right into them while the gas attack was on, what shall I do?"

"*Stop* them," Owensford said. "You *know* where they are, you still outnumber them, just *stop* them. Don't let them through, and it won't be long. Henderson, I gather you went to their support. Report."

"Sir. Fifteen percent casualties."

"Gas situation?"

"We're all right. The Third Brotherhood took some heavy losses. Lot of them down, still alive."

"Leave 'em for the medics. If you don't hold that position, they'll all be dead anyway. Running away just gets you killed, you and everyone you left behind as well."

"Aye, aye, sir."

"Consolidate your present position, mop up those hostiles who are giving the Third trouble, then push directly south down the valley towards me, keeping the armored cars on your western flank as close to the forest as possible. Hit the force that's blocking McLaren, and roll in on the rear of the people attacking the Eighteenth Brotherhood's old encampment from the valley."

"Sir."

"Morrentes here, Colonel, the rebs are over the wire, they're over the wire, I've lost two of my observation outposts and Firebase One isn't reporting, they're using some sort of precision-guided light missile, laser or optical or something they're flying them right through the *firing slits* of our bunkers—"

"It's a damned good thing you're not in them, then. Calm down, Morrentes." Peter watched as data flowed into the map table. The scouts were doing their job, the river base was sending data. A wedge, right through the eastern perimeter of the base, driving straight for the CP and the artillery.

"You can't let them get the artillery, or we've all had it. I know we scattered your troops, now collect what you've got left and get ready to counterattack. Defend those guns. You're to hold them until Barton gets there. Less than an hour."

"Yes sir."

"Good man. Out. Ace?"

"On the river, Pete. They tried to stop us, but we had a surprise for them. ETA as per."

"Thank you."

More bomblets rattled against the command caravan. "The great thing," Peter said to no one in particular, "the great thing is not to lose your nerve."

The third wave of enemy rockets had stopped. The ridge outside was almost swept clean of snow, littered with dead men and mules—others were limping or running through the emplacement, adding their element of horror and chaos—but the flanking infantry companies were moving, deploying and heading south. There were figures moving and muzzle flashes all over the Eighteenth's former position. It was time.

Whunf. The 106mm recoilless gun crashed, igniting the brush behind it. The shell hammered up a gout of dirt two hundred meters ahead, and a platoon of Helot infantry threw themselves forward on the position.

"Keep moving, keep moving!" Niles said again; his throat was hoarse, but it was not safe yet to take off the gas filters; water seemed like a dream of paradise, and rancid sweat soaked his uniform inside the armor, chilling when it came into contact with the outside air.

He dashed forward himself. His troops were firing wildly, charging forward, in among the enemy bunkers—

No one was shooting back. The Royalists must have been stunned by the artillery bombardment.

"Kolnikov!"

"Platoon Leader ben Bella here, sir. Company Leader Kolnikov's dead."

Oh, sodding hell. He had been one of their CD men; only a Garrison Marine officer, but competent in a humorless Russian way.

"Are you in contact with Sickle elements?"

"Yes, sir. They're considerably disorganized, sir, the Fifty-first Brotherhood mauled them pretty bad before they withdrew."

"Well, *get* them organized, man!"

CRUMP. Shockwave, another, like hammer blows. Downslope a dozen more tall flowers of dirt with sparls of fire blossoming at their hearts. The enemy 160mm's were back in action—astonishing, with the intensity of the bombardment they'd just gone through—*and that used up the last of our rocket ammunition. Bloody hell.*

The last Helot elements burst out of the wood, a wave a hundred men strong. Niles grinned to himself; it was the right time, but also an interesting way to get men to advance—have the enemy shell them into it.

"INCOMING!"

The troops ran to the enemy bunkers.

"Fuck all, there's nobody here!"

"Empty! No bodies, nothing!"

"INCOMING!"

"Take cover!"

Nlles ran toward the nearest bunker, then stopped. "Stay out of those bunkers!" he screamed. "Stay out, it's a trap, it's a trap!" Too late. His men were diving into the bunkers as the enemy artillery came in.

He dove to the ground and tried to make himself small, as bomblets and VT fell around him.

Empty bunkers. Royalist artillery registered on this position, ready to fire as soon as he got here. They'd known he was coming, and that meant that the bunkers—

A bunker ten yards to his left exploded in fire. Then another. And another.

Mines. Command detonated mines. The artillery bombardment continued, as one by one the bunkers exploded in fire and white phosphorus, and Niles's command disintegrated.

Skida Thibodeau dodged behind a lacework of fallen trees and turned her binoculars on the main enemy base down below at the river. Floating curves of fire reached out towards her. While Icepick fought its way through the valley, the

headquarters guards units had moved parallel to them. At
the last moment she came in from the North in the only
helicopter available, flying low to the ground, a terrifying
experience but it wasn't likely the distracted enemy would
spot the machine before it dropped her off and went back
to the base camp.

The Spartan river base was a semicircle backed on the river,
lit like day now by burning timber, smashed wagons, the fires
from the barges anchored by the shattered piers. Lights sparkled
all around the perimeter of it, bulging inward here and there,
bulging in furthest from the west, a wedge cut out of the half-
pie. The wedge sent out licks of fire, flame-thrower fire, to
the strongpoints holding out in its path. Just beyond the point
of the wedge longer flashes sparked, mortars firing to support the Royalists.

Suddenly fire fell into the wedge. The men dodged into
bunkers, into holes—

The bunkers began to explode one by one, killing her troops.

Kali eat they eyes, it not working, she thought disgustedly.
The Helots had been relying on overrunning the base while the
defenders were still reacting to the gas attack. Something had
gone wrong. The Brotherhood fighters had recovered too fast
and were dying too hard; the Helots did not have the weight
of numbers or metal to overcome the stiffening resistance.

Or worse. *How did they know we coming? Traitors! Royals
must have spies in the Helots, spies, how else could they know?
It was a good plan, can't go wrong, must be spies.*

Suddenly the Royals were on the move. The big unit on
the ridge above, the one that Icepick had fought past, it wasn't
killed at all, and now it was coming down the hill to close
the trap.

There was gunfire behind her. The Royals were moving in
that way, too! *One more push.* It was a good plan, too good
to give up now, just because a few things went wrong. Something always goes wrong.

She swept her binoculars around the hill. Aha! "They got
observation from up there," she muttered. It was the last of
the river base's outposts, the last one holding out.

"Follow me!" she shouted. The reserve company advanced
behind her. The fire from the observation base was still heavy,
and she found the attack squads grouped in the last cover,
huddling against the timber and rock. She rolled into the biggest
hollow.

"Who's in charge here?" she said.

"F-f-field Prime!" A boy, looking pathetically young, none

of the street-tough now. "I am, Field Prime, at least, Group Leader Metakzas is dead. Platoon Leader Swaggart, ma'am."

"OK. Swaggart. Keep calm, fill me in."

Tears of frustration glistened in his eyes, but his mouth snarled. "They . . . it was so *close*, we got the gatling out with the flamethrower and started to pile in, then a mortar round hit right behind Group Leader and they came back at us, pushed us back over the wire. We tried, we really did, Field Prime."

"Skilly know, boy. Quiet." They certainly had; half the reinforced company sent to take this position looked to be out there, hanging on the wire or scattered in front of the Royalist firing positions. Strong positions, with good overhead log-and-earth cover.

She looked up the slope; the gatling was still dead, but there were functioning machine guns in the two bunkers flanking it. The covering wire had been blown with bangalore torpedoes, long tubes of explosives pushed in under it, but there might be live directional mines. *No help for it*, she said, taking a long breath. *Starting out, you knew it come to this.*

"Weapons," she said. The Meijian answered.

"Sanjuki here."

"You got those mortars silenced yet?"

As if in answer, a bright light arched through the sky from the east; it seemed to hesitate and then plunged down toward the burning chaos of the river base. Launched from a stubby melted-looking automatic mortar, and guided by a fiber-optic cable. There was a tiny Tri-V camera in the nose, but only fractions of a second to guide it in.

"One more down. They have excellent overhead protection, Field Prime, and only open their firing slits for a few seconds."

She gritted her teeth; Skida Thibodeau had always hated excuses. You did it, that was all.

"Field Two, how it going?"

"Hard work, Skilly." Two-knife's gravel voice. "We killing them, but the *rabiblanco's* not giving up much."

"Keep at it, I get their eyes off you." Back to the Meijian. "Fire mission, ring Base One," she said.

"Yes, Field Prime—that is very close to your position—"

"*Skilly know!* Skilly says do it, and *now!*"

"All right," she continued, switching to local push. "Skilly is here, *compadres*. What you all waiting for, the Cits to send you enough lead you can open a bullet factory? This way up!"

The rockets crashed down, and the air filled with steel. "Follow me!"

✧   ✧   ✧

"Urrgk."

Private Brother Pyrrhos McKenzie spat, coughed, spat again. The fluid from his lungs seemed to be about half blood and half thick clear *something* that he didn't want to think about. Everyone else in the bunker was dead, he thought—Ken when the gas came, and Leontes with a bullet through the face in the last attack. He hung over the grips of the gatling, blood and brains from the wound and the inside of his helmet still leaking down on the metal; it sizzled, the breech-ring hot enough to fry the matter that slimed it into a hard crust.

Glad I can't smell, McKenzie thought. The radio was squawking, but there was no time to listen to that. Breathe. Deep bubbling sounds, like air going through a coffee maker. Cough, and his mouth filled with the heavy salt warmth. Spit. A little better on the next breath. Up. Impossible to stand, haul yourself up handover . . . handoverhand. Gasping, he stumbled two steps to the firing slit and collapsed over the weapon, knocking the other militiaman's body off it.

"Sorry, Leo," he wheezed; that was a mistake, he went into another coughing fit and something in his chest felt like a hot knitting needle. *Only right.* Leo and he had been ephebes together, candidates for the Phraetrie. He was going to marry Leo's sister Antigone when they both turned twenty-three. The coughing went on a long time, but he felt a little better afterwards, though, and blinked his eyes clear while his hands fumbled at the grips of the gatling. Took up the slack on the spade grips, and the electric motor whined, spinning the barrels with blurring speed. His thumbs rested on the firing buttons on top of the grips.

God, there's a lot of them. Crawling towards him, but he was nearly level with the ground here. Lots of dead people out there, dead mules and horses, the gas had gotten them. Burning stuff, crates.

He depressed the muzzles, stroked the buttons. *Brrrrrrrrt. Brrrrrrrt.* The recoil surged in his arms, and he coughed again; the liquid spurted out of his mouth and hit the barrels, spraying. Rebels dropped, killed, sawn in half by the fire. The enemy scattered, rolling out of his line of fire; he walked the bursts over crates, bodies, anything that might give cover. Wood and flesh and mud exploded away from the solid streams of heavy 15mm rounds, bullets that would punch right through a mule. One hundred rounds a second, and there was a *big* bin of ammunition right there beneath the firing step.

Brrrrrt. They were shouting out there, or screaming or

something. Trying to crawl closer. Closer to him and Leo, closer to Antigone and mom. *Brrrrrrrt.*

Leonidas. Megistias. Dieneces. The heroes of Thermopylae, he'd been a little bored learning that in school. *I suppose they didn't want to die either,* he thought with a sudden cold lucidity; his knees felt weaker, and the corners of his mouth were leaking. *Alpheus. Maro. Eurytus.*

Another burst. Another, swinging wide to cover the full arc of the bunker's semicircular firing slit, there ought to be a couple of automatic riflemen in support. More rebels down, others trying to crawl backward, some dragging their wounded.

Demaratus the lesser, Deonates—

Skida slumped to the ground, panting. The ground under her heaved slightly as the satchel charge they had thrown into the last bunker went off; flame shot out the firing slits all around.

"OK," she croaked, as much to herself as to the survivors, and used her rifle to push herself up to her knees; the wound in the leg was not too bad, just a gouge out of the muscle really. Bullets were cracking by overhead, so she crawled to the edge of the sandbags, rolled over onto the ground.

That put her next to Platoon Leader Swaggart; on an impulse she reached out to close his eyes, then surprised herself even more by bending to kiss his brow.

Shit, she thought. *Maybe Skilly should have stayed in hidehunting and hijacking.*

"Intercept one," she said, paused to swill out her mouth from her canteen. "Field Prime here. Report."

"They got past us."

"*What?*"

"They had a fucking six-tube *rocket launcher* under tarps on all the hovertruck roofs, Field Prime! As soon as we opened up they all turned and let us have it, my company is *dead* and we lost both● the recoilless! I got maybe ten effectives left."

"OK," Skida said. *Think, bitch.* She looked down at the base. "Shit again," she mumbled.

The wedge below was a sheet of fire, white phosphorus and blown bunkers. They weren't going to overrun the Brotherhood artillery positions. Some of the other penetrations had made progress, but even as she looked tiny figures surged out of the headquarters bunkers and struck the extending flank.

Why? Traitors, it had to be. Someone back at headquarters, knowing she was coming in here, someone who wanted her dead, someone who wanted to take over the Movement, that must be it, and now the Royals were moving. *Shit, pretty soon they trap us all!* It was hard to think.

"OK, Intercept One, pull back to rendevous." At the firebase they had overrun, the first one north of here.

"Pull back with what? To what? Dis de Revo*lution*! Fuck the Revolution!"

Her phones went dead.

She changed channels. "Field Two."

"Field Two's down," a voice answered her. "Senior Group Leader Mendoza here. Orders, ma'am?" Mendoza sounded so tired he had almost stopped caring. For a moment Skida did as well.

"*He dead?*" she cried, voice almost shrill. *Two-knife?*

"No, hit pretty bad. We're carrying him." Desperation. "Orders *please*."

No one to talk to. Can't tell this one it's over, time to bug. Skida raised a fist and hammered it into the wound on her leg, using the savage pain to drive her mind back into action.

"Right," she said coolly. "Consolidate, throw back that counterattack. Dig in, put in supressing fire, get your wounded out. I gives fire-control over to you. Sanjuki, got that? Including you special stuff. And get those mortars hopping. All assault leaders," she continued. "Anyone about to break through?"

Silence.

"OK, Plan Beta, prepare. The relief force made it and they going be here soon." *About ten minutes. That fast thinking, those rockets. Skilly must see that officer has an accident.* "All elements on the east side of the perimeter, Field Prime authorize tactical withdrawal." Bug out.

Run. Live to fight another day. "Time to talk."

She touched a preselected sequence on her helmet, one that would blur her voice.

"Colonel, I have a message," Andy Lahr said. "Claims to be the Helot supreme commander."

"Hah." His command caravan was hull-down, two klicks from the former position of the Eighteenth. Forty-kilo shells from the heavy mortars were passed overhead and fell into the Helot positions. The armored cars were coming up in support.

The only thing they have left is their artillery, and they're pretty well out of rockets for that. "Where's the signal coming from?"

"Up on the ridge, where they overran the Brotherhood outpost."

"Hah. Get me Mace."

"Scouts, Captain Mace."

"Jamey, have a hard look at Ridge 503. Figure out how you'd retreat from there toward the enemy artillery base. Put one of your best SAS teams in a good position, and stand by weapons. I think theyll have targets to designate soon enough. And watch for vehicles, someone claiming to be their top leader is up there and they may send something for him."

"You got it."

"Andy, when we put the rebel commander on, I want you to listen. Patch Barton in too. Private comments to me if indicated."

"Yes, sir. Helot field commander, I have the Colonel. Go ahead."

A woman's voice answered, astonishingly enough. Blurred by an antivoiceprint device, otherwise a clear contralto with a lilting Caribbean accent.

"This Spartan Liberation Army Field Prime, proposin' a mutual withdrawal under terms, with temporary armistice," she said.

Owensford felt his lips turn in a snarl. "Interesting. What are you offering in exchange for letting you get away?"

A laugh, cool and amused. "You can't stop us, merc. We get out of here when we want. Look, up there, we gots threes north and south of you. You attack one way, we come the other."

"I see." Peter thumbed the command set. "Get a good fix on that position, and tell Jamey to get his scouts moving."

"And you come both north and south, and we bugs out," she said reasonably. "One part of the Dales just about like another to us, mon. We got enough firepower left to keep you heads down while we be going, too. And you notice something? All your mules be dead, mon. No transport, nohows; hell, you goan have to *hunt* for the *pot.* You got visual from your river base?"

"Yes," he said, switching on a screen with an overhead view.

"Watch this. See the second mortar on the right?"

A few seconds later something like a very quick firefly darted into the spyeye's view, did a double loop and slammed neatly into the steel cover over the mortar's hatch.

"These things got a range of better than thirty klicks," the voice went on. "So you relief force not going to land here. Gots to land downstream, *fight* they way through thick woods we holding and have mined, by the time they get here we gone. You want to chase us through the woods, booby traps and ambush for a thousand klicks? All right with me, mon. No satellites for you, now, either."

"Thank you," Sastri said on the private channel. "We have located the source of that rocket. Out of our range, I fear. I will notify Captain Mace."

"Another thing," the rebel leader said. "We got, oh, two-fifty prisoners up there, another eighty-so in your Firebase One we overrun, and here at the *riv*er. You don't agree, we kill them all."

"Typical," Jesus Alana said. Hah, Owensford thought. Andy must have the entire staff listening to this. Good.

"Typical terrorists," Alana continued. "When things go wrong they threaten hostages."

"I will hold you personally responsible for any violation of the Laws of War," Peter Owensford said.

Laughter "Responsible? Mon, me head in a noose already if we lose! What you do, hang me twice? This no gentlemon war, dis de Revo*lu*tion. All or nothing.

"Too, we figure you got maybe fifteen percent casualties, lots of gas-wounded what die if they doan get regenn soon. We run away, you kill a few more of us, but not much left of pretty-mon army, hey?"

"I'm listening."

"You talk sensible, we let you fly them out."

That could be crucial; the time between injury and treatment was the single most important factor in survival rates. Particularly for the ones with lungs burned by the desiccants.

"Field Prime moves a company or so out into the open, they hostages. Doan expect you to trust we. You wounded, they *me* hostages."

Owensford changed channels. "Get me Kicker Six. Fast." He switched back. "I don't have authority to make deals with you. I'll have to get a political leader."

"Mon you damn well better hurry doin' it."

"That's as may be," Owensford said. "But until I get political authorization, the answer to your request is no."

"How long it take?"

"Depends on my communications," Owensford said.

"I give you fifteen minutes. Then no deal. I call you back."

"Headquarters calling, Prince," Harv said. He held out the handset.

I don't have time, there are a million things happening all at once and I can't keep track of them— He took the instrument. "Kicker Six here."

"I need to speak to Prince Lysander."

"Sir?"

"Political decision time," Owensford said. "The enemy is offering a truce. The bait is about four hundred Brotherhood soldiers, plus letting us fly out the wounded. They'll release their hostages in exchange for a cease-fire. Otherwise they kill them."

"Will—will they do that?"

"They're terrorists. Of course they will."

"What do we lose if we take them up on it?" Lysander asked.

"Pursuit. I've got the SAS teams moving into place, and a new supply of Thoth. We have an overextended enemy, nearly exhausted, with their elite forces strung out in exposed places. They claim they can always get more troops, but that's exactly what they can't do. It takes *time* to train lunatics out of the illiterates they start with. We're the ones who can turn Citizens into soldiers in short order."

"Four hundred Brothers."

"Or Candidates. About half in half would be my guess. If they have that many. They may be lying."

"But you don't know."

"No. Our communications haven't been that good. The figure is possible." Owensford paused. "I'm more concerned about our wounded. Some were gassed. They'll survive with prompt treatment, otherwise not."

"What would you do if they were your troops?" Lysander asked.

"I don't have to say. Every mercenary hates decisions like that. Our troops are our capital."

"What is it, Prince?" Harv demanded. "What's wrong?"

Lysander shook him off. "Colonel, you don't have to decide, but you do have to advise me. What would you do?"

"I'd win the battle. Every one of their elites we let get away is a new hero, someone to train more. But there's something else. Our troops are exhausted. I can harass the enemy as he pulls out, but what we really need is to break past their rear guards and have a real pursuit. That means more hard fighting, maybe desperate fighting. More casualties, maybe a lot more casualties, and the way the troops are placed, most of that will fall on Spartans. Not just regulars, the Brotherhood militia. I can't kid you, if we refuse the truce you'll lose men. The hostages, lots of the wounded, and more."

Lysander swallowed hard. He could hear the fighting around him. The Prince Royal's Own were still moving forward, slowed now, but still moving.

"They planned it this way," Lysander said.

"Something like that," Owensford agreed. "They had their plan, this elaborate scheme to destroy us. When that didn't work they thought to try this."

"We lose a lot if we turn them down," Lysander said. "And our men are tired too." He felt as if his head had been filled with cotton batting, then set on fire. Mostly he wanted to lie down and sleep. "Will they fight if we do? Will the Legion support us?"

"Yes."

Yes. Not maybe. No hesitation, no excuses. Yes. Lysander looked around the command post. Men dead and dying, but men doing their jobs too. And outside. Troops fought. Fought and died, but every one of them, alive or dead, was facing the enemy. He looked at Harv, who stood relaxed, but eager to move on.

Well at least one of them will follow me. And every one of those bastards we kill now is one fewer to kill our women and children, raid our ranches— And then he knew.

"Colonel Owensford, please patch me through to the Helot commander. When I have finished speaking with him, I would be pleased if you would connect me to the command link so that I can address the troops directly."

"Aye aye. The enemy commander is a woman. May I and my staff listen in on your conversation with the Helots? We can make private comments on channel B if you like."

"Please do."

"Stand by—" There were clicks in the earphones. A voice spoke in his left ear. "This is the private channel. They won't hear anything said here." Then, "Go ahead."

"Hello. With whom am I speaking?" Lysander said.

"Dis de Helot Supreme Commander. I figure who you must be if Colonel has to ask your permission to wipe his ass."

"This is Crown Prince Lysander Collins."

"Well, smell you. Dis de Revolution. You want to join it, Baby Prince?"

"I am told you wish to negotiate."

"Truce. Evacuate wounded. Exchange prisoners."

"No."

There was a long pause, then laughter. "OK, you keep my prisoners, I give you back yours. You stay in place, I pull out of here with whoever can walk. You send medics after your wounded, take care of mine."

"I will say this once. There will be no truce. I am willing to proclaim a general amnesty, provided that all of you lay down your arms immediately and surrender. The amnesty will cover all enlisted personnel including war crimes committed if acting under orders. Excepted from the amnesty will be commissioned officers accused of war crimes. They will stand trial for those crimes. You have two minutes to consider this offer."

Shit he one hard nosed bastard. Skilly looked around at the remains of her command. Down by the river the wedge was shrinking as she watched. Not much left there. On the ridge opposite a whole new Royal force, one that was supposed to have been wiped out, was forming up.

Her own forces were scattered across the Valley, exhausted and out of communications for the most part. There would be very little new fire support.

Not much time left. Not much time at all. She tried to keep the mocking tone in her voice when she answered the Prince, but deep in her throat was a tightness. This wasn't working at all well.

And back at the base is a traitor I have to kill, kill for me, and Two-knife, and all these kids. She thumbed off the microphone. "You two, get ready to move out. We going out of here fast and light. The rest of you, dig in, dig in and fight. I go get more troops, I come back for you." She cleared her throat and thumbed the microphone on again.

Mocking laughter sounded in Lysander's headset. "That no offer at all. Prince, you don' take this truce, I cut de throats. With pictures. Lots of pretty pictures for de TV stations, they be happy to show all your Cits what you make happen."

"Typical," Jesus Alana said in his left ear. "Typical terrorist. 'Look what you made me do.' Keep her talking, Highness. They like to talk."

"If you do not accept the amnesty, then all of your people will be dealt with as traitors," Lysander said.

"They already traitors to your government. You goin' punish them for what I do?" A chuckle. "You stallin' me. You ain't goin' to leave all these Brotherhood babies to die. Some of them coughin' their lungs up now, they going to drown in they own snot, and it's all your fault. Come on, let's stop this fight and take care of these people."

A tempting offer.

"Keep her talking," Alana repeated urgently.

"What do you want?"

"General amnesty. Forgive and forget. Peace, the war is over. We all goes home."

"So you can start killing ranchers again next week. No thank you. Lay down your arms and I will spare the lives of all your troops, and your officers."

"I notice you doan say you let ME go. Listen to this." There was a long burbling scream. "I hope you hear that all your life, that what you done to your brotherhoods."

"Make your decision. Accept amnesty or we will hunt you down and kill you."

"You done killed your people," the voice said. "And that *all* you kill." The phones went dead.

And that's that. He tried not to think about the dead and dying. *But it's cowardly not to think about them. I don't want more of this. I didn't ask to be born Prince of Sparta.*

Leonidas didn't ask to be born king, either. The Three Hundred didn't ask to go to the Hot Gates.

He thumbed the microphone button. "Give me all units."

There was a short pause. "You got it. Want me to announce you?"

"If you please."

"All units, stand by. Crown Prince Lysander Collins will speak."

"Brothers. Brothers and Legionnaires, brothers and sisters all. This is not a speech. I don't know how to make great speeches, and I'm too tired even if I did.

"I just want to say that you've won a great victory, and I'm proud of you all, but the day isn't over. The enemy still lives. Now they want to run away, to hide in their caves so they can creep out and kill and maim and destroy. It's all they know. We see what they do and we say that's inhuman. Brothers and sisters! It is inhuman. They do inhuman acts because they are no longer humans themselves!

"For every one of them you kill today you will save the life of a Spartan, of a dozen Spartans.

"You've beaten them, thrown back the best they have, beaten them despite their poison gas and terror weapons. They are beaten as an army. We have a glorious victory—but they are not all dead. Too many live, and while they live they threaten our homes. Every one of them killed is a victory. Every one that escapes is a defeat for us.

"The way will be hard. My advisors tell me we will lose as many of our Brothers and Sisters in this pursuit as we have lost in the battle—but we will win, we can destroy them utterly.

"We have beaten them in war. Now we must hunt them down and kill them. Kill them like the wolves they are. For our homes. For our country. Kill them."

Lysander set down the microphone. There was silence for a moment, then sound, a swelling of sound, sound that drowned out the noise of battle.

From every part of the valley the troops were shouting, some in unison, most not, but across the battlefield the cries arose. "Kill them! For Kings and Country! For the Prince!"

There was a crackle in Lysander's phones, but it was hard to hear. His own headquarters troops were cheering with the rest of them. Even Harv was shouting his head off.

"Yes?" Lysander shouted into the microphone.

"This is Colonel Owensford. Awaiting orders, Prince Lysander."

CHAPTER FOURTEEN

Crofton's Encyclopedia of the Inhabited Planets
(2nd Edition):

Treaty of Independence, Spartan: Agreement signed between the Grand Senate of the CoDominium and the *Dual Monarchy of Sparta* (q.v.), 2062. The Constitution- alist Society's original settlement agreement with the Colo- nial Bureau of the CoDominium had provided for full internal self-government, but the CoDominium retained jurisdiction over a substantial enclave in *Sparta City,* (q.v.), the orbital transit station *Aegis* (q.v.), and the refueling facilities around the gas-giant planet *Zeus*. In addition, during the period of self-government a CoDominium Marine Regiment remained in garrison on Sparta and its commander also acted as Governor-General, enforcing the residual powers retained by the Colonial Bureau, mostly having to do with the regulation of involuntary colonist and convict populations.

In line with Grand Senator Fedrokov's "New Look" policy of reducing CoDominium involvement in distant systems where practicable, negotiations began with the Dual Monarchy in 2060. Under the terms of the Treaty, the Royal government became fully responsible for internal order and external defense of the Spartan system, and all restrictions on local military and police forces were removed. The transit station and Zeus-orbit refueling stations were also turned over to the Royal government. However, the treaty also stipulated that certain facilities were to be maintained, at Spartan expense, for the use of the CoDominium authorities and the Fleet; these included docking, fueling and repair functions, and orbit to surface shuttles. Also mandated was the continued receipt of involuntary colonists at a level to be set by the Bureau of Relocation, and for this purpose the CoDominium enclave in Sparta City was retained with a reduced garrison. Penalty provisions in the Treaty authorized direct intervention by the Commandant of the enclave should the Royal government fail to fulfill these obligations. . . .

"In the long run, luck is given only to the efficient."
—Helmuth von Moltke

The helicopter dipped into the valley. At its lowest point it slowed briefly, just long enough to let Sergeant Billy Washington and his four teammates tumble out to land beside the gear they'd pushed out ahead of them.

The helicopter continued on over the next ridge. Anyone tracking it from a distance would have seen it enter and leave the valley flying just above the nap of the earth, and would have no reason to suspect that it had done anything unusual while out of sight between ridges.

Sergeant Billy Washington and Monitor Rafe Skinner went up the ridge first, taking plenty of time, because they had time and it never hurt to be careful. The best surveillance they had indicated that the ridge top would be empty, but they took half an hour making sure that it was, before Skinner took up a post where he could keep watch, and Washington motioned for the others to come up.

"All clear," Washington said.

"Thank you, Sergeant Washington." Technical Sergeant Henry Natakian, like the two privates who carried the heavy gear, was Spartan, although he was a full Citizen and they were still Candidates. Because of his technical education Natakian had been posted into the communications section, Headquarters Company, of the First Royals. He'd been surprised to find himself subordinate to a Legionnaire sergeant of no particular technical education, but it hadn't taken long to learn why. Now he hoped that the black man would elect to stay with the Royals rather than return to the Legion. Billy Washington might not have all the technical skills Natakian and his Spartans did, but he understood war. Washington and Skinner had saved them from Helot traps four times in the last three days.

Washington located the precise spot he'd been given on his map. As the two privates humped the heavy gear up the ridge, Washington and Natakian set up the base tripod for their relay antenna. Ridge 602 didn't overlook the source of the Helot artillery, but it was in line of sight to a hill that did; and while it didn't have line of sight to Legion Headquarters, it could see another ridge line that did. . . .

The helicopter dropped Sergeant Taras Hamilton Miscowsky and his twelve-man SAS section nine kilometers from the Helot artillery base, which put him four kilometers from the hilltop that overlooked the Helot base area.

Miscowsky wasn't happy with the assignment. It wasn't that he anticipated trouble taking his objective. Miscowsky hoped there would be some of the scumbags up there on the ridge above, but it wasn't likely. The Helots couldn't guard every possible observation point, and there was nothing special about Hill 633, except that it had a line of sight to Hill 602 where Billy Washington would be setting up his relay. Another team would be moving on Hill 712, which was a more obvious place for the Legion to put an observation post. That team would probably run into trouble, but then they were expecting it.

The problem wasn't this assignment. Miscowsky wanted to be somewhere else. He knew better, knew he was the best man for what he was doing, and that helped, but it still bothered him that he wasn't looking after his former Captain's wife. The rescue team sent to her downed airplane had found no survivors. There were four bodies, one a man with his throat cut, but none of them had been Lieutenant Deborah Lefkowitz.

Sergeant Mendota was with the rescue team. He was as good a tracker as Miscowsky. Maybe better. In this terrain, probably a lot better. If anyone could track down the slimeballs, he could. And after all, Mendota had been on Jerry Lefkowtiz's team too, but it still bothered Miscowsky that he wasn't going on that hunt.

Miscowsky didn't think they'd ever find the lieutenant alive, not unless she was here at the Helot base, and he didn't really expect that. Back at the front, the Helots were bugging out all over, abandoning their wounded and killing their prisoners, and there wasn't any reason to believe they'd taken the trouble to transport Lieutenant Deborah Lefkowitz when they left their own wounded behind. They'd probably killed her, cut her throat like her pilot and those Brotherhood prisoners one of the Scout units found. Maybe it was worse than that. Mendota's report had been sketchy, obviously left something out. They'd found something they didn't want to talk about, something having to do with the lieutenant's clothing. Miscowsky didn't want to guess what.

The blood feud tradition was strong among Taras Miscowsky's people on Haven, and he hadn't forgotten despite his Legion experiences. Hatred filled him as he sent his scouts ahead up the ridge. Cold hatred, but it didn't change his actions. The Legion's SAS people were all selected for their ability to use good judgment in high stress conditions. Hatred only fueled caution. Jerry Lefkowitz had been Miscowsky's officer when he first joined the Legion, and had Lefkowitz not placed as much value on the lives of his men as he did on personal survival, Miscowsky would not have lived through his first battle. As it was, Taras Miscowsky expected to live long enough to settle the score for his captain. Not just those who did it. Those who ordered it. All of them.

"Observation teams in place," Captain Mace reported. "Stand by for data updates."

The displays on Peter Owensford's map table blanked out momentarily, then came up again. Many of the large blurred splotches had been replaced by smaller, more precise figures. Owensford bent over the map of the enemy headquarters area. He used a light pen to circle one section. "How reliable is this?"

"Very," Mace said. "Miscowsky has it under observation. That's real time data."

Owensford smiled thinly. "Looks like they're packing up to leave."

"Yes, sir, looks like that to me, too," Andy Lahr said. "Maybe we ought to help them—"

"No doubt." Owensford turned to Jameson Mace. "Jamey, you've got full priority on Thoth bundles one through four, secondary after that. Use 'em when your team on the spot thinks we'll get the most out of them."

"Roger," Mace said. "It's a judgment call. The longer we wait, the more chance the scouts will have of blocking their escape. On the other hand, the sooner we strike, the more we get before they bug out at all. Then there's the business of the Helot commander."

Owensford turned knobs to scroll the map to the ridge above the river camp. "Last traced to this area. I see McLaren's moving in there now. Andy, see if you can get McLaren on the line."

"Aye aye."

"McLaren here."

"Captain, what are you finding up there?"

"Dead and dying, Colonel. Little else. If they can run they've done it. And the usual. Our lads, hands tied, throats cut, or bayonetted. Or worse, I will no describe some of what we've seen. 'Tis no easy on my lads—"

"It's not supposed to be," Owensford said. "That's what the Helots are counting on. They want to turn us into beasts no better than they are. Don't let them."

"Aye."

"Easier to say than do," Andy Lahr muttered.

Owensford nodded. "Captain, any sign of the rebel commander?"

"Now, how would I know if I found such?" McLaren demanded.

"Sorry, forgot you weren't in on that conversation. The Helot commander's a woman," Owensford said. "At least the voice was contralto."

"Och. Well, there are no women up here, Colonel. No women at all, and sights here no woman should see. Except that one, and I suppose she saw it all. She's no here, Colonel."

Geoffrey Niles let the river carry him down past the Spartan encampments. He had lashed himself to the bleeding corpse of one of his troops. The now useless chemical protection gear kept his clothing dry. It also kept him afloat, and the current soon took him out of the combat zone.

I told them it wouldn't work, he thought. *Too complex. I told them.*

There was no place to go. His command was destroyed. There was supposed to be an emergency rendezvous point, but he wasn't sure he wanted to go there. Would Skilly understand there was nothing he could have done? No more any of them could do? Skida Thibodeau wasn't one to take excuses for failure. *Even if the failure was hers? Because of her plan?* But she wasn't likely to admit that.

He thought of surrender, but he was afraid to do that. Gas. War gas. The books talked about hanging officers for using poison gas. *It wasn't my fault! I didn't want to do that.*

He could say they hadn't told him. It would even be true. They'd said non-lethal chemical agents in the planning sessions. Of course everyone had known better. There were no non-lethal agents effective enough for what they'd attempted. Even the war gasses, the lethal agents Murusaki used, hadn't been good enough. Nothing had been good enough.

What could we have done? They'd been good troops, all of them, they'd done all that courage could do, and it hadn't been good enough. We were so close, a little more and we'd have had his artillery, then we could have punished the Brotherhood troops, but it wasn't good enough, the plan, the gas, none of it was enough.

Should it have been good enough? It had seemed so romantic, help the poor against the Spartan aristocracy, overthrow the tyrants, but the Spartan kings weren't tyrants. Not at all. And the poor, the downtrodden—

He thought of what Skilly had ordered. Kill all the prisoners. His troops would have obeyed, but of course he hadn't transmitted that order. Some of them had done terrible things on their own, but at least they hadn't killed all those Brotherhood troops, the wounded ones they'd captured, the ones disabled by gas.

I didn't do that, anyway. But Skilly had ordered it. And worse. That female Lieutenant, the one from the airplane. Jeff hadn't been there, but he'd heard what happened.

I was on the wrong side. This isn't Lawrence of Arabia. No romance here. This isn't anything I want to be part of.

The current carried him around another bend of the river. He was far from the combat zone now. He began to shiver. The cold was seeping in despite his protective gear. It was time to get out of the water. He watched for a sandbar, some place to land.

I want to go home, he thought. But where was home?

Ten' '*hut!*"

"Please," Lysander said. The command bunker was crowded, and everyone was standing to attention. Officers moved out of the way to allow Lysander and Harv to get to the big map table. When he got to the table, Lysander looked to Peter Owensford for help. "Please," he repeated.

"Carry on," Owensford said. "Welcome to the command center, Your Highness. Have you instructions?"

"Colonel, you're in command of this force—"

"Tactical command," Owensford said. "Yes, sir. Shall we review the situation for you?"

"Colonel, you're embarrassing me—"

"Prince Lysander, there's nothing to be embarrassed about," Owensford said.

"Well, I hadn't really intended to assume command—"

"You hadn't intended to, but you did, and that's all to the good," Owensford said. "Highness, unity of command is the most important principle of war. Having you as a battalion commander violated that principle. Nothing bad came of it, but something could have, and I for one am glad it's over."

He shrugged. "Captain Bennington will see to the Prince Royal's Own. No one expects you to take tactical command here. I'll give the orders. You just tell me what you want accomplished."

Lysander nodded. His face was grim. "I want you to make the most of this pursuit," he said. "I've seen—I've been up on the hill where they had over a hundred Brotherhood prisoners. And in the field hospitals with the troops who were gassed." He shuddered. "The only thing worse than doing that to them would be to have done it for nothing."

"You didn't do it, Prince," Harv said quietly.

"Your Phraetrie brother is right," Owensford said. "You didn't do it. That's what these people want you to think, that it's your fault that your people were killed. It wasn't your fault. They're the ones who did this, not you."

"Yes. Thank you. All right, Colonel, what is our status?"

"Quite good, actually," Owensford said. "As is often the case, the bold course has proven to be the best. We lost a number of prisoners to terrorist crimes, but many of them would not have survived anyway. Meanwhile our assault casualties have been surprisingly light, and we have been able to inject SAS and Scout teams into positions to block enemy retreat paths. We have relay units to observers spotting in the enemy camp headquarters itself. Finally, we rescued forty-seven prisoners, all wounded, down by the river. The Helot officer there either didn't get the order to kill the prisoners, or didn't obey it."

"Who was he?"

"We don't know. He's probably dead. That unit was the spearhead of this crazy stunt, and took very heavy casualties. We're sorting through the survivors, but so far no one admits to being any kind of commander."

Lysander nodded. "Find out, please. Assuming it's possible, of course."

"Wilco," Andy Lahr said.

"Please continue," Lysander said. "Sorry to interrupt."

"Yes, sir." Owensford used his light pen to mark a region on the map table. The computer zoomed in on the area. "Their main force was here. They had been advancing prior to the failure of the gas attack. They then halted, milled around a while, and after we rejected their leader's offer of a cease-fire, dug in and resisted."

"Dug in," Lysander said. "Does that make sense? I'd have thought they would run away."

"So would we," Jesus Alana said. "My conclusion is that they were ordered to hold on to cover the escape of their leaders."

"Which worked," Owensford added. "Or something did. We haven't caught anyone higher ranking than their equivalent of a lieutenant, and both of those were wounded. But it cost them. By the time that force was ready to break and run we had not only pounded it pretty bad, but we had scout units across their line of escape. We don't think more than ten percent of their main unit got away."

"Good," Lysander said. "But those ten percent are their officers?" Owensford nodded. Lysander shook his head ruefully. "All right, what about their technical people?"

"Definitely Meiji mercenaries," Jesus Alana said. "We have found three. All dead, of course. We are hoping for more when we assault the Helot headquarters area."

"When will that be?"

"Probably not until tomorrow," Owensford said. "We've been bombarding the area, of course. We had to neutralize their artillery before we could deal with their dug-in forces. Now we're moving units into position for the actual assault."

"Can they escape after dark?"

"Some will," Owensford said. "We've got scouts and SAS units in the area, but they'll never get all of them. That complex of caves is big."

"What about their missing leader? Will she go back there?"

Jesus Alana shrugged. "Quien sabe? But in my opinion, no. There would be no reason for her to risk her neck again. No. Highness, in my opinion she is gone. A pity but there is nothing we can do."

"I wouldn't want her to escape."

Jesus Alana frowned slightly. "Highness, I would pray that if she escapes, as she has, she never returns. But I am afraid we have not seen the last of that one, and I do not think you will have much reason to rejoice when next we hear of her."

Peter Owensford laid down his pointer and looked around the Council Chamber. He had certainly had an appreciative audience as he explained the campaign to the War Council. "That concludes the briefing, Sires, gentlemen, madam," he said. "In sum: thanks to the leadership of Prince Lysander we turned a tactical win into a superb strategic victory."

"My congratulations," King Alexander said. There was a tremor in his voice. "Please, take your seat. Thank you. Colonel, alas, it was unfortunate that you were unable to find more of the technical people at the enemy headquarters."

"Agreed, Sire," Owensford said. "The materiel losses have

put a heavy dent in their schedule, no doubt about that, they've been knocked back into Phase One of their plan, but it would have been a bigger blow to them if we'd captured their technocrats." Owensford shrugged. "Nothing we could do. Apparently they bugged out about the time the enemy commander did. One reason why their field troops crumpled up so easily after Prince Lysander rejected their truce offer. No tech support."

"If I may," Jesus Alana said.

"Please," Alexander prompted.

"We are wondering if this has not produced a certain tension between the Helot leaders and their Meijian employees. Each may feel betrayed by the other. Certainly there must be suspicions. Suspicions, incidentally, which we will certainly try to foster and exploit."

"Thank you," Alexander said.

"Next," Owensford said. "I expect this next item will surprise you all as much as it did me. Captain Alana."

Jesus Alana bowed slightly. He obviously was enjoying himself. "We have identified one of the Helot leaders," he said. He touched a button on his sleeve console, and a cultured British-sounding voice said, "Actually, I've got eight or ten of your men down here, badly wounded I'm afraid. Ten minutes truce—" Jesus thumbed the button and the voice cut off.

"From the events of the battle at the river camp, it was probable that this was the man who commanded the main thrust of the Helot effort. Prince Lysander"—Jesus bowed again—"instructed us to determine the identity of that commander, so we paid particular attention to the record of his attempt to negotiate a truce.

"Some of our officers believed they had heard this man before," Jesus said. "It was then simple enough to digitize his voice and set the computer searching. It found a match quickly enough." Alana touched another button, and a picture appeared on the screen: a handsome man, clean shaven except for a thin mustache. "The Honorable Geoffrey Niles," Jesus said. "Grand-nephew to Grand Senator Bronson."

"Bronson?" Henry Yamaga demanded.

"Aye, my lord," Peter Owensford said.

Someone whistled. *Freiherr* von Alderheim said, in a low voice, "Ach. Now we know who has paid for these Meiji devils to come here. But why? What interest has Bronson in Sparta?"

"I wish I knew," King Alexander said. "I very much wish that I knew."

"It makes one thing certain," Lysander said. "We aren't safe here. It isn't enough to mind our own business."

"I have always thought the CoDominium's masters would not allow us our experiment in peace," Alexander said. "I— but there is a reason why I should not speak to this. Not at this moment. Captain Alana, Captain Catherine Alana, please make your presentation."

Catherine stood. "Yes, Sire. I will now summarize a report we already delivered to His Majesty and His Highness. The King insisted that I inform the Council."

Peter Owensford stared around the room through half-closed eyes and watched for the effects of Catherine's announcement.

"The Council will recall that His Majesty has—not been quite himself," Catherine said.

Actually, he was acting like a raving maniac there at times, Peter thought. He saw that Lysander had put his hand on his father's shoulder. The Prince's mouth was set in a grim line of determination.

"We have determined the reason for this," Catherine said. "The Palace medical supplies have been tampered with. In particular, His Majesty's normal anti-agathic shots." She waited for the buzz of alarm to die away. "Of course the physicians have been testing regularly for poisons, and examining the King after—he began to act strangely. This was something a great deal more subtle than a simple poison. A tailored virus, aimed at the endocrine glands and the hormonal behavior regulation system."

"Devils," the Minster of War hissed.

"Yes, Sir Alfred," Catherine said. "Quite a devilish trick. Meijian technology, we presume. Certainly much of the equipment Jesus found in the Helot field headquarters could only have originated on Mejji, and they are known to do a great deal of genetic engineering."

"What are the effects?" Lysander asked.

"Similar to paranoid schizophrenia."

Alexander drew in his breath sharply.

"As we told you, it is only temporary, Majesty," Catherine said.

"If I may," Alexander said. The room fell silent. "I noticed that—I was not myself, much of the time. And that I tended to improve when away from the city. But I did not suspect— My friends, I wish to apologize. I have been very cruel to many of you."

"Sire—Majesty—Father it's all right—" Everyone spoke at once.

"So," Madame Rusher said. "That's why our friend Croser has been muttering about Regency provisions."

"This is too much. Far too much," Lord Henry Yamaga said.

"Indeed," *Freiherr* von Alderheim said thoughtfully. "Perhaps this will provide the final stimulus needed in certain quarters. Croser has taken advantage of the law. He thought to make himself immune to ordinary law by taking that seat in the Senate. He forgets that there is also Law."

Alexander looked to his counselors. His eyes had a haunted expression. "My friends—My dear friends, I can't trust my own judgment. Therefore, with your permission, I appoint my son Lysander Prince Regent—"

"No, Father," Lysander said. "It's not necessary."

"I agree the formal devolution isn't necessary," Madam Elayne Rusher said. "Triggers far too many formalities in its wake. Sire, if you're concerned about your judgment, you can have the same effect by taking Prince Lysander into your confidence and having him present your will to the Council."

"Do you—do all of you agree?" Alexander asked.

There was a chorus of assent.

"David?" Alexander asked.

"I would never ask you to step aside," David Freedman said. "Welcome back, sir."

"Thank you. Then so be it. In future, Prince Lysander will, acting on my advice, speak for me to this Council in the same way that Prince David speaks for my colleague. In general I will also be present, but if there is a conflict between us, my son Lysander's views shall prevail, this to be so until Lysander says otherwise in a formal Council meeting at which I am not present. I wish this entered as an order in Council with the assent of my colleague. Is this agreeable to you all? David? Thank you."

CHAPTER FIFTEEN

It is not often that historians can determine the exact
moment when history changes, and it would be hubris
for us to assume we know precisely when the intention to attempt the transformation of Sparta from an
isolated planetary state into the Spartan Hegemony
first entered the thoughts of Crown Prince Lysander.
Yet there are those who believe they not only know,
but were present that day.

—From the Preface to
From Utopia to Imperium: A History of Sparta
from Alexander I to the Accession of Lysander,
by Caldwell C. Whitlock, Ph.D.
(University of Sparta Press, 2120).

The lecture theater of the Royal Spartan War College was
an attractive mixture of old and new. The walls were paneled in wood or something indistinguishable from it. The seats
were arrayed in rising tiers, each seat comfortable enough to
avoid fatigue, yet not so well padded as to make the students
sleepy. The lecture podium was behind a large computerized
map table whose controls were duplicated both at the lectern
and in the control booth at the top of the room. Behind the
lectern were more screens, touch-sensitive so that the lecturer
could draw figures that would be automatically copied for later
printout. The acoustics of the room were excellent.

Cornet Alan Brady of the Second Royal Infantry came to
the podium. He spoke in a clear voice, and if he was in awe
of his audience his voice didn't show it.

The room was filled with officers of all ranks, from officer
cadets through General Peter Owensford; and in the center of
the front row sat Crown Prince Lysander Collins, wearing the
uniform of a Lieutenant General of Royal Infantry. The story
was that Lysander hadn't much care for the rank, but that

Major Generals Owensford and Slater insisted that if the Prince wanted to appear in uniform, he had to outrank them; and they were quite prepared to resign the Royal commissions and revert to Legion rank to make their point.

Brady didn't know, and wasn't thinking much about that anyway. He was a good enough actor to play his part without nervousness, but that meant he couldn't vary much from the script.

"Highness, Lords, Ladies, and Gentlefolk, this will be the inaugural colloquium of the Royal Lectures on Strategy made possible by a grant from *Freiherr* Bernard von Alderheim under the patronage of Their Majesties. The first lecture will be presented by Major General Slater, Commandant of the Royal War College.

"General Slater."

Hal Slater limped to the podium from his place in the front row. He set down his black malacca cane with the silver double-eagle head, a present from King Alexander, and touched controls on the lectern. An outline appeared on the lectern screen. Hal didn't like to read prepared speeches, but this lecture would incorporate quoted materials, and he wanted to get those right.

He looked out at the audience. The best and brightest of the Spartan military—young officers posted to the General Staff as well as senior Legion and Royal officers. There were also half a dozen civilians, military history students at the University admitted to the lectures for their education.

Of course there's only one real target for what I'm about to say, but I need to be careful not to make it too obvious. . . .

"Highness, my Lords, Ladies, and Gentlefolk. Many of you have recently returned from what is rapidly becoming known as the Helot War. Much of our army is still in the field.

"The campaign was a success, in that our forces destroyed much of the enemy's capabilities to wage aggressive war and harm our people. We killed or captured many of their cadre and their best troops, and we destroyed or captured a great deal of military equipment, much of it highly advanced, some advanced over anything we have.

"Unfortunately, despite this victory, the war is not over. It is quiet for the moment, but rest assured, the enemy is reorganizing. Having failed at the tactical offensive, he will assume the defensive, hide, lick his wounds, and make ready to try again.

"We may liken this battle to Thermopylae. Certainly our troops do."

There was general laughter, because, as if on cue, they could hear a section of cadets marching to class, singing, "Leonidas came marching to the Hot Gates by the sea, the Persian Shah was coming and a mighty host had he—"

"Moreover, Thermopylae as Leonidas no doubt intended, a delaying action fought to blunt the advance of the Persian army, and delay the enemy while the Athenian fleet made ready, and the rest of Greece mobilized for war. Of course it didn't work that way, and the Three Hundred went on to a glory undimmed after millennia. Yet for all the effect it will have on the future of this conflict, your battle on the Illyrian Dales might as well have ended as did Leonidas and the Three Hundred: covered with glory, but with the enemy still advancing, still able to harm our country, burn our fields, kill our women and enslave our children.

"This is the nature of this kind of war."

And that got their attention. Hal smiled thinly.

"This kind of war is called Low Intensity Conflict, or LIC. The name is unfortunate, because it is misleading. If we are to draw the correct conclusions from our recent experience, and apply the lessons we have learned to the future, it is very important to understand the threat—and to understand that so-called Low Intensity Conflict can be and has been decisive in determining the destinies of nations.

"Low Intensity Conflicts were highly important all during the latter half of the twentieth century; so much so that one prominent military historian concluded that that kind of war was the only decisive kind of war.

"After describing conventional military forces—the sort of thing you are part of, the Legion, the Royal Infantry—after describing conventional forces and decrying their expense, Creveld said:

"'One would expect forces on which so many resources have been lavished to represent fearsome warfighting machines capable of quickly overcoming any opposition. Nothing, however, is farther from the truth. For all the countless billions that have been and are still being expended on them, the plain fact is that conventional military organizations of the principal powers are hardly even relevant to the predominant form of contemporary war [which is Low Intensity Conflict, or LIC.]

"'Perhaps the best indication of the political importance of LIC is that the results, unlike those of conventional wars, have usually been recognized by the international community. . . . Considered from this point of view—"by their fruits thou shalt know them"—the term LIC itself is grossly misconceived. The same applies to related terms such as "terrorism," "insurgency," "brushfire war," or "guerrilla war." Truth to say, what we are dealing with here is neither low-intensity nor some bastard offspring of war. Rather it is WARRE in the elemental, Hobbesian sense of the word, by far the most important form of armed conflict in our time.

" ' . . . how well have the world's most important armed forces fared in this type of war? For some two decades after 1945 the principal colonial powers fought very hard to maintain the far-flung empires which they had created for themselves during the past centuries. They expended tremendous economic resources, both in absolute terms and relative to those of the insurgents who, in many cases, literally went barefoot. They employed the best available troops, from the Foreign Legion to the Special Air Service and from the Green Berets to the *Spetznatz* and the Israeli *Sayarot*. They fielded every kind of sophisticated military technology in their arsenals, nuclear weapons only excepted. They were also, to put it bluntly, utterly ruthless. Entire populations were driven from their homes, decimated, shut in concentration camps or else turned into refugees. As Ho Chi Minh foresaw when he raised the banner of revolt against France in 1945, in *every* colonial-type war ever fought the number of casualties on the side of the insurgents exceeded those of the "forces of order" by at least an order of magnitude. This is true even if civilian casualties among the colonists are included, which often is not the case.

" 'Notwithstanding this ruthlessness and these military advantages, the "counterinsurgency" forces failed in *every* case. . . .' "

"So wrote Martin van Creveld in *The Transformation of War,* published in 1990 just prior to the American adventure in the Iraqi Desert; demonstrating once again that even the most brilliant historians often draw the wrong conclusions. It is certainly the case that so-called Low Intensity Conflicts had been and could be decisive, against both the United States and the Soviet Union; but this should not have been surprising, since most of those conflicts were no more than an extension of what had been called the Cold War. If either power became involved in LIC, the other power would find compelling reasons to aid the insurgents."

Hal tilted his head down so that he could examine the room over the tops of his glasses. *Still have their attention,* he decided. He took a sip of water and continued.

"What was not noticed until the last decades of the twentieth century was that insurgency was quite often nothing of the kind, but a cover for the invasion of one nation by another, with the invading nation supported by powerful allies who enjoyed immunity from military retaliation. South Vietnam did not fall to insurgents in the jungles, but to a modern armored army employing ten thousand trucks and twenty-five hundred armored fighting vehicles; and while North Vietnam was not always a sanctuary—the 1972 offensive triggered massive bombardment of the North by the United States—China and the Soviet Union always were sanctuaries, and none of the North Vietnamese war materiel was manufactured in North Vietnam. By the same token, the weapons employed by the Afghan *mujahideen* were not made in Afghanistan, and the factories producing Stinger missiles and recoilless artillery pieces were quite safe from Soviet attack.

"Military historians like van Creveld, in considering how successful insurgency aided by one Superpower could be used against the other did not, until the end of the Cold War, consider the improbability of the success of LIC against both Superpowers acting in concert.

"Insurgency against a modern state requires powerful allies operating from sanctuary. The allies need not be of 'super-power' status; but they will require that one of the Super-powers, or both of them acting as the CoDominium, protect the sanctuary status of the supplying nation. Unfortunately, given supply of war material from a sanctuary, insurgency can be continued practically forever."

General Slater looked directly at Prince Lysander, and said, "The strategic implications should be obvious."

Afterwards, after sherry and coffee, after the questions and the congratulations, the audience filed out. They were all talking and joking, all but one.

Crown Prince Lysander Collins left the room alone, lost in thoughts no one wanted to interrupt.

PRINCE OF SPARTA

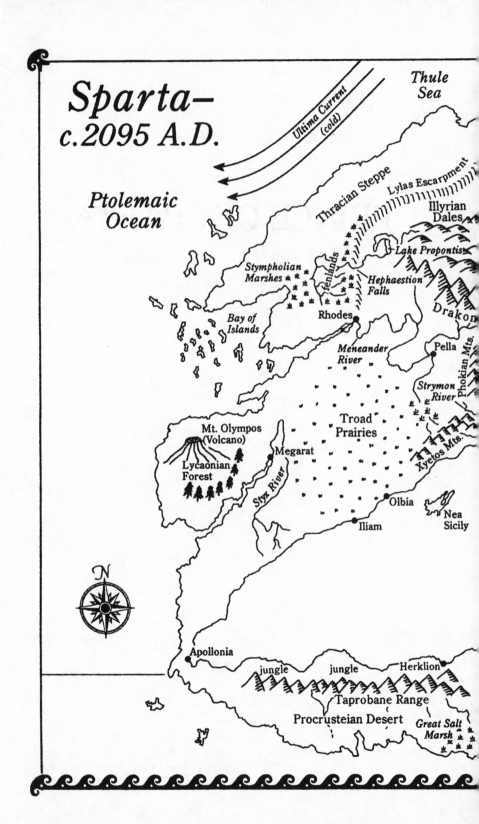

Sparta—
c.2095 A.D.

Thule
Sea

Ultima Current (cold)

Ptolemaic
Ocean

Thracian Steppe

Lylas Escarpment

Illyrian
Dales

Stympholian
Marshes

Fenlands

Hephaestion
Falls

Lake Propontis

Rhodes

Drakon

Meneander
River

Pella

Bay of
Islands

Phokian Mts.

Strymon
River

Troad
Prairies

Mt. Olympos
(Volcano)

Megarat

Xyetos Mts.

Lycaonian
Forest

Styx River

Olbia

Iliam

Nea
Sicily

N

Apollonia

jungle   jungle

Herklion

Taprobane Range

Procrusteian Desert

Great Salt
Marsh

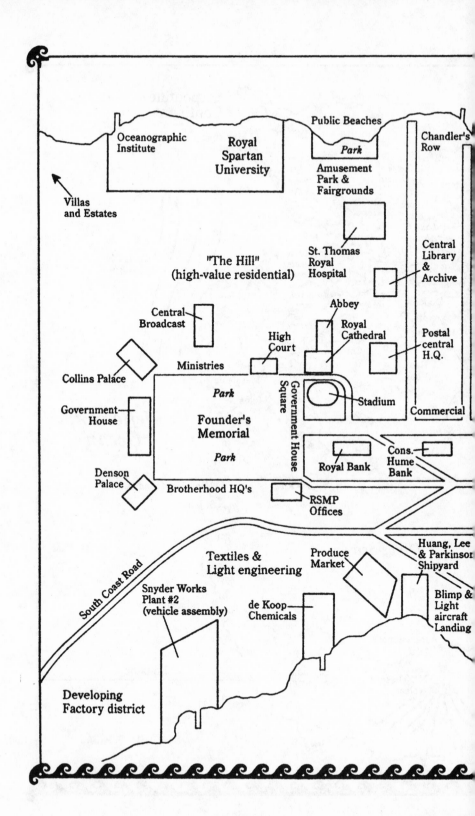

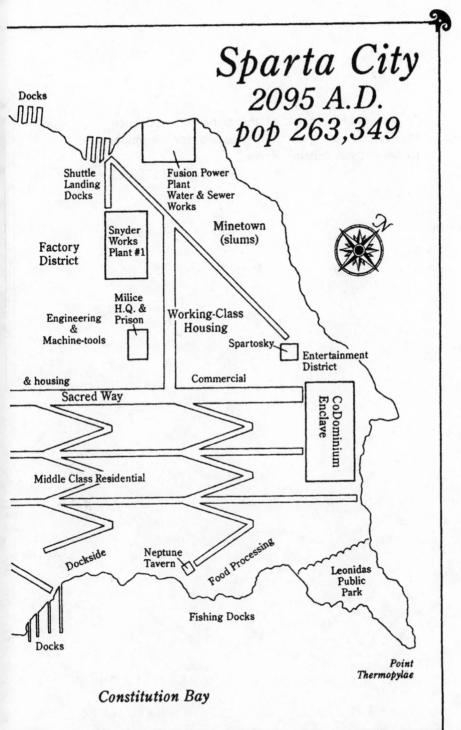

Sparta City
2095 A.D.
pop 263,349

Docks

Shuttle
Landing
Docks

Fusion Power
Plant
Water & Sewer
Works

Minetown
(slums)

Snyder
Works
Plant #1

Factory
District

Milice
H.Q. &
Prison

Engineering
&
Machine-tools

Working-Class
Housing

Spartosky

Entertainment
District

& housing

Commercial

Sacred Way

CoDominium
Enclave

Middle Class Residential

Dockside

Neptune
Tavern

Food Processing

Leonidas
Public
Park

Fishing Docks

Docks

Point
Thermopylae

Constitution Bay

"A well-hidden secret of the principate had been revealed: it was possible, it seemed, for an emperor to be chosen outside Rome."

—Tacitus, HISTORIES, I, 4:

CHAPTER ONE

The soldier stands alone. In the time when he must either succeed or encounter failure that will follow him beyond his grave, he has only a little time and only two considerations—his mission, and what strength he has within himself by which he may accomplish it. Whether he commands a million other men or only the weapon in his own hand, the soldier in the moment of decision is of all men most alone. Whatever of harmony he has achieved in his adjustment to the world as he knows it is the source of his strength. If he has adjusted himself only to chaos, it is in this time that he will dissolve and lose himself in its nothingness.

—Joseph Maxwell Cameron,
The Anatomy of Military Merit

The most important fact of the first half of the Twentieth Century is that the United States and England both speak English. The most important fact of the second half will be that the dominant race in both the United States and the Soviet Union is white.

—*Herman Kahn*, 1960

Crofton's Encyclopedia of Contemporary History and Social Issues (3rd Edition):

CoDominium: The first attempts by the United States to forge a CoDominium alliance were defeated by the failure of an attempted Communist Party coup and the consequent deposition of Gorbachev. The Soviet Union splintered along national and ethnic lines; but when the

865

economic situations of both the former Soviet Union and the United States continued to deteriorate, many in both nations looked back on the Cold War with nostalgia. When a new series of military and political coups resurrected the USSR, the United States was quick to join its former enemy in an alliance that established the supremacy of the two dominant nations over the rest of the world. The alliance was one of convenience rather than genuine friendship. . . .

The Exodus 2015–2050: In the first generation after the perfection of the Alderson Drive in 2010 more than forty planetary colonies were founded, not counting closed-environment mining settlements and refueling stops in systems without Terresteroid planets. While the CoDominium did not encourage governments (other than the US or Soviet Union) to establish direct settlements, corporations or settlement associations clandestinely backed by governments were common. Private colonization ventures were typically either commercial (e.g. *Hadley*, q.v.) or religious-ethnic in nature; see *Arrarat* (q.v.), *Dayan* (q.v.), *Friedland (q.v.)* , *Meiji*, (q.v.), others, spp. During this phase, several million emigrants left the solar system, almost all voluntary—although both the CoDominium Powers offered increasingly strong "encouragement" to politically inconvenient individuals and groups. Thus there are now planets whose population is purely Mormon *(Deseret)*, American Black Separatist *(New Azania)*, Russian nationalist *(St. Ekaterina)*, Finnish *(Sisu)*, and even Eskimo/Innuit *(Nuliajuk)*.

The second phase of interstellar colonization began with the extension of the Bureau of Relocation's mandate to include involuntary transport of colonists (in addition to the already existing flow of convicts, many merely petty criminals). During this period (2040 to date) voluntary emigration has remained roughly stable, but involuntary has increased to levels exceeding fifteen million persons per year; at the same time, more than seventy new planetary colonies have been founded, many specifically by the Colonial Bureau as relocation settlements. Given the sometimes extremely marginal habitability of the planets concerned (see *Haven, Frystaat)* and the endemic shortage of capital in the outsystem colonies, casualties among the transportees are often heavy, with life expectancies averaging as little as three years in some cases.

✧　　　✧　　　✧

Whump.

A globe of violet fire bloomed for an instant against the southern horizon, down in the lowlands, actinic brightness through the gathering dark and the light cold rain. Firefly streams of tracer began to stitch across the ground in long shallow arcs, and the reddish sparks of exploding munitions.

The mercenary sergeant smiled in satisfaction at the picture his facescreen showed. He turned in his foxhole, away from the action to the south and toward the valley below the ridge where his men lay concealed. The twelve-man SAS section was dug in on the low crest, invisible in their spider-holes under chameleon tarps. Only the thread-thin tip of the fiberoptic periscope showed above the sergeant's camouflage.

It was dark, Cytheria was just a sliver on the horizon, but that was no problem with nightsight. The enemy column was spread out down the wooded vale beneath them, winding through the tall grass and eucalyptus trees; the slope was in reddish-brown native scrub and shamboo. Men and mules halted at the sound of the explosion, then scattered to shouted orders.

"Now," Sergeant Taras Miscowsky said into the throat-mike. *Not what the bastards expected,* he thought with a hard grin in the private darkness of the hole.

A heavy droning whistle came through the low clouds overhead. Then: *crump . . . crump . . . crump.* Points of red fire flashed over the valley, proximity-fused 160mm mortar rounds bursting at ten meters up. Circles of vegetation bent away, crushed by blast and flayed by the steel-wire shrapnel. Men and animals screamed or writhed or lay still under the iron flail; faint bitter scent of explosive joined the smells of wet earth and grass. Another salvo came in, and another, the air whistling continuously. The observers called fire on the clumps of guerrillas forming around officers and noncoms, throwing men into panic flight and chopping into dog-meat any attempt to rally.

"That's doing it to them, Captain," Miscowsky said as he threw back the tarpaulin. Then more formally, "Sir, they're taking heavy casualties. I estimate thirty percent casualties on a full company. Better than half the mules are down, too. They're moving, one six five degrees true."

"Roger that. Tracking. We'll get the blocking group in fast."

"Sir. We'll lose most of them if we don't act fast."

"Right. Thank you, Sergeant."

Some of the enemy troops were moving straight west up the slope toward his position; the hill was gentle, and there was good cover. Mortar shells landed closer, probing for them as they moved up toward the ridge. The SAS unit was well dug-in, but they were infiltration scouts, not a line unit, and there were only a dozen of them. Miscowsky flashed a ranging laser at the center of the enemy group.

"Fire mission. Personnel, not armored. Five-fifty-six meters, bearing one hundred seventeen degrees."

"On the way," his commander's voice sounded in the helmet mike. Seconds later Corporal Washington spoke:

"Getting troop movement noise to our rear, Sarge. Multiples, light vehicles and infantry."

"Roger. Cap'n, the Royals are coming in from my west."

"Roger that, Miscowsky; the other side of the trap's moving in from the southeast around now."

Miscowsky turned his head in that direction and switched his facemask to IR sensors. There was a hell of a firefight going on down there a couple of klicks away, at the works the guerrillas had been planning to attack. Small arms, mortars . . . and the lance-shaped blossom of a Cataphract light tank's 76mm cannon. Several of those, coming toward him fast; he could see the faint waver of heat from their engines. Relayed sound-sensor data gave him the push from behind the SAS position. Boots thudding on turf, and a quiet whine from fuel-cell electrics. Then a louder *shoop-wonk* as their mortars opened up, lighter 81mm's and 120mm mediums.

He tapped at the side of his helmet to switch to the Royalist unit's push.

"Miscowsky, Falkenberg's Legion," he said.

A dark machine shape came bounding up the low reverse slope behind him. A cycle, boxy body slung between two wheels that were balls of Charbonneau alloy monomolecular thread. It braked to a stop and a figure in bulky Nemourlon combat armor jumped down.

"Captain Lewis, 2nd Royals," the man said.

Others in the same camouflage uniforms and armor were swarming up the ridge; teams set up machine guns as the riflemen fanned out and opened fire. Behind them light four-wheel vehicles like skeletal jeeps hauled ammunition and heavy weapons, recoilless rifles and rocket-launchers.

Miscowsky straightened and threw a formal salute. "Sir. Falkenberg's Legion presents one enemy column, badly used," he said.

The Royal officer returned the gesture, grinning as he scanned the action below. His night-sight goggles were flipped up, and he was using a blocky pair of sensor-glasses; less efficient than the multitasking facemasks of the Legion, but Sparta was not a rich planet.

"Some of them are putting their hands up already," he said. A signals tech came up behind him and put a handset into his outstretched palm. *"First platoon,"* he continued into it. *"Deploy in skirmish order and advance. I want prisoners, but don't take unnecessary casualties. If in doubt, shoot."* Men fanned out and began to filter into the scrub downslope.

"Well done, Sergeant," he went on, nodding to Miscowsky.

"Next insertion, sir?" Miscowsky said hopefully.

The Royal Spartan Army helicopter was still turning over its turbines behind the SAS squad.

"That's the last of them." Legion Captain Jamey Mace, Scout Commander, twitched his thumb toward the column of enemy prisoners as they shambled past under guard down to the river docks.

The Tyndos flowed north from here into the Eurotas, the great river of the Serpentine Continent. McKenzie's Landing was a riverside town, like most on this world; not much of one, which was also typical. There was an openpit rare-earth mine cut back into a smooth green hill, a geothermal plant and a kilometer of railway down to the loading docks. That and housing for a few hundred people, ranging from tufa-block Georgian houses for the mine-owner down to plastic-stabilized rammed earth for the miners' barracks. A fuel station by the docks, stacked logs for steamers and peanut oil tanks for diesels. A bar, a seedy-looking hotel, a Brotherhood meeting hall, two churches—established and non-conformist—and a tiny Hindi temple, a three-man Mounted Police station-cum-post-office. . . .

Not many of the Spartan People's Liberation Army—Helot—guerrillas had gotten to anywhere useful. Rosie's Bar and Grill was burning, and one of the steamers down at the pier was sinking at its moorings. The rebel plan had probably been to overrun the settlement just long enough to wreck the mine—it brought the Royal government off-planet hard currency—kill the Citizens resident, harangue the convict-transportee section of the labor force. . . .

"Let me go after them, Cap'n."

"Can't do that." Mace shook his head. "Back to training duty, Sergeant. We're going to need every Royal up to the mark—"

"Yes, sir, but—"

"If I thought there was one chance in ten thousand she was still alive I'd *order* you to go look for her."

"You wouldn't have to order me or anyone else. Captain, dammit, I know she's dead. But I want—"

"A head?"

"Balls would do."

"You'll have your chance," Mace said. It was easy to see what Mace was thinking. Taras Hamilton Miscowsky came from a culture that took blood feuds seriously. "Right now we've got a war to win, Sergeant."

'Sir." Miscowsky was silent; obedience, not agreement. Two months ago the war had stopped being a job to him; when Lieutenant Lefkowitz died. Lieutenant Deborah Lefkowitz, wife of Jerry Lefkowitz, who had been Miscowsky's first officer in the Legion. Miscowsky would not have lived past his first battle if Lefkowitz had not put his men ahead of his personal survival. Deborah Lefkowitz had been an electronics tech, not a combat soldier; sheer bad luck had put her observation plane over enemy Skyhawk missiles, in the Dales campaign. Miscowsky hadn't been able to rescue her, nobody had, after her plane augured in still spitting out data. Data that had probably saved the Legion's detachment here on Sparta, but nobody had saved Deborah. They found her torn clothing and some blood, but nothing else, despite the efforts of the Legion's best trackers.

That's the official story, Miscowsky thought. *But Mendota was there, and he's not talking, and I think he found something more. Maybe the skipper has some reason to keep things to himself, but God damn—*

Jerry Lefkowitz was far away, eight months interstellar transit, though only half that for the fastest messages, on New Washington with Colonel Falkenberg and the bulk of the Legion. Sparta had originally been intended as a quiet training assignment for the 5th Battalion and a haven for the noncombatants. He wouldn't even have the news about his wife yet. Miscowsky scowled. At least he wouldn't have to break the news. The chaplain-rabbi would do that. *But I have to write him. And when I do I want an enclosure.*

A man in the uniform of a Brotherhood militia captain came up. "Captain McKenzie, sir," he said to Mace. "Did I hear something about pursuit?" He was a middle-aged man, stocky and sandy-haired. There was a wolfish eagerness in his tone.

"The 18th Brotherhood's authorized to send fighting patrols into bandit country," Mace said, nodding northwestward. There lay the Himalayan-sized Drakon range and the vast forest-and-prairie expanse of hill country known as the Illyrian Dales.

"Not your SAS?" McKenzie said. He looked admiringly at the mercenary troopers squatting stolidly in the rain and leaning on their weapons. "We'd have been royally screwed if you hadn't spotted those terrorist scum massing up in the ravine country. We've only got an under strength company of the Brotherhood here; if they'd hit us without warning . . ."

Captain Mace pulled a pack of cigarettes out of a shoulder-pocket in his armor, offered one to the Spartan. They lit, sheltering their matches from the steady drizzle.

"That's just it," he said. "Look, the enemy *never* attack if they think we know they're coming; they just call it off and split up and concentrate somewhere we're not. And we can't give you long warning . . ."

They both nodded. Legion communications were secure—mostly—but the Brotherhood comm lines were leaky, and there didn't seem to be much that anyone could do.

Most of the three-million population of Sparta was spread out along the nearly ten thousand kilometers of the Eurotas. Most traffic moved at the pace of the riverboat, with the faster alternative being a blimp. There was very little high-tech transport; Sparta saved its money for building its industries, and imported little in the way of personal luxuries. Even military helicopters were still rare, just now starting to come off the lines in quantity. Away from the little towns and scattered ranches of the Valley were mountain, swamp, forest. Easy to hide in, now that the satellites were down. The Helots crept through it like rats in long grass, massing secretly, striking without warning and scattering before the Royalist forces could respond.

"It's like stomping on bloody cockroaches," the Spartan said in frustration. "Can't *find* the buggers. When you do, there are always more of them."

"Mm-hmm," Mace said. "And the Legion doesn't have enough SAS to make much of a difference. We've got to train your own Regulars, your SAS" —which in the Royal forces stood for Spartan Air Service— "to give you a broad-based capacity."

McKenzie nodded unwillingly. "We'll pursue anyway," he said. More softly: "My boy Phyrros was in the Dales. He got the Star of Leonidas . . . posthumously."

"Be cautious," Mace said.

"Sir." Miscowsky leaned forward. "Sir, I've been thinkin'." His provincial accent roughened a little, the Anglic harshened with the tones of Haven, his home planet. "Either the enemy's going downhill, or these were recruits. Prob'ly sent in for a little on-the-job training."

"Yes?" Mace looked at the prisoners thoughtfully.

A lot of them *did* look a little raw, without the stripped-down appearance you got after six months or so in Sparta's heavy gravity. *Transportees.* Convicts and political prisoners from Earth; most of the Helots were, like a majority of Sparta's population. *And they did break up a bit easily.* Not much unit cohesion, as if they were just out of the enemy equivalent of basic training. The Spartan People's Liberation Army probably hadn't expected much resistance here.

"Well," Miscowsky went on, "if this was a training exercise, they had a command group somewhere close watching. Might be worth going after, Cap'n. Maybe even that bastard nephew of Bronson's, the one we got the voiceprint on in the Dales."

That would *be worth it,* the mercenary officer thought. *With Geoffrey Niles in our hands, we'd have more of a lever.* Grand Senator Bronson was illegally backing the rebellion . . . not that anyone on Earth seemed to give a damn anymore about little things like the CoDominium's Laws of War, or treaties, or anything else.

"No." He shook his head. "Niles may be dead . . . or still wandering around the Dales looking for the Helot survivors. We've got orders; mount up, Sergeant."

Crack. A branch broke underneath a boot.

Geoffrey Niles started awake and then crouched lower under the overhang of blue rock. It was screened by tall canes of witch hazel and thick crystalline snow, only feet from the little brook that purled down the shallow valley under a skin of ice.

He forced his breathing to calm, clenching his jaw as it tried to chatter with cold and the effects of malnutrition. The skin on his fingers was cracked where it gripped the rifle; his body felt like an arthritic seventy instead of the twenty-eight Terran years it actually bore. Few would have recognized the sleekly handsome blond Englishman of a scant half-year before in the scarecrow figure that crouched in this cave. The heavy gravity of Sparta dragged at him, as sleep dragged at his eyelids. The air smelled of wet limestone and muddy earth; beyond the stream the first buds were showing on the rock maples, and strands of green among the yellow stalks of grass.

Another crack, and a voice swearing softly. Men dropped past him to stand on the edge of the stream, and another walked up it leading a flop-eared hound. Men in uniform . . .

Royalists, he thought. Camouflage uniforms, Nemourlon armor and helmets, but the shoulder-flashes showed Brotherhood militia. Not Royal Army regulars, and thank *God* not the mercenary SAS-scouts of Falkenberg's Legion. The relief was irrational, he knew; there were a dozen of them, and he had only five rounds left in the clip. The militia were countrymen used to tracking, and well-trained; they would check this overhang eventually. He had escaped from the last battle in the Dales by drifting downstream on a river that eventually fed into the Eurotas. It had carried him far into Royalist-held territory and it had been a long slow journey back into the wilderness.

I can't even blame Grand-Uncle for sending me here, he thought bitterly. He had *asked* to go to Sparta, to serve in the revolution Grand Senator Bronson was clandestinely backing. *I wanted adventure. God!*

"Lost him, Sarge," the man with the dogs said disgustedly. "He went into the creek downstream where it's clear, but I'm damned if I can find where he came out."

The militia noncom grunted. "Everyone, spread out; he may be lying low around here. And keep alert—we've come a long ways west, he isn't the only Helli around here. Sparks, get me—"

Pffft.

The soldier doubled over and fell backwards into the water with a red spot blossoming on his chest. The others went to ground in trained unison, scrambling back up the overhang to return fire. The sharp crackling of their New Aberdeen rifles echoed back overhead, answered by others out in the woods; the silenced sniper weapon fired again, and a light machine gun opened up on the Royalist patrol. A body slid back downslope to lie twitching at the edge of the water next to the bobbing corpse. Branches and scrub fell after it, cut by the hail of bullets; a man was screaming, an endless high keening sound.

Niles flogged his mind into thought. He had been running far and fast ahead of this pursuit; it was unlikely there was another Royalist patrol near enough to intervene. From the sound of the firing the guerrillas outnumbered the government soldiers handily, and according to Spartan People's Liberation Army—Helot—tactics they should . . .

God. If there still are *any Helots—* The attempted ambush in the Dales had fallen apart so fast the Royalists might have mopped up everything but scattered bands.

Fwhump. A rifle-grenade blasting off the muzzle of a rifle some distance away. It landed on the lip of the rise over his head and detonated in a spray of notched steel wire. Then more rifle fire came from the other side of the creek bed, into the backs of the Royalist soldiers, and more grenades. The noise rose to a crescendo and then died away with startling suddenness. Niles waited while the Helots made their cautious approach, waited until their leader whistled an *all clear*. Then he called out:

"I'm coming out! Senior Group Leader Geoffrey Niles, SPLA!" Spartan People's Liberation Army, the formal name of the Helots.

"Out careful," a hard voice replied.

He pushed through the witch hazel, leaving his rifle behind. The tough springy stems parted reluctantly, powdering him with snow. He stood with his hands raised. Half a platoon of Helot guerrillas surrounded him, most busy about their chores. A few leveled rifles at him.

"Police it up good, don't leave nothin' for the Cits," the Helot sergeant was saying. Men moved briskly, stripping the Royalist militiamen of weapons, armor, kit and clothing.

One Brotherhood fighter was still alive, despite the row of bullet-holes across the small of his back. The guerrilla non-com stepped up behind him as he crawled and fired with the muzzle of his rifle an inch from the back of the other man's head. The helmet rolled away in a spray of blood. Then he turned back to Niles.

"Who did you say—" he began, then stopped. His eyes widened as he recognized the scarecrow figure in the rags the winter woods had left of his uniform.

The sergeant was a short man, as were most of the guerrillas, a head shorter than the Englishman's 185 centimeters; virtually all of the guerrillas were transportees from Earth's Welfare Islands, chronically malnourished as children. American, from his accent, and Eurasian by the odd combination of slanted eyes that were a bright bottle green color.

"Jesus and Maria, it *is* Senior Group Leader Niles," he said, saluting and then holding out a hand. "Sergeant Andy Cheung, sir—hell, we thought you were dead meat for sure!"

"So did I for a while, Sergeant, so did I," he said. Relief shook him, and bitter regret. *I wanted out*, he thought. Out of the Helots certainly, after the horrors of the campaign last year; poison gas and slaughtered prisoners, capital crimes under the Laws of War. But the Royalists would hang him; the only chance he had of getting off this world alive was with the guerrillas. Off this world and back to a place where the Bronson power and wealth could buy immunity from anything.

"We gotta get out of here real quick," Sergeant Cheung was saying. "Lost half a platoon to them SAS buggers around here just last week; they're seven klicks of bad news." The non-com grinned at him. "Field Prime will sure be glad to see you again, sir."

Skilly, he thought, with a complex shiver. *Oh,* God.

"Are you telling me, gentlemen, that there is *nothing* we can do to rid our world of these murderous vermin?"

Crown Prince Lysander Collins paced back and forth before the broad windows that looked out over Government House Square; the Council Chamber where the Cabinet met was on the second floor of the Palace. It was a rainy spring day, and the breeze carried in odors of wet vegetation from the gardens, together with a damp salty smell from the Aegean. He was a tall young man in his mid-twenties, with short-cropped brown hair and regular features. Until recently it had been a rather boyish face.

Peter Owensford, Major in Falkenberg's Legion, Major General in the Spartan Royal Army, looked up from his readout and files to the prince. *Not so young as he was.*

A good deal had happened to Crown Prince Lysander Collins over the past eighteen Terran months. Sent to the CoDominium prison-planet of Tanith as unofficial ambassador to Falkenberg's Mercenary Legion; he had "seen the elephant" there, as a volunteer junior officer, and incidentally earned the respect of many of the Legion officers. Owensford suspected Lysander Coffins would have been more than happy to maintain his pseudonym of "Mr. Cornet Prince" and remain in the Legion's ranks. That was impossible, of course, despite Lysander's bravura performance, highjacking the rebel shuttle and the smuggled drugs . . . as impossible as his brief and doomed affair with Ursula Gordon, sometime hotel girl on Tanith. Sparta was too important to civilization, and to the plans of Grand Admiral Sergei Lermontov, for Lysander Collins to have any role but the straight one laid out for him by hereditary duty. *If there's to be any civilization left once the CoDominium collapses.*

Lad's grown up a lot, Owensford thought. Lysander had returned to Sparta to find a full-fledged rebellion in progress. *Did all right, too. Decent as battalion commander. Even better as field commander in chief. I've fought for worse ones.* Now even that was denied him; with his father's judgment impaired by the enemy's viral sabotage he was *de facto* ruler of the Collins half of the Dual Monarchy's executive. *He's seen the elephant with a vengeance.*

"No, sir," Owensford said aloud. "There is a great deal that we can and must do."

The Crown Prince was in uniform at this meeting; as a Lieutenant General, he could be addressed as a military superior rather than sovereign, a useful fiction. "But I am saying for the record that under present conditions it will be very difficult to achieve *swift* and *decisive* victory over the enemy."

He looked over at Hal Slater, the other mercenary present. Commandant of the Royal War College, making him a Major General in the Royal Army. Possibly a more permanent one. Owensford would revert to his mercenary rank of Major whenever the Fifth Battalion of Falkenberg's Legion left Sparta . . . *if* they left; quite probably this would be permanent base for at least part of the mercenary outfit. *And I'm running a whole army here. Challenging.* Long-term if he wanted to stay here and become a Spartan Citizen. *Tempting. Sparta's a good place, and I'm tired of running from planet to planet.* Owensford looked again at Prince Lysander. *He's grown up. I could accept him as sovereign. I think Hal already has.*

Hal Slater wouldn't be filling any active commands. He had gone to the regeneration tanks once too many times, too many bones were titanium-titanium matrix, and his wounds would keep him behind a desk for the rest of his life. Running the War College was a good final berth. One he would do well; Hal Slater had taught Owensford and many another young officer, back in his days with the Legion. His son George was a Legion Captain, and a Brigadier in the Royal forces.

And Hal Slater is Falkenberg's oldest friend. If anyone knows what Falkenberg's game is, Slater will.

Lysander halted at the window and looked out over the square. "I had hoped to get more out of the Illyrian Dales campaign," he said bitterly. "We certainly paid enough for it."

Owensford nodded. The battles against the Helots in the northwestern hills had been bloody. Bloodily victorious, in the conventional sense . . . and a good deal of that was due to Crown Prince Lysander's refusal to accept a truce offered by the enemy when the battle was won. That had cost the Royal Army, but they had harried the enemy units into rout with a relentless pursuit. Lysander, he knew, was still haunted by the casualties. They'd lost some of those wounded in the enemy's poison-gas attacks, because many couldn't be flown out while the battle continued.

"We paid, but never doubt it was worth it," Owensford said. He looked to Slater and got a nod of agreement. "I doubt if one in five of the enemy escaped on the southern front. High cost in their trained leaders."

"Not enough to break them," Lysander said.

"No, sir. But we stopped them. Sir, they were in a fair way to taking and holding a good part of the Dales. That would have given them a sanctuary area. More than that. It would have given them a territory making this an actual planetary war instead of an insurgency. They could have called on the CoDominium to intervene. Depending on CD politics that might even have worked. Instead, we got most of their leaders, maybe half of their lower ranking Meijian technoninjas, a lot of their equipment. Some of their units evaporated. Lots of deserters. One unit surrendered just about to a man."

"Good recruits?" Hal Slater asked.

Owensford nodded.

Prince Lysander frowned. "You're accepting *Helots* as military volunteers?"

Owensford grinned slightly. "Not for you, sir. For the Legion. We'll get them part trained and ship them off as reinforcements for Colonel Falkenberg on New Washington. The point is, sir, don't doubt that you made the right choice. We not only robbed them of their victory, we came close to breaking them."

Slater said, carefully, "It should have been enough to break them."

"But it didn't."

"No, sir," Peter Owensford said. "They've got too much off-planet support."

"Not just off-planet."

"No, sir." A sore point: Sparta hadn't yet suspended constitutional civil rights, and the Helots had allies in the Senate and elsewhere.

"Look at it this way. You forced them back to classical Phase One guerrilla operations," Hal Slater said.

"Vigorous Phase One operations," Owensford said.

"Well, yes," Slater said. "It hurts, but Phase One can't win if you keep your nerve."

Lysander slammed the heel of his hand against the stonework. That was the antiseptic Aristotelian language of a military professional; "Phase One" meant ambush and sabotage, burnt-out ranches and civilians killed by land-mines, every sort of terrorist atrocity.

He looked at Slater. "This is what you meant at the first Royal Strategy Lecture, isn't it?" He quoted: "'Insurgency against a modern state requires powerful allies operating from sanctuary. Unfortunately, given supply of war material from a sanctuary, insurgency can be continued practically forever.'"

"Yes, sir," Hal Slater said. "Under the present circumstances, patience is as important a weapon as explosives." He shrugged. "It's also all we have just now."

Lysander nodded curtly. Both the professionals were older than he—Owensford in his thirties, Slater over fifty—and between them they had a generation's experience. He would use that accumulated wisdom.

"I agree. I don't have to like it," he said. "What else can we do?" He held up a hand. "Not tactics, that's obvious—what can we do to bring the war to an end?"

Slater smiled thinly; it was not every man Lysander's age who could keep the need to have strategy driving tactics firmly before his mind.

"There are essentially three ways to defeat an enemy," Slater began formally. Teaching had been a large part of his military career, even before he became head of the Spartan War College. "Physically smashing them is one—killing so many that the remainder give up in despair. We can only do that with the Helots if they are obliging enough to gather in one place where we can get at them. They *nearly* made that mistake last year in the Dales, but I doubt they will again. Their leaders are evil men—"

And women, Owensford thought; he remembered the mocking contralto voice of the Helot field commander in the Dales, with its soft Caribbean accent. By the look on his face, so did Lysander. Neither of them had forgotten the helpless prisoners slaughtered on her order.

"—evil to the point where 'vile' is an appropriate term, but they are not stupid. Inexperienced in real warfare, but they are cunning, they have experienced mercenary advisors, and they learn quickly."

Slater sipped water and continued. "As is often the case in war, we cannot force battle on the enemy if they are not willing to meet us; the ratio of force to space is too low. There is nothing they must stand and die to defend; they have no towns, farms or families as the Royal forces do, and no base of supply." Slater paused. "None within our reach, anyway."

Sparta had three million people, a tenth of them in the capital; the Serpentine Continent had eighteen million square miles of territory. Even the heartlands along the Eurotas River were thinly peopled.

"Particularly with the limits on surveillance, we are unlikely to catch large numbers of them at any one time." Skysweeper missiles had knocked down every attempt to loft more spy satellites; observation aircraft were impossible, of course, and even drones were high-cost and short-lived if the enemy had countermeasures. In addition, the Helots' Meijian hirelings were simply better at electronic intelligence and counter-intelligence than anything the Dual Monarchy of Sparta could afford, and they were running rampant through every computer on the planet with the exception—he devoutly hoped—of the Legion's. At that, his own electronics specialists were spending a counterproductive amount of time checking for viruses and taps, and vetting Royal Army machines. The Royalist forces were back to what scouts and spies could discover, and whatever the Legion computers could massage out of the data.

"Of course there's an unpleasant implication to our lack of surveillance," Slater said. "Low orbit satellites they can knock down fairly easily, but geosynchronous? They had to have cooperation from the CD Navy for that."

"Are you sure?" Lysander demanded.

"Near enough," Slater said. "The CD may not have knocked our geosynch out, but they had to look the other way when it happened. And you'll note they haven't offered to replace it."

"No. When we ask for cooperation, they never say 'no,' but nothing happens. Delays, red tape, forms not properly filled out . . . Do you think they're actively against us?"

Slater shrugged. "Or tilted neutral at best."

"What can we do about that?"

"I presume you've filed a formal protest."

Lysander nodded. "And you?"

"We've done what we can," Peter Owensford said. "I've sent off urgent signals to Falkenberg and Admiral Lermontov. With any luck Lermontov can use this to order active CD intervention on our side."

"How did you send the message?" Lysander asked.

"With your permission I would rather not say," Owensford said.

Lysander nodded quickly. "That's probably best. Do you think we can get CD Navy support? When?"

Hal Slater shook his head. "It won't be soon. CD politics is thick soup." His voice went back to lecture mode. "The second method of defeating an opponent is to strike at their rear—at the sources of their supplies and support. Unfortunately, we cannot for the same reason we can't locate them. As long as they have even tacit CD support, their rear area is off-planet."

"Bronson," Lysander said; he made the word an obscenity.

"Exactly. Grand Senator Bronson. Somehow Bronson's people are still landing supplies. His shipping lines regularly transit Sparta's system, and the supplies get here. It's like the geosynchronous satellites. We have no proof, but it's hard to imagine any other explanation."

The Treaty of Independence had left spatial traffic control in the hands of the CoDominium forces, and the Grand Senator was a power in the CoDominium. So were Sparta's friends— Grand Admiral Sergei Lermontov and Grand Senator Grant, the Blaine family . . . and the result was deadlock. No new thing. It was a generation since the CoDominium as a whole had been able to *do* anything of note. The Soviet Union was dissolving again—but so was the United States. Between them they ruled the world, but neither nation remembered why they had wanted to.

"Bronson," Slater went on, "is also behind most of our economic problems."

Sparta's main exports were minerals and intermediate-technology products for planets even less industrialized than she. Markets had been drying up, contracts been revoked, suppliers defaulting, loans being called due. The planetary debt was mushrooming, and Standard and Poor's had just reduced the Dual Monarchy's credit rating once more. The financial community was more and more jittery over the situation on Earth, in any case. Capital was flowing out to the secure worlds, places like Friedland and Dayan, and sitting there.

"What does Bronson want?" Lysander demanded.

Hal Slater shook his head. "We don't know."

"He seems to have an active hatred for Falkenberg."

"Yes, sir," Slater said. "But that's a very old story."

"Falkenberg ruined his Tanith operation," Lysander said.

"Yes, sir. With your help." Slater shrugged. "Bronson never forgets an enemy. You'll have noticed that he hasn't even tried to negotiate with you. But given the resources he's putting into this operation, there has to be more at stake than personal animosity. Unless—"

"Unless?"

"Unless he's feeling old and useless and has nothing left but his hatreds," Slater said.

"Whatever his motives, this has to stop." Lysander stared out at the Spartan landscape. "Even if we called out every Brotherhood militiaman," he said slowly, "we wouldn't have enough to finish this quickly. Would we?"

"No, sir," Owensford replied flatly. "They'd disperse, go to earth and wait for new supplies. We can't keep any militia unit in the field for more than a month or so. Helot attacks are planned long in advance; if we detect them concentrating and mass to defend or counterattack, they simply call off their assault and pick another target somewhere else. They never attack without a locally superior ratio of forces, and we don't have enough mechanical transport to respond quickly in such cases."

There were a million Citizens; the first-line militia of their Brotherhoods could field a quarter of a million troops. Unfortunately, when they did the entire planet had to shut down; the Citizens were over a third of the total labor force, and a much higher percentage of the skilled and managerial classes.

"We're keeping fifteen battalions under arms at any one time as regional reaction-forces, and we're building up the standing forces of the Royal Army to twenty-five thousand troops," Owensford said. He ran a hand over his short-cropped brown hair. "Whatever else the Dales campaign did, it certainly gave us plenty of combat-tested men." Action was the best way to identify potential small-unit leaders. "And the cream of the newcomers as recruits, too. Everyone wants to fight for a winner. We'll keep grinding at the enemy."

Hal Slater grimaced slightly. "Now you see why professionals hate guerrilla wars, sir," he said. "It's pure attrition, unless we can kill or capture their top leaders."

Lysander smiled sourly. "I've known mercenaries who liked that kind of thing. A long war and no resolution—no, of course I don't suspect that of Falkenberg."

Slater didn't say anything.

"All right," Lysander said. "Attrition with Grand Senator Bronson sending the Helots weapons and money, and the CoDominium Bureau of Relocation sending convicts and involuntary transportees for them to recruit from. It takes twenty years to produce a Citizen, gentlemen, and only eight months to ship a transportee from Earth to Sparta. And yes, I know, you can recruit among those as well as the enemy. But damn it, no offense intended, Sparta needs Citizens, not more mercenaries."

He moved his shoulders, the unconscious gesture of a man settling a burden he means to carry. "We can also proceed on the political front," he went on. "Breaking up the enemy's clandestine networks. And nailing Croser."

For a moment all three men shared a wolfish grin. Senator Dion Croser, head of the Non-Citizen's Liberation Front . . . and almost certainly leader of the whole insurrection. Almost all the insurgents were transportees and non-Citizens; Croser was the

son of one of the Founders, and there was as yet no smoking-
gun proof of his involvement with the insurrection.

"He won't be the last," Lysander went on softly. Even the
mercenaries were slightly daunted by the look in his grey eyes.
"We can't attack a man who's a power in the CoDominium—
we can't even *defy* the CoDominium—yet. But Croser we *will*
get; and eventually, beyond him, those responsible for backing him. As God is my witness, I'm going to see that nobody
is ever in a position to do this to Sparta again. Or," he went
on, "to anyone else, if I can help it."

"Meanwhile," he continued more briskly, "we should prepare for the War Cabinet meeting."

The rain had been hitting harder as the Helot patrol moved
northwest. The horses hung their heads slightly, wearily placing
one hoof down at a time. For Geoffrey Niles the trip was rest
and recuperation, after starving and freezing for the better part
of two months. By the end of the second week he was strong
enough to curse the cold drops that flicked into his face as
they rode and trickled down inside his camouflaged rain-
poncho, to realize how much he detested the constant smells
of wet human and horse. The forest thickened as they moved
closer to the foothills of the Drakons, spreading up from the
low swales and valleys to conquer the slopes of the hills,
leaving only patches in the tallgrass prairie that was so common
elsewhere in the Illyrian Dales. Occasionally they passed other
patrols—once they nearly tripped an ambush—and more often
saw foraging parties, out cropping the vast herds of game and
feral cattle.

"Not many enemy in this far?" he asked the Helot NCO.

"No, sir," the man replied he kept his rifle across his
saddlebow, and his eyes were always moving. "Leastways, not
big bunches of 'em. Sometimes they send in fightin' patrols,
battalion or better, but we scatter an' harass and they go away.
Hard to supply this far in, too. They got no satellite recce
now, can't put aircraft anywhere near us. Keep tryin' t'locate
our bases, though. Lots of infiltrators. Ambush and counter-
ambush work—helps with training the new chums, anyway."

Niles nodded. They were riding up a long slope; the rain
had a little sleet in it now, they must be at least a thousand
meters above sea level. Well into the foothills, and Sparta's
1.21 G gave it a steep atmosphere and temperature gradient.
The slopes on either side were heavily wooded with Douglas
fir and Redwoods, oaks and beech; the genetic engineers and
seeders had done their work well here. Branches met overhead,

and the hooves clattered through gravel and broken rock. They turned a corner; it took a moment's concentration for Niles to pick out the bunkers that flanked the pathway. They were set deep in the lime, with narrow firing slits hiding the muzzles of 15mm gatlings. His shoulders crawled slightly with the knowledge that Peltast heavy sniper-rifles had probably been trained on them for the better part of an hour.

"Sir," an officer said, as he swung down from the saddle. "We've got transport for you. Field Prime is anxious to debrief you herself."

Niles raised a brow at the sight of the jeep; it was a local model, six balloon-wheels of Charbonneau thread, but the Helots had had little mechanical transport before. *We're coming up in the world,* he thought.

The new base-headquarters was a contrast to the old, as well. It was a rocky bowl several kilometers in extent, a collapsed dome undercut by water seepage. That was common in the Dales, with multiple megatonnes of water coming down off the Drakon slopes every year and hundreds of thousands of square kilometers of old marine limestones to run through. The edges of the ring were jagged fangs thrusting at the sky; his eyes widened at the sight of detection and broadcast antennae up there, and launching frames for Skyhawk and Talon antiaircraft missiles. Cave-mouths ringed the bowl, busy activity about most, but the rolling surface itself was occupied as well.

Not afraid of aerial surveillance any more, he thought. Neat rows of squared-log cabins, and troops drilling in the open. More troops than he expected, many more, but what was really startling was the equipment. Plenty of local make, everything from rifles and machine guns up to the big 160mm mortars that were the local substitute for artillery; Dion Croser had been siphoning off a share of local production and caching it in cave-dumps here in the Dales for a full decade before the open war began. But there was off-planet material as well, in startling quantity, items he remembered from Sandhurst lectures. A dozen stubby 155mm rocket-howitzers, Friedlander-made, with swarms of Helot troopers around them doing familiarization. Six Suslov medium tanks, slab-and-angle composite armor jobs with low-profile turrets and 135mm cannon in hydraulic pods. *Those* were CoDominium issue, made on Earth.

And bloody expensive, he thought.

The jeep pulled up at one of the cave entrances. A man was waiting for him. Niles recognized the figure; 190 cm tall and broad enough to be squat. Skin the color of old mahogany, a head bald as an egg, and a great beak of a nose in the round face. Over his shoulders were the twin machetes that had given him his nickname, and dangling from one hand was a light machine gun looking no bigger than a toy rifle in the great paw. The only change he could see was a certain gauntness to the face.

'Two-knife," he said, nodding to the Helot commander's right-hand man.

"Niles," the other answered, equally polite and noncommittal. The big Mayan had not minded when Skilly took the Englishman as her consort; that was the *Donna's* privilege. Niles was privately certain that he would also have no hesitation in quietly killing an unworthy choice. . . .

The caves were larger than the old Base One that had fallen to the Royalists last winter, but the setup within was similar, down to the constant chill and smell of wet rock. Glowsticks stapled to the walls, color-coded marker strips, occasional wooden walls and partitions, rough-shaping with pneumatic hammers. There seemed to be a lot more modern electronics, though. He passed several large classroom-chambers with squads of Helots in accelerated-learning cubicles, bowl-helmets over their heads for total-sensory input. Then they went past alert-looking guards into a still larger chamber, where officers grouped around a computer-driven map table. One looked up at him.

"Hiyo, Jeffi," she said quietly when he was close enough to salute.

Geoffrey Niles' throat felt blocked. He had *thought* he remembered her, but Skida Thibodeau in the flesh was something different from a memory. Very tall, near two meters, much of it leg. Muscled like a panther and moving like one, a chocolate-brown face framed in loose-curled hair that glinted blue-black. High cheekbones and full lips, nose slightly curved, eyes tilted and colored hazel, glinting with green flecks. His nostrils flared involuntarily at her scent, soap and mint and a hint of the natural musk. And the remembered thrill of not-quite-fear at meeting her eyes, intelligent and probing and completely feral.

"Skilly is glad to see you back," she said.

"Glad to be back, Field Prime," he said. Realized with a slight shock of guilt that it was true. *God, what a woman.*

She smiled lazily, and sweat broke out on his forehead; then she dropped her gaze to the map table. "We having de post-mortem," she continued. "Little training attack go wrong, a bit."

He cleared his throat, looked around at the other officers.

Many he recognized: von Reuter, the ex-CD major; Sutchukil, the Thai aristocrat and political deportee, a man with a constant grin and the coldest eyes Niles had ever seen. Kishi Takadi, the Meijian technoninja liaison. Another man he almost did *not* recognize. Chandos Wichasta, Grand Senator Bronson's troubleshooter. That was a shock; the last time he had seen the little Indian was back on Earth, during the humiliating interview with great-uncle Adrian at the Bronson estate in Michigan. The Spartan mission had been a last chance to redeem himself . . . *Which means Grand-Uncle has managed to get two-way communication going.* There were big glacial lakes in the Drakon foothills where high-powered assault shuttles could land and take off.

"Brigade Leader Niles," Wichasta said discreetly. Another surprise; Niles had been Senior Group Leader—roughly a Major—in the SPLA in the last campaign.

Skilly smiled and shrugged. "You was right about Skilly's plan last time, Jeffi," she said. "Too complicated; or maybe we have de intelligence leak here. Or both; Skilly think both. Howsoever, de wise mon learn from mistake."

"Ah . . ." *Come on, you bloody fool, don't sound like a complete nitwit* " . . . things seem to be well in hand."

Skilly nodded. "Numbers back up some," she said judiciously. "Lots more fancy off-planet stuff coming in—" she nodded to Wichasta "—and money, *lots* of money. The Royals, they doan' know how much we have hid, too. We bleeding them pretty good now, gettin' ready we give them the real grief."

"Hmmm. Won't the CoDo naval station on the Aegis platform—" He broke off at the ring of wolfish grins around the map table.

She laid her light-pencil down. "Field Prime think that enough analysis," she said. "Von Reuter, you breaks up that group and uses the personnel at you discretion." She looked at Niles, and the pulse hammered in his temples. "Brigade Leader Niles need a debriefing."

CHAPTER TWO

Crofton's Essays and Lectures in Military History
(2nd Edition)

Professor John Christian Falkenberg II:
Delivered at West Point, June 17, 2073

The soldier and the spy have always been uneasy bed-fellows doomed to unwilling cohabitation. First and fore-most among the military virtues is loyalty, above all to one's salt. Correspondingly, the most despised military sin—beyond even cowardice—is betrayal of the oath of service. There are, of course, sound and obvious functional reasons for this ethic; the primary emotional cement of armies is and must be, trust. Without it, no military force can operate for a moment. The spy proper—the clandestine operative—is above all one who wears a mask, who dons a uniform and takes an oath under false pretenses, who abuses trust to pass vital information to the enemies of those whom he infiltrates. Accordingly, none of the protections of the Laws of War apply to the spy. Indeed, historically some military forces have hesitated to use information from such "tainted" sources.

Yet there is no substitute for HUMINT—direct intelligence of the inner councils of an opponent. Even where the full panoply of technical intelligence-gathering is available, HUMINT is priceless; it gives direct access to the *intentions* of the enemy, always the most difficult aspect of military intelligence-gathering. Just as important, the knowledge that one's own ranks have been infiltrated is a powerful tool, sowing suspicion and dis-solving the bonds of mutual loyalty that sustain the operational capacity of a military unit.

✧   ✧   ✧

Both principal intelligence officers of Falkenberg's Legion sat at the table. Captain Jesus Alana was a short man, dark and slim with a well-trimmed mustache on his upper lip. His wife Catherine was two fingers taller and flamboyantly red-haired, and also a Captain. As the joke ran, virtually everybody in the Legion was; the chain of command depended on your job, not your pay-scale. Apart from them the office in Fort Plataia was empty The spring rain was falling, mild here only a few kilometers outside Sparta City; it carried a smell of wet adobe clay through the slit of open window. Over that came a sound of boots splashing down on wet gravel and a voice counting *heep . . . heep.* Cadence for another group of recruits; they were pushing them through as fast as possible. Three Legion battalions now, spawned by the 5th, and the Royal army had doubled and redoubled.

"Not very hopeful," Jesus Alana said.

The files lay in front of him, in hard copy. Only two names . . .

"Not very hopeful, that one, eh, *mi corazon?*"

"Thick as a brick," Catherine replied. "He could take the biofeedback, but he's hopeless for anything requiring an imagination. With luck, he'll make a passable rifleman."

"That leaves the young woman."

"From the file, much more hopeful. Finished basic training, and non-com school. Very reasonable to make her an officer. Higher IQ. Also, lots of determination, with that background."

"I know. Yet—"

"Yet you're a romantic, Jesus. She got out of a Welfare Island."

"Yes," he sighed, and touched a control on the table. "Recruit Talkins, please."

Margreta Talkins was a young woman. The russet eyes were harder than her twenty years would justify. Medium height, olive skin and dark-mahogany hair cropped to a short cap of curls, with a wary edge to her expression. Looking a little weary; neither the Royal army nor the Legion accepted women for combatant positions, but their basic training didn't reflect that. *We may not want them to fight, but it happens often enough,* Jesus thought. *Firm body, looks good on her. She will have no difficulty seducing her targets.* Talkins returned Jesus's hard look, then her eyes darted to the equipment on the table, a set of flat screens and a few crackle-finished milspec electronics modules.

"Sir. Ma'am." Her Anglic was North American, almost-but-not-quite Taxpayer class, the voice of someone who carefully copied the upper-class accents on the Tri-V.

"Please sit, recruit Talkins," Catherine said. "Now, I'm going to ask you a series of questions. The answers aren't important in themselves—just say what comes into your head.

"First, how do you feel about the Helots?"

When the interrogation finished an hour later, Talkins' hair was plastered to her forehead, although her face was still calm.

"Perfect," Catherine said. "Not only can she do it, she'll volunteer to do it."

"Volunteer for what, ma'am?" Talkins said.

Jesus Alana leaned forward. "Clandestine operations. Very secret, very dangerous."

"Will this hurt the Helots?"

"If it works, it'll be very damaging to the enemy. We need your agreement, first."

Silence stretched; then she nodded with a bitten-off: "Yes, sir."

"Why?" Captain Jesus Alana said to the young woman in recruit coveralls. "The machinery—" he indicated the book-sized display unit, open on the table "—tells us you mean it. But that doesn't tell us why you are willing to take the risk."

There was a trace of anger in her voice; Alana frowned slightly at that, then recognized it. She was volunteering, and she had the slightly bitter self-accusatory air of a veteran cursing himself as he volunteered for something he knew was stupid. The young woman spoke at last.

"My brother," she said flatly.

"Killed in action," Catherine Alana said. "Revenge?" she went on, keeping half an eye on the Voice Stress Analysis readouts. There was plenty of data to be authorized in more detail later.

"I told George not to enlist," she said. "Look, sir . . . ma'am. We both came from Columbia Welfare Island, you know?"

Jesus nodded. He did know; he'd heard that something like half the population of the US lived in places like that now. Of course the intentions had been good. Make the cities safe, get the festering legions of the underclass out of the downtown ghettoes, put them where they can be educated, learn to be somebody, leave the underclass. And, incidentally, put them in controlled areas. Let them riot, they couldn't get at the wealthy.

Now the Citizens—some bureaucrat seventy-five years ago had a sickly sense of humor to name them that—sat and rotted, and the Taxpayers paid for it, and paid more for the police who guarded them from the Citizens. Borloi from the convict-worked plantations of Tanith kept the Welfare inhabitants pacified, that and cheap booze and the Tri-V. But some escaped. It was possible, barely.

"Yet you managed an education," Catherine said. "How? Or perhaps better, why?"

"Sister Mary Margaret cared. After a while, I did too."

Catherine smiled reassurance. "Not unlike me, then."

"You're from Welfare? Ma'am?"

"The Legion cares no more where you came from than Sparta does," Jesus said. "Nor do either of us usually care why you joined, but in this case we must know more." He touched the personnel forms on the table. "Edison Technical School in Pittsburgh. No record of drug use. Minor crimes—I assume you were intelligent enough to avoid being caught at anything major. You and your brother did well on Earth. With your education you should have been welcomed into the—normal society."

"As trained seals," Margreta said. "Our sosh worker was proud of us. Offered us a shot at civil service."

"Which is the dream of half those in the Islands," Catherine said. "So why are you on Sparta? It says you were voluntary emigrants."

"Didn't seem like a lot of future on Earth. What's the use of reading books if you don't think? Clear to us, United States wasn't like what the history books said. We wanted—" She stopped. "Damn if I know, ma'am. I guess it seemed like a good idea at the time."

"Your intentions here?"

"Start a business. Own our own life. Make Citizen. That was why George enlisted—I told him it was better I do it, less dangerous. George and I always looked out for each other. There was nobody else but the two of us, but I couldn't in the Army. He thought the stats looked good, but *somebody* has to be unlucky."

The Alanas nodded. Private George Talkins had been in the field one week, as a communications tech, when the truck he was riding in went over a land mine.

"Anyway," Margreta said, "George and I . . . George made it sort of personal. I was always for the Royalist side—I like the way this place is run—but George, that makes it personal."

Talkins looked up, and the Alanas both felt a slight cold chill at the intensity. "Sir, what is it exactly you want me to do?"

"Infiltrate," Jesus Alana said. "Both sides have been trying that, of course. And we've combed out a lot of people from the Royalist organization with this." He reached out a finger and tapped the Voice Stress Analyzer.

"The problem is, the enemy evidently have something like this too. They also have better computer equipment and more and better technicians than we do; the Meijians are expensive but they have the best there is, a slight edge even on Fleet Intelligence standards. They've been running rampant through the local computer nets, and only the fact Legion equipment is ROM-programmed has saved ours from penetration—we hope. *Per Dios,* every time we compare hard copy with government or Royal Army computer files, we find discrepancies! Any operation we *really* want to keep secret is to be word-of-mouth only."

Talkins blinked. "How can I help you beat their screening, if they have that, sir?" she said, nodding to the equipment.

"Well," Catherine said, "it *is* possible to beat voice-stress detection. Not without elaborate hypnoconditioning and biofeedback training, and even then only a very small minority can hope to get through more than a superficial scan. Then, only a small minority of *that* minority is qualified for the job in other respects."

Talkins closed her eyes in thought for nearly half a minute. "And I fit? Must be. And the Legion is handling this because of security. Does this count for Citizenship?"

"Assuredly," Jesus Alana said.

"It's dangerous, Margreta," Catherine said. "If you want to walk out of here, no one but us will ever know we talked."

"How long?"

"A year. Perhaps two. No more than that. But understand, it will not be easy. For one thing, the Helots are certain to require your participation in an atrocity. To prove your loyalty to their cause."

"You mean like—"

"Like shooting prisoners," Catherine said. "Perhaps not so clean as shooting."

"Jesus. Like back in William Penn Island." She was quiet for a moment. "I can really make a difference?"

"Yes."

"And Citizenship when it's over."

"Yes."

"Okay I'll do it. What happens next?"

"You'll be sworn in to the Legion—that's plausible, we need people with your sort of educational background, and we've started recruiting locally for a lot of positions. You have been through the Royal non-com school. Assuming you can get past our OCS, you will become a Cornet, a very junior officer in training."

"That counts for Citizenship?"

"In your case, certainly. Whatever your Legion rank on discharge, you will have been a commissioned officer in the Royal Army."

Margreta nodded thoughtfully.

"It will all appear to be entirely natural. We train you, then send you on temporary duty to the University. It is certain that the Helots will try to recruit you once you are there."

"You've tried this before."

"Yes."

"What happened to—my predecessors?"

Catherine grinned. "Not what you think. She married an exchange student, and went to Friedland with him."

"You let her go without finishing her hitch?"

"Special circumstances," Catherine Alana said.

"I don't see that happening to me. Not that I wouldn't do it if the right guy asked. Or was that last one really special?"

Jesus shrugged. "We will cross that bridge when the chickens are hatched. For now, you will be transferred to the Legion and sent to officer candidate school. Understand, you must do well there, your instructors will have no hint that you have any special status. When you are commissioned, Catherine or I will speak with you again. No one else will know of your assignment, not now and not later."

"No records?"

"When next we meet we will tell you how to prove your status in the event that both Catherine and I are unavailable. Otherwise, no, no records. Now, we meet again in six weeks' time."

Good tradecraft, Cornet Margreta Talkins thought, as the waiter brought her lunch, with a sideways glance for her blue and gold Legion walking-out uniform. *Nobody's going to suspect* this *as a Helot dropshop.*

She very much doubted the owners knew that the underground arranged rendezvous here. Half the patrons in the courtyard tavern were in Royal Army uniform, mostly recruits out on their first post-basic furlough, sitting with their buddies or girlfriends or both; there was a sign outside offering them a discount. Many of the rest were machinists or fitters from the Works, in grease-stained overalls. Von Alderheim was running three shifts now, with the war effort.

The Cock and Grill was on Burke Avenue just off the Sacred Way, not far from the CoDo enclave at the northern end of Sparta City's main avenue. West of here and stretching to the edge of the Minetown slums was working-class housing, two or three-story buildings divided into modest apartments; within easy walking or bicycle distance of the docks, the big von Alderheim plant to the south, and the tangle of small factories that had grown up around it. Many of the buildings had shops or service industry trades on the ground floors, like this one. A brick-paved courtyard facing the sidewalk across a low wall, set with wrought-iron tables and wooden chairs under umbrellas; even on an early spring day like this, Sparta City's climate was comfortable enough, so long as the rains held off. The traffic in the sidestreet beyond was light, an occasional van or horse-drawn dray, bicycles and electrocars.

"Here you are, Miss," the waiter said. "One garden salad—" a heaping bowl of greens and vegetables, colorful and neatly arranged "—one mixed grill—" a wooden platter of spiced steak strips, pork loin and lumps of rockcrawler claw with mushrooms and fried onions "—and a wine seltzer."

She reached into her belt-pouch for the tenth Crown piece; about what a dockworker made in an hour, fairly steep by local standards.

"No charge for Falkenberg's Legion, Miss," the waiter said. He looked about seventeen, with a pleasant freckled face and was probably the son of the owners. "Compliments of the proprietors."

"Thank you," she said sincerely; he reminded her of George, a little. More naive, but then, on Sparta a kid could find time for childhood. And the Legion was popular in this district. She remembered the clinegraphs from briefings at Fort Plataia; about a quarter Citizen around here, and most of the rest established family people, ones who hoped to see their children make Citizen, or were saving to homestead in the outback. The Non-Citizen's Liberation Front didn't route demonstrations through here, since the inhabitants tended to turn out with baseball bats and shotguns to stand in menacing silence.

She took a bite of one of the steak strips; beef still tasted a little odd to her. Few enough on Earth ate much meat these days. *Taxpayer food,* she thought. A far cry from the endless starches, synthetic protocarb and bacteria-vat protein they issued in the Welfare Islands.

Still no sign of the contact when she had finished. *Waiting. Soldiers and spies, they both spend a lot of their time waiting.* Students evidently did, when they could afford to actually attend a University and not cram the study in where sleep ought to go. At the University of Sparta she had met Mary Williams; conversation had led to talks about her background on Earth, the squalid poverty of the Welfare Islands. That made a bitter radicalism plausible—plausible to the children of privileged who seemed to make up the Non-Citizen's Liberation Front at the student level.

Idiots, she thought contemptuously. *Wealthy enough to despise money.* She—*and George, God damn them to hell*—had worked their butts off to get *into* the middle classes, not overthrow them. Casual meetings had led to the legal NCLF organization, and then to the clandestine.

Mary had hinted that this would be a *real* contact, someone she couldn't reach herself except through a series of blind drops and cutouts. No listening bug woven into her uniform, that was far too risky against opposition of the quality the Alanas suspected. There *was* a team observing her, a reaction-squad and snipers with heavy Peltast rifles, so she was probably quite safe. And she had the biofeedback training that made it possible to baffle detectors. Had that, and her native wit.

Datamonger, soldier and spy—and all before my twenty-first birthday. What's next, the circus?

Swallowing the last of the food turned out to be a little difficult. She concentrated, breathed deeply, used the trick Catherine Alana had taught her of thinking of a pool of still water, it was quicker and less de-energizing than the techniques she had used to overcome fear back home. *No-Nose Charlie was nerve-wracking enough.* They had never been part of the Organization back on Earth, but they had been contractors. Too many licenses for legit operation, too much paperwork and graft and pull. Everything outside the Welfare Islands was sewn up tight by the guilds and the unions and the big government-favored corporations. *Who else was there to work for,* she thought. All No-Nose cared about was whether you could make computer systems sit up and beg. She and George could do *that,* any day of the week.

After a moment her pulse slowed and the muscles in the back of her neck relaxed. Margreta sighed, ordered coffee and pulled some lecture notes out of the attaché case she was carrying. They were on software design, the University was trying to resurrect that, along with a number of other sciences. The problem was that the CoDo Intelligence people had made more effort to corrupt those files than any others, even to falsifying the early history of its development; BuInt's attempts to suppress all dangerous science—which turned out to mean all science, period—had been all too successful. Reinvention had to go back almost to the beginning to do anything more than assemble the standard premade blocks in new positions. Xanadu and Meiji were rumored to have made a good deal of progress, but if they had nobody was talking.

A shadow fell across the paper. "Yes?" Margreta said, looking up and around. It was the waiter; the place had grown a little more crowded, extra tables set out for more soldiers and the afternoon shift from the factories. "I'm sorry, I was expecting someone; I'll leave if you need the table."

"No problem, Miss," the waiter said. He smiled shyly. "Besides, I may need to keep on your good side." At her raised eyebrows. "Just accepted as an ephebe of the Brotherhood last week, Miss, and reporting to Fort Plataia for training with the 7th Royal Infantry Monday next. Anyway, your friend called. Says they'll be by any time now."

"Thank you. And good luck in the army; I hope you haven't been listening to too many romantic stories. It's hard work." Even by her standards; still, it would be very useful to have a scientific understanding of combat. The Talkins' twins had learned a good deal on the streets, and there was teaching available there if you could pay, but the Legion was a different category altogether.

"You're welcome, Miss, and my brother's in the 1st, he fought in the Dales—you'd think they crawl up cliffs pulling themselves along by their lips, to hear *him* talk."

Margreta smiled and shook her head as the young man bustled away, catching a tray of beer steins at the serving window and weaving between the tables to a boisterous party in high-collared gray tunics and stubble-shave haircuts. Imagining himself one of them, she supposed, as she clipped the attaché case closed. *Babies,* she thought *All overgrown babies.* Trying to prove how tough they were.

She started slightly when the dark man in the conservative brown tunic and tights stopped at her table.

"Do not be alarmed," he said, moving forward with fluid smoothness. He took her hand in a grip like a pneumatic clamp, as impersonal as a machine too.

"We have now," he went on, seating himself and laying an attaché case on the table, "eliminated the obvious; police tailing efforts, implanted electronics, and the rest. Passive observation is possible, of course."

The man was about 175 centimeters, brown-skinned, Latino from the cast of his features. Unusually fit, not massive but broad-shouldered and moving lightly as a racehorse. Not a native Anglic speaker, she judged; an ear for the nuances of language was another thing common to her new profession in Intelligence and her old life on the fringes of the illegal. The mystery man had no trace of a regional or planetary accent. That was rare. Definitely not a Spartan, their dialect was so archaic that it was almost English; it retained the final "g," differentiated between "c" and "k," and had fewer of the Spanish and Oriental loanwords that made up so much of the modern language. This man's Anglic had a pellucid clarity like a very good AI language program or someone high up in the CoDominium information services.

"I should think the information I've delivered over the past weeks would be proof of my *bona fides,* sir," she said; a combination of respectfulness and firmness was best here.

A slight chuckle. "Yes, but as we both know, Miss Talkins, it is often worth the sacrifice of real data to plant a double agent who can feed disinformation into an opponent's information-bloodstream. Granted that the files you have contributed are mostly useful, and all have been corroborated independently, this possibility remains."

Margreta allowed herself to lick her lips; they tasted of salt. "Paranoia is also a threat in this business, sir," she said.

A quaver? No, too much. He's got to think I'm valuable, and an agent with weak nerves is a walking invitation to disaster. "Properly safeguarded, an agent in place in the Legion's intelligence section would be a priceless asset."

"Quite. But an exceedingly risky occupation for an agent with a comfortable position elsewhere," he said dryly.

"I'm scarcely comfortable where I am, sir," she said coldly. "My origins . . . I have abundant reason to sympathize with the Movement."

A skeptical silence. *All right, girl, time to really act.*

"All right. Sir." A calculating viciousness in her tone now. "I've seen enough to know the Helots stand a good chance of winning. If I get in on the ground floor, I can really get somewhere—all the best jobs in the Legion go to Falkenberg's cronies, and you can't get ahead unless you hold a line command and women can't. I don't want to spend thirty years being a glorified commissioned clerk, or marry some po-faced whiskey-swilling mercenary and breed a litter of officerlets. I want to *be* something, *myself.*

"And," she added, panting slightly, "I want the satisfaction of seeing those bungling incompetents who got my brother killed stood up against a wall and *shot.* All my life—all my and George's life—we've had to wade through wet cement to get a living, while morons without a tenth our brains sat fat and happy up on top, rigging the game against us. We couldn't break in back home because we didn't have parents in the business—bad as bloody India. And here, these so-called generals couldn't figure out anything better for a man with George's brains to do than carry a field computer over a minefield."

Amazing what buried resentments you can find, she thought with a slight tremor of distaste, turning her head aside and controlling her breathing. *Be what you want to seem, as Socrates said.*

The unseen man laughed. "Better. Altruists are unreliable, while resentment and spite are the unfailing twin engines of conspiratorial politics." A long silence, while he looked into the briefcase. "Sincerity, or so my equipment assures me. Well.

"However, another problem arises. You have made yourself an object of suspicion to your superiors by associating with members of the NCLF which is popularly—" a shade of irony "—suspected of having links with the People's Liberation Army. 'No politics in the Legion' will scarcely stretch to cover that."

"I never joined," Margreta said. "Just hung around with them and didn't win many arguments." *God, don't let the deal be queered by its own camouflage!* Gradual disaffection was much more credible than a Saul on the road to Damascus conversion; those were rarer than hen's teeth had been before genetic engineering.

"I've staged some quarrels with the NCLF people at the University"—*which was no problem, what a group of geeks, Mary apart; she's quite nice in a spoiled-brat way*—"and made friends with Royalists. They've welcomed me back like a strayed lamb."

"Perhaps. Although I have a healthy respect for the Captains Alana. The Legion is a small organization and tightly-knit, its officer corps very difficult to infiltrate; particularly as they also have access to voice-stress equipment."

Another pause. *Who were these people?* She thought. Not Spartans, not part of the NCLF's underground *apparat.* Off-planet hired specialists—she almost snorted at the irony. *Mercenaries.* Meijians, from the captured equipment—although possibly other Orientals, say from Xanadu or even Earth, trying to make everyone *think* they were Meijians. Clandestine ops were like that.

"You are correct, though," the man continued. "Such an asset is too precious to risk. Continue to use the present dropoffs;

a call to this number—" he slid a slip of paper across the table "—will give you an emergency contact. Please remember that emergency is the operative word. Please also remember that you are now committed; refuse to carry out orders, and we will simply let your Legion superiors know what you have been doing." The Legion's punishment for treason was hanging.

"We won't use this location again?"

"No, its utility is at an end. Good-bye, Cornet Talkins. Leave the location quickly, please."

He nodded and rose to go, brushing past her. She waited a safe ten minutes, then rose and packed the satchel, remembering to leave a decent tip, and flagged a taxi.

"Definitely Meijians," she said, sliding into the back seat. "They've got voice-stress equipment, too."

"Good to have confirmation," Captain Jesus Alana said from the front seat. "It would be splendid," he went on wistfully, "to pull in that son of ten fathers and sweat out what he knows. Not with a Meijian, though."

Margreta nodded; the technoninjas used a suicide-conditioning process, they could stop their hearts by willing it. And would; if captured.

"Feeding them disinformation will be even better," he said. "And now . . . debriefing."

Julio McTieran grinned to himself as he saw the young woman hail a taxi-van and drive away.

God, talk about cute, he thought *Walks like a palm swaying in a south breeze. On her, red hair looks good.* It was very *dark* red, of course. His younger sister had an orange thatch, and in his private opinion she was homely enough to stop a clock. *So that's one of the terrible slave-driving mercenaries Mike's always moaning about.* He'd have to tell his brother about *that* one when he came back from Mandalay on leave.

"Julio, you good-for-nothing, stop dreaming and help me with this!"

"Yes, mother," he said resignedly, throwing the towel over his shoulder and taking the trays.

A big order for the new bunch of soldiers and their dates; five roast chicken, six burrito platters, seven orders of home-fries, ice-cream to follow, three sarsaparillas, a carafe of the tavern red, two half-liter steins of Pale Brewmaster. This bunch weren't recruits; they had the Dales campaign ribbon, and one ferret-faced trooper with monitor's stripes had the Military Medal. Yellowed teeth showed as he sprawled back in his chair, stein in one hand and the other arm around the waist of a girl.

Transportee, Julio thought. He lifted one tray on each hand, corded forearms taking the strain easily; Julio believed in being prepared, and he had been working out more than the Brotherhood training required. Running up and down Thermopylae Point with hand-weights fifteen times every morning, then back home through the streets before the traffic started. *If a transportee can get the Military Medal, I certainly can.*

His mother was laughing and talking with the soldiers; some were from the neighborhood, some from the Valley, a few even from the Minetown slums, but they were all enjoying her banter. Julio felt invisible as he held the trays for her to serve, watching the way the soldiers' girls clung to their arms, smiling and looking pretty and fresh in their thin print frocks. *Only one more week,* he thought doggedly. *One more week till I report.*

He was turning with the empty trays when he noticed the bicycle stopping outside. Nothing unusual about it, a two-seater commuter model, thousands like it. The two men on it were dressed in ordinary clothes, except that they were wearing white Carnival masks weeks and weeks before the season. The young man recognized the shape one drew from beneath his cloak easily enough; the Walther 10mm machine-pistol was part of the training program for his Brotherhood. It was the fact that it had no place *here,* that it was so *strange,* that was what kept him standing and staring blankly while the man raised it, finger tightening on the trigger.

One of the soldiers had better reflexes. The snaggle-toothed monitor kicked the table over for a barricade and drew his sidearm in the same motion, firing without even getting out of the chair. The terrorist gunman lurched backward off the bicycle, and most of the burst went high, cracking into the rooftiles. Diners were shouting, trying to get to their feet, but they were blocked by the table and their chairs and the screaming, milling patrons, bottles and food and wine and blood. The soldier fired again, not quite quick enough to stop the second man on the bicycle as he jerked the pin from a grenade and lobbed it into the Cock and Grill's courtyard. Julio's eyes followed its arc.

Five second fuse, he thought with detachment. The men on the bicycle were both down now; the soldier who had shot them was prudently behind the heavy oak of the table, and his hand reached up to jerk down the girl who had been sitting beside him. Few of the other patrons had that training, most had not even seen the weapon land.

Three seconds. The oblong grenade clattered to the brick not far from him, spinning on its side like a top. *Fragmentation model*, he realized; that was part of ephebe training too. Lined with coils of notched steel wire, kill-radius of fifteen meters.

It detonated less than a second after he dove onto it and flattened himself to the ground.

CHAPTER THREE

Croftons Encyclopedia of the Inhabited Planets
(2nd Edition):

Terraforming: techniques whereby an extrasolar planet
is rendered more habitable for humans and/or other Terran
life. Prior to the discovery of the *Alderson Drive* (q.v.),
terraforming referred primarily to hypothetical projects to
render planets such as Mars and Venus inhabitable. While
technically practical, the discovery of worlds with oxygen-
nitrogen atmospheres and carbon-based life cycles has
made such endeavors non-cost-effective. Habitable planets have proven to be relatively common, and the basic
similarities in their biologies—e.g. the prevalence of close
analogs to DNA—has given considerable support to the
'panspermia' hypothesis that the basic building-blocks of
life are introduced from space, where complex hydrocar-
bons and amino acids are formed spontaneously. Differences in detail, for example the "handedness" of sugars
or, less seriously, the presence or absence of various
vitamins, pose severe problems to human colonization.
A random introduction of Earth bacteria, plant life and
simple animals is an excellent trial indicator of the suit-
ability of a roughly Earthlike world for human settlement.

As a general rule, the less advanced the ecology, the
easier the introduction of Terran forms will be. On *Tanith*
(q.v.), which contrary to surface appearances is in a post-
Miocene, post-mammalian stage of evolutionary progress,
only intensive protection by man allows any Terran plant
or animal life to survive at all. The native species are
simply more efficient. Most oxygen-atmosphere planets are
less formidable, and selective introduction of higher
animals is possible once the native ecosystems are disorganized by human activities. Most favorable of all are

900

worlds like *Meiji* (q.v.), *Xanadu* (q.v.), or *Churchill* (q.v.), where the native ecologies are notably simpler than the Terran; here the introduced forms, with some simple genetic engineering to compensate for factors such as differences in length of year, often replace the local life-forms spontaneously.

An extreme example is *Sparta*, (q.v.), where the relative youth of the planet and the great rapidity of continental formation and subsidence meant that the local ecology had barely begun to colonize the landmasses at all. Faced with an entire planet of virgin ecological niches, the introduced plants and animals exploded across the continent, completely replacing the meager native species (analogs of mosses, lichens and ferns, with some amphibious insects) almost overnight. In turn, the introduced species have engaged in complex and fluctuating interactions as plant-herbivore-predator associations are worked out to fit the patterns of a world never *quite* like Earth. A stable ecology may take millennia to form. . . .

"Excellent," Dion Croser said, lighting his pipe. *Thank god the geneticists got the gunk out of tobacco,* he thought absently. *Greatest aid to concentration ever invented.* "Excellent work." He was a tall man, 180 centimeters, rangily athletic; his face was mostly Anglo-aquiline, and the eyes were blue. Their slant and the high cheekbones were a legacy from a California-nisei mother, but Croser was Sparta-born, the second generation after the Founding. "Particularly getting someone inside the Legion's Intelligence service.

"Not a high-ranking source; and our contacts through the Royalist secret service indicate the double agent may be under suspicion already. We are developing plans to replace this agent, and to extract maximum asset-value in the meantime."

The man sitting across from him in his study did not look much like Kenjiro Murasaki, head of Special Tasks Inc., of New Osaka; more like an American of *mestizo* background, if anything. But then, he had seen Murasaki in his own *persona* only once—if that. *A knight of ghosts and shadows indeed,* Croser thought. Mercenary technoninja, an ironic ally for the Non-Citizen's Liberation Front. Politics made strange bedfellows, and Bronson's money even stranger ones.

"Still, we've gained valuable information already," he said aloud.

Kenjiro made an expansive gesture; even his body-language

had changed with the disguise. "Largely a confirmation of material from other sources, Capital Prime," he said. "We are still working on cracking the control codes for the computers of the Legion itself; even that will be of limited utility, since they are ROM-programmed. Best to proceed very cautiously, very cautiously indeed. Our probes have positively identified CoDominium Intelligence security and counter viral systems, Fleet HQ level. Excellent work, if unsubtle; BuInt has been keeping many of the people they 'disappeared' over the past century working in their own research institutes."

"Certainly," Croser said. "Well, Earth Prime was right, they are working hand-in-glove with Lermontov. Damn the CD anyway."

Once the Democratic Republic's established, I have to get a priority effort going on computers. We can't depend on foreigners. He glanced up, into the mask of North American affability that Murasaki was wearing. *And I'm uneasy at the extent I depend on this one already,* he mused. Meijians had a reputation for fanatic loyalty to their employers. *But Bronson—Earth Prime— is the employer here, and what does the Senator really want?*

Murasaki inclined his head. "Even so, Earth Prime is not without influence on the CoDominium. More may come of that. As for now, Capital Prime, I would recommend certain selective assassinations."

Croser frowned. "I thought you'd started on the regional governments?"

"Yes. I was referring to key personnel in the upper structures of the enemy."

"Not the kings, I hope?" That would be a little too much, at this point. For that matter, he intended to exile rather than execute them, after he won.

"No." Murasaki spread his hands. "David I is a very competent administrator and economist, but is emotionally incapable of adjusting to harsh conflict. We would not wish him replaced. As for Alexander—" a thin smile "—he is still too popular and trusted, among many non-Citizens as well. Removal would be counterproductive. His judgment is still uncertain" —the news of the viral psychopoisoning of the King had come out some time ago— "and Prince Lysander is alarmingly capable, and has a wide following among the young. A heroic soldier-king is not our need at this point. No, I was referring to technical personnel; the Royalist government's mobilization is proving alarmingly effective."

"Agreed," Croser sighed, rubbing thumb and forefinger on the bridge of his nose. *I wonder if the fear aroused by*

Alexander's poisoning was worth the anger? "Try to be a little less sloppy than you were with the Arrnstrongs, won't you?"

He had felt a little sick, when the pictures came in. Oh, Senator Steven Armstrong was a bull-headed reactionary of the worst sort—typical new-money greed and pushiness—but Alicia had been charming. It was a pity about the children, as well. Wife, children and hard-won ship all destroyed in an afternoon; it was no wonder the man had gone crazy.

Murasaki's bow was slightly out of the character he was playing. "Still, Capital Prime, Armstrong's Secret Citizen's Army has been of immense value to us," he pointed out.

"Feh," Croser said, using a pipe cleaner to tamp down the tobacco. "Mad dogs, the lot of them, even if they are throwing more and more of the non-Citizens our way."

Two more bombings this week, one of a group of transportees just off the shuttle and heading for the CoDo enclave, the other of a meeting of the new Migrant Farmworker's Union, the first all-non-Citizen labor organization. Armstrong's group was mad with fear and hate, but their actions might as well have been dictated from Movement headquarters.

"We'll have to dispose of them all, first thing after we take over," he said. *Actually, there are an uncomfortable number of people to be disposed of. I should take some time to think about this; granted you can't make an omelet without breaking eggs, no point in beheading the chicken.* He could not govern Sparta without *some* of the old ruling class. "Still, they help our recruiting considerably. Beautiful symmetry." He grinned. "'See, the Royalists have their extremists too, and they can't control them any more than the NCLF can the Helots.' By the way," he added, reminded. "Field Prime says that she needs more of your people if they're going to get things rolling again after the Dales campaign."

The Meijian bowed again. "We sacrificed a number of assets," he said judiciously. "But an early breaking of the myth of Citizen invincibility is some compensation. Granted that the Royalists held the field, we demonstrated that our troops could fight the Royal Army."

"Well, the dice rolled that way. Could have been much better, could have been *much* worse." Sitting by the receiver during those crucial hours had aged him a year. Unbelievable exultation, when it looked like the mercenaries and the Royal forces had walked into a trap, then the savage disappointment of seeing it close on his own people instead. The combat experience of Falkenberg's people had been enough to offset Murasaki's penetration of the Royalist intelligence computers.

"My next political move," he went on, "is a direct assault on the legitimacy of the Royalist government. Best to get it done before they proscribe the NCLF and me, personally; that's coming, although we'll fight to delay it. Here's how the open and clandestine wings can help—"

"Don't you have to be at the meeting, Lynn?" Melissa von Alderheim said.

"No, they've put it off until tomorrow," Prince Lysander replied to his fiancee; loudly, as the noise from the factory floor was fairly heavy, even up here in the control booth. "They've brought in some political analyst from Earth that Falkenberg's people think will get to the bottom of our problems; he'll be addressing the War Cabinet."

This was the new von Alderheim works, barely a decade old and on a greenfleld site on the southeastern fringe of the city, with its own dock on Constitution Bay. From this station they could see out over the huge machine-littered concrete bay of Assembly Hall Three. The vehicles were moving down the length of it on wheeled pallets guided by the central Works computer, stopping at each team station while groups of overalled machinists swarmed around it. Overhead trolleys lowered sheets and components, welding torches flashed, pneumatic tools shrilled. The air was full of a low electric humm, the smell of ozone and oil and hot metal.

All like something out of a historical documentary on the First Industrial Revolution, Lysander thought wryly. *Something to be proud of, nonetheless.* Most worlds had a thin scattering of modern equipment over a mass of hand-tools. He extended an arm around Melissa's waist as she came to stand beside him; she was wearing overalls too, but the contents were very pleasant.

"Lynn!" she said, in mock protest, as his hand wandered slightly. "Not here!"

"We've got to stop meeting like this, then," he said, straight-faced. "People will begin to suspect, if we keep traveling to the same factories." They had been friends from childhood, their eventual marriage an understood thing. Lately it had been something he looked forward to more and more. *Melissa's not just smart and pretty, she's a real friend, and someone who wants the same things I do.*

"Forgotten your hotel girl?"

"Yes."

"I don't believe you."

"Melissa—"

"It's all right. It's nice that you say it. And we have our duties." Suddenly she was all business. "I have a surprise for you."

"Pleasant, I hope."

"The war isn't going well."

"Depends on what you mean by well. We're not losing." He waved expressively at the factory. "But we're putting effort into the war that ought to go into building civilization."

"Have you thought of negotiation with—with Croser?"

"Sure," Lysander said. "All he wants is for us to dismantle everything that brought us here. Build a welfare state and all that implies. No thanks. But the worst of it is, I think we're just a sideshow," Lysander said.

"Sideshow?"

"Something like that. The real war is political, and it's being fought in the Grand Senate. If the CoDominium would help us—hell, just stop helping the God damned enemy!—we'd end this damned war and get on with our lives. Including our wedding."

"It's bad, then."

He grimaced. "Bad and getting worse," he said. "The enemy can move faster through the Dales than we can down in the lowlands, and they're starting to stick their heads out again. Nothing decisive, but they're killing ranchers— We've got to move faster and hit harder, or there won't be a ranch standing within a day's ride of the hills come summer."

"Well then, come see the present I've made for you," she said, leading him down another staircase into Bay Six, past a bank of humming fabrication machines. "We made, I helped."

He spared the machines a glance. Smooth man-high shapes, with nothing on the exterior but a console, screen and the ingress and egress ports. Put your metal in one end, program, and any possible shape came out the other, formed by everything from powder-deposition to an ultrasonic beam, untouched by human hands. Earth-made by Hyundai, bought forth or fifth-hand, and still representing an investment so huge that the Finance Ministry had had to handle it. Here they were the tiny heart of the great plant; making machines to make machine tools that human operators could use to do the actual production work. *Some day . . .* Some day Sparta would have real factories, robot-run.

They went through a big sheet-metal door with two armed company guards. Inside white-coated technicians were working around an armored vehicle, with parts of several more nearby. "Here it is!" Melissa said. "Behold: the *Cataphract*."

She stood to one side and clapped; there were good-natured cheers from the technicians doing the final testing.

"Your Highness, Miss von Alderheim." A bow from the chief engineer.

"Sorry to interrupt, Mr. Azziz," Lysander said absently. Suddenly even the woman at his side receded from consciousness for a moment as he looked at the sleek gray-green bulk of the machine before him. "I didn't think you could actually come up with a tank worth building," he said.

"More of a light armored gun system, sir," the engineer demurred; his swarthy face split with the smile of a professional who sees a difficult problem solved. "We're just not up to cermet composites, and no realistic thickness of steel is much use. Miss here did it, on that CAD-CAM machine over at the University."

Melissa made a dismissive gesture. "Just playing with the program," she said, blushing. "Thank Andre Charbonneau."

"Charbonneau?" Lysander said.

He knew the name, a French materials engineer arrested for illegal research and sentenced to transportation by BuInt thirty years ago. The Frenchman had been lucky enough to be sent to Sparta, and had been a fixture of the von Alderheim industrial empire for two decades. The single-crystal iron-chrome alloy he had developed was one of Sparta's few really cutting edge products and a staple export.

The new vehicle was a box about six and a half meters long and three and a quarter wide, no more than two and a half tall, sharply sloped in the front and sides. Suspension was on broad treads with seven road wheels and drive sprockets at the front; the wedge-fronted turret mounted towards the rear of the hull carried along cannon and coaxial machine gun.

"The armor's a sandwich," Azziz said, slapping it affectionately. "Twenty mm of steel, then a layer of interwoven Nemourlon and iron-chrome thread in insulac, then another 20mm of steel. With this on top." He held up a square of some hard glossy material, on a sheet-metal backing. "High-stability explosive. Fire a shaped-charge warhead at it, and it explodes and disrupts the plasma jet. Old Dayan idea."

"From Earth, really," Melissa said, smiling indulgently at the enthusiasm of the men. "But I dug it out of a big load of datadump we bought as part of a job-lot from them with those used shuttles."

Azziz nodded and dropped the plate of explosive casually to the deck of the Cataphract.

"Whole thing is bulkier than cermet, and gives about 75% of the protection for the same weight," he said. "It'll stop most light antitank weapons if they hit on the frontal slope. Thirty tons total weight; the track's woven Charbonneau thread again, with inset tungsten cleats, the suspension's hydrogas units taken from our heavy mining truck, and the engine likewise—seven hundred horse-power turbocharged diesel, top speed of 80 kph and a range of 700 klicks. Three versions, this one with the rapid-fire 76mm gun, one with a 125mm rocket howitzer, beam-guidance, and an infantry fighting-vehicle.

"Nothing but basic four-way stabilization on the weapons and a laser range finder, I'm afraid," he continued, with gathering excitement. "But if we could get modern electronics and sensor kits to upgrade them, I swear there'd be a big export market. Not quite as effective as the stuff North American Motors or Daimlerwerk Friedland AG put out, but a lot cheaper—a fifth the cost, and hell of a damn sight easier to maintain on a nonindustrial planet."

"Toys for the boys," Melissa said. At their surprised glances: "It's just machinery to me, Lynn. I don't get that, ah, sensual satisfaction from it. We've done up a set of duplicate jigs, by the way, for the plant in Olynthos, and we're starting series production immediately. We can—"

Whunnnnng. The explosion seemed to go on forever, vibrating from the pressed-metal internal partitions and off the high ceiling of the plant.

"Where was that, where *was* that?" Lysander barked, hand clearing the sidearm he was wearing with his undress grays. Nobody was down, nothing burning. But close. The communicator on his belt squawked:

"On the way. Prince!" Harv, with the headquarters reaction squad. *Thank God I let him talk me into bringing them,* Lysander thought.

The technicians had taken cover; an alarm klaxon was blaring. Melissa had vanished. A moment's panic, before he saw her head emerge from the Cataphract's turret. *Smart girl.* Probably the safest place in miles. The prince cocked his head; his ears were still ringing, but he knew where those screams were coming from. Azziz was at his side, one hand clutching a piece of steel bar stock.

"Stay back, man," Lysander snapped.

"Stay back, hell," the engineer said, although he did drop behind a little. "I didn't sell everything I owned on Earth and move here to lose it all to convict scum."

They dodged through the door to the next bay. "My God!" Azziz exclaimed in horror.

Lysander did not think the emotion was for the two workers lying on the ground; Harv's reaction squad was there, spreading out to search and giving first aid to the wounded. The object of the engineer's attention was the first of the four Hyundai fabricators. The exterior telltales had gone dead, and one side of the boron-fiber outer sheathing was bulged and blackened.

"Ruined!" he screamed, slapping his hands to his head. "Two million CD credits and a year's shipping time, and it's *ruined.*"

His piece of bar stock clattered to the floor as he rushed over to the machine. Harv rose from beside one of the wounded technicians and went over to a robot trolley stacked with sections of 75mm steel-alloy square beams, bent to examine them and lifted the end of one, then another.

"Think I've found it, sir," he said, saluting. "Quick work, Sergeant," he replied. Harv Middleton, body guard and Phraetrie-brother, would never qualify for a commission, but then he wouldn't want one. All he wanted was to stay close to his Prince.

"Sabotage, Prince. The operator there, he said he and his buddy came round and fed the square steel billets there into the machine every half-hour or so, and saw that the bin of parts moved off."

Lysander walked over and looked at one of the neighboring fabricators. There was a feed-arm that gripped the raw stock, with an automatically adjusting chuck to hold it while the interior mechanisms got a firm grip.

"They had a fresh trolley here. They put the first one in, turned away to check on the finished parts, and just when they walked around behind it blew. Must be something in the steel, sir."

"Probably," the Prince agreed grimly. His sidearm was still in his hand; he slapped it back into the holster with a sense of angry futility. "Cordon it off, until the Milice get here. Don't disturb the site, the forensic experts will want it that way." *Probably was the bars,* he thought. *Which either came from the smelter right here, or down from Olynthos on a barge. The barge, I'd bet; thousands of klicks of opportunity to substitute.*

"Sorry to spoil your furlough, Sergeant," he continued.

Harv smiled broadly and tapped the butt of the rifle slung over his shoulder. "We were figuring on doing a night-patrol exercise around your hunting lodge," he said. "To see that you and Miss weren't disturbed, sort of."

"That won't be necessary; we won't be using the cottage,"

Lysander said flatly "Neither of us will be leaving the Palace."

The NCO's face fell slightly. Lysander forced a smile and clapped him on the shoulder; Harv could be a bit of a trial sometimes, but he was a good man and a Brother.

"Visit your own girlfriend, Sergeant," he said.

"Which one?" Harv said, returning the smile. Then he looked to his men: "Excuse me, sir?"

The officer nodded, turned and walked back through the doors, brushing aside the crowd of frightened technicians and their questions. Melissa was sitting on the side of the Cataphract, waiting.

"Bad?" she said.

"Two men injured," Lysander replied. "One of the Hyundai's is wrecked."

She winced. "That *is* bad." He explained, and she shook her head ruefully.

"Don't tell me we're going to have to inspect every shipment of raw stock!"

"I'm afraid so," he said. Softly: "I'm afraid it's too risky for us to visit the Theramenes. Personally, the Palace will do me quite well, and to hell with appearances." He held out his hand.

CHAPTER FOUR

Confusion is often apparent in discussions where the terms *guerrilla, partisan, insurgent, terrorist,* and *mercenary* are used. *Guerrilla, partisan,* and *insurgent* are interchangeable. These three words refer to one whose aim is to overthrow a government by armed force, largely through use of indigenous resources. International conventions provide for the treatment of guerrillas, insurgents, and partisans. They must bear arms openly, wear an identifying symbol that is recognized at a distance, and conform to the laws of war. Compliance with these simple rules places the insurgent, guerrilla, or partisan in the category of a legally recognized combatant, one who is due prisoner-of-war status if captured.

Terrorists enjoy no legal protections. They normally conceal weapons, mingle with the civilian populations for personal protection, and may take hostages to achieve their aims. Defying international conventions, they are usually treated as common criminals. Terrorist methods often involve armed and illegal coercive propaganda. The most typical terrorist goal is to achieve widespread recognition for a cause through outrageous actions that compel international attention.

One term, *mercenary,* is apt to be much in evidence during the 21st Century, and it may be used as inappropriately then as it is now. Commercial contractors currently maintain some weapons systems, perform housekeeping duties at military and naval installations, and conduct military training. They have even drafted military plans. The use of commercial firms in military affairs is growing, and their staffs are often composed of ex-military and -naval personnel. But are these companies and their employees properly labeled as mercenaries?

The word *mercenary* is more often used in pejorative descriptions. The term usually has more to say about the writer or commentator's political orientation than it does about the person described. A true mercenary's sole motivation is financial reward, the acid test being whether he would switch sides for more money. In other words, the mercenary does not discriminate between political causes or nations to which he offers his services. His work simply goes to the highest bidder. As a practical matter, most people who are described as mercenaries are actually adventurers who discriminate between the political causes they support. . . .

—Rod Paschall
*LIC 2010: Special Operations and
Unconventional Warfare in the Next Century*
(Institute of Land Warfare,
Association of the US Army, 1990)

Letter found in War Office general delivery box, Sparta City:

Dear Major-General Owensford:

Hiyo, Petie! This Skilly dropping you a line to thank you for the seminar in operational art you give us Helots back in the Illyrian Dales. That will teach Skilly not to make she plans so fancy! Skilly, now she understand more of what Clausewitz write about friction and other thing as well.

Expensive lesson, Petie, but as old Socrates say, knowledge be a treasure nobody can take away.

We Helots love the knowledge, so we want to learn everything you can teach. We be coming back for more. Again . . . and again . . . and again. As many times as it take until we get it *right* and pass Final Victory exams. Protracted Struggle, hey?

Give Skilly's regards to Baby Prince. He getting so hard-nose, pretty soon maybe he go into her line of work? But he right not to care nothing about those prisoners and wounded.

You and you gunboys was lucky, but you earned it.

Skida Thibodeau
Field Prime, Spartan People's Liberation Army

PS: Maybe you be lucky again. Maybe twice. But we only need be lucky *once.*

"The important thing," Peter Owensford said, "the great thing, is not to lose our nerve."

There were murmurs of approval around the Council table. "Are you going to give that letter to the press?" someone asked.

"I don't know. Would it be more likely to stiffen resolve, or frighten people?"

"Both, I think." Alan Hruska, Milice chief for Sparta City, looked thoughtful. "Me, I'm for telling the Citizens everything we can."

"Right," Owensford said. "It's our major advantage. Citizens are our partners, not our slaves. Besides, she could send a copy to the press herself. All right, I'll hand it to Harold Preston at the *Tribune.* We owe him—that was a good job he did on the Cock and Grill bombing."

Hruska nodded. "I'd say so."

"How's the boy?" someone asked.

Hruska shrugged. "No change. He'll be months in the regenn tanks, but they figure they can rebuild him. I want him on the force when he gets out—"

"And we could use him in the Army," Owensford said. *Pancake on a bomb and get a choice of careers.* "Whatever happens with him, he's got a medal coming. I take it his medical's paid—"

"Sure, his phratrie took care of everything."

"That's good—ah." Owensford stood to greet a newcomer. "Dr. Whitlock. Gentlemen, Dr. Caldwell Whitlock, political consultant."

There was a flurry of greetings. Horace Plummer, secretary to the War Cabinet, stood. "I will inform their majesties that we are ready to begin."

Roland Dawson, Principal Secretary of State, indicated a place at the table next to Owensford, and Whitlock went to it. He bowed slightly. "Madame Attorney General. Gentlemen. My pleasure to be here." He spoke with a thick Alabama accent.

"I wish that were true." Attorney General Elayne Rusher

looked more like a society lady in her thirties than a grand-mother of fifty-five, or would if there hadn't been so many worry lines at the corners of her eyes. "But it's nice of you to say so."

"Ma'am." Whitlock took his seat. He was a tall lean man in his early fifties, looking younger from careful exercise and expensive regeneration treatments; even under Sparta's heavy gravity he was loosely relaxed. A blond mustache and trimmed goatee set off long carefully-arranged yellow locks, and he was dressed with foppish care, in multihued tunic, tooled boots, black-satin tights, broad sash and an emerald stickpin in his cravat, the height of Earth fashion.

"How long will you be here?" Peter Owensford asked.

"I won't be leavin'. Closed out my affairs on Earth before I came."

"Good God."

"Not easy," Whitlock said. "My family settled Montgomery, you know. And we've had the Jacksonville plantation ever since the Yazoo Purchase."

"It's that bad on Earth, then?"

Whitlock looked up to see that everyone was listening, and nodded. "I'll have a few words about that in the meetin'. But yes, things are happening on Earth. With John Grant dead, I wouldn't be surprised to see Unity out of office next election. If things last until then, which—"

The door at the far end of the chamber opened. "Gentle-men, ladies—their Majesties."

Everyone stood as the kings, Alexander and David, entered with Lysander.

The King looks better, Owensford thought with relief. Lysander had told him that Melissa and the Prince's mother Queen Adriana had been working on him in relays to take a vacation at the summer palace on the island of Leros. Two weeks among the orange trees and olive groves had worked wonders in speeding the cure; Alexander's skin was tanned and firmer, his eyes had lost most of the desperate hunted look, and he moved less like a man carrying a double-weighted pack. By contrast, his co-monarch David looked as if he were still in mourning. He'd been Crown Prince Regnant for years until his near-invalid father quietly died. *At least the Helots had the decency to let us bury the king without incidents.* David's rather low key coronation was marred by three car bombings and an attempted riot. The riot was suppressed with casualties to the rioters; relatives of the police were killed by the car bombs. *Another incident of oppression for the oppo-sition to exploit.*

*On the other hand. David Freedman always looks like that
when we have to increase taxes.* The Freedman kings had
been economics professors of a very laissez-faire bent, back
when Sparta was the dream-child of the Constitutionalist
Association on Earth. Every regulation or tax was like tearing off a piece of skin, to them. One could sympathize,
but that money was buying what his men needed to fight
and win.

The royal party took their places at the center of the table.
Alexander nodded to Horace Plummer. "Mister Secretary."

"Your Majesties. Your Highness. The first order of business
is a report on the current situation. General Owensford."

" . . . so by the end of spring, we'll have better than thirty
thousand people under arms in the Royal Army, under the
Emergency Program," Owensford concluded. "In addition we
have a full two regiments of the Spartan Legion. We've got
four companies of Helot deserters trained and heading out
to New Washington as reinforcements for Colonel Falkenberg."

"Tell us about that," Attorney General Rusher said.

"Not much to tell," Owensford said. "We offered amnesty
to any captured enemy enlisted troops who'd join the Legion,
and got about two thousand. Half that many made it through
training. We turned the others, the ones who wouldn't volunteer, over to the Milice."

"What happens to the washout volunteers?" Roland Dawson
asked.

"Turned over to the Milice same as those who told us to
go to hell," Peter said. "Provides an incentive to finish training."

"They go to the far end of the island," the Milice chief said.
"Separated from the ordinary POWs. Right now both groups
have enough work just building their camp and raising their
own food, but we hope to have an education program for those
that stay out of trouble and want to get back into mainland
life." He shrugged. "One more thing to do, and we're in no
big hurry to do it, not until the war's over."

"So none of your trained Helot warriors will stay on Sparta,"
Elayne Rusher asked.

"That's correct, ma'am, we couldn't trust them here. Off-
planet—" Owensford shrugged.

"Legion's been making troopers out of that sort forever,"
Dr. Whitlock observed.

"All true," Owensford agreed. "And finally, we've reinforced
the Fifth Battalion, Falkenberg's Legion, almost to full regimental strength, mostly with recruits just off the CD transports.

Unavoidably, this means temporary compromises with unit quality but we're working on that."

"Nothing like combat to sharpen up the troops," Whitlock said dryly.

"Quite true," Owensford said. "Especially NCOs. Of course we've accelerated officer and NCO training. We're combing the CD transports for men with Marine experience. But the best training is still live fire. Unfortunately we're getting all too much of that." The map wall sprang to life.

"Notice the pattern of incidents." He called up an arrow and traced the line of southern Drakons, south and east from the Rhyndakos toward the coastal town of Colchis. "Attempted infiltrations, here and here. And too many successes, because we have no satellite reconnaissance, and not much aerial."

"Dr. Whitlock," Alexander said. "Do we dare renew the satellites? The local CoDominium commander won't answer. Says the question is insulting. But we haven't infinite resources—"

Whitlock nodded. "I wouldn't, just yet. Admiral Lermontov is aware of the situation, but his efforts to make some changes here were blocked by Vice Admiral Townsend."

"Townsend?"

"A Bronson grandson," Whitlock said.

"That sounds ominous," Hal Slater said.

"Ominous indeed, Colonel Slater. Excuse me. General Slater," Whitlock said. "Control of the Fleet is very much in dispute just now, and unfortunately there are other critical situations demanding Admiral Lermontov's attention and influence."

"Such as New Washington?" David Freedman asked.

"Yes, Majesty," Whitlock said. He looked around the room. "Do you want that report now, with all these people?"

"Yes, I think so," Alexander said. "If we can't trust this group, we're finished."

"All right. But with your permission, Sire, I'll let General Owensford finish telling us how he sees the situation before I begin."

"All right," Alexander said. "I take it that we won't be getting a new satellite."

"Maybe not just yet, Sire."

"I see. General—"

"There's not a great deal more to report," Owensford said. "There have been actions here, up the valley of the Jason and into the Lycourgos Hills. We know they've gotten small forces into the foothills of the Pindaros and Parnassus ranges east of the river. Meanwhile, activity of all sorts is increasing throughout the Middle Valley; their latest trick is to drop mines into the river. We've recovered a few. Big box of plastique with a simple pressure trigger; blows the bottom out of a river boat quite thoroughly."

Lord Henry Yamaga, Minister of Interior and Development, made a sound of disgust. "What's the *point,* beyond sheer sadism?"

Owensford shrugged. "The same *point* as putting small units into the Lower Valley," he said. "We have to divert resources to sweep for mines, and every man we keep in the Lower Valley is another we don't send to the Middle."

"The plan was to keep them bottled up," Yamaga said. "That's not working."

"No, my lord. I haven't enough troops for that. Actually, Alexander the Great and Julius Caesar together couldn't seal that area air-tight, not with a *million* foot-infantry. Controlling guerrilla warfare of this type sops up soldiers the way a sponge does water."

"So what will we do?" *Freiherr* von Alderheim affected a monocle and looked very Prussian, but his voice was friendly. He'd been suspicious of the Legion mercenaries when they first arrived, but lately had become one of their chief supporters.

"We hold on," Owensford said. "And continue to build strength. Majesties, my original assignment here was to train mercenaries you could hire out off-planet for hard currency. That we're doing. As Dr. Whitlock observes, there's nothing like live fire training to cement unit cohesion. In that sense this war has actually helped us get ahead of schedule—"

"At fearsome cost," David Freedman said.

"Yes, Majesty, but the costs of recruiting and training this many soldiers would have been fearsome anyway. When this is over, we'll have trained cohesive units under battle tested leaders. I should think they would command a good price."

"Perhaps," David said. "But I never liked that scheme to begin with." He shrugged. "Of course if we hadn't begun when we did, we wouldn't have had troops ready to fight this— rebellion. We might have lost already. Your pardon, General. Please continue."

"Majesty. Some things go well. The Coast Guard Reserve, our brown-water navy, has got control of a lot of our rivers, and contests the rest with the rebels. They used to get nearly a free ride. Not any more.

"Production of Thoth missiles is up. We don't have as many as I'd like, but the pace accelerates. *Freiherr* von Alderheim's factories are ahead of schedule in helicopter and small aircraft production. We don't have aviation company up to TO&E in every regiment, but at least they all have some kind of aircraft, and brigade levels have more. That gives us considerably more strategic mobility.

"We can't use those for tactical engagements, of course. The rebels have quite enough anti-air to prevent that. On the other hand, having to carry air defense missiles cuts down on their mobility and complicates their logistics, and they don't have air capability.

"The result is that we've cut way back on their ability to resupply from our arms factories. They used to steal us blind, but they can't do that any more. The bad news is they stockpiled a great deal, and they're still receiving off-planet supplies from somewhere. Every time we cut into their quantity, there's new increase in the quality of what they get. Almost as if it's a game."

"Ah," Whitlock said. "And there's where you put your finger on it."

"Sir?"

"In a very real sense, it is a game. Very high stakes game, but a game right enough."

"I expect you're going to explain that," Owensford said.

"Yes. I'll have to lecture."

"Dr. Whitlock, I assure you, you have our full attention," King David Freedman said. "Perhaps you should begin your report now."

"Sire. Well. All along, it must have been obvious to y'all that this rebellion hasn't got a coon's chance without help from off-planet."

"Yes, of course," Alexander said.

"And not just a little help. I don't know what all Bronson has put into this, but it's got to be more than a billion credits."

"That much," David Freedman mused. "Yes, I believe that— but Dr. Whitlock, *why?*"

"That's the question," Whitlock said. "What could he want that's worth that much? There's only one answer that makes sense. Empire."

There was a long silence. "With himself as emperor," Alexander said at last.

"Himself, an heir, a whole group of heirs," Whitlock said. "Yes."

"Why in God's Name would he *want* the job?" Alexander demanded.

"'Cause he thinks it's got to be done, and he's sure he and his people are the only ones that can do it," Whitlock said.

"I know y'all think of Bronson as purely mean and selfish. I can understand Spartans seeing him that way, but I'm surprised you two—" he indicated Peter Owensford and Hal Slater—"bought into that. Colonel Falkenberg always knew better."

"Bronson? A misguided idealist?" David Freedman asked.

Whitlock shrugged. "Call him a patriot if you prefer. He'd think of himself that way."

"And we stand in his way," David said. "Why? Because we— the Collins kings anyway—early on chose to be part of Lermontov's scheme? Is that why our people are being bled to death in a filthy little war we can't win? Because of this ill conceived alliance with Lermontov?"

"David," Alexander said gently. "Please excuse my colleague, Dr. Whitlock. Still, he has a point. Have we merited Senator Bronson's attentions because of our support of his enemies? Could we have avoided all this by remaining neutral?"

"I very much doubt it, Sire. And now I really will have to lecture. If you'll excuse me, I think better on my feet." Whitlock rose and strode to the map wall, where he paced back and forth. "Always did like blackboards," he said absently. "I take it that everyone in this room is cleared for—for everything."

"Yes, of course," Alexander said.

Whitlock was silent as he looked at them one by one.

"You can proceed," Hal Slater said.

"As General Slater says," Lysander said carefully.

Whitlock nodded to Slater, then bowed slightly to Prince Lysander. "Thank you, Highness. All right, let's start from the beginning. The CoDominium's coming apart. When it does, there'll be war on Earth, and it won't stay confined to Earth. Enough of the nationalist elements on Earth have close ties with their colonies that the war will spread beyond the solar system. We have a name for that. Interstellar war. But we don't know much about what that means. Just that it'll be pretty bad, bad enough that it's worth a lot to stop it. We okay so far? Good.

"So. The Grants and the Blaines saw this coming twenty years ago. Earlier, probably, but that's when they hired me to study their options. Problem was, there weren't many options. Too many colonies hate each other. Some areas, the Fleet's all that keeps the peace. Remove the Fleet, war starts like that." He snapped his fingers. "Obvious conclusion is that the Fleet, or a good part of it, has to keep operating if we're to have any chance of holding onto civilization.

"That'll cost money. A lot of money, and a Fleet's no good

without bases, recruiting grounds, retirement homes, home ports for families. You going to keep civilization, you got to have a civilized home base. You need forward bases, too, out among the barbarians. Outposts, listening posts, refueling facilities, bases. Some of those can be enclaves, but it's better to have whole planets.

"That takes soldiers. Long time ago, man named Fehrenbach said it, you can fly over a territory, you can bombard it, you can blow it to hell, you can even sterilize it, but you don't own it until you stand a seventeen year old kid with a rifle on top of it. So. Where to get soldiers? Can't hire 'em. Not enough money, but worse, when you hire mercenaries, what have you got?"

Everyone looked at Slater and Owensford, then looked away.

"'Course there's mercenaries and mercenaries," Whitlock said. "They ain't all alike by a long shot. Take Falkenberg's outfit. It started as the 42nd CoDominium Line Marines. Decorated all to hell, elite outfit even before Falkenberg took it over. No surprise that it stayed together after the CD ordered it disbanded. Lermontov helped find 'em work. Figures. Falkenberg and Lermontov go back a long way. Lot of loyalty in both directions. You can think of Falkenberg's outfit as a kind of Praetorian Guard for Lermontov, except that Lermontov's no would-be emperor.

"But that's one regiment. Need a lot more troops to hold things together. Where to get them?"

"Sparta," King David said. "You and my father—"

"Let's don't get ahead of ourselves, Sire," Whitlock said. "What we've established so far is a need for bases, and troops to guard them with. There's another need, planetary governments interested in civilization. Places without any grudges to work off, no ambitions to drive them. That's Sparta. Not much wonder you were one of the first they tried to sign up."

"There was no commitment. Then," Alexander said. "We were friends with Lermontov and Grant, and we got some trade concessions, favorable interpretations of regulations—"

"All of which ended when the Grants and Blaines lost control," David said.

"Sure, but anyone could foresee that would happen," Whitlock said. "You had to know it, there wouldn't have been no need for this conspiracy if it hadn't been clear things were going to hell and nobody could stop the trip. What were your alternatives? Join up with Bronson?"

Alexander shrugged. "That was never offered to us. If we had—"

"If you had, you'd have ended up with no independence at all," Whitlock said. "Bronson planets have puppet governments, with a Bronson resident calling the shots. Can't see Sparta going along with that."

"Nor I," Baron von Alderheim said. He looked thoughtful. "But is this what will happen if Croser and his people win?"

"Yep."

"Do they know this?" Sir Alfred Nathanson asked. Nathanson was Minister of War, but that was an administrative rather than a command position. Under the Spartan constitution the Kings were the commanders in chief, and could issue orders directly to their generals. For all practical purposes, Crown Prince Lysander was the actual War Minister, with Nathanson handling administration and details.

"I doubt it," Whitlock said. "Y'all know Croser better than me. Would he find the role of puppet very attractive?"

"Attractive, no," Alexander said. "But I really don't know if he would accept it. I knew his father well, but Dion is a bit of an enigma. Would he take the trappings of power without the substance? Probably. He would persuade himself that this was for the best, would serve some higher good."

"And that he'd be able to use his position to take charge some day," Roland Dawson said. "Yes, I think that's how his mind would work. But surely he expects to gain both substance and trappings."

"Well he sure ain't got much chance of it," Whitlock said. "Not given who he's running around with." He clicked the screen controller, and an image formed on the wall screen.

"Field Prime. That's what the Helots call their military commander, just like Croser is Capital Prime, and Bronson is Earth Prime. Interesting set of designations, no? Don't show any one of them subordinate to any other. Anyway here she is."

The woman on the screen was in her early thirties, clearly Eurafrican. 175 centimeters, according to the scale beside the image, with a high-cheeked, snub-featured handsomeness and a mane of loosely-curled hair. Startlingly athletic-looking. An insolent half-smile was on her lips.

"Ms. Skida Thibodeau, aka 'Skilly,' born Belize City, Belize, 2061; mother Mennonite, kidnapped into prostitution, father a pimp. Orphaned at six, primary education in a Catholic charity school. Transported by the Belizian gov'mint—gallows-bait themselves—for 'offenses against public order' in 2083. Better lookin' than your average terrorist, but hoo, lordy, look at that record! Arson, insurance fraud, illegal substances trafficking, assault, intimidation, murder, racketeerin', you name it and she's dabbled in it. When your police people closed in on her accounts and suchlike, they found she'd managed to accumulate better than six million crowns."

"No small sum," Lysander said dryly.

"Right. Got most of the money out, too. Presume it's stashed where she can get at it if she has to vanish fast. She was an, ah, *intimate* friend of your good Citizen Dion Croser fo' six years, but no trace of political ties. No paper trail."

Chief Hruska nodded sourly. "No criminal record, except for the one assault charge that got her in jail. We've known she was a criminal for years, but no evidence. She moved around a lot, but she stayed with Croser every couple of months. They openly went to night spots together."

"And of course Croser is simply shocked to discover she was involved in criminal activities," Attorney General Rusher said.

"The point is, she's not likely to knuckle under to anybody," Whitlock said. "Doesn't fit her personality. So here she is, out there carryin' water for Croser, and if Croser's not smart enough to see what Bronson has in mind for Sparta, this one is. Leavin' us with the question, just what in hell is her game?"

"Do you have an answer?" Alexander asked.

"Only the obvious, she thinks that when the fightin's over, Field Prime'll be runnin' the show and Capital Prime and Earth Prime can dance attendance." He shrugged. "If she can out-maneuver Bronson she's a rare bird for sure."

"Devious, but inexperienced," Hal Slater said. "Inexperienced at this kind of intrigue, that is. She will have been the cleverest around where she came from. Able to outsmart anyone. Look at her battle plan in the Dales campaign. Intricate, fine tuned, clever—and utterly unworkable. I suspect it's the same thing here. She simply has no experience at dealing with really clever people, people served by an equally intelligent general staff. Her experience with Croser probably has done little to disillusion her—and of course Bronson's people aren't going to."

"Until it's too late," Whitlock said. "Yeah, I reckon that's the size of it. She figures when it's over she'll be in charge with Croser to help her, and he reckons the same thing only reversed."

"They really do intend to become the government," David mused. "They *want* to govern."

"No, Sire, they don't want to govern. They want to *rule,*" Caldwell Whitlock said. "Not quite the same thing. And as

General Owensford's report shows, they've made a fair bit of headway."

Alexander shook his head in wonder. "How could people like that put together an army, an army capable of fighting real troops, right under our noses?"

"Careful plannin'," Whitlock said. "An eye for conditions. And a lot of help from off-planet. Conditions first. I was just remarking to General Owensford here, this isn't the sort of war he's used to. It's revolutionary war, the type they had on Earth a hundred, hundred and fifty years ago. You see, you're the victims of your own success. Oppression and despair don't produce revolution; there's been exactly *one* successful slave revolt in all of recorded history. No, what produces revolutions is *hope*—combined with a certain amount of social disorganization. Defeat in war will do it but BuReloc's given you the equivalent—and frustrated ambitions. The underclasses may furnish the troops, but it's people on the make who lead them.

"Places like Meiji or Churchill, they're too homogenous and stable for this kind of war. They'd have to be outright invaded. Frystaat, say, or Diego are quite effectively oppressive. They'd have shot your Croser years ago. You, I'm afraid, are stuck right in the middle. In most places civilization is a thin crust on a sea of barbarism; Rome had her Goths and Saxons, Earth bred 'em in its own guts. Still, the system's had a certain stability. The masses never get to *see* the rulers, mostly they're left to rot while dangerous ones are shipped out, or recruited fo' the Marines and the Fleet; the productive workin' minority is kept in line by the threat of the—pardon me, usin' Earth terminology—Citizen hordes. An' the tiny oligarchy that runs things is secure. Except from itself, which is where the system's breakin' down there, a lot like old Rome.

"Now," he went on, drawing on his cigar, "out here, you've got problems from the bottom *up*, instead. Y'all understand, you've got an unusual rulin' class here. A full third of the population, and *visible*. Then the CD sends you Earth's barbarians. And what do you do? You give them a chance. You give them no excuses. None. You make it plain, their failures are their own fault, and you rub it in by making the rewards of success visible and believable.

"That worked fine so long as you didn't get overwhelmed. Lots of them made good, you've achieved a remarkable and admirable social mobility. But a lot just don't make good. Too many generations of failure, too long away from even suspecting what citizenship is. They see you as rich slavemasters, and they get told all they got to do is take what's coming to them. Okay, you can handle that if you don't lose your nerve, but nobody ever said it was going to be easy."

"We give them every opportunity to get ahead. Become Citizens, or, more likely, their children will," Lord Yamaga said. "My grandfather was a transportee!"

"Yessir, but don't forget how things change. First generation transportees got here into a working society, lots of opportunity. No opposition to speak of. Now you get floods of these barbarians. Most raised in cesspits ruled by two-legged rats. Example, Skida Thibodeau, of Belize. Only difference there between the street gangs and the gov'mint is firepower. Miz Thibodeau grew up in an environment where there's no law nor morals either; she's got enormous ability, and the moral outlook of a hammerhead shark." Another meditative puff.

"Of course, the demographic mix here doesn't help. The surplus of males, that is. Big concentration of young, socially alienated and sexually frustrated males with no prospects of startin' a family is a recipe for trouble. Recruitin' them into an army and sending them offworld was a good idea, only too late. Because of the next factor: who's taking *advantage* of the conditions."

"Croser," someone said; they made the word sound like a curse.

"True. Typical in Utopian settlements to get a rebellious element in the second generation. Your bad luck to get one who's perversely brilliant, with a childhood grudge against your whole social system: Knows history, knows the weak points of your society—I've read some of his papers from his university days. Also a charismatic leader who can win loyalty, not afraid to delegate, and he knows how to pick able people.

"Been plannin' this for the better part of two decades, I'd say. Accumulatin' funds—does it shock you if I say he controls more money than *Freiherr* von Alderheim here?"

The industrialist *did* look shocked.

"Lot of debts," Whitlock said. "But lots of power, too."

"Where did he get it?" van Alderheim demanded.

"Lots from off-planet," Whitlock said. "Easy to guess the source."

"So Bronson has bought him? Why? What does Bronson want with us?" Alexander demanded.

"Regiments. Same thing Lermontov wanted," Whitlock said. "You set out to build a regiment factory. That was fine by Bronson. He'd figured on Croser doing that anyway, you might as well get a good start. Then two things happened. Ms. Skilly got anxious to start things movin'—don't know why, maybe she's beginning to feel her age—and you brought in Falkenberg's Legion to train these troops. That was enough to get Bronson's attention."

"Because he hates Falkenberg," David said.

"Well, Sire, that's a piece of it, but if you bet on Grand Senator Adrian Bronson gettin' carried off by his emotions, you'll lose every time. Not that he minds indulging his grudges when he can, he's got a hell of a streak of mean, but think on it. If you'd built normal mercenary regiments for use off-planet, who'd they be loyal to?"

"The paymaster, I presume," Lysander said quietly.

"Exactly. But Your Highness was with Falkenberg's Legion on Tanith. Who are they loyal to?"

"Falkenberg. I see," Lysander said. "Suddenly what Bronson saw as an asset—mercenary regiments he could subvert— became a possible threat."

"That's about the size of it," Whitlock said. "Before that, his support for Croser was nominal, the kind of thing he does lots of places for insurance, a way to keep his hand in. Sparta didn't look like having any special ties to Falkenberg and Lermontov. Then all of a sudden, Prince Lysander here goes to Tanith, where Falkenberg and one of the Blaines are in cahoots to mess up Bronson's plans to get more control over the Fleet. Crown Prince Lysander becomes Mr. Cornet Prince, and that right there would be enough to take notice of."

"Why?" David asked.

"Reckon you never met Falkenberg," Whitlock said. "If you had, you wouldn't ask. Anyway, pretty soon he don't have to guess whether Prince Lysander's going to choose the Lermontov side in the upcoming struggles, 'cause Mr. Cornet Prince goes and ruins Bronson's whole operation for him."

"Game. You said game," Lysander said.

"Up to not long ago that's what it was," Whitlock said. "Bronson didn't want Croser to win and consolidate his position, but he didn't want him to lose, neither. So he sends just enough to keep him going. But that all changed last year. Now it's all out."

"And so he sent the technoninjas," Slater said. "And stepped up his off-world support by a lot."

"So what will happen now?" Lysander asked.

"Not to get ahead of ourselves," Whitlock said. "First look at what you're facing. For twenty years Croser's been laying a political framework without much opposition. After all, it didn't occur to anyone that organizin' the non-Citizens was anything but an exercise in futility. Developin' an ideology: I mentioned this was an archaic sort of place? Well, you've got something *really* old-fashioned here. A real, honest-to-god Leninist-Maoist vanguard party that believes in itself. Oh, not strictly Marxist—elements of that—more like National Socialism, really. Then he started buildin' up an army. The brigadier here knows more about the ways that might be done."

Owensford nodded. "We've put together something of a picture from the prisoner interrogations," he said.

"You'd start small, with some committed partisans. Get them military educations, and bring in small parties of people with training—there are plenty of good officers and NCOs on the beach on Earth, and the NCOs would be more valuable than the officers, at first. Not all that many who'd be willing to link up with this gang, but enough. Send others off to enlist in merc units on other worlds, which would get you combat-experienced men. Use all those to train selected local recruits who're committed to your cause. It would start small, but once you got well started expansion could be geometric. We've also determined that they—presumably Croser—started stockpiling weapons and equipment, in the Dales and elsewhere, a full decade ago. Skimming export shipments, mostly. Croser's companies would get export orders, over-order enough to cover the five or ten percent they'd take, then use the profits on the real sale to cover the excess. Complicated, but workable, and you wouldn't have to have many people in the know."

Alexander rolled a pen between his fingers. "But surely Croser—if it is he—couldn't think that such a force could overthrow the government? After all, the Brotherhoods can call out hundreds of thousands of troops in an emergency."

Whitlock waved the tip of the cigar to emphasize his point. "Not attack and displace—but you're thinkin' in terms of modern warfare, small decisive campaigns, your Majesty. The enemy is usin' an older model. Their target isn't really your armed forces, it's your society as a whole. They give you nothing to attack, while you have to guard *everything.* You can't call out the Brotherhoods *en masse* for long; too much shuts down. And many of them are scattered on farms and ranches miles from anywhere when they're not under arms. There's a military saying—"

"Frederick the Great," Owensford supplied. *"Who defends everything, defends nothing.* Quite true."

"And a Chinese saying," Whitlock continued, "which sums up the method: death by a thousand cuts." Another puff.

"Won't work, not the way Croser had it planned original. The rebels are underestimatin' the solidarity of your Brotherhoods; also how mad they're getting." A bleak smile. "Ruthless people don't understand how mean good folks can get when their codes are violated. But he has outside help now, an that makes all the difference.

"'Death of a thousand cuts' applies politically as well as militarily," Whitlock continued. "This referendum he's pushing, for example."

David snorted. "A farce. A referendum on universal suffrage, when we don't *have* universal suffrage? Nothing but an opinion poll."

Whitlock chuckled. "Thing is, you people have made a big thing of votes. Back on Earth, not three countries left where votin' means a thing; doesn't in the US, certainly. Here, it's a jealously guarded privilege. Rest of the population figures since Citizens put so much store in it, vote must be a good thing to have. Since most Citizens won't go within ten yards of Croser's poll, give you odds it'll be done scrupulous honest and still win big. No legal force—but it'll polarize the population even more. Who's going to come right out and admit: *yes, I'm lower than a snake's belly in a wagon rut and don't deserve a say?* There'll be some appeal to those workin' towards Citizen status for themselves or their kids, too.

"It's psychological-political jujitsu. After he wins, he'll claim a popular mandate. Then again, some of the measures you're being forced to adopt will push the fringe of the Citizens towards Croser. Higher taxes, fo' example. Then, limitin' access to firearms. Necessary, but many of yourn have what amounts to a religious taboo against regulation of guns; 'armed men are free men.' Likewise war regulations of all sorts. Those who don't go to Croser will be pushed towards the radicals on the other fringe, that poor fool Armstrong and his Secret Citizen's Army, or the radical Pragmatist Party crowd. Lot of pure self-interest there, too. Frontier planets with labor shortages always have a tendency towards bound labor systems, slavery or indentured. Thin profit margins, an' with full employment, workers tend to be mobile. Real, real temptin' to use extra-economic means to get secure supplies of workers at a price that leaves some margin. Most of your Citizens've shown commendable restraint, but they're getting mad and scared. And every move in that direction frightens the non-Citizens still more."

"Wage slavery. Enserfment," Alexander said. "I know it happens, but it is contrary to every principle on which this government was founded."

"Sure," Whitlock said. "But the enemy of every free man is a real greedy successful one. Biggest enemies of capitalism are successful capitalists. That's why you got to have governments, but just havin' one ain't enough either. There's plenty of people start at the bottom, get rich on freedom and hard work and then try to take over the government so they don't have to work any more.

"Fact is, when all this is over, I got some advice for you on tinkerin' with your system. Give your individual workers a bit more power and union bosses and owners a bit less. But that's for happier times. Right now, this random terror campaign gets you tightenin' the screws, giving more power to the owners 'cause they're loyal, scaring the little guys. That, and showin' the Royal government can't offer protection even to the Citizens. Goin' after non-Citizen loyalty and Citizen morale."

The ring of faces around the table was set in grim anger; they had known the outlines of it, but the Earthman's dispassionate assessment was a shock.

Owensford turned his uniform cap in his hands.

"It shows in their military approach," he said meditatively. "Puzzled the hell out of me, at first. They didn't seem to be *fighting*, as I understood the term. As Dr. Whitlock said, we've become accustomed to a certain style of warfare. Essentially limited, careful not to damage the prizes we're fighting for, in societies too fragile to stand the strain of mass mobilization. War between *condottieri* captains; maneuver warfare, we're prepared to fight, but only until one side has an unbeatable advantage. Then we make terms. Soldiers are few and expensive and very carefully trained, and the mercenary captains don't expend them easily.

"Our enemies here," he said, "aren't fighting that kind of war. At all. And they're willin' to expend troops, 'cause they got more than you do."

Dr. Whitlock ground out his cigar. "The details are in my report, gentlemen," he concluded. "Sorry I couldn't be more optimistic. You got some real problems. Nothin you couldn't handle by muddlin' along if they didn't have offworld help, but they've got that. Lordy, do they ever."

"And Bronson really wants to be emperor," Elayne Rusher said.

"More likely Chairman," Whitlock said. "But yes."

"Emperor of what?" David Freedman demanded.

"As much as possible, Your Majesty."

"That's impossible," Peter Owensford said.

Whitlock shrugged. "Maybe. Maybe not. Look at it like this. Sparta's neutralized. Far from having an army and the beginnings of a fleet, you won't have control of your own planet. Get the Grand Senate to depose Lermontov before things come apart, while people are still listening to the Senate, and put a Bronson man in as Grand Admiral—"

"Would the Fleet permit that?" Alexander asked.

"They might. Strong tradition in the Fleet, obey orders and stay out of politics. And stay together. As long as Bronson is careful about who he puts in, there'll be a lot of pressure to go along, stay together. The last thing most of those captains want is war with each other."

"Will that happen?" Lysander demanded.

"Probably not. First place, he hasn't got the votes to depose Lermontov, won't so long as Grant hangs on."

"We can presume you have done all you can do on that score," Lysander said. Whitlock nodded. "So. Since there's no more we can do, we concentrate on our own problems. You can prove that it's Bronson who's aiding the rebels?"

"Yes, Highness, and not long ago that would have been enough. Grand Senators aren't supposed to be pursuin' wars of their own. But the fact is, the CoDominium's coming apart fast. It's every senator for himself. Or herself. And Bronson will offer what it takes to get what he wants."

"Because he doesn't intend to honor his debts."

"Maybe, but don't count on it. Good politicians keep promises, and he's been in politics a long time. Don't matter anyway, what's obvious is that Bronson's got massive resources on and off Earth. The Bronson family's disposable income is certainly greater than the Dual Monarchy's."

"And he's willing to spend billions supporting our enemies," Alexander said.

"Sure. He needs a regiment factory. You have one," Whitlock said. "When the CoDominium collapses, it'll be like the fall of the Roman Empire. Bronson's Earth-side money'll be gone anyway. Right now it's use it or lose it time."

"New Washington," Lysander said. "What about that?"

Whitlock nodded. "That's going well. Falkenberg and his employers have a good half the planet under control, and a handle on the rest as long as the Fleet doesn't interfere. It won't, because Lermontov's seeing to it, but that's using up a lot of the Blaine and Grant clout."

"Leaving none for us, which is why we can't count on the local CD fleet to protect our recon satellites," Lysander said.

"That's the size of it, Your Highness. On the other hand,

the New Washington situation won't last forever, and when that's done, you're the top order of business." Whitlock shrugged. "All you have to do is hold on. We got us a political war here, and we going to have to make some political plans. I'll be talkin' with y'all about that another time."

"I just realized," David Freedman said. "If we hadn't become involved with Lermontov, this would have gone on anyway. Croser would have built his strength, with help from Bronson, and we'd never have known it was happening."

Lysander's voice was not much above a whisper. "And no one cares about Sparta. We're just a catspaw in a larger game."

Whitlock nodded gravely. "Wouldn't put it quite that way, Highness. I do see what you're driving at. Both Lermontov and Bronson think they're protecting civilization, civilized values in a world going to hell. Difference is, Falkenberg and Lermontov ain't quite so certain they're the only ones who know what's best for the universe. Hell, they like free people. They're looking for friends and allies, not just subjects."

"I wish I could believe that," David said.

"What choices have we?" Alexander asked. "The whole basis of civilization is collapsing."

"No more law," Owensford said.

They all looked at him.

"The Laws of War and the Mercenary Code—we've been able to enforce them because everybody who mattered believed in them, and those who didn't were militarily contemptible; we could *force* them to abide by the customs. Dr. Whitlock mentioned our internal barbarians; that's where our armies are recruited from, but they've been under the command of civilized men. Now we've got an army—not a mob, but a real army—whose *leaders* are barbarians themselves. For a lifetime, we've managed to make war a limited thing. Putting a wall of glory around it, making it terrible but splendid. Now it's going to be terrible and squalid."

Lysander didn't say anything, but Peter Owensford felt a chill when the Prince looked at him.

CHAPTER FIVE

Crofton's Encyclopedia of the Inhabited Planets
(2nd edition):

Treaty of Independence, Spartan: Agreement signed between the Grand Senate of the CoDominium and the *Dual Monarchy of Sparta* (q.v.). 2062. The Constitutionalist Society's original settlement agreement with the Colonial Bureau of the CoDominium had provided for full internal self-government, but the CoDominium retained jurisdiction over a substantial enclave in *Sparta City* (q.v.), the orbital transit station *Aegis* (q.v.), and the refueling facilities around the gas-giant planet *Zeus*. In addition, during the period of self-government a CoDominium Marine regiment remained in garrison on Sparta and its commander also acted as Governor-General, enforcing the residual powers retained by the Colonial Bureau, mostly having to do with the regulation of involuntary colonist and convict populations.

In line with Grand Senator Fedrokov's "New Look" policy of reducing CoDominium involvement in distant systems where practicable, negotiations began with the Dual Monarchy in 2060. Under the terms of the Treaty, the Royal government became fully responsible for internal order and external defense of the Spartan system, and all restrictions on local military and police forces were removed. The transit station and Zeus-orbit refueling stations were also turned over to the Royal government. However, the treaty also stipulated that certain facilities were to be maintained, at Spartan expense, for the use of the CoDominium authorities and the Fleet; these included docking, fueling and repair functions, and orbit to surface shuttles. Also mandated was the continued receipt of involuntary colonists at a level to be set by the Bureau of Relocation, and for this purpose the CoDominium enclave in Sparta City was retained with a reduced garrison. Penalty provisions in the Treaty authorized direct intervention by the Commandant of the enclave should the Royal government fail to fulfill these obligations. . . .

"Leader selection and development in Western special operations forces began a departure from military norms after a perception of battlefield failure during the Malayan Emergency in the 1950s. The leadership of the SAS, dissatisfied with the unit's performance against communist terrorist bands, determined that a revision of the induction and initial training of SAS personnel was warranted. The program that was developed not only applied to the enlisted ranks; officers were also included in a demanding and wholly new selection process.

"The SAS selection system eliminated candidates who are physically inferior, cannot exhibit sound independent judgment under stress, and lack determination. The system involves several weeks of arduous, individual land navigation treks. The candidates carry heavy rucksacks. Each man plots his own lonely course day after day and cannot rely on others to make the decisions. During the trial, candidates are not encouraged, but instead given every opportunity to drop out of the course, an action that would eliminate their chances to join the unit. Normally only about 15 to 25 percent of candidates are able to complete the course and be selected for membership in the regiment. The qualities of those who pass the trial include a high IQ, superb physical condition, and demonstrated ability to choose wisely despite conditions of great fatigue and mental stress. Only the determined, self-reliant, and quick-witted are selected to serve in the SAS. . . .

—Rod Paschall
LIC 2010: Special Operations and Unconventional Warfare in the Next Century
(Institute of Land Warfare,
Association of the US Army, 1990)

. . . at the beginning of the war it was easy, we could walk into Kabul and attack where we wanted. We had our bases 2 to 3 kilometers from the enemy positions, even at 6 to 7 kilometers from the biggest Soviet base of Darlahman . . . In 1982, they had a 3-kilometer security belt, but it wasn't very effective . . . eventually we received 207mm rockets with 8-kilometer range, and targets inside the capital were constantly under fire.

. . . eventually, they spread out around their belts of outposts, trying to control an area around the city wide enough to keep it out of range of our rockets. In spite of the three rings of defensive positions they built, we are still regularly slipping through and our operations are still going on . . . Of course we have to be very professional now. All operations have to be carefully planned. We have to have a lot of protection groups because all positions in their area must be engaged . . . routes must be clearly known. Alternative retreat routes have to be studied. We have to take care of mines, booby-trapped illuminating flares that give away our positions, even dogs.
                        —Mujahideen commander, Afghanistan, 1985

The tiltrotor engine changed pitch. The plane circled the military base before landing.

"Good to see the Battalion again, Prince," Harv Middleton said.

Lysander smiled briefly before turning back to the window "Regiment, now. Or will be when we leave." Below, the First Royals, Prince Royal's Own, was encamped on and around three small hills set in the endless grasslands. They were supposed to be on light rear area security duty, a kind of working rest and recreation. Soft duty, but Lysander was pleased to see that hadn't stopped them from building a fortified camp, with perimeter wire and plowed minefields, and mutually supporting fields of fire. They were doing good work. He was eager to talk with them. There'd been a lot of personnel changes in the First Royals since Lysander had been Major Collins in command of the Scouts in the Dales campaign, but the Regiment would remember him.

"Good campaign, Prince," Harv said.

Reading my thoughts. Yep, we didn't do bad at all. He laughed softly as he caught himself thinking how much simpler his life had been in those days. *Simpler, maybe, but it sure got frustrating.* It had been a monumental violation of the principle of the unity of command to have the Crown Prince serving as a unit commander, and as soon as he'd proved himself to the men, Owensford had moved him out, back to politics and staff schools and desk work and pretending to coordinate the entire war. It was important work, but Lysander was glad of any excuse to get out among the troops. *When this war's over I'll let David run the economy. I'll take military affairs. Maybe even lead the Spartan Legion off-planet.*

The hold of the tiltrotor transport plane was crowded with a full platoon of the Life Guards. All Citizens or advanced candidates, they were theoretically under the command of an aristocratic young lieutenant, although Sandy Dunforth was unlikely to contradict Staff Sergeant Harv Middleton in a conflict. When the plane touched down, Harv would be first off, and the Guards would take stations all around the field, as if it were dangerous for the Prince Royal to visit his own regiment.

Hell, I'm safer here than walking the streets of Sparta City, he thought mordantly. *The Helot assassination campaign has to be stopped. We can only guard so many of our people. Death of a thousand cuts, but we don't have to die. As Owensford keeps saying, the great thing is not to lose your nerve. They can't win by killing teachers and administrators. Not as long as we're willing to fight back.*

The sound of the turbines deepened as the plane came in toward the hilltop and the engine-pods tilted backward. The pilot was an artist; the big craft touched down with scarcely a jar, and the guard platoon fanned out as the rear ramp went down with a sigh of hydraulics. Lysander waited obediently until Harv signed the all-clear. Harv was Lysander's oldest friend, a Phraetrie-brother, but also playmate and companion when they were children. *Not that we're all that older now.* Middleton knew he wasn't intellectually gifted, and didn't care: Prince Lysander could do the thinking for both of them, about everything but Lysander's safety. When it came to protecting his Prince, Harv's humorlessly intense sense of duty gave him a monomaniacal intelligence.

Lysander blinked at the bright sunshine outside. Sentries and messengers were scurrying all over the field. A group of three officers came out of the Headquarters building to stride briskly toward them. The leader was Major Bennington, a short competent-looking man, Spartan-born, Citizen, an engineer turned soldier. When he saw who had come, he shouted back into the orderly room. Bugle notes sounded, and a company hastily formed as an honor guard.

Bennington saluted. "Highness, they told us to expect visitors, but not who. Apologies—"

"No problem," Lysander said. He returned the salute, then went over to clasp Bennington's hand and clap him across the shoulder. "It's good to see you, Jamie, my Brother," he said formally. He raised his voice, "And all of my Brothers."

"And you, Brother." Bennington was careful to clasp hands with Harv as well. Then he led the way to the waiting troops.

They walked past the leading ranks of the honor guard. Lysander stopped. "Sergeant Ruark. Good job spotting that minefield in the Dales," he said. "Saved my arse."

Ruark grinned, and so did the men around him.

Lysander stopped to talk with several more of the men he recognized, before letting Bennington lead him away.

"It's good to see you, sir," Bennington said. "But you should have told us—"

"Our communications have been leaky, and headquarters thought it better not to say who was coming. Surprising you wasn't the purpose, but no way to avoid it."

"Yes, sir."

"You look tired. So do the troops."

"A bit, sir. It was tough out there. But we've had three weeks to rest up, and it's getting time to go back into the line. But first—With your permission, we'll have 'dining in' at the mess tonight. Not often we have our Battalion Commander with us."

"'Fraid it will have to be 'dining out,'" Lysander said. "Owensford and some of the staff will get in shortly. Please see they're invited—Who's mess president?"

"Captain Hooker, sir. Preston Hooker. Demartus Phraetrie."

"Ah. Platoon commander in heavy weapons support."

"Company commander now. Yes, sir."

"Lots of new faces," Lysander said. "I don't get here often enough. I know I'm only nominal commander but dammit, I ought to know my officers, all of them in this regiment anyway!" He grinned. "Yes, I said regiment. First Royal Cavalry, Prince Royal's Own. You'll get the official word soon enough, along with a promotion."

"Thank you, sir."

"Not much of a surprise, the way we've been adding to your duties, but I thought I should bring The Word myself." He looked around the compound. "Yep. New faces, now, more coming. I've got my work cut out learning them all. I knew all of Falkenberg's people when we had them showing us how. Things working all right without them?"

"Yes, sir. We miss their technical skills sometimes, but this is a Spartan regiment now."

Lysander nodded, pleased at the pride in Bennington's voice. "Right. Sparta needs—our own people. Now show me around. Only you'll have to indicate where we're headed, else Harv will have kittens."

Bennington led the way to the edge of the raw-earth berm. They looked out over the rolling lands below. The 1st Mechanized Battalion, 1st Royal Spartan Infantry, was encamped on three hilltops near the working parties they were helping to guard. The hill camps were leaguered behind earth berms thrown up by 'dozer blade. The troops were in undress uniforms, weapons stacked, a few doing useful things, but most seemed to be just enjoying the mild weather. They were a hundred kilometers inland and north of the Aegean, but the gentle hand of the sea lay across the rolling volcanic hills. This district was warm enough that there were palms in some of the sheltered swales along the Aegean coast.

"Good land," Lysander said.

"Sir." Bennington grinned. "Like most of Sparta. Hasn't quite made up its mind what to be."

"Grassland, I think," Lysander said. He used his binoculars to scan the terrain around them. A few trees, some scrub brush. An occasional live-oak. "Grass. I bet you get some spectacular fires come summer."

"Yes, sir, that we do."

Long rolling hills faded into haze on the distant horizon of a planet larger than Earth. The pale three-quarter sphere of Cytheria sat on the edge of the world. Something moved out at the edge of what he could see. Antelope, he thought, running free in the knee-high mutant kikuyugrass on the hilltops. Bluegrass in the rocky areas, higher growths on the slopes and flats, feathery pampas grass, sloughgrass and big bluestem taller than a man's head. Everything was vivid green from the cool-season rains, starred and woven with cosmos and crimson meadow rose. The scent was as heady as chilled white wine.

"God, I love this planet."

"Yes, sir. Wish everyone did," Jamie answered grimly. "The Prince Royals have been taking it on the chin. We needed the rest. Thanks for getting us this assignment."

Lysander nodded. A rest from the brutal late-winter campaign in the northwest, trying to stop raids out of the Dales. A war of ambushes and burnt-out ranches and endless cold and mud and low-level fear, seasoned with continuous frustration and spiked with moments of raw terror. Always wondering if the next step would be onto a mine, if that clump of trees held a sniper. Too many recruits and never enough time to teach, as the Royal Army doubled and redoubled and units were mined for cadre; newcomers making stupid newbie mistakes, rushing in straight lines towards a noise, showing lights, walking against the skyline. Getting drunk alone in an Olynthos cathouse and ending up knifed in an alley, for that matter.

"The problem is, the rest gives people time to think," Jamie said. "Everyone was feeling fairly good after the Dales campaign; we'd whipped their butts. The men were walking tall. Then we landed on a greased slope and spent the whole winter running as fast as we could to stay in one place."

Lysander ran a hand through his short brown hair. "Don't I know it, Jamie," he said. "Look, that's one reason I came out here to talk to you. We've got to start thinking beyond the next year; beyond settling this war, come to that. We both know the Helots wouldn't last six months without outside help. Hell, without the CoDo shoveling their human refuse on our heads, there wouldn't *be* any Helots."

"True enough," Jamie Bennington said, narrowing his eyes slightly. "Meaning?"

"Meaning we're in this mess because we're helpless. Not just against Earth. Whitlock says the CoDominium won't last five years. Without the Fleet—"

"Yes, sir," Bennington said. "That gets discussed in the mess of a night. Friedland's friendly enough now, but—"

"Or Meiji. Look at what's happening to Thurstone and Diego, and that's with the CoDominium still trying to keep order. Without it there'll be no order at all out here any more."

"And so, Lysander my Brother, you are saying that we should not plan on soft garrison life after we kill off the Helots."

"More than that."

"More than that," Bennington mused. "More than that, my Prince. So. You will want more than just the Spartan Legion ready for expeditionary duty. And we are chosen?"

"I've thought of it. What will the men think? Will they follow orders?"

"Depends on who gives the orders," Bennington said. "They'll follow their Prince. Just about anywhere, after the Dales."

They went back toward the orderly room. Inside were the duty sergeant and two corporals. The sergeant jumped to his feet. "Sir. I'll inform the officer of the day that you're here."

Before he could do that, a corporal came in from the next room. "Sergeant, urgent message from—" He stopped when he saw Lysander and Bennington.

"Carry on," Bennington said.

"Sir. Urgent signal, sir. Message through the Rural Emergency Network from the Halleck ranch at Three Hills. Oldest son and three hands missing. Suspicious tracks. The local constabulary requests assistance."

"Right," Bennington said. "Sergeant, alert the ready team—"

"Halleck?" Lysander asked.

"Yes, sir."

"Damn," Lysander said. "Would that be Aaron Halleck's place?"

"Sergeant?" Bennington asked.

The duty sergeant typed at a console. "Says here Roger Halleck, let's see, Roger Halleck, Divine Twins Phraetrie, son of Senator Aaron Halleck, sir."

"That's torn it," Lysander said. "Senator Halleck's grandson missing. Major, I'd count it a favor if you sent the best you have on this one."

"Right." Bennington conferred with his duty master sergeant. "Who've we got?"

"Sir, the ready platoon is Lieutenant Hartunian's scouts. About as good as we have for this sort of thing."

"Get them moving," Bennington said.

"Sir." The sergeant turned to his console.

"What's the situation out there?" Lysander asked.

Bennington activated the map wall. "We're pretty sure there aren't any big gangs operating around here—they'd love to get at the road to Colchis before we finish it, but there's no cover south of the Drakons." He waved toward the mountain chain to the north and west. "Snow up there. Hard to get through without leaving tracks. But there's canyon country over here. Anything could hide in those caves."

"Hartunian's ready to roll, Major," the sergeant said.

Benington eyed the map. "Lousy roads. Sergeant, tell the chief constable we'll have troops there in about two hours."

"No planes?" Lysander asked.

"Only have three," Bennington said. "All down for maintenance. Try not to let it happen, but sometimes there's no help for it. Sergeant, you'd best have them speed up the work on those ships—"

"Just did, sir. First plane operational in ninety minutes."

"Right."

"I can speed things up," Lysander said. "Sergeant, have Lieutenant Hartunian load his men into my tiltrotor. You sending anything else?"

"Yes, I thought I'd send a troop of light armor," Bennington said. "The exercise won't do them any harm, and Hartunian may need help."

"Whose?"

"'B troop. Captain Reid."

"Thank you. OK, mount them up and get them on the road. Mind if I tag along with Hartunian?"

"Is that wise, Highness?" Bennington asked.

"Given it's the Hallecks, it might be," Lysander said. "We won't get in the way." He went to the orderly room door. "Harv!"

"Prince!"

"Pick a squad of Life Guards and load up. Alert the pilot we're moving out. We're going hunting."

Harv grinned wolfishly. "Yes, *sir!*"

Three Hills Ranch was typical of the Colchis Gap district, a fairly small operation. Not in area—the Hallecks had patented better than two thousand hectares—but in scale. Most of the rangeland the armored column passed through might never have known the hand of man. Except that the grass itself, the grazing herds of buffalo and impala, mustang and onanger and pronghorn, even the wild geese migrating north in sky-darkening flocks, were all of them a sign of man's presence; Spartan evolution hadn't produced much native life on land. Closer to the ranch headquarters they saw black-coated Angus cattle and shaggy brown beefalo under the guard of mounted vaqueros, and around the ranch house itself waving strips of contour-ploughed cropland. Not much, because there would be little market here; what cash-money this spread saw would be from herds driven down to the slaughterhouse in Colchis town on the coast, or wool hauled there by bullock wagons.

The Senator's younger son, setting up on his own. And looking to make good as a farmer. There were new fields under cultivation, sprouts showing green against the raw-red soil. Beets and sunflowers and soyabeans, some cotton; powered vehicles on Sparta ran mostly on alcohol or vegetable oil, and the new road would provide a market. The ranch house was single-story and not particularly large, with whitewashed walls of rammed earth, roofed in home-made tile that supported a satellite dish. Half a dozen vaquero cottages nearby, and a bunkhouse; much like the rancher's dwelling except for size. Outbuildings were scattered, sheds, barns, a set of windmill generators and a stock-dam fringed with willows. Modest but carefully cultivated flower beds and lawns and tall trees surrounded the houses to make an oasis in the huge rippling landscape.

Exactly what we're trying to build here. Frontier people. The frontier of humanity, and the bastards won't let us alone. It's not Spartans *who are destroying us.*

A windsock marked a landing area near the house, an open pasture beyond a row of big gum-trees. Better than thirty people and two light armor vehicles awaited them there, which was quick work in a district as spread-out as this. Most were in militia cammo uniforms and body armor. A couple of the vaqueros were in their normal leathers, probably non-Citizens, but their rifles were as much a part of their working equipment as their clothes, and they looked just as determined as the rest. Off to one side a pack of hounds that looked to be more than slightly mixed with gray wolf lay in disciplined silence.

"Junior Lieutenant Cantor, 22nd Divine Twins Brotherhood Battalion," a man introduced himself, as Lysander swung himself down from the tiltrotor. Nobody jumped distances like that in Sparta's gravity. Except new chums, who wondered why they ripped tendons and sprained ankles. "Brother Halleck," the militia officer went on, introducing the owner. Roger Halleck was a stocky rancher in his forties with gray in his shag-cut brown hair, a finger missing from one hand and a bulldog determination to his square face. *A lot like the Senator, actually,* Lysander thought.

"This is Lieutenant George Hartunian, Prince Royal's Own," Lysander said. "And Lieutenant Sanford Dunforth, Life Guards."

"Highness—" Cantor began.

"And for the moment I'm Colonel Collins, First Royals Regimental Commander," Lysander said. "No point in getting too formal, Citizens. Now what's our situation?"

"My boy Demetrios was up north about six klicks, scoutin' for a new watering dam. Had a handset, reported all well at sundown yesterday. Nothing this morning, so I sent my top hand out. Miguel?"

"Don Roger," the vaquero said, nodding with dignified formality. "My Prince, I took young Saunders with me"—a big-boned blond youth, another of the vaqueros, shuffled his feet in acknowledgment—"to the stream where the camp was. We found a campfire still warm with unburied embers; this Don

Halleck's son would never do, he was well taught. Also we found this."

He handed a small object to Lysander. A spent cartridge case, standard 10mm magnum caliber. He brought it to his nose. *Recent.* Sparta City Armory marks on the base, which meant little . . .

"See," the vaquero said. "The firing pin imprint is a very little low and to the right of center? The young Don Demitrios's gun, *veridad.* Also we find this, a thousand meters north." A ring. Lysander's brows rose.

"It's his," Halleck said "His grandmother left it to him."

"Twenty horses, maybe more, came during the night from the south," Miguel continued. "Before the rain, because the marks were almost washed out. Only in the mud by the stream we see them, you understand." Lysander nodded. The grasses which had claimed this countryside so quickly after the terraforming package made a deep tough sod. "They paused, then went on with the young Don's horses as well."

Lysander started to speak, then stopped and turned to Lieutenant Hartunian.

George Hartunian straightened. "Not much doubt about what happened," he said. "Lieutenant Cantor, what do we know of enemy activity in the area?"

"Sporadic. Largest group we've seen was a dozen, on horseback. This group may be twice that size, but they shouldn't be any problem, no heavy weapons. Except—"

Except they've got the squire's son as hostage, Lysander thought.

"Anyway," Cantor said, "we had instructions to call on the regulars, and since I don't have any experience with hostage situations—"

"Neither do I," Hartunian said. He hesitated, clearly looking to Lysander for orders he wasn't going to get. "A troop of scouts will be here in an hour," Hartunian said. "Send them after us. I guess it's time for the rest of us to move out." He looked to the dogs. "Is that pack well trained?"

"They can follow a scent," Halleck said. He looked at Hartunian and shrugged, a gesture that clearly said he didn't believe that waiting for the regular troops had been worth the delay. "Colonel, the best thing will be for us to get on the trail, and you look with that tiltrotor. That way we just might find something."

Lysander glanced up at the sky. "Three hours of daylight, maybe a bit more." He projected a map onto the ground. "Dunforth, you'll take the tiltrotor. Cover this area, but stay

away from the canyons. I don't have to tell you the whole
purpose of this just could be to lure that plane into range
of a missile."

"Sir. Shouldn't I stay with you?"

"No. Now get looking, and be careful. Keep Regiment up
to date on your location." Lysander looked to the available
transportation. Two Cataphracts, and three von Alderheim 6x6
trucks. Little enough. "There'll be a light armor cavalry column coming up before dark. Send it after us. And I'm ordering
Regiment to send another cavalry troop."

"Fuel," Hartunian said.

"I'll authorize air resupply," Lysander said. *Expensive.
Damned expensive, but Senator Halleck's always been one of
the team, and by God we can take care of our own.* "Now
load up."

"I'll be going," Halleck said quietly.

"And me." A girl not more than twenty. Freckles, strawberry
blond hair and furious blue eyes, in militia gear. *"I trained
those dogs, as much as Demetrios did, Dad. I ride and shoot
as well as he does, and he's my brother."*

Lysander raised his brows at the rancher. Unwillingly, he
nodded. "Lydia is the best hunter on the place, next her
brother. My family," he added, nodding to two mutinous
looking boys of about fourteen, "runs to twins. And no,
Isagoras and Alexias, you're not going."

"Load up, then," Lysander said. He waited until the Hallecks
were in the trucks. "You go with her," he told Middleton.
"Hartunian will take the lead Cataphract. I'll be in the other
one until Reid's troop catches up."

Harv started to protest and thought better of it. "Yes, Prince."

"Missile attack. Taking evasive action."

Lysander noted the tiltrotor's location on his map projection. "OK, you've found them," Lysander said. "Now get well
back, refuel, and stand by. If they had one missile they'll have
more."

"Yes, sir."

"OK, driver, push it," Lysander said. They rolled onward.

"Bloody hell," Lysander cursed quietly. "There goes the
chance of using the IV sensors."

The hills to the west were aflame for better than a kilometer to either side; there was a strong easterly wind, enough
to move the fire briskly despite the early season. Tall grass
will burn even when green, if the fire is set with torches and

fanned by moving air. The higher partial pressure of oxygen
on Sparta made it even more deadly than prairie fires on
earth. . . . Haze and smoke and the pale-yellow disk of the setting sun made it difficult to see the mountain peaks beyond.

"Halt." The burbling roar of the diesels sank to a low
murmur, no louder than the roar of the fire approaching them
from a kilometer away. He could smell the thick acrid smoke
of it, over the hot metal of engines and the overwhelming
sweetness of crushed grass.

The tracking force was advancing along a front as wide as
the fire itself, Cataphracts in the lead with the trucks a hundred
meters behind. He swiveled to look around; nothing, except
the clouds of birds fleeing the grassfire, and the twin-track
marks the armored vehicles had beaten through the turf. They
were tending south of west, up into the higher country on
the fringes of the Drakons. Not the nine- and ten-thousand
meter peaks of the midrange, but still more than high enough
to carry eternal snow and glaciers. The hills here were already
several hundred meters higher than the Gap country proper,
unclaimed land, with tendrils of brush and forest down the
valleys. Perceptibly colder than the Halleck ranch, too.

"Regimental command push," he said.

"Bennington here," the Major replied after a second.

"Collins here. We're getting closer, but they set a grassfire.
We'll have to stop and find the scent again on the other side."

"They were laying mines back here," Bennington said grimly.
"New wrinkle. Anti-vehicle mines in the track, as a decoy;
laser trigger rigged to a directional mine off to the side. Lost
two of the sappers."

"Goddam!" Lysander said.

"My sentiments exactly. Not to mention a farm wagon further
down the road, another fatal. Get them, sir."

"Will do, Jamie."

The 6x6 jounced up, with the dogs and the Hallecks. The
trucks had excellent cross-country mobility, Charbonneau-thread
tires gripped like fingers, but the ride was rougher than the
broad treads and hydrogas suspension units of the Cataphracts.
Miguel, the chief vaquero, swung down, wiping at his soot-
streaked face with a bandanna.

"The *hijo de puta* picked the spot for their fire well, my
Prince," he said. "No deep valleys, the ground only rolls. More
broken country beyond. Someone among them must be himself
an *llanero*, a plainsman. Donna Halleck says that the forest begins
only ten kilometers beyond, very bad country with many ravines
and cliffs; oaks, firs, deodar cedar and rhododendron thicket."

"I've hunted leopard there," she said from the bed of the truck; her father and Harv were beside her. "Tricky. Pumice soil and rock, pretty steep. Landslide country in the rains."

We'll never get them in there, Lysander thought. His speed advantage would be lost; ambush country, and easier for the bandits to disperse. Roger Halleck was looking grimly furious.

"Backburn?" the vaquero asked, looking at the approaching fire.

"Nix that!" Lydia Halleck said. "Too long—look, we can run it, if a couple of your lobsters go through first right ahead of us. We'll only be in the flame-front for a second or so and nothing flammable will be touching the ground. Hose everything down, and the dogs will be able to take it."

Hell of a risk, he thought. Then: *God damn it, these are my people, I'm not going to let their kinfolk be dragged off by those scum.*

"OK," he said. "Citizen, Miss Halleck, if you'd prefer to ride in one of the Cataphracts?" A family muleishness confronted him.

"The dogs need me to stay with them," the girl said. *Well, not much chance her father won't stay with* her, Lysander thought.

"Sir?" Harv, standing next to the Hallecks. "Sir, if we cover everything with a couple of ground sheets and soak it, we'll be safe enough under."

Lysander blinked in surprise; he had expected another polite-but-firm request that Harv ride in the Cataphract with him. "Carry on, Sergeant." He looked west. An hour of daylight left. "Let's move."

Lysander buttoned the hatch down and looked at the wall of smoke ahead of them; it towered into the sky, and the flames were twice the height from the ground to the top of the Cataphract's turret.

"Goose it!" he said.

The armored vehicle gathered speed with a pitch-and-yaw motion like a boat beating through a medium sea. For a moment there was darkness shot with red outside the vision-blocks, and his ears popped as the overpressure NCB system pumped air into the fighting compartment through its filters. Then they were through, on a broad expanse of smoldering black stubble kilometers wide. The truck was through as well, covered in soot and smut but still functioning; as he watched the tarpaulin over the rear deck was thrown back, revealing grinning humans and hysterical dogs pulling against the short-staple leashes tied down to the railings.

The column pulled to a halt on the unburned grass, the familiar *shhhh* against the hulls replacing the popping crunches of the burn. The Hallecks and Miguel moved efficiently to quiet the dogs; the cycle-mounted scouts pulled up from their wide circle west of the fire. As steady in their way as the humans, the dogs soon settled down and began to cast about, tails high and wagging furiously; they had been following the on-again, off-again trail all day, and they were getting into the spirit of it. *Well-trained pack, too,* Lysander thought, studying the ground ahead. *No yelling off after something else once they've been given a scent.*

The land was rising again, the ridges getting sharper. It suddenly occurred to him how different it would have looked in his grandfather's time. Olive green pseudomoss then, and scraggly patches of semibamboo, scarred by the erosion the introduced vegetation resisted so much better. Grass and brush all mixed in, just beginning its long march to conquest. One long human lifetime, an eyeblink in the history of a world. Even the insects and bacteria beneath his feet were of strains that had come here less than a century ago.

"Message, sir," his driver called.

Lysander frowned. "Right." He retrieved the head-set from the Cataphract. "Collins here."

"Suggestion."

Owensford's voice. *And he's not using honorifics because there's only one person out here he would say "sir" to. OK he thinks someone is listening. Someone with our scrambler codes . . .* "Yes, sir," Lysander said.

"Wait five right where you are."

"Dammit, they'll get away—"

"Strong suggestion."

Lysander started to protest and thought better of it. "Roger."

The tiltrotor landed on a level spot close by. A dozen men, led by Owensford in combat dress. "Like to talk to you for a minute, sir," Owensford said.

Lysander let himself be led away from the others. "What's all this, General?"

"Highness, do you know what the hell you're doing?" Owensford demanded.

"I'm chasing down those scumbags—"

"No, sir, you're making certain that the Senator's grandson is killed, and probably endangering everyone around you,"

Owensford said evenly. "You don't think this was a coincidence, do you?"

"Eh?"

"Senator's grandson gets kidnapped. Not killed, kidnapped, just before the Crown Prince visits the regiment assigned to security duty here. The Prince Royal's Own regiment to be exact. May be coincidence, sir, but more likely leaks in the Palace."

"To what end?'

"God knows," Owensford said. "But they run to complicated plans. My guess is they hoped you'd be sucked into this operation."

"Am I that easy to predict?"

"Senator's grandson, kidnapped in your regiment's sector, plain trail to follow." Owensford shrugged.

"I see. So now what?"

"They plan a surprise for us, I think," Owensford said. "Just maybe we have one for them." He turned to the group who had come with him in the tiltrotor. "Miscowsky."

"Sir." Sergeant Taras Hamilton Miscowsky was a stocky man, dark, clearly of Eurasian descent.

"Got a reading?" Owensford asked.

"I think so, sir." Miscowsky squatted and used his helmet to project a map onto the ground in front of him. "They'll be here, in canyon country. They'll have split up into smaller groups, but there'll always be an obvious main body—"

"It's been that way so far," Lysander said.

"Yes, sir. Point being to get you to divvy up your force while they lead you by the nose." The stocky sergeant grinned slightly.

"By the nose," Lysander said. "You mean the dogs."

"Yes, sir."

"So what do we do now?"

"Chase 'em," Miscowsky said. "The trail will divide somewhere about here, where you'll be just about at dark. You'll want to follow on after dark. Don't. Instead, make camp, but not on the main trail, off here somewhere, like maybe you're going to follow the wrong branch. Keep a good watch, and I mean good, sir."

"You expect them to attack us? In the dark?" Lysander asked.

"Be more likely if you was to camp in the obvious place," Miscowsky said. "But they might try and hit you anyway. And they'll sure as hell send out scout parties to look you over. What they'll want is to get you chasing them out there in the canyons and woods in the dark. I don't suppose I have to tell you, don't do it?"

"I see. And then?"

Miscowsky shook his head. "Then comes the fun part," he said, but his grim look denied the words.

The dogs barked in glee, then milled in confusion, casting along two diverging trails. Lysander cursed loudly. "Bring us up level, Delman," he said to the driver.

The Cataphract quivered and flowed forward with an oilbath smoothness; there were grinding sounds as the tungsten cleats of the treads met an occasional piece of pumice rock.

"Six horses that way, sir." Sergeant Salcion pointed to the left, southwest over a small hillock. "The rest went straight west."

Lydia Halleck squinted into the vanishing sun. "West over that ridge is the beginning of canyon country," she said.

Miguel had been quartering the ground while the others spoke, occasionally stopping and going to one knee to part the grass gently with his hands; it was over a meter high here, new green shoots mingling with winter's pale gold straw.

"Here," he said, indicating a spot of bare wet reddish earth between two tufts. "This horse is shod by the Three Hills farrier; the others have machine-made shoes." He looked up at Lysander. "Ours are hand-hammered from bar stock," he explained.

"It's nearly dark," Lysander said.

"We're gaining on them!" Lydia said. "Come on!"

"Right," Hartunian said. "Mount up!"

"No, I think we make camp," Lysander said. "Cancel that order." *An hour ago I'd have been right with them. There's so damned much I don't know, and it can get my people killed.* He looked at his map. The trail divided almost precisely where Miscowsky had said it would.

Lysander pointed southwest. "We'll camp on that hill. Full perimeter. Get set up while there's still daylight."

"But we can catch them!" Lydia shouted. "No, you can stay if you're scared of the dark, but some of us aren't! Who's with me?"

Peter Owensford had been talking quietly with the girl's father. Halleck said, "Not enough, Lydia. Not enough."

"But—" She stood defiantly. "Miguel—"

The vaquero looked to the rancher.

"You'll stay here, and that's an order," Lysander said. "Owensford!"

"Sir!"

"See that they stay and camp is made."

"Sir."

"Damned cowards," Lydia said. "I never thought I would have to say that about a Prince of Sparta. Coward."

The hilltop was largely dirt, with some boulders, which they used as part of the fortifications Owensford insisted on. Foxholes, trenches, ramparts; tanks hull down in earth bunkers, truck revetted. The work wasn't finished until well after dark. Finally Owensford was satisfied. "Larraby, you'll take first perimeter patrol."

"Sir."

"Highness, Mr. and Miss Halleck, there'll be hot tea in the command bunker. Care to join me?"

The command post was more trench than bunker. Owensford's orderly handed out mugs of tea and left them.

"This is crazy," Lydia said. "We could have caught up to them—"

"Very likely," Owensford said carefully. "At least they certainly hoped we would."

"They—" Lydia's eyes widened. "Oh." She turned to Lysander. "Highness—I'm sorry, really, I didn't—"

"It's all right," Lysander said.

"Better than all right," Owensford said. "I just hope they were listening."

"Real earful," Halleck said. He put his arm around his daughter. "Somebody had to protest," he said. "Knew you would, and it came more natural if you didn't know."

"I should have guessed." She blushed. For just a moment, embarrassment overcame her frantic concern for her twin. Embarrassment, and something else, fear of a loss greater even than her brother.

"I didn't," Lysander said. "It took General Owensford to show me. And that sergeant. Mis—"

"Miscowsky," Owensford said. "Havenite. Grew up thinking like a bandit." He glanced at his watch. "Another couple of hours, if they're coming."

"Coming. You expect them to attack us here, then?" Lydia asked.

"Ma'am—"

"I'm Lydia, General Owensford," the girl said quietly.

"Lydia. You put it stronger than we would. We don't exactly expect an attack, but if they have the strength we think they do, it's one of their options. We need to be prepared, that's all. My guess is they won't. We built a fortified camp in a place they didn't expect, and one thing we've learned about the Helots, they don't do much on the spur of the moment. They like complicated plans, and they won't have time to make one up. Hartunian will see to the watch. I think what we should do is try to get some sleep."

"That won't be easy," Lydia said.

"For any of us," Lysander said. "Good tea. Now I think I'll take General Owensford's advice."

It was dark outside. Two hours until moonrise. Lysander paused to let his eyes adjust, and heard steps behind him.

"Not much chance for my boy, is there?" Halleck asked.

"I don't know," Lysander said.

"Probably dead already."

"Maybe not," Lysander said. "Miscowsky thinks they'll use him as bait."

"For what? For you," Halleck said. "God damn—Highness—Oh God damn it. Well, we can't let them do that."

"Prince."

Lysander woke from a pleasant dream. Dawn light, hardly bright enough for shadows. "Right, Harv."

"General Owensford's respects, he's in the command bunker with coffee," Harv said.

"Right." Lysander pulled himself out of the bedroll and pulled on his boots. Owensford and Lydia Halleck were seated close together in the command bunker. Lysander wondered if she'd been there all night. He got his coffee and sat across from them.

"Good morning," Owensford said. "There are over a hundred of them. With heavy weapons. Big mortars. Rocket launchers. Maybe more. Well dug in, too."

"Christ."

"I'd have walked right into that," Lydia said. "Worse, I'd have taken you—"

"The point is, it didn't happen," Owensford said. "Anyway, now we know what we're facing, the news gets better."

"Such as?"

"They have three live prisoners. The bad news is they know how many we are, and they didn't run away," Owensford said.

"How do we know all this?" Lysander asked.

Owensford grinned. "They're not the only ones who can sneak around in the dark."

"Miscowsky."

"Followed their scouts back, of course. This is an eyeball report."

"That *is* good news. All right, what next?"

Owensford looked pointedly at Lydia Halleck. She stood.

"Whatever happens, thanks, Highness," she said. "And—thank you, Peter, for explaining things."

"Wish I had more hope for you," Owensford said.

"Yeah." She climbed out of the bunker, leaving Lysander and Owensford alone.

"You asked what's next," Owensford said. "I can make a suggestion."

"Make it."

"Order me to handle the situation, then get the hell out of here."

Lysander frowned. "I can't do that—"

"With all respect, Highness, you should do that. There's a lot at stake here—"

"Damned right—"

"A lot more than Senator Halleck's grandson," Owensford said. "Look, this situation is all fucked up. We're out here in the middle of nowhere. We have one ace in the hole, but otherwise we're outnumbered and outgunned. If we bring up reinforcements they'll kill their hostages and run for it into the badlands. If we go straight in they'll likely cream us. The whole deal is tailor made for a defeat, and the biggest disaster of all will be that the Prince Royal was in charge and fucked it up! Bluntly, Highness, losing that kid will be bad enough, but it'll be a lot worse if it makes you look incompetent. Which, by the way, I'm pretty sure was one object of this exercise in the first place."

"How the hell could they have known I'd be here? For long enough that they brought in all that stuff?" Lysander demanded. "Damn it, I didn't know myself I was coming until last week!"

"Yes, sir, but your favorite regiment was here long enough," Owensford said. "The original objective would have been giving the Prince Royals a bloody nose. For that matter, it was predictable you'd visit when the Battalion was upgraded to Regiment. Then they heard when you were coming, and that made it all the better."

"And I took the bait," Lysander said. "I see. But damn it, Peter, I can't just abandon that boy! His grandfather is one of my father's oldest friends! Even if he wasn't—they're my people! This, this ranch, this is what Sparta is *for!* I can't let them take risks I won't take—"

"You can, and you will," Owensford said. "Remember the enemy's objectives, Highness. They can't defeat us as long as we keep our nerve, but if they can make the people lose confidence in the government, they're halfway to winning. And for all practical purposes right now, *you are the government.*

You're already the good luck charm for half the soldiers in the Royal Army. That doesn't mean you can't risk getting killed, but it sure as Hell does mean you've got to be careful not to look like a fool."

"I'll work on that." Lysander said. "Now show me the situation, and tell me what you think we should do."

"That still doesn't work," Owensford said. "I may have it all wrong too." He grinned suddenly. "Hell, neither one of us should be here, come to that. This is a job for a captain." He projected a map on the bunker wall. "An expendable captain."

Lysander didn't answer. After a while Owensford said, "Here's the situation. They're dug in, here, a natural redoubt, with heavy weapons. They won't want us to get close enough to spot for artillery and missile fire, so they'll try to intercept us well short of their main area, probably here. They don't know Miscowsky's group has them under surveillance, which means we can pound them with Thoth missiles."

"We didn't bring any Thoth missiles—"

"I took the liberty of using Legion communications to send for the SAS support unit," Owensford said. "I didn't have them report to anyone in the Royals, but they're out there. Anything Miscowsky can see, we can hit without warning."

"You suspect a traitor in the Royals?"

"I suspect leaks in the Royals," Owensford said. "Not necessarily a traitor, but that's possible. Those Thoths are our main advantage, and we'll want to use them properly."

"So we can kill them any time," Lysander said. "If we don't mind killing the hostages too."

"Something like that."

"What happens if we wait for the rest of the regiment to come up?"

"Don't know," Owensford said. "But they have to worry about that. My guess is if they get worried enough, they kill the hostages and scatter."

"But if they think they have a chance of getting me—"

"They'd take risks for that," Owensford agreed. "But they're not fools. They aren't going to wait until you have a whole battalion of armor here—"

"What if we don't bring the reinforcements here at all," Lysander said. "Suppose I send the regiment around behind them, here. The main body won't be in position until dark, but a scout platoon can be in position a lot earlier than that."

"And then we go in after them?"

"More or less," Lysander said.

"They outnumber us, you know," Owensford said.

"Sure. But it's what you'd do if I weren't here, right?"

Owensford shrugged. "It's what I'd expect from my hypo-thetical captain who ought to be in charge of this cockamamie deal."

"Then we'll do that."

"An expendable captain."

"So we're not expendable," Lysander said. "We'll be care-ful. Now let's go."

Nearly dusk. Peter Owensford used the command tank's optics to peer into the shadows ahead. *Christ, here I am acting like a captain again.* He grinned slightly. *At least by God I've got someone to fight. Not just chasing ghosts. And someone to fight for . . .*

Just ahead would be the enemy's redoubt. This would be the tricky part. "They see you coming," Miscowsky's voice said in his ear. "They're all spread out, waiting."

"Command push," Peter said. "Halt the column."

The two lead Cataphracts slowed, stopped. The infantry fanned out to both sides. Ahead lay a four-hundred-meter escarpment topped with a dense stand of trees, the sun already lost behind it. Somewhere along the base of that escarpment, no more than two kilometers away, was the rebel ambush. Minutes ticked by.

"They're getting nervous," Miscowsky said. The signal was faint but clear. "Timing's gonna be tricky."

"The great thing," Peter said aloud, "is not to lose your nerve." His driver grinned slightly, then nodded. Five long minutes . . .

"Here he comes," the driver said. He opened a port in the armor of the tank, and brought in a thin cable which he handed to the communications sergeant who sat in the loader's seat.

After a moment the sergeant handed Peter a headset and microphone. "Secure communications, sir."

"Right. Thank you. Report by sections. Report."

"Section One set and loaded, sir."

"Section Two in place and loaded sir."

"Armor units ready."

That would be Lysander, of course. *If I let that kid kill himself, John Christian will have my hide. Christ, he's all that's holding this goddam planet together, and here we are playing company commander.* "OK. Here's the situation. They don't suspect the SAS team is observing them. They know we're here, and they're stirring around, wondering why we've halted. It's a war of nerves."

"It will be dark soon enough." A female voice. *I might have known Lydia would be talking for her father.*

"We'll give Mobile One a little more time," Peter said.

The wait seemed endless.

"There's a group moving out. Riflemen. One grenade launcher. I count eleven, moving toward your position," Miscowsky said. "Bearing one niner five at four five zero meters relative my position. They're moving out now. Call it vector niner zero."

Somewhere out there, miles away near the horizon, a Legion SAS signal section had sent up a balloon and tethered it in line of sight to Miscowsky. It would be able to receive Miscowsky's narrow beam signals without any possibility of interception. Of course signals the other way to Miscowsky wouldn't be secure at all, but there was nothing they could do about that. Owensford plotted the enemy patrol's position on his helmet display. "Visitors coming," Peter said. "Call it a dozen, moving due east. If they continue on course that will put them right on top of Section One."

"Scout Section Four moving to intercept."

"Roger that."

"Getting dark, General."

"Scout Four here. We see them. They'll have Section One in sight in six minutes."

And here we go. Peter punched in codes. "Thoth Daddy, fire mission, roll four anti-personnel," he said. "I say again, Thoth Daddy, roll four anti-personnel. Relay to SAS One they're on the way." Then without waiting for acknowledgment he changed channels. "Scout Four. Intercept and destroy that patrol, Scout Four."

"Will intercept and destroy. Scout Four out."

"Sections One and Two load concussion. Armor units stand by."

"Acknowledge four birds on the way," Miscowsky said. "They do not appear to have intercepted the alert to me, I say again they are not reacting. Thoth Daddy, give me four more, anti-personnel, I say again, four anti-personnel."

"Thoth Daddy here. On the way."

Timers on Peter's console began their countdowns, flickering sets of red numbers.

From ahead and to the left came a sudden stammer of rifles and machine guns, then grenades. Contact. "Execute alpha," Peter said. "I say again, all units, execute plan alpha, I say again, execute plan alpha. Move out!"

The Cataphract engines were loud in the falling dusk. There

were more shots and the bright flash of grenades to Peter's left. Then the Cataphracts moved over the ridge.

"Incoming!"

Something burst overhead. Cluster bombs rained around Owensford's position. Any uncovered infantry out there would be in trouble. More bombs fell around them. *They're using their big stuff. Good.*

Peter stared at his console. There was nothing he could do now, it was up to the computers. Green lights flickered. Antennas they'd spent the afternoon putting out a klick to each side backtracked the enemy's artillery shells. Pulses came into the command computers. Analysis. A light flashed. *Locked on.* More lights, as information went at the speed of light from the command unit to the tiltrotor aircraft twenty kilometers away, then to Miscowsky and his missile control unit . . .

"Got it," Miscowsky said. "Four missiles acquired. Guidance set. Locked."

There were flashes from over the ridge. Four missiles, lofted from the aircraft named Thoth Daddy, landed among the enemy's heavy weapons with an accuracy better than one meter.

"Thoth Daddy, give me more," Miscowsky said. "Anti-personnel, stream it."

"On the way."

"Rebel commander, Rebel commander," Owensford said.

He looked down at the screen, split to offer him views from any of the vehicles. Not much to be seen. The Helots were well dug in among their boulders. *No artillery left. No perimeter guards left. Not likely to have much communications, they may not hear me.* Peter touched his console to change communication channels. "Move in fast."

"Sergeant Cheung, Spartan People's Liberation Army," a voice replied. "You got something to say, Cit?"

Sergeant. "Let me speak to your commanding officer."

"That's me, Cit." A laugh, that might or might not have been cut off short. "What you want?"

Officer dead, or escaped? No time for that— "You're surrounded, your heavy weapons are destroyed, and we have you located. Surrender now and you'll be treated as prisoners of war."

"Well, well, Baby Prince—"

"This is Colonel Ford," Peter said.

"Where's the Prince?"

"Not here." *Jesus Alana says keep them talking. About*

anything. "Do you want to talk to the Prince? He's coming, he'll be here shortly."

A nasty laugh. "No need to wait for him. We got the rancher's boy," the rebel said. "Give us twenty hours headstart, and we'll let him go."

"Twenty hours? That's too much," Owensford said.

"How long?"

"Well, not twenty hours—"

"Hell, you don't mean to give us nothing," the rebel said.

"Not true," Owensford said. "Give up and you'll be well treated. Killing hostages gets you hanged."

"Yeah, well, worth just one try," the guerrilla said. "OK, we're sending him out."

Like Hell you are. Owensford switched to his command channel. "All units, stand by. Section One. Section Two. Make ready. SAS One, stand ready." Back to the enemy leader. "Don't do anything rash."

"Me? Rash? Nah, never." A figure was pushed out from behind one of the jagged boulders. Owensford upped the gain to maximum, and the face sprang out at him. Lydia's face, in a square-jawed male version. The hair was darker blond, plastered to the side of his head with blood, and one eye was swollen almost shut. The young man limped; his hands were bound behind him . . . with barbed wire.

"You see him, Cit?"

"Execute, all units execute," Peter said. Then to the rebel, "No, see what?"

Demetrios Halleck was walking upright, with care, watching where he put his feet but moving as quickly as he could.

"You see him?"

"This is Crown Prince Lysander Collins. Stand by, Sergeant Cheung, I'm coming up to talk to you."

"What the hell?" the rebel said. "Where? Show yourself—"

"I'm right over here, Sergeant."

"I don't see you—"

Mortar shells fell around the rebel position. The blast of a concussion grenade knocked the Halleck boy flat. Something moved in the shadows near where he fell.

"Pour it on," Peter ordered. "Go for it, all units, go for it, go, go, go!"

"Go," Lysander said. The sweat under his armor turned suddenly cold and gelid; like those nightmares where you waded through thick dank air, unable to turn and see what chased you.

Breaching charges flew through the air like blurring snakes;

the soft *whumps* of their explosions across the minefield were lost in the hammer of the 76s and the thumping crash from the rocket howitzers. The Cataphract was tossing as they drove forward; out of the corner of one eye he saw the 6x6 truck pacing them. *That wasn't supposed to happen.* They reached the rocks, and armored men leaped out among the rebels. Another flurry of shots. Then silence.

So quickly, Lysander thought. Silence fell, broken only by the crackling of small grass fires and shouts, and moans from the wounded. Lysander halted the Cataphract and climbed down slowly. Bodies everywhere.

"Hey Sarge, maps!" someone shouted.

"Don't touch nothing! It'll keep till morning."

Shots and a grenade off to the left. Someone was running, and half a dozen Royals led by a sergeant gave chase.

Lysander carefully made his way back down the hill, out to where medics hovered over two figures.

Two. "Status?" Lysander asked.

"This one's stable," the medic said. He indicated the Halleck boy. "Broken ribs, but I think nothing internal. The other one will make it if we get him in the tanks in time, but it's going to be close."

"Who is he?" Lysander asked.

"Corporal Owassee," a voice said from behind him. Lysander turned to see Sergeant Miscowsky. "Mine. He put his flak jacket over the kid, and they shot the shit out of him. Sir."

Lysander touched his helmet. "Dustoff. Get in here *now.*"

"Already on the way," the aerial dispatcher said.

"Sergeant, whatever that man wants, we'll get it for him," Lysander said. *Rewards and risks. Statecraft.* "We owe him. *I* owe him, big."

"Yes, sir."

"Now. Where's the rebel leader?" Lysander asked.

Sergeant Miscowsky jerked his head toward the row of boulders behind him. "We got him. Up yonder. Sir."

Lysander started forward, but Miscowsky was in the way and didn't move. For a moment Lysander stared at the man. "Let me by."

"Well, sir—"

"Prince," Owensford said from behind him.

"What's going on?" Lysander demanded.

"Maybe you don't want to know," Owensford said. "You can go, Sergeant."

"Sir." Miscowsky ambled off into the dark.

"All right," Lysander said quietly. "Just what is this? Mutiny?"

"Of course not, Your Highness. You're in total command here. Anything you order will be done. Any question you ask will be answered," Owensford said.

"The Laws of War—"

"A good officer knows what to see, and what not to see," Owensford said. "And the Laws of War apply to prisoners of war. A status this group lost when they refused to surrender while holding hostages."

"General—"

"Yes, your Highness?"

Lysander looked up the hill in time to see Miscowsky vanish behind one of the boulders. "I hate this war," Lysander said.

"We all do."

"Will they learn anything?"

"If there's anything to learn. The important thing now is to keep him drugged so he can't suicide before the Alanas can talk to him."

"He called himself Sergeant Cheung—"

"Yeah. We think he's a bit more than that," Owensford said. "You may not know it, but Croser has a bodyguard named Lee Cheung." Peter shrugged. "It's not an uncommon name, but Lee Cheung is known to have a brother who's a major in their equivalent of special forces. At the least we may find out how they knew you were out here, traitor or leak. You'll notice he did ask for you."

"I want to see that man," Lysander said. "I want to talk to him, find out why—"

"In due time, Highness." Owensford flashed a light on the trail. "Nothing more to do here, and the medics would rather we were out of the way. The cleared path is marked, stay on it and be careful."

The sounds of battle had faded, and now came the inevitable aftermath, the smells of blood and death, screams and groans of wounded and dying. "They've done this to us," Lysander said. "We can't even walk in the forest without worrying about mines. The mines will be here for fifty years, a danger to foresters, children, animals—they don't care. General, what do civilized people owe to barbarians?"

"Sir?"

"We owe them nothing, General Owensford. We owe them nothing."

CHAPTER SIX

New York Times, May 17, 2094:

Luna Base. In a speech before the Grand Senate today, Grand Senator Adrian Bronson denounced anti-CoDominium partisans in both the United States and the Soviet Union.

"No man," Grand Senator Bronson said, "has done more than I to curb the CoDominium's excesses. No longer does the CoDominium pretend to be an omnicompetent government, a veritable interstellar empire. Therefore extreme measures such as this [referring to the proposed 50% cut in Fleet appropriations] are not appropriate at this time."

In other matters, Grand Senator Bronson's motion to instruct the CoDominium commander in the Sparta system to investigate terrorist activities against Fleet personnel and agents of the Bureau of Relocation was passed by acclamation. "We cannot tolerate such activities," Bronson said. "They must be uncompromisingly suppressed."

I love to see a lord when he is the first to advance on
horseback, armed and fearless, thus encouraging his
men to valiant service; then, when the fray has begun,
each must be ready to follow him willingly, because
no one is held in esteem until he has given and
received blows. We shall see clubs and swords, gaily
coloured helmets and shields shattered and spoiled, at
the beginning of the battle, and many vassals all
together receiving great blows, by reason of which
many horses will wander riderless, belonging to the
killed and wounded. Once he has started fighting, no
noble knight thinks of anything but breaking heads
and arms—better a dead man than a live one who is

useless. I tell you, neither in eating, drinking, nor
sleeping do I find what I feel when I hear the shout
"At Them" from both sides, and the neighing of riderless horses in the confusion, or the call "Help! Help!,"
or when I see great and small fall on the grass of the
ditches, or when I espy dead men who still have
pennoned lances in their ribs.

—Bertran de Born,
A Poem of Chivalry, 11th Century

" . . . and we're not happy at all with the way things are
going, Major Owensford," Beatrice Frazer said.

There were nods down the table of the Battalion Council
Meeting; the Legion commander sighed slightly and kneaded
the bridge of his nose with thumb and forefinger. This was
not a staff session. It was a meeting of the ruling body of
the Fifth as an autonomous community, just as the Regimental
Council governed Falkenberg's Legion as a whole; still nothing resembling a democracy, but considerably more political
than a strictly military meeting of the unit's officers alone.
Beatrice Frazer and Laura Bryant represented the civilian
women and children; Sergio Guiterrez sat at the far end with
the senior NCOs.

"We were looking forward to Sparta as a permanent base;
the wives and children came here to set up real homes while
the Legion was dropping into a combat zone on New Washington. Now we can barely go into Sparta City."

Everyone nodded; there had been no terrorist attacks on
Legion civilians yet, but that was as much because of caution and careful planning as anything else.

"And the worst of it is," she went on, "that otherwise it's
close to ideal here. Not just the weather and the food—" That
brought some chuckles; Tanith's perpetual steambath had been
driving everyone berserk, the Legion's civilians worst of all
"—but things in general. The Education Ministry's people have
been a great help with the children; they have *good* schools
here, and on Tanith we had to do everything ourselves. No
borloi, either."

Nods; Tanith lived by the drug trade. Drugs grown by slaves,
at that, and the general social atmosphere was about what
you would expect. Nobody had been at ease with the prospect of their children growing up in a place like that, and
you could only isolate from the surrounding environment so
much.

"In fact," she went on, "we've made more friends here than on planets we've stayed on for years. If it wasn't for the war . . ."

"We wouldn't be here," Owensford answered dryly. "We'll coordinate with the RSMP and try to see the civilians can visit town safely, Mrs. Frazer. I'd also appreciate it if the defense drills for the women and children were stepped up. In fact, I'd like to appoint a standing committee of you, Mrs. Savage, and, hmm, Mrs. Fuller, together with Veterans Smith, Puzdocki and Shaoping, to review the procedures and suggest alternatives. Any objections?"

"We'll need access to the planning computers," Beatrice Frazer said.

"Coordinate with the Captains Alana," Owensford said. "Objections? In favor?" A unanimous show of hands. "Battalion Sergeant Guiterrez?"

The stocky chicano smiled. "Sir," he said, "with the men, we've got almost the opposite problem. They like this place too much."

Owensford frowned; like the CoDominium Marines from whom the Legion had grown, and the French Foreign Legion before *them*, desertion had always been one of Falkenberg's Legions' problems. Soldiers like soft duty, but you have to let warriors kill something once in a while. You can use men who like to polish equipment in barracks, but you'd better have some warriors, too. . . .

"Not going over the hill, exactly, sir," Guiterrez said. "Plenty of fighting. Gets downright personal. But most of our long-service people could get permanent ranks in the Spartan army a couple of jumps up from where they are, commissions even. The pay's good, they could get Citizenship, and hell, the people here *like* soldiers, sir. These are good men we're training, too, not people you'd be ashamed to serve with. And since the Legion'll be retaining a base here, it wouldn't be like cutting themselves off. You can expect a drop in reenlistments as contracts come due. This is a place we can belong."

Owensford nodded. "The CoDominium Fleet likes this place for retirement, for that matter. But we have to *win*, first, Top," he said. "Otherwise this won't be a place anyone can live."

"Win. Yes, sir. Major, dammit, they won't let us win! Major, we know who's behind most of this—"

"We've been over this already, Top. Comments noted. Now, we've received a communiqué from the Colonel—" A rustle around the table. "None of you need worry. I've given the casualty list to the chaplains.

"Came in an hour ago with the CD courier ship. The message is just short of ten Earth months old. The Regiment landed safely, took its initial objective, and has moved on Allansport; they expect some fighting there. Colonel Falkenberg approves our measures to date—" just after he landed and found out how rapidly the situation had deteriorated. *God, we thought* that *was bad.* "—but warns that mobilization on a larger scale may be needed and authorizes the necessary reassignments."

A chuckle, especially from the officers. Exactly what you'd expect from Christian Johnny.

"And a message for all of us." Owensford touched the console in front of him.

Falkenberg appeared on the screen at the far wall. The colonel was seated at his field desk and wore field uniform. "We're moving ahead of schedule here," Falkenberg said. "Light casualties. Good local support. Details attached.

"Your reports say things are rough there," Falkenberg said. "I'm sorry to hear it, but I have to say I'm not greatly surprised. I did hope you'd have some time before our enemies built up strength, but Sparta is important to Bronson and his people. It's even more important to us, the way things are developing. It's vital that you keep Sparta independent. I know you'll do that, whatever it takes.

"Administrative matters. Major Owensford is herewith promoted to Lieutenant Colonel, and authorized to accept whatever Spartan rank he feels is justified.

"Colonel Owensford will now assure himself that this room is secure and all present are authorized and cleared for discussion of regimental business."

The screen went blank. Owensford looked at each person in the room, then typed in a phrase on his console. Falkenberg reappeared.

"As all of you know, there's more happening than we can usually discuss in Council meetings. I regret that, because you're being asked to endure hardships without knowing why. I can only say, what you're doing is important to us all. To the Regiment, and to whatever future civilization has out here. That future is uncertain. The CoDominium is breaking up, but it's not dead yet. It still has great power. That power is divided. Our group, the faction loosely headed by the Grants, the Blaines, Admiral Lermontov—"

"—Bloody blunt about it," George Slater said.

"—controls part of the Fleet. A smaller group is loyal to the Bronson faction in the person of Vice Admiral Townsend.

Most of the Fleet is trying to stay neutral: 'No politics in the Fleet, the Fleet is our fatherland.' We can all sympathize with that view. We've all held it. It's now an obsolete notion. There is no Fleet, and we'll have to build a fatherland, a fatherland for ourselves and a home for the Fleet.

"What you're doing is significant to that effort. If things go well here, we'll have influence in New Washington, enough influence that we should be able to base naval and marine units here. That won't be enough. We'll also need bases on Sparta.

"The question inevitably arises, who do I mean when I say 'we'? I don't know. Clearly some entity larger than the Legion, and for that matter larger than whatever part of the Fleet joins our faction. I confess I don't yet know what that entity will be. I have my hopes. I think you may be in a position to know better than I do.

"We face a very uncertain future. I'll do what I can to take some of the pressure off you, but frankly, I can't do much just now. The situation here will require all our political resources until we have New Washington stabilized. Don't feel ignored, though, because what you're doing is vital. You're distracting our enemies, the enemies of the Legion, and, for that matter, the enemies of civilization. What they throw at you there they can't throw at us here. You're helping grind them down. It won't be easy, that kind of campaign never is, but I know you can do it.

"We're going to win. Never forget that. Godspeed and God bless you." The image faded.

"Bloody hell," someone said.

"A war of attrition," George Slater said. "Major—Colonel, I have a request. I won't put it as a motion until I see what you think."

"Very well," Owensford said.

"I propose that we ask my father to sit on this Council. With all due respect, none of us here is very experienced in Fleet politics—"

"And General Slater has been with Falkenberg longer than anyone else," Owensford finished. "As you all know, Colonel Falkenberg is very sensitive to the principle of unity of command. He was therefore careful not to imply that General Slater was in any way associated with command of Legion units here. I much appreciated that. However, I agree with Captain Slater. The situation here is not what we expected. Events have moved much faster than we expected. I think we can use the experience of retired Lt. Colonel Hal Slater on this Council, and I will entertain a motion to that effect."

"So moved."

"Second."

"Moved by Regimental Sergeant Gutierrez and seconded by Mrs. Frazer. All those in favor say aye. Nays? I hear none. Let the record show the vote was unan—"

There was a brisk knock at the door. Owensford frowned. "Come."

The door opened. Owensford looked up, felt his face freeze into blankness at the junior lieutenant's expression.

"Sir," the young man said. "Sorry to interrupt. Priority message from Sparta City. The transportee shuttle has been sabotaged. There are over a thousand dead, and the . . . Sir, the CoDominium enclave Commandant has summoned all heads of government and armed forces to a meeting. Immediately, sir."

Owensford started to rise. "Wait a minute," he said. *"Heads* of armed forces? Plural?"

"Yes, sir. The summons includes the Helots . . . and they're under CoDominium safe conduct. Any action against them for the duration of the conference period or twenty-four hours thereafter will be treated as an attack on the CoDominium."

Peter looked down the table at the shocked faces as he tried to control his own. "Gentlemen, ladies," he said formally. "I'm afraid we'll have to adjourn."

"Skilly will be back in a minute."

Geoffrey Niles raised himself on one elbow to watch her go. There was a relaxed pleasure in the way the muscle clenched and relaxed in her buttocks as her hips swayed, shadowed in the dim light. *Not at all what you'd expect in some ways,* he thought. She was fastidious as a cat, when there was opportunity. One of the most frequent punishment drills for Helot recruits was for not washing; the offender was scrubbed down by their entire squad, using floor-brushes. . . .

The cave air was still chill, but he ignored that now, not pulling up the coverlet despite his nakedness; he had learned the trick of that, these last few months, of being indifferent to how you felt physically. *Learning a good deal from Skilly,* he thought with a sour grin, running over the last hour in his mind. Even exhausted, it stirred him. *God, what a lay!*

"Lot of fun, all around," he murmured to himself. Which was odd again, considering that he was still working like a slave; no harder than she, of course. Less if anything . . . "But it's rarely boring."

The thought of England and the eternal petty round, traveling in to Amalgamated's offices in the City, vacationing in the Alps or the family's private island in the Caymans. . . . *Brainless debs and endless bloody boredom.* Now *there* was something chilling. Not that there was anything wrong with inherited wealth, except that it tempted you to *waste* yourself. You couldn't really enjoy nothing but enjoyment, and once there were a certain number of credits in the account adding more was just numbers. Not many of the people he had known on Earth had anything approaching Skilly's diamond-hard concentration and single-mindedness; they scattered themselves instead, a little bit of this and that. No way to accomplish anything.

Adventure isn't the thing, he mused. He'd learned that, floating down the river holding onto the corpse of one of his men, after the Dales battle last year. Adventure was like happiness, not something you could set out to find; that way lay safaris and pointless risks that were simply bigger amusement-park rides. What really mattered was *accomplishing* something. Something big and worthwhile, and putting everything you had into it, that was what people like Grand-Uncle Bronson or Murasaki or Skilly did. Starting off with nothing and aiming to win a war and rule and reshape a planet; *that* was something worth spending your time on.

He yawned again. *Well, Grand Uncle, maybe I'll surprise you and find my own career on this little junket,* he thought. He stirred uneasily at the thought of going home now; his Sandhurst classmates wouldn't understand. . . . *I had no choice! Not really, and then it was too late—*

There was a notebook on Skilly's side of the bed, one of hundreds she kept neatly shelved, a 20cm x 10cm black-bound volume. That was another surprising thing, the way she hated to waste time. If there was nothing else to do she'd whip out one of these and start writing, thoughts and observations and plans. . . . Idly, he flipped open the front cover.

Postwar #7, he read. There were plastic markers on the side, dividing it into sections: *pers., polit., miltry., econo.*

Personal first, he thought.

Freehand pencil sketches. Of himself, nude or in fanciful uniforms, or with Skilly. *Are we really that acrobatic?* Notes for insignia, flags. Floor-plans and elevations of houses and gardens. One picture of a ragged, big-eyed urchin, and it was several moments before he recognized a younger Skilly. A last series, showing him and Skilly and a baby; in a cradle, at her breast, playing with Niles. . . . Touched, he closed the notebook and set it down again. *Maybe she fancies the dynastic connection. Marriage into the Bronson clan. Cadet branch, but still quite a step up from Belize. And what would Grand Uncle think? But it's something to think about.*

"Definitely," he murmured, closing his eyes for a moment. In fact, it was an exciting thought. *A dynasty,* he mused. Not that Skilly had ever said anything directly against Croser, but . . . *Most dynasties start with ruthless pirates,* he reminded himself. *Or lucky soldiers, or barbarian invaders. No reason they can't become enlightened in time. Civilizations have been founded by enlightened barbarians . . . Could Skilly think that way? With a Bronson connection, could she be a satrap in a real social order? Would she accept that?*

"Up again? Jeffi really *be* a mon of iron," Skilly laughed, sliding back into the bed. Her feet were cold when she entangled them with his—they were nearly the same height—and so were her fingers as she trailed them down his chest and stomach.

"God, woman, you must be slipping something into my drinks," he said in mock-horror.

"Lots of red meat and fresh air," she said, kissing him and kneading. "But we spare you poor knees and elbows this time," she went on, rising and straddling his hips. "Skilly good to her Jeffi, hey?" she said, looking down at him heavy-lidded as she lowered onto him with taunting slowness. "Enjoy while you can, we in the field soon."

"Soon? *Ah!*" He ran his hands up to her breasts.

"Hmmm. Mmmm, nice. We been spending de winter make life miserable for the kings, now they getting good and mad. We gots to make them spread out—" she grinned "—so they not get it together for a concentrated thrust." Her hips gave a quick downward jerk. "Too many of us to stay pure guerrilla anymore, so."

Niles laughed a little breathlessly. "You're thinking strategy at a time like *this*?"

She leaned forward against his hands, locking her own on his shoulders. The mane of curled black hair fell over his face as they began to rock together, but he could see her teeth and eyes glint through.

"Skilly is always thinking, Jeffi," she gasped. "Always."

Skida Thibodeau slid herself a little to one side and picked up the notebook, sparing a fond glance for the man sleeping beside her and hooking up the coverlet to warm his feet. She pulled a pencil from the spine and licked the point as she flipped the book open.

Polit. The first section was a list of books on internal-security technique; she ran down them and added another note: *secr pol.—own budget—labr cmps. profit—see R. Conquest, details.*

Important to be thrifty. Also—*Rival grps.—balance.* But it would be easy to go too far. *see Anat. der SS-Staat.*

On to *miltry.* The first page of that carried an abbreviated star map centered on Sparta's sun, with transit-times radiating out like the spokes of a wheel. Underneath it was a note: *conscr. army—10/15 div.,* and a list of planets. She put a checkmark beside Thurstone, then stopped for a moment.

Them first, but who next? Haven? she asked herself; it was not nearly as close, but the shimmerstone trade was valuable. On the other hand, it was still CD, and pretty worthless otherwise. Not enough people to serve as a recruiting ground for further expansion. It *did* have a refueling point . . . The pencil moved: *Haven poss. next.; CD goes; expl. beyond?* Time enough to think about that when the Democratic Republic started building up its navy. *Build or take. So much easier to take than build.*

She slipped the pencil back into its holder and sank down on the bed, pulling up the blankets. Niles shifted closer in his sleep, and she smiled to herself as she yawned and prepared to drop off.

Life is good, she thought contentedly. A light began to flash beside the bedside communications unit; she frowned at it, then swung out of bed and belted on a robe. *This better be important,* she thought.

"Well, we know how it was done," General Desjardins said. "Those *fools* in the SCA thought they could terrorize the CoDominium into stopping involuntary transportation. They smuggled a suicide bomber on the shuttle; through the Aegis station." Most spaceships with cargo or passengers docked at the orbital transit-station, and boarded the surface shuttles there.

"Mingled with the transportees, and managed to get close enough to a coolant pump during reentry. They didn't *notice* that there were CD officers on board the shuttle as well as eleven hundred convicts!"

Owensford nodded tautly. The Royalist party was sitting in one corner of what had once been the Officer's Mess of the CoDominium Marine garrison; the dry, slightly musty air of

the big dimly-lit room carried a faint ghost of banners, of
raucous celebrations with bagpipers and Cossack dancers, a
lingering sadness. The remaining staff of the enclave rattled
around like peas in a very empty pod, and the junior officers who had brought the two parties here had been men in
their forties . . . *There, but for luck, go I,* the mercenary thought
with a shudder. Stranded here in a lost outpost of a dying
empire. He glanced up at the group across the room, around
a hastily-dusted table of their own; Dion Croser and his NCLF
gang. Croser was talking with one of them, laughing and
slapping the man on the shoulder.

Bastard.

There was a stir at the entrance; the honor guard there was
not giving the same carefully neutral salute they had accorded
the Spartan kings and their Legion officers.

The Helots, Owensford thought sardonically. *Meet the
enemy.*

They had come under CoDominium safe-conduct, in a heavily
armed Marine shuttle.

Pity, he thought savagely. *Otherwise they'd never get out of
here alive. They may not anyway, once I drop my little surprise into the meeting.* Then: *Observe. Know the enemy.*

The CD Commandant had insisted on seeing all parties to
the civil war, including those that did not recognize each other
as belligerents and those claiming neutrality. The Royal government had spent three days protesting the safe-conduct for
the Helots; the Marine commandant had been sympathetic—
no doubt where the CoDo garrison's sympathies lay, particularly
after the violations of the Laws of War—but standing orders
left no latitude, not with a Grand Senator breathing down their
neck.

The CoDominium might be tottering towards its grave, but
the walking corpse of it still possessed a power no planet without
space-navy capacity could ignore. Even now, a blatant violation like the shuttle bombing could not be ignored. Not even
when Sparta's friends included influential Senators and Grand
Admiral Lermontov. Especially then, when those friends fought
for their lives and any excuse might serve their enemies to bring
them down. There were so many enemies, Kaslov's murderous
neoStalinists in the USSR, Harmon's demented Patriot Party in
the US, both openly courting nuclear war with nihilistic relish.
Bronson and his opportunists playing both sides against the
middle for private gain. . . .

Take a good look, he reminded himself, studying the half-
dozen rebel leaders. They were in camouflage jackets and

leather trousers and boots, but neatly pressed, brasswork and the badges on their berets polished. A touch of *bandido*-flamboyance here and there, a brass earring or long braided hair, a bit of swagger. Skida Thibodeau was in the midst of them and her eyes flicked over him with a steady considering look as she passed, like a predator in hot jungle thoughtfully eyeing a wild boar.

Owensford straightened slightly, feeling an instinctive bristling. *The dog and the wolf,* he thought ironically. He had studied the records and the pictures carefully, but they had not prepared him for this sleek exotic handsomeness, the graceful deadliness of a fer-de-lance.

It must have taken considerable courage to come here, anyway; there were more than a few Spartans and some Legionnaires who would have risked the CoDominium's anger to kill the enemy leaders. This was a bitter war, and the reason for it was right here. Owensford studied them carefully; one or two might not be aware of the danger they were in, several of the others were slightly stiff with the knowledge of it, under their bravado. Skilly was completely relaxed, even slightly amused. The mercenary officer felt his teeth show slightly. Most soldiers endured danger by an act of will. He had known some who enjoyed it . . . and a few who were simply not much affected one way or another, icemen. He had never liked them; there was something missing inside in someone like that, and the Helot leader looked to be a prime example. There was a mind behind the big dark eyes. . . . *But no soul,* he decided. *None at all.*

Ace Barton leaned close and whispered: "Notice Niles," he said.

That must be the tall blond man; he felt their eyes and turned to give them a false and toothy grin as the Helots seated themselves. Skilly leaned back in her chair with arms and legs negligently crossed, and went instantly to sleep.

"Doesn't look much like the pictures." They had extensive video files on the Honorable Geoffrey Niles, and despite the unmistakable Nordic cheekbones and male-model looks, this was a different man. "Our little sprig on the Bronson family tree isn't nearly so much the silly-ass Englishman, these days," Barton replied thoughtfully.

"Can't say that it's altogether an improvement," Owensford said. Nearly two Earth years in the wilderness had thinned him down, and given him something of the feral look the others at the Helot table had. "Keeping bad company and all."

"Gentlemen, ladies." The CoDominium lieutenant called from the inner door; he had a flat Russian face, ash-blond hair turning gray and body stringy under the blue-and-scarlet dress uniform. "The Commandant will see you now."

"Ten-*'hut*," the garrison Sergeant-Major said. "This meeting will come to order."

There was a rustle, the military men standing to and the civilians a little straighter; the kings had already been seated, of course, being heads of state. David I looked no more worried than usual; the improvement in Alexander I was as night and day.

Colonel Boris Karantov returned the polite nods of the Spartan and Legion soldiers and ignored the Helots. He sat carefully, lowering himself down by his hands; he was in his seventies and looked older, regeneration treatments or no.

"Be seated, gentlemen, ladies." His Anglic was still slightly Russian.

"We are here to discuss violations of the Treaty of Independence governing relations between this planet and the CoDominium. And of the Laws of War. Let me first establish that the CoDominium is strictly neutral in the current conflict; I am uninterested in the rights or wrongs of that struggle as you perceive them. I remind you that this meeting is being recorded, and the records will be made available to the appropriate offices of the CoDominium Authority as well as to the Grand Senate."

There was a flat weariness to the tone, the voice of a man who has excluded everything but the performance of a job in which he no longer really believes.

"Now, a shuttle—a civilian vessel—" he pronounced it *wessle* "—under charter to the Bureau of Relocation, carrying both involuntary colonists not yet transferred to Spartan jurisdiction, and off-duty officers of the CoDominium Fleet, has been destroyed by an act of criminal terrorism. I have called all possible parties here to account for this crime. Your Majesties?"

"We, the Dual Monarchy's government denounce this abhorrent act." Alexander looked sternly toward Skida Thibodeau. "It is quite possible that this was an operation organized by this person as a provocation to discredit us. However, we are fairly sure that a dissident group called the SCA is responsible, and if—when—we catch the individuals responsible, they will be subject to trial and execution. Or turned over to you for punishment, Commandant. Sparta values its relations with the CoDominium." A subtle reminder that they had powerful friends in the Grand Senate.

Karantov nodded non-committally, his fingers rolling a light-pencil. "Still," he said judiciously, "this SCA is believed to have links to your own security *apparat.* You say this is entirely a matter of disaffected individuals, but this would be claimed in any case."

His eyes rose to Croser. "Mr. Croser, your organization has also been linked to terrorist activities. You have to say?"

Croser's nod was politely deferential. "Sir, firstly, the NCLF is purely a peaceful political party. It's true we hope to form the government after the illegal Royalist regime is rejected by the people in the upcoming referendum" —David I snorted, and Alexander almost rose in his fury, with General Desjardins laying a hand on his arm— "but we seek to use only legitimate means."

Karantov made a slight bored gesture, as if waving the Spartan through the necessary pieties.

"More to the point," Croser continued, his face and voice taking on a flatter, harsher tone. "The NCLF draws its strength from the oppressed classes—that is, from the transportees oppressed by the Royalist regime. Every transport which lands increases our just strength. It would be suicidal for us to interrupt the flow, even if we would stoop to such an atrocity as this.

"No," he went on, the mellow voice taking on a ringing quality, "the only logical candidate is the Royalists themselves— lashing out in their desperation, now that the whirlwind they created by their own actions is out of control. Through this false-front SCA, which they use to disguise actions too repulsive even for them to openly admit to. Certainly the SCA has claimed responsibility."

Bastard. Owensford thought. *But a* smart *bastard.* No way to prove that wasn't true.

Karantov's head turned toward the Helots. Their commander was sitting with one fist supporting her chin, watching the byplay between the others with lazy enjoyment.

"These NCLF *rabbiblancos* be getting some thing right every now and then, even if they be wuss weaklings," she said lightly. "The Spartan People's Liberation Army *be* a transportee army. Why we kill our own recruits?"

The CoDo officer nodded grimly; obviously loathing the speaker to the point of physical distaste at listening, equally obviously accepting the argument.

Alexander shook off the police commander's hand. "I repeat, as a provocation, of course. You would very much like to ruin our relations with the CD."

Skilly grinned insolently and leaned back with one arm hooked around the back of her chair. She examined the nails of the other hand.

"Tsk, tsk," she said, with mock-kindness. "Old man be having de fantasies. He need the doctor, bad."

"Silence!" Karantov rasped. After a moment: "Under the Treaty, I have the right to resume command of the Aegis station if the Spartan government fails to perform its duties. This will be done. Lunabase informs me that heavy shipments of involuntary colonists will be received shortly, and I will *not* allow anyone entrusted to my care to be endangered!"

"Colonel?" Skilly's voice was chocolate-smooth this time; Owensford glanced aside at her, narrow-eyed. She was keeping her own on her nails, the long black lashes drooping. "Maybe be better you land the convicts somewhere else. Safer than this dangerous city which be too big to secure, hey? Also city is full of legitimate military target place, maybe we attack it soon."

A brilliant smile. "We Spartan People's Liberation Army promise solemn not to attack any place the shuttles land, if no Royal troops be there."

The Royal government delegation tensed; this was the real rebel ploy. Karantov pursed his lips thoughtfully, calling up the map-function of the table. It blinked from steel-gray to transparent, showing an overhead view of the Serpentine continent.

"Where would you suggest?" he said.

"Well, anywhere on the river do OK," she said blandly. "Howsomeever, all the towns have the same objection as Sparta City."

She reached over and tapped a spot on the south shore of Lake Alexander, where the railway from Olynthos circled around the Vulcan Rapids.

"This be the best spot, I think. Plenty open water, already docks for the mineral barges, and not much town. We agree not to attack there or anywhere within five kilometer."

"Commandant, that would cause considerable administrative difficulties," David I broke in.

"Three of my officers and a thousand people whose only offense was to be there when the Bureau of Relocation came through *died* just now, Your Majesty," Karantov said frostily. "This is considerably more than an administrative matter."

He glanced at the map again, then at the guerrilla leader with unconcealed suspicion.

"I and my staff will consider this matter. Provisionally, we will seal off all portions of the Aegis station dealing with

BuReloc. The shuttles will take transportees to the surface—"
he tapped the Lake Alexander location "—and nothing more,
no other traffic."

The Spartans winced slightly; that would cost them heavily,
especially in the CD credits BuReloc would no longer pay for
services on Aegis, and in the foregone lift-capacity of the
shuttle's surface-to-orbit runs.

"Furthermore, I am referring this matter to my superiors.
I warn you that there will at the least be heavy fines, particularly if the culprits in the murder of my officers are not
found; I am asking for reinforcements." Presently there were
only about a company of Garrison Marines on Sparta. "Possibly a CoDominium blockade of this planet for violations of
the Laws of War will be ordered."

This time faces paled. Bronson's aid to the Helots was
already clandestine, and would not be affected. The Royal
government would face riots and collapse, particularly in the
cities. Sparta was only semi-industrialized, it simply could not
function without off-planet supplies; was more vulnerable than
a truly primitive world.

Time, Owensford thought, and cleared his throat.

"Colonel Karantov, if you please. I have a further complaint
with regard to violations of the Laws of War."

Karantov raised his eyebrows, and the Helots' eyes turned
to the Legion officer like turrets tracking.

"As to offenses committed against civilians, or among indigenous armed forces, that is beyond my jurisdiction." Karantov
looked wistful; he was old enough to remember times when
a CoDominium officer's word was law in such matters, and
had been a grown man when the Fleet was still arbiter of
all conflicts.

"The offense concerns a member of Falkenberg's Legion,"
Owensford said.

He felt a chill satisfaction as Skilly leaned over and spoke
rapidly to a subordinate, who began to tap frantically at an
opened laptop. A buzz broke out from Croser's party, until
he cut it off with a knife-hand gesture; the Spartans leaned
forward like hounds on a leash. Owensford slipped a message
cube into the receptor.

"Lieutenant Deborah Lefkowitz, Falkenberg's Mercenary
Legion 11A7732-ze-1," he said. A picture of her flashed up,
together with her service history. Another shot of her with
her husband and their two children, ages four and six. Then
a full-length of her mostly-naked body, lying spread-eagled and
open-eyed with its throat cut from ear to ear.

"Gene typing, finger and retina prints give positive ID," Owensford said, keeping his voice even with an effort. The Legion was very much a family . . . *And I have to explain this to Jerry.* "She went MIA from an aircraft downed near this site during the battle of the Illyrian Dales last year. The cave was being used as a C3 post; our counter battery fire hit an ammunition dump, and the survivors evacuated quickly. Evidence that it was being used by the rebels follows."

Karantov's gray pug-dog face was motionless as he turned it from the screen to the Helots. Owensford saw Skilly's own go equally blank, like a mask from an Egyptian grave, but the fingers of her right hand moved slightly, flexing. Everything took on a diamond clarity as he realized with an icy shock that she was calculating. On whether Karantov would order her arrest, and on how many she could kill before the guards shot her down. Geoffrey Niles was pale, looking at the photo on the screen.

The woman spoke, softly. "Skilly did not order that. If she had, Skilly would have seen that the body was disposed of with a thermite charge. And if you get she the genotypes—" sperm samples from the rapists would have yielded that "—Skilly will give you the bodies. With confessions. *Because Skilly does not like to be left holding the bag.*"

For a moment something with teeth looked out from behind the smooth features.

"Our investigation into this matter will require the perpetrators alive," the CoDominium commander said. His face and voice were near expressionless; Skilly's were as well, but her eyes flicked sideways to Owensford, and her head inclined slightly.

Good move, he translated mentally. There was nothing he could do now, after launching this torpedo.

"Field Prime has read your Laws of War, the old version and the new," Skilly said; left unstated was the shrinking field of application, as the CoDominium's power faded. "And the Mercenary Code." The influence of the free companies had grown with every passing year, particularly if you counted the armies of planets like Covenant who made their living from hiring out their fighting men. "Conducting internal trial and punishment fulfills the letter of both," she went on. "And we has no intention of doing more."

One of Karantov's fingers tapped at the table. "I did not know you were a . . . practitioner of the Code," he said with heavy irony.

Beneath the expressionless mask there was the hint of a cold snarl when Skilly spoke, an ancient anger and contempt.

"Field Prime doesn't give a pitcher of warm spit for you Code, or some dead bitch," she said, in the same soft voice. "Never no laws or codes to protect Skilly where *she* came from . . . but she doan pick fights she can no win, either. No point in paying no atteention to Spartan laws; them or us go to the wall, anyways. But only a fool get into a new battle when this one not won yet. Skilly Thibodeau be no fool. SPLA complying with your Code this time, and that all you going to get. Colonel."

"Punishment of individuals is not sufficient if the violation was policy set by leaders," Karantov said. "My investigators should be involved." The threat of detention was unspoken.

"Skilly regrets that not possible," she said; then she grinned like a wolf. "Skilly also give standing orders anything she say when under a gun be disregarded. Can no play dis game without you willing to lay down the stakes, mon. You safe-conduct is unconditional . . . and Skilly have certain friends on Luna."

Karantov made a small wave of dismissal. "I expect the transcripts and the executions promptly," he said.

The Helots stood. "Oh, very prompt," Skilly said; the fingers of her gun-hand made that small unconscious gesture again. "You get all you ask for, Colonel, and more."

"I request that my evidence be presented to the Military Affairs Committee of the Grand Senate, and that copies be sent to the commanding officer of every registered military organization within the CoDominium," Owensford said formally. Someone involuntarily drew in a breath. It was impossible to determine who, but Peter thought it might have been Geoffrey Niles.

"Skilly don't see any need to do that. She will find your criminals. If this be record, then make the record clear, Skilly have nothing to do with that, and neither do any of her allies." The heavy-lidded eyes swept the others at the table, before she turned on her heel and left.

"Your comments are noted," Karantov said. "Colonel Owensford, your request is reasonable and will be granted. Copies of the relevant portions of this hearing will be furnished to all registered military organizations.

"We now adjourn meeting until I and my officers can consider this matter. That will be all, gentlemen, ladies, Your Majesties. Stay for a moment if you would, Lieutenant Colonel Owensford." The CD commander emphasized his role by using Owensford's rank within Falkenberg's Legion, a registered military organization. . . .

"Please be seated, Piotr Stefanovich." Karantov touched a button to summon the steward. "Vodka and tonic, please. And you, Colonel?"

"Whiskey and water, thank you." They raised their glasses.

"*Spacebo,* Colonel. And congratulations on your promotion."

"Cheers, Colonel Karantov. May you not regret yours." Owensford sighed. "You played that pretty hard-nosed, Boris," he said. "On the Spartans, I mean."

The older man shrugged. "No more than I must." He looked to be certain that the recording cameras were turned off. "Of course, Piotr Stefanovich, it is clear that this is Armstrong's Black Hand *apparat,* no connection to the Spartan government. But this I cannot say in public. No more can I say Grand Admiral wishes most earnestly that you put down this revolt quickly." He paused, looking into his vodka and then snapping it back with a flick of his wrist. "No politics in the Fleet. Bah. Now is all politics."

"Maybe it's time for you to choose sides."

"Sergei and I wish you victory; Grant too, but we Russians most of all," the Russian CD officer continued softly. "This Croser, we Russians know his kind all too well; and the Thibodeau woman, yes. The True Believer, mad and brilliant, and the bandit killer follower . . . too many times has our suffering country seen the like of them." He crossed himself in Orthodox fashion, right to left. "We must hope that sin does not lie so heavy on Sparta as it does on the poor *rodina.*"

"So why are you—"

"My friend, this is not the time. Some power remains, to the CoDominium, to the Senate. Enough to have me removed here if I give cause. Another time—"

"Another time may be too late."

"I think not. Your war goes badly? Surely you do not lose."

"Let's say we're not winning. Boris, the Fleet holds all the power out here."

"Power? Power to destroy, perhaps. Not to build. Not yet."

"Dammit, certainly enough power to intercept off-planet supplies to the rebels!"

"Yes, probably."

"So why—"

"Commodore Guildford has Navy command here. He is typical of new Fleet officers," Karantov said. "He chooses sides, not by principle, not by which is right side, but which side wins, which is how he is Commodore when sector like this would not rate more than Captain of Fleet."

"And he thinks Bronson will win?"

"He thinks he does not know. He thinks that by doing nothing he will anger neither side, be able to deal with winner." Boris Karantov shrugged. "Sometimes that tactic works."

"It also ensures that whoever does win will have no use for you," Peter said carefully.

"Agreed. Is this warning, Piotr Stefanovich? I tell you again, I do all I can. More and they will remove me."

"More a warning to Guildford, I think. Dammit, Boris, a surveillance satellite would make a lot of difference!"

"I will speak with Captain of Fleet Newell. You will understand, Piotr Stefanovich, there is much sympathy for you in Fleet units here. Many have families here, many have retired here, many more think to retire here. Is not popular to watch this planet destroy itself."

"We are *not* destroying ourselves. We are being destroyed. There is a difference."

"*We*, Piotr?" the CD man asked ironically.

"Yes. It's as much my fight as the Spartans. I've found something worth fighting for—dammit, it can be your fight too."

"Da. I know."

"Then for God's sake help us."

"I tell you again, it is not yet time." Karantov reached into his attaché case, and pulled out a message cube. "The latest from our observers at New Washington; somewhat more recent than official channels." A CD Fleet courier could take a direct route, through unsettled systems with no refueling stations, if there was need.

"In brief, Astoria has fallen to the Legion, and your Colonel is tearing up the Columbia Valley to meet the Friedlanders." He smiled wanly. "A swift campaign, glory or defeat, and an honorable enemy. It seems like a vision of paradise, no?"

"So Falkenberg has won?"

"When this message was made, he was winning his war," Karantov said. "He will hold the important parts of the planet. After that—" He shrugged. "Is politics, again."

"Thank you for the message."

"And is this. From Grand Admiral Sergei Mikaelovitch, news so secret that it cannot be sent except by word of mouth. The Grants have done all they can to make Bronson relinquish this feud. He will not."

"What does he want?'

Karantov shook his head. "Some say he is mad. Me, I believe not. But whatever his plans, he is spending fortunes, and we dare not come to an open break with him. Not yet."

"We can tie him to the murder. That was his Grand Nephew there with Thibodeau! I can't think Adrian Bronson wants to be associated with atrocities."

"Nor I. Your pictures will go to Sergei Mikaelovitch, and to Grand Senate. I can do no more than that."

"It may be enough."

"And it may not. My friend, Earth's life hangs in this balance. Sergei Lermontov is no longer sure that we have *one* year, much less the ten we have all planned. Certainly we do not if things come to open fight with Bronson faction. My friend, we have done what we could!"

"It's nice to know you tried," Owensford said dryly.

Karantov snorted laughter. "Still *ami*, thinking the problem will yield to 'can do,' eh, my friend?"

"Boris, I'm beginning to doubt I can do bloody *anything*. This war . . ."

The other man nodded. "Some help I can be, perhaps. The Admiral sends you Fleet Intelligence report on Kenjiro Murasaki; we are certain now that he is mercenary Bronson has hired for Croser."

"Bronson hired him directly?" Owensford said, balancing the message cube in his fingers and then slipping it into a pouch on his belt.

Karantov nodded. "Which may yet be cause of great regret to Croser. Be careful, Piotr Stefanovich, be very careful. The Meijians have some of best computer personnel in all settled worlds, and Special Tasks, Inc. hires only best of those. Murasaki is like ghost; rumored to be here, to be there, never proven. He commands highest fees, and his chosen field is the undermining of an opponent's own weapons and personnel. I read from report. 'Subtle to a fault. Treacherous as a snake, and bound by no soldier's honor, not even as Meijians understand it. His only scruple is loyalty to his employer for the term of the contract.'" Karantov shrugged. "From this I suspect primary motivation is aesthetic—he is artist, artist of assassination and subversion and death."

"That about describes the way things have been going," Owensford said feelingly. "All right. It's a war of attrition. The great thing is not to lose your nerve. But bloody Hell, I could still use an observation satellite."

Karantov nodded, tapping his fingers against the table. "Request has been noted. Now. Grand Admiral also sends you help, twenty computer specialists recently retired from BuInt. Experts in counter viral work. This is, you understand, of most extreme secrecy."

Owensford smiled. "Boris," he said, "it's also extremely welcome. We need them, our own people have enough to do with the Legion systems and a few here in the capital; it's getting pretty bad out there."

"Interesting," the dark figure in the corner said. "Very interesting information. Not vital, of course." Keys clicked as he scanned forward through the data. "Interesting. They have discovered our origins from Fleet Intelligence. Ah, they are sending technical specialists to help the Legion. Fascinating, and incriminating if my principal could use this before the Grand Senate, which of course he cannot. No access codes, I see."

"Murasaki," the Helot commander said. "Skilly did not appreciate that little surprise back with the CoDo."

Geoffrey Niles took another drink from his canteen; water, unfortunately. *I could use a drink right now,* he thought. *God, those pictures . . .*

"Bloody right," he rasped. "Our plausible deniability is running too sodding thin for comfort, Mr. Murasaki. If the Grand Senator has this pinned on him—and I'm pretty conspicuous—he'd lose half his influence in the Fleet, and every second merc on all the hundred planets would be taking potshots at his people and interests—"

"Jeffi," Skilly said, without taking her eyes from the Meijian.

The meeting was taking place in a farmhouse northwest of Colchis; the Movement had financed the owner, decades ago. Land on the Eurotas was cheap, and mostly free once you were a day's ride away from the river, but equipment was expensive. A few thousand Crowns had made the difference between peasant misery and modest comfort for the owner and his family, enough for ploughs, harrows, a satellite dish for the children's education. In return couriers had a safe place to stop. . . . The sound and smell of cooking came up through the floorboards of the attic. It added an unreality to the meeting, Niles thought: death and conspiracy to the scent of fresh bread and a roast.

"Jeffi," Skilly went on, "in case you not notice, mon, you working for Skilly now, not Earth Prime." She turned back to the Meijian. "Well?"

He shrugged. "Operational security in the combat zone is your responsibility," he said.

Skilly shifted slightly; the Meijian did not tense, but the chilly air of the attic was fully of a coiled alertness.

"Yoshida was in command of that post," the woman said. "He responsible, Murasaki; should have his head, too."

"No," Murasaki said flatly "I do not abandon my people."

"Neither does Skilly," the woman said. "Ones who offed the merc fucked up by not hiding de evidence, and they pay." She smiled at the ghastly pun. "But Yoshida commander on site—he should have checked."

"Field Prime," Niles said. "If we just tightened the behavior of the troops up—"

"*Jeffi, shut up,*" Skilly said. She turned her head toward him; a slight trace of fear crept down the Englishman's spine. "This the Revolution, Jeffi; we be fighting by your *rabbiblanco* rules, they kill us all in a month. That the reason their stinkin' Code there at all."

Niles fell silent; usually it was a teasing joke when Skilly referred to him as a *rabbiblanco*, white-ass. Not this time.

Murasaki chuckled softly. "Not the way our enemies would put it, but moral considerations aside, quite accurate. The Law of War certainly has a conservative effect, making it difficult to fight wars with large or radical aims. It favors established, regular forces."

He turned his attention to Skilly once more. "I would remind you that Earth Prime's main goal is to humiliate the Legion. Not merely to defeat it, but to make Falkenberg and its individual members *suffer,* to cause them pain and anguish. So I was ordered."

"Good, OK, *absolutemente,* once we win you can have them all fucked to death by donkeys—but not while it can backfire on we. Mon, Falkenberg got influence! He winning his war, too. We get him mad enough before Helots holding the planet, we gets the Legion an' twenty thousand mercs from Kali knows where, them riding down in CD assault boats pretty likely. Nobody off-planet except maybe Lermontov much care what we do to Spartans, not enough to do much, but the mercs be a different story."

"Is it certain that won't happen now?" Niles asked. "Those pictures. Properly used, they might get quite a few volunteers."

"Why?" Skilly asked. "Not they fight."

"Not everyone would agree," Niles said.

"Jeffi, you crazy. Falkenberg, maybe he get mad enough, he talk them mercs around, but it not they fight unless they get paid."

"Yoshida shall be reprimanded," Murasaki said.

Skilly snorted. "And all you people, they out of the chain of command in my area," she said flatly. "No operations without regular Helot clearance."

"As you wish, Field Prime," Murasaki said, inclining his head. The two leaders stared at each other with mutual respect and equally absolute lack of trust. The Meijian rose and left without further word.

Niles looked from the technoninja's back to Skilly's face. *Alike,* he thought with an inward shudder. *How could I have missed it? What did that old book say about Kritias, the pupil of Socrates who had become one of the Thirty Tyrants?*

"When a man is freed from the bonds of dogma and custom, where will he run? He has gotten loose, of the soul if you like the word, or from whatever keeps a man on two feet instead of four. And now Kritias too is running on the mountains, with no more between him and his will than a wolf has."

When Niles was a child he had loved Turkish Delight; on a visit, Adrian Bronson had grown tired of his whining and bought him a whole box while they were at a county fair on the estate. Niles could remember the exact moment when pleasure turned to disgust, just before the nausea struck; he had never been able to eat the stuff again. No lessons like those you teach yourself, his grand uncle had said to his mother. . . .

"Sometimes Skilly think that one, he a sick puppy," she said meditatively, looking after the Meijian. "Likes to hurt people. But terror only effective if it be used selective . . . Or maybe he not care so much who wins? Maybe he bossman doan care?" Then her gaze sharpened, fixing on the Englishman's face.

"Ah, Jeffi, Skilly think you maybe getting second thoughts, maybe think Skilly not been telling you everything," she said, grinning at him. "Too late, me mon." She stepped closer, over the piled trunks and boxes, puffing a hand under his chin. "River of fire and a river of blood between you and de old life now. You be Skilly's now, Jeffi. Skilly's and the Dreadful Bride's. Come on, we got a long ride ahead and a battle to fight."

"You know, George, I'm breaking the Code," Barton said to the other officer beside him in the lounge of the blimp. "The unwritten sections, at least."

"Oh?" The other man looked up from his laptop.

The sunlight was fading outside, even from two thousand meters altitude; below the oblong shadow of the lighter-than-air craft had faded as darkness fell. They were two hundred kilometers west of Mandalay now, angling north across the bend of the Eurotas to reach the lands north of Olynthos. Below them were the vast marshes around Lake Lynkestis, not a light showing in all the area from horizon to horizon. The lounge was walled in clear plastic, a warm bubble of light in the vast black stillness; somehow the throbbing of the diesels was a lonely sound as they leaned back in their chairs with tobacco and coffee and brandy. Behind them, the riding beacons of the other five aircraft were drifting amber spots.

"Yeah. Gettin' emotionally involved with the clients."

"I know how you feel," Slater said. "Homelike here, isn't it?"

Barton pulled on his cigarette and nodded; they had a lot in common, despite Slater being half a generation younger. Both from the American southwest, he by birth and Slater by heritage. Their families were from country areas that had changed little since the coming of the CoDominium; where as recently as their teen-age years it had still been possible to pretend they lived as free men in a free country. Barton had been born in Arizona, and George Slater had visited kin there often enough. Slater's mother was a colonial from a largely American-settled planet as well.

"Better than home, if it weren't for the war," Barton said. "After we—there I go again, after the *clients* win—I'm giving serious thought about buying back my contract from the Legion and making a go of it in the Royal Army."

"Can't resist being a brigadier, eh?" Slater said, laughing silently. His face creased, leathery with long exposure to strange suns; he was a tall whipcord-lean man, brown hair sun-faded.

"It doesn't hurt," Barton said frankly. *The pay isn't spectacular,* he reminded himself. No better than what he'd been getting as a Captain in the Legion, considerably less than he'd usually made as an independent merc commander with Barton's Bulldogs, if you factored in the foreign-exchange difficulties. The opportunity to use his skills on a larger canvas was more important: it had not been easy, going back down the scale after having his own outfit. Before Falkenberg smashed it back on Tanith; that had been just business, of course. *Business, and I was on the wrong side. Didn't used to be so clear cut, right side, wrong side. Now—*

Now it's important.

"I'll be hanging up my guns in another few years no matter what," he went on, discarding a frayed toothpick and fishing another out of a pocket. He had picked that habit up on

Thurstone, when tobacco was unavailable. "I'm damn near sixty, George. Long past time to think of settling down." Even with regenn, it was half a lifetime.

"Me too," Slater replied. Barton glanced over at him in surprise. "Cindy doesn't think dragging the kids from one base to another is all that good an idea," he explained. "Wants them to have a home before they leave the nest. I always wanted land of my own; anyway, it's what I was raised to. Dad doesn't talk about it much, but he still remembers losing the ranch."

And you'd waited long enough, Barton thought, with a certain wistful envy. Slater's father had been with Falkenberg since before he took over the 42nd CoDominium Marines, the unit that had followed him to become the Legion. His wife was a colonial, country-born. They had four children, from three to ten.

"For that matter," Barton said, "I think Pete Owensford wouldn't mind having a home. He may have found someone to share it with—"

"That Halleck girl?"

"Well, I notice he found reasons to visit the Halleck ranch, and now Lydia Halleck's in Sparta City for a year at University—"

"Well, well," Slater said. "Hadn't heard that last part. Hell, Ace, we're none of us getting any younger. And this is a good world, good in lots of ways."

"Can't fault the Spartans for their terms," Barton said meditatively. Lateral transfer at their brevet ranks was the least of it; automatic Citizenship, landgrants . . . with their Royal Army pay and partial Legion pensions thrown in, they would be well-to-do men by local standards.

"Mmmm-*hm*. And," Slater went on, "this place is one of the few I've seen whose government doesn't make me want to pinch my nose and 'holdeth aside the skirt of the garment.'"

Barton's face went bleak. "Yeah. I like the people, too. Which is why I've started wanting to win even more than usual." *You always did; a matter of self-respect, the Code, and of course you lost fewer men that way.*

"Agreed." A shrug. "Of course, we're getting a lesson in what Christian Johnny always said, remember? 'Soldiers are the cleanup crew.'"

One of Falkenberg's history lessons was on how seldom military men had much say in how their efforts were applied. Armed force was a blunt instrument in politics, liable to do more harm than good unless aimed with extreme precision. At best, it bought time and space for the political leaders to repair the political mistakes that had left no choice but violence in the first place.

The other man nodded and sipped at his brandy. *Damned good,* he thought.

"Well," he said, "at least this time we aren't hired by the ones who screwed up." *To bury the evidence under the bodies.*

"Dad's looking into another matter," George Slater said. "Loyalties. It's easy to see what holds the Spartans to their cause. The Helots are another matter. Whitlock's working on political persuasion. We should too."

"Sure," Barton said. "How?"

"Oh, maybe remind them just what their leaders do. Left their troops and ran like hell at the Dales, saved their skins by sacrificing everyone else. Get that story across, and the first time they get a setback it's every man for himself." Slater tamped tobacco into a pipe. "It's not as if the people they're following are admirable. In any way."

"Maybe their troops don't know that—"

"I'm sure they don't," Slater said. "If they did, would they stick?"

"Maybe some would. Revolutionaries. I learned all about fanatics on Thurstone, hell, before you were born. But it's something to think about." He looked at his watch. "Another day's work in Olynthos," he said. Slater would be taking over there; it was the second-largest city on Sparta, center of the Middle and Upper Valleys of the Eurotas. "And then on to the wilds of the north for me. Should be interesting."

"Are you all *right,* Margreta?" Melissa asked. She had to lean close and put her ear to the young soldier's, given the noise level. "You're pale as a sheet."

"I'm fine," Margreta shouted back. Her fingers were shaking slightly as she put on her helmet; the noise level dropped immediately, as the sonic sensors automatically filtered out the background. "It's just . . . the news about Lieutenant Lefkowitz, you know? Everyone in the Legion is—" *Mostly mad enough to rip out veins with their teeth,* she thought. *With me, it's more personal. I've got to work with the animals who did that.*

Melissa nodded and gave the younger woman's shoulder a squeeze. Margreta smiled back. *Be here. Be ready for possible extraction,* were all the orders that had come from her clandestine Helot contact.

It had run through Fort Plataia like fire through standing grass, and the execution of the four Helots had done little to calm the anger. The CoDominium authorities had little alternative but to accept that as sufficient; the Legionnaires would not. *The Brotherhoods seem to be almost as angry,* Margreta thought. There had been a delegation of condolence, and a new rush of enlistments. Frightening to have the enemy's nature driven home so thoroughly, but there was something in knowing you had a big family to protect you . . . or at least avenge you.

The new vehicle assembly bay was even louder than usual. Armored vehicles were moving down the conveyor, and the air was full of the ugly howling rasp of heavy-duty grinding machines, the ozone-smelling flash of electrowelders and the whine of pneumatic tools. Each light tank started the line as an open frame; as it passed down computer-controlled overhead cranes swung in, first with sections of hull-armor to be welded on, then with components and engines and transmissions. Lighter parts like the roadwheels and tracks ran on trolleys up to the sides of the line, and the last thing to be added was the turret with its basket, lowered onto the Cataphract. These particular models were SP guns, with 155mm gun-howitzers in big boxy turrets.

"Just shows what you can do if you have to," Melissa said again, smiling and waving about at the vast extensions which had nearly doubled the area of von Alderheim Works #2. This time the Legion helmet delivered it in conversational tones. "After the war, we'll have twice the capacity we did going in. Of course, most of it will be for tanks."

They had become friendly, after meeting at the University's software department. Melissa von Alderheim was more than the daughter of Sparta's wealthiest industrialist and fiancee to Lysander Collins; she was the best CAD-CAM designer on the planet. That was a rare art, these days, when design changes were mostly a matter of styling and BuInt suppressed all real change. Much of the new output of war machines was her doing.

"Two fifty per month of the AFVs, and fifty of the SP howitzers?" she said.

Melissa nodded. "It's the stabilization and optics that's the bottleneck," she said. "We're getting the Friedlander stuff through now. And an inquiry about what we're using it for."

A natural worry; Daimlerwerk Friedland AG had lucrative markets for armored fighting vehicles all through this sector, and hiring out their panzer units was even more important to them. Vehicles were parked outside, several hectares of them waiting to be driven down to the plant's docks on Constitution Bay, everything from jeeps and trucks to the self-propelled guns she had seen under construction inside. The landing platforms were busy, barges and steamboats and diesels unloading metals and forms, loading with vehicles and engines and general goods for transshipment upriver.

"This is going to cause the enemy hard trouble," Margreta said. Then shivered. *Why am I frightened?* she thought. It was just a routine consulting trip . . . and Major Owensford said a hunch was your subconcious telling you something.

The main gate of the factory was on the other side of the complex, facing the main road into town; von Alderheim Works #2 had been built on a greenfield site, with plenty of room for expansion.

FAMP. Almost too loud to be an explosion, a pillar of flame reaching for the sky. *Truck-bomb*, she thought numbly. Lots of big articulated trucks driving up there all the time, although *how* they had got a bomb past the checkpoints and inspections . . . *Of course. Use a legitimate load of explosives. And a suicide driver*. Who would look for a bomb in a ten-kilo load of shell filler? Even this far away the blast was perceptible, and the two Royal Army troopers guarding them wheeled, their rifles coming up automatically.

God, please, God, Margreta prayed, an atheist's desperate reflex as she cleared her pistol.

"Wait a minute," she said to herself, crouching and looking around. Nothing, except the normal work of the docks grinding to a halt as everyone turned to look at the pillar of smoke. The explosion was spectacular, but not really damaging. No secondary blasts . . . "*It's a diversion!*" she shouted. "Get—"

KRAK. A Peltast rifle; the massive 15mm round smashed through one soldier's spine and out the front of his chest in a shower of bone and blood, ignoring his body armor as if it were tissue. Impact sledged him forward with his limbs flopping like a rag doll's. Margreta drew and dove for cover; her armored torso struck Melissa at the same moment, sending the slight Spartan woman four steps back on her heels toward the shelter of an APC. The Legionnaire's free hand was reaching up to drag the other woman down into safety and—

KRAK. The 15mm round, which would have punched through Melissa's center of mass if Margreta had not moved her, struck and skimmed all along her arm from shoulder to fingertips instead, shattering bone and tearing muscle. She went down with limp finality, her head thudding into the tungsten-steel cleats of the personnel carrier's treads. *KRAK*. Into the leg of the downed soldier, blasting it off at the shin.

"God *damn!*" Margreta shouted, pulling her communicator free and dropping the useless pistol from the other so that she could fumble a hypo from her belt and slap it against Melissa's neck. Gray skin, rapid breathing, sweat . . . shock.

"Medic, dustoff, Ms. von Alderheim is down, repeat, dustoff soonest," she said. "Wound trauma, internal bleeding, multiple fractures of the right arm." The other Spartan trooper rose from his crouch and fired.

"Talkins, Capital Seven here," a calm voice said from her hand unit. Her chest seemed to turn tight and squeeze; that was her Helot contact's codename. "Make sure of the von Alderheim woman if you can. Quickly."

God damn, she thought to herself. It seemed to come from some distant part of her mind, while her body and mouth did things on their own.

"Guard Graffin von Alderheim," she said sharply, drawing her pistol and moving forward into the maze of parked vehicles. The soldier shouted uselessly behind her, and there was the heavy *bwanggg* of a Peltast round ricochetting off armor, sending him back to cover.

"God *damn.*" Dangerous, but she had to get out of the vicinity of Melissa. Otherwise, it would be difficult to explain her survival.

And there were some things that you couldn't do even to keep your cover.

"God damn, we Legionnaires are supposed to *stop* this sort of thing." That stopped *her,* for a moment. *We.* We had always been her and George, after Mother went away. A helicopter went by overhead, and she shook herself back to awareness.

CHAPTER SEVEN

Thomas Cook & Company: Almanac of Interstellar Travel:

Transit times for standard merchant charter:
(Standard Terran month of 30 days)
Earth–Sparta (via Tanith): **6 months**
Tanith–New Washington/Franklin system: **4 months**
New Washington–Sparta (via Tanith): **9 months**
—*all travel times may be reduced by 50% or more for naval couriers, warships or assault transports.*

When bad men combine, the good must associate;
otherwise they will fall, one by one, an unpitied
sacrifice in a contemptible struggle.

—Edmund Burke,
Thoughts on the Cause of the Present Discontents

Further, war, which is simply the subjection of all life
and property to one momentary aim, is morally vastly
superior to the mere violent egoism of the individual;
it develops power in the service of a supreme general
idea and under a discipline which nevertheless per-
mits supreme heroic virtue to unfold. Indeed, war
alone grants to mankind the magnificent spectacle of a
general submission to a general aim.

—Jakob Burkhardt,
Reflections on History

"The bones in the arm and shoulder were severely damaged.

Shattered would not be too strong a word," the doctor said, with the impersonal sympathy of her craft. "Massive edema and tissue damage as well, from hydrostatic shock."

Lysander listened, but most of his attention was elsewhere. Melissa's face was barely visible through the quartz view port in the regeneration tank universally known as a mummy case. Her head was covered with a white surgical bandage but it looked more like an old fashioned night cap. There was no makeup, but she seldom wore much anyway, and enough remained of her tan to give some illusion of healthy color. She looked relaxed, even peaceful, but very helpless, and very still. *She's always been so active. And now—*

A nurse shouldered through, studied displays and touched a few of the controls around the cocoon-like capsule of the regeneration tank, and left silently. There were half a dozen Life Guards outside the door, and a sandwich-armor slab closed off the window, but otherwise the small private room in the St. Thomas Royal Hospital was nothing out of the ordinary. Every ward was overcrowded with war casualties, and the regeneration clinics more than any.

Lysander swallowed, holding his helmet awkwardly in hands that suddenly felt too big. *Freiherr* von Alderheim was there, looking somehow deflated; Lysander's father was there as well, holding himself erect now, but with an effort that showed the stoop lurking beneath it. Recovery from the enemy's virus attack was proceding, but still slowly. Queen Adriana stood by, holding her husband's arm, almost visibly willing strength into it.

God, I hate hospitals, Lysander thought. There was the smell, of course, but that wasn't as strong as in a battlefield surgical unit. Mostly there was a *feel* of sickness to them, a concentrated misery that soaked into the walls themselves.

"That's fairly straightforward regenn work, though," Dr. Ruskin continued; her fingers touched the scanner equipment tucked into the loops of her green gown slightly nervously. This *was* rather distinguished company for a sickroom. "At least seventy-five percent, possibly complete recovery. It's the neurological damage that had us worried most of the morning. Ten hours of Sir Harlan's best work. It was, well, what he was able to do was wonderful, that's all."

"She will recover?" von Alderheim asked.

"Yes, we think so."

She doesn't sound very sure, Lysander thought.

"And she can still have children?" von Alderheim insisted.

"Yes, there were no injuries of that kind," the doctor said. This time she sounded much more confidant.

"Does she know we're here?" Queen Adriana asked.

"No, Madame," Dr. Ruskin said. "We're using a neurological hookup to keep her asleep until the regeneration stimulation process takes hold."

"So there's no point in her father and my son staying here?"

"I wish they wouldn't," Ruskin said. "We're terribly crowded, and some of the staff are awfully young; they want to see His Highness close up, and that can be disruptive. It really would be better if you go back and wait at the Palace. We'll let you know in plenty of time before we wake her up."

"She shouldn't be alone," Lysander said. "We failed her. I failed. Her and the whole planet, I can't protect them and—"

"Nonsense," the Queen said. "You can't be everywhere at once."

"I know, Mother, but—"

"And the doctor is right, Lysander. We are in the way."

"How long? Until she wakes up?" Lysander demanded.

"Nine days minimum. More likely eleven."

"Hmm. You're certain there's nothing we can do here?"

"Nothing but get in the way," the doctor said. "You could go say a few words to anyone off duty in the staff lounge. They all want to see you. But otherwise—" Her voice softened. "You needn't worry that she'll be neglected, Highness. There's no one here who doesn't love the Princess. Soon to be Princess. We'll have her well in time for the wedding, Prince Lysander. I swear it."

"Thank you. And there's work to do." He started toward the door, then went back inside the room alone after the others left. Lysander, Prince of Sparta, put both hands on the tank and spoke quietly. "I'm sorry," he said. He straightened and looked at the blocked off window as if he could see through to the city outside, to the city and the countryside beyond. "I'm sorry." He stood that way a long time. When he turned to leave, his face might have been carved from stone.

Dion Croser stepped to the edge of the dais and raised his hands. Silence fell across the stadium like a ripple through the ocean of forty thousand faces, all turned toward him. Behind him his image stood, fifty meters high on the great screen; he flashed his famous grim smile and leaned his hands on the lectern. It was full night, but the blazing rectangles of light all around the upper tiers made a white day of the sloping seats, shutting out the dark and the stars. Searchlights stood between them, shining vertical pillars thousands of meters up into the sky until they merged into a canopy of white haze;

between them were giant Movement banners, the black circle on red with the red = sign in its midst.

"Victory!" he said.

The word rolled and boomed back from the ampitheatre, and the crowd roared. A wave of pure noise that thudded into you like a fist in the gut. Terrifying, if you were the crowd's enemy. Exhilaration beyond words when the adoration of the many-throated beast struck. The stadium was just off Government House Square; they would be hearing it in the Palace . . . hearing it in every house in Sparta City.

Power, he thought. *This* is *power.*

The sound went on and on, building until the ground shook with it; the white-noise surf of it gradually modulating as the disciplined blocks of NCLF militants chanted.

Dion the Leader! Dion to Power!" More and more falling in with the chant. *"DION THE LEADER! DION TO POWER!"*

He listened, waiting for the peak moment; they were like some smooth sculptor's material under his command, and he could feel threads of unity stretching out from his mind to each of theirs. The sound was unaltered, but he could feel a moment's smooth pause inside himself, like the hesitation of water at the top of a fountain's arc. He raised his hands, and silence fell like a curtain into an aching void.

"My people," he said, and there was a sigh like a vast moan.

You are my people, he thought. *Foolish and brutish and short-sighted, you are what others have made you. Made you, and then despised you for it; but you will follow me, and I will give you back your pride. Make you worthy of yourselves.*

"My people—the people of Sparta! Tonight we come here together to celebrate a great victory, a victory over oppression, over arrogant elitism. For half a year, we have campaigned together in the Constitutional referendum. Peacefully—"

—except for the riots and so forth—

"—we have gone from neighborhood to neighborhood, from town to town, explaining our just cause—the cause of democracy, of universal suffrage and human equality. Not once have we forbidden those who oppose us, those who have usurped the People's power, from arguing against us. Tonight we see the results!"

It was a warm early-summer night, and the lights and crowd made it a hot one; he could feel the thin film of sweat on his face fighting with the makeup artist's powder, and trickling down his flanks. Smell it as well. That did not bother him; it was a sign of honest labor, of the labor that had earned him this prize. He made a small motion with the fingers of his left hand, and behind him numbers sprang out across the simulacrum of his own face.

"Two thirds have voted *yes* to the great question of our day: *Should all Spartans share equally in the sovereign franchise of citizenship as their inalienable right?* The People have spoken! Let those who dare deny their voice and their right!"

Another roar, harder this time, with an undertone of guttural menace that bristled the hair along his spine.

"Fellow Spartans—fellow *citizens*—" another crashing bark of cheering "—our struggle has been long and difficult. I must confess," and he lowered his eyes, "there was a time when I too, was heedless of the sufferings of the people—better than the corrupt clique around the self-appointed kings only because I was ignorant rather than callous."

Another wash of sound, denial this time.

"Yes! But I went to *the People*, learned from *the People*—" he raised his face, letting humility slide into an expression of iron determination "—and together, we built the Movement. Only a few of us at first, but more and more as the years went by. The vanguard of the People, building their power brick by brick."

He gripped the sides of the lectern, leaning forward and letting his voice go low and confidential. The sound-system here was excellent.

"The kings thought they could stop us with bribes and lies, by having the Milice and the RSMP break heads. Many of our brave comrades—" he shot one hand out towards the NCLF contingents, with their Party banners inscribed with the names of the martyrs "—have fallen. Yet not once have we answered their provocations in kind, despite the brutalities, the brutalities that have driven some poor souls into the hills. Helots in truth, ground down under the heel of militarism—and while we cannot condone their actions, we understand only too well their reasons.

"And that is how we'll build the New Order—brick by brick, with discipline and patience. First, we'll present the results of the people's will to the kings. Then, whether they agree or not—because those same results show that *ours* is the rightful authority—we'll hold elections for the Constitutional Convention, and there we, the People's choice, will make a new Sparta, one that will produce something besides the endless taxes and war and poverty the kings and their flunkies have brought us. And then we'll elect a *government of the people!*"

"DION THE LEADER! DION TO POWER! DION! DION! DION!"

This time he let it go on much longer, falling away raggedly into silence.

"But," he said, then paused while the quiet built. *"But.* If the Royalist clique refuse to heed the people's will *then*—if they try to turn the guns of the bandits and misguided youngsters they call the Royal Spartan Army on us—why, *then*—" His lean, slab-and-angle face contorted, and a fist crashed down on the podium. *"They'll feel the people's anger!"*

A chopping gesture cut short the answering howl. "I make not threats," he continued blandly. "United, we'll carry the people's cause to victory. You have done a great deal, and there's a great deal more to be done. Tonight, enjoy your well-earned victory."

He drew himself up, and gave the Movement salute, fists clenched and wrists crossed over his head, then wheeled and walked briskly through the door beneath the huge overhead display screen.

"Congratulations, Leader!"

He waved to the crowd of NCLF functionaries; his bodyguards closed in around him, protecting from all but a few of the hands thrust forward. Croser walked slowly, grabbing the proferred hands and calling people by name, he made a point of knowing as many as could. Fragments reached him: *best speech ever* and, *inspiring.* It was that, he thought critically; a first-rate professional job of work, if he did say so himself. Oratory and organization were the basic skills of the revolutionist, and he had both.

There were only a few of the inner circle in the room where he sat to let the specialists sponge off the makeup. One of them was Murasaki, he thought—it was difficult to tell, with the Meijian—but most were section-heads and the analytical staff, going over the effect of the referendum campaign and the meeting tonight on public opinion.

"That should throw about one percent of the Citizen body to us," the senior statistician was saying. "About two percent to the SCA. Unfortunately, it'll also firm up most of the rest with this new Crown Loyalist Party."

Croser scowled slightly, holding out his fingers for a cigarette before he stripped off the tunic and began to towel down his torso; his neck and shoulders were beginning to ache slightly with the leftover tension of his performance. The Loyalist-Pragmatist merger was not unforseen, but it was still a negative development. So was the tightening loyalty of many non-Citizens to the Royalist cause; loyalty to their Citizen employers, in many cases. Particularly out in the long-settled parts of the countryside, where it was becoming a serious embarassment to the Helots. Bad enough that most of the Lower Valley had either given the referendum a "no" answer, or boycotted the whole operation. *Too many boycotted the election, and the Royals know that, know we faked it, but they aren't saying anything. Why?* But it didn't matter. Numbers didn't count. What counted was strength. *And we're gaining, and they're losing, because we know we're going to win.*

Croser's image faded from the television screen. Dr. Caldwell Whitlock stared at the set for a moment. "Man could charm the scales off a snake," he said. He turned off the set and looked up at his visitor. "Drink? You look like you could use one."

"I suppose," Lysander said absently. "But it doesn't do any good."

"No, reckon not, and good thing you know that," Whitlock said. "But this time I think no harm done. Bourbon all right?"

"Sure. Dr. Whitlock, we've got to do something about that man."

"Well, yeah, you surely do," Whitlock said. One section of the book case behind his desk was hinged. It swung out, books and all, to reveal a small cabinet. Whitlock poured two drinks, added water, and handed one across his desk. "Cheers. Yes, sir, your Highness, you surely do. So why don't you?"

"What should we do?" Lysander asked.

"Turn him over to Jesus and Catherine Alana," Whitlock said. "I doubt he knows everything, but he'll sure know enough you could put a big dent in their operations."

"Just arrest him? Question him with drugs, or worse? We can't do that."

"Well, you *can* do that," Whitlock said. "Least for now you can. Give him more time and maybe you won't be able to. But right now you can, and you'd save lives by doin' it." Whitlock sipped at his drink and looked over the top of the glass at Lysander. "For instance, I expect he approved that attack on your lady."

Lysander looked as if Whitlock had struck him. "You believe that."

"Surely do. Can't believe that wasn't approved at their highest levels. Tell you another thing. I hope you got real good people watchin' that hospital. Real good, and a lot of 'em, 'cause they're likely to try again."

"Why? What did Melissa do to them?"

"She did plenty," Whitlock said. He ran his stubby fingers through his mane of white hair. "Plenty. Designed those tanks for one. Snubbed Mr. Croser and that Skilly woman at a night club for another."

"I didn't know they'd met."

"Happened when you were off-planet," Whitlock said. "People tell me things maybe they don't tell you. Story got back here you were on Tanith all set up with that hotel girl, Lady Melissa took to being squired around by the youngest Harriman boy. I guess I'm not surprised no one told you."

"No, no one did—"

"Don't reckon it mattered a lot either," Whitlock said. "Far as I can see she was pretty careful 'bout where they went, public places, avoid scandal. Sensible lady, even when she's madder'n hell at you. With good reason, too. 'Course her whole point was that you'd find out, bit of irony there you never did. Anyway, one night they went to a charity thing, and Croser was there with that Skilly. He got drunk, started talking to her about you and what you'd be doing on Tanith. I don't know what all was said, but it ended up she slapped Croser hard across the face and walked out. Looked for a minute like Croser was going to do something about that, but nothing came of it. But he sure didn't like it, and neither did that Skilly."

"I never knew— But that's not reason to have her killed!"

"Might be to him," Whitlock said. "Just might be, and if she said the wrong things about that Skilly person, there'd be another. But the real reason to kill her is to get at you. If they thought she didn't like you, thought she was goin' through with this marriage for politics, she'd be safe enough, they'd purely love to have you in a bad marriage where you're likely to do something stupid. But the way you two been carryin' on, like love birds, it's pretty clear you made up whatever problems you had, and that's not so good, the way they see it."

"What the hell is it to them?"

"Come off it, Highness," Whitlock said. "You got to know, for all practical purposes right now you *are* the nation. Oh, sure, people love your father, but they think of him as the old king, nice old man, symbol of the nation and all that, but still, he's the old king. And they trust David to do what's best if there's peace, but there ain't no peace, and they don't see there'll be any peace without you make it happen. Now most times maybe it's best you don't act like you know all this, but this is a time for some plain talk. Whatever future this experiment in the good society has got, right now it pretty much rests on you."

Lysander didn't say anything. Whitlock nodded. "So, we got that straight. Now, about Croser."

"But— Dr. Whitlock, he's been careful, there's no evidence to connect him or his political movement with any of this. No criminal acts."

"Well, that's right, and if that's what you're waiting for, you'll never get it," Whitlock said. "Son, a long time ago a man named Burke said that for evil to win all that's got to happen is that good men do nothin'. That's happening here. You're in a war, and you got to fight it like a war."

"And if we get like the enemy what's the point of winning?"

"That's what King David's always sayin'," Whitlock said. "Your father, too, sometimes, not so much now. Lysander, let me tell you something, you couldn't in a million years be like them even if you was to work at it." Whitlock studied papers on his desk for a moment. "You better think about it. I'll go on plannin' the politics for you, and Pete Owensford will go on fightin' the enemy for you, good men will go on dyin' for you, and hell, it may be enough, Prince Lysander, it just may be enough, and maybe you got a point. You've got a decent government, and Lord knows I'd hate to see it turn mean, but you better think, Your Highness. Just how many of your people are you willing to see killed just so Citizen Dion Croser can have his legal rights?"

CHAPTER EIGHT

To be a general it is sufficient to pay well, command
well, and hang well.
                              —Sir Ralph Hopton *circa* 1689

The discipline enforced by firing squad or pistol is
inferior to that accepted, self-imposed discipline which
characterizes good soldiers. Regulations designed to
keep dull-witted conscripts together on the shoulder-
to-shoulder battlefields of the blackpowder era are
inappropriate in an age when weapons and tactics
demand dispersion on the battlefield, and when the
initiative may be more important than blind obedience. In the last analysis fighting spirit centres on the
morale of the individual soldier and the small group of
comrades with whom he fights.
                    —John Keegan and Richard Holmes; *Soldiers*

If I learned nothing else from war, it taught me the
falseness of the belief that wealth, material resources,
and industrial genius are the real sources of a nation's
military power. These things are but the stage setting:
those who manage them but the stage crew.
The play's the thing. Finally, every action large or
small is decided by what happens there on the line
where men take the final chance of life or death. And
so in the final and greatest reality, that national
strength lies only in the hearts and spirits of men.
                              —S.L.A. Marshall

Crofton's Encyclopedia of the Inhabited Planets (2nd Edition):

Stora Mine: Mining settlement in the southern foot-hills of the *Kupros Mountains* (q.v.), north of *Lake Alexander* in the Upper Valley section of the Eurotas river, on the planet *Sparta* (q.v.). The initial CoDominium University survey of Sparta indicated that the eroded volcano later christened *Storaberg* contained unusual concentrations of metallic ores. Researchers hypothesized that during the original uplift process which produced the Kupros Mountains, a "plug" of freakishly mineral-rich magma was extruded through a fissure. Over time, the rapid erosive forces produced by Sparta's 1.22 G stripped away the covering of softer rock, exposing the core and depositing alluvial metal deposits extensively in the area. The rock of northern slopes of the mountain contains up to 8% copper, 6% lead, 2% silver and significant quantities of platinum, palladium and thorium group metals; locally higher concentrations are studded through the mass of the mountain and nearby deposits of "ruddle" hematite have iron contents of up to 83%. Exploratory mining began during the period of CoDominium administration and full-scale exploitation commenced with the chartering of Stora Mines Inc. in 2041. Both open-pit and shaft mining is carried on; facilities include a geothermal power plant, smelters and concentration plants, the 215-kilometer electrified railway to Lake Alexander, and miscellaneous support, maintenance and repair industries.

Description: The settlement of Stora Mine lies on an eroded peneplane at the northeastern edge of Storaberg Mt. Built-up areas are largely confined to "ribbon" developments along the valleys of the northeast-southwest tending ridges. The central town is laid out on a grid basis, forming an H surrounding two public squares, and includes a business district, public buildings and the railroad station. Total population (2090) is 27,253, including many temporary workers housed in company barracks. Climate is severe, roughly analogous to northeastern Minnesota or southern Siberia; the longer seasons make this a loose comparison, however. The silt-filled basins and rocky hills of the piedmont zone running down to the lakeshore have been extensively developed to supply the mining labor force and enjoy more moderate temperatures . . .

✧　　✧　　✧

There is a semi-facetious classification of officers
long familiar to many of the military fraternity. It does
credit to the understanding of its unknown originator
as well as to his sense of humor. Its lightly sketched
implications when further explored and a little amplified approached conclusions that are not so humorous.
Using the terms "brilliant," "energetic," "stupid," and
"lazy" and applying them to a selected group of people
of whom the stupidest and laziest may still be well
above the average of brilliance and energy in the general
community, a scale for measurement of certain aspects
of individual military potential may be constructed. . . .
     The Class Four officer we must study diligently, to
devise the means of identifying him in, and eliminating him from, the military services. The combination
of stupidity and energy is the formula of ambition
other than a laudable kind. The ambition generated is
too often entirely personal and totally unconcerned
with any elements contributing to the general welfare
that are not also an occasion of individual prefer-
ment . . . Morally courageous he is not, since this
quality is all too often incompatible with personal
ambition. Given experience, he may be to a degree
learned. He may be cautions, crafty, cunning, and is
seldom lacking in decisiveness, but he can never be
wise, just, loyal, or completely honest. All too often he
achieves a personally successful military career.
Energetic stupidity, once invested with authority and
allowed to accumulate experience, can do a convincing imitation of a hard-driving professional soldier . . .
                              —Joseph Maxwell Cameron,
                              The Anatomy of Military Merit

Winter still lay heavy on the southern slopes of the Kupros
Mountains. The dawn was bright but hard, and the cold wind
sighed mournfully through the branches of the dark pines and
leafless birch-trees. These mountains were not as high as the
Drakons; the quick erosion of a heavy-gravity world had
scoured them down, although the peaks were still glacier-
crowned fangs four thousand meters high. The lower slopes
were a wilderness of canyon and gully badland, tumbled
boulders larger than houses, rushing torrents and new forests
just gaining a foothold amid the shattered granite and volcanic scree.

Skida Thibodeau sat looking thoughtfully down the long slope toward the foothills; Lake Alexander was invisible beyond. Cloud-shadow moved across the huge chaotic landscape, and the young sun tinged the snowdrifts with pink. An orderly handed her a cup of coffee, and she chewed on a ration bar, a leather of fruits and nuts. It was cold enough to make the hairs in her nostrils stick together when she inhaled, but snow might begin to melt by midafternoon; weather turned quickly this time of year in the Upper Valley.

"OK," she said after a moment. "Von Reuter, how are the troops?"

"Those in the latest wave from the Dales are now fully rested. The first arrifals are restless." The German-born ex-CD officer had been in charge of keeping the inflow inconspicuous until she arrived. "Some attempted to desert."

"We doan allow no deserters."

"Ja, we know how to deal with those." The German shrugged. "We have done so. But these are not regular soldiers, and we are short of non-commissioned officers. Too many were lost covering our retreat in the Dales."

"Hard fight, but we win in the Dales," Skilly said. "Victory there. Show we can stand up to the Cits."

"I agree. And so we tell the recruits," von Reuter said evenly. "But they were also told they will win soon. They believe this, but one does not learn patience in Welfare Island. The war goes on, for many longer than anything they have ever done in their miserable lives."

"You knew what kind of recruits you were getting," Skilly said. Her voice hardened. "You tell me you know how to make soldiers out of them. You say CoDo's been doing that for fifty years, taking gang-banger homeboys and making them Marines."

"And so we have, Field Prime. But we do not also hide from police while we train CoDominium Marines, ja? When they graduate they parade, people cheer, pretty girls admire uniforms. Not here." He straightened formally. "Field Prime, if you are not satisfied with my performance—"

"You not thinking of quitting on Skilly?" Everyone in the room stiffened, and tension mounted. Then, suddenly, she grinned wolfishly. "You doin' fine. Doan worry so much. Everything goin' just like we want."

The Helots had been moving men and supplies from the Dales to the Kupros in dribs and drabs since the midwinter battles. It was a long way from the Dales, north and east along the foothills. Longer when you had to move in small bodies and take extreme care not to be observed. The Kupros held few people away from the mining settlements, but there were ranches in the hill-and-basin country of the piedmont, and the odd trapper elsewhere.

"You want fighting, we do that, all right. Now listen up, everyone." The dozen or so commanders leaned closer. "Operational plans you all got, so Field Prime will tell you the general stuff again. We not trying to hold what we take, but this be no hit-and-run, either. Two overall objectives: temporary economic damage, maybe some loot, but mainly we demoralize the militia. Then it easier next time."

She dusted her hands, set the cup down on the pine needles and wrapped her arms around her knees. The hard wolfish faces about her were intent. Everything seemed very clear: von Reuter's methodical clock-mind making notes, Two-knife's rock solidness, Niles still with a little of the detached air—*not as much, maybe he getting over it; this fight show it one way or the other*—the others frowning a little. One of them raised a hand.

"Field Prime, the original planning called for maximum attack on off-world mining equipment. May I ask why that's been changed?" They were all aware of the importance of denying the Royalists foreign exchange to buy weapons systems.

"Because, Hernandez, due to our, ah, consultants, and other things which you got no need to know, the overall schedule been moved up. We be needing CD credits and Friedlander marks someday too. And maybe von Reuter getting them parades he wants sooner than we think."

Predatory grins at that. None of these men intended to live in caves for the rest of their lives.

"OK," Skilly continued. "So you got the schedule of targets, stuff they can replace but not quick. Now, basic, this is a terror raid. Remember, though, it *selective* terror. We has to show the workers they should be more afraid of us than the Royalists, and the Cits that fighting us is no way to protect their households—just the opposite, that the fact. *Useless if they think we kill everyone no matter what they do.* Understand me? We want to demoralize, not make cornered rats. Collateral damage in the course of operation be fine; any unauthorized murder, rape, looting or arson, I want punished quick and public and hard. Skilly will hang anyone not understand that.

"So," she went on, after meeting the eyes of each. "Next, we gots to have real careful timing. Troops, they full of beans and think they can lick the world, we convinced them we won the Dales fight. They believe that, doan matter what really happen." *And they do fight good. All of them.* For a moment she remembered the provisional companies left behind to protect the retreating leadership. *No omelets without eggs. Too many eggs that time, but Skilly learn.* "Good they got confidence, bad if they be getting the stuffing knocked out. Better we not believe our own propaganda; we still no able to fight the enemy on their own terms. We make them fight on *our* terms. First—"

"It's a good computer system," the milita staff chief of Stora Mine said; the commander was out with the troops. "Only as good as the input, of course, but it does help us coordinate things on the security side."

"I see." Ace Barton was deliberately noncommittal.

They were a very long way indeed from Sparta City—seven thousand kilometers or more by river, about half that as the crow flew—in an area crucial to the war effort. The windows on one side of this room showed the reason why. The great openpit mine had been operating for fifty years, but it had only just begun to make a mark on the jagged side of the mountain, itself a lone outlier of the Kupros range that stretched across the northern horizon. A semicircular bite had been taken out of its side, stepping up the striated rock in smooth terraces; there were huge diesel-electric trucks at work there now, hauling down the ore blasted free from the face. Another charge went off, and hundreds of tonnes slid slowly down to lie in a rubbled pile. As the dust clouds settled, hundreds of overalled figures swarmed forward with pneumatic hammers, while others waited with scoop-loaders.

The manager—her name was Olafson—nodded when she noticed the direction of his eyes.

"Bit archaeological, the technique, but it's actually cheaper than sonic crushers and robots," she said cheerfully. "Cheaper than asteroid mining, even, *if* we watch the costs carefully. This is an unusual formation: copper, silver, thorium and platinum, iron, nickel. Mechanical crushing, then powdering, chemical separation, magnetic; we ship the easier stuff in ingot form down the railway to the lake, south to the Vulcan rapids by barge and then down to Olynthos over the railway around *those*. Powdered slurry along the same route for the more refractory materials. We run some shaft mines underground as well, and this is the collection point for a lot of independent outfits up in the hills." A scowl. "Or was, before the bandits got so bad."

She indicated the jagged line of the mountains. "We've got a geothermal power station here as well, about 400 MW, so what with one thing and another we've become the second center of the Upper Valley, after Olynthos."

Anselm Barton had been examining the retrieval system; it was like much else on Sparta, a cobbled-together compromise. Bulky locally-made display monitors, rather than the thin-film liquid crystal units made elsewhere, and multiple terminals routed through ordinary laptops into the mainframe unit. That was a featureless cube about three times the size of a brief-case, hooked in turn to a databank about the same size.

"Earth-made?" he asked.

"Earth's systems are overpriced junk," Olafson replied with a snort; her civilian hat was deputy vice-president for operations of Storaberg Mines Inc. "No, from Xanadu. Thirty years old, and still works like a charm." She nodded again at his unspoken question. "Yes, we check for viral infiltration regularly, and we've had your people up on the link too, once a week. That what brings you here?"

"Part of it. We've brought some technicians along with us," Barton said. He was nervous about that. However careful these people were, they were working with old equipment and they were provincials. The Legion's own computers had Read Only Memory programming; efficient for military use, but not flexible enough for a civilian operation. *And Murasaki's technoninjas are just too damn good with computers.*

"Part of it. What's the rest of it?" she demanded. "You're here with your headquarters groups, Legionnaires at the landing field, and two battalions more on the way. Something's up?"

"Well, not really. Bit of paranoia. Here, show off your system."

"No problem," Olafson said. "Here's how we've managed it. This system's got lots of capacity; we got it cheap, that's why we've got a central unit rather than a dispersed network."

She called up a map of the mine and area. "There are about six thousand people working for the Company, a thousand or so Citizens and long-term employees, the rest casuals. As many again in dependents, service industries and so forth. We've always had a Company police"—Storaberg Mines Inc. was owned by the managers and skilled employees, mostly—"we've expanded to about five hundred men, with Citizen officers and light infantry weapons. Your Captain Alana's people checked them; we spotted half a dozen Helot plants among the recruits, and hanged them to discourage others."

"This perimeter?" Barton asked, drawing a finger along a dotted line.

The whole installation was spread out over kilometers of

rough country, patches of housing or machinery sheds in pockets of flat ground separated by forest and rocky hills.

"Well, that's the problem. It's hard enough to get people to live up here anyway, you couldn't at all if you tried to cram them in cheek-to-jowl. We've got first-rate all-weather roads, though." A true rarity on Sparta, outside the capital and some of the larger towns.

"The perimeter guard is sensors and detectors, with block-houses here"—points sprang out—"manned by the security force and by militia on rotation. If there's an alarm, all the Citizens and the reliable non-Citizens and their families concentrate here, in the Armory, or at assembly-points throughout the settlement, and move to where they're needed. All the real non-combatants, kids and so forth, head for the Armory; it's massive, mostly underground, with a cleared field of fire all around. Not that we expect an attack *here,* of course, the Helots haven't been within fifty kilometers of us, but we're also the coordinating point for the other mining settlements, and the farmlands and ranches all around the north shore of Lake Alexander. There are more of them than you'd expect, with the mines to feed. There's good land up here, it just doesn't come in big blocks like it does down in the Valley.

"And then," she continued, "we've got the woods all around the mine sown thickly with disguised sonic and visual sensors; anything suspicious is routed directly through here and to the relevant perimeter posts. Minefields all around; multiple-use, they can be set for command detonation or sonic, thermal or vibrational triggers—cost a fortune."

Barton nodded. "Okay. Now let's look at that perimeter."

"Now?"

"No time like the present." He led the way outside the room and down the corridor toward the coffee room. When they got there he ushered her inside despite her surprise, and closed the door behind him. A Legion sergeant had set up equipment on the lunch table.

"Secure, Andy?"

"Yes, sir. There was a bug, but I sort of stepped on it."

"Bug? In here?" Karen Olafson stared at the red-haired headquarters sergeant. "Are you sure?"

"Damn sure. You put it there, right?" The sergeant stared menacingly at her.

"What? General Barton—"

"She's okay, sir," Sergeant Andrew Bielskis said, continuing to study the console he had set up on the table. "That's genuine shock reaction."

"Right. Was there a bug in here, Andy?"

"Not in here, sir. But there's a couple in the corridor, and I'll bet my arse the computer system's been penetrated. Ma'am, if you'd just put your hand on this plate for me. Now the other hand here. Excellent. How's the weather outside? Know any Helots?"

Fury and curiosity were fighting it out on Karen Olafson's face. Curiosity won. "All right, General, what *is* this?"

Barton got another nod from Sergeant Bielskis. "They're planning something," Ace said. "Something big, from the number of troops they've been infiltrating into this area. Damned near a regiment."

"I—how do you know that?"

"Luck. Good and bad luck. The good luck was one of their deserters got to sleeping with a local girl, one night tried to warn her to get away before this week. Bad luck was local intelligence decided not to risk sending it on the wire—"

"Or telling me," Karen said indignantly.

"Yes, ma'am. But it took a week for the report to reach Captain Alana. Since then we've seeded some of Mace's scouts into the area. Something's up, all right. Something big and ugly."

"Oh, God— You said 'this week.'"

"Yep. So. First thing I want you to do is shut things down," Barton said. "Close off all mine operations while we do some security checks. Do it slow, make it look like routine maintenance, but start buttoning up and getting your irreplaceables secured, and I mean start right now. I'm particularly worried about that computer system. You rely on it too much."

"We can't operate without it—"

"Exactly. Andy, I want Jenny and her techs to go over this place and put in manual backups for the security stuff, especially all the control systems. That bloody computer is a point failure threat, and I don't like it. It goes down, we have a hell of a job controlling things."

"Yes, sir. We'll start in the morning—"

"No, Sergeant, you'll start tonight," Ace Barton said. "And we'll just damned well pray it's not too late."

Warrant Officer Jennifer Schramm poured coffee and sprawled in a plastic chair that couldn't have been very comfortable. It was well after midnight.

"You look like you can use a break," Ace Barton said.

"General, that's a fact."

"How much have you got done?"

"About half of it," she said. "I've got manual activation lines for the mine fields. Some bypass communications, but we're running out of optical fiber."

"More coming in tomorrow," Barton said. "What does the computer know you've done?"

"Nothing, sir. Well, it knows we shut down its access to some controls for a while, but as far as it's concerned everything's normal again. What we did, we've jury rigged a manual control console. Throw a couple of big switches and the computer's bypassed, you've got manual control." She sipped coffee. "Frankly, General, I'm amazed at how much they trusted to that damn computer."

"Think it's been penetrated?"

"I *know* it has been."

Ace frowned. "How do you know?'

"Well, I don't really, but I feel it. Fault logs. They're squeaky clean, General Barton, and I don't like that. It's like something was erased, maybe. Same for access records. Some of them are missing."

"Missing?"

"Yes, sir. Again, it just looked too damn clean so I got Andy to have a talk with a couple of the techs, and of course they were playing war games on the damn computer—and there's no record of it. Like someone wiped the access record files."

"The techs—"

"No, sir. Look, playing games might get them docked an hour's pay at worst, if anyone really gave a damn, but erasing logs, that's a firing offense, and they bloody know it."

Barton touched his communication card. "Wally."

"Honistu here."

"Wally, take a break. Come drink some coffee and put your feet up."

"Well, a little busy, but that sounds right, sir."

Jennifer looked a question.

Barton smiled. "Right. Wally's been with me a long time. My adjutant in Barton's Bulldogs. Way I asked him made it an order."

"You really think they're listening to everything?" Jennifer asked.

Ace shrugged. "This room's secure, don't know about the rest. Tell you this, if the computer's bugged, the control room is. And Andy found a bug in the corridor. It shouldn't have been there, not smart to put one there."

"Too easy to find?"

"Something like that. Not obvious, but not that hard to find

either. Almost like maybe it's an early warning? Maybe so when
we disable it they know we've found it? I don't know. I can't
think the way the rebels do."

Major Honistu came in and closed the door. "I'm damn busy,
General. What's up?"

"Sit down, Wally, and let's talk a minute. Jenny doesn't like
what she's finding in the computer. More like what she's not
finding."

Honistu nodded judicially. "I got the same ugly feeling,
General. Add in the intelligence reports, and we got problems."

"Right. What you're doing out there is important, but so
is doing a bit of thinking while we have the chance. Let's
talk."

Alarms rang in the corridor.

"That'll be it," Ace Barton said. "OK, Wally, get moving.
I'll be in central control." He led Warrant Officer Schramm
up the corridor while Honistu ran off in the other direction.

Karen Olafson sat at the central console. An alarm *wheeped*
softly, and one screen blinked red. She looked up as Barton
came in. "Emergency Network. The Torrey estate is under
attack."

The screen showed a man in combat armor thrown on over
indoor clothes. Tall, with rather long brown hair and a flam-
boyant mustache, in his thirties.

"Alan, this is General Barton."

"Barton. Alan Torrey here," he said; he spoke with the accent
of an American of the taxpayer class. "I'm definitely under
attack, by a company or better. They overran the RSMP post
up at the Velysen place, then hit here. We stopped them butt-
cold."

A grim smile; Barton decided that he rather *liked* Citizen
Alan Torrey.

"All my people are armed, I won't employ anyone I can't
trust. That gives us nearly a hundred guns, and we've been
preparing for this. The problem is the Militia reaction-force
from Danniels Mill; they came running, and hit an ambush
about four kilometers south of here. Had to fight their way
off the road and onto a hill; they've taken better than fifty
casualties, and they need help bad. I can't do it, we're holding
in our bunkers but if we come out their mortars will slaughter
us."

A man burst through the door of the operations control
center. He was hastily buckling on armor. "General alert, Karen.
General, we're sure glad you're here."

"My husband and partner," Karen said.

"Karl Olafson, general co-manager and Major of the 22nd Brotherhood, for my sins. Alan, can you give me a relay?"

"Here."

This time the screen split. "Captain Solarez here, Major Timmins is down." The new figure was crouched in a shallow hole behind a rock, with a wounded communications tech lying beside him and operating the pickup. Small-arms and explosions sounded from the background.

"Report, Captain," the militia Major said.

"I've got thirty dead, sixty wounded and three hundred effectives, that counts the walking wounded. We had to leave most of our heavy weapons with the transport. The enemy have us under visual observation and they're sending us heavy fire, medium mortars, 84 and 105mm recoilless rifles, heavy machine guns. Nothing fancy but they've got plenty of it. We've beaten off one attack already, in company strength."

A map of the militia position came up; squares indicated possible enemy dispositions. The Brotherhood fighters held a dome-shaped rise, as high as anything in the vicinity; the road wound past it, following the low ground up from the shores of the lake. The gap into the sedimentary basin that held the Torrey estate was still two kilometers north and west, but the picture-pickup showed columns of smoke from that direction.

"Major, I can hold here but not forever," the captain went on. "We've no water except the canteens, very little in the way of other supplies, and I'm taking steady losses. Either someone tries to pull us out, or we'll have to fight our way through to the Torreys'. This is obviously bigger than we thought."

"Hold," Karl Olafson said. "We'll come get you."

Ace Barton spoke. "What do you have on hand, Major?" he asked.

"Our security battalion, Brigadier," the miner replied. "There's another Brotherhood reaction-force battalion here, mobilizing now, I'll leave those. We've got a little surprise, a six-gun battery of 155mm gun-howitzers, just up from the von Alderheim plant in Olynthos. And plenty of trucks, we'll take the mine vehicles. Pick up more infantry at the rally-point at Danniels Mill, and mounted scouts to cover our flanks."

Barton picked his words with care; interfering in the local chain of command was not something to be done lightly. "This isn't going to be anything you can handle," he said. "They're risking too much for just a raid. They've got something much bigger in mind. The mine itself, for a guess. You go out there and they'll ambush you just like they did the original relief force."

Major Olafson nodded. "We'll be careful. And counting the second-line people and the perimeter guardposts, that still leaves the equivalent of a complete rifle-regiment here. It's a chance, sir," he said. "But one we've got to take."

Barton signed agreement; that instant concern was a weakness of these friends-and-neighbors militia outfits, as well as a strength.

"Hell," the militia officer went on, "with nearly a thousand men and artillery, I don't think we'll have much trouble chewing up anything they send at us."

Barton had been writing on a pad of engineering paper. He handed that to Olafson. DON'T REPLY TO THIS. THIS ROOM IS BUGGED. GO FIND MAJOR HONISTU AND PAY ATTENTION TO HIM. "I expect you're right," Barton said aloud. He tapped the paper again. "Not much can happen to a force that size. Godspeed, then. Who'll hold operational command here?"

"I was hoping you would, sir."

"Right." Barton wrote quickly. VITAL YOU SEE HONISTU. He watched Olafson leave and turned back to the console. *Bad luck. Not enough time to make a real plan. I've got a bad feeling about this one.*

"Good," Skida murmured to herself.

Her face-shield was showing the input from a pickup three kilometers south. An armored car led out the gate between two pillboxes, trailed by a huge boxy mine-clearing vehicle. Trucks followed it, 6x6 models crowded with infantry in mottled-white winter camouflage and Nemourlon armor; they towed heavy mortars or two-wheel carts with ammunition and supplies. A string of them, and then two of the big ore trucks. Those pulled cannon, medium jobs with the long barrels turned and clamped over the trails, riding on four-wheeled carriages. More trucks . . .

She turned to the Meijians clustered around their equipment. "This had better work," she grated.

One of them looked up and bowed slightly. "We are downloading into the enemy mainframe even now, Field Prime," he said politely. "There will be too little time for the enemy to react."

As was explained before, went unspoken. The Legion techs were doing random sweeps of the more vital Royal Army machines, of which the Stora Mine was one. No way to leave the pirate taps in for any length of time.

She grunted assent and turned to a display table showing an overview of the mine and town. Too much here depended on the Meijians; too much on the NCLF's secret apparat. Neither the technoninjas nor Croser's people had ever failed her seriously before . . . but this was the first time so large a Helot force had depended on them so totally.

And we not just fighting the hicks. Barton. Barton suspected something. *What was he doing here? How much could he know?* She tried to remember what she'd been told about Brigadier Barton. Older than Owensford but subordinate, could something be made of that? *Bad sign he here. Shouldn't be here. Not now, not when things critical.*

Even in the Dales battle there had always been the option of pulling back; they had never been so deeply committed that the enemy could have destroyed them all, although it had been necessary to sacrifice the better part of two battalions to get the leadership cadre out. Now they had to attack, attack an immensely strong defensive position with forces that were barely superior to the Royalists even with the diversion drawing off some of their strength.

No way Skilly can win a straight fight here, she thought. *She would need five times the troops and more equipment for that.* But if they lost this time, the Movement's edge would be blunted, perhaps forever. The thought of losing the instrument she had worked so long and hard to forge made her stomach feel tight and sour; with an effort of will, she made her hand stop its instinctive desire to rub soothingly. . . . *Armor would stop it anyway.*

Niles gave her a grin and a thumbs-up; he looked better now that combat was near and there was no time to brood. That was another anxiety, she had serious doubts whether the Englishman had thought through the implications of her orders.

He toughen up a lot, she thought. *Now we see if it enough.*

Where's Fatima, Eddie?"

The mechanic jerked at the voice and rolled his trolley out from under the truck. The sirens were still wailing across the maintenance compound parking-lot.

"Ah, she's sick," he said, looking up and wiping his hands on an oily rag. "I came down to see the vehicle park was ready."

Christ, I hope I didn't hit her too hard, he thought. She was a good boss, and no more a Citizen than he was. Had been the one to get him the assistant maintenance chief's job, too. But you didn't retire from the Movement, and when it gave you the word you obeyed. Or died, and your family with you, wherever you tried to hide.

Christ, how did I ever get into this? Shit, shit, shit. *I don't want to kill anybody. Not even the Cits, hell the ones here haven't been so bad—*

The man in militia uniform looked around; fifteen 4x4s, another ten 6x6s. Stora Mine was lavishly equipped with mechanical transport by Spartan standards, since you couldn't haul ore by horse-drawn wagon; even with the mobile Brotherhood force gone, there were still scores of trucks and vans in the settlement, a fair number of private cars as well. The emergency plan called for his two ready companies to billet here, able to reinforce anywhere in the sprawling complex.

"They OK?" the Citizen-soldier said, jerking his head toward the transports.

"Sure, sir. Ticking over normal, but I just wanted to check. You know what's happening?"

"Goddam rebels've attacked a ranch, the boss took some people out to put them down," the militiaman said.

More militia were coming up, and at a wave from the commander began loading prepositioned packs of weapons and equipment on the trucks.

"Nothing wrong here?" the mechanic asked; a man with a wife and a new baby had a right to sound worried.

Why did I listen to that bastard Sverdropov? First it had been little things, turning a blind eye to a crate on a run down to the lake, passing messages, just more union work Sverdropov said, and he'd been sore-headed back then after the last outfit he was with broke a strike with scabs. The Movement had gotten him his first job here . . . Then bigger things, and when he baulked they threatened to turn him in, then it was hanging offenses and he *had* to keep going.

"Nah, just playing safe," the militiaman said; he looked worried, but not very. "You'd better get to your shelter station, but thanks for checking, Eddie. Give my regards to Mary."

"No problem, sir," the mechanic said, zipping the equipment bag and walking toward the office with a friendly wave to the nearest troops. Sweat trickled down his ribs from his armpits despite the cold, as the left-over bombs clinked in the duffle.

Legion Corporal (Headquarters Adjutant Staff) Perry Blackbird was in his last enlistment before retirement. He'd been too old to go with the Legion to New Washington. In fact he was plenty old enough to rate a desk job at headquarters, but Andy

Bielskis had asked him to come along on this job. "Got a feeling on this one, Perry. Can use your nose," Bielskis had said.

And Andy had the best nose in the Legion. Perry had watched Andy grow up in the Legion. He and Andy's father had been sergeants together. Of course that was back in Blackbird's drinking days, when he went up to sergeant and back down to PFC with seasonal regularity. Now with his seniority he was paid as much as a sergeant, and he didn't have any command responsibilities, which was the way he liked it. What with Jeanine married to a farmer and Clara dead these five years, he lived alone and he'd been getting crustier and more set in his ways. "Do me good to get out," he'd told Andy. "Hell, somebody's got to watch out for you."

And there was something wrong here. Perry Blackbird wasn't sure what, but things didn't feel right. *Maybe it's I know Major Barton is worried sick, and Andy ain't too happy.* His instructions were to nose around, see how these militia carried out procedure, watch for anything suspicious, see what he could improve.

Now he watched as the mechanic went into the office. Then he turned to the militia sergeant. "Is that standard, a civilian mechanic workin' your motor pool?"

"Well, sure, this is a mine, not everyone is militia. Eddie's a sorehead sometimes, but he's all right." The Citizen sergeant's voice had an edge to it. Plainly he didn't think they needed any outsiders to tell them how to operate.

"Standard procedure during an alert is nobody's alone with a truck he ain't going to ride in," Blackbird said. "Don't you do that here?"

"Well, sure, but who the hell follows procedure all the time? Never get anything done that way."

"You like this Eddie?"

"He's all right."

"Trust him, do you? With the lives of your troops?"

"Sure—what are you getting at?"

"Why isn't he militia?"

"I don't know, never asked. What the hell do you think you're getting at?"

"Nothing, Sarge, nothing at all. But I sure am glad it ain't me getting into one of them trucks. Have fun, Sarge." He touched his comm card. "Andy, I'm going into the maintenance office, I may need help. Send me a couple MPs, and maybe you better come a-running."

He left the militiaman staring at his back.

✧ ✧ ✧

"Captain Mace," Barton said.

The Scout commander looked up from the plotting board. The Legion techs had set up their own battle tech system in the computer center that doubled as militia HQ. "Sir."

Barton typed at his own console. "HAVE THEY FOUND THE BUGS IN HERE?"

"TWO."

"THINK THATS ALL?"

"NEGATIVE."

Aloud he said, "How long would it take to string landlines of our own between the perimeter bunkers, HQ, and the main interior points?"

"About a day, using all the men, sir," Mace said.

"I think we should get on that as soon as this fracas is over," Barton said.

"Sir."

Christ I'm no goddam actor. "FIND THOSE DAMN BUGS!!!" he typed. "Meantime, collect our spare communicators, and send one to the commander's bunkers. And the power and communications buildings."

"Aye, aye, sir."

Barton turned to the screens. The local militia had mobilized with smooth efficiency, fanning out to their duty posts. Second-line Brotherhood personnel were seeing the families and children to the Armory; an immensely strong position, dug into solid rock and surrounded by pillboxes. *And I don't like this one damned bit.*

"Get me the relief column."

Karl Olafson's face showed, looking up from the tail of a truck set up as a command post. From somewhere outside the field of vision came an unmistakable *booooom,* heavy artillery in action.

"Report, Major."

"Light resistance on the way here, sir. Mines, and snipers, a lot of them with Peltast rifles"—which had considerable antivehicle capacity—"we lost the armored car, and the mine-clearing vehicle is damaged. We had to stop and deploy several times, but we've pushed through to within firing range of the trapped reaction force, and with them to observe we're shooting the rebels out of their positions."

"Are you in ground contact?"

"I think so, at least, my forward patrols are running into them. Infantry screens."

"Resistance?"

"They're giving a stiff fight and then pulling back. Laying mines as they go." The militia officer grimaced, and the mercenary nodded. That was something of a Helot trademark. "But they don't have time to set complete nets, or equipment for air-delivered stuff."

Odd, Barton thought. The enemy had repeatedly shown they *did* have some capacity in that field. Not an unlimited one, but this was a fairly important action. Certainly the largest battle in the Upper Valley so far. One of the few where the Helots had operated in battalion strength.

"And they're keeping their mortars on the reaction force position, mostly."

More understandable. Causing maximum Citizen casualties seemed to be a strategic aim of the enemy high command, and the pinned-down force was a concentrated, sitting target. *And I still don't like it.* "All right, Major, carry on, but keep me in the loop."

"Yes, sir. I expect to break up the enemy concentration within the next few hours, and pursue their elements as they split up and withdraw."

Barton leaned back in the chair. *That ought to be that,* he thought. The screens showed orderly activity, the last of the children going down the elevators at the armory . . .

His Legion console screen lit. "SERGEANT BIELSKIS REPORTS REACTION FORCE VEHICLES MAY BE SABOTAGED. POSSIBLY BOMBS ABOARD. IT IS CONFIRMED THAT BOMBS WERE PLACED IN MOBILE RESERVE VEHICLES."

"Jesus Christ," Barton said.

"Sir?" Olafson said.

"Major, this computer's showing something odd. I've got a terrain plot. You see that secondary road off to your left there?"

"Yes, sir?"

"Dismount your men and go investigate it."

"Sir?"

"Now, Major. Go take a look yourself."

"General, that will delay us—"

"Major, indulge me. It won't take five minutes. I don't quite know what this thing is trying to tell me, and I'd rather have you go in strength. Now get moving, please. And stay on line with me."

Olafson reacted to the tone of command. "Yes, sir. Captain, dismount the unit, please—"

Dear God, let them get out of those trucks and I'll buy the biggest damned Easter candle— Bloody Hell. That perimeter

*monitor's repeating, I saw those rabbits move exactly the same
way last time I looked.* His hand reached for a button. It was
1045, exactly.

"OK, shut it down, just leave the pumps working," the
foreman said. "We'll pop that rockface when the alert's off."

He had half-turned when the prybar struck him behind the
ear. Then he was staring at the wet stone of the tunnel floor;
there was time for a moment of surprise before something hit
the back of his head. The last sound he heard was crumpling
bone.

"Come on, we gotta get everything in place before 1050!"
the man who had struck him hissed. The six men in hard
hats and overalls began taking bricks of *plastique* from their
carryalls. Two of them began shoving extra loads of dynamite
down the holes bored into the glistening black stone of the
stope-face.

"Pumps, transformers and the conveyor," the man continued, looking nervously back over his shoulder at the long
tunnel that led towards the cage of the mine's shaft-elevator.

"Won't nobody notice the body?" one of the workers asked.

"No way, when we pop her they'll be boiling mud all
through here." He glanced at his watch. "Come *on,* we've only
got five minutes!"

"Here, you, what're you doing there?" the power-plant
supervisor asked. "This isn't your workstation."

The turbine room was quiet, except for the ever-present
humming of the rotors, but that was more felt than heard.
He was the only one of the supervisory staff here, most of
the rest were in the militia . . .

The overalled figure at the steam inlet rose and turned.
Consciously the supervisor felt only surprise; drilled reflex
made him draw his sidearm as he saw the man pull a
machine-pistol from his carryall. Brotherhood training brought
it up two-handed, *crack-crack-crack* and the worker was
spinning away with red blotches on his clothing. Hands came
around the turbine housing behind the muzzle of another
submachine gun, and the supervisor dropped flat as 10mm
bullets slapped through the air where his chest had been,
whined off metal.

Jesus God, that'll blow the steam pipe! he thought, returning fire, looking at the brick of plastic explosive. The whole
floor would be flooded with superheated water from the
boreholes that slanted down into the magma.

More bullets, and feet were moving off on the floor somewhere.

Two of them, he thought, snapping a new magazine into the pistol and scuttling backward. The pulse hammered in his ear, but there was no time to be dazed. *Got to report.*

There was five meters of open space between the turbine he was using as cover and the control room. The supervisor took a deep breath and leapt, rolling the last two meters. Lead flicked pits from the concrete at his back, and shattered through the windows as he sprawled through the door of the control room and slammed the metal portal behind him. Glass starred and shifted above him as he crawled to the communicator console and reached up from below; fragments cascaded over him when he reached it, as one of the attackers put another clip through the windows. He shielded his face with his gun arm and keyed the unit.

"Mine Central, Power house One, rebel attack, rebel attack!"

"I am sorry, your call cannot be completed as sent. Please indicate your call direction and try again."

"God damn you!" Panic button. The Legion guys had put in a panic button. It was just over there. His legs didn't want to work, but he could still drag himself across the floor to the desk, reach up and slap the button.

Alarms hooted. Somewhere off in the distance he heard shouts.

"Move, damn you!"

"God damn it, there wasn't 'sposed to be any mother fucking alarms," someone shouted. "Let's get the fuck out of here!"

"Hey you, shithead, get your ass back here—"

"Fuck off."

"Who's there? Sergeant, what the hell, get the Old Man! There's rebels in here. Officer of the Guard! Powerhouse!"

There were shots, and more people shouting, and it all faded away.

It was a thousand meters of rocky open field from the bunker's lip to the beginning of the woods. Brotherhood Lieutenant Hargroves squinted through the IR scanner and frowned in puzzlement.

"Brother Private Diego, you *sure* the audio sensors don't pick up anything? I got stuff moving around out there. What's on the visuals?"

"Nothing, sir. Birds, deer . . . big herd of deer. Sound and sight."

"Yeah, that might be it, but I'm not counting on it. Anything from the patrol?"

"Regular check-in blips, sir."

"Get me Central."

He picked up the microphone. "Central, this is Lieutenant Hargroves. I've got some funny readings on my direct view sensors but they don't match with the stuff through you. Could you check it? And I'd like to send out another patrol."

"Report acknowledged," a voice said. *Captain Olafson, right enough,* the militiaman thought.

"Yes, ma'am, but can I send out the patrol?"

"I'm sure you can handle it, Lieutenant?"

He frowned, uncertain. "But the *patrol,* ma'am?"

"I have full confidence in you, Lieutenant. Remember to maintain radio communications silence under all circumstances." A click.

Bullshit. There's something damned wrong here. "Hell—get me the Captain."

"No answer, sir. It's ringing through but nobody's picking it up."

"The *hell* you say!" Nobody answering in the company command bunker? "Fire up the radar! Get the damned lights on!"

"Sir, standing orders—"

"*Do* it, Diego! Everybody, stand to your guns. Markham, get on the minefield circuit."

"Shit! Sir, multiple metal contacts within three thousand meters. Multiple!"

He keyed the helmet radio. "Captain, are you there?"

"Hargroves, what the hell are you doing calling me on the hailing frequency *again*?"

"Captain, I didn't— Sir, the landlink's down and I've got radar traces—"

"Down? You reported in on it not five minutes ago!"

The desperate voice of the communications tech broke in. "Sir, we're being targeted, designator lasers and—"

Something blinked out of the sky at them behind a trail of fire. There was an explosion on the roof of the bunker that threw them all to the floor, loud enough to jar the senses.

"Radar's gone, radar's gone!"

Hargroves leapt up and to the observation slit. Men were coming out of the woods. Rocket trails slammed down out of the sky to his left and right, and more from positions among the trees. The bunker shook under repeated impacts, and he could hear screaming in the background.

"Open—"

Another streak of fire. He had time to drop down and wrap

his arms around his head, before there was a slamming impact and a violet light loud enough to show through his clenched eyelids. Powdered concrete made him choke and gag, while savage heat washed across the backs of his hands. Blast bounced him back and forth in the right-angle of wall and floor. When he opened his eyes a single tear-blurred glance showed that there was nobody else alive in this chamber. He staggered erect, head and shoulders out of the gaping semicircle that *something* had bitten through the observation slit of the bunker, and keyed the helmet radio again.

"Perimeter six, under rocket attack! Answer me, somebody, *please,* they're through the wire—"

A high-pitched jamming squeal drove into his eardrums. Armed men were swarming out of the woods; a long blade of flame showed as a recoiless rifle fired, and the bunker shook again. None of the gatlings was firing. Bangalore torpedoes erupted beneath the coils of razor wire, and the enemy poured through as the earth was still falling back. They came running, screaming.

Hargroves slapped the audio intake of his helmet to zero, leaving the mike open as he wiped at the blood running down from his nose. "Minefields inoperative," he shouted, bringing up his rifle. *Aim low. Fire. One down.* "Perimeter five and four not supporting." A saw-edged *brrrrrrt. brrrrrt.* came from his left, then ceased. "Correction, five still maintaining fire. Enemy is in at least battalion strength. The mine fields are inoperative. I have no reaction for—"

CHAPTER NINE

If one has never personally experienced war, one
cannot understand why a commander should need
any brilliance and exceptional ability. Everything looks
simple. Everything in war is very simple, but the
simplest thing is difficult. The difficulties accumulate
and end by producing a kind of friction that is incon-
ceivable. Countless minor incidents—the kind you can
never really foresee—combine to lower the general
level of performance, so that one always falls far short
of the intended goal.
                                        —Clausewitz, *On Strategy*

"Field Prime, Attack Force one here. Bunker secured," Niles
said.

And I'm glad, he thought fervently. Running forward across
a minefield that might be activated any moment had not been
one of the more pleasant experiences of his life, with only a
piece of intrusive software between him and being shredded
into a dozen pieces.

The bunker listed as six on his map was more of a tangled
depression of earth and crumbled ferroconcrete now, the sappers
had made sure with a cratering charge centered right on the
twisted wreckage of the radar pickups. There were more
thumping crashes behind him, as they laid strip charges to
clear real as well as virtual paths through the mines.

"This Field Prime. Proceed with Phase Two."

Niles stood, waved his hand in a circle around his head and
chopped it south; the jamming that bolixed the enemy's small-
unit push was unfortunately affecting their own, as well. The
off-world helmetcom systems could filter it, but there were only
enough of those for senior commanders. Squads rose and dashed
by him, heading into the open parkland that separated the

perimeter bunkers from the interior villages of the Stora Mine. The men were bowed under their burdens, bundles of Friedlander target-seeker missiles, satchel charges, flamethrowers. Others were swinging right and left, lugging machine guns and portable gatlings, setting up blocking positions to prevent the intact bunkers from sortieing and closing the quarter-arc wedge the Helots had driven into the north face of the mine's defenses.

"Am advancing. Phase Two in progress," he said. The headquarters company had formed about him. "Follow me!"

"Broadband jamming, sir," Legion Signal Corps Corporal Hiram Klingstauffer said cooly, hands dancing across his controls. "I can filter it."

"Right," Barton said. *Breath in. Breath out. Surprise is an event that takes place in the mind of a commander.* No antiradiation missiles available to him up *here,* though. The replacement shipments for the ones lost in the Dales were still on their way. The enemy's logistics seemed to operate much faster . . .

He strode over to the window and used a chair to smash out the thick double panes; cold air flooded in, and the sound of explosions and small-arms fire. Most loudly from the north, but there were flashes and crumping sounds from all around the perimeter, and that was the most accurate information he was likely to get for a while. Lights flashed and died over the mine-works south of the town as the 24-hour arclamps went off. Barton wheeled and looked at the computer displays.

Power Central. A peaceful, unmarked control booth, distance shots of humming machinery and workers attending it.

Perimeter. A light blinked on, and a militia major's voice shouted: "Long live the Revolution!"

Karen Olafson recoiled as if it had bitten her.

"Turn it off," Barton said. She looked at him blankly. "It's in enemy hands, nothing but disinformation. Forget the damned thing." He went to the Legion console and threw the big switch at the top. Lights winked. "I'm taking manual control of the defenses." *Of what Jenny's crew managed to rig, anyway. God damn it, we needed another week.* He pushed that thought aside. What he needed didn't matter any more. It was what he had that counted.

First things first. Puzzle out just what did which. There was a crude map above the manual console. Right. Infiltrators attacking the power house. Activate the minefields, detonate on contact. North side first, that's where the noise is. He threw the switch.

The response was instant. A dozen blasts, lights flared near the power house, along the whole north periphery. More explosions. Blasts all along the inner perimeter swath. Then more, in the park areas.

"What's happening?" Karen Olafson demanded.

"Somebody was where he shouldn't have been," Ace said absently. "Some of those were secondary explosions. Think you can get that thing working again?"

"I can try. I'll dump it and reboot from WORM."

WORM. Write Once, Read Many, Barton remembered. Computers weren't his specialty, but this was supposed to be a way to make sure nobody tampered with data because once it was burned into a glass disk it didn't get written over.

"Security systems only. *Now!*" Her hands moved, with gathering speed. Blood trickled down her chin from a bitten lip. The screens went blank, flickered, came back up with nothing but a red = sign in a black circle, the Helot banner. Then they flickered again and stayed blank.

"Sir," Klingstauffer said calmly. "I'm getting radio from all the militia units. They're questioning withdrawal orders they've received, demanding confirmations. The Captain in charge of Perimeter 10 through 14 registers that he is withdrawing as ordered but under protest."

"Give me a broadband override. In clear."

"Sir."

"Karen, turn that damn computer off. Never mind trying to restart it. Shut it down so it doesn't send out anymore orders."

"Right," Karen said.

"Here's your general channel, General. No problem with the direct wires, but they're jamming hell out of radio."

"Right. No harm trying." Ace keyed the mike. "ALL UNITS, ALL UNITS, THIS IS GENERAL BARTON." *Calm, Ace, they won't hear any better if you shout. Or will they*—"Klingstauffer, send for some bull horns." He keyed the mike again. "All units, you are on your own, I say again, all commanders, ignore any other instructions, take command of your units. Act as you think best under the circumstances. The central computer system is compromised, I say again the central computer is compromised. Look around you, react to what you see, and kill the sons of bitches. Relay these orders to any other units you can find."

"Klingstauffer, get that message going on a continuous loop, general broadcast."

"Sir."

"And get runners going with bull horns to repeat it any-where and anyhow they can."

"Right."

Barton went to the Legion direct line console. It was difficult to tell what he had there. Direct lines, but to where—He keyed one. Nothing. A second. "This is Barton, Command Central. What do I have?"

"Captain Trent, vehicle reserve. God damn, General, I'm glad to hear from you!"

"What's your status?"

"We're on foot, sir. Vehicles sabotaged, your man found out just in time, lost a truck and some troopers, it was real bad, real bad, but—"

"TRENT!"

"Yes, sir."

"Get hold of yourself. What's your status?"

"Sir. Sir, I have two companies of dismounted infantry. Five percent casualties."

"Right. Like it or not, Captain Trent, you have the only effective force I can communicate with. Captain, the mine's under attack. The perimeter's been penetrated at the north sector, possibly elsewhere. We have unreliable communications, and many of the militia have been given false orders by the central computer. Do you understand?"

"No, sir."

"Good man. I'll explain it. The central computer was briefly taken over by the enemy, Captain. God knows what it told your people to do. We have shut it down."

"Oh—"

"Right. So the one thing we do know is, they're inside the perimeter in the north sector, possibly stations 10 through 14 as well."

"Yes, sir?"

"So you've got to do something about it. First thing, get the word to all unit commanders. Two items. Item one, the mine fields are active again. Chase the bastards into the mines. Item two, all unit commanders are on their own. Act as they think best. You got that?"

Captain Trent sounded scared, but he said, "Sir. Instruct all units, disregard previous orders, act on their own judgment. And the mine fields are active again."

"That's it, son. Now take a deep breath, think about what you're going to do, and do it. You'll be fine."

"Yes, sir."

"Are any Legion people there?"

"There's a sergeant—"

"Get moving on your instructions, then put him on. And leave a communications squad to man this line at all times."

"Sir." Trent left the mike activated when he put it down. Ace Barton could hear him shouting orders in the background.

Scared as hell, but he's making sense.

"Major Olafson, weak signal," Klingstauffer said.

"Barton here. Olafson, the mine is under attack, the perimeter's penetrated, north side for certain, possibly other areas. Your vehicles may have been sabotaged. Check for bombs. Then cancel your present mission and defend the mine. I say again, the mine's under attack, your vehicles may have been sabotaged. Your instructions are to abandon your present position and return to defend the mine. Did you get all that?"

Hissing and buzzing. "— penetrated. —under attack—"

Nothing about checking vehicles. Damn. Ace repeated his instructions.

"Nothing," Klingstauffer said.

"Did we get through?"

"God knows."

"Repeat those orders, and pray." Jesus, I could go broke buying candles and altar flowers.

The direct line squawked. "Sergeant Bielskis, sir."

"What happened down there, Andy?"

"Turncoat, sabotaged the trucks. Blackbird smelled a rat. We've got him. Captain Trent's scared but he's steadying down."

"What I needed to hear. Andy, about that traitor. Keep him. I want him alive, Andy. That's really important."

"Yes, sir. He's scared, keeps talking about how they'll kill his family, wife and little boy—"

"Name?"

"Edward L. Bishop. Wife is Mary Margaret Ryan Bishop. Son Patrick James Bishop, age 2 months."

"Can you get his family into protective custody?"

"No, sir, they're with the other noncombatants in the main bunker."

"Best place for them. OK, Andy, you're on your own. I got other problems."

"Record this, sir. Bishop was recruited by one Leontin Sverdropov, a shop steward. I'd guess Sverdropov has biofeedback conditioning."

"Got it. Have your MP's pick him up if he can be found. Anything else, Andy?"

"No, sir. Blackbird and I'll help get The Word out to the other units."

"Do that. Command Central out." Barton took a deep breath. "Olafson, any progress?"

"There's some sort of viral bit floating around in the system RAM, every time I power down it drags in a trickle current and reboots from the infected config when we come back on line, instead of from the ROM backup."

"Right. Turn it off. Just shut it down, then go through and fix it right. For now we'll rely on manual and what the Legion installed."

"Yes, sir."

"Klingstauffer, can you get Mace?"

"Stand by one. Here, sir."

"Jamey, what's your status?"

"I've just got to my command, sir. From what I can see, they didn't expect the mine field to activate." Mace's words were punctuated by distant explosions. "They've got troops still out there in the mines, both rings."

"Serve them bloody right," Barton said. "Okay, Jamey, make me the best estimate of the situation you can and report back."

"Roger."

"Sir," Klingstauffer said from the plotting table. "Incoming, multiples, bombardment rockets, heavy mortars too from the trajectories. Target zones follow."

Lines swam over the plotting table, and red circles marked the impacts. *Lot of those are empty space,* he thought. Then: *Of course. Air-sown mines. They're trying to immobilize us.* The sky howled outside, but the *bop* sounds of the bursting charges were not followed by the surf-roar of bomblets or the crunching detonations of HE warheads. Instead there was a multiple fluttering whirr, as the rockets split and scattered hundreds, thousands of butterfly mines. Over the blimp haven where the men of the Fifth were moving out, over the wrecked vehicles of the reaction force, around the perimeter garrisons, down the main streets.

"Incoming, bombardment rockets and mortars, multiple," the sergeant said tonelessly.

"Rather a lot, isn't it?" Barton said. He whistled softly. "Rather a lot indeed. Where'd they get it all? Like they're going for broke. Klingstauffer, can you get me General Owensford?"

"Ms. Schramm's working on the antenna now, sir. Five minutes."

"Right." *Stop. Breathe deep. Now go to the window and look out—* Secondary explosions in the mine-fields. Someone was taking some real punishment. *So are our people, with all that artillery pouring in, but the Helots have to be losing more, they're in the open.*

"Legion Headquarters, Fort Plataia sir."

"Owensford here."

"Barton. Uploading situation report." There was a warble of data. "Feed complete."

"Received." A long pause. "Jesus, Ace, what's going on up there?"

"This one's it, sir. I'd say they've committed damned near everything they have. Not just troops, look at how much ordinance they're expending."

"So why are you talking to me?"

"If you'll look close at the situation report, General Owensford, you will discover that you are God damned near the only person I *can* talk to."

"Oh. Lahr! Andy, get Jesus and Catherine in here on the double, then start looking into what direct communications we have with any unit in General Barton's Command. Move! OK, Ace, what you got from where you sit?"

"One hell of a mess, Boss. I got a bad feeling on this one. No command, no control, no communications, and no bloody intelligence."

"They any better off?"

"Some," Ace said. He took another deep breath.

"Actually, things can't be going so good for them, either. They penetrated the computer system here, good move, everything was tied to it. Used the computer to disable the mines and security systems. Had some inside help, too, saboteurs, God knows what else. But we turned the mine fields on with manual. I don't know how many of their troops are out there, but a lot of mines are going off and there's a lot of secondary explosions."

"Ace, are you telling me you have most of the Helot army trapped inside your perimeter?"

"Skipper, we just may, but it's not clear just who has who trapped. I doubt their command elements are in here. They don't much go in for Rommel style. More like Hitler."

"Well. Clarifies your objective, doesn't it?"

Barton laughed. "General, just at the frigging moment the objective is to live through all this! But yeah, I see what you mean. We got them in a killing zone. Only problem is, we don't have a lot handy to kill them with, and they seem to have plenty to do unto us."

"You have two battalions coming."

"Up river and up those roads. This'll be long over by then."

"Royal Cavalry in Olynthos. Prince Lysander went up there yesterday. I could send that. The Air Cav units could be there in a couple of hours."

"Maybe not," Ace said. "They've got bugger all equipment up here. They must have known that Air Cav was down there. This is typical Skilly. Devious. Started with a small attack on an outpost to lure out the reaction force, an ambush for the relief column to make Stora Mine commit *their* mobile force, an ambush for *that,* then the main attack—sure as God made a mule ornery, they've got something that can take out the airborne troops, and it's *already in place.*"

"Good thinking, Ace. Still, I will have to report to the Prince."

"Yes, sir, but make sure he understands. Christ. He's there with the Air Cav? I didn't know that, but bugger all, it doesn't mean *they* didn't."

"It doesn't mean they did, either, Ace. Thanks to Major Cheung we plugged that Palace leak."

"They could have another. Dammit, Peter, they get me thinking they're ten feet tall—"

"The great thing—"

"Is not to lose my nerve. Yes, sir. Wilco."

"Right. You're in charge, Ace. I'll see what I can organize from here."

"Thanks. It's heating up, I better get back to it. Don't let them suck the Prince into anything stupid."

"Godspeed. Out."

Something was happening outside. A line of massive explosions slammed their way across the open space outside the control building. One struck a parked ore-hauler, throwing the hundred-tonne machine onto its side; a moment later it pinwheeled across the gravel again, as a fuel dump went up in a soft *whomp* of orange flame and black smoke. The *crump . . . crump* sounds echoed off the mountainside, were joined by others throughout the settlement as more explosive fell out of the sky.

Ace Barton took a deep breath. "Sergeant, feed counterbattery data to the perimeter posts and the armory." The armory at least had light artillery in revetments, and heavy mortars of its own. "Do what you can to get communications so we have a decent situation report. And anybody you can get to, tell them we win if we hold on. They haven't accomplished dick yet, and their surprise is over. Now all we have to do is live through this."

✧   ✧   ✧

"We got to get out of here!" someone was screaming.

"Keep moving, keep moving," Niles barked into the speaker.

They were supposed to be destroying the town, planting explosives everywhere, making the Citizens' homes uninhabitable. *If I take time to do that, we won't get out of here at all,* Niles thought. *And the mine fields are active again.* He shuddered. A few minutes earlier and he'd have been in the middle of that field when it activated. As it was he'd lost a fifth of his command to the mines. *Dead or run away and there'll be more of those. Just vanished. Where do they think they can run?* There was no safe place. If the Royals didn't find you, Skilly would. *But Skilly won't hold this area after tonight, so all they'll have to worry about is the Royals.*

Groups of infantry were moving, but it wasn't a very orderly maneuver. They were supposed to fan out and make contact with the other Helot formations that would be pouring in through the breached defenses, but not all the defense system was breached, and it wasn't at all clear just what part was. Somewhere out there he should find reinforcements, but he didn't know where. *This is becoming one monumental cock-up.*

His force was divided. He had led some across the greensward while the mines were off, but not all had made it before the field was suddenly activated. Not only had he lost men, he'd lost contact with a third of his force, who were back there in the perimeter, trapped between two mine fields. Paths would have to be cleared before they could advance or retreat, but there was no one to clear them.

"Incoming!"

Niles hit the dirt. There was a nightmare of explosions, some close, some distant. He scrabbled with his radio. "Cease that artillery on north sector, I say again, cease, you're dropping into areas we hold."

There was no acknowledgment, but eventually it stopped. Niles got up to look at the situation. Men were cursing. They knew where that barrage had come from and they didn't like it at all. "Who's fucking side are they on?" someone shouted. There were answering curses.

Niles put that out of his mind, and tried for a calm assessment of the situation. He was near a residential community. The houses were shuttered, but they weren't all empty. Fire spat from a house half a kilometer away. Helot fighters dove for cover like reeds rippling in the wind. Some returned the enemy fire, shooting wildly, while others hugged the ground and waited. The black stone blocks of the shuttered house eroded under the return fire as if they were being sandblasted, in a shower of sparks and ricochets, but it didn't stop the Spartan sniper. Finally two Helot rocketeers came up. They snapped open the collapsible fiberglas tubes, came up to kneeling position and took careful aim; these were the light unguided bunkerbusters. *Whooot*-crash. A house half a block from the target showed a spurt of flame. There were more rifle blasts and the Helot went down. His partner cursed and got the rocket launcher.

Niles tried to shout to the man to move to a different location, but he wasn't listening. He got the launcher loaded, raised up, aimed. Another *whoosh,* and this time the windows of the house blew out in a spectacular shower of fire and shards. A burning figure staggered out the door to lie and twitch for a second. One more obstacle out of the way, but it had cost them time.

Ask me to give you anything but time. Who said that? Doesn't matter. "Keep moving! Up, up, move, move," Niles urged. "You can't stay here!"

"Sir, jamming's off."

Niles cursed silently; that meant the Royalists had communications again. Continued Helot jamming would hinder their own side now more than the enemy. *And I'm in a pocket, and I don't know what I have in here.* The timetable was shot all to shit. Niles had never believed much in that timetable. Too damned complicated, too many units to get to different places, too many things had to happen at the same time. Skilly kept insisting it was a simple plan, just a simple wedge attack, breach the defenses, seek out and destroy, but it hadn't looked simple to Niles. It was hard enough just to get one unit to move on a schedule, under fire or not, and this had dozens. Niles had tried to get von Reuter to discuss it, but the German wasn't about to criticize Skilly's plan. *No one would. Afraid to sound like defeatists. So we went with this, and now—*

"Over to standard radio com," he said. "Codes. Who have we got contact with?" He punched the first channel button.

"Group Leader ben Bella here."

"Situation?"

"Codes CORNUCOPIA an' HEPHAESTUS." The warehouse and smelter areas. Forces advancing but objectives not secured. "We can't find the underground Movement liaison."

"Keep looking, have to evacuate our people."

"Sure, sure, I'll keep looking. Bloody god damn hell!"

"Problems?"

"Half my troops are dead in the fucking mines! The mines were supposed to be off!"

"Yes, I know, we took losses too," Niles said. "What else?"

"They were supposed to be off, damn it!"

"Get hold of yourself. Report."

"We've got sniper fire and infiltrators from the residential districts, and somebody's spotting for that goddam artillery of theirs, it's too damned effective, they must have their computers up again!"

Likely, actually. "Follow standing orders." Those called for blasting down any building from which hostile fire was received. He winced; a little severe . . . but what else could they do?

"Standing orders —" His subordinate broke off with laughter.

"Ben Bella? What the hell?"

"Standing orders, sir? HALF MY FUCKING MORTARS AND ROCKET LAUNCHERS ARE OUT IN THE FUCKING MINEFIELDS! I don't know where the rest are. I don't know where the ammunition is. Sir."

"Sir, sir," his communications sergeant said. "Group Leader Martins."

"A moment. All right, ben Bella, link up with the Movement people and do what you can to get back on schedule—"

He heard more laughter from ben Bella. "Schedule! That's great! Schedule." More laughter, then silence. *Can't say I like that much.* "Go ahead, Martins, Niles here."

"Sir, Code WHITE GUARD." *Heavy resistance, cannot advance.* Martins was supposed to be securing the main smelter complex. Niles looked down at his map; about half a kilometer west of the blimp haven, in a tangle of workers' bunkhouses and maintenance sheds. "I've identified Legion troops, and Brotherhood first-liners, I think they're from the reserve force."

Damn, Niles thought. The truck-sabotage was supposed to have knocked them out of the fight entirely. *Well, everything couldn't work. But had anything worked since the mine fields came back on? How many survived, and how much are they worth?* His head pounded, and it was hard to think. *No way to know the situation. And back up there in central control, they had the computers back on, they knew where everything was. Barton—Barton, what the hell was Barton doing out here anyway, Barton wasn't supposed to be here, this was supposed to be provincials, amateurs, and now we're fighting Barton and the Legion and those damned SAS units will be out there waiting for us.* He shook off the feeling of hysteria. "Martins, can you get through? Answer in clear."

"No, sir. Every time we punch a hole, they fire the buildings and fall back, or pinch us off behind the neck of the penetration. I don't have enough edge in numbers, and these are good troops. Too many civilians running around getting in the way, too."

Another amateur, has to explain everything. But I'm not much more than an amateur myself, and these Legion types, this is their business, they do this all their lives. "Code STALINGRAD." Dig in and hold.

"Bullshit."

"What?"

"I'll do what I can, but everything's fucked up," Martins said. "You better figure something fast, or it's going to be bugout boogie and there won't be fuck all I can do about it. Sir."

"Field Prime," the communications sergeant said.

This ought to be secure. Ought to be. "Marlborough here." *Stupid code name.*

"Report."

He worked to keep his voice calm, and not to give irrelevant complaints. Like ammunition in one place, and guns in another, troops separated from their commanders— "Heavy losses averaging thirty percent due to unexpected activation of the mine field. Ben Bella's still advancing but hasn't secured objectives. Martins is pinned down, unable to advance at all. Part of my troops are with me at Sugar Mike Two, but the rest are still out at the bunkers with the minefield between us, and I don't have a good estimate of what's with me and what's behind. Troops are complaining that the mines weren't supposed to detonate, and some of them are unhappy about taking friendly fire."

"Field Prime know that. Our friends don't have any explanations, they still looking. You ought to be finishing Phase Three, mon!"

"Field Prime, that timetable cannot be kept. It doesn't even make sense any more. The surprise is over, they're organizing, their computers are up, their artillery counterfire programs are starting up, and our whole force is exposed!"

There was a pause. "You sayin' you want to run now?"

"Field Prime, I am suggesting that it is impossible to complete the mission."

"Field Prime will consider that, but not time to give up. Perimeter Ten to Fourteen pulled out when we jimmied the comm, and we overran they bunkers, now we using them." The outer defense positions had all-round fields of fire. "Swing a couple of companies up they ass, see if we can nutcracker them. We rendevous at Objective A-7, eh?"

"I will comply, but my advice is to get out before we take more losses. We've hurt them, and so far we still have an effective force, but—"

"Field Prime will consider recommendation. Now do nutcracker."

"Roger wilco."

Niles looked up. "Sutchukil, you will take A and C companies and swing east against those garrison johnnies," he said. *What's left of them. Between them there's not a full strength company, and I have no idea of what they're facing.* "Da Silva, you're in charge here. Remainder of the reserve, follow me."

He led the way, at a steady wolf-trot rather than a sprint; they had better than a klick and a half to go. The troops followed by platoon columns, spaced out along the verges of the road on alternate sides. The composition soles of their boots rutched steadily on the light snow-covering of the roads and sidewalks. Noise was increasing from either side, small arms fire and explosions. Mortar shells went overhead, making everyone hunch their shoulders involuntarily. They landed to the east, fire support against Royalist militia probing at the Helots. Return fire went *shoomp*-whirrrr overhead in the opposite direction. The garrison was getting its heavy weapons into use.

They ran through a section of park, where pine-trees were blazing like torches, with an overwhelming stink of tar.

"Mines!" someone screamed. A butterfly mine popped up, and half a squad flopped. A leg lay improbably in the center of the path they'd been running on.

"Keep moving," Niles ordered. "Come on, we're going home!"

The men moved ahead, but cautiously now. Niles tried to hurry them.

"Fuck off," someone shouted. "You want to run through mines, you come up here in front and do it." There were shouts of agreement. "Damn right." "This de revolution! Officers to the front!"

"Incoming!"

A box pattern of high explosive fell around them, and several mines detonated. One man screamed, but no one else seemed to be hit. "They clearing the mine field for us!" someone shouted. Others laughed and the units began to move forward again. Another round of artillery, this time behind them.

There's luck, Niles thought. "Move out, move out." He wondered how many were following him. Not as many as started. There were gaps in the ranks. *Damn fools, don't they understand, they can't stay here.* He ran on.

Finally they were through the park and into a business district. Artillery flashed in the distance, but nothing was falling on them at the moment. Buildings were burning on either side; larger ones now as they came closer to the center of the dispersed settlement, flames licking up from the windows to soot-stain the white stucco. Heat drove out the day's chill, turned the uniforms under the armor sodden-wet; the smoke was thick and choking, billowing just over head-high. Bodies lay crumpled; he saw one half-out of the driver's door of a scorched van, pistol still in its hand. A woman dangled from a shattered shop-window, lying on her back with spears of glass through her chest, long blond hair falling a full meter to the sidewalk to rest in a pool of blood.

A bullet went overhead with a nasty *krak.* More, and a man dropped.

"Take cover!" the platoon commanders were shouting. Two men sprinted out to retrieve the wounded man. "Crew weapons, set up weapons," Niles shouted.

A machine gun crew got into action, then another crew opened up with suppressing fire against the sniper. A non-com ran from one clump of troopers to the next, assigning target sectors. *Good man. I need to get his name.*

Niles put himself behind a bullet-riddled electrocar; the Company Leader in charge of the area came sprinting across the open street with his radiotech and a squad at his heels. They dashed into the cover of the car body and crouched beside the Englishman, panting.

Nobody spared a glance for the two dead militia fighters sprawled beneath the body of the car; a man in his fifties, and a boy who probably had never shaved, both in bits and pieces of uniform and armor. The bullets that killed them had probably been a mercy after the burning fuel drained out and down.

"Situation?" Niles said.

"Hell of a fight for this district, sir," the Helot officer replied; Steve Derex, Niles remembered. He was a tall lanky man, heavy-featured, with the fashionable guerrilla braid down his back and a nasal Welfare accent; one arm had a stained bandage around it. "We rushed them out, but they kept comin' back through the sewers and snipin', thicker'n crabs inna hoor's cunt. Got the cure for *thet,* right enough."

As if on cue, there was a massive *thump* under their feet, a sound that shuddered up through the soles of their boots into the breastbone rather than to the ears. Manhole covers all along the broad concrete roadway sprang into the air with a belch of sooty fire.

"Took a fuelin' station and jist ran the hoses down, sir," the guerrilla said with vindictive satisfaction. "Wit' youz troops, maybe we kin clear an' hold this sector."

Niles looked across the street. Two and four story buildings, offices mostly. Perhaps a laboratory or assay office. Nothing of any great importance, certainly nothing worth losing a whole battalion for. From beyond that came a steady booming sound, rolling and echoing off the cliff-line of the open pit mine just to their south. The armory, and the gun-batteries around it.

Clear and hold for what? But that's the Plan— "Let's do it, then," he said, looking at his watch. *1130 hours,* he thought. The timetable was shot all to hell, and there wasn't anything to accomplish. *What did Skilly expect to do?*

"We rendezvous at Objective A-7, eh?" Skilly said, listening to the ripping canvas sound across the sky.

"Roger wilco." Niles' voice sounded hard and flat, tightly confident.

"Incoming!"

Skida went flat along with everyone else in the headquarters unit. The shot fell a thousand meters behind them, crackling echoes through the jagged hills. Then there was a flash visible even in bright noonlight, and another explosion that shuddered the ground beneath her. Secondary explosion, as piled ammunition went up.

"Goddam, that counterbattery too good!" she said. That was the fifth heavy mortar they had lost in the last fifteen minutes. There weren't many left.

"The Legionnaires are feeding the plotting data to the Royalist gunnery computers," consultant Tetsuko said, not glancing up from his consol. "Falkenberg's troops use Xanadu milspec multiband radars, difficult to jam, and their passive sensors are also very good. And the artillery is dug-in and has armored overhead protection. Not very vulnerable even to precision-guided munitions."

"Field Prime don't need explanations, Field Prime need results," Skilly said.

Crump. Crump. That heavy-mortar battery was down to two tubes, but they were maintaining fire. Skilly felt a stab of warmth; they might have been gutter-scum once, but she had shaped something different, as proud and deadly as a King Cobra.

"Report from Olynthos?"

"The Royalist airborne is not scrambling."

Sheee-it. The little Fang missiles were in perfect position, and the Royals couldn't know about them. The air cavalry was a serious problem in her Upper and Middle Valley operations already, and the Spartans were training more. Half the purpose of this raid had been to lure the helicopters out where they could be killed. "Maybe we outsmart us, cut communications too good so they don't know we here yet," she said. "We hurt them enough here, they come." And maybe the Prince, too, there was a report that he'd been seen in Olynthos. *If he there, he will come running, not like him to send his troops out and not go. We get him and this war is half over. If we stay here, punish the Cits, maybe they send that air cav, maybe they send the Prince, we win it all.* Getting rid of the airborne would be worth taking heavy losses, getting the Prince worth even more. *We could still win, win big.*

But suppose he didn't come? If the air cav didn't come? Then she grinned. *They will come next time. Next time they send everything they have, even the old king.*

"OK, the Mjollnir ready?"

"As instructed, Field Prime. We have it set up on the bunker line in the center of your penetration through the enemy defenses."

She touched her helmet. "Von Reuter?"

"Fallback complete and standing by," he said stolidly.

Von Reuter was a comfort; the man didn't give a damn for the Movement, but cared a great deal about doing his professional best. When it came to making a pursuit as costly as possible, he had a certain sadistic imaginativeness as well; anyone who came after them—*assuming we gets away at all*—would get a very bloody nose, while the Helot forces broke up into dozens of small parties and made their way to prepositioned hiding-places and supply caches. And when it was over, the Kupros Mountains would be a second place the Royal forces would be extremely cautious about entering, would have to guard continuously. It was still a good plan.

"Right," she said. "Let's go."

This time they would ride in style; the first people back out had dropped off transport. Someone had even taken time and a spray-paint can to sketch a red = on the sides of each. Skilly led the slide down the hill to the vans and trucks. As they boarded and drove bumping and crashing down the rock-strewn streambed they passed other captured vehicles heading north into the wadi-and-gully country. They were loaded with sedated wounded, or with boxes and crates of refined silver and platinum and thorium, from the looted warehouses, or medical supplies, food, clothing. . . . Money to slip off-planet through Bronson's outlets to pay for weapons, to pay troops and bribe and buy and intimidate here on Sparta. Supplies to help sustain the expanding Helot forces. They would drive the vehicles to destruction, then transfer the loot to muleback and scatter it.

"*'Make War support War,'*" Skilly quoted to herself, as they drove onto the ringroad of the base. *That chink Sun Tzu knew he business.* The background chatter hummed in her helmet-phones, and the sound of combat was a continuous diffuse stutter all around, louder than the roar of engines. Behind a fragment of wall the Meijians had erected the Mjollnir, a squat two-stage rocket shaped like a huge artillery shell twice the height of a man.

"Faster," she said.

There must be at least a thousand, maybe as many as two or four thousand armed Citizens within the perimeter, besides the formed units in the bunkers and the Legion soliders. Speed and the air-sown mines and disrupted communications had kept them from concentrating, but that would not last long. The trucks and vans careered down the streets, veering between wrecked and burning vehicles. The lead car went over a body with a sodden *thump*; a howling dog dashed by, its coat ablaze. Not only houses and cars were on fire, the wooded tongues of ridgeland between the built-up areas had caught as well, and smoke was drifting in billowing clouds.

Helot soldiers with MP brassards and light-wands were directing traffic, most of it people on foot moving at a run. More vans and trucks with wounded and loot passed them; parties of Movement undergrounders clung to their sides or ran back toward the perimeter, those too compromised to stay even with this degree of confusion, and the scores of transpor-tee recruits they had picked up.

Most of those not on pickup or guard duty were laying boobytraps, everything from grenades taped to doors to huge time-detonated mines in the sewers; a lot of them were wired into the settlement power systems, and there was going to be a *very* unpleasant surprise when they got the turbines running again.

Skilly grinned like a wolf at the thought, opening the door of the van and dropping out at a run as it slowed down beside the block of buildings she wanted. The guides waved them in through doors that had been blasted off their hinges with a recoilless-rifle shell, up steel-framed stairs that sagged and creaked, into a corridor slashed and pocked with the remains of close-quarter fighting with grenade and bayonet.

"Down," the man at the head of the stairs warned. "Under observation." The building was flbrocrete, but the tall rectangle of window at the south end looked out onto enemy-held open ground and the armory-fortress. "Peltast snipers."

They squatted and duckwalked down the transverse corridor; the floor was wet and sticky, and the blanket-wrapped form of a Helot trooper lay in one doorway, the hole blasted through his helmet showing why. The corridor turned, and they were in a long room looking out over the open space. More Helots sprawled on the floor, forming heads-in starfish circles amid maps and plotting tables and a tangle of communications lines.

"Yo, Niles," Skilly said; it was safe to come to a crouch here, and she scuttled quickly over to his side. "Crack this nut yet?"

"No, Field Prime," he said. "Here, take a look." They moved to one side beyond the last of the tall narrow windows, and he offered her the thread-thin jack of a pickup camera one of his troopers was holding over a window on an extension grip. "Careful with that, Yip."

The guerrilla commander flipped down her face shield and plugged the jack into her helmet. A view of the field outside sprang into being on the inner surface of the shield's complex materials. The Brotherhood fortress had taken advantage of the proximity of the big open-pit mine a kilometer further south; nothing showed of the main bunker but a low mound of turf set in a dozen hectares of landscaped park. The plans Intelligence had stolen—Movement Intelligence and the Meijians both—showed an underground wedding cake, fibrocrete and steel running down six stories; generators, air-filtration systems, the works. The Spartans had always known it was a dangerous universe. The bunkers radiating out from it were newer, but also knitted into the park's contours, from the little gatling-pillboxes to the round covered gunpits. As she watched a hatch slid open and the barrel of a light gun appeared, a 155mm with a double-baffle muzzle brake. It fired, a pale orange flash against the noon sun, and the hatch was closed again in smooth coordination with the recoil of the cannon.

"Slick," she said.

About a second all-told, the hatch must be keyed to the lanyard of the cannon, not a practical interval to hit it with a PGM. Somebody had gotten lucky; one of the gunpits was a crater blasted open to the sky, but they could peck at them all day and not do that again, and now the Helot army was taking losses.

A van exploded, taking with it two trucks and some motorcycles, tossing men and loot in all directions. Something else exploded.

"Stop that bunching up!" Skilly screamed.

Niles looked at her, then away.

Getting hot, here, not quite like what Skilly expected. She had hoped for better results, hoped the Brotherhood gunners weren't quite that good. If they could have knocked out the bunkers and gun emplacements, a Helot force squatting on the armory roof would have eleven hundred civilians under its boots. The Royalists talked a good line about not bargaining for hostages, and held to it fairly strongly when it came to their own men . . . but it was another thing to say "go ahead" when someone had a gun in your child's ear.

She was aware that Niles was saying something.

" . . . and a lot of our people are still in there inside the perimeter."

"Pull them out."

"As I just told you, the Royals have managed to activate a number of their mine fields, and their artillery is highly accurate. We can't pull out. Much of our force is pinned down." Niles waved behind them, at the trucks going by. "I hope that loot is good, because we paid a heavy price for it."

She was still studying the gun emplacements. She seemed distracted. Then she touched a button on the side of her helmet. "Anything from Olynthos?"

"Two choppers rode out, down river."

Down river. Away from the action, and away from her missile emplacements. *Where could they be going?* "Nothing else? Nothing? All right. We'll make them come here. Now we use the Mjollnir."

Niles frowned. "Well, that will take out one of the gun emplacements—"

"Do the big central bunker pretty good, though."

"No military targets in the central bunker. Just noncombatants."

"You thinking like a *rabbiblanco* again, Jeffi." He frowned, a little insulted. *I've gotten beyond the naive stage, I think,* he told himself. "What do you mean?" he said stiffly.

"*Noncombatants.* Am no such, just enemies with gun and enemies without gun. Get that Mjollnir ready."

"Sk—Field Prime, they've got close to four hundred women and—well, nearly a thousand children in there, and—"

"Get me the fort, Jeffi. They get just one chance, like everybody."

"You *can't—*"

She was standing between him and the others in the room, whose eyes were on the windows or the corridor in any case. Geoffrey Niles froze as the muzzle of her Walther jabbed like a blunt steel finger into his left side, exactly where the armor latched under his armpit. Her face leaned closer to his, and she flipped up the shield; there was tension in the green-flecked brown eyes, and her voice was pitched soft.

So that nobody else will see or hear, he knew with a distant corner of his mind. *For my sake, if it comes out right.* If he passed what he suddenly realized was a carefully contrived test.

"Jeffi, Skilly want you with her when we win. But Skilly going to *win,* Jeffi my sweet." A slight smile, tender. "Welcome to Skilly's world, my mon, where she live all her life. This the real world, *and it like this everyday.*" The high-cheeked brown face went utterly cold. "I doan give me order twice, mon."

He was already one over the limit.

"Jesus Christ, what's going *on* back there!" Karl Olafson barked. "We've been out of com link for better than half an hour!"

"Major," Barton began, "please listen closely." He waited for a second, until the man in the screen nodded.

"The enemy partially penetrated our security systems, used them to disorganize the defenses, and launched a major attack on Stora Mine in conjunction with internal sabotage. They've overrun substantial areas of the settlement. They have taken heavy losses, and we've stopped them, but they're still out there."

Emotion rippled across the square blond-bearded face, fear, rage, astonishment. Then nothing but business; Barton nodded in chill approval. There was no *time* for anything else.

"We've relieved the Torreys, but they've abandoned the attacks. And thanks to your warnings we found the bombs in our trucks."

"Glad you got that message," Barton said. "Wasn't sure you had."

"Just heard part of it, something about sabotage, decided to look into the trucks. Thank God. All right. We're 120 klicks from you. I can be back there in two hours, three at most."

"No you can't," Barton said. "The road's mined, and I'm sure there are ambushes set up all along it."

There was a long pause. "Our families are back there, in the armory bunker."

"I know. It won't do them a bit of good for you to get killed, though."

"All right, what do you want?"

"They're beginning to realize they can't hold here," Barton said. "They'll start to retreat—and they don't have all that much choice about the route they'll take if they want to get away with the loot they've been scooping up. They have truckloads of stuff they've stolen."

"Christ. From where? Our homes?"

"Probably," Barton said. "Keep hold of yourself. The best thing that can happen right now is for them to load up with loot they won't want to give up. Loot will slow them down as much as all the mines they've been scattering. I don't know this area all that well, but from the map it sure looks like you can cut across the ridge line and show them that two can play this ambush game."

"Christ Almighty! Harry, give me that map. Who knows this area? Yeah, get him—General, I think you have something. Davis? What's this ridge like? How long would it take to get over to here—"

Another voice. "No road, but there's good trails. Let's see, maybe fifteen klicks. Four hours? Three for those in real good shape."

"They may be past by then, but maybe not," Barton said. "I don't think they quite appreciate how hard a retreat under fire can be. Get over there and see what you can do," Barton said. "Be careful, you're not trying to stop them, just punish them as they go out, and that's *all* you do. Don't try pursuit. Don't try anything fancy. Just get where you can see them, dig in and hurt them, no need to close with them."

"Roger. OK, we're on the way."

"It's the Royalist commander," Geoffrey Niles said hoarsely.

Skilly touched her helmet. "This Field Prime, Spartan People's Liberation Army."

"Major Bitterman here." A woman's voice. The central armory would be held by administrative troops. "What do you want?"

"You getting one chance to surrender, or we crack you like the egg," Skilly said flatly.

"You haven't been doing much cracking as yet, rebel." There

was confidence in her voice; the armory bunker would withstand most things, short of a nuclear weapon.

"So far, Field Prime be *nice.* Major, de kids and all in there you responsibility. You put them in military zone. Better you left them out, nobody out here get hurt who not fighting. Last chance."

"I've seen what you did to our homes," Bitterman said. "And this is not a military zone. There is no military force here. This is a hospital and bomb shelter."

"Well, too bad," Skilly said. "'Cause it military to me."

"What do you want?"

"You surrender."

"You know what you ask is impossible. I don't have the authority. I tell you this is a hospital and shelter. There are no military units here."

"They all around you out there."

"Well, yes—"

"General Barton here. Who is this?"

"Calls herself Field Prime, General," Major Bitterman said.

"Field Prime, this is General Barton."

"Good. Surrender, and I don't smash in that Armory."

"The Armory is a hospital and shelter for noncombatants," Barton said.

"I don't believe you, but I don' care much either. You surrender or we crack it open."

"General, she's bluffing," Bitterman said. "This place would withstand anything up to nukes."

"Field Prime don't bluff, as you going to find out. I give you your chance. You don't get another."

"Suppose the hospital did surrender?" Barton demanded. "What does that do for you?"

"Oh, fuck off," Skilly said. She cut the connection. "Hey, Jeffi, that bunker be one big military target. Skilly not to blame if the Cits put people over the ammo and power supply, hey?"

He nodded. "Yes . . . I suppose that's true," he said. His shoulders straightened. *It is. A damned sight more of a military target than Dresden was, after all.* Not that it mattered, the Royalists already had evidence enough to hang them all six times over for violations of the Laws of War. *Unless we win. Winners* write *the laws.*

She touched her helmet again. "Tetsuko. Do it."

Barton looked down at the plotting table. The Helot attack reached through the perimeter of Stora Mine like a knobbly treetrunk, with branches reaching out to touch objectives, twisting around obstacles or strongpoints. He was starting to get an accurate picture; also starting to put serious pressure on the attackers. *Daring. Bold. But they depended on their electronic edge too much. If we'd been here another week—*

If we'd been here another week they would have found out and called off the attack. Attack? Or raid? Did they have an objective other than loot and generally smashing things up?

Information was flowing in now. Disorganized as they'd been, the Brotherhood had put up a good defense, which was what Barton had intended. Defense in place was a lot simpler and easier than a coordinated attack, and these Brotherhood troops all knew each other, had worked with each other, knew what to expect. The enemy had pummeled them in a few places, but by and large the Brotherhood forces had held, and that was all they needed to do.

There was one coherent enemy force around what had been defensive post 12, and many pockets of disorganized Helots, some in minefields, others in old bunkers, but all cut off from the enemy's main body. Put screening units out to keep those groups disorganized and make sure they didn't rally, because some were in a position to do some real damage if they broke free, but otherwise leave them alone for the moment. They'd surrender soon enough when they saw they were abandoned.

That left the rest of the Helots, an organized force of fewer troops than he had in total, but larger by far than any integrated force he could put together. The Helot main body was dug in and holding, but rear elements were already withdrawing, and they were sending back a stream of heavily laden vehicles. Concentrate artillery fire on that group, especially on their escape routes. Every possible shelter, and every crossroads, had long ago been added to the target data base, so it was a matter of picking targets for indirect fire and feeding in their coordinates. Drop rounds onto the roads, knock out vehicles that would have to be cleared away before anything else could get past. Make the enemy think he was being cut off. It took steady veterans to go on advancing when they were afraid their line of retreat was cut.

Right. The artillery fire plan could be left to the local militia officers. They could read maps as well as he could, and they'd seen the terrain.

And that would be wearing the enemy down something fierce. *Which is about all I can do just now.*

Aggressive patrols to make the enemy bunch up, and aggressive artillery to pound them when they did bunch up, and meanwhile gather enough troops to mount a real counter attack. *Time's on our side now. . . .*

"Sir," the technician said. "Launch, from one of the perimeter bunker locations under enemy control." The sergeant was frowning as he tracked. "Very odd trajectory, sir. Straight up, almost. Several—better than five clicks."

Some sort of suborbital? he thought. Then: *Oh, Christ.* The whole purpose of the attack was suddenly plain. Not just to shatter the mine, to demoralize the Citizens of Stora Mine and the northlands around it. Some wounds anger, but there are others that break the spirit. *That's what the enemy intended. Had intended all along.* His hand stabbed out toward the communicator, then froze. There was nothing he could do, nothing at all.

"Sir, it's a two-stage. Computer says antifortress penetrator, heavy job. Apogee. Coming down under thrust. Coming down *fast*. Jesus, Mach 18! 20! Jesus, it's—"

The ground shook beneath their feet.

"Prepare to pull out," Skilly said, raising herself to her knees and wiping blood from the corner of her mouth. The explosion had been more like an earthquake, this close.

The bunkers around the underground fortress were intact, but there was a gaping hole near the entrance to the main bunker. Smoke rose from it. It looked bad, looked terrible.

Baffles and multiple armored doors had protected the weapons posts. The steady fire continued, then the Spartan defenders realized what had happened behind them, and then every remaining weapon opened up, firing continuously with no thought of maintaining concealment. Wire-guided missiles lashed out in return from the Helot positions, beamriders. The savage exchange of fire continued for a minute, then died away. The Helot troops couldn't take the losses and dove for cover. Someone screamed near by.

"Fuck this shit, fuck it, fuck this motherfucking shit!"

"Steady," Skilly shouted. "General comm, Phase—"

RAK. Yip had raised himself to reel in the surveillance camera; the sniper bullet punched through his shoulder, upper lungs and out the other side without slowing much. Everyone dove as it whined around the room, pinging off concrete with that ugly sound that told experienced ears the thumb-sized lump of flattened metal might hit anyone from any direction. The guerrilla NCO's heels drummed briefly on the floor, as blood flooded out from nose and mouth and the massive exit wound under his left armpit.

"—Phase Five, say again, Phase Five," Skilly repeated.

Almost on the heels of her words the first of the huge demolition charges the guerrillas had cobbled together from captured blasting explosive went off, with a jarring thump that was loud even a kilometer away. The remaining militia could be expected to press their pursuit with reckless courage, and the Helots intended to make them pay for it. With explosive and steel rather than close-quarter fighting, where possible; with ambushes where it was not.

"Now, Jeffi. Now we run, and they come after us, and we kill them."

CHAPTER TEN

No battle plan survives contact with the enemy.
—Helmuth von Moltke

"All day for nine hours we ran. It was the contagion of
bewilderment and fear and ignorance. Rumour spread
at every halt, no man had his orders. Everyone had
some theory and no plan beyond the frantic desire to
reach his unit. In ourselves we did not know what to
do. Had there been someone in authority to say,
'Stand here, do this and that'—then half our fear
would have vanished. So I began to realize, sitting in
my swaying car, how important the thousand dreary
things in an army are. The drill, the saluting, the
uniform, the very badges on your arm all tend to
identify you with a solid machine and build up a
feeling of security and order. In the moment of danger
the soldier turns to his mechanical habits and draws
strength from them." Alan Moorehead, on the retreat
from Gazala, June, 1942
—Quoted in John Keegan and
Richard Holmes, *Soldiers*

**Crofton's Encyclopedia of the Inhabited Planets
(2nd Edition):**

Olynthos: town at the head of navigation on the *Eurotas
River* (q.v.), *Sparta*, (q.v.). Established as Fort Tanner
during CoDominium administration, 2030. Communication
with Lake Alexander and its mining settlements by rail
and slurry-pipeline (2060), followed by rapid growth; riverport, fitting out point for outback expeditions, and industrial center. Power supplied by hydro developments on

Vulcan Rapids (potential in excess of 1000 MW.). Smelters, refineries, direct-reduction steel mill, mining machinery,
building supplies, explosives, general manufacturing. Pop.
(2090) 66,227 not including part-time residents.

Description: The town lies on the southwestern bank
of the river immediately below the Ninth Cataract of the
Vulcan Rapids, in an area known as Hecate's Pool. Most
buildings are constructed of limestone blocks from nearby
quarries; notable features include . . .

Melissa was down, hurt and bleeding, and shells were
falling all around them, but Lysander couldn't get to her.
His legs were paralyzed, and when he tried to crawl filthy
hands came out of the ground, reached up with slimy fingers to drag him down. Melissa moaned softly, and Lysander
shouted to her, shouted that he was coming, but he couldn't
move, and—

"Prince."

"I'm coming! I swear it—"

"Prince."

Lysander sat bolt upright on the cot. "Harv. I'm awake. God,
what a horrible dream. Melissa, she was— What is it, Harv?"

"Urgent signals, Prince. You're needed in the orderly room.
Helots attacking the Stora Mine complex."

"Right. I'll be there in five minutes." He suddenly realized
where he was. "My compliments to the colonel, and can he
alert the regiment."

"Already being done," Harv said. "Choppers winding up and
they're rolling the armor out."

"Right. Thanks."

Colonel Bennington and his senior officers were in the staff
room clustered around a map table. "Attention, please," Captain
Larry Sugarman, the adjutant, said. They fell silent as Lysander
came into the room.

"Carry on, please. Jamie, what's happening?"

"Sir, it's an all-out assault on the Stora Mine complex,"
Bennington said. "We don't have direct communications, we're
getting everything on relay through the Legion Headquarters
in Sparta City. General Owensford is on line and would like
to speak with you when you have a moment."

Lysander leaned over to study the displays on the map table.
"There's a hell of a lot more 'maybe' and 'probable' and 'could
be' and plain rumor than real information here."

"Yes, sir, the Helots seem to have disabled the main computer at Stora. Disabled or worse; there are indications they got control of it."

The circles, solid, shaded, and dotted, blinked as the table was updated. Some of the dotted circles vanished, others moved to shaded. A few shaded turned solid as sightings and identifications were confirmed, but there was still more rumor than fact reported on that map table. "Better let me speak to General Owensford," Lysander said. "I'm not learning much here. I presume you're getting the regiment ready to respond."

"Yes, sir. Sergeant, see if you can get General Owensford, please."

"On line and holding, sir," the sergeant said. He handed a headset to Lysander.

"Lysander here."

"Owensford, Highness. Urgent request. Do not send out any air cav reaction force. I'll explain, but that's an urgent advice, sir."

Lysander stared at the map. New data flowed in. The impersonal circles moved or changed sizes, with bright flashes indicating battles. Friendly units shrank as he watched. Confirmed casualties. "Our people are taking a licking," Lysander said. "And they need help. I suppose you have reasons."

"Sir. This is an all out assault, regimental to brigade strength, carried out with full intelligence. They have to know where your units are. Possibly even that you're commanding them. Therefore—"

"I see," Lysander said. "Therefore they've already factored in the First Royals and think they can deal with us."

"Exactly, sir."

"Isn't that called taking counsel from our fears, General? Paralyzing ourselves because of what might happen?"

"Yes, sir, but in this case it may be wise. We don't know nearly enough. What we do know is they were willing to commit in strength to this operation knowing your force was there and ready. The plan was complex: initial attack to draw out the reaction force, ambush that, sabotage the mobile reserve, infiltrate saboteurs—"

"Jesus, and all that worked?" Lysander demanded.

"More than ought to have."

"Skilly," Lysander said.

"Yes, sir, I believe so. I have only intermittent contact with General Barton at the mine, but it's my impression he believes so, too."

"Devious," Lysander said. "So it could be a bluff to keep us from sending reinforcements."

"Sir, she's devious all right, but I can't think the Helots would risk this much on the hope that you'd think it through and not send a reaction force."

"Point taken." Lysander grinned wryly. "And she probably thinks this was a simple plan, not much to go wrong. Advice?"

"Keep your options open. You're our reserve, don't commit yet. You're closer than I am," Owensford said. "And you won't be cut off from direct contact with Barton at the mine forever. You can decide what to do when you have a better idea of what the situation is."

Lysander considered the map again. "Barton's in command at the mine?"

"Yes, sir. Local commander asked him to take over."

"All right. We'll be his reserve until the situation develops. You'll keep me up to date, and get me contact with Barton when that's possible."

"Anything we know, you'll know," Owensford said.

Lysander studied the map table. *I'd give a lot for satellite observations. Have to do something about that, there must be a way to convince the CD. And what the hell am I doing, acting like I'm in charge? But it's my job, and no one else is going to do it, whether I get it right or not. And right now—* He turned to Bennington. "Jamie, get your two best pilots. Load up two ships with scouts. Have them duck out this way, down river, then swing wide and angle back, one out to each side of the valley. Straight recon mission, with the option of committing the scouts if that looks worth doing. If they've gone to this much trouble to set up an ambush of the air cav, I can't think they'll give it away attacking one ship, but the pilots should be careful anyway."

"Yes, sir. If the Helots can infiltrate a big unit they can have a couple of small ones, too."

"Good point. And any scouts they do drop will need full rocket support. But you know that."

"I'll see to it, sir."

The First Royal scouts were not as well trained as the Legion's SAS units, but they'd been trained by the Legion, and had some combat experience. *Training's over. Time to get some use out of them. For that matter it's about time for Sparta to stand up independent of Falkenberg's Legion.* "Jamie, General Owensford estimated regiment to brigade strength committed at the mine."

"Yes, sir."

"Then they can't have much left to block the roads."

"Well—"

"How much could they infiltrate up here?" Lysander demanded. "We've had regular air sweeps. Jamie, if they're good enough to have another regiment beyond what's committed already, we're going to lose anyway. Now are they that good?"

"I see your point. No, sir."

"Get the ground units moving upriver. Usual precautions, recon units lead, watch for mines, but get them moving. Keep the aviation units grounded until we figure out what Miz Skilly has in mind. Next thing, get your Intel and aviation people together and figure out where they're planning on engaging the air cav."

"Engage with what?"

"I don't know. Assume something effective."

"Missiles," Bennington said. "Right." He turned to his adjutant. "Larry, who've we got for this?"

"McCulloch and Levy, sir?"

"Good choice. And Captain Flinderman, I think. Give them the assignment and have them report when they've thought of something."

"Yes, sir."

"And get the ground units moving."

Captain Sugarman spoke quietly into his headset. Lysander turned back to the map table. After a few moments the displays changed again. Friendly unit reports became more reliable, although there was still a lot of confusion about enemy strength and locations. Lysander studied the situation carefully. The entire Stora garrison, nearly a full regiment of well equipped and trained Brotherhood troops, reinforced by Legion units, and they were reduced to ineffective and disorganized pockets. What could do that to them? Whatever it was couldn't be small, and he became more certain the enemy had committed all they had. The Helots couldn't possibly have any large strategic reserve, and not much else either. *Anti-aircraft missile units, infiltrated and—*

Infiltrated where? "Jamie?"

"Highness?"

"Have your experts consider this: a small anti-aircraft missile unit in hiding somewhere along the route from here to the mine, probably close to this base. Not so close they can't get away once they launch their birds, but close enough to observe what we're doing. Preferably with a good escape route through terrain that would halt armor."

"Put that way, Highness—" Bennington manipulated the map controls.

"Right. I see it." Lysander increased the gain on the Decelea

Forest, a university experimental arboretum and park north of Olynthos Base. It was easily large enough to hide a company of missileers, it overlooked the Valley road north, and the broken terrain and gullies extended down to the river.

"Hit us, bug out to the river. Without air we couldn't stop them crossing, and that gives them a hell of a head start in getting away," Bennington said. "It's sure where I'd put an ambush for air cav."

"Can't do any harm to send some scouts up there. We might get lucky," Lysander said. He pointed to the map table. "It's about time some luck fell our way, because it looks like we're getting lunched up there."

"Right." Bennington studied the map. "And I think I'll send some artillery units north along the main road, on up past the Decelea turnoff, but not too far past, say to about here, where they'll have that park in range—"

Lysander grinned agreement.

Bennington called his adjutant. "Larry, please ask Lieutenant Arnold to alert his men, then report here. We have a job for him."

Such a simple thing to do. Sending men off to crawl around in a forest until they can bring in artillery shells onto other men. He looked at his hand, and remembered a line from a poem. Just a line. *'The hand that signed the paper . . . these five kings did a king to death." Why do they obey me? They're older and more experienced.* He remembered Owensford, during the Dales battle, and later in the rescue of the Halleck boy. *At least they try to tell me when I'm making a mess of things.* He turned back to the map table.

"Royal Leader, this is Arnold. I have located our objective. We have an enemy unit under observation. They are unaware of our presence, but I can't guarantee that for long if we attempt to close. Visual and IR observation. Data transmission follows, stand by."

Images on the map table swam, dissolved, and reformed as update data flowed in. Lysander and Bennington eagerly bent over the display.

"Missiles, all right," Bennington said. "I don't recognize the type. Let's see if we have a visual." A blurred image appeared on one of the wall screens. "Still doesn't mean anything to me. You, sir?"

Lysander shook his head. "Afraid not. Okay, let's buck this back to the Capital. Maybe the Legion has something in its data base."

"Right." Bennington made adjustments. "Whatever they are, they're anti-air. Give 'em any capability you like, they were looking right down our throats here. If we'd sent the air cav out in a body to follow the highway, or even the river—"

"Yeah. How long will it take Arnold to get into position to attack them?" Lysander asked.

"We'll have to ask him, but I'd give him at least half an hour."

"Please see that your artillery is in place and ready to fire at that time."

"Yes, sir." Bennington sounded enthusiastic.

They studied the map as they waited. The First Royals regiment was poised and ready, all they needed was assurance that they could move safely. *And the right objective. If we can find the enemy we can kill them. Definitely need to talk to the CD people. There has to be a way to get some satellite observations.*

"Urgent signal from General Owensford for Prince Lysander," Sergeant Roscius said.

"Put him on the speaker. Lysander here."

"Sir—" The word was choked off. Everyone in the command room looked up, puzzled.

Owensford was quiet for a moment. Then his voice turned cold and impersonal. "Sir, the mine garrison is engaging in a spontaneous all out counterattack. It is expected that when the attack makes contact with the enemy it will be repulsed with heavy losses. The counterattack began when the garrison learned that the Helots had used an earth penetrator rocket to attack the hospital and civilian shelter area. General Barton is attempting to halt the attack and reorganize the garrison troops, but he has had limited success. The enemy is retreating. General Barton is worried about ambuscades. He is attempting to halt the pursuit until our forces are better organized.

"Civilian casualties were heavy, amounting to sixty percent in the hospital and may be as high as fifty percent among women and children in the shelter."

The command room fell silent. Someone made a deep growling sound.

"Can you get me a direct link to Stora?" Lysander asked.

"Yes, sir, but I thought I'd better tell you this first."

"Quite correct, General Owensford. I suppose there's no chance this was an accident?"

"No, sir, they threatened to attack the central shelter unless it surrendered. The attack was an earth penetrator missile, specially designed to attack hard targets. It was launched instantly after the Helots ceased communication. There was no time for evacuation. It was deliberate, sir." Owensford's icy calm was beginning to fray.

Cold fury gnawed at Lysander's stomach, but he felt a preternatural calm. "All right. Get me General Barton."

"Yes, sir, I'll patch him through."

"Barton here."

"General, this is Lysander. Peter told me."

"Yes, sir."

"It's not your fault. You couldn't have prevented it."

"I don't see how I could have, sir. But we have five hundred dead children here, and I was in command."

"Can you get me a general circuit? I want to speak to everyone there."

"Klingstauffer, His Highness wants a general circuit. Shall I announce you, sir?"

"Yes, please."

There was a pause, then, "All units. This is General Barton in command center. His Highness Prince Lysander Collins will speak to you now. Your Highness—"

"My people. My sisters and brothers. Please listen. I share your grief, and together we will mourn Sparta's dead. That is later. For now, I have a command. I order you to live. Wherever you are, whatever you are doing, stop, take heed, think. You are what the enemy wanted you to be, enraged citizens seeking vengeance, vulnerable to their treachery.

"And THAT IS NOT ENOUGH. You shall be avenged, but you will not be avenged through haste and madness! Vengeance demands victory, and victory demands that we act together, as a disciplined army! Brothers and Sisters! Organize. Organize and obey your officers.

"People of Sparta. I am coming, I am bringing the instruments of vengeance and destruction. Wait for me. And know that this will not end today, not today, and not tomorrow. It will not end until we are avenged. More than avenged. Together we shall pursue these creatures wherever they go, relentless pursuit, until we have killed them all, killed them not only for revenge but to cleanse this land, we shall cleanse this land of all memory of these creatures. They do not deserve to breathe the same air as free men and women, and by God Almighty I swear it, they shall not!

"We came here to this empty land, and we made a home. We built a land of honor, and we offered to share it with anyone worthy, and this is their answer. They cry for their rights. We will give them their due. We will give them justice.

"My brothers and sisters, listen. Do not throw your lives away. Halt and think. Man your assigned stations. Find your officers. Obey them. Organize, make ready, and wait for me. I am coming, my people. Never doubt it. I am coming. God may have mercy on these wolves but we shall not."

"Legion headquarters has identified those missiles, sir. Something new, but the Legion data base has specs on them. Fucking bastards," Captain Tyson said.

Lysander's look silenced him. "Good. Feed the performance data to the air ops commander. What I want is a good feint. Send the choppers out as if they're headed north, but turn away before they're in danger."

Tyson straightened. "Can do."

"Lieutenant Arnold reports enemy alerted," the communications sergeant said. "They're setting up their birds, like they expect us."

"They heard the speech," Lysander said. "Or someone up north heard it and sent an alert. Doesn't matter. They expect us to come running. Arnold in position?"

"Five minutes, sir. Artillery's targeted. Rockets in place."

"Get those choppers going, then. Colonel Bennington, you'll take command of this operation. Hit them, neutralize them, take some live prisoners able to tell us how they got here, then let the constabulary finish them off. I want this regiment headed north as soon as possible."

"Yes, sir. You want me to command?"

"Yes. As soon as we've defeated the ambush, I'll take the air cav and get up to Stora."

"This may not be the only missile force they have."

"May not be, but it probably is. Jamie, they can't cover the whole countryside. We're scouting alternate routes, I'll take one of those, but by God I'm going. They need me up there."

"Aye," Jamie Bennington said. "That they do, my Prince."

Twenty officers and as many civilian leaders were gathered in the command center of the Stora Mine. They greeted Lysander with grim satisfaction. "We waited, Highness," someone said. "Now lead us."

Ace Barton rose wearily to attention and saluted. "Highness. You'll be taking command now. I'd like to go back to the Legion."

"Denied," Lysander said. "General, you will continue in command here." He looked at the grim faces around him.

"You'll need an expert," he said. "This is General Barton's work, and he is good at it."

"Not good enough."

"I forbid that," Lysander said. "Until now we didn't know, couldn't know, the true nature of our enemy. Blaming ourselves for not foreseeing this criminal act is pointless. General Barton, you will organize the pursuit. The objective is to harass and punish the enemy, of course, but that's not the main objective. It is far more important that you avoid their traps, avoid casualties. Preserve our people, so that we can win this war and rebuild."

"Speak for yourself," someone said. An elderly captain. "We lost a daughter and two grandchildren. I don't care what happens to me as long as I take some of them with me."

"How many others feel that way?" There were mutters, but before they could answer, Lysander shouted, "That is *treason,* Captain Caldon." He paused to let that sink in. "I said treason, and I meant it. Sparta needs you alive, not dead."

He strode into the crowd, and stood among them. "We will cleanse this planet," he said. "To do that we must win this war. Not just kill a few hundred, a few thousand, while their leaders skulk off to do this again. We have to defeat them completely, defeat their soldiers and hang those who ordered this. Anything less lets them get away to kill more women and children."

There were mutters of agreement. "How, then?" Karen Olafson asked.

"It won't be easy," Lysander said. "You can't do it alone. A retreat is always faster than the pursuit unless the retreating force is utterly routed, and these weren't. They were prepared to retreat. You've already run into ambushes."

More muttered agreement. "And so did they," Karen Olafson said.

"Yes. That was good work," Lysander said. "Major Olafson hammered them well, but still they were able to screen him out and slip past. This is what they're best at."

"But— Highness, what can we do, then?" Karen demanded.

"Harass them, yes, but carefully, avoid their traps, avoid their ambushes. Kill and capture anything they leave behind. We've already cleaned them out of the Valley behind us. Four different pockets poised to ambush us, and we have destroyed them all. You can do the same. Keep them moving, make them split up into small groups and disperse. Harass them. Many will desert their cause. The rest will be so dispersed they can't do much harm. You'll have this army neutralized, and this is their main force. Brothers, sisters, you do this, and I'll do the rest. Together we'll win this war."

"What about the others? Some of our workers joined this rebellion. We've found them dead, wearing their Helot arm band," Karen Olafson said. "And that awful little man who put the bombs in the reserve force trucks. They have spies everywhere."

"We'll take the prisoners back to Sparta City and wring them out, and we'll send technicians to screen the others here," Lysander said. "But be careful. We don't want to force anyone to join the conspiracy. In fact—General Barton, you're authorized to issue a general amnesty for anyone not directly involved in atrocities."

"But—"

"He's right, Mrs. Olafson," Barton said. "Of course the amnesty won't apply to those we caught in the act."

"No, they'll go back to the capital. The important thing is to win, win and rebuild. End this war once and for all, and leave it behind us. We can do that."

"How?" Captain Caldon asked.

"We have to deprive them of their bases. We need surveillance satellites. We must halt their off-planet supplies. None of that can be done here, and most of it I'll have to do myself. I'll have to go back to the capital. It's time to win this war, but I can't leave this Helot field army intact. It has to be made ineffective, and for that I need your help. All of you, doing the best work you can. Will you help me?"

The old captain studied the prince's look, looked to his comrades, and turned back to Lysander. "As you command."

CHAPTER ELEVEN

Forms of government change. Long ago James
Burnham, following Hobbes, pointed out that while it
is easy to convince people that government is valuable, it is not quite so obvious that any particular form
of government is best. The belief that fifty percent plus
one will best look out for the interests of the whole is
as much a myth as the Divine Right of Kings, and
certainly no more compelling than the notion that the
state may be best placed in the hands of those educated to the task. Alexander Hamilton, himself "the
bastard son of a Scots peddler," argued for a strong
hereditary component to the United States Constitution on the grounds that an aristocracy would look to
the future and not merely to the next election. Clearly
he expected an open aristocracy which could be
entered on merit, but he was not shy in defending
hereditary rights for those who had won admission.

By the Twentieth Century it had been repeatedly
proved that the qualifications required to obtain the
office of chief of state were not optimum for actually
performing the job; and this regardless of whether the
state was a constitutional republic like the United
States, or the kind of revolutionary anarchy favored by
its southern neighbors. . . .

If the ancients from Aristotle to Machiavelli were
agreed on one thing, it was that when a state required
strong armed forces for its survival, those armed
forces had better be commanded by a single person;
that the political crimes of one bad ruler were infinitely preferable to the dangers of dividing military
command. Better Tiberius than a committee. The first
two hundred years of the United States of America
seemed to disprove that thesis, partly because prior to

1950 the United States would never have dreamed of keeping a large army in time of peace, and even had it done so, that army would have been conscripts, not long service volunteers.

The events of the Twenty First Century demonstrated that the ancients may have been wiser than the moderns thought . . .

—From *Utopia to Imperium: A History of Sparta from Alexander I to the Accession of Lysander,* by Caldwell C. Whitlock, Ph.D. (University of Sparta Press, 2220)

Crofton's Encyclopedia of Contemporary History and Social Issues (3rd Edition):

Interdiction: The CoDominium Grand Senate has always reserved the right to declare an *interdiction* of space travel to or from any solar system or body therein, as punishment for actions contrary to laws which the Grand Senate regards as outside the jurisdiction of even sovereign planets. The most usual cause for such action is an attack on CoDominium citizens, particularly on Fleet personnel, or a violation of the Laws of War (q.v.). Many independent planets regard interdiction as an intolerable infringement of their sovereignty, and an attempt to reduce them to the quasi-satellite status of most Earth governments.

It is noteworthy that interdiction has never been attempted against a planet with significant naval strength . . .

But perhaps naval warfare best illustrates the effect of both permanent and contingent factors in limiting the scope, intensity, and duration of operations. Specialized warships are probably quite recent in origin. The first navies may have been antipiratical in purpose, though there are grounds for thinking that the advantages conferred by the ability to move forces along rivers or coasts first prompted rules to maintain warships. But at any stage of economic development, navies have always been expensive to build and have required handling by specialized crews. Their construction and operation therefore demanded considerable disposable wealth, probably the surplus of a

ruler's revenue; and if the earliest form of fighting at
sea was piratical rather than political in motive, we
must remember that even the pirate needs capital to
start in business.
　　　—John Keegan "The Parameters of Warfare"; *MHQ:*
　　　　　　The Quarterly Journal of Military History,
　　　　　　　　　　　　　　Vol 5:2, Winter 1993

The house stood on large open grounds. The entry drive
led past a gatehouse manned by Royal Regiment soldiers, and
through a small grove of elm trees. Beyond that was half an
acre of well tended grass leading up to the Georgian style
house. The porch was as large as many military houses.

Hal Slater answered the door himself, and waved his visitors inside. "Come in, please, Colonel Karantov. Welcome to
my home. I think you met my wife some years ago?"

"Welcome, Boris," Kathryn Slater said. She wore a simple
black dress of elegant design, with a firestone pin. Her earrings flashed with a shade of green that could only have been
greenfire; it was clear that Kathryn Malcolm Slater was not
worried about money.

"Mrs. Kathryn Slater, General Slater," Karantov acknowledged.
"I present Captain of Fleet Clayton Newell."

Newell, like Karantov, wore civilian clothing, and there was
nothing to indicate that they were two of the highest ranking CoDominium officers in the Sparta system. Karantov kissed
Kathryn's hand, and after a moment Newell did likewise.

Hal Slater leaned on his cane to bow stiffly, and ushered
them across the entry hall toward the rear of the house. "We're
meeting in my study," Slater said. "It's as secure as the Legion
can make it."

"I would say trustworthy, then," Karantov said.

Captain Newell stopped in the entry hall and looked around
the room, at the parquet floors, columns and mirrors, original paintings on the walls. Twin curved staircases led up to
a musician's balcony above the entry. "Very nice," he said.

"Mostly Kathryn's design," Slater said.

"Impressive," Newell said. "And very lovely."

"Thank you," Kathryn Slater said. "Hal was offered an official
residence as Commandant of the War College, but we decided
we'd rather build our own. We've lived so many places, and
this will probably be our last."

"You are pleased to live on Sparta, then," Boris Karantov
said.

"Very. I don't think anyone has ever appreciated us quite so much. Now, if you'll excuse me, I'll leave you to your work," Kathryn said. "You won't be disturbed. Pleased to meet you, Captain Newell."

Hal Slater led the visitors into his study. Karantov and Newell went into the room and stopped short at the sight of several others already there. Karantov bowed stiffly. "Your Highness. I expected to meet you, of course. But—Anatoly, Samuel, you I do not expect."

"I'll explain," Hal Slater said. *Russians never consider a meeting friendly if it doesn't open with a drink.* "But first, may I get you anything? I've let the servants go for the day, but we have just about anything you would like."

"Cognac, perhaps," Karantov said.

Hal opened a paneled cabinet and poured brandy from a crystal decanter into small glasses which he handed around to everyone. They all lifted them formally. "To Sparta," Slater said.

Boris Karantov looked quizzically at Slater, but raised his glass and drained it. "Sparta, then." After a moment Captain Newell did the same.

"Excellent cognac," Karantov said. "Terran?"

"Yes, from the Crimea," Hal said. *To Russians, all brandy is cognac no matter where it comes from.* "Do you care for more?"

"Not just at moment."

"Please, be seated," Slater said. "I believe everyone has met? We will have one more visitor—ah, I believe that's him now." Hal left, and came back a few moments later with Dr. Whitlock.

"Dr. Caldwell Whitlock. You'll remember him as a political consultant to Colonel John Christian Falkenberg. Dr. Whitlock is now also in the employ of the Dual Monarchy. Dr. Whitlock, Colonel Boris Karantov, CoDominium Fleet Marines. Fleet Captain Clayton Newell, CoDominium Navy. Captain Anatoly Nosov, formerly of the CoDominium Navy, retired, now a Captain of the Royal Spartan Naval Reserve. Captain Samuel Forrest, also retired as a Captain of the CoDominium Navy, now Rear Admiral, Royal Spartan Naval Reserve. And of course you know Crown Prince Lysander. Caldwell, we just toasted Sparta's health."

"We'll say I join you in the sentiment," Whitlock said. "Highness." Whitlock bowed slightly, and turned to the others. "Gentlemen, I'm proud to meet y'all."

"Also in the employ of Sparta," Karantov said. "May I ask, Doctor, to whom do you give primary loyalty?"

"There's no cause to choose," Whitlock said. "No conflicts."

"None at all?" Karantov frowned. "Interesting." The study was large and comfortable, lined with book cases. The furniture was leather, massive couches and chairs. Everyone found a seat. "Pleased you could all come," Hal Slater said. "I hope no one will think I am rude if we plunge right in."

"Please do," Fleet Captain Newell said. "I confess I am intrigued to learn that two of my former shipmates are now officers of the Royal Spartan Navy. Matter of fact, I didn't know Sparta *had* a navy." If you listened closely you could still hear a bit of American New Englander accent in Newell's careful speech. "Doubtless all will be explained."

"I could have introduced them as Citizen Nosov and Citizen Sir Samuel Forrest," Slater said carefully. "Citizenship was bestowed with their naval commissions, and His Majesty was pleased to confer the Order of the Golden Fleece on his new Admiral."

"Ah," Newell said. "And this offer—it is an offer, isn't it?"

Lysander smiled slightly. "It is indeed, Fleet Captain. The Kings in Council have authorized extending Citizenship to CoDominium personnel willing to serve the Dual Monarchy. And honors, as deserved, of course."

"I see," Newell said.

"To be brief," Dr. Whitlock said, "we can offer commissions, and generous pay to our Navy Reserve, leastwise to those who join up early, being as how we don't have much Navy. Citizenship. Land. Damn good pensions, and a chance of honors, on retirement from the Spartan Navy." He looked at Karantov. "We can use experienced Fleet Marines, too."

"You have naval personnel but not ships," Newell said carefully.

"Well, that's right just at the moment," Whitlock said. "But you know how things are back around Earth. That could change pretty fast. You never know what happens to ships when a fleet starts coming apart."

"Or where Sergei Lermontov orders ships to go," Karantov said. "I take it I am included in offer?"

"Well, yes," Hal Slater said. "You'll need a place to retire in a few years anyway, Boris. Your family is already here. You can retire from the CD any time you like, and take service with the Royal Spartan Navy. And if the CD stops your pension, we'll pay it. In addition to your Spartan pay, of course."

"Is this the deal you have, Samuel?" Newell asked.

"Yes." Samuel Forrest was a big man, large enough that he must have had difficulty getting around in CD warships without bashing his head. "They guaranteed our CoDominium pensions. Did quite a bit better than that, actually. Certainly better than I expected."

"What do you want from us, Samuel?"

"We like it here," Forrest said. "The only thing wrong with Sparta is the war. Dr. Whitlock—"

"Well, everybody knows the war would end like that—" Dr. Whitlock snapped his fingers "—if the CoDominium fleet did its proper job of intercepting arms smuggling into Sparta. That and protecting our observation satellites. Give us our satellites and stop the enemy bringing in weapons, and we'll finish the war right enough."

"I see," Newell said. He looked significantly to Karantov, then back to Lysander. "You do understand, Your Highness, that we are not in command here? Commodore Guilford does not want to be committed, to either side. He turns a blind eye to the smugglers. To his credit, he has not given Bronson's people direct assistance."

"Merely stops the rest of y'all from doing your jobs," Whitlock said. "Well, thank the Deity for small favors even so. But gentlemen, not to rush you, but where the hell did you think of running to when the CoDominium breaks up?"

Karantov inhaled sharply. "You use strong words."

"Situation calls fo' strong words," Whitlock said. "You got to be hearing the same things I am. So many factions in the Grand Senate nobody can get a coalition together. Budget crisis in the United States. Political crisis in Russia. Already had one mutiny in the fleet, ship's crew didn't want to be transferred." Whitlock shrugged. "That's what we know about. Now, here we got a good planet, stable government that *wants* y'all, wants y'all enough they're willing to give you some land, pay good money, and guarantee your CoDominium pension to boot—I don't need to tell you, if there ain't no CoDominium there ain't likely to be no CoDominium pensions. So you got all this you can look forward to."

"And all you want is—"

"All we want," Prince Lysander said softly, "is for you to do your duty. You have the reputation of men of honor, and you have done your duty to the CoDominium. Now—now you have a duty to civilization. Make no mistake, gentlemen. We're going to win this war, and once we have won it, we will take measures to see we are never again dependent on anyone else for our protection. We will have a Navy."

"And y'all can be part of building it," Whitlock said. "You could start in any time. And of course if you retire here, it makes sense to keep this place as healthy as possible. It's goin' to be your home, so the sooner this war is over, the better for everybody—including you."

"Da," Karantov said. "But Highness will excuse me if I say we do not see you wish to *win* this war." He shrugged.

"That can be remedied," Lysander said. He stood, and the others scrambled to their feet although there was no need to. "If that is your objection, I think it will be met soon enough. Dr. Whitlock, you have full authority to negotiate for me," Lysander said. He bowed slightly. "I'll leave the specifics to Dr. Whitlock. But rest assured, rest assured, gentlemen, we do intend to win this war, and we will do whatever we must do. *Whatever* we must do. Good afternoon."

"Our Prince has grown a very great deal," Dr. Whitlock said softly after Lysander left the room. Everyone nodded.

"Negotiate," Boris Karantov said.

Caldwell Whitlock smiled broadly. "Negotiate indeed." He nodded to Slater, and Hal went to the bar and poured their glasses full of cognac again. Whitlock passed them out. "Now, what y'all want is homes, good land, good positions for your families. Education for your children and grandchildren. Let me point out, gentlemen, that one, two, maybe five percent of the developed land on Sparta belongs to rebels. Worth a whole lot. All that will come to the government when we win. We have land, honors, titles, a decent place to live. We need a navy." He raised his glass. "Here's to you."

Karantov looked to Newell, then back to Whitlock. "Falkenberg makes no mistake in choosing you as his representative," he said. "I have always thought to retire to raise horses, perhaps sail small boats on a suitable lake. What say you, Captain Newell? Lord Admiral Newell has a pleasant sound. As does Baron Karantov. To Sparta."

Clayton Newell looked at the others, then around the room. He hesitated for a long moment before he spoke. "You speak for both Falkenberg and the Dual Monarchy." Whitlock nodded. "Which means you speak for Lermontov and the Grants, even if you do not acknowledge that."

"Oh, I reckon I can say I do," Whitlock said. "Long as it's strictly among us friends. Blaines too, for that matter. But you will understand, Captain, what with the communications difficulties, sometimes we don't have orders, but we still got to act."

"And you have that authority?"

"We really are layin' all our cards on the table," Whitlock said. "Well, it's this way. Colonel Falkenberg values King

Alexander and Prince Lysander a lot, and of course anything purely havin' to do with Sparta is goin' to be decided by the Spartans. Anything else is sort of up to me, and Lieutenant Colonels Slater and Owensford, acting collectively."

Newell sat in an overstuffed leather chair. "And you see no conflict of interest? Between Lermontov's interest and Sparta's?" He looked to Forrest and Nosov. "Nor do you?"

Samuel Forrest shook his head. "Not really. You have to be aware that King Alexander has been a Lermontov ally for a long time. Right now, under the CoDominium Treaty, Sparta isn't even supposed to have a foreign policy, let alone a navy, so how can there be a conflict over external matters? But the simple answer is that King Alexander and Prince Lysander are aware of the situation, and they've left Dr. Whitlock to negotiate for them, so they must not see much conflict."

Newell stared at each one in turn for a long time, then contemplated his still full glass. Finally he said, "Clearly Boris is convinced that your Prince Lysander, and all of you, may all be trusted." He spoke slowly and carefully, measuring every word. "I will confess, what we hear from Earth is alarming, and little would surprise me. War, a coup by Admiral Lermontov, perhaps more likely a coup *against* the Grand Admiral. No one knows what to expect." He shrugged. "Look, I find your offers attractive, I'd be a fool not to. But what happens if you don't win? Suppose Boris and I help you, and you lose? We'd be gambling everything."

"We are now," Hal Slater said carefully. "We don't intend to lose."

"No one does," Newell said. "But it's not entirely in your power. You must know what you're up against. Bronson's got money, power, ambition. He has his own shipping line, and enough money to arm those ships. You could win your war, and still find this planet destroyed, with no CoDominium force to avenge you."

"Which is why we need a fleet," Samuel Forrest said. "It need not be a large fleet, just enough to take on armed merchant men. A squadron would do. I believe there is a squadron here, now." He raised his glass. "To Sparta."

Anatoly Nosov stood and held out his glass for a refill. "Let us be specific. You have four warships here. One is frigate *Volga*, Commander Vadim Dzirkals, very much a Lermontov supporter. One is cruiser *Vera Cruz*, your own, and we presume your officers will follow as you lead. One is frigate *Kirov*; I do not know Commander Chornovil, but I understand he is intelligent, and certainly he was promoted by Lermontov.

More to the point, four of his bridge officers formerly served with me in *Moscva*. Fourth is destroyer *Aegir*, with American commander. I believe Captain Forrest knows him—"

"Harry Clarkson," Forrest said. "A Townsend man, but I think most of his wardroom has other sentiments."

"A fleet," Karantov said. "Perhaps sufficient no matter what Bronson sends."

"You're suggesting mutiny," Newell said. His eyes darted around the room.

"I suggest nothing," Nosov said. "But it is very much possible that soon there is no CoDominium, and it is to advantage of us all that we consider possibilities." He raised his glass. "To Sparta."

"If there is no CoDominium, those with control of naval power will have great power indeed," Newell mused. "Much could be done with a squadron of warships. Not just here."

"Well, I suppose," Dr. Whitlock said. "But then there's this. One time, Napoleon was admirin' his troops on parade. 'See the bayonets of my Guards, how they gleam,' he said. And Talleyrand said, 'You can do anything with a bayonet, Sire, except sit on it.' I'd think the same thing might apply to your warships, Captain. You can blow hell out of a planet, but where you goin' to set down? You want to face the kind of war the Spartans have been fighting? Spend your lives wondering when someone's going to kill your family? Long time ago, a man named Ortega y Gasset pointed out, rulin's not so much a matter of an iron fist as it is of a firm seat." He raised his glass. "To Sparta."

"I will drink to Sparta," Newell said. "And perhaps when Spartans have achieved that firm seat, we will continue this discussion. Until then—" He raised his glass. "To Sparta."

CHAPTER TWELVE

It will be agreed that the aim of strategy is to fulfill the objectives laid down by policy, making the best use of the resources available. Now the objective may be offensive in nature (e.g,. conquest or the imposition of severe terms), it may be defensive (e.g., the protection of certain areas or interests) or it may merely be the maintenance of the political *status quo*. It is therefore obvious straight away that formulae such as that attributed to Clausewitz, 'decision as a result of victory in battle,' are not applicable to all types of objective. There is only one general rule applicable to all: disregard the method by which the decision is to be reached and consider only the outcome which it is desired to achieve. The outcome desired is to force the enemy to accept the terms we wish to impose on him. In this dialectic of wills *a decision is achieved when a certain psychological effect* has been produced on the enemy: when he becomes convinced that it is useless to start or alternatively to continue the struggle.

—Général D'Armée André Beaufre,
An Introduction to Strategy, 1965

From this time Cataline turned his back on politics because it involved envy and strife and was not the speediest and most effective means for attaining absolute power. He obtained quantities of money from women who hoped their husbands would be killed in a revolution, conspired with a number of senators and knights, and collected plebeians, foreigners, and slaves. Lesser leaders of the conspiracy were Cornelius Lentulus and Cethegus, then praetors. To the Sullans

1062

up and down Italy who had squandered their profits
and were eager for similar doings he sent messengers,
Gaius Mallius to Faesulae in Etruria and others to
Picenum and Apulia, and these quietly enrolled an
army for him. These facts were still secret when they
were communicated to Cicero by Fulvia, a woman of
position . . .
                        —Moses Hadas, *A History of Rome*

The Senate Chamber was unusually quiet. High marble walls,
a dais for the speaker, benches encircling it. The Chamber had
been designed as a romanticized version of the best description they had of the place of government of ancient Sparta.

Two thrones, one to either side of the rostrum, stood empty
as the Senators took their places around the room. There was
an electric air, which made Senator Dion Croser nervous. What
did they plan?

There was a thundering knock at the door. The Sergeant
at Arms opened it, looked out, and closed the door again. "My
Lord Speaker, the Kings ask admission."

The Speaker's name was Loren Scaevoli, a dry stick of a
man nearing his hundredth year and looking it even with
regenn; he had been the youngest of the Founders. His voice
had an unusual inflection to it this day, almost of glee. "Senators, the Kings ask admission to our chamber. What say you?"

"Aye and welcome!" a hundred voices shouted.

"Three cheers for His Majesty Alexander I!"

The cry ran through the chamber, and the crashing *hurrah*
echoed from the high marble walls of the big semicircular room.
One hundred twenty-three Senators lined the benches that
encircled the dais; one hundred seventeen cheered. Dion Croser
stood politely with his handful of supporters, waiting for the
sound to die.

"Three cheers for King David!" If there was any less enthusiasm it was hard to notice, but when someone shouted "And
for Prince Lysander!" there was no mistaking the renewed
enthusiasm.

"It is the will of the Senate that the Kings be admitted,"
Scaevoli said formally. The Sergeant opened the door to allow
them in, then closed it to exclude the Life Guards. By tradition the Kings of Sparta were guarded only by Senators when
they entered the Senate chamber, and they entered only by
permission, not as a matter of right.

They came down the center aisle together, walking slowly.

Something unusual, Croser thought with a prickle of interest, looking down at the Speaker's dais. He had developed a certain affection for the mock-classical atmosphere in this room, and even for the cut and thrust of Parliamentary debate. Decadent and doomed, of course, but he would miss it; even the smells of tobacco and the leather cushions.

The Kings took their places in the twin thrones on either side of the Speaker's chair. David I, solemn and grim faced, as if he dreaded what was about to happen. And Alexander, smiling, looking very healthy indeed, compared to a few months ago. *Damn him.* The waxing insanity of the Collins king had been a large part of his plans. Behind the dais the display wall was set to show the crowned mountain of the Dual Monarchy.

For now, Croser thought. *For now.*

The Privy Council, led by Crown Prince Lysander, filed in, taking their seats in the horseshoe-shaped area surrounding the thrones. That *was* unusual, except for the Budget Debates and the yearly Speech from the Thrones. Then the five Ephors, the direct representatives of the Citizens. Croser raised his eyes to the spectator's gallery that tinged the upper story of the chamber, just under the coffered ceiling. One of his supporters was arguing with the guard.

Trouble, he thought, looking down at his fingers arranging the papers on the table before him. Black folders against the creamy stone, the whole interior was lined with it . . . He tapped at the terminal built into it; the library functions were active, but not the communicator.

The senators who had escorted the Kings to their thrones filed back to the benches. The Sergeant at Arms carried in the mace of office on its crimson cushion, and the Senatorial Chaplain delivered his invocation, ending as always, "God save the State," but it seemed more than perfunctory today.

"This one hundredth seventy-eight session of the Senate of the Dual Monarchy of Sparta will now come to order. This is to be an Executive Session; I remind all members of this august body that there exists a state of apprehended insurrection."

Croser pressed a key. "Point of order, Mr. Speaker," he said, and the computers relayed his voice until it seemed to come from everywhere and nowhere. "Is this to be a closed session? Pursuant to the Senatorial Rules of Procedure and the Constitution, Article XXI, Rights of Assembly and Information Access, I protest that such action is highly irregular if not unconstitutional without prior notice."

The Speaker's eyes were almost hidden by their wrinkled pouches.

"Senator Croser, you are not recognized."

"I protest!"

"Protest is noted; please be seated, sir."

The Speaker raised the amplification. "Senators, I spy strangers. The Sergeant at Arms will clear the Senate Chamber of all who do not belong here."

Something squeezed at Croser's stomach, as the clerks and secretarial staff left their posts. Shouts came from the galleries; Guard troops were clearing them, and though their uniforms were the gray and blue and silver of ceremony, their rifles held magazines and fixed bayonets. He half-rose and chopped one hand down across his chest; above him his bodyguard Cheung relaxed from the beginning of a move that would have ripped out a soldier's throat as he sprang to seize a weapon. The visitors were led away, out of the galleries, out of the chamber.

Croser keyed the circuit that connected him with the other NCLF representatives in the Senate. "All to be detained," he murmured. "So that nothing can get out. Although silence is a message in itself."

"Leader, what shall we do?" one of his supporters hissed in his ear.

"Shut up."

"But, Leader—"

"Shut up and *stay* shut up. Not one word, any of you; not under any circumstances whatsoever."

Croser forced his lips to stop curling back from his teeth, tasting sweat as he reached out calmly to take a sip of water. *What was it that old tombstone said? "I expected this, but not so soon."*

The Speaker rapped his gavel. "I recognize the President of the Council of Ephors," he said.

Citizen Selena Borah Dawson, wife of the Principal Secretary of State, and very popular in Citizen Assemblies. The Ephors functioned largely as ombudsmen, but they had certain formal duties as direct representatives of the Citizens. "Senators, I ask for a resolution which under the Constitution the Kings may not request, but which you may grant."

There was a ripple of movement. Croser hit the *record* and *playback/scan* functions. "Ah, interesting," he murmured. "See, there are the ones who knew it was coming." Excellent security on this measure, if Murasaki hadn't picked it up. A damaging blow, despite all the preparations.

"Senators, I make no speeches," Selena Dawson said. "The Speaker will show the evidence on which the request of the Citizens will be based."

The Speaker touched buttons, doing the work of his vanished clerk. The crowned mountain faded from the giant display screen above the dais, to be replaced with a close-up shot. Croser recognized it; the Velysen ranch, with the dead bodies displayed.

"Senators, bear witness," the old man said.

The image faded, to be replaced by another. This time a bleeding child, screaming by the corpse of its mother outside a burning building.

Hmmm. Croser thought. *Oh yes, the Hume Consolidated Financial Bank bombing.*

More. Burnt out ranches. A playback of Steven Armstrong's engine crew drowning before the camera as their ship sank, of his family burning in their car. Chaos and blood in a restaurant, and a young man with his ribs peeled open by the grenade he had smothered. The frozen body of Deborah Lefkowitz, as the Helots and the scavengers had left it. More still; after fifteen minutes Croser leaned back in his chair and let his eyes slide down to the panel before him, flicking through shots of the other Senator's faces. Even a few of his own NCLF appointees were looking gray; there were tears elsewhere on the benches, and not only among women. A few were looking away also, swallowing. Colleagues moved to assist one elderly representative who fainted.

"And the final horror," the Speaker said. The wall was filled with the image of the shattered bunker at the Stora Mine. The camera moved inside, to hospital beds thrown over, then came to a halt on a tangle of broken and bleeding children shielded by dying women. "A deliberate act, done with equipment imported for the purpose," Scaevoli said. "Imported from off-planet, brought all this way to be used to kill our women and children. Madame President, do the Ephors have a request of this body?"

"We do, My Lord Speaker. The State is in danger. We ask for the Ultimate Decree."

Lars Armstrong leapt to his feet. "At last!"

I might have known, Croser thought. Steven Armstrong's brother, and his successor as representative of the Maritime Products Trade Association.

Scaevoli looked to the Ephors. "Is this the request of the Ephors? Do each of you agree?" Three nods of assent. A fourth, a young man thought to be a radical fireball, stood staring in horror at the screen. He looked from that to Croser, looked defiantly to the Speaker. "Aye," he said.

The Speaker bowed, and turned to the chamber. "I recognize Senator Armstrong."

"My Lord Speaker, I move that the Senate instruct the Kings to take all measures necessary to ensure the safety of the state, effective as of this date and to run for one Spartan year before expiry or renewal."

"Mr. Speaker!" Croser said, shooting to his feet.

"I recognize Senator Croser."

"If the honorable Senator moves the Ultimate Decree—" essentially a drastic form of martial law, with the suspension of civil rights "—then surely there must be debate beyond mere assertion! Is this a deliberative body, or a rubber-stamp whose assent is secured in advance by conspiracy?"

Or a lynch mob, he thought, looking at the faces glaring at him from every corner of the chamber.

"Mr. Speaker."

"I recognize Senator Armstrong."

"Mr. Speaker." Armstrong was a tall blond man like his brother, perhaps a little heavier, with hair that was thinning on top. His smile was much like that of the carnivore piscoids his family's ships hunted. "I can best reply using words other than my own.

"How long, O Croser, how long," he began, in a calm conversational tone.

"How long will you continue your abuse of our forbearance? What bounds will you set to your display of reckless contempt? Are you not affected by the alarm of the people, by the rallying of all loyal citizens, by the convening of the senate in this safely-guarded spot, by the looks and expressions of all assembled here? Do you not perceive that your designs are exposed? The Senate is well aware of the facts, but the criminal still lives. Lives? Yes, lives; and even comes down to the Senate, takes part in the public deliberations, and marks down with ominous glances every single one of us for massacre.

"As to why—" Armstrong pointed silently to the screen.

Croser waited out the applause. *You'll envy your brother before I'm through with you,* he thought coldly.

"Mr. Speaker," he said quietly.

"I recognize Senator Croser."

"My compliments to the Senator on his ability to paraphrase the Classics; however, he is not Marcus Tullius Cicero. Nor is this Rome. Nor am I," he went on, letting a slight sneer into his tone, "the brother of the man whose agents destroyed a shuttle with over one thousand men, women and children aboard—an atrocity I note is *not* among the disgraceful collection of demagogic propaganda to which we have been exposed! An atrocity which has imperiled the independence of Sparta."

One of Armstrong's friends gripped him by the arm as he began a lunge forward.

"If this assembly," Croser went on, "wishes to emulate the Senate of the late Roman Republic—and court the same fate at the hands of ambitious generals and mercenary armies— then at least my voice will have been heard in warning!"

He sat. *Not bad,* he thought. Not that it would make any difference, but it would be there on the record. Another Senator asked for the floor.

"I recognize Senator Hollings."

"Mr. Speaker. While I agree that a grave emergency confronts the State, I am disturbed by the reckless haste with which the Ultimate Decree has been proposed; in fact—"

Croser glanced at his wrist; a half-hour since the session began. *Longer the better,* he thought.

At last the Speaker's gavel fell. "Senators, do I hear a second for Senator Armstrong's motion?"

"I second."

"Senator Makeba seconds. Senators, a motion is before this assembly. The Ephors acting in their capacity as Protectors of the Citizens have requested the Ultimate Decree, authorizing the Kings to take all necessary actions to safeguard the State, and it has been duly moved and seconded. Duration is one year from this date, subject to renewal by vote. A two-thirds majority is necessary for the passage of this Decree. Senators, you have one minute to register your will."

A thick silence descended; despite the ventilators, Croser could smell the sweat of fear and tension. At last Scaevoli looked up from his desk and smiled at him.

"For, one hundred seven votes. Against, eight votes. Eight abstentions. The Decree is in force, as of this day, April seventeenth, 2096, and this hour."

The old man rose, moving with careful dignity. There was a slight gasp as he lifted the Mace of the Senate from its cushion; the procedure was laid down in the Constitution, but Sparta had never seen it done in all the years since the Founding. Scaevoli turned, bowing as he laid the symbol of representative power on the empty plinth equidistant between the two thrones.

"Your Majesties," he said, bowing to the left and right. "Into your hands we yield the Sword of the State. May God preserve and guide you."

"Amen," Alexander said.

He stood. After a moment David I stood as well.

"Our first act shall be to appoint Crown Prince Lysander as Master of the Forces," Alexander said. "He shall act in the name of the Kings with the authority of the Kings until such time as we shall rescind those powers." He bowed toward David.

David said, "So be it," and sat.

Alexander was still on his feet. "Senators," he said. "One man is the author of our miseries; one man is responsible for the unspeakable conspiracy which has caused so much suffering and death among Our people." He paused, as all eyes turned to Croser. "From respect for your august assembly's immunity from executive action, I now require that you place under arrest Senator Dion Croser, on charges of High Treason, and take him from this place to be delivered to duly appointed officers who shall place him in custody and hold him at our pleasure."

Croser stood; something seemed to pass from his face, as if an invisible mask had been removed.

"Very well." His voice cut through the buzz of excitement that filled the chamber, clear and carrying enough not to need amplification; half a dozen Senators were elbowing their way toward him.

"Treason?" he said coldly, then laughed. "I too have an appropriate quotation. "Why is it that treason never prospers? Why, if it prosper, none dare *call* it treason!'"

Silence fell for a moment. "And if this is treason, rest assured I shall make the most of it. *I'll be back.*"

"Attach the leads here and here, please," Jesus Alana said.

They had selected a small staff office in the Palace for the interrogation; the chair to which Croser was strapped was already secured to the floor, and the equipment had been easy to set up.

"As you can see, gentlemen," Alana went on, "this is a completely non-intrusive technique. No pain or drugs. The subject condemns himself."

Alexander and David seated themselves in one corner, determination and distaste on their faces; the Senators joined them, and Scaevoli, who watched with bright-eyed interest. Prince Lysander entered in full uniform.

"About time," he said softly, smiling at Croser. "About bloody time."

"Catherine?"

"Ready to calibrate," she replied, looking up from the desk.

"Senator Croser," Jesus Alana said politely. "You realize this system doesn't require your collaboration? Your body and nervous system cannot lie to the machines; even if you don't say a word, 'yes' and 'no' will come through as clearly as if you had shouted. Why don't you cooperate now, and save us all time and trouble, and yourself some discomfort?"

Croser could not move in the padded clamps, but he managed to spit with fair accuracy at the Legionnaire's feet. Jesus Alana sighed.

"Is your name Dion Croser?" he asked.

"Got it, positive," Catherine said.

"Are you a dolphin?"

"Negative, Jesus."

"Are you leader of the conspiracy to overthrow the Dual Monarchy?"

"Positive, ninety-seven percent. Fear reaction, aggression. Ambivalence; he's been wondering if he's still really in charge."

This time Croser spoke: *"Om."*

"Do you know the woman known as Field Prime?"

"Om mane padme hum."

"Does she work for you?"

"No—"

"Uncertainty," said Catherine.

"With reason," Jesus answered. "You have been engaged in warfare against the Dual Monarchy. Are you in the employ of anyone off-planet? Are you in the employ of Grand Senator Bronson?"

Catherine shook her head.

Jesus Alana smiled thinly. "Have you received material and financial assistance from Grand Senator Bronson? Thank you. Do you receive much assistance from that source? Was one item of that assistance a large missile designed to penetrate and destroy fortresses? Ah, you remember that missile. Were you aware that this missile was to be employed in the attack on the Stora mines?"

"Not for that!"

"Not for what, Senator?" Jesus asked pleasantly. "You were then aware that there would be an attack on the mine. Did you approve that attack?"

"Om mane padme hum."

"To whom did you give that approval? Did you give approval to Field Prime? Thank you. Is Skida Thibodeau the person known as Field Prime?"

"Om mane padme hum."

"Where is Field Prime now? Do you want to see her? Shall we bring her to you when we have captured her? Perhaps you would care to be in the same cell?"

Croser looked as if he had swallowed a serpent. Catherine held up her thumb and forefinger joined in a circle. Her smile showed wicked glee.

"Does Senator Bronson have representatives on this planet? Ah, does he have more than one? Ah. Thank you, we will return to that point later. For now, does the term technoninja mean anything to you? Do the technoninjas work for you?"

"Doubt again, Jesus," Catherine said.

"So. Ms. Thibodeau calls herself Field Prime. Do you have a title in this movement? What is that title? Are you called President? Chairman? Something Prime? Ah. Sparta Prime? Political Prime? Movement Prime?"

"Om mane padme hum."

"City Prime? Not city but closer. Ah. Capital Prime? So. You are known as Capital Prime," Jesus said. "You see, Senator, it does you no good to evade, and I fear your bio-feedback training is not up to this task. Do you know where Field Prime is? Do you know where her primary base is located? Thank you. Do others around you know? Does the bodyguard known as Cheung know?" Jesus smiled wolfishly. "You may be pleased to know that the Cheung brothers are reunited, in the basement of the Palace. We will soon know all that they know."

"So much for your legalities," Croser said. "Lee Cheung has committed no crime. I didn't know he had a brother."

"Both lies," Catherine said.

"Ah, but under the Ultimate Decree we need not prove a crime to detain someone," Jesus said.

"It wasn't passed yet when you arrested him."

"True, but he was seen to be armed in the Senate Galleries. He was detained for proper identification, but before his release—you see, Senator, you are not the only one who can employ the law for his own purposes. We now require confirmation of information we already have. Is the primary base camp in the Southeast? Here, on this map."

"Om mane padme hum."

"Do you ever eat dogfood for breakfast?"

"Om mane padme hum."

"Was your mother attractive?"

"Om mane padme hum."

"In this sector then? Ah. In this river valley?"

"Om mane padme hum."

"How far from the river is the entrance to that cave known as Base One? More than two hundred kilometers? More than three hundred?"

"*Om mane padme hum.*"

"Did you order the assassination of Alicia Armstrong?"

"*Om mane padme hum.*"

"Ah," Catherine said. "Reaction damping a little . . . Negative. He didn't."

"Was the bombing which killed Alicia Armstrong done on your orders."

"*Om mane padme hum.*"

"Positive, with some ambivalence, Jesus. Remarkably good control over his pulse rate," she added. "Congratulations, Senator. I've worked with few better."

"Did you intend the bombing to kill Senator Steven Armstrong?"

"*Om mane padme hum.*"

"Positive, he did."

"Is Senator Hollings a member of your conspiracy?"

"*Om mane padme hum.*"

"Negative on that, but there's some ambiguity."

"Do you consider Senator Hollings to be an unconscious supporter of your conspiracy?"

"*Om mane padme hum.*"

"Yes-no."

"A dupe?"

"Positive."

"Would you call him a useful idiot?"

"That's it," Catherine said.

"Is the moon made of dog droppings?"

"*Om mane padme hum.*"

"Is the base camp more than thirty kilometers from the bend in the river? Ah, is it more than fifteen? More than ten? More than ten but less than fifteen, then . . ."

"I'm glad that's over," Alexander said as the guards took Croser away. A look of distaste bent the Spartan king's mouth for a moment. "It's necessary, but I don't like it."

Lysander's face showed no emotion at all.

"Over for the moment, Sire," Jesus Alana said, looking up from his notes. He punched a key. "There, the RSMP and the Milice can act on the new information. There's a great deal more information yet to be got out of Croser," he added. "*Madre de Dios,* I'm happy we didn't have to beat it out of him; that one, you could pull his toenails out and get nothing."

"I can still hardly believe it," David said, shaking his head and looking at his hands. "All these years, he was . . . and this was inside him, this sewer. How could, he was meeting people and smiling at them and talking and all along . . . Is he mad?"

"No, Sire," Catherine Alana said, beginning the shutdown on her equipment as she went on:

"Thibodeau may be, technically, from the profile we've built. Human beings have a capacity to learn speech, and to develop a conscience; if they aren't taught at the right stage, conscience atrophies, and you get a feral child or a sociopath. She could be a borderline sociopath. Croser's as sane as any of us here— and as bright, IQ of about one hundred fifty-two—he's just too bloody evil to be allowed to live."

"Amen," Alexander said grimly. "And he'll hang, along with the others we catch."

"And his property goes to reward loyal Citizens," Lysander said. He leaned forward to study the form his father held in his hands. It was a proscription notice, bearing the Royal seals and signatures, describing the individuals' crimes and ending with an identical proclamation: *to be cast out from all protection of law; declared to be among the enemies-general of human kind, to be dealt with as wolves are.*

"Suitable," he said. "I just hope we catch them all."

"We won't," Jesus replied, calling up some of his notes. "They had plans; cut-outs, dispersal plans, duplicate facilities, you name it. Friend Croser was smart enough to arrange not to know a lot of details, and a lot of them will be going to ground right now. We'll sweep up a good many of the big names, and any number of the dupes who didn't know the NCLF was in the rebellion."

"We must be careful of those," Alexander said. "They have committed no crime—"

"Sire, they were at best very stupid," Lysander said. "And while we can't proscribe stupidity, we don't need to reward it. I take it, Captain, you do not consider this morning decisive."

"On the contrary, Highness, I believe it is the most decisive act since the war began. We have undoubtedly hurt them very badly, and if we can keep them on the run we may be able to end this war."

"The leadership," Alexander said. "We need Miss Thibodeau."

"And Murasaki," Jesus Alana said. "He perhaps more than the others, Sire."

"We shall proclaim rewards for both of them," Alexander said. "One million crowns, payable in CoDominium credits if so desired, for the head of Skida Thibodeau. Two million if she is delivered alive. Half a million for Murasaki dead, one million alive. Half that for information leading to their death or capture. We'll set up ways to make it easy to tell us."

"That should prove interesting," Jesus said. "Some of those gutter scum would sell their entire families for much less. I foresee interesting times for their leadership."

"What will you do now?" Alexander asked Lysander.

"Melissa will recover," Lysander said. "I'd like to stay with her, but you've just made me Master of the Forces, and I don't suppose I'll have a free moment. I'm not protesting, it's what I asked for."

"Be careful what you wish for," Catherine Alana said softly.

"Exactly. We will need to marshal our forces against this Base One of theirs, and this time we will destroy it. It and all the equipment in it. But that isn't going to be simple."

"Indeed," Jesus Alana said. "The Legion will assist, of course, particularly with the artillery, but most of this must be primarily a Spartan effort."

"Yes. And that, I have to say, is quite satisfactory. It's not that I don't value the Legion's contributions—"

"But it's nice to have your destiny in your own hands," Catherine said. "We understand, Highness. Maybe better than you think."

CHAPTER THIRTEEN

Guerrillas required a base. Although they traditionally lived partially at their enemy's expense—because of their raids against supply depots and convoys—guerrillas still needed a place that provided them an assured source of supplies, such as Mina's secluded area and powder factory. Without such a base, the need for food, fuel, equipment, and ammunition would dominate their operations, place a severe constraint both on their movements and their choice of objectives for their raids, and could drive them from one raid to another in search of supplies until they had exhausted their physical and psychological resources. In addition, a base provided a place for rest and recuperation and a point to which they could retreat. Thus, the base had to be reasonably secure from enemy attack . . .
—Archer Jones, *The Art Of War in the Western World*

One of the surest means of making a retreat successfully is to familiarize the officers and soldiers with the idea that an enemy may be resisted quite as well when coming on the rear as on the front, and that the preservation of order is the only means of saving a body of troops harassed by the enemy during a retrograde movement. Rigid discipline is at all times the best preservation of good order, but it is of especial importance during a retreat. To enforce discipline, subsistence must be furnished, that the troops may not be obliged to straggle off for the purpose of getting supplies by marauding.
It is a good plan to give the command of the rearguard to an officer of great coolness . . .
—Baron Antoine Henri de Jomini, *The Art of War*

✧   ✧   ✧

The helicopters skimmed in low over the hilltop. The long twilight of Sparta's northern-hemisphere summer was settling over the Dales, throwing purple shadows over the forested vales between the hills. Gathering dusk made the muzzle flashes huge belches of leaf-shaped flame as the howitzers bellowed from their laager, six 155mm cannon on light-tank chassis. They and their supporting vehicles were dug in behind a two-meter berm gouged out by the engineering vehicles. A line of trucks snaked back to the south, bringing up heavy shells to feed the iron appetite of the guns. A radar vehicle stood a little to one side, its big golf-ball shaped tracking antenna rocking slightly on its gimbals; other vehicles were spotted around the enclosure, APC's for the crews, communications tanks, trucks, a field-kitchen.

Peter Owensford stood in the open doorway of the aircraft; the moment the skids touched down he tumbled out, followed by his Headquarters group. Then the lead helicopter whirled away, and the second touched down briefly to disgorge its load. The dark machines sped south, hugging the nape of the earth, the low slicing sound of their silenced blades fading quickly. The soldiers' boots swished in grass, sank into the soft fluffy purple-brown earth thrown up by spades and earthmoving machinery or simply ripped free of the sod by treads and wheels; it smelled as rich as new bread, under the overpowering sweetness of crushed grass and the diesel-explosive stink of war.

Five tubes firing, he thought, remembering to leave his mouth slightly open so the overpressure would not damage eardrums. The sixth must be deadlined for maintenance, about par for the course. The artillery barrage halted, an echoing silence broken by the squeal of bearings as the self-propelled guns shifted targets. Off on the horizon to the north light flickered, lighter weapons firing. Owensford tapped into the battalion push as he walked toward the command table set up at the rear of an APC. Sastri had just acknowledged a request for counterbattery fire; as they walked up he could see a spyeye or RPV surveillance camera view of the target, two batteries of heavy mortars firing from within a narrow erosion-cut gully in the limestone rock. Sastri's singsong voice murmured as the little Krishnan bent over the table.

Muzzle flashes came from the enemy 160s. The table was Legion-standard equipment, either what they had brought to Sparta or one of the shipments of Friedlander battle electronics just coming in; looking down was like being suspended in an aircraft observing the Helot battery. The silence was eerie, you expected to hear the CRUMP and whistle of heavy mortars . . . giddy-making, as the viewpoint shifted. Definitely an RPV about a kilometer to one side. The muzzles of the mortars dipped as the hydraulics lowered them into loading position.

"Fire mission. HE and anti-personnel equal measures," Major Sastri said. He touched controls and a grid sprang out on the table-screen, and then a red dot centered on the enemy position. "Bearing and range, mark."

Another voice sounded, calm and flat, the battery commander. "Received and locked." Clangs and rattles from the guns as the autoloaders cycled. "Loaded basebleed HE standard. Gun one, ranging fire. Mark. Shoot."

A short massive sound, slapping dirt and grit across the firebase in a hot puff as the first gun fired and gas shot out of the twin-baffle muzzle brakes. The gun recoiled, and the vehicle rocked back on its treads slightly, digging the spades at the rear of the chassis deeper into the dirt. A sound like heavy cloth tearing faded across the sky to the north. The mortars on the screen were firing when the shell exploded eleven seconds later, on the lip of the crevasse in which they were emplaced and directly above them.

"Correction," Sastri said. He read off numbers from the map table. "Execute fire mission, battery, fire for effect," Sastri said.

Almost on the heels of the words the other guns of the battery opened up, cycling out the heavy shells at one every seven seconds. On the screen the narrow slit in the earth vanished; most of the 155mm rounds dropped neatly through it, to gout back out in white-light flashes. Several struck the rock lips on either side and penetrated before exploding, sending multitone cascades of chalky rubble down into the depths of the canyon. Smoke and dust billowed back, silent and dreadful; then the ammunition with the mortars detonated in a string of secondary explosions that lifted the whole hillside up in a crackle-finished dome of smoke.

The image jiggled. An operator spoke:

"Acquisition on the drone. Tracking. Evasive action." The surface rushed up and the viewpoint was jinking down a valley. Suddenly camouflage nets showed between the trees, IR-sensor enhancement. Owensford leaned forward in sharp curiosity, and then the screen went to pearly-gray blankness.

"Battery, fire mission," Sastri said thoughtfully. "Three rounds. Penetrator and impact-fuse, mark." His fingers touched a portable keyboard. "Whatever was under that net is deserving a tickle."

He looked up and saluted. "With you in a moment, sir. Captain Liu, take over. This way."

They walked downslope and south, speaking quietly; the helmet earphones filtered the huge thudding noise of the guns.

"Not having much trouble?" Owensford said.

"No indeed, sir. The preliminary artillery duel went as expected, and now they have nothing with the range to reach us, while we can hit them as we please. The drones provide good observation, and the Spartan scouts are proving very effective as well. This is a very one-sided battle, and so long as we have ammunition it will continue to be."

"Just the kind I like," Owensford said. "Well done."

"Thank you, sir. Ah, here we are." The secondary laager was a little apart from the regimental artillery battery; one vehicle was a trailer, from which a tent had been unfolded.

They ducked inside the tent, flipping up the visors of their helmets. There were four men inside; George Slater, commander of 1st Brigade, the spearpoint force of the Royal Army columns heading north into the Dales. The Royal Army colonel commanding the 2nd Mechanized Regiment . . . *Morrentes*, Owensford remembered, he'd been a Brotherhood militia officer last year, transferred to the Field Force shortly after the first Dales campaign. A Royal Army interrogator, a sergeant; tall, wiry-slender, beak-nosed and thin-faced, with steady dark eyes. And a Helot, in the dentist-style chair, his head and limbs immobilized by clamps; his face had the glazed, wandering look of someone under questioning drugs.

Not really truth drugs, the mercenary reminded himself. All they really did was make you not give a damn, and feel very, very chatty. Individual reactions varied widely, as well, unless you had time and facilities to do up a batch adjusted to the subject's personal biochemistry. Spartan biochemists had the knowledge to do that, but the proper equipment was rare outside the University.

"Carry on," Owensford said. He caught the sergeant's eye. "Important prisoner?"

"Equivalent of colonel, sir," the interrogator said. "I've got a transcript . . ." He bent to the captive's ear. "Is it your fault, Perrez?"

"No," the man muttered, his eyes roving the room without seeing the faces around them.

For a moment he tailed off in a mutter of Spanish. Spanglish, actually; Owensford recognized the dialect, common in the tier of states south of the Rio Grande which had once been part of Mexico. The sergeant's gentle urging brought him back to something more generally comprehensible.

"That maricon kraut von Reuter, he no pull back fast enough. If Skilly were here, no esta problema, the Cits wouldn't comprende where we were. Little shits, sneaking through the trees and spying, Skilly would get them. Two-knife would. Reuter doesn't have half the cojones Skilly does." He giggled, speculating obscenely on where she kept them.

"So where is Skilly?"

"She run off, she and Two-knife both. Gone. Bug out, baby."

"Leaving you behind with von Reuter."

"Yeah."

"Why?"

"She got a plan, that one."

"She didn't tell you the plan, did she? Ran off, leaving you behind. How do you know there was a plan, that she wasn't just saving her own skin?"

"Naw, she wouldn't do that. She wouldn't!"

"What do your troops think about the plan?"

"They don't believe no plan. They think what you say, she run off, save hide. Hey man, you got any agua?"

"Sure. Here you go. Where did you say Skilly went?"

"Didn't say. You trying to fool me! But I didn't say because I don' know where she went. Bugged out, that one, say she got a plan, and off she goes. With that Jap."

"What Jap?"

"Crazy one. Murasaki-san. Nothing working the way he expect, not any more. He go off mad, that one." The prisoner began to sing obscenely.

The sergeant got up and came over to them. "Probably not a lot more today," he said. "That stuff tires them out fast."

"Is this one guilty of atrocities?" Owensford asked.

"Not that I know of," the sergeant said. "He wasn't at Stora at all. Want me to work on atrocity stories?"

"Actually, no," Owensford said. "If he's not obviously guilty of a hanging offense I'd as soon keep it that way. Tell you what, Sergeant, you see what else you can get, then wrap him up good and turn him over to my headquarters people. I'll take him back to Sparta City. Sort of a present for His Majesty."

"Yes, sir."

Owensford led the way out of the tent. Outside he turned to Morrentes. "So we're not going to catch their leaders."

Morrentes shook his head. "This is independent corroboration," he said. "Most of the Helot high command just aren't here. Nobody's seen them in days."

"That must upset the hell out of their troops," Owensford said.

"Well, yes, sir, I'd say so, because when we advance we find abandoned equipment, weapons even, and whole platoons ready to surrender."

"Good. Keep pushing," Owensford said. "And we may even have a surprise for you. A pleasant one."

"Sir?"

"It looks like Prince Lysander has talked the CD into making sure our next satellite stays intact."

"Now that's good news."

Owensford stood for a time listening to the artillery bombardment. *What the hell plan has Skilly got this time? Whatever it is, we can see she pays like hell for it.* "Good work, Morrentes. Very good work indeed. Carry on, and Godspeed."

Brigade Leader Hans von Reuter raised himself to his hands and knees, then staggered to his feet wiping at the blood at the corner of his mouth. Around him his headquarters staff were doing the same, righting pieces of equipment that had toppled when the salvo landed practically right outside the cave. His ears were ringing, and he worked his mouth carefully and spat to get the iron-and-salt taste out of his mouth.

"Location," he said. His face was impassive, a square chiseled blank. *Now I know how von Paulus felt in Stalingrad,* he thought. *Duty is duty, however.*

There were screams from outside, from men and the worse sounds of wounded horses. They grew louder as wounded were dragged inside and carried over to the improvised aid-station on the other side of the big cavern, laid down amid the glossy stalactites that sprouted from the sandy floor. Corpsmen with red M symbols on their jackets scurried among them, sorting them for triage and slapping on hyposprays of anesthetic. Outside a slow series of rifle-shots gave the horses and mules slashed by shrapnel or pulped by blast their own peace.

"Here, ah, here, sir," the plotter said, drawing a black circle on the plastic cover of the map, once the easel was back up.

"Hmmph," von Reuter grunted. *Too far.* The Royalist position was twenty kilometers back, and the only weapons he had available that might reach that far were twisted scrap under a hillside half a kilometer away.

Infiltration? he thought. *Again, no.* The enemy had gotten much better at that sort of thing; also, there were just too *many* of them, and clearly they intended to pound him to bits before advancing. They'd be inserting those SAS teams across his retreat routes, too. No dangerous subtleties or daring sweeps, just a straight hammerblow, rolling northwest and then veering northeast toward the exact location of Base One. The Royalist columns were coordinating well, with intensive patrolling between. *He* was having enough problems stopping them from infiltrating his own positions. Mostly they were bypassing or punching through any screen he put into place, the lead elements encircling the Helot blocking forces for the foot-infantry marching up behind to eliminate.

This is the set piece battle the Royals have always wanted. Now they have it.

It shouldn't have happened. When the Senate passed its Ultimate Decree the Helot army should have dispersed, disbanded if necessary. Let the Royals have the bulk of the equipment and stores, take the irreplaceable equipment and retreat to the hills and wastes with the even less replaceable trained officers and non-coms— *We did not do that in time. Field Prime was certain that we would have more time, but there was no time at all. The Legion SAS forces, then Royals, both with those damned missiles, were in place in hours. We could have fought past them if we had sent everything immediately, but Field Prime tried another plan, then another when that failed, and now I am defeated.*

Doubly defeated, because it had taken all his skill to preserve the Stora Commando as it attempted to retreat from the determined attention of the Brotherhood forces and militia. When he was ordered to return to defend Base One, the Commando was doomed as an organized force. *Except for those already extracted. Some of the best of the Commando. And many of the politicals. And it was the same here, many of the best gone before I arrived. Gone to I do not know where.*

Doubtless Field Prime has a plan, and doubtless it will be brilliant, and complex as usual. Amateurs believe simplicity means that a few things can go wrong and the plan will still work. She has no concept. Falkenberg's people well understand that no battle plan survives contact with the enemy. Field Prime has heard the words but they have no meaning to her.

Yet she has come close to success. Perhaps this time it will work.

She only has to win once.

And none of that was important. His mission now was to delay the enemy as much as possible. He could use anything left of the equipment, and delay was more important than preserving his force. *Of course they must not know that, or they will simply run away. Already they resent that Field Prime is no longer here.* Von Reuter sighed. He had taken no part in the attack on non-combatants at the Stora Mine, but he was quite certain to be tried as a war criminal for his part in the poison gas attack in the Dales; and even if he could surrender he would not. He had his professional honor to consider.

The orders are to delay. I am not told why, merely that it is important. It is not easily done. His forces simply could not move as fast as the Royals, not at foot and animal-transport speeds; it was difficult even to break contact once the Royals advanced. His heavy weapons were outranged, and could be used once and once only: then they were destroyed by the suddenly excellent enemy artillery.

They find us easily. Almost as if they have a satellite. Surely they do not, Field Prime would have told me?

Small arms fire crackled; he looked up sharply, estimating distances.

"Evacuate," he snapped. "Company Leader Gimbowitz." The chief of the field-hospital looked up. "You have the enemy wounded here as well?"

The doctor nodded, swallowing; he knew as well as the commander what came next.

"We cannot take prisoners or wounded with us," von Reuter said regretfully. "I must ask for medical volunteers to remain with them until the enemy arrives. They will have permission to contact the Royalist commanders once their troops are in the immediate vicinity."

That made it unlikely the Helot wounded would be slaughtered. Individual soldiers of both sides were as likely as not to shoot out of hand individual soldiers of the other who tried to surrender, but the Royalist senior officers were sticklers for the Laws of War. For that matter, wounded men and medics in an organized setting were reasonably safe.

He turned. "Quickly, please," he said. "Group Leader Sandina, please see to the demolition charges on the equipment we cannot remove."

CHAPTER FOURTEEN

There are two central causes of the generally poor
Western military record in the field of counterinsurgency. The first is that Western armies are either
not large enough or do not consider it important
enough to maintain a full-time, well-qualified cadre for
counterinsurgency tasks. This is perhaps a good
choice, because the main task for these organizations
is to ensure an adequate response in the event of
higher forms of conflict. The resulting cost, of course,
is to occasionally field partially qualified novices in
counterinsurgency situations where professionals are
required. The second cause of lackluster Western
military performance is that Western peoples will not
long tolerate the use of their soldiers in suppressing
rebellions in a distant land, whether their soldiers are
in a direct combat role or serving as advisors.

An international corporation composed of former
Western officers and soldiers skilled in acceptable
counterinsurgency techniques would largely solve
both of these Western counterinsurgency problems . . .
Considering the record of most Western governments
in the field of counterinsurgency, the corporation
would not have to work very hard to achieve comparatively superior results. And a commercial concern
would likely attain those improvements at considerably less cost.

—Rod Paschall
*LIC 2000: Special Operations and
Unconventional Warfare in the Next Century*
(Institute of Land Warfare,
Association of the US Army, 1990)

If, in the future, war will be waged for the souls of
men, then the importance of extending territorial
control will go down. Long past are the days when
provinces, even entire countries, were regarded simply
as items of real estate to be exchanged among rulers
by means of inheritance, agreement, or force. The
triumph of nationalism has brought about a situation
where people do not occupy a piece of land because it
is valuable; on the contrary, a piece of land however
remote or desolate is considered valuable because it is
occupied by this people or that. To adduce but two
examples out of many, since at least 1965 India and
Pakistan have been at loggerheads over a glacier so
remote that it can hardly even be located on a map.
Between 1979 and 1988, Egypt spent nine years of
diplomatic effort in order to recover Taba. Now Taba,
south of Elath, is a half-mile stretch of worthless
desert beach whose very existence had gone unno-
ticed by both Egyptians and Israelis prior to the Camp
David Peace Agreements; all of a sudden it became
part of each side's "sacred" patrimony and coffee-
houses in Cairo were named after it. . . .

Another effect of the postulated breakdown of
conventional war will probably be a greater emphasis
on the interests of men at the head of the organization, as opposed to the interest, of the organization
as such . . . Individual glory, profit, and booty gained
directly at the expense of the civilian population will
once again become important, not simply as incidental
rewards but as the legitimate objectives of war. Nor is
it improbable that the quest for women and sexual
gratification will re-enter the picture. As the distinc-
tions between combatants and noncombatants break
down, the least we can expect is that such things will
be tolerated to a greater extent than is supposed to be
the case under the rules of so-called civilized warfare.
In many of the low-intensity conflicts currently being
waged in developing countries this is already true, and
has, indeed, always been true.

—Martin van Creveld
The Transformation of War, 1991

❖   ❖   ❖

The Council Chamber was colorful, and for the moment buzzing with informal chatter. Most seats at the big conference table were taken. The conspicuous exceptions were the cabinet secretary's console at one end, and a single large arm chair at the center. The War Cabinet was already at the table. Rear Admiral Samuel Forrest, as senior Naval officer, sat between Generals Owensford and Slater, the deep midnight blue of his Navy tunic contrasting with the more colorful army garrison uniforms. Madame Elayne Rusher, the Attorney General, was next to General Lawrence Desjardins, Chief of the Royal Spartan Mounted Police. Roland Dawson, Principal Secretary of State, chatted with Lord Henry Yamaga, Secretary of State for the Interior and Industrial Development. Eric Respari of Finance listened to them with a sour expression. Everyone knew that Respari had been an avid student of the late King Jason's economics theories; now he resembled the Freedman King in expression as well. Sir Alfred Nathanson, called Minister of War even though his office was administrative rather than part of the chain of command, was hard at work on his notebook computer. At the far end of the table Dr. Caldwell Whitlock sat alone. He had been invited by Prince Lysander, and if some of the regular members of the War Cabinet resented his presence, none of them were going to say so, especially not today.

In addition to the principal officers at the conference table, another dozen chairs along the walls were filled with experts: Legion Captains Jesus and Catherine Alana, Alan Hruska, the Milice chief for Sparta City; Spartan and Brotherhood military; Legion officers; civilian officials, most carrying notebook computers.

The room fell silent as Horace Plummer, Secretary to the Cabinet, came into the conference chamber and stood just inside the door. "My lords, ladies, gentlemen, His Highness Crown Prince Lysander, Master of the Forces by order of the Kings acting under the Ultimate Decree of the Senate of Sparta." Everyone stood. The military acted from habit, as perhaps did some of the others, but some were reacting to the solemn formality of Plummer's announcement.

Lysander wore the military uniform of an officer of the Royals but with no insignia of rank. He looked older than his years as he took his place at the center of the big conference table. There was only one chair there. Previously there had always been two, and Lysander had sat across from them, where General Owensford was now. Lysander nodded pleasantly to everyone, but took his seat in silence. After a moment the others sat down as well.

"The agenda is on your screens," Plummer said.

"With his Highness's permission," Roland Dawson said, "the agenda will endure a brief wait. We understand there is good news from St. Thomas's."

Lysander frowned for a moment, then suddenly his smile returned, as if he had remembered to wear it again. "Thank you. Yes, very good news indeed. Graffin Melissa is recovering well."

"Well enough to have enjoyed a brief visit to the Palace last evening. Her father mentioned it this morning. And, Highness, I have heard that we may have better news shortly," Dawson continued relentlessly. The Principal Secretary of State was the leader of the majority party in the Senate, and by definition a politician, and not even the Ultimate Decree would change that. "I understand the Queen is consulting the Archbishop to reschedule the wedding. I understand and appreciate that Your Highness would prefer this to remain a private matter, but the Citizens will be overjoyed at the news, and I ask permission to make the announcement."

Lysander looked around the room at the eager faces. Even the dour finance minister was smiling agreement with Dawson.

"Time we had some good news to announce," Elayne Rusher said.

"The Citizens will certainly want to celebrate," Sir Alfred Nathanson said.

Lysander nodded. "I expect you're right. I'll leave the details to you, then. Now—and thank you, Roland—Mr. Plummer, if we can get back to the agenda?"

"Item One. A report from the military field commands," Horace Plummer said. "General Owensford."

"Highness. My lords and ladies. You've seen the overall figures, and the rest are in the conference room computer. I can summarize in two words. We're winning."

"Thank God," Roland Dawson said. The Principal Secretary of State mopped his brow with an already damp handkerchief. "How soon do you think this will be over?"

"Not as soon as you'd like, I'm afraid," Peter Owensford said. "We're stretched pretty thin, no reserves to speak of. Nearly everything we've got has been thrown into the two campaigns, the Stora pursuit, and the reduction of their main base. We're winning, but it isn't all that easy, there are complications. Full details are in the reports on your consoles there. Unfortunately, I must ask you not to remove electronic copies of those reports from this room. We know the computers here are clean, and they have no physical connection whatever to any other system."

"General?"

"General Desjardins?"

"Does this mean we still can't rely on our computer systems?"

"Correct," Owensford said. "We captured a fair number of Helot technicians in training at Base One, and we've learned a lot from them. Murasaki's people were deeper into our computer systems than I would have imagined. We learned that much mostly by inference and skilled questioning of Helot officers and trainees." Peter Owensford nodded acknowledgment to the Captains Alana. They smiled briefly. Both looked both overworked and triumphant.

"Unfortunately, we didn't get a single live technoninja," Owensford said. "The four we did apprehend were dead when captured, or died before they could be drugged. Interestingly there was one already dead, killed by torture, apparently by Helot experts. No one seems to know anything about that, unless Captain Alana has learned something since I last spoke with him. Yes, Jesus?"

"We have one Helot officer who said the execution was personally ordered by Field Prime, as punishment for failures during the Stora Mines operation," Jesus Mana said. "Apparently this was demanded by the senior survivors of the Stora Commando. They felt they had been betrayed, and someone should be punished."

"So," Lysander said. "The vipers are fanging each other."

"So it would appear, Highness," Owensford said. "We're beginning to see fair numbers of defecting officers. Especially in the Stora Commando group, where we got a colonel, one Hamish Beshara, code name Ben Bella. Incidentally, his *spetsnaz* brigade commander was our friend Niles." Owensford stopped. Prince Lysander's face had frozen into a mask of hate. "Ben Bella had nothing to do with the missile attack, Highness. Jesus?"

"No, my prince. To the best of my skills, no one we have captured had any notion that the missile would be used against a non-military target. Colonel Ben Bella thought its purpose was to destroy the geo-thermal generating system if, as happened, the sabotage effort failed." Jesus shrugged. "I am certain I could find evidence to convict him of wanton destruction of civilian property, but I would not care to argue the case in a CoDominium court martial. Especially since the man surrendered on promise of amnesty for all except deliberate atrocities. He has a different conception of atrocity than we, but he is convinced he committed none—and that the missile attack *was* an atrocity. He insists that he would not have allowed that had he known, and while I may doubt he would have risked his life to prevent it, it is certain he believes he would have."

"Which brings us to a decision item," Owensford said when Lysander didn't answer. "We have captured a number of Helot soldiers, and in the base camp we took prisoner other rebels. The Helots have no conception of non-combatant status. All their membership are rebels, and would be expected to fight. They are nearly all armed, and some of their women and children were killed bearing arms against our forces. Others threw away their weapons. In any case it is difficult to think of a ten year old child as an armed enemy."

"Nits make lice," someone said.

Owensford frowned. "That has been said in every revolutionary war in history," he said. "And it's no more appropriate here than it was in Palestine or Kurdistan. Your Highness, we will need policies and procedures. What shall we do with captured Helot soldiers and their non-military adherents?"

"We can't just let them go," Yamaga said. "They won't work. They wouldn't work before they became Helots, and they won't work now, and now they've got a taste for rebellion. And training with weapons. Let them loose and they'll turn criminals even if they don't rejoin the rebellion."

"They have to be taught to work," Madame Rusher said. "Work habits."

"*Arbeit macht frei,*" General Desjardins said. "A much abused slogan, but I believe Madame Elayne has the essence of it. They must become convinced that work is a better alternative than banditry."

"We can use some of the soldiers in expeditionary forces," Hal Slater said. "And the Legion. But that requires transportation. I can't think we want them armed and at large on Sparta until they've been obedient for a few years." He chuckled. "Pity we can't make them involuntary colonists to somewhere else. Send them to Byer's and let them buy the criminal life in Hell's-a-comin'."

"Now there's a thought," Yamaga said. "Pity indeed we can't do that."

"But the question is, what do we do with them *now*?" Owensford said. "We've got the island camps. The Legion training program worked all right. Last time we had transport we shipped over five hundred retrained Helots to reinforce Falkenberg on New Washington, and last I heard they were doing well enough. Of course that's the cream of the crop, the ones with enough gumption to stick it."

"You sent back a thousand more who'd volunteered and couldn't finish your course," Sir Alfred Nathanson said. "And they're something of a problem. For the moment we've been able to keep order on the Island, even have them growing their own crops. But we can't maintain concentration camps like that forever!"

"Bit of a mess for the Coast Guard," General Desjardins said. "We've been worried that the Helots would try to rescue those people. So far the only reason they haven't has been the physical isolation, but we're using resources I'd like to put to other uses. We lose a few of those wet navy craft and all those Helot soldiers are available to the rebellion again."

"We can't just shoot them," Elayne Rusher said.

"No, Madam," Finance Minister Respari agreed. "Leave aside the ethics, none of the others would ever surrender if we did that. General, Sir Alfred, I'm afraid your island camps are the only solution we have. And the camps are cheaper than the war, by a lot."

"Actually, there are two problems," Yamaga said. "There are the prisoners of war, of course. And although we can't send off the criminals as colonists to a pleasant place like Hell's-a-comin', the CoDominium keeps dumping involuntary colonists on us. I grant you they're not quite the same situation, some of the new colonists fit in well enough, but all too many are nearly as much trouble as rebels." He shrugged. "And for a lot of them it's only a question of time before they go from being useless mouths to joining the rebellion and killing our people. Bread and circuses, that's what they want."

"Every democracy in history has wanted bread and circuses," Roland Dawson said. "Not our party, of course, but there are Citizen groups who'd rather try bread and circuses than continue the war."

"Danegeld," Hal Slater said. "Never a very wise thing to give anyone, certainly not to criminals."

"It is not what they will get," Lysander said. His voice was low, but the room became quiet when he spoke. "Build that kind of welfare state and we corrupt our own people. This government will not pay people to be poor, nor will we set up paid officials with an incentive to have poor and idle clients. General Desjardins, I take it your RSMP doesn't find Island duty pleasant."

"They hate it, Highness. So would you."

"I expect I would. Let me point out that there are advantages to this. No one wants to make a career of administering the camps, so there is no one who has a good reason to retain those camps if we find a better solution."

"No one I'd want in the RSMP," Desjardins sniffed.

"Keep it that way," Lysander said. "Too many nations have destroyed themselves by allowing potentially fatal changes to their institutions as an expedient for winning wars or settling domestic crises. Every institution you build has people who want to keep on doing what they do. It's the nature of government, to build enduring institutions, structures that stay long after their purpose is over. If you pay people to help the poor, you have people who won't be paid if there aren't any poor, so they'll be sure to find some. Sparta was created as the antithesis of that kind of welfare state, and by God it will stay that way. I'd rather lose the war than change that."

There were mutters of agreement around the table.

"Hear, hear," Whitlock said.

"That's clear, then," Lysander said. "Now let me point out that when we win this war we will have far more Helot prisoners, some of them genuine war criminals."

"Hang them," Desjardins said.

"Those we can convict of atrocities, certainly. But how many will that be?"

"Rome crucified a rebel at every milepost from Vesuvius to Rome after the Spartacus rebellion," Madame Rusher said. "That's what? No more than a thousand, surely, and it's remembered to this day. I suppose if we top that we'll get a place in the history books, but I'm not sure it's a place we want."

"Nor I," Lysander said. "I'm not sure what to do with those merely swept up in the rebellion, but there's a simple solution to what to do with the active participants in the rebel cause. They wanted to try the barbarian life. I propose to give them their wish. Turn them loose on the island. Wolf Island. They get hand tools, seeds, and a few farm animals. No weapons, and no technology. If they don't work, they starve. After a few years the survivors can try to negotiate a better deal."

"Stark," Roland Dawson said.

"It's better than they planned for us," Lysander said. "Sir Alfred, this will be your concern. Please see to it."

"Yes, Highness."

"Sir?"

"Admiral Forrest."

"This is my first cabinet meeting. I'm not certain of the procedure," Forrest said.

"We're fairly informal, Admiral," Lysander said. "If you believe you have something we should know that's relevant to the discussion, it's quite proper to speak up."

"Yes, sir. I was going to say, the news from the CoDominium is confusing and contradictory. Rumors of mutinies in the fleet. Ships beached for lack of money to repair and fuel them. Stories of rivalries, along with official documents that don't acknowledge that there's anything unusual happening at all. One thing is certain, the BuReloc transport is overdue. It may be that we won't be getting so many involuntary colonists."

"A consummation devoutly to be wished," Hal Slater said carefully. "I hear much the same as Admiral Forrest. The CD's having trouble finding enough money to operate all their ships. It's probable we won't have as much trouble with involuntary colonists as we thought we would."

"Or that it will all happen at once, with a number of ships coming simultaneously," Lysander said. "But thank you for bringing that up. I presume everyone here knows that Admiral Forrest has persuaded the local CoDominium Fleet Commander to safeguard our observation and communications satellite. We're told that they're also intercepting the clandestine arms shipments to the rebels."

"We very much owe Admiral Forrest a vote of thanks," Elayne Rusher said.

"Indeed," Lysander said. "Those Fang missiles could have been a lot of trouble. Still can be, but at least there aren't infinite supplies of them coming in. And the other high tech gear. From all of us, and from me personally, Admiral, thank you. We won't forget."

"Thank you, Highness," Forrest said. "Of course I had considerable help from Dr. Whitlock. He can be extremely persuasive."

"Well, thank you," Whitlock said. "Most important thing is to convince the local CD people they'll be better off with us as a strong and peaceful place to call home, and the best arguments for that are Admiral Forrest and Captain Nosov."

Lysander nodded agreement. "General Owensford, please continue your report."

"Yes, Highness," Owensford said. "As I said earlier, we're winning. The renewed satellite pictures have been extremely useful, especially in the pursuit of their northern group, the force they called the Stora Commando group. I am pleased to report that the Stora Commando is no longer a threat to anyone. For a while they retreated in an organized and disciplined manner. That gave General Barton a lot of trouble, but shortly after the Ultimate Decree they became little more than disorganized stragglers.

"The change was sudden and dramatic. We have since learned that most of their leadership was evacuated, leaving the rest on their own, which was pretty demoralizing when the word spread among them. Many who hadn't taken a personal part in atrocities surrendered very soon after that. The rest are disorganized, mostly city punks in the wilderness, relentlessly pursued by outdoorsmen who enjoy their work. You could almost feel sorry for them."

"No you couldn't," Lysander said. "They demanded their rights. They'll get justice. How many criminals have we caught?"

"Not so many as I'd like, because of course the ones we could prove to be war criminals don't surrender. On the other hand, over six hundred have accepted the amnesty. Of those, nine were easily proven to be war criminals, thirty-four probably are, and four were traitors, actual Citizen supporters of the rebels."

"Probably," Roland Dawson said. "What means probable, given your—techniques?"

Jesus Alana shrugged. "It is expensive and time consuming to question every captive," he said. "And are we so certain we want the answers? If we know someone is guilty of war crimes, we must make a decision as to what to do with him."

"What happened to the Citizens?" Lysander demanded.

"The traitors are in the Capital prison, Highness, awaiting Their Majesties' pleasure. Or yours," Owensford said. "They're a different case. The Helot soldiers we let go to the Island after interrogation, but we know who they are if we really want to find them again."

"Mutilation," one of the Brotherhood intelligence officers said. "We should chop off a finger. Or toes. Make it a lot easier to find them again."

Lysander didn't answer, and there was an awkward silence. "It's much the same around their Base Camp," Owensford said at last. "Better organized, but most of their leadership has bugged out. The troops left behind were supposed to sell their lives dearly. Some did, but it's beginning to sink in that they're fighting for a lost and dreary cause, and leaders who've run away. Once again we're seeing both individuals and organized groups looking for amnesty. Others have scattered into the wastelands, but this time with not much more than they can carry." Owensford shrugged. "Frankly, I'd rather be on the Island than on the run. Better soil, and I wouldn't have to worry that Mace's Scouts were looking for me."

"But we still haven't caught their leaders."

"Other than Croser and his Capital gang, no."

"General, every one of them seems to believe Skilly has a plan," Lysander said. "Do we have any notion of what it is?"

"No, sir."

"I keep remembering the Dales," Lysander said. "Where they had a plan that couldn't possibly work, only it very nearly did, because we certainly were not expecting poison gas. Captain Alana, you saw through that one just in time. What can they be planning now?"

"I confess to thinking much on that subject," Jesus Alana said. "Alas, my prince, with little result. Nor has Catherine been more successful."

"We're winning, but they're not giving up. Not trying to make terms," Lysander said. "I take that to mean they still believe they can win."

"Clearly," Hal Slater said.

"But they're losing. Losing badly. There's no way they *can* win."

"Well," Owensford said. "Perhaps. We can hope so, but in any event there is one thing I must remind you of, Highness. It may or may not have anything to do with Skilly, but it's clear that every gain we have made could be wiped out by the CoDominium. Give the Helots enough off-planet support and we wouldn't be winning any longer."

"Admiral, is this likely?"

"No," Forrest said. "Likely, no. But of course it's possible."

"Some day," Lysander said, but he said it so softly that Peter Owensford didn't think anyone else had heard.

CHAPTER FIFTEEN

Crofton's Encyclopedia of the Inhabited Planets
(2nd Edition):

Corinth: Town at the head of the *Corinthian Gulf,* (q.v.), a long (700 kilometer), funnel-shaped inlet on the north-eastern portion of the Serpentine Continent. Corinth, founded by settlers from New Newfoundland in 2053, is primarily a collection point for nearby ranches and a fishing-base. The Corinthian Gulf, with its deep and nutrient-rich waters, is a spawning-ground for several important species of large piscoid hunted for their leather, oil and pharmaceutical derivatives; among these are the *Mammoth Daisy,* the *Tennisnet* and the *Galleybeak.* Galleybeak caviar is noted as a delicacy on several planets, having an exotic flavor and mild stimulant and euphoric qualities. Tennisnet glands are processed for a well-known anti obesity drug. Corinth's facilities include deep water docks, small-scale ship repair facilities, warehouses and marine processing plants. Population (2091), 6,753 not including transients.

Another characteristic of the year 2010, familiar to those who will have lived through the last quarter of the 20th Century, is that most of the world's low-intensity conflict will probably be insurgencies. Terrorism, in and of itself, is a weak reed when it comes to effecting political changes. On the other hand, governments have been brought down by insurgents . . .

One aspect of insurgency that promises to be a bit different in the year 2010 has to do with a shift in demography. The continued movement of Third World

Geoffrey Niles woke at the sound of voices, but from long habit he lay still, eyes closed, as if still asleep. It was a habit developed at school to avoid persecution by older boys, but this time it saved him from far worse. He lay still and thought about where he was.

They were in the ranch house of a farm Skilly had bought years before. The nominal owners were a couple Skilly had found in the slums of Minetown. As usual her instinct for choosing the right people served her well: Hildy and Rose Wheeler had quietly tended the farm, increasing its value and drawing no attention to themselves, quiet non-Citizen farmers who ignored politics like many in this Corinthian district a thousand kilometers northeast of the Capital. Yet when Skilly had appeared, nearly alone and on the run, they were eager to help. Geoff had been amazed at the facilities they had quietly built up in a cave driven into the cliffs behind the ranch house. Offices, storage for weapons, residence, all waiting until Skida Thibodeau should need them.

They could relax here. Back in Sparta City they'd been in a different house every night, welcome in some, grudgingly accepted in others, flatly refused admission twice, and always afraid of betrayal even by those who seemed gladdest to see them. It had been an enormous relief to leave the capital even though that required traveling in disguise on the public rail system. Skilly had a dozen disguises, papers, business travel documents, and they'd needed them. In this time of the Ultimate Decree it wasn't enough just to buy a ticket and get on a train. You had to convince the police that you had a legitimate reason for travel, and they wrote it all down to be fed to the computer system. But they'd got here, safe for the first time in weeks. . . .

He was alone in the big bed. Skilly, dressed in a tee shirt and nothing else, sat at her communications console. She had the speaker volume low and spoke softly as if trying not to awaken him, but Niles wondered why she didn't use the headset if that was what she really wanted. For that matter there was a console in the next room.

Testing? he wondered. She had done a lot of that since the Stora incident. She still didn't trust him completely. *That was close. I could have got myself killed, and for nothing, there was nothing I could do, nothing at all.* He shuddered at the memory, Skilly's cold laugh as she launched the missile, the impersonal way she looked at the results. The worst was when she told him later that he'd been right, it hadn't been such a good idea after all. "Should have listened to my Jeffy, sometimes he got good instincts." No remorse except that it hadn't worked as she intended. *And she still thinks to found a dynasty. My God, I've got to get out of here.* He'd thought that many times since the Stora campaign, but there was no place to go. The Royals would cheerfully hang him if they could catch him, and the only places he knew to hide from the Royals were controlled by Skilly.

He lay still and listened. Skilly was talking to someone, and she wasn't happy at all. "You supposed to be working for Skilly," she said.

"My sincere apologies. I am afraid my employer neglected to tell me that." Skilly had the volume set low, and the voice was very low and quiet, so that Niles barely heard it, but he was certain that it was Murasaki. "I was told to consider your interests, as well as those of Capital Prime, but not to the neglect of my primary mission. Indeed, now that Capital Prime is regrettably detained, it is not certain that your interests and my employer's are the same."

"Why you say that?"

"Let us say that my employer had known Capital Prime for many years, and thus understood him. He has never met you. Alas, while I have great admiration for your talents as a leader, a bald narrative of events does little to justify that to someone who does not know you well. All due to bad luck and misfortune, of course, but it does not appear that you have enjoyed great success."

"Skilly told Capital Prime it was time to go underground," Skilly said. "But Capital Prime trusted you to warn him in time. Not Skilly's doing."

"Ah, no, of course not," Murasaki said. "But perhaps had you more thoroughly considered the implications of your use of our earth penetrator? Capturing the mine and its town was a boldly conceived goal, admirable in concept, possibly decisive if combined with suitable political strategy. The CoDominium will often act to aid an actual government in possession of territory. Using the earth penetrator as a means of bringing the Stora garrison to battle on favorable ground was also an admirably bold notion. Alas, it did not have the proper effect."

"That bad luck too," Skilly said. "You don' tell me that Prince Baby is up there. Everything fine until he rallies the troops, make them go back to their holes and organize. That Prince one real piece of bad luck. Best we kill that one. Him and that whole group of his. He put a price on my head, I put one on his. You kill him, now."

"Ah, I was under the impression that you were thoroughly aware that Prince Lysander had gone north. My mistake. As to his demise, this is not so easily accomplished as it would have been earlier," Murasaki said. "The Royals are, after all, very much alerted."

"They still meet sometimes," Skilly said. "Report to the Senate. Broadcast to the people." She looked around, but Geoffrey Niles had never opened his eyes fully, and she saw him apparently still asleep. Her voice fell even lower, so that Geoff didn't hear all of what she said next.

" . . . whole damn place while they in it."

"There are few reliable ways to accomplish that."

"One sure one."

"I had thought you were opposed to using that."

"Skilly not like it, because it cause trouble for the future. But right now, maybe she don't got a future unless something drastic happens."

"That is of course most unfortunate," Murasaki said. "But I have only the one device, and there is some question of where to use it. Indeed, you have been persuasive in arguing against using it at all. Certainly it will greatly upset the CoDominium elements, and it is never wise to do that without powerful reasons."

"Yeah, I understand that," Skilly said. "But think, you don' do something soon, Skilly facing the ugly, ugly jaws of defeat."

"No one understands that better than me," the soft voice said. "But we have sent you vast resources, and I fear we have very little to show for all that huge expenditure. We have embarrassed the Legion, but it seems to have survived the experience, perhaps did not even notice. The Royal Government is stronger than ever. I regret I must point this out, but you do not seem to have much to offer now. Have you established control over the politicals in Sparta City?"

"Yes."

Geoff suppressed a shudder. Regaining control of the political apparatus after the mass arrests following the Ultimate Decree had been a nightmare. There had to be secure cutouts, discontinuities in the command structure, or the entire apparatus would have fallen in the first hours; but once the known leaders were removed, making contact with those remaining was extremely difficult, and proving that you were entitled to give them orders, and that they should continue the fight, was more difficult still. Niles's admiration for Skilly had increased enormously but his horror at her methods had grown equally. Her energy was boundless, and she had set up a number of contingency plans just in case this happened. She was particularly skilled at blackmail, and she had enough evidence to hang most of the political leadership three times over. And one of those who had refused to take her in was found the next day with his testicles stuffed into his eye sockets.

So we have control of the politicals. It takes a lot of personal contact to do it, and we can't do that easily because Skilly insists on moving from place to place all the time. Afraid someone will try to collect the bounty, I suppose. I wonder how long she'll stay here? Its safe here, but she's not getting much done.

"You blow de Palace when the government is all there," Skilly said. "Give Skilly a week warning, hell, six hours, and it'll be all over, Skilly will own this place. No Kings, no Senate, no government. Just the organization."

"Well, it is a possibility to consider," Murasaki said. "But I think we first stay with the original plan. Let us see what that will accomplish before we attempt your way. If that fails, perhaps there is another."

"You just be sure to give Skilly notice first. Those politicals not so easy to control, not trained troops. Maybe both together? Between CD and your stuff, we knock out the government, Skilly does the rest. We take over the Capital, we win, and we only got to win once. . . ."

The girl was about twenty, and she had been pretty in an unsophisticated way. Now her hair had been cut off with a bayonet, her swollen lips oozed blood, and she was missing at least one tooth. The nose was swollen as well, probably broken, one eye was black, and there were other bruises, particularly on her thighs. She was sprawled naked across a couch, and one of the Helot soldiers was fastening his trousers.

Geoffrey Niles looked at the scene with distaste. "Seems a bit of a waste," he said. *Soldiers. Warriors. My God. First the Lefkowitz girl, those pictures! Pictures sent to Luna Base and*

*every mercenary outfit registered with the CD, and they still
don't learn, they think they're going to win and then they can
make the rules. Rules! And everyone knows my family is
associated with this.*

"Waste, Brigade Leader? We're supposed to kill her, but there
wasn't nothing said about not having some fun first."

Niles shook his head. "Odd notions of fun. In any event,
I need confirmation of some information she probably has.
Get her dressed. I'll bring her back when I'm through."

"They say she don't know nothing. The Legion types never
told her anything much, she's no use," the Company Leader
said. He finished fastening his trousers and grinned. "Course
it depends on what you want to use her for, but being as
what you're gettin', you sure don't need any of this."

Niles's look silenced him. "There are things we have to
know. People she's seen, map locations. They weren't supposed to give her to you until we were finished. Just get her
clothes. Can you dress yourself?" he asked the girl.

"Yeah." Her voice was distorted.

"Then do so."

She lay still for a moment. The Helot officer smashed his
hand across her mouth. "You call him sir, and you do what
he says now, bitch."

She pulled herself into a sitting position with an obvious effort. Niles watched as the girl pulled on trousers and
a shirt. She had no underwear, and Niles wondered if it
had been destroyed in the process of undressing her. Her
only shoes were boots, and he waited for her to get those
on. Although she moved slowly and carefully, nothing
seemed to be broken. As she finished with her boots, Niles
swiftly lifted her to her feet, pulled her hands behind her,
and snapped on handcuffs. "Do you want her back?" he
asked.

"Well, it might be fun to have her again before we kill her."

"We'll see. If she cooperates with us. All right—Talkins, isn't
it? Come along." He pushed her out into the corridor of the
cave.

"Watch her," the Helot called. "She bites. Or did. Taught
her not to do that."

The passage led to cellars of the farmhouse, but halfway
along it was a side passage. Niles opened that door, pushed
Margreta Talkins through and followed her, carefully closing
it behind him. "All right," he said. "In a minute I'm going
to take those cuffs off, but I want you to be sure you understand what's happening."

"And what's that?" Margreta's speech was slurred by her swollen lips. She spat blood.

"We're getting the hell out of here," Niles said.

Her eyes widened. "We. Why?"

"Look, we don't have a lot of time," Niles said. "I want to surrender to the Royals, and I need bargaining chips. You're one of them. Now we have about an hour, maybe two, before Skilly calls in asking for me, and as long after that as it takes for her to figure out what's happened. By that time we'd better be a hell of a long way from here. Can you run?"

"A little. I'm pretty bruised. If I'd known I'd have to run, I wouldn't have fought so hard."

"Look, I'm sorry."

"Yeah. It could have been worse. All right, I'll try to keep up. Look, I don't know what's going to happen, but do me this, don't let them get me alive again, all right? OK, let's go."

"All right, we can stop for a few minutes," Niles said. "I've got some clothes and equipment stashed under the rocks here. We'll take five minutes to let you change. There are weapons here, too."

She stumbled forward and sat heavily. "I guess I'm not in as good shape as I thought."

"How'd they catch you?"

"I think they were always on to me," Margreta Talkins said. "At least since Graffin Melissa lived through that assassination attempt. They were pretty sure I could have killed her. Ever since I think they've just been using me to pass false information back to the Legion. The last thing they did was send me on a wild goose chase, so I'd give the wrong story about where they were hiding. I really thought I'd located Skilly, and getting that information out was worth anything. I guess they'd decided I wasn't any more use, because that was a setup."

Niles lifted a flat rock. "Here we are. Canteens, to begin with. Water or whiskey?"

"Water. Whiskey would be great at first, but I don't think it will help for long." She drank deeply. "Let me have the whiskey," she said suddenly. Niles handed the other canteen to her. She took a sip and gargled heavily, then spat it out. "That helps. Now if you'll hand me that bandanna and look the other way—" She laughed. "Or don't, Jesus, you'd think I'd be over any kind of modesty."

Geoff fished in the crevice under the rock, carefully not looking at her.

"Ow. That stings," she said. "I don't suppose you've got some milder form of disinfectant?"

"No. I do have some more clothes. Including underwear. Jockey shorts, a bit large for you, but better than nothing." He held them out behind him and felt her take them. "And some clean trousers and shirt. I made this cache when I heard they were bringing in a Legion prisoner, but I didn't know you'd be a girl."

"Girl," Margreta said. "Lord, man, if this hasn't made a woman of me, nothing will. But thanks, I think. You still haven't explained what this is all about."

"Actually, I did. I want out. Out of all this. Amnesty and a ticket off Sparta."

"Look, we both know I'm not worth that much, not if you were part of anything serious."

"I wasn't. Not Lefkowitz, not Stora. I was in the Dales, poison gas, technically a violation of the Laws of War, but that was against military targets."

"And the anthrax?"

"Anthrax?" Geoff said. "No, I didn't know about that."

"They used it. Ruined a whole farm valley. Look, I still don't see where I come in."

"You can talk to them. I know some things they will want to know," Geoff said. "But if they shoot me before I can tell them that, it won't do anyone any good. You they'll listen to, and I presume you have ways to make contact with the Legion. They might even provide you transportation."

"Sure, if you get me to a telephone. All right, you can turn around now. And thanks for turning your back."

She looked better, but still awful. He found a bandanna and wet it from the water canteen, then added a dash of whiskey. "Hold still, I'll clean your face. And here's a comb."

"If you have a mirror—"

"I do, but let me clean you up a bit first."

"Oh. That bad?"

She tried to laugh, but he could see tears at the corners of her eyes. He wiped off the worst of the dried blood and semen from her face. It was hard to do without hurting her, and he winced as badly as she did when he had to touch some of her bruises.

"There were four of them," she said. "One managed twice."

"Miss Talkins—"

"I think under the circumstances, Brigade Leader Niles, you may call me Margreta," she said solemnly.

"Margreta. Jesus, I'm sorry, Margreta. Uh—and I'm Geoffrey or Geoff, of course."

"Not Jeffy?"

"My God no, never again. Speaking of which." He held up a mini-uzi. "The moment of truth. I'm going to give you this now. If you want to shoot me in retaliation for what they did to you, please make it quick. I deserve that much. Margreta, I'm very sorry they did this to you, and if I could have prevented it I would have, but there was nothing I could do. God damn it! It was like Stora, nothing I could do! I could get killed and it still wouldn't have changed anything! They'd have shot me and the rocket would have gone on schedule, and the same thing with you, until Skilly left I couldn't interfere with—Sorry. You're the one who was hurt, and I'm shouting about it."

She didn't say anything. After a moment, Geoff handed her the machine pistol. He stood and watched as she checked the loads. "They're not blanks," he said. "I'd invite you to fire a few rounds, but it might attract unwanted attention."

"I'm not going to shoot you," she said. "Back there in the cave I would have, you and them and then myself, but— Geoff, are we really going to get away?"

"I surely hope so. Now, how much of this can you carry? We still don't have a lot of time. And I hope your Legion people think enough of you to come get you."

"So do I. All right, find me that telephone."

"Oh, that's no problem. I have a communicator," Geoff said. "All we have to do is get to a place where it's safe to use it."

"Let's go, then," she said. She sounded very small and vulnerable, and Geoff Niles had never hated the war so much. He took her hand to lead her, and after a moment she let him.

CHAPTER SIXTEEN

The advantage which a commander thinks he can
attain through continued personal intervention is
largely illusory. By engaging in it he assumes a task
which really belongs to others, whose effectiveness he
thus destroys. He also multiplies his own tasks to a
point where he can no longer fulfill the whole of them.
　　　　　　　　　　　　　—Helmuth von Moltke

**Crofton's Encyclopedia of Contemporary History
and Social Issues (3rd Edition):**

The Ban: The proudest achievement of the CoDominium
era was the near absence of employment of nuclear
weapons in an era of nuclear plenty. The one issue that
united the Fleet, from the lowest Line Marine recruit to
the Grand Admiral was insistence that the Fleet and only
the Fleet had the right to possess nuclear weapons, and
only the Fleet could use them: and it would not do so
except under nuclear threat. Not even the Grand Senate
could order nuclear bombardment.

Nuclear weapons remained a theoretical last resort to
the Fleet no matter what the opposition, but the only times
they were ever used was in retaliation for first use by
others; on those occasions the vengeance of the
CoDominium Navy could be terrible . . .

The Royal Messenger had a grim expression. "General
Owensford, Prince Lysander's compliments, and can you come
to the war room right away."

"Certainly," Peter said. Something in the Messenger's tone
made him send for his chief of staff.

Peter was almost finished dressing when Andy Lahr came in. "Trouble at Fort Plataia. Good morning, sir."

"Trouble?"

"There's a CoDominium squad at the gate, with an official order that no one is to enter or leave the Fort without CoDominium permission."

"Jesus Christ. What did Captain Alana do?"

"Nothing," Lahr said. "Didn't acknowledge, pending orders, but he has told everyone to stay inside, and put the Fort on alert."

"Sounds good. Tell him to hang onto that until I know what's going on."

"Already did. You got any idea of what's going on?"

"No, but I expect I'm about to find out."

Both Kings and Prince Lysander were in the war room.

"Good morning." Peter bowed. "This looks serious."

"It is," Alexander said. He held out a document. "This appears to be authentic," he said. "It's an order from the CoDominium Sector Headquarters, In the name of Vice Admiral Townsend but actually signed by General Nguyen. Sparta is directed to surrender all units of Falkenberg's Mercenary Legion to the CoDominium, for transport from Sparta to a neutral world to be agreed to after the Legion units are disarmed and embarked."

"I see. That's ridiculous," Peter said. "It's invalid on its face. Vice Admiral Townsend hasn't that authority, and certainly no Marine general acting in the admiral's name does! For that matter, the CoDominium hasn't the authority to order you to do any such thing, even if it's enacted by the Grand Senate."

"They may not have the authority," King Alexander said, "but they have the power. They brought a battle-cruiser and a troop transport with a regiment of Line Marines. The Marines are to be stationed on Sparta ostensibly to protect our independence from foreign invaders—which means you. You're to be taken off-planet in the troop transport."

"What does Clay Newell have to say about this? Or Commodore Guildford for that matter? He's a trimmer. If he obeys this order he's thoroughly committed to Bronson and he knows it. I can't think he wants that."

"We don't know," Alexander said. "I've sent for Admiral Forrest. The whole War Cabinet and Privy Council. But the fact is, we've been unable to talk to anyone in CoDominium headquarters except this newcomer, a Colonel Ciotti, who is coming here shortly to present his demands. His regiment is landing now. They didn't ask permission, they sent us a courtesy information, and that after they'd landed the lead elements."

"There's more," Lysander said. "We're also directed to cease all fraternization with CoDominium personnel, and dismiss from our service any CD officers who retired less than five years ago. Some new regulation. Henceforth all communications with CoDominium personnel are to be official business through the proper channels, and no informal contacts allowed. A full interdict is laid on Sparta until we—" he found a place on the paper he was holding and read "—demonstrate good faith efforts to comply with the directives in paragraph two, to wit, to disarm and surrender to the proper CoDominium authorities all persons at present enrolled in or in the direct employ of the organization known as Falkenberg's Mercenary Legion, sometimes known as the Forty-Second, and paragraph three relative to fraternization and employment of retired CD officials. All CoDominium Marine units stationed on Sparta are directed to cooperate in enforcement of these orders."

"This can't last," Peter said. "When Lermontov hears about this, he'll rescind it."

"And by then Sparta City may be a battlefield," King David said. "I don't even know how to send a message to Grand Admiral Lermontov. They seem to have blocked all our communications. Nothing acknowledges."

"Is our satellite still working?" Peter asked.

"Interesting question," Lysander said. He lifted the phone and spoke briefly, then set it down with a puzzled look "Yes. Which must mean something, but I'm damned if I can figure what."

"Maybe Forrest will have a suggestion," Peter Owensford said. "Now if you'll excuse me, I'll have to inform Commandant Campbell at Fort Plataia."

"Interesting that you named it that," Lysander said.

"Yes, sir." *Plataia was the site of a major Spartan victory over Persia, the place where Thermopylae was avenged, but it was also a city: an Athenian ally, under the protection of Athens. A faithful ally. And was destroyed when the Athenians refused to come to its aid. And how much of that story does Lysander know?* "It seemed like a good idea at the time. If you'll excuse me?"

"Sir, I have my orders," Marco Ciotti said.

The colonel of the 77th CoDominium Marines was a weathered man in his forties, with a blue-jowled aquiline face and eyes black enough that the pupils disappeared in them. His skin was pale from time under a faint sun, and he looked comfortable enough under Spartan gravity. But not comfortable at all with this final conference in the Palace audience chamber overlooking Government House Square. He stood at the end of the Council Chamber, facing the kings and their advisors. "I'm not supposed to even talk to you while you're employing CoDominium people in your armed services." He indicated Admiral Forrest and Captain Nosov. "I'll use my judgment on that, but I don't have any choice about the Legion. Falkenberg's Legion will disarm and surrender, and there aren't any alternatives."

David Freedman looked withering contempt at the CoDominium colonel. "You have no alternatives," King David said. "When a stupid man is doing something he knows is wrong, he always claims it is his duty."

"It may surprise you that I read Shaw too, King David," Colonel Ciotti said. "But it doesn't change my orders."

"Highly irregular orders," Alexander said.

Outside the window Sparta City lay at midsummer peace on a clear morning, a quiet humm of traffic no louder than the sound of birds in the parks below, drifting in with the scent of roses and warm dust. *Unbelievable,* Alexander thought. *That all this can be shattered in a moment.* As if to echo his thought, the double *crack* of a hypersonic transport coming in sounded. Not a commercial flight; all such had ended when the interdict was laid on. This would be the last of the transports bringing down the CoDominium's troops. A full regiment, and the former CD people said a very good one.

Another transport snapped past, startlingly close. Two of the Brotherhood representatives, a banker and the owner of a chain of clothing stores, looked at each other with ashen faces. They stood with the other Phraetrie leaders, middle aged men, a few women. Serious people; it was a high honor on Sparta. Most of them had children up at the front, with the Royal Army or the mobilized Militia, and all of them had families and homes here in Sparta City.

"The orders are unusual. I grant you that," Colonel Ciotti said, regretful firmness in his voice. "But I have no grounds for questioning their validity."

"You don't?" Lysander asked. "Sealed orders, in the name of the Vice Admiral but signed off by a Marine General, from a Sector Command HQ. All communications as well as commerce interdicted. Colonel, you know as well as we do that this is a political move by Grand Senator Bronson, and those orders will be rescinded the instant that Grand Admiral Lermontov hears of them."

"I don't know anything about politics," Ciotti said.

"Don't you, Marco?" Samuel Forrest asked gently. "Then you've forgotten a lot since the High Cathay campaign. You didn't used to be anyone's dupe."

"My orders forbid me even to talk to you," Ciotti said. "And I won't."

"This is a violation of the Treaty of Independence," David said. "Interference in the Dual Monarch's internal affairs."

"That's politics too," Ciotti said. "And I won't be involved in politics. Look, Your Majesties—Major Owensford—I didn't ask to be sent here; my men and I were doing difficult work on Haven, and necessary work at that. I strongly suspect, hell, I *know*, we're being used to pursue some Grand Senator's private vendetta, and I'm pretty sure I could name the Senator. It certainly wouldn't be the first time that's happened to the Fleet. The way things are going, it may well be the last. But that's all irrelevant. The 77th has a valid order, and as of 1800 hours, the troops of Falkenberg's Legion will be in defiance of the CoDominium. If that happens, appropriate action will be taken. Please don't make it worse than it has to be by trying to get in the 77th's way, because anyone who does is going to die, and it's as simple as that. Majesties, gentlemen, ladies, good day." He rose, clicked heels and inclined his head to the monarchs, and left with his aides at his heels.

There was a moment of silence, then everyone tried to talk at once. Peter Owensford listened for a moment, then called, "Attention!" in a parade ground voice. The room fell silent for a moment.

"So. What does it mean?" Lysander demanded. He turned to Admiral Forrest. "What is happening?"

"I don't know. It doesn't make any sense at all," Forrest said. "They've cut off all communications with Karantov and Newell. I can't even get through to Commodore Guildford! Some of this is pretty obvious. Nguyen's motives are clear. He's been in bed with the Bronson faction forever, and Bronson can be pretty generous. Immunity, pardon, or hell, a new identity and a lot of money on whatever planet he likes."

"And what planet will want him after this?" King Alexander demanded.

"Majesty, there are places Bronson stands high," Anatoly Nosov said. He shrugged. "And not so many places that would welcome Nguyen in any event, but this is not important. I agree with Admiral Forrest, problem is to understand why Ciotti does this. My guess is he thinks there will be no rescinding order from Lermontov."

"But—" King Alexander's eyes widened.

"I don't think I'm going to like this, but please explain," Lysander said.

"If Grand Admiral Lermontov is alive and still holds command, he will rescind that order. Ciotti knows this. Inference is obvious."

"I agree," Admiral Forrest said.

"You're saying Lermontov is dead?" King David asked.

"Dead, or deposed, Majesty," Nosov said. "I fear so."

"Which raises other questions," Forrest said. "Just what does Ciotti know, and how does he know it?" He shrugged. "But what's important is, what will we do now?"

"What should we do?" David said simply. "Fight, or obey? Ordinarily the Kings are required to seek counsel on such matters. With the Ultimate Decree in effect I suppose we don't have to, but perhaps it's better."

There were murmurs among the councilors and observers.

"Perhaps you have a choice," Peter Owensford said. "We don't. Once we're disarmed we're helpless, and while I doubt Ciotti would be party to our slaughter, he could sure as hell deliver us to someone who would be. If they can do something this raw, God knows there's nothing they can't do—or that Bronson won't do."

"So you'll fight," Alexander said. "The Legion will fight."

"We'll try. Our fighting strength is supporting Spartan operations at Base One and Stora. Ciotti knows that, and he'll make it plenty tough for any of them to come home. What we've got left is retired troops, staff officers, some military police, the dependents, against a Line Marine regiment. Before we can get any strength transferred from the front, he'll be at the gates of Fort Plataia demanding surrender. Once he has our base and our dependents, it'll be easier to deal with the rest of us. He already has guards posted around the Fort. They're not letting anyone leave, not without a fight anyway." Owensford shrugged. "We can't even run away. Not our people at the Fort, anyway. I suppose some of the field units could disband and hide out, but they'll put a lot of pressure on you people to help them hunt us down, and nobody's going to want to abandon our dependents to Ciotti anyway."

"But what will happen?" someone asked.

For answer, Owensford pointed to the main screen. It showed Marine equipment rolling up from the shuttle docks to the CoDominium enclave; tank-transporters and personnel carriers, artillery, general cargo. The men marched behind, in battledress of synthileather over armor. The harsh male sound of their singing crashed back from the walls of the deserted streets:

> "We've left blood in the dirt of twenty-five worlds
> We've built roads on a dozen more,
> And all that we have at the end of our hitch
> Buys a night with a second-rate whore.
> The Senate decrees, the Grand Admiral Calls
> The orders come down from on high.
> It's 'On Full Kits' and 'Sound Board Ships,'
> We're sending you where you can die."

"It would have been easier to stop their landing, of course," Owensford said conversationally. "Once they're down and sorted out into their units they're a lot stronger."

"Except we don't have any way to control what lands on Sparta," Lysander said.

> "The lands that we take, the Senate gives back
> Rather more often than not,
> But the more that are killed, the less share the loot
> And we won't be back to this spot."

"And if we fight them?" Alexander asked.

> "We'll break the hearts of your women and girls
> We may break your arse, as well
> Then the Line Marines with their banners unfurled
> Will follow those banners to hell—"

"What will happen? We'll probably lose," Peter Owensford said. "Ciotti's heart won't be in it—he'd never have started this if he'd thought we'd resist—but he'll fight because it's what he's done all his life and he doesn't know what else to do."

> "We know the devil, his pomps, and his works,
> Ah, yes! We know them well!
> When you've served out your hitch in
> the Line Marines,
> You can bugger the Senate of Hell!"

"Of course the Bronson people are counting on knocking Sparta out once we don't have your help any more," Lysander said.

"I expect so," Owensford said. "Actually it's rather late for that. You've learned well. Still, you'll be hurt. Murasaki's technoninjas will have your communications in knots once they round up all the former CD technicians. You've got good universities here, but they're not prepared for what Murasaki does. Not many are. Still, we've done a pretty good job on the Helots, at Base Camp One, and the Stora Commando operation. If they'd tried this stunt a couple of months ago, who knows, they really might have knocked you out of the war. Now—" He shrugged. "You've got a better chance than we do. Preserve your strength, take it slow and careful, I think you'll be all right in the end."

> *"Then we'll drink with our comrades and*
>   *throw down our packs,*
> *We'll rest ten years on the flat of our backs,*
> *Then it's 'On Full Kits' and out of your racks,*
> *You must build a new road through Hell!"*

"General Owensford," Lysander said. "I think you are laboring under a misconception."

"Highness?"

Lysander stared at the screen. Rank after rank of Marines swung by the pickup. The tempo of the song changed, to a flurry of drums and horns.

> *"The Fleet is our country, we sleep with a rifle,*
> *No man ever begot a son on his rifle,*
> *They pay us in gin and curse when we sin,*
> *There's not one who can stand us unless*
>   *we're downwind.*
> *We're shot when we lose and turned out*
>   *when we win,*
> *But we bury our comrades wherever they fall,*
> *And there's none that can face us though*
>   *we've nothing at all!"*

"You seem to think we're going to abandon you," Lysander said.

"It's the sensible thing to do," Owensford said.

"No, by God," Alexander said. "Do you think that little of us, Peter Owensford? What have we done that you think that?"

"Sire—" For some reason Peter Owensford couldn't talk.

King David raised his head from his hands. "We here in this room have no choice," he said. "But—you all know what we have here. The Life Guards, some training units, and little else. All the first line Brotherhood units are up north. There's nothing left but the second-line Militia units. Old men, and boys and women. Enough to put down riots or fight terrorists, but can we ask them to fight that?" He pointed at the screen. "General Owensford, the Freedman Life Guards are at your disposal, and me with them, but I can't order the militia to face Line Marines."

"There's no need to order them," Lysander said. He turned to the Brotherhood representatives. "Citizens and Brothers. The Kings will lead their guards in defense of the allies of Sparta. Will the Brotherhoods join us?"

"Yes, Highness." Allan Hyson, the banker, looked scared, but his voice was firm. "How could we not?"

CHAPTER SEVENTEEN

There is a paradox in the study of individual military merit inasmuch as people generally believe that the fundamental strength of soldiers is derived from the mutual dependence of comradeship and its assurance of being never left to fight alone. This is superficially true, but only in the sense that the strength of mutual dependence is an end product itself. Nothing can be derived from mutual support among a group of nothings. The man in a unit who has nothing within himself of any positive value is at best a vacant file. Unit strength is built of individual strength in positive quantities, however small. The approbation of his companions in arms is the greatest reward of a soldier's life. He never wins it by relying wholly on the efforts of others to assure his survival. In battle, when a man is not acting by reflex and retains a moment for introspection, the sensation of aloneness is most vivid. It is not to right or left or backward that he looks for strength of survival, but within himself. He is lost if there is nothing there of substance.

— Joseph Maxwell Cameron,
The Anatomy of Military Merit

"Urgent signal, sir," Andy Lahr said. "Captain Catherine Alana."

"Is this circuit secure?"

"Yes, sir, direct line of sight systems, the Palace to Plataia. I mean, with Murasaki I suppose we can't be sure about anything, but I'd bet on it."

"It will have to do. OK, Andy, put her on screen."

Catherine was in battle dress, armor and leather, her hair hidden under a combat helmet. "New intelligence report," she

1112

said. "Cornet Talkins has reported in. We've arranged a pickup, but I prefer to send her to the Palace. The CoDominium might or might not let her in here, but it wouldn't be much of a favor to put her in the middle of a battle after all she's been through. They were pretty rough on her. Anyway, I told her to ask for you, code Jehosophat."

"All right, I'll arrange to have her brought in. We can send her over to St. Thomas Hospital. Any reason I should talk to her myself? Andy Bielskis is here."

"She knows where Skilly is."

"Jesus. Tell me, quick."

"Unfortunately, it's where Skilly was. A farmhouse up near Corinth. Worth raiding, but you won't get anyone important. Talkins didn't exactly escape, General, she was rescued."

"By whom?"

"Sir, you're not going to like this. By Geoffrey Niles. He's with her, and will be at the Palace shortly."

"Niles. Under some kind of amnesty?"

"Safe conduct," Catherine said. "We didn't have much time, the Helots are looking for them, and so it was kind of a package deal, I had to bring in both."

"I'll do what I can. That Stora business really got to Prince Lysander. If we can show Niles had any connection to that, Lysander will hang him and there won't be a thing I can do about it. Or want to do about it for that matter."

"Yes, sir. Anyway, I told Niles he could walk out with a reasonable head start. General, he did rescue Margreta Talkins."

"Yeah. All right, I said I'll do what I can."

"There's more. The reason Skilly isn't at the farmhouse is that she's in Sparta City, Minetown to be exact, organizing the Helot revolt to take over when the CoDominium Marines kill off the government of Sparta. When the Marines march on us, she'll start a general uprising."

"How truly good," Owensford said. "I have to face the 77th Line Marines with all my forces up north, nothing here but secondary militia, and I get to deploy for a general uprising as well. Actually, I expected it. Nice to see that effort wasn't wasted. Any idea of just what strength she's got?"

"No, sir, and I don't think she knows either. The Ultimate Decree caught them off guard, and a lot of their politicals have deserted the cause now that it's dangerous. Of course if she looks like winning they'll be back. General, that's not the worst of it."

"Captain, just what can be worse?"

"Murasaki. He's got an atom bomb."

"Oh, boy. Do we know what he plans to do with it?"

"No, sir. Niles may know more about that. He was being cagey, holding back some information to bargain with. Of course he maybe wrong, but I'd bet a lot that he believes he's not wrong, that Murasaki has a bomb and Skilly has worked out a way to use it to her advantage. Maybe you can find out more when he gets there."

"I'll try. Wish I had you here."

"Use Andy. He's better than me, almost as good as Jesus," Catherine said. "OK, sir, I'll get back to defense organization."

"Yeah. How's morale."

"Not good, but how could it be?"

"Right. Tell them to hang on. Ciotti may want to carry out his orders, but he doesn't want his bright and shiny regiment all bloodied either. I'm hoping that when he realizes he has a real fight he'll reconsider."

"Yes, sir. Well, I'd best get to work. Alana out." Catherine didn't sound as if she believed that Ciotti would reconsider, which was all right, because Owensford didn't really believe it either.

The gates of the CoDominium compound swung open. Almost silently, two Suslov tanks flowed out, sensors scanning as their turrets swung the 135mm autocannon back and forth. The scouts had gone over the wall earlier; infantry followed the armor, deploying into open formations.

Lysander felt his palms sweat as he watched through the pickup from the lead tank. *God I wish I was there. Like hell I do.*

The plan was to keep the CD Marines in the urban areas, prevent their full deployment. Try to keep them from winning quickly. Every hour's delay was another chance Lermontov would send countermanding orders. *Or something. Hell, the horse may learn to sing.*

The tanks moved forward. *God, I'm glad I'm not there.* Those were better machines than his men had, and crewed by soldiers everyone called the best in the human universe.

He had put the Spartan-made armor in the forward positions, holding the Legion's handful of modern tanks and AFVs back to contain penetrations. The first of the Marine tanks was nosing down the avenue leading south, with a screening force of infantry fanned out ahead, shadowy figures darting from one piece of cover to the next.

"Now," he said.

The pickup monitor shuddered, and buried blast charges

dropped the fronts of the buildings on either side into the street.
A barrier of rubble slid down across the pavement in a cloud
of dust and brick that billowed out to obscure the nightvision
scope's view. Overhead the freight-train rumble of artillery
passed, and seconds later the lead element of the 77th Marines
fell under the hammer of airburst shells. Automatic weapons
opened up, streams of tracer from well-covered positions further
down the street killing or pinning the Marine foot soldiers.
The first Suslov accelerated, rising up over the rubble that
blocked the street.

The monitor shuddered again, this time as the 76mm gun
of the Cataphract opened up, hammering five shells into the
thinner belly armor of the medium tank. The flashes were
bright; the heavier vehicle slewed around and halted. An instant
later it exploded, a muffled *whump* sound and belches of
yellow-orange flame through slits and hatches.

"Got him, got him!" the Cataphract's commander was saying.
"We got—" The pickup went blank.

"Switch to secondary," Lysander said.

"Captain Porter here."

"Collins here."

"Highness, the rebels are making their move concurrently with
the Marine attack. Power's down except for buildings with
auxiliaries." That meant the whole city was dark, no streetlights,
probably no water. "City com lines are completely garbled. Heavy
jamming on the air. Firing in the streets, and fires, from what
sensors I have left. Seems to be centered in Minetown."

Lysander nodded grimly. Every Field Force soldier and
militiaman was needed to contain the Marines; so were the
Milice. The unorganized reserve of the Brotherhoods would
have to contain the Minetowners. That might be difficult; there
were sixty thousand new chums in there, many of them hungry,
and there had been no time to root out all the rebels.

"The third line will have to handle it," he said. *That's all
there* is, he thought. *Ordinary people.*

Another light flashed. "Sir! Major Donald here. The Marines
are—"

"Where do you think you're going?"

Thomas McTiernan sucked in his gut and managed to fasten the armor; a decade as a tavern and restaurant keeper
had left him a good deal heftier than he had been when
he last wore the Brotherhood militia equipment. Behind him
an open window looked out over a street dark except for
the light of a three-quarter Cytheria and the ruddy glow of

burning buildings a little further north; the low-rent district was ablaze from end to end. No fire sirens sounded, not since the rebel snipers slaughtered the first response of the amateur fire companies. He could see the flashes from shells exploding near the CoDo enclave, as well, and the staccato echoes of small-arms fire. Both were increasing, and even as he watched Marine artillery opened up from inside the enclave, firing south against the Royal guns dug in near Government House Square.

"Didn't you hear the King?" he said, turning on her. Their bedroom was plain enough; there was a hologram of a serious-looking young man in Royal Army uniform. Another of a younger man; that one had the simple starburst of the Order of Thermopylae laid across it. "I'm going to help stop the rebels, the Marines, get the bastards who hurt Julio—"

Then he took in the hunting clothes on her stout body, the shotgun firmly clutched in her hands.

"Not without me, you aren't, Thomas McTiernan," she said. "And don't say it. All the young, strong, fit ones are off with the Army, like Mike—" they both glanced toward the picture of their son in uniform "—and we're what's left."

He stared at her in silence for a moment, then snorted. "Startin' to remember why I married you, Maria," he said.

The arms case was in the back of the bedroom closet. A Peltast rifle lay there, massive and ugly-handsome and shining with careful maintenance. He threw the bandoleer over his shoulder, then ducked his head through the carrying strap, grunting as he came erect. *These mothers are* heavy, he thought. One of his knees gave a warning twinge, legacy of an ancient soccer game. *Hope I don't have to sprint much.*

His daughter was waiting at the head of the stairs, a gangling buck-toothed girl with a mop of carrot-colored hair, just turned thirteen and adding pimples to her mass of freckles. She was wearing the brown cotton-drill uniform of the Royal Spartan Scouts, complete with neckerchief, and carrying the scope-sighted .22 rifle they trained with. Her father opened his mouth, hesitated.

"Just keep your head down and don't do anything damn-fool, understand?" he growled.

"Yes, Papa," she said.

Damn sight more respectful than she usually is, he thought, working his mouth to moisten it. *Christ, I wish was twenty again.* A young man didn't think he could die. A young man didn't have responsibilities . . . *A young man didn't see his son after he'd thrown himself on a grenade in his own home.*

They came out into the courtyard that was the patio of the family business, and a shadowy figure leaped back with a cry.

"Jesus, Thom!"

"Ah, Eddie," McTiernan said, recognizing the neighbor who had the appliance-repair shop down at the corner. "Sorry."

They walked out into the street. A crowd was gathering; he recognized most of them, but it was odd to see the same faces you passed the time of day with milling around with guns in their hands.

"Thom, we're putting up a barricade at the end of the street. Mind if we use your van?"

He winced—that was three years scrimping and saving—then nodded and threw the man the keys.

"Hey, sprout, get your bike," a younger voice said. "Mr. Kennedy says we gotta be couriers to the other parts of the neighborhood."

His daughter gave him a brief kiss on the cheek and dashed away; Maria McTiernan came back out of the door, her shotgun slung muzzle-down along her back and two large hampers in her hand.

"Sandwiches," she said, to his unspoken question. "They'll need sandwiches at the barricade."

"Eddie," he said, struck with a thought. He hoisted the Peltast rifle up with the butt resting on one hip.

"Yeah?"

"Get me a couple of people, will you?" He pointed to the library at the end of the street with his free hand; it was a neo-Californian period piece, with a square four-story tower at one corner. "With someone to watch my back, I could do a lot of good from up there with this jackhammer."

"Yeah! Hey, Forchsen, Mrs. Brust, c'mon over here!"

Somebody pedaled up, breathless, shouted in a voice just beginning to break.

"Hey, I'm from Jefferson Street! My Dad sent me to tell you the Minetowners are coming right up Paine Avenue, must be thousands of them, molotovs and guns and all, they've got some trucks covered with boilerplate, too. Coming through where the Marines blew down the buildings."

A growl ran through the householders, mechanics, storekeepers, clerks. The crowd flowed toward the barricade, into firing positions in upper floors; McTiernan heard window-glass being hammered out with rifle butts as he lumbered wheezing toward the library, gasping thanks as Mrs. Brust the schoolteacher came up to take some of the weight off his shoulder.

Her machinepistol clanked against him with every stride, to a mutter of *"sorry, sorry."*

On Burke Avenue, on scores of others like it, the Battle of Sparta City had begun.

"Report, Group Leader Derex?" Kenjiro Murasaki said, indicating the map table. The commander of the Helot regulars infiltrated into Sparta City looked exhausted, his armor dark with grime and smoke.

"Not so good, sir," he said. "Here." The map showed Minetown as a solid splotch of Movement red with long tangled pseudopods reaching out across the city; there was another, smaller block on the other side of the Sacred way, and a scattering like measles almost to Government House Square. From the CoDominium enclave a single broad straight arrow drove south, overlapping the Movement forces.

"Trouble is, them Minetowners ain't gettin' out as much as we'd like," the Helot said regretfully. "Well, not surprisin'. Handing 'em guns don't make them fuckers soldiers, sir. Too many barricades and Cits with guns. Not milishy—the milishy fightin' the Marines—just Cits, but they kin shoot. Nearly got me, b'God; snipers thicker'n dogshit out there. Peltast rifles, too, them armored cars ain't worth jack shit against them fuckers." A look of grudging respect made the Helot's face longer than ever.

"Well, anyways, when the Minetowners *do* git out, 'n overrun places with Cits in 'em, they just stops to loot, rape and burn and drink anythin' they kin find, transmission fluid included. Then the Milice flyin' squads hits and drives 'em back. Our own fires is getting so outa hand they're blockin' us too. Too many of em round the edges of Minetown."

"Flying squads?" Murasaki said thoughtfully "How do they coordinate, without communications?" Much of the Royal Army equipment was still functioning, but the ordinary city facilities were frozen.

The Helot officer brayed laughter. Murasaki frowned, and it sobered the tall man down to a grin.

"They ain't using the com, sir. They's usin' Evil Scuts."

"Eagle Scouts?" the Meijian said, baffled.

"Little motherfuckers're on rooftops and in attic winders all over town, anywhere Cits live, blinkin' at each other with flashlights. Morse code." This time the admiration was ungrudged. "Runnin' messages by bicycle, too."

"Dispose of them."

"How, sir? I ain't got but the one Group, seven hundred

countin' every booger and ass-wipe. Y' Movement gunmen will
have to do it."

Murasaki nodded thoughtfully. *Surprising,* he thought.
Analysis had indicated the blockade and CoDominium intervention would frighten the populace into sitting this out.

"Recommendations?"

"Sure, sir. Them Minetowners don't have the discipline to
overrun even weak forces, but they got more'n enough numbers and firepower, with what we handed out. Your cell-
leaders—" he jerked a thumb at the men and women behind
him, in civilian clothes but armed and wearing = sign
armbands "— keep tryin' to lead from the front. Like tryin'
to stiffen up a pitcher of spit with a handful of buckshot,
just wastin' men who're willing to fight. Put automatic
weapons teams *behind* the crowds. Fire on anyone who
retreats. Set the fires in the *center* of Minetown, big ones.
They'll charge the barricades if you get them too crazy-scared
of what's behind them to stop."

The technoninja nodded.

"Do it. Now. Also, detach two companies for the *Endlosung*
attack on Fort Plataia."

The Helot hesitated. "Sir—"

"It is essential."

Orders crackled out.

"Glad to see you, Cornet Talkins," Owensford said. "Highness, I present Cornet Margreta Talkins. She holds commissions in both the Legion and the Royal Intelligence Corps.
Talkins, Crown Prince Lysander."

"I'm proud to meet you, Highness," Margreta said. She
looked down at her ill fitting clothing with embarrassment.
"They didn't tell me I was to meet you—"

Lysander took her hand and kissed her fingers. "I'm very
pleased to meet you. We'll repeat the introduction at a more
pleasant event," Lysander said. He turned to her companion.
"I can't say I'm pleased to see you, Niles. Frankly, I'd rather
talk to a snake."

"I wish I could resent that," Geoffrey Niles said. "But
unfortunately I understand all too well."

"Were you at Stora?" Lysander demanded.

"At Stora, yes, Highness. But I had nothing to do with the
attack on the Armory. I would have prevented it if I could."

"You knew it was to take place?"

"I knew we had an earth penetrator missile. I did not know
its target until less than five minutes before the launch. I

protested the targeting, and was told that if I continued to protest I would be shot. I did not order that target, nor did I pass along any orders concerning that missile."

"Sergeant Bielskis?" Owensford asked.

"No hesitations, and no doubts," Andy Bielskis said. "If he's faking that, he's the best I ever saw. I'd say genuine, sir."

"If you like I'll submit to any questioning technique you want to employ," Niles said. "The only violation of the Laws of War that I have been involved in or condoned was the gas attack in the Dales, and that was against military targets only. There weren't even any civilians in the area."

"All right, we'll hold that one in abeyance," Owensford said. "Cornet, what was promised to Mr. Niles?"

"Free passage out if he didn't talk us into a better deal, and a reasonable head start before pursuit."

"Talkins, you sound exhausted. I suppose it's best you're here as long as we're talking to Grand Senator Bronson's nephew, but as soon as we're done I want you to go check into St. Thomas's," Owensford said.

"Thanks, sir, but I reckon I can still fight."

"There's no need," Lysander said.

"Every need," Margreta said. "Highness, I intend to accept Citizenship just as soon as I'm discharged. This is my home, and I'll sure feel better when we've got these scum cleaned out of it." She touched her bruised cheeks and black eye. "And I reckon I have some personal reasons, too."

"Well, I can't argue that," Owensford said. "All right, Niles, you hinted that you want a better deal than a safe conduct out of here. What do you want and what will you trade?"

"What I want is a free pardon," Niles said.

"Not a ticket off-planet?"

"If I have to take that I'll do it, but I'd rather earn the right to stay here," Geoff said. "Stay here, help rebuild. Help undo some of the damage I've caused." He looked significantly at Margreta. "Marry, work for Citizenship."

"Why this change of heart?"

"It would take a long time to explain, and we don't have a long time," Geoff said. "You learn a lot about a society from fighting it. And about its leaders. And what I learned was to admire you people."

"And what do you have to bargain with?" Owensford demanded.

"Information. I'll give it all to you, and you determine what it's worth. I'll accept your valuation."

Lysander look coldly at him for a while. "All right. Spill it."

Geoff told them of the conversation he had heard between

Skilly and Murasaki. "I didn't actually hear the word 'nuke,'" he said, "but I can't think what else it could be. Murasaki has one, but only one, nuclear weapon, and he intends to deploy it either to destroy the Palace, or Legion Headquarters at Fort Plataia. If it was left to Skilly it would be the Palace, but my guess is that Murasaki prefers Plataia."

"But you don't know it's a nuke," Lysander said, "and in any event you don't know where it is. Where it is now, or where it is going to be. Who would know?"

"Skilly, and Murasaki," Geoff said. "And maybe not Skilly. Murasaki is crazy. Apparently Grand Uncle gave him the assignment of undermining Sparta, and the secondary but almost equally important goal of punishing Falkenberg's Legion."

"Sounds a bit odd," Owensford said. "The Legion's on New Washington. We're just some odd bits and pieces."

"Including the families," Niles said. "Murasaki would delight in the anguish it would cause Falkenberg and his people on New Washington if they heard their families were killed. Or captured by Bronson people."

"That must take real hate," Owensford said. "Is Bronson that crazy?"

Niles shook his head slowly. "General, I don't know. I used to think he was crazy like a fox. That's still the way to bet it."

"All right," Lysander said. "General, your evaluation? Is his information worth what he asks?"

"It's close. Talkins, have you a recommendation regarding this man?" Owensford said.

"He saved my life," she said. "And he—was very much a gentleman."

"Well, you have a large favor coming from the Crown," Lysander said.

"Oh. Well, if it's large enough to cover his pardon, I'll ask for it," Margreta said.

Lysander nodded. "So be it. Geoffrey Niles, you have a free pardon for all acts committed since you arrived on Sparta to this moment. Cornet Talkins, you've still got a favor coming, you didn't use more than half your credit on this."

"So," Owensford said. "Sergeant, take Mr. Niles to a conference room and see if he remembers anything else worth knowing. Particularly clues about where this Gotterdammerung is going to go off."

Lysander stood. "I don't suppose I can be much help with

that. Cornet Talkins, please go to St. Thomas's. It won't be any picnic. I'm afraid the hospital is going to end up as part of the defense system."

"The next push with their armor may get through," Lysander said bluntly, to the officers grouped around them. "We're sopping up their infantry, us and the Citizens, but we've got to get more antitank teams out there—"

It had been only five hours since the attack began. *Five hours. God.* He could hear his own words as he briefed his men, but somewhere beneath it was running a stream of memory, smashed buildings and men gaping in death around burning iron. *Only five hours and we're already back to Government House Square.* The St. Thomas Hospital had been the only building suitable for a redoubt.

"Sir, rebels, they're in the main ventilation shafts on level four!"

Lysander jerked his head up from the map. "Bloody hell! Come on—not you, just the riflemen."

The machine gunner at the window nodded, tapping off another expert short burst at the shadowy figures darting between the burning cars in the lot below. *God Damn.* The CoDo Marines were not cooperating with the Helots deliberately, but the *effect* could be the same.

Lysander led the way out of the orderly room they had taken over as tactical HQ at a pounding run. Wounded men and the sick evacuated from the lower levels looked up at him as he passed, slalomed off the wall at the axial corridor with the rifle squad at his heels. This *was* level four; his redoubt. And Melissa's room was quite close to where the main airshaft branched off from the service core.

"There!" he shouted.

There was movement behind the grillwork screen, across from her door. He fired from the hip as he ran, walking the bullets up the wall and into the meter-square grille. More movement, a jerk. A flash of white light, and suddenly he was lying against the door and the door was open, and Melissa was looking at him. Smiling. Then horrified, and beginning to struggle out of bed. She had a pistol in one hand, and a book in the other. Some distant part of him recognized it; the Church of Sparta *Book of Hours.*

"No, stay there, darling, *please.*"

"Bastards," he wheezed, levering himself over so that he faced the corridor. The door swung shut behind him. Thin, no protection.

Pain stabbed into his ribs, making him cough. That was a mistake, because white light ran behind his eyelids and the world rocked, and vomiting would *really* be a mistake if his ribs were in the state he thought they were. *Already* in *hospital, nothing I can do.*

"Bastards," he gritted again, and used the rifle to climb to his knees. *"Bastards!"* The men who had followed him here were down, moving or still but down. An arm dangled out of the black hole up near the roof where the screen had been, shredded and dripping, a head and shoulders and too many teeth showing where blast had ripped the skin and muscle off a skull like a glove off a hand. The body jerked and trembled. *Not alive. Moving. More of them in the shaft.*

Lysander slumped against the wall, ignoring the gratings under his chest. The armor would hold it for a while. He clamped the rifle between his side and his arm, brought up the wavering muzzle.

"Bastards!"

Bang and *ptank* as a bullet slammed through the thin lath and thinner metal behind it, the aluminum airshaft itself. Hollow booming as something big thrashed around in that strait space, and the hole began to leak red down the gray-white plaster of the hospital wall.

"Bastards!"

Another shot, another, recoil hammering into his side, spacing them down the length of the corridor, the length of the hidden shaft. Someone came up behind him, another rifleman, firing with him, slow and deliberate. Then a thunderclap; fire shot out around the body stuck in the hole like a cork in a bottle, and plaster showered down as the metal ballooned. Harv came trotting down the corridor reloading his grenade launcher, calling over his shoulder for stretcher-bearers.

Lysander looked to see who his companion was. "Well, Cornet Talkins. I think you've earned another favor. Now do me one. Stay with Melissa."

"Aye aye, sir."

Harv brought the medics up. "Lady, I sure thank you," he said. "It was supposed to be me with the Prince, and—" He gestured to the medics.

"I can stand," Lysander gritted. "I can't sprint but I can command. Get me up. Back to the war room. *Now.*"

Centrifugal force kept the outer rim of the space station at .9 gee, which was comfortable compared to Sparta. Everyone knew that high gravity was much better for your health, people in high gravity planets lived longer due to the increased exercise, but .9 gee was still a relief. Sergeant Wallace and the 77th Captain whose name Boris Karantov couldn't remember had remarked on it. They'd talked about many things in an attempt to be pleasant, and to take Karantov's mind off the fact that he was a prisoner in his own office.

After a while they turned on the television screens. They showed the battles in Sparta City from the view of the Marines of the 77th. The battle wasn't going smoothly. In five hours they'd made a wreck of part of the city but they hadn't stopped the city resistance at all. And now there were other scenes, of rebels attacking the citizens although they carefully avoided fighting any units of the 77th.

Boris Karantov watched the battle with horror. He maintained a chilly silence until the Marine lieutenant had left the room. Then he spoke to the polite Line Marine sergeant. "Sergeant Wallace, good men are being killed down there. Your comrades, Legionnaires, Spartans. And you are illegally detaining legitimate CoDominium authorities who could end this madness."

The Line Marine sergeant didn't like his situation at all. "Sir, the Captain told me—"

"Sergeant, do you deny that I am senior CoDominium Marine officer in this system?"

"No, sir."

"Then forget your captain. I am giving you orders: assist me in regaining control of this station."

"Colonel, I can't do that—"

"Sergeant, you will do that. Or shoot me now. If you disobey this order and I am alive when this is over, Sergeant Wallace, I will have you hanged in low gravity, and the last thing you will see will be recordings of that." He pointed at the screens. "Or do you tell me you join military services to accomplish that?"

"Jesus, Colonel, all I know is they tell me—" He lowered his voice. "Colonel, the story is you're all Lermontov people, and Lermontov is out. Arrested. Admiral Townsend is in charge now."

"And you believe Fleet will go over to Townsend, which is to say, Bronson?"

"God damn, Colonel, we don't know jack shit about politics, I know I got my orders."

"Which are rescinded," a voice said from behind him. "Sergeant, if you reach for that weapon I will cheerfully cut your throat. Colonel, if you'll relieve him of that sidearm— there. Thank you."

"Thank you. Now who are you?" Karantov demanded.

"Master Sergeant Hiram Laramie, SAS, Falkenberg's Legion, at your service, Colonel. When we couldn't raise communications, Colonel Owensford sent us up to have a look."

"How the fuck did you get here?" Sergeant Wallace demanded.

"I confess curiosity myself," Karantov said.

"Navy helped," Laramie said. "They was getting worried they couldn't reach Captain Newell or any of their own officers, sir, so they was glad to help us come take a look. Lieutenant Deighton's looking to help Captain Newell, sir."

"What have you done with the others of the 77th?"

"Got 'em handcuffed outside," Laramie said. "Sergeant Wallace, if you'll put your hands behind you—careful, now, and nobody gets hurt. Thank you. Colonel, General Owensford would like mightily to speak with you. Shall I get him for you?"

"Yes, please, Sergeant. And please to find out status of Fleet Captain Newell, if you will . . ."

Marine Captain Saunders Laubenthal slid up behind the windowsill and looked out onto the street outside. The dead from the last Spartan counterattack littered it; many were down below, where his men had had to clear them out with grenades.

We took the street, he thought bitterly. *And now there's another bloody street to take.*

"Irony," he muttered to himself.

"Sir?" Sandeli said.

The black was the senior sergeant now, and second-in-command of the company since Lieutenant Cernkov had been carried back to the enclave and the regeneration stimulators. The unit had taken twenty percent casualties in the night's fighting.

"I was planning to retire here," Laubenthal said absently. "Gods, if these are militia we're fighting, I'd hate to see their best. They just don't give up."

From another window fire stabbed out across the street toward the Spartan positions. A body pitched forward to tumble off a balcony and forward to the pavement two stories below, a rifle rattling beside it.

"Got them pretty well suppressed, sir," Sandeli said.

Hint. "All right; tell first platoon to—"

A sound interrupted him, a high-pitched shrieking from further down the street to the north, back along their path. Then a scatter of running figures; they were pushing a handcart before them, with a uniformed Spartan wired to the front of it and a thicker mob behind. The uniform was on fire, and the mob behind fell on the Spartan wounded in the street below the Marine position with clubs and tools and bayoneted rifles. More screams rose, and the flood of ragged humanity spilled over to the building the Royalists still held; the Marines had done their work of suppressing fire all too well.

"Kaak," Sandeli muttered in his native tongue: *shit.*

Captain Laubenthal stood and touched the side of his helmet. *"The last bloody straw,"* he muttered. *"Damned* if I'll see good soldiers murdered."

"Sir?"

"It appears that we're out of touch with HQ, sergeant," he said. "I do not seem to hear a thing. A Company! Open fire, selective. Drive off those jackals and rescue the Spartans."

"Sir?"

"You heard me, soldier!"

"Fucking A, sir! Carruthers. New targets! Clean house!" He turned back to his captain. "Sir, I hope you never get that mother fucking radio working again."

"Owensford here."

"Deighton here, sir. I have Fleet Captain Newell and Colonel Karantov with me."

"Thank God. Boris, what's happening up there?"

"Ciotti's people had us under house arrest," Karantov said.

"Thought it was something like that. Guildford too?"

"Sir, they've taken him somewhere else, possibly aboard that battlecruiser *Patton,* sir," Lieutenant Deighton said.

"Thank you. But you have returned control of the CD space station to Fleet Captain Newell and Colonel Karantov?"

"I can do that now, sir. Fleet Captain, Colonel, any time you'd like you can relieve my troops with those you've selected."

"I will see to this," Boris Karantov said. "I also wish to see that my landing craft is made ready. Piotr Stefanovich, my thanks. We will speak again."

"General Slater, let me add my thanks as well," Newell said. "I can't say I enjoyed being under arrest."

"No, sir. If you'll pardon me, Captain, what the hell is going on? Has Ciotti lost his mind?"

"Not quite," Newell said. "According to the sergeant who was holding Colonel Karantov prisoner, Ciotti got, along with his orders to come here and arrest you, a message to the effect that Lermontov has been deposed. It doesn't seem to have been an official order signed by the Grand Senate, but a message from someone at Fleet Headquarters. There was another from the Grand Senate, or maybe from a Senate Committee."

"Or an individual Grand Senator?"

"Possibly. Since Ciotti's the only one we know who read it, I don't have the details. All I know is, we got word Ciotti was coming with special orders, and as soon as he got here he used his troops to take control of this station. We didn't suspect a thing. I couldn't figure out what was his hurry, but then not long after Ciotti's takeover here, Signals got a long coded message from Fleet Headquarters. Ciotti's people can't decode it, and my people said they couldn't, but that may have been a story for Ciotti. I'm checking on that now."

"From Fleet Headquarters, but can't be decoded by Fleet signal officers," Owensford said. "Captain, if all else fails, perhaps Colonel Karantov can decode it. Or King Alexander."

"Hmm. I see," Newell said. "All right, I'll have a copy sent down to you. If you can read it, I expect you ought to."

"Meanwhile, what do you intend to do?" Owensford asked. "With Guildford out of communications, you're the senior Fleet official in this system."

"Until Guildford shows up again," Newell said. "Or we get authenticated orders from Fleet Headquarters."

"And if Lermontov has been thrown out in a Bronson coup?" Owensford asked.

"I'll think about that. Now, if you'll excuse me, General, I thank you for the rescue, but there are serious matters demanding my attention. I want to get to my ship!"

"Certainly. When you get the urgent parts done, Admiral Forrest and Captain Nosov would like to speak with you."

Newell grinned. "I just expect they—I have an intercom light, Colonel Karantov wants to be patched in. Just a moment. Boris?"

"Da. Piotr Stefanovich?"

"I'm here, Boris."

"Do not surrender. I am departing for planetary surface," he said. "Godspeed my friend."

"Are we going to die, Mrs. Fuller?" the girl said.

Juanita Fuller looked around the bombproof shelter at the sea of faces; there were fifty children here, and hers was the ultimate responsibility. A dozen shelters like this . . . The one who had asked the question was just too young to be up above helping with the last-ditch defense, around eleven. Her face was grave behind the CBW suit's transparent visor, but some of the others were sniffling back tears.

Mark! something wailed inside her. But Cornet Mark Fuller was with Aviation Company of the Legion on New Washington. *Lieutenant by now. If he's still alive. We didn't have enough time!* A few months, just enough to begin healing from her horrible captivity in the escaped-convict settlement on Tanith. Now she was supposed to face danger like an officer's lady . . . *I'm just a girl, I'm only nineteen.*

"Of course we aren't going to die, Roberta," she said, putting a teasing note into her voice. "*You* just want a chance to get up there and fire a gun." The miniuzi hung heavy on her hip. *I did all right on the firing range. Could I use it on a man?*

"Let's have a song, everybody," she said. "Because there's no school today . . .

> *Little bunny froo-froo*
> *Hoppin' through the forest—"*

Roberta began to sing, and then the others took it up:

"Pickin' up the field mice
Whackin' 'em on the head!"

"Jodie! Do *not* whack Angie on the head!"

"Something funny that I didn't notice, Kinnie?" Captain Jesus Alana asked. The motion sensors said a company level attack was coming out of them through the fire and smoke of the night; the Legion had pulled back to its original encampment, setting incendiaries in the huge Royal Army logistics buildings that made up much of the base.

Base commander, he thought. *Base commander of a rifle platoon.* Adult hands were far too few in Fort Plataia to spare anyone from the firing line.

Hassan al'Jinnah chuckled again. "Just reminds me of old times, sor," he said, stroking the stock of his machine gun. "Ah, here they come." The Berber had been a long-service man when the Legion was still the 42nd CoDominium Marines and John Christian Falkenberg III had been a junior captain; for the last twenty-five years his job had been chief mess steward. "Reminds me of Kennicott, sor."

A very good steward, since he was devoutly Muslim and never touched alcohol. The cocking lever of his rifle made a *tch-clack* sound as he eased it backward and chambered a round.

Jesus Alana pressed his eyes to the vision block. The dark

outside slipped away, replaced by a silvery day like none waking eyes had ever seen. The vast stores area in the western extension of the base was a pillar of flame behind the advancing Helots; two light tanks in the lead, and an infantry screen following. They came at a cautious trot, the AFVs taking advantage of each building, and the foot soldiers moving forward by squads and sections.

"Pretty drill," he said, and pressed the stud. The ground erupted in a line of orange fire. He blinked; when he opened his eyes again his wife was beside him, whistling through her teeth.

Cathy only does that when she's really *nervous,* he thought, unslinging his rifle. Her grenade launcher spat out its five rounds, *choonk-choonk-choonk-choonk.*

There were no living targets when he brought up his weapon. "Doubt they'll try that again," he said thoughtfully. "And it can't have been their whole effort."

The posts reported in, except for one. "Three?" he said. "Post three?"

Mortar shells whistled overhead. *Landline cut?* Possibly, and he had no one to spare to look.

"They'll be back. At least once," he said.

"Twice," al' Jinneh said. "Care for a bet, sor? Bottle of Cavaret Zinfandel?"

"Against what?"

"Blue Mountain coffee, sor. Half a pound."

"Done. Though you win either way, Mess Steward."

Lieutenant Colonel Scott Farley studied the map table, then looked up to Colonel Marco Ciotti. "Six companies fail to report, Colonel."

"The communications environment is very bad," Ciotti said. "But this is strange. Send messengers with new equipment and orders to report instantly."

"Yes, sir." *Is it that he doesn't know, or he doesn't want to know? Six companies don't report. We know two went over to the enemy! Could it be all six? Six companies of Line Marines gone over to the enemy! Nothing like that has happened in thirty years. Of course they haven't exactly gone over, but they're helping the Spartans put down the Minetown rebellion, and a damned good thing, too. Surely Ciotti knows?*

"The assault on Fort Plataia has been repulsed," Ciotti said.

"Yes sir."

"Have them regroup and wait for assistance. Sergeant Kramer, get me Captain Donovic on the *Patton.*"

"Yes, sir. Have to relay through the space station, sir."

"That's all right."

"Yes, sir. It'll be a minute."

Scott Farley watched the map display, but his attention was on the colonel. He had a very good idea what Ciotti had in mind, and he didn't like it.

"Here's Captain Donovic, sir."

"Ciotti here. Captain, I'm losing far too many men in this operation. I need your help. Please set up to bombard designated targets in the Government House and Fort Plataia areas."

"You really think that's necessary?" Donovic asked. "Guildford isn't going to like it."

"I see no point in telling Commodore Guildford until the battle is over," Ciotti said. "I also see no point in continuing to take casualties from these people. They were given every opportunity for honorable surrender, but it is clear they intend to fight long after the result is inevitable. Why should I let our Marines be slaughtered in this senseless action?"

Senseless. It's senseless, all right, Lt. Col. Farley thought. *But not the way you think! God damn, God damn, damn—*

"Colonel, I'm not sure this is wise," Captain Donovic said.

"What is unwise is holding off any longer," Ciotti said. "You know what is at stake here, and time is not on our side. Now please make ready for kinetic energy weapon bombardments. I will designate targets. It will not take long, and we will finish the resistance, at Fort Plataia and in the city itself. We can then proceed with our plans."

"All right," Donovic said. "I don't like it, but I like failure even less, and as you say, time isn't exactly our friend here. Sound general quarters. Battle stations. Prepare for planetary bombardment." Alarm klaxons hooted in the background.

"Captain Donovic."

The voice was strange. Everyone in the map table room looked up, startled.

"Who the hell is that?" Donovic demanded.

"This is Fleet Captain Samuel Newell. I am apparently the senior CoDominium officer present. Captain Donovic, I forbid you to use your ship to take part in this battle. You will please secure from general quarters and report to me in person. You will find me aboard *Vera Cruz.*"

"How the hell—" Ciotti said.

"You're not the system commander," Donovic said.

"No, I understand that Commodore Guildford is a guest

aboard your ship, Captain Donovic," Newell said. "I trust he is better pleased with that status than I was in my own offices on the space station. I have not heard you order your ship secured from general quarters, Captain, and I am waiting."

"Be damned if I'll take orders from you."

"Very well," Newell said. "Commander Taylor, sound general quarters. Battle stations. Divisions report when cleared for action."

"*Vera Cruz.* A cruiser," Donovic said. "This is a battle cruiser. You're bluffing."

"Am I? Taylor, general signal to the squadron. Continue previous deployment. Battle stations, prepare for fleet action against the battlecruiser *Patton.* All units to report when ready for action."

"*Volga* on station and ready for action, sir!"

"*Kirov,* cleared for action, will be on station in five minutes, sir!"

"Newell, you've lost your mind! Are you going to fire on me? We need unity in the Fleet, not this!"

"Exactly, Captain Donovic," Newell said. "And you're going to achieve unity by bombarding an independent planet against the direct orders of the system commanders? Ever think that our families are down there on Sparta where you've helped start a God damned war?"

"*Aegir* sounding general quarters now. On station in twenty minutes."

"You're not Commander Clarkson!" Donovic shouted.

"No, sir, this is Lieutenant Commander Nielsen."

"Where's Clarkson?"

"He's not available, sir," Nielsen said. "Proceeding with general quarters, Captain Newell."

"Thank you. Captain. Donovic, I am still waiting."

There was a long pause. Then: "You know, there's never been a fleet action like this, four smaller ships against a battle cruiser. I think we can take you, Newell."

"Plus the space station. All units, prepare for general engagement."

"But we'd be hurt pretty bad. And what the hell, we might not win. Robbie, secure from general quarters. Captain Newell, you'll understand if I decline your invitation to join you aboard your ship, but I agree we'll need to continue this conversation without so many eavesdroppers.

"Colonel Ciotti, I regret that your request for fire support has been overruled by the acting system commander. I fear you're on your own. Good luck."

The speakers went silent. Ciotti cursed quietly. "All right. We'll have to do it on our own." He looked at the map table. "Maybe we won't have to take the Palace. It looks like the rebels are about to do that."

"GO!" Group Leader Derex was screaming like a madman. *"Go! Go! Go!"*

The Helots streamed toward the palace steps. One unit dashed to the flagstaff to haul down the crowned mountain of the Dual Monarchy. Their leader had begun to unfasten the halyards when a group burst out of the palace.

An old man, and ten of the ceremonial Life Guards. They didn't look ceremonial at all though, as they deployed on the huge steps, hiding behind Doric columns and the great lion statues.

Someone fired four times. The elderly leader of the Guards took another step forward, stumbled, and fell. For a moment there was a lull in the fighting. A woman burst out of the palace and ran to bend over him. She was still for a moment, then she stood.

"Spartans! They have killed the King! The Helots have killed the King!"

A moment of hushed silence; then a roar. From the palace, from the buildings around the square, from tunnels, seemingly from the sky itself, the cry was repeated. "Spartans! The Helots have killed the King!"

And another cry, wordless, an animal sound of rage. The Life Guards charged forward, firing coldly and efficiently and rapidly. They reached the party around the flagstaff, and the only Helots still standing were battered to the ground. One of the guards fell on the Helot soldier and beat him with his rifle butt.

And from the square came militia, wounded soldiers, old men and women, children barely old enough to seize weapons from the fallen. They came out and they came out to kill.

Derex watched his command dissolve, vanish, not so much beaten as destroyed. Men threw down their weapons to run, and that was no good either. The enemy was out now, out in the open, out where they could be killed, but they weren't dying, it was his men who were being slaughtered, shot, stabbed, strangled, beaten to death with baseball bats. A woman sat on a Helot's chest and pounded at his head with an iron frying pan.

Derex stood to rally the men, and a grenade landed nearby. He threw himself away from it, to the ground, but the world had turned to slow motion, he couldn't fall fast enough, and the sound of the grenade was louder than anything he had ever heard in his life.

The screens panned down a street where outnumbered Spartan militia battled a Helot mob. The pickup was back far enough that it didn't show all the details, but there were enough.

Farley looked at the others in the room, Colonel Ciotti, looking unhappier by the minute, like a man out on a limb with no way off it. Major Bannister, staring at the map table with tears in his eyes, unable to look at his colonel. Sergeant Major Immanual Kramer, who didn't look much better. Lieutenant Beeson, who kept looking at the monitor screens as if he hoped they'd go away.

We're on the wrong side, Farley thought. *And I'm senior man except for the Colonel. I should do something. But—* The cry came through the speaker system. "Spartans! They have killed the King!"

Ciotti looked up from the map. "Sorry to hear that."

"Sorry to hear that," Lt. Colonel Farley said. Something burst inside his head. "Sorry to hear that! Sorry to hear that!"

"Control yourself, Scott," Ciotti said.

Scott Farley stood stiffly for a moment. He looked to the others in the room. They didn't move. He put his hand to his pistol. Ciotti stared in disbelief, and still no one moved.

"Colonel," Farley said. "We're on the wrong side here."

"How dare you—"

"I dare because I'm right," Farley said. "And you know it, Colonel. I don't know what was in those goddam coded messages, I don't know what Bronson promised you, but Colonel, it couldn't possibly be worth this!"

"Spartans! They have killed the King! The Helots have killed the King!"

"Thank God!" Lieutenant Beeson said.

"Beeson?" Ciotti said.

"It wasn't us, it was the Helots," Beeson said. "Colonel Farley's right, sir, we're on the wrong side."

"Farley, I will overlook—"

"No, sir, no you won't, because I won't back off," Farley said. "Colonel, I can't take this. I'm relieving you of command. Bannister, general orders, all units. Cease operations against the Spartans, and assist the Spartans against those barbarians."

Bannister stood frozen.

"Do it and I'll have you in a cell with this mutineer," Ciotti said. "Sergeant Major."

"Sir?"

"Please conduct Colonel Farley to the Provost Marshal for confinement. Bannister, order the renewed assault on Fort Plataia."

Bannister didn't move.

Neither did Sergeant Major Kramer.

"Spartans! They have killed the King!"

Ciotti looked around wildly. His pistol was hung neatly with his uniform tunic in the cloak room. "Sergeant Major—"

Kramer shook himself, as if to wake up. "No, sir."

"Sergeant, you've been with me twenty years!"

"I'm with you now, Colonel. I'll always be with you. But— we're on the wrong side, Colonel, it's the wrong fucking side, and you know it, sir, you have to know it."

Farley nodded slowly. "Sergeant Major, I think Colonel Ciotti has had a mild stroke. He needs rest. Please take him to his quarters and look after him. Major Bannister, please send that order."

Bannister nodded slowly. He raised the microphone. "All units," he said. "Attention to orders."

When Colonel Karantov and his Fleet Marine guards arrived ten minutes later, he found the 77th in full cooperation with the Spartan forces. The battle of Sparta City was over.

CHAPTER EIGHTEEN

A well-hidden secret of the principate had been
revealed: it was possible, it seemed, for an emperor to
be chosen outside Rome.
> —Tacitus, *HISTORIES, 1,4:*

Surveying this watershed year of 1941, from which
mankind has descended into its present predicament,
the historian cannot but be astounded by the decisive
role of individual will. Hitler and Stalin played chess
with humanity. In all essentials, it was Stalin's personal insecurity, his obsessive fear of Germany, that
led him to sign the fatal pact, and it was his greed and
illusion—no one else's—which kept it operative, a
screen of false security behind which Hitler prepared
his murderous spring. It was Hitler, no one else, who
determined on a war of annihilation against Russia,
canceled then postponed it, and reinstated it as the
centerpiece of his strategy, as, how, and when he
chose. Neither man represented irresistible or even
potent historical forces. Neither at any stage conducted any process of consultation with their peoples,
or even spoke for self-appointed collegiate bodies.
Both were solitary and unadvised in the manner in
which they took these fateful steps, being guided by
personal prejudices of the crudest kind and by their
own arbitrary visions. Their lieutenants obeyed blindly
or in apathetic terror and the vast nations over which
they ruled seem to have had no choice but to stumble
in their wake toward mutual destruction. We have
here the very opposite of historical determinism—the
apotheosis of the single autocrat. Thus it is, when the
moral restraints of religion and tradition, hierarchy

and precedent, are removed, the power to suspend or
unleash catastrophic events does not devolve on the
impersonal benevolence of the masses but falls into
the hands of men who are isolated by the very totality
of their evil natures.

—Paul Johnson, *Modern Times:*
The World from the Twenties to
the Nineties (rev. ed. 1991)

There is danger that, if the Court does not temper its
doctrinaire logic with a little practical wisdom, it will
convert the Bill of Rights into a suicide pact.

—Justice Robert Houghwout Jackson,
Terminiello v. *Chicago* 337 US 1, 37(1949)

As with any complex event, many factors were
important in the transformation of Sparta from a
nation founded by university professors seeking to
establish the good society to the nucleus of what is
formally called the Spartan Hegemony and which in
all but name is the first interstellar empire; but analysts are universally agreed that much of the change
can be traced to the will and intent of one man,
Lysander I, Collins King of Sparta. It remains for us to
examine how Lysander, originally very much in agreement with the Spartan Founders that the best policy
for Sparta would be an armed neutrality on the Swiss
model, came to embrace the necessity of empire.

We must also understand that although Lysander
did accept the necessity of an empire uniting a number of planets, he did not come to it willingly. Indeed,
it was thrust upon him in a surprising manner . . .

—From the preface to *From Utopia to Imperium:*
A History of Sparta from Alexander I
to the Accession of Lysander,
by Caldwell C. Whitlock Ph.D.
(University of Sparta Press, 2220)

The war room was nearly deserted. Harv sat motionless at
one end, and Lysander was in the center, his head bowed over
the displays, although it was doubtful that they gave him much
information. Two orderlies and a communications technician

were still on duty. The lights flickered off, then back on, as Peter entered.

"Sire."

Lysander stared at him.

"Victory, your Majesty. The CoDominium forces have changed sides, and the Helots are defeated. More than defeated. Annihilated for the most part."

"Thank you." Lysander tried to stand, but his legs wouldn't hold him. He cursed. "Another hour—If the battle's over I should go to Mother."

"She's under sedation at St. Thomas's, sire," Peter said. "And while the battle is over, there are a great many things to be done. Beginning with evacuation of the Palace. I've come to escort you."

"You really believe in that atom bomb?" Lysander demanded.

"I don't disbelieve in it," Peter said. "I'm also ordering Fort Plataia evacuated. Just in case."

"Good idea. A bomb here would get Government Square. St. Thomas's—"

"Yes, sire, I'm working on that, too. We don't have much transportation, though, and it's not going to be easy. The Queen Mother and Graffin Melissa will be out of there in five minutes. A couple of hours to get everyone."

"I suppose it's best. All right, General, where shall we go?"

"With your permission, Sire, I won't tell you until we're on the way. We've checked this room many times, but still—"

Lysander shuddered. "Won't we *ever* be free of those vermin? General, you have no idea how weary I am of living this way, scared of the very walls—anyway, let's go. I trust you'll have good communications and status displays where you're taking me."

Owensford led him out through the Palace. The corridors were mostly deserted. Peter tried to steer Lysander toward the back gates, but that wasn't possible. Lysander broke free and went to the front gates. "Where?" he demanded.

Peter Owensford sighed and led him to the place where King Alexander had died. A blanket still lay on the marble steps. "It was there, sire. The Helots were going to raise their flag, but the King brought out his guards and prevented that."

Lysander knelt and lifted the blanket to reveal the bloodstained marble. He stared across the public square, to the flagstaff where the Crowned Mountain proudly flew. "Get lights on that flag," he said. "I want it to stay there until we can put up a statue. All right, General, let's go."

✧   ✧   ✧

The command caravan was parked ten kilometers from the Palace. Most of both the Legion and Spartan military staff officers were there. Admiral Forrest waited impatiently as Lysander limped in, leaning heavily on a cane, and was seated with the assistance of two orderlies.

"Highness—uh, excuse me. Sire. General Owensford," he began eagerly.

"I gather Ciotti is talking," Owensford said.

"Oh, yeah. It was this way. Ciotti got the order to arrest the Legion and pronounce an interdict on Sparta. It looked legitimate enough, even though it was signed by Nguyen in Townsend's name. What made it suspicious was the other messages he got.

"First, there was a long report on the breakup of the CoDominum. The Grand Senate is dissolved, but there's not enough stability on Earth to have another election, and a lot of places aren't even stable enough to appoint new Senators."

"Jesus," Owensford said.

"There's more. The Senate dissolved, but apparently a small group of Senators got together again in the Senate Chamber, and declared the adjournment invalid on some technical grounds. That meant this Rump was in theory a legitimate Senate, or at least could call itself that. It proceeded to pass a number of resolutions, one of them the order to imprison all mercenaries on Sparta, another deposing Grand Admiral Lermontov and ordering his arrest.

"Then there was another message, apparently from Bronson himself as the new Chairman of the Naval Affairs Committee. It promises Ciotti promotion to Lieutenant General in command of this system, provided that he gains control here."

"So the swine wasn't just following orders," Lysander said.

"Well, Sire, he can plead that he was," Forrest said. "He did have orders. I'd have questioned them, myself, but he can plead that he considered them valid."

"So what's his status?'

"Karantov has sent him up to the space station under guard. Lieutenant Colonel Farley is confirmed as commander of the 77th. My guess is that Ciotti will be sent off on *Patton*."

Lysander turned to Owensford. "General, I want you to request that Karantov turn him over to us for trial."

Peter shook his head. "Sire, I don't think that would be a good idea. I don't think Karantov will do it. He's not going to put a CoDominium regimental commander up before a mercenary court martial, and if he turns Ciotti over to you, what's to prevent Sparta from demanding the heads of every

CD officer who ever did you harm? As Admiral Forrest says, Ciotti can plead that he had valid orders. Sire, if you do make that request it'll come better through your government than through me. My advice is that you don't ask at all."

"I'll consider that advice," Lysander said.

"He's lost his regiment because of what he did," Peter Owensford said.

"I suppose. He's getting off easy. General, what's the status of that atom bomb?"

"We're searching," Owensford said. "Of course we don't know there is one."

"But you think there is."

"I think we can't take any chances, Majesty. Now we have another problem. Do you have the passwords to your late father's computer system? In particular, where he kept his codes?"

"Possibly," Lysander said. "When the fighting started he gave me a disk."

"We have a long message from Fleet Headquarters that no one seems able to decode," Owensford said. "We suspect it's from Grand Admiral Lermontov, in which case your father might be the only one in this system with a key."

"You don't?"

"No, sir, nor does Karantov. Whitlock may have one. Or Slater. We're trying to find them now."

"Are they missing?"

"Unfortunately," Owensford said. "When last seen, General Slater and his cadets and instructors were driving a Minetown mob off their campus, and we think Whitlock was with him."

"You think they're all right?"

"Yes, Sire," Peter said. "Hal Slater has been through more battles than anyone on this planet, and they weren't facing what you call first class opposition."

"And he'd have code keys you don't have?"

"It's possible," Owensford said. "Lermontov has known Hal nearly as long as he's known Falkenberg. But our best bet is to see if you can find your father's codes."

"All right. I suppose the simplest thing is to start with this disk. Where do you have your code equipment?" Lysander got to his feet and leaned heavily on his cane. "Harv, I can use some help. Let's go, General."

"General, I have someone calling for you. It may be the rebel commander."

Lysander looked up from the code machine. "Perhaps you should talk to her. On the speaker, please."

"Yes, Sire. All right, put her on." He lifted the microphone. "Owensford here."

"Hiyo, Petie. You be remembering Skilly, I think."

"I remember you."

"You sound cold, Petie. Like you don' like me."

Owensford made frantic hand signals. The technicians nodded agreement. *Keep her talking.* "I presume you have a message for me."

"Sure, I want to know if you wan' take up that job offer I make you. Or maybe you want to hire me? That's what you done with Barton after you defeat him, no? So maybe you hire me."

"Well, we could discuss it," Owensford said.

There was a long hard laugh. "Why, Petie, you tryin' to stall me! Lyin' to me, too. But I don' be on here long enough for you to trace where I am, Petie, so maybe we ought to talk serious. I guess Jeffi told you about Murasaki's big surprise."

"What would that be?'

"Oh, come on, now," Skilly said. Her chuckle was loud in the handset. "I know you talk to him, because we see him go into that palace, him and that spy chick you send us. So he tol' you about Murasaki's bomb, which is why you frantic to get everyone out of Government Square and your Fort. Ever stop to think I know you evacuate those people? Maybe I even know where you are. If I don' know now, I find out soon enough, and you can't keep running all the time. Can't govern no country when you can't stop long enough to go to the pot.

"Now you think you goin' find that bomb, or find Skilly, and you maybe right. Maybe right. Skilly down to the triarii now, not many Skilly's people left, who knows, maybe one turn she in for all that money."

"So what do you want?' Owensford asked.

"Skilly want what Niles gets, a ticket off this planet," she said. "You give me that, I give you the bomb. Murasaki too, if you fast enough to catch him, but I don' promise Murasaki. He clever and he fast. But you get his bomb."

"You ask for too much," Owensford said. "You and Niles aren't the same case."

"Yeah, he white ass *gentl*eman," she said. "But I suppose what you mean is Stora Mine. Skilly sorry about that. Bad thing, but if it end the war, kindness after all. Thought it work, thought North Valley would surrender, but your people tougher than we think. And Baby Prince up there to rally the troops, too. Anyway, that water over the spilled milk. Question now is, maybe you catch Skilly and maybe you don't, and meanwhile you going to lose a lot of Citizens and a lot of that city, cause Skilly got nothing left to bargain with."

"We don't even have a way to get you off-planet," Owensford said. "Just at the moment, space is controlled by elements of the CD Navy and it's not certain just who they're loyal to. They like us some, but they hate you a lot, and I doubt we could talk them into letting you leave Sparta even if we wanted to."

"Now, Petie, you wouldn't lie to Skilly, would you? Damn I wish I have one of those gadgets you like so much, but I bet you got your phones jiggered same way I do, filter out all that overtone stuff before it goes out, no? Anyway, I make you one last offer. You take the price off Skilly's head, and you stop looking for Skilly. Outlaw Skilly, that all right. Skilly take care of herself. Any cop on or off duty shoot Skilly on sight, that all right, it happen anyway. But you don' send police tracking me. Or Legion either. Skilly sorry about that Stora Mine business, but nothing she can do."

"We take the price off your head, and you're no longer officially wanted, but you remain an outlaw, to be dealt with as wolves are."

"Right. Without that reward, people get tired of looking for Skilly after a while. They hate Skilly, but they get over it, get on with their lives, if they don' get rich chasing she. Skilly like a better deal, but time getting short. I take that one."

"And in return?"

"I give you that bomb and the last place I know Murasaki at, and we quits."

"I have to refer this to His Majesty."

"Yo. And Petie, you tell His Majesty, Skilly not order anyone to kill his father. That fortunes of war, Dreadful Bride claim him, maybe, but it was nothing deliberate."

"Right. I'll be back in a few minutes."

"Don' take too long," Skilly said. "And don' be delaying thinking you track this call. You track it, all right, but when you get there you find it first relay and you got more tracking to do. Skilly can talk until that bomb go off, you not find she that way, but you lose a lot of you city."

"All right. Be right back." He turned to Lysander. "Sire, you heard."

"Yes. I presume she means it."

"I certainly wouldn't bet most of the Capital on it being a bluff," Owensford said. "And that's exactly what you would be doing."

"I hate letting her get away," Lysander said.

"Maybe she won't."

"Whatever. All right. I hate this, but I don't see what else we can do. Tell her I'll issue the proclamation rescinding the reward, and we'll both issue orders to our forces not to expend official effort in hunting for her. That's as soon as we find the bomb, of course."

"Right." Owensford activated the communications set. "You got it," he said. "Reward called off, no official efforts to find you."

"Legion too," Skilly said. "Your word on that."

"Legion too. Our word, mine and His Majesty's. That's as soon as we find the bomb."

"Yah, I figure you do it that way. All right. At the southeast corner of Government Square, keep going southeast you come to the King Jason Hotel. It probably surprise you a lot, but I own that hotel. Well, someone else name on the papers, but I pay for it. The Royal Arms restaurant there, in the basement, there's a big meat locker. The far wall of that meat locker opens up, there's another room behind it. You'll find the bomb in there, and I think you better hurry, I don't think Murasaki leave much time. That was last place I know him to be, too, but I don't think he there now."

Owensford thumbed off the microphone. "Deighton! Get bomb disposal and a tac unit moving to the King Jason Hotel, southeast corner of Government Square. There's a nuke there, details after they're on the way. Murasaki was last seen there, but I don't expect you to catch him."

"Nuke. King Jason Hotel. On the way, skipper."

"Why won't we catch Murasaki?" Lysander asked.

"He'll have a way off planet. Bronson has agents here, they'll be on their way. The interesting part is they didn't take Skilly. I don't think they like her." He thumbed the microphone back on. "All right, bomb disposal is on the way."

"Aww, Petie, I thought you go yourself. That way, if the city go up, I know you with it. Anyway, Petie, Skilly wish she never start this. Too bad I can't stay around and watch you hang Croser, but I probably see it on TV."

"Miss Thibodeau."

"Who's that? That you, King Lysander?'

"Yes."

"Well, Majesty excuse me, but I don' have long to talk. You take that reward off like you promise, you hear?"

"I will keep my promise," Lysander said.

"An' you don' know why you want to talk with me. It okay,

Majesty, it okay to be curious about such like me. You want
to stare into that empty empty abyss, and you doin' it, and
the abyss stares right back, your Majesty. I tell you this, Skilly
means it when she say she sorry she start this, and sorry she
not listen to Jeffi about that business with the rocket. Now
Skilly gone."

"Signal lost," a technician said. "Carrier lost."

"All right, General," Lysander said. "I've stared into the abyss,
and I'm not about to become like that. We gave her a promise.
Presuming your people find and disarm that bomb, we'll keep
our word."

"Of course, sir. No reward, no official pursuit."

"So why are you looking so smug?" Lysander demanded.

"Well, sir, you may remember Sergeant Taras Miscowsky from
the incident at the Halleck ranch?"

"Indeed. I remember more than him. I'm reliably informed
that you've been seeing quite a lot of the Senator's grand-
daughter."

"Yes, sire. But back to a less pleasant subject. Sergeant
Miscowsky has been on campaign for a long time now.
Accumulated considerable leave. He served with Jerry Lefkowitz,
Sire, and he doesn't need any promise of reward to keep him
on her track until he can send her head to Lefkowitz. I've
sent for him. He'll be on leave status from the time he lands.
That's not an official act. Nor is it official if the Officers Mess
wants to take up a collection to help Miscowsky enjoy his
vacation."

"Sir, I've got some leave coming too," Sergeant Andy Bielskis
said from the doorway. "Excuse me, Colonel, didn't mean to
eavesdrop, but if it's all the same to you, Taras and I get along
just fine, and I think we'd enjoy taking a vacation together."

"You were at Stora, weren't you?" Owensford asked.

"Yes, sir, that I was."

"We might need you—"

"I don't suppose it will take Taras and me very long," Andy
Bielskis said. "Not long at all."

"Where the devil have you been?" Owensford demanded.

Hal Slater grinned sheepishly. "Well—"

"He was chasin' rebels," Caldwell Whitlock said. "Doin'
pretty good at it, too. General Slater's got a pretty good shootin'
eye for a busted up old geezer who can't walk without a cane."

"Why, Professor," Hal said. He eyed Whitlock's ample stomach. "Apparently Dr. Whitlock chose to swallow his enemy.
Anyway, Peter, have you decoded Lermontov's message yet?"

"No, we don't seem to be able to."

"You wouldn't. King Alexander had the code."

"We thought of that, and we think we have his codes, but I'm afraid Lysander hasn't been able to figure out how to use it."

"I'll show him," Slater said. "We need to go tell him about this, but it might be better if we talk about the situation first."

"All right. Coffee?"

"Yes, please, I could use some."

"I'll make it myself." Owensford closed the door and latched it. "Coffee, Caldwell?"

"Yeah, sure. Peter, we have got ourselves a first class mess, and it doesn't help at all that King Alexander's dead."

"Have a seat and tell me about it." Owensford spooned coffee beans into the grinder. "No Sumatra Lintong. No Jamaica. Just local, I'm afraid."

"Right now I'll be grateful for anything," Hal said. "Peter, it's hard to know where to start."

"Start at the—"

"Beginning, go through to the end, and then stop. Yeah," Whitlock said. "Beginning. Lermontov's truly deposed. In gaol if not dead, and my guess is dead. This message was recorded and coded and set up to be sent in the event anything happened to him. It's updated with some other last minute stuff. Oh. Falkenberg won, by the way. New Washington campaign is over, Franklin gave up, and whatever passes for a government on New Washington has proclaimed John Christian Falkenberg as Protector."

Owensford whistled. "Won and won big, then. Wait a minute. Protector. Anything about that political girl, Glenda Ruth Horton, I guess her name was?"

"Yeah, I think so, but we're still decoding the Falkenberg reports. They were included in this message from Lermontov, so they didn't break in clear."

"You think the Colonel married her?" Hal Slater asked.

"You know him better than I do."

"It's certainly a possibility," Slater said. "Which makes things interesting, since we're all pretty well settled *here*. Kathryn isn't going to move again."

"Miriam Ann likes it here," Whitlock said. "Took her a while to get used to the gravity and the short day, but she likes the company. Take a powerful lot to move her now. Me too, of course."

"I never did ask where you finally settled in," Owensford said. "Sorry, been so busy."

"That's all right. I bought a spread near Hal's new place, off that park area the War College uses sometimes. Interesting neighbors. After we had that meetin' at Hal and Kathryn's, Captain Newell started looking around there. He hasn't bought in yet, but we've got, what, Hal? Maybe a dozen CoDominium navy families settled around the area. Makes for good company. I hear you're gettin' pretty serious, you staying on Sparta?"

"Yes. Lydia likes the outback. So do I. We'll keep a ranch out in the Valley, but there's too much work here. We've been looking for something near the Capital."

"Bring her out to meet Miriam Ann," Whitlock said. "I expect Miriam Ann and Kathryn can help her find a place she'll like. Better do it quick, though, I hear there's more CD people looking at land around there, you'll want to get 40 or 50 acres before the prices get too high."

"I'll do that. Thanks." Peter poured more coffee. "All right. Back to work. So Lermontov is definitely out."

"And these are his final orders," Hal Slater said.

"Call it his will," Whitlock said. "Grand Admiral Sergei Mikaelovich Lermontov's legacy to the Fleet."

"I hate to think that," Owensford said. "One damned good man. All right. What are the Grand Admiral's last orders?"

"Lots of stuff addressed to the Fleet, about loyalty, and what the CoDominium Fleet was for," Whitlock said. "Pretty damn good, too. Political scientists will be mining that for a century. But it boils down to this. The CoDominium existed to keep the peace. Now it's broken up, gone, and those who tore it up don't want peace. They're going to come around demanding loyalty from the Fleet, and they don't deserve it. Factions are going to try to use the Fleet, but it'll be to start wars for their own purposes."

"Jesus, that's prophetic enough," Owensford said.

"Right. By the way, there's another message encoded inside this one, encoded in the authentication code Lermontov used to send messages to the Fleet, and of course it's addressed to the Fleet. I sent that up to Boris," Hal said.

"Think his nose will be out of joint that you had the key and he didn't?" Owensford asked.

"Don't know," Hal said.

"I expect yes, but not too bad," Whitlock said. "We put a lot of stress on Hal being one of Lermontov's oldest friends—"

"So was Boris," Hal said.

"And one of Falkenberg's oldest friends, and that's going to be real relevant," Whitlock said. "You see, once he got through warning the Fleet what evil people would do to get control of them and their ships, he gave his last orders. He ordered them to obey his successor as they would him. But he didn't know who his successor would be. Let me read some of that.

"Brothers and sisters in arms, we cannot name my true successor now. We can be certain that the Rump of the Grand Senate will attempt to name a successor. We can be certain that successors will name themselves. How shall we choose among them? I do not believe that we can, yet we—you, for if you read this, I will not be with you—you must stay together. You must have unity. To that end, you can form a council of captains to advise your new commander, and I urge you to do that, but I do not believe that a council of captains can long govern, or even name a commander for you.

"I cannot name a commander for you.

"I will name a group that you can obey with honor. It consists of people you know. Two are young, but you will understand why they are named. The third is older and you will understand that choice also. The fourth some of you will know and some will not. My brothers and sisters in arms, I command you: until they themselves shall name a successor to me, you will accept your orders from John Grant; Carleton Blaine; John Christian Falkenberg; and King Alexander of Sparta. They do not always agree, and that is well, for they can work together and they will, and when they are together they have great wisdom. When they speak together you must obey them as you would me.

"Farewell. We have done our best, for civilization, for the human race. We have not failed in our duties. Those to whom we owed obedience failed us. We have not rebelled against legitimate authority. The authority vanished. Now there is no legitimate authority.

"John Grant. Carleton Blaine. John Christian Falkenberg. Alexander of Sparta. They are my heirs, and they will find you an honorable path to follow. Stay together. Act in honor.

"Good-bye, and Godspeed.

"Sergei Mikaelovich Lermontov, Grand Admiral."

"Holy Christ," Owensford said. "That's Lermontov all right." He wiped at something in his eye. "I guess the Old Man's really gone. But Alexander is dead. What do we do?"

"Don't leave much room for maneuver," Whitlock said. "Four was an unwieldy number anyway. Now it's three. A Grant, a Blaine, and Christian Johnny. I think the Fleet will like that."

"Then you think the Fleet will obey that order?" Hal Slater asked.

"Some will," Whitlock said. "Let's look here at this system. Karantov will. Newell will think about it for a while. He's got all that Navy power, and he can see the potential, but he's pretty smart. He understands you can bash a planet, but you can't take it over, not with any four ships. Life by blackmail isn't much of a life. Besides, down deep he's a good man. He'll come around, and he'll bring those others who stood with him.

"Donovic, now, he's not going to accept this. He'll head off toward Earth. He's that kind, he'll go to see if there's anything worth picking left on the bones of his mother. So figure, that's one out of five here won't accept Lermontov's heirs. Say two out of five on average, but they won't all defect in the same direction. Some'll sell their services to the highest bidder. Hell, that's about what's happened here, it's just we got the bids in early."

"Only now this comes," Hal Slater said thoughtfully.

"So maybe one in five goes over to Bronson?" Owensford asked.

"Sounds as good a guess as any," Whitlock said. "And two in five stick with us. I presume it's us? We all together in this?"

"One for all," Hal Slater said.

"And all for one," Owensford added. "Except where does he come in?" He jerked his thumb toward the door. Whitlock looked at each of his companions.

The flags of Sparta stood at half mast. All but one. Outside the steps of the Palace the Crowned Mountain stood out proudly at the peak of the flagstaff. At night a dozen spotlights illuminated it.

Most of the wreckage had been cleaned up in Government Square. Many walls would be pockmarked for decades, but the debris was gone. Traffic was thin, but commerce had begun again in the two weeks since the battle ended. Sparta had buried a king, and had yet to crown his son, but Lysander was still Master of the Forces, and had more work to do than ever.

"Prince."

Lysander looked up from his desk. There were a million details to attend to. During the battles he had given orders to the soldiers, and things happened. Now he hardly saw the soldiers. He gave orders to civilians, and something might happen or might not.

"Aw hell, excuse me. King," Harv said. "You'd think I'd get used to it."

"Maybe I should issue a special edict," Lysander said, smiling. "Permitting you to use any title you feel like. You've earned it."

"Don't know about that. Sorry to disturb you, but there's a bunch of military people to see you. Officers, and they brought some enlisted people too, sergeants and like that. About fifty. Say they'd like to see you in the audience chamber whenever it's convenient, and they'll wait."

Lysander frowned. "Well, all right—"

"I think maybe I want some of the Life Guards with us when we meet that crew," Harv said.

"Whatever for?"

"Prince—Majesty, I plain don't like it. All these military and navy people, most of 'em in CoDominium uniforms, General Owensford dressed down as a light colonel of the Legion, General Slater in Royal Sparta uniform like Admiral Forrest, and they come with petty officers and sergeants and every one of them wearing sidearms. I been watching them, the last week they been thick as thieves, Majesty. Talking to each other, but not to you."

"Well, Harv, if that group has come to demand my resignation, a dozen Life Guards won't change anything. Among them they've got enough power to slag this planet. Tell them I'll be pleased to receive them in the audience chamber in ten minutes, and don't bother with the Life Guards."

"Well, if you say so, Prince—"

"I just did, Harv."

"Yes, sir."

Lysander found Melissa and Queen Adriana in the family quarters. "I seem to be scheduled to hold an audience," he said. "Actually it's not scheduled, it's more that it's demanded. Right now. By all the military officers in the system. Mine, the old CoDominium, the Legion—"

"Surely the Legion is ours," Melissa said.

"I thought so," Lysander said.

"You look worried," Queen Adriana said.

"Mother, I don't know. Harv's worried, and I guess that's got me thinking."

"That they're here to depose you?"

"Mother, I don't know. I have no reason to believe that, but I never had the military demand to see me in a body before, either. Anyway, I don't think I ought to keep them waiting. Melissa, take Mother to the country lodge. Harv has a driver waiting—"

"I'll do no such thing," Melissa said. "I'm coming with you."

Queen Adriana laughed. "I think you've got the wind up for nothing, boy. They probably want something, titles and honors and promotions. Soldiers like that sort of thing. But I'll tell you this, whatever they want, those Helots couldn't chase me out of this palace, and I'm certainly not going to run from our own soldiers. Now let's go see what they want. But first, you change to your best tunic, and put your orders on. If we're going to be deposed, we may as well be dressed for it!"

The delegation filed in. There were nearly fifty of them, and as Harv had said, they wore many different uniforms. Hal Slater in Legion dress, but still wearing a Royalist shoulder badge, seemed to be their leader, followed closely by Fleet Captain Newell and Colonel Karantov in CoDominium. Just behind them was his own Rear Admiral Forest. Then Colonel Farley of the 77th. The Captains Alana. Legion Senior Sergeant Guiterrez, and other Legion Officers. And last of all, behind the enlisted men, in clothing more colorful than the military uniforms, Dr. Whitlock came in carrying a briefcase.

Lysander received them sitting, with the Dowager Queen and Melissa seated next to him. When they had all filed in, Lysander stood and acknowledged their bows. "I regret that King David is not in the city," Lysander said.

"Sire, it was you we came to see," Hal Slater said. He bowed, then bowed again to Queen Adriana. "Madam. Graffina Melissa."

"General, we are pleased to see you, but this is unexpected."

"Yes, sire, we know it is," Slater said. "We'll be as brief as possible, but the matter is a bit complex.

"Sire, everyone here is familiar with the long messages that constitute Admiral Lermontov's last will, and of course you have read the copy addressed to your late father."

"Yes, General."

"That document named a council of four to succeed Grand Admiral Lermontov. With King Alexander deceased that left three. The purpose of the council is to hold the Fleet together until some new governing structure can be formed to keep the peace." Hal Slater spoke carefully, as if lecturing at the War College rather than speaking to his sovereign.

"That left us all with a problem," Slater said. "Two problems, actually. The first is that a council that's physically dispersed across lightyears of space can't command. Decisions are going to be needed. Right here in this system we have a divided command. I hold a commission as an officer of the Royal Army and as such I am responsible to the Dual

Monarchy; under the Ultimate Decree, to your majesty personally. However, I also have another office. With General Owensford and Dr. Whitlock I am a spokesman for Colonel Falkenberg, and meanwhile he has become Protector of New Washington, as well as a member of the Grand Admiral's succession council.

"Fleet Captain Newell finds himself under orders to obey a council that has never met. One of its members is dead, and no other member of that council is present in this system, yet it is in this system that his interests lie. Owensford, Whitlock, and I know that this system was important to Lermontov, and to Falkenberg. We know that Carleton Blaine as governor of Tanith offered alliance to Sparta. We're certain that Captain Newell and his squadron should stay here and protect Sparta. But whose orders do they follow?"

Lysander shook his head in wonder. "Are you asking me, General Owensford?"

"Permit me, sire," Dr. Whitlock said. He came forward. "There's a sense in which I don't belong in here, but maybe I better explain something. King Lysander, if there's one thing history shows us, the worst kind of government anyone ever had was a council of soldiers. Maybe one soldier can govern and maybe not, but investing supreme power in a council of military officers is about the worst thing that can happen. Lermontov knew that. He made up a council of two officers and two politicians in the hopes they'd balance off, but you'll note he cautioned them to name someone as commander as soon as they could. What he didn't put in that public last will he put in private messages to me and Hal Slater. I've shown those to the other Fleet people here. What he told us to do was use our judgment on whether to offer command to King Alexander. We also know Colonel Falkenberg approved hailing King Alexander as commander if the necessity came up."

Before Lysander could react to that, Hal Slater began to speak. "The CoDominium is gone. Something has to take its place, and we have no time to build anything," Hal said. "There aren't many people we can follow. Falkenberg has always made it clear that he won't accept supreme command. So we've been discussing this, and we've all agreed, and we've come to tell you that agreement."

Hal Slater limped forward. He was joined by Peter Owensford, then Fleet Captain Newell. Boris Karantov and Colonel Farley. Admiral Forrest. They stood in a row.

"This is just a little awkward," Hal said. "We've lost the ceremony for this over the past thousand years. But we mean every word of it." He raised his arm, not outstretched as Germans once did, but high, palm forward. "Hail. Ave. Ave, Lysander, Imperator."

The greeting was said carefully, self consciously at first, then repeated, this time with more enthusiasm. "Ave Lysander, Imperator."

It was echoed by the others in the room, officers and petty officers, representatives of the Fleet, voices blending together into a mighty shout that rang through the palace, and was echoed back to the audience chamber. The words washed over him, and Lysander stood, his expression unreadable.

"AVE, LYSANDER. AVE,
LYSANDER, IMPERATOR."

"Bring us together," Caldwell Whitlock said, his voice low and almost unheard, and then the cry rang through the palace again.

"AVE. AVE LYSANDER, IMPERATOR!"